ANDY PELOQUIN

DARKBLADE

AWAKENER

Caminante, no hay camino; se hace camino al andar.

— Antonio Machado

Part One:
<u>Sojourner</u>

Chapter One

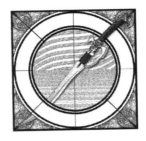

The Hunter dreamed of darkness.

Amidst a sea of golden grass and rolling hills stood a tower of the deepest midnight black. Its surface shone with the light of a thousand thousand shimmering stars, at once bright yet devouring all light around it. Serpentine threads of green and violet entwined around its base and oozed into the ground, turned the lands around it barren, consumed earth and rock and creatures with a rot no living thing could withstand. All in its environs turned to ash and dust and decay. Life extinguished by an insatiable hunger and darkness both fell and unnamable.

For within lurked evil. Boundless, eternally ravenous, like the great maw of a creature as immense as Einan itself. The force of its desire emanated outward with such force it set the shimmering black walls throbbing. Pulsing with the steady rhythm that might have been not one, but *two* vast heartbeats.

Ukuhlushwa Okungapheli.

The name rang in his mind, shivered down his spine, pierced him to the marrow. He could not tear his gaze away, could not retreat. For it held him fast, dragged him ever closer.

Ukuhlushwa Okungapheli.

It called to him, too. Whispered in his mind, seeped into his thoughts, filled his head with incomprehensible pleas, demands, and entreaties. The twin heartbeats called to him with a voice that resonated to the core of his being. To his very soul. Inexorable, insistent, ever-shifting between subtle invitations and incessant commands.

He ached to do its bidding. Recoiled from the voices. Sought to hear them clearer. Fought to keep them out of his mind. An inner war raged, the essence of his being torn in half.

Ukuhlushwa Okungapheli.

It wanted him. Needed him.

"Hssht!" A sharp hiss pierced the Hunter's mind, and an elbow dug into his side.

The Hunter's eyes snapped open, instantly awake and alert. His hand dropped to the weapons on his belt, ready to draw Soulhunger or the Sword of Nasnaz at the first sign of danger. Only to stop upon recognizing the woman hovering in the darkness before him.

Kiara's dark eyes shone with a glint of excitement so bright it rivaled the stars sparkling in the heavens above. A smile split her face from ear to ear, and she radiated the eager energy of anticipation.

"It's here!" she hissed, though her voice was barely audible above the deafening roar of falling water.

The Hunter's eyebrows shot up. "What?"

Kiara nodded, every muscle in her lithe, well-formed body quivering with elation. She jerked a thumb over her right shoulder. "Look!"

The Hunter rose from where he'd been reclining against the stone wall of the narrow trail they'd used to descend from the top of Zamani Falls. He hadn't intended to fall asleep, but the last weeks of restless nights, plagued by torrid dreams, had taken a toll on him. Kiara's pronouncement, however, banished any lingering trace of slumber. He *had* to see it for himself.

Kiara didn't go far. On her hands and knees, she crawled across the narrow trail and settled onto her belly overlooking the basin into which the thunderous Zamani Falls emptied. The roar of hammering water grew louder as the Hunter peered over the trail's edge. His eyes traced the seven cascades rising a full five hundred paces into the air, followed the water plunging from the clifftop into the deep pool that it had carved out of the rocky earth over thousands of years.

And there he saw it. First, he spotted the single glow of its lone eye. A deep blood-red, darker than the light that emanated from Soulhunger's gemstone, yet emanating from an immense orb as large as his torso. Though he could not hear it over the cacophony of the waterfalls, he had no trouble imagining the metallic clinking and clacking of the thousands of coppery scales that stretched along the length of its body.

The Hunter watched in dumbfounded amazement as the creature slithered forth from the depths of the waterfalls' pool. Coil after coil of gleaming reddish-gold thicker than he was tall, propelled by muscles so immense they were said to have cut the Inyoni River out of the earth to carve a path fifty paces wide and a hundred leagues long.

Keeper's teeth! Icy feet danced down the Hunter's spine, and his mouth went suddenly dry. He slid a hand to Soulhunger's hilt; the solid metal came as scant comfort, for he knew even the Sword of Nasnaz would fare poorly against such an immense creature.

Kiara turned toward him, her face aglow with an exuberance that bordered on childlike wonder. "*Indombe!*"

The Hunter nodded. "You were right." He mouthed the words, unable to bring himself to voice them aloud for fear the enormous metallic serpent would somehow overhear him. Even from a hundred paces away and thirty paces above the pool from which the monstrosity was emerging, the Hunter felt far from safe. Nothing but empty air and the tiniest stone ledge separated him from…that.

He tried to call to mind everything Kiara had told him in the week since she'd first insisted they make this detour on their journey northeast to Ghandia. A *short* detour, she'd sworn, just a day out of their way. For all his recalcitrance, the Hunter had ultimately relented. The delay would be worth giving her the chance to see the Zamani Falls—a place spoken of in Drashi myths as the birthplace of *Ach'nalo,* the World-Eater, and in Ghandian lore as the home of *Indombe,* Serpent Fire-Mother.

The Hunter hadn't *truly* believed the legends. Couldn't believe that a creature of such immense size and power could actually exist on Einan for thousands of years and only been sighted a handful of times. Still, he'd gone along in part to humor Kiara, and in part to distract himself from the memories of what lay behind and worries and uncertainties over what lay ahead.

Now, the evidence before his eyes drove all thoughts of past and future aside, fixed him firmly in the present. He stared spellbound at the enormous copper-colored serpent emerging from the depths of the Zamani Basin. Indombe's enormous form circled the entire circumference of the pool once, and still more of the creature's powerful coils rippled beneath the water's surface. The glow emanating from its lone eyeball lit up the entire basin, turning the waterfall into a cascade of a hundred thousand glittering ruby droplets. Wisps of steam rose as its

8

immense internal heat evaporated the water on its scaly body. In the seconds—no, the Hunter realized, it had been *minutes*—since Indombe began emerging, the air around him had grown noticeably warmer.

That was part of the creature's legend, he remembered from the previous night. Kiara had prepared them for what she hoped they would see at the falls—including the dangers they might face.

Ghandian lore held that Indombe had been the first to gift mankind with fire, bestowing upon them a portion of her own soul and earning the title of "Fire-Mother". Hundreds of scholars had attempted over the years to study the creature, but few had actually seen it. Much of what Kiara had learned was little more than a patchwork of local rumors and folk tales.

Yet somehow, she'd been utterly certain about the time and day when Indombe would appear. She'd insisted that every legend spoke of the "final harvest night, when the moon's fire kisses the hunter's star". Except those who came hoping to see Indombe failed to take into account that "the final harvest night" had nothing to do with the date of the *actual* harvest, but the last night of the year that the constellation known as the "Harvester's Sickle" appeared in the sky over Zamani Falls. The same night the largest star in the constellation the Drashi called the "Stalwart Hunter" shone bright enough to rival the moon's light.

And by the Keeper, she was right!

The Hunter stared in wonder at the leviathan creature emerging from the fathomless depths of the pool. How could such a thing exist? What sustained it? The handful of unfortunate travelers said to have vanished around the Zambesi Basin over the last few hundred years could scarcely suffice to feed such a creature. Even the towering Stone Guardians he'd encountered in the Empty Mountains would serve as little more than a mouthful for the colossal beast below.

And what called it up to the surface on *this* night of all nights? What could cause one such as Indombe to leave the lightless recesses?

Even as the question formed in his mind, Indombe's monocular serpentine head reared high. The Hunter nearly scrambled backward in shock, and only his iron will kept him firmly in place. He could not risk drawing the creature's attention, had to stay perfectly still as Indombe rose before him. Up, up, up, a hundred paces into the air, propelled by muscles immense enough to snap a ship in half. And there it stayed, its enormous body undulating as if blown by a gentle breeze, or in mimicry of the rippling sheets of water cascading off the Zamani Falls. Its enormous ruby eye pointed straight up to the sky, as if seeking out the luminous face of the full moon shining in the heavens.

Again, Kiara's words from the previous night sprang to mind. "*Every Indombe searches for her children, for the moon and stars, borne of her fire and her undying love for Ingwe All-Father.*"

The Hunter gave no credence to that portion of the lore, yet in that moment, he could not deny the feeling of strangeness. Emanating among the heat rippling off Indombe's enormous form, driving back the night's chill, it felt like longing. Sorrow. Anguish that ran bone-deep.

Those feelings, he knew all too well. He had lived with them for as long as he could remember. The faint memories of Taiana had filled him with that longing. Cradling Farida's little body in his arms, he'd felt that raw sorrow piercing every fiber of his being. And the anguish had grown nearly overwhelming when he'd learned that he had a *daughter* alive somewhere in Einan, and with Taiana locked in the Chamber of Sustenance, the task of finding Jaia was left to him alone.

Whether the emotions truly came from Indombe or merely from within himself, the Hunter did not know. Yet the tears that sprang to his eyes were no less real than the monstrous form of the coppery serpent glittering in the moonlight in front of him. It was not the heat alone that choked him, thickened his throat.

He felt the urge to scream rising within him. Dragged up from the depths of his soul by a force he could not control. He wanted to leap to his feet, to throw his head back, and howl his anguish at the moon. Even if it meant his death, he ached to do it. To unleash the torrent of emotions swirling within him.

Movement at his side drew his attention. Tears streamed from Kiara's eyes, too, and a look of the purest misery twisted her beautiful face. She felt what he felt, what he saw. The same overwhelming surge of grief and loss, the compulsion to rage at the heavens. And the call to rise. She had pushed herself up onto her arms and knees and begun to do just that.

For the briefest moment, fear pierced the maelstrom whirling in the Hunter's soul. Not fear of the serpent—how could he truly be afraid of something that *felt* so deeply?—but fear for Kiara. In that glimmer of lucidity, the Hunter summoned the presence of mind to reach up and seize Kiara's arm. He dragged her down and onto him, into his embrace. Wrapped his arms around her and held her tight.

She struggled in his grip, writhed like a serpent, but he clutched her with all his inhuman strength. Clasped her to him while the waves of Indombe's anguish roiled through them both. He could not give in to the serpent's compulsion, couldn't let Kiara, either. He fought to save their lives against the ancient beast's strange power.

Indombe shrieked. A sound as powerful as the one bubbling up within Hunter burst from the creature's mouth. No serpentine hissing or spitting, but a scream as primal, raw, and human as any the Hunter had ever heard. It rent the air with ear-shattering force, piercing even the roar of the Zamani Falls, drowning out the water's thundering.

The cacophony nearly split the Hunter's head open. He felt it resonating within his skull, setting his mind trembling, nearly ripping away his consciousness. Only the solid warmth of Kiara in his arms kept him from losing the fight to the darkness. He had to keep her from yielding to whatever terrible power Indombe exuded, could not lose her to the compulsion.

On and on the scream went, seemingly forever, rising in volume until it consumed the entire world. Amplified by the roaring thunder of the falls, reverberating off the stones and setting the very ground beneath the Hunter trembling.

Until it stopped. As abruptly as it had begun, so suddenly it left the Hunter's ears ringing and his head swimming. The utter silence deafened him, disoriented him. Even the Zamani Falls seemed to have fallen deathly still, as if the water dared not shatter Indombe's power.

In that frozen moment, in the space between heartbeats, the Hunter heard the faintest sound. A faint splashing, coming from far below.

It was drowned out a moment later by the falls' thundering, gone so quickly the Hunter almost thought he'd imagined it. He blinked, forced himself to peer out over the lip of the trail.

There, splashing about in the pool at the bottom of the waterfalls, was a young man. Flailing at the water with increasingly panicked frenzy, limbs thrashing, head dipping again and again below the water.

The Hunter's heart leaped into his throat.

Tarek!

Chapter Two

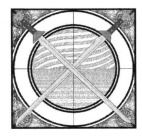

The Hunter leaped to his feet, eyes fixed on the pool thirty paces below him. Hours earlier, before fatigue had dragged the Hunter into sleep, Tarek had chosen to remain on a switchback section of the trail above and slightly to the west of the ledge Kiara had decided on for the vantage point to watch for Indombe. The young Elivasti had wanted to remain far enough back to occasionally check on their horses while still having a view of the Zamani Basin on the off chance Indombe actually emerged.

So how in the Watcher's name did he end up in the water?

The Hunter's heart hammered a furious beat. Had Tarek fallen, a section of the trail giving way beneath him? The force of the serpent's screams had shaken the stone beneath the Hunter and Kiara hard enough that it might have widened existing fissures or been the final crack to weaken an existing weakness? Yet the Hunter hadn't heard the rumbling of any stones falling past their positions.

Or had the young man given in to whatever arcane magic the serpent emanated? Had he answered Indombe's call and leaped into the water?

Whatever the case, the young Elivasti was clearly in trouble. Between the shimmering waves of heat rising off the pool, the copper-scaled serpentine coils rippling beneath the water's surface, and the clear fact that he couldn't swim, Tarek's life hung in the balance.

As if the situation hadn't already been dire enough, Indombe's enormous broad-snouted head shifted, and its gleaming crimson eye turned downward to fix on the figure splashing and flailing in its pool. Its mouth stretched in a massive, hideous reptilian grin. Its maw opened to reveal a long tongue that ended in a razor-sharp fang. With speed terrifying for a beast of such immense size, Indombe dove for its hapless prey.

And the Hunter dove with it.

He'd acted without thinking; his arms slid from his cloak of their own accord, a single step brought him to the edge of the trail, and he leaped away from the cliffside with all the strength in his powerful legs. Only once he was plummeting through the air did reality truly sink home. By then, there was no turning back.

The dark waters of the pool rushed up to meet him, and he hit the surface with spine-jarring force. Only the fact that Indombe's enormous head broke the water's tension saved him from grave injury. Still, the water hammered him with the force of a charging aurochs, and darkness reached icy tendrils to swallow him and drag him into the depths of unconsciousness.

Only the sizzling heat of the pool saved his life. The pain snapped him awake, his mind instantly aware of the danger. If Indombe didn't swallow him, the water would boil him, cook the meat off his bones. He had no idea if his Bucelarii healing could save him from that fate, or for how long. Tarek, however, stood no chance at all.

The Hunter kicked toward the surface, pumping his arms and legs with all the force he possessed. All around him, Indombe's enormous body churned up the water. Around and around the vast serpent swirled, and with it, the pool began to swirl, too. That was *another* of the details about which Kiara had spoken the previous night. The legends of Indombe told of the vast whirlpool that occasionally formed in the Zamani Basin to drag fishing boats, swimmers, and wildlife into the bottomless depths forever.

The Hunter broke the surface with a gasp, but he had no time for relief. He swam toward Tarek with powerful strokes. The young man's struggles grew weaker as his muscles gave out and the water filling his lungs suffocated him. In the seconds it took the Hunter to reach his side, Tarek had gone under and resurfaced twice. When his head once more vanished below the dark, frothy waters, the Hunter knew the young man wouldn't be coming back up a third time.

Sucking in a great breath, he dove for the young man's body. The rapidly accelerating current carried Tarek farther away from him, dragging him into the depths. The Hunter swam for all he was worth. Hand over hand, legs pumping, he pursued Tarek underwater. The young man's eyes were wide and panicked, yet glazing over quickly. When he caught sight of the Hunter, he thrust out a hand with the desperation of a drowning man.

The Hunter seized the outstretched hand and hauled for all he was worth. Tarek's weight dragged him down, but he kicked at the water, propelling them both toward the surface. Slowly—so Keeper-damned slowly—his efforts hindered by the weight of his armor and weapons, and the current whipped up by Indombe's massive body. His lungs soon began screaming, his muscles protesting, but still the Hunter fought on. Wrestling against the swirling water and the weight threatening to pull him forever into the pool.

When finally he broke the water's surface, the kiss of the heated air on his face set his skin prickling. He'd only been in the pool for a few seconds, but he didn't have long. Tarek, either. In a minute, perhaps two, the heat would cook them. Or Indombe would snap them up in its enormous maw and swallow them whole.

The Hunter kicked out for the edge of the pool. Though it was just a dozen paces away, he might as well have been trying to swim the breadth of the Frozen Sea for all the progress he made. His muscles burned with the exertion and still the sandy shore seemed impossibly far. The current grew faster, too. His forward progress stalled, slowed, then he felt himself being sucked backward.

His powerful right arm thrashed at the water with every shred of strength he could summon, his legs kicking out again and again in a desperate effort to fight the current. More than once, his booted feet struck something hard and smooth directly beneath him. Even his iron will faltered at the mental image of that gaping mouth with its fang-tipped tongue opening up beneath him.

Piss on that!

The Hunter gritted his teeth and swam for all he was worth. He could make it if he released Tarek, he knew, but he'd no more let the young Elivasti go than he would allow Indombe to snap him up without a fight. And so the Hunter roared his defiance with what little breath remained to him and swam as if his life depended on it. Because it bloody well did.

One moment, it seemed he was fighting for his life, then the next his hand brushed scalding hot rock. His fingers closed around the stone and he dragged himself forward and up, out of the pool, onto the ledge that ran beneath the cliff from which he'd jumped. Boiling hot water splashed around him, and he felt the current tugging at his boots, his clothing, Tarek's limp form. But he would not let Indombe take them. With a wordless shout—little more than an animal howl of rage and determination—the Hunter scrambled backward, pulling Tarek with him. Up onto the stone, then back, back, back, away from the water.

The moment Tarek's legs were clear of the pool, the Hunter released the young man's still form and leaped to his feet. Though his flesh sizzled and every fiber of his being felt tender, the Hunter bent, scooped up the Elivasti, and slung him over his shoulder. Then he turned and ran along the rocky promontory.

Away from the water. That was all he could think. Away from the water, and from Indombe.

Behind him, the thunder of the waterfall quieted a fraction. The Hunter risked a backward glance and, to his horror, found the swirling current had slowed, the water farther from the falls itself settling. A sick feeling of dread surged in his belly. That could only mean—

Indombe's enormous head erupted from the surface in a spray of water that glittered like rubies in the light emanating from its eye. Up, up, up it rose, its coppery serpent's body looming fifty paces above the Hunter. Its single eye fixed on him, and its immense muscles coiled in anticipation.

The Hunter did the only thing he could. He hurled Tarek's limp form in one direction, then dove in the other. He didn't look where he was diving, just leaped with all the strength he could summon.

Not a moment too soon. Indombe's broad-snouted head slammed into the rocky promontory where he'd just been standing with force enough to shake the earth. The Hunter landed in knee-deep water, splashing onto his belly, but staggered upward as the serpent recovered and reared up once more.

The gleaming ruby eye shifted from him to where Tarek lay face-up on the rocky ledge where the Hunter had thrown him. The Hunter saw the giant snake preparing to strike. The fang-tipped tongue flicked out like a whip, again the colossal copper-clad body coiled for another attack.

"Hey, you big bastard!" the Hunter shouted with all the force he could muster. To his ears, his words sounded faint, all but drowned out by the thundering of the water roaring off the falls and the blood rushing into his ears. Yet he shouted again anyway. "You hungry? Come and get me, you big ugly earthworm!"

Not the most creative of insults, but he didn't exactly have time to think clearly. He was too busy waving his arms over his head and slogging through the boiling water back toward shore to put much thought into his taunts.

To his relief, the gleaming red eye turned to regard him. His stomach bottomed out as the serpent's enormous body shifted toward him, coils rattling like a thousand copper bits, tongue flicking out as if in anticipation of tasting his blood.

This time, the Hunter was ready when Indombe struck. The serpent's huge head darted toward him in a blur of shining red light and metallic scales. The fanged tongue led the way, driving at his chest like a dagger's fatal thrust.

His watered steel sword slipped from its sheath with a ring of metal on metal. The Hunter darted to the side, spun, and swung in a single smooth motion. The Elivasti-forged blade sang through the air on its deadly path toward Indombe. He braced himself for the moment of impact, gritted his teeth against the inevitable agony.

Indombe's head crashed into his arm a split-second later. Blinding pain exploded through the limb as the strike shattered his bones. Yet he'd felt the bite of razor-sharp metal carving into soft flesh. Even as he staggered back, gasping at the searing anguish in his crushed arm, Indombe

13

reared up with another fierce shriek. Only this one held no compulsion, no magic, merely the sound of an enormous creature in terrible pain.

Blood and boiling water sprayed all over the Hunter as the serpent recoiled. The broad-snouted head thrashed about in a blinded frenzy, its gargantuan body whipping the pool into a churning mass of white foam. Yet Indombe did not immediately attack again. Its half-severed tongue hung limp from its enormous maw, bright golden fluid leaking from the wound to glow on its coppery scales. Its single eye focused on the Hunter and its head snaked back and forth.

A creature of such immense size had likely never known fear before, yet now it regarded the miniscule two-legged prey who had harmed it with uncertainty.

"Come on, then!" The Hunter snatched the sword from his shattered right hand, held it aloft in his left and waved it back and forth in a movement to match the bob and weave of Indombe's huge head. He backed out of the pool until his water-sodden boots crunched on the sandy beach surrounding it but didn't stop retreating.

From the corner of his eye, he spotted movement from where he'd tossed Tarek. Kiara had abandoned the relative safety of the trail and raced down into the basin, then over to the unconscious Elivasti. She'd managed to rouse him and get him on his feet, but the young man was still staggering and reeling like a drunken sailor. Nearly drowning had a way of stealing the wits from any man.

The Hunter had to keep Indombe's focus on him, buy Kiara time to drag Tarek away from the water. Nowhere in the basin would be truly out of Indombe's reach, but hopefully the serpent would be distracted enough that they could take shelter behind one of the many rocky outcroppings at the base of the cliffs encircling Indombe's pool.

He racked his brain desperately. What else had Kiara told him about the serpent? Nothing sprang to mind—not that it would do much good. None of the myths and lore surrounding Indombe had ever spoken of how to *kill* the damned thing. A creature of this immense size, shielded by such thick scales—scales that very well might be made of copper, as they appeared—would be nigh impossible for any mortal human to kill. Even a demon would be hard-pressed to hold its own. The Hunter suspected only the Serenii with their arcane magic truly had the power to defeat Indombe.

Time slowed to a standstill as he stared into the glowing ruby eye of the massive serpent. A being as old as Einan itself, legends told, with immense power the Hunter had witnessed for himself. There was no doubt in his mind that Indombe *could* kill him. If those massive jaws snapped shut around him and dragged him into its belly, he would be turned to ash by whatever caused it to emit heat enough to boil the entire Zamani Basin. Or those coils could wrap around him and pull him down, down, down to a watery grave.

This was one fight he had no chance of winning. He could evade only so many attacks before his strength gave out or he made a mistake. Eventually, Indombe *would* claim him, as it had so many others.

So why had he leaped into the pool? Why had he *chosen* to risk his life for Tarek, a young man he barely knew? That question haunted him in those final heartbeats. Consumed his thoughts as he braced himself for the inevitable renewal of Indombe's fury.

And then he heard it. A shrill, piercing sound that sliced through the waterfall's thundering. Like the cry of some great bird, it resounded off the rocks with a force to match Indombe's scream.

Memories flashed through the Hunter's mind. His gaze snapped up, eyes instinctively searching the night sky for the glow of fires flying on the current. For that sound was known to him. It was the sound of a *tayrnahr*. Of *Alsaaeat Aldhahabia,* once more returned to him from across the Advanat.

Indombe, too, responded to the cry. Its enormous broad-snouted head whipped toward the sky, its ruby eyeball shining up at the stars as if searching for a predator.

But the questing gazes of man and serpent alike found only empty sky, pale moon, and shimmering stars. No gold-and-orange flames wreathing vast avian wings.

The sound came again, and now the Hunter recognized its source. It came from *Kiara!*

Kiara stood between the kneeling, dazed Tarek and the edge of the Zamani Basin, feet planted, face staring defiance up at the sky. Her hands pressed a long bronze flute with a round-bellied end to her lips, blowing it with all the strength in her lungs. Again, the phoenix's shriek resounded off the cliff walls, piercing the ferocity of the waterfall's thundering.

Indombe hissed into the sky, and its enormous muscles bunched as its serpentine head dove for the waters. Coil by coil vanished into the pool, plunging into the darkness of the basin's deeps with terrifying speed.

Just before Indombe vanished, its massive tail whipped about, scything through the darkness in a broad arc. The Hunter, acting on instinct, threw himself flat onto his belly on the soft sand. The coppery scales whistled past a hand's breadth above him.

But Kiara had not the Hunter's speed. Her gaze was fixed on the water's surface, attention riveted on the strange flute that had mimicked the phoenix's cry. She didn't see Indombe's tail lashing toward her until it was too late.

Chapter Three

The Hunter tried to cry out a warning, but the waterfall's roaring drowned out his voice. Not that it would have done any good. Only his Bucelarii speed and reactions honed over decades of combat had saved his life. For all her fierce spirit, Kiara was only human. She had no chance of evading the tail whipping toward her.

The enormous copper-scaled tail slammed into Kiara's chest with force enough to lift her off her feet. She flew through the air like a hurled javelin and vanished between two mammoth boulders at the base of the cliff. The Hunter felt more than heard the terrible *thump* of her body striking the cliff walls. Felt it to the core of his being.

"Kiara!" Springing to his feet, he sprinted across the sandy shore, past a half-dazed Tarek, still on hands and knees, and toward the spot where Kiara had been thrown. Dread knotted his belly tighter with every step. His mouth felt dry, and his limbs grew heavy, leaden. Keeper alone knew what he'd see when he finally reached her side. Ribs caved in like kindling snapped by the force of Indombe's enormous tail. Skull crushed by the impact with the unyielding stone. Her beautiful face a mess of blood and agony.

Please, no! He didn't know if he had the strength to witness that. To see the woman he loved dead or dying before his very eyes. To hear her last gasps of breath and watch the light vanish from her dark eyes.

The Hunter was not one for prayer—he had no one to pray to, no faith in the so-called gods of Einan—but in that moment, he fervently wished something, *anything* could grant his request and *let. Her. LIVE!*

Through the boulders the Hunter ran, eyes scanning the darkness of the cliffside for Kiara. Only it wasn't dark, not truly. An eerie golden glow lit up the night, filled the air with a strange warmth. The light came from the dozens of crystalline protuberances that lined the edge of the cliff. The sharp, jagged stones emanated their own internal brilliance—just enough light that the Hunter could finally see Kiara lying face-down atop one of the patches of glowing crystal.

No! Horror thrummed in his body and froze the air breath in his lungs at the sight of Kiara's limp, hanging form. She didn't move, made no sound, not even the gasp of labored breath. Nothing to indicate she still lived.

"Kiara!" The Hunter raced toward her, scrambling across rocks slicked by the water whipped up by Indombe's thrashing, vaulting over the glowing crystals, boots crunching across the sand. "Kiara!"

He threw himself to his knees at her side and reached for her arms, only to remember his shattered right arm. Pain flared through the limb, but he paid it no heed. Instead, he sheathed his sword, seized her wrist in his left hand, and placed two fingers against the underside. The *thump, thump* of her pulse, though faint, sent relief cascading through him. She lived!

"Kiara?" He released her wrist, moved up to stand beside her head. "Talk to me, Kiara." Blood glistened wet on her glossy raven locks, but far less than would have been present had the impact split her skull. More likely, she'd struck the back of her head on a rock.

He placed two fingers to the rear of her neck, walked them down her spine. She didn't moan or cry out—a good sign, when combined with the feeling of intact muscles and bones beneath his fingertips. The collision with the cliff and subsequent fall hadn't shattered her neck.

She *had* lost consciousness, however. He needed to get her awake and talking. "Kiara, can you hear me?" He moved to stand by her head, lifted her long hair away from her face. "Kiara?"

A faint groan escaped her lips. "Hun…ter?"

Relief washed over the Hunter. She could at least recognize him.

"It's me!" He knelt to look up at her face. "It's me. I'm right here."

"Hurts…" she gasped.

"I'll bet it does!" He tried for a laugh, but it came out tight, forced. "I need to get you down, get a better look at you."

She tried to speak but could only manage a weak nod. That was a *bad* sign.

"Just hang on. Stay awake and tell me what hurts." The Hunter stood, shifted to take up a position beside her torso, the part of her draped over the jagged rock patch.

That was when he saw the blood trickling down the glowing crystals. Dark rivulets of crimson stained the golden stones, leaking from where they pierced the armor over her belly and the soft flesh beneath.

Fiery hell! Fear rose acidic and sharp in the Hunter's mouth. If the crystals had gone too deep, they could have damaged her organs, torn open her intestines, or shredded one of the great blood vessels. He *had* to lift her off the crystal to get a closer look at the damage, yet in so doing, might remove the only thing keeping her from bleeding out. Death loomed down both paths. But the Hunter had no choice.

He turned to Kiara. She was mumbling something he couldn't hear over the sound of the thundering waterfall and the pulse hammering in his ears. Her eyes remained open, though, and she appeared lucid enough.

"Look at me." He knelt before her, looked up into her face. "This is going to hurt. A bloody lot. But I have to do it. I have to know how bad your—"

"Just…do it…already." She gave him a wry smile, though it was edged with pain. "I don't…have all day."

The Hunter wanted to laugh and cry and shout in rage and frustration all at once. By the Keeper, she was strong! Jesting at a time like this, in her condition? But that meant her mental faculties remained intact, and she was still herself. If he moved fast enough and stopped whatever bleeding he encountered when he lifted her off the crystal impaling her belly, she had a chance.

A gasp sounded from behind him. The Hunter glanced over his shoulder, found a pale-faced Tarek staring wide-eyed and open-mouthed at them. Horror splashed across the young Elivasti's face.

"Get over here!" The Hunter backed up his command with a beckoning gesture. "Help me lift her off—"

To his dismay, Tarek spun on his heel and took off in the opposite direction.

What in the fiery hell?

"Tarek!" the Hunter shouted. "Tarek! Where in the Keeper's name are you going?"

But the young Elivasti could not hear him over the falls' thunder—or merely chose not to. Within seconds, Tarek vanished from the Hunter's sight, swallowed by the darkness.

The Hunter stared aghast at the empty air where the Elivasti had been standing moments earlier. The Tarek he'd met on the rooftops of Malandria four weeks earlier hadn't been a coward. The man had risked his life to save the Hunter's. But had the near-encounter with Indombe shattered his mind and courage? Was this the callowness of his youth coming to the fore, spurring him to seek his own safety above all?

A groan from Kiara snapped the Hunter from his thoughts. He banished all thoughts of Tarek—he had no time to consider the Elivasti's apparent cowardice, not while Kiara's life hung in the balance.

He turned his attention inward, focused his mind on his right arm. The shattered bone had already begun to re-knit, the pulverized muscles rebuilding fiber by fiber. He needed only accelerate the process. He bent his iron will to the task, *compelled* his body to restore the damage. Lightning arced up and down his arm. Sizzling pain, searing to the bone, setting every nerve alight. Yet he gritted his teeth and bore the pain. He *had* to, for Kiara's sake.

He didn't heal the arm completely; he merely mended the bone and muscle enough that it would work. He didn't have much time and needed all his strength to aid her. Pain, he could handle.

"Get ready." The Hunter slipped his shoulder beneath her chest, braced his hands against her hips. "I'm sorry about this, Kiara."

He heard the intake of breath as she prepared to speak, but whatever retort had been forming on her lips died in a scream of purest agony as he shoved against her hips with all his strength. Crimson light blossomed to life from Soulhunger's gemstone at the sound, and the Hunter could feel the dagger's confusion at encountering no life energies to consume. Yet his attention was riveted on Kiara, on lifting her free of the spiked crystal piercing her belly. Her screams galvanized him, fueled his still-healing muscles with inhuman strength. One hard push, and he had her lifted free of the crystal. Swiveling, he lowered her onto her back on the rocky ground as gently and quickly as he could manage.

His hands flew to her belly, pressing against her wound in a frantic attempt to stop the blood welling up there. Panic clawed at his mind. There was so much blood. Too much! The crystal had damaged an artery or vein. Without his Bucelarii healing, a wound this grave would kill her.

He fought to stanch the gushing, but nothing he did slowed the flow. Kiara cried out in pain, but her struggles were weak...so terribly weak. Finally, in desperation, the Hunter shoved his hand into the wound and reached for the lacerated blood vessel. He was no physicker or chirurgeon, but he'd killed men enough to know *exactly* what sort of injury would cause such voluminous bleeding. He merely had to locate the site of the damage and pinch it tight to stop the flow of blood.

Hope surged within him as his questing fingertips found the torn vessel. He squeezed hard, and instantly the bleeding lessened.

Yes! Relief washed over the Hunter, bringing tears to his eyes. He remembered the last time he'd knelt over Kiara like this. The morning the Hunter had finally caught up with the First of the Bloody Hand. Kiara had taken the Hunter's side against her former master, and in revenge, the whoreson had driven one of the Swordsman's blades into her side.

A lifetime ago, it seemed. They'd been enemies then, yet now—

"This…is new." Kiara's quiet words drew the Hunter's gaze to her face. A ghost of a smile flitted across her lips, a hint of amusement leaking into her visible pain. "Not what I pictured…when last I thought…of you being inside me."

The Hunter's jaw dropped. He could do nothing but stare at her, at a loss for words.

"What?" Her grin grew fractionally larger. "I thought…it was…a pretty great joke."

The Hunter blinked. "Good to see that nearly getting your head split wide open hasn't dented your sense of humor."

"Split open…huh?" Kiara reached a hand up to touch the back of her head. "So you're not…*really* glowing, then? Just a…head injury?"

The Hunter was about to shake his head, but stopped when his gaze followed hers. She was staring at his chest and arms, where, to his astonishment, light emanated from what looked like tiny crystals formed on his water-sodden clothing and leather armor.

The Hunter sucked in a breath. He instinctively slapped at the crystals, and they fell away from him like dust blown off one of Graeme's messy shelves. They *hadn't* sprouted from his skin, as he'd feared. But where had they come from?

Then he remembered. His attack against Indombe had cut the serpent's tongue, and when the great beast reared up, it had sprayed blood and boiling water over the Hunter. Those droplets of its aureate blood had hardened to shards of crystal—crystal the same gleaming gold as the one that had pierced Kiara's side.

He didn't know what to make of that, or what that could possibly mean. All that mattered now was Kiara. He had to keep the pressure on her wound, keep her from bleeding out, and somehow figure out a way to repair the damage. He had none of Graeme's healing potions—he'd used his last in Malandria, weeks earlier—and the few alchemical supplies he'd managed to purchase in Drash remained tucked in his saddlebags, with Elivast at the top of the trail.

Which left him…what? He had neither needle nor catgut thread to stitch the wound—he'd never had need of it, given his Bucelarii healing. That left him only one option: cauterizing the injury. He had knives enough for the task, but there was no way he could strike a flint one-handed. Nor did he have any fuel for a fire close at hand. There were no trees in the Zamani Basin, and the few bits of driftwood that had come over the falls were too far away to be of any use. And even if he'd had fuel within reach, his alchemical firestrikers would be sodden and useless after his swim.

Again, he felt panic clawing at his mind. He couldn't remove his hand from Kiara's wound; she'd bleed out within a matter of *minutes* if he released the blood vessel.

How he wished their roles were reversed! That *he* lay bleeding out at Kiara's feet. But for all his legendary immortality and demon-granted healing ability, there was nothing he could do to help her.

He stared down at her, tears welling in his eyes. Despair and hopelessness settled like a leaden blanket over him, seeped down his throat to choke his breath in his lungs.

In that moment, a terrible thought settled into his mind with crystal-clear certainty. He was about to lose her. He'd lose her, just as he'd lost Taiana. He was helpless, powerless to do anything to keep the Long Keeper at bay.

Chapter Four

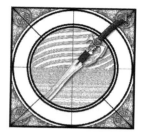

Suddenly, a sound echoed through the waterfall's thundering. Boots crunching on the sand.

The Hunter tore his eyes from Kiara, glanced over his shoulder. Tarek barreled into view between the two boulders. Though the young man was visibly out of breath, his jaw was clenched and his face set in grim determination. He held something clutched to his chest as if it were the most precious thing in the world to him.

"Here!" The young Elivasti all but threw himself to one knee onto the rocks beside the Hunter. He slapped the object—a leather-wrapped bundle of some sort—on the ground before him and hauled at the string to loosen the knot holding it shut. With deft, brisk movements, he unrolled it to reveal dozens of glass jars, oilskin-wrapped packets, and bundles of sticks and dried herbs tied together with twine.

He snatched up what looked like a bundle of dried flowers that might have once been a violet as vivid as his Elivasti eyes, but had lost most of their color once withered. "Take this." He shoved the flowers into Kiara's mouth, stem and all. "Swallow."

Kiara was too weak to protest. Almost too weak to swallow, too. Blood loss had sapped her strength and drained the color from her cheeks. The mere effort of closing her mouth around the dried flowers and gulping them down verged on superhuman. Yet somehow she managed. Distaste twisted her mouth into a grimace.

"Tastes like razor grass, I know." Tarek sounded surprisingly calm despite the incessant movement of his hands. He snatched up a bundle of what looked like ordinary twigs, though from no tree the Hunter recognized, and rubbed the spindly sticks together with a pinch of red-ochre dust from another pouch. Finally, he poured a splash of some deep orange liquid onto his hands and the dust-covered twigs. "But the taste is worth the numbing effects." His expression grew grave. "Because this is going to hurt worse than anything you could possibly imagine."

The Hunter wasn't certain about that—he *had* been carved, sliced, impaled, and all but eviscerated by the Warmaster, had every bone in his body broken over and over by the Third of the Bloody Hand. He could imagine a great deal of hurt, indeed. Yet *he* had suffered it. Seeing Kiara in such agony caused him a new manner of pain he had never before experienced.

Tarek turned to the Hunter, his jaw muscles tightening and brow furrowing in precisely the same way Hailen's did when worry plagued him. "When I give you the word, pull your hand free and shift to hold her down. With luck, she'll pass out from the pain."

"Tarek—"

The Elivasti cut him off with a shake of his head. "We don't have the time for protests. *She* doesn't have the time."

Again, the Hunter was struck by Tarek's level composure. It was a far cry from the panicking, drowning man flailing in the boiling waters of Indombe's pool, or the horror-stricken youth who had, by all appearances, turned tail and run. Only he *hadn't* run away in fear or abandoned the Hunter and Kiara. He'd raced up the trail to fetch the bundle the Hunter had seen him tuck with care and reverence into his saddlebags every morning as they broke camp. For that effort alone, the Hunter decided he owed the young man a chance.

Nothing he does now could make the situation any worse, he thought, staring down at his hand buried to the knuckles in Kiara's belly. The Hunter's skill lay in *ending* lives, not saving them. Kiara's only hope lay in the possibility that Tarek had some manner of talent in the healing arts.

Still, he couldn't bring himself to trust blindly. He didn't know Tarek well enough for that. "What are you going to do? Explain it to me simply."

Tarek set the soaked bundle of dust-covered twigs onto a rock beside Kiara, and drew forth another twig, which he placed apart from the others. "Only way to stop her from bleeding out is to cauterize the wound. This will not only seal the laceration to her portal vein, but also stave off infection and accelerate healing."

The Hunter wasted a single moment studying the young man, searching for any hint of uncertainty, evasion, or deceit. He found none, as expected. Though he'd only known Tarek for a few weeks, he'd gotten a decent sense of the young Elivasti. At least enough of a sense that he knew with a fair degree of confidence that Tarek truly believed every word of what he'd said. Just as he believed that *this* was their best hope of keeping Kiara alive.

"So be it." The Hunter nodded. "On your signal."

Tarek drew out flint and steel and set them next to the twig. One final examination of the three objects, and he looked up to the Hunter. "On three."

The Hunter tensed, muscles coiling in anticipation of what came next. He had to hope Tarek was fast enough to accomplish what felt like an impossibility. He'd seen countless men bleed out from a wound to the large vein feeding their organs—hell, he'd *killed* dozens with a thrust that cut the vessel in the same place where the crystal had wounded Kiara. But he forced himself to trust. To give Tarek a chance to prove himself and save Kiara's life.

Tarek sucked in a great breath, picked up the bundle of soaked twigs. "One, two, three!"

The Hunter acted without hesitation, relaxing his fingers and slipping his hand free of Kiara's belly with a single smooth motion. The instant he was clear, he leaped toward her head, pivoted on his heels, and seized her shoulders to press her into the sandy beach.

Tarek moved, too, inserting the strange bundle of twigs into Kiara's belly, then snatching up the flint and steel. Two quick strikes and a spark landed on the one stick he'd set apart. Instantly, the wood caught alight as if doused in oil. Tarek inserted the burning stick into Kiara's belly even as the blood came gushing up from the severed vein. There was a loud, angry *hiss*, a searing bright light, and the stench of burned meat. Kiara's scream resounded off the cliffs so loud it drowned out the roar of the falls. It cut off a half-heartbeat later as the blessed release of unconsciousness claimed her.

Every muscle in the Hunter's body tensed as Kiara went slack beneath his arms. Yet a moment later, once the light and stench emanating from Kiara's wound faded, he saw the flow of blood had slowed. No, stopped altogether.

"Did it work?" He scarcely dared bring himself to ask, yet he had to know.

Tarek leaned over, frowned down at Kiara's wound. Another expression identical to Hailen. The boy always looked that way when poring over some dusty, archaic tome Father Reverentus gave him. After a few seconds, he looked up. "It did, ancestors be praised."

The Hunter nearly wept in relief. His fingers tightened around Kiara's shoulders, digging into her flesh as if they alone kept her from the Long Keeper's embrace. He'd come so close to losing her; it left him far more shaken than he'd expected.

Yet he lifted his head and nodded to Tarek. "Well done," he managed.

Tarek grimaced. "It's just a temporary measure." The shadows that darkened his violet eyes had nothing to do with the odd glow emanating from the golden crystals around them. "The bleeding has been stopped, but one wrong move, one jostle, and it could begin anew. And there is no telling what manner of infection she may face, what impurities may have entered her bloodstream."

The Hunter didn't like the sound of that. "Then we get her someplace she can rest and recover." He couldn't shake the sense of urgency that had lodged in his mind since the moment he'd communed with Kharna in Malandria, but Kiara *had* to come first. Once he knew she would heal fully…

"Would that I had two doses of *ephrade* here, I could accelerate her body's natural restoration process." Tarek shook his head. "As it stands, the spoolwood twigs and powdered gillflower will have to suffice."

"*Ephrade?*" The Hunter cocked his head. "What is that?"

Tarek frowned. "I believe the people of Drash know it as azure hellebore. In Ghandia, it is called *ndleleni,* flower of the wayside. But Kanna always called it *ephrade.* Loosely translated from the tongue of our ancestors, the name means 'succor for the traveler'."

The Hunter sprang to his feet. "Khafra is but a two-day ride from here. I've coin aplenty, and you can ride ahead to fetch it and return with it." His Hidden Circle contact in Drash had told him how to locate a fellow alchemist in the Ghandian capital.

Tarek bent once more over Kiara, placing his ear first to her chest, then over her mouth. "I cannot go. Not until I know for certain she will live." His expression grew grave, somber—a strangely familiar look, but not one that had been passed down from the father he shared with Hailen. No, this reminded the Hunter of the stubborn, sharp-tongued old herbalist he'd met on Kara-ket. It had the same unyielding, inflexible certainty of a mountain that refused to be moved or a river that could not be dissuaded from traveling its course.

"You learned from Kanna?" he asked. "All of that?" He gestured to the assortment of herbs and remedies contained in the unrolled leather bundle.

Tarek nodded. "Far from the kindest teacher, yet a truly brilliant mind. Our people are far poorer for her passing. The knowledge she failed to pass on to us…it is a fortune truly terrible to lose to the *maistyr's* cruelties."

Anger flared in the young Elivasti's eyes. And with good cause. Most of the True Descendants present on Kara-ket during the Hunter's time there had been slaughtered—apart from a few children and one caretaker saved by the Hunter, Keleos, and Syndine. Kanna, Master Eldor, Belros the smith, Tejet, the Quintariad, and countless more, all slain at the Sage's command.

The Hunter felt the young man's anger directed at *him*, too. From the conversations they'd shared over the past few weeks, the Hunter had gotten the sense that Tarek—along with others of his people—blamed the deaths of their fellows on him. That it had been *his* arrival in Kara-ket that brought the Sage and Warmaster's rivalry to a head and triggered the chain of events that ended with both demons dead, the Masters of Agony and their Menials eradicated, and Kara-ket once more in the hands of a decimated Elivasti people.

The Hunter couldn't exactly fault that rationale. He'd done his utmost to stir up the enmity between the two Abiarazi. Ultimately, his actions had led to all-out war on Kara-ket, and the Elivasti casualties had been high, indeed. But the *other* outcome of his decisions was the Elivasti's freedom. They no longer answered to a demon. For all they had suffered and lost, that *had* to be worth something. The Hunter suspected that factored heavily into why Tarek had been sent by Itan to accompany them, and why the young Elivasti endeavored to keep his anger in check.

But for how long? It *would* boil over, if not today or tomorrow, someday soon. The Hunter had seen it countless times before. The impetuosity of Tarek's youth would win out over his desire for restraint. He and Kiara had discussed how to address the matter without taking the approach he'd used with Tassat and the Cambionari knights—letting them take out their anger at him physically in the way of warriors. Thus far, they had no simple solution. Time would either temper or inflame the young Elivasti's emotions.

Yet none of that mattered now. Only Kiara mattered.

"Can she ride?" the Hunter asked. "Is it safe, given her wound?"

"Tonight, no." Tarek shook his head. "Tomorrow, we shall see." He cast a nervous glance toward the pool. Though the waters were dark and quiet, the memory of Indombe lingered in both their minds. "If you can get her up the trail, we can fashion a bed for her to rest. And perhaps, a litter to carry her. That way, she need not risk re-opening the wound riding."

"Good thinking." The Hunter studied Kiara's face in the gold light of the strange crystals—crystals possibly formed by Indombe's blood. Was it his imagination, or had she begun regaining a hint of color?

"Go," he told the young Elivasti. "Get her bed ready. I'll bring her up."

Nodding, Tarek bent to collect his supplies, rolling up the leather bundle and securing it with the cord once more.

The Hunter noted the dark look on the young man's face—though what brought it on, whether guilt, worry, anger, or the horror at his near-death, he didn't know. He said nothing; clearly, Tarek was in no mood to talk further. Nor was he, truth be told. He just needed to get Kiara to safety, make certain she lived through the night.

Bending, he gathered her into his arms, and cradled her to his chest. Despite the armor and weapons on her belt, she was far from a burden to his Bucelarii muscles. To him, she was everything, and he couldn't imagine life if he'd lost her.

Hang on, Kiara, he told her silently, willing strength to pass from his body into hers. *You have to stay strong, have to live. I can't lose you, too.*

He clung to her, held her close, and set off toward the switchback trail that ascended away from Zamani Falls and the monstrous horror that lurked in the fathomless depths of its pool.

Chapter Five

"Ikh manashar!"

The Hunter started, gaze snapping up to the figure looming over him. His mind steeled in expectation of the blow he knew was coming. He'd have no time to draw his sword, to stop the iron-edged blade from rending his flesh and flooding him with poison. Yet he tried anyway. With all his inhuman speed, he reached for Soulhunger.

Only to freeze when he finally *saw* who had spoken.

"What?" the Hunter croaked, his voice tight.

Tarek frowned. "I just said, have some of this." He again thrust toward the Hunter a small portion of trail biscuit and dried boar—*not* a weapon, then. He'd changed out of his sopping wet clothing, into a form-fitting vest, trousers, and flowing coat of light grey. *Not* gleaming plate mail armor.

After a moment's hesitation, the Hunter removed his hand from Soulhunger's hilt, reached up, and took the proffered food. "Thank you." This, he managed in a voice akin to normal, accompanying it with a nod.

Tarek eyed him askance, a look somewhere between confusion, concern, and apprehension on his youthful face. But he said nothing, merely inclined his head in response and moved over to where his pack sat open on the ground beneath an overhanging baobab tree. The Elivasti sat and tucked into his own food. Whether he enjoyed it, he showed no sign—he never had, truth be told. He merely ate with the dispassion of one who treated food as sustenance rather than pleasure.

The Hunter wished he could do likewise. The dried boar was as tough as old boot leather but nowhere near as tasty, and every third bite of the Drashi trail biscuit flooded his palate with overpowering hints of dill seed and yellow peppercorns that should have been crushed far finer if intended for human—or Bucelarii—consumption. Even the water in his canteen couldn't save the meal; it had gone tepid under the bright sun of the Kgabu Plains.

Still, the Hunter choked the food down. Between the days of travel, the lack of sleep, the fight with Indombe, and carrying Kiara back to camp, he needed all the energy he could get.

His eyes strayed to where Tarek sat eating his own meager meal. Though he no longer heard Soulhunger's voice—hadn't heard it in more than three years, since the day he stepped foot in Enarium—he knew what the dagger would have wanted. To consume the young Elivasti's soul, send the power of his life force to Kharna. Oh, it would have been wrapped up in the promise to replenish the Hunter's strength and banish his fatigue, but in the end, all it wanted was blood.

The Hunter no longer fought that urge the way he once had. He understood it, understood the reason for its existence. Kharna required the strength in his fight against the Devourer of Worlds, and the Hunter alone remained to sustain the Serenii imprisoned in his crystalline tomb beneath Enarium.

He had given Kharna sustenance aplenty. He'd placed his own wife into one of the Chambers of Sustenance—both to save her life and to bolster the embattled Serenii. Cerran, Taiana's Bucelarii companion, had been consigned to a similar fate. The brutish Abiarazi Lord Apus and his cowardly brother Lord Chasteyn lay side by side in an eternal prison from which they would never escape, their entwined life forces consumed by Kharna. The Hunter had begun fulfilling *one* of the two oaths he'd sworn in Enarium.

But the other?

He pushed thoughts of Jaia aside—he already had worries enough for the moment without letting the memories of their only encounter plague him—and focused his attention on Kiara. For an hour, since he'd settled her onto the pile of blankets Tarek had spread out as her bed, she'd slept. Or, at the very least, remained unconscious. The Hunter had bandaged her himself, wrapping soft cloths around her head and torso, using a spare shirt of his for additional padding to soak up the blood that still occasionally trickled from the wound in her abdomen. His cloak, which Tarek had retrieved on their way up the trail, served to cover her.

He hovered his face over her stomach, inhaled deeply through his nostrils. Her scent cascaded over him, drowning out the dryness of the dust-laden air, the slight sweetness of the long plains grass, and the tartness of the baobab tree flowers. She smelled of leather, steel, trumpet lilies, and peonies—a mixture somehow soft and strong at once, just like her.

Her scent was thick with the blood soaking her bandages, but to his relief, he smelled no hint of rot or putrescence. Yet. He'd have to watch carefully, change her dressings regularly, check the wound a few times a day. At least in the beginning. With luck, Tarek's Elivasti alchemy had repaired the worst of the damage. Now it was up to her body to do the rest.

Kiara stirred, and for a moment, her eyelids fluttered open. But only for two long heartbeats. Her eyes closed once more and her breathing grew deep, steady.

The Hunter let out a long breath and leaned back against the gnarled trunk of the baobab tree he'd chosen for a seat. He closed his eyes and let the smell of the night flowers blooming in the branches above his head envelop him. The scent was sweeter than jasmine and tarter than any rose, with a freshness akin to morning dew in the Maiden's Fields. It wouldn't last, though. When morning approached and the flowers reached the end of their life cycle, the sweetness would turn cloying, the tartness growing thick and choking. Akin to carrion, he'd heard it said. He'd smelled corpses aplenty in his time, and none of them had smelled like this.

Then again, he thought grimly, *when have I ever stuck around long enough for them to rot on me?*

"*Ikh manashar!*" The words echoed in his mind again, but they sounded faint, distant, failed to elicit the same violent reaction he'd had when Tarek interrupted his mind's wanderings. They, along with so much else, had haunted every step of his journey away from Malandria.

He still didn't understand what had happened. Even after replaying the events in his mind a thousand times throughout weeks of sleepless nights, he could not comprehend it.

One moment he'd been fighting beside Sir Benoit, comrades in arms united in their battle against the two demons. They'd *finally* triumphed, finally imprisoned the Abiarazi in the Chambers of Sustenance beneath the Monolith at the heart of Malandria. But in the seconds—or minutes, he wasn't certain—the Hunter had spent communing with Kharna, Sir Benoit had changed. He'd driven his iron-edged greatsword into the Hunter's chest and hissed those words, the war cry of the Elisionists, at him over and over.

25

The fool Cambionari had given him no choice but to kill him. The iron from his blade would have poisoned the Hunter, rotted him from the inside out. The primal urge to survive had compelled the Hunter. Feeding the knight's life force to Soulhunger in order to save his own.

How the Hunter *hated* that choice! Not because of the choice itself—he'd have made the same decision every time, he could do nothing less—but because the knight had left him no choice but to make it. The man he'd considered a comrade-in-arms had forced his hand.

But why? That question more than any other haunted him. From the moment Sir Georges' connection to the Elisionists had been revealed, Sir Benoit had made clear his sentiments on the matter. He had shown visible aversion to the extremist views of those members of the Enclave who wanted to purge anything they considered unholy—including, but far from limited to, the Bucelarii. Indeed, the Hunter had felt that he and the knight were actually becoming *friends*. Their conversation in the Forgotten Ward had left him feeling certain that he knew where Sir Benoit's true feelings lay, and the knight had been willing to fight and die at his side in their efforts to eliminate the two Abiarazi.

Right up until he'd stabbed the Hunter and put a grim end to their comradeship. He'd been consumed by the hatred ingrained in him by decades of Cambionari teachings and training, had allowed it to override common sense. Everything he'd learned about the Hunter had meant *nothing* in the face of the acrimony fueled by Elisionist doctrine.

Was I so wrong about him? That question, too, lingered long after he'd washed Sir Benoit's blood off his hands. *Or was I so desperately hoping that I could sway them to my cause like I did Kiara, Graeme, Father Reverentus, and the Night Guild that I was blind to who they really were?*

Again, his gaze slid sidelong toward Tarek. Or where Tarek *should* have been. The young man had apparently finished his meal, for his pack sat neatly tied on the ground next to his saddle. Of the Elivasti, the Hunter saw no sign. Perhaps he'd gone to relieve himself in the bushes between their small camp and the edge of the cliffs over which the Zamani Falls plunged.

There I go again! The Hunter cursed himself for a fool. *When did I stop seeing enemies in every shadow, and start thinking the best of people?* He'd survived as the legendary assassin of Voramis for decades by suspecting everything and everyone of duplicity and ulterior motives. As soon as he'd begun to let go of that mistrust and cynicism, he had wound up stabbed in the back—literally—betrayed by a man he believed he could trust.

He hardened his mind. *No more trusting.* He clenched his fists at his side. After what the Cambionari had done, he was a fool to open himself up, to allow himself to be vulnerable. *Everyone is suspect until I have sufficient proof otherwise. And even then…*

A quiet snore rose from Kiara, drawing his attention to the woman sleeping at his side. Did that include her, too? She'd been one of the Bloody Hand's Five Fingers, instrumental in his betrayal. Though years had passed since that day, could he truly believe she no longer had it in her to turn on him when it suited her?

He dismissed that thought. No, he couldn't believe that. She still had all the cunning and ruthlessness that had made her suited to the role of the Fourth, but she wouldn't turn on him. She'd proven that much time and time again.

Then what of Hailen and Evren? Evren's years with the Lecterns and living on the streets of Vothmot had hardened him, shown him the extents to which a man had to go to survive this life. Hailen was *Melechha,* one of the few beings alive whose power could very well one day exceed the Hunter's own. Would the day come when the boy he'd attempted to raise turned against him in the name of wielding that power or amassing more?

No, he determined. That was foolishness. He couldn't believe that the young men with whom he'd spent the last three years would do that. That wasn't the Hailen or Evren he knew.

And what of Graeme? The Hidden Circle alchemist cared for information above all else. He now possessed the truth of the Hunter's Bucelarii heritage—and its intrinsic vulnerabilities. Would he sell the secret of iron to the highest bidder?

After long moments of contemplation, he decided that was unlikely. Graeme was more than just a resource, he was an ally. A friend, even. For all the endless barter-and-trade of their relationship, the Hunter felt certain he knew the alchemist's mind on the matter.

And just like that, I'm vulnerable again! The Hunter's mouth twisted into a bitter grimace. *Because if I can trust them, it means there have to be others I can trust. But how can I possibly know who those others are?*

He'd have staked his life that he could count Father Reverentus among that number. Until Jaia drove Soulhunger into the old priest's back and fed his life force to Kharna.

Tassat, too, in the end. The Praamian assassin had sacrificed his life to save the Hunter's. Jarl, Mak, and Bover had gone far beyond just the lengths to which their hired service compelled them. The Hunter had counted on them to watch his back. But was that foolishness? Had he merely *believed* the best of them, as he had attempted to do with the Cambionari? Had their Guild Master ordered them to finish him off, how much would they have hesitated out of respect for his skill at arms, and how much out of their genuine loyalty?

In that moment, the Hunter felt like a man adrift in a vast, storm-tossed sea. He had attempted to rebel against his very nature, to show the truth of himself, and that vulnerability had nearly gotten him killed. Yet it had saved his life, too.

So which was it to be? Did he dare risk a knife in the back in the faint hope that, in at least a handful of people, a measure of goodness could somehow outweigh the cruelty, avarice, hatred, and fear inherent in human nature?

He could find no answer. *Had* found no answer over weeks on the road. He couldn't bring himself to speak of it to Kiara, but she didn't press. She'd no doubt believed his moroseness and withdrawn moods stemmed from his grief over the deaths of Tassat and Father Reverentus, or the aftermath of his encounter with Jaia. He'd recounted every agonizing detail of coming face to face with his daughter, and she had no doubt seen the pain in his eyes. But that was far from the *only* pain squirming in his heart. And this one, this doubt and uncertainty, only compounded the rest.

"H-Hun…ter!"

Kiara's faint, labored gasp snapped the Hunter from his gloom. She had opened her eyes and now stared up at him with a look of mingled pain and determination.

"I'm here," he said, moving to kneel at her side and scooping up her hand. "I've got you, Kiara. Just rest. Sleep, and regain your—"

"Where…is…it?"

The intensity burning in her dark eyes surprised the Hunter. "Where is what?" he asked.

"The…*ebroq!*" Kiara gasped.

The Hunter's brow furrowed at the unfamiliar word. "The—" His mind registered. "Oh." He frowned. "Your flute?"

Kiara's head bobbed. "The…*ebroq!*" Her voice grew labored, as if she struggled for each breath. "Where…"

"I don't know." The Hunter shook his head. "Must have fallen somewhere down in the basin." He'd all but forgotten about it, so focused he was on Kiara nearly dying.

"Have to…find it!" Kiara tried to sit up but collapsed before she managed even to raise her head.

27

"Easy, easy." The Hunter held her down gently. "Don't move. The wound to your skull is bad enough, and your belly—"

"Find...it!" Kiara's hand closed around his, her fingers squeezing with a force to match the blaze in her eyes. "Have to...find it!"

The Hunter had no idea why the instrument mattered to her so much—she'd only purchased it a couple of weeks back on their way through Drash—but if it meant she wouldn't try to get up, he'd acquiesce.

"I will, I swear." The Hunter nodded. He glanced around; still no sign of Tarek. "In the morning, when—"

"Go!" Kiara tried to shove him, but she was still weak from blood loss. "You must. It is..." Her voice trailed away, her eyelids fluttering closed.

For long moments, the Hunter didn't move. He remained sitting at Kiara's side, eyes fixed on her pale, pain-pinched face. He watched her until her expression relaxed and her chest rose and fell in a steady rhythm.

Only then did he rise. He had no desire to leave her alone, not in her condition. But if she awoke again and he hadn't found the strange instrument, she might take it upon herself to try—in vain, given her condition—to get up and search for it herself. Better he leave her alone for a few minutes so he could have the instrument close at hand when she regained consciousness. Whatever facilitated her recovery, he'd do it.

He searched the surrounding darkness, eyes scanning the bushes for any sign of movement. Nothing. Not so much as a hint of the young Elivasti in the shadows. The Hunter drew in a deep breath through his nostrils, tasting the scents on the air. He wouldn't detect Tarek that way, he knew. The man had no scent; something about the Expurgation ritual he and his fellow Elivasti underwent eradicated their unique odors. But he searched for any sign of predators stalking toward their camp.

He smelled only the baobab blossoms, prairie grass, the dust on the wind, and their horses. Elivast and Ash stood in the shade of a gnarled baobab tree twenty paces away, cropping grass placidly and enjoying the coolness of the late night. Tarek's horse, a stocky black Hrandari-bred horse he called *Nayaga,* a name he said meant "swift as an arrow" in the language of the plainsmen, dozed with its head hanging low, ears occasionally twitching as it listened for any hint of danger.

The horses' visible relaxation and the lack of any detectable scents convinced the Hunter to leave Kiara. *Just for a few minutes*, he told himself. *Just long enough to find that damned flute for her.*

Still, as he strode toward the switchback trail leading down into the Zamani Basin, he couldn't help casting glances back to where she lay. Worry for her squirmed like worms in his stomach. He hated how helpless he felt seeing her like this. There was nothing he could do for her, no way to help her. He had to rely on Tarek's alchemy and the meager supplies left after weeks on the road. Khafra was still a day-and-a-half away, perhaps longer, if they had to slow their pace for her sake.

He tried to swallow the knot in his throat, turned away from Kiara and hurried down the trail. He had to hurry, had to fetch her damned flute and return before she awoke.

He had barely stepped onto the path when something below and off to his left caught his gaze. A dark figure clad in light grey clothing stood at the edge of the trail, with one foot planted on solid ground, the other dangling over the precipitous drop into the Zamani Basin.

Chapter Six

The Hunter's mind raced. *What is Tarek doing?!*

Did the Elivasti plan to jump? From that height, nearly a hundred paces above Indombe's murky pool, the fall would certainly kill him.

The Hunter dared not shout at the young man for fear of startling him and sending him over the cliff. But he quickened his pace, descending the switchback trail at a full run. Instinct screamed at him to hurry. He had to reach Tarek in time to stop him from doing something foolhardy. How he'd accomplish that, the Hunter had no idea. He only knew he needed to try.

To his relief, the young man did not leap—though he didn't step back to the safety of solid ground, either. He remained standing frozen in place, foot extended out over empty air. What thoughts roiled in his brain, Tarek alone knew. But the Hunter could not shake the chill dread settling over him like an icy cloak.

He slowed as he drew nearer the young man on the trail below him but made no attempt to be quiet. On the contrary, he scuffed his boots on the stony trail, kicked rocks clattering into the cliffside, *anything* to alert Tarek of his approach.

When the Elivasti didn't look his way, the Hunter ventured to speak aloud. "Tarek?"

Tarek did not startle. Nor did he look the Hunter's way. His face was screwed up in a look of confusion, uncertainty, and intense concentration. His gaze locked on his outstretched foot—or, perhaps, on the dark pool far, far below.

"What are you doing?" The Hunter kept his tone gentle, though it felt forced, unnatural.

Tarek's answer came so quietly the night breeze all but carried it away. "I can't figure it out."

The Hunter edged closer, his steps cautious, wary. With no idea of what Tarek was thinking, he had to treat the young man as he would any creature of prey. Slow, quiet approach, making as little sound as possible, no sudden movements.

"Figure what out?"

"Why." Still, Tarek's eyes remained locked on whatever held him spellbound.

The Hunter frowned. "Why what?"

Only now did Tarek's head turn toward the Hunter. "Why I leaped."

The question surprised the Hunter. He blinked, momentarily at a loss for words.

"My whole life, I've avoided deep waters." The confusion twisting Tarek's scruffy-bearded face deepened, the corners of his mouth pulling downward and eyes narrowing. "Not much chance to learn to swim up on Kara-ket, or on the Hrandari Plains. Even after Itan chose me to travel with him, there never seemed opportunity." He looked the Hunter squarely in the face. "So why would I leap into that pool knowing I couldn't swim? It makes no sense."

Ahh, of course. The Hunter nodded understanding. One so young—Tarek couldn't be far into his second decade of life, barely more than an adolescent by the measure of the Elivasti's long lives—wouldn't have likely experienced magic akin to that Indombe had wielded. Only the Hunter's exposure to similar compulsions during his encounters with Garanis, the Illusionist Clerics, and the mind-altering power of Kharna himself had prepared him to recognize the great serpent's subtle weavings. For all Kiara's strength of spirit, she'd been overwhelmed by Indombe's compulsions. He alone had resisted, and even that, barely.

"It makes no sense because you didn't leap," the Hunter said.

At those words, Tarek's confused frown deepened to a scowl. "I bear the burns and the pounding head to prove it." He turned fully to the Hunter—blessedly placing *both* feet on solid ground—and held out his arms to reveal flesh reddened and blistered by the pool's scalding heat.

The Hunter chuckled. "Oh, no doubt that you did end up in that pool. But you didn't leap. Not in the way you think." He tapped a finger against one temple. "It was the voice in here that made you do it. You felt it, didn't you? Not so much coherent words, just an urge. An urge not your own, yet somehow too powerful to ignore. Does that sound right?"

Tarek stared at him for a full ten seconds, his expression somewhere between incredulous and astonished. Finally, he nodded. "Yes, that's it!" Words tumbled from his mouth in a rush. "It was like a part of me knew that I should stay on the trail, but the rest of me, *most* of me, wanted to leap into that pool. To fling myself off the cliff and let the waters drag me under. It was like I wanted it more than anything else in the world, more even than…" He cut himself off, as if realizing what he'd been about to say. He swallowed his words and finished lamely, "…anything."

The Hunter took note of the young man's near-slip—though he couldn't begin to guess what Tarek had nearly blurted out—but let it pass. For now. He'd have time to pry into whatever secrets the Elivasti tried to keep hidden on their journey eastward.

"It's a strange sensation." The Hunter nodded. "Having a voice or presence inside your head compelling you to do something you know you shouldn't. And in truth, it never gets easier, no matter how many times you triumph."

Tarek's eyes widened. "You…you've encountered something like this before?"

More than you could possibly realize, the Hunter thought grimly.

He'd spent decades wrestling against the voice of Soulhunger, the dagger's incessant urgings and cajolings, the endless demands for blood. The day he'd refused to kill Brother Securus, another voice had manifested. A crueler voice. Wicked, insatiable, bloodlust personified. At the time, he'd believed it the demonic half of his nature, the darkness compelling him to kill. Only in Enarium had he come to understand its true purpose: it had been implanted in his mind by Kharna as a reminder of the oath he'd sworn thousands of years earlier. The Hunter had agreed to kill to sustain the Serenii, and the voices had merely been used to remind him of that promise even after the Illusionist Clerics wiped his memories time and time again.

But the Hunter did not speak of those. Instead, he said, "Aye. I met a demon who wielded the power of the Illusionist, who could break the minds of even strong men and compel them to evil. He compelled a pack of thugs to turn against their master, a demon just like him. He nearly gained control of me, too. Only I killed him before he could put me fully in his thrall."

Throughout, Tarek's eyes grew steadily wider. But at mention of killing the demon, the young man's face grew crestfallen. "Not much chance of us killing *that* thing." He jerked a thumb toward the pool below. "But surely you felt it, too? That compulsion. How did you not succumb to it like I did?"

"I very nearly did." The Hunter would *never* have admitted that aloud to most of the world, yet in that moment, it felt like precisely the sort of thing Tarek needed to hear. And for all his recent misgivings and determination to grow more cynical and suspicious of the people around him, the Hunter found he couldn't help trying to settle the young man's visible turmoil. Precisely as he would have had Hailen or Evren come to him with a problem. "Kiara, too. That's what stopped me, in truth. Seeing the danger to *her*. Knowing that she was about to get herself in trouble was the only thing that grounded me, kept me from losing myself to Indombe's magic."

Tarek frowned, his expression pensive. "Because you love her."

The question made the Hunter more than a little uncomfortable. He'd barely spoken the words to her a few weeks back, and only the once. He was far from the emotional sort. His life hadn't exactly been conducive to romance and saccharine sentiment. And yet, he knew the truth.

"Aye." It was simply said, the first time he'd voiced it to anyone. But it felt strangely right. "I love her. And I suppose that love is a power greater than even Indombe's magic."

He groaned inwardly, hearing the words even as they left his lips. *By the Keeper, I sound like the worst of the Taivoro romances!* Next, he'd be composing terrible poetry that spoke of Kiara's eyes "sparkling like gemstones" or far worse. The mawkishness of those lines from the Taivoro that he and Evren had deciphered to find the way to Enarium still lingered even after all these years.

But Tarek seemed not to notice or mind. His thoughts turned inward, his expression darkening. "And for those with no one to love? How do *they* resist?"

This question, too, caught the Hunter by surprise. It was strange yet strangely profound from one so young. Clearly, there was more to it than mere expediency. This went beyond a simple desire to survive should Tarek encounter Indombe—or a similar magic—again in the future. There was something more, something the young Elivasti had kept carefully hidden in the weeks that they'd spent on the road together. A piece of himself he reserved and shielded deep beneath the mask he showed to the world.

Oddly enough, the Hunter understood the young man's instincts. He kept that part hidden for his own sake. To shield *himself* from the world that could hurt him. He'd done the same for decades. Only in the last few years, since Kiara had become a part of his life, had he begun opening up and allowing those parts of himself to show. And because of it, he'd built for himself something greater than just his solitude as the legendary Hunter of Voramis. He had a family now, patchwork though it might be. Friends, too. Few, certainly, but a handful of staunch allies was worth more than ten thousand comrades whose camaraderie ran only skin deep.

"You find people who matter to you," he said. "And they become your reason for resisting. They become enough."

The sight of Tarek's youthful countenance brought to the Hunter's mind another face, one which bore startling similarity to the Elivasti before him.

How many times had his fear for Hailen saved the Hunter's life? It had driven him to resist Garanis' power, had fueled his efforts to break free of Imperius' restraints, given him the fortitude to press back against Kharna's all-encompassing will. The boy who had given the Hunter a reason to fight now served as the answer to a question posed by the half-brother he'd never met.

The strangeness wasn't lost on the Hunter. Nor was the irony of his answer. Minutes ago, he'd been trying to convince himself that trusting and opening himself up to others was weakness. Now, however, he had just told Tarek the weakness was, in fact, a strength. A strength that had saved his life—not just tonight with Indombe, but countless times in the past.

31

And so, despite what he believed was his better instinct, the Hunter *compelled* himself to do what he believed to be foolish and give Tarek a glimpse beneath his mask. To let the young man see a part of who he really was, to be vulnerable though everything screamed at him to protect himself.

He stepped forward and placed a hand on Tarek's shoulder. "I don't know your story, Tarek, just like you don't know mine, not truly. But for as long as you're with us, you will never fight alone." *Alone,* as the Hunter had been for so many years before Farida, before Hailen and Kiara and Graeme and Father Reverentus and all the others. "Whether it's a giant serpent or a *maistyr* with the power to break the minds and wills of men, you've got Kiara and me to stand at your side. For whatever that's worth."

He added this last because his words left him feeling strangely naked, exposed. Like he'd just removed the mask of the hard, ruthless, inexorable assassin of Voramis and revealed the mortal man beneath. The façade that had saved his life so many times before, now stripped away, and only the Hunter stood before Tarek. A man who loved, feared, doubted, and worried just as the young Elivasti did.

"Thank you." Tarek's words were quiet, but a hint of relief shone in his eyes. "Truly."

"Of course." The Hunter clapped the young man's arm, cleared his throat, and broke off Tarek's gaze. He'd had awkwardness enough for one night. "Now, if you're done here, get yourself back to camp. Kiara's sleeping, but I need you to keep an eye on her while I'm gone."

"Gone?" Tarek raised an eyebrow. "Where are you going?"

The Hunter jabbed a finger over the edge of the cliff, pointing straight downward.

Tarek's eyebrows shot up. "What in the ancestors' name for?"

"Kiara asked me to retrieve her *ebroq.*"

The young man's jaw dropped open. "You'd risk yourself...for an instrument?"

The Hunter shrugged. "When the person you love asks you do to something, even if it puts you in danger, you do it." A wry grin broadened his face. "Besides, have you met Kiara? Between facing Indombe's fury and her anger, it's no contest every time."

Tarek broke out laughing, a rich, hearty sound that resounded off the cliffs and swelled with the roar of the Zamani Falls. A moment later, the young man clapped a hand over his mouth, stifling his laugh as if afraid it would rouse Indombe from its slumber.

It was a good sound, just as the smile that had broken out on Tarek's scruff-covered face was a good sight. It reminded the Hunter a great deal of Hailen. That smile had the same open-hearted, good-natured gleam that never failed to lift the Hunter's spirit. In that moment, the similarities between them were undeniably apparent.

The Hunter turned away from the young man before the sensation of homesickness grew too great to ignore. It had been nearly two months since last he'd seen Hailen and Evren.

"Ancestors be with you!" Tarek called after him.

The Hunter didn't respond. He merely hurried to descend the switchback trail, clinging to the hope that whatever the two boys—*his* boys, as he'd begun to think of them—were up to in Shalandra, they were safe.

Tarek

Chapter Seven

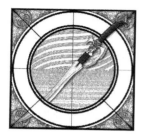

The roar of the Zamani Falls echoed through the basin, drowning out even the thundering of the Hunter's racing heartbeat. He knew there was no chance he'd *hear* the giant serpent emerging from the depths, so he kept one eye fixed firmly on Indombe's pool and stayed as far from the water's edge as possible. He had the distinct impression Indombe wouldn't emerge *twice* in one night—otherwise, sightings would have been far more common—but he'd take no chances all the same.

The light emanating from the glowing crystals had grown dim, as if their gleam followed the serpent whose blood had given them life into the belly of the earth. Yet there was illumination enough for the Hunter to pick his way across the rocky basin to the spot where he'd found Kiara wounded and bleeding out. As good a place as any to begin his search for the *ebroq*, he'd figured.

Worry twisted in his belly at the sight of Kiara's blood still staining the sharp-tipped crystal that had impaled her. He'd seen far too many strong men succumb to such a wound before. They always died in agony, bowels rotting their flesh from within. The odds of survival were dangerously slim. He could only hope he and Tarek had gotten to the injury in time. They'd know soon enough. Either fever claimed her and dragged her in a downward spiral toward death, or she regained consciousness and remained clear-headed.

The Hunter tore his eyes from the bloody crystal and bent his attention to the task of finding Kiara's peculiar instrument. Anything to divert his mind from his anxiety over her condition.

He searched the area around the spot where she'd struck the cliffside before falling into the sharp crystal. Nothing. No sign of the bronze flute with its strange pot-bellied end.

Drawing in a deep breath, he closed his eyes and called to mind the memories of their near-fatal encounter with Indombe. He had to fight to think clearly; the rush of adrenaline from that moment left his recollections hazy, the details vague. He went farther back, retracing the course of events as best he could.

Lying on the trail watching Indombe emerge. The strange magical compulsion that had tried to pull him and Kiara into the water. Hearing the *splash* marking Tarek's plunge into the pool. That split-second decision to dive after the young man.

A foolish decision, he knew. Fiery hell, he'd known it even as he'd leaped. But he'd acted on pure instinct. Hurled himself into danger to save Tarek, just as he would Hailen, Evren, Kiara, or anyone else close to him. Even though he'd known the young Elivasti for only a few weeks, he hadn't been able to stand idly by while the man's life hung in the balance. It merely wasn't his way.

Perhaps it had to do with his near-immortality and invulnerability. Weapons capable of bringing low even the mightiest mortal human inflicted what amounted to no more than a scratch on him. He'd endured the worst agonies and wounds imaginable over his decades of life. It had made him confident—some might say *over*confident, though he never allowed himself to take an enemy lightly. Enabled him to take risks like hurling himself into a scalding pool churned to whitewater by a serpent large enough to swallow him and a hundred full grown men whole.

Realizing his mind had begun to wander—fatigue really *was* taking a toll on him—the Hunter marshaled his thoughts to the matter at hand. He retraced his steps. Diving into the pool. Dragging Tarek to shore. Hurling the Elivasti out of the way and drawing Indombe's attention toward him.

He opened his eyes and traced his path along the rocky promontory and the sandy shore. His finger settled on the spot where he'd made his stand and struck back at Indombe. The spot where he'd barely managed to throw himself to the ground to evade the giant sweeping tail.

From there, he could triangulate the place where he remembered Kiara standing. She'd been helping Tarek out of the water and moving toward the trail when the blow struck.

No, that's not right. He shook his head, as if that would clear away the fog of fatigue. *She let go of Tarek and was playing the ebroq.*

The piercing avian shriek resounded in his ears. The sound, at once familiar and terrifying, evoked memories of *Alsaaeat Aldhahabia,* the phoenix that had been his companion during his years as Nasnaz the Great, conqueror of Al Hani. The Hunter had only the faintest recollection of that part of his life, yet he knew without a shred of doubt that somehow, impossibly, the flute had replicated the *taymahr's* cry to near-perfection.

He focused his mind on that sound, and on the vivid memory of Kiara blowing the flute. She'd been standing near the water's edge, and the tail had swept into her from her right side. With the *ebroq* held chiefly in her right hand—her left pressed against the holes set into its pot-bellied tip—the impact that hurled her toward the wall could very well have sent the flute flying…

There! The Hunter picked his way toward an outcropping of rocks. Boulders, really, larger than he was tall. They appeared to have broken free of the cliffs hundreds of years past and found a new home in the Zamani Basin. Though there were no glowing crystals to illuminate the area, the light of the pale moon sufficed to see where he was going.

And to spot the shine of metal glinting in the darkness. Not the silvery-white of steel, but a softer, aureate gleam that could only be bronze, brass, or gold.

The Hunter hurried toward the object and knelt to retrieve it. To his delight, it *was* the *ebroq.* What remained of it, at least.

A long fissure ran down the entire length of the flute's bronze shaft, and the mouthpiece had been bent and twisted beyond any hope of salvage. But it was the pot-bellied end that had suffered worst of all. The bronze bulb had crumpled beneath the impact of Indombe's tail. Not even the finest smith could hammer that flattened metal back into shape.

The Hunter's heart sank. *Kiara's not going to be happy.*

He didn't know why the flute mattered so much to her—she'd never shown any inclination to other musical instruments in the past. When he'd asked her about her purchase back in Drash, she'd given him an enigmatic smile and the promise of an explanation later. Only later had never come. He'd been so consumed in his own maudlin thoughts and brooding that he'd forgotten entirely about the *ebroq* until its shrill bird call had scared off Indombe.

He stared down at the ruined carcass of the bronze instrument. Hard to believe something so innocuous had saved his life. Had Kiara *known* it would make a cry like a phoenix?

35

He supposed she had, otherwise she'd never have pulled it out in the heart-stopping moments before Indombe's enormous jaws closed around the Hunter. But was that *all* its value?

He turned the flute over and over in his hands, studying it intently. It appeared utterly ordinary, nothing more than bronze painstakingly fashioned into the sort of simple woodwind found in virtually every city around Einan. Indeed, the only irregularity in its design was the pot-bellied end. The fist-sized bulb was akin to those utilized in the bamboo reed *pungi* of the Kurma Empire far, far beyond the northern edge of the Ghandian plains. Yet instead of featuring the bulb in the middle of the flute, the *ebroq's* was set into its end.

Perhaps *that* was how it had generated such a powerful sound. He knew only the rudiments of aerophones and other instruments akin to flutes—he'd had to learn for his façade of the jongleur Gladrin Silvertone—but it was possible that the over-sized chamber at the tip of the flute somehow amplified the air resonating through its wide bronze belly.

He couldn't exactly test out his theory, though. Not with this particular *ebroq*, at least. It was worthless now.

So why in the fiery hell was Kiara so insistent I fetch it now? The Hunter frowned. *She had to know it was likely damaged or destroyed by—*

His thoughts cut off as something caught his eye. He'd been turning the flute over in his hands, studying the cracked and crumpled metal from all angles, when he'd spotted the patch of metal darker than the rest on the flattened bit that had once been the pot-bellied bulb. He held it up to the moonlight, but the pale illumination was far too faint for him to make out the details. Yet as he ran a finger over it, he felt the unmistakable contours of *something* solid. Some shape he couldn't intuit by feel alone.

The Hunter's pulse quickened, curiosity setting his mind aflame. Tucking the flute into a pocket of his cloak, he hurried back the way he'd come, up the switchback trail that rose away from the Zamani Basin. For a moment, all trace of fatigue was forgotten by the interest that held him gripped in a fist of iron.

After everything he'd encountered—Serenii magic brought to life by songs and chants, power to harness and channel the power of the sun itself, arcane machinery that consumed souls and transformed them into energy enough to repel an entity as mighty as the Devourer of Worlds—he had fuel enough to set his thoughts running rampant. His imagination conjured up wild speculations as to what other secrets the *ebroq* concealed.

To his delight, when he reached the top of the trail, he found Tarek had started a small fire from the branches and sticks fallen from the baobab trees that served as their shelter. The Hunter flung himself to one knee by the fire and all but tore the *ebroq* from his pocket.

He turned the instrument over and over in his hands until he found what he sought. As he'd initially suspected, the object was made of a different metal than the bronze used to fashion the flute. It wasn't iron—its touch didn't set his skin crawling the way the poisonous metal always did. Steel, perhaps? He hefted the flute. No, the weight was all wrong. It was lighter than steel. Stronger, too. That small bit of metal alone had survived the impact of Indombe's tail utterly unscathed. While the rest of the flute had been all but destroyed, the metal held its shape.

But what shape *was* it? The Hunter studied it from all angles. When looked at from the top, as if his lips were placed against the mouthpiece, the metallic shape appeared like an X with *eight* arms rather than simply four. From the side, it almost reminded the Hunter of Serenii runes. None he'd ever seen, though.

He was about to show it to Tarek and ask if the young man recognized the shape, but a low groan from Kiara cut him off. Springing to his feet, he darted toward her and knelt at her side.

"Hey," he said, his voice soft. "You're supposed to be resting."

Her eyelids fluttered halfway open, and her lips moved in a quiet whisper. "Did…you…find it?"

"I did." The Hunter pressed the ruined instrument against her chest and folded one of her hands over it. "Just like you asked."

Though Kiara's eyes never opened, her expression relaxed, as if in relief. "Good," she murmured. "I couldn't…stand…to lose…" Her voice trailed off, her head settling back against the blankets once more. Yet she curled her arm tighter around the instrument and clutched it to her breast with all the limited strength remaining to her.

The Hunter watched her, and the tension drained from his muscles as she settled once more into sleep. He thought she might have regained even more color, though the flush on her cheeks could also be fever. To his relief, when he settled a hand against her forehead, he felt only warm flesh. Neither cold and clammy nor burning up.

With a breath, he settled back against the baobab tree where he'd been sitting earlier and let out a long breath.

"She'll live." Tarek spoke from where he sat tending the fire. He sounded confident, though the effect was ruined when he added, "I think."

"She'll live." The Hunter spoke the words with a certainty he didn't truly feel. Yet saying it aloud would *have* to make it so. "There's not a man alive today tougher than her."

Tarek raised an eyebrow, but if he thought anything of that statement, he did not say it. He merely nodded and settled back against his baobab tree. He closed his eyes and settled his breathing to a deep, steady rhythm—a practice the Hunter had noted the young man repeated every night, as if it facilitated sleep.

Fatigue settled over the Hunter's body, but his mind would not slow. He couldn't shake thoughts of the *ebroq* from his mind. What was the meaning of the strange metal symbol or shape hammered into its bulbous tip? Why had it been so important to Kiara?

Tired or not, he knew he'd get no sleep as long as the mystery of the peculiar instrument remained unsolved.

Chapter Eight

The baobab flowers heralded daybreak. The scent filling the air deepened from tart sweetness to the cloying scent that evoked the stink of rotting carrion as the short-lived blossoms died. Worry twisted in the Hunter's belly. He could only hope that didn't presage a similar fate for Kiara.

The smell, and the golden sun rising over the eastern horizon, banished any hopes the Hunter might have had of sleeping. Fatigue dragged on his limbs, but he could find no rest. Not until he knew Kiara would pull through. Her wounds had pained her throughout the night, pulling little groans and moans from her lips, but the morning light on her cheeks revealed no febrile flush.

The Hunter woke her just long enough to drink, though she managed no more than a few sips of the tepid water before falling back asleep. In an effort to keep from worrying overmuch, he set about examining his gear.

His unthinking, headlong dive into the pool had saved Tarek's life, but the impact with the water had torn two of the leather straps holding his concealed daggers in place on his forearms. He had no spare leather with which to mend the damage, forcing him to remove them and stow the weapons in his pack. Fortunately, his sword belt and baldric had escaped unscathed. The Sword of Nasnaz in its plain scabbard seemed none the worse for the wear. Master Eldor's blade, too, remained intact. Just to be safe, the Hunter polished the weapons with a dry cloth and applied a fresh coat of oil along their entire length. He'd have to re-wrap the leather around the watered steel sword's hilt, he saw. Regular use had worn it down so much it had already been on the verge of cracking. The water had merely finished the job that age had begun.

Had his armor been *ordinary* leather, it would have grown stiff, inflexible, and more easily cracked. Fortunately for him, Graeme had insisted on applying alchemical treatments that fortified it against both enemy foes and the elements. Rather than soaking into the leather, the last remaining droplets of water sluiced off the armor like rain off glass.

The Hunter carefully checked over Soulhunger. Not the dagger—he doubted even Indombe could scratch the Serenii-forged *Im'tasi* blade—but the specialized scabbard in which it rested. The sheath itself was ordinary enough, a construction of oiled wood wrapped in hide, but it featured a unique addition: a cable of braided steel ran from the sheath to the egg-sized sphere that now enclosed the dagger's gemstone. The sphere's steel exterior protected the Hunter from its inner lining of thin-hammered iron. That lining obstructed the dagger's magic, prevented it from being detected by the Cambionari's strange ability to sense and locate the gemstones forged from the souls of demons.

The Hunter had insisted they spend an extra two days in Drash for the sole purpose of procuring that particular item. The locksmith he'd paid to craft it had been intrigued by the design, but the hefty purse of gold the Hunter placed in the man's hand forestalled any questions as to its intended use. The wait had been worth it. With a flick of his thumb, the Hunter triggered the mechanism that released the latch holding the sphere closed. It popped open like petals of a flower and fell away from the gemstone to swing lazily from its cable.

Satisfied the water hadn't damaged the delicate internal workings of the lock, the Hunter placed the now-open sphere back on the gemstone and closed its four metal "petals". The pieces connected with a faint *click* to indicate the sphere once more encapsulated the magical gemstone.

The Hunter didn't know exactly how well the device functioned—he had no Cambionari close at hand to test it out. The fact that he hadn't seen a single Beggar Priest or demon-hunting knight on his trail since leaving Malandria was the closest he could come to proof that the iron sufficed to block the gemstone's magic. Still, he'd made certain to steer well clear of Drash's temple district, just to be safe.

His frown deepened as the spherical device brought back memories of the *reason* he'd had it forged. For the hundredth time since departing the Monolith of Malandria, he questioned his decision to leave Sir Sigmund and Remi alive. Three weeks was far from time enough to heal the damage he'd done to the Nyslian knight's face. The burly, bearded knight apprentice had endured terrible torment at the hands of Lord Apus, including broken ribs and torn-out fingernails. Both Remi and Sir Sigmund would require time to recover.

But that didn't mean they wouldn't send *other* Cambionari after him. Though they'd have no idea where he was headed—and couldn't follow him across Einan with the gemstone's magic sealed within the iron sphere—that last look of pure hatred in Sir Sigmund's swollen, bloody eyes had made it clear the giant knight wouldn't be satisfied with anything less than the Hunter's death. For the Hunter was *demonspawn*, an abomination that their order of Beggar Priests had dedicated their lives to exterminating.

The Hunter gave a disgusted grunt and slid Soulhunger back into its sheath. He had no desire to deal with priests and their machinations. The Enclave and their lies. The rift between the Elisionists and those like Father Reverentus who wanted to spread the truth of the so-called gods of Einan. The "divine mandates" of those like Sir Sigmund or Illusionist Cleric Imperius that only caused *him* suffering.

If he never saw another priest again, he'd die happy. Fortunately for him, where they were going, priests were as much a rarity as giant serpents or magical weapons thousands of years old.

"How is she?" Tarek's quiet voice drew the Hunter's attention upward. The young man had awoken before dawn and vanished into the hazy darkness without a word. Now, he'd returned with a pair of grassland hares slung over one shoulder. Just *another* of the Elivasti's skills, in addition to tracking, navigating by the stars, reading the weather in the clouds, and his knowledge of herbal remedies.

"Sleeping," the Hunter said, keeping his tone low so as not to disturb Kiara's rest.

Tarek dropped the game onto the grass beside the ashes that remained of the previous night's fire, then came to kneel at Kiara's side. "She drink at all?"

"A few sips." The Hunter watched the young man examining Kiara: counting the beats of her heart, placing a hand against her forehead to check for fever, and gently lifting the bandages around her wound. "She any better?"

Tarek nodded. "No sign of infection. Her pulse is steadier than last night. If we can get some food into her, it will give her body the strength to heal." He thrust his chin toward the two hares. "Those will make a decent soup. Meat for us, broth for her."

When Tarek stood, the Hunter noted the grimace that twisted the Elivasti's face. At first, he suspected injury—the young man had leaped into the pool from a great height—but then he spotted the blister on the side of Tarek's neck, just at the collar of his pale grey tunic. Another had formed on the back of Tarek's right hand, which suggested there were more elsewhere, covered by his clothing. The water in Indombe's pool had been on the verge of boiling when the Hunter dragged Tarek out.

"How are you?" the Hunter asked. He stabbed a finger at Tarek's neck and hand. "How bad are the burns?"

"Not bad." Tarek pulled up his collar to hide the blister, turning away quickly as if seeking to conceal his chagrin. "Kanna taught me how to make an ointment that will soothe and heal soon enough." The redness of his face had nothing to do with embarrassment, however. He had the appearance of a man who'd spent too many days under the bright sun.

The Hunter didn't press the matter. If the Elivasti wanted to put on a brave face, so be it. He said nothing, and Tarek seemed in no mood to talk, either. The young man first tended to his blisters—applying a foul-smelling unguent he insisted would accelerate his recovery—then moved on to their meal. He skinned, gutted, and butchered the hares in silence, his movements deft and confident. Within minutes, he had a new fire lit and the meat in the cookpot.

While Tarek tended to the meal, the Hunter continued his examination of his gear, going over the contents of his pack. With his blankets and spare shirt used for Kiara's bed, his backpack held only two pairs of trousers, a roll of linen bandages, and the canvas-wrapped bundles that contained their trail rations. Tucked safely at the bottom, however, were the items of greatest value: the purse that contained a fortune in gemstones, and the twin blades of iron in their cloth wrappings.

A grunt of amusement escaped the Hunter's lips. Sir Sigmund had handed him the Swordsman's blades before their assault on Lord Apus' mansion, doubtless believing he'd retrieve the weapons once the demons were in chains. Neither he nor the Hunter could have foreseen the events that led to the violent dissolution of their short-lived alliance.

Now, the Cambionari had *double* incentive to hunt him down. Those blades were ancient holy relics of the Beggar Priests—and, as the Hunter had discovered in Enarium, keys utilized to activate the Illumina and turn the power of the Serenii against the Devourer of Worlds.

But was that *all* they did? Deneen, the Serenii who'd fashioned them, worshipped by humans as the Swordsman, hadn't wielded them as weapons of war. Instead, they had hung around his neck like some prize jewelry. If they were created as keys to bring the Illumina to life, could they do likewise to *other* Serenii handiworks?

The Hunter had never considered that idea before Malandria. Then again, he'd had no idea that the Serenii had built Chambers of Sustenance anywhere outside of Enarium. But what he'd seen in the Monolith had changed his way of thinking. It was possible—likely, even—the Serenii towers dotting Einan functioned to enhance or amplify the power of the Illumina. That structures like the Black Spire of Voramis and the Monolith of Malandria, perhaps even the *Dolmenrath* spread around Einan, could actually be some sort of vast spider's web network to draw in magic from every corner of the continent.

The idea hadn't been his, not truly. Only days after leaving Malandria did he realize the truth: he'd first had the vague notion after being ripped from his communion with Kharna. Had the Serenii implanted it in his mind? It wasn't much of a stretch; the god-like being had implanted the subconscious imperative to kill that led to the manifestation of his inner voices. And the vision the Hunter had seen of similar crystalline towers around Einan—including *Ukuhlushwa Okungapheli*, the tower of star-dotted midnight black that awaited them in Ghandia— only served to reinforce his belief.

Did Kharna want him to activate *all* those towers he'd shown the Hunter? It made sense, in its own bizarre, arcane way. The entombed Serenii needed more power to repel the Devourer of Worlds, to seal the rift in reality. If he could gather that power from every corner of Einan, he stood a better chance of survival—perhaps even triumph. The conviction had blossomed and taken firm root in the Hunter's mind. He'd heard no "voice of god", received no "divine mission", yet he felt the certainty to the marrow of his bones

Of course, Kharna hadn't managed to tell him *how* to pull off that impossibility. The bastard Serenii had implanted the notion in his mind and left him to figure out the particulars for himself. In that sense, Kharna was very much like the gods of Einan. Interfering in the ways of mortals whenever they saw fit, yet remaining aloof and uninvolved when they were most needed.

Leaving me to figure it all out for myself. A scowl twisted the Hunter's lips. *Real helpful, you are!*

"Food's ready."

Tarek's voice drew the Hunter from his thoughts. He looked up, found the young Elivasti standing over him with two bowls in hand. One held a generous portion of boiled hare—which the Hunter knew would doubtless be utterly unseasoned and devoid of any flavor, given the Elivasti's ascetic sense of taste—the other a small measure of watery broth.

Still, the Hunter took the bowls with a nod of thanks. He set his down—he could eat later—and rose to kneel at Kiara's side.

"Help me with her," he told the young man. "If we can get her to eat, mayhap she'll be strong enough to ride."

The sooner they got on the road, the sooner they'd reach Khafra—and a healer to help speed along Kiara's recovery.

Chapter Nine

With Tarek's help cradling Kiara's head, the Hunter managed to get most of the bowl of watery, bland broth down her throat. When finally he finished, rather than falling back asleep, she managed to remain awake. Her eyes took in the sunny morning, the Hunter's worried expression, Tarek's scalded skin, and the horses standing nearby.

"Why...aren't we...already on the road?" Her voice grew stronger and her wry grin broader with every word. "Lazy, good-for-nothing louts...too busy lounging in the shade."

The Hunter chuckled. "Says the one still abed halfway to the noon hour." He shook his head with a look of mock severity. "Keeper's teeth, Woman, if I'd known you intended to delay us so, I'd never have agreed to this detour."

Though he'd meant the words to sound joking, he heard the biting edge to his tone. She'd sworn to the high heavens that they'd be well out of harm's way. That she only wanted the chance to see Indombe from afar. The Hunter hadn't truly believed the giant serpent would appear—he'd been half-convinced it was as fictional as the so-called gods—and now kicked himself for allowing it.

"Agreed?" Kiara snorted, a measure of her usual sardonic strength returning. "You're cute, Hunter. Thinking you actually had a choice in all this." She fixed him with a sharp gaze. "Because we both know that when I bend my mind to something, I get it."

He couldn't argue that. When set on a course, she was as intractable as a mountain. He'd have better luck convincing the Frozen Sea to boil than trying to talk her out of one of her plans. She numbered among the *very* few people alive whose tenacity rivaled his.

A sharp retort formed on his lips. Wisely, he kept the "And see how that turned out!" to himself. Instead, he shrugged and said, "Think you can bend your mind to riding?"

Kiara shot him a scornful look. "Of course I can." She struggled to rise, but when the Hunter offered his hand, she waved him away. "I can do this."

She bloody well couldn't—the Hunter knew it, for the wound to her belly had been truly grievous—but offering her help again would only irritate her. He had to let her try until the truth sank home and she ultimately relented and asked for his aid.

Which she did in a matter of seconds. On her third vain attempt to rise, she slumped back to her makeshift bed with a groan, hand pressed to her stomach. "Fine!" she gasped, shaking her head. "I'll let you help me."

"How gracious of you," the Hunter said in a flat tone, earning himself another sharp look. Yet Kiara didn't protest as the Hunter helped her to sit up and lean back against the baobab tree where he'd been watching over her all night. "Stay here. I'll be back in a few minutes."

She was too busy panting for breath and dripping sweat to reply, merely fluttered her free hand in a vague gesture of acknowledgement.

The Hunter hurried toward Ash. The desert pony pranced up to meet him, blowing a breath in the Hunter's face and whickering in greeting. A night of rest had done the sturdy mount well. His dappled grey coat seemed even more lustrous under the bright sun, and his long, lean muscles rippled with eager anticipation. The desert pony wanted to run free and fast, as was his nature. He barely managed to restrain himself long enough for the Hunter to strap the saddle onto his back.

While the Hunter struggled with the restive pony's tack, Tarek came to join him. The young Elivasti used the task of saddling Nayaga as cover to say in a low, furtive voice, "I do not think it is wisest for her to ride. She is far from recovered."

"You want to be the one to tell her that?" the Hunter asked out of a corner of his mouth.

Tarek shot a glance at Kiara, then shook his head. He'd been traveling with them long enough to have taken measure of the woman's obstinacy. For all her reason and empathy, she'd proven herself obdurate enough to rival even the most indomitable mule.

"We'll watch her." The Hunter moved on to saddling Elivast while he spoke. "First sign of fatigue, we'll stop and rest. Worse comes to it, we'll make a litter. But we *have* to get to Khafra. Soon."

"Agreed." Tarek's tone was somber. "It is the only place we can find the *ephrade* needed to speed her recovery."

The Hunter stroked Elivast's mane, glad for the distraction from his worries over Kiara. The chestnut gelding had traveled far with him—crossed an entire continent—and endured many adventures. He couldn't imagine embarking on any journey without the horse for a companion. Elivast seemed to share his feelings. The horse nuzzled against him and gave a contented snort.

"You'll help me watch over her, won't you?" he whispered into the horse's ears.

For answer, Elivast bumped his long-nosed face against the Hunter's chest.

The Hunter made quick work of preparing the horses, strapped his and Kiara's packs in place behind their saddles, and finally returned to where she sat reclining in the shade of the baobab tree. "Ready?"

She nodded, though even that cost her visible effort. "Just get me on the horse, and I'll be good as new. Might even race to see which of us can reach Khafra first."

"You really want to lose that badly, eh?" The Hunter bent down and wrapped his arms beneath her arms and around her back. "You're many things, Kiara, but a champion rider isn't one of them."

She snorted in his ear. "Say that again when I'm in the saddle, and we'll see who's laughing."

The Hunter couldn't help a chuckle, but it was more relieved than amused. At least she had the strength to crack jokes. She knew as well as he which of them sat a horse better.

His smile faded as soon as he set her on her feet and her legs gave way beneath her. Expecting this, he'd held on to her, and reacted fast enough to catch her before she could fall. He winced at her hiss of pain. The wound in her belly would be agony, he knew, and every movement would tug on the still-healing flesh.

"Allow me, my lady." The Hunter released one arm from behind her back and, before she could protest, swept her up in his arms. "A gentlewoman of your caliber should *never* exert herself more than absolutely necessary. You must conserve your strength for the pursuits befitting your station. Embroidery, knitting, and the like."

43

A growl echoed in his ear. "Say that again, and I'll show you where a gentlewoman of my caliber sticks her dagger when some foppish prick insults her." Kiara's expression was mock severe, but she was too weak to even reach for her weapons to put actions to her threat. She made no further protest as the Hunter carried her in his arms to where Ash stood eagerly waiting.

But the Hunter didn't lift her into Ash's saddle. The desert pony was far too restive, and its high-spirited pace would only compound Kiara's pain. Instead, he settled her onto Elivast's back. The chestnut gelding had fire in his belly to equal Ash's, but it was tempered by a more placid nature. Elivast would be just as happy to spend the day cropping grass in a sunny field as racing across the rolling desert.

Ash appeared to take offense at this, for he came over and nudged his nose forcefully into Kiara's left leg.

"Easy, Ash," Kiara chided. She began to reach down to pet the horse, but stopped with a groan when the movement pulled on the torn muscle and flesh of her belly. The Hunter caught her before she toppled over from the pain, held her steady until she gave him a nod to indicate she'd recovered. Hand pressed to her side, she rubbed the side of Ash's neck with one toe of her boot. "We'll be racing again in no time, you'll see. We've got to show *this one* what true spirit looks like."

The Hunter ignored the gibe; he was too busy keeping an eye on Kiara and adjusting the reins and stirrups to match her shorter frame. When finally he finished, he hesitated before leaving her side.

"Away, you!" Kiara nudged him with one booted toe, though with far less affection than she'd shown Ash. "Stop hovering like a mother hen. I told you, I'm—" Her face spasmed with pain and her jaw muscles clamped down hard. "—fine!" The word escaped in a hissed breath.

"Of course you are." The Hunter couldn't keep the sardonic edge from his tone. "Fighting fit, as always."

Kiara had no answer to that; she struggled visibly to keep from losing her fight against the pain of her wound. To her credit, her obstinacy triumphed and she managed to stay upright and seated until the agony passed. Her face relaxed, her shoulders lowered, and her jaw unclenched.

"As always," she half-said, half-gasped. "Now, let's go! Sunlight's wasting."

The Hunter didn't waste time arguing. If she could out-stubborn her own body, she damned well wouldn't relent to his fussing over her.

He hurried back to where the pile of blankets lay beneath the baobab tree, rolled them together, and tied them in a bundle behind Ash's saddle. Then, with a smooth leap, he vaulted into his seat on the desert pony's back. Ash was two hands shorter than Elivast, its compact frame somehow sleek and powerfully built at once. The Hunter could feel the horse's eagerness to ride, to stretch its legs and race across the grasslands. A part of him wanted to give Ash his head and gallop for Khafra in all haste. No doubt the beast sensed the urgency humming within him, the burning desire to fetch the *ephrade* and other alchemical supplies that would help restore Kiara. It took concentrated effort to keep both of them under control.

But the Hunter managed. Pushing back the worry mounting within him, he tapped his heels lightly against Ash's side.

He turned to Tarek, who had mounted and now sat waiting for them. "Lead the way," he told the young Elivasti. "We've spent enough time on this detour. Best we get back to our *true* purpose for traveling here."

The young man's expression grew serious, somber, his nod grave. "As you say." With that, he turned Nayaga's head toward the path that led *away* from Zamani Falls—and northeast toward the city of Khafra and Ghandia beyond.

* * *

By noon, it was clear Kiara could not go on. The heat of the day bordered on unbearable, the sun beating down so bright it nearly blinded the Hunter, all but suffocating him within the depths of his dark grey hood. The air became choked with dust kicked up by Nayaga's hooves so that every breath seared and scraped his lungs like shards of red-hot metal. With the shade of the baobab trees and the cool air rising off Zamani Falls far behind, the weather turned torrid. The Hunter couldn't decide which was worse: the fires burning within Indombe, potent enough to heat the serpent's pool to boiling, or the arid heat of the Kgabu Plains.

Kiara fought to remain in her saddle, her jaw clenched, sweat streaming down her face, spine rigid. Yet even though Tarek slowed their pace to a walk, she simply could not keep up. She swayed as if lightheaded from dehydration no matter how often she drank from her canteen. Even the slightest jostle and jolt threatened to unhorse her.

Finally, the Hunter had had enough. "Tarek, make for that tree!" He had no need to specify *which* tree; a single umbrella thorn acacia stood head and shoulders above the shrubs and swaying grasses, a lone sentry providing shade and rest from the burning sun.

Kiara didn't protest; she hadn't the strength. They'd barely covered half of the five hundred-pace distance to the tree when she toppled sidelong from her saddle. Had the Hunter not been watching her like a hawk, she would have fallen, doubtless reopening the wound.

But he *had* been watching, and pulled Ash up beside her so she collapsed into his outstretched arms.

"I'm sorry," she murmured weakly. "I…tried." Her eyes fluttered and fell closed.

"I've got you." He clutched her to his chest, wrapping both arms around her as if he cradled a prized possession. Which she was. Few things in the world mattered more to him than this woman. He'd give *anything* to see her whole once again.

Chapter Ten

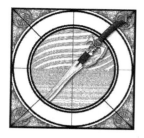

One moment the Hunter was alone beneath the tree with Kiara; the next, Tarek appeared without the faintest sound or a hint of scent to herald his return. The Hunter startled up from where he'd been lying trying to sleep, instantly recognizing the worry clouding the young Elivasti's expression.

"What is it?" he asked, his belly twisting into knots.

"Company." Tarek jerked a thumb over his shoulder, indicating a hill to the southwest, the direction from which they'd come.

The Hunter sprang to his feet, fear rising sharp and bitter in his mouth. His mind conjured images of heavily armored knights mounted on warhorses charging toward him, lances lowered, iron-edged greatswords swinging toward his head. The Cambionari *couldn't* have caught up to him already, could they? That was impossible!

Yes, he told himself, drawing in a long breath to steady his nerves, *it is impossible. There's absolutely no way they could have found us.* Even if the demon-hunting Beggar Priest had somehow figured out where the Hunter was headed, they had strayed far off the main highways connecting Drash and Khafra. The road they traveled was little more than a half-overgrown path meandering through the Kgabu Plains, used chiefly by the people of Nkedi, the farming village a day's journey upstream from the Zamani Falls, and those rare sightseers who traveled to the Zamani Basin in the hopes of spotting Indombe.

All of this flashed through his mind in the space between heartbeats. He steeled his composure and kept his voice calm as he asked, "Any idea who?"

"Couldn't tell." Tarek shook his head. "Dust enough to be horses, maybe a wagon or three. They'll be on us before sunset."

The Hunter glanced at the sky. After Kiara had passed out on their ride, he and Tarek had both agreed she needed a few hours of rest. They'd chosen to rest through the heat of the afternoon and resume their journey once the day cooled.

So what do we do? He mulled over his options. *Ride out now and risk Kiara collapsing once more, or wait for whoever's passing to catch up and ride on?*

His concern was not for himself. If the approaching travelers proved hostile, well, they'd find no easy victim. Tarek, too, could handle himself. The Hunter and Kiara had both engaged in friendly sparring matches with the young man. His fighting style resembled that of the Elivasti the Hunter had faced on Kara-ket. Where the Sage's men had wielded iron-tipped staves adorned with tassels, Tarek's carried a steel-headed Hrandari spear decorated with the feathers of a Hrandari kite hawk. Yet he wielded the weapon with precision and grace impressive for one his age, moved with a warrior's confidence, and had the composure and restraint of a much more seasoned man paired with a youth's spryness.

No, the Hunter worried about Kiara. Collapsing after just a few hours of riding proved she had a long way yet to go on her path to recovery. For all her protests and insistence, the wound left her weak enough that she'd remained soundly asleep for the three hours they'd been sheltering under the umbrella thorn acacia. She could be worse off than either he or Tarek suspected, the wound graver than first appeared. She could yet succumb to fever or wound rot.

She could ill-afford any delay, yet she was far from ready to travel. The more she slept, the more strength she'd regain, and the sooner she'd be restored.

The Hunter didn't take long to reach a decision. "We wait."

Tarek's eyes narrowed a fraction. "And conceal ourselves?"

The Hunter shook his head. "We don't know what manner of travelers they are. Should they mean us ill, they'll have already spotted our tracks leading here." Not expecting to run into any other travelers, neither the Hunter nor Tarek had made the slightest attempt to cover their back trail. "And should they merely be travelers who have the means to lend us aid, I doubt they'll react well to us simply appearing as if from thin air." Besides, though he, Tarek, and Kiara could hide in the tall grass, there was no way to conceal the horses.

Tarek's expression grew pensive as he considered the Hunter's words. Finally, he inclined his head. "As you say." One jaw muscle twitched. "Though if it's all the same to you, I believe I'll take cover, just in case they decide they're after more than just a friendly chat."

The Hunter couldn't fault that logic. A surprise attack from the rear could level even terrible odds. "I'll handle greeting our fellow travelers. Watch for my signal." He patted Soulhunger's hilt. "I make a move, you know what to do."

A fierce grin broadened Tarek's face. That smile, framed by the wisps of sparse fuzz dotting his youthful features, brought to the Hunter's mind a single thought. *So that's what Hailen will look like in ten years or so.*

Tarek turned and dropped low into the tall grass, vanishing in a matter of seconds. *One more skill he'd picked up among the Hrandari, no doubt,* the Hunter thought.

His mind flashed back to the explanation the Sage had given him, of how his trusted Elivasti ruled the many plainsmen clans from behind their masks. Even after weeks of traveling together, he hadn't yet asked Tarek which clan he'd ridden with. He resolved to bring up the matter when opportunity next presented. It behooved him to get to know the young Elivasti riding at his side.

The sight of the distant cloud of dust dragged his thoughts away from his companion. His instinctive worry that the Cambionari had caught up to him had been nothing but a trick of his mind, but that didn't mean whoever was approaching would be any friendlier than the demon-hunting Beggar Priests. The Kgabu Plains were an inhospitable place, yet the villagers of Nkedi had warned them to be watchful for the bands of reavers known to roam the grasslands.

Bandits and highwaymen, he had no need to fear. But the Order of Mithridas was a different matter. According to Nashat al-Azzam, Graeme's Hidden Circle colleague in Malandria, rumors held that the secret organization were actively operating in the region. Al-Azzam's note hadn't offered concrete details, which meant he had no real idea of where they could be found or what manner of "operations" they commanded.

One thing he knew for certain: the Order of Mithridas had attacked his convoy south of Malandria and slain more than half the Beggar Priests traveling with him.

Far too many nights, when dreams of Tassat and Sir Benoit and Sir Georges haunted him, so, too, came the memories of the men who'd died that night. Roget, lying slumped on his side with two crossbow quarrels driven deep into his back. Giles, staring at a sky full of stars he would never again see. Louis, clinging to Giles in death. Antoine, the youngest of the Cambionari, with a bolt embedded in his eye. Brother Penurius, burned by the very fire over which he'd prepared a fine dinner only hours earlier. Brother Solicitous, his notebook pinned to his chest by the quarrel that had ended his life. Pale-faced, wide-eyed, and deathly still, one and all.

The Hunter might not have liked them all—certainly didn't *trust* them fully—yet they hadn't deserved to die like that. For those deaths, the Hunter felt only burning enmity and a desire to extinguish the Order wherever they could be found.

It might be argued that the priests and Cambionari had merely been unlucky casualties, fallen in the attack intended to free Lord Chasteyn. The Hunter refused to take that appearance at face value.

Father Reverentus' warning still rang in his ears every time he pondered the nighttime attackers in their black drake scale masks. *"According to the writings of early Cambionari, they were a plague upon this world for the better part of three millennia. Stirring up unrest, inciting civil wars, toppling kingdoms and empires, turning nation against nation, even fomenting discord among the priesthoods."*

The Hunter's research into the Order had yielded a number of upheavals attributed to them—the Dajashah Revolt that destroyed the kingdoms of Luthra, Suramanish, and Aarsuhi, paving the way for the Kurma Empire to rise; the civil strife that broke a once-united Nysl into the Principalities that existed to this day; and the Cleric War that set the priestly orders at each other's throats for nearly two hundred years, spilling blood all across Einan.

But all of those were ancient history. The organization had been said to be extinct, destroyed root and branch. However, the reason for their actions remained unknown.

"The ultimate aims of the Order of Mithridas have always been a mystery," Father Reverentus had explained. *"All of the Enclave's attempts to ascertain their true purpose failed. Those of their agents who were captured and subjected to questioning died without revealing a word. What they intend to do with an Abiarazi— whether to use him, ransom him off, sacrifice him in some dark ritual—I cannot be certain. But what I do know is that they pose a threat that cannot be ignored."*

Had the Hunter not personally witnessed the Sage being ripped apart and consumed by the Devourer of Worlds, he might have chalked it up to the Abiarazi's cunning. Such manipulation certainly fit the demon's methods of operating.

Yet the Sage had been dead for three years, and if the Order of Mithridas was only *now* resurging, it suggested someone else pulled their strings.

Their presence alone wasn't enough to compel the Hunter to make the long journey northeast. Yet Itan had sent Tarek to accompany him out of a fervent belief that a demon would be found in Ghandia. The Hunter hadn't seen any mention of a demon on the Sage's map, but if there was even a chance one existed, the Hunter had to investigate. He'd vowed to the True Descendants of Kara-ket that he'd free them of their servitude to the *maistyrs*. Adding to that Kharna's insistence that he visit *Ukuhlushwa Okungapheli,* circumstances conspired to force his hand.

He did not know who approached—be they friend or foe, man or demon—but whatever happened, he'd face them head on.

At that moment, Kiara stirred behind him. The Hunter glanced over his shoulder and found her shifting beneath her blankets, face twisted in pain, the occasional restless groan escaping her lips. But only for a few moments. To his relief, she quickly drifted off into undisturbed sleep.

Good, he thought, letting out a long breath. *The more she rests, the better.*

He hoped she'd have strength enough to travel through the night—to have any chance of reaching Khafra soon, they had to cover a lot of ground to make up for their slow pace.

With Kiara once more settled, the Hunter returned his attention to the road southwest. The cloud of dust had appeared over a distant hill, drawing closer at a steady pace. Horses and wagons, as Tarek had believed.

The Hunter frowned as a *second* cloud of dust broke off from the first. This one approached at a far faster pace, and soon a quartet of riders appeared on the meandering trail through the grasslands. He'd been spotted, he knew. They were heading straight for him. No doubt their minds had run in a similar direction to his; these four were sent ahead to ascertain whether the two travelers sheltering beneath the umbrella thorn acacia tree would prove a threat.

After a moment's consideration, the Hunter pulled back his hood so his features were plainly visible. As were the hilts of the two swords jutting over his shoulders. He kept Soulhunger hidden beneath his cloak—only a fool would display the gemstone set into the dagger's pommel so brazenly—but ensured he could reach the weapon at a moment's notice. No telling what these riders intended. He trusted his dark cloak, visible armaments, and stern countenance would prove deterrence enough. But if not…

He shrugged. *If they're foolish enough to attack a pair of travelers, they deserve the only reward I have to offer them.*

The four riders approached at a gallop. Details about them grew clearer beneath the bright afternoon sun as they closed the distance. All four were men, though none from the same part of Einan. One had the lustrous golden skin of a Vothmoti, another the pallor common among Drashi, and a third wore his blond hair and beard cropped close to his skin in a fashion much in style in the courts of Voramis.

It was the fourth man, however, who most drew the Hunter's attention. His skin was a deep ebony, his head shaved to the scalp, and his long, loose robes of the vivid red, orange, and lavender hues favored in Ghandia streamed behind him like a cape flying in the breeze. This man, at least, belonged on the Kgabu Plains. But the other three?

Even from afar, the Hunter could see they were men of action. All wore the same weapons on their belts: a mid-length sword with a slightly curved blade and a hilt that gave it the appearance of an oversized dagger. The Hunter had heard of such a weapon—the *kriegsmesser,* as it was called among the people of Odaron where it had originated, or the "greatknife" as it was better known around Einan. It was a practical, sturdy soldier's weapon, a far cry from the *schlager* fencing saber utilized by the wealthy and aristocracy of Odaron. What it was doing on these men, hundreds of leagues away from the "City of Steel" that sat at the eastern extreme of the Chasm of the Lost, the Hunter didn't know. But he bloody well intended to find out.

He stepped into the path, standing like a shield between the sleeping Kiara and the oncoming riders. Slowly, deliberately, he spread his arms wide to reveal empty hands. A gesture that bespoke peace despite his own prominently visible weapons.

Twenty paces away from him, the riders slowed their horses from a gallop to a trot. Interestingly, it was the Ghandian who acted first to rein in his horse, and the Drashi, Vothmoti, and Voramian followed suit without hesitation.

This, then, is the leader. The Hunter fixed his attention on the ebony-skinned Ghandian. He was larger than the others, taller even than the Hunter and nearly as thick in the chest as Jarl had been. His flowing multi-hued robes accentuated the breadth of his shoulders and barrel torso, which were barely concealed by the steel-studded leather vest he wore. A necklace of what looked like eight small finger bones dangling from a leather thong hung from his neck.

His features proved as intriguing as his choice of jewelry and clothing. Three vertical scars marked each of his cheeks, with two more running down the middle of his clean-shaven chin like twin tusks. No battle scars, these. They had been carved into his skin with deliberate precision. Their meaning, the Hunter didn't know any more than their purpose. None of the villages in Nkedi had sported such marks, nor had the few Ghandian merchants and travelers they'd met on their way northeast.

"Greetings, fellow travelers!" The Hunter chose to speak first. "A fine day on the road, is it not?" Better to play friendly to mask his innate suspicions of any armed men riding in such an out-of-the-way region of the Kgabu Plains.

"It is, indeed," the Ghandian answered, his voice deep and rich, with only the faintest hint of accent. "My companions and I spotted your horses, and decided it was best we introduce ourselves. All the better to avoid any misunderstandings, of course."

The Hunter smiled. "Of course!" Clearly the man had been of the same mind as he and Tarek. This tete-a-tete served for both parties to gauge the potential for danger. "Hardwell of Praamis, at your service." He gave the man a stiff, military nod, as befitted the persona of soldier-of-fortune he'd crafted so many years ago. "I and my wife—" He swept a hand toward the pile of blankets where Kiara slept. "—are traveling to Khafra in the hopes of standing at the edge of the Great Chasm and renewing our vows of marriage." The Hunter plastered a beaming smile on his face. "We've long heard of the beauty of the Spear of Khafra, and on this, what will soon be our tenth anniversary, it felt like the perfect excuse to make the journey."

He, Kiara, and Tarek had come up with this particular tale on their journey from Malandria. It made perfect sense for him and Kiara to pose as husband and wife, Tarek either as Kiara's nephew or younger brother, depending on what suited the situation best. The "renewing of vows" had been Kiara's idea, and Tarek had added the detail of the Spear of Khafra—a stone ledge that jutted sixty paces out over the Chasm of the Lost and offering peerless views. People from all around Einan journeyed to the Ghandian capital to the Spear. Some to offer prayers to their god, others to capture its beauty in paint or charcoal, others to hurl themselves into the canyon. Not exactly the most romantic destination on Einan, but it served their tale well enough.

"And your wife?" The Ghandian's eyes slid past the Hunter, alighting on Kiara's blanket-covered form. "She sleeps soundly."

The Hunter allowed a fraction of the worry twisting in his belly to show on his features. "Alas, the heat of the day has taken its toll on her. She suffered a spell of dizziness, so it was decided we stop and rest in the shade until the day cools."

"Ahh, a wise choice." The man nodded. "Crossing the Kgabu Plains can prove difficult for *alay-alagbara* unaccustomed to its ferocity."

Alay-alagbara. The Hunter had heard the word before—used by the villagers of Nkedi to refer to them—but didn't know its meaning.

"And what brings you so far from the main road, Hardwell of Praamis?" The Ghandian leaned on his saddlehorn and stared down at the Hunter with barely concealed suspicion.

"The Zamani Falls, of course!" The Hunter pretended wide-eyed ignorance. People rarely suspected treachery from the less-intelligent and naïve. "The stories fail to do it justice, truth be told." He shook his head sadly. "Though I was desperately hoping we would catch a glimpse of Indombe during our visit."

"Indombe?" The ebony-skinned man threw back his head and laughed, a jovial sound that resonated across the plains. "You believe such legends?"

50

"Legend?" The Hunter bristled. "Such a mighty creature cannot possibly be the stuff solely of stories. Surely it is real, otherwise, why would the story have traveled all the way to us in Praamis?"

In all honesty, he'd have reacted much the same two days earlier. He'd written the giant serpent off as nothing more than myth until seeing it with his own eyes.

"Perhaps, perhaps." The man's dismissive tone and wave made it clear how likely he believed it to be. With that same amused smile on his face, he turned to his companions and said a few words in Ghandian. That earned a laugh—no doubt at the Hunter's expense—from the three armed men.

"And you are?" Again, the Hunter feigned ignorance of the mockery aimed at him. "I have introduced myself and my wife, but you and your companions remain strangers."

"But of course." The Ghandian dipped his head. "I, Hardwell of Praamis, am called Gwala. These good men are Thrax—" At this, the Voramian nodded. "—Ahmoud—" The Vothmoti touched one knuckle casually to his forehead in the greeting of the city far to the north. "—and the aptly named Slant."

The Hunter raised an eyebrow; it was far from clear why that name was "apt" to describe the Drashi.

"My companions and I belong to the Vassalage Consortium," Gwala said, bestowing a beaming smile on the Hunter. "Perhaps you have heard of us on your journeys north?"

The Hunter shook his head. "I'm afraid the name means nothing to me."

"Interesting." Gwala shot Slant a look, and the Drashi grinned back.

That smile instantly explained the origin of the man's name. When he smiled, one corner of his lip pulled up, but the other remained frozen, as if the muscles were paralyzed. The lopsided expression was, indeed, slanted.

The Hunter was about to ask about the Vassalage Consortium when a sight behind the four riders stopped him cold. Over the hill, in the distance, the source of the dust cloud had come into view. Twenty more riders, each clearly armed, rode alongside a column of six wagons pulled by the long-horned raya cattle native to the Kgabu Plains and the southern extremities of what had once been the Empire of Ghandia.

But these were no ordinary wagons. Larger, sturdier, and longer than the average cart found in the south, these had large metal cages set upon their backs. And filling each of the cages were dozens, perhaps even *scores,* of figures with the same swarthy skin tones as Gwala.

Bitter bile rose in the Hunter's mouth. The Vassalage Consortium…were *slavers*.

Chapter Eleven

The practice of slavery had been abolished across the majority of Einan—at least officially. Most monarchs and rulers outwardly condemned the practice as inhuman. All the while, they bled their people dry with exorbitant taxes and kept them in line through overly stringent edicts that ensured their power to govern was preserved at all costs. Nevertheless, the poor unfortunates who cleaned their homes, tilled their lands, and worked their mines were given titles like "serfs" and "indentured servants", all in the name of maintaining the façade of sophistication and civility.

But nothing truly stopped the slave trade. Even in cities that pretended to be hubs of culture and wealth, there was always the need for flesh to stock the brothels and whorehouses, cheap labor to save the nobility and landed gentry's precious fortunes, and chattel to be despised and abused by the jumped-up men and women who fancied themselves the world's "betters".

The Hunter had witnessed it with his own eyes in Voramis time and time again. His war with the Bloody Hand had begun in earnest the day he killed Captain Rothos of the *Medora*, a ship trafficking children and youths from all around Einan—and beyond. Runa and her Iron Sisters had been among those brought into Voramis to satiate the endless appetites of the Bloody Hand and their noble clientele.

There were few things the Hunter despised more than slavery, and the men who profited off the foul practice. Men who took advantage of the weak and vulnerable—more often than not, children and youths barely able to defend themselves from violent, trained brutes like the men before him—deserved the cruelest deaths he could contrive. He'd repaid the Fifth of the Bloody Hand for his role in trafficking by stringing the man up by his own entrails. A fate that still felt too kind for all the misery the bastard had caused.

In Voramis, slavery had been practiced in secret, always under cover of darkness. But here, in the middle of the Kgabu Plains, the slavers operated in broad daylight, calling themselves the Vassalage Consortium—a filthy, tawdry name that could no more hide their true cruelty than whitewash could mask a sepulcher's stench.

The Hunter's eyes narrowed as he caught sight of the figures packed into the foremost wagon. Even through the haze of heat and dust kicked up by the hooves of raya and horses, the Hunter recognized the women weeping and clutching their children to their breasts. He did not know their names, but he knew their faces.

One, an aged woman with her snow-white hair pulled up into tight braids that clung to her sun-darkened scalp, had called them *alay-alagbara* and shaken her head as they rode through Nkedi. Another clung to the two young girls who had pursued their horses through the village's streets with laughter and shouts. Two more, daughter and mother, had offered them water at the well. Now, they appeared parched and on the verge of collapse. Blood stained their faces and the ripped vestiges of their once-colorful robes.

The Hunter's eyes darted to the next wagon, which held *more* of the Nkedi women. A third and fourth transported the young men and boys of the village. Not a single one of the captives, however, were the strong warriors who had silently watched them while sharpening their steel-tipped spears from beneath the shade of their thatched huts. Nor did the Hunter see the trio of toothless old men who had cackled when speaking of Indombe and the Zamani Basin, or the chieftain who had greeted them with terse words, a stern expression, and the admonishment to ride on without delay.

Nausea swirled in the Hunter's stomach, but it quickly turned to anger. His fists clenched at his sides, his spine going rigid, his jaw muscles clenching. So consumed he was by the sight of the wagons and the armed men riding escort that he only noticed Gwala when the Ghandian was nearly upon him.

The Hunter's eyes instantly darted to the man, but Gwala's expression remained friendly. Too friendly by far. He was a man of striking features, his cheekbones and chin chiseled as if by a master sculptor's hand from the finest onyx, and his smile set his dark brown eyes dancing with a humor that might have been jovial on anyone else, but which made him look even harder and sharper. His scent filled the Hunter's nostrils: citron, myrtle pepper, and iron.

The Hunter took an instinctive step backward, his eyes searching the man for the source of that foul stench. Gwala's curved sword and the metal spikes studding his vest shone with the brilliance of steel, and he wore no other hint of metal the Hunter could see.

"Be at peace." Gwala raised both hands. "I intend you no harm."

The Hunter found that statement impossible to believe. The wagons filled with the Nkedi—and other prisoners from origins unknown—belied the Ghandian's words.

Yet his attention was drawn to the glove on Gwala's left hand. A strange affectation, a single glove of black leather that covered his hand to the forearm. A hand, the Hunter saw, that did not move even when Gwala raised it, and which had an unnatural stiffness to it.

This, then, had to be the source of the iron stink.

Gwala seemed to notice his gaze lingering and gave the Hunter a grin and a shrug. "Hazards of a hard life." He lowered his hand, and his eyes slid past the Hunter toward where Kiara lay. "Just as it seems the hazards of the road have left your companion unwell. Allow me to offer some water." He turned and barked to one of the slavers riding past. "Djineza, water!"

The rider who broke from the column was a diminutive woman, short enough the Hunter guessed she'd barely reach his shoulder. Her skin and facial features had the cast of a Shalandran, complete with the thick rings of *kohl* around her eyes and the heavy paints on her lips favored by women of the southern city. She looked as if she'd only just passed her teenage years, but there was something dangerous about her. Perhaps it was the thick black lines painted down her cheeks and chin in imitation of Gwala's scars, or the way even Ahmoud and Thrax eyed her warily and moved their horses away from hers. She alone wore no greatknife. Instead, strapped beside her saddle was a wrapped bundle the Hunter suspected contained a sword—one large enough to rival even those wielded by the Cambionari.

Her choice of weapon was as much a curiosity as her presence and her unique scent—a mixture of rose, pistachio, chestnut, and something akin to steel yet like no steel the Hunter had encountered—but he had no desire to consider her further. Nor accept Gwala's offer of water. He wanted *nothing* from any slaver.

"That won't be necessary." The Hunter cursed himself; in his loathing of these men, he'd responded too quickly, his tone too harsh. Such a reaction was sure to arouse the man's

53

suspicions. He hurried to add, "What I mean is, she's already had water, and it's better she sleeps until such a time as we're prepared to resume our journey."

Djineza held the waterskin casually, looking between the Hunter and Gwala as if awaiting some manner of signal.

Gwala raised an eyebrow, and the corners of his mouth quivered—in a smile or frown, the Hunter couldn't tell. But he merely inclined his head. "Of course. She is your wife, after all."

Something about the way the man said it sent a chill down the Hunter's spine. There had been no implication of threat, yet the Hunter had no doubt that this Vassalage Consortium would have reacted to his presence far differently had he been unarmed and a goatherder alone on the empty plains.

Even now, he sensed the four riders around Gwala eyeing him, sizing him up. The wagons were rumbling closer and would draw abreast of the umbrella thorn acacia in a matter of minutes. Surely all the armed men riding in the column sufficed to subdue and take him captive. He could all but see the Drashi, Slant, running calculations on how high a price the Hunter would fetch on the slaver's block.

How the Hunter wished the men would be foolish enough to try something! If they forced his hand, he would kill every Keeper-damned one of them without hesitation. Tarek could watch over Kiara while he fed these slaving pissants their own entrails.

To his dismay, Gwala merely inclined his head and smiled broader. "We will keep you from your wife's side no longer, Hardwell of Praamis." He touched the first fingers of his good right hand to his left cheek and slid them down to the tip of his chin, then repeated the gesture again on his right cheek. "May *Nuru Iwu* see you safely to Khafra."

The Hunter bowed his head. "Swordsman guide your journey likewise." He had no idea who or what *Nuru Iwu* was, and the last thing he wanted was for this man and his slaver companions to arrive at their destination—he'd much rather they ended up as food for a pride of Kgabu lions. But he had begun the charade as a hapless if amiable traveler, and so said the words for the sake of maintaining his façade.

With that, Gwala turned his back on the Hunter. The Ghandian emitted a loud clicking sound, and his horse responded by trotting toward its master. Gwala swung smoothly up into his saddle with the grace of a man born to ride. Once settled, he turned his horse away and, without a second glance for the Hunter, set off down the trail. Djineza fell in behind Gwala, no more interested in the Hunter than the man she followed. Thrax, Ahmoud, and Slant all eyed the Hunter as they rode past, but their leader was so supremely confident that he didn't look back once. As if the Hunter and his sleeping wife were now beneath his notice.

The Hunter returned to his place at Kiara's side, his stomach in knots and heart in his throat. Yet it was not fear that twisted in his belly as he watched the twenty armored riders approach. Their steel greatknives posed little threat to him. No, he felt only disgust and bone-deep loathing for these men who had taken captive the peaceful people of Nkedi. Those fishermen, hunters, and cultivators had been ripped from their homes and now were being transported like chattel to the slaver's block.

Sorrow welled in the Hunter's heart as he watched the wagons rumble past. Through the dust and haze, he saw the bloodied, battered faces, the hollow-eyed stares, the tear-soaked cheeks, the terror etched into the features of children who had only days before known a lifetime of peace and joy. Hunger, fear, thirst, and suffering would consume the rest of their days. Their lives would be doubtless short and filled with pain. Soon, they would know only the sting of the whip and the endless horror of the prison to which they had been condemned through no crime of their own.

Such was the true cruelty of slavery. Always the innocent and weak suffered, and the *true* criminals, the monsters like Gwala and his companions, profited off their torment.

It took all the Hunter's self-control to remain seated when he wanted nothing more than to rise and butcher the slavers. Had Kiara been on her feet, he might have risked it. But he couldn't take the chance that one of the armed men survived his assault long enough to kill her where she lay. Still, his guilt grew with every whimper and sniffle that reached his ears, every pair of desperate, tear-filled eyes that met his.

In that moment, he vowed to himself that he *would* make these men pay for what they'd done. The Vassalage Consortium had just made an enemy of the Hunter of Voramis. And by the Watcher in the Dark, god of justice, he would return upon them the anguish they caused the people of Nkedi a hundredfold.

His jaw muscles remained tight and his fists clenched until long after the wagons rumbled past. He did not take his eyes off the column until they vanished from sight and only the cloud of dust rising from the wagon wheels and horses' hooves remained.

Only then did Tarek emerge from the long grass where he'd been hiding. His face revealed his thoughts plain, and they mirrored the Hunter's own. The young Elivasti spat in disgust and muttered under his breath words the Hunter did not understand. Curses in the tongue of the Hrandari plainsmen, or perhaps even the tongue of the Serenii.

The Elivasti had suffered under the Warmaster and the Sage for decades, possibly even *generations*. Though he was young, Tarek, like all his people, knew the sting of the slaver's whip keenly.

The Hunter met the young man's eyes. "Their time will come," he said, his voice hard.

Tarek's crisp nod spoke volumes. With that simple gesture alone, the Hunter knew without a shred of doubt that when he moved against the Vassalage Consortium, the young man would be at his side.

Chapter Twelve

A tense silence hung over the Kgabu Plains in the wake of the slavers' departure. Save for the distant cry of birds or the whisper of the wind in the umbrella thorn acacia's widespread branches, nothing disturbed the eerie stillness. The sun steadily progressed toward the western horizon, the shadows relentless in their conquest of the sky, until finally darkness settled like a blanket over the plains.

And still Kiara did not wake. She slept lightly, chest rising and falling in shallow rhythm, sweat pricking on her brow. But even when the Hunter attempted to rouse her to pour some water down her throat, she could not keep her eyes open long. Her skin had begun to grow hot—from the searing sun and oppressive humidity, the Hunter hoped.

Tarek returned from his hunt shortly after dark, empty-handed, his expression grim. The Hunter made no mention of the youth's failure to catch game, but simply reached into his pack for his trail rations. Tarek accepted the food with a nod and finished the stringy salt deer in a few bites. After finishing the last of the tepid water from his canteen, he moved to kneel beside Kiara and examined her condition.

The Hunter's stomach twisted in knots at the sight of the frown forming on Tarek's lips. "That bad?"

"I don't know," Tarek said, though a little *too* quickly. He pressed a hand to Kiara's forehead, counted her heartbeats, listened to the rhythm of her breathing. "She pushed herself too hard, no doubt about it. Either it's exhaustion or..." He shook his head. "We'll know before too long."

The Hunter swallowed hard, fighting down the worry rising within him. "We rest here, then, and continue when she's strong enough to ride. I'll take the first watch." For all his fatigue, he doubted he could bring himself to rest until he knew for certain Kiara would pull through.

Tarek made no argument. He merely bundled himself up into his cloak, lay on the grass beneath the shade of the umbrella acacia thorn, and fell asleep in a matter of minutes. The Hunter envied that. He'd always been a restless sleeper, his dreams tormented, his nights haunted by the faces of his victims. After Enarium, he'd found a measure of peace, consoled by Kiara's presence at his side and the knowledge that he killed for a purpose beyond simply silencing the voices in his head. But since leaving for Praamis, the old, familiar disquiet had returned.

And why wouldn't it? For the three years following his return to Voramis, he'd existed within a strange cocoon of peace. The cruelties of the world around him had never touched him, never invaded the oasis of peace he'd created with Kiara, Hailen, and Evren. He'd largely managed to put aside concerns of demons, Serenii, and world-devouring beings of chaos in his focus on the two young boys he'd taken under his wing.

But all that had changed. He could *never* go back to that impossible state of serenity. It had been nothing more than a temporary reprieve from the harsh reality of his life.

Once again, a whirlwind of turmoil swirled around him. He felt like a man swept up in a great tidal wave, tossed about by forces far beyond his control. So much had happened since the day he rode out of Voramis' gates on his journey to Praamis.

His clash with the Night Guild. The capture of Lord Chasteyn. Meeting Sir Sigmund, Sir Georges, Sir Benoit, and the knight apprentices. The journey to Malandria with Father Reverentus. The attack by the Order of Mithridas. Their clash with Lord Apus. The discovery of the Monolith's secrets. His communion with Kharna. His fateful meeting with Jaia—which had ended in Father Reverentus' death.

He grimaced as the memory played again through his mind, as it had a thousand times since that day. Every time, he felt the sharp bite of steel as Soulhunger pierced the old priest's chest, saw the priest fighting against the dagger's power before ultimately choosing to give in and sacrifice his life for Kharna, heard the scream of anguish and agony. He could not forget that day—any more than he could forget whose hand struck the death blow.

Jaia had killed Father Reverentus. Almost casually, as if the priest's life meant no more to her than a cockroach squashed beneath her heel. That look on her face…so cold and hard, it reminded him of himself the night he pinned Captain Rothos to the *Medora's* mainmast with his own sword. The look of a dispassionate killer. A butcher. A *monster.*

What had happened to her to make her thus? What great sufferings had transformed her from the child Taiana loved more than anything else in the world—more even than *him*—to a woman who could kill a priest so readily in cold blood?

Her final words to him echoed through his mind. "Until we meet again, Hunter." There had been so much scorn in those words, in her smile, as if she'd *delighted* in his misery.

He didn't understand anything about that encounter. Where she'd come from, how she'd found her way into the Monolith, how she'd arrived at *precisely* the moment when he was present—none of it. It made no more sense than why she'd want Father Reverentus dead.

No, that wasn't fully true. He *could* think of a reason, an answer that made sense. He simply didn't want to. Didn't want to believe that she'd been watching him, had waited until precisely that moment to make her move. That she'd known exactly how killing the old priest with *his* dagger would look.

Kiara had told him they'd arrived and found the way into the Monolith open. The Hunter had turned that over and over in his mind. *If Jaia opened it, why not close it?* The question had burned in his mind. She couldn't want the power of the Serenii falling into just *anyone's* hands. Whatever she had done, she'd activated the Serenii tower. So why not seal the way behind her?

Because Jaia had made certain Sir Sigmund and the others could follow her into the bowels of the Serenii structure and come upon the corpses of the slain Father Reverentus and Sir Benoit.

He had no desire to believe that Jaia was actively working *against* him. That the daughter he'd sworn to find was now his enemy—an enemy who had turned the Cambionari knight who had been his ally only hours earlier into the bitterest of foes. For what reason, and to what end, the Hunter had no idea. She had vanished before he'd had the chance to speak a single word to her. And in her wake, left only sorrow, grief, and bewilderment.

The Hunter had told Kiara of what transpired but hadn't found the strength to speak of the feelings now roiling within him. Words had failed him every time. And so, he'd done the only thing he could.

Reaching into his pack, he drew out the small roll of vellum and charcoal writing stick he'd procured in Drash. He unrolled the parchment and stared down at the crude lines etched upon its surface. A pathetic attempt to put down what he remembered of Jaia's face. He was no artist, he knew. His skill with a blade exceeded that of any chirurgeon alive, yet when it came to wielding a tool to *create* instead of destroy, he felt as clumsy as a toddling infant.

Still, he *had* to try. Her face—so consumed by scorn, so cold and callous—had been irrevocably burned into his mind. But he could not track her down alone. He needed help, Graeme's help and that of the Hidden Circle, and so needed an image that could be used to identify her wherever she had vanished to after leaving him in the Monolith.

The strokes of his charcoal stick felt crude, his fingers thick and stiff, but the Hunter drew each line with care. Even if he went through a dozen such rolls—as many as he carried in his saddlebag—he'd repeat the effort until he got it just right.

Heat stung in the backs of his eyes, his throat grew thick, and his heart thudded against his ribs. Every time he saw Jaia's face, the memory of Taiana returned, too. How alike they looked, mother and daughter. The same arrow-straight hair, black as a raven's feathers. The same well-muscled leanness of their build. The same midnight black eyes that marked her as Bucelarii—*his* daughter, as well as Taiana's.

He relived the moment Taiana had nearly collapsed before the Chamber of Sustenance in which Jaia had been imprisoned by the Warmaster centuries earlier. Felt the agony and despair radiating off his wife, followed by the hope and relief upon realizing Jaia was still alive. What would Taiana say now if she saw their daughter? Would she feel as torn as the Hunter did, trapped between the love of a parent for their child and the abhorrence at her actions?

"Hun...ter?" A weak whisper pierced the gloom filling the Hunter's mind, snapped him from his concentration on his work. His head whipped up and around toward Kiara. Her eyes had halfway opened and fixed on him. Her lips moved but no sound came out.

The Hunter dropped the charcoal stick and vellum onto his pack and turned toward her. "I'm here, Kiara. I'm here." He moved to kneel over her, lowered his ear to hear her faint words.

"Thir...sty."

"Of course!" The Hunter reached for his canteen where he'd left it beside his pack after swallowing his dry rations, removed the lid, and tipped it up to her lips. "Drink."

She managed a couple of mouthfuls, but a cough seized her, spraying half the water across the Hunter's hands and shirt. He paid it no heed. Instead, he poured a smaller trickle into her mouth, barely a few drops at a time.

Kiara took a few more swallows then shook her head. "Enough." Her voice, though weak, had grown audibly stronger. It had lost its parched croak and rose above a feeble murmur. Her eyes opened all the way and she stared up into his face. "How bad...is it?"

"Not bad at all," the Hunter said, forcing a smile.

"Liar." Kiara scowled at him.

"Really," the Hunter insisted. "Pretty sure you just overexerted yourself riding, so we decided to stay here a little longer, give you time to rest up. Come dawn, we'll push on for a few hours."

Kiara's dark eyes searched his face. "Tell me...the truth."

"I am." The Hunter squeezed her hand tightly. "I know how stubborn you are. You won't let a pesky wound like this stop you from getting back on your feet." He chuckled. "Someone's got to order me around."

A smile cracked Kiara's face. "Damned right!"

She drew in a deep breath, let it out in a long gasp, then inhaled again. No pain marred her features, which the Hunter took as a good sign. He watched her, attuned to every miniscule expression, every twitch of her mouth. Anything to indicate whether she had begun recovering or worsening. He couldn't stand to see her so weak; she was among the strongest people he knew, and he'd need her strength for what lay ahead.

"I had to, you know?"

Kiara's words caught the Hunter by surprise. "Had to?" He frowned. "Had to what?"

"Come down…and help Tarek." Kiara's jaw muscles worked, her eyes drilling into his. "I had to."

The Hunter's eyebrows shot up. How could she have possibly known the question of "why" had echoed in his head a hundred times since the previous night?

"Kiara—" he began. They could speak on the matter once she had regained her strength.

"No, listen to me." She reached a hand up and pressed a finger to his lips. "I know you, Hunter. I know that you threw yourself into danger without thinking because somewhere, deep down, you believed that helping Tarek was the right thing to do." Her voice grew strong, confident, the weakness of her condition receding before the force of her certainty. "You leap into action knowing you can survive. But the rest of us have to think before we act. Have to consider all the consequences of our actions, knowing we could die."

"And you did that?" The Hunter heard the bitter edge and bite of fury to his voice. "You thought, 'Oh, that's a snake large enough to swallow an entire village whole, just the sort of thing I should get *closer* to rather than run away!'"

He hadn't realized how angry he was—not at Tarek, for the young man had been bewitched by Indombe's magic, but at *her*. The irony wasn't lost on him; she'd merely done exactly as he had. But she had no Bucelarii healing to keep her from the Long Keeper's arms.

"Watcher take it, Kiara," the Hunter growled, "don't you dare try to tell me that wasn't a bloody stupid thing to do!"

"It might have been stupid, but it was still *right*." The Hunter started to retort, but Kiara spoke over him. "Hailen deserves to meet his brother."

Whatever the Hunter had been about to say died on his lips. Trust her to think of the *one* argument that he couldn't refute. She'd made the choice not out of instinct as he had, out of self-preservation as he wished she would, or even out of some moralistic impulse that compelled her to do what was "right". She'd done it out of her love for Hailen. Had been willing to risk her own life to give the boy she'd come to think of as her own a chance at some measure of happiness she knew she couldn't provide.

"I know you worry." She dug her fingers into his beard, toyed with the long, coarse hair on his cheek. "And I love you for it."

The Hunter allowed her to pull his face down to hers and planted a soft, tender kiss on her lips. When he broke off, she smiled up at him.

"Now, you and your worries leave me alone." She playfully pushed him away. "I've got to get more beauty sleep if we're to be off at dawn."

The Hunter grinned. "So commanding." He clucked his tongue scornfully. "I take it back. I'd much rather have you lying around all day than trying to order me around."

Kiara muttered a reply, but it was too faint for the Hunter to hear. Closing her eyes, she turned her head to the side and buried her face once more in the blankets. Within seconds, the faint sound of snoring echoed through the still night.

The Hunter's smile grew, and a warm glow suffused the core of his being. She'd not only begun regaining her natural domineering imperiousness, but her physical fortitude, too. Her push had been surprisingly strong.

Relief flooded him, and it felt as if a weight lifted off his shoulders as he settled back against the trunk of the umbrella thorn acacia. *She's on the mend,* he told himself, his spirits soaring. *She'll be back in fighting shape in no time.*

Chapter Thirteen

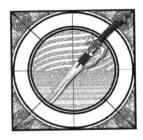

Midnight came and went, and still Kiara slept. The Hunter distracted himself from his worries for her wellbeing by bending his attention to the tasks of keeping watch on their surroundings while also working on his sketch of Jaia. The former proved a simple task; save for the distant growl of a plainswolf or the chirruping warble of nightjars, the night was calm and quiet. The latter, however, troubled him. Try as he might, he could not command his fingers to illustrate the image of Jaia burned into his mind's eye. His efforts yielded only the crudest of drawings. Her features were all wrong, the proportions of her face utterly imbalanced. No way he could truly capture her as he remembered her from their encounter.

He wanted to abandon the effort—to blame the poor moonlight for his lack of success rather than admit any dearth of skill—but his innate stubbornness won out over his irritation. Growling low in his throat, he set aside yet *another* ruined parchment and pulled out a fresh one from his saddlebags. He had just two left, and he'd used more than half the charcoal stick, leaving a stub barely long enough to grip.

The Hunter set parchment and charcoal onto his lap and leaned back against the tree. Closing his eyes, he massaged his cramping right hand with his left and focused on taking long, deep breaths. Fatigue hung on his body like leaden weights, bowing his shoulders and filling his head with cotton. Yet he refused to cede this battle. He would not give up until he had it *just* right. He needed that sketch of Jaia to pass off to the Hidden Circle contact he planned to meet in Khafra. That meant he had no more than a day or two to finish it.

The sound of rustling fabric and crackling grass snapped his eyelids open. But it wasn't Kiara awakening from deep sleep. Tarek rose from where he lay to his feet in a single graceful movement, unfurling his cloak from around him and turning toward the Hunter.

"My watch." He spoke quietly, careful his voice didn't travel across the flat, quiet plains.

The Hunter answered with a grunt and nod. He was in no mood to sleep, but handing off the duty of watching for dangers in the night meant he could focus fully on the art. While Tarek settled on an exposed root of the thick-trunked tree that served as their shelter, the Hunter set to work on yet another attempt to depict Jaia.

Within the first few lines, he knew he'd already gotten it wrong. The nose was unnaturally straight and the shape of the eyes inhuman verging on monstrous. He cursed inwardly and struggled to swallow the frustration swelling within him.

How in the fiery hell is this so hard? He fought the urge to close his fist around the charcoal stick that refused to heed his commands. *The artist in Voramis made it look so easy.*

"What is that?" Tarek's voice drifted over to him.

The Hunter turned, found the young man regarding him with eager curiosity.

Tarek leaned closer, as if trying to get a better look at the image on the Hunter's parchment. "Are you drawing Indombe?"

The Hunter scowled, both at the young man and his artistic failure. "It's supposed to be a woman."

"Oh?" Tarek's gaze darted to Kiara. "Something for her?"

The Hunter shook his head. "It's…" He found himself reluctant to say the words "my daughter". Instead, he settled for, "A woman I met not long ago. Someone important."

"Important." Tarek echoed the word with a deadpan expression. "Important, how?"

The Hunter's eyes narrowed. "Don't the Elivasti teach their children to mind their own pissing business?" His retort came out sharper than he'd intended.

"They do." Tarek's scruff-covered face hardened and his spine went rigid. "They do, indeed."

He turned away from the Hunter, fixing his attention on the surrounding darkness.

The Hunter cursed himself. He'd responded harshly to the young man's harmless interest, his temper shortened by his artistic inadequacies. Drawing in another breath and tamping down his irritation, he attempted to remedy his exasperated retort.

"She's someone important to me," he said quietly. "To both of us. Someone I haven't seen in a long time."

Tarek sat stiff and unmoving, back squarely turned on the Hunter.

The Hunter sighed inwardly. He'd earned that response, the way he'd gone off on the Elivasti.

Once, he would have been perfectly content to let the young man stew in his silence, never caring what hurt his words caused. But the Hunter wasn't that same callous bastard. The years with Kiara, Hailen, and Evren had changed him, in more ways than one.

Tarek's reaction was familiar; he'd encountered it on those occasions when he'd unleashed his temper on Hailen. The boy had withdrawn into himself, gone quiet, and it had taken days—or Kiara's gentle concern—to draw him out once more. And the Hunter had wanted to draw Hailen out. He'd actually *apologized* in an effort to make amends with the boy he'd grown to love. The gentle, caring, empathetic, sensitive boy who was quickly growing into a man—one who might end up much like the half-brother who now sat mere paces away from the Hunter.

Though it went against his nature, he'd tried with Hailen and Evren. He supposed he ought to try with Tarek, too. If the young man was to accompany them to Ghandia—and face whatever awaited them there—it made more sense to keep the peace between them.

"I'm sorry," he said. The words tasted bitter in his mouth, but he still said them. Meant them, too. "I'm not accustomed to being terrible at things. I had sort of hoped that in all my past lives, during the thousands of years I've spent alive, at least one of me would have been an artist." He hefted the parchment aloft. "Turns out that's not the case."

Still, Tarek said nothing. The Hunter could almost feel the sullen anger radiating off Tarek in tangible waves. For all his skill and warrior's confidence, he was still young, his skin not yet fully thickened by the hardships of a long life. And no one of *any* age enjoyed being spoken to the way the Hunter had—

Tarek's voice pierced the fraught silence. "Not easy, art." He shook his head. "You can spend years practicing, and still you'll never truly be good." Only now did he turn to look at the Hunter. His expression remained tight, but the anger was visibly fading from his face. "May I see them?"

The Hunter hesitated. The last thing he wanted was for *anyone* to glimpse his terrible handiwork. He'd kept it a secret even from Kiara. Yet he knew that for the sake of mending the damage his harsh words had done, only one course of action lay open to him.

"Here." Before he could reconsider, he thrust the parchment toward Tarek. The rest of them, too, including the truly terrible sketches that appeared like some crude cave painting or the drawings of an Illusionist-touched madman.

Tarek took the parchments and considered them with a curious eye. His expression grew decidedly neutral. "Not bad," he said, in a tone that belied the words. One of the Hunter's drawings actually earned a grimace, albeit a faint one.

Heat flushed in the Hunter's cheeks, his face burning hot. He was glad for the darkness to cover his chagrin. He couldn't believe he'd allowed the young man to see his failures. He opened his mouth to mutter some excuse—blaming the poor moonlight, the quality of the charcoal stick, even the parchment—but Tarek spoke first.

"Can I try?"

The young man's words caught the Hunter by surprise.

Tarek looked up from the parchments, fixing the Hunter with a look midway between eager desire and a youth's appeal for permission. "Kanna always insisted I sketch out the leaves, flowers, and stems of every plant she showed me. Said that was the only way a clod-headed fool would learn to tell poison hemlock apart from wild parsnip."

The Hunter chuckled. "That does sound like her." The woman had been possessed of a barbed tongue sharper than even Master Eldor's watered steel sword.

A faint grin appeared on Tarek's face. "And that was on one of her *good* days." He brightened, shoulders lifting a fraction. "Master Eldor once told me she could scold a mountain into a canyon and cuss the hard off a rock."

The Hunter's smile broadened. He'd seen the subtle interplay between the First Blade of the Elivasti and the old herbalist; that had doubtless been spoken out of his affection for the woman. If anyone could weather her scorn, it would have been Master Eldor. The Hunter could only hope that they had found each other in the Long Keeper's arms or whatever afterlife or paradise the Elivasti believed awaited them.

"She was hard, but I think I became better for it." Tarek continued, the words pouring from him as if some invisible floodgate had been opened and the pressure building within him finally released. "Because of her, I learned as much as I did about plants and herbs and remedies. It's why Itan said he chose me to ride with him even though I was one of the youngest to undergo the Expurgation. He wanted someone who could do more than just sit a horse or swing a sword. He wanted someone who could think and use their head—even if I was too young to do it at the time, he'd mold me into the sort of man who would."

The Hunter nodded. "Seems like he did a fine job of it."

Tarek's blush was visible even in the pale moonlight, and he ducked his head too slow to hide the embarrassed smile that blossomed on his lips.

"As I was saying," he hurried on, "Kanna insisted I learn to draw, not just plants, but insects and animals, too. I found I enjoyed it enough to take it up outside of my lessons with her. I started drawing some of the others in the enclosure with me whenever Kanna brought me more supplies." He gave a self-deprecating shrug. "I think if you could describe this woman to me, I could try to draw her. It might not be any good. But it's worth a try, right?"

The Hunter saw the eagerness in the young man's expression, heard it in his tone. It reminded him of Evren's sidelong grin after the young Vothmoti landed a particularly clever punch, or as Hailen's excited countenance when explaining some new marvel or secret Father Reverentus had shared with him. It was an unconscious bid for approval or acknowledgement—a reminder of just how young Tarek really was.

"Absolutely." The Hunter handed over the charcoal stick. "I'll do my best to tell you what I remember, and between us, we might just come up with something halfway accurate."

Tarek beamed. "Let's do it."

The Hunter had never been good with words, but he tried to give Tarek a clear description. The arrow-straight, raven-black hair and dark eyes were easy enough. Her build, so akin to Taiana's, with lean musculature that spoke of a warrior's strength. He still didn't know what material had comprised her armor—it appeared like no metal or leather he'd encountered—but describing her cloak and the Legion-issue short sword and fencing blade she'd carried proved a simple matter.

Yet his tongue tied in knots when he attempted to convey the cold, hard scorn that had twisted her lips, the disdain in the look she'd fixed on him, the mockery that edged her final words to him before she vanished into the secret passage. Finally, he gave up the attempt.

"And that's all I can remember," he said lamely.

Tarek didn't even nod; his attention was fully fixed on the parchment. The charcoal stick flew in his hands, his strokes surprisingly confident and determined. His face had the same scrunched-up look that appeared on Hailen's whenever he wrestled with a particularly difficult problem or complex passage from one of Father Reverentus' books.

The Hunter let the young man concentrate on his work and turned his attention to Kiara. She hadn't stirred once since falling asleep hours earlier.

He touched a hand to her forehead. Warm, certainly. Perhaps even hot. The night hadn't fully cooled, though, so he banished the worries from his mind. As long as she slept peacefully, she had a chance of awakening stronger and ready for at least a few hours of travel.

"Finished!" Tarek's proclamation echoed across the plains.

The Hunter turned back to find the young man holding up the parchment, a triumphant grin on his face.

"Tell me what you think," Tarek said, handing him the picture.

The Hunter took the parchment and studied it. "Keeper's teeth!" He blinked, stunned by the young man's skill. He looked up, found Tarek staring at him with an expression of mingled worry, anticipation, and hope. "Tarek, this is bloody magnificent!"

A massive smile sprang to Tarek's lips, spreading so wide his face looked ready to split in half. "You think so?"

The Hunter looked down at the parchment. The young Elivasti had gotten the details almost perfectly right. Any error lay in *his* descriptions, or the lack of thereof, not in Tarek's skill. "Absolutely." He lifted his head. "I've seen the works of some of the finest artists in Voramis, Praamis, and all of Einan, and I can say without a doubt, you've got a talent."

Tarek's expression grew bashful yet his face shone with a delighted glow. "I've wanted to draw more, but haven't had the time over the last few years. It's not exactly the sort of skill that comes in handy when riding with Soaring Hawk Clan."

The Hunter shook the parchment at him. "It's a skill you'd damned well better pursue as long as you're traveling with us. I swear, when we reach Khafra, I'll buy every scrap of parchment and every charcoal stick I can find. You keep this up, and I have no doubt that within a few years, your works will be good enough to grace the halls of any nobleman or king in the south of Einan."

Tarek appeared ready to explode with satisfaction at the Hunter's words. His face glowed so brightly it rivaled the moon and stars shining in the night sky. So overcome was he that he could not respond, merely stared down at the charcoal stick, which he turned over and over in his hands.

The howl of a nearby plainswolf shattered the fragile moment. The Hunter and Tarek both sprang to their feet, hands on the hilts of their weapons. They scanned the darkness in search of the predators, but none appeared. The only indication that the creature had approached at all was a more-distant call echoing a full minute later.

The Hunter let out a low breath and removed his hand from his hilt. Tarek did likewise, settling back onto the exposed root that had served as his seat.

"I've got watch," the young man told the Hunter. "You get some rest. I'll wake you before dawn, and with luck, Kiara will be strong enough for us to cover a few miles before the day gets too hot."

The Hunter nodded. "Good idea." He was far from tired, yet the idea of closing his eyes and letting his mind wander for a few hours now came as a welcome relief from the worry and tension of the last day.

Without a word, he settled once more into place at Kiara's side and wrapped his cloak around himself. When he leaned his head back against the tree, his eyelids quickly fell shut of their own accord, fatigue finally overcoming him. He gave in to the inexorable tug of sleep that crawled over him with irresistible determination. He needed rest. Needed to let go of the concerns and guilt that dogged him. Even for just a few short hours. When tomorrow came—

"Hunter!"

The Hunter's eyes snapped open, and he found himself staring up into Tarek's face. He was about to shout at the young man for disturbing him when he'd *just* relaxed, but stopped at the sight of the first rays of dawn shining over the eastern horizon. He'd actually fallen asleep and remained sleeping for hours, not seconds, as it felt.

His mind, still trapped in slumber, took a moment to register the worried look on Tarek's face. When finally it did, he jerked upright.

"What?" His hand reached for his sword.

"It's Kiara." Worry darkened the young man's expression. "She...she's dying, Hunter!"

Chapter Fourteen

Any lingering traces of sleep evaporated like the morning mist, and the Hunter was instantly awake. He was on his knees at Kiara's side a moment later. Even without touching her forehead, he could feel the heat of fever radiating off her. The early morning light accentuated the pallor of her cheeks and the sweat rolling in sheets down her face.

Fiery hell! The Hunter stared down at Kiara, paralyzed by uncertainty. How had she gotten so bad in a matter of hours? Worse, what could he possibly do to help her?

"The fever hasn't been on her long," Tarek was saying, though his voice sounded distant through the pounding of the blood rushing in the Hunter's ears. "But she's fading fast. The rot is settling deeper and spreading to her organs. She needs that *ephrade*, now!"

The Hunter's head snapped up toward the young man. "Khafra's still a day's ride away. And there's no way she can get there in this condition."

Tarek's expression was solemn, his eyes dark with worry. "I know." He met the Hunter's gaze with his own. "Which means we need to get her as close to the city as we can before it's too late."

"What?" The Hunter recoiled. "Too late? No!" He shook his head violently. "No way I'm letting this be the end of her. Not a bloody chance!"

"Neither am I." Tarek's tone turned earnest. "One of us needs to ride for Khafra and procure the *ephrade*. The other one needs to tend to her and cover as much ground as possible."

The Hunter had no doubt as to which role he was better-suited. "I'll go." The look on the young Elivasti's face made it clear they'd both reached the same conclusion. "You get her as near the city as you can." He gripped Tarek's shoulder in an iron vise. "Stick to the main roads, and I'll find you. Just keep her alive!"

Tarek nodded. "I will, I swear it." His voice echoed the determination etched into every contour of his youthful face. "But hurry!"

The Hunter wasted no time. He sprang to his feet and whirled in a single smooth motion, raced toward the horses, and set about untying the knots securing Elivast's tether to the trunk of the umbrella thorn acacia tree.

"Take both horses!" Tarek called out from where he knelt at Kiara's side. "Two will get you there faster than one. And Nayaga can carry the two of us."

The Hunter didn't argue. Once finished saddling Elivast, he hurried to do likewise with Ash, then sprang onto the desert pony's back. Tarek was right; he'd have to ride both horses for all they—and he—were worth if he wanted to reach Khafra and finding the *ephrade* that would save Kiara's life.

He swung the horses' heads around, pointing them northeast toward the dirt trail up which the slavers' caravan had disappeared the previous night. He spared a single glance for Kiara—how pale her face, how frail she looked, shivering in her sweat-soaked blankets, it tore at his heart—but wrested his gaze away and steeled his heart.

"Keep her alive!" he shouted to Tarek as he dug his heels into Ash's flanks.

The young Elivasti's response, if he'd offered one, was drowned out by the clatter and clamor of the two horses springing into motion. Ash responded to the Hunter's urging with all his usual alacrity, muscles coiling and unleashing with the speed of a striking whip. The stocky desert pony went from a standstill to a gallop in the space of three heartbeats. Elivast was only a moment slower, but soon the three of them were charging through the scrubby bush, away from the umbrella thorn acacia tree and out into the brightening daylight of the Kgabu Plains.

The Hunter refused to look back. He already knew what he'd see; the image of Kiara's feverish face was burned into his mind. All his willpower bent to the task of riding with all the strength within his mighty limbs.

The city of Khafra lay roughly a day's ride to the northeast, but the Hunter determined to reach it far sooner. He'd push himself and the horses to within an inch of their lives if it meant he got to Kiara in time. In that moment, nothing else mattered to him.

The Kgabu Plains rushed past him in a blur of dull browns, greys, and yellows still shadowed by the early morning clouds. Spindly trees thrusting their widespread branches toward the heavens, scrubby bushes clinging to the arid soil, tall grasses swaying in the breeze—he saw it all and yet none of it. His nose brought him the scent of myriad wildlife: a pack of plainswolves, no doubt stalking the herd of antelope charging along a rising hill, foxes, long-horned oryx, and more. The smells were carried away by the wind and forgotten in a moment.

All he saw was the sinuous track carving a path northeast through the plains. His nostrils and mouth filled with the dust kicked up by his galloping horses, his ears ringing with the report of eight steel-shod hooves pounding against the rocky dirt trail. Every sinew and nerve in his body thrummed with the adrenaline-amplified fire of a man hell-bent on achieving the impossible.

Beneath him, Ash seemed to sense his urgency, his resolve. The stocky pony was bred to run, and run he did. The narrow track through the Kgabu Plains offered footing far more solid than the sand of the Advanat Desert. The horse's powerful musculature propelled its compact frame up the trail at speeds surpassing even the fleetest of Il Seytani's *Mhareb* or the shaggy steppe ponies of the Hrandari plainsmen.

The first rays of sun peered over the eastern horizon, blinding bright on the Hunter's right side, yet he merely squinted against the brilliance and rode on. His legs ached from the effort of clinging to Ash's saddle and pain shot up his spine with every jolting step. Yet he paid it no more heed than the sweat streaming down his back from the growing heat of the day or the relentless advance of thirst and hunger.

Soon, the sun rose higher and higher, until he could no longer see it overhead, bent low as he was over Ash's streaming mane. The heat worsened, growing unbearable, the brilliant plains sun searing through his dark cloak, threatening to suffocate him within his leather armor. His tunic grew sodden and clung to his aching body. Sweat poured down his face, stung his eyes, turned the dust on his face into mud.

The Hunter rode on, heedless of his mounting fatigue and the fire coursing through his exhausted muscles. He did not slow until he felt Ash tiring beneath him. Even then, he halted only long enough to give the horse a minute to recover his breath while he tottered on shaky, unsteady legs toward Elivast. The chestnut gelding had matched the desert pony's pace well enough, but without the Hunter's weight, hadn't drained his strength fully.

It took the Hunter three tries to spring onto Elivast's back—his knees buckled on the first attempt, and his head swam so violently on the second he lost his balance and ended up sprawled in the dirt of the road. Exhausted, caked in dust, he still clawed his way once more to his feet and mounted the chestnut gelding's back. Though every fiber of his being ached for rest, he dug his heels into Elivast's flanks, setting off once more at a run.

Hours passed in a blur of heat and haze and blinding sunlight and vague landscape. When the horses tired, he paused just long enough for them to rest, then mounted Ash to give Elivast a rest. His mind registered and catalogued every detail of the Kgabu Plains, but discarded everything not immediately threatening or important to the matter at hand. He recalled only the most nebulous minutia of his ride: the low-hanging branch of a *sterculia* tree that nearly swept him from Ash's back, the sharp-tipped rock the horse barely avoided, the shallow depression in the path that remained of a stream long ago dried up, the pack of spotted hyenas that yipped and cackled alongside him for a quarter-league before vanishing into the brush.

Hope surged within him as he caught sight of the main trade road to the east. To the south, a caravan of wagons covered with brightly colored canvas rolled northward, pulled by long-horned raya that filled the air with their deep-throated lowing. Headed in the opposite direction, a train of twenty camels hauling cargo on their humped backs lumbered at a steady pace down a steep hill—the last obstacle blocking his view of Khafra.

Of the slavers' convoy, the Hunter saw no sign. But even had he come upon Gwala and his companions, the Hunter would not have stopped. Nothing could deter him from procuring the means of Kiara's salvation.

As if sensing his elation, Ash poured on a fresh burst of speed. Elivast panted but gamely attempted to keep pace with the swifter desert pony. The Hunter knew he'd pushed them too hard—he owed both horses a long rest and all the sweet, juicy apples they could stomach—yet did not slow. Not when he was so close.

The Hunter thundered onto the broad, well-maintained trade highway, steering Ash hard to the north. The camels groaned a strident protest, but he rode past the line of towering, twin-humped beasts without paying them or their shouting, cursing drivers any heed. His eyes fixed on the flat peak of the hill ahead. Just a few hundred paces up that steep incline, and he would see it. His mad race across the Kgabu Plains would be almost over once he crested that rise.

Every muscle and bone in his body ached, his tongue was as dry and dusty as a Legionnaire's boot after a ten-league march, and though his clothing was sodden with sweat, he could feel the onset of dehydration. The horses, too, were on the verge of collapse. Ash had borne his weight for much of the trip, and the desert pony was lathered and snorting heavily. Even without a rider in the saddle, Elivast struggled to match Ash's pace as they raced up the hill. Yet somehow, impossibly, they continued on. Their stubbornness matched his, and for that, he loved them. They were giving him everything they had. Whether they understood why or merely sensed the urgency, the two horses heeded his commands to press on out of their devotion to him. Just as his devotion to Kiara impelled him along on this mad ride.

Up, up, up they rode. One step at a time, the three of them straining to labor on despite the crushing weight of fatigue, fighting the chains of exhaustion that grew inexorably heavier with every beat of their hearts. The top of the hill seemed impossibly far, seemed to grow farther away as the Hunter's vision swam. He reeled and swayed with such violence that only sheer determination kept him from falling. Yet somehow, he clung on. Fought through the fatigue and regained control of his senses.

His eyes cleared just as he crested the rise and rode onto the hill's flat top. Had he not already been gasping for air, the sight that spread out before him would have stolen the breath from his lungs. He couldn't help reining in Ash to take a moment to stare.

On the far side of the hill, the land descended into a verdant swath of grasslands and forests fed by the water of the Inyoni River, which dumped its contents off the edge of the cliffs and emptied in the Chasm of the Lost just to the west of Khafra. It looked like a glittering emerald nestled in a sea of dull yellow grain, an oasis amidst the arid sparsity of the Kgabu Plains.

But it was Khafra itself that held the Hunter spellbound. The first city ever built by human hands, so the histories told. Long ago, it had served as the seat of power of the mighty Ghandian Empire, Einan's first true empire, comprised of twenty kingdoms united under the rule of Zaqala Eusas, who marched at the head of an army eighty thousand strong.

For centuries, Ghandia had offered the only place in the continent's eastern hemisphere to cross the Chasm of the Lost. The city stood on the sole land bridge to span the northern and southern edges of the canyon that bisected Einan from the Endless Ocean in the west to the Hurab Sea far to the east. Until the construction of the Godsbridge two thousand years ago, it had served as the primary hub for the majority of the commerce that flowed around Einan. The wealth of Ghandia was once said to rival that of Aegeos itself.

Looking at Khafra from afar, the Hunter had little doubt of the claim's veracity. The city was a halcyon paradise—three leagues from east to west, two towering walls encircled countless thousands of sandstone homes, which stood nestled amidst a forest of towering stelae that dated back to the earliest days of Einan, after the War of Gods split the world asunder. The sprawling metropolis glittered like a mountain of gold that spanned the terrain for three leagues from east to west and extended half a league from the Chasm's southern edge.

The Hunter nearly wept in relief. He'd never seen anything so beautiful in all his life. Not only because of the sense of antiquity and timelessness the city radiated, even from far off. Relief washed over him like a cool breeze. He felt his spirits lift, his strength replenished.

"Come on," he urged, nudging Ash into a trot. With only a snort of protest, the desert pony took off down the hill. Elivast followed tiredly along behind. The Hunter couldn't blame the horses for their reluctance. He had pushed himself to the point of collapse and only realized it because he'd allowed himself to stop. Now, the simple act of setting off required a monumental effort, akin to rising to his feet with the weight of a mountain atop his shoulders.

Yet he had no choice. Khafra was still at least a two-hour ride away, likely more like three given how winded the horses were. He could afford no delay in his efforts to find the *ephrade* and return with it to Kiara.

Tarek's words had made one thing perfectly clear: the woman he loved was running out of time.

Chapter Fifteen

From afar, the city of Khafra had resembled a gleaming pile of gold. Yet as the Hunter drew nearer, its tarnish grew ever more evident.

The city walls, made of a brilliant, fiery yellow sandstone, had spent so many decades—perhaps even centuries—crumbling without repair that they would no more repel an invading army than a row of ripe wheat stalks. A few dust-covered moldering planks lying in the shadow of the wall were all that remained of the once-mighty city gates. The Hunter rode into Khafra unchallenged, not a single guard in sight.

The chaos beyond only served to accentuate the degree of decay that gripped Khafra. Mud and dirt clogged the rutted streets. A thick layer of fine ochre dust covered everything, kicked up by the stomping feet of playing children, the hooves of oxen, and the wheels of the wagons trundling through the messy disarray of ever-narrowing lanes that wended in a haphazard labyrinth deeper into the city. Patched stone walls, sagging thatched roofs, and doors hanging askew and ajar greeted the Hunter's gaze everywhere he turned.

What had once been the first great triumph of humankind now struggled in its final death throes.

The Ghandian Empire had dissolved nearly nineteen hundred years earlier, its political might waning as its primary source of power—revenue from the trade flowing through its gates—dwindled from a vast stream to a mere trickle. One by one, the tribes comprising the empire had split off, cutting off access to their resources. Now, all that remained of Ghandia was a mere shade of its former glory.

Indeed, the only thing keeping it from utter extinction was its location. The merchants traveling Einan's eastern hemisphere certainly *could* choose to spend a fortune traveling weeks out of their way to the Godsbridge, where they would pay the exorbitant toll charged by the Drashi Bridgekeepers for the privilege to cross the Chasm of the Lost. But for many, the land bridge in Ghandia was their best, cheapest, nearest option. Expediency alone staved off the kingdom's dying gasp.

As the Hunter rode through the former capital of the Ghandian Empire, he could see how glorious it had once been. The myriad stelae erected in every square and plaza of the city stared down like silent imperial sentinels. The images etched into their golden stone surfaces depicted scenes of war and conquest dating back thousands of years. Warriors locked in combat with men and great, impossible beasts—among them, the Hunter saw, a monstrous serpentine creature that could feasibly have been Indombe. Kings riding proud steeds. Emperors basking in the adoration of their subjects while fending off the attacks of their enemies. Brave deeds the subject of myths and legends brought to life through the ancient art.

The beauty lay not only in the age-old, either. The streets were a riot of color—every scrap of fabric visible had been dyed brilliant shades of red, orange, violet, blue, and green. Women wore loose-flowing handwoven dresses displaying intricate interplays of multi-hued threads, while the men wore more muted yet no less eye-catching variations on the complex patterns. Their bright garments stood in sharp contrast with their deeper skin tones, a diverse array of ebony, onyx, copper, umber, and *kaffe*-dark brown.

The interior of the city was as alive as the lands surrounding it, too. A system of elevated aqueducts delivered fresh water from the Inyoni River throughout city. Long lines of men, women, even children carrying buckets and clay jars were seemingly everywhere the Hunter looked. Some collected water for their cookpots—which emanated a sizzling mélange of spicy scents that delighted the Hunter's senses and set his stomach rumbling—while others tended to the lush gardens that seemed to fill every home. How odd those patches of verdant greenery looked against the backdrop of decay that permeated the crumbling city of stone.

The Hunter was struck by the sharp contrast within Khafra. The city itself was a model of decaying antiquity, a neglectful abandon he'd seen from the moment he first drew within eyeshot of the walls, no visible sense of order or any tangible reminder of the codices that had once governed the Ghandian Empire. Yet the *people* themselves still flourished, still lived and loved and found meaning in their families and professions.

His interest in the ancient city was tempered by the memory of Kiara's pale, sweat-soaked face. He spurred Ash to ride faster and forced his way through the dense crowds of colorfully dressed Ghandians swirling up the street toward a marketplace a few hundred paces to the east.

The Hunter called to mind the instructions he'd been given by Grytch, the apothecary and Hidden Circle member he'd visited during his stay in Drash. *Through the south gate, then due east until you hit the first market square,* she'd told him. *After that, turn north and look for the sign of The Blind Pig.*

One look at the marketplace told the Hunter he'd never reach his destination heading that way. He doubted even a trickle of water could find a path through the thick crush of people clogging the streets. Besides, he had no desire to deal with a parade of vendors and merchants attempting to hawk some goods he "simply couldn't live without" or refuse to purchase "the finest" of whatever particular item was offered for sale.

Confident he could find a way around the marketplace, he turned his horses into a narrow side street that led north, away from the main avenue. And came to regret that decision within a matter of minutes. He'd barely gone a dozen paces into the side street when it narrowed to barely more than the width of his hand where a stone building had been expanded close to its neighbor. He was forced to back Ash and Elivast out into the street once more and continue eastward.

His next attempt to bypass the marketplace proved marginally more successful. The muddy alley ran for a full twenty paces before splitting into three diverging paths. The one that led farther east ended in a lush garden with no way through, while the north-leading avenue simply terminated at the back of a stone wall. The west-headed lane led him on a winding route that *occasionally* circled eastward and to the north, but drew him ever farther from his destination.

He was about to give up the attempt and return to the main avenue to brave the marketplace when the narrow alley ended at a small circular plaza. A single towering stela dominated the heart of the open square, but set at its four corners were small stone statues no taller than the top of Ash's head. Unfortunately for whoever had been depicted thereupon, the effigies had suffered the ravages of time. One had been truncated at the neck, not so much as a trace of rubble remaining of its missing head. Two more had a head but were missing their arms. The final was nothing more than a pair of legs with nothing above it. No names or inscriptions remained, nothing to indicate who they may have been or what deeds had earned their being immortalized in stone.

Beyond the square, the Hunter spotted a smaller road that ran to the northeast. To his delight, he found it *didn't* lead to a dead end or a twisting maze. It seemed to travel fairly straight—surprising, given his journey through Khafra thus far.

As he rode, his eyes never stopped moving, roaming the shadows, open doors, and rooftops for any hint of threat. He had his hood pulled back and his weapons clearly visible as a warning sign to all that he was not a man to trifle with. Between the steel he carried and the absence of saddlebags, he doubted anyone would give him grief. He'd spent years enough walking the harsh streets of Voramis not to take that for granted. His wariness never lessened though he never got even the faintest whiff of danger.

The men and women he passed eyed him askance, though more curious than suspicious. In a city such as Khafra, traders and travelers were common fare, a source of interest and tales from the wider world. His lighter skin tone, leather armor, and his swords garnered him attention that once would have made him uncomfortable—well, *more* uncomfortable. Yet the curious looks often turned to friendly smiles and greetings in both the tongue of Ghandia and Einari.

The Hunter answered with polite nods and tight smiles of his own, but his attention was fixed on the way ahead and his search for The Blind Pig. To his relief, the road soon intersected with a broad avenue lined on either side by trees, with a row of hundreds of stelae running down its center. This *had* to be the way leading north from the marketplace—it was just as Grytch described it.

He scanned the road in search of the signpost that would lead him to the Hidden Circle contact. He spotted it a hundred paces up the avenue—it boldly proclaimed "The Blind Pig" in broad white letters, both in Einari and what the Hunter suspected was the written language of Ghandia. The three interlocking rings of the Hidden Circle at the bottom of the sign were unmistakable even from afar.

The Hunter's heart leaped. He clapped his heels to Ash's flanks and charged up the broad, tree-shaded, stelae-lined thoroughfare. He was forced to slow less than five heartbeats later when a column of wagons coming in the opposite direction congested the road. When he tried to navigate between the stelae to approach on the other side of the avenue, he found the way blocked by a crowd gathered around a trio of women playing instruments unfamiliar to the Hunter—a hand drum hanging from a strap over one's shoulder, a metal trumpet nearly as tall as the woman who played it, and what looked like an oversized lyre with ten strings. The jovial sound of their music would have lifted his spirit on any other occasion. Now, it only served to enhance his frustration, for he knew he could not navigate the crowd easily.

He was forced to pull Ash and Elivast to the side of the road and wait for the wagon column to pass. The raya cattle's glacial pace infuriated him, and it took all his willpower not to shout at the Drashi drivers herding them slowly along.

Finally, the way was clear, and the Hunter galloped up the avenue. He leaped from the saddle before The Blind Pig, wound Ash and Elivast's reins around the hitching post, and stalked through the open doorway into the building where he hoped to find the means to save Kiara's life.

The moment he entered, he was struck by *two* things.

First, the smell. He'd recognize the stink of fermenting grain anywhere, but this was unlike anything he'd encountered in the breweries, distilleries, and taverns elsewhere. The sour odor reminded him almost of decaying corpses mingled with a compost heap left unturned far too long. His stomach somersaulted and acid burned up the back of his throat at the assault on his delicate nostrils.

Yet all thoughts of the stink faded as the second detail registered in his mind. His eyes, accustomed to the brightness of the afternoon, took a moment to acclimate to The Blind Pig's dimness. When they finally did, he saw the ten armed men with drawn swords staring straight at him.

Chapter Sixteen

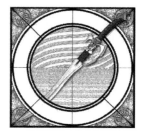

The Hunter took in the details of The Blind Pig's interior at a glance.

Four enormous copper tanks connected by an intricate network of pipes bearing valves, spigots, and levers dominated fully two-thirds of the vast chamber. Along the southern wall, row upon row of clay, porcelain, ceramic, wood, earthenware, and glass bottles sat upon stone shelves—some empty, some brimming with the brew that permeated the building with the yeasty scent of fermentation. A dozen wooden trestle tables and benches occupied the remainder of the space, making clear its use as a taproom to seat those who came to sample The Blind Pig's wares.

The tables and benches were utterly empty of patrons; the only people present stood clustered around the strange ornament that occupied the heart of the taproom. Ten men wearing steel-studded leather vests and holding naked swords pointed at the odd-looking fellow perched upon what appeared to be a grand throne fashioned from the multi-hued shards of broken bottles from his collection.

Grytch, the Hidden Circle alchemist in Drash, had spoken of her companion in Khafra as being "a quirky sort." That, the Hunter immediately saw, was an understatement. The man, Indigo, was dressed entirely in indigo-colored robes—either the source of his moniker, or a reflection of it—cut in the loose, flowing style common to Ghandia. Unlike the people of Ghandia, however, his skin was the color of fresh-driven snow, made even whiter by the broad streaks of indigo either painted or tattooed on his face, head, arms, legs, and chest.

As if that wasn't strange enough, he wore his ash-white hair in a single thick lock that jutted from the top of his head, held perfectly stiff and upright by some waxy substance that set it glistening in the light shining in through the square skylight set into the taproom's flat roof. He carried no weapons the Hunter could see, yet he regarded the ten armed men before him with an air of calm only encountered in the most confident warrior or maddest lunatic.

So bizarre was the alchemist that the Hunter barely noticed the men menacing him with swords. They, however, noticed him.

"Taproom's closed!" came the hard, gruff call.

The Hunter tore his gaze away from Indigo and regarded the speaker. The man was clearly a southerner—Praamian, most likely, given his sharper accent and the coarseness of his curly black hair and beard. Among the others surrounding the alchemist, the Hunter recognized two Drashi, an Odarian, one might have been from either Shalandra or Vothmot, and a Fehlan. The remainder were from Ghandia, though from which region or tribe, he could not tell. A mismatched outfit, yet united by steel-studded vests and curving knife-hilted swords the Hunter found familiar.

"This is Consortium business," said the Praamian, scowling at the Hunter. "Whoever you are, do yourself a favor and piss off."

"Consortium?" A smile tugged at the Hunter's lips. "As in, the *Vassalage* Consortium?"

The Praamian gave him a look that made it clear he suspected the Hunter of being thick in the head. "There any other?" His mouth twisted into a sneer. "And if you know what's good for you, you'll do as I said and Piss. Off!" He added menace to his words by taking a threatening step closer and bringing his sword swiveling around to point at the Hunter's chest. His scent—unwashed armpits, almonds, and boot rot—couldn't begin to compete with the foul-smelling breath wafting out of a mouth filled with rotting teeth.

The Hunter gave each of the ten men a closer look. Gwala wasn't among their number. Nor were Djineza, Slant, Thrax, or Ahmoud, or any of those who'd been riding alongside the wagons filled with the captive Nkedi villagers.

A pity, he thought, his smile widening. *But I suppose these will have to do.*

"You won't know this about me," he said in a calm, conversational tone, as if the Praamian held a bouquet of flowers rather than a sharp sword, "but I've made a terrible habit of never doing what others tell me is good for me."

He took a step toward the man, until the tip of the greatknife touched his chest.

"Here's the rub, though." The Hunter met the man's eyes levelly. "He's got something I need. By the looks of things, there's something you need of him, too. Best for all of us that you let me get what I'm after, then you can keep on with…" He waved his hand in a vague circular gesture. "…whatever manner of entertainment this is supposed to be. All you lads with your fine little *swords* out might not be my cup of wine, but if that's what you're into, who am I to judge?"

The Praamian's face went through an amusing transformation. First, astonishment that his threat hadn't served to terrify the Hunter, which transformed to scorn, then confusion a moment later. Finally, outrage as the Hunter's derisive barb sank home.

"Listen here, you goat-sucking prick!" the slaver snarled. He took a threatening step toward the Hunter. "When I say—"

The Hunter didn't even bother slapping the man's sword aside; he simply shattered the Praamian's teeth with a single punch. The slaver's head snapped back and his spine gave an audible *crack*. His body crumpled to the taproom's rush-strewn earthen floor in a sodden heap.

For a moment, the remaining nine Consortium men stood paralyzed by surprise and disbelief. All carried steel. Not so much as an iron cloak pin among them. Had this been any other encounter, the Hunter would have enjoyed baiting them, mocking them and drawing them into a fight he could enjoy. He'd take nine-on-one odds any day.

But the Hunter was in a hurry. Kiara needed that *ephrade* now. And so, instead of allowing his new enemies to recover from their astonishment to put up a fair fight, he drew his weapons and charged without delay.

His watered steel sword hacked through the Odarian's neck, sending his head flying in a spray of blood. The Hunter spun with the momentum of the swinging blade and drove Soulhunger into the Fehlan's temple. When he tore the dagger free, taking brains and bits of skull with it, he thrust it into the armored chest of a Ghandian. Razor-sharp steel punched through the studded vest like a red-hot knife through freshly fallen snow. Flesh parted, bones *snapped,* the dagger's tip tore through smooth heart muscle.

The dying man's scream of agony and terror resounded through the taproom. The gemstone set into Soulhunger's pommel flared bright, and power surged through the Hunter. His fatigue evaporated, pushed back the searing heat coursing through his veins, setting his nerves alight and his heart galloping. He felt the invisible finger of fire carving a new scar into his flesh, but paid it no heed. After what he'd witnessed on the plains, the suffering the Vassalage Consortium had inflicted on the people of Nkedi, these men had earned their fate. Guilty by association, the crimes of their companions now paid for in their blood.

The Hunter relinquished his grip on Soulhunger, leaving it embedded in the Ghandian's chest, and spun toward the next armed men. The two Drashi had recovered enough to raise their weapons, but they put up only a pitiful defense. Again and again he hammered at their defenses, his watered steel sword striking at them from too many directions to anticipate at a speed they could not hope to match. They fell before him in a matter of seconds, cut them down like stalks of wheat before a whirlwind.

Instinct warned the Hunter of danger to his left. He spun and brought his sword up, just in time to parry a blow aimed at his head. He snarled into the Ghandian's face and punched his crossguard into the man's mouth. Once, twice, three times, over and over until the ebony-skinned man collapsed unconscious in a bloody heap.

"Behind you!" came a shout.

The Hunter spun, found the Vothmoti—or was he Shalandran?—behind him, sword poised to thrust into his back. Too late to bring his own weapon to bear, the Hunter could only step into the man's attack and twist his torso to avoid the strike. The sword hissed a hair's breadth past his armored belly. Before the Consortium man could recover, the Hunter seized him by the neck and crushed his throat with a single flexion of his fingers. The greatknife fell from the man's fingers and clattered onto the earthen floor. The man himself followed a moment later, choking and clutching at the ruins of his neck. His breath came in terrible wheezing gasps. His face had already begun to purple. He would not live long.

"Do not move, or he dies!"

The words came from the Hunter's right, spoken in a thick Ghandian accent. He spun toward the sound. The last two of the Consortium's men stood beside Indigo's throne, sword tips pressed against the alchemist's sides. One look at their faces made it clear they wouldn't hesitate to drive the blades home. Unless Indigo's flowing bright-colored robes were treated with some alchemy that made it immune to swords, his life hung in the balance.

"You'd kill him?" The Hunter turned to face the two men—both Ghandian, skin the same dark copper of the vats dominating the area behind the alchemist's throne—and raised his bloody sword to point at Indigo. "Seemed to me like you wanted something from him. Hard to get whatever that was if he's too dead to talk."

At that, the most horrifying sound broke out in the room. Mirth blossomed on Indigo's face and from his lips emerged a noise that was somewhere between a donkey's braying, the gurgle of a dying man, and a hacking akin to the cough of a man dying from the Bloody Flux. Both Ghandians flinched instinctively, and even the Hunter's skin crawled at the sound. It took him a moment to realize Indigo was *laughing*. At what, he didn't know. He hadn't said anything particularly amusing.

One of the Ghandians, a tall, sturdily built man with a long sword scar running the length of his left forearm, recovered first. "You would dare to interfere with Consortium business?" He tried to sound outraged, but it came out as more uncertain. No surprise, given he'd just witnessed eight of his companions rendered unconscious or killed in a matter of seconds.

"The better question is, does the Consortium dare interfere with *my* business?" The Hunter made no move, but his eyes studied the two men, watching, waiting for his moment. One instant of hesitation or distraction was all he needed.

76

"You are fool to raise a hand against the Consortium." The second man had regained some of his pluck, too. "All power in Khafra is ours. And beyond. All of the Ghandian Empire will soon be—"

There it was, the moment he'd been searching for. The man, caught up in whatever he'd been about to say, lowered his arm just enough the tip of his sword shifted away from Indigo's side. The Hunter snapped his left wrist outward and a dagger slid out of his concealed forearm sheath into his palm. With a single fluid motion, he hurled the throwing knife at the *other* man, the one whose blade still menaced the enthroned alchemist. He didn't watch it fly—there was no need, for his aim had been true—but hurled himself at the last man standing.

The slaver, caught by surprise, had no time to react. His eyes went wide as his gaze locked on the tip of the watered steel sword darting toward him with the speed of a striking serpent. His muscles bunched, preparing to drive his own blade into Indigo's side. Too slow, the Hunter knew. He'd reach the man before—

The head of a spear exploded out of the front of the Ghandian's throat. Blood splashed warm and hot over the Hunter's face and outstretched sword hand. So surprised was he, he barely felt his sword pierce the Ghandian's neck, just above the collar of his studded vest.

The spear was pulled free a moment later, dragging the dying man backward. He collapsed, gagging and choking, drowning in his own blood.

And in the shadows between Indigo's throne and the vast fermentation tanks, a single pace behind where the Consortium man had been standing, the Hunter spotted another figure. A woman with skin darker than any Ghandian he'd encountered, silver piercings in her nose and eyebrows, face blazing bright with fury and hatred, teeth pulled back in a snarl. In her hands were a long dirk and a short-handled spear, its head still dripping red with the slaver's blood. She spat on the man bleeding out at her feet and snarled something in an unfamiliar language.

When her gaze snapped back up to him, the Hunter took an instinctive step back, brought his sword up between them. Something about her eyes—dark as Vothmoti *kaffe,* yet seeming to burn with their own inner light—sent a shiver of fear down his spine.

"Wait!" came another voice from a few paces to the Hunter's right. The same voice that had called a warning to him in the heat of battle, he realized.

A second figure appeared between the copper tanks, a young man with a long sword in his right hand. But his empty left hand was held up in a gesture of peace.

"Just wait!"

The Hunter's eyes narrowed. Something about that voice was familiar. He'd heard it before today. But where?

"You remember me, don't you, Hunter?"

The young man emerged into the light streaming from the glass skylight, and the Hunter recognized the handsome features and dark hair. More than anything, though, he recognized the confident bearing. He'd know it anywhere; it had so impressed him when he'd first met this young man's mother months earlier in Praamis.

"It's Kodyn, of the Night Guild."

Chapter Seventeen

The Hunter stared at the young man for a long moment. It *was,* indeed, Master Gold's son, no doubt about it. Kodyn's scent—lemon rind and oak with a hint of fresh rosemary, the same scent he'd detected when first they met on the rooftops overlooking the Gatherers' hideout—didn't lie.

The Hunter's eyes darted to the snarling, fire-eyed figure who'd killed the last of the Consortium's slavers. Her, he recognized as well, even without inhaling her unique scent of musk, wild lavender, lemongrass, and beechwood. Aisha, the Guild Master had called her. She'd fought with equal ferocity on the day he and the Night Guild had executed the last of the Gatherers, a match for the Ghandian warrior woman who'd guarded Master Gold with such devotion.

"I remember you." He raised an eyebrow. "What are you doing here?"

Kodyn's face smoothed into an unreadable mask. "Traveling." He'd clearly inherited his mother's preference for keeping his thoughts and intentions concealed behind a façade.

Yet that, in and of itself, communicated more than the young man realized. His evasion only made it all the more apparent that he was here for some purpose beyond merely exploring the oldest city on Einan. And the way his eyes shifted to Aisha as he pronounced the words spoke to the fact that they'd traveled thousands of leagues from their home in the Praamian underworld to what appeared to be Aisha's homeland.

For all his curiosity, the Hunter couldn't spare the time to delve further into the matter. "Your warning, I appreciate it." He turned to Aisha. "Your intervention, however, was unnecessary."

Aisha seemed not to register his words. Her gaze was fixed on the slaver who now lay motionless in a puddle of blood at her feet. Her shoulders rose and fell in time with her heavy breathing, as if she'd fought a days-long battle. A strange energy rolled off her in tangible waves, setting the Hunter's skin prickling.

He took a step back, eyes narrowing. He'd never encountered such intensity, such white-hot rage. Whatever internal war raged within her, it consumed every shred of attention, every fiber of her being.

"Aisha." Kodyn moved to stand beside his companion, resting a hand on her shoulder. "Aisha." He spoke her name more firmly. "Aisha, focus!"

The whip-crack of his voice seemed to snap Aisha out of whatever held her transfixed. Her head snapped up and she blinked at the young man standing in front of her.

"He's dead." Kodyn spoke in a calm, soothing tone. "They're all dead."

"Dead." She repeated the word in a dull, wooden monotone. Then, drawing in a deep, shuddering breath, she seemed to emerge the rest of the way back to sanity. The hand gripping her dirk in white knuckles went to something hanging at her neck, and the last traces of feral rage drained away. Once again, she became the young woman the Hunter had met in Praamis—no less a warrior, but somehow more restrained and in control of herself. "Good riddance."

Kodyn gave an enthusiastic nod. "Good riddance, indeed!" His hand slid along her shoulder, up her neck, to cradle the back of her head. "You good?"

"Yeah." Aisha gave him a wry smile, a hint of embarrassment etched into her strong features as she sheathed her weapons. "There were...a lot of them here."

"Here?" Kodyn looked around, but not toward the slavers' corpses. Instead, it was as if he scanned the shadows for hidden enemies. "Strange. Not the sort of place I'd expect."

Aisha shrugged. "I just know what I felt. And it was..." She let out a long breath.

"Hate to interrupt...whatever this is." The Hunter waved vaguely at the space between the two youths. "But I've got to chat with my friend here."

"So do we," Aisha shot back. "And we *were* here first."

"That so?" The Hunter cocked his head. "Way I remember it, I came on him surrounded by all these fine fellows." He gestured to the bloody corpses littering the rush-strewn floor. "No sign of you two."

"He instructed us to hide while he talked with them." Aisha's jaw set in a stubborn cast, and she stepped up to square off with the Hunter. "We were just about to hit them from the shadows when you walked in."

"Which means *I* am the one to whom he owes his life." The Hunter turned away from the Ghandian and stepped toward the still-seated Indigo. "And I carry this." From within his cloak, he drew out the silver medallion bearing the three interlocking rings of the Hidden Circle.

Indigo's crimson eyes widened as he caught sight of the jewelry. But he did not reply. Instead, his hands lifted from where they rested on the strange armrests made of glass, clay, and porcelain and began to gesticulate wildly.

The Hunter frowned. "I trust you've heard of me from Graeme." His alchemist friend in Voramis had long ago sent word to every corner of Einan that the Hidden Circle was to cooperate with the Hunter—albeit, not for free. He still had to pay the alchemists in the coin they most valued: information.

The albino's gesticulations grew more frantic, which only served to confuse the Hunter further. He couldn't follow the movements, couldn't look in every direction Indigo's fingers indicated.

Then it hit him. *Of course!* His mind flashed back to three years earlier, when he'd traveled with Sirkar Jeroen's caravan from Malandria across the Advanat Desert. Among those in the caravan had been a young boy named Wyllis who communicated not in words, but hand gestures. That certainly explained why Indigo had laughed when the Hunter spoke of being "too dead to talk".

The Hunter racked his brain, trying to remember the signals Hailen had taught him. Only one sprang to mind. He doubted Indigo would understand what he meant by "I'm fine", and other than that—

"He's asking what you want." This came from Kodyn, who stood next to Aisha.

The Hunter regarded the young man. "You understand what he's saying?"

Kodyn shrugged. "Mostly."

"How?" The Hunter narrowed his eyes.

"Picked up a thing or two." Again, with the evasion. Clearly there was a great deal the Guild Master's son had no intention of saying.

The Hunter let it go. He had more important matters to attend to. "Will you translate his answers to me? I don't have time for confusion. What I'm here for, it's a matter of life and death." That appeal would be hard even for one of the Night Guild to ignore.

Kodyn's eyebrows shot up. "Whose?"

The Hunter scowled. "Will you, or not?"

Kodyn and Aisha exchanged glances. Their hands moved quickly, too, though out of the still-enthroned Indigo's line of sight. After a moment, Kodyn turned back and nodded. "Ask him what you want."

The Hunter turned back to the albino. "I need *ephrade.* Do you have it, and if not, where can I get it?"

Confusion twisted Indigo's pale, blue-stained features. His hands flew, fingers dancing in his silent language. Every movement accentuated his unique scent, the one the Hunter could only describe as *blue*. Hints of blueberries mingled with cornflower and an edge of some mint that called to mind the scent of snow falling from a clear blue sky. An odd mixture of aromas for a man as odd as the indigo-robed alchemist himself.

"Never heard of it, he says," Kodyn translated. "Any other names for whatever it is? A description?"

The Hunter cursed under his breath. He'd been so focused on tending to Kiara then racing for Khafra that he hadn't even bothered to ask Tarek what the plant looked like. He racked his brain for the other names the young Elivasti had used for it.

"I think it's something like *nele...*" That sounded wrong. He tried again. "*Lend...*" Still wrong. He growled low in his throat, frustrated. "*Nendel—*"

"*Ndleleni?*" Aisha spoke the Ghandian word with ease.

"That's it!" The Hunter whirled on Indigo. "Do you have *that,* what she said?"

Indigo nodded, and again his hands moved.

"Why do you want it?" Aisha asked, her voice hard, a frown tugging at her lips.

The Hunter looked between the two youths, uncertain whether that had been the translation of Indigo's hand signals or a question from Aisha. Judging by the way Kodyn glanced sidelong at his companion, it was more likely the latter.

"Like I said, a matter of life and death." The Hunter met her gaze levelly. Whatever light had once shone in her eyes was now gone, but her stubbornness had waned not at all. For all her youth, he suspected she could give both Kiara and the Guild Master a run for their money.

"He says he has," Kodyn translated. "But only a small amount. The rest is in there."

The Hunter followed Indigo's pointing finger to one of the four enormous copper tanks occupying the back of The Blind Pig's high-vaulted taproom. The alchemist's hands moved again, and Kodyn relayed the meaning of his gestures. "*Ndleleni* adds a pleasant kick to his teff beer."

Indigo crossed his eyes and stuck his tongue out, head wobbling on his shoulders. An odd, if accurate, depiction of a man drunk off his wits.

"Whatever you have, I'll take it." The Hunter reached into his cloak and drew out a purse. "I don't care how much it costs."

The alchemist's indigo-painted white face scrunched up into a worried look, and his eyes darted toward Aisha. His hands flashed a few quick signals.

"Bloody right that'll be a problem," Aisha growled. She stepped between the Hunter and the alchemist, defiance blazing on her strong-featured face. "Because he was just about to sell it to us."

The Hunter raised an eyebrow. "Why do you need it?"

Aisha just stared up at him, lips pressed tightly shut.

Anger surged in the Hunter's chest. He had no quarrel with these youths—indeed, he owed the Night Guild a great debt, one he could never repay—but he'd be damned if he let them interfere with his efforts to save Kiara's life.

"Listen—" the Hunter growled.

"Aisha." Kodyn's voice drew the attention of both the Hunter and the young Ghandian woman. His hands flashed, his expression grew somber, and his eyebrows moved as if to emphasize the silent words formed by his fingers.

Aisha's jaw clenched and she gestured back something with emphasis. The square of her shoulders and set of her jaw showed her determination—which the Hunter might have admired under any other circumstance.

"But you know I'm right," Kodyn said emphatically.

Aisha scowled but threw up her hands. "Fine," she snapped. She looked to Indigo and moved her fingers in the silent hand language.

The Hunter was about to snarl something angry, to demand an explanation, but Indigo's sudden movement silenced him. The alchemist produced a fist-sized pouch seemingly from nowhere and held it up cradled on his open palm. An herbaceous, sweet, slightly acidic scent emanated from the pouch, and the Hunter's heart leaped. He reached out to take the pouch, relief coursing through him.

Aisha snatched it from Indigo's hand first. "Not all of it's for you." She clutched the pouch of *ephrade* to her chest as if it were the most precious thing in the world. "We'll split it. Half each."

The Hunter bared his teeth in a snarl. He had no idea how much *ephrade* was needed to purge the infection from Kiara's veins, but he'd take it all just to make certain—

"And know that the *only* reason we're doing this is because Hailen and Evren would insist on it."

"Especially if it's to save Kiara's life," Kodyn added. "The two of them would never forgive us if we let anything happen to her."

Chapter Eighteen

The Hunter's jaw dropped. *Hailen and Evren?* He looked between the two youths. *How...what?* His mind struggled to comprehend how these two, who he'd last seen in Praamis, had crossed paths with Hailen and Evren. According to Kiara, the boys had been on their way to Shalandra.

Shalandra. Something clicked in the Hunter's mind. *The same place where the Gatherers were from. And that girl...what was her name? Briana!*

He was suddenly possessed by a burning desire to ask them how his boys fared. Before he could, however, Aisha dug her hand into the pouch and held a handful of dark green dried leaves up to him.

"Well?" she demanded. "Do you want it or not?" The *ephrade's* distinct smell—thicker and sweeter than lavender, yet with a citric hint akin to bitter lemon rind—drifted up from the leaves piled on her upturned palm.

The Hunter nodded. "Aye." Sheathing his sword, he drew out a strip of cloth and used it to carefully collect the leaves from Aisha's hand. "Thank you."

"As he said," Aisha jerked her head toward Kodyn, "it's what Hailen and Evren would have done."

"And," Kodyn added, prodding Aisha with one elbow, "after what we went through in Shalandra together, we owe them at least this much."

The Hunter longed to know more—since departing Voramis, he'd wondered about his boys a hundred times—but the urgency of Kiara's condition compelled him to depart with all haste. Already, time could be running out. Every second mattered.

Still, he couldn't stop himself from asking, "Are they alive?" Pain twisted in his heart. "Are they well?"

"They are." Kodyn's handsome face creased into a wry smile. "Though it was a close thing on more than one occasion."

Knots tightened in the Hunter's shoulders. He could only imagine what sort of mischief Evren had gotten into, which meant *Hailen* had likely been dragged into it as well. Yet Kodyn's answer filled him with immeasurable relief, too. As long as they'd come out the other side, he could ride away without guilt.

He turned to Indigo. "What do I owe you for the *ephrade?*" He drew out a purse heavy with golden imperials and silver half-drakes. Though Khafra and what remained of the Ghandian Empire stubbornly refused to abandon its ancient currency—the *kubu*, coins minted from brass and bronze, bearing the face of the mightiest of their emperors—the Einari standard currency was accepted here, too. "The full measure." The least he could do was cover the cost of the youths' portion of *ephrade*; the information on Hailen and Evren was worth a far greater fortune than the alchemist could charge.

Indigo's hands moved, fingers flashing at blurring speed.

"No charge," Kodyn translated. "You arrived before those men made the decision to use those big, sharp swords on me"—at this, the albino's face creased into a sultry smile, as if the innuendo amused him to no end—"but I have no doubt how things would have ended up had you not been here." Indigo gestured to both the Hunter and the two youths.

The Hunter considered the tableau that had greeted him upon entering The Blind Pig. "What were they after?" He looked to the enormous copper tanks behind the enthroned alchemist. "Your recipe for making fine beer is truly worth killing over?"

Indigo nodded so emphatically the Hunter didn't need Kodyn's translation of his hand signals.

"Absolutely! Nowhere else in Ghandia—nay, the entire world—can you find teff beer to rival mine. Nor as old." Kodyn's eyebrows rose in surprise, as if finding interest in the words he relayed to the Hunter. "He says he recreated the recipe used for the very first beer ever brewed in history."

Had that statement come from anyone else, the Hunter might have doubted it. But Indigo was a member of the Hidden Circle. Any such claims from them were often backed up by alchemical prowess that rivaled that of the Secret Keepers. If Graeme's alchemy could save him from the magical rot inflicted by the First's sword, was it so impossible to believe Indigo had somehow unlocked the oldest brewing secrets in the world?

Indigo's colored face darkened, his crimson eyes narrowing as his fingers continued speaking.

"But that's not why they came after me," Kodyn translated. "They have other uses for my alchemy, but I have no intention of letting my creations be turned to their evil."

"What other uses?" Aisha asked the question out before the Hunter could.

"Beer was first brewed for both the purpose of intoxication—" Again, Indigo acted this out by reeling in his seat like a drunkard and clutching the throne's arms as if it alone held up upright. "—and as a form of combining liquid and solid nourishment. A single sack of teff grain could sustain five times as many working men when brewed into a beer like this." The albino gestured to the copper tanks. "When enhanced with a few extra herbs of my own concoction, just one mouthful is enough to keep a man working for a full day and night."

The Hunter had tried some of Graeme's concoctions and could personally attest to the veracity of that claim. A single vial of the Voramian alchemist's energy tonic had similar effects as Indigo described. Though their ingredients would likely be different, the end result was the same.

A memory from the previous night brought acid rising to the Hunter's stomach. "They wanted your alchemy to enhance the strength of their slaves. Or keep the guards transporting them awake for days at a stretch."

Indigo shrugged. "I did not ask," he said, through Kodyn, "but it did not take the full capacity of my brilliant mind to deduce as much."

The Hunter's gaze strayed to the ten bodies lying on the floor of The Blind Pig, and his jaw muscles clenched. The latter guess suggested the Vassalage Consortium planned to step up their slaving efforts significantly, while the former hinted at some purpose beyond merely selling their captives on the slaver's block. Neither was a pleasant outcome for the people of Nkedi and the other villages, homesteads, farms, and towns upon which they intended to prey.

Indigo's fingers moved again. "By your intervention here, you have made a powerful enemy."

The Hunter snorted. "Let them come after me. Their anger means nothing. Indeed, it is *my* wrath that should worry them."

Indigo made a loud sound like a half-cluck, half-whistle, as strange as his laughter, and shook his head. His hands moved, almost too fast for Kodyn to translate.

"They are more powerful than you realize. No mere band of slavers. The Consortium has considerable political and financial backing, including—" Kodyn's face scrunched up. "I don't recognize what those hand signals mean. But there was something about queen. Blood hand. Smart man. Maybe sage?"

The Hunter's blood ran cold. "The Sage?" It wouldn't surprise him to learn the bastard demon of Kara-ket had carried a significant stake in an enterprise that caused such suffering and misery in Einan. "And the Bloody Hand?"

Kodyn nodded hesitantly. "I...think so?" His brow furrowed. "It makes sense, given what mother—er, Master Gold—used to say about them."

The Bloody Hand had trafficked women and girls from not only around Einan, but Fehl across the Frozen Sea. An alliance with the Vassalage Consortium would certainly prove beneficial in their efforts to stock the brothels and flophouses of Voramis.

Indigo looked between the three of them. "But they will not have me, nor my alchemy." His jaw muscles clenched as Kodyn spoke his words aloud. "A fact I knew long ago, and prepared for."

For the first time since the Hunter had entered, he leaned forward and rose from the throne where he'd sat as placidly as if he entertained guests of honor. The moment he stood, a loud *click* echoed from some mechanism set into the base of the throne, accompanied a heartbeat later by angry hissing emanating from all four copper tanks.

Indigo's hands flashed at blurring speed.

"Fiery hell!" Kodyn cursed. "He says we've got thirty seconds to get out of here."

The Hunter's heart sprang into his throat. "Let's go!" He could feel the room already growing hotter, the smell of fermentation thickening as whatever fail-safe Indigo had tripped set the tanks boiling. He spun away from the alchemist and raced for the door, only pausing long enough to retrieve his throwing knife and Soulhunger from where they remained embedded in the dead Consortium slavers' corpses. Aisha and Kodyn raced at his heels, both fleet of foot and spurred on by the hissing that rose in volume with every passing moment.

But through the rising noise, the Hunter heard only *two* pairs of footsteps at his back. Turning, he cast a glance behind him, searching the taproom until he spotted the alchemist still standing by the base of his great throne of bottles. Indigo had thrown off his robe, and now wore nothing beyond an equally colorful loincloth that encircled his emaciated waist. The indigo paint or tattoos swirled in a mind-boggling pattern around every inch of his spare frame. In the light of the sun streaming through the glass skylight, they seemed to glow with their own internal brilliance. Almost like the runes of the Serenii or those etched into the Sword of Nasnaz. Yet their color was like nothing the Hunter had ever seen before.

Indigo knelt beside the throne and pulled open a wooden door in the floor the Hunter had not seen, so carefully it was concealed. A strange indigo light shone from within, silhouetting the kneeling alchemist. As if sensing the Hunter's gaze on him, Indigo turned and gave the Hunter a sly smile and wink. Then dove head-first through the door into the brilliant light beneath. The door fell shut behind him with a resounding *clang* and once again became indistinct from the hard-packed earth around the throne.

A particularly loud, angry hiss emanated from one of the copper tanks, and the other three soon joined in. The Hunter could almost see the metal swelling, as if about to burst from the pressure mounting within. With one last glance toward the bizarre throne where the odd alchemist had vanished through that hidden door in the ground, he spun and raced away from The Blind Pig.

Kodyn and Aisha were only a few steps ahead of him, racing south down the street at a full sprint. The Hunter sprinted toward the hitching post, unslung his horses' reins, and vaulted onto Ash's back. Within seconds, he and the two horses were galloping down the broad, tree-lined avenue at breakneck speed. His heart hammered in time with Ash's flying hooves, his mouth as dry as the arid sandstone buildings. He had no idea how much time had elapsed, how much longer he had before—

BOOOOOOM!

A blast wave of sound rolled over him with the force of a thunderclap, followed a moment later by a hot wind that buffeted with such ferocity it nearly knocked him from the horse's back. Only Ash's innate agility and his own stubborn tenacity kept him seated. Still, his horses joined every animal within a thirty-block radius in rearing up and shrieking in terror. It took the Hunter long seconds to calm the beasts. Only then could he glance back at what had caused the sound.

Where The Blind Pig had once stood, only a smoking hole in the earth remained. Gone were the four walls, the vast copper tanks, the throne of glass, porcelain, and clay bottles, even the wooden signpost. Only a thick column of stinking grey smoke that rose a hundred paces into the sky. Looking at the destruction, the Hunter found it difficult to imagine Indigo had escaped. Yet something about that strange, glowing door left him uncertain. The alchemist could very well have been prepared for an explosion of such immense size caused by his own concoctions and planned an escape that carried him safely away.

A loud, shrieking hiss drew the Hunter's attention upward. His eyes widened in surprise as he spotted the object plummeting toward him. He clapped his heels into Ash's flanks, and the horse sprang away. Not a moment too soon. The copper tank hurtled from the sky and crashed into the ground where the Hunter had been, crumpling into a twisted, smoking pile of scorched metal and spraying clouds of hissing, foaming super-heated beer in every direction.

The Hunter stared in dumbfounded amazement at the wreckage of the tank—all that remained of The Blind Pig. He could only begin to imagine the immense power of the alchemical explosion that had hurled it so high into the air it had only just *now* landed. And a good fifty paces away from its starting point, too.

Damn, he thought, shaking his head. *Must have been some bloody fine beer!*

The destruction of The Blind Pig plunged the street into utter chaos. A pair of horse-drawn chariots had capsized as the draft animals rioted at the tumult, and a team of raya cattle was backed against a wall, lowing angrily and swiping their long, sharp horns at the drovers attempting to herd them once more into line. A few unlucky bystanders had been caught by the invisible blast and heat wave, and their shrieks and cries of pain only added to the clamor. It took the Hunter nearly five minutes to get Ash and Elivast once more under control and extricate himself from the crush of people surging toward the smoldering ruins of The Blind Pig to gawk at the destruction.

When he finally did, however, he found himself confronted by two riders blocking his path.

"We're coming with you." Kodyn spoke in a matter-of-fact tone. Oddly self-assured for one so young, especially given who he was speaking to. His certainty wavered a fraction when he glanced to Aisha, as if for reassurance or support. She looked far from pleased—had he talked her into it—but didn't back down before the Hunter's gaze. On the contrary, she set her jaw all the more stiffly and squared her shoulders as if daring him to argue.

The Hunter fought the urge to laugh. "You are, are you?" The sight was almost comical, the two youths attempting to dictate terms to *him*. "And where exactly do you think that is?"

"We don't know, but don't care, either." Kodyn shrugged. "What we *do* know is that you're here for something important, something bigger than anyone else in the world realizes. And whatever that is, we're going to be part of it. That's why we're here right now." Again, he looked to Aisha as if for confirmation. "It can't just be a coincidence the *Kish'aa* sent us to The Blind Pig at that precise moment."

Aisha's face tightened almost imperceptibly, the lines at the corners of her eyes deepening.

The confidence in the young man's words surprised the Hunter. He'd told Kodyn's mother of his true purpose for being in Praamis—hunting Abiarazi masquerading as humans, in this case, one Lord Chasteyn—but the way Kodyn spoke, it was clear he and Aisha knew far more than even his mother. If there was any doubt that these two had crossed paths with Hailen and Evren, it evaporated in that moment.

"So be it." The Hunter shrugged. "You can come."

Both Kodyn and Aisha's jaws dropped slightly. Clearly, they'd expected him to put up more of an argument.

In truth, he had, too. He had no desire to be saddled with the care of two callow youths, nor be slowed on his mad dash back to Kiara. Yet they had horses of their own—sturdy mounts, well cared for—along with ample packs, full waterskins, weapons, and the skill to wield them. He'd seen them both fight the Gatherers in Praamis. If they were anything like the Guild Master and her Ghandian protectress, they'd be less of a liability than he feared.

But the *true* reason he had agreed lay in their mention of Kiara. Only someone who had intimate knowledge of Hailen and Evren would know that name—or what it meant to them and the Hunter both. These two youths, though they were half a continent away, were his best source of information on his boys. For that, he welcomed them…for now.

"But I warn you now," he said, waggling a finger at them, "I'm riding hard to get the *ephrade* to Kiara. You either keep up or find your own way."

Without waiting for an answer, he clapped his heels to Ash's flanks and set off at a gallop southbound along the main avenue. He had no time to delay, no time to take two wayward lambs under his wing. They would either sink or swim, match his pace or be left behind.

All that mattered now was reaching Kiara's side before the rot stole away the woman he loved.

Chapter Nineteen

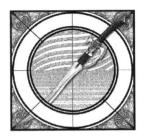

The Hunter rode for everything he was worth. The image of Kiara's pale, sweat-soaked face spurred him to push himself and the horses as fast as he dared through the streets of Khafra. Only once did he glance back to see if the two youths followed him. To their credit, they managed to *almost* match his pace—they emerged from the throng of travelers and carters entering the city gates only a few dozen paces behind him.

Once out on the verdant grasslands encircling, the Hunter had nothing to impede his progress, so allowed Ash to truly stretch his legs. The desert pony and Elivast would soon tire—they had rested too little after riding too hard for far too long—but for the moment, both horses seemed to have recovered a second wind. When finally they reached Kiara, the Hunter vowed to give their mounts ample opportunity to rest and graze.

But he had to reach her. Worry tightened like a bowstring in his gut, his nerves thrumming with a nervous anticipation amplified by his mounting dread. The sun had already dipped low toward the horizon; nearly a full day had elapsed since he rode away from Kiara and Tarek. No telling what had happened in that time.

Had Kiara survived her wounds only to fall prey in her weakened state to one of the Kgabu lion prides roaming the plains? Or had the spotted hyenas the Hunter had seen screwed up the courage to attack the two riders traveling alone? Had the heat of the day, fatigue, or fever sapped the last of Kiara's strength? Was she even now lying cold and lifeless somewhere in the middle of nowhere, breathing her last gasp while he was far, far away?

No! The Hunter gritted his teeth and pushed that thought from his mind. *No bloody way she's died. Not Kiara.* She numbered among the strongest people he'd ever met, in spirit, temperament, and force of personality if not in physical strength. If anyone could prove stubborn enough to endure and survive despite terrible odds, it was her.

Please let her be alive! It wasn't exactly a prayer; there were no gods to listen, he knew, and even had they existed, he put little trust that they'd care enough to hear him. But the silent plea was all he could do for her now. He could only hope she felt his presence from across the vast distance separating them and it lent her strength. There was nothing more he could do.

Nothing except ride with every shred of strength he could demand from Ash and Elivast. He pitied the horses—both were soon gasping and straining—but he could not allow them to slow. They were his *only* hope of reaching Kiara in time.

As if sensing his need, Ash poured on a fresh burst of speed. The desert pony's mane streamed and his hooves flew in a deafening thunder that beat in time with the Hunter's stampeding heartbeat. Across the vast swath of emerald grass and up the hill upon which the Hunter had sat to take in the view of the city for the first time.

Cresting the rise, the Hunter scanned the way ahead for any sign of Tarek and Kiara. The road was busy at the late afternoon hour—with the final rays of sunlight already vanishing behind the western hills, the caravans and carters too far from Khafra had begun pitching tents and building campfires, preparing to settle down for the night. No sign of Tarek or Kiara, however.

The Hunter charged down the hill, but he could feel his strength waning. Every muscle was drained, every joint pounded to mush, his reserves of strength all but depleted. The horses, too, were on the verge of giving out. Sweat lathered both Ash and Elivast's flanks, and the Hunter knew neither could sustain the mad pace. Twin waves of frustration and hopelessness washed over him as he felt Ash slowing beneath him. His throat closed up and his breath burned in his lungs. He wanted to scream, to howl his fury into the darkening sky. He would not make it in time. Could not—

Then he spotted them. Far to the southwest, barely visible along the narrow dirt trail the Hunter had traveled hours earlier, two figures swayed atop the back of a stocky black horse. From this distance, the Hunter could not tell the two hooded, cloaked figures apart, but there was no doubt in his mind. It could *only* be Tarek and Kiara.

A wild, half-mad whoop escaped his lips, and he clapped his heels to Ash's flanks. The desert pony groaned beneath him but somehow managed to summon one last effort from within some deep, hidden reservoir. Down the hill they raced, past the startled caravaners and carters, and down the narrow dirt trail.

"I'm coming!" the Hunter shouted. A futile effort, for the wind carried away his voice. Yet he *needed* her to know. Needed her to hang on just a little longer.

Horror twisted in his belly as the rearmost of the two figures swayed dangerously to the side and toppled from the saddle. The Hunter felt the *thump* of the cloaked body striking the rocky trail, even from hundreds of paces away. Panic and fear sank icy claws into the back of his mind as he watched the other figure—Tarek—leap out of the horse's saddle and kneel at Kiara's side.

A roar of fury burst up from the depths of the Hunter's soul and echoed across the plains. The kneeling figure's head whipped up and around toward him. The Hunter's keen eyes spotted the relief blossoming on Tarek's face, driving back the worry. The young Elivasti sprang to his feet and raced toward the Hunter. His lips moved as he shouted something, but the wind rushing past and the blood pounding in the Hunter's ears drowned out Tarek's words. He did not waste energy trying to answer, merely bent lower in the saddle and galloped toward Tarek at full speed.

The moment he drew abreast of the young man, he leaped from Ash's back, hit the ground in a roll, and came up staggering to his feet. His legs nearly gave out beneath him, but somehow, he managed to stay upright, to stumble toward Tarek. "I have it!" he shouted. With fingers gone leaden and numb from clutching the reins in a death grip, he fumbled in his cloak for the small cloth in which he'd wrapped the leaves. "I have it!"

His body finally lost the battle against fatigue when he was just five paces away. He collapsed to his knees but thrust the pouch out and up toward Tarek. "Take it! Save her!"

Tarek said something, but the Hunter didn't hear the words. He barely felt the young man snatch the *ephrade* from his hands. The world swam around him, the darkness encroaching on his vision, until it seemed the sky swirled in a mad melee of chaos and color. The Hunter fell forward, barely catching himself before his face crashed into the ground. He'd exhausted even the strength Soulhunger had fed him after consuming the slaver's life. Now, it was all he could do to lie face-down and draw in a single, shaky breath when every part of him wanted to simply *stop*.

But he couldn't. Not when he was so close.

Kiara! He had no strength to say her name but called out to her in his thoughts. *I've come back for you.*

After long seconds, he summoned just enough energy to push himself up to his hands and knees. He could not rise—his legs would not sustain him—and so crawled toward her. One hand in front of the other, heedless of the sharp rocks grinding against his knees. His vision narrowed to a single point of focus: *she* was all he saw. A seemingly endless distance away. Yet he went to her. Though it strained him to the point of shattering, he did not allow himself to stop until he was at her side.

"I'm here!" The words came out in a croak, barely more than a whisper. "I'm here, Kiara. I'm here." It was all he could say, the only thing his mind could conjure through the bone-deep exhaustion. He clutched her hand as if he could somehow transmit what little vitality he possessed to her through the grip.

But she did not answer. Did not so much as stir. She reeked of rot and putrescence, a smell so strong it twisted his stomach. Her face was deathly pale, her hand clammy. Her pulse was weak—so terribly weak, barely more than a flutter beneath his fingers. He wanted to shake her, to shout at her to wake up, to open her eyes, but he did not. He merely held on to her and willed her to keep breathing. Just a little longer, until Tarek could use the *ephrade* to save her life.

"Hunter!"

The shout came from nearby, right at the Hunter's side. The urgency in the word drew the Hunter's attention away from Kiara. Lifting his head required a near-superhuman effort, yet he forced himself to meet Tarek's gaze.

"I need you to hold her mouth open," the young Elivasti said. "I'll pour it down her throat, and as long as she can swallow it, she's got a chance."

The Hunter nodded, though his head drooped. He struggled to sit up, leaning on Kiara's limp form for support, and slid his numb hands up her neck to clamp on her jaw. She did not resist as he pulled her mouth open.

Tarek appeared at Kiara's other side, kneeling by her head with a small wooden pestle and mortar clutched in his hands. He leaned over Kiara and tipped the wooden vessel to her mouth. Within, a dark, viscous, greenish-brown mixture—more paste than liquid—flowed like treacle along the mortar's curved sides at an agonizingly slow pace. Collected at the edge, forming into a large gobbet that dripped into Kiara's mouth.

"She *has* to get it down," Tarek insisted. "Close her mouth and tilt her chin to her chest. It'll keep it from choking her."

The Hunter did as ordered. Too slowly. Kiara coughed and gagged, spraying droplets of dark greenish-brown from her nostrils. Yet the Hunter held her mouth closed, and there was nowhere else for the alchemical mixture to go but down. To his relief, he felt the muscles of her throat contracting.

"There!" he gasped, relaxing his grip on her mouth. "She swallowed it."

Tarek nodded. "Good." He sat on his back leg, arm resting on his bent knee. "Now we wait." His violet eyes fixed on Kiara. "Mixed with the powdered gillflower, the *ephrade* should purge the infection from her veins."

"Should?" The Hunter heard the worry and uncertainty in the young man's voice. "What do you mean, *should?*" The fire of anger flooded his veins, pushed back a measure of his fatigue. "You said this would save her!"

"And it will, if it's enough." Tarek's jaw muscles clenched and he raised a hand protectively between himself and the Hunter. "The amount you brought me was so small, I can't be certain."

The Hunter's eyes widened, red rushing in his vision. "It *has* to be enough!" He'd gotten as much as Indigo could spare. The rest had gone to—

To Aisha!

He spun to look back the way he'd come. In the distance, he could see the two youths riding toward them. In his mad dash to reach Kiara's side, he'd left them far behind, Ash's speed far outstripping their mounts. Yet they *had* kept pace enough to follow him up this trail.

Hope surged within him. Reaching deep within himself, he summoned a burst of strength and labored to his feet. He tottered, unsteady on shaky legs, but willed his trembling muscles to hold him upright. Staggering back up the trail, he fumbled for the sword at his hip.

"Hunter!" Tarek called behind him. "What are you doing?"

The Hunter ignored the young Elivasti. His gaze fixed on the young woman riding toward him. Aisha had more *ephrade*—the rest of what Indigo had possessed. He'd ask her for it, politely at first. But if that failed…

His fist tightened on the hilt of his sword. She *would* give him her share of the *ephrade,* one way or another.

The Hunter's strength returned in force, his muscles growing stronger with every step. Desperation and determination propelled him onward. He had no desire to raise a hand against the two youths, but he would if it proved necessary. He had no other choice. Not with Kiara's life on the line.

Kodyn and Aisha reined up as they approached. "Did it work?" Kodyn called. The young man was breathless and flushed with exertion, sweat soaking his long, dark hair.

"I need more!" the Hunter shouted back. He fixed his gaze on Aisha. "I need your share of the *ephrade.*"

Aisha appeared equally exhausted after the hard ride, yet at the Hunter's words, she went instantly rigid and her hand darted to the short-handled spear strapped to her back.

The Hunter took an unsteady step toward them. "It's the only way," he said, his voice hard. "The only way to stop the rot from killing her."

"I…can't." Aisha's jaw clenched, a shadow filling her dark eyes.

"Aisha—" Kodyn started.

"Don't, Kodyn!" The Ghandian girl rounded on her companion. "Don't you think I *want* to help her? Knowing what she means to Hailen and Evren." Her shoulders tensed and her face set in a stubborn cast. "But I can't give him the *ephrade.* You know what that means to me. What it will do for…" She cut off, swallowing her words.

The Hunter had no idea what she needed it for. Nor did he care. "Please. I can't let her die. I won't let her." His fist clutched the hilt of his sword so tightly his knuckles creaked. "I need the *ephrade.*"

Aisha's eyes narrowed. "You would take it from me?" Her hand, too, went to the dagger at her hip.

The Hunter said nothing, but didn't slow his advance.

"Aisha—" Again, Kodyn attempted to speak.

Again, she cut him off. "No!" She didn't look at her companion; her eyes were fixed on the Hunter, her expression hard. "I want to hear him say it. What he'll do if I don't give it to

90

him." She dropped lightly from her saddle and planted her feet in a battle-ready stance. "Say it, Hunter."

Sorrow panged in the Hunter's belly. How unfortunate circumstances would turn out thus. But if Kiara's life—

"Aisha!" Kodyn's voice cracked like a whip, so hard and sharp it set nightjars flapping away from a tree fifty paces away. "You can save her *and* keep the *ephrade* both! You just have to do what you did for me at the Heartspring."

At that, Aisha's eyes flew wide. Her gaze ripped away from the Hunter and she whirled on Kodyn. "What?"

Kodyn thrust a finger toward the spot where the Hunter had left Kiara lying on the ground. "You heard the Hunter. He said *rot* is killing her. Not a battle wound or damage to her organs. *Rot*." He emphasized the word as if it held particular meaning. "You can save her. The *Kish'aa* can save her!"

Aisha froze, paralyzed by Kodyn's words.

The Hunter, too, stopped advancing. He looked to Kodyn. "Can she truly—"

"I swear it, on my love for my mother and Ria." Kodyn sprang down from his horse and moved to stand beside Aisha, resting a hand on her shoulder. "She can save Kiara. But you have to trust her." He fixed the Hunter with a piercing gaze. "Can you do that, Hunter? Can you trust us with Kiara's life as Hailen and Evren would?"

Chapter Twenty

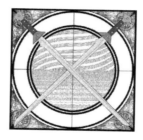

The Hunter hesitated not at all. Perhaps it was Kodyn's oath invoking the Guild Master and her fierce warrior protectress, or the way they'd spoken again and again of Hailen and Evren with a familiarity that bespoke friendship, even affection. Or maybe it was just that the Hunter was desperate and had no real desire to harm these youths to get his hands on the *ephrade*.

But whatever the reason, he had only one answer to give. "Do it!" He moved his hand away from his sword and stepped aside. If there was any chance they could stop the rot from killing Kiara, he'd take it in a heartbeat. "Whatever you have to do, save her."

Kodyn strode toward Aisha, an expression of pure confidence and trust on his face. Not in himself, but in *her*. It reminded him of the way Kiara looked at him. His faith in her was unshakeable, as solid as the ground beneath their feet.

The same could not be said of Aisha. At Kodyn's words, a look of uncertainty and hesitation crossed her umber-colored features. Everything from the sudden tension in her shoulders to the way she half-retreated from Kodyn bespoke doubt.

"Kodyn," she began, shaking her head, "this isn't like the Wellspring. It's—"

"It's *exactly* the same." Kodyn planted his feet and gripped her shoulder firmly, as if attempting to impart his assurance to her through his touch. "It's poison that must be burned away. And you can do that, just like you did for me."

The Hunter stared between the two, eyes narrowing. His own doubt mirrored Aisha's. *Burn* away the poison? Did she intend to use fire to cleanse Kiara's wounds? If that had been possible, surely Tarek would have attempted it already.

But Kodyn had eyes only for Aisha. "Trust yourself on this, Aisha. Trust the *Kish'aa*. This is what you've been working toward for all these weeks." He took her free hand in his. "You can do this!"

At the young man's words, Aisha's uncertainty waned a fraction. She appeared far from confident, yet her jaw set in a stubborn cast and she gave a slow nod of her head.

"I can do this." Her voice lacked Kodyn's certainty, but she repeated the words. "I can do this." Again, stronger and more forceful. "I can do this!"

"Do what, exactly?" the Hunter had to ask. He'd been willing to put his trust in the two youths, but Aisha's momentary hesitation had caused him to question the wisdom of that decision.

Aisha turned and marched toward Kiara, not meeting the Hunter's gaze. The Hunter made to move in her way—he felt less certain by the moment that he should allow Aisha to do...whatever it was Kodyn believed she could—but Kodyn slid smoothly toward him.

"Trust her!" the young man said, his eyes filled with the steadfast resoluteness so much like his mother's. Her force of will commanded the Night Guild, and clearly the young man had inherited a measure of her strength. "Aisha can save Kiara. She *will* save her."

Despite himself, the Hunter found he actually believed Kodyn. How desperately he wanted to—he wanted Kiara whole and on her feet—and the confidence in the young Praamian's voice instilled in him the faintest measure of hope. He stepped fully aside for Aisha to march past, then followed the two youths to where Kiara lay.

Tarek shot him a curious glance, but at a look from the Hunter, moved out of Aisha's way. He joined the Hunter and Kodyn in watching as Aisha knelt beside Kiara and placed her left hand on the unconscious woman's chest.

Kiara barely lived. Her breath came in shallow gasps, her face all but drained of color. Even the sweat that had once dripped down her forehead and soaked her clothing had dried up. She was all but gone. In a matter of minutes, the Long Keeper would collect her into his arms. The Hunter had no choice but to hang his hopes on Aisha doing the impossible and bringing Kiara back from the brink of death.

Aisha's right hand went to her throat—to a pendant that had been hidden beneath her clothing. The Hunter couldn't see the object, but when Aisha closed her eyes and drew in a deep breath, he could all but feel its power. Its subtle throbbing presence set the very air around her crackling like lightning. Faint at first, but growing stronger with every hammering beat of his heart.

Suddenly, light brightened the darkness. A blue-white glow emanated from the object clutched in Aisha's right hand, shining even through her grasping fingers. Sparks of similarly colored light danced around her left hand, up her arm, around her head in a luminous crown of sizzling power.

The Hunter sucked in a breath, took an instinctive step away from the magic. For it could only be magic. One he'd never encountered before, yet as real as the arcane sorcery the First had utilized to open a portal into the fiery hell or the energy harnessed by the Illumina. Every hair on the Hunter's arms and neck stood on end. He could feel the aura around Aisha growing stronger and spreading outward, saw the blue-white sparks dancing around her hand solidifying into concentrated beams of lightning—but lightning *she* summoned and commanded.

An eerie serenity had settled over Aisha. All trace of her earlier uncertainty had vanished, replaced by an air of utter calmness and control. Only the faintest hint of strain showed at the corners of her mouth and eyes as she drew more of the lightning to her. More, more, more, until she almost glowed with her own internal light.

With no visible motion the Hunter could see, Aisha directed the corona of energy undulating around her into Kiara's body. Kiara cried out, her voice so weak yet ringing with purest agony. Her back arched, the muscles in her neck contracted, and her body began to writhe and spasm on the floor as the power blazed through every fiber of her being.

The Hunter wanted to go to her, yet dared not for fear of interrupting whatever Aisha was doing. The Ghandian girl's magic was Kiara's *only* hope. If it didn't kill her first.

"Almost…" Aisha growled the word, her voice tight with strain. Sweat pricked on her brow and her muscles, too, corded like a hundred bowstrings snapped taut at once. Yet she did not remove her hand from the glowing object at her neck or Kiara's chest. She merely gritted her teeth and leaned into the effort—literally bowing forward at the waist, until her forehead nearly touched Kiara's chest.

The blue-white lights vanished as abruptly as they had appeared. Aisha slumped forward, as if utterly drained.

"Aisha!" Kodyn shouted, springing to her side.

"Kiara!" the Hunter called in the same moment. He dashed around the two youths and threw himself to one knee next to Kiara. "Kiara, can you hear me?"

Nothing happened. His heart pounded a furious staccato against his ribs. Dread twisted a dagger in his belly as he watched, waited, hoped. Whatever Aisha had done, would it—

Kiara's eyelids fluttered slowly open and her gaze fixed on him. "Hunter?" Her voice was weak—so terribly weak, barely above a whisper—but lucidity filled her eyes. She reached for him with a trembling hand, and he took it in his.

"I'm here." Tears stung at the backs of his eyes, and he wanted to shout, weep, and laugh all at once. Elation coursed through him like a tidal wave sweeping across marshlands. "I'm right here." He cupped her cheek, searched her face. "How do you feel?"

Kiara grimaced and gave a weak grunt. "Like I ate one of Graeme's spicy tamarind balls. Everything hurts. But..." She drew in a deep breath, then another. "But it's not the same pain. A better pain, if that makes sense?"

The Hunter swept her into his arms, relief washing through him. Her cracking jokes at Graeme's expense sent his spirits soaring heavenward. He cradled her, rocking back and forth, finally letting out the laugh that had been bubbling up within him since the moment she'd opened her eyes. "It makes perfect sense!" It didn't, but he didn't care. He only cared that she still lived.

His gaze darted to where Aisha now sat leaning heavily against Kodyn. She looked as if she'd just run across all of Einan, a pallor of exhaustion on her umber-toned features.

"Is it..." He scarcely dared to voice the question aloud for fear of the answer. Yet he *had* to know. "Is the rot gone?"

"It is." Aisha gave a slow nod of her head, as if that mere effort cost her greatly. "I burned away the last of the putrescence. Her wound should heal on its own."

The Hunter sensed the unspoken worry in her voice. The shadows in her dark eyes didn't only come from exhaustion. "But?"

Aisha winced. "Even after the rot was destroyed, something else remained. Something I could not burn away."

The Hunter's eyes narrowed. "What kind of something?" He glanced at Tarek. "Surely we removed all the shards?"

The young Elivasti stood frozen in place, staring wide-eyed at the empty air between Aisha and Kiara, as if reliving what they'd all just seen.

"Tarek!"

The Hunter's sharp tone snapped the young man out of his stupor. He blinked, regained his wits. "What?"

"We got all the shards out of her, right?" He gestured to Kiara's belly where the glowing crystal had pierced her.

"I-I believe so," Tarek stammered. He swallowed, scrubbed a hand over his eyes. "Yes, I'm all but certain we did." He sounded more confident now, once again in control of himself. "I checked the wound twice and saw no fragments."

The Hunter looked back to Aisha. "What remained?"

Aisha looked to Kodyn, who responded by nodding his encouragement. "It felt...like fire." Uncertainty edged her words and twisted her face into a frown. "A fire far hotter than the power of the *Kish'aa*. It remains within her still."

The Hunter's heart sprang into his throat. He tensed, worry once more stringing his nerves taut as a bowstring. "We have to get it out!" He looked down at Kiara. "We can't let it—"

"I don't think it will hurt her." Aisha's voice drew the Hunter's attention once more. The young Ghandian woman had recovered strength enough that she attempted to rise. Kodyn sprang to his feet and reached down a hand to help her stand. She managed to remain upright, though her legs trembled visibly with the effort. Her gaze returned to the Hunter. "I don't know *how* I know this, but when the *Kish'aa* encountered the fire, it did not repel them." Her frown deepened. "On the contrary, it drew them in, as if they fueled it. Made it burn brighter and hotter. But it did not hurt her. Instead, it made her stronger. Almost as if it was now a part of her."

The Hunter stared at Aisha. He could barely make sense of what she was saying—he'd seen enough magic to have the scarcest understanding of what he'd just witnessed, but so much was far beyond his comprehension. How it all worked—the Ritual of Cleansing, Garanis' Illusionist powers, the runes in the Hall of Remembrance, the magic that had opened the way to Enarium—he didn't know.

But he *did* know what he could see and feel. Kiara's eyes were open and color had begun to return to her face. Her pulse was stronger, too. She'd even attempted—albeit weakly—to extricate herself from his embrace and sit up. If Aisha believed she would recover her strength, the "how" of it came only of secondary importance.

"Thank you!" The words burst from his lips, backed by the force of the immense relief sweeping through him. "Truly, thank you. I am in your debt."

"We both are." Kiara had shifted in his arms, turning to look up at the two youths standing over her. "Whoever you are, I owe you my life."

Kodyn grinned. "I'm pretty sure that with everything Hailen and Evren did for us, we're even."

Kiara's eyes flew wide and she sat up with a gasp. "Hailen and Evren? You know them?"

"Know them?" Kodyn laughed. "You could say that." He looked between Kiara and the Hunter. "And after listening to them talk about the two of you, I feel like I know you." His gaze settled on the Hunter. "Even more so than what I saw in Praamis."

The Hunter and Kiara exchanged glances. "Tell me of them!" Kiara asked, a pleading tone to her voice. "Tell me of my boys."

"Our boys," the Hunter said in a tone of playful chiding.

Kiara ignored him, save to claw at his arm in her efforts to sit upright. "Are they well? Have they been eating properly? Staying out of trouble? Evren has a knack for getting into trouble—which I'm certain you saw for yourself—and dragging Hailen with him. Tell me they are unharmed, and that they fulfilled the mission to which Father Reverentus set them."

Kodyn's smile grew so wide it occupied the whole of his handsome face. "I'll be glad to tell you all about them, and what they got up to in Shalandra. But I think for this story, we'll need a fire, someplace comfortable to sit, and dinner." He looked to Aisha, chuckling. "Because it's a long tale better told over a hearty meal and a bottle of fine Nyslian wine."

Chapter Twenty-One

Half an hour later, the five of them sat around the small campfire Tarek had built. The Hunter had only left Kiara's side long enough to tend to the horses—Elivast and Ash had both earned a good rub-down and wet compresses for their legs made with the last of the water from the Hunter's canteen before being let free to crop the long grass. The Hunter swore that when they passed through Khafra, he'd purchase the finest fruits and largest sugar cubes he could find. It was because of the two horses that he'd arrived in time to save Kiara.

Though the meal of dried boar and gritty trail biscuits they had to offer Kodyn was far from hearty, the young man surprised them by producing the aforementioned bottle of Nyslian wine. Far from the best vintage—a young, sour *Vin Vert* from Renové—but after weeks of mostly drinking tepid canteen water, it tasted as good as the Sage's treasured Filaine Rouge.

When finally they settled back to listen to the story, Kodyn opened with a disclaimer. "I know that what I'm about to tell you may sound utterly insane and impossible." A wry grin broadened his face. "Honestly, looking back, it certainly *feels* that way. But it's all true, I swear." He gestured toward the Hunter. "You more than anyone should know just how many tales written off as legend and myth are, in fact, based largely on fact."

The Hunter inclined his head. "Understood." Few people had the capacity to believe even just the events of his journey from Voramis to Enarium, much less comprehend his half-demon heritage and the countless lives he'd lived over his millennia roaming Einan.

Kiara lay motionless in the Hunter's arms, still wrapped in blankets, but the Hunter could feel the eager anticipation setting every muscle in her body quivering. She'd been as worried about Hailen and Evren as he, just better at hiding it.

With bated breath, they listened to Kodyn's tale. Calling it fanciful would have been an understatement of the highest magnitude. Had he not lived through his own share of impossibilities—the ritual to summon a demon from the fiery hell, an ancient scimitar he'd wielded centuries ago, magic that encased the Elivasti dead in a tomb of stone, a power so mighty even the Serenii could not withstand it—he might have written it off as the conjurings of a truly imaginative mind.

Yet looking into Kodyn's eyes, seeing the young man's animated expressions as he told the story, the Hunter could not doubt it was all true. Every word of it, with Aisha's occasional nod, grimace, and interjection to support the tale.

The Hunter and Kiara clung to every word out of the youth's mouth, listening as he told of their journey to Shalandra to return Briana, the girl they'd rescued in Praamis, to her father—who just so happened to be the highest-ranking Secret Keeper in the City of the Dead. He spoke of his plan to steal the Crown of the Pharus and complete his Undertaking, which seemed like some sort of Night Guild coming-of-age ritual. Of Aisha's reason for accompanying him, he spoke little. The Hunter suspected it had something to do with whatever in the fiery hell those dancing blue-white lights had been.

Kodyn recounted how their paths had crossed with Hailen and Evren, who'd been masquerading as servants in Briana's household. How they had found Hailen holding a Serenii artifact alive and glowing with arcane magic.

At this, the Hunter's heart sprang into his throat. Of all his concerns for Hailen's wellbeing, few fears proved as terrifying as the promise of what Hailen's *Melechha* blood could do. How it could be used as the Sage had intended, to activate the Serenii mechanisms around Einan and wield the ancient race's magic. In the wrong hands, Hailen could be a weapon of terrible destruction. His life would forever be in danger because of that blood.

"Truth be told," Aisha interjected, "when I first saw him standing there, I thought he was an assassin come to kill Briana. Evren certainly had the look. But Hailen…" She shook her head, a hint of a smile tugging at her lips. "There was something instantly disarming about him. The way he answered Briana's questions without a shred of deceit or malice."

Kiara craned her head to beam up at the Hunter. "That's Hailen." Pride shone in her eyes and set her face glowing.

The Hunter grinned back at her, squeezing her arm. The boy's innocence had been what first compelled the Hunter to protect him all those years ago. Despite everything he'd endured, he hadn't lost it, hadn't been hardened by sorrow, loss, or suffering.

"Now Evren, that's a different story." Kodyn chuckled. "I've met few people warier and more suspicious in my life. And that's saying a lot, given the sort of criminals I grew up around."

The Hunter couldn't help a chuckle of his own. Evren's street smarts had been earned through hard experience, and his innate mistrust of *everyone* had kept him alive over years of living on the streets of Vothmot, dodging the city guard and Lecterns hunting him.

"It made sense, though." Kodyn's smile faded and his face grew serious, a solemn look in his eyes. "He told us what happened to him. In the Master's Temple, on the streets. How he ended up traveling with you into the Empty Mountains and joining you on your return to Voramis."

The Hunter's eyebrows rose. "He must have *truly* trusted you." He found it hard to imagine Evren would willingly share that part of himself with just anyone.

Kodyn exchanged a glance with Aisha, and both youths nodded. "In the end, he did," Kodyn said.

"And we trusted him, too." Aisha gave a little shrug of her shoulders. "Hard not to when you're all fighting for your lives side by side."

Kiara sucked in a breath. "Fighting? Fighting who?"

Kodyn settled back against the gnarled flat-top acacia that served as a makeshift shelter for their camp and continued with his story.

He told of the grim fate that had befallen Briana's father, how she had been cast out of her golden palace to live among the commoners of Shalandra, how they'd been attacked by the Gatherers.

"The *same* Gatherers that we eradicated in Praamis?" the Hunter asked, surprised.

"Sort of." Kodyn tilted his head to the side. "They were as mad as the ones serving Necroset Kytos, raving about the Final Destruction. But rather than murdering children in some strange ritual, they were after the Serenii artifacts that Briana's father had taken from the Temple of Whispers."

The Hunter noted the way the young man's eyes darted toward Aisha. To the pendant she'd been gripping earlier, he realized. The trinket had been tucked away beneath her clothing once more, out of sight. Yet the Hunter had seen the glow emanating from between her fingers. Save for its blue-white color, it could have been twin to the gemstone set into the hilts of the *Im'tasi* blades like Soulhunger and Deathbite. Questions roiled through his head, but before he could ask them, Kodyn continued his story.

"Anyways, once Aisha found out where the Gatherers were hiding—" The young man's dark eyebrows shot up. "In the Keeper's Crypts, of all places!" He shook his head, his expression incredulous. "—Issa and Hykos wiped them out."

The Hunter frowned. "And they are?"

"Oh, right." Kodyn looked to Aisha. "Did I forget to mention Issa?"

Aisha nodded. "You did."

Kodyn blushed. "Sorry." He turned back to the Hunter with an apologetic grin. "Issa was the Keeper's Blade assigned to guard Briana."

"A Keeper's Blade?" The Hunter let out a low whistle. "Briana was *that* valuable to the Pharus?" Though he'd never crossed blades with the Shalandran elite warriors, he'd heard tales of their skill with their enormous flame-bladed greatswords and their nigh-unbreakable armor forged of some unknown metal.

"Her father wasn't just a Secret Keeper," Kodyn said. "He was also one of the Pharus' chief advisors. Until he was murdered by Gatherers attempting to assassinate the Pharus."

That surprised the Hunter. He knew only a little of Shalandran politics, but he was given to understand that "Pharus" was more than just a monarchical title. Among his many honorifics was "Chosen of Hallar," conveying that his right to rule came from his long-dead ancestor and the founder of Shalandra. Few had the power and audacity to attempt to strike down that particular potentate. It would be much like assassinating the Grand Reckoner of the Coin Counter's Temple or the highest-ranking Warrior Priest of Derelana.

Then again, he thought, *the Gatherers in Praamis were pretty much insane, driven by their dream of the Final Destruction, whatever the fiery hell that is. Not hard to believe they'd go after the Pharus if they believed he somehow impeded its arrival.*

Kodyn recovered, the shadows vanishing from his expression and his face lifting. "Anyways, as I was saying, Issa and Hykos—"

"Another of the Keeper's Blades," Aisha interjected. "Issa's trainer, of sorts."

"Yes, that." Kodyn swept his hand in a vague gesture of acknowledgement. "While they were dealing with the Gatherers, more attacked us in Briana's home, so we had to flee to the Temple of Whispers for shelter. Hailen was there with us—"

"In the Temple of Whispers?" Kiara bolted upright, so abruptly she all but hurled the blankets off her. "With the Secret Keepers?!"

The Hunter heard the worry ringing in her voice and felt its match churning in his belly. The thought of Hailen falling into the clutches of the Secret Keepers sent a shiver of fear rippling down his spine. The servants of the Mistress believed their holy duty lay in not only uncovering the hidden truths of the world, but concealing those they deemed too dangerous to fall into others' hands. Which was why they had banned alchemical practices and hunted down those like Graeme and the others of the Hidden Circle who flouted their proscriptions.

"Don't worry!" Kodyn held up both hands in a pacifying gesture. "Everything worked out in the end, I promise."

Despite the young man's assurances, every muscle in Kiara's upper body remained as taut as braided cable and she emanated an air of concern nearly as potent as the glowing aura that had encircled Aisha earlier. But only for a few more heartbeats. Her strength soon gave out and she slumped back against the Hunter, exhausted.

He wrapped his arms around her from behind, elated. The fact that she'd managed to sit up at all filled him with hope. Her wound was already healing in the wake of whatever magic Aisha had wielded, the flesh once again pink and free of any trace of rot. She was on the mend, but had to take it easy the next few days to regain her stamina.

While Kodyn continued his story—telling of Evren's encounter with the blacksmith Killian and their war against Blackfinger and the Ybrazhe Syndicate that ruled Shalandra's underworld—the Hunter's gaze strayed to Aisha. She sat at Kodyn's side, leaning against him with a comfortable familiarity that bespoke the true nature of their relationship. Yet though she watched him recounting their adventures, her mind appeared to be far off. Every so often, her left hand strayed to a bulge in one of her pockets, her right hand playing with the outline of the pendant barely visible beneath her shirt.

Thus far, Kodyn had spoken little of *her* involvement in their adventures in Shalandra, keeping his story centered largely on himself, Hailen, Evren, Briana, and the Keeper's Blade, Issa. But the shadows filling her eyes hadn't been there when their paths had crossed in Praamis, during their clash with the Gatherers. Nor had that burning light he'd seen back in The Blind Pig after she killed the slaver. There was a great deal about the Ghandian woman hidden beneath the surface. Kodyn's friendly demeanor only highlighted the contrast between them.

But could the Hunter blame her? He'd done everything in his power to shield the truth about Hailen from the world. It was clear she possessed some manner of magical ability, though its true nature remained a mystery. Perhaps to her, too. She'd been hesitant, uncertain when Kodyn spoke of using her power to save Kiara's life. It had taken *his* confidence to bolster her enough to act.

As Kodyn continued—telling of the unrest stirred up and the riots tearing through the streets of Shalandra, the attack on the Temple of Whispers that Hailen had repelled using the Serenii artifacts—the Hunter watched Aisha carefully. Watched the way her face grew tighter, her mind retreated farther inward. Almost as if reliving the events in Shalandra amplified the magnitude of whatever internal war raged within her soul.

In that moment, he felt a strange sense of kinship with her. He, too, had fought his own inner battles, wrestled against demons both real and imagined. For years, he'd struggled against Soulhunger's demands. Though he'd found freedom from the dagger's voice in Enarium, he now grappled with the dilemma presented by the magic fueling the Sword of Nasnaz, the bloodlust that surged within him whenever he drew the blade.

Though he did not know what ghosts of her past haunted her or what turmoil churned within her, he determined that if he could do something—*anything*—to help her find even a measure of peace, he would.

He owed her that much for saving Kiara's life.

Chapter Twenty-Two

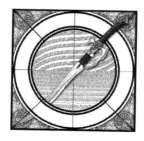

"Wait, wait!" Kiara's insistent voice drew the Hunter's attention away from Aisha and back to Kodyn's story. "You're saying that Hailen, *my* Hailen, was spoken of in this Hallar's Prophecy?"

The Hunter frowned. *Prophecy?* He'd clearly missed something truly important.

Kodyn nodded. "Truth is, we *all* were." He gestured to the young woman sitting at his side. "Aisha, too. And Issa and Briana. Even Evren."

"Evren!" Kiara gave a little cry of delight and twisted to look up at the Hunter. "Evren, too!" A smile of purest joy wreathed her face. "I always told him he was special."

The Hunter tried to smile back, but confusion turned his grin lopsided. "What prophecy?"

Kiara's smile cracked. "Weren't you listening?" Her lips turned down into a frown that looked to be well in its way to a scowl.

The Hunter tried to play it off. "I was savoring the wine." He took a sip from his long-forgotten cup. The heat of the night had warmed the wine, and it was halfway to vinegar, but it gave him cover. He doubted either Aisha or Kodyn would be delighted to hear he'd been scrutinizing the Ghandian woman. "But what was this prophecy you mentioned?"

"The Prophecy of the Final Destruction." Kodyn's expression grew serious. "It foretold that all six of us would bring about the end of days."

The Hunter grimaced. "Sounds...delightful." Truth be told, he *hated* the idea of such prophecies. The notion that some ancient somebody might actually be able to foretell the future felt a lot like imprisonment. He'd struggled his entire life against anything resembling "destiny" or "fate." Even the remote possibility that Hailen and Evren were tied to any sort of divination or foretelling left him uneasy. He put no stock in coincidences, and these things had a way of ending in the worst possible outcome for those involved.

"Which we did," Kodyn added.

To the Hunter's surprise, the young man's face broke out into a beaming smile. Aisha, too, grinned, as if at some grand joke only they understood.

"You brought on the Final Destruction," the Hunter said in a flat voice. "Just like that?"

Kodyn chuckled. "That's the thing. It wasn't actually *destruction.*" He leaned forward and his eyes sparkled as if he prepared to share some great secret. "Whoever translated it originally mixed up their Serenii runes. They read it as 'destruction, the end of all things', sort of what the Devourer of Worlds intends for all living things."

The Hunter sucked in a breath. Had Hailen and Evren told them of the Hunter's quest? Or had Kodyn's knowledge been passed down from his mother, the Master of the Night Guild? *One less earth-shattering revelation to worry about explaining, I suppose.*

"But really," Kodyn continued, not noticing the Hunter's surprise, "according to Briana, based on what she learned from her father, the rune actually meant 'destruction that heralds a rebirth'." He looked to Aisha. "How did she explain it?"

"Issa said something about burning farmlands to make the ground fertile for new crops to grow," Aisha said.

"That's it!" Kodyn snapped his fingers, a triumphant look on his face. "And that's what led us to unlocking the Vault of Ancients and finding Hallar's final resting place." Wonder shone in his eyes as he turned to look at the Hunter. "Did you know that he was a Bucelarii?"

The question caught the Hunter by surprise. "What?"

"Yeah!" Kodyn nodded, his expression mirroring the Hunter's astonishment. "That's what I thought, too, when Evren first told us. But the Pharus said his father had told him the same thing. That Hallar, Shalandra's founder, was Bucelarii. Which, it turns out, is the same kind of half-demon you told my mother you were."

The Hunter had no answer to that. He'd known that *he* had lived other lives, roamed across Einan throughout his thousands of years. Yet the only other half-demons he'd encountered had been in Enarium. The Beggar Priests had hunted his kind to extinction long ago, he knew. Yet the idea that his fellow Bucelarii could have legends written about them—just as the legend of Nasnaz was about him—had never once crossed his mind.

"And he had one of those *Im'tasi* blades." Kodyn gestured to Soulhunger, sitting on the Hunter's belt. "Which, I guess, Evren now carries."

The Hunter felt Kiara inhale sharply. "He *what?*" she demanded.

"That's why he traveled to Shalandra in the first place, so he said." Kodyn looked between the Hunter and Kiara, as if confused by their surprise. "He came to collect the Blade of Hallar for the Beggar Priests in Voramis, but he intended to bring it back to *you* all along. Said it was how he intended to contribute to your efforts to uphold the oath you swore to Kharna."

The Hunter sat back heavily against his own acacia tree trunk, his mind awhirl. "He...said that?"

Kodyn nodded. "He and Hailen both, they were so intent on doing whatever they could to help you. They saw how heavy a burden it was for you, and though you'd never allow it to weigh on them, they *wanted* to help." A shy smile sprouted on the young man's face. "They wanted you to know you weren't in it alone."

Warmth glowed like a smith's forge in the Hunter's belly, and tears pricked at the Hunter's eyes. "They're good lads," he said, his voice rough, hoarse with emotion. He turned away quickly and covered his emotion by taking a sip of his wine, then used his sleeve to roughly scrub any hint of moisture from his cheeks while pretending to wipe his mouth. Kiara's hand squeezed his leg reassuringly. He didn't need to see her face to know that she, too, was aglow with maternal pride.

"And it was Evren's idea to trap the demon in the Chamber of Sustenance where we found Hallar," Kodyn continued. "He said—"

"*Demon!*" Kiara bolted upright again. "There was a bloody *demon* in Shalandra and you're just telling us this now?"

"Oh, shite, did I forget that, too?" Kodyn's face flushed red and he shot an embarrassed look at Aisha.

"You did." Aisha's expression remained flat, but the corners of her eyes crinkled as if she struggled to conceal her laughter. "Go on, Kodyn. Tell them about the *demon* who nearly killed us all."

"Yes, Kodyn," Kiara said through gritted teeth. "Tell us." Her fingers gripped the Hunter's leg with such force her fingernails nearly clawed holes in his trousers.

"I told you, it all worked out in the end!" Kodyn held up his hands like a shield before him. His words came in a rush. "We only realized it was a demon once Evren got a good look at him. The eyes, he said." He tapped his cheek for emphasis. "Blacker than night. Blacker even than yours." He pointed to the Hunter's face. "But we put the bastard down. Issa had the Blade of Hallar and Evren had an iron dagger. Between them, they incapacitated the demon long enough to put him in the Chamber of Sustenance. By then, Aisha and Hailen had already activated the Serenii machine and unleashed the Final Destruction across the city. It was over at that point—"

"Wait!" Now it was the Hunter's turn to startle. "Activate the Serenii machine? Did I hear that correct?"

Kodyn's cheeks darkened to a deep crimson. "Y-Yes, you did. But Hailen didn't bleed a lot. Just a finger-prick, I swea—"

"When?" The Hunter's voice cracked like a whip. He leaned forward, eyes drilling into Kodyn. "When, *exactly*, did this happen?"

Kodyn's face screwed up into a frown. "I, uh—"

"Think, Kodyn," the Hunter insisted. "It's important. Can you remember the day and time?"

"I can." Aisha's voice pierced the blood rushing in the Hunter's ears. His head snapped toward her, found her once more possessed of an inhuman calm. Her face was serene and once more faint sparks of blue-white light glowed in her eyes. "Twenty-four days and five hours ago."

The Hunter didn't need to count backward to know *exactly* when it had happened. He had seen the magic flickering to life even from thousands of leagues away.

"The Monolith!" Kiara breathed in a voice tinged with wonder. "The day we attacked Lord Apus." She'd come to the same conclusion as the Hunter.

Now it was Kodyn's turn to look confused. "What?"

"When you turned on the Serenii machine," the Hunter said, "it did something to another Serenii structure in Malandria. It turned it on, but only for a few seconds. And I think…" He hesitated. "No, I'm *certain* I saw the moment when it happened."

Kiara turned to regard him. "How?"

The Hunter's jaw muscles worked. "In my communion with Kharna, I saw it."

His mind flashed back to the image. He described it as he'd seen it. "It was a chamber with two large, round windows that overlooked the city, wasn't it?" He still recalled the vast city of gold spreading out all around the six youths in his vision. "And you were there, Kodyn. The wings of a great bird spread out in the air above you. Like an eagle or…of course." He snorted softly. "A hawk."

Kodyn's jaw dropped.

The Hunter turned to Aisha. "You were there, too. Surrounded by an aura of blue-white—the same aura I saw when you healed Kiara."

Aisha, too, appeared stunned.

Now the Hunter saw the vision more clearly, began to make sense of it. "There was one that gave off an air of wisdom despite his youth." He beamed down at Kiara. "That was Evren. And Hailen was there, too. Blazing with golden light as bright as the sun."

"That's my boys." Kiara's smile matched the Hunter's.

The Hunter turned back to Kodyn and Aisha. "The other two—one shrouded in secrets, the other holding both a great sword and a scepter—those were your companions. Issa and Briana?"

Kodyn looked to Aisha with an expression of wonder shining on his handsome face. "Briana, daughter of the Secret Keeper. And Issa, daughter of—"

Aisha pressed a finger to his lips. "That's not our story to tell, Kodyn." She turned back to the Hunter. "But if you saw all of that, then you know why we did what we did. To fulfill the vow Hallar made to the Serenii to protect Shalandra."

That caught the Hunter by surprise. "A vow Hallar made to the Serenii?" He frowned. He had known of *his* oath to Kharna, sworn thousands of years earlier. But he had no knowledge of any other oaths made by his kind. "How do you know he swore an oath?"

Aisha recoiled as if he'd just ripped open her belly. Every muscle in her strong shoulders tensed, her posture instantly going rigid.

The Hunter saw her defenses going up—he'd felt it within himself countless times in the past. Always his reaction when he felt endangered, or when uncertainty and self-doubt threatened to undermine him. Every time, he'd told himself he did it out of a desire for self-preservation, to keep the ugly, monstrous parts of himself hidden from those around him. And in the end, every time, it had earned him nothing but grief.

Not that revealing those parts of himself had always ended well, either. Sir Sigmund's baleful glare and dire words still rang in his mind, even weeks after leaving Malandria. The hatred twisting Sir Georges and Sir Benoit's faces into monstrous masks haunted him, as did their snarled Elisionist mantra of *"Ikh manashar!"*

Kiara had helped him to see the truth: opening up to others *might* drive them away, but closing himself off and building walls between them *definitely* would.

"Tell us, Aisha." The Hunter spoke in as gentle a tone as he could manage. "You know our worst secrets. You know I am half-demon, that I am sworn to kill to sustain Kharna. Whatever you are afraid to say, it cannot possibly be worse than that."

"You are safe," Kiara said, her voice ringing with the same maternal note that had always soothed Hailen and Evren. "You know my boys well enough that I believe they trusted you. Evren wouldn't have told you all of that unless he truly did." She stretched out a hand toward Aisha, leaned forward so she could rest her fingers lightly on the young woman's knee. "Trust us, like you trusted them."

Still, Aisha remained silent. Her jaw muscles clenched so tight the bones creaked and her teeth ground. Her shoulders tensed as if fighting a battle, one that raged in her mind.

"Aisha." Kodyn's voice echoed with a tenderness reflected in the comforting touch of his hand on her shoulder. "They've already seen it for themselves. There's no point in hiding it." He squeezed gently. "And Kiara's right. We trusted Hailen and Evren. We can trust them, too."

For a long moment, Aisha remained utterly motionless, hard and stiff as the stony earth beneath them. Then she seemed to crumple like a sail on a becalmed ocean. Her head slumped to her chest as if exhausted and she leaned heavily against Kodyn's hand.

Silence hung in the camp. The Hunter and Kiara stared at the woman, waiting, expectant. Kodyn's grip tightened on her shoulder, offering wordless reassurance of his touch and presence.

When Aisha spoke, her voice was half-muffled by her chin pressing against her chest. "I know of Hallar's oath to the Serenii because I spoke to him." Slowly, she lifted her head, eyes downcast. Finally, she looked at the Hunter and Kiara. "I spoke to Hallar as I spoke to all the *Kish'aa* in Shalandra."

The Hunter's mind raced. He'd heard Kodyn mention that name, had wondered about it. He'd almost asked about it while watching Aisha retreat into herself during Kodyn's story. But now, she spoke of it of her own free will, though it clearly cost her effort.

"What are the *Kish'aa*?" Kiara asked gently.

"The spirits of the dead." Aisha's jaw set, her head lifting. "That is my ability—though I once saw it as a curse, I now know the truth. I am *Umoyahlebe*, a Spirit Whisperer, and my gift is to commune with and command the dead."

Chapter Twenty-Three

The Hunter studied Aisha's face. The Ghandian's expression was defiant, as if daring them to scorn or challenge her. But he just nodded. "Interesting."

Aisha seemed taken aback by his response, almost at a loss for words. No doubt she'd expected ridicule or disbelief. But acceptance?

The Hunter smiled. "There was a time *I* saw the dead, too."

Aisha's eyes narrowed and her lips tightened into a thin, angry line.

The Hunter held up a hand. "That is neither jest nor pretense." He held her gaze, let her see the truth written in his eyes. "Once, years ago, I was exposed to alchemy that allowed me to hear and speak with the spirits of those slain by the Bloody Hand. I doubt you are suffering under the effects of the same poison that nearly killed me, but I suspect the spirits you see are no less real than mine felt at the time."

Aisha's jaw dropped. Kodyn, too, appeared utterly shocked to speechlessness. The Hunter hadn't spoken of his visions of Farida, Bardin, Old Nan, and the others he'd lost with Hailen or Evren. Kiara alone knew. He'd told her one night two years earlier as they lay in bed together. It had been a test of how much he could trust her with his heart, his secrets. She'd responded with tenderness and empathy, as was her nature. The Hunter had felt the weight lifting off his chest, his very soul made lighter by her acceptance. If he could do the same for Aisha...

He leaned forward and said in a gentle tone, "I understand, at least in small part, what that must be like for you."

A profound and instantaneous transformation swept over Aisha. Before his words, she'd sat stiff and wary, her anger flaring like a torch, a defensive measure to shield herself in the moment of utter vulnerability. Yet in the wake of his pronouncement, she seemed to inflate, her shoulders lifting, the worry and fear and hesitation draining from her eyes.

"It has been...trying, to say the least." Aisha managed a small smile, one tinged with a generous measure of relief. "But over the last few weeks, I've started to make more sense of things, to gain some semblance of control over it. The spirits are loud and insistent, but *this* helps to clarify things."

She drew out the pendant from beneath her shirt and showed it to him. It was a simple stone of purest black—the same black as the *Dolmenrath,* perhaps—with not a trace of the glow the Hunter had seen emanating from between Aisha's fingers. Yet he could feel its power faintly, like the merest whisper of an early-morning zephyr gliding through the leaves of a distant tree.

"Serenii?" the Hunter asked, his gaze sliding from the pendant to Aisha's face.

Aisha nodded. "It is called the *Dy'nashia.* Meaning—"

"Repository."

The word out of the darkness startled the Hunter. His head snapped toward the spot where Tarek sat to his left, just within the ring of firelight. The young Elivasti had spoken not a word throughout Kodyn's recounting of events. Due to his stillness and utter lack of scent, the Hunter had all but forgotten about him until this moment.

Tarek sat hunched low in his cloak, wine cup clasped in both hands, his violet eyes cast in shadow. "A storehouse for magical power," he said, his voice low and expression solemn.

"That's it." Aisha looked to the young man. "You know the language of the Serenii?"

"I ought to." Tarek's scruffy face tightened.

"How?" Aisha cocked her head, a curious look on her face. "Thus far, the only people I've met who know *anything* about them are Briana, the daughter of a Secret Keeper who dedicated his life to studying these artifacts—" She held up the pendant once more. "—and Hailen. He said he met some in Kara-ket and Enarium."

Mention of Hailen knotted the Hunter's belly. He felt Kiara tense in his arms, too. They had both agreed to tell Tarek the truth about his blood kinship with Hailen when the time was right. But this *definitely* wasn't that time.

"Tarek is Elivasti," the Hunter said. "He, like all of his people, are descended from the Serenii themselves."

Aisha and Kodyn both sucked in sharp breaths, exchanging excited glances.

"Truly?" Kodyn leaned forward, eagerness sparkling in his eyes. "Can you read *all* of their runes, or just some? And how much do you know about their creations? Briana and Aisha managed to figure out the rudiments of the *Dy'nashia's* functions, but if there is more to be learned—"

"I am not an expert on the Serenii," Tarek said. "I only know what I was taught by my elders among the Elivasti. There are far too many runes for any one person to learn them all—not even Kanna claimed to know all, and she lived close to two hundred years—but I have learned enough of the written and spoken language to keep alive the traditions we True Descendants cherish."

The young man's response surprised the Hunter. He'd expected Tarek to clam up, as he'd been about to. Yet something had drawn the Elivasti out and kept him talking. Was it the presence of *other* youths? Kodyn and Aisha were roughly of an age with Evren, he knew, but Tarek couldn't be many years older. After months of traveling with Itan, a man easily three or four decades his senior, and now weeks on the road with the Hunter and Kiara, the presence of people around his own age had to be a welcome change.

"Fascinating!" Kodyn's handsome face shone bright in the firelight. "It's strange to think that we've lived around the works of the Serenii our whole lives, but there is so much that we don't know. So many secrets yet to be unlocked—and countless more already lost to time." He looked to Aisha with an eager smile. "It's exciting and terrifying to think about."

Aisha nodded. "Indeed."

The Hunter looked between the pair. There was clearly more to their presence in Khafra than merely what they'd discovered in Shalandra. They had journeyed thousands of leagues, far from the only home Kodyn had known, but for what purpose?

"This gift of yours, the ability to speak to the dead, it isn't truly linked to that Serenii pendant, is it?" Kiara sat up, leaned toward the two youths. "You said the *Dy'nashia* clarifies things for you. But the power itself, where is it from?"

The question took everyone, even the Hunter, by surprise. Yet it was precisely the question he'd been wanting to voice aloud since he'd first seen the sparks of blue-white light dancing around the young woman's strong hands.

Kodyn and Aisha exchanged glances, but neither of them spoke. Tarek stared at Aisha with curiosity blazing on his face.

Kiara pressed on. "I've spent a great deal of time discussing what little is known of magic with…a friend."

By her hesitation, the Hunter suspected it was either Graeme or Father Reverentus. To his knowledge, Kiara had gone to the alchemist for answers pertaining to the creatures spoken of in myths and legend, but Graeme's knowledge tended toward the scientific and quantifiable. Magic was far more the priest's area of expertise. Perhaps *that* had been one of the subjects of their discussion the day Kiara joined Father Reverentus in his carriage—one of the final days of their fateful journey that ended in the old cleric's demise.

The Hunter shoved aside the thoughts of Father Reverentus. The inevitable upswell of guilt he felt at the grim memories would make it difficult to focus on the matter at hand.

"From what we've been able to determine, there are really only *two* types." Kiara held up a pair of fingers. "First, there is the magic accessed through the mechanisms and artifacts crafted by the Serenii. Soulhunger. The towers of Enarium. The Monolith. Whatever it was you encountered in Shalandra. The second is the magic inherent in blood. Some would call it *abilities*. Like the ability of the Bucelarii and Abiarazi to recover from wounds that would kill any mortal man." She gestured to Tarek. "Or the Elivasti's long lives could also be considered such."

The Hunter could see the truth written on Aisha's face from the moment Kiara mentioned *blood*.

"Yours is the latter, isn't it?" Kiara's question was gentle but firm, as inexorable as a river seeping through cracks in stone. "The Serenii-crafted Repository could give you access to whatever power it stores, but that's not how you described it." Fascination echoed in her voice. "This is a power in your blood. Something you inherited. The question is, from who?"

As Kiara's spoke, Aisha's mien had grown more solemn, the shadows spreading across her strong features. Her shoulders grew hunched and her fists whitened in her lap. *This*, then, was the true burden weighing on her.

"Tell them, Aisha." Kodyn spoke softly, laying a gentle hand on her shoulder. "If anyone can help, it's them."

Sorrow twisted Aisha's face. She looked to her companion, as if seeking strength from his touch, his presence at her side. When she finally found her voice, her words came out slow, heavy, as if each cost her an immense effort.

"The gift of the *Umoyahlebe* was passed down to me by my father." Tears welled in her eyes. "For him, though, it was a curse. It untethered his mind from reality, set his thoughts adrift. When last I saw him, nearly five years ago, he lived more among the spirits than his own family."

Kodyn's grip on her tightened, but instead of sinking deeper into herself, something about that memory strengthened Aisha's resolve. She sat straighter and lifted her head.

"I am here to return to my people." Aisha's voice rang with a certainty and confidence that stood in stark contrast with her earlier hesitation. "I have learned much about what it means to be *Umoyahlebe*, and found a means of preventing the curse from claiming any more Spirit Whisperers. Including my sister."

The Hunter felt the pain in Aisha's words, saw it reflected in every muscle of her face and knotted shoulders.

Aisha's eyes locked with the Hunter. "*That* is why I could not give you the *ephrade.*" She tapped the pocket where the Hunter had guessed she carried the pouch of dried herbs Indigo had given them. "It was the final missing ingredient in an alchemical potion Briana and I discovered could stop the *Inkuleko,* the Unshackling of a Spirit Whisperer's mind from their body. It is too late to save my father, but there are countless more *Umoyahlebe* who I can help. I go to my people to do what I can for those like me."

"And I'm going with you to watch your back," Kodyn said. When Aisha turned to regard him, he grinned widely. "Hey, I may be just a humble Journeyman of the Night Guild, not a potential savior of all the Issai, but we're in this together." He took her hands in his and held them with the tenderness that could only be borne of true love. "Whatever happens."

"Whatever happens," Aisha echoed.

Kodyn leaned forward and kissed her gently. A quick, almost shy kiss, one that brought color rushing to both their cheeks.

Kiara grinned up at the Hunter, and he knew what she was thinking. Theirs was a love still in its infancy. They would have time to explore its true depth and breadth over the years to come, through the hardships and challenges that lay ahead.

He found himself hoping it weathered the inevitable storms, though. There was something so genuinely *good* about the two of them together. Two people from vastly different backgrounds thrown together by circumstances he couldn't begin to understand, finding some measure of solace and strength in the other's presence. Much like him and Kiara, he supposed.

"You say that there are others among your people with the same power?" This question came from Tarek, who had again been listening silently.

The Hunter glanced over. The young Elivasti's expression was pensive, bordering on worried. But over what?

"Others of these…" Tarek fished for the word. "*Umoyahlebe?*"

Aisha nodded. "Yes. I do not know how many, or to what extent they can speak with or command the *Kish'aa.*" She twitched her shoulder in a shrug. "But there are more."

Tarek's face darkened. "That was what I feared."

The Hunter's eyebrow rose. "Feared?" He didn't understand the young man's concern. "What would—" Then it struck him. The *true* reason Tarek had been sent to accompany them to Ghandia.

Kiara voiced the words aloud. "You are afraid the Abiarazi are seeking to harness this *Umoyahlebe* power for themselves?"

"Aren't you?" Tarek sprang to his feet, all trace of calm vanishing in a moment as he rounded on the Hunter. "You saw what she can do!" He jabbed a finger toward Aisha. "She may have used the power to *help* Kiara, but if one of the *maistyrs* somehow figured a way to turn it to their evil ends, there is no telling how it could be misused."

A chill ran down the Hunter's spine at the mental image of the Sage or Warmaster marching at the head of an army of people who could tap into whatever magic Aisha had used to burn away the rot within Kiara. The aura of power she'd exuded had been awe-inspiring, and she was just *one*. But if the Abiarazi collected every *Umoyahlebe* from around the vast lands that had once been the Ghandian Empire?

"The truth?" Aisha's face was hard, her anger only tightly reined. "*Any* power can be misused in the wrong hands. Be it the power to speak to the spirits or wield a sword, where it is wielded with ill intent, the outcome is the same."

The Hunter had seen evidence of that far too often in his own life. Those with power—physical might, wealth, or arcane magics—rarely chose the path of kindness and compassion. Always it was more profitable to exert influence and control over those without.

"But to my people," Aisha continued, leaning forward and lowering her voice, "the gift of speaking with the *Kish'aa* is used to bring comfort, to gain wisdom and insight, to learn from our forefathers and mothers. The dead speak, and the *Umoyahlebe* listen."

Tarek looked as if he wanted to say more, to press the matter. A look from Kiara stopped him. He appeared far from mollified, but at least he took his seat.

"That's not all, though." This from Kodyn. "Tell them what you told me."

Aisha shot the young man a hard glance, but it had no effect on him. He merely gave her an encouraging nod.

Aisha let out a slow breath. "To manifest the *Kish'aa* as I have…" She shook her head. "I know it is possible—my father has spoken of it—but never have I seen him do what I have done. I do not know if it is beyond him, if he does not know how, or if he merely has never done it in my presence. But for most *Umoyahlebe,* their gifts are restricted to communing with the spirits." She fingered the Serenii-crafted pendant. "Perhaps with this, I will find out if I am alone in what I can do, or if there is more to my abilities—*our* abilities—than was believed possible. I know that what I have done is beyond what I believed possible, so perhaps…"

She let her words trail off; no more was needed, in truth.

The Hunter considered what she'd said. To hear that the ability to manipulate the magical energy of the *Kish'aa* in such a tangible way was unique to her didn't exactly settle his worries. If she had learned how to do so, the Hunter had no doubt *others* could, too. Especially one as old and cunning as an Abiarazi. A demon who had dedicated centuries or millennia to unlocking this singular power stood no less chance of discovering the power's full potential than a young woman not much older than Evren. It *could* have been mere coincidence—the Abiarazi in Ghandia could be seeking something else entirely, with no knowledge of this magical ability to command the *Kish'aa,* these spirits of the dead. But the Hunter couldn't take that chance, not if there was even the remotest possibility a Keeper-damned *demon* was involved.

He fixed Aisha with a hard gaze. "Looks like we'll be joining you on your journey."

Aisha's mouth opened, a protest forming on her lips.

Kodyn spoke first. "No, they're right."

Aisha's teeth snapped shut with a click and she rounded on Kodyn. "Excuse me?"

Kodyn didn't back down, despite the forcefulness of her tone. "You were there in Shalandra, Aisha. You know how hard it was to take down that demon. Fiery hell, had it not been for Hallar's spirit, we might *all* have died." He gestured to the Hunter. "And if there's any chance we might run into one of them, who better to have at our side than the bloody Hunter of Voramis?!"

Aisha's brow furrowed, her expression darkening. The tension in her face returned as she wrestled with the notion.

"Aisha," Kiara said, her voice sweet and gentle yet commanding, brooking no argument. "We're coming with you. I owe you for saving my life. Whatever we can do to help you, we will. Even if that just means making sure you return to your people in one piece, so be it."

She stretched out a hand and gripped Aisha's knee. "It can't be a coincidence your path crossed the Hunter's when and where it did. Somehow, two of the only people in the world who know the truth about Hailen and Evren ended up right here with us. Call it destiny, fate, prophecy, the will of the gods, the work of your *Kish'aa,* anything you want. But there's no denying it. We're *meant* to travel together, meant to face whatever lies ahead together."

Aisha did not immediately relent. The stubborn look persisted for long moments. Yet the Hunter could sense her resistance weakening. Kiara could be damned persuasive when she tried.

"Fine," she growled. "But you must know that my first priority is to *my* people." Her strong jaw muscles clenched and her fists balled tight. "I will save my sister from the grim fate that claimed my father. I have come this far, and nothing, and I mean *nothing,* will stop me."

Looking at her face, the Hunter did not doubt it for a moment.

Chapter Twenty-Four

Their group—now consisting of *five* horses and riders—set off for Khafra shortly after noon the following day.

No one had argued about the late departure. Kiara slept a full eight hours, until well after the sun's rise, but even after she awoke, the Hunter refused to ride on. Ash and Elivast needed more rest, he told her. Not *exactly* a lie. Both horses showed signs of lingering fatigue after their hard ride the previous day. The Hunter had given them extra salt cubes to restore their strength and rubbed them down with the last of Tarek's water. Yet he took care to drag on his ministrations to give Kiara more time at ease. She was just stubborn enough to try and push herself too hard, too soon.

Tarek spent the last few hours before sunrise hunting and returned with the rising sun carrying a scimitar-horned oryx slung over his shoulder. At the Hunter's insistence, the young man had skinned and dressed the kill, butchering half to cook and eat now and the other half to sell while in Khafra. Not that they needed additional coin, with what the Hunter had stashed away. But there was no sense letting so much fine meat go to waste.

Kodyn proved an able hand with the cooking. He added enough salt to bring out the meat's taste, along with a few spices Aisha produced from her pack. The smell alone was enough to set the Hunter's stomach rumbling. Anything was better than hard, dried trail rations and Tarek's flavorless cooking of recent days.

Only after the last of the cooked meat had been gnawed off the bone or wrapped up for later consumption did the Hunter *finally* saddle the horses and prepare to ride. Getting Kiara up into the saddle proved a daunting task. His desire to aid her was matched by her sheer loathing of what she deemed "an unnecessary fuss and bother" when she waved him away. He refused to leave off, however, and was glad of his own stubbornness when she couldn't climb onto Ash's back unaided. He all but lifted her into the saddle, armor and all, and stoically bore the angry invective she hurled at him for "treating me like some Keeper-damned noble lady".

Throughout the ordeal, Kodyn, Aisha, and Tarek paid careful attention to their own mounts and studiously kept their eyes away from him and the obstreperous Kiara. More than once, the Hunter caught glimpses of grins and shared glances of amusement passing between them. One more thing for him to ignore as he finished packing up his gear and climbed onto Elivast's back.

He set a slow pace, keenly aware of but pretending not to notice Kiara's condition. She no longer swayed in the saddle, but he occasionally caught the faint grunt or gasp signaling just how much the effort of staying upright cost her. The still-healing wound had to be paining her badly. But, he knew, she'd rather collapse from exhaustion than show the toll it was taking on her.

111

The Hunter had inspected her injury before setting off. All trace of infection had vanished, and the wound had developed a thick crust that no longer bled. So long as Ash didn't break into a gallop, she ought to survive a day's travel without re-opening the injury.

Neither Ash nor Elivast appeared to be in the mood for another mad ride. Elivast plodded along with his head hanging down low, each step more sluggish than usual. Ash had lost his effervescence and the spring in his step.

Kodyn and Aisha's horses, too, showed signs of fatigue. They hadn't been ridden nearly as hard as Ash and Elivast, but they'd come close to matching the Hunter's mad pace. The youths seemed strangely worn out, too. Aisha had slept little—less even than the Hunter—and dark circles showed around her eyes. Kodyn, on the other hand, had fallen asleep in seconds, but woke up frequently throughout the night to seek out Aisha. He was clearly worried for her, which did him credit. As did the fact that he'd apparently come all this way for the sole purpose of supporting and guarding her back as she endeavored to help her people.

They crested the hill obstructing the view of Khafra when the sun was halfway to the western horizon. The Hunter made no complaint as Kiara paused to drink in the view. In truth, he wanted to see the ancient city again, this time *without* the possibility of Kiara's death looming over his head.

In the reddish-gold sunlight of late afternoon, the myriad stelae seemed to glow with an otherworldly radiance. Though they could never match the towering magnificence of the Serenii's handiwork, they stood testament to human ingenuity that had withstood the passage of time. For thousands of years, these stones had guarded the people of Khafra and served as testament to the greatest feats of the Ghandian Empire. They were as central to the history of Einan as the Lost City of Enarium and the Bridge of Ilyerrion.

They reached the unguarded gates of Khafra shortly after sundown. That had been the Hunter's intention, part of the reason for delaying their departure. He had no idea what manner of consequences the previous day's events might have. Thousands of Ghandians had witnessed the destruction of The Blind Pig—and some might have spotted him riding away. And if the Vassalage Consortium truly was as powerful as Indigo had claimed, they certainly wouldn't let the deaths of their men go unanswered.

So it was with significant apprehension that the Hunter rode through the streets of Khafra. His eyes darted around, ever wary, searching every shadowy alleyway and side avenue for any sign of danger. Even now, daggers could be lurking in the dark, waiting for him to pass to strike out in vengeance for the ten slavers killed in The Blind Pig's destruction. The chances that anyone could identify him as being present at the time were slim, but not nonexistent. Caution and attentiveness to every minute detail of his surroundings had saved his life countless times in the past.

Fortunately, his route through Khafra led *away* from the path he'd taken to reach The Blind Pig. Instead of turning east toward the grand marketplace, he turned west on the grand avenue that led directly toward the Spear of Khafra and the land bridge that spanned the Chasm of the Lost. He saw no hint of threat, no eyes paying overt or excessive attention to his small group.

Though the sun had set, Khafra remained a hive of activity. Lanterns of bronze and glass shone in every window and brightened every doorway. It seemed as if every man, woman, and child who moved through the streets carried a torch of woven reeds. In the soft, flickering glow, the flowing, vivid-hued robes of the Ghandians seemed to come alive in an intricate dance of light, color, and movement stirred by the evening breeze.

The commotion of commerce had faded, but the sound of the joyous music he'd encountered earlier seemed to come from every direction. Here, a crowd of women wearing bright headscarves stamped their feet and clapped their hands in time to the steady, throbbing rhythm of hand drums. There, men shouted and sang in the Ghandian tongue, their voices all but drowning out the warbling tone of a reed flute. The high, piping voices of children echoed above it all.

The Hunter found within himself a growing desire to stay awhile longer, to bask in the life and exuberance surrounding him. For all the city's ancient grandeur, its people seemed more alive than the reserved southerners. Even the most opulent of Lord Dannaros' balls paled in comparison to the gaiety and mirth resounding throughout Khafra. The stuffy mansions and swirling frocks of lace and silk could never come close to the free-spirited ebullience on display. And to his knowledge, this was no grand festival or city-wide celebration, but a night like any other.

We could all use a great deal more of this vivacity, he thought, a smile spreading slowly across his face.

But he knew he could not stay. Tarek's fear held a great deal of merit. The Abiarazi rumored to be present in Ghandia could very well be seeking to use the *Umoyahlebe* to their own wicked end. Whoever they were, the Hunter *had* to find and put an end to their schemes. For the Elivasti, who would be compelled to swear fealty to a new *maistyr*. For Aisha's people, who she had crossed half a continent to help. And, of course, for the sake of Einan itself.

The journey north through Khafra took the better part of three hours. Kiara insisted they pause at every stela they passed so she could examine the artwork and the stories it told. The Hunter stopped at the first marketplace he found to procure as many fresh apples as he could find. Apples, it turned out, were in scarce supply in Ghandia. Fortunately, Ash and Elivast proved as delighted by the mangoes available in abundance. One bite, and the Hunter agreed the horses had good taste. The fruit somehow struck the perfect balance between rich, sweet, and tart, with a heady aroma that enchanted his keen nostrils.

Meanwhile, Kiara slipped away to procure the charcoal sticks and parchment the Hunter had promised Tarek. He didn't explain why but she knew him well enough to trust he would when the time proved more opportune. Once she saw the sketch he'd done of Jaia—her first true glimpse of his daughter's face—she'd agree that it was worth nurturing the young Elivasti's artistic skills.

But the *real* delay proved the crowds of dancing, singing, clapping, stomping, and leaping Ghandians. More than once, the Hunter had to duck down a side street to navigate around a throng too swept up by their revelry to notice they were blocking the broad thoroughfare. For all his frustration at the constant detours, the Hunter found a measure of comfort in knowing anyone attempting to follow them would find it equally impossible.

Finally, they reached the edge of the Chasm of the Lost, and the Spear of Khafra. Torches lined the entire length of the stone spar jutting out over the vast canyon, illuminating its sharp-tipped shape. It did, indeed, resemble a spearhead, rising in a steep incline and narrowing to a point nearly a hundred paces out above empty air.

The Hunter glanced over his shoulder at Kiara. "Shame we won't get to renew our vows of marriage here."

"Our *what* now?" Kiara's eyes narrowed.

The Hunter just laughed. "I'll tell you about it later."

He turned away from the Spear of Khafra with only a little reluctance. Years ago, he'd stood on the Bridge of Ilyerrion and stared down into the depths of the Chasm of the Lost. It was a truly memorable and awe-inspiring experience. Just as standing at the base of Shana Laal or riding across the Whispering Waste had been. These grand sights had driven home just how

113

small and insignificant a single human—or Bucelarii—was in comparison to the vast majesty of Einan.

Yet for all his desire to share that experience with Kiara—and, he supposed, Tarek, Kodyn, and Aisha—he couldn't shake the sense of urgency thrumming within him. Kharna had set him on this journey to *Ukuhlushwa Okungapheli*, though to what end, he didn't yet know. The possibility of encountering both the Order of Mithridas and an Abiarazi left him uneasy, eager to come to grips with the dangers he *knew* awaited him ahead. Better to face his enemy head on and drive his sword down their throats than wait for them to come after him. And better to leave the Vassalage Consortium far behind him. He could deal with the slavers when he returned. One foe at a time, though.

The land bridge upon which Khafra had been built stood a half-league to the east of the Spear of Khafra. At this spot, the Chasm of the Lost narrowed until the north and south walls stood just thirty paces apart. The bridge itself was nearly four hundred paces wide at its center, but only twenty paces broad where it adjoined the southern rim of the canyon.

At this late hour, there were few making the crossing—a pair of covered wagons drawn by raya, a train consisting of six malodorous camels, and a smattering of people riding horses or journeying on foot. The Hunter nodded in satisfaction; his decision to travel later in the day had paid off once again. Grytch had warned that traffic could grow thick at the bottleneck, causing hours-long delays.

Yet the Drashi *hadn't* alerted him to the presence of armed men barring the way onto the land bridge.

The Hunter's eyes narrowed as he spotted the thirty torches arrayed in a flickering line behind at least an equal number of guards. It struck him as odd—the city had no official lawkeepers or enforcers who would take command of directing or controlling the flow of people crossing the canyon.

As he approached, the details of the armed men became clearer. He got a clear view of their studded leather vests and the curved knife-hilted swords at their hips.

Fiery hell! His heart sank, his stomach tightening. *Not the Keeper-damned Vassalage Consortium again!*

Chapter Twenty-Five

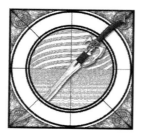

The Consortium guards blocking the way across the land bridge were as motley an assortment as those the Hunter had encountered on the road away from the Zamani Falls and again in The Blind Pig. Drashi, Nyslians, Voramians, Shalandrans, Vothmoti, even a couple of Hrandari fleshed out their ranks. Despite their disparate origins, all wore the armor and carried the weapons of the slaving company. Whatever lives they'd led in the past, whoever they might have once been, all the Hunter could see was their complicity in the enslavement of the Nkedi villagers.

His fingers tightened around Soulhunger's hilt. It would be so easy to draw the dagger and paint the stone bridge red with the blood of these men and women who made a living preying on those weaker than they. He wouldn't even need to call on the magic in the Sword of Nasnaz; none of the slavers wielded weapons of iron.

It took all of his willpower to relax his muscles and release his grip on Soulhunger. The sense of urgency ringing in his mind bade him hurry to reach his destination and uncover whatever Kharna intended him to find. He might never reach *Ukuhlushwa Okungapheli* if he got swept into a war with the Vassalage Consortium. There would be foes aplenty awaiting him ahead—among them the Order of Mithridas and the Abiarazi Tarek had been sent to locate—without making new enemies here in Khafra.

The traffic to cross the land bridge was sparse at the late hour. The covered raya-drawn wagons and stinking camel train passed the Consortium line with only minor delay, and the few riders and foot-bound travelers were ushered through at a steady pace. Always with a few stern words from the Consortium man who appeared to be in charge—a large Drashi with bushy black whiskers and long sideburns, a shaven chin, and a perpetual scowl on his sun-weathered face—and the offering of coin in payment.

The Hunter sneered inwardly. *Armed men demanding a toll from anyone they can. How original.*

Over the years, the Hunter had encountered bandits and highwaymen on the roads leading away from Voramis. The fools had attempted to extract similar payment from him—*him!* None had gotten so much as a copper bit out of his purse. A lucky few had escaped with their lives. The less-fortunate had fed Soulhunger's ravenous appetite. Those deaths, the Hunter had never once lost sleep over.

"Let me do the talking," Kiara said, nudging the Hunter's leg with her knee.

"Worried I won't play nice?" the Hunter muttered out of the corner of his mouth.

Kiara snorted. "To say the least."

The Hunter shot her a dark look, but she answered with a smile. Before he could retort, the Drashi slaver shouted, "Next!" and it was their turn.

Kiara set Ash into motion with a cluck of her tongue, and the desert pony walked toward the line of Consortium guards. The Hunter followed, with Aisha and Kodyn riding behind and Tarek bringing up the rear.

"Good evening." Kiara graced the Consortium man with a pleasant smile. "Lovely night for a ride."

The Drashi just scowled more deeply. "How many?" His eyes roamed over the four riders behind Kiara.

"Five," Kiara held up the correct number of fingers. "I take it we owe you fine gentlemen a toll of some sort for making the use of *your* crossing here?"

The saccharine politeness of her tone sickened the Hunter, but he had to admit she handled the situation well. Calling it "their" crossing showed acknowledgement of their authority, unjustified and unmerited as it might be. The lack of grumbling or fuss would ingratiate her to them. The beauty of her smile and her dignified manner certainly didn't hinder her efforts, either.

Not that it made much difference to the scowling Drashi. "Thirty *kubu* each," he barked, his tone utterly devoid of patience or good humor. "And another ten for each horse."

Kiara gave him a blank look. "I'm afraid I'm not familiar with the exchange rate. Not being from the region, as you no doubt guessed." She gestured to her clothing, visibly cut in the style common in the south of Einan.

The Consortium guard rolled his eyes. "A golden imperial each for you, half-drake each for the horses."

The Hunter resisted the urge to point out that those particular sums couldn't possibly be correct. But it would do little more than anger the man—and doubtless raise the toll. Careful to keep his expression neutral, he dug into his purse and produced the requisite number of coins.

"And this for you gentlemen," Kiara said, dropping a *sixth* golden imperial into the man's hand. "As a token of our appreciation for your efforts in keeping this crossing safe."

The man's scowl never softened as he closed his fist around the coins and tucked them into his pocket. "On with you, then." He snapped his fingers, and the line of torch-bearing Consortium guards opened to make way for them to ride through.

The Hunter's jaw muscles twitched, his teeth grinding as he touched his heels to Elivast's flanks. The whole experience left a bitter taste in his mouth. He was glad to ride on; better to leave Khafra and the Consortium behind before—

The Drashi slaver suddenly turned toward him. "You there!" He held up a hand. "Stop!"

The Hunter was forced to rein in to avoid trampling the man. Elivast snorted and stamped a forefoot in displeasure. The Hunter didn't blame the horse, yet he had to keep his face a mask of neutrality as he asked, "Yes?"

"Lower your hood," the Drashi barked.

The Hunter's pulse quickened, his mind on full alert. "Excuse me?"

"You heard." The slaver stepped toward him, scowl growing deeper still. "Lower. Your. Hood." His bushy whiskers and thick sideburns seemed to bristle. "That's an order."

The Hunter considered that. He was tempted to invite the man to step close and *make* him comply; he'd love nothing more than an excuse to kick the Drashi's face in. But that wouldn't go over with the remaining Consortium guards. A fight now would do them no good—and it could actually put the still-recovering Kiara in serious danger.

"Of course," the Hunter said in a voice only marginally less pleasant than Kiara's had been. Reaching up, he pulled the hood of his cloak back to fully reveal his face to the Drashi. "Any particular reason?"

Outwardly, he cut the picture of serenity. Inwardly, however, worry gnawed at his gut. His eyes darted across the ranks of guards standing nearby. Gwala wasn't among them, nor either of the three who'd ridden at his back. But could any of them have been riding beside the wagons bearing the Nkedi villagers? Had they recognized him from that brief glimpse?

It *shouldn't* have mattered, even if they had. There was no way they could connect that man sitting beneath the shade of the acacia tree to the one who'd ridden away from the explosion that leveled The Blind Pig. None of the Consortium had emerged from Indigo's tavern alive.

The Drashi studied him for a long moment, his eyes narrowed—though in suspicion or mere curiosity, the Hunter couldn't tell. The man's single facial expression made it difficult to decipher the inner workings of his mind.

"Toll just went up," the Drashi finally barked. He stabbed a finger at the Hunter. "You've got the look of trouble about you, and trouble costs *double.*"

The Hunter's eyebrows shot up. He'd already paid a ridiculously exorbitant price, and now the man had the gall to extort further payment based on his looks alone? He was bloody right about one thing: the Hunter *was* trouble. The ten Consortium corpses burned to ash in the ruins of The Blind Pig proved that much.

The Drashi held up a leathery hand. "Double." He gave the Hunter a look daring him to argue. No doubt he'd only raise the bribe further the more fuss the Hunter put up. That was the way of such men. They wielded what miniscule measure of power they could amass to the fullest, always at the expense of the powerless.

Though it went against every grain of the Hunter's nature, he reached into his purse, plucked out another golden imperial, and bent to drop it into the man's hand. "No trouble here," he said in a calm tone.

For a moment, the Consortium guard's scowl flickered and a look of disappointment flashed across his sunbaked features. Almost as if he'd been *hoping* the Hunter tried something. With a grunt, he pocketed the coin and stepped back. "Off you ride."

The Hunter kicked Elivast into motion before the guard could change his mind and rode through the line of Consortium guards without a backward glance. None of the torch-bearing slavers stopped him or even paid him a second glance. The lack of scrutiny proved comforting. The slaver hadn't truly seen anything amiss about him or somehow connected him to the commotion the previous day. He'd merely wanted more coin and found a convenient excuse to justify his demand.

To his relief, Kodyn, Aisha, and Tarek passed through the Consortium line unhindered. They rode in silence, keeping well away from the line of rush lanterns that marked the safe edges of the stone land bridge. The crossing proved short—a few minutes later, they were riding through the sea of small, crude wattle-and-daub huts that surrounded the land bridge's northern end.

The Hunter's gaze wandered to the south, toward the place where the Spear of Khafra jutted up in the darkness. The stone itself was a black even deeper than the night sky above, save for the thin line of illumination cast by the torches outlining its contours. It proved a strange and beautiful sight—a massive shape rising high into the sky, somehow both utterly solid and as indefinable as a great ship traversing the oceans on a starless night.

"Easy, Aisha." The wind wafting up from the depths of the Chasm of the Lost carried Kodyn's quiet words to the Hunter's ears. "Breathe."

The Hunter cast a glance over his shoulder. Kodyn's eyes were fixed on Aisha, who sat rigid in her saddle, her shoulders tense and her umber-colored face set in a look that could only be described as primal fury. Sparks of blue-white light danced around her fists and blazed in her eyes. She was looking right at him yet saw him not at all. She seemed a thousand leagues away, reliving some painful memory.

"Just breathe," Kodyn urged. He reached for her hand but hesitated to touch her as if afraid of the sparks dancing around her fingers. But only for a moment. He clenched his jaw and grasped her hand firmly. "Focus on my voice. Come back to me."

His touch and calm words seemed to draw her out of whatever depths she'd gotten lost in. The sparks faded, the light in her eyes dimming, and the tension in her shoulders relaxed. She let out a long breath and slumped in her saddle as if exhausted.

The Hunter turned away quickly before either of the youths noticed him watching. Whatever had happened to Aisha, he doubted it was something they'd want observed or commented upon. There would come a time when he'd want an explanation—if her *Umoyahlebe* powers and control of the *Kish'aa* were somehow out of control or could endanger Kiara or Tarek, he needed to know. For now, however, he'd give them their space. Such matters couldn't be rushed. He'd learned that with Hailen and Evren—both boys had needed time to work up the courage to confide in him and Kiara.

He just hoped that whatever internal war raged within Aisha didn't endanger her—and the rest of them with her—or imperil the mission that had brought them all this way.

Chapter Twenty-Six

The largest, grandest parts of Khafra occupied the lands to the south of the canyon, whereas the city that spread north of the land bridge proved little more than a collection of wattle-and-daub huts, with only a few buildings built of stone or sun-baked clay bricks. Hard to believe that this part of Khafra had once housed the grand palace erected by Zaqala Eusas himself. Not a single stone remained of the vast Imperial complex, said to once be home to hanging gardens unrivaled anywhere else in the world. Centuries past, in the wake of the Ghandian Empire's collapse, the palace and every other grand structure north of the Chasm had been torn down to reinforce the southern wall against the armies seeking vengeance against the vast kingdom that had enslaved and oppressed them for thousands of years.

As the Hunter rode through the muddy, deep-rutted streets of what had become known as "Imperial Khafra," he found little evidence of what had once been a truly splendid metropolis. The ramshackle buildings reminded him of the Wandering, the twisted maze of streets that wandered through a sea of tents and hastily erected temporary shelters emanating a sense of transience. Gone were any demarcations that once might have suggested the order for which Einan's first empire had been famous. All that remained of the grand city fortifications that had repelled the empire's northern enemies for millennia was a knee-high wall—the sort of simple barrier erected around a sheep's pen or cow pasture.

Once through the city, only the vast expanse of the Ghandian Plains awaited them. There was not a single sign of human life as far as the Hunter's eyes could see. A fitting depiction of what had become of the empire that once ruled these lands.

During their visit to Drash, the Hunter had obtained a book by Ingiyab Yengwayo, one of the foremost historians and experts on the Ghandian Empire. The volume had gone into lavish detail chronicling the empire's rise to power but contained far less information on the current state of affairs in the vast Imperial lands.

To most of Einan, the lands were simply and collectively called *Ghandia,* all that remained of the mighty empire. This, the Hunter had learned, was in truth a misnomer. Ghandia was but one of the tribes that called this land home. They ruled Khafra and a few score villages to the east and south, and it was only their control of the land bridge that kept them from extinction.

The bulk of the lands south of the Chasm of the Lost were occupied by the *Dalingcebo,* a loose association of towns and villages—like Nkedi—that belonged to no true tribe. Once across the land bridge and away from the ruins of Imperial Khafra, the division of power grew far more nebulous.

Close to four score tribes had once been part of the Ghandian Empire. After its fall, some few had united to form newer, stronger tribes, while others fell to ruin or were subsumed by their rivals. According to Ingiyab Yengwayo, anywhere between four and six dozen of those tribes remained to this day, living on the ancestral lands of their people.

Some of the tribes prioritized animal husbandry, roaming wherever their herds of raya cattle, wildebeest, buffalo, and sheep could find fresh pastures among the arid savannas. A select few excelled in agriculture, caring for vast fields of sorghum, millet, teff, fonio, and other hardy grains capable of growing in such high temperatures with minimal water supply. But the majority were migratory, moving from water source to water source, hunting ground to hunting ground, living off the land with no agrarian practices to speak of.

War between tribes was common practice. Pitched battles between large armies was virtually unheard of, but small-scale raids provided both access to much-needed resources and training for younger warriors. Rarely did the bloodshed escalate beyond this, but Yengwayo had noted four significant instances in the last century alone where once-powerful tribes had been brought low and ultimately exterminated by their rivals. In a land where water was precious and the threat of hunger eternally loomed, even one poor breeding season or drought could cause a drastic shift in the tides of fate.

On the Ghandian Plains and the vast jungles and forests beyond, there were no kingdoms as the rest of Einan knew them. Boundaries were defined only by what each tribe could hold and defend against their neighbors. Arid terrain that served of little use remained uncontested and used only as traveling grounds by the tribes who staked their claims to the more fertile regions. According to Yengwayo's descriptions, entire kingdoms could fit into the many uninhabited areas of Ghandia.

It reminded the Hunter a great deal of the Hrandari clans. They, too, had once gathered to form a mighty host, warring under the single banner of a great ruler who sought to conquer all of Einan. Now, both the Hrandari of the north and the peoples of the Ghandian Plains lived free, as if in defiance of those who had once sought to yoke them.

The five-man party rode in silence, with only the wind and the sound of their horses' hoofbeats for company. They traveled through the night and into the early hours of the morning, stopping only when the heat grew intolerable. Taking shelter beneath a yellowwood tree—which bore the sweet-scented, bright golden blooms from which its name was derived—they spread out their blankets and prepared to rest.

Kiara fell asleep quickly. Though she'd made not a single protest, the ride had exhausted her, drained what little strength she had recovered. She slept soundly, for which the Hunter gave silent thanks. He owed *actual* words of thanks to Aisha, he supposed, but she appeared in no mood to hear them.

The young Ghandian woman sat in silence, staring off across the emptiness of the Ghandian Plains with a shroud of gloom hanging over her. Shoulders hunched, arms wrapped around knees pulled up to her chest, fingers toying with the handle of her short spear, she seemed lost in her own grim thoughts. After attempting—unsuccessfully—to press some food and water on her, Kodyn retreated to give her space and fell asleep, too.

Curiously, Tarek did not immediately fall asleep. He, too, sat staring off across the plains, his brow furrowed and nose scrunched up in a look of intense concentration that reminded the Hunter a great deal of Hailen. He didn't lose himself in whatever melancholy gripped Aisha, yet *something* weighed on the young Elivasti's mind.

The Hunter looked between the two, uncertain what to do—or even *if* he should do anything. They weren't his responsibility. They shared the road with him and Kiara, certainly, but they had their own families and people to watch over them. Their problems didn't have to be his problems.

But he had only to look at Kiara sleeping peacefully nearby to know what she would do. And what she would want him to do. Sighing inwardly, he moved over to take a seat beside Tarek.

"Copper bit for your thoughts," he said, speaking quietly so as not to startle the young man or disturb Aisha.

Tarek looked up, and though his expression smoothed, the weight on his mind remained fully evident in the stiffness of his shoulders and spine. "Nothing interesting," he said, too quickly.

The Hunter merely raised an eyebrow and held the young man's gaze.

Tarek's eyes dropped away after a moment. "Fine, you got me." His jaw muscles worked as he stared out once more across the plains. "It's just…"

When the young man trailed off, the Hunter didn't press, didn't insist. Better to let Tarek speak in his own time.

Nearly a full half-minute passed in silence before Tarek spoke once more. "Do you know where we're headed?"

The question surprised the Hunter. "Do you?"

Tarek shot him an irritated look. "I'm serious, Hunter."

The Hunter met the young man's eyes—the same deep violet as Hailen's—without hesitation. "So am I." He gestured to Tarek with a flick of one finger. "You're the one sent here to find the *maistyr*. Surely Itan gave you more to go on than just 'somewhere in Ghandia'."

"He did," Tarek snapped. After a moment though, his glower faltered. "Sort of."

Again, the Hunter held his tongue and waited.

Tarek let out a long breath and threw up his hands. "Truth be told, Itan had very little concrete evidence to act on. News of the *maistyr* reached us from outside our usual sources. People we can trust, mind you, but not one of our people."

"Not Elivasti?" The Hunter cocked his head. "Or not a True Descendant?"

"Neither." Tarek's expression grew grim. "Under ordinary circumstances, one of the Quintariad would be dispatched to ascertain the truth in person, or even the Second Blade. But these are far from ordinary circumstances. In the wake of the chaos on Kara-ket, there are too few left to guard our people, and only a handful of us can be spared to roam the world in search of *maistyrrah*."

"Which is how you ended up being sent by the Second Blade to lead us." The Hunter had reached that conclusion weeks earlier. He knew little of the Elivasti's operations, but he knew how *he* would treat a problem of this scale—the discovery of an Abiarazi who might assert control over the Serenii's descendants. For all his skills, Tarek was still very much a young warrior, far from the veteran who the Hunter would dispatch in such a situation. Which meant that Itan simply couldn't be spared to attend to the matter personally.

"Indeed," Tarek said, nodding. "But for weeks, since we left Malandria, I have tried everything to collect further information on this *maistyr*—their identity, where they may be found, and the like—and come up empty-handed every time. Somewhere out here"—his gesture encompassed the vast plains to the north—"awaits a nameless Abiarazi who could be the downfall of my people, and I am no closer to finding them than when Itan dispatched me."

The Hunter understood the young man's pain all too well. He'd traveled across Einan in search of Taiana knowing nothing about her. All he'd had were the few fragmented memories the Illusionist Clerics hadn't ripped from his mind—including the recollection of when she'd put a dagger in his chest in the name of saving their daughter.

He considered how best to respond. "You worry that you will fail your people by not finding the Abiarazi? Or, worse, find them and be compelled by the oath of your people to swear fealty to them?"

Tarek's eyes darkened. He did not answer, but his shrug spoke with eloquence aplenty.

A memory sprang to the Hunter's mind—a strong voice speaking solemn words that had followed the Hunter across the decades. The recollection brought a smile to the Hunter's lips. *How appropriate.*

"Tell me," the Hunter said, "if you were starving, you would hunt for food, yes?"

Tarek shot him a scornful look. "Of course!" His chest puffed up. "Soaring Hawk Clan are proudly the finest hunters among the Hrandari, and I learned their ways from Itan himself."

"Good." The Hunter gestured toward the vast, empty plains. "But do you know where out there your quarry is? Right this very moment."

Tarek frowned. "Of course not!"

The Hunter grinned. "Then how do you find them? Not knowing where they are?"

Tarek stared at him as if he were a madman. "Surely you don't need me to explain the tricks of tracking game and hunting to *you*." He gestured to the Hunter. "Unless the name 'the Hunter of Voramis' has some other meaning."

The Hunter laughed. "Humor me. A brief explanation of how you would go from this very spot"—he jabbed a finger to the ground between the young man's feet—"to locating your quarry."

Tarek launched into an explanation of how he'd read the terrain, searching for the lower areas where water was more likely to collect into pools and ponds. There, animals would be shielded from the eyes of their predators and the wind wouldn't carry their scent as far. He could also search for regions where the trees grew thickest and tallest, also an indication of water, even pinpoint potential interruptions in the plains signaling the location of rivers or streams. In the arid grasslands, water was the key.

"Precisely." The Hunter inclined his head. "A hunter must know his prey before ever he takes aim. A hunter must also know his surroundings, for even the most minute terrain feature can be turned to advantage or disadvantage in an instant." He recited the first and second tenets of the Way of the Hunt in a voice as solemn as the one he heard in his memories.

Tarek's jaw dropped, his eyes going wide. "You know the *Elohas id'Arzaian?*"

"I do," the Hunter said. "They were taught to me by Master Eldor, the First Blade himself."

Tarek's chin nearly hit his chest, so surprised was he. He stared speechless at the Hunter for long seconds.

"Finding an Abiarazi is no different from finding any other prey." The Hunter tapped his temple. "You simply need to understand them. Every demon I have ever met shares two things in common: a lust for power, and the willingness to do *anything* to achieve their ends. Understanding that is the key to finding them wherever they hide."

Tarek recovered from his astonishment, his expression growing sober as he considered the Hunter's words.

"Wherever cruelty abounds, where the bloodshed and suffering are greatest, that is where you will find an Abiarazi." The Hunter clapped the young man on the shoulder. "Remember that as we continue onward."

"But onward to *where?*" Tarek asked. The doubt remained a dark shadow in his eyes. "We can ride north and west for thousands of leagues and come no closer to finding the *maistyr.*" He scanned the horizon, as if seeking an answer beyond the farthest hill. "I have no idea which way we should go."

"But you do." The Hunter smiled at the young man. "We owe Aisha our help because she saved Kiara's life, which means our path is now entwined with hers." For a short time, at least. "And there is still the matter of *Ukuhlushwa Okungapheli.* I, at least, am compelled to seek it out. Perhaps we will find the *maistyr* there. For wherever the power of the Serenii is, there are Abiarazi seeking to claim it."

He'd seen as much in Voramis with the First's ritual to summon the demons, and again in Kara-ket, Enarium, even in Malandria. Demons could not truly create magic of their own, but they were ever determined to harness the immense power of the Serenii for themselves.

"And if not," the Hunter continued, "if we find no trace of the Abiarazi there, trust that my oath to the True Descendants still holds true and I *will* aid you in ridding the world of the *maistyr.*" He held out a hand to the young man. "Can you believe that?"

Tarek stared down at his open palm for a moment, then clasped it. "I can." He shook, his grip firm, a new light of confidence blossoming in his eyes. "Thank you, Hunter."

The Hunter smiled. "Any time. Now, what say we get some rest? We've got a long night of travel ahead."

"Good idea." Tarek settled back into his bedroll, closed his eyes, and, within minutes, was fast asleep. The faintest hint of a smile showed on his lips, though.

Glowing warmth filled the Hunter's belly. He delighted in the change that had come over the young man; his words had actually helped to lighten the burden on Tarek's soul. It seemed Kiara wasn't the only one who could make things better.

His joy tarnished a fraction when he glanced over to Aisha. The young woman still sat staring into the distance, barely blinking, her shoulders hunched up around her ears. Whatever she wrestled with, it hadn't diminished along the hours of travel away from Imperial Khafra.

He considered trying to talk to her, but discarded the idea a moment later. He'd gotten lucky with Tarek—Master Eldor's teachings of the *Elohas id'Arzaian* had given him a way to reach the Elivasti. He knew so little about Aisha that he couldn't begin to hope he could understand her troubles.

At least not now. He sat next to Kiara and reclined against the trunk of the yellowwood tree. A few hours of rest would do them all some good. With luck, Aisha would pull out of her gloom. And if not…well, that was a problem he could deal with far more effectively when he was clear-headed and refreshed.

He closed his eyes, listened to the sounds of the wind rustling the grasses and the yellowwood leaves overhead, and gave in to the inexorable embrace of sleep.

Chapter Twenty-Seven

The Hunter was dragged from sleep by a gentle caress. Yet the touch was not on his body, but his mind. A presence called to him. Intangible and inaudible but no less real than the wind rustling the leaves overhead or the golden rays of sunlight bathing the plains.

He started upright, instantly awake and alert. Yet it appeared he alone felt it. The rest of his companions slumbered on around him. Even Aisha had succumbed to exhaustion and slept so deeply she did not so much as stir when a fly settled on her closed eyelid.

The touch came stronger now. Calling to him, beckoning him to rise. He obeyed, eyes scanning the vast expanse around him, searching for its source. He saw nothing, heard nothing save the gentle wind and the beating of his heart. Yet the sensation of being watched grew stronger with every beat of his heart.

And then he saw them: two creatures racing across the grasslands just at the farthest range of his vision. Indistinct shapes at first, barely more than blurs of color standing out against the afternoon sky, but growing closer. Approaching him at impossible speed.

He blinked, and suddenly the creatures were a dozen leagues closer. Close enough he could make out more details.

One was unmistakably equine, graceful and powerful as it raced across the plains. Its brilliant white coat and streaming mane and tail gleamed in the daylight. Even from afar, the Hunter knew it stood nearly twice as tall as Ash, its body rippling and heavy with muscle. A majestic beast flying free in its native element.

The other, however, was like nothing the Hunter had ever seen. It seemed to slither and run at once, with a sinewy, elongated frame borne along by six short, thick legs. Its undulating head and tail each extended nearly again the length of its body. The monstrosity seemed to pursue the horse, its powerful reptilian jaws snapping open and closed in anticipation of tasting its flesh.

Again the Hunter blinked, and now the two creatures had closed to within a stone's throw of where he stood rooted in place. Now he could see *every* detail in crystal clarity.

Two trails of hair hung from the horse's chin like the twin beards of a goat. Rather than looking foolish, however, it lent the beast an air of solemnity, a wisdom accumulated through ages of life. From its forehead protruded two gleaming horns that rose toward the heavens with only a slight curve. No mere bone these horns, though, but they seemed to be made of purest ruby. As were the hooves that dug great furrows through the grassy terrain with every step.

The creature's ruby eyes fixed on the Hunter. He felt its entreaty, its unspoken plea for aid. It longed for nothing more than to escape the clutches of the monstrosity in its wake. Yet without the Hunter's help, it could not.

Their gazes locked for only a moment, then the strange two-horned horse streaked past him like an arrow loosed from a hunter's bow, a rippling blur of white and glowing crimson.

In its wake came the second creature. An involuntary shudder ran down the Hunter's spine at the sight of the thing. Up close, it was even more hideous. Its scaly body shimmered as if wet, the sunlight dancing off mottled patches of blue and brown. When it reared up before the Hunter, white speckled its soft underbelly, and its claw-tipped, four-toed feet raked at the air. Its reptilian jaw opened to reveal twin rows of razor-sharp fangs. A bony frill stood erect on the back of its head and rippled down its elongated neck like a lizard's spines. Its long tail lashed the air around it as if it sought to strike the sun from its place in the heavens.

It, too, turned its eyes on the Hunter, and the power in its gaze pushed him back a step. Its insistence burned into his mind. The creature it pursued would not escape its grasp. The Hunter saw how it would end—the long tail coiling around the horse-beast's legs, bringing it to the ground and preventing its flight; the stunted, over-thick arms driving down to dig its claws into the pristine white coat; the long fangs sinking into rippling muscle, draining all fight from its prey.

A chill settled over the Hunter. Staring into those eyes, he felt his own strength fading, sucked out of him, consumed until nothing remained but an empty husk. He took another step back, hand dropping toward Soulhunger's hilt. That movement seemed to shatter whatever spell held him fast—and whatever compelled the monstrosity's attention. Its sinewy neck whipped away from the Hunter and it took off in lumbering, slithering pursuit of the fleeing horse-beast.

The Hunter's eyes burned and the need to blink grew stronger with every heartbeat. Yet he refused to close his eyes, to look away for even a moment. He fixed his gaze on the two fleeing creatures and watched them until he could fight the urge no longer.

He blinked, and as he feared, when he opened his eyes once more, the creatures were gone. Gone and yet not. Somehow, he could sense them far in the distance. Their presences were faint yet their touch on his mind lingered. He felt their call—and it drew him to the north and east.

Toward *Ukuhlushwa Okungapheli*. Instinctively, he knew. Or perhaps it *wasn't* instinct. The two beasts had been the conjuring of his mind, yet he couldn't believe they were imaginary. No, more likely they were a manifestation of the battle he'd felt in his vision from Kharna.

He'd seen that tower of black in his dreams, watched the stars shimmering on its surface and felt the darkness permeating the ground around it. A darkness akin to one of the two presences he'd felt within the tower. Two heartbeats. One more ferocious, the other steady, controlled. A struggle for dominance that had lasted far longer than he could imagine. Perhaps longer than he'd been alive.

Whatever inhabited that tower had reached out to him, had pulled him from sleep so he could bear witness to...what? What had been the meaning behind the vision? Had it merely been so the horse-beast could beg for his aid and the monstrosity admonish him not to interfere? That message had been plain enough. But what—or *who*—did those creatures represent? What manner of being needed his help to escape imprisonment? What entity powerful enough to reach out to him from across this vast distance feared him to such a degree that it felt compelled to warn him away?

"Hunter?"

The Hunter spun, startled by the sound of his name. He found Kiara sitting up, staring at him with a curious look.

"Trouble?" she asked, reaching for Deathbite, which lay on the ground at her side.

The Hunter shook his head quickly. "No, nothing like that."

She arched an eyebrow. "Then what?"

The Hunter hesitated. He had no fear that she'd think him insane—she'd heard equally strange things over their years together—but didn't quite know how to explain what he'd seen. At best, he could describe the bizarre creatures and the impression he'd gotten from them.

But before he could respond, Aisha and Kodyn both sat bolt upright—no doubt awoken by the sound of the Hunter and Kiara's voices—and sprang to their feet, weapons at the ready.

"Where are they?" Kodyn snapped.

"And how many?" Aisha's eyes darted around, seeking the enemies they feared.

The Hunter held up a hand. "There is no one out here. We are still alone."

Kodyn and Aisha remained on the alert for a few moments longer. Finally, the Hunter's words sank into their minds, still sluggish from sleep, and they relaxed.

"Oh," Kodyn said, a flush rising to his cheeks. "Right."

Aisha didn't look embarrassed; she merely lowered her short-handled spear and frowned into the emptiness surrounding them.

The Hunter couldn't help being impressed by the speed of their reactions. He'd traveled with soldiers and warriors who'd responded more slowly. The pair might be a tad on the high-strung side, but given what had happened to them in Shalandra, he didn't blame them.

"Sun looks to be setting," Kodyn said, trying to cover his blush with a serious look. "Should be cool enough to travel within the hour."

The Hunter just nodded. "Agreed." No need to mention their startlement now. He could learn what had them—and Aisha, in particular—wound so tight later. "See to the horses. I'll wake Tarek."

Kodyn set off without hesitation, but Aisha remained staring off once more toward the horizon, brow furrowed and face set in a hard cast. She startled when Kodyn called her name and lightly touched her arm, then quickly covered it up by setting off toward the horses. Whatever had her mind in turmoil was clearly growing more prominent.

"You see it, too?" Kiara's voice came from his left elbow, soft and barely above a whisper. The Hunter glanced toward her. She'd risen and stood at his side, eyes trained on Aisha. "She's struggling with something. It's gotten worse since we left Khafra."

The Hunter grunted acknowledgement.

"You going to talk to her?" Kiara asked.

"*Me?*" The Hunter turned to her, surprised. A frown pulled his lips downward. "You're far better suited to it. You understand…" He gave a vague wave, fishing for the word and finally settling on, "…people more than I ever will."

"Maybe." Kiara smiled up at him and nudged him with her elbow. "But you did well with Tarek this morning."

The Hunter's eyebrows shot up. "You were sleeping!"

"Was I, though?" Kiara's grin turned mischievous. "Or did I just let you think that so you wouldn't be too self-conscious about your efforts to help?"

Now it was the Hunter's turn to blush. He turned away from her, cheeks burning.

"I was impressed." Kiara slid her arm through his, leaned against his shoulder. "And proud of you for trying. You connected with him on *his* level." She rose on her tiptoes to place a kiss against the side of his neck. "Reminded me why I fell in love with you."

The Hunter turned toward her, caught her before she settled back onto her heels, and lifted her off her feet to kiss her back. Only to remember her wound too late. She hissed in pain and clutched his shoulder in a white-knuckled grip.

"Sorry," he said, grimacing.

Kiara smiled despite the pain. "Give me another kiss, and you can consider yourself forgiven."

The Hunter obeyed, though he took care to avoid squeezing her or making even the slightest contact with her still-healing belly. She held the kiss for long seconds, holding the back of his head and pressing her lips to his with a ferocity that surprised him.

"I know how close I came to leaving you," she murmured into his ear when she finally broke off. "Just as I know how hard you fought to keep me here. If I wasn't already head over heels for you, I bloody well would be after what you did."

The Hunter cradled the back of her neck and pulled her to him as tightly as he dared. "I'd ride to the ends of Einan and beyond for you, Kiara. I hope you know that."

"I do." She kissed his ear, sending a delicious tingle down his spine. "And I'd be right by your side the whole time." When she pulled back, a mischievous smile twisted her lips. "Because if I wasn't, who would remind you to lace up your trousers?"

The Hunter's gaze snapped downward, to where the drawstring of his trousers hung un-knotted. "Why you little—!"

Kiara danced back, laughing, eyes aglow with delight. "Got you!"

The Hunter growled curses after her, but couldn't pursue until after he'd re-tied the cord she'd pulled loose while he was distracted. It didn't matter that his belt held his trousers in place—it was her little impish game, one that brought her far too much joy for his liking. Always she waited until he forgot about it and seized the moment of his greatest vulnerability.

By the time he finished, Kiara had already awoken Tarek and rolled their blankets into bundles to be strapped behind their saddles. Every time she looked his way, she shot him that sly look he found both terribly endearing and annoying. He vowed to turn the tables on her when the opportunity next presented itself.

Kodyn and Tarek exchanged amused grins, but Aisha seemed incapable of smiling. A frown had permanently affixed to her face, and the shadows filling her eyes grew ever darker by the moment.

The Hunter searched out Kiara, giving her an entreating look and gesturing toward Aisha with his eyes. She raised her hands, palms facing him, then stabbed a finger at him. Her message was clear: it fell to *him* to try and coax Aisha out, to learn whatever plagued her mind. That would prove far easier said than done, the Hunter knew. Talking was far from his strong suit. He'd gotten lucky with Tarek, but Aisha would be a much tougher nut to crack.

Fortunately for him, they had another long night of traveling to attempt it. *Now, let's just hope the opportunity presents itself. Otherwise, I'm going to have to try to draw her out, and there's no telling how many ways that could go wrong.*

Chapter Twenty-Eight

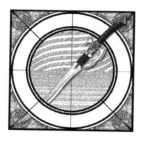

As the Hunter's luck would have it, the chance to speak with Aisha never arose. The young woman remained at Kodyn's side all through the night. During the one respite they took from their hard ride, shortly after midnight, she sat in morose silence, barely looking up to acknowledge when Kodyn offered her food and water.

Kodyn, however, proved amiable enough. He offered to teach the Hunter the Ghandian tongue. "It'll be bloody hard to get by if you don't speak the language." Over the course of an hour, he taught the Hunter, Kiara, and Tarek more than three score words.

The next morning, just before setting off, the Hunter attempted to once again engage Aisha in conversation. "Who do these lands belong to?" he asked. With no formal boundaries or political demarcations to define territory, he had no idea what manner of tribe they might encounter on their journey northeast.

Aisha either didn't hear him or chose to ignore the question.

He tried again. "Aisha."

She startled at the sound of her name, head snapping around toward him. "What?"

The Hunter ignored the edge to her tone, kept his own voice calm. "These lands." He gestured to the moonlit plains and rolling hills surrounding them. "Do you know which tribe rules them?"

Aisha's face hardened. "No." The word came out barely short of a snarl. "I have no idea."

Kodyn interjected. "She has been in Praamis for more than five years. Hasn't returned home in all that time." He rested a hand on her forearm, a calming gesture that didn't go unnoticed. Nor did the Hunter miss the way the young Praamian had spoken up quickly in her defense.

He knows what's bothering her, then, the Hunter thought. He eyed Kodyn, lips pressed into a thoughtful frown. The young man remained at Aisha's side but hadn't once attempted to invade her gloomy thoughts. Either he believed she needed to process matters on her own, or she had pushed him away. The Hunter understood both of those urges all too well. How many times had he retreated from Kiara to brood on grim matters? It had taken years to fight the compulsion to push her away when his thoughts turned dark. Even now, he still found he hesitated to fill her in on his internal struggles—such as his turmoil over Jaia, or his guilt over Tassat's death.

All this flashed through the Hunter's mind, but he kept his expression neutral. "Fair enough," he said, shrugging. "Guess either we'll find out or we won't."

Kodyn fixed him with a curious look. "What does that mean?"

The Hunter raised both hands before him, palms facing upward like the two plates of a scale. "Either we encounter the tribe that rules these lands, or we pass through without running into a single human being." He shrugged. "I know which I'd prefer."

The last thing he wanted now was to fight an unnecessary battle. Kiara was on the mend but still had a long way to go to fully recover. Aisha's distraction and brooding would doubtless prove a liability. And the Hunter had no true measure of either Kodyn or Tarek's skill in an open battle. He'd seen the Praamian youth fight during the attack on the Gatherers, but a scuffle in an enclosed building or alleyway was vastly different from the sort of combat they'd face out here on the plains, facing off against an entire tribe of Ghandians.

Fortunately, they traveled the remainder of the night without ever sighting a single human being. The Hunter never relaxed his wariness, his gaze searching the darkness of the plains for any signs of life, but even his keen eyes found nothing amiss. Every deep breath drawn in through his nostrils carried to him the myriad scents of the plains—the dry sweetness of the tall grass, the pungency of droppings left by passing oryx, the deep musk of wild raya cattle, the occasional hint of wild fruits or berries sprouting from the scrubby bushes, and the dust eternally kicked up by the wind—but not once did he smell humans save for Kodyn, Aisha, and Kiara.

Tarek's knowledge of Einan had brought them all the way to Khafra, but once across the Chasm of the Lost, he had no concrete direction in mind. If Aisha had any way to guide them to her people, she made no mention of it, but kept her thoughts firmly to herself. The Hunter could tell immediately that despite his grasp of the language, Kodyn had no more experience traveling these lands than either he or Kiara. The young man's attention was consumed by worrying over Aisha, though his Night Guild-trained wariness didn't wane as he constantly scanned the terrain for threats, just as the Hunter did.

Thus, it fell to the Hunter to lead the way. He alone appeared to have any idea which way to travel. North and east, deeper into the plains, on what could only be a path leading directly to *Ukuhlushwa Okungapheli*. Kharna's compulsion propelled him onward, and the two presences he'd felt in his vision—and now seen in his hallucination called him inexorably closer. What he'd find when he arrived, he couldn't begin to imagine. That galled him to no end. He *hated* being unprepared. That was the fastest way to die painfully. Foreknowledge and meticulous planning had been crucial for his success as the legendary assassin of Voramis.

But out here on the plains of Ghandia, *only* the unknown and unexpected awaited him. All he could do was ride onward, bracing himself for whatever he'd face at the end of the road.

Through the night they continued, setting as brisk a pace as they could safely manage. He dared not push too hard for fear of injuring the horses, but in the bright light shining down from the pale moon and the starry heavens, his keen eyes could pick out the safest path through the tall plains grass. He felt an odd sense of disappointment when the first rays of morning light brightened the eastern horizon. They'd covered a good distance—at least ten leagues, by his reckoning—and he'd begun enjoying the cool night breeze in his face, the strangely soothing shadows. He'd spent much of his life in darkness, and it felt safe, comfortable. The coming of dawn meant they would soon have to stop before the day grew too scorching hot to continue onward.

Soon arrived less than a quarter-hour later. The sunlight brightening the world shone on thickening trees and denser clusters of bushes, signaling the presence of fresh water. The smell of flowing water reached the Hunter hundreds of paces before they emerged from the trees and into the grass-covered, sloping banks bordering the nameless river barring their way forward.

The Hunter reined in Elivast at the top of the riverbank and studied the obstacle. Even from here, he could tell the current flowed fast, and the river appeared too deep to ford easily.

He had a decent chance of swimming the fifty paces to the far bank. His companions and the horses, however, would find it virtually impossible.

"There's no bloody way we're crossing here," he said, shaking his head.

Kiara looked ready to disagree—she was stubborn enough to believe they might do it, even in her current condition—but the Hunter drove on before she could.

"Best thing to do is ride either up or downriver in search of shallows, or somewhere with a better crossing." He fixed Kiara with a hard look, his tone brooking no argument. "But not yet. First, we rest." She looked well and truly exhausted, though she'd never admit it. "The trees provide both shade and concealment."

To emphasize the finality of his declaration, he leaped down from Elivast's saddle and wrapped the reins around a low branch of a nearby teak tree. Blessedly, Kiara didn't contest his decision, but followed his lead and dismounted. Tarek, Kodyn, and Aisha did likewise. With surprising efficiency, the five of them set about making camp—the Hunter and Kodyn tending to the horses while practicing the Ghandian tongue, Aisha and Kiara arranging their packs and bedrolls beneath the shade of the trees, and Tarek digging into his pack for a wrapped package containing the last of the cooked oryx meat.

Once the Hunter had finished removing Elivast and Ash's tack and saddles, he let them free to crop the grass and set off toward the river. His keen nostrils searched for any hint of life—either human or animal—in the vicinity. He'd heard tales of the vicious *crocodylus* said to make their home in the rivers of Ghandia, had even seen one on display in a traveling carnival that had passed through Voramis close to two decades earlier. After their encounter with Indombe, he was wary of any predator who might threaten his companions.

His questing senses detected only a few small creatures: rodents, hares, meerkats, and others unfamiliar to him by smell alone.

He knelt and reached his hand into the river. It was warmer than he'd expected, even after a night without the sun's rays.

It would almost be perfect for swimming, if only the current wasn't so fast.

Standing, he scanned the riverbank first to the west, then east. To his delight, a few dozen paces upriver from where they had begun making camp, a promontory of earth and rock jutted out into the river far enough to create an eddy in its flow. Shedding his cloak, armor, and weapons, he waded in up to his knees. The current proved slow enough that it would be safe for bathing.

As he slogged his way back to shore, he found Kiara approaching from the camp. A mischievous smile tugged on her lips. "Thinking of taking a bath?" she asked. "And a good thing, too! You were starting to reek." She made a grand show of pinching her nostrils between her fingers.

"Maybe." The Hunter strode toward her, his face a mask of calm. "Or maybe I had another idea in mind."

"Oh?" Kiara arched an eyebrow. "What exactly did you—hey!" She cut off as he bent and swept her off her feet. "What are you doing?"

The Hunter said nothing, just spun and raced back toward the river he'd just left.

Kiara, sensing his wicked intentions, began struggling to extricate herself from his encircling arms. "Put me down this instant, Hunter!"

The Hunter clutched her tighter. Her strength was no match for his, his iron grip on her legs and waist unbreakable.

"Don't you dare!" Kiara shouted, pushing against his shoulders as if that could somehow stop the inevitable. "You do this, Hunter, I swear to all the gods, I'll—"

Her words ended in a splash as he unceremoniously dumped her into the knee-high water. She let out a shriek of rage and hurled herself at him. The Hunter sidestepped her lunge and evaded her outstretched arms, and she fell once more into the water. She came up a moment later, soaking wet, her face red with fury.

"Got you!" he said, grinning at her. "Call that revenge for your trick with my trouse—"

She launched at him once more, and this time the Hunter was too close to evade. He allowed himself to be borne down into the water beneath her, laughing all the while. She clambered atop his chest and held him against the rocky riverbed. But only for a few moments. She let up long before the Hunter's breath gave out, and when he arose, she, too, had a broad grin on her face.

They remained there a while, laughing, splashing each other, basking in the warm water and the cool morning breeze. Tarek joined them, though he never strayed far from the shore. Kodyn stripped down to nothing but his trousers and lay back in the knee-high water until only his face remained above the surface. His long, dark hair flowed around him and he appeared utterly at peace.

Only Aisha didn't join them. When the Hunter glanced back toward camp, he found the young Ghandian woman staring off into the distance once more, oblivious to the merriment of her companions.

A hand rested on his arm, drawing his attention. Kiara had seen Aisha, too. She thrust her chin toward the Ghandian and gave him a meaningful look.

"Really?" the Hunter mouthed. "Now?" He was so enjoying his moment in the warm water.

Kiara nodded and shoved his arm gently.

The Hunter complied. He supposed he'd find few better opportunities to speak to the young woman alone. He felt foolish—surely she'd feel more comfortable discussing matters with another woman—but he supposed he ought to at least make the attempt. If he failed, Kiara could always take a stab at it afterward.

He waded out of the river and slogged along the grassy bank, his boots squelching with every step. Aisha didn't look his way, but clearly registered his approach, for she did not startle when he joined her in staring across the river toward the thick trees obstructing view of the lands beyond.

The Hunter stood there, the silence feeling more awkward with every beat of his heart. Try as he might, however, he could find nothing to say. Words had never been his strong suit. Feelings even less so. Chances were, he'd make things even worse.

Keeper take it! He ground his teeth in frustration. *I don't know why Kiara thinks that I'm the one who should—*

"Is it true?"

Aisha's abrupt question caught the Hunter off guard. He turned toward her, confused.

"Is what true?" Had she said something and he missed it?

"That when you destroyed the Bloody Hand, you strung the Fifth up by his own entrails?" Aisha's dark eyes burned into his, and she radiated an intensity as fiery as the blue-white light he'd seen crackling between her fingers when she'd healed Kiara.

131

The Hunter nodded. "It is." How that was relevant now, he had no idea. At least she was talking, though. He took that as a good sign. He was about to ask why it interested her, but her next question forestalled his.

"And the rest of the Bloody Hand's trafficking operations and slave pens." Her face hardened, lines forming at the corners of her mouth and eyes. "Did you really destroy them and burn the ships they used to transport their captives into the city?"

"I did." The Hunter found her line of questioning curious. That had been nearly four years earlier. Aisha had been in Praamis at the time, and his destruction of the Bloody Hand had *benefitted* her and her Night Guild.

"Good." Aisha's lip curled into a snarl. "It's a fate far kinder than they deserved." Her fists clenched at her side. "One I intend to visit on the Vassalage Consortium when the time is right."

The Hunter's eyebrows rose. "You plan on taking down the Consortium? Just the two of you?"

Aisha's expression grew stony. "If necessary." Her eyes narrowed. "If you won't help—"

"I never said I wouldn't help." The Hunter held up both hands in a placating gesture. "On the contrary, I'd love nothing more than to see every one of those bastards in a grave for what they did to the people of Nkedi—and no doubt other villages." He didn't know why he'd just said that to her, yet it felt oddly right.

Judging by the look on her face, it *had* been right. Her face took on a hard, vicious edge the Hunter had only seen the day she'd killed one of the Consortium guards in The Blind Pig. Blue-white sparks danced in her dark eyes, and the very air around her seemed to grow hotter, thick with crackling energy.

He felt the words pulled forth from within him, as if her power compelled him to speak. "There are few things in the world I hate as much as slavers and traffickers. Ripping people from their homes and selling them like cattle. I have seen many abuses of power in my time, but I despise none so much as the scum who make a living preying on others in this way."

"On this, we agree!" Aisha's words came out in a feral snarl. Her eyes were fully aglow now, the blue-white light crackling like lightning bolts up and down her umber-colored face. "Every one of them deserves to die, and I plan to be the one to kill them!"

The ferocity of her declaration surprised the Hunter. As she spoke, the aura of power he'd sensed expanded outward, encompassing him. The hairs on the back of his neck stood on end and he felt the sizzling energy burning in his lungs, setting his blood pounding in his ears.

"Why?" the Hunter asked. "You said you returned to save your sister and the other *Umoyahlebe* like you." He fought the urge to back away from her, but instead took a step closer, though his eyes stung and the heat radiating off her seared his skin. "Why risk your life trying to take down the Vassalage Consortium instead?"

"Because I owe them pain!" Aisha's voice thundered into him with the force of a hurricane wind. "I owe them suffering in equal measure to my own. They will feel every shred of the anguish and agony I've felt since the day they ripped me from my family and home and hauled me in chains a thousand leagues away to sell as a slave!"

Chapter Twenty-Nine

With Aisha's words, pieces clicked into place in the Hunter's mind. Her reactions in The Blind Pig and on the land bridge made terrible sense now.

"Five years!" Aisha's shout echoed across the river. "For five long years I have lived with the memory of what was done to me and the other Issai taken alongside me. I relive the terror, feel the weight of the shackles dragging on my limbs, smell the stink of the dark, cramped ship's hold that carried us down the Stannar River from Obrathe to Praamis. I hear the cries still—all of us, weeping, begging, pleading to be set free."

Her tight-curled hair rippled as if stirred by an invisible wind. Her silver eyebrow and nose piercings seemed to glow—or perhaps they merely reflected the light seeping through her tunic, emanating from the Serenii pendant hanging at her neck.

"And in those nightmares, I saw only monsters," she said in a voice rising to a furious roar. Such was the intensity that a flock of birds nesting in a cluster of teak trees fifty paces to the south startled and flew away. "Dark, hideous, cruel things with claws and fangs and eyes of burning crimson. But now I know the truth." Her glowing blue-white eyes pierced the Hunter to his very soul. "Those monsters were men. Men wearing the armor and carrying the weapons of the Consortium. I see it now, as clearly as I have seen anything. I know what they did to me. And I will see they suffer for it!"

Though the Hunter's skin prickled from the heat and the very air seemed to scorch the breath in his lungs, he faced her head on. He knew all too well the price of revenge—a cost she might not be prepared to pay.

"And what of your sister? The other *Umoyahlebe*? Would you abandon your efforts to save them in the name of vengeance?"

Aisha's eyes brightened from blue-white to pure white. "The *Kish'aa* demand it! The spirits of every man, woman, and child who died captive or enslaved by the Consortium, they speak to me." She pounded a closed fist against the side of her head as if trying to break her skull open. "Hundreds of memories, perhaps thousands, I have seen and felt and heard what was done to them. They will not find rest until they have been avenged!"

"Even if it means your sister succumbs to the curse of the Spirit Whisperers?" He might not understand the full extent of her powers, but he had no trouble comprehending the horror of watching a loved one descending into madness. He'd nearly lost Hailen to the *Irrsinnon* feared by all Elivasti. This dose of reality might be his best chance of getting through to her.

"I cannot ignore their pleas!" Aisha shook her head. Desperation and determination echoed in her words in equal measure. "The *Kish'aa* must be heard, must be brought peace. This is the gift I was given, the burden I must bear!"

"But not alone!" Kodyn's voice sounded at the Hunter's side, followed by the young man himself a moment later. He was still wet from his swim in the river, and the heat emanating from Aisha turned the water dripping off his long, dark hair and handsome face to steam. Yet he advanced toward her without fear or hesitation. "If that is what the *Kish'aa* want, then we will do it."

Aisha turned toward the young man, and the white light shining in her eyes faded a fraction. "You would risk yourself—"

"I'd leap into the fiery hell for you, Aisha!" Kodyn reached a hand toward her. "I told you the day we left Shalandra, whatever happens, no matter what life throws at us, we face it side by side. You and me, together."

Aisha's hand came up and her fingers intertwined with Kodyn's. At the contact, the heat radiating off her diminished, and her eyes once more shone a cool blue-white, her fury gone and only a burning intensity remained.

For what felt like an eternity, the two youths had eyes only for each other. Some silent communion passed between them. Their shared experiences and mutual love had bonded them in a way only *they* understood. With every heartbeat, the energy surrounding Aisha faded, retreating once more inside her. The heat faded until the Hunter could once again feel the cool breeze wafting across the river. Yet still Kodyn and Aisha stood as immobile as statues, eyes locked, the ferocious expression on Aisha's face a stark contrast to Kodyn's easy, calming smile.

Slowly, the last traces of blue-white light in Aisha's eyes flickered and died, restoring them to their *kaffe*-brown color. The glow from beneath her tunic faded, too. Though her face remained set in the stubborn, grim cast, she was once again *only* human.

A long breath escaped her lips, and her shoulders sagged as if beneath a great weight. Kodyn wrapped an arm around her and held her up. "I've got you," he whispered, though not quietly enough to escape the Hunter's keen ears. Aisha gave him a grateful grin and leaned against him.

In that moment, the Hunter saw the pair in a new light. Kodyn was no longer the same youth he'd met in Praamis weeks earlier. Though only two months had passed, he appeared to have aged a matter of *years*. His eyes had sunken a bit deeper, his cheekbones sharpening, his jaw and shoulders somehow more filled out. An air of solemnity hung around him, a certainty he hadn't possessed in his mother's presence.

Aisha, too, appeared somehow changed. More…herself, was all the Hunter could think of to explain it. The strength evident in every line of her broad shoulders and stalwart build was manifested in the iron determination she exuded. And that power! The Hunter had never felt its like. The Serenii had constructed enormous towers and mechanisms capable of generating magic forceful enough to shatter the world. Yet Aisha's power seemed to come from within, as if generated deep by her very soul. Such a thing was only spoken of in the legends and myths…a magic the gods alone were capable of wielding.

"So the *Kish'aa,* these spirits of the dead, they cry out to you for vengeance?" the Hunter asked.

Aisha lifted her head, though the effort seemed to cost her a great deal. "Some. Not all, though. There are those who cannot find rest until some important task is completed."

"Like the Secret Keeper who had to make sure the antidote she'd created survived her death," Kodyn put in. "Or Briana's mother." A smile broadened his face, accentuating his innate good looks. "She helped Aisha save Briana's life. Only then, once she knew her daughter was safe, could she be at peace."

"Fascinating!" A dripping wet Kiara joined the conversation now. By the look on her face—mingled concern for Aisha and excitement at the prospect of learning more about the *Umoyahlebe* magic—she'd overheard everything. Hard not to, given how powerful Aisha's voice had resonated. "And you can hear them clearly? It's actual *voices,* or just a sense of what they want?"

Her eyes darted to him, and the Hunter knew what she was thinking. He'd told her about his hallucinations resulting from the Watcher's Bloom poison, of hearing the voices of Farida, Bardin, Old Nan, and countless other spirits of the dead. Kiara shared Graeme's curiosity to know and understand. The possibility of deciphering and comprehending Aisha's ability was too tantalizing to ignore, momentarily outweighing her worry for the young woman's emotional state.

"I hear them," Aisha said. Her eyebrows drew together, tugging at the silver piercings embedded in her flesh. "Sometimes I see their final moments, too. I don't control it, though. The *Kish'aa* do. Those with greater strength of will tend to have more…physical effects." She held her hands palms up, and the blue-white sparks danced between them. "For others, it will merely be a sense. But the more spirits I absorb, the more powerful their desires become."

The Hunter's eyebrows shot up. "Absorb…spirits?" That sounded odd to him, far from what he'd experienced. "How, exactly, does one absorb a spirit?"

Aisha exchanged a glance with Kodyn. He gave her an encouraging smile and nod.

"My father once explained it," Aisha said, hesitant at first, but growing more confident as she spoke. "Within each of us is a spark of life, a soul. When we die, it lingers for a time. We *Umoyahlebe* can not only see the sparks, but absorb the energy into our bodies."

"That tracks with what Kharna explained to me." The Hunter looked between Kiara and the two youths. "The Serenii created Khar'nath to absorb the power of one million souls— enough to seal the rift against the Devourer of Worlds."

Both Aisha and Kodyn's jaws dropped. The idea of so many souls was doubtless as staggering to them as it had been for him when he'd first spoken to Kharna.

"How many spirits are absorbed within you right now?" the Hunter asked, unable to help his curiosity.

Aisha frowned. "I…" Her eyes dropped to the ground at her feet, and when she spoke, her voice was quiet. "Too many, I fear."

That surprised the Hunter. "What does that mean?"

"The way one of Father Reverentus' favorite treatises explained it, our bodies were only meant to house one soul," Kiara said. "Enough life force to sustain the body. More souls means too much force. Over time, that would wear away the flesh, yes?" She looked to Aisha as if for confirmation.

The Hunter raised an eyebrow. The mental picture of Kiara and the old cleric debating theology amused him immensely. He smiled, but his humor quickly faded at the memory of when last he'd seen the Beggar Priest.

Uncertainty blossomed on Aisha's face, but she nodded. "I've never heard it explained like that, but yes, that could be it." One of her shoulders rose in a half-shrug. "All I know is that absorbing too many souls killed…" She hesitated, glancing at Kodyn. "…a Spirit Whisperer I knew. And it nearly killed me, too. Would have, if not for this." She drew out the pendant from beneath her tunic. "The *Dy'nashia* serves as a storehouse for the souls. In there, the power can't harm me. Or at least, I thought it couldn't. I don't feel the effects on my body, but their voices, their desires, they can grow difficult to ignore. Maybe even *too* hard to ignore."

135

"Wait!" Kodyn stepped in front of her, fixing her with a serious look. "Are they taking over your mind like Hallar did?"

Mention of the long-deceased Bucelarii stirred the Hunter's interest. He wanted to know more—he could only recall meeting three demonspawn, and he'd been so focused on reconnecting with Taiana and finding Hailen he'd never gotten a chance to ask them about their lives. He'd have to find time to ask Aisha about Hallar, though at a later date.

"Not like that." Aisha shook her head. "There's just so many of them in here, and they all want the same thing." She looked from Kodyn to the Hunter and Kiara. "They're all victims of the Vassalage Consortium. Like me. Torn from their families, their villages and towns destroyed. Succumbing to hunger, thirst, beatings, or merely killed for the slavers' entertainment." The blue-white light crackled in her eyes and her fists clenched. "Now that I know the Consortium were the ones who abducted me, it's all but impossible to ignore the *Kish'aa's* demands because it's exactly what I want. Vengeance for all the years I lost, for everything that was taken from me."

"Even if it means you can't help your sister and the other *Umoyahlebe*?" Kodyn asked. A flush had risen to his cheeks, and shadows darkened his honey-colored eyes. "Surely that has to be more important."

"It is, it is!" Aisha turned to the young man, squeezing his hands firmly. "To me, at least. But every time I think about the Consortium, the anger rising within me is like fuel that feeds the fire of the *Kish'aa*. My rage just makes the voices stronger, and…" She swallowed. "And I'm afraid I'll lose control if I try to resist them."

"Maybe we can help with that."

The Hunter turned to regard Kiara, eyebrows shooting up. What did she have in mind? What could they do to help Aisha manage this ability they could barely begin to understand?

She met his gaze levelly. "You know a thing or two about voices in your head, right, Hunter? And how to silence them?" She shot him a knowing look.

The Hunter read the meaning in her eyes and understood. "Of course." He turned back to Aisha with a wry smile. "How would you like to learn a mental control technique taught to me by the cruelest and vilest demon I've ever had the misfortune to encounter?"

Chapter Thirty

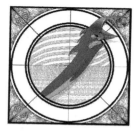

"The most important thing to remember is that you are in control of your mind. Believe you have the power to silence the voices and use that conviction to drive them back."

It felt so strange repeating the words the Sage had spoken to him all those years ago. The demon had only helped him with the intention of using him—he'd needed the Hunter fully in control of himself if there was any chance of eliminating the Warmaster.

Hard to believe the bastard's words would actually prove useful not just for me, but for Aisha.

He studied the young Ghandian woman, who sat cross-legged in front of him, with her eyes closed and face screwed up in concentration.

"Take slow, deep breaths." The Hunter spoke in the most soothing, calming voice he could manage. His words sounded terribly odd in his ears—he was far more comfortable shouting or growling than pretending serenity. Yet he had to try, for Aisha's sake. "As you exhale, picture yourself pushing the voices out of your mind. And repeat to yourself—"

A bark of pain cut into his concentration. Aisha's, too. Her eyes snapped open and her gaze darted toward their campfire, where Kodyn grimaced and held his bleeding thumb. He'd pretended not to watch them, but the Hunter had felt the young man's eyes on them, his concern tangible even from a dozen paces away. His inattention from his task of carving up the last of the oryx meat had cost him.

Kiara scolded the young man—albeit at a whisper too quiet for Aisha to overhear—and waved him back to the task at hand. Aisha gave Kodyn a meaningful look, which brought a flush rising to his cheeks. He quickly turned back to preparing their meal.

"Sorry about that." Aisha turned back to the Hunter with a wry grin. "He can't help himself. He inherited his mothers' protective natures."

The Hunter nodded. "I noticed." Not that he could blame the young man. He'd felt similar protectiveness over Hailen, Evren, and Kiara, though each for different reasons. Aisha's power definitely gave him cause for concern. "Now, back to the task at hand."

"Right." Aisha sat straighter, closing her eyes. "Slow, deep breaths. Push the voices out as I exhale. And repeat to myself…?"

The Hunter thought back to what he'd been about to say before the interruption. "You are in control."

"You are in control," Aisha repeated.

The Hunter was about to scowl, but stopped as he caught the subtle twitching of Aisha's lips. He took that bit of humor as a good sign.

"Now," he continued, as if she hadn't spoken, "exhale forcefully, and as you expel the voices, picture yourself building a wall in your mind. Your will form the bricks, and with each one you put in place, the more you contain the voices."

Aisha's face tightened, lines of concentration forming between her eyebrows and at the corners of her mouth. Her lips trembled and the thick muscles of her shoulders twitched. Yet she did not open her eyes or abandon the effort, struggle though it may have been. Her fists clenched where they rested on her knees and she leaned forward as if pushing against the inner turmoil.

The Hunter remained silent. He'd passed on the instructions, now the rest was up to her. Either she'd master the voices or the control would slip like sand through her fingers. Her willpower alone determined the outcome of the attempt.

Aisha's shoulders suddenly relaxed and her face smoothed out. When she opened her eyes, no trace of blue-white light shone there, and she appeared far more at peace.

"It worked," she breathed. She tilted her head first to one side, then the other, as if analyzing some sensation within her skull. "By the Watcher, it really worked!"

"You sound surprised." The Hunter arched an eyebrow.

Aisha looked mortified. "I…er…I didn't mean to—"

The Hunter chuckled. "I took no offense."

Aisha's chagrined expression transformed into a rueful smile. "Good." She unclenched her fists and let her arms hang limp at her sides, as if setting down an immense burden. "And this wall, how long will it hold?"

The Hunter considered the question. "Truth be told, I don't know." He rubbed his bearded chin with one hand. "The voices in my mind always ultimately overcame my resistance, but I suppose that's what they were intended to do." He tapped his temple with one finger. "They were merely a manifestation of a command implanted by Kharna, one that survived over five thousand years and Keeper knows how many erasures of my mind by the Illusionist Clerics."

Aisha's eyes widened. "Erasures?" She leaned forward. "How?"

The Hunter grimaced. "A ritual of some kind. Using a pendant much like this." He drew out the filthy, tarnished silver pendant from beneath his drying tunic and held it up for her. Even after all these years, he'd refused to clean it. Removing the grime would be like erasing the last piece of Bardin remaining to him. "They call it a kindness. That the curse of a long life is the memory of everything I have done. They treat it as if they're giving us a clean slate."

Aisha's eyes darkened. "Sometimes, forgetting could be easier." She shook her head, her voice quiet. "Watcher knows there are things I'd rather not recall." A shudder ran down her spine at some grim memory.

The Hunter chose his next words carefully. He'd gotten her talking—a massive success by any standards—and as he'd learned during his recent journeys, the more of himself he revealed, the more others would open up to him in return. Perhaps *that* was why Kiara had insisted he talk to Aisha. Doubtless she'd noticed how he'd retreated inward after the events in Malandria. His efforts with the Cambionari had ended only in betrayal and rejection. This was Kiara's way of pushing him to keep trying, despite his instinct to clam up and shield himself.

"Plenty of memories I'd rather forget, too." He spoke quietly, allowing the emotions brought up by his words to show on his face. "I've lost a lot of people over the years. Some who were like family to me, others friends, others…" He swallowed the lump rising in his throat. Thinking and talking about Farida never got easier, even after all this time. "There was a girl. Farida. A Beggared child who grew up in the House of Need with Hailen. She was killed by the Bloody Hand. By a demon who thought he was doing me a favor and ridding me of my attachments to humans—what he saw as a weakness."

Aisha's eyes went wide. "That's terrible."

The Hunter nodded. "Worse than you could imagine." The memories of her body lying abandoned at the edge of the Midden still haunted him. He blinked back the tears burning in the backs of his eyes. "I don't say this to downplay your suffering or paint it as if my pain is worse than yours. Your losses are no less grievous than my own." He leaned forward, fixing his gaze on her. "I share this so you know that, in some small way, I do understand. I've felt the anguish that refuses to go away, that buries itself down deep." He hammered a clenched fist against his chest. "The pain that claws its way to the surface in your nightmares and threatens to suffocate you."

Tears appeared in Aisha's brown eyes. "That, I know all too well." A haunted look appeared on her face. "Kodyn loves me, and he's had his own share of hardships, but he doesn't understand. Not truly." Her fists clenched. "He's never really lost anyone. I don't resent him for it, but sometimes I wish—"

"That he knew just how deeply you hurt," the Hunter said gravely.

"I know that sounds cruel, but it's true." Aisha scrubbed at her cheeks. "And I hate myself for thinking it. He's given up everything to be here with me, and here I am, so fixated on my pain and the *Kish'aa* crying out for vengeance. He deserves better."

"I doubt he thinks that." The Hunter gave her a small smile. "The way he looks at you, there is no better in his mind." A thought occurred to him, and he spoke the words before he could second-guess them. "Tell him how you feel. Everything you just said to me, say it to him."

Aisha's head jerked back. "What?"

"You say it sounds cruel. I say it sounds *honest.*" The Hunter shrugged. "It might not be easy for him to hear, but I think if you tell him, it will bring you both closer." His gaze strayed to where Kiara sat beside the fire, helping Tarek to peel and chop hairy tubers to add into the stew Kodyn was busy preparing. "I know that every time I took the risk with Kiara, it made things better. We wouldn't be where we are now without that."

He felt foolish advocating vulnerability when it went against his every instinct. Yet because of it, he'd turned his one-time enemies of the Night Guild into comrades, even friends. Kiara, the Fourth of the very Bloody Hand that had wanted him dead, was now central to his life. Father Reverentus, head of the demon-hunting Cambionari priests, had become an ally. If it could work for him, he gave it decent odds it would work for her, too. She and Kodyn would begin from a place of love and mutual respect. With any luck, her honesty would only serve to strengthen the foundation of their relationship.

A hesitant look flashed across Aisha's face. "I…guess."

"No way to find out but to give it a try," the Hunter said, nodding toward the young Praamian.

"Now?" Aisha's eyebrows shot up. "*Now*, now?"

The Hunter chuckled. "Something tells me he wouldn't mind a swim and a conversation, just the two of you." He jabbed a finger toward the spot where he, Kiara, Kodyn, and Tarek had enjoyed the river. "Water's pretty damned relaxing after a day's ride."

Aisha's uncertainty faded, replaced by a confident grin. "That does sound good." She rose to her feet and began striding toward the fire. However, after a few steps, she stopped and looked over her shoulder at him. "Thank you," she said, her eyes bright, the weight on her shoulders visibly lessened. "For the lesson." She tapped her temple. "And the advice."

The Hunter shrugged. "Anytime." He caught her eye. "And I meant what I said about the Consortium. Getting to your people to help your sister and the other *Umoyahlebe* is important, but when the time is right, we'll do to the slavers what I did to the Bloody Hand." He slid his thumb across his throat. "Every one of the whoresons."

Aisha's grin widened, took on a predatory edge. "When the time is right."

Chapter Thirty-One

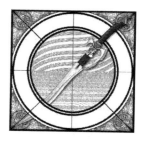

The Hunter lounged against the trunk of a teak tree and fought to suppress a yawn. Perhaps it was the warmth of Kiara curled up against his side, the woody smell of smoke rising from the campfire, or the bellyful of Kodyn's flavorful oryx stew—whatever it was, he hadn't felt this at ease in a long time. For a short while, his thoughts and worries over what lay ahead remained just distant enough that he could truly relax and enjoy the warm wind blowing through the teak trees and the sound of water rushing past.

He cast a lazy eye toward the place where Kodyn and Aisha sat neck-deep in the river, engaged in earnest conversation. They'd been there for at least half an hour already. The Hunter purposely kept his keen sense of hearing attuned elsewhere to give them privacy.

Kiara's chest rose and fell in the steady rhythm of sleep, her head resting on the Hunter's shoulder and her hand warm against his chest. A swim, a hearty meal, and fresh bandages had done her good. The wound in her belly was healing well, no trace of infection remaining.

Tarek, however, appeared ill at ease. He'd spoken not a word since the Hunter joined him and Kiara by the fire, retreating inward and poking a stick absentmindedly at the fire. Lines furrowed his brow and a frown tugged on his lips. His bowl of stew sat abandoned and quickly cooling between his booted feet.

"Still thinking about the *maistyr?*" the Hunter asked, speaking quietly so as not to disturb Kiara.

No response from Tarek. The Elivasti's eyes remained affixed on the dancing flames as if hypnotized.

The Hunter nudged the young man with a toe.

"What?" Tarek's head snapped up, his shoulders straightening. When he found the Hunter looking at him, a flush rose to his cheeks. "Did you say something?"

"I did." The Hunter raised an eyebrow. "And you didn't hear it because you were a thousand leagues off." He cocked his head. "What's wrong?"

"Nothing." Tarek waved the question away with a gesture, shaking his head. "Nothing's wrong."

The Hunter didn't believe that for a moment. "Then what had your mind so far away?"

Tarek's expression remained unchanged, his gaze holding the Hunter's. Only once did his eyes slide away—toward Aisha and Kodyn—but returned a moment later.

The Hunter said nothing, merely studied the young man expectantly. Patience numbered among an assassin's greatest weapons. He'd spent two nights hiding in the private wardrobe of Baronet Uston, a Praamian who'd made an enemy of the wrong Voramian nobleman, all so he could drive a needle into the man's brain and vanish into the darkness without *anyone* ascertaining his manner of death. He had no trouble waiting while Tarek endeavored to put into words whatever troubled him.

Nearly a full minute elapsed before the Elivasti found his voice. "Will your efforts to help her distract from our true purpose for being here?"

The Hunter had no need to ask which "she" Tarek referred to. He couldn't fault the young man's question. They'd traveled all this way in search of a demon—one who could claim the fealty of all the Elivasti in Kara-ket and Enarium—and the notion of getting sidetracked no doubt sat poorly with him.

He considered his best response. Ultimately, he settled on the truth. "It would be a lie to say that it won't, because I don't know for certain."

Tarek's face tightened at his words.

"But trust me when I say that I know the Abiarazi are the greatest threat facing not just your people, but the entire world." He meant it. The Devourer of Worlds sought to *someday* bring about utter eradication of all existence. The demons' rot and evil spread across Einan now, however, affecting all alive today and for generations to come. The Elivasti were living proof of that. "No matter what happens, getting rid of them will *always* be my highest priority. Because in so doing, I fulfill my oath to your people and the oath I swore to Kharna."

As he spoke, the tension drained from Tarek's face. He didn't fully relax, but the worried lines of his brow smoothed and his jaw muscles unclenched.

"Good." The young Elivasti managed a smile—weak but genuine. "I do understand the importance of Aisha's mission. I, too, would help her sister. Just as you helped mine."

The words surprised the Hunter. "As I...?" His mind raced. Tarek had a *sister?* Another sibling for Hailen?

Tarek gave him an awkward smile. "Half-sister. Risia."

The Hunter nearly bolted upright, only barely remembered that Kiara slept on his chest in time to stop himself. He knew that name. "Risia...is your sister?"

Tarek nodded. "She is. And she only lives today because of you."

The Hunter's thoughts flashed back to the night the Menials attacked the Elivasti city below the twin temples of Kara-ket. Goodie Eriath, Belros, Kanna, and others of the True Descendants had brought the children into the Hall of Remembrance to safeguard them. Among them had been a girl named Risia, one of the children who had lived within the Enclosure and played with Hailen.

He drew in a breath, but words escaped him. Finally, he settled on a stunned, "Bloody hell!"

Tarek's smile grew into a broad grin. "She still remembers you. The man who stormed into the Hall of Remembrance bathed in the blood of those who'd tried to kill her, but who cared more about finding his boy than saving his own life. And she knows what you did for us— Goodie Eriath and the others who survived that night made sure all the children did. But what she doesn't know, what only Itan and I know, is how you saved them *again.*"

The Hunter frowned. "I don't understand."

"What you told us about the *opia* in Enarium," Tarek said, a light shining in his violet eyes, "how it will cure the *Irrsinnon* without harming those who take it. Risia will be one of those."

The Hunter's thoughts spun. On leaving Kara-ket, he'd been so fixated on *Hailen's* condition and wellbeing that he'd forgotten about all the other Elivasti children trapped within the shadow of the Serenii, unable to leave the mountaintop. For over three years, while Hailen roamed Einan and lived as close to a "normal" life as was possible for the last *Melechha* alive, Risia, Orpheth, Certon, and every other child with whom he'd shared those happy days had been penned up, imprisoned by the curse of their ancestors.

"That is why I asked Itan to send me with you." Tarek's strong jaw muscles clenched in the same way Hailen's did when his innate stubbornness kicked in. "He wanted to send another more experienced Elivasti, but I convinced him that I was the best choice to accompany you. Because once you knew the truth, there would be no doubt left in your mind that I can be trusted. Not merely because I am a True Descendant and care about the future of my people, but because I owe you a debt for my sister's life and freedom from the *Irrsinnon.*"

The Hunter studied the young man, considering his words. Things began to make far more sense now. But one question echoed in his mind.

"Why wait until now to tell me?" he asked. "Why not tell me our first day on the road? Surely that would have earned my trust faster."

"It would." Tarek nodded. "And in truth, I *did* consider telling you that first day." His expression hardened. "But all I knew of the Hunter of Voramis was what I was told by Risia, Goodie Eriath, and the others who remember you, as well as the information we've gathered about you. It was not enough to tell me what manner of man you are. I decided I wanted to learn that for myself first, and only tell you the full truth when I deemed the time right."

"And?" The Hunter tilted his head to the side. "What manner of man have you determined I am?"

Tarek answered without hesitation. "The kind who will do everything in his power to live up to his word. Who will expend every shred of strength for those who matter to him and risk his own life to protect those who he decides are worthy of his protection. Among them, my sister and those you saved that night three years ago."

Warmth suffused the Hunter's chest and rose to his cheeks. His reaction to the Elivasti's words struck him as odd—why should he care about the opinion of one young man? Yet there was no denying the glow filling the core of his being. It was the same glow he experienced on those occasions when Hailen embraced him—occasions which had grown exceedingly rare over the last year or so, as Hailen grew to a young man—or when Evren looked to him for approval after landing a particularly clever blow during training. Their reactions tapped into the part of his mind that had swelled with delight upon learning he had a daughter.

"Aside from my mother," Tarek said, seeming not to notice the Hunter's reaction, "Risia is the only family I've ever known. My mother went to join the ancestors when I was young, so it's just been me and her. Now, my sister has a chance at a real life." He pressed his hand to his heart. "I, as a True Descendant of the Serenii, swear my sword to always fight by your side, my path to join with yours, my strength to be given freely to your cause. In the name of the ancestors, from this day until my last breath, let it be so."

The young man's words echoed with a solemnity that would have set the stones of the Hall of Remembrance quivering, his violet eyes shining with the same glow that had emanated from the arcane runes. In that moment, the wind around them seemed to still and even the river fell silent, as if all the world paid witness to Tarek's vow.

Again, heat rose within the Hunter. He found himself seized by the sudden urge to speak, but he could find no words. Anything he thought of felt foolish and trite in the wake of the young Elivasti's oath. Master Eldor would have known what to say. Father Reverentus, too. Hell, even Kiara could have found a better response than clueless silence.

142

A thought sprang to his mind. He had something to offer that might very well prove of equal value to what Tarek had given him. The young man had spoken of having no family other than his sister...but that wasn't entirely true.

The Hunter never got the chance. Before he could speak, Kodyn and Aisha returned from their swim. The two youths strode arm in arm, dripping wet but laughing at some private jest and utterly oblivious to everything around them.

"Mmm, that stew smells good!" Aisha pronounced in a loud voice.

Kodyn beamed. "I added cinnamon and cloves, just the way you like—oh, sorry!" He'd spotted Kiara sleeping against the Hunter's chest and quickly dropped his voice to a whisper as he and Aisha talked over their stew.

The Hunter glanced back to Tarek, but the moment had passed. The young Elivasti picked up his bowl and set to work devouring the stew. He glanced once toward the Hunter, only long enough for the Hunter to nod his thanks, then his gaze strayed elsewhere.

Leaning his head back, the Hunter closed his eyes and let out a frustrated breath. That had felt like the ideal time to tell Tarek about Hailen. He supposed another such moment could come again, but if it did, would he second-guess or hesitate?

He startled at the gentle pat of Kiara's hand against his chest. His eyes opened and he stared down at her. Though her eyelids remained shut, the smile that spread across on her full lips left no doubt in the Hunter's mind that she merely pretended to sleep.

Keeper take her! Had she been awake and listening this whole time? The Hunter's jaw muscles clenched. She really was taking this "making him do the talking" thing much too far.

Chapter Thirty-Two

The Hunter shaded his eyes against the sun and stared out across the plains—still as empty and devoid of human life as the first day they'd left Khafra behind. He'd expected to encounter *someone* along their journey, yet they hadn't seen a single soul in the three days following their crossing of the nameless river.

Three days, twenty leagues, and it feels like we're nowhere closer to our goal.

The thrumming in his head had grown marginally stronger as they drew nearer *Ukuhlushwa Okungapheli,* but he had no idea how much farther they had left to travel before reaching the Serenii tower somewhere in the vastness of the Ghandian Plains. Nor did he have any idea whose lands they traveled or how many days remained before they reached the domain held by Aisha's tribe, the Issai.

Aisha herself didn't know. From what little she'd told them, the Consortium slavers had abducted her on Issai lands but traveled far to the east before turning south toward Khafra, heading for Obrathe to sail their captives downriver to Praamis. She'd been too terrified to keep track of days and distances; everything faded into a blur of fear, panic, and homesickness. And that was *before* the slavers had begun dosing them with Bonedust.

The recounting of Aisha's story only reinforced the Hunter's determination to bring down the Vassalage Consortium. Einan would be far better off without their filth.

A small voice nagged in the back of his mind. *Why are you so eager to take on yet another impossible battle?* He had no illusions that bringing down the slaving outfit would be a simple matter. *Are you so afraid of facing your own daughter that you need yet another distraction to draw your focus away from cruel reality?*

Once, he might have called that voice his inner demon, or perhaps believed the grim thoughts came from Soulhunger. But that was no longer the case. That was *his* voice—what Father Reverentus might call his conscience, or Graeme would name as his subconscious. Whatever it was, it spoke a truth he had no desire to hear—but could no more ignore than a stone in his boot.

He watched the sun setting over the western horizon, felt the breeze picking up as afternoon cooled to evening. Sleep had proven even more elusive than usual over the last two nights. His conversations with Aisha and Tarek had put his mind to rest regarding his companions, but that left plenty of headspace free for the turmoil of other dark contemplations.

Nightmares had plagued what few hours of rest he managed. Over and over, he watched Father Reverentus die, saw the bright hatred in Sir Sigmund's eyes, heard the snarl of *"Ikh manashar!"* hissing from the lips of Sir Benoit and Sir Georges.

Memories of Tassat's pale face haunted his dreams, too. Try as he might, he could not shake the guilt over the Night Guild assassin's death. How could he? He'd chosen to save Sir Benoit's life—a life he himself had been forced to end a day later—and in so doing, set Tassat down the path toward the Long Keeper's arms. Had he given the assassin the last of Graeme's healing draughts, Tassat would never have thrown himself in the path of Sir Sigmund's blade. Surely the Hunter could have survived the blow of the iron greatsword long enough to drive Soulhunger into the Cambionari giant's flesh. He'd replayed in his mind the sequence of events in Malandria a hundred times and still could find no peace about the choices he'd made—or the consequences those choices had brought about.

Then there were the apparitions. He'd been awoken an hour earlier by the same touch on his mind, dragged from restless sleep to witness the goat-bearded, two-horned horse racing across the rolling grasslands, pursued endlessly by the ravenous beast with the scaled serpentine body and reptilian eyes. Again, the former's entreaties and the latter's menacing warning had echoed wordlessly in his mind.

He could make no sense of it—he might almost have written off the phantasmal creatures as the product of a fatigued mind had he not felt the beckoning from the Serenii tower pulling him steadily northward. Somehow, the two were inextricably linked to the endless struggle he'd sensed during his communion with Kharna. Yet repeated visits had made their purpose no more comprehensible. If anything, they only deepened his confusion.

Even practicing his sword forms for an hour hadn't sufficed to clear his mind. The heat of the late afternoon didn't help; he was dripping sweat, parched, and hungry enough to eat a stale, dusty trail biscuit, if only they hadn't run out the previous day. Fortunately for him, there were a few strands of meat still clinging to what remained of the fat hare Tarek had caught earlier that morning. The Hunter brought the bone to his mouth and gnawed on it in a vain attempt at quieting the hunger twisting in his belly.

Movement stirred behind him. Rustling cloth, accompanied by a light footfall and the scent of leather, steel, trumpet lilies, and peonies carried to him on the breeze.

He did not look back as Kiara came to stand beside him. "Again?" she asked quietly.

The Hunter nodded. "Again." He'd told her alone about the spectral creatures, hoping she'd recognize them from one of the legends that so fascinated her. In vain. She had never heard of any horse with a gleaming white coat, crimson hooves, two horns, and goat beard. On the other hand, far too many creatures of ancient folklore could resemble the six-legged reptilian monstrosity. Tomes containing Imperial Ghandian myths were virtually nonexistent, and to her knowledge and that of the Hidden Circle, none of the tribes beyond the Chasm of the Lost had recorded writings.

"And still no idea what they want?"

The Hunter shrugged. "Other than to beg for help and warn me not to interfere? No."

Kiara's hand was warm and strong, sliding up his arm to grip his shoulder. "I suppose we'll find out when we find out."

The Hunter turned to regard her. Even fresh from sleep and covered in three days' worth of road dust, she was still beautiful. Not a day went by that he didn't count himself fortunate that their paths had joined together—by the gods, demons, fate, destiny, or pure luck, it didn't matter.

He let out a long, tired sigh. "We could be a league away or a hundred." He tapped one finger against his temple. "No way to know for sure."

"Pretty sure we're not *one* league away." Kiara grinned up at him. "Unless I've just gone blind, there's no great big bloody tower anywhere near that close."

The Hunter rolled his eyes. "You know what I mean."

"I do." She chuckled. "But it's still wonderfully enjoyable to poke fun when you get so serious and broody." She adopted an exaggerated imitation of what she expected him to believe was his expression. There was simply no way he could scowl with his *entire* face the way she did.

The Hunter had a retort ready to growl, but sound from behind forestalled his words. Kodyn, Tarek, and Aisha were in various stages of rising. They'd slept the day away as comfortably as they could beneath the sparse shade of a candelabra tree. The Hunter envied them their rest. Youth had its perks, he supposed.

"Come on," Kiara said, nudging his arm with her shoulder. "Time we prepare to ride." She rose up on her tiptoes to kiss him, then turned away and set about packing up.

The Hunter joined her, and within a quarter-hour, the five of them were setting off into the fading afternoon. Relief came long after the sun set; the heat seemed to emanate from every ant hill, blade of grass, and scrubby bush on the plains, lingering well into the night hours. For the dozenth time in the last three days, the Hunter was tempted to shed his armor. The leather proved bloody stifling and soaked up copious quantities of sweat. Only the knowledge that there were potentially hostile tribes lurking in the darkness around them kept him from divesting himself of the protection. His companions could hold their own well enough, but if it came to battle, he knew the bulk of the fighting would fall to him.

The night dragged on the way the last four had. Hours of riding in the cooling darkness, over gently rolling hills thick with plains grass swaying in the breeze. The distant yipping of hyenas, the growling of far-off lion prides, and the calls of night birds echoing all around him. The steady *thump-thump* of five sets of hooves trotting across the endless grasslands. No road to follow, no true idea of what lay ahead. Only the knowledge that their path led north—though how far, none of them could say.

The Hunter had come to *hate* the journey. On his path to Khafra, he'd had a destination in mind, and at least some idea of what he'd face. Here, he had only the vaguest notions to lead him onward. He rode an unknowable distance toward untold dangers. The lack of information only compounded his worries and threatened to turn his instinctive wariness to paranoia. Even when his companions relaxed during their daytime rest periods, he could not stop his mind racing, couldn't keep his eyes from searching every shadow for even the merest hint of the threat he *knew* had to be lurking somewhere around him. He felt as if he'd go mad from the mounting anticipation.

Yet when the night ended and the sun once more made its appearance on the eastern fringes of the world, he felt no nearer his vague destination. Like a boat fighting a riptide, endless hours of struggle that left him exactly where he'd begun. Only the last twinkling stars fading in the brightening sky told him he'd made any progress at all.

He scanned the horizon in search of a place to take shelter from the day's scorching heat. To his surprise, the rising sun shone down on the first true green vegetation he'd seen since leaving the river behind. To the northeast, the land dipped into what appeared to be a vast basin thick with a verdant forest.

He reined in Elivast and waited for his companions to do likewise. "Any objections to riding a few more hours?" he asked, gesturing toward the distant patches of lush green. "Chances are, we'll find food, fresh water, and shade in there."

Aisha, Kodyn, Tarek, and Kiara all nodded assent, and they set off once again. The Hunter's eyes fixed on the forest—it had to be two or three leagues away, but at their pace, they'd reach it before the worst of the day's heat. And it *would* be worth it if, as he suspected, there was water among the trees. Their canteens were all but empty and their rations were running low. Nothing but stringy dried boar and a few handfuls of nuts remained of the supplies they'd carried out of Khafra.

As the land descended toward the forest in the basin, Elivast picked up speed, as if his sensitive horse nostrils had scented water. The Hunter drew in a deep breath through his nose and nearly fell from his saddle. He hadn't smelled water, but it was *another* scent that surprised him—a sweet, floral aroma he'd only encountered in fragmented memories.

He reined in so abruptly Elivast snorted a protest. But the Hunter paid the horse no heed. Fear crawled down his spine and his eyes darted about, scanning the landscape in search of the smell's source.

"Hunter?" Kiara slowed Ash to a halt beside him, kicking up dust in the process. "What is it?"

The Hunter ignored her, too. He *had* to find it. Had to make sure it truly was what he believed it to be. Surely time had distorted that memory, twisted the recollection of the scent in his mind. Here he was, a world away, and yet—

His stomach bottomed out as his eyes fell on the flowers. Delicate petals of sky-blue crowned stems that sprouted thorny leaves of deep green. The nearest patch of the blossoms grew a hundred paces to the north, but the more he looked, the more he saw.

"Hunter?" Kiara's voice grew insistent. "What's wrong?"

The Hunter turned toward Kiara, fighting against the instinctive dread brought up by the scent of those flowers. "There." He gestured toward the spray of color that stood out bright against the dull yellow-green of the plains. "Those flowers, they're…" His mouth turned dry just thinking of the name. "Watcher's Bloom."

Kiara sucked in a breath. "You mean—?"

The Hunter nodded. "The same." His stomach tightened. "The same Watcher's Bloom Brother Securus poisoned me with. That nearly killed me, and caused the hallucina—"

His words were drowned out in a raucous whooping. He spun to his right, just in time to see Aisha break into a gallop and race in the direction he'd pointed. Kodyn was caught off guard—just as the rest of them—but set off in pursuit of his Ghandian companion.

The Hunter exchanged a confused glance with Kiara, then spurred Elivast to follow. Kiara and Tarek raced along at his side.

Aisha reached the patch of bright blue flowers a few dozen paces ahead of all of them, and to the Hunter's surprise, barely slowed her horse before throwing herself from the saddle and onto her knees beside the Watcher's Blooms. Scooping up an armful of the flowers, she brought them to her nose and drew in a deep breath. She sprang to her feet, whooped once more, and broke out into a delighted laugh that echoed across the plains as she spun toward them.

"I remember!" she shouted, holding up the flowers before them. "I remember my father bringing me here. Me and Nkanyezi both!"

The Hunter, Kodyn, Kiara, and Tarek reined in before her. She had never looked so alive, excitement shining on her face with a brilliance to rival the bright sun.

"She used to love this place." Aisha spun to point toward a small pile of dark grey stones protruding from amidst a nearby flower patch. "She always thought those rocks looked like a gorilla wearing a flower chain. And that!" Her finger indicated a small hollow in the earth twenty paces away. "She *loved* to hide there. She truly believed we couldn't see her, and so we played along, made her believe she was hidden."

Aisha turned back toward them with tears of joy shining in her eyes. "This is it!" Beaming, she shook the flowers in the air with one hand, and with the other, gestured to the land around them. "This is the land of the Issai. We're almost home!"

Chapter Thirty-Three

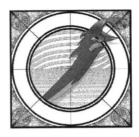

At Aisha's insistence, they paused in their travels to gather as many of the delicate blue blossoms as were in bloom. She seemed not to mind the heat, but flitted from flower patch to flower patch with the eager excitement of a bee. Her enthusiasm proved contagious. Kodyn set to helping her, and even Tarek dismounted long enough to join in the task.

The Hunter, however, refused to ride closer. The memories of what the Watcher's Bloom had done still lingered after close to four years. Brother Securus' poisoned crossbow bolt had weakened him to the point where the First of the Bloody Hand had nearly killed him. Only his suicidal leap into the Midden had saved his life.

But the paralysis had only been the beginning of the effects. On more nights than he cared to count, he relived the visions of the dead, the lifeless eyes staring at him, the silent voices in his mind begging him for vengeance. Not all the specters had been as welcome a sight as Bardin and Farida. He'd danced along the edge of madness because of this little plant.

"You know it can't hurt you like this."

The Hunter's head snapped toward Kiara. She, too, remained in her saddle, regarding him with a small smile. "What?" The word came out angrier than he'd intended.

Her smile never wavered. "After what happened to you, Graeme went out of his way to procure some from the Chasm of the Lost. Wanted to test out its effects for himself and see what it could do."

The Hunter's jaw muscles clenched. Of *course* the fat alchemist would do something like that. Had he not known better, he might have suspected Graeme of trying to concoct a poison capable of finishing him off. But Graeme simply wanted to know. *Damned inquisitive fool.*

Kiara continued as if he'd asked her to rather than lapsing into angry silence. "Distilled into a tincture, it is potent, indeed. Same if the sap comes in contact with a wound and is absorbed into the bloodstream. However, freshly picked, the flowers induce only a slight reaction. No hallucinations or visions. Merely a light drowsiness."

The Hunter scowled. "Still not going to pick them."

Kiara shrugged. "Suit yourself." She swung down from Ash's saddle. "Keep watch while we help Aisha."

"What does she want them for anyways?" the Hunter called after her.

His voice carried far enough that Aisha herself heard even from the farthest patch thirty paces to the north. The Ghandian stood, her arms laden with the sweet-smelling flowers, and looked to him.

"The flowers are a critical component in a potion Briana concocted to help the *Umoyahlebe*." She glanced down at the blue blossoms in her arms, then back to him. "The more I can gather, the more potion I can make, and the more of my tribe's Spirit Whisperers I can help."

The Hunter remembered her mentioning such a potion back when she'd refused to hand over the *ephrade* to save Kiara. Something to do with "*stopping the Inkuleko, the Unshackling of a Spirit Whisperer's mind from their body*". He found it difficult to believe a plant that triggered visions of the dead could stave off any form of insanity, but she clearly understood her own mystical abilities enough to speak from experience.

How mad is that? A wry smile twisted at his lips. *A few years ago, the thought of magic would have been lunacy. Now I'm thinking about it as if it's the most commonplace thing in the world.*

He'd encountered more arcane powers in the last four years than in the previous fifty he could recall. How many other forms of magic and sorcery had he come across in his five thousand years of life? How many had he *forgotten*, lost to his memories and time both?

Graeme would love to hear all about everything I've seen over the last few years. The alchemist would be happier than the fattest pig in the muddiest puddle writing down the Hunter's recounting of the Beggar Priests' ritual of cleansing, the Cambionari ability to sense the *Im'tasi* blades, the Illusionist Cleric powers Garanis and Imperius had wielded, the Elivasti magic within the Hall of Remembrance, the power inherent in Enarium and the Monolith, not to mention the Hunter's communions—*plural*—with the imprisoned Kharna.

Thoughts of the alchemist brought to the Hunter's mind a memory of the night he'd gone to Graeme for help dealing with the wounds inflicted by the First's corruptive magic sword and the Beggar Priest's poisoned darts.

He frowned. According to Graeme, the Watcher's Bloom was supposedly found exclusively in the Chasm of the Lost. One glance around proved how untrue that belief was. It also proved how little the rest of Einan knew of the lands that had once been Imperial Ghandia beyond the walls of Khafra. Keeper alone knew what other discoveries awaited them among the vast plains, known only to the tribes who called them home.

The Hunter remained in his saddle while his companions worked. Though he kept up the pretense of watching for enemies, he was all too glad to keep well clear of the blooms. He took the opportunity to study the basin stretching out below and far into the horizon. In the middle of the huge forest of lush bamboo stood a lake shaped like an enormous serpent curling around its body in a succession of bends and loops. The sight sent a shiver down his spine. Save for its color—a light green-blue rather than shining copper—it could very well have been Indombe itself wending its way through the terrain.

With Kiara and Tarek to lend Kodyn and Aisha a hand, the collection process took no more than a quarter-hour. Kodyn produced a shirt and offered it to wrap the flowers, which earned him a bright smile from Aisha. Kiara helped the young Ghandian tie the bundle tightly in place behind her saddle. Soon, they were all once more mounted.

"You know how to find your people from here?" the Hunter asked.

Aisha nodded. "I do." Uncertainty flashed across her umber-hued face. "That is, I *believe* I do."

The Hunter gestured for her to lead. "We follow you, then." Hesitant or no, she was their best chance at reaching their next destination. Once he deposited her with her people, he would be free to ride on toward his ultimate objective.

For the moment, it appeared their paths led in the same direction. Aisha set off northeast, descending straight toward the forest of bamboo at the bottom of the basin.

The Hunter cast one last glance at the now-desolate field that had been so thick with Watcher's Bloom less than an hour earlier. Not a single blue petal or bud remained behind. Aisha had taken everything—evidently all were needed for whatever alchemy she intended to brew. He could only hope it was enough. There were no more flowers to collect on a second trip.

The descent into the basin took the better part of an hour. Aisha kept the horses at a trot; no sense pushing them too hard after a long night and hours of riding. The day grew hotter with every minute, the Hunter's clothing and armor growing even more sodden with the sweat that seemed to pour from every part of his body. He was all too glad to reach the shelter of the bamboo forest.

Yet the forest offered no relief. Though the towering bamboo rose high overhead—some as tall as forty or fifty paces—and offered ample shade from the sun, the air within the forest was so thick with humidity that the Hunter was tempted to draw Soulhunger to hack his way through. Every breath proved a struggle and his limbs grew heavy. It felt as if an invisible shroud hung about him—a paralysis nearly as total as the effects of the Watcher's Bloom, only there was no antidote. No escape, either. The bamboo stalks were so thick and clustered so tightly together no wind could pass between them.

How Aisha navigated the forest, the Hunter did not know. It seemed as if the swaying bamboo opened before her, then snapped shut at his approach. None of the others appeared to be struggling—though the Hunter caught Kiara repeatedly mopping at her brow with a sodden handkerchief—so he kept his complaints to himself and labored on with his jaw clenched against the frustration welling within him.

For nearly two hours they rode, until the horses began to tire visibly, and the riders drooped in their saddles. Only Aisha's excitement kept them moving forward through the dense bamboo. None of them dared risk falling behind for fear of getting lost amidst the host of yellow-green stalks swaying beneath the weight of their immense height.

Finally, the Hunter'd had enough. Elivast had slowed noticeably and the usually nimble Ash nearly stumbled over exposed roots that should have presented no problem had he been fresh. The Hunter, riding in the rear of their column, couldn't see the faces of his companions to gauge their levels of dehydration or fatigue, but if *his* Bucelarii stamina was flagging, he had no doubts they were on the verge of collapse.

Before he could voice his concern, a gap opened in the bamboo trees ahead, and their small group rode out onto the grassy banks of the lake the Hunter had seen. Up close, it was even more beautiful. The rays of the noonday sun pierced the crystal-clear waters to the depths of the lakebed, revealing the enormous limestone boulders from which the lake derived its green-blue color. A cool breeze wafted across the shore and caressed the Hunter's sweat-soaked face with the delicate tenderness of a long-lost lover. He nearly wept at the relief from the sweltering heat and stifling humidity.

This time, not even Tarek could resist the siren's call of the water. Though he waded in no deeper than his waist, his face showed no trace of fear, only utter delight. Aisha and Kodyn lounged in a shallow pool, floating on their backs with their arms and legs spread wide. Kiara joined the Hunter in swimming out to where the lake was deepest. There, they treaded water and relished the cool sensations rippling over their sore muscles.

"By all the gods," Kiara moaned, closing her eyes and tilting her head back. The water caught up her dark hair and fanned it out like a halo of gleaming raven shadows around her. "I could live here forever."

"Not the worst idea," the Hunter said. He gulped down a mouthful of the water—had anything ever tasted so sweet?—and paddled toward her. "We could build a little cottage out of bamboo, swim in the lake every day. Plenty of fresh water here. Food might prove difficult, but I'm sure there are plenty of roots and grubs to fill our bellies."

"Roots and grubs!" With a scowl, Kiara cupped her hands and splashed water in his face. "You're rich enough for three lifetimes. Should be no trouble to pay for regular deliveries of *real* food out this way." She shot him a stern look. "I expect to be treated like a proper lady."

"Proper lady, eh?" The Hunter's face took on a wicked look. "Proper's the last thing you have ever been, ever will be." The sight of her wet undertunic clinging to her flesh brought warmth stirring in his body.

Kiara laughed and reached for him as he approached, wrapping her arms around his neck and draping her legs over his. "I hope that's not a complaint I hear."

The Hunter kept them afloat by kicking his legs, and allowed his hands to travel over her barely clad body. "Never."

She lifted her head and water cascaded down her glistening raven hair. Everything about her seemed to glow brighter in the sunlight, and the background of the green-blue lake only enhanced her beauty.

When she brought her lips—still broadened by that mischievous smile he loved so much—to his, he could not help but kiss her back. When the kissing didn't stop, but instead grew in ardor, he could only thank all the gods real and imagined that they were far enough away from the shore that Kodyn, Aisha, and Tarek could neither see nor hear the evidence of their passions.

Chapter Thirty-Four

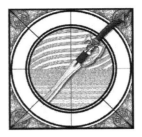

The Hunter was awakened by a truly bizarre chorus of yapping and barking unlike anything he'd encountered. He sprang to his feet and reached for his sword, but stopped himself at the sight of Aisha's upraised hand. The Ghandian sat in a relaxed cross-legged position with Kodyn at her side. No trace of worry or concern, merely the same elated serenity that had gripped her since she first laid eyes on the Watcher's Bloom the previous day.

"The *zabara* are no danger," Aisha said in a quiet voice, a small smile on her face. "The *Uhamaji*, the *zabara's* migration, will not be upon us for two more weeks. For now, in this place, there is no risk of stampede. They will drink and be on their way with the rising sun."

The Hunter looked toward the source of the sound. A herd of easily five or six score four-legged creatures were streaming from the bamboo a few hundred paces to the east, making straight toward the calm, chilly waters of the lake—*Nsukeja*, Aisha had called it. They bore a strong resemblance to horses—the same equine shape, deep torsos and slender legs, though with manes far shorter and tails stubbier—but stood easily twice Ash's size. Coats of mingled white, black, and brown stripes set them apart from any horse the Hunter had ever encountered.

The *zabara* splashed through the water, drinking deep and swimming around to cool off as the Hunter and his companions had a day earlier and again in the final hours before sunset. The sound of their strange yappy-barking echoed across the open expanse, loud enough that Kiara and Tarek both startled awake, too. At Aisha's repeated assurance that the creatures would prove harmless, they joined in watching the creatures.

They cut a strange sight, the Hunter had to admit. When packed close together, the stripes on their compact bodies played tricks on the eye, making it nearly impossible to get an accurate count of their number even from this short distance away.

Perhaps this was where the Illusionist's priests derived the idea for the confusing patterns of their temple and optical illusions, he thought, massaging his temples to soothe the headache that grew more pronounced the harder he tried to identify individual animals amidst the riot of fast-moving stripes.

"We of the Issai believe the *zabara* house the spirits of the greatest warriors and *nassor—* the chieftainesses—of our tribe." Aisha spoke in a quiet voice, never taking her eyes off the swimming herd. "For they are the noblest of the beasts that call these lands home."

The Hunter found it no difficult task to understand where such a belief might have originated. Anyone who had witnessed a herd of horses—be they Al Hani desert ponies, Hrandari steppe horses, or the great chargers ridden by Legionnaire cavalry—galloping across an open field would be hard-pressed to contain their awe. No doubt such the sight of the enormous *zabara* at full run proved equally impressive.

Tension knotted his belly as a few of the horse-like creatures turned to swim toward them. Their immense size made them a possible danger. Should they sense a threat in the Hunter and his companions, cries of alarm could send the entire herd on a stampede course. There would be nowhere to hide amidst the bamboo. No way to outrun the enormously powerful beasts, either.

Aisha, however, remained calm. From within her cloak, she drew out the length of bamboo she had spent hours the previous night carving. Barely more than the length of her palm and the thickness of her pinky finger, she had cut out a small notch into one hollow end. This she placed to her lips and blew.

A shrill whistle emerged from the crude instrument, ringing out across the lake, higher even than the yapping of the *zabara*. To the Hunter's astonishment, the striped beasts responded with a fresh chorus of barking and yipping. Again, Aisha blew a note—the same note—and the *zabara* did likewise, their voices rising in tone. Together, the simple bamboo flute and *zabara* created a song simpler and yet somehow purer than the most complex musical arrangement favored by Voramian composers. For every call Aisha sent, the *zabara* answered back with a different note, the two entwining in a melody that swelled and dipped in time with the horse-beast's head and the splashing of their hooves.

The *zabara* who had been swimming toward their small camp turned back, rejoining the rest of the herd to cut a steady path across the water. Soon, the foremost of the striped creatures emerged from the lake, water dripping off them in great rivulets and droplets glistening on their white, black, and brown coats like diamonds in the morning light.

The Hunter stood transfixed, his gaze locked on the racing beasts and his ears ringing with the chorus of Aisha's flute and the answering calls of the *zabara*. He could only watch in awe as the herd thundered from the lake and vanished into the bamboo forest to the west.

Only once the last of the *zabara* had disappeared did Aisha's flute fall still. The silence shattered the spell, and the Hunter turned to regard the young woman.

"That was…"

"Spectacular," Kiara finished for him. A smile stretched from ear to ear and a transcendent gleam shone from her dark eyes.

Aisha lowered the little instrument from her lips, and the Hunter was surprised to see tears slipping down her cheeks.

"What's wrong?" Kodyn asked. Concern for her darkened his face, and he turned to face her, his expression earnest.

"That song." Aisha brushed the moisture from her cheeks, though that did little to stanch the flow of tears. "*Iloba'si Zabara*. The Chorus of the Zabara, in the tongue of the Einari. My father taught it to me the last time we traveled this way."

The Hunter knew the young woman's pain all too well. *When last I saw him, nearly five years ago,* she'd said of her father, *he lived more among the spirits than his own family.* The Hunter had nearly lost Hailen to a similar malady: the *Irrsinnon* passed down among the Elivasti. The thought of that *still* twisted his gut in knots even three years later. And he'd gotten Hailen—the smiling, joyous, innocent boy so full of life—back after Rothia had cured him with the *opia* that grew in Enarium. Aisha had lost her father to his madness. No wonder the memory brought sorrow.

Aisha waved her free hand dismissively. "I'm fine, I'm fine." She gave Kodyn a smile—tinged with sadness, yet genuine. "I just never imagined coming home would be so hard."

Kodyn didn't answer, merely nodded and squeezed her shoulder. Kiara turned away and caught the Hunter's attention with a little wave of her hand.

"What say we prepare to travel, yes?" she asked. "Tarek, would you help me with the horses? Hunter, you handle the morning meal."

The Hunter understood the meaningful look she shot his way instantly and turned away to set about preparing their breakfast—and to give Kodyn and Aisha a small measure of privacy. It took him only a few minutes to unpack the last of their boot-stiff boar jerky and the trail biscuits that had gone as hard as the round, smooth stones lining Nsukeja Lake. Yet when he finished, he set to the task of packing their bedrolls and blankets.

Kodyn and a once-again dry-eyed Aisha joined them by the time Tarek and Kiara finished with the horses. Aisha shot Kiara a grateful look. Kiara smiled and squeezed the girl's broad shoulder, reassurance in the touch. Kodyn gathered up his and Aisha's share of the meager breakfast and brought it over to her. Tarek joined them, and together the five of them ate their meal in companionable silence.

The food didn't last long—there were no more than a few bites between them, a fact of which the Hunter was keenly aware. He looked to Aisha. "How far are we from your people?"

Aisha's brow furrowed. "I...don't know."

The Hunter frowned. "I thought you said this was Issai land?"

"It is." Aisha nodded, brushing crumbs off her leggings and tunic. "But the lands of the Issai are vast, and my people travel wherever there is grass for the herd to graze."

So the Issai numbered among the tribes that prioritized husbandry. The Hunter tucked that fact away as useful. They would be far more mobile than the agriculture-dependent tribes but move more slowly than the tribes that subsisted on hunting and foraging. "Any ideas where they might be at this time of the year?"

Aisha shook her head. "My mother was *nassor,* chieftainess of the Issai, and she trained me to follow in her footsteps. She taught me to hunt, to fight, to scout for enemies. The matters of caring for the herds were left to the men of our tribe."

Yet another interesting fact the Hunter hadn't read in the pages of Ingiyab Yengwayo's book. Matriarchal societies were far from common among the southern Einari, at least not for the past few thousand years.

"However," Aisha continued, "we will find them. With this"—she held up the little carved bamboo flute—"and with that."

The Hunter followed the direction of her pointing finger. What she might be indicating, he could not see. Nothing but bamboo trees swaying in the early morning breeze met his gaze.

"And what, exactly, is the that I should be—"

He cut off as he spotted what she'd indicated. High up in one of the bamboo trees, nearly fifteen paces off the ground, two lengths of bamboo had been woven together by a third to form a four-armed shape—resembling the Einari letter "X".

"Some sort of marking," he said, realizing what it meant.

"Guiding your way," Kiara added. She, too, was staring at the crossed bamboo, her eyes narrowed in thought. "Your people leave them behind to tell you which way to go?"

Aisha nodded, her *kaffe*-brown eyes sparkling. "The *sikalo* indicates east. The *jaliji*"—she held two fingers up parallel to each other—"signal west." She took away one hand, leaving only her right forefinger up. "The *taide* points north or south."

"I like it." Tarek beamed, nodding his head in what appeared to be approval. "The Hrandari clans use something similar. Stones piled in a pattern only known to the tribe."

"The clans of Fehl do likewise," the Hunter added. "They carve notches into trees to chart paths through their dense forests."

Aisha inclined her head. "Then you know that all we need to do is follow those"—again, she stabbed a finger toward the crossed staves anchored high in the bamboo tree—"and other markings left by my people until we reach them. How far away they are, I cannot say. But as long as I have those to guide my path, I will find our way home."

* * *

It took no more than a few minutes to finish packing their gear onto the horses. Before the sun had fully risen over the lofty bamboo forest, their small group of five were off and riding eastward, following the Issai way-marking Aisha had pointed out.

Within a few dozen paces into the forest, the Hunter understood why Aisha had strongly counseled against departing the lake during the night. At the time, he'd expected her to push on this close to her home. Her insistence they remain at the lakeside until the sun rose made sense now. The bamboo grew as thick as weeds, virtually impossible to navigate even in daylight. Had they attempted to travel in the dark, the spear-like shoots sprouting from the ground would have proven a danger to the horses.

Progress proved slow, the humidity and heat agonizing after the refreshing coolness of the Nsukeja Lake. The Hunter was soon dripping sweat everywhere, his tunic and armor sodden. Even his boots felt full with puddles of perspiration. He was glad they'd taken the time to refill their canteens and waterskins at the lake; he emptied more than half of his in a matter of hours in the effort to replenish the fluid he was rapidly losing.

The day of travel passed in a blur of heat and misery. The towering bamboo hid the sky, so the Hunter had no way to check their progress according to the sun's position. When finally the world began to grow dark, the shadows within the dense forest thickened so quickly it seemed to go from dull daylight to pitch blackness in a matter of moments.

Theirs was a silent camp that evening. A hungry one, too. Aisha had told them the bamboo shoots that made their path so treacherous could be boiled and eaten, but they had no wood with which to start a fire. Raw, the shoots were toxic, not to mention stringy and tougher even than the last of the boar jerky. Besides, the work clearing away enough bamboo to set up a proper camp made the effort of attempting to cook seem daunting to even the indefatigable Hunter.

Few words were exchanged in the darkness—everyone was too sweaty and tired to be social—and sleep came quickly to most. Only the Hunter could find no rest. Exhausted as he was, the sight of the *zabara* herd that morning had brought back the memory of the twin phantasms.

They'd returned again the previous night. The horse-creature's crimson hooves had struck sparks and left fires dancing on the surface of Nsukeja Lake, its twin ruby horns gleaming so bright they lit up the night for a hundred paces in every direction. The reptilian creature had dived beneath the water and emerged without so much as a ripple. Its undulating body sliced through the lake with an agility that should have been impossible given its stubby legs.

He'd wanted to ask Aisha about them—after all, these were *her* lands, and she knew the creatures that roamed it—but couldn't bring himself to do it. After all, the two beings were incorporeal, specters as intangible as the spirits of the dead he'd seen under the influence of the Watcher's Bloom. What they portended, he had not yet determined. Their forms had grown more solid, as if their strength increased the nearer he drew to *Ukuhlushwa Okungapheli*. But until they spoke to him in words, not merely voiceless commands and entreaties, he would no more understand them than the yappy-barking of the *zabara*.

Dawn found the Hunter sleepy, grumpy, and anxious. Fortunately for him, none of his companions appeared in a chatty mood, either. Aisha had tossed and turned, even once calling out in her sleep—though she'd spoken in what the Hunter guessed was the tongue of her people. Kodyn had awoken with every one of Aisha's stirrings. Kiara had joined the Hunter for a few hours, sitting silently in the darkness, until she'd fallen asleep on his shoulder. The dark circles around Tarek's violet eyes spoke plainly of how little rest he'd gotten.

It was a far more morose company that set out through the forest again. Aisha led the way, Kodyn at her back, with Tarek and Kiara in the middle and the Hunter bringing up the rear. Any hopes that the wind of their passing might stir up some sort of cooling breeze proved fruitless; if anything, being at the back of their column seemed to only magnify the heat and humidity clinging to him like a stifling cloak.

To his immense relief, they reached the end of the bamboo forest and rode up a hill at what appeared to be the northeastern edge of the basin formed around Nsukeja Lake. Free of the dense bamboo, the humidity decreased and the wind alleviated a measure of the heat—but only for a short while. Within a few hours, the sun had neared its zenith and the day had grown all but unbearable. Their waterskins were growing dangerously empty, too. Without food, they would soon be in dire straits.

Only Aisha's excitement kept the Hunter from true concern. Again and again, she had identified the waypoints left by the Issai to mark their passage: a pile of stones here, a cracked branch on a scraggly tree there, the skull of what appeared to be a long-horned raya with its sharp-tipped nose pointed to the northeast.

Then came Aisha's shout. "There!"

The Hunter followed her finger and spotted the unmistakable imprint of hooves in the hard dirt and thick plains grass. The tracks were old—at least two or three days, by his reckoning, though it was hard to tell given how dry the plains were—but Aisha took them as a sign that her people were close.

Producing her little bamboo flute, she pressed the instrument to her lips and blew three long, ringing notes. Silence answered her.

"Come on!" she beckoned for them to follow and clapped her heels to her horse's flank. "They can't be far."

The Hunter couldn't summon her enthusiasm, but he followed along behind as Kodyn, Kiara, and Tarek broke into a fast trot to match her pace. He had to trust that she knew her people well enough to guide them to safety. With no food and the water sure to run out within a day, their survival hinged on her now.

Every few minutes, she blew the three long notes on her flute. Though the sound rang across the plains, she received no answer save for the whistling of the wind and the rustling of the long grasses. If that disturbed her, she gave no sign of it, merely continued riding on.

Until, finally, her dogged determination was rewarded. The last trilling note of her bamboo flute had just faded away into silence and the Hunter's gut tightened with the growing concern when the sound came. Distant, so faint it was nearly carried away by the wind, yet unmistakable. A flute similar to Aisha's answered her call.

Aisha's laugh rang out and she blew four sharp blasts on the flute. "We're home!" She bent low over her horse's flanks and drove the beast into a gallop. She raced across the plains, repeatedly blaring out with her flute. And every time, the call answered.

Up a gently rolling hill they rode, and Aisha reined in at the crest of the rise. When she turned back, her face shone as bright as the afternoon sun, her eyes alight with eagerness to match the blue-white glow of her *Umoyahlebe* powers.

For there, nestled in the valley below them, was a smattering of tents and stick shelters that could only belong to the Issai.

They had found Aisha's people.

Chapter Thirty-Five

The Hunter expected Aisha to charge down the hill, whooping and laughing as she had upon discovering the field of Watcher's Blooms. Yet she moved not a muscle. She sat utterly motionless in her saddle, her broad shoulders hunched and spine stiff.

"Aisha?" When the woman didn't respond, Kodyn reached out a hand to rest on her arm. "Aisha?"

"I heard you." Her voice came out strangled, her words tight. "I'm just…" She swallowed and shook her head. "I can't move, Kodyn." She seemed incapable of tearing her eyes away from her people, and tears glimmered in her dark eyes. "They're right there, but all I can think about is that this is a cruel dream and when I wake up, I'll be back in that ship's hold, chained and bound in darkness." Pain echoed in her every word. "I'm afraid even to blink for fear that it will evaporate and it will all be my imagination."

The Hunter glanced to Kiara. Surely she would know what to say to comfort the Ghandian.

Kiara radiated concern, a look of utter compassion on her face. The Hunter had no doubt she felt Aisha's pain; he had only a fraction of her empathy, and even *he* heard the anguish in the young woman's voice. Kiara remained silent, however. She merely returned the Hunter's glance with a shake of her head. There was only *one* person who needed to speak now.

"It's real, Aisha." Kodyn moved his horse closer to hers, took her hand in his. "You're home. Well, *almost.*" He forced a smile and chuckle. "Just a few more steps to descend the hill." He leaned forward. "And we'll take them together."

Aisha's fingers tightened on his and squeezed them back. Gratitude shone in her tear-filled eyes, and she gave him a slow nod. "Together."

Finally she moved, twitching her right leg to nudge her horse with a light brush of her heel. The beast responded by setting off downhill at a sedate walk. Kodyn matched her pace, never releasing his hold on her hand. Kiara, Tarek, and the Hunter set off behind them.

Within a few steps, Aisha's leg moved again, nudging the horse into a trot. She released Kodyn's hand and leaned forward, every muscle in her body straining toward the camp at the base of the hill. Faster she rode now. Her horse picked up speed, goaded on by her eagerness. Soon, she was galloping down the decline at full speed, her tight-curling hair streaming in the wind. Kodyn raced along in her wake, gaining speed to keep pace with her. The youthful pair led the charge down the hill toward the Issai.

The sound of galloping hooves announced their approach long before they reached the nearest of the tents. Before they had raced halfway down the hill, a dozen figures materialized to form a defensive wall between their people and the approaching riders. All wore loose, flowing, sleeveless robes displaying complex patterns and dyed myriad hues—red, yellow, brown, green, and the unmistakable blue of the Watcher's Bloom. In one hand, they gripped short-handled spears with broad steel heads a match for the one Aisha carried, and in the other held shields made of what appeared to be interwoven vines. Their sandals, too, appeared to be made from some thick hide or leather with forefoot, ankle, and calf-high straps fashioned from the same vines, albeit thinner and suppler.

Kodyn reined in first, wise enough to give Aisha space. Aisha, however, only stopped her horse ten paces away from the wall of Issai. Leaping from her saddle, she planted her feet defiantly before them, raised her own spear high, and shouted something in what the Hunter guessed had to be the tongue of her people. Her words had an instant effect on the twelve warriors barring their path. Confused looks passed between them, and one shouted back. Aisha's answer rang with a note of confidence that had not been evident only moments earlier. Every trace of hesitation and doubt had vanished like mist beneath the midday sun. The Hunter didn't understand all the words that passed between Aisha and the warriors—his lessons with Kodyn hadn't advanced his grasp of their tongue far—but their meaning was clear.

The daughter of the Issai's chieftainess had returned home.

A wild, whooping call echoed from one of the warriors in the wall—a woman, the Hunter saw, though her hair had been shorn to the scalp and she wore clothing identical to the men at her side. Another warrior took up the call, and within moments, the air filled with the ululating, joyous cries issuing from twelve powerful throats. The shields lowered and the woman who'd called out first raced forward to throw her arms around Aisha. Aisha returned the embrace with an almost desperate ferocity. The remaining eleven slung their arms around each other's shoulders and bounced toward Aisha in a leaping, whooping line. Smiles stretched across their umber-skinned faces, their delight as plain to see as the bright colors on their clothing.

Aisha didn't break off her embrace with the warrior in time, and was soon swept up by the line of capering warriors. The line moved to close in a circle, her arms joined with the rest of the warriors, and she, too, leaped and gamboled with her fellow Issai.

The whooping cries transformed from wordless ululations to a song that rang out across the valley. Brightly-clad men, women, and children raced toward them, streaming through the tents. If they seemed surprised to find their warriors cavorting about, they did not show it. Instead, they, too, linked arms and united with their fellows in the revelry. More and more and more, until close to two hundred Issai of all ages swirled around Aisha. Their voices added to the rousing song, and everyone from the youngest child to the most venerable white-haired elder joined in the leaping.

The Hunter stared wide-eyed at the jubilant display. He'd had no idea what to expect, but nothing could have prepared him for a celebration on this scale. His companions—even Kodyn—appeared equally amazed. Kodyn's smile was so wide his head looked ready to fall off, and Kiara sat with a hand pressed to her chest, as if overcome with joy for Aisha. Tarek just watched slack-jawed, his youth never more evident than in that moment.

The singing and leaping lasted for long minutes, the Issai getting swept up in the excitement of the moment. Even the Hunter felt the urge to dismount and join in the gaiety. Kodyn actually *did* leap off his horse, though he remained outside the edge of the swirling vortex of brightly-colored Issai. Right until Aisha appeared through the crowd, clamped a hand on his arm, and dragged him into the joyous melee.

When at long last the tumult died and the final note of their ringing song faded across the plains, the Issai continued to press in around Aisha. Some touched her face and arms, others plucked at her strange garb with curious fingers, and others laughed and exchanged excited words in their language. Aisha stood breathless at the heart of the commotion, a flushed and red-faced Kodyn at her side, and returned the embraces, touches, and words of her people. She truly *was* home.

A shout from between a nearby row of tents pierced the commotion, and all eyes turned toward the sound. The speaker was a tall man—taller even than the Hunter—with the lean, lithe build of a warrior. Tufts of snow-white flecked his near-black hair and beard, and deep wrinkles lined the skin around his eyes and mouth, yet he moved with an upright posture and a predatory grace accentuated by the cheetah pelt he wore on his broad shoulders. His deep blue robes swirled about him with every step, cloaking him in an air of unquestionable authority only amplified by the short-handled spear and shield he carried.

The man might not be the chieftain—Aisha's mother held that title—but he clearly held the respect of his people. At his appearance, the Issai around Aisha parted to clear a path for him to approach her.

Aisha, sensing the shift around her, turned to find the way opening. Her gaze fell upon the man marching toward her. Her already-bright smile turned blinding.

"Duma!" she cried, and raced toward him.

The man's stern expression remained fixed for only a moment longer. Then he, too, broke into a beaming smile. His long, muscle-corded arms flew wide, and Aisha sprang into them with a shout of delight. He wrapped her in his embrace and crushed her to his blue-robed chest. She clung to him in return, her arms locked around his waist. Every man, woman, and child around fell silent, save for a few whispers and exchanged words, and watched the joyful reunion between the man and the young woman.

Their embrace lasted only moments. When they broke off and Aisha turned back, tears glimmered once more in her eyes. Every fiber of her being seemed to crackle with a new energy as she led the older man toward where Kodyn stood amidst the watching crowd of Issai.

"Kodyn," she said breathlessly, "this is Duma, *Umdala* of the Issai. *Umdala* Duma, this is Kodyn, my…" She hesitated, a flush rising to her cheeks. "…*oqinywe.*"

At that, a chorus of "Oooohs" arose from the crowd—particularly, the Hunter noticed, the older women. Aisha's blush only deepened further, her umber-hued cheeks shining as bright as the noonday sun. The warrior who'd first embraced her said something in an unmistakably teasing tone, and Aisha hissed something back.

Duma, however, had not taken his eyes off Kodyn. Nor had Kodyn looked away from the older man despite the intensity of Duma's scrutiny. Instead, he stepped forward and held out his hand. "*Umdala* Duma, it is an honor to meet one of Aisha's family." To the Hunter's surprise, he continued speaking in what sounded like passable Issai. The Hunter recognized a few words, but not enough to put together what was said.

Duma appeared taken aback, too. His dark eyes widened a fraction as Kodyn spoke. Then, slowly, he nodded his head and answered something in his own tongue. This time, the Hunter recognized the friendly greeting—referencing the ancestors, or *Kish'aa*—Aisha had said was common to her people. A short exchange passed between him and Kodyn, ending with Duma clasping the young man's arm at the elbow.

Duma's eyes wheeled to the Hunter, Kiara, and Tarek—all still in their saddles—and he asked Aisha what no doubt was a question as to their identity.

"Oh, of course." Aisha turned toward them. "These are our companions. Tarek, Kiara, and…" Her brow furrowed, as if she had no idea what name to give the Hunter. After all, "the Hunter" would be strange to a tribe with countless hunters.

161

"*Umzukeli,*" Kodyn put in. A sly smile twisted his lips, and judging by Aisha's answering chuckle, she'd understood whatever joke that name invoked. The Hunter didn't understand the humor, for neither of the two had taught him that word.

"Umzukeli?" Duma turned a pensive look on the Hunter, his lips twisting down into a frown. "You are *alay-alagbara* yet you carry a name of Ghandia." He spoke Einari well, though with a thick accent and a melodic intonation that sounded odd to the Hunter's ears. No doubt as odd as Issai words would sound coming from his tongue, accustomed as it was to speaking Einari. "I would hear more of—"

At that moment, a shout rang out across the valley in which the camp of the Issai nestled. All spun toward the northwest, just in time to see a figure appearing over the crest of the hill. They were too far away for the Hunter to tell anything about them—man or woman, young or old—but they were spry and agile, racing down the slope at a run that any gazelle would envy. They carried a spear and shield and long robes of black, brown, and purple streamed out behind them.

Again, they shouted, and the moment their word reached the camp, a startling change came over everyone around Aisha. The festive air vanished in a moment, replaced by screams of alarm and panic. Instantly, the warriors gathered up their weapons and turned to race in the direction of the running figure. Duma, too, turned to go, but Aisha stopped him with a shouted question. He called back something in the tongue of the Issai and was gone in a blur of flying limbs and flapping blue robes.

"What is it?" the Hunter asked. Even as the words left his mouth, the answer to his question appeared. A swarm of figures materialized over the rise and boiled down the hill like a horde of ants.

Aisha drew her short-handled spear and dirk and blue-white light blazed in her eyes. "We're under attack!"

162

Chapter Thirty-Six

The Hunter wheeled Elivast toward the charging attackers and drove his heels into the horse's ribs. Elivast took off like a loosed crossbow bolt, breaking into a gallop in response to the Hunter's command.

"Hunter!" Kiara's voice rang out behind him, but the sound was drowned beneath the drumming of Elivast's hooves and the wind rushing in the Hunter's ears. He didn't look back—he could only trust she was smart enough *not* to follow him in his headlong dash straight toward the mass of dark-clad men streaming down the hill.

By now, the onrushing enemies numbered in the dozens, but still more were appearing over the rise. The Hunter reached for his weapons, hesitating only a moment before drawing Master Eldor's watered steel blade. He would not draw the Sword of Nasnaz unless he had no other choice. The risk to the Issai would be too great.

"Come on!" he roared, both to Elivast and the horde barreling toward the Issai camp. The horse responded by picking up speed, and the attackers turned toward him.

The Hunter waved his sword high in the air, catching the sunlight. He was seized by a sudden sense of déjà vu—how many lifetimes ago had he done precisely this, Nasnaz the Great charging fearlessly toward his enemies? Desert sands or rolling grasslands, it mattered not. Only the thrill of battle and the adrenaline coursing through his veins.

He raced toward the vanguard, the fastest of the warriors streaming down the hill. The closer he drew, the louder the sound of their approach became. A terrible clacking like a thousand wooden sticks striking in cacophonous staccato echoed in time with the ululating war cries loosed from their lips.

The Hunter roared in reply, a wordless, bestial snarl backed by all the force of his inhumanly powerful lungs. When he was but five paces away, he flung himself from Elivast's saddle and flew through the air to crash into the foremost enemy's upraised shield. The shield was made of some tough, wrinkled hide stretched over a wooden frame, and it snapped as easily as the warrior's arm. The impact of their collision bore both to the ground, but the Hunter rolled off the man and gained his feet in an instant. A vicious thrust drove the tip of his sword into his downed enemy's throat and silenced the man's cries.

A spear drove through the air for the Hunter's chest, and he knocked it aside with a contemptuous sweep of his sword. Razor-sharp watered steel sheared through the wooden shaft to lop off the crude spearhead. A moment later, Soulhunger punched into the man's exposed neck and drove down between his collarbones to pierce his heart.

As the dying man's screams filled the air with the crimson light that streamed from the dagger's gemstone, power washed over the Hunter and the world slowed to a crawl. He had but a moment to take in his enemies—their armor, fashioned out of hardwood carefully inscribed with decorative details and studded with jagged stones; the long-handled spears, hide-covered wooden shields, and bronze hand axes; their umber skin, broad facial features, lean muscular build, and the ragged pelts shielding them from the sun—before they surged around him in a tidal wave of flesh and fury. Surrounded on all sides, outnumbered, the Hunter abandoned himself to the mindless frenzy of the battle.

His sword and dagger blurred in the bright light of the sun, a deadly streak of glinting steel that carved through muscle, bone, wood, and hide with unquenchable ferocity. His wordless roaring answered the war cries hurled into his face. Blood misted in the air, splattered his face, soaked into his clothing, seeped down his boots. Some of it his own. He could not hope to turn aside every spear, evade every axe. Yet he met each attack with three of his own, each more savage than the last. He wove a wall of metal about him, and everywhere his sword touched, wooden-armored attackers died. Soulhunger fed on enemy after enemy, fueling the fire burning within him and healing the worst of his wounds.

And then, as abruptly as it had begun, the frenzy about the Hunter died. He cut down a woman draped with what appeared to be hyena furs, knocked a spear away before it could pierce his belly, and hacked off the arm of the warrior who'd thrust at him. Yet the man did not fall back screaming in agony. He seemed not to register the pain at all. He merely reached for the bronze axe in his belt with his free hand, determined to fight on. The Hunter opened the man's throat before he could draw. The moment the warrior fell, he realized he was alone.

Through the rush of blood filling his ears, the Hunter registered the sounds of battle. It came from *behind* him. He spun and found the bulk of the attackers rampaging through the camp. Encircling him, corpses piled five and ten deep where he'd stood, an immovable bulwark amidst the carnage. The rest of the wooden-armored warriors, however, had merely swirled around him and now fell upon the Issai.

Keeper take it! The Hunter dashed toward the camp. Pain twinged from fresh gashes on his hands and face, inflicted *after* Soulhunger's last victim. He felt the phantom aches in a dozen places where his armor had turned aside the blades of his enemies but not the bruising force of the blows. Yet all the sensations faded beneath the battle rush coursing like molten steel through his limbs.

Smoke billowed up from deep among the sea of tents and stick shelters, filling the air with dark clouds of noxious grey. Shouts of rage, screams of panic, and ululating war cries rang out on all sides. The lowing of cattle and bleating of panicking sheep joined the cacophony. And underscoring it all was that eerie wooden clacking of the attackers' armor.

The Hunter charged into the camp, cutting down the slowest-moving of the attackers from behind. Barely past the first row of shelters, he came upon a pair of Issai warriors defending against thrice their number of enemies. The Issai had thrown off their robes and faced their foes in only thick wrappings of a fibrous cloth—what passed for battle armor or undergarments among their people, the Hunter didn't know. What he *did* know was that the Issai's short-handled spears were no match for their enemies' longer weapons. Only their fighting style—a uniquely agile, graceful flow of movement that kept them continually on the move and evading attacks while remaining protected behind their shields of interwoven vines—had kept them alive thus far. At any second, however, the Hunter knew the battle could turn against them.

Silent as death, he charged toward the swirling knot of combatants. The attackers never saw him coming, never had a chance to turn to face him before he was among them. His sword struck out to the right and left. Blood fountained from severed arteries, a warm mist dark beneath the bright blue sky. A scream of agony sounded from one of the Issai, and the woman went down with a spear buried in her belly. The Hunter cut down the one who'd killed her a

164

moment too late. He never even got a look at his enemy's face before his sword separated the warrior's head from their neck.

The remaining Issai warrior finished off her enemy with a thrust of her spear. The long, sharp steel head punched into flesh just above the wooden breastplate, finding the attacker's throat. Crimson gushed from the wound, but still the warrior fought on. His spear swung for the Issai woman's head, and only the Hunter's quick reflexes kept it from finding flesh. He knocked the weapon out of the dying warrior's hand and shoved him to the ground. The Issai warrior tore her spear from the falling enemy's throat and sprang backward. Her weapons came up as if to defend herself from the Hunter.

The Hunter held up his empty hand—far from the most peaceful gesture, given that it was spattered with blood. The woman spoke to him in Issai, her tone sharp, but the Hunter shook his head and took another step back to widen the space between them. The moment he was out of reach of her spear, he turned and raced away from the warrior. No sense wasting time trying to explain himself when there were still enemies in the camp.

His eyes fixed on the two pillars of smoke rising from the camp, and he dashed toward the nearest. Doubtless he'd find enemies aplenty there. Plenty more in his path, too. Some were engaged in combat with the Issai, others tearing through shelters and tents intent only on destruction and despoilment. Any who stood in his way died. Many never even saw death coming, cut down from behind as they pawed through the Issai's belongings or clashed with their warriors. Those who faced the Hunter fared little better. Their wooden armor and hide-bound shields couldn't stand before his watered steel sword and the force of his fury.

He did not know who these attackers were or what grievance they might have had with the Issai, but that didn't matter. All he cared about was the promise he'd made to Aisha to do what he could to help her people. *This* hadn't been the help either of them had envisioned— Aisha had been intent on bringing a means of saving the *Umoyahlebe*—but now was far from the time to split hairs. Drive back the attack first, quibble over fine details later.

A chorus of ululating war cries echoed from just beyond the next row of tents, accompanied by the *clack* of wooden armor and weapons. The Hunter barreled around the shelters at a full run and came upon a fierce battle between two lines of struggling warriors. On one side, the attackers in their dark-colored armor shoved their hide-bound wooden shields against the interwoven vine shields of Issai garbed only in their sparse, fibrous wrappings. Behind the Issai warriors, bright-robed men wielding an assortment of crude weapons—staves, axes, hoes, and mattocks—lent their strength to the defense of their homes.

There was no room for dexterity or swiftness of movement in such a shield wall. Here, only brute strength and grim determination mattered. While the Issai fighting for their homes might possess the latter in abundance, their attackers outnumbered them easily three to one. Their superior numbers slowly pushed the defenders back toward the pen of long-horned raya cattle they guarded.

Here, however, the Issai's short-handled spears gave them an edge. Again and again, they struck from behind their shields, their shorter weapons ideal for close-quarters combat. Soon, the ground was strewn with their enemies' corpses. But more than a few of theirs bled out into the grassy plains, too. The battle would be over in a matter of minutes at this rate.

The Hunter hurled himself into the attackers from behind. Soulhunger whispered from its sheath, and he laid about him with a weapon in each hand. Together, sword and dagger carved their way through the ranks of attackers. He gave Soulhunger no chance to feed—he could not slow for even a moment, outnumbered as he was—but the blade's keen edge dealt death in measure equal to his sword. The wooden armor was light and sturdy yet could not fully cover its wearer. The Hunter exploited every vulnerability, driving the dagger into every bit of exposed flesh he could strike at. His sword merely carved through wood or shattered bone beneath.

A few of the attackers registered his presence and turned to face him. In vain. Packed tightly together as they were, pressing forward into the Issai's shield wall, they could not bring their long spears to bear on him. One managed to draw a belt axe, but the Hunter put his sword through the warrior's eye before he could swing. The remainder died without ever realizing death fell upon them from the rear.

The Hunter broke off his attack when only a handful of attackers remained standing. These pressed forward, unaware that they fought alone, the comrades who'd once supported them now lying dead at the Hunter's feet. The Issai, however, saw the truth. They responded with a push of their own, catching the few attackers remaining off guard. The wooden-armored warriors fell beneath the Issai's fury. The last the Hunter saw as he raced off to find new enemies, the short-handled spears were making quick work of the downed foes.

The Hunter ran through the camp, but in the few minutes he'd spent fighting near the cattle pen, the ferocity of the battle seemed to have abated. A few of the attackers remained, but now *they* were outnumbered and surrounded. Whether any attempt was made to surrender, the Hunter didn't know. None lived long. The Issai showed no mercy to those who had violated their lands and destroyed their homes.

"Hunter!" A familiar voice rang out from the Hunter's left.

He spun, and relief washed over him like the cool water of Nsukeja Lake at the sight of Kiara. Crimson trickled from a cut in her forehead and another on her left cheek, but she appeared otherwise unhurt as she ran toward him. For a moment, he feared much of the blood staining her armor and clothing was hers. Had her belly wound re-opened, the stitches torn? Yet the way she moved, upright and free of pain, he knew she had escaped unharmed and her wound intact. Deathbite's hilt was stained and dripping blood, but its blade, of course, was utterly clean, as if fresh from the forge. The Hunter caught a final flickering glimmer of light fading from the gemstone. Her last kill must have been only moments earlier.

"Have you seen Tarek?" she demanded. "I lost sight of him."

The Hunter shook his head. "Aisha and Kodyn?"

"Here!" came a familiar voice. Kodyn lurched toward them, half-carrying, half-dragging an Issai warrior with him. Copious amounts of blood gushed from a wound in the woman's belly, and her face was pale. Yet she stumbled on with her jaw clenched against the pain and her spear gripped firmly in hand. "Aisha's right behind me."

The young woman appeared on Kodyn's tail in the company of three more Issai warriors—among them, the towering Duma. The older warrior, too, had thrown off his colored robes and wore only his cheetah pelt and thick fibrous wrappings, which displayed an impressive physique despite his advanced age. He carried a shield to match his height, but instead of a short-handled spear like the rest of his tribe, he wielded a sword with a thick double-edged blade and a half-moon-shaped tip. The Hunter recognized the blade at once; he'd gone to great lengths to procure a Ghandian *ikakalaka* for his collection of Einari weaponry. Favored by the Ghandian Empire, it was well-suited to hacking and chopping, heavy enough to sever limbs in the right hands. The abundance of blood staining its blade, crossguard, and the arm of its wielder spoke of Duma's prowess.

Kiara turned toward Aisha. "Have you seen—"

Before the words left her mouth, Tarek's voice echoed from the Hunter's right. "Help!"

The Hunter, Kiara, Aisha, and Kodyn all looked toward the sound. Duma and a handful of the warriors, too—those who spoke at least *some* Einari, the Hunter suspected.

166

A soot-stained, blood-spattered Tarek appeared between two tents, coughing heavily. His spear was gone, abandoned or lost in the melee, but his face revealed no panic or fear. Only concern for the warrior lying in his arms.

"Help her!" Tarek shouted, stumbling toward them.

Aisha, Duma, and the Issai reacted first. All of them raced toward Tarek, but it was long-legged Duma who reached the Elivasti first.

"*Zalika!*" The single word—or name—burst from his lips, and he all but snatched the limp figure from Tarek's arms. He lowered the warrior woman to the ground and knelt over her, touching her neck, her arms, her chest.

The Hunter and Kiara were only two steps behind Aisha and the Issai warriors in reaching Duma's side. One look at the warrior woman was all the Hunter needed to know there would be no helping her. Her face was bloodless, pale despite the umber hue of her skin, and her eyes were wide in panic. Blood sluiced down her leg from a deep gash in her bared thigh, more gushing from a spear wound in her neck. She tried to speak but no words escaped her lips. Only bubbling, crimson-tinged froth.

Duma took her hand in his and held it tight. He bent low over her and pressed his forehead to hers. If he spoke, it was in a voice too quiet for even the Hunter's keen ears to hear.

The Hunter's heart lurched. He'd recognized the warrior. She was the one who had first greeted Aisha—greeted her with the excitement of a long-lost sister.

He looked to Aisha. Tears glimmered in her eyes, but she did not let them fall. Instead, she joined the rest of the Issai warrior women in throwing back her head and loosing a wailing cry into the air.

More echoed from around the camp. They came from every direction, carried aloft by a hundred voices. The sound twisted the Hunter's stomach in knots and filled his belly with lead.

Where there had been joy only minutes earlier, now only grief and anguish remained.

Chapter Thirty-Seven

The Hunter felt a nudge against his elbow. He turned to see Kiara looking at him. Her eyes darted toward Tarek, who stood just beyond the edge of the crowd gathered around Duma and the fallen warrior. The young Elivasti's face was as pale as the woman he'd carried, all color drained from his cheeks, his eyes wide. His mouth moved but no sound came out.

"Tarek." The Hunter moved toward the man. When he received no response, he tried again, more forcefully. "Tarek!"

Tarek's eyes snapped toward him, yet they held a faraway look. "I-I tried!" Words poured from his mouth in a torrent. "I tried to get to her, but there were too many. And they didn't stop coming. Even when she cut them, they kept on. Like they were mad! Too many of them. Too many."

The Hunter's heart went out to the man. For all his skill, he was still young and lacking the experience of an older warrior. Experience like watching a comrade fall in battle or die in his arms. He'd lost his mother not long ago—she'd died during the Menials' attack on the Elivasti city below Kara-ket—but he'd been far away at the time and thus spared the pain of seeing her corpse. This must have been the first person who had died in front of him...what he clearly took to be *because* of him. That guilt was a burden the Hunter knew all too well. Just as he knew it could drag Tarek into darkness if he let it.

"Listen to me, Tarek." The Hunter sheathed his weapons and gripped the young man's shoulders in bloodstained hands. The look in Tarek's violet eyes remained distant, unfocused, so the Hunter shook him. "Listen to me!"

Tarek's eyes narrowed on him with visible effort.

"There was nothing you could do." The Hunter spoke in a firm, commanding voice. "Hard as that may be to accept, that's the truth. People die in battle. Always have and always will. What matters is that *you're* still alive. You lived. That may feel like a betrayal, or the act of a coward, or Keeper alone knows what else, but that's just a lie your mind tells you to try and make sense of what happened. Understand this: there is no sense to it. It simply *is*. And the sooner you wrap your head around that, the sooner you'll be able to move past it."

Tarek opened his mouth, and his voice came out in a croak. "But—"

"There is no but!" The Hunter cut the young man's protest off with a slash of his hand. "You are no more deserving than she, no more fortunate than she, no more blessed by the ancestors or the spirits. It is merely happenstance that you lived and she died. All you can do now is make the most of the life you still have because she gave hers."

Suddenly, the Hunter was struck by the profound irony of his words. For weeks now, he had been wrestling with guilt identical to the burden now plaguing Tarek. He'd blamed himself for Tassat's death, even though the assassin had *chosen* to give his life to save the Hunter's. In his attempt to help the young Elivasti, he'd just talked himself into understanding the truth of how to accept Tassat's death—and how to move past the guilt.

The Hunter glanced at Kiara. How had she known that it would work out this way? *Had* she even known, or was it mere happenstance? The knowing smile tugging at her lips answered his question. *Damn, she's good!*

He turned back to Tarek. "But now isn't the time to think about all that." He knew the full weight would crash down onto the young man soon enough. Better to offer a distraction to take his mind off the turmoil that would even now be raging in his mind. "I need you to go collect the horses. I ditched Elivast somewhere over there." He gestured to the spot where he'd leaped from his saddle onto the attackers. "Track down Ash, your horse, and Kodyn and Aisha's horses, too. Gather them together, make sure all our gear is intact. Can you do that?"

Tarek nodded, though the gesture was as dull as his expression.

"Go." The Hunter emphasized his words with a gentle push on Tarek's arm. The young man didn't resist, but stumbled off, his steps dragging. The Hunter could only hope the task kept Tarek's mind and body busy for a while.

A fresh chorus of wails emanating from the crowd around Duma and the fallen warrior drew his attention once more. Aisha knelt beside the white-haired man, and Kodyn had passed the injured woman he'd been helping off to one of her comrades and now stood behind Aisha, a hand resting on her shoulder in silent comfort.

168

"Duma!" A strong, commanding voice cut through the cacophony. Through the smoke strode a woman wearing a long robe of black, brown and purple. She bled from a trio of wounds on her belly, shoulder, and right leg and her woven-vine shield was twisted and bent beyond all use, yet the blood staining the head of her short-handled spear demonstrated that she'd given at least as good as she'd gotten.

As she approached, the Hunter realized he'd seen that specific interplay of colors on her robes before. Only minutes earlier, in fact. *She* had been the figure running down the hill shouting warning of the impending attack.

The newcomer rattled off a string of words in the tongue of the Issai—they sounded questioning, though they were spoken too fast for the Hunter to piece together. The elderly man bent over the fallen warrior did not so much as look up. He remained as motionless as the now-silent, lifeless woman lying before him.

"Siyanda?"

Aisha's question seemed to catch the woman off guard. Her eyes scanned the warriors surrounding Duma, searching for its source. When Aisha rose, the woman's confident stride faltered mid-step, and she froze as if a blast of glacial wind had turned her to ice.

"*Sa'bone*, Siyanda." Aisha slipped out from beneath Kodyn's hand and moved toward the newcomer.

The woman sucked in a breath. "A-Aisha?" She spoke the word as if naming the ghost of someone long-dead.

Aisha responded in Issai, and the woman's jaw dropped. Then her brow furrowed and a frown twisted her lips. She snapped out something that sounded as angry as she looked.

Now it was Aisha's turn to falter mid-step. She stopped five paces away from the woman and stood staring, silent.

The Hunter frowned. *Could they be…?* The similarities between the two were startling. Both had the same tight-curled hair, though that was common to many of the Issai around them. They wore silver piercings in the same side of their nose and both eyebrows, though the woman had another in her lower lip. The shapes of their noses, lips, and strong jaws were alike enough they could have been sisters. But Aisha had called this woman *Siyanda*. Back in the field of the Watcher's Bloom, she'd called her sister *Nkanyezi*.

Some manner of family, though, the Hunter decided.

"Aisha?" Kodyn's tentative question shattered the momentary silence that had descended between the two women and the warriors around Duma. "Is this—?"

"My cousin, Siyanda." Aisha's voice was clipped—though she sounded confused more than angry. "Daughter of my mother's older sister."

"Oh." Kodyn seemed to sense the same tension emanating from Aisha, but he managed a genial smile and stepped forward to hold out his hand to the woman. Again, he spoke in the language of the Issai with surprising ease.

Siyanda stared at Kodyn as if at a venomous serpent, and she did not take his hand. After a moment, her eyes strayed to the Hunter and Kiara.

"Who are these outsiders you have brought to our home?" she demanded. She spoke Einari with only a hint of accent, the words rolling off her tongue as easily as Kodyn spoke her language—perhaps even more so. She rounded on Aisha, scowling. "Whoever they are, they are no more welcome here than—"

"Siyanda!" Aisha's voice drowned out her cousin's. "I will not have you speaking so to my *oqinywe*." Again, a flush rose to her cheeks at the words, though slighter than the first time.

169

Kodyn's lack of reaction suggested either he didn't know the meaning of the word or accepted it without the same embarrassment she did. "Or to the companions who have traveled a long way to see me safely home."

"Companions?" Siyanda's upper lip pulled back to reveal teeth a bright white against her umber-hued skin. She turned back to Aisha with a scornful look and shook her head. "Have these years away turned you into an *alay-alagbara*, then?"

The Hunter recognized the word—or at least he *thought* he did. It sounded suspiciously like the word Gwala had called him. He suspected it was some slight used to refer to those foreign to the lands that had once been the Ghandian Empire. Her tone certainly made it seem thus.

Aisha didn't rise to the bait. "I am Issai to the marrow, just as you are, Siyanda." She stepped toward the woman and stood taller. "Though I was taken far away, I have returned to my people. *My* home."

Siyanda squared off in front of Aisha. She stood shorter by a finger's width but her shoulders were wider, her musculature more pronounced. She looked roughly of an age with Aisha, at most two or three years older.

"Tell me, Siyanda." Aisha spoke in a calmer, more equitable tone. "Where is my mother?" She looked around. "I did not see her in all the chaos. Is she on a hunt? Is that why the Tefaye chose to attack now?"

Siyanda's face tightened. "Your mother..." The woman's jaw muscles worked, her eyes narrowing. "She is not here. Nor are your sister or father."

Aisha switched to her native tongue and rattled off what sounded suspiciously like a demand for answers. The Hunter watched Siyanda's face shift through myriad emotions—anger, frustration, even fear—before finally settling on a chilly imperiousness the Hunter didn't understand.

At her answer, Aisha's face drained of color, and her hand shot up to cover her mouth.

"Keeper's balls!" Kodyn cursed.

"What is it?" the Hunter asked, stepping forward.

"Her family—"

"This is not a matter for the *alay-alagbara!*" Siyanda's voice rang out through the valley in which the camp nestled. She stomped her right foot once, kicking up a puff of dust, and glared at Aisha. "You say he is your *oqinywe*. So be it. But *they*"—her short-handled spear jabbed toward the Hunter and Kiara—"do not belong among us. For all you know, they could be the ones that led the Tefaye right to us."

"Not bloody likely!" the Hunter snarled. He held up his crimson-stained hands. "If we *had* led those bastards here, would we have just joined in the fight to drive them off?"

Siyanda sneered at the Hunter, but the retort forming never left her lips. For in that moment, Duma straightened from where he bent over the fallen warrior, and Siyanda's eyes rested on the woman's face. Her eyes flew wide and she staggered back as if a dagger had been driven into her breast.

"*Um'zala?*" Aisha took a step toward Siyanda.

Siyanda ignored Aisha, casting aside her shattered shield and rushing past to fall to her knees beside Duma. A great wailing sob burst from her lips. "*Zalika!*" She dropped her spear and wrapped her arms around the unmoving woman. Tears streamed down her face to drop onto the pale, lifeless cheeks of the slain warrior. She bent forward and pressed her forehead to the woman's just as Duma had.

170

The elderly man looked up, and though his cheeks were dry, sorrow shone dark in his eyes. "My *ala'indokazi* and our *nassor* were *ingani*. Heart-sisters, in your tongue."

A dagger twisted in the Hunter's belly. His *daughter?* No, that wasn't quite right. The *indokazi* part referred to daughter, but there was something more to it, the *ala,* he didn't understand. But he understood pain etched into Duma's lined face all too well. The sight struck a chord within him. He'd lost a daughter, too, in a way. For thousands of years, he had lived without knowing she even existed. Then he'd found her, only to lose her again. *After* she'd murdered Father Reverentus in cold blood.

He nodded to the warrior. "My condolences, *Umdala* Duma."

The white-haired man inclined his head. "Zalika was as much my daughter as if she were my own flesh. I loved her with all my heart. Now, she is with the *Kish'aa.*" He reached for a stone lying on the ground beside his daughter's corpse, dipped it into her blood, and tucked it into a pouch on his belt. Then he stood, slowly, with great solemnity. "And the *Kish'aa* are with us always. So she is not truly gone. Merely awaiting the day I, too, cross over to join with the ancestors."

"*Nassor?!*"

Aisha's exclamation was so out of place in this moment of profound sorrow that it caught the Hunter by surprise. He turned to find her stalking toward Siyanda.

"You call yourself *nassor,* yet you do nothing to help our people?" Aisha's shout rang out with force amplified by the blue-white light that had flickered to life in her eyes. "My mother is not dead. You said so yourself!"

Siyanda muttered something back in her native tongue without rising from the body of the woman the Duma had called her heart-sister—a title that spoke of a connection far deeper than mere friendship or siblinghood.

"Yes, this is the time!" Aisha stopped just beside the kneeling Siyanda and planted her feet, glaring fury down at her cousin. "Tell me exactly how this happened, and in the language of the *alay-alagbara* so they, too, can understand it." She gestured toward the Hunter and Kiara. "Because if anyone can help us to free my family and the rest of our people from the people you say have them prisoner in *Indawo Yokwesaba,* it's them!"

171

Chapter Thirty-Eight

Mention of *Indawo Yokwesaba* set the Hunter's mind racing. Graeme had believed the Order of Mithridas in Ghandia, though he'd found nothing concrete as to what held their interest. Nashat al-Azzam had believed the masks worn by the Ordermen who'd attacked their convoy on the way to Malandria had come from slashwyrms, drake-like creatures said to inhabit the exact forest where Aisha now said her family was being held prisoner.

No way it's a coincidence!

Whatever the Order wanted in the forest, it had to go far beyond merely harvesting slashwyrm scales for their masks. An organization dedicated to toppling empires and kingdoms and fomenting discord across Einan *had* to have greater purpose for being here beyond such a trivial detail. How it involved Aisha's mother and whoever else they had prisoner, the Hunter didn't know, but he bloody well intended to find out.

All this flashed through the Hunter's mind in an instant, so quickly Aisha's shouted question still hung in the air as he reached his conclusion.

Siyanda pressed a kiss to Zalika's forehead and, in one smooth motion, gathered up her spear and rose to her feet. She shouted a few words in the Issai tongue, and the handful of warrior women around her sprang into action. For the first time, the Hunter got a good look at them from up close. He was surprised to find none were older than Siyanda herself. Most appeared younger even than Aisha. For all their determination in battle, they now stood staring down at Zalika's lifeless body with the same wide-eyed look that had stained Tarek's face. Only Siyanda's commanding voice snapped them from their stupor and set them scurrying away to obey whatever order she'd given. Had this been their first battle, too?

His thoughts were interrupted when Siyanda rounded on them. "Come," she snapped, her voice curt, eyes hard as obsidian points. "We will discuss this in private." Her gaze flicked to the Hunter and Kiara. "If you insist, the *alay-alaghara* may come, too."

"I insist." Aisha's sharp tone matched her cousin's.

Siyanda's jaw clenched, but she had no response for Aisha. Instead, she turned to the tall, white-haired warrior who now stood silently watching. "*Umdala* Duma, your counsel is welcome as always."

"I am honored, *nassor.*" Duma placed his right hand on his heart and inclined his head.

"This way." Siyanda spun on her heel and marched off, her multi-colored robes swirling around her.

Aisha, Kodyn, Kiara, and the Hunter all followed the woman. Duma brought up the rear, his steps now visibly laborious and his body stooped beneath the effort of carrying his broad sword and shield. Through the pall of smoke that now pervaded the camp, the Hunter caught

172

wind of the man's unique scent—steel, Ghandian blackwood, and a deep, meaty musk that could only come from the cheetah pelt draped over his shoulders.

Siyanda led them through the camp…what remained of it. Stick shelters had been kicked over or pulled down as the attackers clawed through the meager belongings within. Tent ropes had been severed, the light cloth rent and slashed, and the supports shattered. At the heart of the camp, smoke still rose from the remnants of what appeared to be a tent large enough to serve as some sort of communal space—a shade from the heat—beneath which meals and gatherings took place.

The pen the Hunter had helped the Issai warriors defend had been broken, too. A few of the warrior women had re-donned their colorful robes and set to directing the men—many twice or three times their age—in the task of rounding up the long-horned cattle that had escaped. More were already hard at work dressing the cattle butchered senselessly or maimed too grievously to be treated.

Long, ululating wails echoed from every direction, the sound of grief borne aloft on the clouds of smoke and the voices of those who had lost friends and loved ones. Everywhere the Hunter looked, his eyes fell upon corpses clad in brightly colored robes shredded by enemy weapons, stained with the blood of the fallen. Men, women, and children knelt beside the deceased, some whispering silent words, others pressing their foreheads against those of their kin, many more merely sitting in stupefied horror and numb disbelief.

Acid rose in the Hunter's gut. He had witnessed death aplenty, but sights like this…well, they never grew easier. For every warrior who had given their life in defense of the camp, five more noncombatants had fallen. Hunters, herders, foragers, weavers, grandmothers and grandfathers, sons and daughters. Such slaughter was always senseless. The innocent and peaceful suffered most of all.

Siyanda strode stiffly, her back as straight as the spear she carried, her battle-torn and bloodstained robe flapping about her lithe warrior's frame. More than once, she paused to call out a command, to press the hands of and offer words to some grieving Issai, or to kneel at the side of a fallen warrior to pay her final respects. But always she continued on with only brief delay, driven by purpose. Or, equally likely, the need to keep moving in the desperate hope of outrunning her sorrow. A futile endeavor in the long run, the Hunter knew all too well. For a short time, however, purpose kept her from succumbing to the crushing emotions.

Once free of the camp, the wind gusting down the hill carried to the Hunter's nostrils the woman's unique scent: cloves, ginger, bamboo, and hibiscus. A curious, complex mixture of aromas—perhaps emblematic of the woman herself.

Siyanda only stopped once she reached the top of the hill down which she had raced bearing warning of the impending attack. From there, she had a clear view of the plains stretching for dozens of leagues in all directions. The basin containing Nsukeja Lake was no longer visible to the southwest, obscured by rolling hills. Far to the north, however, the Hunter caught sight of a smudge of dark green that *might* have been a forest. *Indawo Yokwesaba,* perhaps?

"Enough delay, *um'zala.*" Aisha's patience had evidently reached its limits. She had carried her spear all this way in a grip so tight her knuckles had long ago whitened, and her jaw muscles creaked with the strain of her clenching. "Speak, now! How is it that my *mother,* the fiercest of the Issai, was captured? And how were *Nkanyezi* and my father taken, too? And where are the rest of our warriors?" She stabbed a finger toward the camp below them. "Why do the *unkgaliwe* fight for our home?"

Siyanda endured the barrage of questions with ever-growing stiffness, her powerful muscles knotting and relaxing as if she fought to restrain herself. "You will address your *nassor* with—"

"You are not *nassor!*" Aisha shouted. She stepped toward Siyanda, so close her face hovered mere inches from her cousin's. "Unless my mother is dead, that title is hers alone."

Siyanda's free hand tightened into a fist. For a moment, the Hunter believed she might actually strike Aisha.

"Siyanda," Duma said, a warning in his voice. Evidently he'd come to the same conclusion as the Hunter.

Siyanda tore her gaze from Aisha and looked toward the elderly warrior. Duma said nothing, but the frown and slight shake of his head spoke volumes. With a frustrated grunt, Siyanda unclenched her fist and stepped back, opening a space between her and Aisha.

"It happened four moons ago," she said, clearly struggling but winning the battle to control her temper. "Enemies came in the night and attacked us in the Zwelibani Valley. Your mother and the other *amaqhawe* drove them off, but when they gave chase, they were led into an ambush and captured."

Aisha's eyes narrowed. "Ambush?" She shook her head. "The *nassor* would not be fooled so easily."

"Nor was she." Siyanda's head lifted, her spine stiffening. "The ambush had been carefully laid out days before. The night attack was a trick to draw her and the rest of the *amaqhawe* in. She and the others were clapped in chains and taken to *Indawo Yokwesaba*."

"And these ambushers?" the Hunter asked. "Who were they?" If she mentioned men in black masks, he would have his answer as to the Order of Mithridas' location.

"Our people call them *Gcinue'eleku awandile*." Siyanda's lip curled up, anger blazing in her eyes. "But among your people, they are called the Vassalage Consortium."

The Hunter's stomach clenched. *Those Keeper-cursed bastards again?*

Kiara growled a curse under her breath, and Kodyn's hand dipped to the sword on his belt. The very air around Aisha seemed to come alive. Power emanated from her in an aura as tangible as the wind rolling off the plains, and sparks of blue-white light danced around her hands.

At the sudden blaze of magic, Siyanda retreated a half-step, her eyes flying wide. She stared at Aisha in utter shock—mingled with a hint of what might have been dismay.

Duma, however, dropped to one knee. "*Umoyahlebe*," he intoned, bowing his head. "Beloved of the *Kish'aa*." When he straightened, a smile tugged at his lips. "As your father hoped you would become."

Instantly, the power around Aisha extinguished. Her fury remained blazing bright and hot, but it was now *human* anger, not that of whatever spirits appeared to her.

"Where is he?" she looked between Duma and Siyanda. "You said the Consortium took my mother and the *amaqhawe*. But father was not *amaqhawai*. And Nkanyezi cannot be old enough to embark on her *uhambo loguquko*. So where are they?"

Siyanda glanced at Duma. The elderly warrior had climbed to his feet, and now stood with shoulders heavy beneath a burden of sorrow. "We do not know," he said.

"What?" Aisha rounded on Siyanda. "How do you not know?"

"Your father and sister vanished two days before the *Gcinue'eleku awandile*. They went walking together as they did every day, and never returned. The *nassor* had sent people to find them." She swallowed, a sudden tension in her face. "Zalika and I were sent to find them. We lost their tracks in the Gwembashi River. By the time we returned, the battle had ended and your mother and the rest of the *amaqhawe* were already prisoner."

"And you did not go after them?" Aisha demanded. Again, sparks flared to life around her hands, and blue-white light shone in her eyes. "For four months, you have done nothing to—"

"I have not done *nothing!*" Siyanda's voice cut into Aisha's, anger evident in every shouted word. "I have done everything I can to keep our people alive. Zalika and I are all that remain of the *amaqhawe,* and Duma is the last of our *Umdala.* We cannot go to hunt and leave the *ekhaya* undefended, so we are forced to go where the food and water are. But to do so would make it easy for our enemies to find us. We believed the *ekhaya* would be safe here, but somehow the Tefaye found us." She cast a sharp glare at the Hunter. Somehow, she'd gotten it into her head that he had led their attackers here, and rationale be damned.

"And they are not the only threat we face," Siyanda continued, her voice rising in intensity, eyes blazing brighter. "For months, we have fled to escape the Buhari, the Ujana, even the Mwaani. Us, afraid of the Mwaani!" Scorn dripped from her lips and a look of utter distaste twisted her face. "If I cannot even depart to feed our people, what chance could I possibly have of liberating your mother and the *amaqhawe* from *Indawo Yokwesaba?* And now, with Zalika—"

Her voice cracked, and she turned away so fiercely her colorful robe whipped Aisha's face.

A tense silence settled between the two Issai women. Siyanda stood with her back turned to Aisha, and though her shoulders did not shake, the Hunter didn't need Kiara's finely attuned sense of empathy to feel Siyanda's pain. Aisha stared at her cousin's back, fists balled, yet at Siyanda's outburst, a fraction of her anger had vanished.

Then, slowly, Aisha's tense muscles relaxed and her hands unclenched. The energy crackling in the air around her diminished and once more went calm.

"I'm sorry, *um'zala,*" Aisha said in a quiet voice. She stepped close to her cousin and placed a hand on the woman's shoulder. Siyanda flinched, as if intending to jerk away, but stopped and remained motionless. Aisha squeezed Siyanda's shoulder. "I'm sorry. I have just dreamed of the day I would return home for so many years, I did not expect—"

"I have dreamed of this day, too!" Siyanda again spun about, this time facing Aisha. Tears glimmered in her eyes. She took Aisha by both shoulders. "Every day since you were taken, *um'zala,* I have prayed to all the *Kish'aa* that you would return safely to us." She swallowed. "I did not expect things to be this way when you returned, either."

Aisha surged forward, pulling her cousin into a crushing hug. Siyanda's arms wrapped around Aisha's shoulders and held her tight. For long moments, they stood locked in the embrace. All trace of their earlier animosity faded beneath the joy of their reunion.

The Hunter felt a warm, strong hand slide into his. Looking over, he found Kiara staring at him with a bright smile and a hint of moisture forming in her eyes. *"We did this,"* her look told him.

He smiled back and squeezed her hand. For at least a few seconds, the two women could forget the death behind them, the pain over lost and missing loved ones, and the suffering they had endured over the years since last they saw each other.

Even the Hunter, a lifelong cynic who had seen the worst of mankind, couldn't help feeling pleased knowing he had played some small part in bringing about this fleeting moment of happiness between Aisha and her cousin.

Chapter Thirty-Nine

Siyanda broke off the embrace a moment later, wiping brusquely at her face. Her demeanor sobered and her shoulders drooped as if beneath a great weight.

"I cannot leave the *ekhaya* undefended, Aisha." She shook her shaven head and tightened her grip on her short-handled spear. "Your mother would do the same in my place. You know this as well as I."

"I do." Aisha nodded slowly. "And you're right. You cannot leave. But *we* can." Her gesture encompassed Kodyn, Kiara, the Hunter, and herself.

"The four of you alone?" Siyanda looked at Aisha as if she were mad.

"Not alone." Aisha turned the palm of her free hand upward, and sparks of blue-white light danced around her fingers. "The *Kish'aa* travel with us."

Siyanda's eyes went fractionally wider, and she stared at the cavorting glimmers in open wonder. But only for a moment. She tore her eyes from the power manifested in Aisha's hand and recovered her poise. "You are the *Umoyahlebe* that *Umalume* Lwazi believed you could be— and clearly a great deal more than he or *Umamkhulu* Davathi could ever have imagined. But even with the *Kish'aa* at your command, you cannot believe yourself capable of defeating hundreds of *Gcinue'eleku awandile*. Remember, you did not complete your *uhambo loguquko*, either. You are not *amaqhawai*."

"I am not." Aisha's lips pressed together in a thin, hard line. "But even the full might of our *amaqhawe* could not prevail against the Consortium. What is needed here is something else." She turned and gestured to the Hunter. "What is needed is *Okanele.*"

At the word, Duma and Siyanda both recoiled away from the Hunter as if he had the Bloody Flux. They stared at him in horror and disbelief. Duma raised his heavy sword in both hands and Siyanda dropped into a crouch, spear held at the ready.

The Hunter raised his hands, showing them empty, albeit bloodstained. "Would you believe me if I claimed to be a friendly *Okanele*?"

He'd first heard the word from the lips of Ria, the fierce warrior who had guarded the Guild Master, one of Kodyn's mothers. She had said the *Okanele* were death-bringers and soul-stealers sent by *Inzayo Okubi*—no doubt some evil deity akin to what most Einari believed Kharna to be—to consume the spirits of mankind.

"*Okanele!*" Siyanda hissed. "He is a man!"

"Well, not quite." The Hunter considered how best to proceed. He had a good idea of what Aisha intended—proving she had a demon on her side would no doubt convince Siyanda to tell them how to locate her mother and the others captured by the Consortium—he merely had to do it in a way that left no doubt in Siyanda or Duma's minds that he, the embodiment of their monsters, could be trusted.

In Praamis, he'd demonstrated his transformation abilities, shifting the structure of his face before Master Gold's very eyes. He'd let Tassat drive a sword through his belly—the act doubled as irrefutable evidence of his regenerative capacity and a means of letting the man work off some of his anger over the accidental death of his fellow Night Guild assassin, Kindan. Words had sufficed to persuade Graeme, though the alchemist had doubtless already suspected there was more to the Hunter than met the eye.

Finally, he settled on what seemed like the fastest approach to address the issue.

"Kiara," he said, turning to her. "Would you mind terribly stabbing me?"

Four pairs of eyes flew wide. Duma and Siyanda froze, weapons at the ready yet caught off guard by the Hunter's request. Surprise sprouted on both Kodyn and Aisha's faces.

Kiara, however, just smiled. "With pleasure."

Perhaps a bit too much for the Hunter's liking. At least she made it quick. Her dagger slid along the side of his neck, not quite hitting the jugular vein but cutting deep enough into his flesh that the wound bled profusely.

The Hunter gritted his teeth against the sudden flash of hot pain. "Really?" he muttered. "You had to go for the neck?"

Kiara's grin widened. "You wanted me to cut someplace else, you should have said so."

The Hunter tamped down his irritation and instead focused his attention on mending the damage. He shifted his focus inward as Queen Asalah had taught him all those years ago, directing his mind to the severed flesh and muscle. A quick exertion of his will mended the laceration in a matter of seconds.

The surprise remained plastered on Kodyn and Aisha's faces. Siyanda hissed like a feral cat and growled something in the Issai tongue. She looked on the verge of charging, her eyes fixing on the Hunter's exposed throat, just above the collar of his leather armor. Duma's eyes narrowed; from up close, he had a clear view of the Hunter's neck as the blood slowed to a trickle, then ceased, the skin re-knitting and becoming whole once more.

Aisha said something sharp in Issai, and Siyanda glanced her way. Suspicion blazed in the *nassor's* eyes and twisted her face. Yet she did not attack, merely looked back to the Hunter.

"You are bound to Aisha by *isithembiso*?" she demanded.

Aisha translated. "An oath." She held his gaze levelly, an intent look on her face. "You said when the time is right, you would aid me in destroying the Consortium." She gestured with the tip of her spear toward the camp below them. "*This* happened to my *ekhaya*, my home, because of them. Look at that and tell me the time is not right!"

The Hunter didn't need to look. "If they have your family and the rest of your *amaqhawe*—" He had no idea what the word meant and knew for certain his tongue mangled its pronunciation but didn't care. "—then you're right." He placed a hand over his heart. "I will uphold my oath to you. My *isithembiso*."

Aisha looked back to Siyanda. "Just tell me how to find them, and we will see to it that the *Gcinue'eleku awandile* are punished. We will bring back my family and make our people whole once more."

Siyanda's expression remained hesitant. She stared at the Hunter with naked suspicion etched onto her face—a face so alike Aisha's. Siyanda's features were lined with worry for her people where Aisha's bore the lingering memories of her grim experiences as a captive of the

177

Consortium, yet they both spoke with the confidence of proud, skilled warriors. One, the daughter of the true *nassor*, the other temporarily serving the role and leading her people.

"You trust him?" Siyanda demanded of Aisha, though she never took her gaze off the Hunter or lowered her spear. "Knowing he is *Okanele*?"

Aisha shot a sidelong glance at the Hunter. "I do." The certainty in her voice surprised the Hunter—and filled him with a warm glow. "He helped me. In more ways than one. And some people very close to me trust him…with their lives." Her eyes lit up at a happy memory. The Hunter suspected those "people" of whom she spoke were Hailen and Evren. "You believe it is impossible to defeat the *Gcinue'eleku awandile*. Well, what is impossible for even the mightiest *amaqhawai* may prove far less difficult for an *Okanele*."

Siyanda still looked far from convinced. She studied the Hunter in tense silence, her features twisted in concentration. In that moment, the façade of assertive chieftainess cracked and the truth of her age showed through. Had she been more experienced—both in the ways of the world and leadership—she might have reached the decision more easily. But by her own account, she had been *nassor* for only a few months. That could feel like a lifetime when the survival of an entire tribe hinged on her decisions. The Hunter could not remember his life as Nasnaz the Great, but he recalled this feeling, this burden of knowing every misstep had the potential to lead to death, every misspoken word might end in bloodshed.

Duma's voice broke the silence. "Siyanda." He spoke briefly in the Issai tongue—the Hunter thought he caught the word for "forest", though it might have been "sunset", he wasn't certain—punctuating his statement with a gesture toward the camp, then toward the smudge of green near the northern horizon.

Siyanda glanced at Aisha before responding. Duma's answer was short—just two words, accompanied by a shrug of his broad shoulders.

"I acknowledge that you are *nassor*," Aisha joined in, "at least until my mother returns. And while I am Issai, they are not." She indicated the Hunter, Kodyn, and Kiara with a nod of her head. "They do not need your permission. But they could use your help." She stepped forward and gripped her cousin's right bicep with her free hand. "I need you, *um'zala*. So do my mother, father, and Nkanyezi. Help us! Tell us where to go."

The confident façade cracked further as emotions swirled on Siyanda's face. Dread, doubt, hope, fear, worry, sorrow, and anger swam across her features in equal measure. She looked into Aisha's eyes, and she looked as if she wanted to pull Aisha into another hug—not one of joy this time, but one seeking comfort.

The moment passed in an instant. Siyanda regained control of herself and the mask of command slipped once more into place.

"Very well, *um'zala*." Siyanda squared her shoulders and lifted her head. "I will take you where you must go."

Aisha looked taken aback. "But you said—"

"I know what I said." Siyanda's jaw muscles clenched. "I have not dared to leave the *ekhaya* undefended by the *unkgaliwe* alone. They are young and still lack training. For all their bravery, they have not yet undertaken the *uhambo loguquko*. But they will not be alone." She turned to Duma. "You will command in my absence. You will lead the herd to shelter west of the Unathi River. Close enough to *Indawo Yokwesaba* that if there is any trouble, you can send a runner to me. Ntombi, for she is the fastest of the *unkgaliwe*. But I can guide Aisha and her *alay-alagbara* companions"—her eyes darted to the Hunter and a hint of her former suspicion returned—"to where our true *nassor* and the *amaqhawe* are being held."

178

Duma raised no protest. "Yes, *nassor*," he said, bowing to her. His acceptance came so easily the Hunter suspected that he'd already determined that was the best course of action. A man of Duma's years would have seen many battles akin to the one they'd fought today, and would have lived through decades of turmoil, skirmishes, and raids. Even in a tribe ruled by women, the voice of one so experienced had to carry some measure of respect. Matriarchal societies throughout Einan's history often allowed—or even encouraged—males to hold advisory positions.

Siyanda turned to Aisha. "I will inform the *omama* of what I have decided, what must be done. They will see that the *ekhaya* departs with the night. After the fallen are commended to the *Kish'aa*." Her face tightened at this. "But we will leave before the sun begins its descent. Make ready." She never glanced at the Hunter or the others, but nodded respectfully to Duma and hurried down the hill toward the camp.

Aisha watched her cousin go, and the Hunter noticed new lines furrowing her brow and the corners of her eyes. Not exactly the joyful reunion she'd been expecting, it seemed. Or was it the fact that Siyanda intended to accompany them into what had the potential to be a truly dangerous mission to free her parents? Perhaps some other concern he didn't understand.

Kodyn stepped up beside Aisha. "You good?" he asked, his voice barely above a whisper.

She looked to him, and the worry lines deepened. "That is the Siyanda I remember...and yet not."

The Hunter glanced at Kiara. She, too, looked as if she wanted to say something, but had no more idea of what to offer than he did.

Duma's deep voice broke the silence. "Even the cheetah may feel small stepping into the lion's footprint. Yet once the cheetah understands the lion cannot outrun it, it finds peace."

With those words, the tall warrior slung his heavy sword onto his shoulder and strode down the hill toward the camp.

Siyanda

Chapter Forty

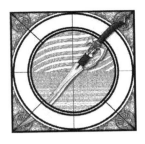

The Hunter found Tarek leading the horses up the hill, away from the smoke and wailing and corpses. The animals were skittish and restive in the wake of the attack, but the young Elivasti had calmed them down enough that they only snorted and reared once at the Hunter's approach.

Shadows darkened Tarek's face. His violet eyes were hooded, deep lines furrowed his brow, and he moved sluggishly, stiff as one of Juliuss de Langstaff's renowned toy automatons. The Hunter had to call Tarek's name thrice to get the young man's attention, and upon hearing of the change to their plans, Tarek just nodded and climbed into his saddle. Not a single word of protest that they were no closer to locating the *maistyr* or that this new challenge would bring them no closer to completing the mission to which the Second Blade had set him. Merely mute acceptance.

The Hunter wanted to speak to the young man, but what could he say? His earlier words had poured forth without conscious thought. Now, anything he considered felt trite, hollow. Nor did he have the time to expend on the slow, measured approach he'd taken before. They had a long day of travel to reach the forest where Aisha said her family were being held by the Vassalage Consortium. The Hunter resolved to find a moment when next they rested to try and speak to the young man. *After* discussing with Kiara how best to approach the matter.

He and Tarek skirted the perimeter of the camp on their way to where Kodyn, Aisha, and Kiara awaited them. Kodyn had insisted on inspecting the wound Aisha had sustained in the battle—a gash to the right shoulder left by an enemy spear. When the Hunter rode up, the young man was poking at Kiara's cheek.

"It'll be fine," she said in an irritable voice, waving him away. "They're just scratches."

Kodyn snorted but stepped back. "Watcher's teeth, you sound just like mother."

The Hunter grinned. "Jarl said the two were alike."

Kodyn nodded. "I see it." He looked Kiara up and down. "Stubborn, determined, commanding, too proud to let anyone offer help."

"She sounds utterly delightful." Kiara shot the young man a mocking smile. "Looking forward to the day I meet her."

Kodyn looked over to Aisha. "Wouldn't that be a sight?" His grin faded as he realized she wasn't looking his way. Instead, she stood sideways to him and Kiara, staring down at the camp spread out below her. The fingers of her left hand tugged absentmindedly at the cloth Kodyn had wrapped around her shoulder.

Kodyn turned to Aisha, reaching a hand up toward her. Kiara caught his wrist before he could touch the young woman.

"Give her a moment," Kiara whispered.

Kodyn hesitated a moment, then lowered his hand with a nod.

Kiara graced the young man with the same smile that appeared whenever Hailen or Evren shared some great success or accomplishment with her. "Not the homecoming she imagined."

"No, it's not." Kodyn shook his head sadly.

"Mount up," Kiara said, inclining her head toward Kodyn's horse. "She'll be ready soon enough."

With a worried glance over his shoulder toward Aisha, Kodyn hurried to swing up into his saddle.

The Hunter inwardly nodded his approval. For all the young Praamian cared deeply for Aisha—and clearly wanted to do or say something to help her—he'd instantly recognized the truth behind Kiara's words and heeded her advice without argument or protest. That spoke of a degree of maturity rarely found in one so young.

Kiara moved toward Ash, calming the restive desert pony with a few gentle words, and mounted. The Hunter did likewise, until only Aisha remained standing. She moved not at all, save for her fingers twitching at the fabric of her bandage.

The Hunter shifted his gaze from the young woman to the object of her focus. A flurry of activity consumed the camp of the Issai. The men sent to retrieve the cattle that had fled during the battle were returning, joining the others corralling the herd at one corner of the broken pen. All throughout camp, women dismantled tents and lashed the sticks used to form their simple shelters into bundles that could be carried on their backs. A group of white-haired elders kept a stern eye on a group of the children old enough to walk on their own feet, while toddling infants were secured to their mothers' chests with the same flowing, colorful fabric of their robes. The wounded, ill, and lame were helped or loaded onto sled-like constructions woven from vines much like those used for the warriors' shields.

Half of the Issai warriors stood on the crest of the hill, forming a defensive ring around the camp. Their watchful eyes scanned the grassy plains surrounding their valley for any sign of an enemy. The remainder of the warriors, however, bent to the task of preparing the dead. The bodies were stripped bare, their colorful robes removed and passed on to their families. The warriors fallen in battle were placed atop their shields with their spears resting on their chests. The rest were laid out side by side. High in the sky, the dark shapes of crows had already begun to gather in expectation of a feast.

It was there, beside the dead, the Hunter caught sight of Siyanda. The *nassor* knelt at the side of a warrior—even from this distance, the Hunter had no doubt it was Zalika—but rather than bowing her head as so many other cultures did, Siyanda's face was turned up to the sky and her arms thrown wide. Her lips moved, but her words were drowned out beneath the commotion of the Issai breaking camp. Some prayer to the gods her people worshipped, perhaps? Imploring the *Kish'aa* to look after her?

Whatever it was, it didn't last long. Siyanda's arms lowered and she bent to touch her forehead to the dead warrior's. After a few seconds, she straightened, climbed to her feet, and shrugged out of her colorful robes until she stood only in the fibrous cloth wrappings all the Issai wore—a curious mix of battle garments and underclothes, apparently. She laid her loose-flowing robes atop Zalika's face, then turned and strode through the camp on her way to where the Hunter and the others awaited her.

Without her robes, the strength inherent in Siyanda's physique was unmistakable. She had the lean, long-muscled build of a runner, but with power in her arms and leg muscles developed over years of martial training and combat. A warrior, no doubt about it.

Just before Siyanda reached the edge of the camp, however, one of the warriors stopped her. A brief exchange ensued; the warrior said something that surprised Siyanda, and pointed a finger to where the Hunter sat on his horse. The Hunter wasted a moment trying to figure out what might have drawn the warrior's attention. Perhaps the Issai had seen him ride straight at the enemy or witnessed Soulhunger's magic as it devoured the soul of the Hunter's victim. Doubtless she was warning her chieftainess to be wary of the *alay-alagbara*.

A grim smile twisted the Hunter's lips. They had no idea just what he was capable of. When he finally let loose the Sword of Nasnaz against the Vassalage Consortium, they would know the true meaning of *Okanele*.

Siyanda bounded up the hill toward them at a run, shield and spear in hand, a grim expression on her face.

At her approach, Aisha snapped out of her brooding and moved to intercept Siyanda. "Will you ride with me, *um'zala?*" she asked, holding out a hand.

Siyanda shot a scornful look toward the Hunter and the others seated on their horses. "My feet will carry me well enough. I am no *alay-alagbara*." Her words dripped disdain, aimed squarely at Aisha.

If Aisha was bothered, she hid it well. "We will reach *Indawo Yokwesaba* more quickly—"

"I will run." Siyanda's eyes flashed, her lip curling upward. "If you cannot match my pace, I will await you at the Unathi River crossing."

So saying, she pushed past Aisha and set off northward at a run.

Aisha watched her cousin depart, and a glimmer of confusion and frustration flashed across her face. The emotions vanished as quickly as they had come. Her strong features once more smoothed, save for the lines furrowing her brow, and, with a shake of her head, she sprang into her saddle and set off after Siyanda.

The Hunter exchanged a glance with Kiara. The look in her eyes told him that she'd made note of the *nassor's* behavior, too. The Hunter found it difficult to understand why Siyanda wasn't more overjoyed at her cousin's return, but he was far from an expert on matters of family. He'd never had one to speak of until only recently. And after what had happened with Jaia…

He shoved the thought aside. Time for such grim contemplations later. Right now, they had a task to be about.

A nudge of his legs turned Elivast to face north, toward the smudge of dark green of *Indawo Yokwesaba*. Even as he did, he felt the familiar call of *Ukuhlushwa Okungapheli* pulling at his mind. Perhaps helping Aisha to rescue her family wouldn't be a detour from his mission for Kharna at all, but a stepping stone that led to where the Serenii needed him to be.

He clenched his jaw and tapped his heels against Elivast's ribs. *I suppose I'll find out soon enough.*

* * *

They rode the remainder of the day. The Hunter had to admit Siyanda did an admirable job of matching their pace. The Issai's long stride ate up the grasslands at an impressive speed, and she ran for hours without slowing or showing signs of tiring. And that *after* she'd run Keeper-knew-how-far to warn of the attack on the camp and joined in the battle to defend the *ekhaya*. Such stamina could only come from a lifetime spent traveling long distances on foot. In a way, he understood the woman's disdain for riding. He'd seen countless Praamians and Voramians made soft and weak by their reliance on horses.

On the other hand, no amount of human indefatigability could ever compensate for a horse's speed. They caught up to Siyanda within minutes, and Aisha slowed the pace to a jog-trot to keep pace with the running Issai. Siyanda never once looked their way. She merely kept her face pointed straight ahead and bent her focus entirely to her run.

Hours passed, the sun descended toward the horizon, and still they continued on. The grasslands' rolling hills rose and dipped in undulating waves of dull green around them. The brilliant rays of the afternoon sun bathed the world in a mélange of bright reds, golds, and oranges.

Just before the sun vanished behind the western hills, the land descended toward a sinuous furrow that looked to have been carved into the earth by a giant's finger. Thirty paces wide at its broadest point and easily as deep at the center, it must have once been a great river wending through the Ghandian Plains. All that remained was cracked earth and stones worn smooth by water.

Siyanda led the way across a spot where the furrow was shallowest—likely once a crossing point—and turned northward to follow the river's remains toward the forest. Even after running for hours, she showed no intention of slowing down or stopping to rest for the night.

If Aisha felt even the slightest fatigue after their long journey and battle, she was too stubborn to show it. Kodyn labored gamely onward, clearly determined to keep up with Aisha, but the Hunter could see the young man was tiring just from the way he bounced about in his saddle.

Tarek had lived for years among the Hrandari—most of them spent on horseback—but his shoulders were hunched and his head hung low as he wrestled with the inner turmoil that had consumed him since the battle.

The Hunter glanced at Kiara. She'd recovered from the wound in her belly, but her strength had not yet fully returned. Of course, she would never let him or the others see that. She, Siyanda, and Aisha all had that relentless tenacity in common. It made them strong, empowered them to push through their pain, but it could also be a weakness. Pushed too hard, even the toughest steel could crack.

He made the decision knowing it was best for *everyone* in his company.

"Hold up!" he shouted, reining in Elivast.

His voice resonated off the stones of the dry riverbed loud enough to demand the attention of his companions. All glanced back and, seeing him slow, did likewise. Even Siyanda.

The Hunter leaped down from his saddle and made a show of inspecting Elivast's back right hoof. When he straightened, he shook his head. "He can't keep on like this. I'll need some time to tend to him if we're to keep riding."

Kiara raised an eyebrow. Aisha and Kodyn exchanged glances. Tarek barely registered the words; his violet eyes remained dull, his gaze unfocused. Siyanda snorted and muttered something in Issai the Hunter had no doubt was derisive.

"I won't be long, I promise," he said, an apologetic tone in his voice. "We'll be back on our way soon enough."

He returned to bending over Elivast's hoof, but watched his companions from the corners of his eyes. They hesitated only a few moments before dismounting—or, in Siyanda's case, jogging back toward where the horses stood. Kodyn and Tarek both slumped to the ground, the former from exhaustion and the latter burdened beneath his grim thoughts. Aisha dismounted and turned to her cousin, but Siyanda spoke first.

"I will not wait." The *nassor's* tone was curt, her words clipped. "You remember how to find *Uhumi Wolandle?*"

"Of course!" Aisha snapped, eyes flaring with a glimmer of blue-white light. "I am still Issai!"

But Siyanda was already running off into the darkness. Aisha watched her cousin go, frustration lining her face, fists clenched at her sides.

A quiet snort echoed from the Hunter's shoulder. "Clearly, he's in bad shape."

The Hunter's head whipped around. Kiara had dismounted and slipped toward him, coming around on his other side. She cast a glance down at Elivast's upraised roof and raised an eyebrow.

The Hunter met her challenge with a shrug. "They need a rest," he said quietly, nodding his head toward Kodyn, Tarek, and Aisha. "Couldn't think of any other way." No sense telling her that *she* had also factored into his decision.

A smile broadened Kiara's face. "I thought as much." She patted Elivast's rump gently and winked at him. "Take good care of him. Hopefully we can be on our way before midnight."

The Hunter grinned back. "That's the plan."

After the day they'd just endured, a few hours of rest would do them all good.

Chapter Forty-One

The Hunter studied the three youths from the corners of his eyes while he "tended" to Elivast. Aisha continually glanced in the direction Siyanda had gone, as if expecting her cousin to return. Kodyn lay back on the grassy earth and tried not to be too overt in the way he watched Aisha. Tarek's eyes remained closed, but the Hunter knew the Elivasti wasn't sleeping, for he could sense the turmoil roiling within the young man.

Kiara, too, watched their younger companions. She kept her thoughts to herself, though. If she was concerned, she didn't show it. She merely sat on the bank of the dried-up river and enjoyed the few minutes of silence and rest.

Less than a quarter-hour into the break, Aisha rose to her feet and began stalking back and forth along the riverbank. Deep lines of worry etched on her face. Her gaze shifted endlessly between the darkness concealing her from Siyanda and the Hunter. With every passing minute, her impatience grew more visible.

The Hunter shot a questioning glance at Kiara. "Walk?" he mouthed.

Kiara gave a little shrug and nod, rising to her feet without a word.

"Come on," the Hunter said, calling to the youths. "Elivast's not quite ready to run, but a bit of walk will do him good. Better we at least make some progress in the right direction, even if it's slow, right?"

Aisha looked ready to snap some angry retort, but she managed to restrain her impatience and merely gave a stiff nod. Kodyn climbed to his feet far too slow for a spry young man his age. He placed each step gingerly and with a slight limp in his right leg. Either he deemed the wound or injury not serious enough to mention, or he hid it from Aisha to spare her from additional concerns. With her tribe under attack and her parents held captive, no doubt the young man believed she had worries enough to occupy her mind.

The Hunter resolved to speak to Kodyn and ascertain the extent of his injuries before long. If the Praamian truly wanted to be of aid to Aisha, he'd need to be at full strength. And from what the Hunter had learned countless times over the past three years with Kiara, shared burdens grew easier to bear.

Tarek was on his feet in a moment and heading toward his horse before the Hunter finished speaking. Though the darkness cast his violet eyes in shadow, the pale starlight illuminated the tension written in the clench of the Elivasti's jaw and the furrows deepening his brow. The wary alertness he'd demonstrated along the road to Khafra had vanished, replaced by a deep, gloomy introspection and heavy gait.

The Hunter frowned. Rest had done *some* good, but clearly the youths needed more than just a few minutes off their feet. Unfortunately, he doubted any of them would have much time to sit and process everything that had happened over the last day. Not with Aisha so fiercely determined to free her family and bring down the Vassalage Consortium.

Let's just hope they don't crack under the growing strain of everything we've got to do.

Aisha led the way northward along the riverbanks. The dried-up waterway carved a sinuous track through the plains, but the low ground proved easily navigable, the sandy earth long ago deposited by the river soft underfoot. The few river rocks large enough to offer any serious obstacle were easily bypassed with little effort.

The Hunter kept a moderate pace, though he had to call out to Aisha a few times to slow down. Her impatience rivaled her cousin's. She looked on the verge of riding off on her own, and doubtless would have, if not for the fact that none of them knew the way. Even from the middle of the column, the Hunter could hear her teeth grinding over the plodding of their boots and horses' hooves on the yielding earth.

Less than an hour into their trek, the horses' ears pricked up and their noses lifted into the air. The Hunter smelled it a few moments later: fresh water from up ahead. Soon, the faintest sound of trickling wafted toward him, carried on the night breeze. A few hundred paces farther north, they reached its source. A small creek—barely more than a rivulet of water—cut eastward away from what had once been the grand river, channeled off-course by an obstacle formed of large stones upon which a mound of clay-heavy earth had been piled.

Aisha frowned as she approached the obstacle. She glanced over her shoulder and shook her head. "This wasn't here six years ago."

The Hunter eyed the stones. In the dark, it was hard to tell unless he approached to within touching distance, but they didn't have the look of boulders naturally carried downstream by the river's flow. First off, there was no real river to speak of—the tiny creek couldn't so much as shift one of these immense stones. Second, their shape was too uniform and their placement too precise.

Kodyn voiced aloud the thought on the Hunter's mind. "Someone placed them here."

Aisha frowned. "That was my thought." She turned to look at the empty riverbed behind them. "The Unathi River was mighty in the days of my grandfather's grandfathers, but as the land grows hotter, the water recedes. Yet always it flowed through the lands of the Issai, until now." She gestured to the rivulet diverting from the water's main course. "That flows into the lands set apart for the Tefaye. Once, they would never have dared steal from the Issai. I cannot believe that in so few years, our tribe has grown so weak."

Mention of the Tefaye caught the Hunter's attention. Aisha and Siyanda had both referred to the warriors who'd attacked the Issai camp by that name.

He was about to ask about them when a shout rang out.

"Stop!"

The Hunter spun toward the sound. It had come from Kodyn. The young man stood staring at the ground beside Tarek, eyes narrowed, left hand outstretched in warning.

The Hunter followed Kodyn's gaze, and his gut twisted as he spotted the cause of alarm. A sinewy, serpentine shape wavered in the air, forked tongue flicking in and out of a fanged mouth. Its two vertical-slitted eyes fixed on Tarek's left leg as it descended straight toward where the snake lay coiled. Moonlight shone off twin ribbons of bright crimson running down its spiny back, marking it an imp adder, one of the deadliest venomous snakes on Einan.

Kodyn's shout *should* have frozen Tarek, but the Elivasti, lost in himself, seemed not to hear it. His foot continued on a direct course in the snake's direction. In response, the serpent opened its mouth wide and snapped forward at blurring speed toward Tarek's leg. Even as the Hunter reached for a throwing dagger, he knew he would be too slow.

Steel blurred in the darkness and intercepted the darting snake. The flat-snouted head spun one way, the body another, and a thin blade buried into the grass with a quiet *thunk*.

Only then did Tarek react. He jerked back, nearly stumbling as he recoiled. Then he rounded on Kodyn. "What in the fiery hell are you doing!?"

Kodyn stood with his right hand—his throwing hand—still extended, a second knife appearing in his left hand. Tarek's outrage surprised him, and his brow furrowed in confusion.

"I—" Kodyn began.

Tarek's hand dropped to the hilt of his sword. "You could have—"

"TAREK!" The Hunter's thunderous shout echoed through the darkness. His voice rang with a note of command that even the startled Elivasti couldn't ignore. When Tarek whipped around toward the Hunter, surprise and alarm sprouting on his face, the Hunter stabbed a finger toward the spot where the snake's severed head still lay quivering on the ground a hand's breadth from his foot.

Tarek's eyes snapped downward, then flew wide. All color drained from his face and his jaw hung open. He blinked, speechless. Blood returned to his cheeks in a rush, and even in the pale moonlight, it was clear to see him reddening to his hairline.

"Kodyn, I…" He swallowed. "I-I'm sorry."

The apology appeared equally surprising to Kodyn. But only for a moment. He lowered his hand, let the tension drain from his shoulders. "No, it's fine." He gave Tarek an awkward smile. "When you didn't stop, I just had to act."

"Yeah." Tarek's eyes once more wandered to the snake's body lying near his boot. A shudder ran down his spine. He, too, must have recognized the danger he was in from the imp adder.

"There may be more near the boulders," Aisha said. She retrieved Kodyn's knife then quickly backpedaled to put plenty of distance between herself and the riverbed. "They like to sun themselves during the heat of the day and stay near the water where there's easy prey. Better we stay deeper in the grass until we're well clear of here."

No one argued that. One brush with near-death was enough for today, and this had been *twice* now.

A tense silence descended over their group as they followed Aisha up the incline that led up a hill away from the riverbank. They continued on without speaking for the better part of a quarter-hour, until Aisha finally decided they had put enough distance between themselves and the boulders that there would be no imp adders. Only then did she lead them back down toward the low ground along the bank of the river.

This far north, the creek had widened to a stream, the water flowing faster and about as deep as the Hunter's ankle. A glance at the stars told the Hunter he had dragged on the charade of "tending to Elivast" long enough. Better they quicken the pace and cover some real ground. He had no idea how far they were from *Uhumi Wolandle,* whatever that was, but he had no doubt Siyanda would only grow more impatient the longer they delayed.

But first, he gave the horses a chance to drink. They had traveled a great distance that day—hard to believe they had only left the bamboo forest that very morning—and still had plenty of ground to cover before they reached *Indawo Yokwesaba.* He bent to refill his canteen, and his companions did likewise. However, he noticed Tarek moving away from their small group, heading a few paces upstream. The Elivasti's inner turmoil hadn't lessened since his near-

188

death-by-serpent. If anything, it had only grown worse. The Hunter supposed now was as good a time as any to speak to Tarek. The young man's inattention had come close to costing his life—and there was no telling how much higher the price could be once the time came to take on the Vassalage Consortium.

He had just taken his first step toward Tarek when he spotted another figure heading in the same direction. Kodyn moved easily, his step calm and unhurried. He hadn't noticed the Hunter; his gaze was fixed on Tarek, the same concerned expression on his face.

Surprise slowed the Hunter's approach. After a moment, he stopped. Curious, he knelt in the pretense of filling his canteen, but he pricked up his ears to overhear what passed between them.

"Hey," Kodyn said in a gentle voice. "You good? That—"

Downstream, Elivast snorted and splashed his hooves in the water, drowning out the sound of Kodyn's voice. The Hunter wanted to growl at the horse, but that would only draw attention to him. Worse, the ever-playful Ash took that as a sign to dip his long nose beneath the water's surface and splash Elivast and Nayaga. When Kodyn and Aisha's horses joined in the frolic, the Hunter gave up any hope of hearing the conversation.

Yet still he watched out of the corner of one eye. At first, Tarek's posture was defensive, but whatever Kodyn said caused it to shift to apologetic. Then the young Elivasti's shoulders slumped and his hands began to tremble. The tremor soon spread up his arms until his whole upper body was shaking, sweat pricking on his brow.

Kodyn responded by stepping closer and gripping Tarek's shoulders in both hands. Quiet words passed between them, Kodyn's confident, Tarek's hesitant, shaken. Slowly, Tarek's quaking stilled, his hands fell to his sides, and his posture relaxed. The darkness drained from his face. He offered Kodyn an awkward smile and a nod of visible gratitude. Kodyn answered with something that made Tarek chuckle, then he turned and headed back toward the group.

Inevitably, the horses chose precisely *that* moment to end their play, their noise fading away too late for the Hunter to make out even the tail end of the conversation. Yet one look at Tarek's lightened expression spoke clearly enough.

Kodyn smiled at the Hunter as he approached. "Almost ready to move on," he said, his tone bright, as if he hadn't a care in the world. "Just have to fill my canteen, and—"

"Thank you." The words escaped the Hunter's lips before he realized it. He'd been about to ask if Tarek would be able to continue on, but somehow that hadn't felt right. This did.

Kodyn ducked his head. "It's nothing. I just know how he feels. Wasn't long ago I killed my first enemy. Lost someone for the first time, too."

"No, it's not nothing." The Hunter spoke in a serious voice. "Doing what you did, caring for the wellbeing of those around you, that's what makes a great leader." It felt foolish—what did *he* know about leading anything?—but the way Kodyn's face brightened told him his words held meaning to the young man. "I saw the way your mother inspires the loyalty of her people. Some may fear her, but more love her. And *that's* why." He gestured toward Tarek, indicating the conversation that had passed between them. "You may have lived most of your life among thieves and cutthroats, Kodyn of the Night Guild, but that has not stopped you from becoming a good man."

Kodyn colored all the way to the roots of his dark hair. He stammered out something incomprehensible.

"But a word of caution. Caring for others is a strength, but you must take care of yourself, too." He gestured with his chin toward Kodyn's injured leg. "I know you want to be there for her. But you cannot help her if you are too hurt to help yourself."

Kodyn reddened so deep his face matched the bright crimson of the imp adder he'd killed. Neither of them needed clarification as to which "her" the Hunter was talking about.

"Remember," the Hunter said, his voice pitched low for Kodyn's ears only, "sometimes sharing your troubles with others helps them forget their own. Or, at least, lightens them for a few moments. You need not always carry *both* of your burdens."

Kodyn inclined his head. "I-I'll remember that," he stammered.

The Hunter smiled. "Good." He clapped the young man on the shoulder. "Now, get that canteen filled, and let's be off. Sunrise comes early on the plains, and we've got a lot of ground to cover before we can rest again."

Chapter Forty-Two

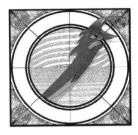

They rode through the rest of the night without stopping. Aisha guided them steadily northward along the curving ribbon of water that cut through the plains. Farther upriver, the stream had grown wider, turning once more into a proper river, though it was far from the thirty-pace-wide waterway it had once been. The flow was sluggish enough the Hunter had no doubt they could easily wade against its current except where the riverbed cut deepest into the earth. Crossing would be no great difficulty should the need arise.

However, Aisha kept them on the western bank of the river. By morning, the Hunter understood why. East of the river, the plains rose toward sharp bluffs formed of multiple layers of stone that shone a vibrant mix of reds and oranges in the brightening daylight. The bluffs plunged straight down into the once-mighty waterway. More cliffs rose on the land west of the river, but the riverbank was broad and flat enough the horses could navigate the gorge carved through the stone. The sound of rushing water and the clatter of their horses' metal shoes sounded loud in the Hunter's ears.

Atop the cliffs, the dense forest that had looked like a smudge of green from the Issai camp now stretched as far to the east and west as the Hunter could see. He was tempted to ask Aisha why they had chosen to enter the narrow gorge rather than ascend the cliffs toward *Indawo Yokwesaba* if the forest was their ultimate goal, but kept his questions to himself. Aisha had shown herself capable enough in the days they'd traveled together. He could put at least a measure of trust in her. She'd displayed a remarkable amount of confidence—enough to settle his initial misgivings.

Worse comes to worst, he thought, eyeing the cliffs towering high overhead, *I can always climb up and pass down a rope.* The stony faces were pitted and worn by weather. The ascent looked to be easier than his climb in the Empty Mountains, and this time, he was neither being pursued by Cambionari or hunted by demons.

The closer they drew to the southern edge of the forest atop the cliffs, the muddier the river grew and the faster it flowed. The water also drew creatures to make their home in the gorge. Once, the Hunter and his companions were forced to halt as a handful of lizard-looking animals with narrow snouts, enormous jaws, stubby legs, and spiny protrusions along the length of their undulating bodies emerged from a dark cave near the riverside and waddled down toward the river. The Hunter had seen a *crocodylus* once before, brought to Voramis by a traveling menagerie. The creature had snapped a goat in half with a single crunch of its mighty jaws, then finished it off in a few powerful bites.

Farther up the gorge, creatures with barrel-shaped torsos, wide-open mouths, long canines, hairless bodies and legs like four great pillars rolled and splashed on the muddy riverbank. Aisha kept even farther back from these beasts, which she named *imvubu,* than the

191

crocodylus. The Hunter saw no reason for the fear—they resembled fat cows, absent the horns—but Aisha warned that the *imvubu* could grow aggressive if provoked and had the strength to crush a full-grown horse in its immense jaws.

The Hunter watched the Ghandian unobtrusively. Though she tried to maintain her calm, she chafed at every delay, her frustration mounting with every moment not spent riding to free her family. The Hunter couldn't fault her—he'd have felt the same were he in her place—but worried that impatience would cost her in the long run.

Tarek appeared more at ease since his conversation with Kodyn. He'd emerged from his inner turmoil still burdened but no longer consumed by the war within his mind. His wariness had returned; even as they sat waiting for the *imvubu* to move on, he scanned the clifftops in search of enemies or attackers waiting to strike at them from above.

Kodyn just looked tired. He'd spoken to Aisha of his injury—a blow to the knee had left an ugly bruise, though the bone was thankfully intact—and she'd spent a few minutes wrapping it with cloth to brace it. But the effort of posting in his saddle to match his horse's pace was clearly beginning to take a toll on him. Not that he'd say anything aloud; he'd clearly inherited his mother's stubbornness.

Kiara concerned him. The raven-haired woman rode at his side in silence. She'd been awfully quiet in the last few hours. Ever since daybreak, when she'd gone suddenly rigid in her saddle. The Hunter had feared the return of the weakness that had lingered for days following her injury, or perhaps the lack of rest and food had taken their toll on her after the day's rigors. She had recovered quickly and ridden for hours without visible fatigue, but the Hunter still worried for her. He'd have to ask her what had happened the next time they got a moment alone.

Finally, the last of the barrel-bellied *imvubu* waded into the river and began floating downstream, and Aisha gave them the signal to ride on. They had not far to go—within a few hundred paces, the gorge cut sharply eastward, and from around the bend the Hunter heard the unmistakable roar of a waterfall.

Compared to the Zamani Falls, the cataract was anemic, ten paces across at its widest and falling only thirty paces to splash in the shallow pool at the base of the cliffs. The water was also a muddy brown and emanated a reek the Hunter could only compare to a marsh or swamp, thick with rotting vegetation and stagnation. Even the water droplets hanging in the air left a grimy film on his skin and filled the air within the gorge with an uncomfortable, cloying humidity.

Inevitably, Aisha rode straight toward the malodorous waterfalls. They drew so close the water falling into the pool splashed over them all. The water was far too hot to be cooling, and the Hunter's nostrils curled at the growing stink. It was as if someone had dumped the contents of a cesspit or the Praamian sewers into the river at the top of the falls.

The rest of his companions were no more immune to the stink than he. Kodyn grimaced and wiped his nose with his sleeve, as if trying to scrub away the bad smell. Kiara's lips twitched down into a frown. Tarek shielded his face with the hem of his cloak. Even Aisha shook her head.

"I had forgotten the smell." Lines appeared on her umber-hued brow, her *kaffe*-colored eyes narrowing. "But I do not recall it ever being this bad."

"So why are you leading us right toward it, then?" Kodyn asked, his voice half-choked in a cough.

For answer, Aisha just clapped her heels to her horse and rode along the riverbank, circling the pool and vanishing around behind the waterfall. The rest of them followed suit—fighting to breathe through the stench—and found themselves riding into a cave that tunneled far into the cliffs. Water droplets glistened on the walls and ceiling, turning the crimson stone slick and feeding the moss that grew there. It was a strange world of bright red and dark, dull green, like the mottling of a leper's flesh.

Aisha leaped down from her saddle and led her horse off to one side of the cave. "We'll need to leave the horses here for now. The rest of our journey will be on foot."

The Hunter and the others followed her lead, dismounting and leading the horses off to the side of the cave. They didn't tether their mounts—the horses would need freedom to move about, to drink from the pools of much cleaner-smelling water that had formed within depressions in the stone. The Hunter made certain to pour the last of the grain they'd brought into two neat piles for Ash and Elivast. It wouldn't last more than a day. Should their efforts to free Aisha's family drag on more than a couple of days, the horses *could* eat the moss off the stones or wander outside to crop the sparse patches of grass that grew around the pool.

"Be good," the Hunter said, rubbing Elivast's long face. "And try not to get eaten by anything while I'm gone, yeah?"

Elivast just snorted and nudged the Hunter sharply with his nose.

With the horses settled, they turned toward the darkness that marked the way deeper into the caves. From within his bag, Kodyn produced a pair of stones—one red and one blue—and handed them to Aisha. She nodded and stuffed them each into a pocket before leading them into the shadows away from the faint light seeping through the waterfall.

"Feel your way along either wall," Aisha instructed. "There are grooves carved into the stone at roughly waist height. Follow them, and you'll never get lost."

The Hunter ran his fingers across the smooth stone to his right as instructed. Sure enough, his fingertips brushed against a fissure that had to be man-made—only tools could carve a line with such straight edges and always at roughly the same height. With one hand on the wall and the other resting lightly on Kiara's back just ahead of him, he followed deeper into the darkness.

As always, the gloom beneath the ground quickly grew thick and all-consuming, not a single shred of light remaining once the mouth of the cave was hidden from view. The stink of the waterfall hung thick and stifling, and the Hunter had to focus on controlling his breathing despite the instinctive tightening in his chest. It took continual effort to remind himself that Aisha knew the way ahead.

Occasionally, a flash of red and blue light shone in the darkness ahead—the stones Kodyn had handed Aisha. The glimmer lasted only for a brief instant, enough for Aisha to get her bearings, then was quickly extinguished. Why she didn't just keep them shining the entire time, the Hunter didn't understand. The Night Guild had used similar glowing stones during his visit to Praamis, but only sparingly. Perhaps whatever alchemy caused them to glow had limitations. Graeme would no doubt be able to offer some form of explanation—once he thoroughly dissected the stones and analyzed their workings.

All thoughts of alchemy faded from the Hunter's mind when Kiara bent nearly double in front of him. He ducked just in time to avoid the looming presence he sensed in the darkness. His fingers found the stone ceiling sloping downward so sharply he was forced to walk bent double just to fit beneath.

As if that wasn't bad enough, the walls grew narrower, too. The Hunter had to twist at a terribly awkward angle to squeeze his broad, armored frame through the gap. Once, his face rammed into Kiara's behind—which would have been an otherwise pleasant experience under other circumstances, but which earned him a curse from the woman and a throbbing skull when he jerked upright in surprise and cracked his head against stone.

Fortunately, the confines lasted for only a few paces. A flash of light from up ahead revealed the narrow aperture widening and the roof rising. One by one, they emerged from the passage through stone and into a world unlike anything the Hunter had seen before.

Everywhere around him, the cavern glowed. Not the magical rune brightness of the Hall of Remembrance or the eerie pulsing crimson from within Khar'nath, but a natural, soothing gleam emanating from what looked like tendrils of mossy vines creeping along the walls, floor, and ceiling of the cave. A gentle blue-green illumination bathed the entire space in a calming radiance, and the air smelled faintly of the ocean's brine mixed with the sweet scent of a flower the Hunter couldn't name.

"Wow!" Kodyn breathed.

Aisha grinned and nudged him with an elbow. "I thought you'd love it." She gestured to the glowing cavern around them. "Welcome to *Uhumi Wolandle,* the last of the ocean's gifts to Ghandia."

Chapter Forty-Three

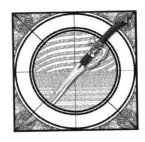

"According to Issai legend," Aisha explained, "when the Great Ocean *Wolandle* fled from the war of the *okulukulu*—the beings of great power that are our equivalent of your Einari gods—they left behind the *intambelu*." She knelt and ran a finger along the back of one glowing moss-like vine snaking across the floor at her feet. "The Great Ocean did not want to abandon mankind, so the *intambelu* were their gift to provide light in the darkness."

The Hunter marveled at the luminous plants. Graeme would have *loved* to see them. No doubt he'd have some overly complex explanation as to what caused them to glow when the sunlight never reached this deep into the stone.

Aisha rapped her knuckles against the stone underfoot. "The *intambelu* feed on what remains of *Wolandle's* essence—the salt in the rocks—and thus, Wolandle's gift lives on even after thousands of y—"

A voice cut into Aisha's. "There you are!"

All in the cavern jumped, save for Aisha. She merely looked toward the silhouetted shape that had appeared deeper into the glowing cave. Siyanda slipped toward them silent as a shadow, her bare feet padding noiselessly on the stone. Her umber-hued skin blended with the darkness and the sweet, briny smell of the *intambelu* had concealed her scent even from the Hunter's keen senses. The Hunter forced his hand to release its grip on Soulhunger's hilt and took a deep breath to calm his racing heart.

"I expected you hours ago, *um'zala*," Siyanda said, her tone curt, brusque. The Hunter could not make out much of her face in the dim light leaking off the glowing vines, but she radiated impatience. "Did you get lost?"

Aisha bristled. "No, I did *not* get lost!" she snapped. "One of the horses—"

"It doesn't matter." Siyanda dismissed Aisha's words with a wave. "We must move quickly if we are to enter *Indawo Yokwesaba* before the setting of the sun."

"Surely you don't believe what we were taught as children," Aisha scoffed. "The stories we were told of *Indawo Yokwesaba* were intended to keep us from wandering into the forest and getting lost. There are no vengeful *mashetani* spirits hungry to feast on the souls of children who stray from their parents."

"And how do you know that?" Siyanda's tone was sharp. "You may have returned *Umoyahlebe*, but you have not entered *Indawo Yokwesaba* since we were very young. Bear witness to what Zalika and I saw, and only *then* tell me we have nothing to fear." The *nassor* drew herself up to her full height and folded her arms across her chest. "I will not bring further misfortune upon our people by angering the forest. We enter before sunset, or we wait until sunrise."

"Fine!" Aisha threw up her hands. "Have it your way, Cousin." A single spark of blue-white light flashed in her eyes, gone again as quickly as it had come. Beneath her anger, however, the Hunter almost imagined he sensed a subtle undercurrent of hurt. Apparently, she no more understood the hostility coming from Siyanda any more than he did.

"This way." Without waiting, Siyanda spun on her heel and padded off noiselessly into the darkness. The light of the *intambelu* cast her well-muscled frame in silhouette, outlining the tension in her posture and the hunch of her shoulders. Was it fear of the forest that had her on edge? Worry for the safety of her people in the wake of the Tefaye attack? Or something else the Hunter couldn't begin to understand? The subtlety of human emotion was not his area of strength.

The Hunter wanted to ask Kiara what he wasn't seeing—why Aisha's cousin *wouldn't* be overjoyed at their reunion baffled him—but the moment didn't seem quite opportune for that discussion. And so he consigned himself to curious silence as he and the others followed Siyanda through the glowing vine-laden cavern.

The cave continued on for another two or three hundred paces—hard to tell in the darkness—until the walls closed in around them and the ceiling dipped low. But instead of a wall of blank stone, the cavern connected to a fissure in the rock slightly wider than the breadth of the Hunter's shoulders and nearly thrice his height. This, too, was lined with the *intambelu*, illuminating the way clearly for the Hunter to see that the crack ran deeper into the earth.

The air around them remained cool, though the humidity increased. Soon, they emerged from the crack into a chamber roughly five paces across, with a pool at its heart. Here, the smell of ocean brine hung so thick the Hunter could all but taste the salt in the air. The concentration of *intambelu* increased, too, almost as if *this* place served as the origin point for all the vines growing outward and filling the cavern.

On the opposite side of the pool, another crack continued onward through the stone, and it was there Siyanda led them. The Hunter tried to guess how far they'd come since entering the cavern behind the waterfall. A quarter-league, by his estimate, though he couldn't be certain. All that mattered was that Aisha and Siyanda appeared confident in their way forward.

They squeezed through cracks, climbed over boulders, and crawled through a hole no higher than the Hunter's knees. The *intambelu* guided them onward, providing just enough illumination to break up the darkness and light their way deeper and deeper into the bowels of the earth.

Finally, after what felt like hours, the fissure seemed to reach a terminus. The way ahead simply ended, nothing but blank stone on all sides. Above, however, the Hunter felt only empty air. And high, high overhead, a narrow beam of diffuse daylight was just barely visible.

"We climb," Siyanda said tersely. She stepped up onto a rocky ledge and was just reaching for a handhold when Aisha grabbed her arm.

"Wait!"

Siyanda looked down at her cousin, annoyance plain on her face. "What now?"

"Before we enter the forest," Aisha said, "I have to know the truth."

"What truth?" The glow of the *intambelu* made Siyanda's scowl appear ferocious.

"The Tefaye. What happened to them?"

A drastic change came over Siyanda. Her eyes darkened and her expression grew strained, tense.

"The Tefaye were always the weakest of the tribes," Aisha continued. No way she'd missed Siyanda's reaction, which meant she realized she'd been right to question. "Save for the occasional raid or the snatching of stray cattle, they were never a threat to the Issai. So how is it that they are attacking in such numbers? And why are they fighting as if possessed by the *mashetani?*" She turned to Kodyn. "You saw it, too, didn't you? They were mindless, like the Stumblers we faced in Shalandra."

Kodyn nodded. "More than once, wounds that would have dropped any normal man did nothing to slow them down." He grimaced and shook his head. "Nearly got me killed a few times because they just kept coming! I thought it was strange but didn't know for sure."

The Hunter thought back to the attack on the Issai camp. He'd hacked off one enemy's arm but the man hadn't been slowed any more than if he'd been stung by a gnat. There had been a certain measure of relentlessness about the Tefaye. At the time, he'd written it off as the rush of battle drowning out the sensations of pain. Now, however, he could understand what both Aisha and Kodyn had seen.

Mirroring nods from Kiara and Tarek made it clear they'd reached similar conclusions.

"The Tefaye are…" Siyanda paused, her face cast in even deeper shadows by the blue-green light of the glowing vines. "No longer the Tefaye."

The Hunter frowned. "Clear as mud, that explanation."

He had to stifle a hiss as Kiara elbowed him in the ribs. Evidently, she believed the situation warranted a far more delicate touch than his brute approach.

Judging by the furious scowl Siyanda shot him, Kiara was right. "I owe you no explanation, *alay-alagbara!*" she snarled.

"But you do owe me one," Aisha said, squaring off in front of her cousin. "What does that mean, the Tefaye are no longer the Tefaye?"

Siyanda drew in a sharp breath. Her fists clenched at her sides, her broad shoulder muscles tensing. "Always, the Tefaye have been those our people do not want—the thieves, the murderers, the troublemakers, those who do not heed the will of their *nassor* and are banished from their tribes. Yet now, they have become something wicked, as if the *mashetani* themselves spoke in their minds. They do more than just attack us now—they hunt us as if we are their prey. Those they kill, they devour. They even feast on their own dead. They have become as the *Okanele!*" She glared daggers at the Hunter.

The Hunter met her gaze calmly. "Been a long time since last I ate anyone." He couldn't help himself. The remark earned him another elbow from Kiara, sharper and more forceful this time.

Mention of the Tefaye devouring their kills brought back what he'd read in Nashat al-Azzam's message. *"Travelers venturing into the plains of Ghandia have vanished, and travelers from Ghandia have diminished to barely a trickle. All bear tales of ghastly monstrosities lurking in the darkness, of creatures feasting on the flesh of men and slaughtering warriors by the dozens."* That lent a great deal of credence to the rest of the information the alchemist had passed on.

"How long has this been so?" Aisha asked, as if the Hunter hadn't spoken. "When did this happen? And how?"

"To that last, I have no answer." Siyanda's jaw clenched. "Before she was taken, your mother had begun investigating the matter. After the first Tefaye raid on the *ekhaya* six months ago, she was determined to learn the truth. To see if, as Nkanyezi told her, there was any connection to the presence of the *alay-alagbara* in *Indawo Yokwesaba.*"

"What?" Aisha recoiled, shock echoing in her voice. "What do you mean, as Nkanyezi told her?"

Siyanda fixed Aisha with a look that *might* have been triumphant. "Surely you did not think you alone inherited your father's gifts? Or did you believe yourself so important that you would be both *nassor* after your mother and *Umoyahlebe* after your father?"

There was nothing ambiguous about the enmity in Siyanda's tone now. Her every word dripped venom and scorn.

Aisha reeled and leaned against the stone wall as if she'd had too much to drink. When Kodyn reached out to steady her, she did not push him away.

"Enough delay," Siyanda snapped. "We must reach the forest before the sun sets. And the climb is long." She turned and began scaling the rock wall. She was lithe and strong and seemed familiar with the ascent. Within moments, she had climbed far enough that the Hunter's keen eyes could barely make out her form against the light of the *intambelu* vines.

The Hunter glanced at Kiara, found her staring with a frown up in Siyanda's direction. Even *she* seemed not to understand the Issai *nassor's* animosity toward Aisha.

"Easy." Kodyn's soft voice reached the Hunter's ears. The young man stood close by Aisha's side, gripping her arm. "We knew this was a possibility. That's what brought us back, remember?"

Aisha couldn't answer; the blue-green glow made her face appear deathly pale.

"Tarek," Kiara said into the young Elivasti's ear. "Go."

Tarek didn't need to be told twice. He delayed only long enough to shoot a concerned glance at Kodyn and Aisha before beginning the ascent after Siyanda. Kiara set off after Tarek, but not before giving the Hunter a look that warned him to follow quickly. Aisha had told them of the steep cost paid by those who wielded the power of the Spirit Whisperers, and of her fears that her sister would follow in her father's footsteps.

The Hunter hurried to climb after Kiara. When last he looked down, Kodyn had Aisha wrapped up an embrace, and the young woman clung to him with the desperate strength of one whose fears had been confirmed in the cruelest way possible.

Anger swelled within the Hunter. He'd come to like Aisha over their time traveling together. He admired her strength of spirit and determination to return to help her people, especially after learning how she'd been ripped from her home and everything she'd endured in the years since. He couldn't deny that her power to control the *Kish'aa* was truly impressive.

More than that, he'd promised he would do what he could to help her. If that meant putting her arsehole-of-a-cousin in her place, so be it. Siyanda would find out the hard, painful way what happened to those who hurt the few who could claim to be the Hunter's friends.

Chapter Forty-Four

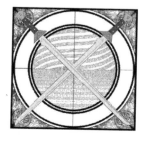

The ascent took the better part of an hour by the Hunter's reckoning.

At first, they had the *intambelu* to light their ascent and offer convenient hand and footholds. However, the vines only stretched a few dozen paces upward before branching out into thin tendrils that burrowed into the rock. Almost as if they *feared* the dim sunlight shining high above.

Even without the vines, however, the rock face had fissures and protrusions aplenty that the Hunter climbed with little difficulty. His inhuman muscles propelled him upward at a speed none of his companions could hope to match. He was forced to slow his pace to stay two full arm's lengths beneath Kiara—far enough to catch her in case she fell, and to evade any stones dislodged by her efforts.

Kiara was strong and stubborn, but the weight of her armor and weapons made the climb more difficult. Tarek, too, appeared to struggle. His long spear clacked against the stone wall every time he shifted to his right foot, and more than once, the ash shaft nearly tripped him up as it swung about on his back.

A glance downward revealed Kodyn and Aisha only a few paces below the Hunter. They dripped sweat and panted from the exertion, but they seemed far more at home on the rock cliff than either Tarek or Kiara. Kodyn's Night Guild training and the years he'd spent running across the rooftops of Praamis had prepared him well for this ascent. The anger and determination blazing on Aisha's face kept her moving steadily onward through any fatigue.

The Hunter looked up once more, just in time to see Siyanda vanishing from sight at the top. The Issai woman had raced ahead without waiting for them. Not once had she looked down, as if Aisha and the rest were beneath her notice. Never mind the fact that they had come to save *her* people, too. Siyanda's contempt sat poorly with the Hunter. At the moment, however, he would bear it for the sake of fulfilling his promise to Aisha.

When finally they reached the top, Tarek slumped onto his hands and knees. He sucked in great gasping breaths, wiped away the sweat dripping from his brows, and fought to keep his quivering arms from giving out beneath him. Kiara was far less obtrusive about her exhaustion, but the way she hurried to sit against the trunk of a sturdy mahogany spoke clearly enough. Though Kodyn and Aisha remained on their feet beside the Hunter, their faces showed plain the strain of the climb.

Even Siyanda appeared drained by the ascent. At their emergence, she did not immediately leap to her feet from where she reclined in the shade of a Ghandian blackwood. Sweat streamed down her bare shoulders, belly, and legs, soaking into the fibrous battle-wrappings girding her chest and loins.

The Hunter took the moment while his companions recovered to examine their surroundings. Overhead, the sky was barely visible through the intertwined branches of towering trees. Beneath the dense canopy, the light of day was twilight-dim, the forest around them a mess of dark greens and browns thick with shadows. The humidity was so oppressive the Hunter felt as if a steaming blanket had been wrapped around his head. Every breath seemed to fill his lungs with the moisture that hung on the air.

The smells of the forest were equally overpowering. There were a few pleasant scents—green leaves, a few bright-colored flowers sprouting from vines high above his head, and the loamy aroma of earth covered in a thick carpet of vegetation—yet they were all but drowned out beneath a thick stench of decay that seemed to emanate from every tree, bush, moss patch, and blade of grass around the Hunter. As if the entire forest rotted from lack of sunlight, strangled slowly, inevitably, toward deterioration and putrescence.

The Hunter's keen nostrils caught the occasional whiff of predators slinking through the foliage. He could not pick out the scents exactly—he had no way of knowing what manner of creatures dwelled here—but the familiar stink of carnivore set his senses on full alert.

He tried to listen for any sound to warn him of approaching danger and was struck by the absolute stillness within the forest. Where there should have been the song of birds and the rustle of ground disturbed by the small feet of forest-dwelling rodents and ruminant beasts, only stifling quiet met his ears. Even the sound of the trees swaying and leaves rustling in the faint breeze seemed somehow muted to little more than a susurrus.

Despite the heat, a chill ghosted down the Hunter's spine. *So this is Indawo Yokwesaba.* Somewhere in this jungle lived the slashwyrms, the creatures from whom Nashat al-Azzam surmised the Order of Mithridas had obtained the drake scales used to craft their gleaming black masks. Perhaps the Order themselves called this desolate place home, too. The possibility of running into the mysterious assailants who'd attacked him on the road to Malandria filled him with a mixture of dread and grim anticipation. He owed them for the lives taken that night— among them eight knight apprentices, the portly Brother Penurius, so adept in the culinary arts, and the young Brother Solicitous.

Then there was the matter of the Vassalage Consortium, who Siyanda had said held Aisha's mother and the rest of the *amaqhawe*—a word he'd guessed referred to the tribe's experienced warriors—prisoner. The Hunter had no qualms about eviscerating that particular organization. He'd gladly kill every slaver he encountered, even if he hadn't promised Aisha vengeance for what they'd done to her years earlier.

"Enough delay," Siyanda snapped, impatience plain in her voice and on her features. She sprang to her feet and glared at the five of them as if they were the reason she hadn't continued on, not her own exhaustion after the climb. "We have much ground left to travel before the light is fully gone."

Tarek had recovered enough he could find his feet, though he accepted Kodyn's help to rise with a brief nod of thanks. Kiara stood, too. Her face was tight and paler than usual, even after drinking from her canteen. The Hunter kept the worry from his face—she wouldn't want him "fussing over her like a mother hen", as she'd put it—but resolved to keep an eye on her. The heat and humidity within the forest could sap even *his* strength. Further exertion after the relentless pace of their travel over the last day-and-a-half might very well push her beyond her limits.

Siyanda fixed Aisha with a scornful look and said something in Issai. The Hunter *definitely* caught a derisive tone to the words; insults needed no translation to understand their intent. Aisha's jaw muscles clenched, and her eyes darted toward Kodyn, then the Hunter and Kiara.

"What is it?" the Hunter asked.

Siyanda's gaze flicked to him, but she gave no other indication she'd heard him.

The Hunter's fist clenched at his side. He was growing rather tired of the woman's—

"Your armor." Kodyn gestured to the Hunter and Kiara. His expression was stiff, as if he struggled to restrain his own temper. He spoke enough of Aisha and Siyanda's tongue to understand whatever barbed insult had been hurled their way. "She says it will kill you faster than a red constrictor boa."

The Hunter raised an eyebrow. "How's that?"

This time, Siyanda responded to his direct question. "Should you blunder foolishly into quicksand, blind and clueless as you *alay-alagbara* are, the weight will drag you under. Your sweat, too, will drain your bodies of much-needed water, withering you like *kola* fruit under the noon sun."

The Hunter glanced down at his leather armor. He had no doubt she was right—the thick material was sodden and heavier than ever, and even his healing abilities could only stave off dehydration so much. But the *way* she said it rubbed him entirely the wrong way.

"I'll be fine." He bared his teeth in a wicked grin. "We *Okanele* don't suffer the same weaknesses you puny humans do."

He suspected he'd said the wrong thing even as the words left his mouth. Antagonizing Siyanda would do nothing to soften her ire or turn away her scorn. On the contrary, he saw the anger flashing in her dark eyes—the same deep *kaffe* color as Aisha's—and her well-built frame stiffen. She snarled something in Issai and stalked off into the forest.

Aisha shot the Hunter an indecipherable look, then hurried to follow her cousin. Kodyn and Tarek looked somewhat pleased the Hunter had answered back to Siyanda—they enjoyed her derision no more than he did.

Kiara, however, clucked her tongue. "Really?"

The Hunter grimaced. "A man can only hold his tongue for so long. It'd be one thing if it was only aimed at me, but…" He gestured toward Aisha's retreating form.

Kiara snorted. "We both know how you'd respond to that. Fist to the face or dagger to the throat."

The Hunter couldn't argue that. He'd never been known for his equanimity or cool temper.

Kiara spoke in a voice low enough only the Hunter could hear. "I love that you feel protective over her." She placed a hand on his arm. "But this is *her* battle to fight. All we can do is have her back."

"You know I'm no good at that," the Hunter said, wincing.

"Lots of things you were no good at initially." Kiara gave him a coy smile. "But with the right training and patience, you learned. Like how to talk to people without attempting to kill them first."

"Yeah, about that." The Hunter glared down at her. "Don't think I haven't noticed that you're pushing me to—"

"Hunter!" Tarek's voice echoed through the trees. "Don't fall behind. It's easy to get lost."

Sure enough, when the Hunter turned toward the sound, he saw no sign of the young Elivasti or any of the others. They had vanished into the dense jungle in a matter of seconds.

"To be continued," the Hunter promised Kiara.

Kiara just grinned. "Can't wait."

They hurried off in the direction their companions had gone and caught up within a few moments. Their path cut through a series of towering trees supported by root systems that bore a strong resemblance to the buttresses of the Coin Counter's Temple in Voramis. The roots snaked along the ground and rose as high as the Hunter's waist and even his chest, forcing them to navigate around or climb over the obstacles.

Soon, they were pushing through a maze of vines that hung in such dense tangles the Hunter could barely see his companions a few steps ahead of him. Some were thick enough he could not push them aside, but had to squeeze his armored form through or force gaps by moving the thinner vines around them. Tiny thorns cut into his hands, face, and neck.

The swords strapped to his back didn't make the going any easier. Their hilts, jutting up above his shoulders, got caught on branches or entangled in vines. He wanted to stop and shift them onto his belt, but doubted Siyanda would entertain even a few minutes' delay. Thus, he was forced to endure the constant frustration of trying to navigate the snake-like vines—among which he spotted a few *actual* pale-colored snakes dangling down in search of easy prey.

Eventually, the vines thinned and the path forward proved easier. For all of fifty paces, before the ground sloped sharply downward and descended into knee-high marsh water. The thick clay mud made the trek even more laborious; the weight dragged on the Hunter's legs and the water seeped into his boots. The moldy stink rising from the stagnant mire twisted his nostrils. The decay around him increased, until it appeared as if every tree encircling the marsh was rotting from the inside out, and only the web of creeping vines kept their carcasses standing.

To make matters worse, the shadows began to lengthen and a thick blanket of gloom settled over the forest. Soon, the world was consumed by darkness as the sun finally set far to the west. Only the faintest of starlight penetrated the dense canopy. The Hunter's keen eyes could barely make out Kiara directly in front of him. Were it not for the sound of her feet slogging through muddy water and the quiet curses rolling off her lips between labored breaths, he might have lost track of her altogether.

He entertained the idea of fashioning a torch, but ultimately surmised that finding dry wood in this damp environment would prove nigh on impossible. If Aisha chose not to use those glowing alchemical stones Kodyn had given her, she had good reason for doing so. Even if it was just proving to her cousin that she was still as much at home in the lands of the Issai as the cities of the *alay-alagbara*.

Still, as the night wore on and their journey through the dark marshlands continued, the Hunter's patience began to wear thin. Surely they would make better progress with at least some sort of illumination. Enough to see the way ahead without blundering into upraised roots or deeper stretches of marshland impossible to see beneath the faint starlight.

Before he could raise the matter, however, a hiss from up ahead drew his attention. The sound of splashing water and boots slogging through mud stilled, signaling the rest of his companions had stopped. He did likewise just in time to avoid bumping into Kiara.

"What is it?" Kiara whispered.

"Lights," came Aisha's answer.

The Hunter's heart leaped.

"Quietly." Siyanda managed to put an immense amount of scorn into that one word. He caught sight of her moving through a patch of pale light ahead, and joined the others in following her up a short hill.

They had not far to go. Within a few paces, they reached the top of the hill and the Hunter saw the lights Siyanda had mentioned.

There were *hundreds* of them, torches and alchemical lanterns lighting up the darkness as bright as day. Running around the perimeter of a sharp-tipped palisade wall, set between stick huts and canvas tents, held in the hands of armed and armored men. Even from this distance, the smell of burning wood penetrated the scent of decay and rotting vegetation that filled the forest.

A grim smile twisted the Hunter's lips. He recognized the studded leather armor and the curving greatknives each of the torch-wielding men and women below wore on their belts.

They had found the Vassalage Consortium's stronghold.

Chapter Forty-Five

The Hunter surveyed the slavers' camp. He didn't know what he'd been expecting, but certainly not *this*. What he saw before him looked like a veritable fortress built over the course of months with an immense amount of effort—and gold—invested.

At the heart of the camp stood a wooden structure ten paces tall, easily fifty long, and twenty wide. Smoke rose from four stone chimneys jutting up from the building's sloping roof, foul-smelling clouds of black that blotted out the light of the stars. Figures clad in Consortium armor stood guard at the southern end of the building, keeping a watchful eye on the seemingly endless stream of men and women shackled to heavy covered carts flowing in and out of the south-facing double doors. More armed men guarded two smaller entrances set into the east and west sides of the building. As to what lay on the north side, the Hunter couldn't see from this vantage point.

Dozens of smaller structures stood to the east of the main building. Most were two stories tall and large enough to serve as barracks. One single-floor building had the look of a stable—a paddock adjoined it, and a large mound of dried grass had been piled up against the outside of one wall.

To the south and west, however, deep furrows and pits had been gouged out of the earth. Even at this late hour, the repetitive *chink, chink* of pickaxes striking hard stone reverberated through the camp. Occasionally, the *crack* of a whip resounded sharply. Hundreds of filthy figures clad in ragged remnants of what might once have been bright-colored, loose-flowing robes akin to those worn by the Issai and Ghandians were hard at work. Those not digging were engaged in filling barrows or loading what looked like dark-colored dirt onto the carts that would then be hauled up the steep slope toward the central building.

A chill ran down the Hunter's spine as he caught sight of the cages that occupied the northern edge of the camp. Hundreds of them, fashioned from metal and wood, some so small they could barely hold a full-grown bloodhound, others the size of a house. Sloppy-looking roofs had been erected on tilting wooden poles, a last-minute addition to keep the elements off the cages—and the people housed within.

Fewer than a third of the cages were full. Men, women, and children thrown together with no care for comfort or safety. The sound of the work going on in the camp drowned out the inevitable sounds of whimpering children, squalling infants, and weeping, terrified men and women. Many of the cages' occupants lay sprawled on the ground in states of visible exhaustion—no doubt worked to the bone by the whip-wielding, armored figures moving among those within the pit.

Surrounding the camp on three sides, a palisade wall five paces high formed a defensive barrier against enemies and a prison from which the captive Ghandians could not escape. A sluggish, swampy river bordered the camp's northern edge.

None of the slavers patrolled outside the camp's palisade walls. Then again, reasoned the Hunter, what need had they to fear enemies from without? Not only was it a well-guarded, heavily fortified secret, but the tribe to whom the lands belonged—the Issai—had no warriors to threaten and attack. Their *amaqhawe* was chained and working within. The guards' watchfulness was turned inward, to prevent their prisoners escaping.

The Hunter's mind registered all these details in the space of a few moments. In that time, his heartbeat quickened and the fire of fury coursed in his veins. His fingers dug into the loamy earth beneath him and he growled a silent curse. The hissed Issai words pouring from Aisha's lips no doubt echoed the Hunter's abhorrence of the cruelty perpetuated before them. Even Tarek growled something in the Elivasti tongue that held the razor-sharp edge of obscenity.

He crawled back down the hill, not stopping until the camp was hidden from view and his boots once more splashed in the marsh water. All but Siyanda joined him. The Issai *nassor* did not move, didn't even glance back toward them, but remained at the crest of the hill, watching in silence and shrouded by shadow.

"Rot them in the foulest hell!" Aisha's entire body trembled with fury, and sparks of blue-white light danced in her eyes and around her clenched fists. She looked to Kodyn. "Give me one good reason why I shouldn't unleash the *Kish'aa* against them right now?"

"Aisha—" Kodyn began.

"No!" Aisha's whispered hiss set the air around her crackling. Waves of heat rolled off her. "There are *hundreds* of them down there, Kodyn. Hundreds of *Kish'aa*. All of them killed by the Vassalage Consortium—either by their hands, worked to death, or killed by hunger and thirst. Not just Issai, either. From every tribe, and from beyond the edges of Ghandia, too." Lightning sparked between her silver eyebrow and nose piercings. "Even from here, I can hear them cry out for vengeance."

"And they will have it." The Hunter stepped closer, within range of the dangerous energy swirling around Aisha. He was the only one who could withstand that power should she unleash it—or, worse, lose control. That meant it fell to him to keep her from unwittingly harming the others. Especially Kodyn. "But not if you join them."

Aisha whirled on him, and a wisp of the blue-white energy slammed into the Hunter. Pain shot through his face, his muscles spasmed, and his joints threatened to lock up. Yet he had felt pain like this before. Every time he shifted his features, lightning coruscated through him, setting every fiber of his being sizzling. This small dose of her power hurt—Keeper's teeth, how it hurt!—but it was not beyond his ability to endure.

"Listen to me!" The Hunter forced his seizing muscles to propel him forward. His arms snapped up, his hands closing around her muscular arms. "Right now, we are the *only* chance those people have of getting out of this. If you die, then you do them no good. And the *Kish'aa* will never have their vengeance. Is that what you want? Do you want the pleas of the spirits to go forever unanswered because you let your anger and hatred override your common sense?"

Again, Aisha's eyes blazed, and this time the power seared through the Hunter's hands, up his arms, and rippled through his chest with such force his heart nearly stopped its beat. But it lasted for only a moment before the agony passed and the aura of blue-white light encircling Aisha dimmed.

"You've come to save your family." The Hunter's words sounded slurred; that last blast of power had locked up his jaw, turned his tongue thick. "To do that, you've got to first be sure they're there. Them and the Issai *amaqhawe.* Tell me, did you recognize anyone from that quick glimpse? Did you see your mother? Your father? Nkanyezi?"

At mention of her sister, sparks danced between Aisha's piercings anew. The Hunter gritted his teeth and braced himself for another surge of lightning. But Aisha remained in control. Though her eyes still shone bright blue-white, she did not turn the power of the *Kish'aa* against him.

"You know how Ria would approach this," Kodyn spoke up now, coming to stand beside the Hunter. "She trained everyone in House Phoenix how to think like both a Ghandian warrior *and* a Night Guild thief."

Mention of *phoenix* caught the Hunter's attention, but he tucked the thought away for a later time.

"I can't even begin to imagine how this feels," Kodyn said, his voice warm and compassionate. "Just the thought of someone doing this to either of my mothers sets my blood boiling. But if it was me, I'd want you to stop me from rushing in and getting myself killed."

The Hunter released Aisha's arms and slid smoothly aside, making space for Kodyn to stand in front of the furious young woman.

"Please, Aisha, let's do this right." Kodyn held out his hands toward Aisha, his supplicating expression matching his tone. "Between the five of us—including the Hunter of bloody Voramis—we can come up with a plan that will give us a proper chance at this." His face tightened. "I know how powerful your *Umoyahlebe* gifts can be. I saw it firsthand back in Shalandra, and I've seen it again and again in the weeks since. But the *Kish'aa* don't make you invincible. They can't stop a sword from tearing open your belly or a spear from piercing your heart."

Aisha looked ready to argue, but Kodyn drove on over her.

"No, let me say this. Because I have to get it out before we go any further." The young Praamian drew in a deep breath, steeling himself. "I told you before, you mean more to me than anyone else in the world. Which means that the idea that you could get hurt terrifies me. I know that ours isn't a safe life—especially now, more than ever before—but that doesn't mean I can stand by and let you throw yourself into danger unprepared. I have to accept that you'll be in harm's way, just like you have to with me, but we can still do every bloody thing we can to watch each other's backs."

He swept her hands up in his and gripped them tight. "Right now, coming up with a plan is the best way I can watch your back. You've got the *Kish'aa,* but all I've got is what my mothers and the Night Guild taught me. Let me use what I know to help you make the most of your powers without getting yourself killed. Please."

The Hunter wrestled a smile under submission. Kodyn's impassioned plea was more than impressive; it displayed a measure of sagacity beyond his years. The Hunter understood the desire to protect the woman he loved—Kiara had scolded him for those same instincts countless times in the past—but Kodyn had found an appeal that held an immense degree of merit.

The appeal worked. The light didn't fully fade from Aisha's eyes, but the heat around her dissipated and the blue-white sparks stopped dancing between her piercings.

"Very well." Aisha's words came out clipped, her jaw and shoulder muscles still tight, yet she gave Kodyn a nod. "We'll do it your way."

Kodyn beamed. "*Our* way." He squeezed her hands. "We come up with a plan together."

Nodding, Aisha turned and once more ascended the hill, Kodyn at her side.

Tarek looked slightly embarrassed, as if he'd just interrupted some private moment between the pair. "Uhh…a plan, yes." He hurried back up the hill, too.

"Damn." Kiara's whispered word drew the Hunter's attention. The pale light of the stars illuminated the look of pride on her face—the same look she got whenever watching Evren train with the Hunter or Hailen poring over some ancient manuscript. "He really cares."

The Hunter nodded. "And so does she." Kodyn's logic had been sound, but it had been his unmistakable love and respect that had gotten through to her. "Let's just hope our boys can find something like that. Someone as perfect for them as she is for him. And you are for me."

"Charmer." Kiara winked up at him. "I'll remember these flattering words next time we've got a moment alone to ourselves." She reached up and kissed him—a long, lingering kiss filled with promise that set blood racing in the Hunter's veins. She broke off with a mischievous smile and nodded her head toward the hill. "Come on."

A slightly out-of-breath Hunter followed her back to join their companions watching the Consortium camp. They arrived in time to hear the tail end of a conversation between Siyanda and Aisha.

"…certain you saw them?"

"Of course I am!" Siyanda snapped. "Your mother lived, and at least forty of our *amaqhawe* with her."

Aisha nodded. "And Nkanyezi and my father?"

Siyanda shook her head. "Of them, I saw—"

As she spotted the Hunter, she switched to Issai. Only a few more words passed between them, then Aisha turned grim-faced back toward the camp. Siyanda shot the Hunter and Kiara a sidelong glance—one rife with her evident disdain for the *alay-alagbara*, or perhaps them in particular—but that was all the attention she spared. Her eyes were fixed on the camp below, her face shadowed by dark emotions.

The Hunter paid the Issai woman no heed. If she was determined to dislike him, so be it. She had gotten them this far. Now, it fell to him and the others to figure out a way to do what she had been unable to do thus far: free her people.

At least Aisha knows her mother is down there. That was a start. And forty Issai warriors were definitely a good number to work with.

He studied the camp, searching for any vulnerabilities. That marshy river on the north side of the camp *might* have been an easy way in, but the utter absence of guards along the banks suggested otherwise. The Consortium had guards patrolling the length of the palisade wall, stationed at the entrance to the central building, and watching over their captives. They wouldn't be careless enough to leave such an obvious means of escape unguarded unless it wasn't, in fact, a means of escape.

The Hunter's eyes traced the outline of the wall encircling the camp. It appeared sturdily built, though it was hard to tell from this distance. It had at least *one* apparent weak point: the enormous gate that exited the northeastern corner of the camp. A broad dirt road ran directly from the central building to the gate, and a path had been carved through the forest beyond.

The Hunter raised an eyebrow. *Wonder where that leads.* Whatever the Consortium was doing here—some form of mining or excavation, he couldn't tell—they had made certain to have a way out.

"What lies in that direction?" the Hunter asked Aisha in a whisper, thrusting a finger toward the northeastern path leading away from the camp.

"I…" Aisha frowned. "I do not know."

Siyanda said something in Issai, causing Aisha's head to snap around to regard her cousin. "You are certain?"

Siyanda responded to the question again in Issai, her expression growing tight.

When Aisha turned back toward the Hunter, a strange look had overtaken her face. A look of mingled wonder, fear, and uncertainty. Her eyes locked on Kodyn. "Remember what I told you, the day we decided to leave Shalandra?"

Kodyn hesitated. "About…"

"The place where my father took me," Aisha said, her voice a breathy whisper. "The place with stones that glowed the same blue-white as the *Kish'aa.*"

"Oh, yes." Kodyn nodded. Then, as if the meaning of her words had suddenly dawned on him, he asked, "Wait, you're telling me it's in *that* direction?"

"Yes." Aisha's eyes took on a faraway look, as if at a memory. "That is the way I must go. Not today, but soon. Once my family is safe. I have to get to *Ukuhlushwa Okungapheli,* for only there can I fulfill the promise I made Hallar."

Chapter Forty-Six

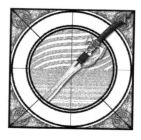

Aisha's words set the Hunter's mind racing. "What promise?" Curiosity blazed within him. What could a long-dead Bucelarii want from her?

Aisha met his gaze steadily. "To safeguard our world, as he did. By activating the Serenii machines that have somehow gone dormant."

The Hunter's eyes flew wide. "You're sure?" His words came out barely above a whisper. "You're sure *Ukuhlushwa Okungapheli* was built by the Serenii? That it houses one of those machines?"

He'd seen the midnight black tower dotted with shimmering stars in his communion with Kharna, and even now the Serenii's compulsion propelled him onward, driving him toward the structure he could vaguely sense to the northeast. The Hunter had heeded Kharna's call to travel because of the vow he'd sworn in Enarium—and the vow he'd sworn to Master Eldor and the True Descendants to eliminate any *maistyrs* he could find so they would never again be enslaved. Yet he hadn't known for *certain* what awaited him.

But if Aisha had seen the tower, had heard from Hallar's lips that it was home to another of the mechanisms like he'd encountered in the Monolith—

"No." Aisha's words dashed his momentary hope. "I'm not sure." She shook her head, glancing at Kodyn. "All I know for certain is that Hallar swore to guard the machinery in Shalandra, and after I accepted the task of carrying on his oath, I dreamed of the time my father took me to *Ukuhlushwa Okungapheli*. I feel there is a connection"—she tapped her temple—"but it is no more than that, a feeling. Which is why I will first make certain my family and my people are safe before I go to learn the truth for myself."

Siyanda gave a snort, so soft Aisha missed it. But the Hunter noticed. He noticed the look on Siyanda's face when Aisha said "my people", too.

"Before *we* go to learn the truth," Kodyn insisted. He rested a hand on Aisha's arm. "There's no way I'm letting you have all the fun on your own."

Aisha shot him a smile—tight, but bright with gratitude. "Of course."

"Damned right you're not going alone." Kiara nodded to the young woman. "Our path leads to *Ukuhlushwa Okungapheli*, too. We will all make the journey toge—"

An angry hiss from Siyanda cut her off. Kiara bristled, but Siyanda pressed a finger to her lips and gestured with her other hand toward the Consortium camp.

All eyes turned in the direction she indicated. For a moment, the Hunter didn't see what she'd deemed important enough to interrupt Kiara. His annoyance flared—he was growing bloody tired of Siyanda's open hostility. The time would soon come when his patience ran out and, *nassor* of the Issai or not, Siyanda would learn a lesson in respect.

208

Then he saw them. A team of long-horned raya cattle lumbering down the northeastern path, pulling a covered wagon toward the gate that led into the slavers' encampment. Two figures sat on the wagon's bench—one holding the reins, the other watching the forest around them. Their long cloaks concealed whatever clothing or armor lay beneath, and their hoods were pulled far forward to hide their faces. From this distance, the Hunter couldn't tell if they carried weapons beneath their cloaks, nor catch even the faintest whiff of their scents through the pall of smoke that hung over the camp.

The newcomers did not travel alone. From the trees behind them emerged a second covered wagon, then a third, and still more, until fifteen cattle-drawn vehicles were visible on the path carved through the forest. Three of the wagons bore more hooded figures, but the rest were driven by men and women clad in the studded leather and carrying the curve-bladed greatknives of the Consortium.

Another angry hiss tore from Siyanda's throat, echoed by Aisha a moment later as more dark shapes emerged from the trees behind the wagons. These moved on their own two feet, and instead of wearing armor, they were clad in loose, flowing robes much more akin to the Issai garments than the Consortium leather. Their clothing lacked the bright hues and eye-catching patterns worn by Aisha's people, however, and even from afar, appeared more ragged and threadbare. Every one of the warriors—for warriors they were, as made evident by the spears, bows, and odd round-tipped, jagged-toothed swords they carried—had a lean, hungry look about them.

"*Ujana!*" Siyanda spat the word with enough venom to kill all thirty-odd warriors trailing behind the wagon train.

"I don't understand." Confusion showed plainly on Aisha's face, in the deep furrows in her forehead. "Why would the Ujana align with the Consortium?"

The Hunter could guess the answer to that question, and it sickened him. "Perhaps because if they didn't, *they* would be the ones wearing the shackles." His eyes strayed to the mass of chained men and women working within the encampment. "They chose to throw their lot in with the Consortium rather than suffering their lash."

Siyanda snarled a torrent of Issai words that needed no translation. Her fist clenched around the haft of her short-handled spear and her face twisted into a look of utter loathing and fury that she'd thus far reserved only for the *alay-alagbara*. Aisha said nothing, but her face had gone a shade paler, her mouth tightening into a thin line.

The five of them watched the convoy of carts and Ujana warriors approaching the camp from the northeast. The raya moved slowly, and the hooded and armored figures driving the wagons did not lash them to greater speeds—which stood in stark contrast to the slavers within the encampment, who plied their whips mercilessly. Anger burned brighter and hotter in the Hunter's belly with every angry *crack* and every answering cry of pain. His determination to eradicate every Consortium bastard below only hardened. Pathetic palisade walls could not keep him out.

But he had to bide his time, he knew. Between the wagon drivers and the Ujana, that meant an additional sixty armed enemies would soon stand between him and the slaves. Better he watch and learn more about the operation before he made his move. He'd need to come up with a plan—not for his own sake, but for that of those fighting at his side.

He once again scanned the palisade wall in search of vulnerabilities. His examination proved as fruitless the second time. Only straight, sturdy trees had been used in its construction, lashed together tightly enough there were no cracks he could slip through. The earthen berms supporting the wall had been built high enough that the wall could not be pulled down from within or without, and the sharpened tips would make it difficult for a man to climb over.

An *ordinary* man, that was. The Hunter bared his teeth in a feral grin. *Not a chance that'll keep me out.*

He had no doubt he could scale the palisade wall, but once inside, the torch-carrying men ceaselessly patrolling the interior perimeter of the camp would prove problematic. Oh, he'd have little trouble cutting his way through them—their studded leather armor couldn't turn aside Soulhunger or the Sword of Nasnaz, and their steel greatknives posed little true threat to him. But doing so *without* an alarm being raised, that was a different matter.

Had he faced this battle alone, his plan would have been mostly straightforward: cut his way through his enemies, and keep on cutting until every one of the slavers lay dead at his feet. But there was a problem with that particular plan—and it went by the names Kiara, Aisha, and Kodyn. Aisha would insist on fighting to free her family, and wherever she went, Kodyn would go, too. Kiara wouldn't even bother entertaining the possibility of the Hunter going at it alone, either. She'd just draw Deathbite and dare him to stop her.

Which meant that his plan *had* to account for their mortality. They didn't have Soulhunger to restore them, nor a Bucelarii healing ability to pull them back from the brink of death.

Then there was the matter of the captives. The Hunter suspected the Consortium would have no qualms about killing their slaves to spite anyone audacious enough to attack them. The moment anyone recognized Aisha and Siyanda as Issai, they'd doubtless round up and begin executing the Issai captives. Starting with the Issai's true *nassor*.

For their plan to have the maximum chance of success with the fewest casualties possible, the Hunter had to keep all eyes focused on *him*. If the Consortium saw him as a lone enemy—easy prey—they would swarm him, use their numbers to bring him down. He'd keep their attention focused on him long enough to buy the others a chance to scale the palisade wall, overwhelm any slavers left to guard the captives, and liberate the Issai warriors. That led the Hunter back to his original plan: slaughtering the Consortium to a man.

The question is how soon we can move, he thought, focusing his attention once more on the convoy approaching the gate. *That will depend on whether these bastards are here to stay, or just visiting.*

From what the Hunter could tell, the covered wagons were empty. That suggested they were here to collect whatever was being dug up by the slaves and transport it elsewhere. He *hoped* that meant the convoy would be here only long enough to gather the load and be off again within a few hours. The efficiency of the slavers' operation would determine how soon the attack against the encampment could be launched.

The sound of creaking metal hinges drew his attention to the gate, which were swinging open to allow the approaching wagons to enter the encampment. Five Consortium guards labored against the immense gate's weight. It would be no simple matter to throw it open to allow the liberated captives to flee, but with luck, the strength of their numbers would suffice. As long as they had someone keeping the Consortium guards from cutting them down from behind, that was.

The plan began to take shape in his mind. First, they needed rope—or, in its absence, vines tough enough to bear his companions' weight. That would allow Aisha and Siyanda to scale the palisade wall. Once inside, they'd blend in among the captives, locate Aisha's mother and the *amaqhawe*. When the Hunter launched his attack—a very loud, very attention-drawing one— they'd be in place to throw open the cages.

Kodyn and Tarek could remain in the shadows outside the gates, ready to climb over the walls and join in the attack from the opposite side. Kiara would scale the walls where Aisha and Siyanda had to lend her skill and strength to the effort of freeing the captives. After that, it was just a matter of arming the liberated warriors—taking weapons from the downed slavers, even fighting with picks and shovels—and letting the weight of numbers turn the battle in their favor.

No doubt Kodyn would have suggestions of his own—the young man *had* learned the ways of thievery and subterfuge from the Guild Master herself. Kiara, too. Knowing Siyanda, she'd find some way to mock or deride their plan, though whether she'd have anything useful to offer remained to be seen. Tarek was far out of his element here in the forests, but he'd proven himself adept at a number of skills and might have something to contribute. And Aisha…well, this attack stood the best chance of success if she could call on the *Kish'aa* power and unleash the blue-white lightning against the Consortium.

He had just opened his mouth to relay his initial plan to his companions when a sight within struck him momentarily dumb.

The foremost of the wagons had rumbled up the dirt road and stopped just before the northern entrance to the central building. As the two hooded figures driving the vehicle climbed down, one's hood slipped back, exposing his face.

But what the Hunter saw was no face. Instead, it was a black mask that gleamed in the light spilling off the torches in the hands of the Consortium guards moving to greet them. Even from this distance, there could be no mistaking it. The Hunter didn't need to get close to know the mask bore the facsimile of a four-horned creature with a long nose, wide-set nostrils, and bestial fangs.

A chill ran down his spine. The Order of Mithridas was here, *now.* And they were in league with the Vassalage Consortium.

Chapter Forty-Seven

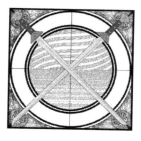

A sharp intake of breath from beside the Hunter told him Kiara had spotted the Orderman, too. They'd been expecting the possibility that they would encounter the Order of Mithridas in Ghandia—Graeme's message had told them as much—but finding them entwined with the Vassalage Consortium set the Hunter's mind racing.

According to Indigo, the Consortium had powerful backers. Once, they had counted the Sage and the Bloody Hand among that number. The Hunter had cut off those financial and political relationships—literally—but doubtless they had more. Was it so surprising to imagine that an organization said to be capable of toppling empires and kingdoms would pull the Consortium's strings? Even if they were not *directing* this undertaking, whatever the fiery hell it was, the Hunter had no doubt the Order benefited from it somehow.

Nashat al-Azzam had suggested the Order was obtaining the black scales used to craft their masks from the slashwyrms said to live in this very forest. But had it only been about slashwyrm scales, they could have paid the Consortium to deliver the cargo for them. No, there had to be some greater reason for their physical presence here.

The Hunter turned to Kiara. One look into her eyes told him she'd reached the same conclusion. The question was: how did they proceed? They alone knew the significance of those black masks. Kodyn, Tarek, Aisha, and Siyanda merely saw new enemies no more or less important than the Ujana or the Consortium.

The Hunter raised an eyebrow. Kiara understood the unspoken question and, after a moment's consideration, nodded once. "They need to know."

The Hunter agreed. The youths traveling with him—under his protection, as he'd come to think of it—had to be aware of the danger posed by those men in the black masks. If the Ordermen could kill Beggar Priests and knight apprentices of the Cambionari without compunction, they would not hesitate to slaughter the son of the Praamian Night Guild's master, the daughter of an Issai chieftainess, or a young Elivasti warrior.

Drawing the attention of his companions, the Hunter pointed out the figure in the black mask—who now followed the Consortium guards into the central building, along with the rest of the hooded wagon drivers—and told them of the Order of Mithridas. He recounted the legend of King Mithridas of Aegeos as Father Reverentus had told it to him, though he no more knew how an ancient fable connected to the Order any more now than he had that night on the road to Malandria. He then spoke of the attack on the Beggar Priests' convoy and the lives lost in the battle.

Kodyn and Aisha exchanged stunned looks, and even Tarek appeared surprised to hear of the Order's actions over the past thousands of years—stirring up unrest, inciting civil wars, meddling in the fate of nations. The Hunter didn't know specifics, but he spoke the same words Father Reverentus had, with the same gravity that had weighed on the old priest's shoulders.

"We still don't know what they wanted with Lord Chasteyn," the Hunter said, after explaining how they'd ridden off with the demon in tow, only to be savaged—and, in one Orderman's case, devoured—by the Abiarazi when he got free. "In truth, no one knows a great deal about them. Why they do what they do or what their ultimate goal us. But one thing is certain: whatever they're up to here, it can't be good for the Issai, the other tribes, Ghandia, fiery hell, all of Einan."

He thrust a finger toward the camp. "Right now, we have a chance to take one or more of them alive and put them to the question. I don't plan on asking politely, either. One way or another, we're going to find out what they're doing here, what they want with this place, and anything else I can cut out of them."

Siyanda snorted and muttered something in Issai. The Hunter heard the word "*alay-alagbara*" but understood nothing else.

Aisha, however, did understand. She rounded on her cousin, eyes blazing blue-white. "This is more than just *our* problem." Fury rendered her words hard as steel. "Those are *our* people down there, Siyanda. My mother, my father, my sister, my tribe."

Siyanda's expression grew scornful, but before she could muster a retort, Aisha drove on over her.

"Take a good look, *um'zala,* and you will see it is not the *alay-alagbara* who wear the chains down there. Buhari, Nyemba, Mwaani, Ghandians—they may not belong to our tribe, but they are no more deserving of what the *alay-alagbara* have done to them than our people." She shook a clenched fist under her cousin's nose. "You don't want to help, so be it. Return to the *ekhaya* and we will deal with this alone. I am not afraid of the *Gcinue'eleku awandile!*"

"Nor am I!" Siyanda's anger flared in response to Aisha's furious words.

"Good," Aisha snarled. "Then shut your mouth until you have something productive to contribute."

Siyanda bristled. "Have you forgotten I am *nassor?* Such disrespect—"

"Show yourself worthy of respect, and I will give it!" Aisha's tone was razor-sharp. "But since the moment I returned, all you've shown me is contempt and enmity. You've treated my companions—my *oqinywe*—with hostility when they have done nothing but help our people. I do not know what has happened to you to cause you to hate me, Cousin. But I have no time for it, not while my family is in chains and the tribe I have crossed a world to return to is in danger."

The two young women did not rise from where they lay on the hill overlooking the Consortium camp, but the Hunter had no doubt that one wrong word from either of them could end in spilled blood. And that would help no one, least of all the Issai and the rest of the Ghandians held captive below.

"Listen to me, both of you." The Hunter never raised his voice, but his words resonated with a force of command they could not ignore. Both pairs of *kaffe*-brown eyes swiveled toward him. Kodyn and Tarek, too, looked his way. "I have a plan to get in and get to your people. It's risky yet there's a good chance we can pull it off. But *only* if we all work together. And that means you two in particular!" He skewered the two young women with a glare so baleful Aisha flinched and Siyanda actually recoiled.

"You are our best shot of getting your people free and paying back the Consortium for all the suffering they've caused—not only to the Issai, but all the peoples of Ghandia." His lip curled upward into a sneering snarl. "Now can you put aside whatever differences you may have with each other and us long enough to be useful, or am I going to have to do this all on my own?"

Siyanda's face took on an expression that was half-sulk, half-glare. She had no response—neither acknowledgement of the Hunter's words or muttered retort in Issai or Einari—which the Hunter took as a good sign.

Aisha nodded curtly. "Fine by me." She shot a furious glance at her cousin. Fortunately, Siyanda didn't notice.

The Hunter outlined the plan he'd formulated. "Right now, we've got darkness to provide cover. The Consortium is also occupied with its guests." In the last few minutes since the Ordermen and their Ujana had arrived, many of the slavers had made their way toward the central building. Some herded slaves—likely to fill the fifteen wagons driven into the encampment—but many more appeared merely curious. "If you time it just right, the two of you can slip over the walls and slip in among the captives with no one noticing." He turned to Aisha. "Though you'll have to go in without your armor or weapons."

Aisha's jaw muscles clenched, but she didn't argue.

The Hunter continued speaking, though he addressed Aisha chiefly. Siyanda was too busy glowering at him for the Hunter to expect she'd truly heed his words. "Once inside, find your mother and the rest of the Issai warriors. Find a way to free them, too. Because when I make my move, things are going to happen fast, and we'll need the weight of numbers on our side in order to pull this off."

Together, the Sword of Nasnaz and Soulhunger could slaughter their way through every Consortium slaver, Orderman, and Ujana warrior within the encampment. But the Hunter risked losing control to the bloodlust amplified by the sword's magic. If things turned truly ugly and he had no choice but to use the scimitar, he needed to know the captives would be far from the path of destruction unleashed through him. The very notion that the men, women, or children penned up in those cages might die because he could not withstand the power of the Sword of Nasnaz sickened him. He would not become the monster his ancestors had bred him to be.

"What do we do?" Kodyn asked.

Tarek's mouth snapped shut, as if he'd been about to ask the same question.

The Hunter told them of their role as diversion and sneak attack from the rear. "But first, we'll need some way to get over the walls." He jerked a thumb back the way they'd traveled earlier that evening. "There are plenty of vines we can fashion into—"

"Oh, that's not necessary." Kodyn opened his cloak and pointed down at his belt. "I've got rope enough here for all of us."

The Hunter looked closer. In the faint starlight, it was hard to see what Kodyn was pointing at. His belt appeared ordinary—some sort of hemp-like material braided together—and nowhere near long enough for even *one* of their groups to scale the five-pace-tall wall, much less both.

His confusion must have registered on his face, for Kodyn chuckled and set about removing his belt. "Night Guild special, this." He tugged at a knot on one end, and the braided length suddenly unwound into a long black cord no thicker than the Hunter's pinky finger. "It's thin, light, but strong enough to support even Jarl's weight." He grinned. "Trust me, I made sure to test it."

The Hunter's eyebrows rose. If it could support the hulking man's bulk, it would more than suffice to handle any of them.

"Well done." He nodded to Kodyn, who beamed. "That's one problem solved."

"If you don't mind," Kodyn said, almost hesitantly, "but I've got a slight twist to your plan."

The Hunter cocked his head. "Oh?"

Kodyn blushed but spoke anyway. "Tarek and I are to wait outside the gate, ready for when you give the signal, right?"

"Aye," the Hunter said. He was curious to see what the young man could offer. Keeper knew his Night Guild training could come in handy now.

"Why not plan for *many* diversions?" Kodyn asked. "Split the Consortium's focus and keep them confused."

"What, exactly, did you have in mind?" A wicked gleam shone in Kiara's eyes. She appeared as excited by the prospect of assaulting the slavers' camp as he was.

Kodyn's smile was equally nasty. "Mother always said, 'Find a man's fear, and you have the simplest means of compelling him to your will.'" He gestured toward the camp. "The Consortium wouldn't build high walls just to keep the captives in. They have chains and whips and weapons for that." He shook his head. "That wall is as much to keep people out. People who might be coming to do exactly what we're doing: rescue their captives."

The Hunter's eyebrows rose. "So your plan is to pretend you're an army come to attack?"

Kodyn nodded. "Pretty sure between Tarek and me, we can make enough noise to be convincing." He glanced to the young Elivasti as if for confirmation.

Tarek made a show of clearing his throat. "The Hrandari war cries carry for leagues across the steppes. The forest is thick, but if we get close enough, I'm sure we can strike some fear into at least a few hearts."

"Add to that a few well-placed fires," Kodyn added, "and we'll draw their attention toward us. At least long enough that when you launch your attack, they'll be off-balance and disoriented. When we strike at them from the northeast and Aisha and Siyanda hit them with all the freed prisoners, they won't know their arses from their elbows."

The Hunter considered the suggested adaptations. They certainly would help to throw the Consortium into disarray. The more confusion, the better his chances of picking off the slavers in bewildered groups before they could mount any sort of defense. Their focus would also be diverted away from their prisoners—and the two Issai women stealthily moving among them to liberate the warriors.

"One question, though." Kodyn frowned. "You've said what we're doing." He gestured to the Hunter. "But where are *you* attacking from?"

The Hunter grinned and slipped out of his cloak. Better he leave it here with his gear than risk it getting waterlogged as he swam across the marshy river bordering the unprotected north side of the Consortium camp. "The last place they'll be expecting: from among their slave cages."

* * *

"If this doesn't work, your plan's buggered, you know that, right?"

The Hunter glanced toward Kiara, who slid through the jungle at his side.

"Not buggered." He grunted. "Just a bit...complicated."

Kiara snorted. "Sounds like buggered to me."

The Hunter let out a huffing breath. "Yes, we'll have to re-think things if this doesn't work. But that's why we're scouting the way ahead first. This way, we'll know for sure."

Kiara muttered something the Hunter chose not to hear. Instead, he shifted his attention to Aisha, who ghosted through the thick shadows beneath the canopy.

The young Issai—for that was how the Hunter had forced himself to begin thinking of her, not in the broadly generic term of "Ghandian" by which all Einari referred to the people that had once been part of the Ghandian Empire, but as a member of the Issai tribe—led the way around the western edge of the Consortium camp with barely a sound. She might have spent the last five or so years away from her people, but her skill at moving through the dense jungle in silence rivaled Siyanda's. And even though she'd never been to this part of the forest, by her own admission, she'd thus far led them unerringly in the direction they'd wanted to go.

When the Hunter explained his intention to find a way across the marshy river, Aisha had been the first to volunteer to guide them. As much to get away from Siyanda's open hostility as to expedite the rescue of her family, the Hunter suspected. Convincing Kodyn to remain behind had proven as difficult as the Hunter had expected. Only when Kiara had suggested the young man gather the dry wood he'd need to start the fires he'd proposed had he relented. Siyanda had assented to helping Kodyn and Tarek—albeit with great reluctance.

The Hunter had allotted three hours for the task of scouting and preparing for the assault. If, as he hoped, he found a way through, Kiara and Aisha would return to execute the plan as they'd conceived it. Aisha and Siyanda would slip over the wall and wait within the camp until the moment the Hunter attacked. That would be Kodyn and Tarek's signal to unleash their own diversion.

The matter of the sixty additional armed men within the encampment was cause for concern. The Ujana, Ordermen, and Consortium reinforcements would make the battle fiercer by far. But Kiara had agreed with the Hunter's assessment that the risk would be vastly outweighed by the possibility of taking a member of the Order of Mithridas alive. The secrets he could torture out of a captive Orderman would doubtless prove invaluable in his efforts to stop whatever machinations had led them to break an Abiarazi out of the Hunter's clutches. Perhaps they would find the path to the *maistyr* Itan had dispatched Tarek to locate in Ghandia.

Just means I'll have to fight all the harder, he thought.

The prospect of combat filled him with a measure of dread. If things turned ugly—and knowing his luck, they would—he might be forced to draw the Sword of Nasnaz. He'd been fortunate enough that, until now, he hadn't needed the scimitar and its fell magic. But there was no telling what would happen once battle was joined.

"Just a little farther." Aisha's whispered voice drifted back toward the Hunter. "We're passing the camp now."

How she knew that, the Hunter didn't know. When the Hunter glanced eastward, he saw not even the faintest gleam of light outlining the spiked tops of the palisade walls. But he had to trust her. These were *her* lands, after all.

He nodded in satisfaction. The trek this far had taken them less than half an hour by his reckoning. They could be in position and ready to attack before midnight at this rate.

All that remained in question now was what he'd find north of the camp. Marshlands and swamps, he could handle. It would be slow going and a difficult crossing, no doubt replete with quagmires and quicksand pits that would make the way dangerous. But if it got him close enough to slip into the Consortium's camp, he'd deem it well worth the—

A warning sense flared at the back of his mind. Some ancient instinct, honed over millennia of fighting and surviving countless enemies, warned him of danger.

Almost too late.

216

Aisha had just stepped off a grassy mound and into a shallow-looking swamp when the water before her exploded upward and a monstrous form emerged from beneath the surface. Mud, leaves, and rotting vegetation sprayed in every direction.

From the darkness, two gleaming eyes the burning orange of a wood fire with vertical slits for pupil swiveled downward to lock on Aisha, and an enormous maw filled with row upon row of razor sharp teeth opened to swallow her whole.

Chapter Forty-Eight

The Hunter dove forward, tackling Aisha around the waist. Together, the two of them flew out of the path of the monstrosity's descending jaws. Its teeth snapped shut with a fearsome *clack* on empty air and its snout splashed up a spray of mud where it struck the ground.

By the time the Hunter found his feet, the creature was shaking its head violently, as if to clear away the lingering dizziness of the impact. Without glancing back to see if Aisha rose, the Hunter darted toward the giant beast. His watered steel sword swept from its sheath and crashed into the tree trunk-thick leg before him.

And bounced off. The impact reverberated up his arm and sent a twinge through his wrist, but the creature's thick scales repelled the Hunter's attacks as easily as if he'd been a biting gnat. He was forced to backpedal to evade its snout, which swung toward him, teeth passing dangerously close to his chest. Its hot breath, thick with the stench of rotting vegetation and meat, washed over his face and brought acid rising into the back of his throat.

He tensed in anticipation of the next attack—another snapping bite of its toothy maw or perhaps a strike of its foreclaws, paws, or talons, whatever the fiery hell this hideous thing possessed—but in the darkness, he barely saw it coming. He had just time enough to throw himself flat onto his face as a long, sinewy tail whipped around toward him. The crackle of vibrating scales passed barely a finger's breadth over his head. The wind of its passage stirred up the muddy water around him into a terrible frothy foam.

The Hunter sprang to his feet, striking out again at the tail with his sword. Again, the blade bounced off without leaving a scratch. *Keeper take it!* He cursed, springing backward as the thing reared up—nearly three times his height, as tall as the trees around the marsh—and brought its bulk thundering back down in the spot where he'd been standing only a moment earlier. Its gleaming yellow eyes fixed on him, a predatory hunger shining in those vertically slitted pupils. The thing did not *hate* him—hate was an emotion reserved for higher consciousnesses—it merely saw him as food and pursued him with the relentlessness of a starved beast of prey.

The Hunter retreated, but his boots caught in the muck and mire, slowing him. As he moved, he tried to sheathe his watered steel sword and draw the Sword of Nasnaz. Surely the magic would grow strong enough with repeated strikes that it could pierce the beast's scales and—

Something struck the Hunter dead in the chest with the force of a stampeding bull. Air exploded from his lungs and he was lifted off his feet to fly through the air. He careened across the marshes and crashed into a tree with such force it shattered beneath the impact. So did his bones. Searing pain raced up his left side and down his left leg. He crashed to the muddy earth head-first. It was all he could do to curl up his body so he landed in an ungainly sprawl rather than shatter his neck.

He tried to rise, to reach for his weapons, but even as he did, he knew it would be futile. His leg bone was shattered and every movement sent waves of misery coursing through him. He couldn't even draw breath long enough to clear his vision. All he could see was darkness and the spots of light dancing in his vision. But he could *hear* the water being churned to mud and *feel* the thunderous footsteps of the enormous creature bearing down on him. Not quickly—on the contrary, the thing seemed to lumber at a pace slower even than the most placid mule—but the inevitability of its approach was undeniable. The Hunter couldn't get to the Sword of Nasnaz in time. He could barely lift his head to stare the approaching death in the glowing amber eyes.

And then the world turned blindingly bright. Blue-white light burst into brilliance that drove back every shadow within the forest for fifty paces. The illumination seemed to sear the fog from the Hunter's vision. The world crystallized into perfect clarity—clear enough for the Hunter to see the barrage of lightning assaulting the creature from the side.

The power in the air would have burned the Hunter to a crisp had the scaled monstrosity not absorbed the entirety of the blast. Every hair on the Hunter's body stood on end and the smell of burning scales and flesh filled the air. The lightning danced through the creature's enormous form, illuminating it from within, painting every sinew, blood vessel, organ, and bone in stark relief. The creature reared up onto its hind legs and shrieked in a voice so loud and terrible it nearly shattered the Hunter's ear drums. Yet it was a scream of all-consuming agony and a terror borne of deep, primal fear a beast like this could never have experienced before.

The creature's cry rang out through the forest, long and loud, but for all its immense volume, it cut off quickly. A gurgling, gasping sound burst from its throat, accompanied by a spray of black ichor that cascaded over the Hunter, drenching him in the stench of charred blood. Then, like a mighty oak cut off at the base by a woodsman's axe, the beast toppled slowly sideways. Tearing through trees as old as the forest itself, filling the air with a cacophony of snapping branches, before finally collapsing onto the ground with a mighty crash that shook the ground beneath it. For long seconds, the reverberations shuddered through the forest, accompanied by the sound of thousands of birds startled into flight or screeching their protest.

And still, the lightning seared its body. Spears of brilliant, crackling energy rippled forth from the outstretched hands of an umber-skinned figure who stood amidst a brilliant nimbus of blue-white light. Aisha's eyes glowed brightest of all, the magic shining off her bared teeth. The Serenii pendant—the *Dy'nashia,* she'd called it—had slipped out from beneath her clothing in her fall, and it, too, gleamed with a luminescence that nearly blinded the Hunter.

Kiara suddenly appeared from the darkness at Aisha's side, and she shouted something the Hunter could not hear over the thundering of his pulse in his ear. At the touch of Kiara's hand on her shoulder, Aisha finally cut off the flow of lightning. Her hands spat one last crackling spear toward the monstrosity, which now lay smoking, reeking of charred flesh and viscera, then fell slack at her side. The light of her *Dy'nashia* faded in time with the aura surrounding her. The glow in her eyes faded last of all. As if the *Kish'aa* whose power she channeled were reluctant to relinquish their grip on her.

But relinquish, they did. As the flow of power cut off, Aisha's whole body seemed to collapse. She reeled, off-balance, and would have fallen if Kiara hadn't caught her and lowered her to the ground. There she lay, head lolling, eyes open but unseeing.

"Aisha!" Kiara's voice finally penetrated the roaring in the Hunter's ears. "Aisha, talk to me!"

The young woman did not answer. Even when Kiara slapped her cheeks—gently at first, but progressively firmer—she didn't stir, merely laid back on the soft marsh grass, her body slack.

The Hunter struggled to his right knee, groaning with the effort and the agony coursing through him. He couldn't stand, he knew, much less hobble over to help. Not with his damned leg and ribs broken and his head pounding as if he'd just used it to knock down a tree—which he bloody had, thanks to that accursed beast.

With effort, he turned his attention inward to attempt to mend his injuries. The task proved arduous; he could scarcely focus around the throbbing in his skull. Only when he gritted his teeth and focused on the torment ripping through the left side of his body did he finally manage to locate the shards of pulverized bone in his hip and thigh, the sharp tip of broken rib dangerously close to puncturing his lung. He had little energy to spare—the days of travel and combat had taken a toll on him—but what he had, he forced toward his injuries. Bulwarked by his iron will, he commanded what was broken to mend as the Sage had taught him.

He almost welcomed the sensation of lightning coursing through his flesh. It was the sign his body responded to his commands and had begun healing. He stifled his cries and forced himself to keep mending through the anguish. If Aisha had overexerted herself, drawn too much of the *Kish'aa* power within her, he needed to be on his feet and able to get her help. He owed her that much for saving him from that...whatever the fiery hell it was!

When finally the pain in his side, hip, and leg faded that he could stand without passing out, he rose to his feet and hobbled over to where Kiara knelt beside Aisha. The forest had once again gone dark, the light of Aisha's magic snuffed out completely, but the Hunter didn't need to see Kiara's face to sense the worry radiating off her.

"Aisha." Kiara's voice was gentle but firm. "Aisha, keep your eyes open."

To the Hunter's immense relief, Aisha's eyelids were fluttering and her chest rose and fell in steady, if shallow, breath. Her lips moved but only slurred words emerged. She sounded as if she'd drunk too much, or as if a week of sleep deprivation had robbed her of her senses.

"How bad..." The Hunter's voice came out in a hoarse croak; his mouth was dry, his tongue as thick as leather. The healing had drained him far more than he'd realized. He swallowed, tried again. "How bad is she?"

"I don't know." Kiara answered with a shake of her head, not looking up from Aisha. "I don't know enough about her *Umoyahlebe* gift to know exactly what's wrong. Best guess, she used too much power and it's left her drained. I need her to tell me how to help her, but she's too exhausted to speak clearly."

The Hunter chewed on his lip—and immediately regretted it. It, like the rest of him, was covered in the charred blood that had erupted in a gory fountain from the dying creature. He spat to clear his mouth, but the foul taste helped to cleanse the last of the fog from his mind. "If she can't tell us how to help her, maybe Kodyn can."

Now Kiara looked up toward him. "You mean go back?"

The Hunter nodded. "Get her back. See if he can do anything to get her back on her feet." He shrugged. "If nothing else, we've got food and water in our packs. Tarek's likely got something that can help her." The Elivasti's alchemical knowledge had proven useful in the past. Surely he'd know of some remedy to restore at least a measure of Aisha's energy.

"I don't disagree," Kiara said, her expression growing tight. "But I have to ask: what of the plan?" She nodded with her chin toward the way ahead. "One of us could continue that way, scout it out. If there's a chance to get into the encampment from behind—"

"What chance could there *really* be?" The Hunter gestured toward the still-smoking corpse of the enormous beast. "Take a good look at that thing, Kiara. Tell me that's not *exactly* what you'd picture a slashwyrm to look like."

They turned to study the beast. The faint light of the moon and stars streamed through the hole the creature had broken in the canopy as it collapsed and shattered the trees around it, illuminating its hideous form. It had a snout halfway between a serpent and one of the *crocodylus* they had passed on the banks of the river below the waterfall, but its eyes had definitely been reptilian. Its legs were sturdy, thick as trees, yet from its side sprouted two appendages the Hunter hadn't noticed in his fight: membranous wings far too stubby to carry its body aloft. Ridges of bony spikes ran from the crest of its head along its spine and down its tail, which was easily as long again as its entire body. A body, the Hunter noticed, which was covered entirely by black scales that seemed to gleam in the moonlight.

Kiara grunted. "If that's a slashwyrm, then you're right. There's no point in going forward now." When the Hunter turned to her, her face was tight with worry. "Slashwyrms are unlike their cousins in the Empty Mountains. While drakes are solitary creatures, preferring to live far from each other, slashwyrms are far less territorial and more social. They tend to make their nests in marshes like this, far enough apart from each other to prevent overfeeding but close enough that they can still mate and protect each other's young like a wolf pack."

The Hunter's gut clenched as somewhere in the distance echoed the sound of a heavy body crashing through the trees and splashing through the marsh.

Kiara sprang to her feet. "And close enough they can feed on each other when they die." Genuine fear blossomed on her face. "We need to get out of here, now!"

The Hunter didn't need to be told twice. Kneeling, he scooped Aisha up into his arms. She was as heavy as he'd expected, a solid mass of hardened muscle, nearly as tall as he was. But he bore her weight with only the occasional grunt of effort. He refused to let the pain in his still-healing ribs, hip, and leg slow him down, either. The slashwyrms might not be fast, but he had no desire to stick around and wait for the beast—or *beasts*—lumbering his way.

Better we're long gone before they spot us and decide we'll make a tastier snack than their friend here.

The Hunter couldn't help casting one last glance toward the smoking slashwyrm corpse. Aisha's power had stunned him on the road to Khafra when she'd saved Kiara, but this…

He shook his head. *Keeper's teeth, how powerful is she?*

Chapter Forty-Nine

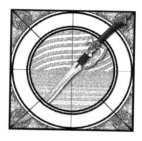

Tarek alone awaited them back at the hill that served as their meeting spot. The young Elivasti tensed at the sound of their approach, hand dropping to his spear. His eyebrows shot up at the sight of Kiara and the Hunter with Aisha cradled in his arms.

He sprang to his feet, rising from where he'd been lying on his belly overlooking the Consortium camp, and hurried toward them, eyes fixed on Aisha's limp form. "Is she—?"

"Unconscious," Kiara said before the Hunter could. "Tell me you've got something alchemical that'll wake her up and restore her energy."

Tarek's face twisted into a frown of mingled worry and contemplation. "I…" He started to shake his head, then seemed to think better of it. "I might." He jerked a thumb toward the marsh to the southwest. "I spotted a few *piniba* shoots back that way that could make a half-decent remedy, mixed with <u>acharia</u> weed."

"Go!" The Hunter pushed past the Elivasti and lowered Aisha to the ground. "We can't make any move with her in this condition. The sooner she's on her feet, the better."

With a nod, Tarek raced off into the marsh and vanished into the darkness to the southeast. Soon, even, the sound of his splashing faded, swallowed by the dense jungle encircling them.

The Hunter pressed two fingers to Aisha's neck. Her heart still fluttered occasionally, the beat weak but growing stronger—he hoped. She'd stirred only a few times on their trek back. Once, her eyes had opened, but fatigue had slurred her words beyond comprehension. The Hunter glanced over at Kiara. The look in her eyes mirrored the helplessness he felt. With no true understanding of her *Kish'aa* magic, they had no real idea how to help her. All they could do was watch and hope she recovered.

"Aisha?" The Hunter gripped her right arm, lifted her head from the ground. "Aisha, can you hear me?"

Her eyelids opened sluggishly, and her eyes—once again the dark *kaffe*-brown, not so much as a flicker of light within—settled on him. Her lips moved but no sound came out.

"Aisha, focus on my voice." The Hunter squeezed her arm tighter. "If you can, tell me how to help you."

Again, the silent moving of Aisha's lips. Only a faint gasp of air accompanied her effort.

"You saved my life, Aisha," the Hunter said, his voice firm. "Don't you dare die on me until I can thank you properly for that."

At his words, a smile tugged at the corners of Aisha's mouth. This time, when her lips moved, the Hunter understood the silent words.

"We...are...even."

Then her eyelids sagged closed once more and her body went limp in his grip. Were it not for the warmth of her skin and the steady rise and fall of her chest, the Hunter might have believed her dead. In truth, he had no idea how far from death she was.

He glanced toward the darkness where Tarek had vanished and willed the Elivasti to hurry. His head swiveled to the northeast, the direction Kodyn had gone with Siyanda to prepare for the attack on the camp. The young Praamian had to be due to return at any moment. Surely he'd know what to do to help Aisha.

"Hunter." Kiara's words were soft, but firm enough that they drew the Hunter's attention. She was staring at him with a look of forced confidence. "She will recover. She is strong."

The Hunter was far from convinced, but he nodded all the same. "Of course." He spoke the words as if trying to convince himself as much as her—as she'd done.

"Focus on what you *can* control," Kiara said. She knew him all too well. "The slashwyrms are going to muck up your plan. Which means we've got to find another way to get you into the camp."

With effort, the Hunter dragged his mind out of his worries for Aisha and bent his thoughts to the plan he'd concocted what felt like *days* ago. He was about to chew on his lip, but remembered in time that he was still covered in slashwyrm blood. Instead, he bit the inside of his cheek in contemplation.

"You're sure about the slashwyrms?" He narrowed his eyes. "We *know* there is at least one more out there—"

"I'm sure." Kiara nodded, then added. "At least, as sure as I can be. Everything I know I got from a translation of a replica of a scroll nearly as old as the Ghandian Empire itself. And it's light enough on details that I'm having to make a lot of guesses."

Before departing Malandria, Kiara had sent a message to Nashat al-Azzam requesting more information on the slashwyrms she'd mentioned in her letter. After all, she'd reasoned, if they were to encounter the Order of Mithridas anywhere near the slashwyrms from which they obtained the scales used for their masks, she damned well wanted to know about the creatures.

A book had been waiting for her when they met with Grytch, the Hidden Circle alchemist in Drash. The volume sent by al-Azzam was the work of Jwahir Yengwayo, wife of Ingiyab Yengwayo, the historian who'd chronicled the account of the Ghandian Empire. She had found the replica among her husband's papers and dedicated herself to collecting more information on the creatures found in the former Imperial lands.

Some of the creatures mentioned, they had seen for themselves—the *crocodylus,* the *zabara,* and Kgabu lions, for example. Many more, however, were lost to time. The slashwyrm was one somewhere in between, seen so rarely it was believed to be myth, yet still with evidence enough to maintain that they were still in existence.

Kiara had pored over that volume a dozen times on their journey northward. By now, she knew as much about the monstrous beasts that were cousin to the drakes of the Empty Mountains as Jwahir Yengwayo herself.

"Where there's one," Kiara said, "there are bound to be more. Anywhere between five and two dozen, depending on their size and the size of the marshlands they inhabit."

The Hunter grimaced. "That was one huge bloody slashwyrm!"

Kiara nodded. "Probably about as large as they get; any bigger, and they couldn't find enough food, so they'd starve to death."

The Hunter glanced toward the slavers' camp. "Unless they had a convenient source of food handy." His eyes roamed the northern edge, where a wall was conspicuous by its absence. He'd have gambled good coin the Consortium purposely left that section unguarded. The prospect of freedom would be enough to tempt any number of captives into braving the marshes for the chance at escape. The sound of the slashwyrms tearing apart those few who made the attempt would be deterrent enough for the rest.

Kiara followed his gaze, and seemed to reach the same conclusion as he, for she said, "Despite their size, slashwyrms are fearful, placid creatures. They remain hidden and let their food come to them. The only time they attack is if they feel threatened. When that happens…well, you saw how they defend themselves."

The Hunter struggled to wrap his mind around that. The creature had been easily four or five times his size, so how could it possibly have perceived him as a threat?

"Our plan's not *entirely* buggered, though." Kiara's tone turned musing, pensive. She frowned down at the ground in thought. "They're most active at night, but they tend to sleep during the day. If you can get past them and into position before the sun sets—"

"—we've got a chance," the Hunter finished her thought. His heart sank. "But not until *tomorrow.*"

Kiara inclined her head. "Gives her time to rest." She thrust her chin toward Aisha. "And you."

The Hunter started to argue, to tell her he didn't need rest. She cut him off with a sharp look.

"I saw what that thing did to you." Her face tightened, a glimmer of worry—for *him*—darkening her eyes. "And I know how much healing injuries that grave takes it out of you."

In that moment, the Hunter was struck by a strange realization. He'd spent so much time in the last few weeks worrying over *her* that he'd never once considered her feelings. He'd allowed Tassat to put a sword in his chest, Sir Sigmund to beat him senseless, and Lord Apus to pummel him to within an inch of his life. He'd been run through with one iron-edged greatsword and nearly decapitated with another. He'd danced dangerously close to death first with Indombe, then again now with the slashwyrm. How many wounds had he sustained since he first rode out of Voramis—against the Order of Mithridas, the Sanguinaries, Lord Apus' armed men, the Tefaye, and everyone else they'd fought?

Every injury she'd sustained filled him with worry. He hated seeing her in pain, knowing all too well the full extent of her mortality. But did seeing *him* injured, cut, and banged up hurt her, too? Time and again, he threw himself into danger's path as he always had, never once thinking that her love for him might make the sight of his pain as difficult to bear as her pain was for him.

There wasn't much he could do about it. At the end of the day, he was still the Hunter of Voramis, Bucelarii, demon-slayer, all but immortal. He could recover from wounds that would kill any human. He would *always* hurl himself into the thick of the fray if it meant defending those he loved from harm.

Yet at the very least, he could be aware of how his nature would affect her.

He wrapped an arm around her shoulders, pulled her close, and pressed a kiss to her forehead. If she wondered at the cause for the affection, she didn't question it aloud. She merely wrapped her arms around him in return and held him close. There they stayed for long minutes, until a rustling from the east warned of approaching figures.

224

Siyanda and Kodyn emerged from the darkness. The *nassor's* expression was unreadable, but Kodyn's face shone with triumph. "Wait until those bastards see what we've got prepared for—"

His words cut off in a sharp intake of breath and his triumphant expression shifted to a look of horror as he spotted Aisha lying on the ground beside the Hunter.

"Aisha!" His hissed shout reverberated through the forest. In three long steps, he was on his knees at Aisha's side, pressing a hand to her neck, her forehead, her chest, frantically searching for signs of injury or any indication she lived. After a moment, his head snapped up toward the Hunter and Kiara. "What in the fiery hell happened?"

At the Hunter's explanation, the young Praamian's eyes went wide. "She overexerted herself again! Damn it!"

"Again?" the Hunter asked, kneeling on Aisha's other side, opposite Kodyn. "This happened before?"

Kodyn nodded, worry etched deep on his youthful face. "On our journey upriver from Praamis, she was practicing her *Kish'aa* abilities relentlessly. There was nothing much else to do while on the boat, so she spent every minute she had trying to gain control over her powers. Seeing how many spirits she could absorb into herself and the *Dy'nashia*. Ten days ago, when we finally disembarked in Taitawna, she was having a hard time controlling so many. She tried to hold it in until we got out of the city and were heading toward Khafra, but eventually she lost her grip on the spirits. They exploded out of her in what looked like a lightning storm." His expression grew grim. "It was terrifying and awesome, like nothing I'd ever seen."

The Hunter could agree with that assessment. The immense power she'd hurled at the slashwyrm was breathtaking. She'd burned the creature alive, roasted it from the inside out even through scales too thick for his swords to pierce.

"But she used too much, and it left her drained. Like this." Kodyn touched a hand to her cheek, as if feeling for a fever. "We had to rest for a whole day before she could ride again, and even then, it was slow going for a while." He gave the Hunter a wry grin. "We were supposed to meet with Indigo a full two days before we did."

The Hunter smiled back. "Lucky us you arrived late, then." He clapped the young man on the shoulder, attempting reassurance.

Kodyn's grin brightened to a full beam. He seemed genuinely pleased by the Hunter's words. But his worried frown returned quickly as he turned his attention back to Aisha's limp form. "She promised she'd never do it again unless it was life or death."

"Trust me, it was," the Hunter said. "She saved me."

"She tends to do that, doesn't she?" Kodyn's voice was tender, filled with love. He settled onto a seat at her side. "I'll keep watch over her, make sure she's—"

"Here!" Tarek emerged from the marsh, cradling a bundle of leaves and roots in his hand. "Give her this—oh, you're back." His eyes darted between Kodyn, Aisha, the Hunter, and Kiara, and he hesitated a moment.

"What is it?" Kodyn asked.

"*Piniba* shoots, acharia weed, a few other things I found." Tarek thrust the bundle toward Kodyn. "Get her to chew it all. It'll taste like mud, but it'll help get her back on her feet."

"Thank you." Kodyn accepted the vegetation with a grateful nod. Something seemed to occur to him as he did. His gaze snapped up to the Hunter. "Does this mean our plan's buggered? The presence of slashwyrms so close to the camp?"

The Hunter grimaced. "Maybe." He tried for a nonchalant shrug. "I've got to give it more thought. Either way, we're not making a move until tomorrow."

Siyanda hissed something angry in Issai.

"You're calling him a liar?" Kodyn rounded on the woman. "Both of them?"

Siyanda seemed taken aback by Kodyn's anger, but recovered in an instant. "The *Nsanga* are no more real than the *mashetani!*" A sneer curled her lip up, marring her beautiful, strong features. "Tales told to children to—"

Kiara moved toward the Issai *nassor* in a blur of motion, her hand rising and driving forward into Siyanda's chest. The woman was caught off guard and stumbled backward. But Kiara hadn't struck Siyanda, merely pressed something into her arms. Something dark, hard, and gleaming.

"See for yourself," Kiara's voice was calm as ice and just as sharp.

The Hunter's eyes widened as he recognized the object. He hadn't seen Kiara pick up a slashwyrm scale, but he'd been so focused on hauling Aisha and ignoring the pain of his still-healing bones he could have easily missed it.

Siyanda stared down at the black scale with a look of mixed disbelief, bewilderment, and stubborn anger.

"The *Nsanga* are bloody real." A hint of anger crept into Kiara's voice. Perhaps she'd finally grown tired of Siyanda's scorn. "And they're going to be a problem until we can figure out a way around them. If you know anything about the creatures that can help us, we're all ears. Otherwise…" She shook her head with a growl. "I'm getting some sleep."

She marched a short distance away, lay back on the ground with her arms folded, and rolled onto her side. The Hunter *knew* she was far from rest—she couldn't fall asleep as easily as Tarek—but the message was clear.

Tarek slid away, too, moving to lie on his belly on the hill overlooking the Consortium camp. The Hunter turned sharply on his heel and stalked over to join Kiara, leaving a stunned, speechless Siyanda standing alone.

The woman's jaw hung open and her eyes were wide as she stared down at the enormous black scale belonging to a creature she couldn't believe existed—yet whose existence she could no more deny than the grass beneath her feet.

The Hunter turned his back on the woman and wrapped an arm around Kiara. The last thing he heard was an angry hiss of breath and the soft, fading footsteps as Siyanda stalked off into the forest.

Chapter Fifty

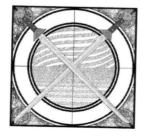

The Hunter awoke to cold, empty ground. His spine ached from hours spent in the same uncomfortable position—had he truly been so exhausted he hadn't moved once?—and his head felt stuffed with wool. Opening his eyes, he found the world around him a gloomy grey. The sun hadn't yet risen high enough to drive the shadows beneath the forest canopy away.

His back gave a loud *pop* as he rose to his feet, and he rolled his head from side to side to work out the kinks. Looking around, he found Kiara standing just below the crest of the hill that had served as their vantage point to spy on the Consortium's operation. Oddly, she was turned *away* from the slavers' camp. Her gaze lingered on the dense forest to the northeast.

The Hunter slid up beside her. "What do you see?" he asked as quietly as he could so as not to disturb Aisha and Kodyn sleeping nearby.

At the sound of his voice, Kiara startled and spun toward him, hand dropping to Deathbite's hilt. For a moment, her eyes locked on him but did not see him. Instead, she seemed to be looking *through* him—but at what, he could not know.

"Kiara?"

Her dark eyes focused on him, and the tension drained from her posture. "Not wise, creeping up on a woman like that." She lowered her hand from her sword and gave him a strained smile. "More than a few of the Bloody Hand earned themselves a dagger in the bollocks trying that."

The Hunter raised both hands like a shield between them. "Didn't try to creep. Just my natural predatory grace, I suppose." He grinned. "Stealthy as a ghost, is the Hunter of Voramis."

Kiara snorted. "Easy, ghost-man." She waggled a finger at him. "Don't go getting a big head over it. I was just…distracted."

The Hunter noted the odd hesitation in her voice. She didn't elaborate further, and before he could ask about it, she changed the subject quickly.

"She's looking better." She gestured toward the spot where Aisha lay on the ground, with Kodyn beside her, his arm draped across her chest.

The Hunter studied the young woman. In the light of day, dim as it was, she did, indeed, appear to have more color in her cheeks, her breathing steady and deep as she slept. The truth of her condition would only be ascertained once she awoke fully, but the Hunter felt a shred of optimism.

"We're missing two," he said, frowning. Siyanda had stomped off the previous night— what couldn't have been more than four or five hours earlier—but if she'd returned, she must have left again, for she was nowhere in sight. Tarek, too, was conspicuously absent. "Any idea where they went?"

"Siyanda, no." Kiara shook her head. "Last I saw Tarek, he was headed that way." She gestured east, toward a thicket of trees. "Pretty sure he was off to relieve himself in the bushes. I doubt he'll be gone much longer."

The Hunter nodded. He couldn't help glancing northeast, following the line Kiara's gaze had traveled. What had consumed her attention so completely she'd been startled by his— admittedly quiet—approach?

He scanned the Consortium camp. Of the fifteen wagons that had entered the camp the previous night, only four were visible outside the central building. They had been loaded overnight, though the heavy sheets of canvas covering them obscured whatever now filled their beds to bulging. The Ordermen were nowhere in sight—likely either inside the building overseeing the loading or taking their ease elsewhere before their eventual departure. The flurry of activity in the camp made it clear that the wagons were in a hurry to depart, but the process of filling the wagons was time-consuming.

The Ujana warriors had not followed the Ordermen inside; they sat cross-legged in the grass beside the wagons, shoulders hunched and heads hanging down in rest. Perhaps they even slept. In the light of day, he could make out more details about the tribe. Their robes lacked the colors characteristic among the Issai, but they wore a heavy assortment of bracelets, earrings, anklets, and necklaces fashioned from a material that gleamed a rich mahogany red in the growing light. Whether they were carved from wood or stone, the Hunter couldn't tell from this far.

He'd seen nothing of interest in the forest beyond the camp. If no one else had arrived or departed—she would have made mention of it, for certain—he had no clue as to what had commanded her interest.

"You saw something?" the Hunter asked, looking sidelong at her.

Kiara's face scrunched up into a frown, her nose wrinkling. "I…thought I did."

That piqued the Hunter's interest. "What did you *think* you saw?"

Kiara rubbed a hand over her eyes. "Nothing, really. Probably just tired."

The Hunter frowned. She was tired—that much was evident in the dark circles around her eyes—but this could be more than that. He was reminded of the previous morning, when she'd gone rigid in her saddle. Had the wound she'd sustained at Zamani Falls been exacerbated?

Or was it that *something else* Aisha had mentioned? Her words echoed in his mind.

"Even after the rot was destroyed, something else remained. Something I could not burn away. It felt…like fire. A fire far hotter than the power of the Kish'aa. It remains within her still. I don't know how I know this, but when the Kish'aa encountered the fire, it did not repel them. On the contrary, it drew them in, as if they fueled it. Made it burn brighter and hotter. But it did not hurt her. Instead, it made her stronger. Almost as if it was now a part of her."

The Hunter didn't understand it now any more than he had then, but if it was affecting Kiara, he had to try and—

His thoughts cut off abruptly as the rustling of leaves drew his attention to the west. He and Kiara both spun toward the sound, hands dropping to their weapons. Only when Siyanda emerged from the dense forest did they relax and release their hilts.

The Hunter opened his mouth to ask where she'd been when the stench struck him like a physical blow to the face. "Keeper's teeth!" he hissed, covering his face with his arm to shield his sensitive nostrils from the reek of burned flesh she emanated. "Did you actually go *see* the *Nsanga* corpse for yourself?"

"Yes." Siyanda met his question with icy disdain. "The word of an *alay-alagbara* is never to be trusted. My people have learned that the hard way far too many times." To illustrate her point, she stabbed a finger in the direction of the Consortium's stronghold. "But my eyes have witnessed the truth. We must find another way for you to get inside the camp. Unless you wish to risk the *Nsanga's* teeth once more."

The Hunter scowled. "Not if I can bloody help it." The slashwyrms hadn't been particularly fast, but between their enormous size, their long, powerful tails, and the thick marsh mud to slow him down, his chances of making it through the beasts' territory uneaten were on the far side of slim. "Did you and Kodyn find anything that might make getting into the camp easier?"

Siyanda regarded him and Kiara with a look that stopped just short of contempt. However, she kept her antipathy restrained enough to manage an indifferent tone. "There is a

228

great tree near the camp." She swept a hand in a vague gesture toward the eastern perimeter. "It will fall with our help, and its weight should bring down a section of the wall."

The Hunter nodded. "Good." That would make noise enough the Consortium guards would have to investigate, splitting their forces even further. "And the fires?"

"Too much damp." Siyanda's face tightened. "Though if we are waiting until nightfall, we could gather some wood—"

All three of them spun at the crackling of twigs and crunching of leaves from the east, in time to see Tarek stumbling into view, fumbling at the string of his trousers. When he felt their eyes on him, he blushed all the way to his hairline.

"Sorry," he said, a strangely contrite look on his youthful face. "Got distracted."

The Hunter didn't know what the Elivasti had to apologize for, nor did he want to know what had distracted the young man. He dismissed the words with a wave. "We're figuring out our next steps. Siyanda said she and Kodyn found a tree they could bring down to collapse a section of the wall. But if we want fires, we'll need to find dry wood somewhere."

"Not going to be easy," Tarek said. He finished tying his trousers and hitched up his belt. "Not a lot of dry spots in this marsh. Only place anything looks close to suitable is there." He gestured toward the forest northeast of the camp.

Upon close examination, the Hunter realized the young man was right. The path the Order of Mithridas' wagons had traveled the previous night appeared dry almost to the point of dusty. The ground was higher, too, and the trees less verdant, with patches of discolored leaves showing among the dense green.

The Hunter turned to Siyanda. "Do you think you, Tarek, and Kodyn can get around to that part of the forest?"

Siyanda looked as if he'd asked if she knew how to walk or say her name. "Of course!"

The Hunter nodded. "Good. Then we'll make use of the day to collect what wood we can. Gather at least enough for *one* fire—" He scanned the wall, then pointed to the southwestern corner. "—there, as far from the gate as possible."

Siyanda followed his pointing finger. "That will suffice."

The Hunter studied the camp, chewing on his lip. He could go over the wall with Aisha and Siyanda, but most of the places where they'd make the climb would be heavily patrolled by torch-carrying guards or near enough to where the captives were digging that the whip-cracking slavers would be watching. He'd have to wait until *after* Kodyn and Tarek brought down the tree on the wall before attempting it. And there was no guarantee he'd get where he needed to go— the cages on the northern side of the camp—before he came under attack.

He glanced at Kiara, but she seemed to have no other solution to offer. The Hunter didn't bother asking Siyanda—she'd be about as helpful as the slashwyrms, and no less likely to bite his head off. Instead, he moved toward the sleeping Kodyn. The young man's Night Guild training might come in handy. Surely all the years he'd spent learning the secrets of breaking into the mansions of Praamian nobility would give him some insight into how best to approach this task. At the very least, his input now could inspire some idea in the Hunter's mind.

He'd taken just two steps when Kiara's voice hissed behind him. "Hunter! Look!"

The Hunter spun back toward her and was at her side in a moment. He followed her pointing finger. The Ujana had all risen to their feet, and the four wagons that had been stationary since he'd awoken were now preparing to move. The drivers—all clad in Consortium armor—were clambering into their seats and gathering up the reins.

More of the covered wagons emerged from the central building. The foremost were being driven by the figures in the dark cloaks with the hoods pulled forward to hide the black masks they wore beneath. These wagons, too, were covered by heavy sheets of canvas secured with ropes, concealing their bulging contents. Without slowing, the Ordermen led the way in a beeline toward the gates, which were even now being pulled open by a quartet of Consortium guards.

Watcher take it! The Hunter's mind raced. The Order of Mithridas was departing, taking their mysterious cargo—and the secrets locked up behind those masks—with them.

He felt torn. On the one hand, their departure meant the camp would be far less fortified, fewer defenders for his small group to deal with in their efforts to liberate the Issai and the rest of the captives. That minimized the risk to his companions and increased the chances of their success.

On the other hand, the thought of losing track of the Ordermen rankled. He'd come all this way—at least in part—to put an end to whatever wicked machinations had them operating this deep in Ghandian lands, hundreds of leagues away from the nearest city. If they were in league with the Consortium, it meant they, too, were a threat to Aisha's people—people they'd already had a hand in enslaving. He could fulfill his oath to help her *and* learn more about the Order of Mithridas' plans in one fell swoop.

But did he dare attack *now?* Within the walls of the Consortium camp, they had easy access to reinforcements. All they had to do was throw off the shackles of the Issai *amaqhawe* and the other captive warriors and the odds would tilt drastically in their favor. But out in the open forest, with only the six of them, what were their *true* chances of carrying the day?

Indecision froze the Hunter in place. He knew what the *smart* play was here: to let the Ordermen ride away, to wait until dark and attack the camp. Yet he hated the idea of standing by and doing nothing when he was so close to the enemies who had killed the Beggar Priests on the road to Malandria—and in so doing, put Father Reverentus in Lord Apus' clutches, leading to his death in the Monolith.

Before he could make up his mind or move a muscle, a *new* sound reached his ears. A sound so faint he almost missed it through the hammering of his heartbeat in his ears. But it came again, and this time he heard it clearly. A bright, cheerful warbling like some forest bird far in the distance.

Siyanda spun toward the sound, every muscle in her body immediately going rigid. From beneath her robes, she drew out a small bamboo flute—much like the one Aisha had carved on the road—and clapped it to her lips. When she blew, it emitted a trilling whistle in answer.

Again came the whistle, closer this time, and Siyanda responded with her own. Within minutes, the sound of splashing feet drew nearer, and from the trees emerged a young woman clad in the same fibrous cloth battle-wrappings as Siyanda.

"Ntombi?" Siyanda called.

At the sight of her *nassor,* the young woman—who couldn't have seen more than fifteen or sixteen summers—fell to her knees in the marsh, gasping and struggling for breath. A torrent of Issai words poured from her lips. The Hunter thought he recognized the word he'd heard Siyanda shouting when she raced back to warn of the Tefaye attack.

Siyanda's face went instantly pale. She barked a few words back, and at, Ntombi's reply, her fist clenched around the haft of her short-handled spear.

"What is it?" the Hunter asked. Dread rose in the pit of his stomach, and from the fear evident on the young warrior's face and on Siyanda's face, he already knew the answer before the Issai *nassor* choked them out.

230

"Enemies…attacking the *ekhaya!*"

Chapter Fifty-One

The Hunter's heart leaped into his throat. "When?" he demanded. "How long ago?"

He didn't know how long it had taken Ntombi to travel all this way from wherever Duma had moved the camp to, but by this point, the damage would be done. If the attack had been Consortium-led, there could be a whole new batch of slaves on their way here even now. If it had been the Tefaye, no telling how many Issai had been slaughtered by the lunatic, cannibalistic enemy tribe. All that Siyanda could do now was return to bury the dead—what remained of them—and seek vengeance on those who'd perpetrated the attack.

Siyanda shook her head. "Not attacking now. Soon!" She turned back to Ntombi, speaking again in Issai.

The young warrior's words came out in a torrent. The acrid stench of fear all but overwhelmed her unique scent—hyssop, hyacinth, acacia, and dried palm fiber. Drenched in sweat and visibly exhausted from her run, she looked on the verge of collapse.

Siyanda sucked in a sharp breath. "Ntombi spotted enemy warriors traveling toward the *ekhaya*. Not a hunting party; too many, and armed for battle. She ran straight here with all speed, praying to the *Kish'aa* she would find us in time to return and fight off the attack."

The Hunter stared at the young woman on her knees in the marsh. He could demand an answer as to where the enemy had been sighted or how she knew they were on the way to the Issai camp, but her answer would likely do him little good. He had no idea how far west of the Unathi River Duma had led the tribe, or how far upstream. Only one question mattered now.

"Can you reach the *ekhaya* in time?" he asked, both Siyanda and Ntombi though only the former understood him.

Siyanda's jaw muscles clenched. "Even if I have to run until my lungs can no longer draw breath and my feet are worn to my knees, I intend to try."

"As do I."

The Hunter and Siyanda both spun at the sound of that voice. Aisha's eyes had opened, her gaze locked on Ntombi and Siyanda. She'd evidently heard the entire conversation, for her face was set in a determined cast and she struggled to rise.

"Aisha—" Kodyn began.

She silenced him with a sharp look. "Help me or step aside, Kodyn. They are *my* people."

For answer, Kodyn reached down and helped her to her feet. Worry darkened his face as she wobbled in his grasp, but he wisely kept his thoughts to himself. One look at Aisha's expression made it clear that she would not be dissuaded from her purpose.

"*Um'zala*," Siyanda said, raising a hand to forestall Aisha. "You are too weak to—"

"Do not tell me what I am!" Aisha's eyes flashed blue-white. It was little more than a spark—a far cry from the blaze that had burned there the previous night—yet there was no mistaking it. She had not used *all* of the *Kish'aa* power at her command. "I am going. There is no argument."

"We are going," Kodyn said.

Kiara stepped up beside the Hunter. "All of us."

At those words, the Hunter's heart sank. He'd *known* it was the right thing to do—it wasn't in his nature to stand by and allow Aisha's people to get slaughtered—but he'd allowed himself to momentarily consider remaining here to launch an attack on the departing Ordermen. Alone, he could draw the Sword of Nasnaz and unleash its power against the three-score warriors and drivers in the convoy of covered wagons without fear of his companions getting hurt in the melee.

It was more than that, though. He felt pulled to the northeast, toward *Ukuhlushwa Okungapheli*. Kharna's silent urging had drawn him all this way. He'd crossed half of Einan to find out what the entombed Serenii wanted him to discover—or, according to Aisha, activate. The thought of turning back when he was so close to both the tower of midnight *and* the Order of Mithridas together sat like a stone in his belly.

He cast but a single glance over his shoulder at the wagon train wending northeast along the path through the jungle. Though he could not pursue them now, he knew which way they had gone. When he returned, he would pick up their trail—so many men and draft animals would leave a clear scent, not to mention hoofprints, footprints, and wagon ruts in the dirt and mud—and follow it wherever it led. He would visit upon them just punishment for what had been done to the Beggar Priests and the knight apprentices.

But not yet. Not until he fulfilled the promise he'd made to Aisha.

When he looked back, he found Kiara's gaze on him. Pride shone in her eyes and she gave him a little nod of approval. She alone could guess what had passed through his thoughts—she knew him too bloody well sometimes—and acknowledged the choice he'd just made.

At Kiara's words, Aisha had pushed off Kodyn and tried her best to stand straight. She managed, though she still sagged beneath the weight of exhaustion. To his credit, Kodyn didn't try to help her further; he was smart enough to know fussing like a mother hen would only irritate her. Instead, he turned to gather up her pack along with his own and slung both over his shoulders.

"No." The Hunter stepped toward the young man, shaking his head. "Leave them. They'll only slow you down."

"Leaving them here leaves proof of our presence," Kodyn argued. "Just because the Consortium hasn't yet sent out scouts or patrols to examine the area, that doesn't mean they won't."

The Hunter nodded. "I know." From the moment he'd determined to return to the Issai camp, he'd considered how best to proceed. "But Tarek will make sure none of our belongings are spotted."

At the sound of his name, Tarek's head whipped toward the Hunter. "What?" He stood from where he'd bent to retrieve his own pack.

"You're staying here," the Hunter said.

"Staying?" Tarek's eyes flew wide and his spine went as stiff as the spear strapped to his back. His gaze darted to Kodyn, then back to the Hunter. "Why?"

"Because we need someone to watch the Consortium camp while we're gone." The Hunter spoke in a matter-of-fact tone. "If the wagons return, how soon, if they get reinforcements, anything that could prove problematic when we attack."

Tarek's mouth worked soundlessly.

The Hunter gathered up his and Kiara's packs and set them on the ground before Kodyn. "Leave them," he ordered, shooting a pointed glance at the packs still slung over the young man's shoulders.

The sound of angry footsteps brought him around, just in time to see Tarek planting his feet directly in front of him. The Elivasti directed a burning glare up at him.

"You think that I'm too weak to fight, is that it?" he hissed. An ugly look twisted his face and fury radiated off him like waves of desert heat. "Yes, that was the first time I'd ever killed anyone in battle, but I wouldn't be the first warrior to struggle with that. And for a matter of *hours*. Tell me, have I shown any indication since the river that I am anything but fully present and capable?"

The Hunter met the Elivasti's blazing intensity with icy calm. "Tarek—"

"I am not weak!" Tarek all but shouted. He jabbed a finger into the Hunter's chest. "You want me to prove that, I will show you. But at least be man enough to tell me the truth to my face."

The Hunter growled low in his throat. "Now's not the time for this, Tarek. We've got—"

"Now is *precisely* the time!" Tarek shook his fist in the Hunter's face. "I am a warrior of the Elivasti, trained by the Second Blade himself, horse-blooded *daichin* of Soaring Hawk Clan, True Descendant of the Serenii. Just because I do not slaughter my enemies by the thousands without remorse, that doesn't make me either a coward or weakling!"

"Tarek!" The Hunter had grown tired of the young man's tirade. "Shut your Keeper-damned mouth and listen to me."

The Elivasti looked ready to throw a punch—indeed, he actually began drawing back his right arm, shifting his left foot forward into the combat stance Master Eldor had called the Woodcutter—so the Hunter did the only thing he could: he moved first.

He sprang forward, slipping into Tarek's guard before the young man could stop him, seized Tarek by the shoulders, and shoved backward. His left foot slid around behind Tarek's and collided with the back of the young man's knee. Off-balance, Tarek toppled backward and would have fallen were it not for the Hunter's firm grip on his shoulders.

"Enough!" the Hunter snarled into the young man's face. "Despite what you think, I am not punishing you because of some perceived failing. Never *once* have I thought you are either weak or cowardly. You would not be the first young man to struggle after taking his first life or losing his first comrade in battle, nor will you be the last."

Tarek's eyes went wide in a combination of fear and shock.

"I am not treating you like a child and demanding you prove yourself to me," the Hunter continued, his words coming hot and fast. "I am not your father, nor am I your mentor. What I am is someone who needs a competent warrior with a sharp eye and a keen mind to remain behind and observe the camp of my enemy. Because when I return, I need to know exactly what I'm facing so I can figure out the best way to rip that enemy to pieces without losing any of my friends and allies."

Tarek's mouth opened, but no words came out.

The Hunter was far from done. "I also need someone who is capable of thinking fast on his feet and adapting as the situation demands. Someone who can survive on his own for as long as it takes for us to get to the Issai, fight off the attack—an attack that is drawing ever-closer as we debate this—and return."

He straightened abruptly and pulled the Elivasti back onto his feet.

"Look around you, Tarek," the Hunter snapped. "You're the *only* one who can stay. You have to know that."

It didn't take a genius to figure that Kodyn would go wherever Aisha went, be that into the jaws of an army or into the deepest, darkest hell. Deathbite gave Kiara an edge in battle that Tarek's well-crafted Elivasti spear simply couldn't match—*and* sustained Kharna with every life she took. That left only the Hunter himself, and not even the most clod-headed idiot would expect him to remain behind in the face of a potentially impossible battle.

The Hunter softened his tone. He'd gotten his point across clearly enough. No need to ram the rest of what needed saying down Tarek's throat.

"I'm asking you to stay because I trust that you'll keep your head, keep out of sight, and keep a close eye on the camp below." He leaned closer, lowered his voice. "You've more than proven yourself to all of us, Tarek. No one is questioning your worth or doubting that you can be trusted to handle yourself where and as needed. And right now, where you're needed most is right here. Can you accept that?"

For a long moment, Tarek remained speechless, staring at the Hunter open-mouthed. Finally, he managed a nod and stammered out. "Y-Yes. I-I can."

"Good." The Hunter clapped the young Elivasti on the shoulder. "We'll be back as soon as we can, but until then, we're counting on you to make sure that when the time comes for the attack, we've got the best shot at success."

"I won't let you down," Tarek said.

The Hunter hid a grimace. Clearly the young man had missed the part about not needing to prove his worth. But he merely nodded. "So be it."

With that, he turned and joined Kiara, Aisha, Kodyn, Ntombi, and an impatient Siyanda in racing off through the marshes back toward the camp of the Issai—and the attack they could only *hope* they'd arrive in time to repel.

Chapter Fifty-Two

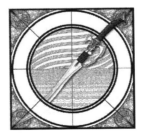

The Hunter ran at the back of the pack. He could outpace every one of his companions, he knew—none of them could match his Bucelarii speed—but doing so would serve little purpose. Without Siyanda, Ntombi, or Aisha to guide him to the Issai camp, he could spend years wandering the Ghandian Plains and come no closer to his end goal. Thus, he forced himself to match the pace set by the group's slowest member.

Aisha struggled gamely on despite her exhaustion. She did her best to keep up with Siyanda and Ntombi, but the Issai were fleet of foot and far more familiar with the route through the marshes than she. Within a matter of minutes, she was stumbling more often than not, her legs dragging with fatigue. When Kodyn finally slung her arm around his shoulder to help her keep on, she made no protest. She had neither the breath nor strength to spare.

The Hunter was familiar with stubborn people—he numbered himself among the most bull-headed, single-minded people alive, and had fallen in love with not one, but *two* women whose tenacity was a match for his own. Determination and persistence could only carry them so far; the steeliest of wills would always eventually succumb to the limits of mortality. The Warmaster's tortures had proven that even one with his inhuman grit could be broken.

Aisha *might* make the journey to the hole in the ground that descended into *Uhumi Wolandle*, but there was simply no way she could climb down in her condition. Even once they'd made the descent, they still had to navigate the tight *intambelu*-lit stone passages to reach the cavern behind the waterfall where their horses awaited. Then would come the mad gallop toward the Issai camp. She would arrive too exhausted to raise her spear in defense of her people, much less her own life.

He couldn't talk her out of making the journey—she'd made that much crystal clear—but perhaps there was a means of hastening their arrival, or reducing the exertion required. Ideas spun through his mind only to be discarded in a moment. Riding behind Kodyn wasn't an option; the horse would fatigue faster carrying both of them. Strapping her to her saddle to give her a chance to rest while they rode? Her warrior's pride wouldn't suffer that indignity. At most, the Hunter hoped to convince her to allow him to lower her into the underground passages using Kodyn's rope. Perhaps *all* of them could make the descent that way. It would prove faster to simply climb down—

Climb down! He cursed himself for a fool. How had he not seen it sooner?

He picked up his pace, racing past the laboring Aisha and Kodyn, Kiara, and the two fleet-footed Issai. Only then did he stop and turn to face the group.

"Wait!" he shouted, holding up both hands.

Ntombi slowed—she might not understand the Einari word, but the meaning was evident enough even without translation. Siyanda looked as if she wanted to merely run through the Hunter, but she, too, slowed. Though Aisha's labored breathing drowned out some of Kiara's huffing and puffing, the Hunter could see the run—going on an hour now, scrambling over rocks, splashing through waist-high marshes, and squeezing between thick vines—was taking its toll on her.

"What?" Siyanda snapped, though her anger was meaningless, for the Hunter was already speaking.

"We can't go through *Uhumi Wolandle.*" He spoke quickly, not giving the Issai *nassor* a chance to argue. "It'll take too long making the climb down and navigating those tunnels in the darkness." He rounded on Kodyn. "How much rope do you have?"

Kodyn wiped a stream of sweat from his forehead and gasped, "Thirty…paces."

The Hunter turned to Aisha. "And how tall do you think that waterfall was?"

Aisha sucked in a breath—really, more of a heavy pant—and considered for a moment. "Maybe fifty paces."

The Hunter glanced at Kiara. She gave a little shrug, confirming the guess he'd made based on his recollections of the previous day.

"That's how we get down in a hurry," he said, looking between Aisha, Kodyn, Kiara, and, finally, Siyanda. He could already see the retort forming on her lips, the disdain twisting her features. He drove on before she could protest. "I'll hold the rope, lower you down as far as I can, then you jump the last distance into the pool. The water will break our fall, and rather than spending an hour climbing down the way we came up and squeezing through the passages, we're down in a matter of *minutes.*"

Three heads nodded in agreement. Even Siyanda's mouth snapped shut. She couldn't argue with his assessment or the efficacy of his plan. Ntombi just looked bewildered, but when Aisha translated, her eyebrows shot up in the universal look that said "why didn't I think of that?" without the need for words.

The Hunter looked to Siyanda. Their plan hinged on her cooperation. "Can you get us to the upper edge of the falls? Do you know the way?"

Siyanda's lip curled upward. "These are *my* lands."

The Hunter took that as her way of saying "yes". "Then let's go. With luck, that'll cut enough time on the journey we can reach your people in time."

If Siyanda was at all grateful, she didn't show it. Instead, she merely turned an icy shoulder and ran around him as if he were nothing more than another rock or tree—or, perhaps worse, as if he were a venomous viper to avoid like the plague.

The rest of them set into motion, running on in pursuit of the *nassor.* Kodyn shot the Hunter a pleading look as he struggled past laboring under Aisha's weight. For all his devotion to her and desire to support her, he, too, was reaching the limits of his strength. He might have been trained to run across the rooftops of Praamis, but the muddy marshes made the going far harder.

"Allow me," the Hunter said, stepping into the youths' path.

Aisha looked ready to protest, but the Hunter cut her off with a glare.

"You'll do your people no good if you arrive at the *ekhaya* too tired to fight. Either you let me help you, or I throw you over my shoulder and haul you the rest of the way there."

Aisha snorted. "I'd…welcome…you…to try." The ferociousness of the statement was undermined by the fact that it came out in a series of barely audible gasps. Her knees chose that moment to buckle beneath her.

The Hunter caught her before she fell. "That being hauled over my shoulder doesn't sound too bad about now, does it?"

Aisha's eyes wobbled, her head lolling on her shoulders for a minute. "Not…too…bad." She managed a weak grin.

"Come on, then." The Hunter ducked to sling her arm over his shoulder, bearing her weight beneath him. He looked to Kodyn, who appeared only fractionally steadier on his feet than Aisha. "Get that rope ready. The second we reach the waterfall, I want you heading down to get the horses ready."

Kodyn tilted his head. "Yes, sir." He spoke with a measure of new respect, and gratitude shone in his eyes as he took off behind Ntombi and Siyanda.

Kiara smiled at the Hunter as she passed. "Race you!" she called over her shoulder.

The Hunter chuckled and glanced down at Aisha. "You hear that, Aisha? We're being challenged. We've got to win for the honor of the Issai, right?"

237

"Honor!" Aisha gasped. She lurched forward into a run, stumbling but stubbornly refusing to give in to exhaustion. The Hunter did his best to bear as much of her weight as he could, matching his pace to hers, but in truth, he could do little more than grit his teeth in sympathy and cling to her as they raced through the marshes. It fell to her to endure the exhaustion and exertion long enough to reach the waterfall.

The forest passed by in a blur of green leaves, thick shrubs, dangling vines, gnarled trees, and muddy brown water kicked up by their racing feet. With every step, the Hunter could feel Aisha's strength waning, but she refused to succumb to the frailty of her mortal body. Somehow, impossibly, she managed to keep on. The Hunter knew her legs had to be leaden and her feet heavy even without the mud clinging to her boots. In her state, only inertia kept her from utter collapse.

So he did the only thing he could: he gave her a distraction to take her mind off her exhaustion.

He told her of his earliest memories—of arriving at the gates of Voramis with nothing but Soulhunger at his hip—and how he'd survived his first few years on the city's streets taking on the occasional job as muscle-for-hire, then a blade-for-hire. He spoke of how he'd earned the name "the Hunter of Voramis", then how he'd gone about building his legend as the Hunter of Voramis, paying good coin to disseminate rumors among the citizenry and nobility of his superhuman abilities.

Soon, he, too, was laboring for breath, but he did not stop talking. Could not, for once she remembered how exhausted she was, her strength would fully give out. He told her of Farida and her death at the hands of the First. It might have been his imagination, but he thought he saw the blue-white light dancing across her fingertips as he described how he'd gone about eliminating the Bloody Hand root and branch in vengeance.

He had just begun talking about the night the First and Third had opened a portal into the fiery hell to summon one of their brethren when a shout echoed from ahead. He lifted his eyes and, through a break in the trees, saw clear skies and naked rock ahead. A new sound pierced the pulse hammering in his ears: rushing water.

"We're…there!" Aisha gasped, half-sobbing, half-laughing.

"You did it!"

The Hunter helped her the last few hundred paces, then passed her off to a panting, profusely sweating Kiara, who stood just beneath the shade of the last tree. Kodyn had already raced out onto the rocky ledge beside the river plunging over the falls and set about unwrapping the dark coils of thin rope from around his waist.

"Get the horses and bring them out from the cavern," the Hunter instructed as he took one end of the rope from the young man. "I want them beside the pool and ready to ride the moment I'm down."

"Understood." With a nod, Kodyn tossed the other end of the rope over the falls and followed it a moment later. The Hunter had just time enough to brace his feet and wrap the rope around his waist before Kodyn's weight yanked hard on it. Gritting his teeth, the Hunter clung on to the finger-thin line with all his strength.

Kodyn's descent took only a matter of seconds. He must have sped down the rope nearly as fast as he'd been running, for within ten labored heartbeats, the Hunter felt the line go slack so suddenly he nearly stumbled backward. A few seconds later, a loud *splash* echoed from below.

"He's down!" The Hunter spun around. His gaze settled on Siyanda and Ntombi. "You two, you're next."

For once, Siyanda didn't protest or sneer her disapproval of him. Instead, she just called to Ntombi in Issai, and together they ran toward him.

At the *nassor's* insistence, the younger woman went first. She might have been a warrior—or, more likely a warrior-in-training of some sort—but her lithe, lean frame weighed so little the Hunter barely had to brace himself to support her. She climbed down at nearly the same pace as Kodyn, and soon Siyanda began making the descent. The *nassor* had a bit more meat on her bones, and she proved far less adept at descending the rope. Judging by the occasional jerks on the line, she must have stopped every few seconds—to rest, catch her breath, or merely to adjust her position, the Hunter didn't know. He just clung to the line and willed the woman to hurry.

When, finally, the line again went slack and the third *splash* echoed from far below, the Hunter spun toward Kiara and Aisha. "Last two!" he called.

Kiara had kept Aisha standing, though her legs were wobbling and she looked on the verge of collapse. It took all her strength just to take two tottering steps onto the ledge. Then she sagged in Kiara's arms.

"I-I'm sorry!" Tears streamed down Aisha's cheeks. "I...can't!" The look on her face tore at the Hunter's heart. So much shame, self-recrimination, and guilt the Hunter could feel it even from this distance. She had come so far, but her body had gone well beyond its limits.

"Yes, you bloody can!" The Hunter turned to Kiara. "Go down first."

Kiara shot him a questioning look, raising an eyebrow.

"I've got this," he told her gently.

Kiara hesitated only a moment before nodding and lowering Aisha to the rocky ledge. There, the young woman lay gasping for breath and trying to quell the tremors that stole the strength from her legs.

The Hunter braced himself in anticipation of Kiara's descent.

"Oh, rot you! I'm not that heavy!" were her last indignant words to him before she vanished over the ledge.

The Hunter chuckled to himself as he clung to the rope, leaning back against Kiara's weight. He was tempted to shout down "Yes, you bloody are!" but thought better of it. He had enemies enough on all sides without angering *her*.

Once Kiara jumped clear, the Hunter set about gathering up the dangling rope as quickly as he could. Reaching the end, he turned back toward Aisha, knelt beside her, and set about tying the free end around her waist.

"Here's what's going to happen," he told Aisha as he finished the knot, lifted her into his arms, carried her toward the ledge. "You saved my ass back there with the slashwyrm. So that means I owe you *two* now—one for my life, one for Kiara. So you can bet your muddy boots that I'm getting you to your camp in time. All you have to do is swim once you hit the pool below. Can you do that?"

Aisha looked up at him, her umber-skinned face twisting into a worried frown. "What about you?"

"Don't you worry about me," he said, giving her a confident smile. "Just focus on recovering enough to ride." He lowered her to the ledge and gripped one shoulder. "We both know which of us is more powerful. You proved that last night. Which means that it's on you to turn things around for your people. To do that, though, you've got to recover."

For a moment, the hard, determined look on her face slipped, and the young, vulnerable woman beneath showed through. "I'm so tired," she whispered, clutching his arm as if he were the only thing keeping her from passing out. "I can barely keep my eyes open, and my head's spinning so wildly I can't tell if there are three or eight of you."

"One is more than enough," the Hunter said, chuckling.

She smiled, but it was a tired, wan, weak thing. It lasted only a moment before fading to a look of tearful desperation. "If I stop, my people die. My family dies." Her voice came out in a whisper. "I came all this way to save them and I'm too weak to do anything."

"Right *now* you are." The Hunter spoke in a firm voice. "But you won't always be. You'll be as strong again as you were last night." He gave her a confident smile. "Just keep fighting through the pain and exhaustion. Do that, and I promise you'll once again have the power to save everyone."

He didn't understand her *Kish'aa* abilities—did absorbing the spirits of the dead reinvigorate her the way Soulhunger did whenever it consumed a soul?—but he suspected that was what she needed to hear at the moment.

It seemed to work. She lifted her head, her shoulders, and her spine stiffened with new resolve. "Just keep fighting," she whispered. "I've done that my whole life. What's one more fight?"

The Hunter grinned. "Well, maybe *two* more."

He helped Aisha to scoot toward the edge of the rock, lowering herself over the lip. "I've got you," he told her. "Just hang on to the rope and get ready to swim."

Aisha nodded. "I can do that."

The Hunter lowered her as quickly as he could without knocking her against the rocks. It didn't take long before he ran out of rope. He waited a moment, hoping she would sense what was to come, then released his grip on the thin black cord. A satisfying *splash* echoed a moment later from below, accompanied by a triumphant shout of "I've got her!" from Kiara.

Letting out a long, relieved breath, the Hunter stepped up to the edge and looked down. *Fifty paces, eh?*

He studied the pool far below, where Kiara was wading out toward the place where Aisha was splashing to the surface. He'd made a similar jump at Zamani Falls, but Indombe's pool had been so deep he couldn't have seen the bottom even had the water been crystal clear. This pool appeared more like a puddle—perhaps as deep as he was tall, not much more.

Nothing for it, the Hunter thought, grimacing inwardly. He'd had no other way to help Aisha down; she'd been far too weak to make the climb herself. Now, he had to live with the consequences of his decision, however painful they might be.

Retreating three steps, he braced himself for what was to come, dashed toward the edge, and hurled himself out into empty space.

Chapter Fifty-Three

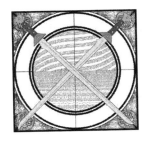

The Hunter knew the fall would hurt even before he hit the pool, but knowledge did little to diminish the pain of impact. Though he kept his legs extended to break the water's surface, it still felt as if he'd slammed into solid stone. Worse, he actually *struck* solid stone at the bottom of the pool feet-first. His feet and legs shattered instantly and searing pain raced all the way up to his hips.

He couldn't stifle a scream, though it was blessedly muffled by the water. Darkness surged at the edges of his vision and it was all he could do to remain conscious against the anguish shivering through his pulverized bones. He clawed his way to the surface using only the power in his arms, though that proved difficult, for his body was on the verge of shutting down to prevent the pain from overwhelming his mind.

He sucked in a shuddering breath as his head broke above the water, and through the anguish consuming his lower body, he heard Kiara's shouted "Hunter!" Then her hand was gripping his collar and dragging him toward the pool's edge.

The Hunter fought to keep from crying out as the water rippling against his shattered legs sent fresh waves of pain. He nearly lost his gorge when he looked down and saw shards of bone jutting through his flesh. A scream burst from his lips as he shoved the bones back into place. He nearly lost the battle to remain conscious and would have no doubt drowned if not for Kiara's grip on him.

Through a superhuman effort of will, the Hunter turned his focus inward and sought out the damage to his body. So much damage! Torn flesh, severed nerves, ripped muscle, and mangled bone from his feet to his thighs. Another hissing cry slipped past his clenched teeth as he set to work repairing the damage. The lightning coursing through every fiber of his being was no worse, just another layer of pain atop the torment wracking him.

His body mended slowly—so slowly he could feel his muscles re-knitting, his bone ossifying, the nerves reconnecting one tendril at a time. Every fresh repair brought a new wave of pain jolting up his spine and searing through his brain. His breath came hard and fast, tears streamed down his soaking wet face, and his teeth ground against each other, so tightly clenched was his jaw.

The pain receded, one agonized heartbeat at a time. In truth, it couldn't have taken more than a few seconds in all—he was still in the water, being dragged toward the shore—but it felt as if an eternity of torment had transpired in that short space. When he opened his eyes, he saw the trail of blood streaming from his now-healed legs toward the center of the pool where he'd landed.

When finally he felt hard stone grinding against his back, he tried to stand. Fresh agony rippled from his hips to his toes, though it was more a remnant than anything real, his mind's recollection of the pain he'd just endured. His legs wobbled as violently as Aisha's had, and he had to lean heavily on Kiara to remain upright.

Aisha lay sprawled on the rocks just beyond the pool's edge, staring up at the sky, too exhausted to move. Siyanda and Ntombi, however, stared at him in wide-eyed astonishment. The *nassor's* face had gone pale, horror etched into her features. The younger woman, however, was more stunned than horrified. She had no idea of the Hunter's true nature, and thus had no understanding of what she'd witnessed.

The clack and clatter of horses' hooves on stone drew the Hunter's attention toward the roaring waterfall. Kodyn rode out of the cave behind the waterfall with their four horses in tow. He brought the mounts to a skittering halt five paces from where Aisha lay and vaulted down from the saddle with impressive agility. He was at Aisha's side and helping to lift her to her feet in the space of two heartbeats.

"I'm fine," the Hunter gasped, pushing off Kiara. He could stand unaided, though the pain had not yet fully faded, and the effort of mending his broken body had sapped his strength. "Go help Kodyn get Aisha into the saddle."

Kiara gave him an unconvinced look, but she didn't argue. A few quick steps brought her to Aisha's other side, and, together with Kodyn, set about helping the exhausted young woman toward her horse.

The Hunter twisted to look at Siyanda and Ntombi, who still stood staring wide-eyed at him. "Can you ride?" he demanded.

Ntombi's expression didn't change—she continued gawping at him, uncomprehending of his Einari words—but the question snapped Siyanda out of her stupefaction. Her expression shifted from astonishment to disdain in a single instant. "As I told you before," she spat, "my feet will carry me well enough."

"But not fast enough." The Hunter fought to keep the furious snarl from his voice. Now wasn't the time to entertain her stubbornness, but he'd make little headway coming at her head-on. "You can run longer than horses, but you cannot hope to match their speed. And speed is of far greater importance at the moment. So I ask you again, Can. You. Ride?" He failed to fully conceal his annoyance, his final words coming out clipped, sharp as iron.

Siyanda's expression hardened, but the Hunter could see his words had the desired effect. "I will ride," she said, nodding. "But Ntombi cannot."

"Then she will have to catch up as best she can," the Hunter said, shrugging. "But we *have* to reach your *ekhaya* before your enemies attack, and the only way we'll do that is if you ride Nayaga." He gestured toward Tarek's horse.

Siyanda eyed the stocky black steppe pony, and even her antipathy toward him could not fully mask her admiration of the Hrandari-bred mount.

The Hunter didn't wait for her to explain the situation to Ntombi. He staggered toward Elivast, seized the saddlehorn, and half-dragged himself onto the horse's back. The twinges of pain were fading from his legs, the muscles once again responding to his command, but he was not yet at full strength. Fortunately for him, the horse would be doing most of the work for the next short while.

Elivast danced beneath him, energy quivering through his body. A full day of rest had done the horse good. He wanted to run now, to stretch his long legs and feel the breeze through his mane. That would serve the Hunter's purposes just fine. He'd have need of every bit of Elivast's speed.

He glanced over his shoulder and found Kiara climbing into Ash's saddle. Kodyn had mounted behind Aisha, gripping her firmly around the waist with one hand and holding the reins

242

with the other. A good thing, too, for the young woman was half-slumped, her eyelids sagging in exhaustion.

The Hunter knew the horse could not sustain full speed for long burdened by two riders. But they only needed to ride until Aisha recovered enough from the run that she could sit the saddle on her own. How she'd fare when they reached the Issai camp and joined the battle to come, he didn't know. Her iron-willed obstinacy had carried her this far. With the help of the *Kish'aa,* she might stand a chance of recovering enough to face her enemies on her own two feet. And if not…

He pushed the thought aside. They had worries enough for the moment. All he needed to do was focus on the ride ahead, and deal with whatever came next whenever it came.

A tug on the reins turned Elivast's head south, toward the rocky path that led alongside the Unathi River. Already, Ntombi had set off at a run. Siyanda sat mounted, appearing terribly uncomfortable in the saddle. Nayaga didn't fight her, either, but seemed to accept her presence without hesitation. The Hunter didn't have time to wonder at the strange contradiction—a woman who'd disdained riding as a practice of the *alay-alagbara* skilled enough to control even a restive Hrandari-bred steppe pony. He merely clapped his heels to Elivast's flanks and set off at a gallop along the riverbank. He didn't need Siyanda's guidance yet; there was only *one* way out of the waterfall's basin.

The Hunter set a breakneck pace, galloping along the riverside path as fast as Elivast could safely manage. Within half a minute, he drew abreast of Ntombi. The young Issai was running fast, but she couldn't hope to match the horses' speed. She moved aside to make way for them to ride past. The Hunter didn't look back, but had no doubt she'd set off at her best possible speed in the hopes she would arrive at the Issai camp in time to tip the balance of the impending battle in favor of her people.

Rocks were strewn across the trail, but Elivast was fleet and sure of foot, and sensed the Hunter's urgency. He galloped past the spot where the barrel-bellied *imvubu* waded in the middle of the sluggishly flowing river, never slowing even as they drew abreast of a pack of *crocodylus* sunning themselves in the heat of the day. Fortunately, the bright sun made the reptilians lethargic, and they did little more than open their vertically-slitted pupils and hiss in the Hunter's direction.

The sight of the lean, spiny-backed creatures brought back memory of the slashwyrm and sent an involuntary shiver down the Hunter's spine. He still had to figure out another way to reach the northern side of the Consortium camp *without* trespassing on the monstrosities' territory. One close encounter with those massive jaws and powerful tails was enough for a lifetime.

A part of him hoped it was the Consortium attacking. He'd welcome a chance to unleash carnage on the slavers. They more than deserved to sample a taste of the suffering they had heaped upon the Issai and others captive within their work camp. With any luck, the Order of Mithridas would be present to direct the attack, and the Hunter wouldn't lose his opportunity to get his hands on one of the masked bastards and put them to the question.

Ntombi had made no mention of *Gcinue'eleku awandile,* however. Granted, there existed the possibility he'd missed it—his grasp of the Issai tongue was nonexistent, and fear had dragged the words from her mouth at an impossibly fast speed. He hadn't heard mention of the Tefaye, either.

Does that mean some other enemy is attacking? Who else could want to spill Issai blood?

Then he remembered what he'd read in the histories of Ghandia as penned by Ingiyab Yengwayo of the raids carried out by the endlessly warring tribes. Even the maddened Tefaye hadn't just attacked the Issai to slaughter their rivals; they'd specifically gone after the pen holding the *raya* cattle. Did some *other* tribe now seek to take advantage of the Issai's vulnerability to steal the tribe's most valuable resource? If so, the already-reduced tribe could very well find themselves on a slow, inevitable march toward extinction. The capture of the *nassor* and the *amaqhawe* meant there would be no warriors—aside from Siyanda, Duma, and a handful of young women in training—to steal back what was taken. Without the *raya* to provide precious food and milk, they would be in dire straits.

Whoever was attacking—the Consortium to enslave, the Tefaye to slaughter and feast, or some rival tribe to steal—the end would be much the same for the Issai. Aisha's people would be left with nothing. They would wander the plains in search of resources, slowly wasting away from hunger and thirst, to either die out or be subsumed by a larger, stronger tribe. The Hunter had no particular love for the Issai, but he *had* made a promise to Aisha. He owed it to her to fight for her people. And fight he would, with every shred of strength and ferocity he possessed.

The sun wheeled overhead and time passed in a blur of stone cliffs, sunlight glinting off the water, and dust kicked up by the horses. Sweat streamed down the Hunter's face, trickled in great sheets down his spine. The air clung to him like a choking blanket, the humidity made far worse by the leather armor and the sodden garments beneath. It felt as if he could not draw breath, yet could not slow, either. Not with the fate of Aisha's people hanging in the balance.

To his immense relief, the cliffs bordering the river sloped downward, and the terrain once more descended toward the gentle, rolling hills of the plains. The Hunter slowed Elivast just enough to allow Siyanda to race past on Nayaga. She was the only one who could get them where they needed to go in time. She bounced painfully in the saddle but managed to hang on through sheer stubbornness alone.

The Hunter glanced back—Aisha and Kodyn still shared a saddle, and their horse was tiring visibly. Kiara rode behind them, and even from this distance, the Hunter could see the worry etched onto her dust-caked face. Aisha had recovered enough that she could hold her head upright, but she was far from fighting shape. The mere effort of sitting in the saddle and matching the horse's rolling gait exhausted her.

Gritting his teeth, the Hunter returned his attention to the path ahead. He had no idea how much farther remained to ride, nor what they'd find when they reached their destination. All he knew was that when they finally drew within sight of their enemy, Aisha would be in no shape to fight—yet fight she would, for that was in her nature.

But what could he do? He hadn't been able to dissuade her from making this arduous trek, so what made him think he'd have a chance of talking her out of leaping into the battle spear-first?

He had no time to consider it further, for in that moment, Siyanda charged up a steep, rocky hill that rose from the riverbank toward a flat-topped peak. The Hunter followed, and as he reached the top, he came in sight of what they had raced all this way for.

The Issai *ekhaya* was nestled in the middle of a secluded hollow that had, like the southern edge of the Unathi River, once been home to a vast waterway. Only this waterway carved far deeper into the earth and had formed a canyon twenty paces across guarded on the west and east by cliff-steep stone walls. It was a suitably defensible position, with only a narrow, winding approach on the northern side and rock-strewn, uneven ground that had once been a riverbed to the south. The *raya* cattle were huddled together at the heart of the camp, with every able-bodied Issai defending them. Some, like Duma and the *unkgaliwe*, wielded weapons of wood and steel, with their woven-vine shields for protection. Others carried hunting bows and arrows. But there were far too few so armed. The rest—men, women, even children—held mattocks, picks, axes, hoes, flails, staves, and any other improvised weapon they could find.

But it was the mass of dark bodies on the clifftops east of the *ekhaya* that drew the Hunter's attention. Easily a hundred of them, clad in a mess of hides, cloth robes, and pelts, carrying spears, sickle-shaped swords, and shields that from afar could have been made of solid wood or dark hides akin to those they wore. Their shouts and ululating cries of battle reverberated across the plains as they flooded toward the narrow pathway that descended into the canyon.

The sight of them shocked him. Instead of the umber or copper hue of the Issai and Ghandians, their skin was a rusty vermillion. He instinctively drew in a breath through his nostrils; could there be an Abiarazi among their ranks? He was too far away to know for certain—the wind was blowing in the opposite direction, carrying his scent toward them—but it didn't matter.

He dug his heels into Elivast's flanks and spurred the horse into a gallop. Elivast might have been tired from running—for what felt like hours—but summoned the strength for one last burst of energy. He passed Siyanda in seconds and barreled toward the horde of warriors ahead of him.

The Hunter let go of the horse's reins and reached for his weapons. Soulhunger slid into his left hand with the familiar eagerness that no longer came from some dissonant voice, but the depths of his own mind.

His right hand closed around the gold-wrought hilt of the Sword of Nasnaz. He felt the needle-prick pain as he slid the scimitar free of its sheath, and the hunger began to rise within him. He did not look at the runes that sprang to life along its curving blade; his gaze fixed on the enemies ahead, at the warriors who would soon taste the wrath of the sword's ancient magic.

In some dim recess of his mind, he hoped Kiara would somehow find a way to keep Aisha, Kodyn, and Siyanda back from the battle. But the thought was fleeting, consumed by the surging bloodlust and the tide of adrenaline that coursed through him at the promise of bloodshed and death.

As he had so many centuries before as Nasnaz the Conqueror, the Hunter howled a furious, wordless battle cry into the bright sky and set his horse charging straight at the enemy.

Chapter Fifty-Four

The Hunter bore down on the horde of vermillion-skinned warriors as fast as Elivast could gallop. Yet it felt far too slow—he hungered to wade into the fray, to bathe in the rivers of his enemies' blood, to revel in the chorus of their screams. Far too much time had passed since he'd been let loose to kill without compunction or hesitation. How he *ached* for the carnage, the chaos, the death!

Another wordless cry ripped from his lips. The sound echoed across the plains and down into the canyon, clashing with the ululating howls of the oncoming horde. Startled, they spun toward him, spears and swords coming about, shields rising.

Time slowed to a crawl and the world narrowed into razor-sharp focus. Everything around him disappeared—the cloudless blue sky, the rippling plains grasses, the rocky cliffs, the distant thunder of horses' hoofbeats from behind him—and in that moment, nothing else existed but him and the enemy drawing ever closer with every steady *thump, thump* of his heart.

He drank in the details of his attackers in an instant. Their shields were made not of interlocking vines like the Issai's, but a thinner, reed-like frond entwined into a tighter weave. Their spears were nearly as long again as their wielders were tall—similar to the lances utilized by Legion cavalry or Nyslian knights, though made from a supple wood that bent and flexed as they moved. Their swords might have once been sickles, a harvester's tool in a land where few crops grew. Every figure the Hunter's eyes settled on was male, powerfully built, and draped with the furs, jaws, manes, and claw-tipped paws of lions. Proud warriors one and all.

Dark eyes locked on him; some going wide, others crinkling in mocking mirth. Spattered laughter rippled through the horde—he saw their barrel chests rising and their bellies convulsing, though he could not hear the sound over the thunder in his ears. Fully half turned away from him, their attention returning to the Issai camp they had come to attack. After all, what had they to fear from a lone rider?

The Hunter bared his teeth in a furious snarl. They would know the true meaning of fear this day.

Closer and closer he drew, until he could see the whites of his enemies' eyes, their teeth shining bright against their skin—skin he saw was merely *painted,* tinted with some strange substance that covered every bit of exposed flesh. Protection against the sun or some superstition believed to imbue them with power to shield them from enemy weapons, he didn't know. Nor did he care. The red staining their forms heralded the rivers of crimson soon to flow.

The spears came up toward him, their razor-sharp heads—nearly the length of his forearm—wobbling at the end of their flexile shafts. Confidence etched the faces of the warriors. A few even appeared amused. His wild ride would end impaled on their polearms, and his fury would be for naught.

Now it was the Hunter's turn to smile. A cruel, cold expression, one that had graced the face of the Hunter of Voramis he had once been. It had not been seen since the day he stood his ground in the *Dolmenrath* in the Advanat Desert and slaughtered the *Mhareb* of Il Seytani in scores.

With one final roar, he pulled his feet from the stirrups, planted his boots on his saddle, and launched himself up as high and far as his powerful legs could propel him. His strength, backed by the speed of Elivast's charge, sent him sailing dozens of paces through the air. Over the upraised spears and the lion's mane-clad heads of the enemy warriors.

He came down in their midst in a blaze of fury and bloodshed. The Sword of Nasnaz struck to the right, Soulhunger slashing left, then he spun and brought the two blades swinging across his body. High and low, forward and backward, stabbing, slicing, thrusting, hacking, and chopping in a terrible explosion of violence. He was a blur of motion, blades weaving a wall of shining, magic-imbued steel around him. Faster and faster, his innate agility and strength augmented by the power of the Sword of Nasnaz, his stamina restored with every life Soulhunger claimed.

Wherever he struck, vermillion-painted warriors died. Howled war cries cut off in agonized screams as Soulhunger devoured their life essence, leaving only husks of flesh to fall to the grass. Terror sprouted on the faces of warriors bred to battle, the crimson light leaking from the Hunter's ensorcelled weapons bathing them in a hideous light and filling them with a fear they could not understand—a fear that sapped their will and stole their courage.

They fought—oh, how they fought! Their spears darted in, sickles slashing for his head, daggers biting at his flesh. More than a little of the blood misting in the air was his own. Yet for every wound they inflicted, Soulhunger claimed *two* lives. For every upraised shield that turned aside a thrust of Soulhunger's ravenous blade, the Sword of Nasnaz hacked through lion furs, hides, woven shields, armor, flesh, and bone. He was a whirlwind of death and fury that could no more be stopped than a thunderstorm or fierce storm winds. Those who stood before him died. Those who turned to flee died. Some banded together in threes and fours to defend against him—they died, too. He was inexorable, the very incarnation of destruction.

All the while, his wordless howls ripped through their ranks, heralding his fury and promising blood. So much blood! Great spurting gouts spraying from slashed throats, sluicing down red-painted bellies, gushing from sheared limbs and necks. The ground beneath the Hunter's boots turned so soft and thick with it he could barely stand.

More than once, he tripped on spilled guts, severed heads, weapons fallen from lifeless hands, and the corpses of his enemies. Yet even on the ground, he did not stop killing. His scimitar carved through ankles unarmored save for bright strings of lion's teeth and calves clad only in the woven armor. He clawed his way atop his fallen enemies and hacked their throats open, drove Soulhunger into their yielding flesh, even tore at them with his teeth. Lost in the battle madness, the blood fury amplified by the Sword of Nasnaz's magic with every swing of the scimitar.

The power was intoxicating. What had started out as a surging rush became a swelling tide, then a thundering roar that drowned out everything else. He was lost in the madness, in the haze of crimson, in the excitement shivering through every fiber of his being. There was no fighting it—it was too powerful—and in truth, he had no desire to resist. *This* was living! This was the reason for which he had been created. Destroyer, reaver, conqueror!

He sprang to his feet, wiping blood from his face, but suddenly he no longer stood in the land of the Issai.

Golden desert, blinding bright on all sides, with his army behind and the host of Tel Khalah before him. Thousands of enemies, tens of thousands, clad in glittering bronze that reflected the blazing sunlight. All-consuming heat that clung to him, soaked through his armor, and set the blood boiling in his veins.

"Nasnaz, Nasnaz!" The cry swelled with every thundering beat of his heart. Fully half of his army remained motionless, awaiting his call to join the battle. They did not stand silent, however. Their voices rang out across the field of combat. They shouted his name. Cheered his victory to come. For there was no doubt in his mind—victory was his.

Already, he could see the men of Tel Khalah on the verge of breaking. Their lines had begun to bow at the center, their right flank slowly buckling beneath the pressure of his onslaught. Their left flank, decimated by his first charge, would not last much longer beneath the withering fire of his archers. Not once he cut through the heart of their army and tore through their ranks with his own two bloody hands.

"Nasnaz, Nasnaz!" The chant reverberated across the Advanat, pounding in his ears, burned through his veins. They called his name. They followed him. He was their conqueror, their general, their king. He would carve for them a kingdom and water the sands in the blood of their enemies.

His eyes fell upon his true *enemy. Tel Khalah, proud and tall, clad in bloodstained armor and swinging a sword dripping crimson. Even surrounded by his chosen elites, it was all he could do to keep on his feet, so thick was the press about him.*

"Tel Khalah!" The shout pierced the din of battle like a hurled spear.

The warrior-king who had defied him and refused to bend the knee turned at the sound of his name. Olive-colored eyes narrowed and white teeth bared in a snarl.

"You are mine!" His arms rose of its own accord; Thanal Eth'Athaur hungered for blood, and Ibad'at Mutlaqa sang its song of death in his ears. "You die this day, and your kingdom with you. As your blood stains the sands, I will erase your name from history. I condemn you to be forever forgotten by—"

Lightning ripped through the Hunter. Agony coursed through every fiber of his being, and his muscles seized up. He toppled forward to crash face-first into a puddle of blood. There he lay, jerking and writhing as the crackling power sizzled up and down his arms, his legs, searing in his brain.

He could not draw breath through the convulsing of his lungs. Darkness washed over him and the day grew as dark as night. Panic clawed at his mind. He could not fall now. Not before he claimed Tel Khalah's head and eviscerated his army. He had to rise, had to return to battle before his own army's courage wavered.

"Hurry!" a voice sounded from afar off, so faint he almost thought he imagined it. A voice at once familiar yet impossible for his agony-numbed mind to recognize. "I can't...hold...much longer!"

A new pain joined the anguish searing through his body. Something hard struck his right hand, nearly shattering his fingers. He felt *Ibad'at Mutlaqa's* hard, leather-wrapped hilt flying from his grasp.

Suddenly, he could breathe. The fist of iron squeezing his chest loosened its grip, and he filled his lungs with fresh air. With air came blood, so much it set him coughing. He curled up on the blood-soaked Advanat sands and tried to recover.

"Hunter?" Another voice, also familiar, one he knew so well.

His heart leaped at the sound, yet his mind could not fully place it. The army of Nasnaz had no women, yet this was unmistakably a woman's voice.

"Hunter?" More urgency now. Worry, too. "Talk to me! Are you still in there?"

He opened his eyes. Bright sun beat down on his face, blinding him. He could barely make out the blurry form of a woman hovering over him. He pushed against the golden sand, only to find crimson-soaked grass beneath his hands.

Then it all came back in a rush of realization. Kiara's face. The Issai lands. The red-painted enemies.

He sucked in a hacking breath. He blinked away the tears—no, he realized, it was blood in his eyes. He tried to wipe his face, but his hand was dripping wet with crimson, too. He spat a mouthful of metallic-tinged spit and rasped out, "Ki...ara?"

Something struck his arm—her fist—and sent a jolt of pain shivering from his shoulder to wrist. "Damn you, Hunter!" Kiara snarled. "You gave me a proper scare for a second."

The Hunter finally managed to wipe his eyes clean enough he could focus on her face. Only then did he register the utter stillness where there should have been the din and clamor of battle.

"What...happened?" he asked, looking around.

"You happened." Kiara's answer, spoken in a tone of grim severity, chilled him to the bone. "You, and that sword."

The Hunter drank in his surroundings. He'd seen death before, but this...this was something else. Corpses lay strewn about him by the dozens, perhaps scores. Many were in pieces or hacked open as if by some giant's cleaver. Guts spilled from torn bellies, blood trickled from severed limbs, and the acrid tang of vomit joined the stench of bowels and bladders loosened in death.

Looking at it, the Hunter could scarcely believe it. *He'd* done this, he knew. Yet it felt as if someone else—some*thing* else—had been in control.

If only it was that simple. If only he could blame his inner demon or Soulhunger. In the Advanat, the night he slaughtered Lord Knight Moradiss and his fellow Cambionari, he'd lost control to the voices in his mind. But the truth then, as now, was that this was *his* doing. *His* bloodlust and battle-rage amplified by the magic of the Sword of Nasnaz.

Ibad'at Mutlaqa. The name came to him again, as crystal clear as it had been the day Khalid al-Waziri—an Abiarazi in human flesh—had first gifted him the scimitar and promised that with it in hand, he would conquer the world.

The Hunter turned and found the blade lying in a pool of blood. He was tempted to leave it where it had fallen—after Kiara kicked it from his hand, and in so doing, severed his connection to the blade's magic—where it couldn't harm anyone else. Yet he knew that he could not. For all its evil, the scimitar *had* to serve a purpose.

It had served today. The corpses around him accounted for no more than a quarter of the enemy force, at most a third. Likely, they had broken and fled from the blood-frenzied monstrosity in human flesh carving through their ranks.

His actions today, sickening and sobering as they might be, had saved the Issai *ekhaya*. He had to cling to that knowledge. If he didn't, if he let the truth of what he'd just done sink home, he might never be able to live with himself.

Chapter Fifty-Five

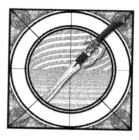

A furious shout shattered the momentary silence that had settled over the field of battle. The Hunter turned to find Siyanda stalking through the blood-soaked, corpse-laden grass toward him. Though her face was pale and her expression stained with horror, anger blazed in her dark eyes and the torrent of Issai words she hurled at him had the sharp edge of invective.

The Hunter didn't have the energy to deal with her; though Soulhunger had restored the strength consumed by *Ibad'at Mutlaqa's* magic, he felt strained, as if his soul had been hammered crystal-thin and was now on the verge of shattering. He turned away from the enraged *nassor* and stooped to collect his fallen scimitar.

"No!" This, Siyanda shouted in Einari. A short-handled spear whistled past the Hunter's head, so close it nearly grazed his cheek, and stabbed into the ground between his outstretched hand and the Sword of Nasnaz.

The Hunter whipped around toward the woman. "What in the fiery hell are you—"

"*Okanele!*" Siyanda hissed, her face contorted in rage, disgust, and a generous measure of fear. She stalked toward him, finger stabbing like a lance at his heart. "Accursed creature of *Inzayo Okubi*, sent to destroy us."

"Destroy?" The Hunter arched an eyebrow. He couldn't fault her for being afraid of him, even disgusted at what he'd done—he felt more than his fair share of revulsion at the moment— but her anger made little sense. "If I was planning to destroy you, why would I have just killed the tribe coming to attack your *ekhaya?*"

Siyanda moved to stand between him and the Sword of Nasnaz, planting her feet and snarling up at him. "This attack, as you call it, was a raid! These were Buhari, not Tefaye. They did not want us; they wanted the raya."

The Hunter's jaw clenched. "And I just stopped them from getting what they wanted." He'd been right about the reason for the attack, which made Siyanda's reaction all the more confusing. "Seems like instead of shouting at me, you ought to be thanking me."

"Thanking you?!" Siyanda's pale face turned apoplectic. "Such are all *alay-alagbara*, doing whatever they see fit and never thinking about the consequences!" She stepped up to the Hunter and, despite him standing nearly a head taller and drenched in the blood of dozens of warriors, she jabbed a finger hard into his armored chest. "You believe you have saved us? What you have done is condemn us to certain death!"

The Hunter opened his mouth to retort, but Siyanda drove on over him.

"The Buhari came to raid, to steal our cattle. That is our way here on the *amathafa*. The strong take from the weak! With our warriors captive, they saw the opportunity to make off with our cattle. They would have taken, but only some of the cattle. Perhaps half the herd. We would

250

have suffered, but the Issai have endured worse hardships before. And when we finally freed the *amaqhawe*, we would have raided them in return and retrieved what is ours. That is how it is, how it always has been among our people."

Siyanda jabbed a finger toward the corpses littering the ground in a wide swath around them. "But now they will be coming for blood. You killed their warriors, and they will kill ours in return. And when they find no warriors, that will not matter. Blood for blood, that, too, is the way of the *amathafa*. Our hunters, our foragers, herders, women, children, the *Umdala*." She shook her fist in his face. "No one is safe once Jumaane hears what was done here this day."

"*Um'zala—*" Aisha spoke up, her tone rational, attempting to placate Siyanda. She was on her knees, Kodyn holding her upright by the arm, but at least she no longer appeared on the verge of collapse.

"And you!" Siyanda rounded on her cousin. "This is *your* fault! You are the one who brought these *alay-alagbara* into our home, yet you did not tell them of our ways." She stalked toward Aisha, who leaned on Kodyn to rise to her feet. "Now I must take the *ekhaya* into hiding. The herd must be protected and we must flee Jumaane's wrath. You have doomed us, *um'zala.*" She sneered the last word like a curse. "It is as I told you before, you are no true Issai. You have become weak like them—" Her angry gesture indicated Kodyn, Kiara, and the Hunter. "—as weak as the child who was taken all those years ag—"

Kodyn's fist whipped out and across, so fast Siyanda did not see the blow coming. His punch caught her on the edge of the jaw and snapped her head around to the side. Her legs buckled beneath her and she sagged, her body *thumping* onto the grass before Aisha.

A shout echoed from the plains behind Aisha. All spun to see one of the *unkgaliwe* racing toward them, her arm raised to hurl her short-handled spear at Kodyn in vengeance for striking her *nassor*. Aisha stepped between them, raising a hand and roared something at the warrior. Whatever she said stopped the warrior from hurling her spear, but could not convince her to lower it. The young woman's eyes locked on Kodyn, blazing with open fury and hostility. Kodyn just stared right back. The young man's anger was far less prominent, but the Hunter knew him well enough to recognize the fury that set his body quivering.

A sharp, barked Issai word echoed from where Siyanda lay on the ground. The *nassor* spat a mouthful of blood and pushed herself to her feet, shaking her head to clear away the disorientating effects of Kodyn's blow—a well-laid blow, the Hunter had to admit.

Siyanda spoke a few terse words in the warrior's direction—the Hunter heard "*ekhaya*" and "*Duma*" and what might have been "*warn*" or "*warning*". The young Issai hesitated, but finally lowered her spear, and with one final glare at Kodyn, spun on her heel and raced off in the direction of the path that wended down into the canyon where the Issai *ekhaya* sheltered.

"*Um'zala—*" Aisha tried again; this time, her tone rang with a faint note of pleading.

Siyanda cut her off with a furious retort in Issai, shaking her head and slashing her hand in the air in a gesture of finality. Her words poured forth far too fast for the Hunter to begin to understand. But Aisha understood clear enough. Her face paled and tightened, and her right hand rose to touch the silver ring piercing her nose.

Her answer had no effect on Siyanda; the *nassor* just turned on her heel and stalked toward the Hunter. She did not address him directly, however. She merely stooped to pluck her spear from the ground, spat on the Sword of Nasnaz, spat again at the Hunter's feet, then stalked off after Ntombi, spine as stiff as the weapon in her hand.

Aisha's left hand rose a fraction as Siyanda marched past her, but little more than a faint flutter before falling quickly back to her side once more. A weight seemed to drag her downward, steal the breath from her lungs. She wobbled and leaned heavily against Kodyn. Kodyn tried to speak to Siyanda in Issai, his tone entreating, but the *nassor* just ignored him and marched past.

In silence, the four of them watched Siyanda stride away from the battlefield. Only once the *nassor* had vanished down the path into the canyon did Kodyn manage to speak.

"Aisha, I-I'm sorry," he stammered. "I know I shouldn't have hit her like that, but the way she was talking to you—"

"No." Aisha turned a weak smile on Kodyn. "I'm glad you did. Had I the strength, I would have done it myself."

"Still." Kodyn's face colored, and he hung his head. "What just happened—"

"Hush, Kodyn." Aisha gripped the young man's shoulders, pulled herself upright. "As I told you, I do not understand what happened to the cousin I knew and loved so many years ago, do not know what has changed her into this..." Her lips twisted as if at a bitter taste. "...person I don't recognize. But since my return, I've felt her watching me, as if waiting for me to fail, to give her proof that I am no longer Issai. This is just the excuse she's using."

"Aisha," the Hunter said, moving toward the young woman—leaving the Sword of Nasnaz lying on the ground behind him. "For what it's worth, I'm sorry. Had I known—"

"Things might have turned out different here," Aisha said, shaking her head, "but in the end, Siyanda would have found something else that proves her hatred for me right." Pain shone in her eyes, etched deep lines into her face. "I get the feeling that banishing me from the tribe is what she's wanted all along."

"Wait, what?" The Hunter frowned. "She just *banished* you? From your own people?"

"She is the *nassor*," Aisha replied simply. "It is her right." She touched her piercing again. "She could have demanded these from me, if she'd wanted. But she wanted me to wear them, so I would remember who I had once been, and the cost of what I did here."

"Piss on that!" The Hunter's fists clenched. "You said that the banished are sent to join the Tefaye, but right now, the Tefaye are half-mad flesh-eaters who will kill and devour you on sight. Not a bloody chance I'm letting that happen."

"I have no intention of joining the Tefaye," Aisha said, her jaw tightening. "I would rather return to Praamis than remain here, cast out from my people, cut off from my family, my sister."

"So what, then?" Kodyn asked, narrowing his eyes. "You said it yourself, it's her right as the *nassor.*"

"She is the *nassor* now. But only so long as my mother, the true *nassor* is held captive." Aisha lifted her head, standing a little taller. "So that is what I must do. I must free the *amaqhawe* and restore the strength of the Issai. My actions will prove to my mother—and to Siyanda—what I already know: that I am worthy to be Issai. And in so doing, I will regain my place among my people."

The Hunter didn't for one second doubt she would. "Then let's get going." He forced a smile. "If we hurry, we could be back at the Consortium camp before dark—just in time to attack."

Kodyn shot a worried glance at Aisha.

"I will be fine, Kodyn," Aisha said in a patient tone. "Already, I can feel my strength returning as the power of the *Kish'aa* flows through me."

The Hunter made a mental note of that. It was good to know that her *Umoyahlebe* powers could restore her just as Soulhunger's magic restored him.

"And there are plenty of *Kish'aa* around to sustain me." Aisha gestured to the corpses littered around them. "Though I might find it hard to restrain their desire to be avenged against their killer." Her attempt at a joke fell terribly flat. When not even Kodyn grinned or chuckled, her smile faded and was replaced by a curious expression. "There are fewer than I'd expect from so many dead." She looked to the Hunter. "Your *Im'tasi* dagger, it is true, then, that it consumes the spirits of its victims?"

The Hunter looked down at Soulhunger, still gripped in his crimson-stained left hand. The pommel and crossguard were covered in drying blood, which would soon turn to a rusty crust, but the blade was clean as if freshly forged and oiled.

"The Serenii call it the 'life force'," he said, lifting his gaze to meet hers once more, "but you could call it their spirit, or their soul. It sends the energy to Kharna, sustaining him in his battle against the Devourer of Worlds." Hailen and Evren had explained that much to them.

Aisha's expression grew grim. "That explains it." She gestured vaguely toward the air above his head. "I count forty-three dead, but only twenty-seven *Kish'aa*."

The Hunter felt a faint pressure forming around him, followed by a gentle tug in Aisha's direction. For a moment, her eyes glowed blue-white and a similar light shone through her clothing and armor concealing the *Dy'nashia* pendant. As the light faded, her expression grew strained but she stood straighter, on her own. Gone was the fatigue that had weighed her down. The burden on her heart remained—Siyanda's words and banishment could not be easily ignored—but at least her body was fortified. The Hunter had no idea how much power could be unleashed from the energy of twenty-seven warriors—a few dancing sparks, or a blast of lightning as powerful as the one that had killed the slashwyrm.

And, he realized, stopped him in his tracks. A single glance at the bodies surrounding him proved correct the thought that flitted through his mind. Not one of them bore the same scorch marks that had been so plentiful on the dead slashwyrm. All of her expended power had been aimed at him. She'd used her strength to momentarily incapacitate him, allowing Kiara to break his connection to the Sword of Nasnaz.

He turned to Kiara, raising a questioning eyebrow. "Was that your idea?" he asked.

"Was what my idea?" She cocked her head.

"Having Aisha hit me with her *Kish'aa* power."

"Oh. Yes." Kiara shrugged, as nonchalant as if he'd just asked her if the sky was, indeed, blue. "The Buhari were running, and I figured, why risk ourselves when there was a simple way to keep you from doing anything you'd regret?"

The Hunter glanced at Aisha. She, at least, had the good grace to appear slightly embarrassed. She quickly turned away and set about helping Kodyn to gather their horses.

"Truth is, it's bloody genius." He shook his head. "Much as I wish there was a better way, chances are, it's probably the best way you could have handled it." He'd been too far gone in his bloodlust, battle-frenzy, and memories that he'd have slaughtered them without pause or even recognizing who he was hacking to pieces.

Kiara moved to gather up the Sword of Nasnaz, holding it out to him by the crossguard so as to keep her hand well away from whatever mechanism drew blood to activate its magic. "It makes sense now," she said in a low voice, for his ears only. "What you told me about fearing becoming a monster."

The Hunter's shoulders knotted. Dread coiled in his belly. She had seen the worst possible side of him—the curse he'd inherited from his Abiarazi father—what would she think? Would she fear him now that she knew the truth? Would she no longer be capable of loving a creature capable of—

"I stand by what I said." Her eyes fixed on his, filled with a confidence—in him—he did not feel at that moment. "You're stronger than any magic. You can fight it. *We* can fight it."

The Hunter wanted to believe her, truly he did. Yet she hadn't felt the terrifying, awe-inspiring, breathtaking rush of power, the feeling of invulnerability as he waded through his enemies, spilled rivers of blood, basked in the screams of agony. She did not understand the bloodlust that burned within him—always beneath the surface, rarely let out, yet eternally ravenous and forever present.

If that monster in his soul broke its chains—or, worse, he allowed it to slip free—it would unleash upon Einan a terrible death and destruction unlike anything seen for centuries, not since the days he strode the earth as Nasnaz the Great and spilled rivers of blood to bring all the desert kingdoms under his heel.

Chapter Fifty-Six

A cloud hung over the plains as the Hunter, Kiara, Kodyn, and Aisha rode away from the field of carnage. Rain threatened, the sky dark grey and a storm loomed ominously on the horizon, yet the true darkness came from the enormous birds circling lower and lower toward the corpses strewn on the battlefield. The Hunter had seen them before, after the Tefaye attack on the Issai camp. He'd thought them crows at the time; now, he could see the truth of them. Birds half again as tall as he was, with a wingspan nearly twice his height, with viciously sharp beaks and taloned feet well-suited for ripping at flesh.

"The *makalala* will feast well," Aisha said, turning her back on the birds and their intended meal. Her face remained somber, but her eyes never strayed once to the bodies littering the blood-soaked grass. No doubt her mind was consumed with whatever Siyanda had snarled in the same breath as she pronounced banishment from the Issai.

The Hunter was tempted to ask Kodyn—he'd clearly understood Siyanda's tirade, no doubt attempted to speak up in Aisha's defense—but decided against it for the moment. The young Praamian's attention was focused entirely on Aisha. He watched her from the corners of his eyes, trying to be mindful of her without the appearance of hovering. His care for her was evident, as was the fact that he hurt in sympathy for the pain tearing at her.

As they passed the trail that descended into the canyon, Aisha cast a longing, lingering glance toward the *ekhaya* below. Already, the Issai were breaking camp and herding the cattle southward, farther into the ravine along the rocky-bottomed, dried-up riverbed. Siyanda hadn't said where she would go. Judging by the deepening slump of her shoulders, Aisha had no idea how to find them. She'd crossed half a continent to reach her people. Now, she was cast out and rejected by her own cousin. A particularly cruel twist of fate, one that would have given the Hunter good cause to hate the gods had they truly existed.

He wished he could do something to help, but he doubted Aisha wanted anything to do with him at the moment. After all, his actions here had been the final straw. Never mind that Siyanda hadn't thought to mention that their attackers were only *raiding* and not intent on slaughtering the Issai. As Aisha had said, her cousin had merely wanted an excuse, and the Hunter had given it to her.

Their journey toward the Unathi River and through the canyon passed in fraught silence. The Hunter rode in the lead, letting the horses dictate the pace. They had been ridden hard and only given a short time to rest and crop the plains grass. Even the usually restive Ash and indefatigable Nayaga moved more slowly, burdened by exhaustion.

Fortunately, they had not far to ride. In truth, the river ran northeast for only a league or so before reaching the waterfall that concealed the entrance to *Uhumi Wolandle*. The pool at the base of the falls was once again crystal clear, no trace of the Hunter's blood remaining. The memory of the pain, too, was erased. Only the fatigue lingered. A tiredness not of body—Soulhunger's magic had seen to that—but of his spirit. *Ibad'at Mutlaqa,* the famed Sword of Nasnaz, devoured bits and pieces of his soul that were not easily nor quickly restored.

The Hunter reined in Elivast just before reaching the waterfall. From his saddle, he studied the cliff wall ascending toward the top of the falls. The rocks near the ground were slick with damp and covered in a thin coat of slimy moss. Not easy climbing, even for him. Had he been able to leave the rope secured to a tree at the top, he might have entertained this ascent. He could certainly *try* to climb this way, slippery rocks or not, but he risked falling. The time he'd need to expend healing himself would delay their return to the Consortium camp further. Plus, he'd arrive drained in body as well as spirit.

Without a word, he rode on up the path that led toward the cave behind the waterfall. The roar of the falling water enveloped him in a strange cacophonic bubble. For a few moments, while he dismounted and removed Elivast's tack, he had no need to think, to dwell on what had happened or to worry over what the future held. He merely existed amidst that swirling rush of noise that drowned out all conscious thought. He moved by rote, content to repeat the exact same motions he'd gone through the last time they'd come this way.

Slowly, as they worked their way through the underground network of tunnels carved into the rock by water and the *intambelu* vines, the waterfall's roar faded and the Hunter was once again confronted by harsh reality.

He stopped abruptly and turned back to the three people moving through the vine-lit darkness behind him.

"Look, I've just got to say this." He *hated* the way he felt—guilty, ashamed, as if he'd somehow failed—and needed to be rid of the weight that had settled over him. "I know it's my fault you're here. You came all this way to help your people, and now because of me, you have no people. I understand if you need to be angry at me, even hate me. But I need you to know that I didn't intend this. I really *was* attempting to do right by your people."

The look on Aisha's face only added to his burden. She was in so much pain, pain he'd caused.

"I knew you were going to ride into that battle," he rushed on, glad for the darkness to hide the rush of heat rising to his cheeks. "Exhausted as you were, you were going to fight for your people anyway. I took what I thought was a calculated risk to keep you out of harm's way while also fulfilling the promise I made to help you." His eyes strayed toward Kiara, who stood silently watching him from the rear of their group. "I've been told I tend to act first, think later"—she loved reminding him of that one—"but this time, it's you who is paying the price. I know it can't make up for what's happened, but anything I can do to rectify the situation, I will. Even if that means that once your mother and the rest of your people are freed, we need to leave Issai land, so be it. Just tell me what you need, how you want me to proceed, and I will heed. I'll do whatever I can not to mess things up for you again or make what's already bad worse."

The flow of words dried up, and he found himself suddenly uncertain what to say. In truth, little could be said that would fix what was broken. But he despised the notion of doing nothing, especially to redress some problem he'd caused with someone who—to his great surprise—he found he'd come to quite like, even admire. For all her youth, Aisha had impressed him many times over.

The silence stretched on for painfully long seconds before Aisha spoke. Yet when she did, her voice rang off the stone surrounding them, echoing with surprising certainty.

"I don't hate you at all." Her eyes locked on his. "You did exactly what you promised you'd do. You saved my people. You rode head-first into battle, charged an enemy that outnumbered you nearly a hundred to one, all because you believed that doing so would save me and the people I love from harm." She stepped up toward him, looked him square in the face. "Nor do I blame you for my current circumstances. That is Siyanda's fault as much as my own."

"More, I'd say," Kodyn muttered, his face twisted into a scowl. "She could have bloody explained who was attacking and what the rules of engagement were."

"Yes." Aisha turned to face the young man, reaching out to lay a hand on his arm. "And the time will come when I face my cousin and demand an answer for why she hates me so." The pain etched into her face deepened, revealing just how profoundly this invisible wound cut. "But until then, I have no time for hate or anger." She turned back to the Hunter, and through her sorrow shone a glimmer of determination. "Nor time for self-pity or wallowing in my own misery."

Her shoulders rose and she stood straighter, head lifting. "The *ekhaya* is safe. Siyanda will take them someplace even the Buhari won't find them. Once we get my mother and the rest of the *amaqhawe,* they will know where to go. Tonight, we restore the Issai to full strength and tear out the heart of the *Gcinue'eleku awandile.*" She shook a clenched fist before her face. "We will let nothing—not *Nsanga,* not the Consortium, not even this Order of Mithridas—stop us. We have no need of Siyanda. We will do this on our own, because together, we're bloody unstoppable."

"Damned right!" Kodyn beamed, clapping Aisha on the shoulder.

Kiara smiled and nodded. She said nothing, but the light of the *intambelu* couldn't shine as bright as the pride glowing in her eyes.

The Hunter bared his teeth in a snarl. "May the gods have pity on the bastards who stand against us, for we will have none."

* * *

The sun had dropped perilously low toward the western horizon by the time their small group approached the hilltop where they had left Tarek. They saw no sign of the young Elivasti—no hint of their packs, not even tamped-down grass where they'd slept on the ground. Before the Hunter could worry overmuch, however, a low, quiet whistle cut through the dense forest to the west.

Twenty paces away from where they'd made camp the previous night, they found Tarek sitting in the branches of a gnarled, vine-covered tree. In truth, they never would have *found* the young man had he not swung down to dangle from his legs and waved his hands to get their attention. The vines winding through the trees formed a knotted web so thick his dull-colored clothing all but vanished in the tangle.

Tarek looked over the Hunter's blood-soaked armor and the muddy-but-unwounded state of the other three, and merely raised an eyebrow. "Siyanda?"

"Back at the Issai camp," Kodyn answered, eyes darting to Aisha. "Making sure the herd is safe."

Tarek's face tightened and he ran a dirt-speckled hand along one sparsely-bearded cheek. "Five of us, then?" He looked to the Hunter. "Think your plan will still work?"

The Hunter opened his mouth to respond but couldn't. He'd spent the last hour struggling beneath his armor, which had grown ever-more sodden with the weight of the muck and mire adding to the dried blood encrusting him from head to toe. The heat and humidity of the day was far worse, too. He found it surprisingly difficult to draw breath.

"One moment," he said, trying to hide the gasp from his voice. "Water first." He drained half his canteen's contents, paused to draw breath, then drained the other half.

As he drank, Siyanda's scornful words echoed in his mind. *"Should you blunder foolishly into quicksand, blind and clueless as you alay-alagbara are, the weight will drag you under. Your sweat, too, will drain your bodies of much-needed water, withering you like kola fruit under the noon sun."*

He'd encountered no quicksand, but he could easily imagine an enormous serpent coiling around his body and wringing all the water out of his body. Much as he wanted to remove the armor, however, he knew he could not. Given what he was about to face, he needed all the protection he could get. *Especially* if he intended to keep the Sword of Nasnaz sheathed and face his foes with only the mundane watered steel blade.

"Better." Though he still felt the drag on his limbs and the weight on his chest that made drawing a full breath difficult, he stood straighter, filled his voice with confidence. "Anything change in the camp while we were gone? Anyone come or go?"

Tarek shook his head. "A few guard changes, but that's it." His youthful face—so much like Hailen's it still occasionally sent a pang of homesickness through the Hunter's heart—tugged down into a frown. "The captives have been working all day without rest, though. A bit of water and a few bites of food, nothing else. Chances are, they'll be too tired to fight."

"Not a bloody chance!" Aisha's voice held not a shred of doubt. "An *amaqhawai* can run for days on nothing more than a few mouthfuls of seeds and grasses." She gripped her short-handled spear in a white-knuckled fist. "Unless they are dead, they will fight."

Tarek inclined his head. "Glad to hear it." He looked back to the Hunter. "I spent an hour or two earlier collecting enough dried sticks to get at least a small fire burning. Throw some damp and green wood onto it, and it'll create a fierce, acrid smoke that is certain to draw their attention."

"Good man." The Hunter clapped the Elivasti on the shoulder. Tarek tried to keep a straight face, but he couldn't fully hide a pleased smile. "Between your fire and Kodyn's tree, we've got enough to drag their attention to the south. Meaning they won't be watching when Kiara slips over the wall and attacks them from the west."

"West?" Kiara raised her eyebrow. "By the dig?"

The Hunter nodded. "Without Siyanda, we've got to change the plan." He'd given it a great deal of thought on the climb out of *Uhumi Wolandle* and their trek across the marshes. "And *because* of her, I know how we can strike hard enough from all sides to keep the Consortium off-balance while still getting to the captives."

Four pairs of eyes stared at him in expectation.

"Because of her?" Aisha asked.

The Hunter grinned. "She didn't know how right she was when she asked if I intended to risk the *Nsanga's* teeth once more."

Kiara understood the meaning of his words first. Her eyes widened a fraction, and she gave him the sharp "you're not *actually* this insane" look only she could muster. Aisha, Tarek, and Kodyn were only a half-second behind. Tarek sucked in a breath, Kodyn blinked, and Aisha demanded, "Are you mad? You still plan to go through the slashwyrms?"

"I do." The Hunter met her gaze and those of his companions levelly. "And you're coming with me."

Chapter Fifty-Seven

If Aisha, Kodyn, and Tarek had been surprised by the Hunter's first declaration, this last left them utterly speechless. The three of them stared at him as if he'd lost his mind. Kiara just gave him that sharp look of hers. After all, *she* had been the one to suggest he still attempt to navigate the slashwyrm territory. The addition of Aisha gave her visible pause, but she didn't raise protest. Yet. She knew him well enough to know he'd *never* suggest anything with such potential for danger—not to himself, but to Aisha—without good reason.

The Hunter continued quickly. "You saw them for yourself," he told Aisha. "They're fierce but move slowly. More than that, they tend to sleep during the day. If we go now, while there's still light out, before they wake up at night, we've got a bloody good chance of getting past them if we run enough."

He saw the look on Aisha's face shift slightly from utterly against the idea to contemplating it. Kodyn's expression, however, grew utterly stubborn.

The Hunter persisted before the young man could give voice to the protest forming on his lips. All he needed was for *Aisha* to be on board with his plan; Kodyn wouldn't argue if she believed it the right course of action, danger or no.

"If, as I suspect, the north wall of the camp has been left open to allow—even encourage—the captives to attempt escape, there will be plenty of *Kish'aa* all over that marshland. Many of them hungering for vengeance against the *Nsanga* that killed them. You will have access to power to blast aside any slashwyrms that get in our path with plenty to spare. By the time we finally reach the camp and start freeing your family, you will be so full of the *Kish'aa* that the Consortium will have no hope of standing in your way. And I'll be there to watch your back and keep the whoresons off you while you free your mother, the *amaqhawe,* and anyone else who can fight."

The Hunter was watching Aisha carefully, and saw the moment she realized the merit of this adjustment to his plan. Without Siyanda, she would have entered the camp on her own. She could more than handle herself, but no plan was without risk, especially one that involved sneaking past chained captives and whip-wielding slavers wary for any hint of dissent, defiance, or escape. There were too many unknown variables. She'd be in danger the moment she attempted to climb the wall. Worse, she'd be alone.

For all the perils of the Hunter's plan—chief among them, the bloody slashwyrms—she would not be alone. She'd have *him* fighting at her side. It wasn't arrogance to say that having the Hunter to watch her back went a long way toward mitigating any risk. The battlefield he'd just walked away from hours earlier proved just what he was capable of.

"We move quick and don't stop," the Hunter said, his voice ringing with confidence. "All we need to do is get past them and we've got a straight path to the camp."

"Through marshlands." Uncertainty shone on Aisha's face, echoed in her voice. "Kind of hard to move fast through waist-deep mud."

"If you don't think you can do it..." The Hunter didn't need to finish that sentence.

Aisha bristled. "It's not *me* I'm worried about." Her voice was curt, a sharp glare in her eyes. "You're carrying a lot of extra weight with all that armor. We hit quicksand—"

The Hunter gave a careless shrug. "We'll be careful not to."

"Aisha, tell me you're not actually considering this!" Kodyn interjected. He came to stand between the Hunter and Aisha, turning to face the young woman he'd followed halfway across Einan. "Don't get me wrong, *if* you can actually get through, it's a damned good plan. But that's a big if, Aisha!"

"I know." Aisha nodded. "But tell me this, Kodyn: what would your mother do if she were here? What would Ria do?"

The Hunter couldn't see Kodyn's face, but he heard the young man's teeth *click* shut. He let out a long breath and shook his head. "Damn it!"

A grin blossomed on Aisha's face—she'd clearly won that little debate—and she rested a hand on his shoulder. "Besides, if I'm to convince my mother I'm worthy to be an Issai once more, running through *Nsanga* territory is certainly proof I have the courage of an *amaqhawai*." Her smile broadened. "Even if the thought of facing those scaly lizards again is bloody terrifying."

"Courage is not the absence of fear," Kiara said, quoting the ages-old maxim. With a slight adaptation of her own, of course. "Courage is staring that icy bastard straight in the face and kicking it in the bollocks."

* * *

The Hunter and Aisha departed a quarter-hour later. The Hunter delayed only long enough to run the other three through their part of the plan, and to leave the Sword of Nasnaz with the rest of his gear. His pack already contained *one* ancient relic—the Swordsman's twin iron blades, wrapped in thick cloth beneath his clothing—and Tarek had done an admirable job of hiding it beneath a dense screen of woven branches and vines to prevent any Consortium patrols from spotting it.

Besides, after what the Hunter had done to the Buhari, he felt better knowing the scimitar was safely out of his reach. He couldn't risk inadvertently drawing it while carving his way through the Consortium camp. They'd come to *save* Aisha's people and free the other captives, not put them in further danger when the sword's magic drove him blood-mad.

He did take a moment to slip a few of Graeme's alchemical tricks out of his cloak's hidden pockets. They'd come in handy to cause confusion among the slavers' camp.

Kodyn and Aisha exchanged a quick, tender, and somewhat awkward embrace. Neither seemed to know how to say goodbye without actually *saying* it in a way that felt their final farewell. Though the Hunter would do his damnedest to see the two reunited, given the danger ahead, it wasn't beyond the realm of possibility that they could suffer casualties.

Kiara's goodbye, however, was more scolding than tender. "You know it's utterly unfair that *you* get to see the slashwyrms up close again, right?" She jabbed a finger into his armored chest. "You're not the one who's read up on them, or who has dedicated themselves to making a study of creatures like them."

The Hunter deflected her next jab. "I'd say you've gotten up close and personal with one too many impossible-yet-somehow-existing beasts for the time being." He jabbed her back, right in the spot where her leather armor protected her belly.

Kiara scowled and pretended to sulk, folding her arms over her chest. The pretense didn't last long. When the Hunter bent to kiss her, she returned it with ardor, wrapping her arms around his neck to hold him close.

"Don't you dare get eaten!" she whispered into his ear. "You do, I'll carve every one of those beasts open until I find the little digested bits and pieces of you."

With that pleasant visual in his mind, the Hunter had joined Aisha in trekking through the marshes in the same direction they'd gone the previous night. Neither of them spoke; the anticipation of what lay ahead weighed on both their minds. For all his bravado and confident talk, the Hunter was far from eager to come face to face with the slashwyrms again. His watered steel sword hadn't penetrated their scales, and he doubted Soulhunger would fare much better. That left him entirely dependent on his speed and agility to evade the beasts. And Aisha's *Umoyahlebe* powers, which had already saved him from being *Nsanga*-food the night before.

He didn't know what burden rested heaviest on Aisha—the banishment from her tribe, her cousin's enmity, her desire to be avenged against the Consortium who had torn her from her people years earlier, or apprehension over the battle to come—but she seemed in a far from talkative mood. That suited him just fine. Better they focus on making steady progress toward the spot where they'd nearly been devoured by a giant lizard monster.

They moved as quickly and quietly as they could. The sun was fast descending toward the horizon—they had at most an hour before nightfall—which meant the slashwyrms would soon be waking up from their daytime slumber and on the prowl for food. The Hunter fully intended to be well out of their reach and hidden in the marshes north of the Consortium camp before sunset.

But they hadn't covered half the ground to their destination when Aisha let out a hiss and gestured for the Hunter to slow. He didn't need her pointing finger to see what had caused her alarm: bootprints in the mud. The tracks headed in the same direction they were.

The Hunter shot Aisha a questioning glance, tilting his head as if to ask, "What do you suggest we do?" In response, she just shrugged and gestured to the way ahead. The Hunter nodded. They couldn't turn back now, not if they intended the attack to happen tonight.

They advanced cautiously, moving slower, ears pricked up for any signs of human life. The bootprints weren't easy to spot—whoever had left them was picking through the marshes and wading across pools—but the Hunter soon discovered that he had no need to search for them. The tracks were undoubtedly heading the same way they were.

Sure enough, a quarter-hour later, the sound of voices reached the Hunter's keen ears. The stink of decay and rot that hung thick in the marshes drowned out the scents of the humans ahead, but the Hunter had little doubt what he'd find when finally he drew abreast of his quarry.

The voices grew louder, until he could make out what was being said. "—a bloody chance this was one of them that did it," said a man, his voice thick with the accent of the Twelve Kingdoms. "The bite marks are theirs, but this?"

"Aye," came another voice, though oddly muffled and nasal. "Unless the scaly buggers truly can do as the legends say and shoot fire from their arses."

"That looks like no fire to me." The third man's voice reminded the Hunter of Darrilon and Rassek, the two Vothmoti trail guides who'd joined him on his trek through the Empty Mountains in search of Enarium. "But it very much looks like a bull I once saw killed by a thunderclap."

Through a gap in the trees, the Hunter spotted the talking men. All three wore the armor and greatknives marking them as belonging to the Vassalage Consortium. Two were crouched over the remains of the slashwyrm Aisha had killed the previous night—or what remained of it. Something with equally massive teeth and sharp claws had torn the carcass open and feasted on the soft flesh and entrails beneath the scales. Flies the size of the Hunter's finger buzzed in a cacophony around and settled in a thick black cloud atop the eviscerated beast. The third slaver stood a few paces back from his crouching companions, holding one hand pinching his nose and the other covering his mouth.

The Hunter's eyes widened. Even in the gloom of the encroaching evening, he knew that man. He'd seen those distinctly Voramian features—pale skin, blond hair, and beard cropped close to his cheeks in the fashion popular among the nobility of Voramis—before. They had leered down at him from atop horseback on the road leading away from Zamani Falls.

Thrax, Gwala called him, the Hunter remembered.

His eyes darted to one of the two men crouching over the dead slashwyrm. His skin was lighter than the other, tinted more Vothmoti gold than the sepia that marked his companion as a man of Al Hani. The Vothmoti, the Hunter knew, too. Ahmoud, another of Gwala's companions.

The Hunter's pulse quickened. Anger burned in his belly, but he made no attempt to quell it. His loathing for the Vassalage Consortium had been born the day he first met these two men among those carting the villagers of Nkedi along the isolated dirt path through the Kgabu Plains. At the time, there'd been no doubt in his mind that they would have attempted to take him and his "wife" captive had they believed they could do so without difficulty. Now, here they were, deep in Issai lands, guarding the slaves they had taken from not just Aisha's tribe, but from Keeper-only-knew which other tribes in the region, or from beyond the borders of Imperial Khafra.

He turned to Aisha, found her staring at the three slavers. Her spine was rigid, her jaw clenched, and her fingers whitening on the shaft of her short-handled spear.

The Hunter nudged her gently to draw her attention. With a fierce grin, he drew a pair of throwing knives and held a finger to his lips. She needed no further encouragement nor convincing. The blue-white fire blazing in her eyes made her feelings on the matter plain.

Her vengeance against the Vassalage Consortium began here and now.

Chapter Fifty-Eight

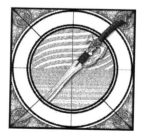

Thrax died without a sound. The Hunter's throwing knife caught the Voramian in the side of the neck, severing his windpipe and jugular vein instantly. His entire body went rigid for a moment, then he toppled sideways to lie gagging and wheezing on the ground, legs jerking as he tried in vain to draw breath.

The man of Al Hani fell a half-heartbeat later as Aisha's short-handled spear, backed by the force of her rage and the power of the *Kish'aa,* hurtled across the space separating them to punch through his armor and the flesh beneath. He staggered sideways and collapsed face-first onto the rotting slashwyrm carcass. His fall stirred up a swarm of black flies, who attacked and set about feasting on him even before his twitching stilled and the dark heart's blood finished gushing from his side.

Fortune turned against the Hunter, however. Ahmoud, startled by his companions' sudden collapse, abruptly straightened from his crouch. The Hunter's second throwing dagger took the Vothmoti not in the throat as intended, but in the meat of the thigh. Ahmoud let out a strangled cry of pain and fumbled for the greatknife hanging at his belt.

The Hunter had no time to reach for a third throwing knife. Instead, he sprang from the bushes and sprinted toward the slaver at a dead run. Ahmoud's dark eyes flew wide, his mouth opened, and he sucked in a great breath. The Hunter's heart sprang into his throat. Whether the man cried out in pain or attempted to shout a warning, there was a chance those within the Consortium camp would hear. Within moments, the forest could be crawling with more slavers, and the Hunter would be forced to either retrace his steps or pick off his enemies in groups.

The Hunter could do it—there was no way the Consortium slavers had the skills to take him down under cover of the dense forest, even fighting in packs of five or ten—but his plan to launch a surprise attack against the camp would be shattered. He'd be forced to fight a foe *prepared* for battle. Things would go far worse for his companions if that happened. There were far too few of them to believe they could triumph over an entrenched enemy on full alert.

A dark blur whistled past the Hunter's shoulder and slammed into Ahmoud's throat. Aisha's dirk struck pommel-first and bounced off without doing any real damage, but the impact was enough to startle the man and knock the wind from his lungs. In the time it took him to draw another breath, the Hunter was upon him. Ahmoud never managed to clear his greatknife from its sheath before the Hunter's fist slammed straight into his face. The Vothmoti's head snapped backward with such violent force his neck gave an audible *crack* and he sagged like a pile of horse droppings.

The Hunter stared down at the three bodies, heart hammering in his throat. *Damn!* He shook his head. *Bloody close call.*

The rustling of branches came from behind him, and a moment later, Aisha moved to stand beside him. "Three down," she snarled, her voice low and angry.

The Hunter nodded. "Good throws." He stooped to retrieve her dirk from the mud where it had fallen. Even if her throw hadn't ended the man, it had been perfectly timed.

While she worked her spear loose from the third slaver's body, the Hunter retrieved his throwing knives from Ahmoud's leg and Thrax's throat. He made sure to clean both blades on the fallen men's trousers. Aisha's dirk, too.

Aisha wrestled with her weapon, cursing to herself in Einari and her own tongue. So invested was she in the effort that, when bone *cracked* and the spear suddenly pulled free, she stumbled and nearly fell to her rear in the muck. Reflex and agility spared her from that particular indignity, and she managed to recover in time to keep her feet. The Hunter made no comment, merely held out the dirk to her. She took it with a nod of thanks and sheathed the clean blade.

"We leave them like this?" she asked, indicating the newly made corpses around the slashwyrm carcass with the bloody head of her spear.

The Hunter considered. He had no way of knowing if these were the *only* three sent out to patrol the area. Tarek must have somehow missed them while he was gathering dry wood for the fire. Were it dark, he could merely leave them as a feast for the slashwyrms. But he couldn't risk their bodies being discovered in the time it took him and Aisha to reach the northern side of the slavers' camp.

He shook his head. "We hide them." A thought struck him as his gaze fell on the slashwyrm carcass. "Someplace no one will ever look."

It took him and Aisha a matter of minutes to drag the corpses into the marsh behind the dead monstrosity and tuck them beneath the trees that the dying slashwyrm had toppled. They would only be found if searchers came upon them directly, but the Hunter was gambling that the dead, half-eaten corpse of a giant lizard monster would keep anyone else who stumbled on the scene occupied. At least long enough for the Hunter and Aisha to get into place for their attack on the camp. By midnight, he intended to make certain not a single slaver within the walls remained alive to come hunting the dead trio.

"You absorb their spirits?" the Hunter asked Aisha once they had finished hiding the bodies. He'd remembered her words from earlier regarding the spirits of the fallen Buhari warriors—or their *absence* in the case of any killed by Soulhunger—and intentionally kept his dagger sheathed.

She frowned. "They're not exactly compliant," she said, her eyes going distant for a moment. "It will take some effort to keep them controlled and compel them to my will, but I believe I can manage." Her jaw muscles clenched and her fingers flexed around the hilt of her spear. But only for a few seconds. Her gaze once more focused on him, her shoulders relaxed, and she nodded. "I've got them in hand."

Myriad questions flitted through the Hunter's mind—how, exactly, did one understand a spirit's wishes, and force compliance should they prove unwilling—but he pushed them aside. Now wasn't the time to interrogate Aisha on the workings of her *Umoyahlebe* gifts. All that mattered now was that she felt certain she could wield the energy gathered from the life forces of the three slavers. She'd need all the power available to her in the battle to come.

Dark had fully fallen by the time they set off again, heading deeper into the marshes—and into slashwyrm territory. The Hunter recalled all too vividly the sounds of the *second* lizard monster crashing through the trees the previous night. It hadn't been more than a few hundred paces off, which had prompted him and Kiara to flee in a hurry. Every step led him closer toward the gaping maw and razor-sharp teeth of that slashwyrm and every other lurking within the marshes.

He tried to recall anything that might give them some way of detecting—and thereby evading—the slashwyrms. So muddy was the water the Hunter hadn't seen the creature's scaly body until it broke the surface. Nor had there been any sounds or hints of movement in the marsh water, not so much as a ripple of its enormous tail. It had merely sprung up from the mud as if appearing by magic.

That, in and of itself, did tell the Hunter something. For all their bulk, the slashwyrms liked to hide in the mud and muck—to escape the heat of the day, to startle prey, or perhaps both. That meant all he and Aisha had to do was stick to the high ground and evade any body of water that appeared large and deep enough to hide a slashwyrm's massive bulk.

He shared his thoughts with Aisha—albeit quietly, so as not to draw the attention of any slashwyrms that might happen to be awake before sunset—and she nodded understanding. "Stick to the high ground, got it."

That proved easier said than done, however. The farther north into slashwyrm territory they went, the waterier the marsh grew. Soon, there *was* no high ground, and they were forced to wade up to their ankles through thick, fibrous reeds that stubbornly grew along the banks of a shallow pond so as to avoid deeper pockets of water.

The shadows of night thickened, and the pale light of the moon and stars failed to fully drive back the darkness. The Hunter had to rely on his keen ears to detect even the faintest sound that could hint at danger, his nostrils sniffing the air in search of the reptilian odor warning that a slashwyrm was nearby. The absence of peril only further frayed his nerves. Every muscle in his body felt tense in expectation of an attack that would not come. Like the breathless moment before the battle, the dread of the unknown all around him had him on a knife's edge.

Minutes passed, and still no sign of slashwyrms. The Hunter glanced skyward. The sun was invisible behind the dense canopy, but he suspected it had already dipped dangerously low below the forest line. Sunset wasn't afar off, and by his reckoning, they still had a quarter-league to go before they reached their destination. No telling how many slashwyrms would soon be stirring from their daytime slumber and prowling in search of food—namely, him and Aisha.

Why the fiery hell did I think this was a good idea? He cursed himself. *I could have just climbed over the wall, pulled down the gates, hell, even dug my way through. Anything would have been better than this insanity!*

It was merely the instinctive fear talking, some dim part of his mind knew. Yet now that he was in the thick of it, he could think of nothing else. He almost found himself wishing a slashwyrm or two would finally appear. At least that way, he'd *see* his enemy. The not knowing was far worse than—

The ground underfoot suddenly gave way beneath him. His right boot sank up to the knee into the mire, and he found himself falling face-first into the filthy marsh water. Before he could regain his balance, the mud had him fast, clamped around his legs with earthen fingers that threatened to drag him under.

The Hunter couldn't help himself; instinct kicked in and he began to thrash in an effort to free himself. All that did was stir up the water to foam around him, but he could not draw his right leg loose. Worse, in his struggles, he merely drove his stuck foot deeper into the mud. He pawed at the mud with his left foot, desperate to find solid ground, but his boots slipped off muck-covered roots. His grasping fingers tore through reeds that bent and swayed yet could not pull him free.

"Stop!" Aisha's hiss cut through the thundering of blood rushing in the Hunter's ears.

The Hunter could not. Panic had sunk its icy claws deep into his mind. His heart felt ready to beat free of his chest and it felt as if a fist of iron closed around his lungs.

Something struck the side of his head hard. His vision wobbled and stars spun before his eyes. He reeled, off-balance, and it was all he could do to keep from collapsing into the water.

Anger flared white-hot in his chest, cutting momentarily through the chill of terror. The Hunter seized upon that fury and clung to it for dear life. *Anything* to focus on to keep himself from panicking.

"Watcher's beard!" he snarled at Aisha.

"You're welcome." She raised her spear, which she now gripped just beneath the steel head. "You need me to hit you again, or are you calm?"

The Hunter growled a curse but nodded. "I'm calm." It was hard to remain so, given that the mud was dragging him deeper under the water's surface with every breath. But he was not alone, he reminded himself. "What do I do?"

"To start, stop moving." Aisha spoke quickly, worry evident on her face. "Struggling only drags you under faster. Mud and quicksand on their own are no great threat, but if you get pulled down far enough your head's under water, you'll drown."

The Hunter was seized by the urge to snarl in annoyance over her stating something so simple and obvious. But that was just his innate fear response, and he had to do everything in his power to *fight* the fear. Through an immense effort of will, he forced himself to stop moving.

"Spread your arms like you're floating," Aisha told him. Her eyes darted around, no doubt searching for something with which to haul him loose. "Keep still, and don't do anything that will cause you to sink. Give the mud time to condense around your feet."

"Condense?" The Hunter's eyebrows shot up. "Won't that just make it harder to drag me free?"

"It will," Aisha said, nodding. "But it'll also give you something to push against. It's the only way you get out of there."

The Hunter growled low in his throat but didn't argue. This was *her* land, after all, and he'd had little experience surviving quicksand. Not a lot of marshy terrain around Voramis, in the Advanat Desert, on Kara-ket, or in the Empty Mountains around Enarium.

He did as she instructed, spreading out his arms, leaning his upper body forward as if he were floating. Though it went against his every instinct, he kept his right leg utterly still so the mud could solidify around his boot. He also had to fight against the urge to paw at the ground with his left foot. If both feet got sucked under, he'd be in far greater trouble.

Aisha's eyes suddenly brightened. "I'll be back!" she said, and took off back the way they'd come. The Hunter couldn't move enough to look over his shoulder to see where she'd gone. Hopefully, she'd found some vine or branch that could get him out. Otherwise, he'd be forced to drag himself clear, and given the weight of the mud pressing down around his right leg, that would be an immensely arduous battle.

Again, Siyanda's mocking words echoed in his mind. "*Should you blunder foolishly into quicksand, blind and clueless as you alay-alagbara are, the weight will drag you under. Your sweat, too, will drain your bodies of much-needed water, withering you like kola fruit under the noon sun.*"

He *hated* that she'd been right about the former. And, he realized, she wasn't far off on the latter count, either. The trek through the marshes had left his armor sodden with mud, water, and his own sweat. With his face a hand's breadth from the pond's muddy surface, he was made suddenly aware of how thirsty he was.

Then he heard it: a rippling of water, accompanied by a wet splashing, the patter of falling droplets, and the crunch of reed collapsing beneath a heavy weight.

The Hunter's heart sank. *As if things weren't already bad enough!*

From the marshes, not thirty paces away from where he was stuck in the mud, the massive bulk of a slashwyrm lumbered into view between two waterlogged trees. Two burning yellow eyes fixed on him and massive fangs bared. With a hungry hiss, the slashwyrm charged.

Chapter Fifty-Nine

The giant lizard creature bore down on the Hunter with terrible slowness yet an undeniable inexorability. Its great lumbering steps shook the very ground, its tail undulated through the water to leave great splashes in its wake, but its long-snouted head never wavered from its course toward him. Another hungry hiss emanated from its gaping maw, sending a chill down the Hunter's spine. He had mere *seconds* before far too many razor-sharp teeth clamped down on him and bit him clean in half.

Aisha had warned him not to struggle, but he couldn't bloody well lie calmly while this *beast* had its sights set on him. His only hope of getting out of this alive was to work himself free of the mud.

Gritting his teeth, he dug his left foot into the muck at the bottom of the pool and strained to pull his right foot clear. The mire had congealed around his boot, clamping down as tight as bands of iron, yet the slashwyrm's ground-shaking steps loosened it up just enough so that he felt himself beginning to slip free. Slowly, so painfully slowly it might have been his imagination, yet it was enough. He strained with every ounce of strength, pitting his inhuman might against the utter implacability of the pitiless muck.

A gut-twisting sucking bubbled up from the water, and the grip on the Hunter's leg suddenly loosened. He hauled himself clear and dove backward. Just in time to avoid the teeth snapping down on the spot where he had been only a heartbeat earlier. The slashwyrm's head passed so close he felt its wide-nostriled nose brush against the side of his mud-encrusted leg. He drove his foot into the top of the creature's snout, using it as solid leverage to push himself back, clear of the mire that had so nearly dragged him under. The impact, however, only enraged the slashwyrm. The huge head snapped up and the burning yellow eyes locked on the Hunter once more. Its maw opened wide and a spittle-flecked hiss and warm breath reeking of rotting meat washed over him.

The Hunter reached for his sword—though he couldn't pierce the beast's scales, the flesh inside its mouth appeared soft and easily shredded. It didn't matter how futile he knew the gesture to be. He simply *refused* to give up and die, even in the face of this immense beast.

His sword had only just begun clearing its scabbard when a searing blast of blue-white light sizzled past the Hunter's head. Instantly, the air grew scorching hot, stinging the Hunter's eyes. The lizard hissed and recoiled, smoke and steam rising from the ruins of its right eye.

"Come on!" A hand gripped the Hunter by the right arm, dragging him backward and hauling him to his feet. Aisha, her eyes still shining blue-white and bright in the darkness, held her spear extended in the slashwyrm's direction. The vine she'd collected to drag him out of the water lay abandoned at her feet, forgotten in the moment's danger. Sparks danced around the steel head and crackled along the wooden shaft. "We've got to pull back before—"

"No!" The Hunter tore his arm free of her grasp. "We knew this was a possibility. We go forward!"

Aisha tore her gaze from the hissing slashwyrm to fix him with the same "Are you mad?" look she'd given him when first he'd spoken of coming this way.

"If they're already awake," the Hunter said, stabbing a finger at the beast, "we don't need to be stealthy any—" He cut off as the slashwyrm spun about on its tree trunk legs and whipped its long, spiny tail toward him. He and Aisha both dropped beneath the tail, which sliced the air a hand's breadth above their heads. "—more!" he finished. "Now we run!"

"But—"

The Hunter shook his head. "Your family's counting on us!"

He didn't wait to see Aisha's reaction. Instead, he took off at a dead sprint, running straight toward the slashwyrm. The lizard creature, still coming out of its spinning tail slash, couldn't see him as he ran between its legs and raced off through the ankle-deep marsh toward a patch of high ground fifty paces north. They had almost passed the camp's northwestern corner, which meant they could soon swing to the east to cross the river that served as the camp's only border to the north. He and Aisha were *minutes* away from reaching those cages filled with captive Ghandians. They had come too far to turn back now!

A loud curse echoed from behind him, accompanied by splashing feet. The Hunter glanced over his shoulder and grinned at the sight of Aisha unleashing another burst of blue-white lightning at the slashwyrm—not enough to roast it alive, but stunning and slowing it so she could race past. Her face was set in a furious, determined expression, and her eyes glowed so bright they all but lit up the settling darkness.

The Hunter burst free of the marsh and raced up the shallow incline onto the mound of soft earth rising out of the swamp. A hundred paces to the west, another dark shape emerged from a deep, scum-covered pond. Doubtless this second slashwyrm had heard its companion's angry hissing—which even now resumed as it shook off the effects of Aisha's blast—and had risen from its swampy hiding place to investigate. The burning amber eyes roved the marshes; it would see the Hunter at any moment and charge.

An idea struck the Hunter. Terrible, desperate, most would say suicidal, yet an idea that could give him and his companions the *true* advantage in the fight to come.

He spun back toward Aisha, who was even now racing up the hill he'd just ascended. She, too, spotted the second slashwyrm, and her eyes flew wide. The sparks dancing around her fingers brightened but she did not unleash the lightning. Like the clever warrior she was, she'd use only what was needed so as not to exhaust what power was available to her.

But they needed it now.

"Blast it!" the Hunter said, jabbing a finger toward the second slashwyrm. "Get its attention."

"Are you mad?" Aisha demanded. "You want it chasing us, too?"

Sure enough, the first slashwyrm was even now lumbering toward them. Anger blazed in its eyes and its long, spiny tail flicked back and forth, destroying vast swaths of reeds and scraggly marsh trees as it whipped at the air.

"Damn right I do!" The Hunter grinned. "They're already hungry, but we want them driven into a rage."

Confusion flicked across Aisha's face. She seemed incapable of understanding why the Hunter wasn't just suggesting doing something utterly insane, but he was *delighted* by the prospect of certain death.

But the Hunter had no need to explain. Realization dawned on her a moment later and she shook her head. "Bloody hell!"

The Hunter's smile widened. "How's that for evening the odds?"

Aisha threw up her free hand. "Provided we don't get eaten first!" Despite her protest, she extended her right arm to level her short-handled spear at the second slashwyrm. A dozen fingernail-sized sparks hissed across the darkening marshes to sizzle on the beast's scaly snout. One landed in its open mouth, and the sizzle of burning flesh was followed by a hiss of rage. The slashwyrm's head snapped around and its eyes locked on the place where they stood.

"Yeah, that worked!" Aisha said, breaking into a run. The Hunter was right at her side, and together they charged northeast along the spiny ridge of soft earth rising from the marsh. The footing was treacherous and the moss and scum clinging to the edges of the pond made for slippery going. However, the knowledge that *two* slashwyrms now lumbered along in pursuit was all the motivation the Hunter and Aisha needed to keep moving as fast as they could.

Two loud, furious hisses echoed from behind them, answered by more from the north and west. The Hunter couldn't tear his eyes off the precarious route he and Aisha were picking through the marshes, but the sound of snapping trees, splashing water, and heavy claw-tipped feet stamping into mud and mire grew louder with every beat of his heart. Something told him that *every* slashwyrm within earshot of the first two had been roused by their fellows' anger and pain.

Abruptly, the ground ahead dropped away into the water, and exploded upward in the form of a massive scaly body encrusted with mud. The Hunter darted out a hand, caught Aisha's arm, and dragged her backward. The slashwyrm's swinging head missed the young woman by an arm's length. She regained her balance enough to join the Hunter in dropping into a crouch to avoid the tail that came swinging around.

"Hit it!" the Hunter shouted.

It wasn't necessary. Even as Aisha's straightened, she thrust her empty left hand forward and a burst of lightning shot from her hands. The blue-white light nearly blinded the Hunter, set every hair on the back of his neck standing straight up. The force of the blast sent the slashwyrm staggering to the side. With its bulk out of the way, the Hunter could dimly make out a marshy stretch of grass beyond ending at the sluggish river bordering the camp.

They had almost made it.

"Come on!" He broke into a run, ducked beneath the stunned slashwyrm's flailing tail and hind legs, and sprinted across the ankle-deep marsh toward the grass that separated him from the river. He could feel the thick mud attempting to cling to him, to drag him under, but his feet were a blur, moving so fast he might as well have been racing across the water's surface. Aisha barreled along at his side, as fleet and sure of foot as if she'd spent her entire life in the dark marshes of *Indawo Yokwesaba.*

Out of the marsh they ran, onto what felt like the first truly solid ground the Hunter had stepped in for hours. The grass was springy underfoot but bore his weight with ease. Elation blossomed in his chest as he sprinted toward the river that separated him from the now-visible northern edge of the slavers' camp.

A cry of alarm and pain echoed from behind him. The Hunter skidded to a halt and spun to see Aisha floundering, her right leg sunk up to the knee in the grass. Water bubbled up from the hole where the grass had given way beneath her. The grass hadn't truly been solid, merely entwined at the roots tightly enough to support a measure of weight.

The Hunter's eyes darted back the way they'd come. Three more slashwyrms had emerged from the murky marshes to join the two enraged beasts pursuing them. The one he and

Aisha had *just* evaded was now ten paces away from stepping onto the grass. If the falsely solid-looking grass had crumbled beneath Aisha's weight, it would *never* bear up under the bulk of the slashwyrm. He and Aisha could very well be dragged under the water's surface and ensnared in the roots. Or end up food for the slashwyrms even now lumbering toward them.

Not a bloody chance!

The Hunter raced back toward Aisha. "Give me your hand!" he shouted, thrusting out his own. She complied. He caught her outstretched wrist and dragged on it with all his might. He could not set his feet to lean into the effort for fear he would break through the grass, too. But his strength, together with her own, sufficed to haul her clear. In an instant, she was springing to her feet and breaking into a run heedless of the blood flowing from long scrapes and cuts in her shin and calf.

Together, they sprinted across the grass, zigzagging side to side in a desperate attempt to place their feet on solid ground. The Hunter felt like a thief sneaking through some ancient vault, painfully aware that hidden traps lurked everywhere but with no idea how to locate or evade them. Here, however, certain death came not in the form of some cleverly concealed pit of spikes or fired missile, but drowning or being torn apart by ravenous monstrosities.

Somehow, impossibly, they made it across without breaking through. Yet they were far from clear of danger. The grass underfoot swayed and bucked violently, and water bubbled up all around them. The Hunter didn't need to look back to know the first of the slashwyrms was even now clawing its way toward them.

"Swim!" The Hunter dove into the river without hesitation, swimming across with powerful strokes of his arms and kicking ferociously with his legs. He reached the far bank two heartbeats before Aisha and clawed his way once more onto ground that he knew was *truly* solid. By the time he gained his feet on the cleared stretch of marshland that marked the Consortium camp's northern edge, Aisha was close enough he could reach down and help her up. She turned, dripping wet and panting with exhaustion, to hurl an Issai curse at the slashwyrms pursuing them.

"Once more, with feeling," the Hunter said, gesturing toward the beast. "Angry and hungry, right?"

"Damned right!" Aisha raised her hand, and a rush of blue-white light shot out from her fingers toward the slashwyrms.

Spinning back toward the camp, the Hunter reached into one waterlogged pouch and drew out two small glass orbs he'd brought all this way from Voramis. He hurled them onto the ground, where they shattered with a crystalline *tinkling*. The instant the glass cracked, alchemical ingredients mixed together and combusted, spewing thick clouds of white smoke into the night. Within seconds, the air around him and Aisha was thick with the foul-smelling haze, which quickly spread to cover twenty paces to the east and west.

"What's that for?" Aisha asked.

The Hunter grinned as he drew his swords. "So the bastards never see the slashwyrms coming until it's too late!"

Chapter Sixty

"Stay behind me," the Hunter said as he turned toward the camp. "And for the love of all the gods, shout when you see a slashwyrm."

"Like hell I'm letting you fight this battle for—" Aisha began.

The Hunter cut her off with a slash of his left hand, which held Soulhunger. "I'm about to make a whole bloody lot more *Kish'aa* for you to absorb. You focus on that, and on seeing if you can spot your mother and the rest of your Issai *amaqhawe*. Trust me when I say there's fight enough to go around, and more besides."

He half-expected Aisha to protest. But as he'd hoped, she saw the merit of his words enough not to argue. In truth, she had to know just what odds they faced—she'd seen the camp for herself, no doubt counted the number of armed slavers within the walls. Before the night's end, her spear would run red with blood aplenty.

The Hunter stalked southward through the camp. He did not run; there was no need, for he had no doubt the ruckus raised by the slashwyrms had attracted the Consortium guards' notice. He spent a moment studying the cages surrounding him. The steel bars and wooden frames strong enough to keep dozens of desperate men and women from breaking free would keep the slashwyrms out—at least long enough for the monstrosities to spot the guards that even now had to be racing through the darkness toward them.

Sure enough, the first pack of Consortium guards appeared through the rows of cages. Eight men, all armed with greatknives and wearing studded leather armor, a hodge-podge of Voramians, Odarians, Malandrians, and Vothmoti. Their faces twisted into various expressions of outrage, anger, and surprise upon seeing the Hunter striding toward them. Teeth bared, curving blades came up, and the eight charged directly toward the Hunter.

The Hunter saluted them with a flick of his watered steel sword. Not that he had any respect for these bastards—to him, they were little better than Abiarazi, equally cruel but far easier to kill. He merely knew the value of a calm façade in the face of overwhelming odds. Such a demeanor would cause at least a few of the guards to question what manner of man could be so composed despite being heavily outnumbered. Questions led to uncertainty, which in turn led to hesitation. And hesitation got men killed more often than any lack of skill or courage.

Three of the Consortium guards—all Odarians, by the look of them—faltered in their charge, their brows furrowing in confusion. That left only five for the Hunter to face in the initial clash. Odds he'd take any day of the week.

He broke into a mad dash at the last moment, closing the distance with the slavers in two long steps. So quickly he moved that they had no time to register his sudden rush before he was

271

upon them. His watered steel sword flicked out like the tongue of a viper, and a Vothmoti fell with a gaping tear in his throat, blood gushing out of a severed vein.

As the Hunter pulled his sword back, he spun and drove Soulhunger's tip into the eye of a Malandrian. He slid the dagger free before the man's scream could bring the gemstone's magic flaring to life, and the man's eyeball came with it. The Hunter flicked the bloody, nerve-tipped orb into the open mouth of a charging Voramian. The man's advanced faltered as he coughed, choking on his companion's eyeball.

The Hunter hacked down the last two in the lead with a single swing of his sword that overpowered their pathetic attempt at defenses and sheared through their necks. Two heads spun away and blood sprayed over the gagging Voramian. In his panic, the man swallowed the eyeball, causing him to choke and retch. The Hunter put the sorry bastard out of his misery with a sword thrust that speared him through the neck, just above the collar of his armor.

Five deaths in the space of five heartbeats. By then, the three who'd faltered had recovered. Too slow to aid their companions, but they hurled themselves upon him in unison. For a few tense seconds, the Hunter was pushed backward by an onslaught of steel. Blows came at him from all sides, striking high and low, and it took all his skill to keep their blades from striking anything vital. As it was, pain flared in his right cheek and left knee from blows that slipped through his guard.

"Hunter!" came Aisha's shout.

The three slavers' gazes slid past the Hunter and their eyes went wide in horror. All color drained from their faces, their swords lowered, and their relentless assault faltered. The Hunter had no doubt what they'd just seen.

He seized their momentary terror and distraction to finish off the battle. He could have killed them easily—they didn't even have their curve-edged blades on guard—but that wouldn't serve his purposes. Instead, he dropped his sword and dagger and leaped upon them with empty hands. His fists and boots struck out in a blurring sequence of bare-handed strikes that would have made Master Eldor proud, hammering into the three guards' knees, elbows, shoulders, and ankles. Bone *snapped*, cartilage *crunched*, and screams of pain rang out as the three collapsed to the ground.

The Hunter turned his back on the slavers, spinning around to face Aisha. Beyond her, the first of the slashwyrms had appeared through the wall of alchemical smoke. Twin eyes of gleaming amber roved over the camp, and upon settling on the cages filled with sleeping, weeping, and exhausted slaves, the monstrosity bared its fangs with a ravenous hiss.

"Draw its attention to a proper meal, if you'd be so kind?" the Hunter shouted to Aisha.

The Issai woman grinned. "With pleasure!" She raised her right hand, extended her short-handled spear toward the slashwyrm, and sent a stream of sparks hurtling through the air. The blue-white lights landed on the slashwyrm's reptilian tongue, searing its flesh and eliciting a shriek of pain. Its head snapped toward Aisha and those burning eyes narrowed at the sight of two-legged meat.

"I think that worked," Aisha called over her shoulder.

"Then we need to move!" The Hunter took off at a run in the same instant the slashwyrm began lumbering toward him. He vaulted the three downed Consortium guards, evaded a desperate slash of the one he hadn't bothered to disarm, and sprinted through the cages deeper into the camp.

Behind him, Aisha let out a shout of "Dinner is served!" before taking off in pursuit of the Hunter. She caught up to him quickly, her eyes shining blue-white with a light both furious and delighted. The screams of the three Consortium guards the Hunter had left as offering for the slashwyrm grew louder, then ended abruptly with a terrible crunching sound that made even the Hunter wince.

Eight down, the Hunter thought with a grim smile. *Only a few score more to go.* According to Tarek's count, close to a hundred and thirty slavers called the camp home, though from afar it had been impossible to get a truly accurate tally. *Near enough* suited the Hunter just fine.

"You manage to collect those spirits?" the Hunter called over his shoulder as he ran.

"Four of them," Aisha called back.

The Hunter grunted. "Get ready for more." He spotted a dozen more enemies racing in his direction. They hadn't yet seen him and Aisha—their gazes were firmly fixed on the wall of smoke and the slashwyrm devouring their comrades—but he made a beeline directly at them. When finally they spotted him, they attempted to form what *might* have been some military formation. Their lack of discipline and any manner of martial training failed in that crucial moment. They were still struggling to coordinate their positions and arrange their lines when the Hunter crashed into them.

His sword struck out in a blur of watered steel, barely visible in the last vestiges of fading daylight. Their superior numbers had no chance of withstanding the sheer savagery and ferocity of his attack. Nor could their human strength stand before the might of the Bucelarii. He had no need of the Sword of Nasnaz; his watered steel sword could cut through their bared flesh, and where Soulhunger could not find gaps in their armor, he merely drove the dagger through the studded leather with the force of his inhumanly powerful muscles.

This time, however, he did not pull Soulhunger immediately free. He relinquished his hold on the dagger, leaving it embedded in a slaver's chest, and swung his sword two-handed. For all the sterling quality of the Odarian steel used to forge the Consortium's greatknives, the men wielding them were little more than dross and dregs. Their strength was used to abuse the defenseless, not fight off a foe far more skilled and ruthless than they. And against the Hunter, a foe that no steel could kill, they stood no more chance than a leaf before a hurricane.

A scream split the air, ringing with pain and terror. Crimson light flared from Soulhunger's gemstone, glowing bright in the darkness. The sudden appearance of the strange, hideous gleam diverted the attention of more than a few slavers. Their eyes sought out the source of the light, and when they saw it came from the dagger buried in the chest of their fallen companion, their courage and determination faltered. The Hunter cut them down before they could regain either.

Yet the Hunter had barely finished off the last of this group and ripped Soulhunger free of the dead man's chest when another pack of slavers raced toward them. A much larger group, nearly thirty-strong, all armed with whips and greatknives. They spotted him instantly and fanned out to close in around him and Aisha from the south, east, and west.

The Hunter took in his enemy at a glance. The majority had circled to the south and west; those heading east had to circle around a trio of kennel-sized cages in which a dozen terrified children huddled. This last group, he could more than handle. But no sense keeping all the fun for himself.

He tore Soulhunger from the dead man's chest and leveled the dagger at the slavers coming at him from ahead and to the left. "Think you can deal with them?" he called over his shoulder.

A derisive snort was all the answer he received. He took that as an affirmative, and sprang toward the seven slavers preparing to attack from his right side. He was among them in a heartbeat, his sword striking out, carving a deadly swath through their ranks.

273

He did not see Aisha's lightning arcing toward the remaining Consortium guards, but he could feel its power rippling through the air behind him. Blistering heat seared his back and the settling darkness grew suddenly bright. The slavers in front of him threw up their hands to shield their eyes from the brilliance. Their surprise cost them their lives. The Hunter slaughtered the seven in a matter of seconds.

Yet when he turned, the devastation behind him was unlike anything he could have imagined. Twenty-three bodies lay on the ground—some deathly still, others twitching from the remnants of power coursing through them. Flesh seared, armor scorched, steel burned and blackened. Not one rose. The power of the *Kish'aa* had killed every last one of the bastards in a single barrage.

Aisha let out a gasp and slumped to one knee, leaning heavily on her spear. The Hunter ran to her side, but she waved him away. "I'm fine," she panted, shaking her head. "Just a little dizzy. Too much…at once."

The Hunter wasn't so certain. When she lifted her face, she was once again pale, covered in sweat, and her jaw clenched tight against fatigue. Still, she managed to rise to her feet unaided. She stretched out her left hand, still clutching her unused dirk, toward the seven the Hunter had killed. The light in her eyes brightened and the blue-white gleam shone from the *Dy'nashia* pendant that had fallen from beneath her clothing. A moment later, the strain of tension drained away, and she nodded. "Better."

"Well come on, then," the Hunter said, baring his teeth in a ferocious snarl. "The night's entertainment is just beginning!"

Chapter Sixty-One

Shouts of alarm, fear, panic, and pain echoed from all directions as the Hunter and Aisha ran deeper into the slavers' camp. Far to the south resounded a thunderous cracking of branches, followed by a deafening *crash*. The Hunter grinned as he spotted the thick pillar of black smoke rising above the palisade's southeastern corner. Kodyn and Tarek had kept to their part of the plan. The few slavers who'd been rushing from the central building turned toward the sound. Some headed southward to investigate, others resumed their hurried dash in the direction of the shrieks and screams coming from the camp's northern edge. Many, however, simply milled around, too confused and disoriented to know what to do.

Precisely as the Hunter had hoped.

Now, we hit them hard and don't stop hitting until every last one of them is dead!

He slipped through the rows of cages at a stealthy run, keeping to the shadows whenever possible. The hissing of multiple slashwyrms filled the air behind him; the rest had doubtless caught up to their companion and now were slithering through the camp in search of the ones who'd stirred their ire. The Hunter purposely evaded clashing with two groups of Consortium slavers, letting them pass him and Aisha unchallenged. They would soon be too busy fighting for their lives against hungry beasts to spare a glance over their shoulders.

The Hunter's gaze fixed on the knot of armed and armored men surrounding the central building. A few had regained some semblance of wits and now called orders to their bewildered companions. Rather than racing off, however, they pulled back, forming a solid defensive line of steel and flesh outside the entrance from which the Order's carts had emerged that very morning. A dozen or so even slipped inside and hauled the heavy rolling door shut.

That drew the Hunter's attention instantly. Something within that structure was important enough for them to *defend* rather than seeking out the source of the chaos and tumult. What that something was, he bloody well intended to find out.

"This way!" he barked to Aisha, gesturing with his crimson-edged sword toward the knot of men.

Her eyes narrowed. "You sure? That's a whole damned lot of them, and I've only got a few *Kish'aa* at my command."

The Hunter slowed his advance, pausing in the shadow between two heavy cages. But rather than giving him space to think, as he'd hoped, it only served to draw the attention of the Ghandians trapped within. Their voices rose in a chorus of what could only be pleas and entreaties in their own tongue. Muddy, bloody, tear-stained faces pressed against the bars and hands reached through gaps in the steel toward him, beckoning him and gesturing toward the heavy padlock securing the gated door that stood between them and freedom.

Though the Hunter barely spoke a few words of their language—enough to recognize the pleas for help—Aisha was born to the Issai, and their cries did not land on deaf or uncomprehending ears. She took a step toward the gated door and raised her spear as if intending to break the locking mechanism with the power of the *Kish'aa*.

"No!" It went against every instinct—the Hunter loathed the idea of leaving these people imprisoned any longer—but at the moment, the cages were the safest place for them. "There are a mess of furious, hungry slashwyrms prowling through the camp right now who can't tell friend from foe. All they see is food." He gestured toward the people within the cage. "In their case, *easy* food."

"But—" Aisha began.

"Think about it." The Hunter threw up his hands. "Much as I hate it, they're better off with those heavy bars between them and slashwyrm teeth and claws." He stepped closer, so close she could clearly see the look on his face. "But I swear to you that we will have them out as soon as it's safe. Once the Consortium is dealt with, we'll open every one of these cages. Not one of them will be in chains by sunrise."

Aisha's jaw clenched, anger causing the blue-white light to flare in her eyes. But she managed a stiff nod. "So be it." She turned and spoke quickly in the Issai tongue to the people in the cages—the Hunter caught words for "safe" and "wait," along with *Nsanga*, what could have been "eating," and a gesture that clearly called for them to be quiet. Their entreaties grew louder and more strident, some even shouting in visible outrage. But she did not relent. She had to know the Hunter was right, though the thought of leaving her fellow Ghandians locked up visibly pained her.

While she spoke to the captives, the Hunter turned his attention back to the group of slavers clustered around the entrance to the central building. He counted roughly thirty, all wielded drawn greatknives, their faces set in a determined—if somewhat uncertain and fearful—cast. Had he the Sword of Nasnaz at hand, he would have charged with the full confidence that he could hack his way through their ranks.

But to what end? He had no idea what lay within the building that mattered enough they prioritized it over their captives. And in truth, he couldn't afford to care at the moment. His first concern was helping Aisha locate her mother and the Issai *amaqhawe*. Once they'd liberated and armed her tribe's warriors, the numbers would be on their side. They could storm around the camp's perimeter to pick off the clusters of Consortium guards attempting to fight off the slashwyrms, hold the collapsed section of southern wall, and likely defend the gate. Every other captive who took up arms and joined their ranks effort would only bolster their strength. When the time came to finally turn on the thirty-odd guards holding the central building, they'd do so with the full weight of numbers behind them.

The Hunter considered his next move carefully. Kodyn and Tarek would be heading toward the gate to deal with however many slavers were positioned there. Given the chaos in the camp, that number would likely dwindle fast as curious or terrified guards abandoned their stations. The two young men could watch each other's backs. Both were also smart enough to choose the right time and place to strike.

Kiara, however, was on her own. She'd even now be fighting through the western edge of the camp, liberating as many of the shackled captives as possible. Those newly-freed would doubtless take up arms against their captors. However, picks, hoes, and shovels couldn't hope to triumph against Odarian steel and armor.

The decision was made in the space between heartbeats.

"This way!" the Hunter shouted to Aisha as he dashed west and south. He had only to listen for the sound of screams, watch for the glow of Deathbite's gemstone. Together, he, Kiara, and Aisha would be unstoppable.

He circled wide around the central building, staying out of sight of those guarding the double doors. He needed them to feel the way he had when creeping through the slashwyrm-infested swamp: terrified, uncertain where the enemy lurked or from where they would be attacked. When the time came to eliminate them, the toll that fear would take on them would leave them drained, exhausted, and easily defeated.

From the south and west came a deafening ruckus. The clash of steel, wood, and fists. Shouts of rage accompanied by screams of pain and panic. A stampede of stomping feet, both bare and booted. Whips *cracking* sharply against flesh. Above it all, the clank and clatter of rattling metal chains. The tumult rose from the depths of the pit, and the hundreds of figures locked in battle therein.

The captives had not been freed from their bondage—all still bore the manacles around wrists, ankles, and necks—yet they fought as if unencumbered by their imprisonment. Leaping onto the slavers, bearing them to the ground beneath the weight of their numbers, tore at them with fingers and teeth. Some fought with the tools of their slavery, swinging picks and shovels with a desperate ferocity.

One look, however, told the Hunter how this battle would end. Nearly thirty men in Consortium armor formed an outward-facing ring, surrounded by overturned wheelbarrows and piles of stone. They hacked and slashed at any who drew too close, and where their fine steel swords cut, men and women died bloody. The bodies had begun to pile up around their improvised defensive position. Soon, the corpses would rise high enough to form a wall that would impede the Ghandians attacking them even further. For all their fury, the captives in the pit numbered barely more than a hundred, far too few to overwhelm the slavers' defenses, not armed as they were. Soon, the freed captives' onslaught would falter, their courage waver in the face of such carnage—so many of their companions dead—and the assault would stall.

"Don't you dare follow me!" the Hunter shouted over his shoulder at Aisha. Then he charged into the pit.

He could not run straight down—the walls sloped too steeply even for him—so he descended in a skidding, slipping slide. Only his inhuman agility kept him from falling and tumbling headlong downward. His feet were a blur, his legs pumping as he leaped downward, sliding in the scree-like rocks toward the ring of slavers fighting near the pit's bottom. In his haste, his foot caught on a stone, nearly flying out from beneath him. It was all he could do to hurl himself into a forward roll to keep from falling. Pain raced up his shoulder as he struck a sharp rock. Yet he ignored it, springing to his feet in time to jump the last five paces toward the flat ledge upon which the Consortium guards had made their stand.

His knees groaned and the impact shivered painfully up his spine, but the Hunter summoned one last burst of speed to dash the five paces to where the chained captives were gathering up their courage for another charge. Slipping through the crowd, the Hunter planted his foot on an overturned wheelbarrow and leaped high into the air. He soared over the heads of the guards to land in a cleared patch of rocky ground in their midst. Spinning, he dropped into a low crouch, weapons held at the ready.

Time to die, you whoresons!

So swift had been his approach that only *two* of the Consortium men fighting in the ring had spotted him. That pair turned, leaving the defense of their position to their companions, and charged him with a wordless yell. The Hunter sprang to meet them in a blur of razor-sharp rage. His sword knocked aside the first greatknife sweeping toward his head, and Soulhunger flashed out to pierce the man's armored chest. Even as his scream brought the gemstone flaring to bright crimson light, the Hunter spun out of the path of the second slaver's sword. The blade whistled harmlessly past his shoulder and swung so low the man—a Vothmoti with dark tattoos swirling around his chin and cheeks—could not bring it back up in time. The Hunter's watered steel blade sent the man's head spinning away from his shoulders.

The dying man's screams had drawn more attention, however. A handful of slavers turned to search for the source of the cry, and their eyes widened at the sight of the blood-red light leaking from the dagger. When their gazes strayed to the gore-splattered figure standing over their comrades' bodies, their confusion turned instantly to anger. Five men charged him from all directions.

The Hunter did not wait for them to close; he leaped toward the first man, sword cleaving into the slaver's thigh just beneath the edge of his armor, then spun about to hack open the second's throat. He dove beneath a vicious slash, seized Soulhunger's hilt, and tore it free in time to bring the dagger up to turn aside a thrust aimed at his face. He sprang forward, slid beneath the last man's upraised sword, and tackled the slaver around the waist. But instead of bearing him to the ground, he lifted the man off his feet and hurled him into the backs of his comrades facing the chained captives. The force of his flying body bore three of the defenders to the ground.

Pain flared in the side of the Hunter's neck, just below his skull. He staggered to the side, his legs wobbling as the greatknife slid free of his flesh. The blow had struck the nerve in his spine but scraped off bone without doing any permanent damage. Though his body rushed to repair the damage, his legs were temporarily weakened, his balance compromised. He couldn't even see straight through the pain to bring up his sword in defense.

Fire lanced through his left leg, his right arm, across his face. The sword in his thigh twisted before ripping free, and the Hunter couldn't help letting out a grunt of agony. His leg buckled beneath him, the muscles and tendons severed, and he collapsed face-first into the mud.

He tried to roll, to evade the next attack he could not see yet knew was coming. In vain. A sword slammed into his shoulder, another into his lower back. His armor held, but the impact sent more pain shivering up his spine. When he tried to rise, his wounded left leg gave out. It was all he could do to lift his arms and bring up his sword to defend himself.

Two slavers towered over him. Both had the pale skin and flaxen hair of the Princelands, both slope-shouldered brutes who loomed at least a head taller than he. Triumph shone on their ugly, blunt-nosed faces as they brought their swords crashing down toward him. The Hunter braced himself for the pain he knew was to come. He could not summon strength or speed enough to deflect *both* attacks, and he had no hope of evading. All he could do was grit his teeth and endure the pain for as long as it took for his body to heal from—

Twin spears of blue-white light shot past his head to impale the two slavers. The very air around the men sizzled, and smoke rose from their wide eyes and gaping mouths. They toppled backward, writhing and jerking on the ground as the lights burned them alive from the inside out.

"Come on!" Aisha was suddenly at the Hunter's side, slinging an arm around him and dragging him to his feet. "Get your arse up, Keeper take it!"

The Hunter managed to rise, though he had to bear all the weight on his right leg. His left was one wrong move away from buckling once more. "I thought I told you not to follow me!" he shouted.

Aisha shot him an incredulous look. "Really?" She brought her spear up and sent another burst of blue-white light hurtling toward one of the slavers who was turning away from the defensive wall. The bolt was small, barely as thick as her pinky finger, but it caught the man right between the eyes. His body instantly went rigid as a corpse, and he toppled forward to land atop the still-twitching corpses of the Princelanders. "You've an odd way of saying thank you!"

The Hunter laughed. "Yeah, yeah!" He brought his sword up to deflect a greatknife attack from the side, and Aisha finished off the man with a thrust of her spear. The way she was breathing heavily, the Hunter could tell she was all but drained, her strength fading as she used up the last of her *Kish'aa* power. "I'll save the thank yous for after we get out of this alive. We've still got—" He cut down a slaver whose sword Aisha dodged, nearly stumbling as his leg threatened to give way. "—a few more of these bastards to…"

His words were drowned out beneath a swelling roar. Triumph echoed in that sound, accompanied by a bone-deep fury. All around him, the defensive ring of Consortium slavers suddenly fell, borne down beneath a tidal wave of enraged captives. And among their midst, the Hunter caught sight of a brilliant, crimson-glowing gemstone set into the pommel of a long sword. That light, and Kiara's blood-spattered face, was the most beautiful thing the Hunter had seen all day.

One slaver turned to flee, only to find himself face to face with the Hunter and Aisha. Panic and desperation blossomed on the Voramian's features. He threw himself into a maddened rush, as if hoping to trample the pair of them in his escape.

He managed just two steps when something hurtled through the darkness and slammed into the side of his head. The impact sent him flying to the side and knocked him to the ground. There he lay, twitching, gasping for breath, blood spurting from his lips. His fingers rose to feel for the steel spearhead embedded just behind his jaw.

A figure sprang from amidst the chaos and strode toward the dying slaver; tall, powerfully built, with shoulders even Lord Apus himself would have envied and legs as thick as the Hunter's. With a snarl, she bent and ripped the short-handled spear from the dying man's neck. She spat something in her native tongue and kicked the slaver in the fork of the legs.

The Hunter's eyes widened as the woman turned toward them and he sucked in a sharp breath. Though he'd never met her, there was no mistaking her features.

Aisha's face lit up as bright as if every *Kish'aa* within a hundred leagues shone in her eyes. "Mother!"

Chapter Sixty-Two

The Hunter barely had time to shift his weight onto his uninjured leg before Aisha threw herself headlong toward her mother. Two long steps were all she needed to cross the distance separating them, and so fierce was her embrace that she nearly bore the woman to the ground. The two of them dissolved into a tearful mess of shouting, laughing, and chattering in the language of the Issai. Words poured from their lips so fast the Hunter would have had no chance to understand them even had he spoken their tongue. That didn't stop a lump from rising in his throat at the sight of their joyous reunion.

For a few precious heartbeats, the world around the pair seemed to fade. Nothing else existed—not the chained captives beating the last of the Consortium guards to death, not the blood staining the rocky ground where they had slaved away, not the threat of slashwyrms or the promise of more battle to come. Only mother and daughter caught up in a moment they had doubtless both imagined a thousand times over the years.

Reality came crashing back down around them a moment later when a slaver stumbled past. The man—Odarian, judging by his olive complexion and neatly trimmed beard—had managed to extricate himself from the captives who had borne him to the ground. Yet he hadn't escaped unscathed. His left arm hung at an awkward angle, his right foot dragged behind him, and both eyes were swollen nearly shut from broken cheekbones. The Hunter almost felt a moment's pity for the man. *Almost.* He knew what the slaver had done—the whip tucked into his belt was still stained with blood—and felt no compunction about stepping into the man's path and driving Soulhunger into his chest.

As the man fell screaming, clutching at the dagger embedded deep within his armored body, light blossomed from the gemstone and the Hunter felt the rush of power coursing through him. In a matter of moments, his wounds had healed, his muscles and tendons re-knit, and a fresh fire burned in his veins. He stooped easily on his now-undamaged leg and tore the blade free of the corpse.

"I was about to say you looked like hammered dog shite, then you go and do that!"

The Hunter straightened and found Kiara slipping toward him. Deathbite's gemstone had once again gone translucent, its magical light fading, and its blade was as pristine as if she'd just drawn it. That stood in stark contrast with the crimson splattering her face, arms, and armored body.

He grinned. "Funny running into you here. I could have sworn that *you* should have been the one fighting in this pit, while I was supposed to be clearing out the northern end of the camp."

Kiara raised an eyebrow. "So the slashwyrms are your doing, then?"

The Hunter chuckled. "I thought it was a nice touch." He winked at her. "Though I'll admit that I'm used to being the most terrifying thing my enemies face. I feel a tad upstaged, truth be told."

Kiara threw back her head and laughed, a high, ringing sound that warmed the Hunter's heart. "Never happy unless you're complaining, are you?"

The Hunter had no chance to answer, for at that moment, Aisha headed their way, pulling her mother by the arm.

"Hunter," Aisha said, excitement pitching her voice high, "I'd like you to meet my mother, Davathi, true *nassor* of the Issai." She turned to her mother. "*Umama*, meet *Umzukeli*. Or, as he's known in the south, the Hunter of Voramis."

Aisha's mother squared up in front of the Hunter, inspecting him from head to toe. Upon first glance, the Hunter had been struck by her impressive physique—she stood half a hand's breadth shorter than he, her shoulders nearly as broad as his. Only now, up close, did he see the true toll captivity had taken on her. Her leather wrappings, torn and soiled from months without changing, hung in loose coils about her, and her torso and leonine face had a gaunt hollowness that only came from weeks of starvation and overwork.

Yet though she appeared on the verge of collapse, fire still blazed in her eyes—eyes the same *kaffe*-brown as Aisha's, without the blue-white light of the *Kish'aa*. The stink of sweat accumulated over months of captivity couldn't drown out her unique fragrance of magnolia, neroli, copal resin, and myrrh. Her muscles appeared hard and lean, like hempen cords strengthened by the backbreaking labor she'd been forced to endure. She also still wore the myriad silver rings piercing her lips, eyebrows, nostrils, and cheeks.

A part of the Hunter's mind wondered at that. That much silver had to be worth a small fortune in the south. Which suggested the Consortium hadn't come here to mine for gold or silver—or, perhaps better said, whatever they had set their captives to digging was worth exponentially more than all the silver worn by the Issai warriors.

He pushed that thought aside for later. First, they had a battle to win.

He stepped forward and extended his hand. "*Sa'bone*, Davathi of the Issai." He'd heard Aisha greet Siyanda that way, and had to hope he'd used it correctly now.

Davathi's expression remained hard, inscrutable. The Hunter thought he saw a measure of Siyanda's disdain of the *alay-alagbara* reflected in her aunt's face. His stomach clenched; he didn't have the energy to deal with hostility from yet another Issai *nassor*.

Suddenly, Davathi's face broke into a smile, and her strong hand gripped his outstretched arms. "*Sa'bone, Umzukeli*. I do not know what brings you and the *ibhubekazi* here—" At this, her eyes flitted to Kiara. "—but you have my gratitude. Not only for giving us a chance to throw off the chains of the *Gcinue'eleku awandile*, but for what my daughter tells me you have done to bring her home to her people. To me."

The Hunter was impressed. Davathi's voice held only a gentle accent, her Einari fluent and easy.

The woman wrapped a powerful arm around Aisha's shoulders and pulled her daughter close against her broad side. "There is much I would hear from you, but now is not the time."

"Indeed." The Hunter looked around. The ring of slavers had been broken; the people living in the pit still wore the chains of bondage, but they shouted in triumph and raised high picks, hoes, and shovels stained with the blood of their slain captors. "The Consortium is far from broken."

"And apparently," Davathi shot a questioning glance at Aisha, "someone led *Nsanga* into the camp?"

Aisha blushed, but she replied with confidence. "We had to tip the balance in our favor."

"It was well done, *indokazi.*" Davathi nodded her approval, which caused Aisha's already beaming smile to widen further. "However, it presents us with difficulty." The Issai *nassor* turned to the Hunter and Kiara. "Most of my *amaqhawe*—my blooded warriors—are within those cages. Though they are exhausted from their day's labor, if we can free them, we will have the strength to crush the *Gcinue'eleku awandile.*"

Provided they don't get eaten by slashwyrms, the Hunter thought, but wisely didn't say. Davathi had clearly been thinking the same, hence her mention of "difficulty".

The Hunter glanced to Kiara. "You saw the men guarding the central building?"

Kiara shook her head. "Too busy trying to get Davathi and as many of the others free as I could." She nodded to Aisha. "Like you said, tipping the balance in our favor."

Davathi raised her arms, rattling the severed lengths of chains dangling from her wrists. "My *amaqhawe* and I have spent every day searching for a way to break the *Gcinue'eleku awandile.* No doubt they expected as much, for they have kept us divided, always working apart." She clenched her fist and drove a heel down on the skull of the slaver the Hunter had killed. "But we would not be broken. The Issai do not break!"

The Hunter had no trouble believing that. He'd seen and heard only a fraction of what Aisha had endured over the last five years, and he had no doubt a weaker spirit would have shattered before even one of her ordeals.

"You have any objection to leaving those bastards for last?" he asked Davathi. "First we get rid of any stragglers, deal with the *Nsanga,* then we cut the whoresons out of the building."

"Whore...sons?" Davathi glanced to Aisha.

Aisha colored but rattled off a few words in Issai.

"Ahh, yes." Davathi's expression grew fierce—almost a mirror to the one the Hunter had seen on Aisha's face, save a few more age lines and battle scars—and a ferocious smile twisted her lips. "A good *alay-alagbara* expression." She nodded. "We leave the whoresons until after I have my *amaqhawe* at my side.*"

"Suits me," Kiara said, shrugging. She thrust her chin toward the spear in Davathi's hand. "We'll likely need a few more of those, though."

Davathi looked down at the weapon. It was clearly well-worn and equally well-maintained, though it appeared oddly small in her large hand. "The *Gcinue'eleku awandile* have all of our *assegai* in there." She gestured with the spear toward the central building. "They took them from us the day we were captured. Only the one who called himself Eomma was foolish enough to carry it around with him as if it were a trophy." Her fist tightened around the spear's wooden haft. "He has paid for the cruelties he inflicted on my sisters and me. As the *Kish'aa* are my witness, the rest will soon follow."

The chieftainess turned to Aisha. "Come, Daughter. Join me. Fight at my side, as I always believed you one day would."

"I would be honored, *nassor.*" Aisha bowed. She spoke a few words in Issai that rang with a tone as solemn as any knightly pledge or priestly vow.

Davathi's face lit up, and fresh tears streamed from her eyes. She enveloped Aisha once more in a fierce hug, which Aisha returned. She, too, was crying with joy.

When finally the *nassor* broke off from her daughter, she scrubbed the moisture from her cheeks and turned to the Hunter. "*Umzukeli. Ibhubekazi.* To battle!"

282

The Hunter raised his bloody sword in salute, and joined the two Issai women and Kiara in racing away from the scene of battle. Already, the captives who'd overwhelmed the Consortium guards were retrieving their fallen captors' swords. Some set about hacking at their chains, attempting to cut through the metal links using the fine Odarian steel. Others caught up the weapons fully intending to use them. These few brave men and women surged up the winding track that ascended from the base of the pit toward the higher ground upon which the central building had been constructed.

One glance at the steep slope he'd rushed down was enough to convince the Hunter *not* to attempt to climb back the way he'd come. He joined Davathi, Aisha, and Kiara in running up the dirt-and-rock path that had been constructed to allow the wheelbarrows to haul loads up from the depths of the pit.

He still had no idea what it was that had brought the Consortium here to the marshy heart of *Indawo Yokwesaba,* but he'd seen nothing of interest in the pit. Granted, he'd had little light by which to see—the torches and lanterns that had once lit up the night had been seized by the captives and used as weapons. But to him, all he'd seen was dark-colored stone and soil aplenty. No twinkling veins of gold or silver. No gemstones or diamonds trapped among the rocks.

Again, he pushed aside the thought. It was of little consequence until *after* the battle was all but won. However, before he killed the last Consortium man, he intended to put the bastard to the question and find out the true purpose for their presence here.

Up the incline they ran, pushing their way through the slower-moving captives, dodging those too wounded in the fight or exhausted from their day of backbreaking work to continue climbing. It took a matter of minutes to reach the top, yet in that time, a dozen worries settled into the Hunter's mind. What if Kodyn and Tarek got themselves injured in the fight? What if the Consortium tried to make a break for it and escaped out the northeastern gate? What if the captives set fire to the central building and burned it to the ground with everyone inside before he got answers? What if the slashwyrms ran out of slavers to feed on and attempted to break into the cages?

As he reached the top of the path and emerged onto the flat ground between the pit and the central building, he saw at least *one* of his fears had come true. A group of armed and armored slavers were even now fighting their way through the crowd of captives that attempted to bar their progress to the gate. The gate had been thrown open, and a small knot of guards were already fleeing out into the darkness of the forest beyond.

Of Tarek and Kodyn, the Hunter saw no sign. He fought down an instinctive wave of fear and tried to think rationally. They *had* to be lying in wait outside or fighting elsewhere inside the camp. He had no desire to watch Aisha weeping over the body of her lover as Siyanda had, nor explain to Hailen that the half-brother he'd never met had died a world away.

His worries vanished a moment later when a massive lizard creature barged into view around the central building. Blood stained its snout, its claws, and its trunk-like legs. Bits of gristle and steel-studded leather hung from its razor-sharp teeth. One eye was missing, its flesh still charred and pitted where Aisha's lightning had struck it. Yet its other eye, that burning amber-colored orb with a vertically-slitted pupil, turned to lock on him. Its huge nostrils sniffed the air once, and the Hunter *knew* it had picked out his scent from among the myriad odors around him.

The slashwyrm's giant, crimson-stained maw opened and, with a gurgling hiss, the enormous creature broke into a lumbering charge.

Chapter Sixty-Three

The sight of the oncoming monstrosity sent the Hunter's heart plummeting. The beast couldn't have possibly chosen a worse time or place to set its sights on him. Nigh on sixty captives—some freed, many still in chains—were within snapping range of the slashwyrm's teeth, and they had little chance of getting out of its way before it bore down on them. Behind him, more were ascending from the pit, among them Kiara and Aisha. He could evade the slow-moving slashwyrm with relative ease, but saving his own hide would endanger the people he'd just gone to such great lengths to free. And if the slashwyrm went over the edge and skidded down the steep slope into the pit below, Keeper help the captives who found themselves trapped down there with it.

No, the Hunter couldn't allow the slashwyrm's attention to shift away from him, not when so many others would be at risk. But what could he do? His watered steel sword couldn't so much as scratch the lizard's thick black scales. Even if he managed to drive Soulhunger into its flesh, it would be little more than an annoyance.

He searched his mind for *any* idea, anything that could give him a chance to bring down the monstrosity lumbering toward him. The vials of sleeping miasmas he'd brought *might* work, but any slaves in the vicinity would be rendered unconscious long before the slashwyrm succumbed to Graeme's alchemy. If it decided to feed on *them* rather than him—

Come on! The Hunter cursed himself—and the slashwyrm—desperately trying to come up with a plan. Precious seconds passed and ever-closer the beast came on, its steps slow but inexorable. Bloody spittle dripped from its bared fangs and its lone remaining eye burned as it fixed on him. Its huge tail flicked out, barely missing a cluster of chained captives trying to escape the monstrosity's path, and slammed into the side of the central building with such force that it tore out a chunk of the wooden structure.

The Hunter sucked in a breath. *Of course!* How had he not seen it until now?

"Hey!" he shouted at the top of his lungs. He waved his swords over his head to make certain the beast saw him. "Come and get me, you ugly cunt!"

The creature hissed its fury at him and lowered its broad-snouted head. Its eye shone with a new hunger as it bore down on him.

But the Hunter did not merely stand waiting to be eaten. He glanced over his shoulder, searching the crowd to find Kiara, Aisha, or Davathi. He spotted the *nassor* towering a full head above the rest of the freed captives. "Get to your warriors!" he shouted, and took off at a run toward the eastern edge of the camp. He never looked back to see if she'd heard him or hesitated at receiving a command from an *alay-alaghara*—he had his hands full with the slashwyrm.

The beast, seeing him run, changed course to pursue him. Two unfortunate captives were knocked down and crushed beneath the slashwyrm's enormous trunk-like legs, and the Hunter spared a silent prayer for their souls. But he could offer no more than that. He had to remain fully focused on his plan if it was to have any chance of working.

"Come on!" he shouted, waving his hands. He turned to face the slashwyrm and jogged backward, keeping just a dozen or so paces ahead of it. "Don't I look a bloody tasty treat?"

The slashwyrm hissed and lowered its head, trying to pick up speed. Its tail whipped back and forth, and its huge reptilian body wobbled from side to side, but on it came, faster now.

"That's it!" The Hunter led the beast first southward, skirting the edge of the pit by a wide margin—he couldn't risk it falling in—then to the east. Steadily away from the captives surging out of the narrow track ascending from the pit, and from his companions on their way northward to the cages. Once, he nearly tripped over a rock, stumbling and staggering in an effort to keep from falling. In the seconds it took him to recover, the slashwyrm drew so close its massive teeth were nearly within snapping range. When it saw it couldn't bite the Hunter, it spun and whipped its tail around to try and knock him down.

The Hunter threw himself flat onto the ground. Just in time, for in the next instant, the huge tail whistled above his head. That tail strike had power enough to crush trees, and even his bones couldn't withstand that impact. He sprang to his feet and raced away, only slowing once he was again a dozen paces away from the slashwyrm. Now he led it northward, away from the pit's edge.

And straight toward the central building's southern wall.

Now he slowed, letting it draw once more nearly within snapping range. At the last minute, when it was so close he had no doubt his scent filled its nostrils, he sprinted the rest of the distance separating him from the building.

"Get out of the way!" he shouted to the Ghandians in his path. Even if they didn't understand him, his message was clear. The enormous beast pursuing him was more than motivation enough for them to scramble away.

The Hunter skidded to a halt so close to the wooden building he could stretch out his arm and place his hand flat on the wall. Only then did he turn to face the slashwyrm.

"Oh, no!" he wailed, affecting a high and terrified pitch—what he imagined a damsel in distress would sound like. "I'm trapped. Woe is me!" For dramatic effect, he pressed his dagger hand to his chest.

His performance was utterly wasted on the slashwyrm, but his voice kept its attention firmly fixed on him. Again, it lowered its head and lashed its tail back and forth faster to gain speed. On it came, charging with the force of a raging bull and the speed of a plodding donkey.

The Hunter waited until the absolute last moment—until the spines on the top of its lowered head were all but brushing his armored chest—before throwing himself out of the way. His agility carried him out of the slashwyrm's path just in time to evade its raking claws. But the slashwyrm was far less nimble. It had no chance of stopping or slowing. The huge beast plowed into the wooden wall at full speed. Planks and beams *cracked* beneath the impact, and the massive beast crashed through the wall to disappear in a cloud of dust.

A grin split the Hunter's face as cries of alarm echoed from within the building—the Consortium defenders had just received a truly nasty surprise. He turned away, brushing splinters off his armor. He could leave that problem for the slavers to deal with. Whatever the outcome, at least *one* of his enemies would now be eliminated.

286

He'd taken just two steps when a new sound echoed from within the building: a thundering, high-pitched squealing shriek. Not a cry of pain, but terror. Like a pig after the butcher's first knife stroke, a howl of pure fear at the knowledge that certain death approached.

The wall exploded outward in a spray of splinters that bowled the Hunter over. He rolled with the impact, coming up to his feet. In that moment, the slashwyrm burst from the building at a pace the Hunter could only describe as "glacial panic". Its taloned feet clawed at the shattered planks and beams in its path in what appeared utter desperation to escape.

The Hunter's jaw dropped. Peering through the gap it had left in the wall, he could see nothing to terrify it. No fiery weapons, no glowing magic, nothing!

He had no time to wonder at the abrupt change that had come over the slashwyrm, for in that moment, its burning amber eye settled on him and it lurched toward him, hunger overcoming its momentary terror. The Hunter's legs tensed, prepared to leap out of the way. Only to stop as the slashwyrm skidded to a halt mere paces away from him. Its head recoiled, air blasted from its wide-set nostrils, and it let out another panicking hiss.

Confusion rooted the Hunter in place. His eyes dropped to the ground—had it stepped on some sharp plank or dropped sword, injuring itself? That was the only explanation that made any kind of sense to explain why it had stopped so close to its intended meal.

There were no slivers of wood large enough to inflict any significant damage. No weapons, either. Only a fist-sized chunk of dark stone—the same stone the captives had been digging from the ground and carting into the very building from which it had just emerged.

Acting on instinct, the Hunter knelt, sheathed Soulhunger, and snatched up the stone with his left hand. He hurled it at the slashwyrm's lone eye. The effect was instantaneous. The creature shrieked once more and recoiled as if from certain death.

The Hunter's eyes flew wide. *The stone?* He had no idea why—what could they fear from inert rock?—but didn't bother asking questions. Instead, he raced toward the massive hole torn in the wooden wall and found more of the same dark-colored stone around the opening, scattered by the slashwyrm's thrashing.

Sheathing his sword, the Hunter collected an armful of the stones and spun to face the creature.

"Hyah!" he shouted, to once again draw the slashwyrm's attention. The moment its eye swiveled toward him, he hurled one of his gathered stones. The beast recoiled, hissing, and lashing its tail in the air. Yet when the Hunter threw a second stone, it lumbered away.

Hope surged within the Hunter. He pursued the slashwyrm, pelting it with the rocks he'd collected. Its squealing hisses grew louder as it fled northward, all but crashing through one corner of the wooden structure in its haste to escape his barrage.

The Hunter experienced a moment of panic as the beast charged straight toward a cage still filled with captives. The door was closed, and only a few of those inside were on their feet. Most lay or sat, too weak from exhaustion, hunger, and thirst to even attempt escape. Racing around the beast's right side, the Hunter pelted it with rocks to send it veering left. Its charging bulk and lashing tail missed the cage by an arm's length.

Farther north, the Hunter caught sight of the rest of the slashwyrms rampaging through the camp. Some were busy feasting on the corpses of the fallen—the Hunter refused to look closely at the bodies, knowing full well many would be captives too slow to flee—while others hissed angrily at the few Consortium guards attempting to drive them away and regain control of the camp. At the sound of the one-eyed slashwyrm's cries, the slavers turned to see what was happening. That inattention cost them their lives. Those who turned had no chance to get out of the panicking slashwyrm's path, while those who remained facing the others were devoured.

"Hyah!" the Hunter shouted, hurling the dark-colored stones at every slashwyrm within his range. The beasts recoiled from their feasts of fresh meat and hissed at him. Yet they, too, soon joined their one-eyed fellow in fleeing before him—before whatever it was about the stones that terrified them. Within seconds, all seven of the slashwyrms that had pursued the Hunter and Aisha were fleeing across the sluggish river, the patch of now torn-up floating grass, and vanishing into the darkness of the forest beyond.

The Hunter hurled the last of his stones at the retreating beasts. "And stay out!" he roared.

An angry, hungry hiss was all the answer he got.

That's one problem sorted out. With a grin, he turned back toward the camp. *Time to mop up the last of the Consortium, then the battle is won!*

Something on the ground caught his eye. A chunk of stone had fallen from the armful he'd carried, and lay next to a pool of blood spreading outward from a trio of dead Consortium slavers.

Kneeling, the Hunter picked up the fist-sized rock and stared at it. He could see nothing of interest—in the darkness of the night, it appeared as ordinary as any other dark grey chunk of rock he'd seen in his long life.

So what is it, he wondered, *that terrified the slashwyrms so?*

Whatever it was, it had tipped the scales of battle firmly in their favor, and saved the lives of countless Ghandians.

Davathi

Chapter Sixty-Four

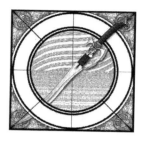

The Hunter spotted Kiara and Davathi hauling open the door to one cage, while Aisha shattered the lock on another with a blast of *Kish'aa* power. The Hunter raced toward Aisha, reaching her in time to help her with the door. The metal hinges squealed loudly but swung open with far less effort than the Hunter had expected. Apparently the Consortium cared more for their makeshift prisons than the shackled men and women captive within.

The moment the door swung open, a dozen women rushed outward and swarmed around Aisha. All bore piercings similar to those she and her mother wore, and they had the lean, muscled look of warriors. The Issai *amaqhawe,* the Hunter guessed. Judging by the delight that shone on their faces, they had recognized her as the long-lost daughter of their *nassor.* Just as the Issai had done the day of Aisha's return, they linked arms to form a circle and bounded into the air again and again, singing and chanting at the tops of their lungs.

Davathi and Kiara soon joined them with another handful of women, all of whom joined in the revelry. However, the joyous celebration lasted only a few moments. Many were soon winded and gasping for breath, others staggering or on the verge of collapse from fatigue. Months of starvation, thirst, beatings, and labor had left a mark on them in the form of gaunt faces, lean frames, cracked lips, bloodstains on their sparse, fibrous cloth battle-wrappings, and whip wounds. At Davathi's shouted command, the warrior women broke off their gaiety and shot questions in the Issai tongue at Aisha's mother.

Davathi snapped a few terse orders. In response, the twenty or so Issai warriors spread out. Before the Hunter could ask what they were doing, the fastest-moving among them bent to retrieve Consortium swords from the fallen guards.

A few steps away from where he stood, one woman wrestled to free her blade from the death grip of pale-skinned fingers enclosing its hilt. The hand was all that remained of its wielder, the rest of it doubtless gone down a slashwyrm's gullet. Farther to the east, a woman tore the greatknife from the mud where a mighty tail had driven it as it crushed its owner into a shattered pile on the ground. Everywhere, the Issai armed themselves using the weapons of their captors.

Davathi's voice drew the Hunter's attention. "We will not stop until we are certain the camp is clear of all *Gcinue'eleku awandile.* Then we will burn every building, tent, and wall to the ground!"

Aisha gestured toward the structure at the heart of the camp. "Last we saw, there were more than thirty of the bastards barricaded in there."

The Hunter glanced in the direction she indicated. No sign of the guards who had once been stationed *outside* the double doors on the building's north face. Either they'd joined their comrades inside or fled through the gate.

He glanced toward the gate. It was still open but no longer under Consortium control. A handful of slavers lay dead at the feet of the four-score slaves who had seized the camp's only entrance. If any had survived, they would be long gone into the dark jungle beyond.

The Hunter nodded. "And that'll be the last of them." He indicated the gate with a nod of his head. "But seeing their way out is blocked, they'll be desperate. And rats are always at their most ferocious when cornered."

Davathi gave him a curious look. "You have a suggestion, *Umzukeli?*"

"I do." The Hunter grinned, drawing his sword and Soulhunger. "Let *me* deal with them. Alone."

The *nassor's* eyebrows rose sharply, a look of surprise blossoming on her face. "Alone?"

The Hunter merely inclined his head. "Thirty-to-one odds aren't too bad, are they, Aisha?"

Aisha gave him a flat look.

Davathi turned to her daughter. "*Indokazi?*"

Aisha let out a breath. "He's not wrong." She sounded almost reluctant to agree with him. "He walks into that building alone, he's got a bloody good chance of walking out again."

The *nassor's* surprise deepened to incredulity, her brow furrowing as she looked between her daughter and the Hunter. She opened her mouth to speak, but a shout from one of the Issai warriors forestalled her words and drew her attention. The twenty or so warrior women had returned, armed with Consortium steel, and the fire of vengeance shone in every one of their eyes.

Davathi's expression hardened. "This is *our* battle to fight." Her large, strong hand tightened around the haft of her short-handled spear. "It was our blood the *Ganue'eleku awandile* spilled, our freedom they stole, our pride they mocked with every strike of their cruel whips." She shook her head. "No true *amaqhawai* could let another face danger in their place. We will show them the Issai strength they could not break." She slammed her clenched fist against her broad chest and barked a word in her tongue—one Kodyn had taught him meant "strength", but of spirit rather than flesh or sinew.

As one, the twenty-odd *amaqhawe* did likewise, and their shout echoed in the night sky. The Hunter noted Aisha did not join in, however. Siyanda's snarled words from days earlier— "*You are not amaqhawai!*"—rang in his mind. She had been absent from her people for years, and thus had not been present for whatever ritual or test the Issai underwent to become a warrior. Yet the Hunter knew the truth. He'd seen it in every action, heard it in every word. She was a true warrior at heart, no doubt about it.

Davathi shouted again to her warriors and, as one, the Issai set off at a loping run toward the central building. Aisha hesitated for a moment, her eyes following her mother and the tribe's warriors. The Hunter was about to offer some word of encouragement, but there was no need. Aisha's jaw set, her shoulders squaring, and she fell in behind the rearmost of the Issai.

The Hunter raced to catch up to the young woman, Kiara right on his heels. "You want to give your mother the best shot at winning this battle, convince her to let you use your *Kish'aa* power on the doors." He thrust his left hand, still gripping Soulhunger, forward to mimic her motion when unleashing the blue-white lightning. "A solid blast will blow those doors off their hinges."

Aisha shot him a sidelong glance, and the Hunter saw the wheels turning in her eyes. There were spirits aplenty for her to collect—the Consortium dead alone numbered in the dozens, and the Hunter suspected more than a few of the captives had fallen to the slashwyrms or the slavers' blades. Sucking in a sharp breath, she broke into a full run, passing the rest of the *amaqhawe* to reach her mother at the front of the pack.

The Hunter didn't wait to hear if Aisha managed to convince her mother. Turning to Kiara, he called "Watch her back!" then took off at a sprint around the building's eastern side. He couldn't talk Davathi out of fighting—the Issai deserved to mete out retribution against the slavers who had captured and tormented them for all these months—but he *could* make their fight marginally easier.

At the very least, he told himself, *I can make bloody certain there are no surprises awaiting them inside.*

He raced around the structure until he reached the gaping hole the one-eyed slashwyrm had made in the wooden wall. To his relief, it had largely gone unnoticed—the Consortium inside the building had their attention focused on the double doors they'd chosen to defend, and the captives were too busy freeing each other from their chains and cages and sealing the camp's gates to pay it much heed. The Hunter slipped unchallenged into the building. Sword and dagger in hand, he stalked through the darkness in search of the enemies he *knew* awaited him within.

Inside, a pile of dark-colored stones that had scared away the slashwyrm loomed over his head, rising nearly twice his height and spreading across fully a quarter of the vast space inside the building. Circling it, careful where he placed his feet to avoid making any noise, the Hunter scanned the rest of the darkened interior. No lamps or lanterns shone on the southern end of the enormous structure; the only light came from the northern end.

The south-facing double doors that had stood open only recently to allow the stone-laden wheelbarrows to flow in were closed and barred. Beside them, the Hunter saw what looked to be a great wheel used to pump water up from a well-like hole in the ground and send it running along a wooden trough that stretched fully half as long as the building itself before emptying into another deep hole dug into the ground. A dozen or so captives were still chained to the enormous winch wheel that operated the water wheel, though they huddled on their knees, clinging to whatever shadows they could find. The Hunter pressed a finger to his lips before moving on.

To the north stood what appeared to be a handful of smaller rooms within the enormous structure. The rooms occupied the northwestern corner of the building, connected by wooden ladders and a series of catwalks that encircled all three levels. More than likely, those were the offices where the operations of the camp were organized by whoever the Consortium had placed in charge.

That'll definitely be the first place I look once this battle is over, he thought. *Perhaps I'll find something that will tell me what the Consortium is* really *doing here, what this operation is all about, and how they're tied to the Order. Depending on how fastidious the Consortium is with keeping records of their undertakings.*

Decades as the Hunter of Voramis had taught him that the wealthiest and most successful noblemen tended to keep meticulous documentation on everything—including, and sometimes *especially,* their more nefarious and illicit enterprises. Those who lacked organization were also typically prone to spendthrift. Extravagance bled their fortunes quickly away to nothing. From what he knew of the Consortium, he suspected they fell into the former category.

But the offices would have to wait. First, he had a handful of Consortium guards to deal with. Not eliminate, merely…soften up in anticipation of the Issai attack.

Fortunately, his enemies were not far off. The thirty-odd men had *not,* as he'd suspected, fled their camp, but remained to hold their position. Six held lanterns aloft and guarded the door to the ground-floor offices and the ladders that ascended to the upper levels. Six more nervously eyed the shadows south of their position to watch for a rear attack. The remainder faced the door, greatknives in hand.

Tension rippled off every one of the slavers in palpable waves. The acrid stink of fear hung thick in the air. They had to know they were outnumbered, their chances of surviving the night virtually nonexistent. So why had they not fled? More than likely, they had barricaded themselves in the building initially intending to protect whatever of value they guarded, only to find their way of escape cut off. They were trapped. The question that was doubtless on every one of their minds was how they would face what was to come.

The Hunter grinned. *Let's have some fun with that.*

Sheathing his weapons, he slipped silent as a wraith through the building, moving ever-closer until he stood in the shadows of a huge wooden support beam not five paces away from the rear-facing guards. He wasted a moment wishing he'd brought his cloak—the sight of a hooded stranger seemingly *appearing* out of thin air tended to have a wondrous effect on already-terrified guards—before stepping out of the shadows.

"I'd say 'good evening', but judging by what's outside these walls, I'm afraid there's not a great deal of good in your future."

All thirty-three of the Consortium guards jumped at the sound of his deep, gravelly voice. A few even yelped, one dropped his sword, and another stumbled back against the ladder he'd been guarding, clutching at his chest. Ten more of the guards facing the door whirled toward the Hunter and raced over to join the six that had been stationed as rearguard.

"How'd you get in here?" snarled one in the harsh, clipped accent of Odaron.

The Hunter grinned. "Is that *really* the question you want to be asking?" He had no need to hurry this along; all he had to do was keep them looking at him until the Issai launched their attack. "Not something more like 'what are the angry Issai outside going to do to us when they get their hands on us?' or 'do I have even a snowflake's chance in the fiery hell of getting through this night without being torn limb from limb?'" He snorted a quiet laugh. "*Those* sound like the kind of questions I'd be asking were I in your position."

"Shut up!" growled one of the slavers. "You can't scare us!"

The Hunter studied the man. Short, slightly on the rotund side, he had a face much like a sloth bear, complete with the long lower lip and furry face. Though he wore the same armor and carried the same weapon as the others, upon closer examination, his studded leather appeared oddly unused, and he held his greatknife in the grip of one not quite comfortable with bared steel. He was also standing in the middle of their formation, his companions forming a defensive ring around him.

"Let me guess," the Hunter said, baring his teeth in a snarl, "you're the one in charge here." He took a step toward the man, causing every one of the slavers between them to bristle and raise their swords. Not that it bothered the Hunter in the slightest. He smelled not a scrap of iron among them. Not so much as a cloak pin or nail to fear.

He clucked his tongue and waggled a finger at the man. "Right now, you've got two choices." He turned his hands palms upward like the plates of a scale. "One, I kill every one of you here and now, leave your bodies for the slashwyrms, and burn down this entire camp."

A few of the slavers tried to laugh or sneer off his words, yet in the lantern light, the Hunter saw sweat trickling down more than a few foreheads, throats bobbing as men swallowed the fear rising within them.

"Two," the Hunter continued, before the pudgy fellow could stammer some form of reply, "the Issai and the others you've whipped and tortured for months get their hands on you, tear you apart, leave your bodies for the slashwyrms, and burn down the camp." He tipped his hands up and down in imitation of taking a measurement. "Like I said, not a lot of *good* in your future."

"Don't listen to him!" shouted the man—who earned himself the nickname of The Sloth in lieu of a proper name. He turned to his companions and waved his arms in a motion not unlike the ineffectual flapping of a rooster attempting in vain to fly. "He is just one man, and we far outnumber him!"

"True." The Hunter nodded. "But think about it. If I really was just *one* man, would I be standing here with my weapons sheathed?"

That seemed to confuse more than a few of the slavers. Those who'd remained facing the door now glanced over their shoulders, searching the darkness behind the Hunter for more enemies. The ones facing the Hunter tensed in anticipation of the attack they could not see coming.

"If I were you," the Hunter said with a wide, mocking grin, "I'd get on with attacking me en masse. Better to die at my hands than wait for the Issai to get through those doors." He thrust a finger toward the heavy barred double doors the slavers had been guarding.

"They cannot!" The Sloth sneered. "This building was built to withstand—"

The Hunter chuckled. "About that." Through a gap in the heavy doors, the Hunter caught sight of blue-white light building in the darkness outside.

"Uhh, Boss—" one began to say.

His words died as the doors exploded inward in a shower of sparks and blue-white lightning.

Chapter Sixty-Five

Aisha's power ripped one door off its hinges and reduced the other to splinters and shards of wood. The Consortium guards had no time to cry out before they were bowled over by the force of the blast. Even the Hunter, standing a full fifteen paces from the doorway, staggered as he was buffeted by the shockwave rippling outward from the spot where her power had struck. The resulting thunderclap set his ears ringing.

He recovered quickly—he'd been expecting it and braced himself, though its power had surprised him—but the same couldn't be said of the slavers. Those nearest the entrance were scythed down by the flying door and the spraying shards and splinters. The ones nearer the Hunter who'd escaped the worst of the blast had no chance to regain their feet before twenty-odd shouting, ululating Issai warriors flooded into the building.

The Hunter took one look at the disoriented Consortium and the enraged Issai, and the outcome of the battle grew abundantly clear. He melted back into the shadows from which he'd emerged without ever once drawing his sword. Better the Issai not see him or sense even the faintest hint of his presence. After what they'd endured at the hands of these bastards, they *deserved* to carry the battle.

Yet he had only gone a few steps when movement above and to his left caught his eye. Three of the Consortium guards had escaped the worst of the blast and, finding themselves under attack, had chosen to flee rather than stand their ground. They had scrambled up the ladders that ascended to the upper-floor offices. No doubt they hoped to lose themselves in the shadows above while the Issai were focused on their comrades below. Their chances of escaping alive were only fractionally better, but desperate men would take those odds.

The Hunter bared his teeth in a snarl. His opinion of the Consortium's men, already low enough, sank even farther. *Cowards!*

He glanced toward the Issai. Aisha's mother fought at their head, wielding her short-handled *assegai* spear with deadly precision and righteous fury. Her warriors battled at her side and guarded her back, no less ferocious than their *nassor*, even armed with the unfamiliar weapons taken from their enemies. None of them had noticed the three slavers attempting to flee.

I suppose that's a job for me, then. He grinned. *Don't mind if I do.*

He dashed across the warehouse, a blur of motion barely visible in the darkness, and sprang into the air with all the force of his powerful muscles. His leap carried him high enough he could grab on to the catwalk encircling the first floor. Within seconds, he was climbing up onto the railing and vaulting up to grab on to the second-floor catwalk. A final burst of effort sent him springing onto the third floor and scrambling over the railing.

Just in time for the first of the slavers to reach the top of the ladder. The Hunter didn't move—better to let them all reach the spot where he stood—but slid Soulhunger silently from its sheath. No point making this a fair fight. He and Kharna could both use the power devoured by the dagger's gemstone.

"Come on!" hissed one of the men, a tall Fehlan with a blond beard and dark blue circles tattooed across his neck, just visible above the collar of his studded leather armor. "Knowing Serran, that bloody skylight was left unlocked. That's our way out!"

The Hunter raised an eyebrow. *Skylight, eh?* So the slavers hadn't just fled to *hide*. Apparently they had a way out. Though that meant going through him.

"And then what?" snarled a second voice, which came from the second man to scramble up the ladder, a fellow with the swarthy complexion and oiled beard common in the Twelve Kingdoms. "We'll be stuck on the roof, with no way—"

The slaver's words cut off in a sharp intake of breath as his eyes settled on the Hunter. His dark face paled and his eyes widened. "Eyvind!" He thrust a finger in the Hunter's direction.

The Fehlan spun, and his sword instinctively swung up in expectation of an attack. Yet as he spotted the Hunter, his light grey eyes narrowed and his bearded face split into a growl. "Come to die, have you?"

The Hunter said nothing, merely tossed Soulhunger from his left hand to his right.

"Kill him already, and let's get out of—" His words cut off in a strangled cry, and he vanished from sight as abruptly as if he'd dropped. Another shout of pain came from below, accompanied a moment later by a whimpering howl of pain.

The Fehlan whirled toward his friend, and the Hunter seized the moment to advance. When Eyvind turned back, the Hunter stood so close his chest all but touched the slaver's. A quick thrust was all it took to drive Soulhunger through the studded leather armor and deep into Eyvind's chest.

Eyvind's eyes went wide, and a terrible, unearthly howl of pain burst from his lips. Instantly, Soulhunger's gemstone sprang to life and crimson light brightened the darkness. Power coursed through the Hunter, a river of fire that washed away any trace of fatigue, exhaustion, hunger, and thirst. Sizzling, searing energy that set his nerves and muscles ablaze. The familiar pain of a red-hot knife carving a line into his chest went all but ignored as the Hunter basked in the sudden rush of vitality. He felt something akin to reluctance when he finally ripped Soulhunger free from Eyvind's chest to let the drained corpse fall to a limp puddle at his feet. The sensations shimmering through every fiber of his being could be far more addictive than even the finest wine or opiate.

He watched the light fade from Soulhunger's gem, the blood absorbed into the steel. Only once the last crimson spark vanished and the gemstone once more grew translucent did the Hunter sheathe the dagger and let out the breath he'd been holding. With the exhalation, a fraction of the power he'd felt drained away, too, and his heart slowed its hammering.

"Hunter?" came a familiar voice from below him. "Is that you?"

The Hunter, still coming down from the euphoric swell of feeling his enemy's life force coursing through his veins, barely had time to recognize the voice before Kodyn's head appeared at the top of the ladder.

"It is!" The young Praamian's face—speckled with blood and what might have been mud or soot—broke into a broad grin. "Fancy meeting you here."

The Hunter frowned. "And why, exactly, *are* we meeting here?" He blinked. "Were you with Aisha and the *amaqhawe* when she blew down the doors?" He hadn't seen Kodyn charge in with the Issai—or Aisha or Kiara, for that matter—but he could easily have missed the young man behind the warriors.

"Nah." Kodyn pulled himself up onto the third floor and stooped to wipe the blood off his drawn sword onto the trousers of the dead Eyvind. "Tarek and I were snooping around when all that happened." He gestured in the direction of the battle below, where the final sounds of fighting were already fading.

As if summoned by magic, the Elivasti himself appeared on the ladder behind Kodyn. He'd drawn his long spear and it, too, was covered with blood.

The Hunter put the pieces together quickly. The two of *them* had finished off the other guards attempting to escape. Which likely meant they'd been on the second floor, rummaging through the Consortium's offices. Doubtless in search of the same information the Hunter had intended to seek out once the battle ended.

"Find anything of use?" he asked the pair.

"Plenty!" Kodyn nodded. He swung a heavy-looking satchel—not *his*—off his shoulder and held it out to the Hunter, showing it was filled to bursting with parchments—*also* not his. "Master Hawk always emphasized the importance of a thorough search. And boy, he was right!" He beamed and patted the bag. "This is everything I could find on their operations here. Who's bankrolling it, what they're after, where it's going, their schedule, *everything!*"

The Hunter was surprised by the force of the emotions swelling within him—relief at finding them alive and pride at their successful endeavor in equal measure. He couldn't keep a smile as wide as Kodyn's from his face. "Bloody fine work!"

Kodyn and Tarek exchanged delighted glances and broke out laughing.

"See?" Kodyn said.

"Fine, fine!" Tarek threw up his free hand. "You were right. There, happy?"

The Hunter narrowed his eyes. "Right? About what?"

Kodyn turned a satisfied grin on the Hunter. "After we took care of our part of the plan—starting the fire and bringing down the tree—we slipped over the wall and got into the camp. That's when we saw the slashwyrms." He shook his head, incredulous. "Slashwyrms!"

"Kodyn saw that the slavers were barricading themselves into this place rather than spreading out to regain control of the camp," Tarek continued. "He figured they were guarding something of value in here, and said you had the *battle* part under control, and that you'd agree the smart choice was to break in and find out what we could in here." He shot Kodyn a look that fell just short of sour. "So yeah, looks like I owe you that silver half-drake after all."

The Hunter raised an eyebrow at the young Praamian.

Kodyn's smile wavered and his expression grew embarrassed, but he didn't cringe beneath the Hunter's stare. "Mother liked to say the things of greatest value aren't always those most immediately apparent as valuable." He swung the satchel over his shoulder once more. "After what you told us about the Order of Mithridas, it was a safe wager that you'd want information more than you'd want us to eliminate a few more of the Consortium." He gestured to Soulhunger with his sword. "You don't really need us for that, but if there was a chance they'd destroy these documents—"

The Hunter held up his free hand. "You chose well." He looked between the young men. Only a few years separated them in age, yet they had both proven themselves quick-thinking and fast on their feet time and time again. "Keeper knows what we'll find when we dig deeper, but thanks to you both, we *will* find something." He gave them a nod of approval. "I won't forget this."

Kodyn and Tarek both blushed and ducked their heads, but they couldn't hide their grins.

"Come on," the Hunter said, sliding between them and striding toward the ladder they'd just ascended. "The battle is all but won. Time to finish this and put the camp to the torch." He paused at the top of the ladder and turned back to Kodyn and Tarek. "You're *certain* you found everything of value?"

The two exchanged glances. "Fairly certain," Kodyn said, nodding. "Every scrap of paper I could get my hands on, every ledger and notebook." He gestured toward the satchel on his back. "We searched as thoroughly as we could without drawing attention." A frown tugged at his lips. "We could always search again if—"

"That won't be necessary." The Hunter shook his head. "I trust you. Your mothers and fellow Hawks trained you well."

In truth, he *could* have gone through the offices one final time just to make absolutely certain they hadn't missed anything. But that would send the wrong message to the two young men. His actions would say he didn't trust them, and that would undermine their confidence far more than any words out of his mouth.

Turning away, he stepped off the edge of the catwalk and dropped to next level down, where lay the lifeless bodies of the last two Consortium guards attempting to flee. He landed hard but his legs absorbed the impact with ease. Eyvind's death had reinvigorated him, banishing any traces of fatigue from the battle. As if to prove as much, he vaulted over the railing to drop the last two stories to the hard-packed earth.

His sudden appearance drew the attention of the Issai nearest the ladder, who spun toward him, bloody swords swinging around to threaten him. A shout from Davathi stopped them from attacking, however. The *nassor* stood from where she knelt over the body of a dead Consortium guard, tore her short-handled spear from the corpse's throat, and stalked toward him with a hard smile on her leonine face.

"Victory is ours, *Umzukeli.*" She came to stand directly in front of him, squaring her shoulders and planting her feet in a wide, confident stance. "My *amaqhawe* and I owe you much."

The Hunter met her eyes. "After everything your daughter has done for me, consider us even." He looked over Davathi's shoulder but saw no sign of Aisha. Or Kiara. He knew he oughtn't be worried—they could take care of themselves—yet he'd expected them to join in the fight.

"My daughter and your *ibhubekazi* are opening the rest of the cages," Davathi said, seeming to read his thoughts. "This was *our* battle to fight." She raised her spear high over her head and shouted in the Issai tongue, and every one of her surviving warriors—nineteen of the original twenty-two—did likewise. "There is much to be done before the sun rises, but the time will come when we speak again. There is much I would hear about how you came to be in the company of my *indokazi* and what your purpose is for being in Issai lands." She gave him a predatory smile. "Men like you do not simply *happen* to be in the right place at the right time."

The Hunter bowed his head. "I have nothing to hide from you, Davathi of the Issai."

Oddly enough, it was the truth. He had no need to lie or offer half-truths, for their desires were all but certainly aligned. The Issai would want vengeance against the Consortium and the Order of Mithridas—who the Hunter suspected Kodyn's stolen documents would confirm were in true command of this operation. If they had encountered the *maistyr* Tarek had been sent to locate, they would doubtless welcome the aid of an *Okanele* in hunting down a creature far more fearsome than even the mightiest slashwyrm.

As for Kharna's urging to reach *Ukuhlushwa Okungapheli*—which the Hunter still felt, albeit faintly beneath the fading battle rush—the Hunter suspected he would find answers among the Issai, too. If not with Davathi, he could always speak to Aisha's father on the matter once they located and liberated him. After all, she'd said that *he* had been the one to take her to see the Serenii tower.

Shouts echoed from the darkness at the far side of the building, calling out in a tongue the Hunter did not understand. The Issai warrior women answered, and a handful carrying lanterns—taken from the dead Consortium guards—hurried off in the direction of the huge water wheel where the Hunter had seen the captives still chained. Davathi went with them, leaving the Hunter alone amidst the carnage.

The Hunter stared at the corpses littering the ground. The pudgy one he'd dubbed The Sloth had died first, brained by the flying door Aisha had blasted off its hinges. The rest hadn't lasted much longer. The Issai had unleashed every shred of fury and hatred that had built up over months of captivity and brutal treatment. The Hunter had known not one of those standing here would survive.

Which was why he'd pursued the three up into the catwalks. He'd intended to take at least one alive. He couldn't blame Kodyn and Tarek for finishing off the first two; of anyone, he ought to blame himself for killing Eyvind when the man might have had answers to offer. Yet he'd been so caught up in the heat of battle he'd given in to the urge to kill. Even without the magic of the Sword of Nasnaz, his innate bloodlust once again left him empty-handed.

It's fine, he told himself, drawing in a deep, cleansing breath. *Kodyn found the Consortium's documents. He's got answers aplenty for—*

"Get away!" A voice from above snapped the Hunter's head upward.

Tarek stood at the railing of the catwalk, leaning far over, his face set in a worried cast as he looked deeper into the warehouse.

The Hunter whirled to follow Tarek's line of sight and found his gaze fixed on the Issai. The warrior women had just drawn abreast of the rock pile, lanterns held high to cast light over the enormous mound of dark grey stones.

"Get away from there!" the Elivasti shouted, waving his arms frantically. Fear blossomed on his face. "For the love of the ancestors, if you want to live through the night, stay away from the stones!"

Chapter Sixty-Six

Davathi was the first to react to Tarek's shouted warning. The *nassor* sprang to the side, backpedaling as if trying to escape a slashwyrm's grasping claws and not an inert pile of stone. A few of the other Issai reacted as well—those the Hunter suspected spoke at least enough Einari to comprehend Tarek's words. The remainder reacted with impressive agility, copying their chieftainess and companions, even though confusion clouded their expressions, and they stared uncomprehending at their *nassor*. At Davathi's translations, their bewilderment only deepened.

Despite Davathi's reaction, she, too, appeared utterly at a loss. She spun to face Tarek, who had leaped down from the last catwalk and hurried toward them. "What is the meaning of this warning?" she demanded.

"The stones!" Tarek stopped at the Hunter's side, staring at the pile with a leery concern. "They're not just ordinary rocks. They're dimercurite!" He uttered the name with the severity of a funeral crier calling out the names of the dead, yet to the Hunter, it meant nothing.

"Di…mercurite?" Davathi struggled to pronounce the word. "And this means?"

"It means every breath we're taking could be flooding our lungs with toxic dust!" Tarek rounded on the Hunter, and words spilled from his mouth in a rush. "Kanna told me about it years ago. Our people hit a vein of the stone as they were excavating to build the Sage's archway. When the dimercurite mixes with water and dries to mud, it turns poisonous. Killed three dozen of our people before they understood the source of the toxin."

The Hunter's eyes widened. "And how do you know this is the same?"

"She showed me a piece she kept," Tarek explained, worry furrowing his brow. "She was determined to study it, to find a cure so that if it ever happened again—"

Davathi growled something in the Issai tongue that could only be a curse. The Hunter and Tarek both looked to her.

"That explains it," she snarled.

"Explains what?" the Hunter asked.

"I will show you." The *nassor's* leonine face hardened, lines forming at the corners of her mouth and eyes. "But first, we must get everyone away."

"Yes, *now!*" Tarek's voice grew insistent. He looked over his shoulder, to where Kodyn had just descended from the catwalk carrying his satchel of stolen Consortium documents. "We need to get out of here!" he shouted, waving the Praamian toward the wreckage of the double doors. "All of us. Every step we take kicks up more dust, and every breath pulls it into our lungs."

Kodyn's eyebrows shot up, but he responded to Tarek's urgings by slipping out of the building. Davathi, meanwhile, had turned to shout orders at her Issai. They retreated from the pile, moving gingerly, placing each foot with care so as not to disturb the dark grey dust the Hunter now saw coated the floor.

In the light of the lanterns held by the Issai, the Hunter got a better look at the stone pile. No longer were they merely inert, dull pieces of rock. They seemed to glimmer like glass, but instead of crystal-clear, they reflected a reddish-orange hue. The Hunter had never seen anything like it—there certainly had been no indication of any such reflection under direct sunlight—yet the young Elivasti's words at least gave some explanation as to the slashwyrms' panic. If even the giant lizard-beasts feared the stones, all the more reason for the frailer humans to give them a wide berth.

As for him? He reached into his pocket and closed his fingers around the chunk of stone he'd picked up from the ground. He felt nothing, not so much as a tickle at the back of his throat. It was only when the dust was exposed to water and left to dry that it proved dangerous. He wouldn't discard the chunk of stone just yet. Not if it could help them understand why the Order of Mithridas and the Consortium valued it so highly.

Danger or no, he joined the others in evacuating the building. Their retreat brought a fresh wave of cries from the captives still chained to the giant water wheel. Yet in that moment, the doors at the southern end of the building were dragged open by the combined might of a cluster of enraged, freed slaves, who flooded into the structure, stolen weapons raised high.

Davathi and her *amaqhawe* called to their fellow captives—now liberated—in the Issai tongue, and clearly the rest understood, for they united to break the chains binding the last few slaves to the water wheel before retreating from the building. A resounding *boom* echoed through the structure as the southern doors were once again thrown shut. The northern doors couldn't be closed—they were little more than splinters and twisted wreckage—but at Davathi's words, six of her surviving warriors remained behind to stand guard at the entrance.

"This way," Davathi called to the Hunter, beckoning to him as she hurried past. Tarek and Kodyn fell in beside the Hunter as they followed the *nassor* northward to where more captives were emerging from the now-opened cages in a tide of shouting, laughing, cheering men, women, and children.

But not *all* of those held captive were fleeing their bondage. Many lay curled on the dusty floor, sprawled on their backs, or slumped against the cages' steel bars, too weak to rise, much less move. The Hunter might have attributed it to starvation, dehydration, and exhaustion, were it not for Davathi's next words.

"Look at them," the *nassor* said, turning to Tarek. "Is this what happened to your people?"

The Elivasti knelt in the open doorway of the largest cage, staring at the six men and four women lying within. Only *two* lived, as evidenced by the weak rise and fall of their chest. The rest had died on the cold, hard ground, their last breaths unmarked by—or simply uninteresting to—their captors.

Tarek listed symptoms without ever looking away from the dead and dying. "Fever and chills. Weakness in the muscles. Vomiting, dizziness, breathing difficulties. Loosening bowels. Blackening of the lips and gums. Slow, agonizing death by dehydration."

"Yes." Davathi's expression grew grim. "From what I understand, that is what happens to those like them. They were set to work inside the building. As were many of my *amaqhawe*."

Tarek stood and when he turned, shadows darkened his violet eyes. "Take me to them."

Davathi led them past toward two cages farther to the east, where another twenty-five or thirty women bearing the lean physiques and facial piercings of the Issai warriors exhibited various states of illness. Some had stubbornly risen to their feet yet were too weak to do more than cling to the bars. Many sat heaving, puddles of vomit—little more than bile, by this point—pooling around them. Some gasped for air, breaths coming in wheezing rasps. Four of the warriors lay among the terrible stink of ordure. Dark stains marred their flesh and stained their simple fibrous cloth battle-wrappings. Their teeth had all but fallen out of gums gone black with rot, and their lips had blackened and swollen to grotesque size. Death would claim them soon.

Tarek swore under his breath. "How long have they been like this?"

"Some, weeks," Davathi gestured to the weakest of the group. "Others, only a few days."

Tarek's face darkened. "Anyone who has been ill for more than a fortnight is already too far gone. They will only worsen, and nothing we do will help them."

Davathi's eyes narrowed. "You are *umuthi?*"

Tarek gave her a confused look.

"One who knows healing," Davathi translated.

Tarek nodded. "I studied under one, learned everything she could teach me. Including about this. She lost her son and daughter to the dimercurite, and that drove her to understand everything she could."

"Can you help my *amaqhawe?*" Davathi eyed him, her expression as sharp as the head of her spear.

Tarek sucked in a long breath, and when he let it out, his shoulders drooped slightly. "Any who can walk with aid, there is hope for them. As for the others…" He shook his head. "I'm sorry, *nassor.* Better they don't suffer more than they already have."

"I understand." Davathi drew herself up to her full height. Her hand tightened around the haft of her spear and her shoulders squared as if beneath a great burden. For in truth, it *was* a burden. The weight of command sat uneasy on even the mightiest shoulders. "I will see it is done."

"And I will do what I can to help the others," Tarek said, bowing to the woman.

Davathi placed her clenched right fist over her heart and said something in Issai. The Hunter didn't understand the words, but the solemnity of her tone and expression made their meaning plain enough. Neither Tarek nor the Hunter spoke when Davathi turned away. She gathered her warriors around her, but her voice was quiet, grave. That gravity quickly spread among the rest of the Issai *amaqhawe.* No doubt their chieftainess had told them what needed to be done.

Tarek's voice drew the Hunter's attention. "I've got some supplies in my pack," he said, his words heavy, his scruff-bearded face somber. "I think I have enough to neutralize the worst of the dimercurite's effects, but it won't be easy to reverse it."

"Just do what you can." The Hunter rested a hand on the young man's shoulder. The muscles were knotted, tense with worry. "It will be enough."

With a nod, Tarek turned and set off toward the northeastern gate, and the forest beyond where he'd left his pack and the rest of their gear.

All this time, Kodyn had remained with them, yet his eyes roved the camp. No doubt seeking Aisha. His concern showed plain on his face.

"She's got Kiara watching her back," the Hunter said, trying for a reassuring tone. "They were opening the last of the cages, freeing the rest of the cap—"

A cry of pure misery and anguish rang out in the darkness. The sound echoed off the palisade walls, rising to a keening wail.

The Hunter and Kodyn's eyes both flew wide. They knew that voice.

"Aisha!" Kodyn shouted. Spinning, he dashed toward the source of the sound.

The Hunter was three steps ahead of the young thief, his feet a blur as he raced in the direction from which the cry had come. That was not the cry of someone who'd suffered a wound or witnessed the horrors perpetrated upon her people. No, that sound rang with a pain that cut to the very soul: the gut-wrenching anguish of loss.

He did not have far to go before Aisha came into view. Her eyes were wild, blue-white light shining in a sizzling halo around her head, sparks dancing around her hands and the head of her short-handed spear. Yet rather than the air of command or fury she'd radiated only moments earlier, she exuded fear that bordered on panic.

"Where are they?" she called in a voice terribly ragged and raw. "Where are they!?"

She stormed toward the nearest cage and, finding it empty, lurched in the opposite direction toward a second, smaller cage in which two child-sized bodies lay.

"Aisha!" Kiara appeared through the cages, racing in pursuit. "Aisha, you don't—"

"Where are they!" Aisha's words started off as a roar, but cracked halfway through and ended in what sounded more like a shriek.

She tripped on a fallen Consortium slaver's corpse and would have fallen, if Kiara hadn't reached her in time to catch her. The Hunter and Kodyn arrived a heartbeat later.

"Aisha?" Kodyn called. "What's the ma—"

Aisha's head snapped up and, upon seeing Kodyn, lunged toward the young man so abruptly he staggered backward as she seized the collar of his light armor.

The light in her eyes blazed brighter. "I can't find them! I've looked everywhere but—" Her voice shattered, and the look on her face grew pleading, desperate as her words came out in a hoarse rasp. "My father, my sister. Why can't I find them?!"

Chapter Sixty-Seven

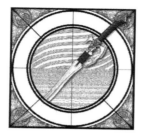

Aisha's strength seemed to give out in that moment, and she slumped onto her knees. "So many dead," she croaked, tears streaming down her face. "I didn't want to search them. Didn't want to believe Nkanyezi or my father were among them." She lifted her eyes to Kodyn. "But if they're not among the living—"

"We'll find them." Kodyn wrapped his arms around Aisha and pulled her to her feet. "I promise we'll find them."

Aisha managed to remain standing, though Kiara lent a hand to steady the young woman. The Hunter felt her pain all too keenly—his heart ached at the agonizing memory of cradling Farida's lifeless body. The sight had all but broken him. Had he believed in the gods, he would have flooded the heavens with prayers that she would be spared the same torment, that her father and sister would still be alive. Yet he couldn't help the dread twisting in his gut. If, as she'd begun to say, they weren't among the living escaping the cages, she would soon suffer as he had that night so long ago.

At least she has Kodyn and her mother, he tried to tell himself. The thought rang terribly hollow. The pain she would soon be forced to endure might very well break her, whether or not she faced it alone.

"Come on," Kodyn said in a soothing voice, pulling Aisha along beside him. Where they went didn't matter, the Hunter knew, only that she got moving. At times like this, *doing* was often the only way to keep from crumbling. "Which cages have you searched?"

Aisha scrubbed the moisture from her cheeks. "All of them." She shook her head, but her expression no longer showed the fearful edge of panic. Only grim determination. "I've checked all of them."

"Then we'll check again." Kodyn sounded confident. Looked it, too. He gripped Aisha's arm in his free hand and squeezed tight. "We'll check every cage, talk to everyone we can. Maybe you missed them in the chaos, or that they got free without you seeing them. Anything is possible, right?"

"Right." Aisha nodded, hesitantly at first, but her uncertainty faded as she gained a new sense of purpose. "And I didn't look in the pit. It's possible they were there when we were busy fighting, and I just didn't see them."

"There you go!" Kodyn beamed. "Then we'll start there."

The Hunter exchanged glances with Kiara. By the look on her face, the young man's response had impressed her as much as it had him. Again, Kodyn had demonstrated a degree of astuteness beyond his age.

Evren and Hailen certainly chose their friends well, he thought, hiding a grin.

"The camp is ours," Kodyn said, his smile widening. "We can take our time to search every corner, every building until we find your father and sister. Wherever they are—"

"Your father and sister are not here." Davathi's strong voice cut in.

The Hunter, Kiara, Kodyn, and Aisha turned to see the *nassor* striding toward them, coming from the direction of the cage in which Issai *amaqhawe* had been held captive. A grim expression and fresh specks of blood cast her leonine face in darkness. The long, sharp blade of her short-handled spear bore a fresh edge of crimson, too. Behind her, the warriors not occupied helping their ill comrades from the cage were busy carrying limp, now-lifeless bodies out into the open air to lay them out in the same way the Issai had done for Zalika and the others fallen in battle. She had fulfilled her duties as chieftainess, and now could attend to her role as Aisha's mother.

"They were taken." Davathi's jaw muscles clenched, a furrow deepening her brow. "They, and every other who showed even the slightest hint of *Umoyahlebe* abilities."

Aisha had been about to speak—no doubt to ask *where* they had been taken—yet her words died in a sharp intake of breath and her jaw fell slack. She stared at her mother for a long moment. "So Nkanyezi truly is…" She swallowed, seemingly incapable of saying the word and confirming what Siyanda had told her.

Davathi inclined her head. "She inherited your father's gift. As, it seems, you have." She gestured toward Aisha's spearhead, around which blue-white sparks still danced.

"How—?" The word came out in a croak. Clearing her throat, Aisha tried again. "How did the *Gcinue'eleku awandile* know?"

"The stone." Davathi swept a hand toward the central building that held the enormous pile of what Tarek had called dimercurite. "Everyone who arrives is subjected to…tests." She grimaced at the unpleasant memory. "Those who are blessed by the *Kish'aa* react to the stone's touch."

An idea occurred to the Hunter. Reaching into his pocket, he drew out the small piece of dimercurite and tossed it to Aisha. She reached out by instinct and snatched it from the air. No sooner had her fingers touched the stone than it began to glow. Like metal heated in a forge, it turned from dark grey to near-black, then began to glow red. Barely a spark at first, but growing brighter with every beat of her heart until the entire stone shone a brilliant reddish-orange.

Aisha stared wide-eyed at the stone in her hand. No sign of pain showed on her face, only wonder mingled with worry—not for herself, the Hunter suspected, but for her sister.

Davathi took a step backward, raising a hand to shield her eyes from the brilliance. "Aisha!" Issai words poured from her lips, spoken in a tone of wonder.

Aisha blinked, looking at her mother in surprise, but shook her head and answered also in Issai. Even as she spoke, she tossed the stone back to the Hunter. The light vanished from the dimercurite in the heartbeat it took to fly through the air. When the Hunter caught the stone, it was once more a dull, inert grey.

Questions seethed in his thoughts, but he pushed them to the back of his mind. He could deal with them later. They had greater concerns to address first.

"You said they were taken." The Hunter narrowed his eyes. "Taken where? By whom?"

"Men in masks carved from *Nsanga* scales took them. As for where?" Davathi turned to thrust her blood-edged spear toward the darkness northeast of the camp. "Though they called it the Bondshold, I am certain they spoke of *Ukuhlushwa Okungapheli*."

A shiver ran down the Hunter's spine. Even as she spoke the name, he *knew* without a doubt that she'd guessed right. Only that could explain the urgency he'd felt during his communion with Kharna. The Serenii had sent him here to prevent whatever the Order of Mithridas—and, likely, the Abiarazi among their ranks—intended to do at the midnight tower. If it involved *Umoyahlebe* with power akin to Aisha's, it could be nothing good.

Aisha pushed off Kodyn, a determined look on her face. "We have to go after them!" She squared her shoulders and, adjusted her grip on her spear as if preparing for battle, set off toward the gate. "I won't leave them—"

"*Indokazi.*" Davathi moved to block her daughter's path. "Look around you."

Aisha made to avoid her mother, but Davathi shifted to again bar Aisha's way.

"Look!" The *nassor's* voice cracked like a whip. She gripped Aisha's shoulder and turned her physically to face the camp.

With visible reluctance, Aisha obeyed her mother's command.

"A great victory has been won this night," Davathi said, her tone as hard as stone. "But this has just begun. There are more battles to fight, for the *Gcinue'eleku awandile* that lie dead here are far from all of those who have invaded our lands. Going after the rest now would be foolish. We are too few, too weakened. We must regain our strength before we—"

"What?" Aisha whirled on her mother. "You'd just leave father and *Nkanyezi* in the hands of our enemies? For how long? Weeks? Months?!"

"I would rip out every one of their hearts with my bare hands," Davathi snapped. The fingers of her free hand flexed into a claw. "For that is *my kwa'indokazi* they have captive, *my* husband." Her teeth bared in a snarl that only heightened her resemblance to the lions of the Kgabu Plains. "Yet getting myself killed will do them no good. For their sakes, and for my love for them, I must turn my back on them. For only when I and what remains of my *amaqhawe* are once again strong will I have any chance of cutting down our enemies to free them." She rested her hand on Aisha's shoulder. "As you have done here."

Aisha softened at her mother's touch and the pride evident in her dark eyes.

"Trust me, *indokazi.*" Davathi leaned forward, touching her forehead to Aisha's. "After all these years, the *Kish'aa* have brought you back to me. I will not lose you again."

Aisha swallowed, and in lieu of an answer, pressed her head against her mother's. Both women's eyes closed and some silent communication passed between them in that moment. Tears slid down their cheeks as they stood like that for long moments.

The Hunter turned away to give mother and daughter a moment of privacy. It was strange, feeling such joy in the midst of so much carnage. But perhaps it was *because* of the suffering surrounding him on all sides that he could bask in the happiness. Despite everything that had happened to both of them, despite half a continent separating them for years, they were finally reunited. What came next, they would face together. That alone made all the blood spilled and hardships endured up until this point worth it.

* * *

The Consortium stronghold burned. So hot was the fire the heat was felt even from a hundred paces away, so large the flames they lit up the darkness for miles in all directions.

The Hunter, Kiara, Kodyn, Tarek, Aisha, and Davathi stood watching the bright flames consuming the slavers' camp. While half of the Issai laid out their dead for the *makalala* and the other half coordinated the escape into the marshy forest, the six of them had set fire to every building, every cage, every log erected to form the palisade wall. There would be nothing but corpses and smoking wreckage left for the Consortium should they return. Which, the Hunter

306

suspected, they soon would. If for nothing else but to gather up the enormous pile of dimercurite they had taken such pains to accumulate.

The Hunter had considered carving great furrows into the ground or staking out the Consortium corpses to send a grim message to whoever was dispatched to inspect the ruins. But he supposed the Consortium and the Order would understand the meaning of what they'd find clearly enough.

And that was just the beginning. Eliminating this camp was just the opening move in what appeared to be a far greater game. The liberation of the Issai warriors left his enemy at a disadvantage. The question was: what would their next action be? And what of *his*? Already, plans had begun formulating in his mind. The Vassalage Consortium and the Order of Mithridas would come to fear him and his allies soon enough.

The Hunter's eyes were drawn past the towering inferno that was the camp, toward the darkness of the northeast. The call of *Ukuhlushwa Okungapheli* had grown stronger now that the battle had ended. The urgency implanted in his mind by Kharna increased with every beat of his heart. The tower beckoned him, and a voice within the core of his soul told him he could not delay much longer. Nor did he intend to. The day was not far off when he'd set out to determine the true reason why Kharna had needed him here, what the Order of Mithridas wanted with the Serenii structure. He had no doubt he'd find the Abiarazi Tarek had been dispatched to locate at the Bondshold. Where there was power, there would be a demon seeking to claim it for their own.

Which meant the Hunter needed power commensurate. At least enough to pose a serious threat to the demons' plans. He also needed information, to learn about the forces arrayed against him. There *had* to be more than just the Ujana and handful of drivers he'd seen leaving the Consortium camp days earlier. He needed to do reconnaissance and see his enemies with his own two eyes.

Information and reinforcements, those were his prime objectives now.

Information, he could not obtain on his own. He'd need someone who knew the lay of the land to guide him toward *Ukuhlushwa Okungapheli*. For the time being, Davathi and her people would be focused on survival—their own, and the two hundred and seventy-three others who had joined them in escaping the camp.

One look at Aisha's face, and the Hunter could see she was torn. On one hand, she wanted to remain at her mother's side, to once more be a loving daughter and loyal Issai. On the other, she had traveled all this way to share the discovery she'd made that could save her sister and all other *Umoyahlebe* from the toll their gift took on their minds and bodies.

At the moment, the Issai side of her was winning. Her mother's words had lodged in her mind, and she appeared content to remain focused on escaping the forest and returning to her people. But the time might soon come when she would be driven to go after her father and sister. When it did, the Hunter would be at her side.

Reinforcements, however, that was a different matter. He needed to speak with Aisha on the subject, but he had an idea as to how to bolster their strength before taking on the combined forces of the Order and Consortium.

For us to have any chance of winning this, we'll have to find allies among our enemies. A grim smile played on the Hunter's lips as he ran a thumb over the hilt of the Sword of Nasnaz, once more sheathed on his hip. *And I've got just the enemy to start with!*

Part Two:
<u>Awakener</u>

Chapter One

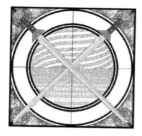

"You're sure about this?" the Hunter asked, shooting a sidelong glance at Davathi. "He's right there. All I need to do is get close enough to put a dagger to his throat and—"

"No." The Issai *nassor* shook her head once. "That is not our way."

The Hunter ignored the biting scorn in the woman's voice. He'd heard it from countless others before. Most Einari disdained assassins, calling them "cowards" and "backstabbing bastards"—though that didn't stop them from making use of the Hunter's skills. It came as no surprise that the Issai warriors shared a code of honorable battle as fierce as any Nyslian knight's.

He shrugged. "As you insist." He'd do things her way...for now. He checked his weapons—Soulhunger at his left hip, the watered steel sword at his right, the Sword of Nasnaz on his back—to ensure they slid smoothly from their scabbards. If battle was to be joined, he would not be caught unprepared.

Davathi barked a quiet order to the ten Issai chosen to accompany her, and as one, the eleven warriors rose from where they'd been hiding among the tall grass. Aisha, Kodyn, and the Hunter rose, too. Silent as shadows, they slipped down the hill toward the camp of the Buhari they'd spent the last hour watching.

Two days it had taken them to find this place. Much of that time had been spent herding the freed captives from *Indawo Yokwesaba*. Most were too weak, exhausted, and hungry to travel far. Tarek had run himself ragged accompanying the stronger Issai warriors in the hunt for enough game to feed such a vast group. The rest of the Issai had been dispatched by Davathi to locate the Buhari. The *nassor*, after learning what the Hunter had done to the enemy tribe—and what he intended for them—had determined to reach the Buhari before they found wherever Siyanda had herded the Issai. They needed to address this problem *first*. What came next depended entirely on the events of the next few minutes.

Davathi led the way through the darkness, moving through the tall plains grass with the stealthy grace of a hunting predator. She and her ten warriors had retrieved their clothing, woven-vine shields, and weapons from the Consortium camp before setting it to the torch. Now, they made no more noise than the night breeze whispering down the hill. To the Hunter's ears, the near-silent padding of his boots and the *thump-thump* of his heart seemed deafening by comparison.

Crouched low, they managed to draw within thirty paces of the camp before Davathi called a halt. Below them spread out the assembled host of the Buhari. Easily a hundred and fifty warriors with skin painted bright vermillion, all wearing some piece of a lion: legs ending in claw-tipped paws draped like mantles around their shoulders, manes and skulls worn as headdresses, jaw and leg bones dangling from their belts like weapons, necklaces and anklets fashioned from lion's teeth, and capes made of fur-covered hides. Every one of them—sitting, standing, even those lying on the grass—kept a grip on their long, flexible spears and within easy reach of their shields.

If the night turned against them, the Issai would find themselves in dire straits facing such an enemy. The Hunter tightened his grip on Soulhunger's hilt. He would play the part he'd chosen, and trust his companions held to theirs. Their lives now balanced on the razor's edge of a blade.

He drew in a deep breath through his nostrils. The scent of so many men hung thick in the air, a mélange comprised of hundreds of individual odors that overlapped too densely for him to make out. Yet he sought one smell in particular: the metallic tang of iron.

His gut twisted as the stink reached him. Far more of it than he'd hoped, in truth. He had no way to know precisely where it came from—there were hundreds of spearheads, dagger blades, even a few short swords visible among the Buhari—yet its presence drove home the reality of the danger they faced. A danger he now shared.

He glanced at Aisha. She appeared outwardly calm, composed, but he felt the worry seething within her. Her anxiety manifested in the form of blue-white sparks that danced around the white-knuckled fingers clutching her short-handled *assegai*.

Kodyn caught him staring and gave the Hunter a nod that clearly conveyed his confidence—in himself, in what they intended to do, and, most of all, in Aisha. His devotion to Aisha did him credit.

Let's just hope it doesn't get him—and the rest of us—killed here.

At a word from Davathi, they all rose from their crouch and strode toward the camp.

"*Jumaane!*" the *nassor* shouted at the top of her lungs. "*Jumaane!*"

The Buhari reacted with impressive alacrity. Those set to watch the darkness in the direction from which the Issai had come seemed surprised by the sudden appearance of an enemy, but quickly joined together to lock shields and raise their long spears. Those sitting or lying around the sparse campfires that illuminated the darkness of the night gathered up their weapons and sprang to their feet. A thunderous tumult, like the sound of a stampeding herd of cattle, filled the night as the Buhari rushed to face the Issai.

Davathi strode toward the line of spearmen at an unhurried pace, each step precisely placed with the leonine grace of a lifelong warrior. The Issai formed a wall to either side of her, like an honor guard escorting their monarch into some grand audience chamber. Aisha, Kodyn, and the Hunter remained in the shadows behind the Issai—their moment was yet to come.

"*Jumaane!*" Davathi called again, followed by some words in the Issai tongue. The Hunter's lessons with Kodyn and Aisha had progressed well over the last few days and being surrounded by so many Issai had advanced his grasp on the language. Yet he had no need of translation to hear the challenge in her tone.

In response, a man shouldered his way through the ranks of warriors. Yet this was no ordinary man. He stood half a head above the tallest of the Buhari, his shoulders broad enough Jarl would have been envious, his legs thick with powerful sinews. But he had none of Lord Apus' hulking, cumbersome musculature; instead, he had the lean, sparse strength of one who spent a lifetime running and fighting. The battle scars on his torso, shoulders, arms, and legs paid testament to his might. One look and the Hunter had no doubt that *this* was the chieftain of the Buhari.

Jumaane stopped two paces in front of the Buhari shield wall, planted the butt of his long spear into the ground, and stared at Davathi with a curious look. He was a handsome fellow, with a thick nose, a strong jaw beneath his curling black beard, thick eyebrows that accentuated the depth of his eye sockets, and a cunning light in his dark eyes. Upon his head, he wore the full mane of the largest lion the Hunter had ever seen, which only served to accentuate his impressive size.

"Davathi." His voice was deep—as deep as thunder rolling in the distant hills—and strong, backed by a certitude that could only come from being undisputedly the mightiest of his tribe's warriors. He spoke calmly, his answer sparse as if he chose each word carefully.

The Hunter didn't fully understand the man's answer, but fortunately, Kodyn had agreed to translate for him, to fill in the gaps in his command of the Ghandian tongue. After all, he needed to know what was being said so he could make his move at precisely the right time.

"I had believed you captive," the Buhari chieftain said.

Davathi leveled her spear at his barrel chest. "Here I stand." She narrowed her eyes. "Come to give answer for your raid on *my heart's resting place.*"

Kodyn's translation of the word *ekhaya* intrigued the Hunter. It spoke of more than just a house or home, but a deep emotional connection. Not to any one place, but the people of her tribe.

Jumaane's thick eyebrows rose. "*You,* come to give answer to *me?*" Anger blazed on his strong face and his huge hands tightened around the grip of his long spear. "Forty-three of my warriors have gone to join their *ancestors.*"

The Buhari chieftain used the word *Kish'aa,* which surprised the Hunter. He'd thought of the *Kish'aa* as nothing more than spirits, yet the word held a note of reverence akin to the way the Einari spoke of the Thirteen. It shed an interesting new light on Aisha's *Umoyahlebe* abilities—one he didn't have time to consider at the moment.

Jumaane lowered his spear to point the long head back at Davathi, a furious yet mocking imitation of her gesture. "My war band"—this, he said as *amaqhawe*—"will have blood. And we will start with yours!"

That was the Hunter's moment to act. Davathi had been certain Jumaane would demand retribution for the deaths of his warriors, as Siyanda had feared. There was only *one* thing capable of stopping the Buhari from killing every one of the Issai where they stood.

The Hunter slipped between the gap Aisha had left between her and her mother just for this moment. He'd worn his dark cloak, all the better to sell the ruse. The Buhari startled as he seemed to appear from shadows. Their eyes widened a moment later when the Hunter unsheathed the Sword of Nasnaz and the crimson runes brightened the night.

Within the depths of his hood, the Hunter gritted his teeth against the rush of fire coursing through his veins. The magic etched into *Ibad'at Mutlaqa's* blade set his head pounding and his limbs trembling with the desire for battle. A lust for blood and death, to hear the screams of his enemies ringing like the Choir of Purity in his ears. He sought out the faces of his victims, chose the warriors to strike down first. They could not stop him. Not even the iron among their ranks could slow him down. Every fiber of his being ached to be unleashed, to wade into the frenzied chaos of combat, to feel the hot gush of his foes' lives washing over him.

He fought it. With all of his steel-hard willpower, he fought the power of *Ibad'at Mutlaqa.* He could not lose control now. Not with Aisha, Kodyn, and the Issai so close behind him. They would die, too, he knew. If the Buhari did not kill them, he would. By the time he carved his way through his enemies, the sword's power would have grown to such an extent he would be unable to stop himself. The people he had fought so hard to protect and to rescue from the Consortium would die at his hands the moment he gave in to the scimitar's magic.

His willpower grew strained, began to fray. In a desperate attempt to diminish the fire building within him, the Hunter raised his voice in a terrible shout. "Lift one weapon against the Issai, and every man, woman, and child of the Buhari will die! I will carve out their eyes and leave their organs for the *makalala* to feast upon."

His tirade was far more theatrical than the Hunter had intended, yet with *Ibad'at Mutlaqa* in hand, the words bubbled up from somewhere within him—or somewhere far in his past—of their own accord.

He gripped the Sword of Nasnaz in both hands and held it in a ferocious fighting posture, letting the glow of the shining crimson runes illuminate his face—a face he had transformed to the hideous, scarred visage he'd fashioned from alchemical masks all those years ago.

"I will burn your lands and leave nothing but a desolate wasteland," he roared at the top of his lungs. "When I am done, not even the memory of the Buhari will remain!"

He took a threatening step toward the Buhari in the pretense of attacking. Though he'd spoken in Einari, understanding—and a generous measure of fear—shone on many of the Buhari's faces. Jumaane wasn't the only one of his tribe who spoke the language of the *Gcinue'eleku awandile,* according to Davathi. And there were doubtless survivors of the Hunter's slaughter among the ranks arrayed in front of him. Every one of them had witnessed the carnage, beheld the Hunter lost in the battle frenzy, and seen that same scimitar with its gleaming runes running red with the blood of their brothers, friends, and comrades.

A hundred and fifty spears came up to point toward him. Even the mighty Jumaane took a half-step back and dropped into a crouch, raising his great spear. The look on the chieftain's face was instantly serious and ready for battle.

"Stop!"

The shout resounded through the darkness, carried across the camp, cut through the tension that hung thick in the air. Just one word, yet spoken in a tone of undeniable command.

The Hunter wanted to ignore it—who would dare to command *him,* give him orders to stand his ground when there was blood to be spilled in such abundance? Yet he could not. Couldn't give in to the scimitar's magic, to the battle lust burning through every sinew. With an immense effort of will, the Hunter commanded his feet to stop moving. Then his arms to remain motionless, to hold the blade before him *without* turning its razor edge loose against his enemies.

His foe was so close; just a few steps, and he'd be among them. Hacking off Jumaane's head. Disemboweling the warriors around him. Slicing and stabbing and slashing until he drowned in the blazing heat of battle.

But he gritted his teeth and held his ground. Fighting for all he was worth to stay perfectly still just one more second, one more heartbeat.

"There is no need for bloodshed," came a familiar voice. Aisha's, speaking Einari. "Put up your sword, *Umzukeli.*"

The strain within his mind and soul nearly ripped him in half as he warred against his own magic-amplified urges. Yet somehow, the Hunter managed to will his arms to move, to raise the scimitar slowly and slide it into the scabbard on his back. He almost thought he heard a scream—a voice much like the demon that had once made its home in his mind—and that only solidified his determination. Defiantly, he rammed the sword home in its scabbard and forced his fingers to unclench from around its hilt.

The instant his fingers lost contact, the fire in his veins faded, so abruptly it left the Hunter reeling. Only sheer stubbornness kept him upright. He refused to show weakness—to

Buhari, certainly, but also to the sword's magic and his own innate demonic nature. He dug his heels into the ground and willed his legs to remain firm despite the swimming in his head.

Slowly, the world coalesced before him, just in time to see Aisha stride out to stand between him and Jumaane.

"Were we here to destroy the Buhari," Aisha said, still speaking in Einari, "I would have given *Umzukeli* the order to finish what he started days ago. But that is not why we are here."

The Buhari chieftain had straightened from his martial crouch, but his spear remained lowered to point toward the Hunter—and now Aisha. His face had smoothed, his expression revealing none of the fear that still showed on more than a few of his warriors' faces. They *had* to have heard the tales of what the Hunter had done.

"Why are you here?" he asked, also in Einari, though with a thicker, harsher accent than Davathi's.

Aisha raised a clenched fist. "Because rather than warring against the Buhari, I would have them fight the *Gcinue'eleku awandile* with us."

Chapter Two

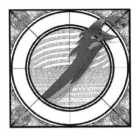

At Aisha's words, Jumaane's thick eyebrows rose even higher. "Fight...*with* you?" He stared at Aisha impassively for a long moment, no shred of expression on his face. Then he suddenly burst out laughing—a big, rich, belly-shaking sound that rumbled around the valley in which the Buhari had camped.

A few of his warriors, those who spoke Einari, laughed with him. When Jumaane spoke in his own tongue, the rest joined in, howling their mockery in Aisha's face.

To her credit, the young Issai woman didn't flinch or shrink back. The Hunter couldn't see her face, but he knew her well enough by now to know her expression would give away *nothing* of her true feelings.

Behind him, however, a few of the Issai warriors tensed, hands tightening on their *assegai*. Only a quiet word from Davathi kept the women from coming to the defense of their *nassor's* daughter—the one who had rescued them from the Consortium camp only two days earlier.

Jumaane stamped the ground with one huge bare foot, settling his lion's teeth anklet rattling. "You fight the *Gcinue'eleku awandile?*" he asked, punctuating his words with a derisive guffaw. "With your mighty army?" Despite his mockery, his eyes darted to the Hunter. He'd evidently heard the stories, too. And no one who saw the magic runes lighting up on the blade of the Sword of Nasnaz would so easily write off its wielder.

"Yes," Aisha said simply, not bothering to raise her voice over the cacophony of the Buhari's laughter. Raising her left hand high over her head, she snapped her fingers.

A piercing whistle echoed through the night, so loud it hurt even the Hunter's ears. A trick Kodyn said he'd learned from one of his fellow Hawks—the boy Sid, he'd rescued from the Gatherers, in fact. The sound was higher-pitched even than Aisha's little bamboo flute and carried much farther.

Seconds later, gasps of alarm rose from among the Buhari. Eyes went wide, spears and shields came up, and the warriors surrounding Jumaane began to shout at each other. The Hunter risked a single glance over his shoulder. At the top of the hill, spreading out in a long line, were *hundreds* of dark figures holding spears and shields.

Jumaane's laughter died in an instant, and his expression went from mocking to suspicious from one second to the next. He barked something in his tongue, sharp, questioning words aimed at Aisha.

"My mighty army," Aisha said in a too-sweet voice.

The Buhari warriors called out to their chieftain, their eyes roaming the armed figures standing on the hilltop. Fear and alarm replaced their contempt.

Aisha swept the head of her short-handled *assegai* toward the hilltop. "Let that serve as proof that I speak in earnest when I say I would rather join forces with the Buhari against our mutual enemies than shed further blood." She took a step closer to Jumaane. "Had I truly intended vengeance for your raid on my *ekhaya,* we would not be speaking."

Jumaane's face shifted through a series of expressions. Suspicion deepened, fear seeping in, transforming to recognition of his situation, then finally settling on curiosity.

"And who are you that we are speaking?" he asked, his voice rumbling up from the depths of his barrel chest. He grounded the butt of his spear beside his red-painted foot and leaned on it, bending to study her from closer. "I do not recognize you." Without straightening or moving his head, his eyes shifted beyond Aisha to seek out the Issai *nassor.* "Why do you not speak for yourself, Davathi?"

"I speak." Davathi's voice was firm, ringing with command. "Through my *indokazi,* Aisha.*"

Jumaane's head snapped up, and his eyes widened. "Your...?" He stared at Aisha as if seeing her for the first time. "You...are Aisha?"

Aisha seemed almost as taken aback as the Buhari chieftain, but to her credit, hid it better. "I am." She straightened, lifting her head. "For five years, I have sought a way to return and exact vengeance on the *Gcinue'eleku awandile* who stole me away from my *ekhaya* and my people. I would have the Buhari and Issai fight side by side as they did long ago, in the days of Falakhe and Jabhile."

Jumaane took a step closer to Aisha, moving to stand directly in front of her—so close the Hunter could smell his unique scent of *zabara* musk, kola nut, and star apple. He loomed a full head taller and nearly twice as broad in the shoulder, a mountain of muscle and intensity, yet he didn't truly dwarf Aisha. She emanated a power that only the few who'd witnessed her wield the *Kish'aa* could understand.

Something about her gave Jumaane pause. Davathi had given her assessment of the Buhari chieftain, one gained over years spent on opposite sides of raids and skirmishes. A man of Jumaane's impressive size and chieftain of a warrior people would doubtless respect strength. Yet one so economical with his words and movements would also admire *control* over that strength. He had watched the dreaded *Umzukeli* with his magical sword respond to her command like a loyal hound and heard Davathi's implicit acceptance of her daughter's authority—both critical components of the façade the Hunter, Kiara, Aisha, and Kodyn had concocted. Her fearlessness in the face of his imposing size and strength would all but clinch the deal.

Save for *one* detail.

"The Buhari have no quarrel with the *Gcinue'eleku awandile.*" Jumaane fixed Aisha with a hard look. "Why would we invite retribution when we could simply wait until the Issai are weakened and vulnerable?"

Which he *had,* hence the raid on the *ekhaya* days earlier. Davathi had spoken of Jumaane as a clever chieftain, his ferocity in battle unrivaled yet his head level when planning his course of action.

Aisha met the larger man's gaze calmly. "Do not believe there are no *Nsanga* just because the water is calm."

Jumaane's eyes narrowed, and he chewed on her words in silence.

In truth, the Buhari chieftain was correct. None of the captives freed from the Consortium camp had belonged to Jumaane's tribe. Most had been brought from the *Dalingcebo* people south of the Chasm of the Lost—including the Nkedi villagers who'd been carted past the Hunter on the road north—but many were Issai, Nyemba, Mwaani, even Tefaye. Absent the madness that had marked the Tefaye who attacked the Issai camp, of course. The Ujana had prevented their people's captivity by aligning themselves with the Consortium. According to Davathi, only the Buhari's status as the most powerful tribe with the largest *amaqhawe* had kept the Consortium at bay thus far.

Aisha's words served to remind Jumaane that the time might come—and soon—when the *Gcinue'eleku awandile* turned their eyes on the Buhari.

"Your people are mighty," Aisha said, inclining her head in a respectful nod to the towering chieftain, "but mighty enough to withstand the Vassalage Consortium on your own?"

Jumaane's huge face creased into a sneering scowl. He slammed his free hand against his chest and shouted something in his tongue. The warriors behind him took up the cry, beating their own fists to chests, and slamming the butts of their long spears against the ground.

"The *alay-alagbara* are weak!" Jumaane roared. "We are Buhari!"

I am alay-alagbara, the Hunter wanted to say, *and look what I did to you*. He wisely kept that to himself. His time to speak—or draw his sword once more—would soon come.

"The Buhari will fall!" Aisha had to shout to be heard over the deafening tumult of shouting voices and pounding spears. "Alone, they are—"

"Enough!" Jumaane silenced the shouts of his warriors and cut off Aisha's words with a slashing gesture of his huge hand. "You are brave to come here, and for that, I will allow you to walk away." He leveled a finger at the Hunter. "But know this, when we find your *ekhaya*, your people will give answer for what this *Okanele* has done."

The Hunter fought to hide a grin at the insult. *If only he knew how right he was!*

Jumaane lifted his gaze to Aisha's mother. "Leave now, Davathi. It is good to know we will soon lock spears."

"Jumaane—" Davathi began.

The Buhari chieftain snarled something in his tongue and turned on his heel to march away. At his command, forty of the warriors nearest Aisha began to advance, spears and shields raised.

The Hunter tensed, hand dropping to Soulhunger's hilt and his watered steel sword. If any one of them made a threatening move against Aisha, they would find out what a real *Okanele* looked like.

But the Buhari never got the chance. They had just taken their first step when Aisha's voice rang out.

"*Impi yechipekwe!*"

Jumaane's stride faltered mid-step. The warriors advancing on Aisha, too, slowed, hesitating.

"*Impi yechipekwe,* Jumaane!" Aisha repeated. She strode toward the warriors, heedless of the spears raised against her, the shields barring her path. "We will do this the way our peoples always have."

Jumaane turned slowly, his expression hard. He addressed her in his tongue—among his words were two the Hunter recognized: "ritual" and "combat"—and she nodded.

"I give you a choice." Aisha spoke without looking at the Buhari in her way, and like grass blown in the wind, they parted before her to let her pass. She strode up to stand before the towering chieftain. A lone Issai surrounded by Buhari, yet as fearless as if she stood within the heart of her *ekhaya*. "Fight me, or my *Okanele*. But you will fight." She leaned closer, lowering her voice so only Jumaane—and the Hunter's keen Bucelarii ears—could hear. "And when you are defeated, the Buhari will join the Issai against the *Gcinue'eleku awandile.*"

Jumaane stared down at Aisha, a look just short of a sneer on his face. He spoke in his own tongue, his words quiet and sharp, but the insult had no effect on Aisha. She merely shrugged and repeated, "Choose."

The Buhari glanced at the Hunter, and naked hatred shone in his eyes. Yet there was a generous helping of doubt, too. If he'd heard the tales from his warriors—seasoned, experienced fighters, not callow youths easily terrified—he'd have good cause to question his odds of defeating the Hunter. After all, the *Okanele* had hacked his way through more than two-score Buhari. Alone. Jumaane was confident, proud, doubtless more than a little arrogant. Yet he was no fool. He would weigh up his chances of not only winning the fight, but coming out of the battle ahead in the eyes of his warriors.

Which meant fighting Aisha wasn't the best option available to him. What had he to gain from beating the daughter of the Issai's *nassor* rather than the *nassor* herself? A girl too young to be a true *amaqhawai,* as Siyanda had made so painfully clear.

Jumaane was in a dangerous position—possible death on one hand, losing face on the other. Now it remained to be seen how he acted when faced with such a quandary. His response to Aisha's challenge would determine whether the Buhari and Issai truly *could* have a future together, as he'd hoped.

Davathi and the Issai warriors tensed as Jumaane raised his spear. However, he did not strike, merely lowered the spearhead—one made of dark grey iron, the Hunter saw in the light of a nearby campfire—to tap Aisha on the shoulder.

He barked something in his tongue, earning a roar from his warriors. Even to the Hunter, the meaning was clear. He had chosen to face Aisha in the *Impi yechipekwe.* The fate of all the people of the plains—the Issai, Buhari, and every other tribe threatened by the Vassalage Consortium and the Order of Mithridas—now rested on *her* shoulders.

Chapter Three

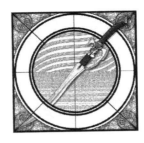

Impi yechipekwe—which translated loosely to "the clash of the chipekwe"—was a tradition as old as the plains themselves, Davathi had explained when they concocted this plan. Typically, warriors challenged the *nassor* of their own tribe to earn the right to lead or to oust an unfit chieftain or chieftainess. But over the centuries, inter-tribe conflicts had also been resolved by single combat.

Never had the combat appeared so terribly unmatched, however.

Jumaane stood in the center of the ring formed by the Issai and Buhari warriors, a giant among men. Gone were his lion's mane headdress and cape, revealing a head thick with tightly curled hair that jutted up in all directions. He wore none of the supple armor crafted from interwoven vines like the rest of his warriors, only a woven loincloth and loose-flowing skirt-like robe that swirled around his tree trunk-thick legs but left his scarred, heavily muscled torso bare. His spear and shield lay behind him; his huge hands gripped a long sword with twin edges, a vicious-looking hook for its pommel, and a flat, blunt tip. Backed by the power of his immense muscles, that blade could chop Aisha in half without slowing. Twin daggers of iron were secured to his enormous calves by bands of fibrous cloth much like those worn by the Issai, though woven of a material akin to the Buhari's shields.

Aisha stood opposite the Buhari *nassor,* far slighter and shorter by comparison, yet her outward calm remained undiminished in the face of her opponent. She had stripped off her *alay-alagbara* armor and now wore only light cloth undergarments and her boots. Her arms hung loose at her sides, holding her short-handled *assegai* and dirk in a light, easy grip.

The Hunter glanced toward the two people immediately behind Aisha. Davathi's expression was smooth, save for a single furrow visible in her brow—a match for the one that appeared on Aisha's face when she tried to mask her worries. Kodyn was far less adept at hiding his concern; the way his hands continually twitched toward the weapons on his belt, the Hunter had no doubt the young man was seriously entertaining the notion of joining Aisha in the combat circle.

But they *all* knew the role they were to play. The Hunter had been prepared to fight—upon hearing of Jumaane's skill, he'd actually looked forward to it—but they'd gone into this confrontation knowing the odds tilted far heavier toward Aisha being the one facing off against the Buhari *nassor*. The Hunter couldn't deny he felt his fair share of worry, yet it was ameliorated by the memory of what Aisha had done within the Consortium's camp. The power at her command gave her an edge here even *he* could not hope to match.

All around them, the Buhari chanted in their own tongue—shouting something about lions, perhaps invoking the spirits of the great beasts of prey whose furs they wore—and banged the butts of their spears against the ground. The Issai warriors stamped their feet and slapped their thighs in a steady cadence, answering the Buhari with defiance shining in their eyes and etched into their expressions. Though they were few, the ten women held their ground and defiantly made their voices heard among the tumult.

The chanting and stamping had gone on for the better part of a quarter-hour, and in all that time, neither Aisha nor Jumaane had moved. They stood staring each other down, studying their opponent, gauging strengths and weaknesses. Some were apparent—Aisha's agility and Jumaane's strength—but many would only become evident once combat began.

Jumaane's left hand suddenly shot up, and in an instant, the Buhari fell silent, their spears slamming against the ground one last time. Still the Issai stamped their feet and slapped their thighs, continuing alone until, nearly a full minute later, Aisha raised her *assegai* above her head. Only then did silence descend over the combat circle.

Jumaane spoke in a loud, powerful voice, his words echoing off the hills surrounding the camp. Kodyn was too far away to translate for him, but the Hunter understood a few snatches, enough to piece together the fact that the Buhari *nassor* spoke some ritual proclamation that was part of the *Impi yechipekwe*. When his hand lowered, Aisha shouted an answer in her own tongue—the Issai word for "Ready!"—and her spear came down once more to hang at her side.

A roar rose from the gathered warriors, and the battle began.

The Hunter had watched Jumaane's every movement and gesture since they first strode into the Buhari camp. His assessment of the big man proved accurate: Jumaane did not roar a challenge and barrel toward Aisha, but hefted his huge sword and advanced at a measured pace. His eyes blazed with the light of battle and an intensity shone on his bearded face, yet he did not lose himself in bloodlust as Lord Apus had. He moved like a looming thunderstorm, slow, inexorable, and threatening terrible violence.

Aisha, however, did not wait for the Buhari to reach her. No sooner had Jumaane begun his advance than she broke into a run, sprinting straight for her enemy. She closed the distance in a half-dozen steps and drove the tip of her short-handled spear straight at his belly.

Jumaane responded by bringing his heavy, blunt-tipped sword swinging across in a devastating arc. She barely had time to throw herself into a forward roll. A gasp rose from the Issai warriors as the iron blade sheared through the air a hand's breadth above Aisha's head. Scattered cheers rose from the Buhari, but turned to angry shouts as Aisha's outthrust spearhead swung around to strike Jumaane's leg. The blow didn't so much as rock the big man, and the flat of the spearhead slapped against the heavy muscle of his thigh. Yet when Aisha leaped backward, the glint of triumph shone in her eyes.

The strike had been intentionally harmless. Davathi's plan to go on the offensive against the *alay-alagbara* would only stand a chance with Jumaane at the head of the Buhari.

Jumaane spun to face Aisha, and a new wariness shone on his face. He pulled his heavy sword up to his shoulder and stalked after his smaller, younger foe with surprising grace for his size. Much like the great lion whose pelt and mane he wore. His eyes remained fixed on Aisha, his muscled body poised for her next attack.

But Aisha did not charge. Instead, she circled to her left, moving in a low, ready crouch. The tip of her *assegai* threatened Jumaane, kept his attention fixated on the outstretched weapon and away from the woman herself. The perfect distraction for her to launch her next attack.

Her left hand flashed forward in a blur of motion, and a dark shape spun end over end toward Jumaane so fast the big man had no time to evade. The pommel of Aisha's dirk *cracked* against his forehead. The throw lacked any real force, but like a well-placed jab, it sufficed to throw the Buhari *nassor* off-balance. Just enough for Aisha to dart forward and slap the flat of her spearhead against Jumaane's forearm.

320

Jumaane's face flushed, and he brought a huge hand up to wipe his forehead as if brushing a fly. His teeth bared in a snarl and he growled something in his own tongue. Aisha allowed a faint smile to form on her lips as she gave answer.

Whatever she said struck home. Jumaane abandoned his expectant pose and instead went on the attack. He threw back his head and loosed a roar that sounded terribly akin to that of a lion, then lunged toward her with terrifying speed. His huge sword whipped around his head and swung toward her chest. Aisha backpedaled, too slow. The Hunter's heart leaped into his throat as the enormous sword kissed Aisha's skin and left a long red line just below her collarbone. Aisha's confident smile wavered as she gave ground. Jumaane pursued her without hesitation. The *nassor* seemed tireless, whirling his heavy blade around and around in vicious arcs that lashed the wind in its passing. His long legs outpaced hers, his advance relentless, his strength unflagging.

When Jumaane advanced another step and brought his blade around for another strike, the Hunter nearly drew his own weapons and launched himself into the fray. Aisha barely managed to throw herself to the ground in time to avoid decapitation. When she rolled away, however, Jumaane took one long step forward and launched a kick at her. His huge foot made solid contact with her chest, and only her desperate retreat kept her ribs from breaking. The impact hurled her sprawling to the ground. For the space between heartbeats, she was entirely at Jumaane's mercy. But Jumaane did not follow up. Instead, he stepped back, raised his sword, and called something to his warriors.

Laughter rippled among the Buhari. Aisha rose to her feet, and in the light of the campfires, the Hunter could see the flush on her face. Her smile was gone now, her face set in an angry cast. The faintest hints of blue-white light danced in her eyes. With effort, she regained control of herself, tightened her grip on her weapons, and shouted to Jumaane, egging him on.

The Buhari *nassor* answered with what sounded like an insult, but Aisha did not rise to the bait. Instead, she sheathed her dirk, turned to her mother, and held out her empty left hand. Davathi tossed her *assegai* to Aisha and gave her daughter a tight nod. Now armed with *two* short-handled spears, Aisha swiveled to face her enemy across the ring.

Jumaane's expression grew sardonic, and he beckoned her with his left hand. But when Aisha advanced, she did not move as she had thus far. No sudden rush or lightning charge to get inside Jumaane's guard. She jumped first to her right, striking the two spears against each other, then darted to her left. Back and forth, her feet always moving, wooden spear shafts *clacking* in front of her, weaving her way forward, then darting backward. Graceful as a dancer, swift as a striking snake.

Jumaane's mocking smile shifted to a frown, which deepened every time she sprang forward to feint a strike and retreating without landing a blow. Again and again, his great muscles tensed in expectation of swinging his sword at her, but she never stayed within his range of attack long enough. When he took a step forward, she leaped to the side. When he pursued, she jumped toward him and slid in the opposite direction before springing away.

As one, the Issai—including Davathi—slung their arms across each other's shoulders and began to sing. It was not the joyful tune that had rung out upon Aisha's return, but a fiercer song of defiance. Calling out a challenge to their enemy, daring him to strike. They leaped high in the air, whooping in a strangely rhythmic, melodic chorus. Even the Hunter felt himself swept up in the excitement. He did not know the words, but he wanted to join the Issai in their energetic bounding, if for no other reason than to spite the motionless Buhari and their *nassor*.

Jumaane growled low in his throat, his anger directed at the Issai. Aisha seized his momentary distraction to dart forward and slap the flats of both spearheads against the side of the *nassor's* right knee. This time, the blows landed with force enough that the big man's leg wobbled beneath him.

With another lion-like roar, Jumaane brought his sword swinging up and across in a strike intended to chop Aisha in half from hip to sternum. Every muscle in the Hunter's body went suddenly tense as the heavy blade carved a deadly arc through the air toward her. But she was too swift, spinning around the sword to bring her spears slapping into the side of his left leg. This time, the Hunter saw the flash of blue-white light springing to life the moment the blows struck home.

Before the big man could recover, Aisha was behind him, driving her fists into the small of his back, then swinging around his right side once more to strike his right knee again. This time, the leg gave out and Jumaane fell to one knee. He lashed out with an elbow, and Aisha barely managed to twist her head out of the path of the attack. Even still, Jumaane's arm glanced off her shoulder and sent her staggering to the side.

Get back in there! The Hunter felt himself straining, his feet urging him to fight. Only with a supreme effort of will did he hold himself back. Yet his heart thundered in his chest, his pulse racing.

The interruption of Aisha's attack gave Jumaane precious time to regain his feet. His leg still trembled and seemed unwilling to hold him upright, but now that he was standing, he had leverage to bring his sword swinging around.

Time froze as the Hunter watched the heavy blade carve a deadly path toward Aisha's side. Off-balance, she had no chance to bring her weapons around to defend herself. Not that it would do her much good. No way the *assegai* shafts, sturdy as they were, could withstand that impact. Her only hope lay in the power she had until now kept hidden.

But before the Hunter could open his mouth to shout, Aisha unleashed the power of the *Kish'aa.* A brilliant halo of blue-white enveloped her entire body and a wave of light erupted from her chest to spray outward in all directions. The blast tore Jumaane's sword from his hand and sent it flying away into the darkness. The *nassor* himself was hurled backward. He tumbled and fell, landing hard, his head striking against the grass.

The Buhari and the leaping Issai staggered as the shockwave slammed into them. Only Kodyn and the Hunter remained unmoved; they had been prepared and braced themselves. Still, the power punched into the Hunter's chest with the force of a hammer blow and nearly knocked the wind from his lungs. The brilliance of the *Kish'aa's* light momentary blinded him. Long seconds passed as he fought to blink the dancing spots out of his eyes.

When finally his vision cleared, he found Aisha standing over the prone Jumaane. She held the tips of her spears pointed at his chest, but the razor-sharp metal heads were far from the greatest threat to the *nassor.* Jumaane's wide eyes were fixed on the sparks swirling like a firestorm around Aisha's outstretched arms, hands, and weapons.

"Umoyahlebe!" The word burst from his lips. Yet it held a ring of respect, even wonder at seeing such a visible display of her powers.

Aisha spoke in a voice too quiet for the Hunter to hear, but whatever she said had the desired effect on Jumaane. His expression grew pensive as he stared up at her silently for long moments. Then he gave a single nod of his head—which had the look of a bow of respect. Only then did Aisha lower her spears to her sides. The dancing light faded and the night once more grew dark.

Jumaane lifted his hand and shouted something to his warriors. They did not answer. Surprise appeared on every one of the faces—not only at their chieftain's words, but at the display of power they'd just witnessed. When Jumaane called again, however, those who'd managed to remain standing thumped the butts of their spears against the ground, and those who'd fallen hammered a fist against their chest.

The Issai took up a new song, and this one rang with the joy of victory. Davathi sang loudest and leaped highest of all. Pride shone in her dark eyes, nearly as bright as the sparks that had lit up the air around Aisha.

Again, the Issai *nassor* had been right about Jumaane. Her Buhari counterpart was a fierce fighter, and had Aisha faced him with skill alone, she would have likely lost. But this battle had never been about winning—at least, not *only* about winning. Aisha's combat prowess and agility would have earned Jumaane's regard, likely kept him from killing her outright. Yet the demonstration of her power—and, more importantly, her control over it—would command his respect.

Though the Hunter understood only a fraction of what had been spoken, the outcome was crystal clear.

Aisha had won the *Impi yechipekwe*...and with it, the aid of the Buhari in the war they intended to wage on the *Gcinue'eleku awandile*.

Chapter Four

The Issai celebration did not spread to the Buhari. Some still stared at Aisha with open-mouthed shock, The demonstration of her *Umoyahlebe* powers stunned them to speechlessness. More looked to Jumaane with naked disbelief, seemingly incapable of comprehending that their *nassor* had been defeated.

But there were those who turned ugly looks on the Hunter. Those nearest him in the ring moved away, their attention focused on *him*—slayer of their fellow warriors—now that the spectacle of the *Impi yechipekwe* had ended. Hands gripped spears and shields tighter, faces hardened, and angry words flew his way.

The Hunter spread his arms wide to show them empty. There had been no doubt that this would happen—all that remained to see was how it played out.

A few of the bolder Buhari began advancing on him. The fear in their eyes made it clear that they had been among those to survive the slaughter, but surrounded by so many comrades, they had regained a measure of their confidence. Perhaps even managed to delude themselves into believing they had a chance of killing him. Men who lived warriors' lives suffered defeat poorly, and now sought retribution for their dead.

Yet even as the Buhari closed in, the Hunter made no move toward his weapons. Inwardly, his stomach clenched at the sight of the dark grey iron spearheads and daggers among those arrayed against him. Outwardly, however, he forced himself to remain calm. This was among the most crucial elements of the plan they'd concocted—he had to give Aisha a chance to play the necessary part.

"Stop!" Aisha shouted in Einari, then shouted again in her own tongue. She raised her spears to level them at the Buhari advancing on the Hunter. Sparks of blue-white light glowed in the darkness again, swirling around her hands and the tips of her two weapons. When she spoke once more, her tone commanding, the warriors stopped. They did not, however, lower their weapons.

One spoke without taking his eyes off the Hunter, his face a mask of rage. He gestured toward the Hunter with his own long spear, which set the head wobbling dangerously close to the Hunter's face. It took all of his self-control not to slap the weapon aside in contempt. That would do nothing to aid Aisha now.

Aisha strode toward them, moving to stand between the Hunter and the nearest Buhari. She seemed not to care that they were surrounded by scores more—her gaze was fixed on those who had raised weapons against the Hunter, the ones most likely to actually carry out their intended violence. Her voice and the lights dancing to her command sufficed to push the Buhari back a single step. Just enough to open a gap between her and the tips of the Buhari spears.

Only then did Aisha turn to Jumaane. "*Umzukeli* answers to me," she said in Einari. "Without him, we cannot hope to defeat the enemies we now face together. If you do as your *amaqhawe* demands and spill his blood, the *Gcinue'eleku awandile* win before the battle is ever joined. Call them off."

By now, Jumaane had risen to his feet, and one of his warriors had retrieved for him the sword Aisha's magic had sent flying into the darkness. He looked between his warriors, Aisha, and the Hunter, his eyes narrowed to slits and his bearded face hard. His fingers toyed with the pommel's hook. His silence stretched on for what felt like an eternity. With every passing heartbeat, the tension in the air thickened, the Buhari warriors grew more restive, and the likelihood of bloodshed increased. Was that his intention? He'd lost the *Impi yechipekwe*, but it wouldn't matter if his *amaqhawe* attacked the Hunter in the name of retribution and the Issai died in the skirmish.

The Hunter's fingers twitched. He needed just *one* second, and he'd have his blades drawn and ready for battle. Those threatening Aisha would die first, followed by any wielding iron weapons, then—

Jumaane barked a single word in his tongue and raised his empty right hand over his head. A few of the Buhari shouted back, hatred of the Hunter evident in their retorts and on their faces, but a deafening lion-like roar from the *nassor* drowned them out. Even the most furious backed down at that. Their chieftain had lost in battle against an *Umoyahlebe* wielding powers few of them had ever seen, yet his prowess in combat had never once been called into doubt. His command of his people remained unquestioned—precisely the reason the Hunter had advised Aisha to end the fight using her *Kish'aa* magic rather than attempting to defeat him with skill alone. A feat that none of them had been certain she could manage, truth be told.

Jumaane shouted orders to his *amaqhawe*, and to their credit and his, they heeded his command. The warriors surrounding Aisha and the Hunter lowered their weapons and turned away, joining the rest of their fellows in stamping out the fires and breaking their sparse camp. The numbers around them dwindled until only thirteen Buhari stood beside Jumaane to face Aisha and her companions. An equal number, more of a token honor guard than any true fighting force. That boded well for their discourse.

One look at Jumaane's face disabused the Hunter of any hopes the Buhari would easily look past the deaths of their fellows. As Siyanda had made abundantly clear, their raid on the Issai would have ended with broken bones and wounds far from mortal, with no more than a few casualties at most. But no leader—be they emperor, king, or *nassor*—could let such slaughter as the Hunter had wreaked go unanswered.

"You call him *Okanele* and *Umzukeli*," Jumaane growled, his voice low and angry. He tightened his grip on his heavy sword. "Then you will pay the price of his actions?"

The Hunter had no need to ask what that price would be. Such things were only ever paid for in blood and agony.

"No." Aisha stood straighter, lifted her head. "The *Gcinue'eleku awandile* will."

Jumaane's eyes narrowed to slits, his umber-skinned face growing as hard and dark as the iron daggers strapped to his legs. "How?"

Aisha stepped to the side, gesturing for the Hunter to step forward. The time had finally come for him to say the words he'd been rehearsing in his mind since the plan to convert the Buhari from enemies into allies first entered his mind.

"I answer to Aisha," he said, pitching his voice low like Jumaane's, though with more gravel and rasp to match the scarred visage he now wore. "My strength and my blades are bound to her cause. And to any who would align with her." He stepped closer, advancing to within

325

striking range of Jumaane's great sword yet making no move toward his own weapons. "I have sworn to cut the rot of the *Gcinue'eleku awandile* from these lands, to drive out the *alay-alagbara* who would sully your *ekhaya*, steal your people, use the *Umoyahlebe* to their own wicked ends."

That last had been most important, according to Davathi. Few of the tribes in the region had their own Spirit Whisperers. Most alive today hailed from the Issai, though the Nyemba and Mwaani had a few among their number. Like the Tefaye and Ujana, the Buhari had none living. Not for two hundred years had any with the *Umoyahlebe* gift been born to the Buhari. This had given rise to a respect bordering on reverence for those blessed with the ability to speak to the *Kish'aa.* After all, without *Umoyahlebe,* the Buhari had no means of communicating with their dead—their *ancestors,* according to Kodyn's translation.

The Hunter thumped a fist against his chest in imitation of the Buhari warriors' gesture. "I am bound to the Issai—and all the tribes who unite in their cause—until such a time as these lands are cleansed and every one of your people held captive are freed. Until you are free of their cruelty and the threat they pose to all who stand in their way." He stood straighter, raised his voice louder. "I will spill rivers of blood in the execution of this task. For every Buhari life ended at my hand, I vow to end *five* of your enemies. For every tear shed by your people over the loss, I will drown the *amathafa* in the cries of the *alay-alagbara.* This I have sworn, and this I swear."

Throughout his speech, Jumaane had watched him carefully, his eyes sharp and scrutiny intense. There was a keen intelligence behind the man's eyes, a mind as honed as his sword's edge. Despite his rough visage and scarred figure, he had not yet reached his third decade of life. Attaining the role of *nassor* at such a young age and among such a warlike people spoke highly of the man. Davathi's assessment of her rival chieftain had only served to cement the Hunter's certainty that they needed Jumaane on their side if they wanted any chance to defeat the foes they would soon face. Which meant he *had* to convince the man to let bygones be bygones, at least until such a time as the Order and Consortium were defeated. If the Buhari still wanted vengeance for their fallen warriors...

We'll burn down that particular bridge when we get to it, the Hunter thought, shrugging mentally.

Aisha seized that moment to step in. "Right now, the *Gcinue'eleku awandile* are holding captive every *Umoyahlebe* they could find." This, they had learned from the Nyemba and Mwaani warriors who'd been among those liberated from the Consortium camp. "What they want with them, we do not yet know. But they are all being held at *Ukuhlushwa Okungapheli.*"

At that, an involuntary shudder ran down Jumaane's spine and his expression darkened. The Buhari were among the most superstitious of the tribes, and for all their aggressive conquest in the past, they had always claimed land *away* from what they maintained to be "a place of evil".

Now Davathi came to stand beside her daughter, lending her authority as *nassor* of the Issai to the discussion. "I will be leading my *amaqhawe* against the *alay-alagbara,* but alone, we stand little chance of victory." She slid an arm around Aisha's shoulders and squeezed. "Of liberating my *umiyani* and *kwa'indokazi.*"

This word, Kodyn had explained before, meant something akin to "beloved younger daughter".

Jumaane's eyebrows rose. "Lwazi is among those taken?" He spoke the name with audible reverence.

"He is." Davathi's face creased into a snarl. "But not for much longer. Not once the Issai and Buhari unite against the enemy we both share." She stretched out her hand to Jumaane. "The enemy who will bring destruction to us all unless we are united."

Jumaane stared down at Davathi's hand, then, with a slow nod, reached out to clasp her arm. "By the traditions of *Impi yechipekwe,* we are united." His huge muscles coiled as he tightened his grip on Davathi. "But this matter of the *Okanele*"—his eyes darted to the Hunter—"will be resolved when the time comes."

Davathi answered in Issai, and whatever she said seemed to satisfy Jumaane. When he pulled his arm back, he inclined his head to Aisha. "*Umoyahlebe.*" Then, turning on his heel, he strode away and joined his fellow Buhari in breaking camp.

Beside the Hunter, Aisha let out a long breath. "Bloody hell!" she whispered.

"Well done, *indokazi.*" Pride echoed in Davathi's voice. She looked over her shoulder and gave the Hunter a satisfied nod. "And you played your part well, *Okanele.*"

The Hunter swept a theatrical bow. "I live to serve."

Davathi snorted. "Two days I have known you, *Umzukeli,* and I needed much less to know that is the farthest thing from the truth."

The Hunter grinned. She wasn't far wrong.

Chapter Five

Jumaane roared out a hearty laugh when he first laid eyes on Aisha's "mighty army".

"Ahh, Davathi, I should have known." The huge Buhari clucked his tongue and shook his head at the Issai *nassor*. "The Old Cheetah taught you well."

Davathi arched an eyebrow at her counterpart. "This was all my *indokazi's* idea."

Jumaane turned to regard Aisha. "Is that so?" He made no attempt to keep the impressed look off his face. "Then I am glad my *nkemba* did not remove your head from your shoulders." For emphasis, he patted the huge sword he now wore hanging suspended from his woven, fibrous armor, which he'd donned in the aftermath of his fight with Aisha. The rest of his warriors were similarly armored, covered from neck to ankle in the same light protective material that comprised their shields. With spears in their hands and more compact versions of Jumaane's *nkemba* sword, they appeared a true fighting force.

Which contrasted sharply with Aisha's "army". Most of those who had joined the Issai warriors atop the hill were too weak to do more than stand and lean heavily on the wooden staves carved to appear as spears in the darkness. Days of traveling eastward into Buhari lands had left the half-starved, overworked people on the verge of collapse. Only sheer determination to escape their captors and return to their homes—some beyond even the borders of Ghandia—had kept them going.

More than a few of the Buhari who'd ascended from their camp below cast dark looks at the ragged, filthy, half-naked men, women, and children surrounding them. Had they known the truth, they would have leaped into battle without hesitation, and they would not be aligned with what appeared to be a tribe near the edge of utter destruction. Aisha's plan—in large part, Kodyn's plan, modeled after some chicanery his mother had pulled off during her younger years in the Night Guild, according to the young Praamian—had ensured the darkness provided ample concealment for the weakness of those accompanying Davathi.

Angry shouts were hurled in the Issai's direction—among them the word the Hunter had come to understand was a slur meaning "coward" that called into question the intended target's intestinal fortitude—but a roar and a few barked words from Jumaane stifled them. He turned back to Davathi and said something in his own tongue. Whatever it was, the Issai *nassor* bowed her head, gratitude visible on her face.

The Hunter caught sight of Kodyn standing beside Aisha. The young man had remained largely silent and in the shadows, content to not only let Aisha take credit for his plan, but to serve as the face of the uprising preparing to move against the *alay-alaghara*. That, in and of itself, was something to be admired. It took a strong man to let another take the lead, when he had proven himself cunning and capable in his own right.

"What'd Jumaane say to Davathi?" he asked, moving to stand behind the two youths.

"'The Buhari abide by their oaths,'" Kodyn translated. "He pledged his strength to the Issai, a marriage made stronger by the cunning displayed here."

Jumaane's words seemed to resonate among his warriors. When they looked at the twenty-odd Issai standing around Davathi or among the captives, their faces held a new respect. Perhaps even a hint of admiration. Such a ruse was the very definition of audacity. The fact that Davathi and Aisha had marched into their camp and put themselves in direct danger—in Aisha's case, likely death at the hands of their *nassor*—earned them more than a generous measure of regard.

Yet when their eyes strayed in his direction, the visible hatred and loathing returned. The Hunter couldn't blame them. So long as none of them were foolish enough to carry out some form of vengeance, he would not begrudge them their vitriolic stares and sullen mutterings.

At that moment, a familiar figure emerged from among the crowd of recently-freed captives playing at being an army. Kiara's hands were covered in blood, with streaks of crimson staining her clothing and speckles dotting her face. She had spent every spare moment over the last two days doing her best to minister to the myriad wounds sustained during months of enslavement and the battle for freedom. Already, nearly a score of captives had succumbed to blood loss, fester and rot, fever, or simply the plains' unforgiving heat. Without canteens or waterskins, they had no way to transport water on their journey. They'd been forced to leave nearly half of their number behind on the banks of the Gwembashi River a day's run east of the place where Sizwe, one of the Issai's older *amaqhawai*, had believed they would find the Buhari.

The Hunter's spirits lifted at the sight of Kiara. Even tired, sweaty, covered in blood, her hair matted, and with dark circles under her eyes, she was beautiful. Perhaps even *more* so.

Her mocking smile lit up the darkness. "I see you managed to keep yourself out of trouble, eh?"

"Not for lack of trying," he said, shrugging.

She laughed—a sound that still melted his heart, three years on—and rose on tiptoes to kiss him gently. The metallic tang of blood on her lips bothered him not at all. "I'm guessing by the lack of lowered spears and shouted war cries that the plan worked?"

"It did." Aisha smiled, looked at Kodyn. "Just like you said it should."

Kodyn raised his hands. "Hey, it took *your* fearlessness to pull it off. Even the best plan could have collapsed without that."

From anyone else, the Hunter might have considered the humility false. But Kodyn appeared genuinely modest. He certainly had his mother's confidence, yet it had none of her—admittedly well-earned, by all accounts—arrogance. His estimation of the young man rose even higher.

Kiara looked over the Buhari. "Friendly lot."

The Hunter chuckled. "You could say that."

The lion-clad warriors on the hilltop remained in a tight bunch, staring around them with suspicion, wariness, scorn, or, in the Hunter's case, tightly restrained fury. Jumaane, by contrast, appeared utterly at ease, speaking with Davathi as if they were old friends. Or, perhaps better said, old *enemies*. If, as Siyanda had said, the raid was merely the way of the *amathafa*, it wouldn't surprise the Hunter to learn that Davathi and Jumaane had squared off across the battlefield before. Indeed, it had been Davathi who advised Aisha on the best tactics to combat Jumaane's strength and reach. There had been familiarity in her words, just as there was familiarity in the way Davathi now spoke to Jumaane. She held her *assegai* in a loose grip, its tip pointed at the ground, her stance relaxed and open.

"How are they?" the Hunter asked. When Kiara turned to look at him, he gestured with his chin toward the bedraggled men, women, and children occupying the hilltop.

Kiara's expression grew grim. "Tired. Hungry. Thirsty." Despite the hard edge, a glimmer of admiration shone on her face. "Determined to return to their people as soon as they can. In the case of our friends from Nkedi, they're already talking about rebuilding their village."

"Like water carving a path through stone, few things are as stubborn as a man resolved to survive." The Hunter surveyed the huddled, exhausted captives. They had come all this way for a chance at freedom and vengeance. Few were warriors, yet they had all joined in without hesitation when the time for battle came. In a way, they *were*, in fact, an army. What they lacked in training and weaponry they more than made up for in resolve. If Davathi's plan to arm those willing to fight succeeded—and their alliance with the Buhari was an admirable first step in the right direction—the Vassalage Consortium and Order of Mithridas were in for a ferocious fight.

Kiara opened her mouth to say something, but the words never came out. Her eyelids fluttered and she swayed as if drunk.

The Hunter reached out to grab her, catching her before she fell. For long seconds, she leaned against him heavily—indeed, it felt as if his arms were the only thing holding her up. Her breath came faster and sweat streamed down her face. A vein on the side of her neck throbbed visibly.

"Kiara?" The Hunter spoke quietly, urgently. "Talk to me."

"What's wrong?" Aisha asked. She and Kodyn crowded around him, staring worriedly at Kiara.

"I don't know." The Hunter pressed one hand to her forehead. "She's a bit hot, but not feverish. I didn't see any wounds that might have—"

"I'm fine." Kiara was suddenly once more herself. She slapped his hand away, standing upright on her own. "Just exhausted, that's all. There haven't exactly been many feather beds and goose down comforters these last few weeks."

The Hunter studied her through narrowed eyes, unconvinced. The pallor of her skin *might* have been merely from exhaustion, or a trick of the moonlight.

"You sure?" he asked. She hadn't collapsed like this since Khafra. "I know your wound's had time to heal, but—"

"I'm sure." Kiara gave him a reassuring smile, turning it to Kodyn and Aisha to assuage the worry evident on their faces. "I told you, I'm just tired." She ran a hand across her brow, wiping away sweat, grime, and speckles of blood. "I'm going to get some proper sleep as soon as I can. And a drink of water and a real meal. But we've had little of the last two and less in the way of time. Too many people on the verge of collapse."

"And you'll do them no good if you collapse." The Hunter tried in vain to keep his own concern for her under wraps. The fact that she'd all but passed out on her feet made it clear that she was pushing herself beyond her limits. "Promise me that you'll get some rest first chance you get. Otherwise, I'll have Tarek put something alchemical and sleep-inducing in your water."

"I'd settle for just the water and a few minutes off my feet." Kiara patted his arm, beaming up at him. "You're adorable when you're worried about me, you know?" She gestured to his forehead. "Your nose goes all scrunched up, like Hailen's, and you get these delightful little wrinkles between your eyebrows." Her eyes lit up. "Yes, like that!"

The Hunter felt his forehead. "I don't get—" He trailed off as his fingertips found the wrinkles she'd mentioned. With a quick effort of will, he shifted the muscles of his forehead to smooth out the flesh. "I don't get wrinkles."

Kiara snorted. "That's cheating!" Her eyes shone brighter, and she reached a hand behind his head to pull him down toward her for a kiss. "But still adorable."

The Hunter didn't fail to note the way Aisha and Kodyn colored and turned their backs on them, suddenly *very* interested in the last of the Buhari streaming up the hill from the camp. But in the next moment, he was fully attentive to the sweet, soft lips pressed against his. The warmth of Kiara's body against his suddenly reminded him how long it had been since last they'd had time alone. The cool, green-blue waters of Nsukeja Lake felt a world away.

When Kiara broke off, she didn't release him. Instead, she shifted so her lips were pressed against his cheeks.

"I'm not the one you should be worrying about," she whispered, her voice pitched low for his ears only.

The Hunter stiffened. That was *not* the "sweet nothings" he'd expected from her lips.

"Next chance you get, find Tarek and talk to him."

The Hunter frowned—and couldn't help feeling the furrow once more returning between his eyebrows. "Tarek?" He pulled back, looking down at Kiara. "What's wrong with him?"

Kiara stared up into his eyes. "That's for you to find out." Her right hand squeezed the back of his neck firmly. "Ask him next chance you get. I don't know what exactly, but I can feel it. There's something going on in here..." She tapped her chest with her left hand, then her forehead. "And in here." She placed her hand against his armored chest, just above his heart. "Talk to him. He needs to get it out before it, whatever it is, gets worse."

Chapter Six

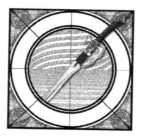

Try as he might, the Hunter could not locate Tarek. That worried him, until Kodyn mentioned he'd overheard two of the Issai talking about the young man's incessant questioning about some plant they called *okhafi*. It seemed the Elivasti had been interested enough about the flower to slip away after the *Impi yechipekwe* resolved. Fortunately, he'd had the presence of mind to take one of the *amaqhawai* with him.

"Naledi will know how to find us," said one of the Issai, speaking through Kodyn. "She knows where we are going and will meet us along the way."

The Hunter had no choice but to accept that. He couldn't exactly go riding off into the plains after Tarek. The Elivasti had no scent he could track, and save for the vague direction of "southeast" the Issai had mentioned, the Hunter couldn't be sure where to find the young man.

A pity, he thought wryly. *I could have used the distraction.* He was growing weary of the hate-filled glares the Buhari cast his way. They had made no move in open defiance of their *nassor,* but he wouldn't put it past them to find some means of avenging their fallen comrades. A dagger in the back when the eyes of Jumaane and the Issai were turned away, he suspected. He'd spent countless nights sleeping with one eye open, so what were a few more?

Fortunately, most of the Buhari were soon too busy to do more than direct an occasional glower at him. Whether of their own accord or at the command of their *nassor,* the warriors fell to the task of helping those weakened and exhausted by their months in captivity. Though none of those held by the Consortium had been Buhari, many came from tribes whose lands bordered theirs: Nyemba, Mwaani, and Issai. Furthermore, the tribes hadn't always been enemies—the occasional raid notwithstanding. Ingiyab Yengwayo had chronicled countless occasions when the tribes had aligned against common enemies.

Which, in part, was where the Hunter had gotten the idea to recruit the Buhari. It had been Davathi who had proposed the *Impi yechipekwe* and Aisha who'd put forward herself and the Hunter both as combatants.

Now, the same Buhari that had intended to raid the Issai to steal their cattle only days earlier joined arms with their fellows and lent aid wherever it was needed. At Jumaane's order, a five-man company ran southeast to bring word to the Buhari *ekhaya* of their newfound alliance with the Issai and to summon the remainder of the *amaqhawe.* More joined the strongest of the Issai warriors in scouting the way ahead and traveling toward the edge of *Indawo Yokwesaba* to keep watch for the first signs of the inevitable reprisal by the *Gcinue'eleku awandile.*

The bulk of the warriors, however, remained to help the captives. They distributed what food and water they could spare, supported or even carried those too wounded or weak to travel. Buhari walked alongside Dalingcebo who had, until only weeks earlier, never stepped foot beyond the Chasm of the Lost, and joined arms with the Nyemba and Mwaani to help them return to the lands of the Issai.

Davathi and Jumaane strode at the head of the long, straggling column marching steadily northwest toward the place where Aisha's mother believed Siyanda had taken the Issai *ekhaya* to hide. Behind them, six warriors from each tribe formed an honor guard that spread out in a semi-circle flanking their respective *nassors*. Aisha had taken up a place between the two chieftains, and to the Hunter, it looked as if *she* was what united the two tribes. She was no *amaqhawai*, yet her *Umoyahlebe* gifts and the power she'd displayed before all made her something else…something greater, perhaps.

The Hunter glanced toward Kodyn, who rode beside him and Kiara on the column's eastern flank, a few dozen paces back from Aisha and the two *nassors*. It was clear the young man wanted to be at Aisha's side, yet he seemed content to remain apart. As if he understood that his place—for the time being—was to give her space to be where she was most needed.

"Tell me, Kodyn, what did you find among the papers you took from the Consortium offices?" The Hunter asked the question both to pass the time and distract the young man's mind, but also out of genuine interest. "Anything to explain what the Order of Mithridas wanted with all that dimercurite, and what they're doing at the Bondshold?"

Kodyn glanced down at the satchel of papers hanging from his saddlehorn. "Truth be told, I haven't had more than a few minutes to dig through what I found." He gave an apologetic shrug. "Saying things have been a bit hectic since we left *Indawo Yokwesaba* is a bit of an understatement."

The Hunter chuckled. "Fair enough." They *had*, after all, traveled virtually nonstop for two days, all the while watching over their shoulders for any sign of Consortium pursuit while also searching for the Buhari *amaqhawe* Davathi had known would come hunting the Issai seeking vengeance for the slaughter the Hunter had wreaked. "Find anything useful in those few minutes of digging?"

Kodyn frowned, scratching at the stubble that had begun to grow thicker on his handsome face. "There's something that *might* be records of some kind of alchemical testing, though my training with House Scorpion falls well short of true understanding of what exactly they're testing for."

"Oh?" This from Kiara. Her voice held an intrigued note. "Mind if I take a look at it?"

Kodyn's eyebrows rose. "You think you can understand them?" As if realizing what he'd just said, he flushed and stammered, "What I meant was—"

"I know no disrespect was intended." Kiara gave the young man a reassuring smile. "I'll admit, I don't exactly look the part of an alchemist." She gestured to her armor and weapons. "But I've got a good friend in Voramis who's made it his mission over the last year or so to teach me as much as he can." Her eyes darted to the Hunter. "Quality time together, and all that."

The Hunter plastered on a mock scowl. "Seems like I owe our *friend* a good talking-to when I get back." He didn't keep up the pretense for long. There was no faulting Graeme for being taken by Kiara's beauty, intelligence, and spirit. The Hunter himself had fallen for exactly that.

Kiara's grin widened to match his. "Don't worry, Hunter. Your place is safe. For now." Her smile grew wicked and sharp. "Though I will admit Jumaane is looking pretty g—"

"So," the Hunter said, turning back to Kodyn, "those tests?"

"Right!" Kodyn colored slightly as if embarrassed at being drawn into their private feud and hurried to dig a pair of parchments out of the satchel he'd carried away from the Consortium

333

camp. "Here." He extended them toward the Hunter, who took them and handed them to Kiara, who rode on his left side.

She glanced at the sky, then held the documents tilted at just the right angle to catch the faint light of the moon. For long minutes, she frowned down at the parchments, her brow furrowed and a look of utter concentration on her face. The Hunter had turned back to the plains ahead—what appeared to be endless miles of gently rolling grass-covered hills dotted with the occasional tree or shrub—when a sharp intake of breath snapped his attention to Kiara.

"By the Watcher!" she said, her face going pale.

"What is it?" the Hunter and Kodyn both asked at the same time.

Kiara's eyes lifted from the parchment, and a look of utter loathing twisted her features. "The Consortium...they were experimenting with the dimercurite. Like you said"—this, she directed at Kodyn—"testing its effects. On *people*."

The Hunter's eyebrows shot up. "Which people?" He glanced past Kiara to where the line of bedraggled Issai, Mwaani, Nyemba, and Dalingcebo struggled to keep pace with the hale, well-fed Buhari. "And what kind of tests?"

"The worst kind." A grim edge sharpened Kiara's words. "The kind that leaves their victims—" She looked down at the parchment and read, "*in a state of high suggestibility and heightened aggression, to the extent that even the slightest provocation led to extreme violence comparable to rabidity, with a near-total lack of response to pain stimuli.*"

A sick feeling settled into the pit of the Hunter's stomach.

"Does it say what poor bastards were the subjects of these tests?" he asked, yet he had a sinking suspicion that he already knew. The description sounded terribly familiar.

Kiara's expression grew grave, shadows dark in her eyes. "The Tefaye."

Not *a* Tefaye. *The* Tefaye. The Consortium tests had been run on an entire tribe of Ghandians. And not just any tribe, but the worst of them. Thieves, murderers, troublemakers, those cast out from the other tribes.

"How is that possible to test on an entire—?" the Hunter began, but a memory from days earlier answered the half-formed question. The sick feeling in his stomach wormed its way deeper. "The water."

"The Unathi River!" Kodyn said at the same time.

The Hunter glanced toward the young man. Kodyn had spoken with such certainty, but how had he known?

"In Shalandra," Kodyn said, "a group of Gatherers tried something similar. Pouring a poison into the Wellspring that fed water to the city's lower tiers. Everyone who drank it fell ill with what they called the Azure Rot."

The Hunter's stomach clenched at the thought. He'd been in Voramis when the Bloody Flux devastated Lower Voramis, left tens of thousands dead on the streets, alleys, and thoroughfares. The idea of unleashing something of that scale *intentionally* revolted him.

Yet the Consortium had done precisely that. It had been *they* who channeled the Unathi River away from its natural course to direct it into the lands set apart for the Tefaye. A clever plan in a disgustingly pragmatic way. None of the other tribes would care if the Tefaye died out as a result of the Consortium testing—they would likely see it merely as just punishment for their crimes, or the way of the *amathafa*. Only when the Tefaye began attacking the other tribes did the consequences of the Consortium's actions become known. And those consequences only served to strengthen their position in Ghandia by weakening every tribe that might oppose them.

Mention of "high suggestibility" lent more than a little credence to the notion that the Consortium somehow steered or controlled the Tefaye.

Still, something didn't quite sit right with the Hunter. "Tarek said nothing about heightened aggression or blood-madness, though." He frowned. "Seems like the sort of thing to mention when everyone is breathing in dimercurite dust."

"That's because it wasn't *just* dimercurite." Kiara was glaring down at the parchments once more. "That was just what they started with." She tapped a finger against a line of text scrawled in a cribbed hand. "Dimercurite alone just made the Tefaye sick, weak. It's clear that's not at all the desired outcome, so they started mixing in other substances. Violet Flagberry. Abstralia. Whispering Lily."

The Hunter had heard of the first two—one was a poisonous berry popular among the nobility of Voramis for its dark purple pigmentation and slight euphoria-inducing effect, the other the herb from which Bonedust was extracted. But the last was unfamiliar to him.

"Whispering Lily?" he asked.

To his surprise, the answer came from Kodyn. "Watcher's Bloom."

The Hunter turned to regard the young man. "You sure?"

Kodyn returned his look with a nod. "In Shalandra, the flowers are called Keeper's Spike. But Aisha called them Whispering Lilies. She recognized them in Shalandra, just as she recognized them again a few days ago."

The Hunter grimaced. He'd experienced the hallucinogenic side effects of the Watcher's Bloom firsthand in Voramis. If the Tefaye were seeing the spirits of the dead *and* succumbing to the same illness that had gripped the Issai back in the Consortium camp, that might explain a measure of their madness. But not all of it.

"Is there anything else?" he asked Kiara. "Any other ingredient mentioned there?" The more they knew about whatever was poisoning the Tefaye, the greater the chance they'd have of counteracting the toxin. Restoring the Tefaye to full health and sanity would serve their purposes two-fold: deprive the Consortium of a tool they had clearly been using since the testing began, and possibly gain additional allies to bolster their forces.

"There is." Kiara's face had gone grey, solemn. "Their last addition to the test was Tangled Gallberry."

The Hunter stared blankly at her. The name meant nothing to him. A glance in Kodyn's direction revealed a similar expression on the young man's face.

"Graeme told me about it," Kiara said, in a slow, ponderous voice. "That night you went to him for supplies to eliminate the Red Fists, you did the thing where you startled him. When I saw him the next morning, he was in a foul mood, railing at you and swearing that the next time he gave you a healing draught, it would instead be Tangled Gallberry. 'Let's see him walk that off!' were his exact words."

Something about her expression filled the Hunter's belly with dread. Not because she believed for a moment Graeme would *truly* poison him. No, it was something about the ingredient itself that had her worried.

"What does it do?" he asked, curious yet somehow dreading her answer.

Kiara's eyes grew shadowed. "In concentrated doses, it shatters the minds of its victims, leaves them nothing more than mindless husks with little will of their own."

"Highly suggestible," Kodyn breathed.

The Hunter's heart sank. The Consortium hadn't just poisoned the Tefaye; with their tests, they had turned an entire tribe of murderers, thieves, and outcasts into a weapon that only *they* commanded. An army that obeyed their masters' commands without question and fought without fear or pain.

That was a foe not even the combined *amaqhawe* of the Issai and Buhari were certain to defeat.

Chapter Seven

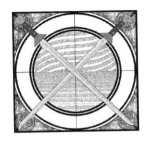

The Hunter's unease mounted with every passing hour. By the time dawn threatened on the eastern horizon and Tarek still hadn't returned, the Hunter was on the verge of genuine worry. He wasn't alone. Kiara's eyes never ceased straying to the horizon, the furrows on her brow growing deeper the farther to the northwest they traveled.

His concern proved unfounded when, finally, the sun brightening the eastern skies shone down on two figures—one mounted on horseback, the other racing on two bare feet—hurrying to catch up with them.

The Hunter breathed a sigh of relief, and thought he heard Kiara doing likewise. It felt foolish—Tarek was, to his own people, a man grown, a True Descendant, the warrior chosen by the Second Blade for a task of this magnitude.

Yet the Hunter couldn't help seeing Hailen whenever he looked at Tarek. It didn't help that they resembled each other so strongly, or that Tarek frequently exhibited the same mannerisms the Hunter had seen from the boy he'd come to love over the years. And for all Tarek's competence and the wide range of abilities he'd demonstrated time and time again over their journey together, the young man was still that: *young*. Not much older than Kodyn and Evren, in truth. The Hunter had grown to feel responsibility for Tarek much the same way he did for Evren and Hailen. Or, over the last few weeks, for Kodyn and Aisha.

Tarek and Naledi caught up with the slow-moving procession two hours before noon. The Issai *amaqhawai* was among the strongest of those freed from the Consortium camp; the months of hunger, thirst, hard labor, and insufficient sleep hadn't worn on her as greatly as some of her fellow warriors. Still, she had the lean, emaciated, hollow-eyed look that marked every one of the captives. Despite the brave façade they put on, the Issai were a long way off from recovering.

The Hunter was astonished by how ragged Tarek looked. Heavy bags hung beneath his eyes, which had grown sunken from lack of sleep. His scruffy beard was matted with sweat, dust, and blood, his lips were chapped from thirst, and he had the appearance of a man who hadn't seen a hearty meal in weeks, not days. When he reined in Nayaga beside the Hunter, he all but collapsed from the saddle.

"Easy!" The Hunter reached out a hand to steady the young man.

"I'm fine." Tarek waved him away, recovering enough to sit up straight. "Long night."

A lot of long nights, the Hunter wanted to say. He didn't. The look in Tarek's eyes reminded him a great deal of Hailen. There had been more than a few times when the boy had refused sleep in the name of completing some task or lesson assigned him by Father Reverentus.

Graeme, too, could be obsessive in his pursuit of alchemical secrets. *But then I suppose the same could be said about me as well when I find something that consumes my attention.*

"Did you find what you sought?" he asked. The hunt for a cure for the dimercurite poisoning had driven Tarek relentlessly over the last two days. Only the need to hunt and tend to the injured and ill had distracted him from the single-minded pursuit. "The *okhafa?*"

"*Okhafi,*" Tarek corrected. "And no, I didn't." A sour expression darkened his face. "It was something else, something…useless." His fists clenched around Nayaga's reins. "Another night wasted, and I'm no closer to finding a solution."

The Hunter narrowed his eyes. Not even the pursuit of the *maistyr* he'd been sent by Itan to locate had consumed Tarek so completely. And that was the future of *his* people on the line, not the fate of a few captives he'd only met two days ago.

No, there was something more to this than met his eye. But what? The Hunter couldn't begin to guess.

"Go easy on yourself," the Hunter said, trying for a gentle tone. "No one's expecting you to solve this overnight."

"I know!" Tarek's voice came out razor-sharp, accompanied by a glare with far too much vehemence. The fire in his violet eyes died in a moment, however, replaced by the shadows of weariness and some deeper, darker emotion the Hunter could not decipher. He scrubbed a hand over his face. "I know," he said again, calmer and quieter now. "It's just frustrating, knowing so little. I thought…" His voice trailed off.

The Hunter saw the opening, the momentary crack in Tarek's façade, and seized the opportunity to dig further. "Thought what?"

Tarek shook his head. "Never mind." He slumped in his saddle. "I'll feel better after a bit of food and some sleep." He eyed the slow-moving column of Ghandians trailing hundreds of paces behind them. "Any idea how soon they'll call a halt?"

The Hunter felt the young man retreating, clamming up, and wanted to press the matter. But he thought better of it. He couldn't force such things; he'd learned that with Hailen over and over. Young men tended to open up on their own time, only showing vulnerability when they felt truly safe.

And so, he allowed the young man to shift subjects to escape discussing the truth beneath the newfound preoccupation that drove him to near-obsession.

"Not a clue." He shrugged. "But by the looks of things, it won't be much longer. The heat's getting worse, people are getting tired, and something tells me *that's* an ideal resting place." He indicated a thick stand of trees a half-league to the northwest. At the very least, they'd have shelter from the blistering sun.

"Good." Tarek let out a yawn, his shoulders and head drooping.

"You'll rest when we stop?" the Hunter asked, trying to keep the concern from his voice. "With what the Buhari have shared, there's food enough that you won't be needed to hunt."

Tarek cast a sidelong glance at the Hunter but nodded. "Aye. Rest." He ran a hand over his face again. "Sleep'll clear out the cobwebs in my brain. Who knows, maybe I'll think up something new." With a nod, he dug his heels into Nayaga's flanks and set off at a fast trot toward the trees, joining the three Buhari and two Issai warriors dispatched to scout the way ahead.

Once Tarek had passed out of earshot, Kiara spoke up from where she rode beside the Hunter. "You're not going to tell him what we found? About the Consortium tests?"

The Hunter studied the young man's retreating back for long seconds, then shook his head. "Soon, but not yet. He's not ready."

"Not ready?"

The Hunter turned to find Kiara giving him a curious look, one eyebrow arched.

"Whatever's going on in his head, it's consuming him, driving him beyond the point of exhaustion." The Hunter shook his head. "Until he can come to terms with it, the last thing he needs is *another* burden."

"He's our best chance of reversing what was done to the Tefaye, if such a thing is possible." Kiara spoke with her voice pitched low for his ears only. With a nudge of her legs, she shifted Ash to ride directly alongside the Hunter until her knee all but scraped his ankle. "It's a lot to put on his shoulders, but if there's any hope—"

"I know." The Hunter let out a long breath. "But it's as if he feels *responsible* somehow, like it's all on him. And in truth, it is. No one else seems to know anything about dimercurite, much less how to negate its effects. That's got to be a weight, which grows heavier every time he fails. Because that failure means someone else dies."

He glanced behind him. Far behind the column of Ghandians, the enormous winged *makalala* circled around four corpses laid out among the tall plains grasses. Two Issai, one Nyemba, and one of the young women taken from Nkedi. More unfortunate souls succumbed to the Consortium's cruelties and dimercurite poisoning. Seeing those bodies could only have added to the burden on Tarek's shoulders—on his soul.

"I don't know *why* he feels like this, but he does." The Hunter shook his head. "And telling him an entire tribe was poisoned with some dimercurite mixture is only going to make it worse."

He looked down at Kiara, half-expecting some rebuttal from her. But she merely smiled at him and rested her hand on his leg.

"You're getting better at this, you know?" Her eyes brightened, her face alight with pride. In *him?* "There was a time you wouldn't have understood simple emotions unless they hit you in the face with a brick. Now?" She squeezed his leg firmly. "I've always known you were a remarkable man, Hunter. Thank you for proving me right once more."

To that, the Hunter could find no answer.

* * *

"That's it!"

The sudden shout from Tarek startled the Hunter awake. He bolted upright, eyes flying open in time to see the young Elivasti springing up from where he'd spread his bedroll in the shade of a thick *swawa* tree.

The noise jolted Kiara from her sleep, too, along with Kodyn, Aisha, and half a dozen of the Issai *amaqhawe* who had surreptitiously chosen their rest positions between the tree beneath which the Hunter's group sheltered and the main bulk of the Buhari warriors—no doubt at Davathi's whispered order.

But Tarek noticed none of the eyes turning his way. He paced with an almost feverish intensity, like a starving greatcat attempting to terrify its prey from a high tree. His eyes remained downcast, and he muttered to himself. Had the Hunter not known better, he might have thought Tarek half-mad. But Hailen had the same tendency when attempting to decipher some mystery or commit some important detail to memory. Some tendencies, it seemed, were inherited, not learned.

"Tarek?" The Hunter rose to his feet and approached the pacing Elivasti with caution, like a hunter advancing on a skittish fawn. "What's it?"

Tarek's eyes snapped up toward him. "I-I…" He seemed to be struggling, fumbling for some word that would not come. After a moment, he growled a curse in Elivasti and punched his balled right fist into his open left palm. "Damn it! I just had it!"

"Had what?" the Hunter asked. "What is it?"

"The…the…the name!" Tarek made a beckoning motion with his hand, as if he could summon the name on command. "The name of this Ghandian plant that Kanna talked about. The one she was certain would counteract the dimercurite poisoning if only she could get her hands on it. The one *maistyr* refused to procure for her."

The Hunter's eyebrows shot up. He wanted to ask "What plant?" but caught the question before it escaped his lips. That would only serve to further aggravate the already agitated young man.

"Can you describe it?" The question came from Kiara, who had risen from her bedroll and now moved to join them. Aisha and Kodyn weren't far behind, joining the small group even as Kiara continued. "Maybe if you can tell us what it looks like, Aisha can translate, explain it to her people. One of them could know where—"

"Of course!" Tarek's eyes flew wide. He rounded on the Hunter. "Parchment!"

The ferocity of the word caught the Hunter by surprise. It took his mind a moment to comprehend what Tarek was saying.

"You said you were going to procure parchment and charcoal sticks in Khafra!" Tarek insisted, moving toward the Hunter with an intent look on his scruffy, sweat-soaked face. "Did you?"

The Hunter sucked in a breath. He'd all but forgotten the promise he made to Tarek, so much had transpired in the days since their journey through the capital of Imperial Ghandia.

Without giving answer, he spun, knelt beside his pack, and dug around until he found the small cloth-wrapped bundle he'd purchased at the marketplace. He stood and thrust it into the young man's hands.

"There!"

Tarek all but ripped the fibrous grass twine holding the bundle closed and tore at the wrappings. A dozen charcoal sticks fell out, so hurried he was to get at the parchments, and only the Hunter's lightning reflexes enabled him to catch them before the delicate sticks struck the ground and snapped. As if nothing else in the world existed, Tarek dropped to a seat where he stood, snatched one of the charcoal sticks from the Hunter's hand, and set about scribbling on a parchment he'd chosen at random.

Kiara, Aisha, and Kodyn stared down at the young man, various incarnations of curiosity and astonishment etched into their expressions. Not even Kiara had seen Tarek so consumed and intent; she'd been unconscious the night the Hunter discovered Tarek's marvelous talent.

Instead of offering an explanation, the Hunter drew out the image of Jaia which Tarek had drawn for him. Kodyn and Aisha's eyebrows flew up at the sight. "Fiery hell!" Kodyn gasped. "It's…wow!"

"Incredible," Aisha said, wonder in her voice. "That is true skill."

Kiara, too, appeared surprised. However, her eyes narrowed a fraction, and she studied the face of the young woman etched onto the parchment. When she looked up at him, a question shone in her eyes. She knew. Though the hard face staring up at her bore little resemblance to him, there was something there, something that only the woman who knew him better than anyone else alive could see.

He nodded. She took the parchment and, holding it before her, moved to sit on her bedroll. Silence descended once more as Kiara studied the sketch of Jaia while Tarek labored furiously at his art.

The Hunter watched the two, scrutinizing their faces for any indication of their thoughts. Tarek's eyes shone with an almost feverish light, and his nose scrunched up the way Hailen's did when deep in concentration.

By contrast, Kiara's face was almost devoid of outward emotion. Her expression revealed little beyond the intensity of her concentration. What she searched for, he didn't know. Some measure of goodness, perhaps? She knew what Jaia had done to Father Reverentus, had seen the body lying motionless on the floor of the underground chamber deep beneath the Monolith. Or was she merely committing Jaia's face to memory in anticipation of when they finally met? And meet they would, as Jaia had made clear with her final mocking words.

"Done!" Tarek's voice snapped the Hunter's attention away from Kiara. The young Elivasti remained seated, but he held the parchment up with a triumphant expression as if he stood over a fallen enemy or sat astride a hard-conquered throne. "I can't remember what it's called, but I swear, that's precisely how it looked in Kanna's drawings."

The Hunter took the sketch and studied the plant Tarek had drawn. It resembled a fern, with the same complex leaf patterns and multiple stems, but far more gnarled with leaves that curled inward on itself like rheumatic limbs. Rather than pure green, the fern was speckled with dots of various sizes—some as large as the Hunter's thumbnail, others smaller than a blood droplet.

"Well done, lad," the Hunter said, offering Tarek an approving nod.

Tarek glowed with pride, and the intensity in his eyes steadily diminished.

"Now get back to your rest." The Hunter held up a finger to forestall any complaint. "That's an order."

Tarek seemed disinclined to argue. With the artwork completed, he seemed to deflate and sag, as if the labor had sapped the last of his strength.

The Hunter rolled up the sketch. "With this," he said, tapping the parchment against his open hand, "you've likely saved a lot of lives. More than you could possibly know."

If it worked, if the strange-looking fern did what Tarek believed it did, the young Elivasti might have given them the means of not only saving the captives suffering from dimercurite poisoning but reversing what was done to the Tefaye. And if they could achieve that impossibility, their army would grow stronger, and the Consortium's position in Ghandia would grow even more tenuous.

Tarek's charcoal sticks could very well have just signed the *Gainue'eleku awandile's* death warrant.

Chapter Eight

"I know of this plant." Davathi said, looking up from Tarek's drawing. "I have seen this before."

The Hunter's spirit soared. He'd half-expected to have to show it to dozens of people until he finally lucked upon one who recognized it. Fiery hell, he'd been prepared to venture among the visibly hostile Buhari on the off-chance they'd know it based on Tarek's detailed sketch. Yet the fact that Davathi, the first person who'd looked at the sketch, recognized it filled him with hope.

"Where did you see it?" he asked, his pulse quickening.

For a moment, Davathi's answering frown threatened to shatter his optimism. The frown quickly turned to a look of understanding and a smile filled with certainty. "Around the edges of *Isigodi Umlilophilayo.* Yes." She tapped the parchment with a strong finger. "It grows among the *umuthi wamatshe.*"

The Hunter gave her a blank look. He recognized the word *umuthi,* Issai for "tree", but the other meant nothing to him.

"Stone trees?" Kodyn translated—the reason the Hunter had brought him along—though his question was aimed at the Issai *nassor.* "Fire Valley?"

Davathi's smile widened. "In your tongue, it would be better said *Valley of Living Fire.* For an *alay-alagbara,* your command of our language is impressive."

"My mother taught me." Kodyn bowed his head. "She is Ghandian, from a small village north of the Great Chasm." He continued speaking, switching languages seamlessly. He and Davathi conversed for a few moments, and her smile grew wider with every Ghandian word rolling off his lips. The Hunter caught snippets of their conversation—he thought he recognized descriptions of a woman, likely the Ria he'd met in Praamis.

"I hate to interrupt," the Hunter said, growing impatient, "but what exactly is this Valley of Living Fire?" He grimaced. "Sounds like a friendly place."

Davathi turned to regard him with a level look. "Far from it." Her smile faded and her expression grew grave. "It is said that the valley was once home to the beating, fiery heart of *Ugunkubantwana* himself, firstborn of Ingwe All-Father. However, when the *Ukujiswa Okhulu* sundered the world and created the Great Chasm, *Ugunkubantwana* fell into darkness. Now, all that remains is the fire-blood that once coursed in his veins, flowing in the depths of *Isigodi Umlilophilayo.*"

The Hunter cocked his head. "And the stone trees?"

"Touched by *Ugunkubantwana's* breath," Davathi explained. "Once living trees, turned to stone. No creatures live among the *umuthi wamatshe,* and few plants can grow in its soil." She tapped the parchment again. "Which is how I remember this even twenty years after my *uhambo loguquko.*"

The Hunter looked to Kodyn for translation, but the young man shook his head. "I do not know those words."

"There is no translation to your tongue." Davathi gave Kodyn a reassuring smile. "The closest would be 'journey of awakening', though that fails to truly convey its depth of meaning. For *uhambo loguquko* speaks of a ritual that all Issai must undergo, a journey away from home, family, and comrades in search of their true selves, who they are beneath." She rested a hand on her powerfully muscled chest, directly over her heart. "The journey is different for each person, even those who share the path. For some, it lasts only a few days, for others, years. Yet always they return changed. Worthy of the title of *amaqhawai* and joining their sisters in protecting our people."

The Hunter nodded understanding. Many cultures had rites of passage to which youths were subjected upon coming of age. Though each varied in form—some vastly so—the intention remained the same: to prove themselves worthy of taking their place in society.

"Not unlike my Undertaking, then," Kodyn said.

The Hunter and Davathi both turned to regard the young man.

"You have completed an *uhambo loguquko?*" Davathi asked.

"After the way of my people, I suppose I have." Kodyn raised his head, stood a bit taller. "I was not born to warriors as your daughter was, but my people are no less skilled at their own trade. Aisha and I journeyed together to the City of the Dead so I could prove myself worthy."

Davathi's eyebrows shot up. "Aisha...traveled to the City of the Dead?"

"She did." Kodyn met the *nassor's* gaze evenly, confidence in his voice. "And there she found the truth of her *Umoyahlebe* gifts, her abilities to commune with and command the *Kish'aa*. There, too, she discovered a means to cure the *Inkuleko* and protect the minds of those who share her gifts."

Davathi's eyes shifted from Kodyn's gaze toward the spot where Aisha had once more returned to sleep in her bedroll. "My daughter..." Her voice came out barely above a whisper. "She said nothing to me."

"Doubt she's had much of a chance, the way we've been running the last few days." The Hunter recognized the look in Davathi's eyes: sorrow, a deep-rooted sense of loss. It was exactly how he felt every time he'd thought about Jaia after learning of her existence and all the years he'd missed with her. "But I've no doubt she has a great deal to tell you when you finally find the time."

Davathi turned back to him. Her *kaffe*-brown eyes, so much like Aisha's, bored into him. Measuring him, assessing the meaning beneath his words. She said nothing, but gave the faintest nod of her head in acknowledgment of what he'd said. Then she looked to Kodyn. "I would hear more of you, too. Clearly, you mean a great deal to my daughter." She gestured toward the spot where she'd been sitting amidst her warriors when the Hunter and Kodyn came to speak with her. "Join me."

Kodyn bowed and said something in her tongue. "But first," he switched back to Einari, "where is *Isigodi Umlilophilayo?* How do we find this plant among the stone trees?" He gestured to the parchment she still held.

"Why?" Davathi asked, eyes narrowing.

Kodyn looked to the Hunter, as if asking for permission. The Hunter nodded. He'd intended to tell Davathi—and Jumaane, eventually—what they'd discovered about the Consortium's tests on the Tefaye.

Kodyn leaned closer, speaking quickly and quietly in the Ghandian tongue. Surprise blossomed on Davathi's leonine face, accompanied by anger, suspicion, and a faint glimmer of hope.

"If it is possible," she said in Einari, for the Hunter's benefit, "then we must see it done at all costs. But the journey is not one to undertake lightly. *Isigodi Umlilophilayo* dwells within the shadow of *Ukuhlushwa Okungapheli.*"

The Hunter's gut clenched. Of *course* it would be there. If not at the bottom of the deepest chasm or upon the summit of the highest mountain, then inevitably it would be near the heavily guarded stronghold of his enemies.

This new discovery only added to the certainty that he was being drawn toward the Serenii spire, and not just for Kharna's sake. Too many threads all wound in a tangled skein with the Bondshold at its knotted heart. The sense of urgency within him hummed all the louder. Soon, it would grow impossible to ignore.

"We will speak on the matter further." Davathi's voice cut into the Hunter's thoughts. His eyes focused on her, found her holding out Tarek's sketch to him.

The Hunter recognized the dismissal in the gesture and her tone. He didn't protest, merely took the proffered parchment. They would have plenty of time to discuss their next course of action. For the moment, he could use a few more hours of rest and relaxation before the day cooled and they resumed their journey.

Bowing to the *nassor,* he departed the cluster of Issai, leaving Kodyn to sit and chat with Davathi while he returned to where Kiara, Tarek, and Aisha slept in the—admittedly far from cool—shade of the *swawa* tree.

* * *

"Umzukeli!"

The Hunter looked up from his task of tightening Elivast's tack to see three Buhari marching stiff-backed toward him. Their spears remained upright, but their eyes were as sharp as daggers, their loathing of him fully evident.

"Jumaane demands you," said the one at the head of the trio in thickly accented Einari. His lion's mane headdress and lion-hide cape were larger and more decorative than his two companions; some sort of leader among the Buhari *amaqhawe,* perhaps?

The Hunter pulled the last cinch on Elivast's saddle tight, then straightened and turned to face the three. "Why?"

His question went ignored. "Jumaane demands you," was all the answer he got.

The Hunter eyed the three warriors. Tall, broad-shouldered, clearly skilled with their long spears and the woven shields they carried. Not a scrap of iron among them, though. Should the situation turn ugly—

He banished that thought. If Jumaane—or any of the Buhari—intended him harm, they would face him in open combat. *He* was the assassin here, the one accustomed to skulking in shadows. Stabbing a man in the back didn't seem the way of the *amathafa.*

The Hunter nodded. "Take me to him, then."

344

The leader stepped aside, gesturing with the tip of his spear for the Hunter to precede him. The other two remained motionless. Until Kiara and Aisha moved to join the Hunter. Only then did they lower their spears to forestall the two women's advance.

"Him," the leader barked, shaking his head. "Him."

Curiosity swelled within the Hunter, accompanied by a hint of suspicion. Jumaane wanted to speak with him *alone*?

Outwardly, however, he remained calm and composed. He shot Aisha and Kiara a wry grin. "Last time we spoke, I remember him saying something about a private moonlight dinner for two. Moon's not out yet, but I suppose the afternoon sky casts a romantic enough ambience."

Kiara chuckled, a wicked light shining in her eyes. Aisha's smile felt more forced, tinged with a measure of concern. But she held her tongue and remained where she was. Apparently she'd come to the same conclusion as he: the alliance with the Buhari was still tenuous, easily broken. They'd do nothing to incur the wrath of either Jumaane or his warriors.

Still, as he strode between the three warriors, the Hunter kept his hands tucked into his belt, easily within reach of Soulhunger and his watered steel sword. No sense taking chances.

He was led toward the tree Jumaane had chosen to rest under. With the afternoon well on its way to evening, the sky splashed with hues of violet and ochre to brighten the grey-blue, the Buhari had joined the Issai and the other Ghandians in preparing to depart. Jumaane alone sat at ease, his long legs extended and his broad back leaning against the even broader trunk of a *swawa* tree.

The three Buhari stopped when they were ten paces away, but gestured for him to continue. Curiosity growing, the Hunter did as instructed.

"*Umzukeli!*" Jumaane's voice rang out in a greeting far more cheerful than the Hunter had anticipated. The *nassor* did not rise, but swept a hand in a gesture inviting the Hunter to sit in front of him. "We must speak."

The Hunter studied the Buhari. Though Jumaane did not smile, his bearded face was composed, relaxed, no tension evident at the corners of his eyes and mouth. His spear and shield lay next to his right leg, his heavy *nkemba* sword beside his left. He seemed no more bothered by the Hunter's hesitation than his presence, as if he'd forgotten the fact that the man standing before him had slaughtered two-score of his best warriors.

Uncertain of what to expect, the Hunter complied with the invitation. He lowered himself gracefully to a cross-legged seat in front of the *nassor*. He plastered a calm look on his face to match Jumaane's, but inwardly, his mind was racing, his keen ears listening for any sound of warriors creeping up from behind him, any scents to warn him of enemies at his back.

Yet the only sound that met his ears was the rustling of the leaves overhead, accompanied by the sound of nearly three hundred Ghandians preparing to travel. Aside from the slightly sweet aroma of the red-and-orange gourd-shaped fruit growing on the *swawa* tree, the only scent he detected in the immediate area was Jumaane's: of *zabara* musk, kola nut, and star apple.

The Hunter gestured to the man. "Speak."

Jumaane did not, merely remained silent, dark eyes fixed on him with the same intense scrutiny the Hunter had felt from Davathi. He was being weighed and measured against some standard he, being an outsider to these lands, could not hope to understand.

When finally he broke his silence, his words remained calm and utterly free of sentiment. "My *amaqhawe* want your head. I am inclined to heed them." His face revealed no more emotion than his voice as he tapped a thick finger against the hilt of his *nkemba*. "My question to you, *Okanele,* is why should I deny them their vengeance?"

Jumaane

Chapter Nine

The Hunter held Jumaane's gaze with total equanimity. The question was far from a surprise—in truth, the only surprise here was that the *nassor* had used words to express his warriors' desires rather than fists or weapons. The last group of armed men who'd had grievance against him had come for blood while he trained with Tassat. Whatever Buhari *amaqhawai* was foolish enough to seek vengeance directly would have stood no better chance of killing him than the Cambionari knight apprentices.

"It is true I have sworn the Buhari to fight alongside the Issai. Our peoples are allied now." Jumaane's gesture encompassed both himself and the tree where Davathi and her Issai had chosen to shelter from the day's heat. The motion ended with him pointing a lazy finger at the Hunter. "But you are neither Issai nor Buhari. My oath to Davathi does not hold to you. So tell me." He leaned forward slightly. "What reason do I have to keep my men from taking out their wrath on you, *alay-alagbara?*"

The Hunter held his silence. The question had a rhetorical ring to it, as if Jumaane tossed it offhandedly at him on his path toward some form of concrete point.

As expected, Jumaane continued without really giving him time to answer. "Do you know what this means, *alay-alagbara?*" He spoke in a slow, languorous tone, letting each word hang in the air between them.

The Hunter shook his head.

A smile broadened Jumaane's bearded face. "There is no exact translation into your tongue." He ran a hand through his great beard as if combing out the knots—fully relaxed, self-assured, and master of all he surveyed. "But it refers to one who is weak, easily sickened by the cold, like a child whose mother must wrap them in blankets. Just as you wrap yourself in armor and thick clothing. You have much to hide, *alay-alagbara*. Secrets and hidden shames and fears you would rather flee than face. But we of the *amathafa*"—he thumped a balled fist against the woven armor covering his barrel chest—"we do not hide from sun or wind or cold. We bare our flesh to prove to all that we are not afraid."

"And yet, your warriors fear me." The Hunter couldn't help himself. "I see it every time they look at me. They think it is hatred and anger—and in truth, there is plenty of both—but it does not disguise their fear." He cocked his head. "Even you fear me."

He half-expected Jumaane to bristle; such accusation laid against the *nassor* of the most powerful tribe of warriors could not go unanswered. He braced himself for a tirade.

But Jumaane just laughed. Not the roaring, belly laugh from the previous night, but a hearty chuckle no less mirthful.

348

"Of course I fear you!" The Buhari threw up one huge hand. "What manner of idiot would I be if I did not?"

The Hunter raised an eyebrow. "But you said—"

"I said we prove we are not afraid, not that we do not know fear." Jumaane raised up a finger. "The difference, though small, is what separates a true *amaqhawai* from *alay-alagbara*."

The Hunter pondered those words. "All men know fear; brave men refuse to submit to it. That is what you mean, yes?"

Jumaane tilted his great, bearded head toward the Hunter. "That is so." He shook a finger at the Hunter. "You are not what I expected when I heard of the *Okanele* who destroyed so much of my *amaqhawe*. More man than beast, if you take my meaning."

The Hunter did. "I am unlike any *Okanele* alive." That was no exaggeration. "And for the time being, I fight at your side." He leaned back, his posture relaxed to mirror Jumaane's. "To answer your question, you should not heed your warriors in their pleas for vengeance because to do so would be to waste their lives. Send them against me in single combat or in a host"—he raised a hand and snapped his fingers—"their ends would be the same."

He had no need to say more. Jumaane had doubtless heard the same account from every one of the Buhari who'd returned from the raid. He had seen the magic of *Ibad'at Mutlaqa* for himself. There could be no denying such power, even if he had not personally witnessed the deaths of his warriors.

"But more than that," the Hunter continued, allowing a smile to spread across his lips, "you will not allow it because the Jumaane of whom Davathi has spoken so much would never be so foolish as to waste such a weapon. No more than he would cast aside his *nkemba* and face his enemy with a twig, or drop his shield to protect himself with a leaf."

A smile grew on Jumaane's face to match his. "Such a man would be a true fool, indeed."

The Hunter had come to understand the intention behind this interaction. Jumaane had wanted to gauge him, to see what manner of man—or *Okanele*—he was. Perhaps he truly had contemplated allowing his warriors to seek redress against the Hunter, or that was merely the excuse he gave to prompt the conversation.

In the end, though, the Hunter knew the truth. "You will keep your men at bay because you are convinced I will hurl myself at the enemy you share with the Issai until either I lay dead or the *alay-alagbara* are destroyed. And when that is done, when these lands are once more yours, you and every *amaqhawai* who has cause to hate me will be free to take up spears and seek my blood. That is the way of the *amathafa*, is it not?"

"It is so." Jumaane's grin broadened. He leaned forward abruptly, seized his *nkemba,* and rose to his feet with impressive swiftness for one so large. But he made no move to raise the great blunt-tipped sword. Instead, he held out his right hand to the Hunter. "There is always tomorrow, *Umzukeli.*"

"Or the following day." The Hunter accepted the proffered hand up, pulling himself to his feet. "But definitely *after* the *Gcinue'eleku awandile* are destroyed."

"After, of course." Jumaane squeezed his hand, the strength of his grip prodigious, impressive. "For today, though, I allow your head to remain where it is."

The Hunter saw the twinkle in the big man's eyes. "You are too kind, great *nassor.*"

* * *

Whatever Jumaane said to his *amaqhawe* in the aftermath of his conversation with the Hunter had a drastic effect on the Buhari. The hate-filled glares directed his way diminished in number, if not intensity. Throughout the long night of travel, the Hunter only occasionally felt eyes burning into his back. The Buhari nearest him fingered their weapons with fractionally less murderous intent written on their faces. Their animosity toward him, if not fully sheathed, had at least been blunted by the *nassor's* words.

Which served to make the following days and nights of travel far easier, at least in that one small regard. Long hours of riding through darkness on their relentless journey northwest passed in a blur of shadows and starlight, interrupted occasionally when another of the ill captives succumbed to the dimercurite poisoning or collapsed from exhaustion. In the latter case, the Buhari and Issai warriors lent a hand, supporting the weak. In the former, the tribespeople of the deceased spoke a few words over the dead, then laid out their bodies for the *makalala* to feast upon.

The Hunter had thought it a barbaric ritual—Einari armies gathered their dead so the crows and vultures would not desecrate the corpses—until Aisha explained its true purpose. The *makalala* were believed to be the winged servants of Ingwe All-Father sent to free the dead from their physical forms. Only once the *makalala* had devoured the mortal flesh would their spirits be free to join the *Kish'aa,* the ancestors revered and worshipped by all Ghandians.

The sight of the freed captives laying out their dead burned into the Hunter's mind, joining the memory of the Issai doing likewise in the aftermath of the Tefaye raid and Davathi's blood-spattered countenance after she put her dying warriors out of their misery in the Consortium camp. The specter of death haunted every land—not even the immensely powerful Serenii had escaped the inevitability—yet this was death on a scale far greater than these people had known in decades, even centuries. Such suffering was the direct result of the Consortium and the Order of Mithridas meddling in places they did not belong. When the time came to mete out justice for the lives snuffed out needlessly by cruelty and avarice, the Hunter would no more hold back than those who had felt the sting of the lash or watched friends or comrades die on their feet.

Despite the steady attrition, the two *nassors* leading the column refused to slow the pace. Davathi was possessed by an iron will to return to protect her people, who were all but defenseless against the Tefaye or whatever other enemy moved against them. Jumaane raised no protest when his counterpart pressed to move faster, travel longer, rest for fewer and fewer hours. Either he understood Davathi's desire to return home or was merely eager to begin the war against the *alay-alagbara.* The Hunter could not decide which was more likely. Nor did he care.

When, finally, they reached the Gwembashi River and were reunited with those who had stayed behind, the mood pervading the column grew even grimmer. Fully one third of the one hundred and fifty had succumbed to the ravages of dimercurite poisoning, starvation, dehydration, or overwork. Of those who remained, fewer than seventy were fit enough to travel unaided.

Kodyn of all people had been seized with an idea: to volunteer their horses to drag sledges fashioned from branches of the wild fig trees that grew beside the river. With the most depleted and gravely ill thus conveyed, they were able to make faster progress. Of course, that condemned the Hunter—along with Kodyn, Aisha, Tarek, and Kiara—to spend the long hours of travel trudging along with the rest of the column.

The Hunter didn't fail to notice the way Tarek's expression darkened and his shoulders slumped when they strode past the field of corpses laid out along the riverbank for the *makalala.* His efforts to locate *okhafi* plants or any other remedy to alleviate the dimercurite poisoning had failed. It didn't matter that he had been far away when these people died; he still saw them as *his* failures. Why, the Hunter couldn't begin to guess, but the grueling hours of travel left him with no opportunity to raise the question to the young man.

The leagues seemed endless. Windy nights gave way to blistering hot days, which were spent attempting to snatch what rest they could, only to end when the day grew cool enough to march beneath the setting sun and the starry night sky. Two full days and nights passed in this fashion, a blur of heat and haze and wind and cold and all-consuming exhaustion. Until finally they reached the trickle that had once been the Unathi River. Far to the north, the shadow of *Indawo Yokwesaba* darkened the horizon, but Davathi led the way firmly south. She did not say where they went—not even to Aisha—but seemed confident that she knew where to find the place where Siyanda had taken the Issai to hide.

While they traveled alongside the barren track that had once been the Unathi River, the Hunter sought out Jumaane and spoke to him of what they'd found among the papers Kodyn had taken from the Consortium offices. The young man had been too exhausted from hours of trudging along and lending the strength of his shoulders to whomever needed it to dig further into the documents. But for the time being, what he'd discovered about the Consortium experiments on the Tefaye was more than enough.

Jumaane's expression grew pensive as he heard how the tribe of outcasts had been driven mad. "I had heard stories of the Tefaye but could not confirm them for certain. The warriors I dispatched to see for themselves returned without ever finding their *ekhaya*. I did not believe it was possible for them to disappear entirely, yet with no proof..." He shrugged. "Besides, we were distracted with far more opportune foes."

The Hunter grimaced inwardly. That, at least, explained how the Buhari had located the Issai *ekhaya* hidden in the canyon.

"And your man," Jumaane said, gesturing to Tarek, "he believes he has a way to cure them?"

"He does." The Hunter tried to sound more confident than he felt. Until Tarek actually found and tested this strange-looking fern—along with whatever else was needed to counteract the other ingredients the Consortium had mixed into their alchemical poison—he could not know for certain. "But to do so, he needs *okhafi* and something from *Isigodi Umlilophilayo.*"

Jumaane grimaced. "He would risk straying near *Ukuhlushwa Okungapheli*?" He shook his head. "It is an evil place. A place of the *Okanele.*"

The Hunter had expected that response from the superstitious Buhari. "Which is why I will be the one to go with him when he seeks it out."

Jumaane studied him from the corners of his eyes. For long moments, they walked in silence, basking in the coolness of the night breeze. "What do you know of the *Okanele?*"

"Soul-stealers, death-bringers, all the usual sorts of evil." The Hunter shrugged. "Sent by *Inzayo Okubi* to carry out his dark bidding."

"To some, yes." Jumaane nodded. "To my people, however, the *Okanele* are message-bringers of something greater. Sent by *Inzayo Okubi*, yes, much like *Nuru Iwu* and *Okadigbo*. Yet they are not all evil of themselves. They are merely a reflection of *Inzayo Okubi's* dual nature, of his three faces: one light, one dark, and one the shadows between."

The Hunter raised an eyebrow. He had no idea who or what *Nuru Iwu* and *Okadigbo* were, but Jumaane's description of *Inzayo Okubi* sounded strangely akin to the Einari concept of Kharna. Kharna had once been a noble god turned to darkness and evil by his own lust for conquest and domination, then transformed into the Beggar God, servant to all. Dual nature.

Three faces, though, that was new to him.

Jumaane continued speaking, taking the Hunter's silence as interest. "We of the Buhari believe the *Okanele* choose what they wish to be. Most choose darkness, it is true, but it is the *Okanele* who choose the light who are the most powerful."

"And what of us who choose the shadows?" The Hunter tried his best to keep the sarcasm from his voice.

"Ahh, that is what most do not understand." Jumaane gave him a knowing smile. "For the shadows are within all—man and *Okanele* alike—even in those who choose light. They are the *truth* that governs all things. For light cannot exist without darkness, and where light and darkness intertwine, the shadows are born."

All the philosophical talk had the Hunter's head spinning. Such things were far more Father Reverentus' domain than his own. Yet something Jumaane had said piqued his interest. "You mentioned message-bringers. What is their message?"

Jumaane shook his head. "To each, it is different. None can know what message the *Okanele* will pass on, but therein lies the true test brought about by their presence. Even the mightiest warrior can fall from light into darkness, just as even the darkest heart can be filled with light." He tapped a hand against his huge, armored chest. "No man ever is finished. Every day, they choose the darkness or light, and the shadows within grow thinner or thicker."

The Hunter stared up at the chieftain. Though Jumaane's words were wrapped up in myth and metaphor, the Hunter found they made a great deal of sense.

"I do not yet know for certain what manner of *Okanele* you are." Jumaane looked down at him, a thoughtful expression on his face. "But I believe that your message will soon become plain. Until then…" He shrugged. "I will wait."

The Hunter had no idea what kind of message he could impart—he certainly wasn't sent by some mythical deity of light and darkness—but didn't believe it was worth trying to convince Jumaane of that. At the moment, the Buhari *nassor* was among the few around who didn't intend him harm. Better to stay on his good side, even if that meant entertaining the man's superstition.

Yet he couldn't help pondering the conversation over and over in his head for the rest of that night, and much of the following day. Try as he might to convince himself otherwise, Jumaane's words had rung with a strange measure of truth.

His companions seemed not to notice—or mind—that he was quieter than usual. Tarek was lost within the darkness in his own mind and the guilt he had taken upon himself. Aisha spent most of her waking hours at her mother's side, while Kodyn occupied himself helping the weaker and sicker members of the liberated captives to keep up with the column. The circles under Kiara's eyes grew darker and her skin paler with every passing day, yet she continually insisted that nothing was amiss. The Hunter was too lost within the turmoil of his own mind to press the matter.

Finally, on the fourth morning after the *Impi yechipekwe,* they reached a tall hill upon which sat piles of enormous rocks. The stones appeared ancient—as old as the plains themselves—and jutted up from the tall grass as if worn away by time and the elements. A *kopje,* Aisha called it.

At Davathi's nod, one of her warriors drew out a bamboo flute similar to the one Aisha had carved—no, the Hunter realized as he looked again, it *was* Aisha's little flute—and blew a series of trilling notes. The sound echoed across the flat plains, and was answered moments later by an equally high-pitched tone. Two umber-skinned figures clad only in the tight fibrous cloth battle-wrappings emerged from the thick trees that grew atop one huge boulder. They waved their arms and spears high into the air, and their joyous shouts drifted across the expanse toward the column.

"We found them!" Aisha's eyes shone bright, her face lighting up. "We're almost home!"

No sooner had the words left her mouth than three more figures appeared, this time at the base of the *kopje*. These, however, did not wave a greeting. Nor were they Issai. The trio had the red-stained skin and wore the light-colored woven armor of the Buhari. Their lion's hide cloaks streamed out behind them and their legs pumped as they raced back to the column.

The Hunter felt it in his gut: something was wrong. Those three might be the warriors Jumaane had sent to scout the way ahead. But what had happened to the two Issai who'd gone with them?

A shout echoed across the plains. The fearful tone of voice was unmistakable, as was the word—one the Hunter had come to recognize as the warning of an attack.

A new sound reached him: a thundering like a stampede of wildebeest or a cavalry charge. The ground beneath his feet trembled, so faintly he might not have felt it had his senses not been on full alert, wary and attuned to even the slightest change.

His heart dropped into his throat when, seconds later, the first of the pursuing figures swarmed into view around the base of the *kopje*.

Chapter Ten

The Hunter's keen eyes could clearly make out the details of the horde pursuing the three Buhari: dark, stone-studded hardwood armor, hide-covered shields, long spears, bronze hand axes, and ragged pelts. The terrible *clacking* reached him a moment later, and a familiar rush of adrenaline surged through his veins.

The Keeper-damned Tefaye, again! More than a hundred of them, all emaciated, grimy, and crusted with dried blood and mud.

The swarm's attention appeared to be collectively focused on the Buhari scouts, but the Hunter couldn't take the chance they'd notice the Issai still standing atop the *kopje's* enormous boulders. The *ekhaya* hidden on the hill had only a handful of defenders—Siyanda, a few dozen *unkgaliwe* who'd seen far too few summers, and Duma. They would be hard-pressed to repel an attack should the Tefaye turn their gaze upward.

Which meant the attack had to be drawn *away* from the hill. Toward the column of freed captives stretching out behind him. United, the Buhari and what remained of the Issai *amaqhawe* stood a far better chance of victory.

The Hunter acted without hesitation. Two long steps brought him to Elivast's side. He whipped his watered steel sword from its sheath and, in a single slash, hacked through the woven fiber cords connecting Elivast to the *swawa* wood sled laden with ill Ghandians. With a mighty bound, he sprang onto his horse's back and dug in his heels to set the beast galloping toward the head of the column.

A handful of the Issai and Buhari warriors surrounding the two *nassors* leading the group lowered their weapons at his approach, yet it was more instinctive reaction than any real belief that he intended their chieftains harm. The rest were focused on the oncoming Tefaye and the promise of battle to come.

The Hunter locked eyes with Davathi. "I'm riding out to meet them. But I need you to keep your warriors *at least* fifty strides behind me."

Davathi's mouth opened, a protest forming on her lips.

"Trust me!" The Hunter shifted his gaze to Aisha. "I need you to explain to them what could happen if they don't."

"You ride alone against such an enemy?" The question came from Jumaane, who had moved closer to Davathi's side. He had his heavy *nkemba* sword in hand and shield already braced for battle.

The Hunter grinned. "Time you see what manner of *Okanele* I am—what manner of *Okanele* fights at your side." He looked back to Aisha. "Please. For their sakes."

Aisha nodded. "I will—"

The Hunter did not hear the rest of her words, for he had already turned Elivast around and dug his heels into the horse's flanks.

Elivast leaped forward as if he had eagle's wings on his legs. After four days of walking, he seemed restive, eager to run. Yet a lack of water and long hours of hauling a heavy sled had sapped his strength. He could only sustain a gallop for a few minutes—just long enough to pull well ahead of the column and close the distance with the running Buhari.

The trio of warriors shouted at him as they passed, but the Hunter did not understand. Nor would he have stopped even if he did. The fate of hundreds of lives depended on him now.

When he felt Elivast tiring, he allowed the horse to slow to a walk, then reined him to a halt. Leaping up, he stood on his saddle and waved his arms high over his head.

"Hey, you bastards!" he roared with all the power he could muster. "Come and get me!"

The foremost of the Tefaye had spotted him riding toward them, but his shout drew the focus of those in the rear. Their attention shifted from the *kopje* to the lone figure standing on horseback. Ululating howls and war cries rose from among the throng as they surged en masse toward him. Spears rose into the air, bronze hand axes flashed, and hide-bound shields bore down on him. The clacking of the Tefaye's wooden armor grew deafening, underscored by the thunder of their racing feet.

The Hunter drew Soulhunger and, dagger and watered steel blade in hand, he braced to meet them. He would not draw the Sword of Nasnaz…yet. He could not be certain Aisha would convince her mother and Jumaane to hold their warriors back far enough to keep them out of danger—not from the Tefaye, but *him*. Once he started killing, it would take everything in his power to break the scimitar's hold on his mind and soul. He could not risk shattering the tenuous alliance between the Issai and Buhari.

Nor could he forget what had been done to the Tefaye. This was the *Consortium's* doing. They had turned the tribe into blood-maddened savages through devious alchemy. They were as much victims of the *Gcinue'eleku awandile* as those chained and forced to labor in the dimercurite pit.

The chances of undoing the damage were slim—Kiara had said Tangled Gallberry turned its victims into "mindless husks"—but if there existed even the faintest possibility, the Hunter *had* to try. Slaughtering every one of the Tefaye before him would be doing the Consortium's dirty work for them.

He tightened his grip on his weapons, drew in a long breath. *This is going to hurt,* he thought, a grim expression on his face. *But no helping it, I suppose.*

Raising sword and dagger high over his head, he loosed a roar of fury and charged straight into the teeth of the enemy.

* * *

The Hunter stood alone. A fist of iron squeezed his lungs, making it nearly impossible to draw a full breath, and his heart hammered with such ferocity he feared it would tear free of his chest. His pulse throbbed in his ears so loudly it drowned out all other sound, save for his wheezing.

Keeper…take it! He fell to one knee, splashing in a puddle of gore, and fumbled at the spear transfixing his chest. It had struck vital organs and torn a hole on his lungs. Bloody hurt, too. The spear's steel head scraped against his spine anytime he moved even a muscle.

He tried to close his left hand around the spear's shaft, but his fingers were thick, clumsy. Still healing from the axe blow that had shattered the small bones and nearly taken off his hand. With a supreme effort of will, he forced his right hand to unclench from around the blood-soaked hilt of his watered steel sword. The weapon splashed into the ever-widening crimson pool seeping in all directions. The wound in his leg was worse than he'd expected. He was losing strength fast, darkness creeping in on him. But with that Watcher-damned spear in his chest, he couldn't concentrate enough to compel his body to repair the damage.

Pain rippled up and down his spine as he closed the cramping, exhausted fingers of his right hand around the spear shaft. Gritting his teeth, he braced himself for the inevitable and hauled at the spear. For a terrible heartbeat, agony flooded his torso as the weapon transfixing his body tugged at muscle, tissue, and bone. A fresh gush of fluid filled his lungs; he coughed red-tinged phlegm, tried to ignore the panic rising in his mind when he could not fully draw breath.

But the anguish lasted only a moment. Blood rendered the spear shaft slick, and his hands slipped, lost purchase. He toppled forward, which only served to drive the spear deeper. A howl of pure misery ripped from his lips.

Come on! He fought to regain control of himself. The pain was blinding, setting his head pounding as if the entire Tefaye host trampled his skull. *You can do—*

His thoughts cut off as a shadow fell over him. Opening his eyes, he found a figure standing before him. Tall, powerfully built, cast into silhouette by the bright sun shining overhead. Yet he recognized the enormous lion's mane headdress instantly. The bloody *nkemba* held in a low grip, too.

The Hunter tried to speak, but a coughing fit seized him. Every spasm of his muscles only drove the spear farther into his flesh and sent fresh waves of fire coursing through his veins. The world swam before him, darkness closing in around him, dragging him toward unconsciousness.

A sound—it might have been a grunt, or a harsh chuckle, he couldn't tell—came from somewhere far away, faint through the throbbing in his ears. A weight rested against his chest, nearly sending him toppling backward.

Then came the pain. Worse than anything he'd felt since…fiery hell, he could not remember anything quite as exquisitely terrible as the torment that consumed him. It seemed to stretch on for eons, an eternity, but must have been only a moment or two. When the Hunter's world finally solidified and the hazy red darkness retreated, he found himself standing on his feet. Strong hands held him upright, kept him from collapse.

The Hunter blinked, focused his gaze on the figure looming large in front of him. Jumaane's striking features swam into clarity after a few dizzying seconds. The *nassor* stared down at a blood-soaked spear, a look of surprise—and was that a hint of respect?—on his bearded face.

"Easy," came a familiar voice from beside the Hunter. He managed to turn his head just enough to see Kiara gripping his right shoulder. "You're…well, let's just say you've looked better."

The Hunter coughed, and again blood rose from his lungs. Yet the cough didn't send lances of pain shivering up and down his body. When he looked down, he found the spear had been torn free. The spear Jumaane now held and admired as if it were some hard-won trophy.

"Heal first," Kiara said. "The rest can wait."

The Hunter was in too much pain to argue. He wanted to collapse, to let the darkness claim him. He'd love nothing more than to lie down in that very spot and sleep for a month straight. But he couldn't. He had to make certain the battle had ended in their favor.

And so, summoning every shred of willpower remaining to his battle-numbed mind, he turned his attention inward. Sent his consciousness traveling along the paths formed by his blood vessels, muscles, nerves, and organs. Lightning crackled in his brain as he compelled his flesh to heal. The deep wound in his leg first—had to stop himself from bleeding out—then the tear in his lungs. The spearhead had also torn open his stomach and lacerated the great vein feeding blood to his liver. More wounds, too minor to do much damage alone but draining in their multitude, were repaired, the flesh mended. The bones in his hand re-knit and the damaged cartilage restored.

He ran out of energy before he ran out of wounds. Those not of immediate concern he left alone. His body's accelerated healing abilities would see to them. He just needed to draw a full breath and stand on his own two feet for the time being.

When he emerged from the depths of his body, the world around him no longer spun quite as wildly, and he found his legs heeded his command to stay upright. He took that as a good sign.

"Not...quite...dead," he rasped out, spitting a gobbet of bloody phlegm.

"Could have fooled us," came another familiar voice from the Hunter's opposite side. Kodyn's. The young man's face was flecked with crimson—as was Kiara's, the Hunter realized— and bore a shallow cut along his forehead. Whether inflicted by axe or spear, the Hunter couldn't be certain. Yet like him, Kodyn, Kiara, and Jumaane, at least, remained very much alive.

"I take it...we won?" The Hunter's voice grew stronger as oxygen flooded his now-healed lungs. He stood straighter.

"*We* won." Jumaane's face twisted into a grin. "A battle unlike any fought in these lands, I must admit."

Only then did the rest of the world shift into focus. The Hunter looked past the three standing around him and realized there were many more. Most were Buhari, their long spears and woven armor spattered with blood. A few Issai numbered among their ranks, including Davathi and Aisha. To the Hunter's relief, Tarek was with them. He appeared no worse for the wear.

The same couldn't be said for the Tefaye.

The Hunter stood amidst a field of blood and carnage. Tefaye lay all around him. So many dead. Necks snapped, throats hacked open, bellies gutted, chests pierced through. Soulhunger's hilt still protruded from between the ribs of one dead warrior's armor. Its gemstone was once again translucent; the Hunter still remembered the moment he was forced to relinquish his grip on the dagger, and try as he might, he had been unable to fight his way back through the crush of bodies to retrieve it. Which was how he'd ended up dangerously close to the Long Keeper's arms. The six lives Soulhunger had claimed during the battle had sustained him only while the power of their life energy lasted. And the battle had continued long after.

Yet not *all* the Tefaye joined the *Kish'aa*. The Hunter couldn't know exactly, but hoped to count at least half his foes among the living. He'd taken great pains to strike incapacitating and debilitating blows, only killing when unavoidable or necessary. Many of the Tefaye would never fight again—severed limbs made wielding a shield or spear difficult—and many more would be out of commission for weeks or months with shattered bones and wrenched muscles. But he could vaguely remember rendering more than a few unconscious with deliberate pommel strikes and kicks to vulnerable spots.

"As soon as I saw you pulling your blows," Kiara said beside him, "I realized what you were doing." When he looked toward her, he saw admiration and approval shining on her blood-spattered face.

357

Jumaane's voice drew the Hunter's attention. "For all that our people revile the Tefaye for their crimes, even they do not deserve this." The bearded *nassor* shook his head, setting his lion's mane waving a furry halo around him. "And if, as the young *Umoyahlebe* says, what was done can be undone, we will deprive our enemies of a valuable weapon—and, perhaps, wield that weapon ourselves."

The Hunter nodded. That was exactly what he'd intended, but there'd been no time to explain. Fortunately for him, Kiara knew him well enough to understand, and with Aisha's help, she could have convinced a mountain to become a valley.

Then he remembered. *The captives!* He craned his neck, trying to look over his shoulder to gauge the outcome of the battle. He'd done his best to take down the Tefaye, but he had no doubt at least *some* had gotten past him. For all the temptation he, a lone fighter, had offered the oncoming horde, there would be those who merely ran around him to attack those he guarded.

At a glance, he estimated at least two score had evaded him. Some lay dead, but many were now being taken captive by the Buhari and Issai who'd remained behind as guard.

"How many?" the Hunter asked. "How many on our side?"

"None."

The word, spoken in Jumaane's deep, calm tone, snapped the Hunter's head back around. "What?" Such a thing couldn't be possible. *Every* battle had its casualties. Some hapless fool whose luck turned against him at the wrong moment, or who made a poor choice in the heat of combat.

But Jumaane just nodded. "Not one," he said, emphasizing each word. He held the Hunter's gaze for a long moment, his expression inscrutable. Then he allowed a hint of a smile to spread across his face. "You were right. I *do* see what manner of *Okanele* you are." He thrust the bloody spear at the Hunter. "Today, we have all seen."

Chapter Eleven

It took all of five minutes for the Hunter to remember why he had never been fond of wielding spears in training or combat. Like all polearms, they were long, cumbersome, and prone to getting in his way. Plus, he couldn't exactly sheathe the thing—it stood taller than he was, and unless he fashioned some sort of back harness, he had no means of carrying it to free up his hands.

But he endured the annoyance in stoic silence. Jumaane had given him the weapon to carry as a trophy—and in truth, he *had* won it by defeating the Tefaye who wielded it. Oddly, the sight of it seemed to have a marked effect on the Buhari. The hatred and loathing on their faces had dwindled and, in some cases, all but vanished. Now, when they looked at him, at the spear soaked with his own blood and the blood of their enemies, they did not cast angry glares his way or mutter to their companions. A few of the warriors even raised their own spears in a silent salute.

The Hunter couldn't help a wry chuckle in his mind. *And all it took to stop them from wanting to kill me was letting their enemies take a stab at it.* He rubbed the wound in his chest, which had all but healed but remained tender still. *Literally.*

It was more than that, he knew. In barreling toward danger—alone—he'd proven his courage to warriors who valued bravery above everything. He'd howled defiance into the face of an enemy they had not expected him to defeat and somehow remained standing despite wounds that ought to have killed him. The fact that they had walked away from this battle with no casualties only served to solidify the true impossibility of what he'd done. No man trained for battle and death could see that and remain unchanged.

He had a long way to go, he had no doubt. The Buhari would not easily forget what he'd done to their fellows. But perhaps, eventually, if his actions saved enough of their lives, turned enough battles in their favor, they might tolerate or even accept his existence among them. At the very least, he hoped it would deter them from seeking vengeance.

Though he stood amidst so much death, he couldn't help feeling strangely optimistic. The blood soaking his clothes and staining his hands had gone a long way toward cementing the Issai alliance with the Buhari—he'd seen as much written in the eyes of both Davathi and Jumaane. They did not speak to him, too occupied directing the capture and binding of the surviving Tefaye or finishing off the dying, but it no longer felt as if they *ignored* him. Indeed, they and all their warriors left a wide space around him as they passed, either out of respect or fear. Likely both in equal measure.

Relief washed over him as Kiara returned, leading Elivast by the reins. The horse nickered and nudged his chest in an eager, happy greeting.

"Hey, Boy." The Hunter rubbed the horse's nose. "Worried about me, were you?"

Elivast snorted and gave him a look that held far more scorn than the Hunter expected a horse could manage.

"Yeah, yeah." He pushed the horse's long face away gently and moved toward his saddle. "I knew you'd be fine, too." A faint hiss escaped his lips as he put his weight down incorrectly on his injured leg. He'd stopped the bleeding but evidently failed to repair the damage done to the knee joint. Every step sent twinges of pain shooting down to his ankle and up to his hip. Along with all the rest of his still-healing injuries and the exhaustion from expending his energy repairing the wounds, he had little strength to spare. The idea of walking the few hundred paces separating him from the *kopje* that hid the Issai held little appeal, thus he'd asked Kiara to fetch him his horse so he could ride.

But even as he climbed into the saddle, a great shout rose up from among the boulders atop the hill, and a stream of colorfully clad men, women, and children streamed into view. When they reached the flat plains surrounding the *kopje,* they intertwined their arms around each other and began to sing, laugh, shout, and leap as they had upon Aisha's return.

A handful of them—Siyanda and her *unkgaliwe*, all wearing their streaming, bright-hued robes—advanced in a dance-like, zigzagging motion. A joyous song rang out across the plains, underscored by a rhythmic cadence of stamping feet and thigh-slapping. In response, Davathi, Aisha, and the Issai linked arms, too, and took up the song. The two lines of warriors drew closer in their erratic, leaping dance, until finally they swirled together into one large ring of singing, shouting, and leaping women.

Even the Hunter couldn't help smiling at that. He could only imagine how tense the last few days had felt for the handful of warriors protecting the Issai *ekhaya*. Seeing their *nassor*

359

returning with the *amaqhawe*, even so reduced, had to come as an immense relief for the young women. Even Siyanda's usually hard, scowling face lit up as bright as the morning sun.

A few of the Buhari—Jumaane among them—stopped to watch the revelry. The rest, however, remained occupied with the task of binding the Tefaye survivors and herding the column toward the *kopje*. The Nyemba, Mwaani, and Dalingcebo looked upon the joyous reunion with a mixture of expressions: delight at the raucous celebration, hope, relief, and, of course, sorrow aplenty, doubtless over lost homes and loves ones.

The dancing, singing, and leaping continued for long minutes, until Davathi finally relinquished her grip on Aisha and Naledi's shoulders and stepped back. Raising her hands, she shouted to gain the attention of her people. When they fell silent, she addressed them in their own tongue. The Hunter didn't understand everything that what was being said—and Kodyn was with Tarek, helping the Buhari bind the captive Tefaye—but pieced together enough to know it had something to do with Jumaane and his *amaqhawe*. Davathi's repeated gestures toward the *nassor* confirmed his suspicion.

Upon seeing Jumaane, Siyanda's eyebrows rose, and the words poured from her mouth in a torrent. Uncertainty and a measure of fear showed on her face, only vanishing when Davathi answered whatever question or concern she'd raised. Surprised expressions blossomed among the *unkgaliwe* as they stared at the Buhari warriors and those liberated from the Consortium camp.

Siyanda's eyes darted toward the Hunter and, with anger creasing her face, she spoke to the *nassor* in a sharp tone. Aisha spoke up, but Siyanda paid her no heed. She never even glanced Aisha's way. Only Davathi's words seemed to elicit any manner of response from the younger woman. "Enough!" the *nassor* barked in Issai.

Siyanda's expression smoothed out, though her hand still toyed with the handle of her *assegai*.

Davathi turned to the Buhari *nassor*, who stood watching the exchange with his thick arms folded over his broad, armored chest. "Jumaane!" She said something in her tongue and beckoned him over.

Jumaane strode calmly toward the group of Issai. In truth, it was more of a prowl, his movements characterized by the fluid grace and restrained fury of the greatcat whose mane he wore. A part of the Hunter wished he could have seen the *nassor* in battle against the Tefaye. That would have been a sight, indeed.

Davathi said something to her people—the Hunter caught the words for "welcome" and "alliance" as well as "enemies" and *alay-alagbara*—and the young women of the *unkgaliwe* raised their short-handled spears in salute to the towering Buhari *nassor*. Jumaane responded by thumping his fist against his chest and loosing a leonine roar.

At that sound, something intriguing happened to Siyanda's face. Her cheeks flushed slightly, her lips parted, and a strange light shone in her dark eyes. The Hunter could have sworn her breathing quickened, too.

"*Nassor* Jumaane." Siyanda inclined her head toward the bearded man.

"Siyanda." Jumaane's face creased into a smile just a tad too large. He said something, which she answered, and a brief exchange passed between them. Because the Hunter could not comprehend their words, he had no choice but to scrutinize their body language. And *both* of their bodies spoke far more loudly than either of them appeared to realize.

A little "*Hmm?*" sounded from where Kiara still stood beside his foot. When the Hunter caught her eyes, a knowing smile tugged on her lips. So, she'd seen it, too.

He had no more time to consider the matter, for another lion-like roar from Jumaane snapped his attention back toward the Issai. Just in time to see a tall, lithe man with flecks of snow-white in his near-black hair and beard striding from among those standing at the base of the *kopje* toward the crowd gathered around Davathi and Jumaane.

"Duma!" Jumaane roared, spreading his arms wide.

Duma's sun-lined face broke into a smile to match the Buhari *nassor's* and he pressed the hand holding his spear and shield to his chest in a greeting at once respectful and oddly friendly given the Issai and Buhari had, until only recently, been rivals.

There was a story there, the Hunter knew, one he was immensely curious to learn. But not now. The time for such tales would come later.

"Come on," he said, turning to Kiara and leaning down to offer her a hand. "Now that all the friendly greetings are sorted, time we get on with the important matters."

Kiara gripped his hand and pulled herself up onto the saddle behind him. Elivast snorted a quiet protest, but rest and a few mouthfuls of plains grass had done him well. Without further complaint, he set off at a trot toward the knot of Issai standing with Jumaane.

At his approach, all eyes turned toward him. Siyanda's expression darkened, but the faces of the Issai—both *unkgalive* and *amaqhawe* alike—revealed a mixture of fear, respect, and curiosity. They had all witnessed him do the impossible. That was the *third* time he'd charged an enemy alone to defend the Issai, which had earned their admiration, and had stated to Davathi, Siyanda, Duma, and the warriors that he was *Okanele*.

It felt odd, being the subject of such scrutiny and interest. It wasn't exactly the first time—he'd told Master Gold and her trusted Night Guild subordinates the truth, and the Cambionari traveling with him from Voramis had known as well. Both had looked at him with the same fear he saw etched into the faces of the Issai and Buhari—in the knights' case, there'd been hatred aplenty, too. Yet there was something different about the way he was being regarded. Interest that bordered on awe rather than dread. Almost as if they wanted to believe he was more man than beast, as Jumaane had said.

He felt the color rising to his cheeks, an uncomfortable heat surging within him. Fortunately, the Tefaye blood hid it well enough. He attempted to keep his tone even, level, but Duma spoke before he could.

"*Umzukeli,*" said the man, with a slight bow of his head. "The name is appropriate, I see."

The Hunter offered a similar gesture of respect. "So they tell me, *Umdala.*" He spoke the title with respect, as was its intent. The honorific was unique to the Issai, Aisha had explained. In the tribe where the women became warriors and the men hunters and herders, only those very few men who'd proven themselves valiant in battle and defense of the *ekhaya* were worthy to carry the name *Umdala.*

Despite that, the Hunter couldn't help cracking a jest. "'Most handsome man on the plains is definitely a title I can agree with."

Duma laughed, as did Jumaane, Davathi, Aisha, and the Issai who spoke Einari. A few cast confused glances around, and when their companions translated, their reactions were mixed—some amused, some scornful, others merely shaking their heads. Siyanda rolled her eyes with such ferocity they nearly popped free of her skull, though she held her tongue. Kiara dug a knuckle into his ribs, though the force was blunted by his armor.

"I am certain my *nassor*—" At this, Duma's eyes darted to Davathi, passing over Siyanda entirely. "—has shown much gratitude." The elder pressed the hand holding his spear and shield to his heart in a gesture identical the one he'd given Jumaane. "But I will show it, too. Three times now, my people owe you much."

Warmth burned within the Hunter's belly, and he felt a beaming smile tugging at his lips. He bowed to keep himself from grinning like a fool. "As I told you, I am bound to Aisha by *isithembiso*. And through her, to the Issai"—he cast a sidelong glance at Jumaane—"and their allies."

Jumaane merely gave him a knowing smile.

"But now that we're all finished with the happy reunions, it's time we discuss war." The Hunter turned to face Davathi. "I would not keep you from celebrating your return to your people, but it has already been six days since we freed you from the Consortium camp. By now, the *Gcinue'eleku awandile* will be planning how best to respond to our opening move. If they have not yet already begun their counterattack, they soon will."

"On that, we agree, *Umzukeli*." Davathi's attention shifted from the Hunter to Jumaane, Siyanda, and Duma. "The *Umkhadulu Iwepi* must be convened. We will speak in council and decide our best course of action. When the *alay-alagbara* come, they will not find us unprepared."

Chapter Twelve

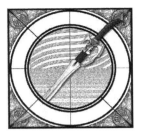

The *Umkhadulu Iwepi*—or, as Kodyn translated, "the Great Council of Warriors"—met on the flat top of the tallest boulder that formed the *kopje*. The vantage offered an unbroken view of the plains for leagues in every direction, as well as the Issai *ekhaya* and cattle penned up among the rocks on the hilltop. At the base of the *kopje*, the Issai had already joined the Buhari in lending what aid they could—in the form of clothing, shelters, even weaponry—to the liberated captives.

Thirteen people formed the *Umkhadulu Iwepi*. Davathi, Siyanda, Sizwe, and Naledi represented the Issai, with Jumaane and three of his warriors to stand for the Buhari. Four more Ghandians sat among those planning for battle—two men of the Nyemba, one Mwaani, and a Dalingcebo—all of whom had evidently proven capable warriors during the recent clash against the Tefaye.

Umdala Duma rounded out the ranks of those called to speak at the *Umkhadulu Iwepi*. Davathi and Jumaane both treated him with deference—the former speaking to him as one spoke to a mentor, the latter more akin to a father. Kodyn had explained to him that *Umdala* was a title given to those who had, through acts of courage, earned their place among the warriors despite not being *amaqhawai* themselves. One look at Duma's sword and the skill with which he wielded it made it clear that he deserved the honorific.

At Aisha's insistence, Kodyn and Tarek had been permitted to join her, the Hunter, and Kiara. She held an interesting place among those gathered here. She was no *amaqhawai*, yet had bested Jumaane in ritual combat. Her *Umoyahlebe* gifts made her arguably the most powerful fighter in their ranks. It was clear that everyone who had witnessed her powers during the attack on the Consortium camp and the *Impi yechipekwe* respected her. Jumaane and his warriors regarded her with a look akin to reverence. Only Siyanda seemed unimpressed by Aisha. On the contrary, animosity blazed visibly in her eyes every time they strayed toward her cousin.

At Davathi's suggestion, Kodyn sat next to the Hunter, Tarek, and Kiara to translate the discussion. Each tribe spoke their own variation on the local tongue, yet the similarities were such they could be easily understood. When the time came for the *alay-alaghara* to speak their piece, Davathi or Aisha would translate for those who did not speak Einari.

Davathi wasted no time cutting to the heart of the matter.

"The Issai and Buhari are united in their desire to drive the *Gcinue'eleku awandile* from these lands," she said, her leonine face stern. "*Nassor* Jumaane and his warriors will fight alongside the Issai *amaqhawe*. We would be honored for the Nyemba, Mwaani, and our brethren from across the Great Chasm to do likewise."

The Mwaani warrior, a venerable-looking man with a shock of unruly curly hair shot through with three broad streaks of grey, and more than a few battle scars, tapped the butt of the bronze hand axe he'd taken off a Tefaye corpse against the stone before his crossed legs. "Our *amaqhawe* is far off, and even before our numbers were reduced by the attacks of the Tefaye and the predations of the *alay-alagbara,* our strength could not compare to the might of the Buhari." The smell of the sea hung heavy about him—coral, algae, and brackish water.

"The Nyemba are a peaceful people," spoke up the Nyemba warrior, who smelled of harsh mountain winds, limestone, and wild heather. "Our *amaqhawe* hunt the great *kitaka* apes of the Mthokozisi Mountains or drive off the packs of wild dogs that dwell among the Nhlanhla foothills."

"We have no warriors," said the one Dalingcebo. "Our people are not reavers, but fishers and weavers." His scent—a mixture of dried reeds, dried trout scales, and clay—made that much clear to the Hunter's keen nostrils. The man's weather-beaten face creased into a dark scowl. "It is for this reason we were vulnerable to attack from the *alay-alagbara.*"

"That is understood." Jumaane inclined his head, which was absent its lion's mane headdress for the time being. Even sitting down, he was large and imposing enough he all but dominated the gathering by sheer presence and volume alone. "But in times such as these, facing an enemy such as this, it is only when all stand united that we have hope of triumph."

"A mighty river is not dammed with one pebble alone," Duma said.

Jumaane's lips quirked into a broad smile and he gestured to the *Umdala* for emphasis. "Precisely." He looked to the Nyemba and Mwaani primarily. "I will send two of my fastest runners with your strongest warriors. Bring word to your *nassors* of what we discuss here today, and of what you have seen and endured. Attempt to convince them of the need for their aid. If you cannot, if your *nassors* choose to ignore my request, I cannot fault you." He leaned forward, placing his huge hands on his knees flaring his elbows out so wide that he all but loomed over the women and men seated around him. "Nor will I forget."

The Nyemba and Mwaani warriors offered hasty assurances that they would convey his message as requested and make every attempt to convince their tribes to join. But the doubt in their eyes was unmistakable.

"As for our southern cousins," Davathi said, looking to the Dalingcebo man, "the *amathafa* is not your home, and you cannot be expected to fight its battles. Your people are welcome among my own until such a time as you are recovered sufficiently to return to your lands. I ask, however, that you at least *consider* joining your strength with ours. Though warriors you may not be, the addition of your numbers to our ranks could mean the difference between triumph and defeat when battle is joined."

The Dalingcebo's expression grew cautious, guarded. He clearly understood just how indebted he and everyone else from south of the Chasm of the Lost were—while among these lands, they depended entirely on the hospitality and mercy of the Issai for survival—yet remained unwilling to risk his people in battle. Besides, *his* people might only number a handful; the Dalingcebo were not a united tribe like the Issai or Buhari, but a loose agglomeration of villages and towns that merely shared similar languages and cultures. Each community spoke for and governed themselves in whatever way they saw fit, independent of outside interference of any kind.

"I ask for no commitments now." Davathi's tone held a placating edge. "Merely speak to your people and consider your best course of action. If you choose to abstain from battle, I would ask that you join my people in tending our cattle, foraging, hunting, and maintaining our *ekhaya* in our absence."

"To that," said the man with a little bow, "I will gladly accede."

"Speaking on the subject of dammed rivers," Aisha interjected. "We have discovered the truth of the Tefaye." Her jaw muscles clenched. "And what was done to them by the *Ganue'eleku awandile.*"

At a nod of approval from her mother, Aisha recounted what Kodyn had found among the Consortium's papers, the alchemical tests to turn the outcast tribe into little better than mindless, ravening beasts.

"Their presence here is of great concern." Aisha's brow furrowed. "How they found this place, I cannot begin to guess." She looked to Siyanda. "Cousin, have you any ideas?"

The question was asked in a tone the Hunter recognized as utterly genuine and free of malice. To his surprise, Siyanda's face flushed a deep, furious red and she sprang to her feet.

"What are you accusing me of, Cousin?" she snarled, hand tightening on the hilt of her *assegai.*

Aisha's eyes flew wide in surprise, and her mouth dropped open. "I—"

Kodyn's translation cut off abruptly as Siyanda roared at Aisha, a tirade of epic proportions unleashed from her lips. She stabbed an accusatory finger toward Aisha's face, and Aisha seemed unable to find an answer, so stunned was she. Only Davathi's sharp shout silenced the younger woman. With a few sullen mutters, she bowed to her *nassor* and returned to her seat.

The Hunter noted the way her eyes darted between Aisha and Jumaane, the color on her face deepening to an angry crimson. Aisha hadn't intended insult, yet Siyanda had heard only accusation, and her outburst had only been made all the stronger by the Buhari *nassor's* presence.

If Jumaane thought anything about the exchange, he kept it from his face. Indeed, his expression remained impassive as if nothing at all had occurred. The Hunter couldn't help wondering whether that was done for Siyanda's sake, Davathi's, or Aisha's.

With a hard glare for Siyanda, Davathi resumed speaking, and Kodyn's translation continued. "The Tefaye's presence here today is, as my daughter said, a cause for great concern. *However* they found the *kopje*"—she threw a sharp, scolding look at Siyanda—"it's clear that our lands are too close to theirs to be safe. Jumaane and I have spoken and agree that it is best that we move our *ekhaya* to join with the Buhari's while we wage war on the *Ganue'eleku awandile.*"

This time, it wasn't just Siyanda who sprang to her feet. Naledi, Sizwe, and two of Jumaane's hand-picked warriors jumped up and began shouting in protest. Kodyn couldn't begin to translate their arguments, but the Hunter had no doubt each tribe had good reason for wanting to keep their camps separate.

A lion's roar from Jumaane's lips silenced the outcry. The sound carried across the plains, startling the Ghandians gathered at the base of the *kopje* and drawing hundreds of eyes up toward them.

"It has been decided." Jumaane's deep voice rang with a note of unquestioned authority. "The Buhari and Issai are united in this war. By combining our *ekhayas,* we bring greater strength both to battle and the defense of our lands."

"And when the war is over?" Naledi demanded. She was one of the younger *amaqhawai,* and apparently on the hot-tempered side, her face flushed and eyes blazing. "The Buhari have long sought to conquer the Issai lands." Her scent was strong with the *makini* nut oil the Issai used to protect their spears from rust, along with the grasses used for their cloth undergarments, aloe, and hyacinth.

Jumaane held up one huge hand. "The Issai will return to find their lands unclaimed. At least by my people. I have given my word. And the word of the *nassor* is the word of the Buhari." He turned a baleful look on his three warriors. "Is that not so?"

The two who had risen looked as if they wanted to argue, but the one who'd remained seated—an older fellow not quite as wizened as Duma, but at least a decade older than Davathi—nodded and spoke. "The word of the *nassor* is the word of the Buhari." He thumped his fist against his armored chest for emphasis.

After a sullen moment, the two standing Buhari echoed the words and mimicked the gesture.

"Then it is settled." Davathi inclined her head to Jumaane, as if conceding victory in some private argument to which only they were privy. "When the sun rises upon the morrow, our united peoples—Issai, Dalingcebo, Buhari, and those of the Nyemba and Mwaani not yet strong enough to return to their own lands—will begin the journey to join with the Buhari *ekhaya.* Meanwhile, Naledi and Dabu"—her gesture indicated the elder Buhari warrior sitting at Jumaane's side—"will lead a portion of our *amaqhawe* to seek out the *Gcinue'eleku awandile,* to assess their strength and bring warning of any attack. Another portion, led by Sizwe and Guduzo"—this indicated the younger of the two who'd sprang to their feet—"will endeavor to locate the Tefaye and learn what we can of them. To know for certain what danger they pose."

It had been Kiara who first raised the question of whether the Tefaye could have been *sent* to attack the Issai. There existed the possibility the Consortium had merely turned the outcast tribe into what amounted to a pack of rabid wild beasts set loose on the plains to weaken their enemies, but she had surmised that the Consortium—or the Order of Mithridas, who the Hunter suspected were truly pulling the strings—would be far more likely to wield direct control of the weapon they had created. *Targeted* attacks would be exponentially more effective at reducing the strength of tribes potentially hostile to whatever nefarious enterprise they had underway at *Ukuhlushwa Okungapheli.*

"And what of the Tefaye?" the Hunter spoke up for the first time since the *Umkhadulu Iwepi* had begun. "What do you intend to do with them?"

Davathi and Jumaane exchanged glances, and similar expressions of concern blossomed on their faces. Nearly three score Tefaye had survived the battle. Already, they had proven problematic to restrain. In their poison-madness, they thrashed and struggled against the fibrous rope and cords used to bind them. Four had broken free, attacked their captors with empty hands and gnashing teeth, and died for their efforts. Yet that hadn't deterred the rest from straining to tear their bonds. Their enraged howls echoed like the cries of wild animals across the plains, audible for leagues in all direction.

It was Davathi who spoke. "For the sake of our peoples, they must die."

Chapter Thirteen

Now it was the Hunter's turn to spring to his feet. "No." He spoke the word firmly, shook his head for emphasis. "I left them alive for a reason! Had I wanted them dead—"

"What you want, *Umzukeli,* is not of utmost importance here." Davathi's expression went flat, her dark eyes as hard and flinty as the stone beneath her. "Make no mistake, we all here recognize what you have done for us. But this decision affects *our* people. It is *our* food they will eat, *our* water they will drink." Her gesture encompassed every one of the Ghandians seated around the circle. "As such, it is *our* choice to make."

Anger flared in the Hunter's belly. Kiara shot him a warning look, yet it did little to deter him from speaking.

"Why?" He looked from Davathi to Jumaane, then to the rest of the Issai, Buhari, Nyemba, Mwaani, and Dalingcebo encircling him. "Yes, food and water are scarce, resources precious. I can understand that you desire to save them for your own people. But why do the lives of your people matter more than theirs? Is it because they have been cast out from your tribes? They are not one of you, and so they are lesser?"

The looks on the faces staring back at him made it clear he'd guessed correctly.

"They are *izigebengu,*" Siyanda snapped. "Murderers and thieves, those who brought ruin to their tribes. They have earned their fate, every one of them."

"Perhaps." The Hunter met the younger woman's gaze with cold calm. "But they are still people. And they do not deserve to be butchered like cattle." His lip curled into a snarl. "Worse than cattle, for I have seen how highly you prize your raya. You would slaughter them because they have been turned into *that* by your enemies."

He thrust a finger toward the Tefaye warriors, who despite their bonds, were still struggling, writhing on the ground, and howling like maddened beasts. "Whatever they did to earn their place among the Tefaye, can you truly say that it is *just* to be rid of them like this? To slit their throats and leave their bodies to the *makalala* rather than attempting to help them?" He folded his arms across his chest. "If you say yes, then you are no better than the *Gcinue'eleku awandile.*"

Anger darkened more than a few faces. Guduzo and the other Buhari who'd sprang to his feet looked on the verge of leveling their spears at him. The Nyemba, Mwaani, and even a few of the Issai stared at him with wrathful expressions.

But the ones who *truly* mattered—Davathi and Jumaane—regarded him with more contemplation than outrage. Jumaane's bearded chin twitched, his eyes narrowing in thought. Davathi's fingers toyed with the shaft of her *assegai.* Though neither spoke, they appeared to at least *consider* his words.

The Hunter took that as a good sign and drove on. "You know the truth of what was done to the Tefaye." He fixed each member of the *Umkhadulu Iwepi* with a glower in turn. "If there is a chance of reversing it, of curing them, surely *that* would be the nobler path. The warrior's path. To kill them here and now would make you as bad as the *alay-alagbara* you hate. It would be the act of *Okanele*, not men."

That sank home. Even Siyanda couldn't help backing down. Her expression remained sullen, angry, yet she had nothing further to say.

Davathi leaned forward, eyes burning into his. "You believe you can heal them?" she asked in a quiet voice.

"I don't bloody know!" The Hunter threw up his hands. "But I know we have to at least *try*."

How strange to hear those words coming out of *his* mouth. Not long ago, he'd have been the first to suggest eliminating even the slightest threat. But after all the death he'd witnessed—and brought about—he could not so easily cast aside human lives. Especially when those lives could very well one day be needed to sustain Kharna and drive away the Great Devourer.

But it was more than that. His time in Enarium had opened his eyes. The people in the Pit had lived entire lives in captivity, had been condemned to die a slow, miserable death by a people who believed such a sacrifice was worth it. The Elivasti had chosen *their people* over the humans they'd imprisoned. They would have fed hundreds of thousands to power *Khar'nath's* magic in the name of saving their own lives. What was happening here today was no different.

"I don't know if there's any hope of curing them." He spoke quickly; he had Davathi and Jumaane at least *entertaining* his point of view, and had to draw them toward what he truly believed to be the right conclusion before he lost them. "I'm no bloody alchemist or healer. I know nothing about what was done to them or whether it can be reversed. But what I do know is that I can't stand by and let them be butchered without having at least *tried*." He fixed Davathi with a hard look. "Just like I couldn't stand by and let your people remain prisoners." His gaze swiveled to the rest of those he'd freed from the Consortium camp. "Or your people."

His words had an instant effect on most of those around him. The Nyemba, Mwaani, Dalingcebo, and Issai who'd suffered under the slavers' lash glanced around, questioning looks on their faces. That was good. Questioning their certainty about what they considered a "necessity" could lead them to a vastly different conclusion.

The Hunter saw Siyanda bristle, start to rise, but drove on before she could speak.

"Give me time," he insisted, again returning his gaze to Davathi and Jumaane. "That is all I ask." He swept a hand toward Tarek and Kodyn. "During our raid of the *alay-alagbara* camp, we found records of what was done to the Tefaye. With that knowledge, there exists at least the possibility we can undo what was done." He looked to Tarek. "Isn't that right?"

The young Elivasti flushed, seeming surprised to be so put on the spot. "I-I do not yet know." He swallowed, and when he spoke again, his voice held more confidence. "As the Hunter said, we need time. Time to study the poisons used against the Tefaye, and to test antidotes." He hesitated a moment before saying, "But yes, I believe we may be able to undo what was done."

Murmured words passed between the Issai warriors and their *nassor*, echoed by Jumaane's Buhari. The Nyemba, Mwaani, and Dalingcebo muttered amongst themselves. Only those on the Hunter's side—Tarek, Aisha, Kodyn, and Kiara—remained silent. Kiara gave the Hunter an encouraging nod, though her face remained impassive. Kodyn's expression was thoughtful, and Aisha's eyes were riveted on her mother and Siyanda. Duma, too, was occupied watching, weighing, measuring. Not just his own people, but all around him.

After a few seconds of turmoil, Davathi quietened her people with a slashing gesture of her hand, and Jumaane did likewise with a low, leonine growl in the back of his throat. Silence descended over the circle, until the only sound drifting between them was the whispering wind and the distant wails of the imprisoned Tefaye.

Davathi looked to Jumaane. Their eyes locked for long moments, and an unspoken conversation passed between them.

To the Hunter's surprise, it was Duma who broke the silence first. "When two *chipekwe* fight, it is the grass that suffers."

All eyes, even Davathi and Jumaane's, turned to regard the Issai *Umdala*.

"The *Gcinue'eleku awandile* have used our own division against us," the elder man said, a somber look on his age-lined face. He stroked his white-flecked black beard with one strong hand. "They know we cannot stand against them while we are occupied with our own concerns. It is only through unity that victory is possible. Issai. Buhari. Nyemba. Mwaani. Dalingcebo." He indicated each of the tribes represented around the circle with one finger, then turned that finger to point toward the struggling, howling captives below. "And Tefaye. All the *amathafa* joined as one." He closed the pointing finger into a clenched fist. "Only when the lion pride hunts together will all be fed."

Duma's words, spoken in his strong, deep voice, rang out around the circle. One by one, every member of the *Umkhadulu Iwepi*—even Siyanda—nodded slowly.

A slow smile spread across Jumaane's face. "The Old Cheetah speaks the truth."

"As always." Davathi inclined her head in respect to Duma. "Your wisdom is welcome, *Umdala*. And heeded."

Duma mirrored Davathi's gesture with a deeper bow of his own, hand pressed to his heart.

Davathi turned back to the Hunter. "You ask for time, *Umzukeli*. It is granted." She glanced to Jumaane, who answered with a barely perceptible nod of his great head. "You will have until we reach the Buhari *ekhaya*. On that day, if you have not found a cure, we will do what must be done. For we cannot wage war on the *Gcinue'eleku awandile* while guarding so many prisoners."

The Hunter's gut clenched. That was far from a great deal of time—the return journey to Buhari lands would be far faster as the Ghandians regained their strength—but it would have to suffice. "Thank you, *nassors.*" He bowed low to both Davathi and Jumaane. They had shown him respect by listening to his argument, even acceding to it, and thus deserved his respect in return.

"And now, let us speak of our plans for the journey to Buhari lands," Davathi said, while the Hunter returned to his seat. "*Nassor* Jumaane, tell us…"

The Hunter stopped paying attention the instant he saw the change that had come over Kiara. In the last few moments, all color had drained from her face, her eyes wobbled, and her head looked on the verge of sagging onto her chest. Her fingers clawed at the ground as if fighting to remain upright.

The Hunter knelt at her side and gripped her shoulder. "Kiara?" he whispered. "Ki—"

Her eyes snapped toward him, and her face regained its healthy glow. So quick was her recovery that he almost believed he'd imagined it, save for the whiteness of her knuckles.

"I'm fine," she whispered back. "Tired."

The Hunter scrutinized her intently. Her voice sounded a little too breathy for his liking, and the bags under her eyes had grown darker, yet he could see nothing else amiss with her. No wounds, no flush of fever. A bit of lightheadedness from fatigue wasn't entirely unexpected.

Kiara had never before shown any such weakness—not even during her recovery from the time she'd spent in the Pit in Enarium—but her current state *could* be explained by everything that had happened since departing Malandria. Fiery hell, they'd spent the better part of the last week incessantly running, riding, and fighting. Rest had been in scarce supply for all of them.

He grunted and released her shoulder, but settled close enough at her side that she could lean against him should the fatigue return. Only then did he return his attention to the goings-on of the Great Council of Warriors. Jumaane was speaking in his own tongue, and worried looks darkened the faces of the others around the circle.

The Hunter raised a questioning eyebrow in Kodyn's direction. The young man leaned over and whispered, "They're talking about another tribe that seemed to have disappeared without a trace. The Bheka, who hold the lands between the Nyemba and Buhari."

"The Consortium?" the Hunter asked.

Kodyn tipped his head to the side. "Likely." He cocked one ear to listen to Jumaane's words, then translated. "He'll send two more of his warriors with the party going to convince the Nyemba to join our war efforts. They'll see if they can find out what happened to the Bheka."

At that moment, Jumaane wrapped up whatever he'd been saying and Davathi climbed to her feet. However, as she spoke, the solemn expression fled her face and a smile replaced it. The mood around the circle instantly lightened. Joy and delight brightened the eyes of all the Ghandians. Every one of them, even Duma, sprang to their feet and spoke in rapid, excited voices.

"What is it?" The Hunter turned to Kodyn and was rewarded with an equally large smile on the young Praamian's face. "What's going on?"

"An *umgubho*!" Kodyn scrambled to stand, his expression ablaze with wonder and excitement. "A celebration of the *amaqhawe's* return home and the alliance between the Issai and Buhari."

The Hunter's eyebrows rose. "A party?"

"Yes," Aisha said, and even her face had brightened at the prospect. "But one I guarantee is unlike anything you'll find outside our *amathafa.*"

Duma

Chapter Fourteen

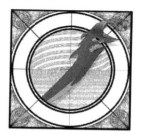

Aisha hadn't been exaggerating. Though the Hunter had attended countless fêtes thrown by some of the wealthiest of the Voramian nobility, none of their extravagance could hold a candle to the Issai's celebrations.

By comparison, the revelry could have seemed a paltry affair. Yet the Issai themselves made it a truly joyous occasion even in its utter simplicity.

Not so much as a lace scarf or silk ribbon decorated their clothing, but the way their multi-hued robes swirled about them as they danced and leaped about filled the night with a riot of color. In place of crystal chandeliers or lanterns burning a small fortune in oil, they had only the stars and the light of small cattle dung bonfires for illumination. Somehow, though, that made it all the more spectacular. Almost as if nature itself played a hand in the grand spectacle.

And grand it was, despite the absence of a banquet table laden with a gluttonous feast. The meal was simple yet satisfying fare: a savory, stiff dough made from sorghum grass ground to fine flour and cooked in sour raya milk, roasted cattle and antelope seasoned liberally with cumin and cloves, a soup thick with root vegetables and clotted cream, and a sweet dish made of stewed raisins, apricots, and nuts housed within balls of the very same sorghum-and-sour-milk dough.

The Hunter ate sparingly—even *he* could see there was far too little to feed the entire Issai tribe, the Buhari *amaqhawe*, and the others—but it warmed his soul as well as his belly. Perhaps it was the broad smiles on the faces of the Issai women who served it to him or the proud looks adorning the tribe's hunters who had brought down the game for the feast.

Or maybe it was the music that truly lent the evening's affair the proper ambience of revelry. The moment the sun dipped behind the western horizon and Davathi announced the celebration's commencement, a fascinating orchestra of instruments had appeared in the hands of the Issai.

A dozen men sat in a broad half-circle facing the central campfire, pounding away at percussion instruments fashioned from hollowed-out logs. When the sticks struck the slits set into the drums' sides, they generated a beautifully resonant tone. The drums ranged from palm-sized and handheld to nearly as large around as a Voramian beer barrel. Each generated its own unique sound, and to the Hunter's ears, it seemed as if they spoke to each other. Not a quarrel or tumult; every drum added a layer to the beat that dipped and swelled in rhythmic cadence.

Accompanying the drummers were women playing what appeared to be brass water jugs with a hole in the side. Every tap of the fingertips against the jars' sides produced a light, percussive sound that added to the beat of the drums. But when they struck the holes with flat palms, the sound was a deeper, hollower base tone. Even merely brushing their palms against the brass sides added a higher dimension to the sound.

Of course, there were dozens of bamboo flutes akin to the one Aisha had carved. Unlike woodwinds common to Voramis, these were capable of producing only a single note. Most curiously, however, the children who played the flutes followed each blown note with a sung note either of the same or harmonizing pitch. The result was a fascinating conversation between the various flute players.

What piqued the Hunter's attention most, however, were the twin gourds tied together with leather thongs. These were played by a few younger women the Hunter recognized as *unkgaliwe*, with one ball held firmly in hand and the other swung around at the end of the thong to *clack* against each other. With every strike, the seeds or pebbles within the dried gourds created a sound like falling sand. The combination was a complex, multi-faceted rhythm that had even the Hunter's toes tapping.

Everyone within range of the music joined in the festivities. Issai, Nyemba, Mwaani, even Dalingcebo and those of the Buhari *amaqhawe* not assigned to guard the prisoners gathered around the fires, food, and musicians. Jumaane's warriors stomped their feet and shouted in time with the music, while the Issai answered with rhythmic hand slaps to their thighs and chests. Some of the Mwaani had found sticks of hardwood that resonated when struck together, while the Nyemba filled the air with ululating cries. The Dalingcebo clapped their hands, shouted encouragement, and lent their voices to whatever songs they knew.

Jumaane and Davathi sat side by side, watching the entire affair with satisfaction and pride written on their faces. The Buhari *nassor* loomed large in his lion's headdress and hide cape, his skin shining even brighter red in the light of the burning fires. Davathi had donned the flowing robes of her people, the fabric a glorious riot of blues, purples, reds, oranges, and yellows. They appeared utterly at ease—almost as if they *weren't* about to march to war against the Vassalage Consortium and the Order of Mithridas upon the morrow.

A small knot of Buhari and Issai warriors clustered around their *nassors,* but instead of remaining apart as they had while traveling, they sat intermingled, sharing their food, stories, laughter, and jugs of rich sorghum beer.

Though Siyanda numbered among their ranks, she appeared far from at ease. The smile on her face failed to reach her eyes and she did not sing, tap, or slap along with the music. More than once, the Hunter caught her gaze darting around, a haunted air about her. The dark circles ringing her eyes spoke of far too many sleepless nights.

Of Aisha and Kodyn, the Hunter saw no sign. Despite their excitement at the promise of the revelry, the pair had vanished immediately following the *Umkhadulu Iwepi* and remained firmly out of sight. According to Kiara, they'd wanted to snatch a few hours of rest away from the hustle and bustle of the Issai *ekhaya.*

Thoughts of Kiara brought back the worry that had gnawed at the Hunter all day long. The way she'd nearly collapsed during the Great Council of Warriors troubled him. She had tried to put on a brave face afterward, scoffing when he'd offered his arm to escort her someplace quiet to sleep, but he'd seen the exhaustion written deep in every line and shadow on her face. It had taken her all of three breaths to fall asleep, and she hadn't so much as stirred when the sound of merrymaking roused the Hunter from his own rest.

She'll be here soon, no doubt, he told himself. *She loves a party as much as anyone.* The mental image of her dancing, leaping, and stamping her feet enthusiastically brought a smile to his face. Few people could light up a room and infuse life into even the simplest celebration like she could.

He sat alone in the crowd of Ghandians, understanding little of what was being said around him, yet he did not truly feel an outsider as he had in so many other soirees in the past. It didn't matter that he was different. He didn't need to be at the heart of the dancers or raising his voice in song. In that moment, in the midst of that revelry, he felt himself drawn into its churning currents of merrymaking as everyone else.

A shadow fell across his face, blocking out the light of a nearby fire. Looking up, the Hunter found himself staring into the face of an Issai *amaqhawai*. He didn't know her name, merely recognized her by her piercings, her swirling robes, and the *assegai* gripped loosely in her left hand. Her right, however, extended toward him holding a bowl of the rich vegetable stew.

When he didn't immediately take the bowl, she said something in her language—the words for "food" and "delicious", he recognized—and all but shoved it into his hands. He had no choice but to accept the gift. She was gone before he could raise his voice in thanks, vanished into the crowd of dancing and leaping Issai.

The Hunter brought the bowl to his lips and took a long drink. Instantly, he regretted it. Liquid fire poured down his throat and stung his nostrils. He coughed, fighting to draw in a breath, but his lungs refused to draw in air. His mouth burned and went numb at the same time.

It was all he could do to keep from retching. He barely managed to summon enough awareness through the blinding pain on his lips to turn his attention inward and focus on the nerve fibers transmitting the tremendous agony from his mouth to his brain. Slowly, the anguish diminished from the blazing inferno of molten steel to a simmering burn akin to a scalded tongue.

As his consciousness returned to the world around him, laughter rippled through the Issai. He looked up to find dozens of eyes fixed on him. Among them, the *amaqhawai* who'd handed him the bowl laced with what he now recognized as Ghandian lion peppers. She laughed loudest of all, slapping her thighs and leaning on Naledi as if too weakened by her mirth to stand.

The Hunter was about to spring to his feet when a deep, rumbling voice reached him.

"Consider it an honor, *Umzukeli.*"

The Hunter's head snapped to his right. Duma sat cross-legged on the grass a few paces away, a bowl of his own in hand and a wry smile on his lips.

"Cebile has played the same prank on every guest of the Issai since the day she was old enough to walk." The old warrior's eyes twinkled. "The more important the guest, the more peppers she uses."

The Hunter tried to speak, but his throat was hoarse, his tongue utterly numb. His gaze went back to Cebile, who was still shaking with laughter. The meaning behind Duma's words sank home then. There was no mockery or disdain on her face, only mischief. She had chosen him because he was an easy target—an *alay-alagbara,* unaccustomed to the vicious fire of the spice native to her *amathafa.*

With a wry smile of his own, the Hunter brought the bowl to his lips and emptied the remainder of the soup. A chorus of delighted and surprised shouts rang out among the Issai and all gathered around, loudest of all from Cebile herself.

The Hunter could feel the molten heat burning its way down his throat—he'd regret that in the morning for certain—but ignored it long enough to stand, stride toward Cebile and Naledi, and hold out his bowl. "Is there any more?"

Cebile's howled laughter was accompanied by those of every Ghandian around. She, Naledi, and a few of her fellow *amaqhawe* closed around the Hunter, slapping his back. The bowl was torn from his hands and replaced by a jar filled with what the Hunter suspected was raya milk. It took all his iron willpower not to drink every last drop to quell the burning in his mouth, nostrils, and throat.

The Issai's laughter echoed louder, accompanied by shouts and cries of *"Umzukeli!"* Hands tugged at the Hunter's armor, and a few derisive expressions appeared on the warriors' faces. No doubt they were saying the same thing Siyanda had told him, albeit with far less scorn.

"Gift!" shouted Naledi in Einari. The *amaqhawe* around her took up the cry, and before the Hunter knew what was happening, a bundle was thrust into his hands. Within was a set of the same robes worn by the Issai, beautifully crafted, brightly colored, and light as air.

Naledi rapped her knuckles against his armored chest. "You go to war with Issai, you dress as Issai."

Joyous cries and cheers accompanied her pronouncement, and again, a round of back slapping nearly sent the Hunter staggering. Judging by the expectant looks on the faces of all those encircling him—not just the *amaqhawe,* but all the Ghandians not occupied in the dancing and feasting—they intended he don the robes at that very moment. The Hunter had never been one for modesty, but the idea of stripping down in front of an entire crowd held little appeal. But he saw no way out of the throng that surrounded him.

"All right, all right!" He had to shout to be heard over the din. "Give me a few minutes to get out of—"

Even as he spoke, he felt strong hands loosening the clasps, buckles, and straps of his armor. It felt oddly personal yet somehow utterly normal at the same time. At once a ritual ceremony and the most commonplace thing in the world.

In a matter of seconds, his leather armor had been stripped off—and, to his relief, laid in a neat pile beside the spot where he'd been sitting. He stood only in his trousers, boots, and undertunic. When he stripped off the sweat-soaked shirt, a chorus of shouts that sounded perilously close to catcalls arose all around him. Some were mocking, accompanied by broad grins—and a few appreciative looks—from the *amaqhawe.* Many, however, echoed with a note of curiosity and astonishment at the sight of his physique and the myriad scars marking his flesh.

The Hunter stood still for a moment, baring himself to the eyes of the people he had sworn to Aisha to defend and protect. They saw him now in a way few ever had, and he felt oddly vulnerable revealed thus. Yet defiant, too. He had nothing to hide from them. They knew the truth of his nature, an *Okanele,* for better or worse.

"Careful, *alay-alagbara,*" called Naledi, a mischievous twinkle on her strong face. "The nights on the *amathafa* grow cold."

At her words, the colorful robes were pulled from his hands and draped over his shoulders. When it was done, the two warriors who'd dressed him joined their companions in looking him over. Cebile called something to Jumaane in her tongue, and both the Issai and Buhari roared in laughter.

The Hunter raised an eyebrow. "What did she say?"

"That though the robes suit you well enough, you are still missing something important." Jumaane's voice answered his question. The huge *nassor* had risen from his seat and now strode toward the Hunter with a broad grin on his face. "Color."

From within the pouch he wore on his belt, he drew out a small container that looked to have been made from the ivory tusk of some great beast. When he removed the lid, the smell of butter and dirt rose up from the reddish mixture within.

Jumaane dipped two fingers into the container and drew out a generous dollop of the odorous substance. This, he smeared down the Hunter's face, chest, and arms. When he stepped back, his grin broadened.

"There, *Okanele!* Now you look like a true man of the *amathafa.* Almost." His face screwed up in concentration and he rubbed his beard with his other hand. "Aha!" The big man's eyes lit up and he called something to his people. From among the crowd of Buhari emerged two of the warriors carrying a set of the light, woven-vine armor worn by Jumaane's *amaqhawe.*

This, the two warriors placed in his hands with curt nods before backing away—though whether this was part of the celebration or they didn't yet trust him enough to turn their backs on him, he didn't know.

One look at Jumaane, however, made it clear where the Hunter stood in the *nassor's* esteem. Warmth spread through him at the approving smile the big man directed his way.

"With this," Jumaane said, clapping him on the shoulder, "you are honorary Buhari and Issai both."

Chapter Fifteen

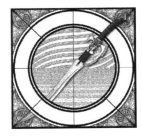

The Hunter sat amidst the swirling, joyous revelry admiring his new vestments.

Contrary to his expectations, the Buhari armor proved exceedingly comfortable. A layer of soft antelope hide was stretched beneath the lattice of woven vines to prevent chafing and add an extra layer of reinforcement. The armor covering his shoulders and torso proved surprisingly lightweight and flexible, allowing him excellent freedom of movement. What remained to be seen was how well it could repel enemy weapons. Just because it could not withstand *Ibad'at Mutlaqa* and Soulhunger's magic-enhanced steel didn't mean it would fail to protect him against the Consortium's greatknives.

The Issai robes, too, were true works of art. Every stitch placed with precision, every colorful thread interwoven with purpose, creating patterns as intricate as those woven into the tapestries that hung in the al-Malek's palace in Al Hani or the throne room of King Gavian of Voramis. The cloth felt soft as goosedown to the touch yet sturdy as canvas. It seemed to flow and billow around him with every movement, drawing air toward his body and allowing excess warmth to escape.

No wonder the Issai can run through even the heat of the day! He fluffed out the robe to feel the cooling breeze once more.

"What have we here?" A familiar voice cut into the Hunter's examination of his clothing.

Looking up, he spotted Kodyn and Aisha approaching. The two strode arm in arm, and they, too, had shed their *alay-alagbara* clothing in favor of Issai garments. Their robes were virtually identical in color—a riot of oranges and reds interwoven with gold and blacks—but the subtle differences in pattern called attention to their respective masculine and feminine aspects. Clearly these had been woven specifically for them. Fast handiwork, given that not even ten days had elapsed since their arrival at the Issai *ekhaya*.

Aisha wore the robes with the ease of one born to such clothing, though Kodyn appeared far less comfortable. Like the Hunter, he was accustomed to the more constricting confines of Einari raiment. His movements were almost exaggerated, as if he tested the freedom of the billowing, loose-flowing robes with every motion of his limbs.

The Hunter stood, and the two youths looked him up and down with approving grins.

"I *swear* I've seen this guy before," Kodyn said, pretending mock contemplation. "I mean, the beard and hair, at least."

"Definitely not all this." Aisha's gesture encompassed the robes, armor, and red vermillion pigment staining the Hunter's skin. "On anyone else, it might be a bit much." She grinned up at him. "But it oddly suits you."

The Hunter smiled back. "I won't lie, these are some of the softest robes I've ever worn." He tugged at one voluminous sleeve. "I can't imagine wearing anything else ever again. At least not in the heat of the *amathafa* or *Indawo Yokwesaba.*"

Siyanda had been right; his armor had proven stifling, chafing, and dehydrating. In these robes, he felt like a new man.

"And did you see these?" Kodyn held out his right arm to the Hunter, tapping one finger against the sleeve covering his elbow. "Aisha was telling me the story about these two creatures. It's a fascinating story, one that dates—"

But the Hunter was no longer listening. Ice froze in his veins, and every muscle in his body went rigid as he recognized the creatures sewn into the pattern of the robes. One, a horse with twin goat beards, two gleaming ruby horns, and shining hooves; the other, a serpentine monstrosity with mottled scales, a speckled white underbelly, and claw-tipped feet.

The Hunter's eyes locked on to the creatures. There was no mistaking it: they *were* the same beasts he'd seen repeatedly since crossing the Chasm of the Lost.

He opened his mouth, yet no words came out. For in that moment, he caught sight of another identical pair embroidered into Kodyn's sleeve. Then another running rampant across his chest, and more slithering up his shoulders, galloping down his legs, clashing at his waist.

When the Hunter's gaze shifted to Aisha, he found the same patterns etched into her clothing, the same beasts depicted in vivid color all up and down her robes. His heart hammered faster, his breath quickening. Looking down at his own sleeves, his mouth went dry as he saw the creatures stitched into his robes, too.

He looked up, and it was as if his eyes had been opened for the first time. Everywhere he looked, he saw them. Stitched into sleeves, woven into belts, painted onto clay jars, even hammered into the brass instruments and carved into the bamboo flutes. Again and again, the same goat-bearded, horned horse and the claw-footed reptilian monstrosity pursuing it, curled around it, even stretching its jaws wide to consume it whole.

"Hunter?" Aisha's voice came to him as if from across a vast distance.

With effort, he tore his gaze from the myriad depictions all around him and forced his eyes to focus on Aisha's face. Worry etched her features and furrowed her brow.

"What's the matter?" She looked him up and down, as if searching for injury.

The Hunter lifted his finger to point at the creatures stitched into her clothes. "Those—" His voice cracked. Clearing his throat, he spoke again. "Those beasts. You know them?"

Aisha looked down, following his pointing finger. "You mean *Nuru Iwu* and *Okadigbo*?"

The names meant no more to the Hunter now than they did when Jumaane had spoken them, yet merely hearing them sent a shiver down his spine. "Yes," he said, his voice coming out in a hoarse rasp. "What are they?"

Aisha's face lifted toward him, and confusion etched her features. "They are...*Nuru Iwu* and *Okadigbo*." She spoke the words as if that alone sufficed to explain.

"Like I was telling you," Kodyn spoke up, bewilderment evident on his face, too, "it's old Issai folklore."

The Hunter looked between the two. "Folklore?" His eyes narrowed. "What exactly does the folklore say about them?"

Aisha glanced to Kodyn, who answered with a shrug. When she began recounting the story, she spoke hesitantly, as if her confusion made it difficult to recall the details. "The legend is as old as the *amathafa* itself." With every word, however, she gained confidence. "It is said they were the youngest sons of Ingwe All-Father, fiercest of friends and bitterest of rivals, as is the way of twin brothers."

Something about the way she said it reminded the Hunter a great deal about her hurt and surprise at Siyanda's scornful reaction to her return. That thought flickered through his mind and vanished in the next heartbeat as Aisha continued.

"Long ago, in the days before the *Ukujiswa Okhulu* split apart the world, the brothers called these plains home, and to them was given rule over every creature great and small. Together, they made the grass grow green, the trees bear fruit, and the rivers flow strong. For a time—what the Einari would call 'an age'—the twins lived in harmony."

"Let me guess," the Hunter said, frowning, "one of them eventually decided he'd be better off ruling on his own?" That was ever the way of such stories. Even Kharna's fabricated legend had accused the "god of destruction" of waging war against the other divinities in the name of power.

"Yes." Aisha nodded. "The younger was content to run the *amathafa,* but the elder sought to claim dominion for himself. He transformed himself into a great serpent beast to lure his brother into a trap. For the younger cherished nothing more than a fight in defense of the lands given him. Thus, he was tricked into battle—a battle the elder could not win, for though he was the cleverer, his younger brother was the greater warrior."

"And what happened in this battle?" the Hunter asked. "Who won?"

"Neither." Aisha shook her head. "For though the younger fell into the elder's trap and was imprisoned by his brother's magic, he struck the elder a grievous wound. That is where the name 'Okadigbo' comes from. It is an old word, translated to 'The Bleeding One'. Meanwhile, the younger brother lies imprisoned, his name forgotten—quite literally. For *Nuru Iwu* was not his true name, but a word as old as *Okadigbo,* meaning 'He Who Is Nameless'."

The young woman's eyes took on a faraway look. "It is said *Okadigbo* dwells deep beneath the ground, biding his time until he is recovered enough he can finish what he began that day. And while *Nuru Iwu* slumbers, his spirit still roams the *amathafa* in the form of a great crimson-horned *abada.*" She tapped the horse-like creature sewn into her colorful robes. "Yet he will never be free, for *Okadigbo* forever pursues him, preventing his escape."

The Hunter contemplated the legend. It had a great deal in common with countless other stories and myths passed down by myriad cultures over the millennia—many of which he'd doubtless heard and forgotten thanks to the Illusionist Clerics' accursed ritual.

Yet there had to be something more to it, some reason these two creatures were so ubiquitous not just among Issai folklore, but their craftsmanship and artwork.

"Why does the story matter so much to the Issai?" he asked, gesturing to her clothing, Kodyn's, and his own. "Why are *Nuru Iwu* and *Okadigbo* depicted everywhere? What's the moral your people want to learn from the story?"

"Not a moral." Aisha's eyes narrowed slightly, a frown furrowing her brow. "More a promise."

The Hunter cocked his head. Even Kodyn appeared interested by that. Had she not told him of its meaning, merely recounted the legend?

"It is believed among the Issai that the day will come when *Okadigbo* will grow strong enough to destroy his brother forever, and *Nuru Iwu* will attempt to make one last escape. On that day, the fate of the *amathafa* will be decided. Either the land will flourish as it once did in the days before the *Ukujiswa Okhulu* or waste away to ruin." She tapped the two beasts sewn into her sleeve. "The legend is told and the brothers depicted for all to see as a reminder that even small decisions can have great consequences. For had *Okadigbo* not chosen to raise a hand against his brother, our lands would still be green and flourishing as it was under their rule, and our people would know peace and prosperity."

Her expression brightened. "The Issai believe we are all descended from Ingwe All-Father. Thus, our decisions may affect the world in equal measure to the decisions made by the two brothers."

The Hunter nodded. "It is a good legend." Powerful gods, sibling rivalry, *and* a moral easily understood even by young children—all the hallmarks of the sort of folklore that shaped cultures. "But what if I told you that I've been *seeing Nuru Iwu* and *Okadigbo*?"

Aisha's jaw dropped and her eyes flew wide. Kodyn, too, looked taken aback. "You've—"

"Aisha!" A loud, feminine voice drowned out Kodyn's question.

The Hunter's gaze slid past the two stunned youths and fixed on Davathi. The Issai *nassor* had risen to her feet and now beckoned toward her daughter. She accompanied her gesture with a few commanding words in her own tongue.

The sound of her name shattered Aisha's startlement. She turned toward her mother. Davathi said something else in Issai, her beckoning gesture growing more insistent.

"Go," Kodyn said, nodding his head toward her mother.

Aisha's gaze darted toward the Hunter.

"We can talk about it later." Kodyn gave her an encouraging smile and made a shooing motion with his hand. "After your mother's speech."

Aisha hesitated, but at Kodyn's insistence, hurried over to where her mother stood next to the still-seated Jumaane and the mingled Issai and Buhari warriors.

With a broad grin, Davathi wrapped an arm around her daughter and turned to face the crowd. Judging by the flush on her face, she had sampled more than a few mouthfuls of the sorghum beer, yet she was beaming with pride and joy as she addressed the people celebrating around her.

"What's she saying?" the Hunter asked Kodyn. He understood bits and pieces, but not enough to piece together the full meaning.

Kodyn blushed. "Oh, right." He scrunched up his face in concentration and translated Davathi's proclamation.

"Today is a day of great joy for all of the *amathafa!*" Davathi raised her other hand high, shaking her *assegai* over her head. "For today, our tribes unite for the first time since the days of Falakhe and Jabhile. Buhari!" She gestured to Jumaane and his warriors with her spear, eliciting a chorus of leonine roars. "Nyemba! Mwaani! Dalingcebo!" Each tribe cheered or lifted their voices in ululating howls as they were mentioned. "Issai!"

At this last, Naledi, Cebile, Sizwe, Siyanda, and the rest of the warrior women around Davathi slapped their thighs and shouted in approval. Even Duma joined in the chorus.

"Tomorrow, we journey to the lands of the Buhari, and from there, we march to war with the *Gcinue'eleku awandile* in vengeance for what was done—not only to us, but to *every* tribe who shares these lands."

A roar of boos, hisses, and angry shouts accompanied the Consortium's name.

"But first, there is cause for joy!" Davathi beamed, delight shining bright in her eyes. "With this celebration, we honor one who gave everything of herself in the name of protecting our people. Who, when faced with impossible circumstances, proved herself worthy of bearing the title of *nassor.*" She turned to face Siyanda and held out a hand. "Come, *um' shana.* Join us. You have earned the respect and gratitude of *all* the Issai."

Siyanda appeared utterly speechless, caught off guard by Davathi's recognition. She remained frozen in place—a place, the Hunter noted, that had grown steadily closer to Jumaane over the last hour of celebration. Only when the cheers and shouts from her fellow *amaqhawe* and every other Issai in attendance swelled around her did she rise. Red-faced with embarrassment yet glowing with unabashed pride, she came to stand beside Davathi opposite Aisha.

"You could not have expected to take up the mantle of *nassor.*" Davathi spoke in a clear voice that carried around the now-silent camp. "Yet you have shown wisdom and experience beyond your years, strength beyond expectation, and courage that would do even the mightiest of our ancestors honor." She lowered her *assegai* and held it out to Siyanda. "You are a true *amaqhawai* of the Issai."

Davathi wrapped her arms around Siyanda, and the entire tribe—and every Ghandian with them—roared approval.

The *nassor* allowed the furor to last for only a few seconds before once more raising her spear high for silence. "But most important of all, on this day we celebrate the return of Aisha." She turned her back on Siyanda and rested a hand on her daughter's shoulder. "Eldest of my womb, cherished *indokazi,* and *Umoyahlebe!*"

More cheers and shouts greeted this pronouncement, loudest of all from those who had witnessed the display of Aisha's powers in the Consortium camp. However, the Buhari lent their voices to the tumult with only marginally less enthusiasms. Apparently the prospect of fighting alongside the *Umoyahlebe* they respected—and one as mighty as Aisha—held a great deal of appeal to them.

All save Siyanda. The young warrior stood in the shadow of her aunt and cousin, and made no attempt to hide the bitter glare she aimed squarely at Aisha's back.

Chapter Sixteen

The louder the crowd cheered for Aisha, the harder the look on Siyanda's face grew. Even from where he sat, the Hunter could all but feel the fury radiating off her.

That was when the thought struck him: *Is she angry at being supplanted?*

In that moment, it made such clear sense he felt foolish for not realizing it sooner. Siyanda had spent the last months as *nassor*—a title claimed under duress, given the absence of Davathi and the rest of the *amaqhawe*—yet Aisha's return all but ensured she would never inherit the tribe's leadership. Aisha was Davathi's firstborn, and though not yet *amaqhawai,* she had proven herself a capable warrior as well as a truly powerful *Umoyahlebe.* When the day came that

Davathi went to the *Kish'aa* and the mantle of *nassor* passed on, it was not difficult to imagine which of the two held a stronger claim.

Aisha was too busy glowing from her mother's words and the cheers of her people to notice. Her eyes shone as bright as the campfires surrounding her, and sparks of blue-white light danced around her hands and in a corona encircling her head. No doubt it was an unconscious manifestation of the emotions welling within her. Yet it only served to accentuate the full truth of her power, and the crowd "oohed" and "aahed" in delighted approval.

When Davathi removed her arm from her daughter's shoulder, Aisha turned toward Siyanda and held out a hand. She said something the Hunter could not hear beneath the roars and cheers. In response, Siyanda's face smoothed and she plastered what appeared to be a clearly forced, strained smile on her face. Her movements were stiff as she reached up to take Aisha's hand in her own.

With a laugh, Aisha dragged Siyanda away from the crowd seated around Davathi and Jumaane and into a cleared patch of grass before the campfire. Raising her *assegai* high, she threw back her head and shouted a challenge into the sky. Siyanda raised her own spear in response.

"Ooh!" Excitement echoed in Kodyn's voice. "Aisha told me about this. She and Siyanda are going to dance the *Kim'ware,* the Issai war dance." His eyes sparkled with eager anticipation and he leaned forward to get a better look. "She used to love it before…well, you know. She said that she, Siyanda, and Nkanyezi would spend hours practicing to get every movement down perfectly. Because if they're not careful, someone can get badly hurt."

The Hunter didn't need to ask how one could get injured dancing, for in that moment, Aisha sprang toward Siyanda with a shout and drove her spear toward her cousin's chest. Siyanda pirouetted with breathtaking grace to let the spear slide past her ribs. In response, she swung her own spear low toward Aisha's knees, and Aisha sprang high into the air to evade. Yet there was no fear in her eyes, no tension in her posture. She laughed as she landed and bounded in pursuit of the twirling Siyanda. Spear flashing, limbs pumping, face alight with exhilaration.

Together, the two moved in a concert of ferocious battle and impressive agility. Siyanda's next thrust glided dangerously close to Aisha's neck, but Aisha was already bending low to slide beneath it and return the attack with a strike of her own. Attacks intended not to kill, but to demonstrate the control and finesse of both dancers.

The Hunter couldn't help marveling at the two young Issai women. Both powerfully built, so similar in features, yet strikingly different in personalities and dispositions. Siyanda's strikes came hard and fast, Aisha's precise and dexterous. The two sprang, twirled, and dipped around the clearing nimble as antelopes. Movements in perfect concert and synchronicity, as if they had spent hours that very day practicing the dance rather than spending the last six years apart. Even Siyanda grew swept up in the rush of the simulated combat and the thrill of the movement. For a few brief moments, the hardness of her face softened, and the glow of youth peered through the stony façade she'd presented since the moment she and Aisha had come face to face.

The music swelled, the singing grew in volume, the slapping accelerated, and the rhythm pounded faster. Faster, too, Siyanda and Aisha moved. Their spears swirled around them, darting through the darkness like striking serpents' tongues, their corded limbs driving each mock attack with greater power and speed.

The Hunter saw the joy fade from Aisha's face, replaced by a look of concentration. Sweat stood out on her forehead and her movements grew wilder as she attempted to match the ever-increasing pace. His heart sank into his stomach. He knew what was coming seconds before it happened. He'd seen it before.

Aisha could not hope to keep up with movements she had not practiced in years. The rising speed bred panic, and panic made control and finesse all but impossible. One wild attack aimed at Siyanda's legs, swung with just a little too much force, was all it took to shatter the delicate rhythm of the war dance. The spear *cracked* against Siyanda's knee before she could leap above it. The impact knocked Siyanda's legs out from beneath her and she *thumped* hard into the grass.

Horror blossomed on Aisha's face. "Siyanda!" She spun out of the next simulated attack stiffly, thrown off-balance by the realization of what she'd done. Lowering her spear, she sprang to her cousin's side, visibly mortified.

"Get away!" Siyanda's face lifted from the grass, flushed red and twisted in bared wrath. Her lips curled upward in a snarl and she swung her *assegai* at Aisha's legs. But this was no mock attack. She lashed out fully intending to harm.

Aisha barely had time to leap back to avoid the short-handled spear. Even her innate agility could not fully save her; the head of Siyanda's spear opened a shallow cut along the top of her right foot.

The Hunter was on his feet in an instant, hand dropping to the hilt of his sword. Kodyn was right there with him. Yet before they could leap to Aisha's defense, Davathi roared something in Issai. The Hunter didn't need Kodyn's translation to tell him the Issai had demanded an explanation of Siyanda's behavior. He froze but did not take his hand from the hilt of his watered steel sword.

Siyanda slowly rose to her feet, wincing and growling low in her throat. The side of her knee had already begun to swell. Yet she gritted her teeth against the pain and turned a bitter, frosty glare on Aisha.

"I will say this in your language to spare you the embarrassment in front of my people!" she spat. Venom dripped from her every word and she thrust her finger at Aisha's face as if wielding her spear. "When I look at you, I do not see the *um'zala* who vanished years ago. All I see is one of *them!*" She swept a hand toward the Hunter and Kodyn. "You are as much *alay-alagbara* as they are."

"Siyanda!" Davathi snapped, also speaking Einari. "That is—"

Siyanda rounded on her aunt. "You cannot see it, *nassor,*" she seethed. "Or perhaps you merely refuse to accept the truth. But I see it. She may wear our clothes and carry our weapons and speak our language all she wishes, but she is no true Issai."

Aisha reached for her cousin. "Siyanda, I don't know what—"

Siyanda slapped Aisha's hand aside. "You were banished!" Her voice rose to a shout. "Cast out from the Issai. You do not belong here."

"What is the meaning of this?" Davathi demanded. Her expression was hard, her jaw muscles visibly clenched. "Explain yourself, Siyanda."

"Ask *her!*" Siyanda thrust her finger accusingly at Aisha's face once more. "Ask her what she did to earn her banishment."

Davathi turned a questioning gaze on Aisha. "*Indokazi?*"

Aisha's face flushed a deep, angry purple. She glared at Siyanda, and Siyanda glared right back. For a long moment, a silent war of wills raged between the two. When finally Aisha spoke, her voice was strained, taut with fury.

"I am to blame for the deaths of the Buhari." Her jaw muscles clenched. "Because I brought the *Umzukeli* into our *ekhaya* and did not tell him the ways of our people, their deaths—and the danger to our people—was my fault."

383

The Hunter's gaze darted toward Jumaane. The *nassor* hadn't risen, but his bearded face had a look of surprise, and his eyes fixed pensively on Siyanda.

"But surely that is all behind us!" Aisha said, a hint of pleading in her tone. "The Buhari and Issai are allied, and—"

"That does not change your banishment," Siyanda snapped. Her voice and mien were as hard as the steel head of her spear.

Aisha's gaze went to her mother and she looked on the verge of speaking.

"Do not look to her!" Siyanda took one long step and planted herself between Aisha and Davathi. "You cannot hide in your mother's shadow as you always did before."

Aisha bristled at that. Her fist tightened around the haft of her spear. "What in the fiery hell does *that* mean?"

"You know what it means." Siyanda took a determined step toward Aisha, as if daring her to strike. "Always you avoided trouble and responsibility because your mother was *nassor*." She came to stand directly in front of Aisha and jabbed a finger into her chest. "Not everyone has a mother to shield them. Some of us actually have to face the consequences of our actions!"

Aisha's eyes widened. She stared at Siyanda with an utterly bewildered look on her face, incapable of understanding the reason for such vitriol.

To her credit, she recovered quickly. "So it does not matter to you that *my* actions have brought our *nassor* and *amaqhawe* back, or that because of *me*, we are now allied with the Buhari?"

"It matters a great deal." Siyanda's voice was cold, her eyes hard. "Yet it does not change the fact that you were cast out." She leaned forward and glared into Aisha's face. "And your mother cannot undo what was done."

Aisha's gaze darted toward her mother.

Davathi raised her hands in a gesture of helplessness. "By the customs of our people, she was rightful *nassor* at the time. I cannot countermand her decision."

A cruel, gleeful grin broadened Siyanda's face. "Only I can." She jabbed a finger into Aisha's chest. "And I say you have not yet proven yourself worthy to be Issai."

With visible effort, Aisha restrained her temper—though sparks danced around her clenched fists—and drew herself up to her full height. "What must I do to prove myself worthy?" Anger clipped every word.

Siyanda sneered. "I will know when you have done it." So saying, she turned on her heel and stalked away through the now-silent crowd.

Aisha stared at her cousin's retreating back, bewilderment and astonishment written plain on her face. All eyes followed Siyanda, too, until she vanished into the darkness of the grasslands beyond the firelight and the *ekhaya's* western edge.

Muttering and murmuring instantly consumed the crowd. Though the majority did not understand Einari, there was no mistaking that something big had happened. Those who spoke the *alay-alagbara* tongue translated, and the Hunter could all but hear the speculation running rampant throughout every Ghandian around him.

"Aisha—" Kodyn began, but before he could take a single step in her direction, Davathi strode from the crowd of Issai and Buhari toward her daughter.

"Come, *indokazi*." Though the Issai *nassor* spoke in a quiet voice intended for her daughter's ears only, the Hunter's keen hearing picked up the words. "There is something we must discuss. Something your father and I have not told you about your cousin."

So saying, she wrapped an arm around Aisha's shoulder and led her daughter in the opposite direction from Siyanda, into the shadows of night and out of the Hunter's view.

Chapter Seventeen

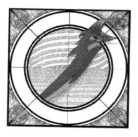

The mood around the fires felt far from festive in the wake of what had happened. Though the instruments played, it seemed the dancers leaped and bounded with less enthusiasm. More than a few of the men and women who had only minutes earlier been laughing and cheering now sat quietly eating or sharing muted conversations. Even the fires themselves appeared to be burning steadily lower, no matter how many dried dung chips they were fed.

Beside the Hunter, Kodyn seemed restive, anxious. No doubt eager to find Aisha and offer what support and comfort he could. He picked at his food, toyed with the embroidery of his Issai robes, and dug the toes of his boots into the grass. The Hunter couldn't fault the young man. He'd wanted to speak up, too, to raise his voice in defense of Aisha, but had understood that any intervention would only lend strength to Siyanda's accusation.

The Hunter found his gaze drawn to Jumaane. The Buhari *nassor* sat amidst the mingled Issai and Buhari warriors, eating and drinking yet oddly pensive, even solemn. The Hunter hadn't missed the way Jumaane watched Siyanda, or how Siyanda's eyes had darted toward Jumaane immediately after being knocked to the ground. Her outrage had been sparked not merely by pain, but embarrassment. Any attempt to restrain her animosity toward Aisha had been shattered when made to look the fool in front of Jumaane.

If, as he and Kiara both surmised, Siyanda was interested in Jumaane, that could, in a way, explain what had struck him as exaggerated outrage over the Hunter's slaughter of the Buhari. His actions put the Issai in danger, true, yet there had been more to Siyanda's reaction. If she'd been *afraid* Jumaane was among the dead, however, that made more sense.

The Hunter watched Jumaane. Time and again, the *nassor's* eyes darted toward the darkness where Siyanda had vanished. He appeared to wear a smile for the benefit of those watching, yet the Hunter thought he recognized a look beneath the surface akin to the one painting Kodyn's face. Concern borne of genuine feelings.

That intrigued him. Now clearly wasn't the time to broach such matters, but the time would come when he'd inquire about inter-tribe pairings. In the rest of Einan, marriages were often used to cement alliances to powerful houses or put an end to war between kingdoms. Perhaps some benefit could come from a similar arrangement here…provided such a notion could even be countenanced.

Beside the Hunter, Kodyn sprang to his feet and hurried through the camp. Davathi and Aisha had been gone for the better part of an hour, and now the *nassor* returned alone. She moved through the crowd of Issai, Nyemba, and Mwaani dancing around the westernmost campfire, greeting her people with a smile that failed to conceal the worry churning within her.

"Davathi—" Kodyn began as he drew near the woman.

"Give her some time." Davathi rested a hand on the young man's shoulder. "My *indokazi* has much to consider."

Kodyn frowned. "But what Siyanda said, is it true? Is she the only one who can undo Aisha's banishment?"

"It is." Shadows crept into Davathi's dark eyes, and her leonine face tightened. "I believe that she can be brought to reason, but after what I have witnessed this night…" She trailed off, letting out a long breath. Then, as if an idea struck her, she turned and scanned the crowd surrounding her. "Duma!"

The *Umdala*, sitting near the fire and working his way through a bowl of stew and raisin-stuffed sorghum buns, looked up at the sound of his name. Upon seeing Davathi, he set his bowl down and rose to his feet with the agile grace of a much younger man, moving toward them with long, easy strides.

He inclined his head in respect to Davathi. "*Nassor?*"

"Find Siyanda." Davathi spoke Einari, doubtless intending to maintain at least a modicum of privacy. "She respects you and may even listen to you."

"Of course, *nassor.*" Duma's lips pressed together. "For all that has happened, I believe she will see reason. I will do what I can to remind her that a real family eats from the same cornmeal."

"Your wisdom is appreciated and welcome, as always." This time, Davathi's smile was genuine, though filled with more relief than joy.

With a bow, Duma hurried off in the direction Siyanda had gone. Jumaane's eyes followed the *Umdala*. He looked as if he, too, wanted to pursue the departed Issai woman. But he gave a little nod to himself and returned his attention to the warriors around him. He'd made plain his respect for Duma—the Old Cheetah, he'd called him. Perhaps he even knew that Siyanda had been *ingani* to Zalika, Duma's daughter. He had to know that Duma stood a better-than-decent chance of getting through to Siyanda. The Hunter suspected Jumaane would seek out the young woman—if not tonight, then *eventually*. They were to share the road together, after all.

"Where is your *ibhubekazi, Umzukeli?*" Davathi's voice and her usage of the Issai name Kodyn had given him drew the Hunter's attention back to the *nassor*. "I have not seen her since our *Umkhadulu Iwepi.*"

"When last I saw her, she was sleeping. Our recent travails have given us little time for rest, her least of all." The Hunter tried for a confident smile. "I am certain she will join us soon." He did not *feel* the words, though. He'd half-expected Kiara to arrive already, yet though the night was far along, she hadn't yet shown her face.

Davathi gestured toward the fire over which the cattle and antelope were roasting. "Perhaps a bit of food will awaken her? It would be a shame for her to miss such a fine feast."

"An excellent idea." The Hunter nodded. "She's going to love the—" He looked to Kodyn. "What was the name of those apricot-stuffed buns?"

"My mother called them *mthokisi*." The young man's face brightened. "They were her childhood favorites."

"Among the Issai," Davathi said, "they are called *mthokosa. Mthokisi* is a name from Imperial Ghandia. I recall you said your mother is of Ghandia, yes?" She gripped Kodyn by the arm and steered him toward the spot where she'd been seated among the Buhari and Issai warriors. "If, as I hear, you are to be my *oqinywe* to my *indokazi*, there is much more I would hear about you. Beginning with your mother and how…"

387

Her voice was soon swallowed up by the din of the music and revelry around them. The Hunter watched for a moment as Davathi settled in her seat with Kodyn—who somehow looked both fully at home among the warriors and terribly uncomfortable in the presence of Aisha's mother—at her side, then turned and moved toward the roasting meat. If Kiara had slept all this time, she'd wake famished and thirsty. He made sure to grab a clay jug of the sorghum beer and carried it along with a generous portion of raya tongue away from the fires and in the direction of the *kopje*.

He'd left Kiara sleeping in a small, hollowed-out nook formed by two of the larger boulders jutting from the base of the hill. They'd chosen that spot specifically for privacy; the massive stones shielded them from curious eyes and muffled the din and clamor of the *ekhaya* as it prepared for the night's festivities. Perhaps that was why she'd not yet awoken. She simply hadn't heard the music, singing, or shouting—at least not loud enough to drag her from slumber.

In a way, the Hunter was glad for that. Though she'd be disappointed to miss the festivities, she needed her rest. The fatigue was getting to her more than she cared to admit. A half-day and full night of sleep would do wonders to replenish her depleted reserves of energy. She'd need her strength in the days to come as they escorted the *ekhaya*, cattle, and the liberated captives back toward Buhari lands and waged war on the Consortium.

He'd just begun climbing the grassy hill when his nostrils detected a familiar scent: musk, wild lavender, lemongrass, and beechwood. A moment later, the susurrus of quiet crying reached him.

The Hunter's head snapped upward. The sound and smell had come from atop one of the huge flat-topped stones near the base of the *kopje*. He wasted a single second looking down at the food and drink in his hands before making up his mind. Placing the bowl and jug in the shadows of the boulder, he began to climb. Kiara's dinner could wait. Aisha was up there, clearly in distress.

Time and the elements had worn the stone's surface largely smooth, but his strong fingers and toes found ample purchase in minute fissures, cracks, and protuberances. He made the climb in a matter of seconds, and only once he'd reached the top did he pause to wonder what he was doing. He almost turned around and descended—Kodyn ought to be the one offering comfort to Aisha—but stopped himself. He was here now. Best he at least *attempted* to ease whatever burden had the usually strong young woman so troubled.

Aisha sat alone in the darkness, arms wrapped around her legs, knees drawn up to her chest, face buried. Sobs wracked her strong shoulders and set her robes fluttering behind her.

The Hunter considered how best to approach, and settled on announcing his presence by clearing his throat. His attempt to *avoid* startling her failed in spectacular fashion. At the sound, she spun around and half-leaped to her feet before spotting him.

Though he'd come with the best of intentions, now that he stared at her tear-and-anguish-stained face, the Hunter found himself lacking anything to say beyond, "I-I'm sorry. I didn't mean to startle you."

Aisha's face hardened. "It's fine. I'm fine. Just…" She brushed the tears from her cheeks. "I just need to be alone."

Not long ago, the Hunter would have loved nothing more than to take her at her word. He'd have turned around and gone back the way he'd come, knowing full well he was ill-equipped to help her in a situation like this. Yet he did not retreat now. Kiara's face flashed into his mind, and the look in her eyes was all the prompting he needed to fight his instinctive urge to flee.

"Want to talk about it?" he asked, his voice gentle. "Or, perhaps better, want to *not* talk about it?"

Judging by the way Aisha's face and posture tensed, the latter option held far more appeal to her.

"Yeah, let's not talk about it." He moved toward her, settled onto the rock a few paces away from her. "We don't have to talk at all, if you don't want to. Nights like tonight are great for not talking." He leaned back on his arms and stared up at the starry sky.

He had no doubt she knew what he was doing, but if she minded it, she made no complaint. Instead, she lowered herself once more onto the rock and mirrored his posture. Aisha said nothing and the Hunter did not press her. For long minutes, the two of them just sat there in silence. The stone was large enough they could hear the revelry below but not see it. Nor could the celebrants see them. Precisely why Aisha had chosen this spot, the Hunter had no doubt.

The Hunter waited until he deemed sufficient time had passed before finally venturing to speak. He had no idea what to say, but began talking anyway hoping the words would come to him once he did. "Aisha—"

"She had a sister." Aisha's voice cut him off. Sorrow dripped from every word. "Siyanda. A sister the same age as me. And she believes it's my fault her sister is dead!"

Chapter Eighteen

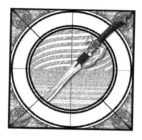

"What do you mean, your fault?" The Hunter fought to keep any hint of emotion from showing on his face. The last thing he wanted was for her to misinterpret his curiosity or concern as condemnation.

Aisha didn't bother to look his way. She was visibly struggling to keep her temporarily stemmed tears from flowing anew. "I was just a child. Barely four years old, too young to remember. But according to my mother, one day I wandered away from the *ekhaya* and Enanela, Siyanda's sister, wandered off with me. We were only gone for a little while, a few hours, no more. But when I was finally found, I was covered in blood. Enanela's blood."

The Hunter's eyebrows shot up—he couldn't keep a lid on his surprise—yet fortunately, Aisha never took her eyes off the stars above.

"They say she was taken by a pack of hyenas." Aisha's throat bobbed, the sound of her swallow loud. "All they found of her was her dress. Bloody fabric, torn and savaged by claws, surrounded by hyena tracks. The *amaqhawe* searched for three days. She was never found. Her father insisted that Enanela was alive somewhere. He never stopped searching for her, and that was what got him killed."

"And Siyanda blames *you?*" The Hunter frowned. "You said it yourself. You were a child. There's no way—"

"My mother believes Siyanda thinks that if I'd never wandered away, Enanela would have never gone with me." Aisha turned her face away from him. "She would never have been taken, and her father would never have died trying to find her." Tears echoed in her voice and pattered softly onto the flat-topped rock beside her. She was crying again. "All these years, I never knew. No one ever told me. Not my mother or father. She's hated me and never said a thing. I thought..." She scrubbed a hand across her cheeks. "We were like sisters for years. After her mother went to the *Kish'aa* and left her alone, my mother and father treated her more like a daughter than niece. Until the day I was taken."

At that, Aisha's voice cracked. Overcome with seething emotions, the young woman—usually so strong and assured—buried her head in her lap and wept. Great sobs shook her shoulders and tears puddled on the rock beneath her.

The Hunter sat in silence, wishing he could do or say something—*anything!*—to console her. Yet he had no idea how to begin or what words could possibly alleviate her visible torment. He'd only truly met her a couple of weeks past. What he knew of her life, he'd only gleaned through snippets of conversation with her and Kodyn.

Yet a detail from one conversation, now long days past, flashed through his mind.

"You said you belonged to House Phoenix, yes?"

The question felt ridiculous, utterly out of place given what she'd just told him. But it was all he could come up with. He had to hope that, tenuous as the thread might feel, it led him to something that actually helped her.

Aisha did not respond immediately, but the Hunter did not press. She'd heard him, he had no doubt, but her crying made it hard to speak. When finally she did manage a response, it was nearly inaudible, a word he could only guess affirmed what he'd heard from Kodyn.

"Is there a reason it's called House Phoenix?" he asked, again grasping at straws. "It's an unusual name, unlike the rest of the Night Guild. House Serpent, House Hawk, House Bloodbear, and House *Phoenix*." He emphasized the name, hoping her answer gave him something he could tie into the idea forming in his mind.

Aisha looked up from her lap, her face tear-stained and eyes rimmed with red. "Ria, Kodyn's mother...she said...it was a symbol." She labored to speak at first, but her voice grew stronger with every word. "Most of us...were those like me, those brought into Praamis as..." Her eyes darkened. "...slaves."

The Hunter knew what manner of slavery had been intended for them. He'd seen countless barges and boats brought into the Port of Voramis transporting young women and girls abducted from their homes by ruthless, cruel, and enterprising men. Men like those of the Vassalage Consortium.

"House Phoenix was created to give us a second chance." Aisha seemed to find comfort and strength in the familiar subject. "Those of us who could not return to our homes..." Her expression grew solemn, her eyes downcast. "...who were not yet ready to return, it gave us someplace safe to forge a new path. To hone new skills and to become new people. Not the weak, vulnerable, scared girls rescued from captivity, but something greater."

"The strong, confident woman you have become," the Hunter said, giving her an encouraging smile. "The one who crossed half a continent to return home—not for her sake, but for the sake of helping her people."

Aisha didn't smile, didn't speak, but she nodded. That, the Hunter took as a good sign.

"Would you believe me if I told you that I've seen a phoenix?" He leaned closer, spoke in a conspiratorial tone. "Not the kind of phoenixes you're familiar with, but a *real* one. A creature of fire and fury. In the Twelve Kingdoms, they were called *tayrnahr.*"

Aisha's eyes widened slightly. "Ria once told me of the legend that gave her the idea for the name. And you *saw* one?"

"Not just saw it." The Hunter's grin widened. "I knew it. It was bound to me, much like..." He paused, fumbling for words. In truth, he didn't know how to describe what he'd felt when seeing *Alsaaeat Aldhahabia* in his memories. "The best way I can put it is that it's like my bond with Soulhunger, and yet not at all the same." He patted the dagger on his hip. "Soulhunger was forged *for* me, and is inextricably linked to my soul by a force beyond either of our choosing. But *Alsaaeat Aldhahabia*—for that was her name, a name that meant 'golden hour' for her gold-and-orange coloring—she was bound to me by her own choosing. She was a mighty creature, far more powerful than even me, yet she chose me."

Wonder sparkled in Aisha's eyes, for a moment replacing the inner turmoil and anguish. Precisely as the Hunter had hoped. Just as in battle, the momentary distraction presented an opening he could exploit.

"I don't remember everything about *tayrnahr.*" He shrugged. "In truth, I have only a few snatches of memory from a life I lived thousands of years ago. But the legend of the phoenix has persisted to this day. Their ability to be reborn not just in fire, but *from* the fire. The hotter the blaze, the fiercer the creature that emerged." He rested a hand on her shoulder. "This is just one more blaze."

Understanding dawned on Aisha's face. His point had been made, at least clearly enough she'd made sense of what he'd been trying to say.

A moment later, however, her expression fell. "I am tired of fires." She leaned forward, hunching her shoulders, wrapping her arms around her legs, and burying her face between her knees. "I have been burning for as long as I can remember." She grunted in frustration and her clasped knuckles whitened. "Even longer, apparently. My life has been nothing but turmoil and anguish."

The Hunter heard the pain in her voice—not self-pity, for that was not her way, but exhaustion. The bone-deep weariness of one who is pushed beyond the limits of their strength. Had it been merely physical, she could have found escape in sleep or let unconsciousness claim her. But this was fatigue of the soul. No amount of rest could prevent an over-burdened spirit from shattering.

"Do you want to know a piece of the legend that few alive today recall?" He did not remember seeing *Alsaaeat Aldhahabia* reborn with his own eyes, yet this one detail had come to him as he spoke of the *taymahr* that had once been companion to Nasnaz the Great.

Aisha gave only the tiniest shrug of her shoulders but didn't lift her head.

"When the phoenix is reborn, the fire burns away all their old feathers, forcing the bird to grow them anew. Every regrowth causes subtle shifts in color and size." In the memory he'd first had of seeing *Alsaaeat Aldhahabia* returning from far off, he'd been surprised by the thick veins of crimson threaded among the gold and orange feathers for which he—Nasnaz—had named the creature. "They are the same bird, yet they are, in a small way, new every time."

Now Aisha lifted her head. She stared at him through narrowed eyes. He saw he had no need to explain his point; she understood clearly enough.

Still, he found he had more to say.

"Your life has been one blaze after another. Every time, you have grown fiercer and stronger. The fire allows you to grow something new, yet parts of the old you remain." He leaned forward, fixed her with an intent gaze. "But you get to decide what you keep and what you cling to. You decide how strong you emerge from the blaze."

Tears flowed down Aisha's face again, but they no longer held the shadows of her anguish. She tilted her head to him. "I'll...think about that," she said in a hoarse voice.

The Hunter nodded. "Whatever happened years ago, that's not who you are now, Aisha. If Siyanda's too small-minded to see past the time you've spent among the *alay-alagbara*, if she won't realize just how much you can help your people, that's on her. All that matters is that you know who you are and what you have to offer. With that foundation to build upon, there's no question in my mind that you'll find a way to make her see—make everyone who has even the slightest doubt about you see—that you are so much more than the girl who was taken away. You have your mother's strength and your father's gifts. You are a true Issai in every sense of the word, for you have the joy, ferocity, determination, and loyalty that has so impressed me about your people since the day I first laid eyes on your *ekhaya*." He squeezed her shoulder. "Never forget that, Aisha. And never let anyone tell you that you're not enough."

For the first time that night, a smile blossomed on Aisha's face. Genuine happiness, gratitude, and relief shone in her eyes. In that moment, the Hunter saw both the young girl and the strong woman. The Aisha who was barely past her eighteenth nameday and the one who had endured more in those years than most others did in a lifetime. The warrior and *Umoyahlebe*, the proud Phoenix and Issai.

392

He stood, turned to leave, but Aisha's voice stopped him.

"Hunter."

The Hunter glanced back. Aisha remained seated, but she had uncurled from around her legs and now stared up at him with a much-lightened expression on her face.

"Evren and Hailen were right about you." She gave him another smile, genuine warmth blossoming on her face. "No one would ever think it by looking at you or watching you most of the time, but in moments like this, I can see what they meant when they said you had a damned good way of showing you care about them." Her smile grew slightly sad, but her shoulders appeared relaxed and the shadows had begun retreating from her eyes. "You remind me a great deal of my father before the *Kish'aa* claimed his mind."

The Hunter bowed—both in acknowledgement and to hide the flush of blood rising to his face. "I'm honored."

"Good night, Hunter." Aisha turned away from him and lay back on the rock to stare up at the night sky. "And thank you."

The Hunter wanted to say "you're welcome" but the words proved strangely stubborn, refusing to form around the lump thickening his throat. And so, in silence, he turned and left Aisha alone with her thoughts and the starry heavens above.

Chapter Nineteen

The Hunter was about to climb back down to the ground when movement to his right caught his eye. It was little more than the flutter of cloth, yet that sufficed to draw his gaze in the direction. To his surprise, he spotted a familiar figure sitting on another of the stones protruding from higher up on the *kopje's* incline. Unlike the one atop which Aisha perched, the boulder was rounded at the top and sprouted a short, stubby tree with a gnarled trunk and thin leaves. It was in the shadow of this tree that Tarek sat. Utterly unmoving save for his tunic flapping in the gentle night breeze, silent as stone, and with no scent to mark his presence. All but invisible to the world, in truth.

The Hunter's eyebrows rose. *What's he doing up there?* It was then the Hunter realized he hadn't seen the young man since the end of the *Umkhadulu Iwepi*. Like Kiara, he hadn't shown his face during the feasting or revelry. *So how long has he been sitting there?*

After a moment's contemplation, the Hunter decided it merited his attention. Tarek wouldn't have missed a hearty meal without good cause. Whatever had caused him to forego the revelry altogether had to be serious, indeed.

The Hunter slid over the side of the boulder and dropped to the ground, then scaled the hill to the boulder that served as Tarek's hidden seat. He made quick work of the climb—its surface was even more weather-worn than the one Aisha had chosen, offering hand and foot-holds aplenty. Tarek must have heard him coming, for when he finished his climb, the young man had risen to his feet and faced the Hunter with a chagrined look.

"F-Forgive me," he said, color rising to his cheeks. "I know you were likely expecting me at the celebration. I just…" He swallowed. "Just got distracted, that's all."

The Hunter held up his hands in a placating gesture. "No expectations," he said, shaking his head. "Just not like you to pass up on a meal. Especially one as grand as that." He jerked his thumb toward the fires and crowd of dancing Ghandians clearly visible from the boulder. "When I saw you here—"

"I'm fine."

The Hunter raised an eyebrow. The young man's insistence had come far too fast, and with too much emphasis.

"Truly." Tarek tried for a smile, but it failed to reach his violet eyes. The darkness in those eyes remained, the shadows that had appeared since the Consortium camp persisting.

The Hunter had intended to seek out the young man and delve into whatever burden troubled him. *I suppose now's as good a time as any,* he thought.

"Way I've seen it," he said, trying to keep his tone gentle so as not to cause Tarek to retreat like a skittish fawn, "you've been far from fine for a few days now. Ever since you saw

394

that dimercurite." He narrowed his eyes. "When you said it killed three dozen of your people, you weren't just talking about random Elivasti, were you?"

The Hunter had recalled his conversation with Tarek the night they'd spent at Nsukeja Lake. The young man had spoken about his half-sister, Risia, and claimed she was the only family he'd had left after his mother went to the ancestors. Given his near-fanatical effort to reverse the dimercurite poisoning, the Hunter had leaped to what felt like the most logical conclusion.

His guess proved correct. Tarek's face fell, and his shoulders slumped. "No." He settled back down where he'd been sitting as if the mere effort of standing proved too much. His violet eyes fixed on the gnarled root of the tree snaking into a crack in the boulder, and for long moments, he did not speak.

The Hunter waited in silence, only moving to take a seat in front of Tarek. He let the young man wrestle with his thoughts until Tarek finally mustered words.

"Seeing Aisha and her mother reunited, it…I don't know, it just reminded me of what I've lost." He lifted his gaze, an almost apologetic look on his face. "I-I don't begrudge her the happiness, of course. I'm glad she found her mother. Just brought back the hurt of seeing my mother wither away before my eyes, too young to do anything to help but old enough to feel every shred of anguish. Even seeing her commended to the Hall of Remembrance didn't help as much as I thought it would. If anything…" He blew out a long breath. "It's been a long time since I felt this way. I believed I was beyond it."

The Hunter shook his head. "It's been almost four years since I lost a little girl I loved more than I had any right to, and it doesn't hurt any less. We never really move beyond the pain. I think we just stop thinking about it as much, and it becomes easier to forget. But every time it comes back, it hurts."

Tears brimmed in Tarek's eyes, though he seemed determined not to let them fall.

"What do you remember about her?" the Hunter asked. Perhaps talking about the woman would help the young man cope with the emotions roiling within him. "What manner of woman was she?"

"She was my mother." Tarek's expression tightened, his jaw muscles working. "I wish I could say she was the most beautiful woman on Kara-ket, or the most intelligent, or the kindest. But that would be a lie. To everyone else, she was just one more of our people. To Risia and me, though, she was our mother. She loved us and that was enough."

"It always is." The Hunter raised a hand to the young man's shoulder and squeezed it once. Then a thought occurred to him. "You said that Risia was the only family you'd ever known. But what of *her* father?" He'd called Risia his half-sister.

Tarek's face scrunched up. "What of him?"

The Hunter heard the hint of snarl in the young man's voice, saw the sneer unborn on his lips. "That bad, was he?"

Tarek looked at the Hunter, as if surprised by the question. He must not have realized how much his face gave away. "What makes you say that?"

The Hunter shrugged. "Call it a hunch."

Tarek's lips quirked into a frown. "I suppose there are worse fathers in the world. Even among our people." He rubbed one hand along a sparsely bearded cheek. "Better, too, though." A flash of anger sprang to life in his violet eyes. "Hard to respect any man who leaves a woman because he doesn't want to raise 'a dead man's bastard'."

The vitriol and fury in those words were unmistakable. The Hunter had seen the look that now twisted Tarek's face before—the day they had met in Malandria, when the Hunter had asked him about his *true* father, Esanne. It had shown again the night after their encounter with Indombe, when Tarek had puzzled over what had caused him to leap into the pool despite his inability to swim.

In that moment, understanding dawned on the Hunter. *That explains so much about Tarek's actions and behaviors since the moment we met all those weeks ago.*

He considered his next words carefully. He had to tread with caution on what he now knew to be fragile ground.

Finally, he settled on an approach. "Did you know I never met my father?" Far from subtle, but when dealing with a warrior, the most direct path often proved most effective. "Never met either of my parents, leastways not as I can recall." He tapped his forehead. "Just one of the things taken from me over the thousands of years I've been alive."

Tarek's eyes widened, though whether in interest, surprise, or a combination of the two, the Hunter couldn't quite tell. He stubborned on anyway. Now that he'd committed to the path, no sense mincing words.

"I've no idea what manner of woman my mother was, but I can say with a fair degree of certainty my father was an absolute cunt." The Hunter gave the Elivasti a wry grin. "The *maistyrrah* aren't exactly known for being solid father figures."

Tarek actually cracked a ghost of a smile. "Can't argue that." He'd met two of them—the Warmaster and the Sage—and knew from firsthand experience just how cruel, ruthless, and bloodthirsty the Abiarazi could be.

"I've wasted a few nights wondering about who he was, though." The Hunter had never told anyone that, not even Kiara. Yet now it seemed precisely the thing Tarek needed to hear. "Wondering what he'd think of me now. Not that I'd give a wet shite about him being disappointed that I'm not a savage flesh-eating monstrosity like him." He shrugged one shoulder. "But still…"

"Still," Tarek said in a quiet voice, "you can't help but wonder."

The Hunter smiled inwardly, relieved and excited both. He'd been right about the cause of the young man's inner turmoil. Now that he understood, he might be able to do or say something to alleviate the anguish.

"I used to think about it all the time, you know?" Tarek shot the Hunter a sidelong glance, a look akin to embarrassment on his face, as if admitting some dark, shameful secret. "All those years Hyeras, Risia's father, lived with us, I'd watch him with her and wonder how my father would have treated me. Would he have loved me, looked at me with pride the way a father should, trained me in the ways of the True Descendants? I'd wonder that if he'd just stuck around after learning my mother had conceived me, things might have been different. That the other children wouldn't look at me the way they did, treat me the way they did. The same way Hyeras treated me."

"As a dead man's bastard." The Hunter uttered the words in a level tone.

"As a dead man's bastard," Tarek repeated. Shadows once again deepened in his violet eyes, and his expression drooped. "Every time, I'd think myself a fool for caring what that man thought. He didn't care enough to stick around for me, so why should I care enough about him to, as you say, give a wet shite about what he thought of me?"

"Only it's never that easy, is it?" The Hunter grimaced. "No matter how many times you call yourself a fool, you can't stop caring." He'd believed himself uncaring of the opinions of others, yet seeing the look of utter horror and revulsion in Ellinor's eyes after she'd watched him slaughtering Breaker Beckett and his Bloody Hand thugs had devastated him. "Just trying to convince ourselves we don't care doesn't make it the truth."

Tarek shook his head. "No, it doesn't."

The Hunter leaned closer to Tarek, lowered his voice. "I told you I never met your father. Yet from what I heard of him, he was a good man. One who died defending his child."

Tarek's face scrunched up into a frown. "He died—?"

The Hunter drew in a deep breath. He'd intended to tell Tarek about Hailen for days but hadn't found an opportune moment. This was that moment. If anything could help Tarek to make sense of his father—and perhaps answer some of the questions plaguing his mind—it was the revelation of how Esanne had died at Syladine's side protecting Hailen from the Elivasti intending to kill the "abomination".

Yet even as he opened his mouth to speak, Tarek shifted in place, and his boot sent something clattering away. The Hunter caught sight of a sheathed dagger skittering across the boulder, and in the next moment, the evening breeze swept up something white and flat from Tarek's side. Instinctively, the Hunter reached out and snatched it out of the air. Even as his fingers closed around it, he recognized it as one of the parchments he'd purchased to encourage Tarek's artistry. He'd evidently been sketching something before the Hunter's arrival and set the dagger down atop the parchment to serve as a paperweight.

He was about to hand the parchment back to Tarek when he caught sight of the image depicted thereupon. Not a face like Jaia's, nor the sketch of any plant like the one he'd drawn of the unnamed fern he believed could cure the dimercurite poisoning.

No, the picture he'd drawn was that of a two-horned horse with a goat-like beard and shining hooves. A picture that exactly resembled the creature the Hunter had seen bounding across the plains, and who Aisha had called *Nuru Iwu*.

Chapter Twenty

The Hunter stared down in surprise at Tarek's sketch. Somehow, the young man had captured every detail as the Hunter recalled it from the many times he'd seen the phantasmal creature racing across the plains. He'd even depicted the same silent plea that had filled *Nuru Iwu's* gleaming eyes.

"What is this?" the Hunter asked when he finally tore his gaze from the drawing.

Tarek's face was flushed a deep red, an embarrassed look once again on his face. "N-Nothing," he said hastily, and reached for the drawing. "Just something I was sketching, but—"

The Hunter pulled the parchment out of Tarek's reach. "You've seen this thing?" He tapped a finger against the two-horned horse creature. Surely it had been *his* imagination alone, and yet…

Tarek's eyes slid away from his, and the Hunter saw the "No" forming on the young man's lips.

"Tarek." The Hunter spoke in a firm, hard voice. "The truth. Have you seen this thing?" The answer *had* to be yes, he knew—how else could Tarek have conceived of its existence and depicted it so clearly—yet still the Hunter needed to be sure.

"Yes. And no." Tarek shook his head. A chagrined look appeared on his scruffy-bearded face. "You're going to think I'm going mad, but I swear—"

"It's real."

Tarek's head snapped up and his eyes locked on the Hunter's. "R-Real?"

The Hunter held the parchment out to the young Elivasti. "I've seen it, too. Every sunrise since the day we first crossed the Chasm of the Lost, I've seen it. A ghostly horse racing across the plains. Does that sound right?"

The way Tarek's eyes widened and his jaw fell slack, the Hunter knew his words had struck home.

"Have you been seeing it, too?" the Hunter pressed. "I thought it might have just been me, but if you've seen it…" He trailed off. "Watcher's beard, I've no idea *what* it means. But it's got to mean something!"

"I have seen it." Tarek's brow furrowed. "Since the first morning in *Indawo Yokwesaba*. That was when I saw it originally, and it's been coming back to me every morning since."

The Hunter's mind spun, toying with the implications of that. "Did you see anything else?" He hesitated a moment before asking, "Any other creatures with it? Pursuing it?"

Tarek shook his head. "No. Just…that!" He jabbed a finger toward the parchment he hadn't yet taken from the Hunter.

The Hunter didn't know what to make of that. He'd seen both *Nuru Iwu* and *Okadigbo*, but if Tarek was only seeing one…

"What is it?" Tarek's question pierced the Hunter's muddled thoughts. "What did you call it?"

"*Nuru Iwu.*" The Hunter called to mind the legend Aisha had told him. "Supposedly, *Nuru Iwu* was one of the two great spirits who ruled the *amathafa* long ago. It took on this form—" He tapped the drawing. "—to run the plains. Until he was imprisoned."

"Imprisoned?" Tarek's eyebrows shot up. "So that's what it means, then!"

"What *what* means?" The Hunter's eyes narrowed.

Tarek's expression grew pensive, and he toyed with his scruffy beard with one hand as he reached out with the other to take the sketch. "At first, I was just seeing it." He spoke without tearing his eyes from the image. "But the last few days, ever since we joined forces with the Buhari, I've begun hearing it, too." Now he looked up, worry dark in his violet eyes. "It's begging me to free it from its prison."

The Hunter's gut twisted. "It never spoke to me, but I got the same sense." He, at least, had seen the monstrosity that eternally pursued *Nuru Iwu*. No wonder the creature pleaded to be freed. "You heard its voice? In your ears, or in here?" He tapped his temple.

"Yes, in my mind." Tarek nodded, mimicking the Hunter's gesture. "Somehow, I had the feeling that even appearing and communicating with me in that way required an immense effort. The creature—this *Nuru Iwu*, as you call it—was desperate. Dying, even."

That fit with the legend Aisha had told him, which he now recounted to Tarek. Of *Okadigbo* seeking to snuff out *Nuru Iwu's* existence, growing ever stronger as he recovered from the grievous wound his brother had dealt. That the day might come when *Nuru Iwu* attempted to free himself from his imprisonment.

"So what if that's what's happening here?" the Hunter wondered aloud. "What if the battle between *Nuru Iwu* and *Okadigbo*—" Whatever manner of creatures, spirits, or ancient beings they were. "—is coming to a head? *Nuru Iwu* is gaining strength and attempting to break out, but *Okadigbo* is recovering enough to snuff out his brother once and for all." It made a strange sort of sense as he put it into words. "And they're reaching out to us for help. Because somehow we're the only ones that can see them."

"But why?" Tarek's brow and nose scrunched up in confusion. "Why us?" He gestured between himself and the Hunter. "We're not Issai, not even Ghandians. Why do these things, whatever they are, believe *we* can help them?"

The Hunter considered the question. He'd been visited by the spirits of the dead, but that had been the side effects of a potent poison, not because of any ability of his. Tarek had witnessed the magic of his Serenii ancestors, but to the Hunter's knowledge, commanded none of his own. Were it simply that *Nuru Iwu* and *Okadigbo* were seeking out those most sensitive to the spirits and possessing of magic, they would have gone to Aisha.

He said as much to Tarek. "Which means we need to find out if Aisha has seen them, too." Then added, "And Kodyn, for that matter. Because if you and I are seeing them, maybe *they're* getting the same visions, or visitations, or whatever you want to call them."

Tarek rose to his feet. "I'll find them and ask."

The Hunter's eyebrows rose. "Just like that?"

Tarek shrugged. "I've said nothing until now because I was afraid *I* was the only one touched by madness, heat stroke, or delusions. But I'm not alone, and that changes things." He lifted his head. "I have nothing to be ashamed of."

"You're right." The words left the Hunter's mouth before he realized their significance. Yet in that moment, he saw the opening and took it. He took a step closer to Tarek and rested a hand on the Elivasti's shoulder. "You have nothing to be ashamed of. Not because you are 'a dead man's bastard' or because you could do nothing to stop the dimercurite from killing your mother."

Tarek had been on the verge of leaving, but he stopped mid-step, frozen in place by the Hunter's words.

The Hunter pressed on. "I can understand your feeling responsible for helping all the people who are suffering here. There's a part of you desperate to believe that saving them now will somehow make up for what happened to your mother, what you see as your failure to protect her."

He locked eyes with Tarek, his gaze burning and intense. "I felt exactly the same way not long ago, when I saved one child's life in an effort to atone for the death of another." He shook his head. "But that's not how life works. Our mistakes remain unchanged, no matter how hard we try to atone."

Tarek's face darkened, and a look of shame flashed across his face.

"But know this, Tarek, son of Esanne." The Hunter gripped the young man's shoulder firmly. "There was nothing you could have done for your mother all those years ago. So put that behind you. Set down that burden of guilt. Easier said than done, I know, but whenever you feel it weighing on you, remember that. There was nothing you could do then. But there *is* something you can do now. And you can give everything you have to help these people—not out of guilt or feelings of failure, but because you know in here—" He tapped Tarek's armored chest. "—that is what you must do. It will be much easier in the doing if you are free of the burden you have carried around all these years."

Moisture sparkled in Tarek's eyes. He opened his mouth, but no words came out.

"I have not known you long, but from what I have seen, there is no doubt in my mind that your mother would be proud of who you've become." The Hunter hesitated, but only for a moment. "And your father, if he still lived, would be proud, too. No question about it."

Tarek turned his head away to hide the tears streaming down his cheeks, but he did not leave. Not yet. He remained standing, the Hunter's hand on his shoulder, as if comforted by the touch. Precisely as the Hunter had hoped. He was neither the young man's father nor mentor—as he'd made abundantly clear days earlier—yet there was no denying the role he had unwittingly begun playing in Tarek's life. That was a responsibility he could not avoid, whether he wished it or not. And in truth, he *didn't* wish it. He had come to like the Elivasti.

"For my part," he said quietly, "I am glad Itan granted your request to accompany me."

"As am I," Tarek said, though his voice came out barely above a hoarse whisper. He scrubbed a hand across his face, and when he turned back, his cheeks were dry but his eyes shone nearly as bright as the stars in the heavens. "I have learned a great deal from you and Kiara. From Kodyn and Aisha, too." His smile lit up his features and pushed back most of the shadows from his features. "I cannot begin to imagine where this latest discovery will lead, yet I know that with all of you at my side, I do not feel quite so alone. Not quite the outcast that I have been among my own people most of my life."

"Or, maybe better said, an outcast like the rest of us." The Hunter grinned wryly. "But together, we outcasts have something special." He clapped Tarek on the shoulder once and allowed his hand to fall to his side. "A family of sorts, if not the one any of us expected."

Tarek's smile nearly split his face in half. "I like the sound of that."

He turned to go, his spine straighter and the weight on his shoulders visibly lightened.

"Wait!"

Tarek spun back toward the Hunter.

"You won't want to leave these." The Hunter stooped to pick up the parchment and charcoal sticks that had joined the pile held down by Tarek's dagger.

"Oh, right." Tarek's face flushed lightly. "Yeah, these are important." He took the proffered implements.

The Hunter did not immediately release the items, causing Tarek to glance up at him.

"You see anything else like this," the Hunter said, his voice growing serious, "you trust us enough to tell us, aye?"

Tarek nodded. "I will."

"Good." The Hunter relinquished his grip. "Because there's something big about this. I don't know what, but I can't shake the sense that our way forward leads there. And we need to figure it out sooner rather than later." He leaned forward, giving Tarek an intent look. "Together."

"Together," Tarek echoed. He clutched the parchments and sticks to his chest and turned to go but stopped halfway. "I came up here because I wanted to get away." He spoke without looking back at the Hunter. "I wanted time to think, to make sense of what was happening, to get a handle on everything I've been feeling." Now he glanced over his shoulder. "But I see now that retreating is the wrong way to handle it. That the more I try to deal with things alone, the more alone I feel."

The Hunter's eyebrows rose. That lesson had taken him years to learn. Fiery hell, he was *still* learning it. Yet Tarek had come to the conclusion so quickly? It spoke of the young man's maturity—*or perhaps,* the Hunter thought wryly, *just how hardheaded I can be, even after all the times Kiara has told me as much.*

"I'll remember that." Tarek tapped his temple, as if lodging the thought firmly in his brain. "I only need to be told a thing once and it sticks." He smiled, and new warmth shone from his eyes. "If I have to be an outcast, I'm glad it's among outcasts like you."

With those words, he slid over the side of the boulder and climbed down, disappearing from the Hunter's view.

Only then did the Hunter remember that he'd forgotten to tell Tarek about Hailen. *Again.* He cursed himself. *Will I never find the chance to—*

"Oh, and I forgot to tell you!" Tarek's voice drifted up from below. "I like the clothing. Makes you look very…"

Whatever he said was drowned out by a roar of laughter and a chorus of cheers from the celebrating Ghandians on the plains below.

Chapter Twenty-One

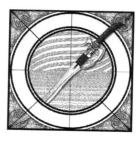

Still sleeping, even after all this time?

The Hunter stared down at Kiara's sleeping form, a frown twisting his lips. In the three years he'd known Kiara, she'd rarely slept a full night through, preferring to be up and busy rather than laying abed. At current count, however, she hadn't awoken for a full twelve hours. She'd fallen asleep shortly before noon, and midnight was fast approaching.

He tried in vain to shake the worry rising within him. She lay on her side, face half-buried in the clasped hands that served as her pillow. Though the night air was cool, a bead of sweat trickled down her forehead and the collar of her light undertunic was ringed with damp. Her health had been steadily deteriorating over the last few days, yet always she insisted she was merely overtired. That *could* be it, but—

"Anyone ever tell you that watching someone sleep comes off as creepy?" Kiara's voice drifted up from her bedroll.

The Hunter startled. "What?"

Kiara's eyes fluttered open and, turning almost lazily onto her back, she stared up at him with a scolding expression. "You. Standing there. Just watching." She shook her head. "Not the sort of thing an upstanding, law-abiding citizen should do."

The Hunter couldn't help a smile. "Lucky me, I'm neither upstanding nor law-abiding." He twisted his features into a leering, lecherous expression and waggled his eyebrows. "Means I can get away with watching you sleep, creepy or not."

"Hard not to love a face like that." A small grin tugged at Kiara's lips, though it did little to push back the fatigue etched into her features. "Any chance you brought me something to eat or drink?"

The Hunter glanced down, found his hands empty. He cursed himself. "I did. But I forgot it." He held up a finger. "Be right back."

He hurried to retrieve the bowl of now-congealed stew and tepid sorghum beer he'd left at the base of the boulder upon which he'd found Aisha. When he returned, Kiara had managed to sit upright, her back and head propped against the craggy stone wall that served as a windbreak for their two bedrolls.

"Loving this new look, by the way," Kiara said, gesturing to his Issai robes and Buhari armor. "Plenty of visible flesh for a lady to enjoy ogling."

The Hunter grinned. "Dinner *and* a view, eh?" He held out the food.

Kiara's face lit up at the sight, and she took it from him and tucked in with visible relish.

The Hunter settled onto his bedroll, sitting cross-legged and facing her. He waited in silence while she ate and drank her fill. After a half-day of rest, the nourishment seemed to do her good. With every bite, more color returned to her cheeks. Every swallow of sorghum beer seemed to infuse her limbs with greater vitality. By the time she'd near-finished the meal, she was looking much more herself.

Perhaps she really was *just overtired,* the Hunter thought. *Not hard to believe, given how hard we've been pushing ourselves these last days.*

"You're doing it again." Kiara's voice pierced his thoughts.

"*It?*" The Hunter raised an eyebrow.

"Worrying. I can see it all right there, in that little furrow your brow gets." Kiara gestured with one finger toward his forehead. "And your mouth does that thing, too." A wicked glee sparkled in her eyes. "One might almost confuse it for a puckered ars—"

The Hunter cut her off before she could finish that particular thought. "Can you blame me? It wasn't long ago you came dangerously close to the Long Keeper's arms, after what Indombe did to you." His gut clenched at the memory of seeing her lying so pale-faced and weak, on the verge of death. Only Aisha's timely intervention had dragged her back from the brink. "I don't believe it's unreasonable of me to worry a little bit."

"A little." Kiara raised her free hand and held her thumb and forefinger close together to illustrate her point. "But I know you, Hunter. You're one cough away from going all fussyboots mother hen on me."

"I've got the swaddling cloths and herbal poultices standing by." He adopted a severe expression that would have been fully at home on the face of any Ministrant or healer. "You so much as yawn the wrong way and you'll be in for the full treatment, like it or not."

For answer, Kiara stuck out her tongue at him.

The Hunter chuckled, and Kiara joined him. The laughter died quickly.

"In all seriousness," the Hunter said, "I am worried. You've never collapsed like that before."

"And I still haven't." Kiara sat straighter, lifting her head and squaring her shoulders. "I didn't collapse. Just got a bit dizzy, that's all. The day was hot, I hadn't had anything to drink for hours, and we were just coming down from the battle rush." She shook her head. "I'm feeling fine now."

"Then why are you doing that?" The Hunter pointed to her left hand.

Kiara looked down at the hand which she held pressed to her belly, directly on the spot where the crystal had transfixed her flesh. She quickly pulled her hand away.

"Kiara," the Hunter said, before she could dismiss it as nothing. "Talk to me."

Kiara's face tightened, her jaw muscles working. For a long moment, she did not look up at him, but her eyes remained fixed on her torso.

"What is it?" The Hunter kept his tone gentle but firm.

"I wanted to believe it was nothing." Kiara finally lifted her eyes to meet his, and worry reflected back at him. "But I don't know that it is."

"What is nothing?" The Hunter leaned closer, reaching one hand toward her belly. "Is the wound—"

"The wound is healed." Kiara snatched his wrist before it could make contact. "But there's this." She pulled his hand closer and rested it on her stomach.

The Hunter's eyebrows widened, and he sucked in a breath. Even through the thin tunic, he could feel the intense heat radiating off her skin.

"Kiara, that's—"

"It's not a fever!" Her voice was sharp, her grip on his wrist iron-hard. "Trust me, I know what fever is like, and this isn't it."

The Hunter looked at her face. She was paler than usual, certainly, but there was no fever-brightness in her eyes, no abnormal flush or flood of sweat.

"And it's *only* right there." Kiara pulled the Hunter's hand a few finger-widths to the side, and her skin was once more its usual warmness. The heat only returned when she replaced his hand on the site of the healed wound. "I don't know what it is. There's no pain, no soreness, nothing but that heat. Radiating from somewhere deep inside me."

The furrow returned to the Hunter's brow. Aisha's words from the night she'd first healed Kiara sprang to his mind. "*Even after the rot was destroyed, something else remained. Something I could not burn away. It felt...like fire. A fire far hotter than the power of the Kish'aa. It remains within her still.*"

Aisha had been unable to tell him what exactly it was—she'd only known that it drew in the power of the *Kish'aa,* absorbing the spirits and growing stronger—but believed it wouldn't harm Kiara. Given how tired Kiara had looked over the last few days, the Hunter couldn't be certain.

When he reminded Kiara of that conversation, her eyes lit up. "She was right! I didn't pay it much heed until just now, but I'd swear that every time she unleashed her *Umoyahlebe* magic around me, I could almost feel the heat building within me. As if it's drawn to whatever...this is."

She released her grip on the Hunter's wrist and her expression grew pensive, the way it did whenever she was discussing some matter of mythology or alchemy with Graeme.

"I know Tarek said he removed all the fragments he could find. But what if he missed one?" Her words came fast and thick, the cogs visibly turning behind her eyes. "The crystal went all the way through me. That's a big bloody wound, and it's possible that a chunk of the stone remained embedded within." She spoke to him yet seemed to see right through him. "And you saw how bright those crystals burned. Almost as if letting off their own internal fire. So what if they had some magical properties, and that chunk that's still stuck within me has magic, like Deathbite's gemstone or Aisha's pendant."

The Hunter tried to keep up. He had to admit her theory made a measure of sense. "What kind of magical properties could it have?" he asked, narrowing his eyes. "Other than making you feel like you're burning up from the inside out and absorbing Aisha's *Kish'aa* magic?"

"I don't know!" Kiara threw up her hands, but her expression was one of exhilaration and eagerness, not frustration. "Isn't that amazing?"

"Sure." The Hunter found it hard to share her enthusiasm.

Kiara gave him a playful slap. "Oh, don't you spoil it for me!" Humor sparkled in her eyes. "You're basically magic yourself. Changing shape, impossible healing abilities, and the way you seem to draw trouble directly toward you as if by the most powerful sorcery."

The Hunter scowled but got no chance to retort for Kiara was already driving on.

"Then there's Hailen, with his *Melechha* blood able to activate Serenii mechanisms." She counted on her fingers. "Tarek and the magic of the True Descendants. Aisha and her *Umoyahlebe* gifts." She raised an eyebrow. "I'm surrounded by all these people who can do truly remarkable

404

things, and now it turns out *I* might be able to do remarkable things, too. There's no way I'm letting you ruin this!"

The Hunter held up his hands like a shield between them. "I'd never want to ruin it for you. Just—"

"Just want to play it safe. *Boo-ring!*" Kiara pronounced this last in a sing-song voice.

The Hunter opened his mouth, but a finger to his lips stopped him from speaking.

"Trust me, Hunter." Her expression went from playful to dead earnest in an instant. "I know the toll exacted by magic. Hailen's blood, your struggles with the Sword of Nasnaz, Aisha's exhaustion after using too much power." She shook her head. "Whatever this is, whatever it might do or be or lead to, I promise I won't take it lightly. There's too much at stake. Too much to lose."

"Damned right," the Hunter growled. He took her hand. "I nearly lost you once because of that stupid giant bloody serpent. Hailen and Evren nearly lost you, too."

"I know." Kiara's face grew solemn. "Had I died that day, I could have gone to the Long Keeper's arms knowing I did the right thing, putting myself in harm's way to save Tarek's life. Just like you did when you dove into the pool and tried to fight Indombe."

"That's differ—" the Hunter began.

"It's not different at all." Kiara waggled a finger in his face. "You didn't know if you could have survived being bitten in half or swallowed by Indombe, much less dragged down into the depths of that pool. You took your life into your own hands just as much as I did."

The Hunter couldn't argue that logic.

"But this isn't that." Kiara met his eyes. "This is something new, something neither of us yet understand, but it's something that we will endeavor to discover as carefully as we can." She raised a hand to his cheek. "I can't do or say anything that will stop you from worrying except trust me. Trust that I'm smart enough *not* to risk myself just because I'm excited by the idea that just maybe there's a bit of magic inside of me right now."

For long moments, they sat in silence, gazes locked. Even as the words left her mouth, though, the Hunter had known she was right. She was a great many things, but fool was not one of them.

"I promise that I will trust you," he said slowly. "But that won't stop me from worrying if I see you looking like you did this morning. And from giving you the fussyboots mother hen treatment the moment I believe you're pushing yourself too hard—be it physically or, and I can't believe I'm saying this, *magically.*"

"Ah hah!" Kiara laughed and clapped her hands in delight. "I knew there was a reason I loved you!" She leaned forward and planted a ferocious kiss on him.

Through the contact between their lips, he could feel the excitement setting every fiber of her being aquiver, the eager energy coursing through her veins. And despite his worry, he couldn't help feeling a measure of it himself. Seeing her so happy, so thrilled at the prospect of some new discovery—one that could very well benefit them in the long run—filled him with joy overflowing.

"Oooh!" Kiara cried in a voice very much like a girlish squeal. "I think I just figured out a great way we can put this theory to the test!"

Chapter Twenty-Two

Never in his life had the Hunter believed he'd need to explain the follies of being struck by lightning—much less willingly. Yet somehow, he spent the better part of a quarter-hour trying to explain to Kiara why asking Aisha to direct a blast of her *Kish'aa* power into her belly was an idea that strayed far beyond the realm of sheer idiocy.

"Just *no!*" He folded his arms over his chest and shook his head. "There's got to be a better first test to conduct, a smarter, safer experiment!"

"If you've got one, I'm all ears." Kiara fixed him with an expectant look.

The Hunter scowled but had nothing to offer.

Triumph shone in Kiara's eyes. "That's what I thought. You've got nothing better—"

"Still doesn't make it a good idea." The Hunter knew how stubborn Kiara could be, but this was one fight he had no intention of backing down from. "Sure, if you were out of other options, I'd consider it. But you haven't tested anything else yet, have you?"

Kiara's elation slipped a little. "No," she admitted. "But that's because I only came to this conclusion just now."

"Then maybe you take more than half a minute to consider a few more options!" The Hunter found it hard to believe *he* had to be the voice of reason on such a simple matter. "I'm sure between us, we can come up with something—anything—that doesn't involve hitting you with the same energy that, if you'll recall, took down a bloody *slashwyrm!*"

"Same power, but not the same quantity," Kiara insisted. "I'd have her start with a very small amount. A spark at first, just enough to see its effects." She turned away and set about rummaging through her pack as she spoke. "Graeme taught me what he calls his 'scientific method'. Establishing a hypothesis, predicting a specific outcome, factoring in variables, conducting an experiment, analyzing results."

Her words were punctuated by items flying out of her pack. Rolled-up clothing, pouches of dried herbs, a purse heavy with gold, another containing gemstones, and more, all dislodged as Kiara searched for...the Hunter didn't quite know what.

"It's all about consistent testing," Kiara said, her voice muffled as her face was half-buried in her pack. "Adapting and adjusting the tests according to the outcomes until you get the one you want. And taking detailed—aha!"

She emerged from her pack, the triumphant look once more on her face as she turned to him, holding up a leather-bound notebook. The plain black leather cover bore only the interlocking rings of the Hidden Circle; a gift from Graeme, no doubt.

"Taking detailed notes," Kiara finished, tapping the notebook's cover with one finger. "That's the only way anything is learned. Physickers, alchemists, blacksmiths, herbalists, poisoners, *everyone!* They all use a similar process of trial and error."

"Yes, but in this case, error could end with your guts fried by magical *lightning!*" The Hunter added extra emphasis on that last word.

Kiara rolled her eyes. "I wouldn't let it get that far. Like I said, start with just a spark, and go from there."

The Hunter's jaw muscles clenched. "And if Aisha won't do it? If she isn't willing to risk hurting you in this harebrained scheme of yours?"

Kiara gave him a too-sweet smile. "I'm *very* persuasive."

The Hunter cursed under his breath. She truly *was,* a part of why he loved her. Yet in this instance, her winsome personality would work against her, put her at risk. Even if he tried to talk Aisha out of it, in the end, Kiara would have her way.

"Kiara—" he began, trying desperately to get her to see reason.

"Don't 'Kiara' me." Her eyes narrowed, a glimmer of anger flashing there. "I'll gladly consider another option, but if you give it more than three seconds of thought, you'll come to the same realization I have. There really isn't any other way of testing how some shard of fire crystal embedded in my body responds to the magical energy of the *Kish'aa.*"

The Hunter growled low in his throat. He hated to admit it—truly loathed the notion to the core of his being—but she was right. Worse, she *knew* it. Certainty was etched into every line on her beautiful, stubborn face.

He threw up his hands in defeat. "Just promise me you'll be careful! And you'll *talk* to Aisha first. Maybe she has some idea of why you're feeling the effects of the *Kish'aa* even though you're not Ghandian, much less *Umoyahlebe.* Or why some piece of Indombe embedded in your body could have this effect."

"Of course." Kiara shot him a scolding look. "Like I said, I know what I'm risking here." She tapped her stomach. "After all, it's my guts that'll be fried, right?"

The Hunter glared. "Not funny in the slightest."

"A little bit funny." A wicked grin split Kiara's face. "Just a wee little bit."

The Hunter muttered a curse too low for her to hear.

"What's that?" she asked, cocking her head. The look on her face made it clear she understood the spirit behind the words perfectly even if not the words themselves.

"I said, 'What in the fiery hell did I ever do to deserve such a fate?'" The Hunter met her gaze. "Somehow, I end up with one of the only women alive who can out-stubborn me."

"And don't you forget it!" Kiara gave his nose a playful tweak.

The Hunter brushed her hand away. He was about to continue his tirade, when a glint of metal caught his gaze. His eyes dropped to the items Kiara had pulled out of her pack and scattered around her bedroll. There, among the mess, lay a familiar object: what had once been a long, bronze flute with a pot-bellied end, but was now little more than crumpled, flattened, and bent scrap.

The Hunter's eyebrows rose. *The ebroq!* He'd all but forgotten about it since retrieving it from the Zamani Basin. Yet as he saw it, the questions he'd pushed to the back of his mind that night now bubbled to the surface.

He plucked up the ruined *ebroq* from the bedroll and waved it before her eyes. "Were you ever going to tell me about this thing?"

A surprised look sprouted on Kiara's face as she focused on the instrument. "Oh." Her gaze shifted to him. "Of course I was. Just had a lot of other things going on the last few weeks. Sort of slipped my mind."

"Understandable," the Hunter said, nodding. "But now that we're thinking about it…?" He waved it in front of her again, almost teasing. "What was so important about it that you insisted I go retrieve it? And did you know it would have that effect on Indombe? And—"

"One question at a time!" Kiara held up an admonishing finger. "To answer your second question first, I *hoped* it would have that effect, but I didn't know for sure." She gave him a look that might have been chagrined on anyone else's face. On her, it just looked delightful. "The merchant who sold it to me *swore* its sound could summon a *tayrnahr.* "

The Hunter snorted a derisive laugh. "And you believed him?"

"Not at first." Kiara didn't bristle at his mocking. "I walked away initially, but he chased me halfway through the market, insisting it was genuine. I wasn't going to give him a copper bit for it until he showed me this."

She took the flattened, bent bronze instrument and turned it over to reveal the solid, dark-colored metal object embedded into its pot-bellied tip. The shape was familiar to him: the outline of a bird with wings of fire.

The Hunter sucked in a breath. *Impossible!* Reaching over his shoulder, he drew the Sword of Nasnaz, careful to keep his hand away from the hidden needle that drew his blood and activated its magic. He held the scimitar up before him, next to the *ebroq.* Sure enough, hammered into its crossguard was a similar fiery-winged bird, only this was wrought in gilt rather than what appeared to be cheap tin. Yet there was no doubt about it. The two were identical.

"*Alsaaeat Aldhahabia,*" the Hunter said, his voice a breathy whisper.

"The *tayrnahr* who was companion to Nasnaz the Great." An excited smile broadened Kiara's face. She tapped a fingernail against the tin-cast phoenix. "The instant I saw this, I recognized it from the hilt of your sword. When the merchant boasted that he'd procured it from a village that stood near the site of an ancient battleground—one where Nasnaz was said to have destroyed the armies of Tel Khalah, one of the first of the first kingdoms to fall to his conquest—I knew I had to buy it. As a gift for you, one I intended to give you at a later date. A piece of your history you could hold and touch and maybe use to remember more of what you lost."

The Hunter was surprised by the tide of emotion surging within him. A lump rose in his throat and heat pricked at the backs of his eyes. That was among the kindest things anyone had ever done for him—just like the rooftop garden she, Graeme, Evren, and Hailen had conspired to create in his absence.

He stared into her eyes and poured into his look all the love he could muster. Reaching for her with his free hand, he pulled her into a tight embrace and pressed a fierce kiss to her lips. "What in the fiery hell did I ever do to deserve such a fate as this?" he whispered when he finally broke off.

Kiara laughed softly. "Flatterer." She pulled back, a beaming smile on her face. "But that's not all, you know."

The Hunter's eyebrows shot up. "There's more?"

"The Sword of Nasnaz and the *ebroq* aren't the only places where I've seen that symbol." Her face took on that excited expression that always appeared whenever she spoke of the myths and legends that so fascinated her. "In my research with Graeme, I kept coming across mention of a creature called Artaxeras."

"What manner of creature?"

"That's the thing. There's *no* descriptions ever given about it. Just the name. Artaxeras." Oddly, rather than disappointment, Kiara's face held only excitement. "This thing, whatever it is, is always mentioned only in passing, and always in books speaking about the oldest myths. Some even dating back to before the War of Gods."

"Whoa!"

"Right?" A delighted smile tugged at Kiara's lips. "Virtually no written records exist from before that time, and what little we do know comes from oral histories passed down for generations. But every time the name Artaxeras comes up, it's written about with great reverence or fear. Often both."

The Hunter studied her, then looked down at the scimitar he still cradled in his right hand. "And this symbol of the fire-winged bird is somehow tied to Artaxeras?"

Kiara nodded. "Graeme found it alongside a mention of a book supposedly written by Oldgar Wildfoot, a Drashi explorer who, more than four thousand years ago, joined a company of Secret Keepers on an expedition to locate Artaxeras. If not the creature itself, then some sort of evidence that it existed. Bones, fossils, anything!" Her expression soured. "Unsurprisingly, the book is locked away deep within some Temple of Whispers—and which, Graeme has been unable to find out. But imagine if we could get our hands on it!"

The Hunter gave her a blank look. "What *if* we get our hands on it?" he asked, curious and confused. "What would that do other than prove its existence?" As they had proved Indombe's existence, with near-fatal consequences.

"Don't you understand?" Kiara's voice dropped to a whisper. "Such a creature could be precisely what you need to fulfill your oath to Kharna."

The Hunter's confusion deepened. "My oath—"

"To collect the power of one million human souls," Kiara said. Her expression grew intent, all trace of humor vanishing, replaced by grave solemnity. "Think about it. If a demon's life force is equal to that of a Serenii, imagine how much power would be contained in the soul of a creature as grand as Indombe, as powerful as the stories of Artaxeras claim him to be!" A fiery intensity blazed in her eyes. "If you could somehow find a way to harness that power, connect it to Kharna, you might actually be able to defeat the Great Devourer—all without the cost of a single human life. Such a creature, or a few like it, could save our world!"

Chapter Twenty-Three

The Hunter stared slack-jawed at Kiara. He'd known of her fascination for mythical creatures like Indombe and *Alsaaeat Aldhahabia*, yet always chalked it up to the commonplace enthrallment for the lost, forgotten, and unknowns of the world. But this...

"Don't look at me like that." Kiara's face tightened.

"Like what?" the Hunter asked, trying in vain to keep the churning in his gut from echoing in his voice.

"Like I'm some kind of cruel monster for having an idea like that."

The Hunter swallowed. Had his feelings been so apparent?

"I don't like it any more than you!" Kiara threw up her hands. "These are fascinating creatures. Many of them beautiful like *Alsaaeat Aldhahabia* or powerful like Indombe." Wonder sparkled in her eyes. "What I'd give to see every one of them with my own eyes and to walk away knowing such marvels exist in our world."

"But?" The Hunter cocked his head.

"But I can't see myself *ever* stomaching the idea of killing a million humans—even just letting a million humans die—for the sake of saving our world." She leaned forward and jabbed a finger into his woven-vine breastplate. "And neither can you. You could have taken the easy way in Enarium, but no, you fought with everything you had to keep the Sage from activating Khar'nath. You swore you would endeavor to find another way—swore an oath to Kharna, and that oath still burdens you to this day. I can see it in your eyes, hear it in your every word, and I know it is written on your heart." She laid her open hand on his chest. "I can think of no other way. Can you?"

The Hunter met her gaze. How he wanted to speak, to give her the answer she longed to hear. But no words leaped to his mind. His endeavors to locate and imprison the Abiarazi around Einan were little more than stop-gap measures. Too few demonkind still lived to provide power enough to sustain Kharna indefinitely, much less empower him to defeat the Devourer of Worlds. Though the next *Er'hato Tashat* would not come for another four hundred ninety-seven years, he was no closer to finding a solution than he'd been that day he stood in the Illumina in Enarium.

But Kiara had. Her brilliant, cunning mind had found a means of salvation that *didn't* involve millions of deaths. At least not *human* deaths.

Kiara must have seen the turmoil in his eyes, for when she continued, her tone turned pleading, as if begging him to see the reason in her argument. "You said that Kharna told you the Abiarazi were resilient enough to endure the drain on their life forces. That they would sustain him without being burned out as the humans and Elivasti who had been imprisoned in the Chambers."

"I did," the Hunter said, nodding slowly.

"So if the Abiarazi could endure, how much more could a creature like Indombe or *Alsaaeat Aldhahabia* or even whatever Artaxeras is?" Kiara took his free hand in hers, clasped them together. "Their souls could give Kharna power enough to defeat the Devourer of Worlds without being utterly consumed. If *anything* alive stood a chance of surviving that—"

"—it would be them," the Hunter finished her thought. It made a grim sort of sense.

Kiara held his gaze, searching his eyes, his face, as if trying to read his mind. For the first time in the Hunter's memory, she appeared *afraid*. Afraid of what he'd think, how he'd react. Because the words she'd just voiced aloud were kindred to those uttered by every Abiarazi the Hunter had encountered. Expediency above decency. Pragmatism above humanity.

"You're right." The words left the Hunter's mouth even before his mind reached the conclusion. He blew out a long breath and squeezed her hands. "Keeper take it, much as I hate the idea, you're right. That *is* a way to do what needs to be done without a million lives being snuffed out."

Kiara's face didn't relax. "But?"

The Hunter considered for a long moment. "But I'm not certain how I feel about it." He fixed his gaze on her. "Nor are you. If you were, you would have come out and told me about it long ago. And you wouldn't be as troubled by it as you clearly are."

Kiara's eyes slid away from his. "I told you, I don't like the idea any more than you do."

"But at least you *had* another idea, and that's worth something." Dropping the Sword of Nasnaz onto his bedroll, the Hunter pulled her to him, wrapped her arms around his neck, and gripped her waist firmly in both hands. "I'm no more convinced that this is the best way forward than you are. You're right to at least *explore* the option. To find these creatures and learn as much as you can about them. Knowledge is power."

Kiara nodded. "And if there's another way, a better way—"

"Then we'll find it." The Hunter spoke in a firm, confident voice. "We'll do our damnedest to exhaust our options. But if the time comes that we have no choice, that it's the lives of one million humans or the souls of these creatures, we'll know where we stand." He pulled her close and held her tight. "And we stand together."

Kiara's arms gripped him fiercely and she buried her face in his neck. "I should have told you sooner," she whispered, her voice hoarse, raspy. "I should have trusted you'd understand."

The Hunter shrugged. "You told me now. We'll call that good enough."

In truth, he was *glad* she hadn't told him sooner. By keeping him in ignorance all this time, she'd allowed him to enjoy recovering his memories of *Alsaaeat Aldhahabia,* to experience the wonder—and terror—of merely seeing Indombe unencumbered by the burden of figuring out how to entrap and imprison such a gargantuan creature.

Now, however, the weight settled on his shoulders. Calling such an effort colossal was as much an understatement as calling Indombe "sizeable". For a human, it could very well be the endeavor of a lifetime, or the labor of many generations. Kiara knew that his efforts would endure long after her passing, and wanted to arm him with the knowledge that would give him the best chance of success. How could he do anything less than love her for it?

Her arms around his neck loosened, and he pulled back from the embrace. "About this symbol." He lifted *Ibad'at Mutlaqa* from where he'd dropped it and tapped a fingernail against the fiery-winged bird gilded onto its crossguard. "You say it's connected to this Oldgar Wildfoot explorer fellow?"

Kiara nodded. "That's what Graeme and I believe." She plucked up the crumpled *ebroq.* "Best we can figure, he went with the Secret Keepers on their expedition, but through fate or misfortune, he was the only one to return. Whatever he found, he used to bargain with the Temple of Whispers for his life."

The Hunter grimaced. The Secret Keepers were fanatical in their devotion to guarding their Mistress' secrets, more than willing to kill for it. The explorer must have brought back something truly valuable to earn himself a stay of execution.

"After that," Kiara continued, "the only other mention of Oldgar Wildfoot we could find was his name among the founding members of a Drashi organization called the 'Brotherhood of Prospectors'. An organization that used *this*—" She gestured to the symbol hammered onto the *ebroq* and the scimitar. "—as their insignia."

The Hunter frowned down at the Sword of Nasnaz, studying the gilt-wrought crossguard intently. "And is there any link between this Brotherhood of Prospectors and Nasnaz?"

Kiara shrugged. "Not that we've found." She held up a finger. "Yet."

The Hunter raised an eyebrow. "You think there's something to be found?"

"I do." Kiara sounded so confident the Hunter had no trouble believing her. "Think about it, a Drashi trader has a Twelve Kingdoms instrument that makes a sound like a *tayrnahr* from the Advanat Desert, an instrument that bears the same Drashi mark as decorates the weapon wielded by the first king of Al Hani. Sure, Oldgar Wildfoot lived easily two thousand years before Nasnaz the Great, so there's no telling how this—" She gestured to the *ebroq*, then the scimitar's crossguard. "—ended up there. Maybe you were a member of this Brotherhood of Prospectors in a former lifetime, or whoever forged this sword was. Or maybe there's some other connection I don't understand. I don't have those answers, but if they can be found, Graeme and the Hidden Circle will find them."

The Hunter pursed his lips. "Does Graeme know why you're interested in these creatures? What you've considered doing once you find them?"

"No." Kiara shook her head. "And in truth, he doesn't need to. Because this isn't going to happen in my lifetime or his." A sad look entered her eyes. "This will only matter once we're gone. But it will matter. To you, and to whoever comes after us. Our boys, and their children, and their children's children."

That caught the Hunter by surprise. He'd never given much thought to the future that awaited Evren and Hailen. Oh, certainly, he'd entertained the vague notion of a *tomorrow* for which they'd need to be prepared—hence all his effort in training Evren and encouraging Hailen to study under Father Reverentus—but nothing concrete. Not once had he pictured falling in love, starting families, leading their own lives, and, ultimately, dying. Perhaps that thought had been too painful to entertain, or he'd been so focused on the here and now that anything beyond had merely escaped his mind.

Yet Kiara's words put that into stark perspective. *She* hadn't the luxury of time, not in the same way he did. The Long Keeper would come for her, if not that day or the next, someday. Even if she managed to defy nature and live longer than any human alive, that gave her no more than a century before age would finally take its toll and her strength would fail. She had to think beyond her today and plan for a tomorrow she'd never see.

Therein lay the advantage of being human, he supposed. While he would continue in his daily existence and labors for what was essentially *forever,* she lived with the ever-looming consequences of her mortality. Her every effort mattered in the moment because it could all come to an abrupt, final halt at any moment.

The Hunter's appreciation for her presence at his side grew with that realization. Because of her, he was forced to act, to *do*. His time with her was finite, so he had to make the most of that time while he still had it.

"Have I ever told you—" he began to say, only to be interrupted by a shout.

"Hunter!"

The Hunter and Kiara both spun toward the familiar voice. Aisha was marching toward them with a serious expression to match her determined step. Kodyn was a step behind her, a look of mingled worry and resolve in his honey-colored eyes. In the rear came Tarek, his face set in a purposeful cast.

Aisha wore full Issai garb, with only the fibrous cloth battle-wrappings beneath her flowing robes. Kodyn, however, wore his armor beneath the colorful over-garment he'd been given. Tarek had received no robes, but his armor appeared freshly scrubbed and cleaned of blood.

Both the Hunter and Kiara sprang to their feet, yet neither was prepared for Aisha's declaration.

"We're leaving," the young woman proclaimed. "Right bloody now!"

Chapter Twenty-Four

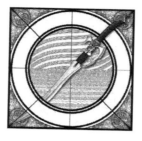

"Leaving?" Kiara asked. She exchanged a curious glance with the Hunter. "I thought we were departing at sunrise."

Aisha stopped in front of the Hunter and Kiara, a hard look on her face. "Not us." She gestured to herself, Kodyn, and Tarek. "We're leaving now. And we're not going to the land of the Buhari. At least not yet."

That piqued the Hunter's interest. "Where to, then?"

Aisha's intent gaze settled on him. "*Ukuhlushwa Okungapheli.*"

The Hunter's eyebrows shot up.

"And before you try to talk us out of it," Aisha hurried on without giving him a chance to speak, "our minds are set. You will not dissuade us from this path."

The Hunter glanced at the two young men behind Aisha. Tarek certainly appeared convinced, but Kodyn's face revealed the merest hint of hesitation. Something told the Hunter he was going along more to watch Aisha's back than out of any real desire to visit the Serenii tower. But trying to talk the young man out of it would have no more success than dissuading Aisha. She had her mind made up.

"But we want you to come with us," Aisha continued stubbornly. "Our chances of succeeding will increase exponentially with the two of you along."

"Succeeding at what, exactly?" Kiara voiced aloud the question that had been forming on the Hunter's lips. "What do you plan to do, just the three of you?"

"Find my father and sister," Aisha said.

"Find the fern," Tarek said at the same time, holding up his sketch of the plant he'd believed could cure the dimercurite poisoning.

The Hunter looked between the two. They both appeared utterly determined to pursue this course of action, reckless though it might be.

"You first," he focused his gaze on Aisha. "Why now? Why not wait until your people are safely in Buhari lands and you've got the *amaqhawe* of both tribes at your back?"

"Because the Issai are no longer my people." Pain flashed in Aisha's eyes, and her fists clenched at her side. "Siyanda made that abundantly clear tonight. Only *she* can reverse that decision, and after what my mother told me about Enanela, I can't think of anything short of a bloody miracle that would give her cause to do so." She blew out a frustrated breath. "Maybe if I can free all the Spirit Whisperers taken captive, that might be enough to prove to her I am worthy to be Issai."

Those last words were spoken in a tone that resonated with deep anguish. She had spent the last years dreaming of coming home, had given up everything she'd had with the Night Guild in Praamis, all to return to her people. Having those people taken away from her and being cast out from her tribe was enough to shatter a weaker-willed person. But, in true Aisha fashion, she was determined to face this impossibility head-on, teeth bared and weapons drawn.

"And you." The Hunter turned to Tarek. "You believe risking yourself in this Valley of Living Fire is the smart play?" He leaned closer, looming large over the shorter Elivasti. "That this fern-thing is the key to curing the dimercurite poisoning—and, with luck, reversing what was done to the Tefaye?"

Tarek lifted his head, his jaw set. "I do."

The Hunter looked from Tarek to Aisha, then back again. "Good." He nodded once. "Just making sure we're all on the same page here." He glanced at Kiara. "We're in."

Kiara tilted her head. "When do we leave?"

Both Aisha and Tarek appeared utterly befuddled by his easy acceptance. Almost as if they'd braced for an argument or prepared to convince him they were right.

It was Kodyn who spoke. "As soon as you're ready." He grinned that easy, charming grin of his. "*Someone*—" His eyes darted to Aisha. "—wasn't certain you'd come. But just in case, I made preparations. We've food and water enough for a week, and the horses stand ready to ride."

The Hunter beamed. "Well, then, no time to be off on a mad quest like the present!"

* * *

"You sure about this?"

Kiara's question drifted over from where she and Aisha stood tending to their horses. Though she'd spoken too quietly for Kodyn and Tarek to overhear, the Hunter's keen ears had picked up the whispered words.

"I am." For all its quietness, Aisha's response rang with grave certainty. "With this one action, we defeat two enemies."

"Surely your mother would—"

"My mother does not command me." Aisha's jaw muscles clenched. "I am outcast. I do not answer to the Issai *nassor* at the moment."

"She just got you back," Kiara pressed. The Hunter didn't know if she actually believed she could talk Aisha out of this action, but she had to at least speak her piece. "I can't begin to imagine how much she's suffered over these last six years, and now you'd leave her again?"

"I am my mother's daughter." Aisha drew herself up. "She taught me to be strong and courageous, through her deeds and her words. She will understand." This last sounded a great deal like she was trying to convince herself.

Kiara inclined her head. "As you say." With that, she swung up into her saddle.

She'd clearly seen the folly of trying to dissuade Aisha from her chosen course of action. By the grim look on her face, she'd determined her strength would now be best expended keeping Aisha—and, of course, Tarek and Kodyn—alive long enough to return to the Issai. The Hunter had come to a similar realization the moment Aisha had first announced her intention. Between the two of them and Kodyn, they had better-than-even odds of pulling it off.

The Hunter, too, climbed into his saddle. Elivast shifted beneath him, as energetic and eager to run as he always was after plenty of rest and feed. He'd spent the day and night with Ash, Nayaga, and Kodyn and Aisha's horses cropping the plains grass and enduring the attention of too-curious Ghandian children who had likely never before seen such small *zabara* with no stripes.

From where they were on the *kopje's* western slope, the tall boulders, grassy hill, and stubby trees blocked out the light and tumult of the distant revelry. Though the night was well advanced—dawn couldn't be more than three or four hours off—the celebration showed no sign of abating. With the storm cloud of impending battle looming large, the Hunter had gotten the sense the Issai and their new allies doubtless needed one final hurrah before the arduous work of waging war began.

With one last glance toward the place where her mother and the rest of her people even now danced, sang, and basked in the glow of campfires, Aisha dug her heels into her horse's flanks and set off into the darkness. Kodyn and Tarek followed close behind, with Kiara at their backs and the Hunter bringing up the rear. Aisha led the way northwest, intent on putting a good half-league or so between them and the *kopje* before swinging eastward and heading toward *Indawo Yokwesaba*. That way, the cloak of darkness would hide them from the watching eyes of the *amaqhawe* set to watch the plains.

Doubt niggled at the back of the Hunter's mind. It felt wrong leaving this way, stealing away into the night like thieves and cutthroats. Which, admittedly, some of them were—or had been, before coming to the *amathafa*. Here, things were different. Or they should have been for at least Aisha and Kodyn. The Hunter, Kiara, and Tarek were outsiders, but Aisha was Issai and Kodyn her *oqinywe*. They should have been welcomed to the tribe with open arms. Yet here they were, skulking and sneaking because of Siyanda's enmity toward Aisha.

Let's just hope Aisha's plan works and she can earn her way back into her tribe. He tightened his grip on Elivast's reins. Whatever was needed to make that come about, he'd do it, no hesitation. Yet he couldn't shake the feeling that their actions tonight and in the days to follow would lead to dire consequences for all the Ghandians they left behind.

It took him the better part of an hour to put his worries out of his head enough to enjoy the late-night ride. The plains were truly beautiful at night, rolling hills of dark grey-green illuminated by the faint light of the stars. No clouds hovered in the sky to obscure the moon's pale face. The wind whipping past them was cool but lacked any real icy bite.

What finally drew the Hunter's attention away from his concerns was his new armor and clothing. The Issai robes streamed behind him, caught up in a swirling dance with the wind. Light, breezy, and immensely comfortable, they offered just enough protection that he felt no cold but remained unencumbered, his limbs free to move. The Buhari armor was supple and supremely flexible, too. If it could turn aside an enemy sword, he might never need to don his suit of leather ever again.

All the same, he'd strapped his leather armor behind his saddle, along with his pack containing the Swordsman's twin iron blades and the rest of his gear. Soulhunger hung from his left hip, the watered steel blade at his right, and *Ibad'at Mutlaqa* bounced against his back. Whatever lay ahead, he would face it with drawn steel and sorcery.

Dawn found them riding hard eastward, the Issai camp left far behind. Aisha pushed the pace, and none of her companions, neither human nor equine, complained. Almost as if even the horses understood the necessity for haste.

The Hunter's eyes roved the eastern horizon. He could feel the call of *Ukuhlushwa Okungapheli* growing stronger with every beat of his heart, as if the Serenii tower sensed his approach. Or, perhaps, Kharna's implanted compulsion urged him on with greater force now that he'd acceded to its demands. Either way, it didn't matter. All that mattered now was that soon he'd come face to face with the ancient site of power he'd crossed half of Einan to see.

Yet it was not the Bondshold he sought. He scanned the lands ahead for any hint of the phantasmal creatures that had appeared to him so many times since crossing the Chasm of the Lost. The horse-like *Nuru Iwu* with its eyes of fire, twin horns, and ruby hooves, and the serpentine *Okadigbo* pursuing his brother relentlessly, impeding escape.

To the Hunter's surprise, they did not appear to him. The plains ahead remained empty save for the rolling hills and the distant darkness of *Indawo Yokwesaba*. The Hunter considered that. Had the ancient spirits—or gods, or whatever they were—given up their attempts to communicate with him? *Nuru Iwu* had appeared to Tarek, had begged for his aid in escaping the prison crafted by his brother. But who, then, received *Okadigbo's* dire warnings and unspoken threats? Had the crueler, more guileful of the twins found a new member of his small group—Kodyn, Aisha, or Kiara—to commune with? Or someone from among the Issai, Buhari, or the other tribes? The thought troubled the Hunter almost as much as the sight of the slithering creature itself.

Over the rest of the day's travel, the Hunter had plenty of time to consider the matter. That, and other matters: the fiery-winged symbol of the Brotherhood of Prospectors on *Ibad'at Mutlaqa's* crossguard and the *ebroq* that had come into Kiara's hands through what struck him as curious coincidence; Kiara's desires to explore what, if any, magical abilities manifested as a result of the crystal shard embedded in her flesh; the labor to locate ancient mythical creatures of immense power to one day feed their life force to Kharna; the mystery of why Kharna had set him on this path toward the Bondshold; the enemies that awaited them ahead, both the Vassalage Consortium and the mysterious Order of Mithridas; and countless more concerns that occupied his mind.

And with every step, the weight of what he had yet to do—the responsibilities he'd taken upon himself—grew ever-heavier, constricting like a noose around his throat.

Chapter Twenty-Five

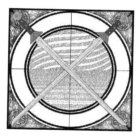

The mood around their camp that afternoon proved subdued. Everyone seemed to have a great deal on their minds. None of them found much sleep, and that had only a little to do with the sweltering, dry heat of the plains—even the sparse shade of the stubby fig tree offered no escape. Fortunately, they'd all had a chance to rest the previous day, and when the time came to move on after sunset, none of them complained.

The last of the fading light bathed the land ahead in a dimming grey glow that somehow made the dense vastness of *Indawo Yokwesaba* loom more ominous. Aisha had led them on a path steadily northeast, intending to skirt around the jungle rather than ride through it. According to her, less than a league from *Indawo Yokwesaba's* northern edge, they would find *Ukuhlushwa Okungapheli*—or the Bondshold, as the Consortium had called it—and just beyond it, the Valley of Living Fire.

The fact that their journey led through the land reserved for the Tefaye had only amplified the Hunter's wariness. He did not know how many of the outcast tribe remained alive or uncaptured—Aisha had not known, and none of them had thought to ask before departing. His eyes never stopped roving the lands all around him, searching for even the faintest hint of enemies. He had no doubt their horses could outrun even the fleetest Tefaye and the Sword of Nasnaz could defeat however many foes came against them. Still, he had no desire for either delay or unnecessary bloodshed. Not if reaching *Isigodi Umlilophilayo* unhindered and finding this unnamed fern could undo what had been done to the Tefaye. Those still alive could very well turn the tide of the upcoming battle in favor of the united tribes.

They reached the northwestern edge of *Indawo Yokwesaba* shortly before sunrise. The Hunter couldn't help peering into the dense jungle and searching among the trees for threats—both two-legged and draconic. He saw only one possible danger—a writhing tangle of what had to be hundreds of snakes slithering around a dried-up basin clogged with fallen trees, each twice the length of a horse, their thick bodies covered in a gleaming mass of silvery scales that reflected the brightening sunlight with every color of the rainbow—and none of his companions were any more inclined to approach it than he. Yet of slashwyrms or humans, he encountered no sign.

After consulting the map he'd created in his mind, he determined the Consortium camp lay at least another half-day's ride to the east, which meant slashwyrm territory was still a long way off, too. With luck, they were far enough to the north that they'd be unlikely to venture too close to the *Nsanga* on their journey.

And when they inevitably encountered humans? The Hunter checked his weapons once more out of habit. He'd face whatever obstacles and dangers the Consortium and the Order of Mithridas had to throw at him with bared steel.

The thrumming of the horses' hooves amplified the throbbing within the recesses of his mind. Kharna's urging grew louder, more ferocious, drawing him toward the Serenii-built tower with a force almost beyond his control. It was akin to the compulsion that had driven him for so many years, the inescapable need to slake Soulhunger's boundless thirst. Only this time, he knew its origin and understood its purpose. And he did not fight it—not the same way he'd wrestled with the dagger's demands. He'd already acceded to Kharna's implanted constraints; every delay merely forestalled what he knew was to one day come.

Today was that day. Today, he would finally lay eyes on *Ukuhlushwa Okungapheli*. He would see for himself the tower of midnight black dotted with stars to rival those shining in the sky. He did not know what would happen when he did—would he feel the sensations he had during his communion with Kharna, that ravenous, hungry evil, the two great heartbeats striving for dominance? All too soon, he would find out.

The lands north of *Indawo Yokwesaba* proved far more mountainous than the gently rolling plains to the south. Indeed, only a solid wall of jagged limestone and granite cliffs had prevented the jungle from spreading inexorably northward. The Hunter and his companions were forced to ride into the rocky hills, where narrow passes cut through crumbling boulders and dirt trails skirted the edges of terrifying precipices. Even the sure-footed Ash and Nayaga struggled with the treacherous footing.

The rest of the day was spent navigating the hills. Aisha alone knew the terrain, and her recollections of this route came from the one visit she'd made to *Ukuhlushwa Okungapheli* alongside her father, more than a decade earlier. More than once, she was forced to slow and study the way ahead. The Hunter suspected she was guessing or relying on instinct half the time. But she never wavered, always forged onward, and she'd earned the Hunter's trust enough that he held his peace. So did the others. The journey was challenging enough without second-guessing the only one who could get them where they all felt they needed to go.

Shortly after noon, they came upon two corpses. Human, clearly, though the flesh had been picked clean and only a few strips of dull brown fabric remained of their clothing. The bones were all but bleached by the sun; the Hunter guessed they'd been lying here for the better part of a year, perhaps longer.

Curiously, Aisha reined in her horse in front of the bodies. She did not dismount, yet she leaned forward, frowning down at the corpses. After a moment, she extended her right hand and closed her eyes, drawing in long, slow breaths. Blue-white light shone from the *Dy'nashia* pendant that hung visible at her neck. The glow lasted only for a few heartbeats, then faded and dimmed once more.

Aisha's eyes opened slowly, and a few sparks of the same light danced around her dark brown irises. "Adeola and Ebere. Those were their names." She spoke slowly, as if every word proved a labor. "They were Tefaye. Among those who were invited by the *Gcinue'eleku awandile* to journey to *Ukuhlushwa Okungapheli* to discuss terms of some arrangement mutually beneficial to their tribe and the *alay-alagbara*. Only they died here, on the journey." She gestured to the corpse on the right. "Ebere succumbed to fever. Adeola was ill, too. She could have traveled on, but she refused to leave Ebere. Joined in life and death." Moisture glimmered in her eyes. "Adeola made certain she and Ebere were both laid out for the *makalala,* then ended her life to join him in *Pharadesi.*"

The Hunter stared down at the bodies. Upon closer inspection, he could see where Adeola's hand draped across Ebere's body. As if even the scavengers that picked their flesh clean could not truly separate them.

"Ebere's spirit remained." Tears tracked down Aisha's cheeks. Her hand crept to her pendant and gripped it tight. "He could not pass on to the ancestors without making certain *someone* remembered the great love they shared."

The Hunter noted the way her eyes darted toward Kodyn's, and his looked firmly back at her. He himself was seized by a sudden desire to reach for Kiara and feel the warmth and comfort of her presence. She looked back at him, and in her smile was written all the emotion he felt welling within him.

Only Tarek did not move. He stared down at the two corpses in silence, his expression solemn.

Aisha removed the hand from her pendant and used it to brush the wetness away from her cheeks. "Ebere has passed on now, but before he left, he gave me a gift." She tapped her temple. "I know the route the Tefaye were using to travel to *Ukuhlushwa Okungapheli*. If we ride hard, we'll reach it well before nightfall."

"Damn!" The Hunter let out a long whistle. "These *Umoyahlebe* powers of yours really are something, aren't they?"

A touch of color rose to Aisha's cheeks, but she nodded. "They truly are a gift, though they have been a curse for some."

By the shadows that darkened her eyes, the Hunter knew she was thinking of her father. She'd told him of what had happened—the *Inkuleko,* the Unshackling of mind and body—and her determination to prevent it from ruining any other *Umoyahlebe* lives. Including that of her younger sister.

"We'll get Nkanyezi back," Kodyn said, his jaw set in a determined expression. "We'll get all of them back."

"I know." Aisha gave the young man a reassuring smile. "I'm just…worried." She looked from Kodyn to the Hunter, Kiara, and Tarek. "After the night we attacked the camp, my mother told me about Nkanyezi. When my sister touched the dimercurite, the stone shone so bright it nearly blinded her. Brighter even than when my father touched it." She frowned. "It only glowed brighter for me."

The Hunter narrowed his eyes. "So you're worried that whatever the Consortium want with the *Umoyahlebe,* your sister is going to be at greatest risk because of her power?"

"Yes." Aisha's jaw muscles clenched. "My father was regarded among the Issai as one of the greatest Spirit Whisperers alive today. Those of the other tribes—the Nyemba, Mwaani, Ujana, and the Bheka—were wise in the way of lore and remedies, but none of them could commune with the *Kish'aa* with the same clarity. And if Nkanyezi's gift dwarfs even my father's…"

She didn't need to finish that sentence. The Hunter could think of no good purpose to which the Consortium or the Order of Mithridas could possibly put anyone who wielded power like Aisha's. They had gone out of their way to identify and remove *everyone* with even the faintest hint of *Umoyahlebe* abilities from all the tribes they'd captured. Whatever they planned, it seemed to involve the Bondshold, and the power inherent in the Serenii mechanisms was far from trifling.

"Well, then?" He forced a grin to his face. "Time to put Ebere's last gift to use and get on with our ride. It's been days since Soulhunger's tasted Consortium blood. Time we remind the *Gcinue'eleku awandile* just who they're dealing with!"

The rest of the day was spent riding through the rocky hills, navigating steep ascents and scree-covered slopes. The journey proved arduous but they covered ground far faster than

420

before, for they now had the final whispers of a dying Tefaye to guide them along a path he evidently knew well.

As they traveled, the Hunter mulled over what Aisha had told them. If the Tefaye had been *invited* to the Bondshold, it suggested the Consortium had attempted to convince them to join their efforts willingly, offering payment in gold, slaves, land, or whatever else appealed to the outcast tribe. So why had they then *poisoned* the Tefaye? Only one explanation made sense: the tribe had rejected the Consortium's offer, forcing their hand.

That proved...interesting. It was possible the Consortium's offer held little interest to the Tefaye, or it was of miserly value. But could it be that the Tefaye had rejected the offer because they did not agree with whatever the Consortium intended?

So why, then, had the Ujana accepted? The Consortium could have merely seen the inefficiency of a legitimate bargain or business agreement and instead resorted to the strong-arm tactics to which enterprises like them were most accustomed. Had the Hunter been in their position, he might have gone the same route. Where gold proved unsuccessful, threats rarely failed. Especially when those doing the threatening had power to back it up with violence.

The possibility filled the Hunter with a measure of hope. *If* the Tefaye had turned down the Consortium, they might willingly join the united Buhari and Issai tribes—and that was before they learned how *Gcinue'eleku awandile* had poisoned them. Their chances of destroying the Consortium could drastically improve. Provided Tarek found a cure, of course.

All thoughts fled from his mind as they rounded the last bend in the rocky pass and the path dropped sharply ahead of them. For it was then, through a gap in the jagged cliffs, that the Hunter first laid eyes on the place he had traveled all this way to see.

Ukuhlushwa Okungapheli.

Chapter Twenty-Six

The sight of the Bondshold stole the Hunter's breath. In the glow of the setting sun, it appeared a shard of blackest night jutting up hundreds of paces from the earth, shadow given form in crystalline glass.

A shudder ran down the Hunter's spine as a memory of what he'd witnessed in the uppermost chamber of the Illumina flashed through his mind. There, he'd seen the Devourer of Worlds encased in a crimson pillar, beheld its inky tendrils of chaos seeping into the world. Where it touched, nothing existed. Its very presence created an absence almost incomprehensible to the mortal mind.

Ukuhlushwa Okungapheli bore a terrible resemblance to the Devourer. Instead of reflecting the vivid, multi-hued glow that splashed the heavens in glorious color, the Serenii tower appeared to drink in all light. Merely looking at it strained the Hunter's eyes. Spots and sparks danced in his vision. No, he realized, that was just an optical illusion. A trick. It was the tower's *surface* that danced with the glittering light of a thousand stars. He could make no sense of it, like the swirling patterns decorating the Illusionist's Temple in Voramis. He tore his gaze away and rested his eyes on the details he could comprehend.

The Bondshold stood at the end of a wedge-shaped plateau, but beyond it to the north, south, and east, the ground fell away into what appeared to be a deep valley. To the Hunter's eyes, it appeared as if a giant had carved out a vast slice of pie from the terrain, and only the tower's deep roots had kept it from crumbling into the depths.

But the Serenii-built tower did not stand alone. Hundreds of wood, brick, and stone structures cluttered the plateau west of the Bondshold, packing every bit of open ground between the steep cliffs to the north and south and the midnight-colored structure and the massive stone wall that protected the camp. From where he sat high up in the hills, every one of the buildings appeared in miniature, but more than a few were multi-storied—including one with a brass dome that reflected the fading sunlight in a dazzling array of colors. In contrast to the small work camp the Consortium had erected in the jungle, this appeared a veritable city, large enough to house easily twenty thousand people by the Hunter's reckoning.

The sight brought to mind the city the Elivasti built in the shadow of Kara-ket's twin temples. Yet something about these felt...wrong.

A hiss escaped Aisha's lips. "What is this?" she growled, her voice low, angry. A scowl twisted his lips. "This was not here when my father brought me. There was nothing but empty lands as far as the eyes could see."

The Hunter frowned. The structures had not been present in Kharna's vision, either. He'd seen barren earth threaded through with rivulets of green and violet. Rot had pervaded the lands encircling *Ukuhlushwa Okungapheli*, consuming the ground, every living creature, and plant in its vicinity, rendering it utterly inhospitable.

Only now life persisted. As stubborn human tenacity always had, this city had been built. Though to what ultimate end, the Hunter could only begin to guess.

Almost certainly it had to do with the Bondshold. The Serenii tower stood at the eastern edge of the camp, but every street and avenue intersected before the enormous structure, every building faced it. And it was around the base of the tower that the flurry of activity was concentrated.

"What are they doing?" The Hunter's eyes were keen, but from this distance, he could only make out the hundreds—perhaps *thousands*—of umber-skinned people moving around the base of the tower, clambering onto what appeared to be scaffolding that descended over the side of the cliff and vanished from sight below. Among them, the Hunter caught sight of men clad in what appeared to be armor, carrying swords that glinted in the fading sunlight. *Consortium, no doubt about it.*

"No idea," Aisha said, "but I bloody well intend to find out."

The Hunter looked toward the young woman. Her face was hard, tight with anger, yet a hint of worry shone there. She had been among those who had brought to life the Serenii machine in Shalandra, had seen firsthand the devastating power it could unleash. There was no telling what would happen if the Consortium and the Order of Mithridas managed to do likewise.

"I'm going down there." Aisha's jaw set in a stubborn cast. "I'm going to find my father and sister."

"After dark, of course," Kodyn put in quickly.

Aisha shot him a look—though the Hunter didn't understand its meaning—and nodded. "Of course." Her fingers twitched on the haft of her *assegai* as if itching to begin the bloodletting sooner. The Hunter couldn't blame her. He'd be just as eager were he in her place.

Which made it all the more imperative she had someone level-headed at her side, someone who she might actually listen to. "And I'm going, too."

Relief flashed in Kodyn eyes. "That makes three of us." Evidently the thief had come to the same conclusion as he. Aisha was driven, angry, and spoiling for a fight. If she got it in her mind to unleash her rage on the bastards who had imprisoned her father and sister, he might not be able to dissuade her. But the Hunter...well, he'd prove harder to ignore.

"I'm going with Tarek." Kiara regarded the Elivasti with a smile. "You're going to need help finding and gathering enough of those ferns to cure the Tefaye."

The Hunter turned his attention toward the lowlands encircling the Bondshold to the south, east, and north. *Valley of Living Fire sounds about right,* he thought grimly. Even from this distance, he could see the veins of acidic green and violet threading through the black volcanic stone, and the steam rising from the depths of *Isigodi Umlilophilayo* filled the air with a sulfurous stench. A forest of petrified trees stood like a silent army of spiny, twisted, and gnarled soldiers, not a speck of green life visible among their ranks. Whatever had given birth to this blasted place had snuffed out every living thing for leagues in every direction in an instant—and forever.

That was when he felt it. Just as he had in his communion with Kharna, the moment his eyes settled on the wracked, twisted valley, the insatiable hunger gnawed at his belly and the darkness of the stone seeped into his soul. He almost imagined he could feel the twin hearts beating beneath his feet even from this great distance. Somehow, he knew: this had to be the final resting place of the twins *Nuru Iwu* and *Okadigbo,* ancient spirits or beings of immense power.

Serenii, perhaps? The thought struck him with the force of a physical blow. Like an arrowhead, once it lodged deep in his mind, the more he could not shake the idea. And the more a fool he felt.

How had he *not* put it together? *Nuru Iwu* had drawn him onward in the same way Kharna's compulsion did. *Okadigbo's* warning had grown more ferocious with every passing day, every league closer he drew to this very place. One longed for his approach, the other threatened by his presence. When he refused to heed their entreaties and threats, they had ceased appearing to him and found other vessels to hear them. Tarek and...

Who? He did not know, and at the moment, it did not greatly matter. What *did* matter was that he had finally come to *Ukuhlushwa Okungapheli* as Kharna had desired.

And if Kharna wanted—no, needed—*me here, then could it be he's on Nuru Iwu's side?*

He considered the legend Aisha had told him. Had *both* brothers been Serenii? Considered spirits or gods by the ancient Ghandians who once dwelled in their shadows, reality giving way to myth and legend in order to make sense of the incomprehensible. If so, one had imprisoned the other within the Bondshold—just as Kharna had imprisoned the Devourer of Worlds in the pillar atop the Illumina in Enarium.

Endless possibilities spun through the Hunter's mind. If learning the truth of the so-called "gods of Einan" had taught him anything, it was that only a kernel of fact ever endured repeated retellings and the passage of time. The only way to know for certain was to enter the Bondshold for himself. Only then would he behold the beings who had been worshipped as the twin brothers *Nuru Iwu* and *Okadigbo*, be they Serenii or something else entirely.

"Hunter?"

The sound of his name snapped the Hunter from his thoughts. He glanced toward the one who'd spoken, found Kiara staring at him—as were Aisha, Tarek, and Kodyn.

"You with us?" A furrow deepened Kiara's brow.

"Yes. And no." He grimaced. "Sorry. Something just occurred to me, and I was mulling it over."

Kiara cocked her head. "Care to share?"

The Hunter looked between her and the three youths regarding him. Not long ago, he would likely have shrugged it off, kept it to himself until he and Kiara could speak in private. But a lot had changed in the last couple of months. His experiences with the Night Guild in Praamis and on the road to Malandria had proven there was benefit to trusting others. Hearing Kodyn and Aisha's account of events in Shalandra, of the bond they'd forged with Hailen and Evren, had instilled in him faith in their abilities. They and Tarek had proven themselves time and again. He had not a single shred of doubt that he could trust the three of them.

Without hesitation, he recounted everything that had passed through his mind. As he did, facts and suspicions began to fall into place.

"What if *that's* what brings the Order all the way out here?" he asked, thrusting a finger toward the Bondshold. "If they believe *Nuru Iwu* is trapped in there, they could be trying to get in and free him." He frowned. "Or trying to finish what *Okadigbo* started and *kill* him for good."

Aisha sucked in a breath. "How does one kill a spirit so powerful?"

"I don't know." The Hunter shook his head. "But I do know that as difficult as it is, it's possible to kill a Serenii." In his visions of the so-called "War of Gods", the clash between the Abiarazi and Serenii, more than a few of the ancient beings had fallen before the ferocity of the demon horde. "Especially if the one doing the killing is another Serenii—or something with equal power."

The Hunter saw Kiara's eyes light up, the wheels in her mind begin to turn. Anything mighty enough to rival a Serenii could very well tip the scales in Kharna's struggle against the Great Devourer.

"Right now, that doesn't matter." The Hunter emphasized his point with a slashing gesture of his hand. "What *does* matter is that we stop the Order of Mithridas from getting in. I don't know if they're trying to free *Nuru Iwu* or kill him to appease *Okadigbo*, but I know without a shred of doubt that we can't allow it to happen. Not after what Father Reverentus told us about the Order of Mithridas."

He thought back to the old priest's words and repeated them aloud. "According to the Cambionari, they were a plague upon our world for nearly three thousand years. Stirring up unrest, inciting civil wars, toppling kingdoms and empires, turning nation against nation, fomenting discord among the priesthoods. They nearly ripped our world apart at the seams and were only stopped when all the priesthoods of the Thirteen united against them." He shook his head. "They can mean no good, which means we cannot allow them to accomplish whatever they're doing here."

"We can't stop them just the five of us," Tarek said. All eyes turned to him, but the young Elivasti didn't back down. "But we *can* gather intelligence, figure out as much as we can and bring that information back to the *ekhaya.*" He looked to Aisha. "The more we know, the easier it will be to convince your mother and Jumaane to move against this place."

"Agreed." Aisha nodded, as did Kodyn.

Kiara smiled proudly at Tarek. "A good plan, then. You and I will see to the salvation of the Tefaye, while those trained to slink through the shadows—" She gestured to the Hunter and Kodyn with a sly grin. "—will do what they do best."

Kodyn beamed. "It's been weeks since I've had a real challenge for my Hawk skills. I'm not going to lie, I'm looking forward to breaking into someplace properly fortified." He cracked his knuckles loudly, and a jaunty twinkle shone in his honey-colored eyes. "Let's see if these Consortium bastards have built a stronghold capable of keeping me out."

Chapter Twenty-Seven

From high up in the hills, the wall surrounding the encampment had appeared impressive. Up close, it was downright intimidating, even for the Hunter.

Oh, he'd scaled barriers taller than the thirty-pace wall before him and in far worse conditions than the dense darkness that now settled over the blasted landscape. Yet there was something ominous about the black stone, which appeared darker and more forbidding than the night itself. And high above it all rose the shimmering tower like an obsidian dagger gleaming with the light of the stars dotting the heavens.

The noxious stench of sulfur on the too-warm wind did little to ease the Hunter's apprehension. From where he crouched behind a boulder fifty paces south of the wall, he was near enough to the edge of the cliff to peer down into the Valley of Living Fire. Below, the threads of acidic green and stark violet lit up the night and turned the air stifling. The Hunter had no trouble understanding why the Buhari treated this as a place of evil. The two vast heartbeats he'd first sensed in his vision with Kharna had grown louder the closer he drew. Now, he could all but feel them *thump-thumping* beneath his feet.

He tore his gaze from *Isigodi Umlilophilayo* and focused his attention on the stationary army of petrified trees beyond. With luck, Kiara and Tarek would be nearly there—they'd been forced to take the long way around to avoid being spotted by the Consortium guards patrolling the camp's perimeter outside the wall—and beginning their search for the strange-looking fern. They would not venture into the caldera itself; according to Davathi, the plant grew among the dead forest.

Kodyn had given them a pair of alchemical lamps he'd called "beamers" to facilitate their hunt. They'd have to be careful to keep the light hidden from watching eyes in the camp, but Kiara's time among the Bloody Hand had taught her a great many things about the art of thievery and subterfuge.

Besides, the Hunter told himself with a wry smile, *they've got the easier and safer of tonight's tasks.* He glanced to where Kodyn and Aisha knelt in the shadows at his side. *Our job carries a great deal more risk.*

As always, his hands moved of their own accord through the motions of checking his arsenal. Soulhunger on his left hip, Master Eldor's sword on his right, the Sword of Nasnaz on his back. Both of Graeme's beautifully-crafted handheld crossbows were holstered and strapped to his thighs. Each of his leather bracers and boots contained a throwing knife, along with a trio of stilettos concealed in his belt.

He'd chosen to keep the Buhari armor—the woven vines moved easily and weighed little—but left the fine Issai robes with the rest of his belongings, strapped to Elivast's back. His dark cloak blended into the shadows of night far more effectively than the bright, multi-hued garments gifted him by the Issai warriors.

Drawing in a deep breath, the Hunter rose smoothly to his feet.

"Watch for the tripwire chain," Kodyn said, his voice barely audible beneath the night's gentle breeze.

The Hunter answered with a nod and set off at a smooth glide forward through the darkness. His soft-soled boots made hardly a sound as he raced across the rocky terrain separating his hiding place from the base of the wall. He didn't even slow as he approached the near-invisible chain Kodyn had somehow spotted during his reconnaissance; he merely sprang high into the air and landed a good three paces past where the young man had pointed out the trap to him.

The remainder of the journey took him all of half a minute, marked by the furious hammering of his heart and his flying feet. Reaching the wall, he leaped high into the air and dug his fingers into the rough volcanic rock. He hung three paces off the ground for only a moment before setting his toes against the wall and pushing himself upward. He'd made no more noise than the passing breeze, his presence utterly unmarked by the patrol now marching northward away from him.

A confident grin split the Hunter's face as he climbed. He made quick work of the thirty-pace ascent, leaping from handhold to handhold and foothold to foothold with the grace of a mountain goat. Not that it was a particularly difficult climb. The stone used in the construction of the wall was so craggy and rough that he never had trouble finding somewhere to grip or dig in his toes. Indeed, the only real threat in this climb was scraping away the skin of his hands, so abrasive and harsh was the volcanic stone.

Five minutes later, he was pulling himself up onto the wall's craggy top. Shrouded in his dark cloak and the shadows of night, he had no fears of being spotted by anyone below—either the occupants of the camp or one of the three guard patrols now marching back in his direction. Nor were there guards atop the wall. The volcanic stone was too uneven and rough to form a proper battlement or parapet, and the eternally vigilant Consortium guards inside and outside the camp appeared more concerned with keeping their captives from getting out to search for anyone attempting to break in.

Still, the Hunter kept his movements slow and surreptitious as he uncoiled Kodyn's rope from where he'd secured it around his torso. The wall offered no convenient anchor points, so the Hunter tied a loop around his waist. He was more than strong enough to bear the weight of the two youths.

Rope in hand, he watched the Consortium guards passing at the base of the wall. Their stink—sweat, poor hygiene, and more than a few diseases—drifted up the thirty paces toward him, accompanied by the creaking of studded leather armor, the clatter of bouncing weapons, and the *tromp, tromp* of their heavy boots. The eight slavers marched at a crisp, military pace, yet the torches they carried at the front and back of their column rendered them effectively night blind. Further proof they were more carrying out the formality of patrolling than genuinely endeavoring to protect their encampment.

The Hunter waited until the patrol reached the far southern end of their route, the cliff's edge, and returned on their way north. The moment they passed the spot where he hunkered atop the wall, he dropped the rope. In the same instant, he spotted Kodyn and Aisha rising from their hiding place and racing toward him. They had less than five minutes before the third patrol reached their position, but for the two Night Guild-trained youths, that was more than enough.

When Kodyn and Aisha reached the wall's base, the Hunter braced himself on the stone in anticipation of their climb. He felt the rope dragging at his waist but had no trouble bearing up against the weight—Aisha's, if he had to guess. She made quick work of the ascent, but Kodyn was quicker. He scaled the rope at a faster pace than the Hunter had climbed the wall, with hardly any jolt or jostle.

The Hunter's mind cast back to the odd rope maze that had given him access to the Night Guild's underground stronghold in Praamis. Judging by the young man's climbing skill, he'd spent countless hours practicing on the contraption.

Once the three of them had reached the top, the Hunter turned his attention toward the interior of the camp. The two patrols marching along the inner perimeter set a pace far slower and more lackadaisical than those guarding the outside. Even now, both groups dawdled in the light of the torches and braziers illuminating the broad avenue just inside the wall's single massive gate, chatting up the twenty guards stationed there, in no apparent hurry.

That suited the Hunter's purposes just fine. Inattentive and inexperienced guards were the delight of any assassin and the—often fatal—bane of the one who paid them. It appeared the Vassalage Consortium was as riddled with ineptitude as any other armed force. In all his years as the Hunter of Voramis, he had yet to see a single outfit, be it military or civilian, comprised solely of competents.

Kodyn's experience apparently taught him a similar lesson, for he shot the Hunter a grin and tossed the rope over the wall. Five seconds was all he needed to slide down and duck into the shadows of a small hut-like building. Aisha followed, albeit more slowly. The moment she hit the ground, the Hunter untied the rope from around his waist and dropped it. While Aisha gathered up the long black coils, the Hunter glanced toward the guards and, finding them still occupied in conversation, began his descent.

Climbing down proved only fractionally more difficult than up. The Hunter's palms and fingers were abraded and bleeding in a few places by the time he reached the ground, but he ignored the discomfort—his natural healing ability would restore the flesh in a matter of minutes—and darted toward the shadows where Kodyn and Aisha now awaited him. In all that time, the patrol hadn't taken a step toward them.

The Hunter gave a derisive snort. Despite the Vassalage Consortium's appearance of a proper martial force, their ranks were riddled with the apathetic and lethargic. For all the power the organization at large supposedly wielded through their gold, political influence, and the sizeable force of armed men at their command, at an individual level, they were far from impressive.

Nodding to Kodyn and Aisha, the Hunter set off at a loping, stealthy run through the camp. At this southern extreme of the wedge-shaped plateau, the buildings were sparse and simple. Dark, too. Oddly silent, even. The Hunter's eyes narrowed as he passed his *third* street without spotting a single torch, candle, or lantern. No snores emanated from the open windows, no doors creaked, and not a single muttered conversation reached his ears. The only sound came from farther west, where the Consortium slavers cracked their whips and drove their captives toward the scaffolding descending out of sight beneath the cliffs.

The Hunter had chosen this part of the city-sized camp intentionally because in the time he and the others had spent watching it from atop the hill, he hadn't seen any movement here. Yet now it felt...odd. A glaring absence of life considering the commotion and bustle closer to the Bondshold.

The farther he went, the more convinced he became that *something* was off. By his reckoning, there was housing enough for twenty thousand. There had been at least two or three thousand near the Serenii tower—mostly the slaves toiling at whatever labor the Consortium had set them to, along with their armored, whip-wielding captors—and the Hunter suspected there would be more sleeping, eating, or taking their ease among the remainder of the city-sized camp. Yet that still left easily *half* the city unoccupied.

Unease settled in the pit of his stomach. Had the encampment been built to accommodate an existing force, or in anticipation of further arrivals? Was the Consortium even now sending more troops to occupy the city? Were more Ordermen on their way to join whatever enterprise brought them to the Bondshold? Or had the city's builders constructed these dwellings on the orders of a commander who believed the local tribes could be swayed to their cause? After all, the Tefaye had been *invited* to *Ukuhlushwa Okungapheli* to "discuss terms of some arrangement mutually beneficial to their tribe and the *alay-alagbara.*" They could have very well intended to offer the Tefaye a permanent home, an offer they doubtless believed would entice the outcasts to consider an alliance against those who had banished them.

The Hunter was snapped from his contemplation by a familiar sound: drunken singing, accompanied by the scuff of heavy boots on stone. A figure staggered into view between two houses just twenty paces ahead of them. A man, visibly inebriated and terribly off-balance from the effects of whatever alcohol he'd imbibed—something potent and foul-smelling that seemed to emanate from every pore, soak every thread of his dull grey tunic. He wore no armor, carried no sword, yet his burly build and scarred knuckles identified him as a fighting man. Consortium, likely.

A thought flashed through the Hunter's mind. *But maybe an Orderman?*

He did not know why the Order of Mithridas had worn those black slashwyrm scale masks the night they attacked him on the road to Malandria—merely to hide their features, to intimidate their foes, or for some religious reason? Again, they'd been masked when picking up their cartloads of dimercurite from the Consortium camp in the jungle. But it wasn't a stretch to imagine they removed their masks in their off-hours.

And if he is an Orderman, he might be able to tell us a thing or two about what they're really doing here.

The Hunter waved a hand to get Kodyn and Aisha's attention, and silently beckoned them to accompany him. They shot him curious looks but followed without hesitation as he slipped down a side street that cut a path parallel to the one along which the drunken man staggered. They kept pace easily with the sot; the fool was so deep in his cups he wouldn't have noticed the three shadows behind him if they'd come up and put a dagger into his spine. His attention was consumed entirely with staying upright and belting out a terribly off-tune drinking song through the frequent interruption of wet belches.

Finally, the drunkard staggered into one of the houses, and the Hunter shot a grin to his young companions. He stopped outside the door and gestured for them to wait. They nodded and kept to the shadows while he slid into the single-story structure.

The sound of snoring greeted his entrance. It did not come from the small cot in the corner of the cramped room, though. The man lay sprawled on the dirt floor just inside the door. He'd lost his battle with gravity and alcohol, it seemed.

The Hunter glanced around the sparsely furnished dwelling. A wooden table with two rickety chairs, the cot, and a small chest were the only comforts the man possessed. If there'd been any question as to his identity—Orderman or Consortium—they were immediately put to rest by the sight of the studded leather vest lying on the table alongside the standard-issue greatknife.

The Hunter's lip curled. *A waste of time.*

He turned to go, then stopped.

Or is it? An idea occurred to him, one he hadn't entertained before, but now held a measure of appeal. He considered it a moment longer, then gave in.

Slipping toward the table, he hefted the armor and held it up. It was about the right size, though a bit stretched in the midsection.

It'll have to do, he thought, and set about stripping off his cloak.

When he emerged from the small house a few minutes later, Kodyn and Aisha's eyes widened at the sight of him dressed in the stolen armor, along with the clothing the drunkard had been wearing. Though the shirt was stained with a truly fetid-smelling alcohol, the trousers remained unsoiled. The gods had seen fit to fortify the drunkard's bladder enough that he'd only pissed himself *after* the Hunter undressed him—then buried a stiletto in his brain.

A truly undignified way to go to the Long Keeper, he thought with a sneer, *but one befitting a slaver.*

Chapter Twenty-Eight

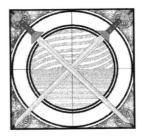

Despite his newly acquired disguise, the Hunter kept to the shadows as he moved deeper into his enemy's encampment. Better to remain unseen for as long as possible and only rely on trickery when necessary. Less scrutiny and interest meant less likelihood of discovery.

Not that he doubted the façade would hold up. The Consortium was comprised of a motley collection of men and women from every corner of Einan. He could easily pass as just one more slaver, even without shifting his features. The only thing marking him as anything out of the ordinary was the dark grey cloak he used to blend into the darkness and conceal his weapons. He'd talked his way out of far trickier situations with far less effective disguises.

Still, decades of hard experience had taught him never to take anything for granted. One wrong word or movement, even the simplest hand gesture, could shatter even the most detailed illusion. Remaining out of sight unless otherwise unavoidable was *always* the smartest play.

Aisha and Kodyn trailed a dozen paces or so behind him. That had been Kodyn's idea, and a clever one at that. The separation made it easier for the Hunter to shed stealth in an instant without risking his companions being discovered.

Not that there's much chance of that happening at the moment, the Hunter thought wryly. *It's a bloody ghost town around here!*

Save for the one drunkard who had kindly provided the Hunter's disguise, they hadn't spotted a single soul as they moved through the darkened streets bordering the plateau's southern cliff. Indeed, were it not for the light shining to the north, nearer the base of the Bondshold, the city could have appeared abandoned.

But the Hunter knew better. There had been plenty of movement among the buildings along the camp's northern edge, and the tumult echoing from around the Serenii tower hadn't diminished despite the late hour.

The Hunter slowed as he approached another intersection of streets, clinging to the shadows and scanning the way ahead for any sign of movement or glimmer of light. None appeared. He sniffed the air in search of any scents. Nothing but the sulfurous stink rising from the Valley of Living Fire filled his nostrils. The stench drowned out any lingering odors that might have been left by anyone who might have once occupied the dark, quiet houses around him.

Anxiety twisted in his belly, tightened the knots in his shoulders. He *hated* when things seemed too easy. It always filled him with anticipation and dread, as if some greater danger would befall him at any moment.

Give me impossible odds to overcome over a stroll in the park any day.

With effort, he drew in a deep breath and forced down the simmering worry. The night was still young. No sense summoning disaster unnecessarily.

He glided from shadow to shadow, silent as darkness and stealthy as a wraith. Pausing at intersections, racing across open spaces, ducking between houses and slipping down side alleys. Always keeping out of sight while hurrying as fast as he dared. Ever-closer to his true destination.

The Bondshold loomed high overhead, terrifying and impressive from up close. The shimmering, twinkling lights dotting its glassy obsidian surface drew his gaze time and again, and always left him reeling, his head aching. Whether it was merely the ever-shifting surface or some innate magic emanating from the tower, he did not know. All he knew was that *Ukuhlushwa Okungapheli* was utterly unlike any of the Serenii structures he'd encountered in his journeys around Einan. Something about it struck him as odd, perplexing even, but he could not quite discern what.

Fortunately for him, he soon had plenty of *human* structures to occupy his attention. The closer he drew to the tower, the thicker the buildings clustered, and the more people moved among them. Lanterns and lamps shone in windows. Shouts, laughter, and the mutter of conversation drifted from what appeared to be drinking houses and eating halls. People both in and out of Consortium armor moved through the city singly, in pairs, and in larger groups. More than once, the Hunter was forced to slow his progress or detour farther south toward the cliff's edge to evade packs of men and women going about whatever it was slavers did in their downtime.

A low whistle from behind him drew the Hunter's attention. Pausing in the shadows of what appeared to be a vacant house, the Hunter glanced over his shoulder. Kodyn and Aisha were just ten paces behind him, all but invisible in the darkness. Even the Hunter's keen eyes could barely make out Kodyn's movements as the young man gestured to the northeast, then tapped his chest.

The Hunter raised an eyebrow, but gave a single nod of acknowledgement. The next moment, Kodyn had vanished completely from sight and Aisha was darting across the empty street toward him.

"He'll meet us back where we entered," Aisha said in a whisper so low it was nearly lost on the evening breeze. "First sign of trouble, he's a ghost."

The Hunter nodded. "Let's just hope he finds something of use."

The young Hawk had insisted on coming along, but not, as the Hunter had expected, to worry over Aisha. Instead, he'd determined to put his Night Guild-honed skills to use breaking into whatever manner of offices the Consortium or Order of Mithridas had established here and add to his collection of stolen documents. No telling what he'd find, but hopefully something of value—details of the operations here, the identities of those backing the immense undertaking, duty rosters that could indicate the size of the force quartered within the city, and more—that could be used to put an end to the Consortium's enterprise here in Ghandia. If nothing else, he might find something to inform the battle strategy in the impending war against the *alay-alagbara*.

The Hunter would help Aisha locate—and, with luck, liberate—her father, sister, and the rest of the captive *Umoyahlebe*. Along the way, he fully intended to capture an Orderman to put to the question. The more he could learn about their mysterious organization, including their intentions here and the ultimate objective that had brought them back from supposed extinction, the better.

The Hunter had just begun to step out of the shadows when Aisha's hand caught his arm and held him fast. He glanced over his shoulder, and found a worried look on her face.

"Something's wrong," she whispered.

432

The Hunter snorted softly. "*All* of this is wrong. You'll have to be more specific."

Aisha didn't smile. She merely lifted her *Dy'nashia* pendant from beneath her tunic and held it up. "There are no *Kish'aa* here." The stone was dark, and if any power radiated from its depths, it was too faint for the Hunter to feel.

The Hunter cocked his head. "What do you mean?"

"The spirits." Aisha shook her head. "The fellow you killed, he's the only *Kish'aa* I've encountered since we crossed over the wall. All of those houses back there, the empty ones, there wasn't a single spirit among them."

"So no one died there?" That seemed the most logical answer.

"Maybe." Aisha shrugged. "But since we came over that wall, I've been searching for any *Kish'aa*, and I haven't come across a single one. You can't say that doesn't strike you as odd."

The Hunter frowned. It was, indeed, odd. Implausible, even. He couldn't begin to predict the behaviors of spirits—that was the realm of priests and Spirit Whisperers—but he'd seen and made enough corpses over his years in Voramis to know that in a city this size, at least *one* person should have died. From illness, a drunken fight gone wrong, even some hapless fool accidentally slitting his own throat while shaving.

"What do you think happened?" he asked. This was her area of expertise.

"I don't know." Aisha's jaw muscles clenched. "And that's what worries me."

The Hunter considered her words. "Maybe that has something to do with it?" He gestured toward the Bondshold. "The Serenii created Soulhunger to consume the life force of its victims. Surely it's not impossible to believe they built a tower with the same capabilities?"

"Maybe." The shadows concealing Aisha's face deepened.

The Hunter sensed her worry, and had no way to alleviate it. "Best way to know for sure is to keep looking." He kept his tone light, adding a nonchalant shrug for emphasis. "Might be we find a simple explanation ahead."

"Agreed." Aisha nodded. She didn't appear greatly relieved, but a hint of the worry had drained from her face.

Without a word, the Hunter set off, continuing the way he'd been headed before Kodyn's interruption. He'd taken just three steps when the smell hit him. A familiar stink, one that brought back memories far more terrifying than he'd care to admit.

Decaying vegetation and meat. The smell of slashwyrms.

It took the Hunter a few seconds to quieten the suddenly quickened beat of his pulse, and in that time, his mind registered the subtle difference between this scent and those he'd encountered in the marshes of *Indawo Yokwesaba*. The meaty smell was sickly sweet and putrid. The stench of rotting flesh.

The Hunter stopped within the concealment of a single-story house and peered around the corner. Thirty paces up the street, half a dozen torches shone within a large, roofless enclosure formed of a circular stone wall closed in on three sides. The wooden gate was thrown open to reveal the occupants inside. Four burly figures clad in butcher's aprons and wielding enormous cleavers and sharp-tipped hooks worked at pulling oily black scales free from the hulking corpse of a slashwyrm.

The Hunter's eyes shot up. He recognized the beast—or the pieces of it. It was the slashwyrm Aisha had killed the first night in the marshes, the same beast that Thrax, Ahmoud, and their nameless companion had found. Not much was left of the ravaged, torn-open body, and what remained was foul with writhing maggots and reeking to the high heavens. The four laboring to pry loose the few scales still clinging to rotted flesh wore thick leather masks that concealed their features—but which the Hunter knew failed to fully drown out the stench.

As he watched, one of the butchers finally pulled free a scale and held it up to the light for scrutiny. It was nearly as large as his chest and thicker than the butcher's cleaver he wielded. Incredibly tough, too, at least it had been while the beast was alive. The man shouted something the Hunter could not hear to his companions and hauled his prize off to one side of the enclosure to deposit it into a wooden crate overflowing with more identical scales. Again the man shouted, this time accompanying it with a wave of his hand. One of the masked figures abandoned their fruitless efforts to pry a scale free of the rotting slashwyrm's spine and came over to help his companion to lift the crate. Grunting and groaning beneath the strain of their burden, they lumbered out of the enclosure.

Excitement surged within the Hunter. *And where might you be going?* A grin split his lips. *A delivery to your masters of the Order of Mithridas, perhaps?*

The Hunter gestured for Aisha to follow him, and the two of them slipped through the darkness in pursuit of the departing butchers. With every step, the Hunter's excitement grew. Thus far, he'd only caught glimpses of the Ordermen, just enough to prove that Nashat al-Azzam's information had been correct but nothing concrete.

But this…this was tangible, undeniable proof!

Those scales could only be headed for one destination: the Order of Mithridas, to be carved into their hideous beast masks.

All the Hunter needed to do now was follow the cargo until it led him to the foes he'd crossed half a continent to find.

Chapter Twenty-Nine

The Hunter's gamble paid off a mere few minutes later. The crate-carrying goons in the gore-splattered butcher's aprons led him straight toward the huge brass-domed building he'd spotted from atop the hill overlooking the plateau. His heart sprang into his throat as he caught sight of the dozen or so figures visible on guard around the vast structure's southern end.

All wore the same gleaming black scale masks carved with the hideous rictus grins of the four-horned, wide-nostriled beast. Beneath their dark grey cloaks, they wore only simple tunics, vests, and trousers, but carried a vast array of armaments between them: Legion-issue throwing axes and Fehlan-style greataxes, swords of all shapes and sizes, spears, halberds, wooden staves tipped with sickle-like blades, clubs, maces, metal-shod quarterstaffs, crossbows, flails, whips, rope darts, and many more the Hunter had never seen before—and that was saying a great deal, given the vast weapon collection he'd amassed over the decades.

The absence of armor did nothing to detract from the professional air they exuded. In stark contrast to the Consortium guards patrolling the wall or stationed at the gate, the Ordermen stood firm at their posts, their masked faces perpetually turning, eyes scanning their surrounding with the wary alertness of well-trained soldiers or guards. Their polished boots, well-maintained weaponry, and unblemished clothing spoke volumes about their competence.

As the crate-bearing goons approached, two of the Ordermen stepped forward to intercept them with lowered weapons—a curved *tulwar* of the sort favored by the Vothmoti and a polearm-mounted axe called a bardiche, popular among Odarians. A handful of words passed between the Ordermen and the brutes, then the weapons were raised for the pair to pass. The masked guards returned to their stations with crisp, precise steps and once more assumed their wary, alert posture.

The Hunter grimaced. *I suppose it was too much to ask for an entire city full of incompetents.* Not that he'd truly been expecting the Order of Mithridas to field fools. Their attack on the Cambionari caravan had taught him they were not a foe to take lightly.

The confirmation of their presence here elated him, but brought a whole new set of questions, too. They had hundreds of Consortium guards at their command, yet they stood watch here in person. What could be so important to the Order that they'd set their own people to guard it?

He got his answer a few seconds later when the double doors set into the huge domed building's south side swung open to admit the two slashwyrm butchers. Through the grand aperture, the Hunter caught a glimpse of the building's interior. A stack of wooden crates identical to the one being hauled by the goons stood just within, piled beside the door as if prepared to be carted away.

But it was what stood *beyond* the crates that drew the Hunter's attention. The interior of the domed building was ringed with columns like some grand temple or palace atrium, but instead of marble or granite, these columns were forged of metal. A single thick chain stretched from column to column, forming what looked like a cattle pen. Only it was no herd imprisoned within. People—men, women, even children, their dark features difficult to make out in the faint lamplight spilling through the open doorway—sat, stood, or sprawled about.

Anger burned in the Hunter's chest. Ghandians. Dozens, perhaps even scores. Locked up inside the domed building and guarded by the Order of Mithridas.

No doubt about it: he had found the *Umoyahlebe*.

Behind him, he heard Aisha's furious hiss, accompanied by the creak of wood. He glanced over his shoulder and found her glaring at the open gates. Her knuckles were white around the haft of her spear, her other hand even now reaching for the hilt of her sheathed dirk. She appeared on the verge of bursting from the shadows and charging the dozen Ordermen standing between her and her fellow Spirit Whisperers.

Quick as a striking snake, he darted toward her, seized her by the spear arm, and dragged her deeper into the shadows behind one of the empty houses. She had no time to respond before he had her out of sight of the domed building and pressed up against a wooden wall.

"Do not!" he hissed, fixing her with a warning glare. "You will do your father and sister no good getting yourself killed!"

Aisha's eyes flashed blue-white and she opened her mouth, a retort forming on her lips.

The Hunter shook his head. "Think!" He squeezed her arm tighter, stopping just short of rendering her weapon arm numb. "We cannot act in haste. Yours is not the only life you would risk by storming in like a hurricane!"

His words—or perhaps it was his iron-hard grip on her arm—seemed to get through to her. Her mouth snapped shut with an audible *click* of her teeth and, with visible effort, she managed a curt nod.

The Hunter released her, but did not step back. "We have found them, but that is not the only reason we came tonight." He spoke quickly, urgency in his voice. He had to convince her not to act. At least not yet. "We came to learn about our enemies' plans. We can learn nothing if we are forced to flee now. First we gather information, then we act. Understood?"

For a moment, he feared she would ignore him. The blue-white sparks still danced in her eyes, growing brighter with every beat of the Hunter's heart. If they formed around her fists or the head of her spear the way they often did when her emotions ran hot, the light would surely draw the attention of the fully alert Ordermen standing not thirty paces away. But what else could he say or do to make her understand that he counseled restraint out of expediency and not fear?

To his relief, Aisha nodded again. "Understood," she whispered through clenched teeth. The blue-white light slowly faded from her eyes and her fists unclenched.

"Good." The Hunter willed his pulse to cease racing, his heart to slow. He was tempted to extract from her a solemn vow not to do anything rash, but discarded the idea after a moment's contemplation. She was once more in control of her emotions. He'd trust she wouldn't give in to her rage, now that she had a moment to consider the best course of action. "We watch and wait."

He was just turning back to poke his head out from behind the house when something to the northeast caught his attention. Two or three hundred paces away, an expansive flat-roofed building similar in design to the warehouse built within the Consortium camp rose high above the rest of the human-built structures, save the one the Ordermen guarded. Neatly arrayed in front of the six-story building were the covered wagons that had visited and departed the jungle mining operation. No sign of their drivers, the raya that had pulled them, nor their Ujana escort. Yet there was no mistake: those *were* the carts.

Curiosity flared within the Hunter. He had wondered what the Order of Mithridas wanted with the dimercurite, or why it was so valuable they had contracted the Vassalage Consortium to capture and transport in the slaves necessary to extract it from the ground.

Time to find out for certain.

He turned to Aisha. "I'm going to explore deeper into the camp, get as close to *Ukuhlushwa Okungapheli* as I can. I'll blend in like this." He gestured to his armor. "But I need *you* to stay here. Watch that building, take note of everything and anything that happens. And when I get back, we'll figure out the best move to make."

Aisha's jaw set in a stubborn cast and her strong shoulders squared. "We have not come all this way to leave empty-handed."

The Hunter heard the threat and promise in her words. One way or another, she was determined to free her sister and father *tonight*. Even if that meant fighting through the entire camp—which, admittedly, the two of them stood a surprisingly decent chance of doing.

"Nor do I intend to." It was no lie. The Hunter planned to come away from this visit with *information,* if nothing else. If they were fortunate enough to get in and out unnoticed, they could enter the camp the next night, this time armed with a well-crafted plan and reinforcements in the form of Kiara and Tarek. Five of them stood a far better chance of achieving the impossible than just *two*. "Just swear to me you'll wait until I return."

Aisha bared her teeth, but growled out, "I swear," in a low, angry voice.

The Hunter had to accept that. She hadn't survived all these years in the Night Guild acting in haste. He had to trust that despite being so close to her father and sister—so close she could almost reach out and touch them—she'd keep her head. At least long enough for him to return.

Swallowing the anxiety worming through his gut, he cast one last glance in Aisha's direction before slipping through the dark, quiet streets toward the huge building where he'd spotted the carts. He drew within fifty paces of the structure before he had to abandon the shadows. Fortunately for him, there were no Consortium guards or Ordermen around. The perimeter was unlit and unguarded—and, it turned out when he tested the huge double doors, unlocked.

He grimaced as the squeal of un-oiled hinges echoed through the night, but slipped inside the huge structure and shut the door behind him before anyone came to investigate. Inside, the darkness was all-consuming and oppressive. Bloody hot, too. The smoky, metallic smell of a blast furnace filled the interior, amplified by the stink of burned hair, scorched steel, charred wood, and burning coal. It reminded the Hunter a great deal of the inside of Belros' smithy on Kara-ket, only instead of stinging iron dust in the air, the Hunter's nostrils detected a smell at once unfamiliar and familiar.

Dimercurite, he thought. *And yet not?*

A faint reddish glow came from the far end of the huge building—the furnace the Hunter had smelled—and cast paltry light on the structure's interior. To his right stood a pile of tar-black coal. Fuel for the fire that now burned low in the furnace. To his left, a knee-high pile of dimercurite was all that remained of the load transported here by the fifteen carts.

So where's the rest?

He slipped deeper into the building, careful not to step on loose coal or chunks of dimercurite. Beyond, ten empty wheelbarrows stood next to each pile, with twenty shovels scattered around. A trail of black dust marked the path taken by the workers—doubtless captive Ghandians—hauling the minerals toward the furnace.

The Hunter's eyes narrowed as he approached the furnace. The fire was low, all but burned out save for the last glowing embers. No smith worth their wages would ever allow so much ash to accumulate within, even the Hunter knew that. That, combined with the tools that now lay discarded around the wheelbarrows, spoke volumes. The furnace had served its purpose and was no longer needed.

But what purpose is that? the Hunter couldn't help but wonder.

He studied the furnace. It appeared much like any other—a main chamber in which fuel was burned, connected to a massive bellows that pumped in air to stoke the fire hot enough to turn solid metal into molten liquid. A line of black dust led from the pile of dimercurite toward the massive smelting pot that hung over the burning chamber.

So they were smelting the dimercurite. The Hunter's lips pursed into a frown. *The question is, what were they mak—*

The squeal of hinges shattered the silence, and the brilliant orange light of a lantern suddenly flooded the warehouse.

"Oi, you!" came a strident shout. "What in the Keeper's 'orny elbows are you doin' in 'ere?"

Chapter Thirty

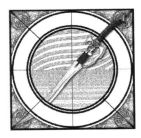

Every shred of the Hunter's willpower went into fighting the urge to spin around and confront the speaker. Such a violent reaction would only cement the appearance of guilt and further inflame the suspicion of whoever had spotted him.

"Doing my duty," he called over his shoulder, adopting the accent and harsh timbre he'd developed for the sellsword Hardwell of Praamis persona. With a slow, unhurried pace, he advanced toward the furnace and crouched down to peer into the chamber with the still-burning coals. After a moment, he gave a satisfied grunt, stood, and turned around. "All good."

He found himself confronted by a man and woman hurrying toward him. Both wore the studded leather armor of the Consortium. The woman held a lantern high to illuminate the enormous building's interior, and the man had drawn his greatknife. Suspicion shone plain in both their expressions.

"Don't worry." The Hunter shook his head. "Furnace is burned down low enough there's no risk of a stray spark catching anything alight."

The slavers' steps faltered, and they exchanged confused glances.

"*That's* what you're doin'?" the man asked. "Checkin' the fire?"

"Aye." The Hunter looked between the pair. "Wait, was one of *you* supposed to do that?" He threw up his hands. "Keeper take it, I'm supposed to be face-down and well into sleep by now, and you're telling me I got dragged out of bed for a duty already assigned to someone else?"

The man and woman stopped a few paces in front of him. The lantern remained high, but the greatknife lowered a fraction.

"Checking the fire," repeated the woman, visibly struggling to believe his words. "In the dark?"

"How else?" The Hunter shot her a look as if she were mad. "Hard to see errant sparks flying otherwise." The idea had sprung to his mind in the desperation of the moment—perhaps not his finest or most plausible, but at least it explained his presence.

Again the perplexed glances passed between them. Then a knowing look dawned on both their faces.

"Saindz!" they said in unison.

A scowl twisted the man's lips. "Of course that cunt Saindz'd be puttin' you up to somethin' like this." He shook his head. "Fussy prick never met a task 'e didn't want double and triple-checked. And for no better reason than 'e don't trust no one to do a 'alfway decent job. Fella spends three years in the Legion of 'Eroes and suddenly 'e thinks 'e's some 'igh and mighty general and the rest of us is so much dog meat."

The Hunter sneered. "Popular fellow, eh?"

"You could say that." The woman nodded, a sour look twisting her lips. "More'n a few of us have come within a whisker's breadth of walking away 'cause of that uppity prick."

"More'n a few of us have contemplated 'elpin' 'im accidentally fall off the nearest cliff," the man added with a growl.

The Hunter chuckled. "And the world would be a far poorer place for his absence!" He mimicked raising an imaginary goblet, earning a pair of sharp grins from the two slavers. "Well, now that's done and dusted, it's back to bed for me. Dawn patrol comes far too soon."

He made to stride past the two, but the man's hand on his shoulder stopped him. "Not to pile on, but while you're 'ere, might be you'd lend Tolla'n'me a 'and?" His smell of moldy leather, charred steak, and the *tabacc* that stained his teeth yellow proved powerfully pungent.

The Hunter gave a theatrical groan. "Oh, for the Keep—"

"Quick as a virgin's prick, I swear!" the man insisted. "Just got a crate as needs movin', and me with the misfortune of throwing out my back crawlin' out of bed this evenin'." With a theatrical groan, he removed his hand from the Hunter's shoulder and pressed it against his lower back. "Tolla's tough, but even she cain't move it all on 'er lonesome."

The woman, Tolla, rolled her eyes. "Not like you can either, Rhodd."

"Aye, aye." Rhodd gave a dismissive wave of his hand. "Look, if it tips the scales, I'll refill your cup next time our paths cross at the ale line."

The Hunter pretended to contemplate the matter, then nodded with a begrudging look on his face. "One crate." He held up a single finger. "And *two* refills."

"Deal!" Rhodd clapped the Hunter on the shoulder. "Crate's back 'ere."

The Hunter fell in behind the two slavers, following them around the furnace's left side. In the light of Tolla's lantern, the Hunter could make out more details of the massive room: a pair of anvils and smiths' tools, quenching barrels filled to the brim with metallic-smelling water, and a small pile of what appeared to be discarded slag of a color not quite as dark as dimercurite. Clearly the stone had been melted down and mixed with some other mineral—but what, the Hunter didn't know.

"This one." Rhodd's voice, accompanied by a heavy thump and metallic clatter, drew the Hunter's attention to a long wooden crate that sat beside one of the two anvils. The lid had been placed upon it but not hammered down, and Rhodd's kick had dislodged it just enough for the Hunter to catch sight of the objects within.

Chains. His gut twisted. *But made with dimercurite?*

His knowledge of steelmaking was rudimentary, though he had an adequate understanding of why carbon was mixed with iron to produce a tougher, more resilient metal. Dimercurite could share similar properties with carbon or result in some entirely new effect altogether. Only a truly experienced smith or alchemist would understand the purpose for the combination. It was possible such a mixture could result in a new and superior form of steel— for example, Shalandran or Odarian steel, each of which contained their own proprietary ingredients.

"Take this," Tolla said, thrusting the lantern at Rhodd. "Less'n you think your delicate back won't bear up under the weight."

For answer, Rhodd shot back a curse favored among the street rats of Voramis. Tolla, too, had the look of a Voramian—she even smelled faintly of netting and the salt brine air that eternally pervaded the streets of Fisherman's End, along with marigold and bitterroot. Fortunately for him, though all in his city knew the name of the Hunter of Voramis, none had seen his true face. Even the one he now wore was the harsher, sterner features he typically adopted for Hardwell.

"Come on, then," Tolla growled up at him from where she crouched and gripped one side of the long crate. "Sooner we get this where it needs to go, sooner you're off to bed and we're off to find some bread that ain't moldy or harder'n Rhodd's skull."

The Hunter snorted a chuckle, more for Tolla's sake than out of any real mirth. Bending, he gave an exaggerated grunt of effort as he helped to lift the crate. His Bucelarii muscles could bear up under the weight with little difficulty, but the two slavers expected to see him struggle, so struggle he did. Indeed, he put on quite the show, sweating and straining and cursing as he and Tolla hauled the crate deeper into the warehouse and out a pair of double doors which Rhodd opened for them.

They exited out of the building's northern end, which led onto a mud road that bore the deep imprints of wagon and wheelbarrow wheels running straight toward the Bondshold.

"We taking it there?" he asked, jerking his head toward the Serenii tower.

Tolla's face creased into a frown. The look she gave him was tinged with suspicion and incredulity, as if he'd just asked a truly stupid question.

The Hunter cursed inwardly. He should have figured the chains could *only* be headed in the direction of the captives laboring on the cliffside scaffolding he'd spotted.

To cover, he quickly added, "Don't tell me that bloody thing don't give you the creeps!" He shuddered theatrically. "Sets my head aching every time I just look its way."

"Aye, so it does," Rhodd spoke up from where he strode beside the sweating, straining Tolla and the Hunter.

"Way I…hear it…place is…some sort of…magic." Tolla's pronouncement was punctuated by gasping breaths. "Some sort…of ancient…foolery. Don't understand it…don't want to." She shook her head. "Just want…to get paid…and do my job. Questions…is for fools…and dead men."

That intrigued the Hunter. He glanced at Rhodd. The man's expression mirrored Tolla's: a generous amount of suspicion and anxiety mixed with the stubborn look of willful ignorance.

They're being kept in the dark? He frowned inwardly. *The Order isn't telling them what they're doing here?*

That certainly fit with what he'd heard of the Order of Mithridas. Father Reverentus had called their ultimate aims a mystery. Indeed, the organization had apparently earned a reputation for going to extremes to conceal their true purposes—even compelling their members to commit suicide rather than break under questioning.

If, as the Hunter had come to believe, the Order had hired the Consortium to run their operations—both here and in the jungle—they needn't have revealed all the details to their paid lackeys. Or, at least not those as low down on the chain of command as these two.

"You don't mind me askin', wha'd you do to get you stuck 'ere?"

Rhodd's question snapped the Hunter from his thoughts.

"What's…that…mean?" the Hunter asked, pretending to huff and puff like Tolla.

"Nothin' meant by it." Rhodd held up his free hand in a defensive gesture. "Just curious, is all." He gestured to himself. "Me, I've got this bum back. Damned thing has a 'abit of actin' up at the worst times. As for Tolla 'ere, well…" He clucked his tongue. "Let's just say she punched a few too many of the wrong people who tried to put their 'ands down the wrong pants."

441

Tolla bared her teeth in a feral snarl. "None of 'em...looked any worse...for the missing teeth!"

"No judgment 'ere," Rhodd continued, his tone innocent, "just can't 'elp wonderin' what a big'un like you did to get left behind. Seems like you're just the sort who'd be marchin' out with the rest, yet 'ere's you, stuck with the likes of us. So I figured I'd ask—"

The Hunter never had time to ponder Rhodd's question, or even to hear the rest of the words out of his mouth, for in that moment, they rounded the last building standing between him and the Bondshold. The tip of the plateau was cleared for a hundred paces around the base of the Serenii tower, with not so much as a storage shed or shack standing there. But it was far from empty.

Under the watchful eyes of whip-wielding slavers, hundreds of umber-skinned Ghandians moved about, hauling buckets, pushing wheelbarrows, carrying tools, or dragging barrels of water. None wore chains, yet every one had the bedraggled, weary, hollow-eyed look of captives. They were even gaunter and more emaciated than those liberated from the camp within the jungle, which spoke of longer months—perhaps even *years*—in captivity.

Yet Ghandians were not the only ones enslaved here. Flaxen-haired Fehlans and Princelanders toiled next to golden-skinned Vothmoti, swarthy men and women of the Twelve Kingdoms, Voramis, Praamians, Malandrians, Drashi, Hrandari plainsfolk, Odarians, even those from the distant Kurma Empire. More than a thousand people were visible on the mud-churned plateau and the tops of the scaffolding built into the cliff. Keeper alone knew how many more were hard at work below.

The sheer scale of the enterprise boggled the Hunter's mind. What he'd seen on the road from the Zamani Falls and in the Consortium camp was just a sliver of the whole. An undertaking of this immensity had to have cost the Order more gold than filled the coffers of King Gavian and the entire nobility of Voramis. And for what? What was so important they'd foot such a gargantuan bill?

Again, his eyes strayed toward *Ukuhlushwa Okungapheli*, at its shimmering, glassy black surface dotted with millions of twinkling lights. But instead of staring up at its immense heights, his gaze was drawn toward where the base of the tower jutted up from the ground into which it had been built. There, he spotted a vast door easily ten paces tall and twice as wide, carved of a stone fractionally lighter in color than the midnight-hued material used in the tower's construction.

A shiver ran down the Hunter's spine. *Dimercurite.* The light of the countless torches, braziers, and lanterns burning around the plateau reflected off the enormous door, reflecting a reddish-orange hue just as the stones in the jungle camp had.

That was when the Hunter spotted the figures in front of the Bondshold. Fifty men and women, all chained and clad in rags, on their knees or lying sprawled on the muddy ground. Lips dark and distended, teeth falling from rotting black gums. Even from this distance, the Hunter recognized the truth: every one of them was dying, the same way the Issai warriors and so many others had been dying the night he freed Davathi and the *amaqhawe.*

Dimercurite poisoning. His heart sank. *It's killing them, slowly, painfully.*

But the fifty dying captives were not alone. A dozen Ordermen stood over them, staring down with pitiless eyes and black-masked faces.

A thirteenth Orderman stood apart from the rest, facing the enormous stone door, hands clasped behind their back. After a long moment, the lone figure turned and gave a single sharp nod of their head.

As one, the twelve drew their weapons—swords, axes, spears, maces, clubs, and more—and set to the grim work of slaughtering the dying captives.

Chapter Thirty-One

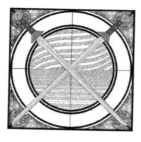

Horror twisted in the Hunter's gut at the sight of the senseless carnage. It didn't matter that the victims were suffering and well on their way to succumbing to the terrible effects of dimercurite poisoning. This was butchery, plain, simple, and utterly sickening.

He nearly dropped the crate then and there. Every fiber of his being shrieked at him to draw his weapons and wade into the Ordermen with bared steel. Soulhunger and *Ibad'at Mutlaqa* would make mincemeat of the black-masked bastards. Even if every one of them wielded iron—he could not tell for certain at this distance—they stood no chance against him and the arcane power inherent in his blades.

With a supreme effort of will, he compelled his fingers to tighten around the corners of the crate. Wood creaked beneath the force of his grip. Yet he did not abandon his pretense. Nor did he look away as every one of the captives kneeling and lying in the muck fell beneath the Order of Mithridas.

Swords thrust, axes fell, maces *crunched* into skulls, and spears pierced flesh with precision. No malice, enmity, or hatred drove them. The dispassion of their massacre only made it all the crueler. They simply killed for killing's sake.

What made it more gruesome and grimmer still was the silence of it all. The dying could raise no protest, no defense. The few who had strength to cry out barely managed weak gasps and pitiful moans before falling into the widening puddle of blood. Had it not been for the commotion of the slaves laboring around the scaffolding and the *crack* of the slavers' whips, the plateau would have echoed loud with meaty *thumps* of steel biting into flesh and the horrible *crunch* of shattering bones.

A low, muttered curse echoed from beside the Hunter. "Bloody animals," Rhodd snarled. His face had a queasy pallor and disgust spelled plain on his features.

Tolla just set her jaw and stubbornly refused to turn around, even when her boot heel struck a deep wheel rut in the road. She would not look at the slaughter but stared resolutely at the Hunter with a look no less revolted than Rhodd's.

Despite his loathing of the cruelty, the Hunter could not help but watch. He scrutinized the masked Ordermen doing the killing, marked the way they moved, the rise and fall of their weapons, the grace, or lack thereof, in their steps. He noted every minute detail he could of their build and their stances. Anything he could use to identify them later. Because when he came for their heads—and by the Watcher, he *would!*—he intended to drag out their deaths. They would die neither quickly nor painlessly. They would scream and rage, would howl in agony, and only after he had dragged every answer he wanted from their lips and made them suffer the way these captives had suffered up until this point, only then would he feed their souls to Soulhunger and send them to the darkest depths of the forgotten hell.

444

To the Hunter's horror, Tolla and Rhodd led him on a direct path toward the slaughter. Their steps carried them just to the edge of the pool of blood—where the Hunter now saw the churned-up mud was stained red with far more crimson than had flowed from these fifty corpses. Tolla dropped her side of the crate so abruptly it nearly slammed down on the Hunter's boots. He barely managed to release his end and step out of the way as it crashed onto the muddy ground. A cacophonous rattling of chains echoed from within and the lid fell free. But neither Rhodd nor Tolla seemed to care. They were hustling back the way they'd come as fast as their feet could carry them.

The Hunter had just turned to follow when a harsh, masculine voice stopped him in his tracks.

"You there!"

He froze, glancing back toward the Ordermen.

The one who'd been standing facing *Ukuhlushwa Okungapheli* had now turned. His eyes, the only thing visible behind his black snarling beast mask, fixed on the Hunter.

"Pick it up." The command was imperious, sharp.

The Hunter blinked. "What?" He had to maintain the façade, play the role of dull-witted slaver.

"The crate," came the voice from beneath the mask. A cruel voice, hard as stone and cold as ice, edged with the crisp accent of a Voramian nobleman. "Pick. It. Up." He pronounced each word with an audible sneer, and everything about him radiated scorn. "That is not where it should be left. It goes *there.*" He finally unclasped his hands from behind his back and stabbed his left forefinger toward something off to one side of the scene of carnage.

The Hunter followed the pointing finger. Close to two dozen long wooden crates identical to the one he'd helped haul all this way stood in a neat stack just a few paces in front of the enormous stone door into *Ukuhlushwa Okungapheli*.

"Begging pardon, sir," the Hunter said, adopting a thick Praamian accent and a heavy, witless slowness to his voice, "but it's heavy. Too heavy for one—"

"I said pick it up!" Anger flashed in the Orderman's eyes, and he stalked toward the Hunter with crisp, furious steps. "You lot answer to *us*. We say run, you ask how fast. We say throw yourself off the bloody cliff, you thank us for the privilege." He stopped in front of the Hunter, and though they were of a height, the man attempted to loom over him. "You are being paid handsomely to do exactly what we tell you. So when I say pick up that crate and put it where it belongs—"

"I do it." The Hunter ducked his head. "Yes, sir." Slowly, he knelt and slid his arms beneath the crate. He made a show of wrestling to try and lift it, sweating and straining, until he finally managed to pick it up off the ground. In truth, though it was heavy, he could have managed it. Yet he wanted the Orderman who'd spoken to feel as if he'd won a great victory, to believe he'd cowed this dull-witted slaver into submission.

But he didn't win. Not truly. The Hunter pretended to stagger under the weight, lurching forward to collide with the Orderman. He put a bit of extra effort into driving the sharp corner of the crate into the masked man's solar plexus, striking it with just enough force to knock the wind from the Orderman's lungs.

He stammered out profuse apologies, plastering a terrified look on his expression, but the Orderman was too busy gasping for breath to stop the Hunter from staggering past. The Hunter had to hide a self-satisfied smile as the man bent over and leaned on his knees, wheezing and struggling to refill his lungs.

A couple of the nearby Ordermen raised their weapons and made to step in the Hunter's path, but the Hunter dissuaded them from action by lurching and stumbling around, shifting the box of chains in his arms as if he struggled to retain his grip on it. After seeing what had happened to their comrade—or was it *commander?*—they gave him a wide berth.

The Hunter put on a truly masterful performance of heaving, grunting, groaning, and wheezing with the visible effort of carrying his load. When finally he reached his destination, he dropped it in such a way that it shattered the sides of two of the stacked crates. More chains of the same dark dimercurite alloy spilled out. Again, the Hunter was profuse in his apologies as he bent to try and salvage his "mistake".

"Enough!" the Orderman roared. "I've half a mind to order you flogged. Or, perhaps, send you off to join the digging with the rest of the *chattel.*"

A shadow loomed over him, and the Hunter looked up from fumbling with the heavy chains to see the furious masked man glaring down.

"What is your name?" the Orderman demanded.

"Hardwell, sir." The Hunter ducked his head. "Hardwell of Praamis."

"Well, Hardwell of Praamis." The masked man sneered his name like a curse. "Pray to whatever god you hold dearest that our paths never cross again. Because if I lay eyes on you again, you will join them!" He stabbed a finger toward the corpses scattered across the blood-soaked ground.

"Sir, yes, sir!" The Hunter sprang to his feet and took off at a run, as if terrified for his life. Smattered laughter, jeers, and shouts pursued him. The two Ordermen who'd moved to intercept him before actually looked as if they'd try to interfere with his flight or trip him up. The Hunter saved them from the attempt by pretending to trip over his own feet. He tumbled forward in what appeared to an ungraceful sprawl, only "barely saving himself at the last moment" by flinging himself into a roll. When he finally regained his feet, he raced away without a backward glance.

But the pretense was merely for the Ordermen's benefit. His tumble had carried him close enough to the two masked men that he'd managed to catch a whiff of their scents. Unlike the man he'd fought on the road to Malandria, these hadn't the fiery reek of Ghandian lion peppers to assault his senses and conceal their unique aromas from his nostrils. There was no need for such precaution, for they couldn't possibly know that the stumbling, fumbling buffoon they'd just humiliated was, in fact, the same Bucelarii. They believed the masks and the power of their gold was all the protection they needed from "just one more slaver".

The Hunter burned their smells into his mind. The Orderman who'd spoken to him had a nobleman's scent to match his pompous voice: lavender, satin, and crabapple. The plain grey tunic and trousers he wore could no more conceal his aristocratic upbringing than the slashwyrm scale mask. As for the other two men, one smelled of tar, spruce, and bridle leather, the second of sea grass, coriander leaf, and boot black.

When the time came for him to repay these bastards for what they'd done tonight, he would seek them out and pay special attention to their torment. They would suffer for—

All thoughts of retribution vanished from his mind as he caught sight of more Ordermen marching his way. There were six of them, all armed and concealed behind the black beast-faced masks. They marched in two columns of three, and between them they herded four youths—three girls, none older than Hailen, and a man roughly of an age with Tarek. Farther back, straggling twenty paces behind the company, another Orderman dragged a white-haired man with deep age lines and sun spots on his face, gnarled limbs, and a sunken-in chest.

All five of the captives were Ghandian, though of what tribe, the Hunter could not tell. None wore the fibrous cloth battle-wrappings or brightly colored flowing robes of the Issai, nor the lion pelts of the Buhari. Instead, they were bedecked in clothes that appeared to be fashioned from straps of some tough leather or hide interwoven with colorful shells. Their garments might once have been lustrous, perhaps even opulent, but now, they were stained with mud and sweat and soiled with far worse. Their wearers were gaunt, raw-boned, and visibly terrified.

Something else about them drew the Hunter's attention. All five of the Ghandians wore bracelets, anklets, and collars of the same dark dimercurite alloy that had comprised the chains. They were not manacles, for no ropes or chains connected them, yet the Ghandians wearing them appeared no less bound for their absence.

The Hunter hurried on, ducking his head to avoid drawing the gaze of the Ordermen escorting the captives. As soon as he was past, he hurried toward the nearest building—a two-story brick structure that was little more than an uncovered enclosure, likely a holding pen of some sort to house the slaves—and slid into the shadows. There he hunkered down and turned back to study the Ordermen and their captives.

The five Ghandians were dragged toward the scene of carnage and hurled to the blood-soaked ground. The Voramian nobleman barked an order the Hunter could not hear to the dozen masked men who'd butchered the captives, and they set about hauling chains out of the crates the Hunter had broken. These were secured to the dimercurite bands on the Ghandians' wrists. But instead of shackling each prisoner separately, they joined the five together.

The Ghandians did not protest; they either hadn't the strength or were too broken to fight back. The only sign of resistance appeared when one of the Ordermen secured a chain to the collar around the old man's neck. A hard cuff to the back of his head put an end to his feeble struggles.

To the Hunter's surprise, the Voramian nobleman pulled up his sleeve to reveal a nearly-identical bracelet on his own right wrist. The only difference between his band and those adorning the prisoners was the large chunk of glittering black stone set into the metal. A sickening sensation twisted in the pit of the Hunter's stomach as the Orderman secured the chain to his bracelet.

This can be nothing good!

The Voramian Orderman stood behind the kneeling Ghandians facing the Bondshold, so the Hunter did not hear if he spoke or shouted a command. Yet as one, the five Ghandians' right hands came up and extended toward the field of corpses scattered before the Serenii tower.

The Hunter's breath froze in his lungs. *It can't be!* He'd seen Aisha stretch out her hand precisely in that way, and always when she—

Keeper's teeth, no wonder she felt something was wrong!

At that moment, the five Ghandians turned toward the enormous door at the base of *Ukuhlushwa Okungapheli* and streams of blue-white lightning burst from their outstretched hands.

The sight drove home the Hunter's realization. Aisha had sensed no *Kish'aa* because there were none to sense. Every single spirit, including those of the recently butchered captives, had been gathered by these *Umoyahlebe* and turned against the Bondshold.

Chapter Thirty-Two

The Hunter couldn't tear his eyes away from the sight of the *Umoyahlebe* assaulting the enormous entrance to the Bondshold. The white-haired elder clearly had the greatest control over his power; twin spears of lightning snaked out from his extended hands on a direct path toward the stone doors barring entry to the tower. The others, however, seemed to struggle to constrain the power. One of the young women sent a blast of blue-white sparks spraying off to her right, while the man's magic burst from him with such force it nearly knocked him from his feet. He staggered backward and only the strong hands of an Orderman kept him from collapsing.

The Hunter could only stare transfixed at the display. It was more than just the power evident—though that proved impressive enough. No, he was consumed and paralyzed by a single grim thought: *the Order of Mithridas have found a means of harnessing the Umoyahlebe power.*

The dimercurite bands and chains linking the Ghandians together somehow gave the Orderman holding their bonds the ability to command them. No way they could have moved in such unison otherwise, and the way they remained immobilized like puppets suspended from their master's strings made that much clear.

The Order of Mithridas did not need magic of their own, not when they could enslave and compel its wielders to do their bidding. That realization sent a chill rippling down the Hunter's spine.

And if they've figured out a way to bend the Umoyahlebe power to their will, what's to stop them from doing the same with the power of the Serenii?

Again, the lightning speared into the enormous stone doors guarding the Bondshold, the barrage renewed as the young man regained his footing and the woman managed to channel a concerted stream of blue-white light into the tower. So bright was it that the Hunter could not stare at it directly for fear of growing night blind, spots dancing in his eyes. While the power raged and slammed into the Serenii tower, the Hunter examined everything else visible on the plateau.

Thousands of chained and roped captives swarmed up and down the scaffolding. When descending, they carried tools for digging and hauling stone. But they did not ascend with laden barrows and heavy sacks. Indeed, always they returned empty-handed, covered head to toe with dirt, soot, and stone.

More men and women were constantly rotated in to replace those who collapsed from exhaustion, hunger, and thirst. Those too feeble to work were kicked roughly out of the way of progress by the whip-wielding slavers, after which they were ignored. When they finally managed to scrape themselves out of the dirt, they staggered on shaking legs toward the stone enclosure the Hunter guessed served as their prison. No doubt to sleep away the hours until they were next summoned to resume the backbreaking labor. Whether they were fed or given water, the Hunter did not know, but saw no evidence of any sustenance. Not so much as a crust of moldy bread or a pile of rotting fruits and vegetables anywhere near the work site.

Such cruelty, the Hunter thought grimly. *If ever I had cause to doubt that humans were as capable of monstrosity as demonkind, this would banish those in a heartbeat.*

Lord Chasteyn's final words resonated through the Hunter's mind. *"Humans raised their hands against their own. My own wife murdered children, for the Keeper's sake. How am I any worse than they? For five thousand years, I have seen what these humans are capable of, and for all they hate us, they cannot claim that we are worse than they. Every single atrocity of which we are accused, they have done the same. Rape, pillage, torture, abuse, all and more. They are as much monsters as we are."*

The words had been a pitiful attempt to stay the Hunter's hand, to delay his imprisonment in the Chamber of Sustenance beneath the Monolith in Malandria. Now, witnessing this cruelty on such a vast scale, the Hunter could not deny they held a ring of truth.

The only difference, the Hunter thought, *is that at least there are* some *good humans. Or, at the very least, some who try to be good.* He patted Soulhunger. *As for those who are truly evil, like those capable of perpetrating an atrocity like this, their fates will be no different from the demons'. Their life forces, too, will sustain Kharna. And the world will be better off for it.*

A terrible shriek of agony snapped the Hunter's attention back to the five *Umoyahlebe.* The cry came from the young man, who had fallen to his knees. Vast streams of lightning forked out of his hands, utterly wild and uncontrolled. His entire body trembled with the power coursing through him. Smoke rose from his flesh, burned his leather-and-shell clothing, set his hair ablaze.

The two young women on either side of him shrank back, terrified, and the flow of power streaming from their hands cut off abruptly. Yet, like a barrel with a broad crack, the young man could not stop the flow of magic. Indeed, it grew more wild with every passing moment, spreading outward in wider, brighter, hotter fingers. The woman to his right took a blindingly bright bolt of lightning to the side of her head and collapsed face-first to the blood-soaked ground. The one to his left managed to raise her hands to shield her face but could not stop the fingers of blue-white light from ripping into her chest and abdomen. She, too, fell to the ground, writhing in the grip of a terrible spasm.

Horror twisted in the Hunter's gut. He could not tear his eyes from the grisly scene, could not stop himself from watching the young man burned alive from the inside. For that was precisely what happened—his hair burned down to the skull, lightning shot from his eyes and wide-screaming mouth, and burst outward from his chest. When finally he fell to the ground, he lay unmoving in a limp pile. Streams of dark smoke rose from his motionless body and he did not so much as twitch.

With the young man's fall, the flow of power cut off entirely. The two remaining *Umoyahlebe* collapsed onto their hands and knees. The old man's arms gave out and he fell to his face. There he lay, gasping for breath, his chest heaving.

But the Ordermen did not let them rest. Cruel as the whoresons were, they kicked the old man and the only young woman still conscious, dragging them back upright. Though they trembled in visible exhaustion and fear, the Voramian Orderman clamped his hand on the back of the white-haired *Umoyahlebe's* neck and, once again, their hands rose and extended toward the door into the Bondshold.

The Hunter had just a heartbeat to glance at the huge stone portal before the barrage of magical energy renewed. He saw no scratch, no scorch marks, not so much as a chunk of chipped stone. A few threads of light shone in a strange swirling, circular pattern emanating outward from the spots where the magic had blasted it, but that was all the effect the assault had had on the stone.

The Hunter's gut twisted. The Serenii were the greatest builders who had ever existed on Einan, their structures truly impressive monuments that stood testament to their ingenuity. Yet as the Hunter had seen before, time and the elements could wear away at even the mightiest constructions. The Order of Mithridas were simply hastening the process. Rather than attempt to understand the Serenii magic or mechanisms that would give them access to the Bondshold, they sought to blast through it. No telling if they'd succeed, but one thing the Hunter knew for certain: they would willingly let *Umoyahlebe* die in the doing.

The Hunter's fists clenched. *That, I cannot allow!*

He'd come all this way to learn of the Order's plans, and what he'd discovered filled him with dread. But now his mission intersected with Aisha's intention to liberate her father, sister, and every other imprisoned Spirit Whisperer. Indeed, this new discovery *demanded* it. If the Order continued unchecked, they would either push every *Umoyahlebe* until they died or succeed at breaking into *Ukuhlushwa Okungapheli*. Neither outcome boded well for Ghandia…or the rest of humanity, for that matter.

Anger burned in the Hunter's gut as he slipped back the way he'd come. He'd seen enough of the Order's cruelty for one night. He promised Aisha he'd conceive of some plan of attack after gathering information. Now, he had all the information he needed—he knew what the Order was doing here, and what lengths they'd go to in order to achieve their ends—so the time for action was now.

He paid close attention to the camp as he returned to where he'd left Aisha. Midnight was not yet past and the majority of the slavers not on patrol, guard duty, or driving the slaves appeared to be either abed or at the ale line Rhodd had mentioned.

That left the Hunter with *three* obstacles to overcome. First, there were the Ordermen standing guard outside the domed building where the *Umoyahlebe* were being held. He'd spotted a dozen or so, which would prove little trouble to eliminate. Eliminating them quickly enough they had no time to raise an alarm, on the other hand, that was more trouble. Fortunately, he wouldn't face them alone. Between him and Aisha, he was confident he could manage it.

With that obstacle out of his path, he'd have a chance to liberate the Spirit Whisperers from within that building. The fact that the Order seemed to *only* trust their own men to guard their prized prisoners would work in their favor. There would be no Consortium to reinforce the Ordermen.

However, the second obstacle was the largest and most problematic: the gate. The obstacle would slow his escape, and the guards holding the gate would prove a hindrance— perhaps even hindrance enough that Consortium guards patrolling the wall's interior would get wind of their attempted flight and intervene. The resulting clangor of battle would alert every slaver and Orderman within the wall. And even if they got through the gate, there was still the matter of the patrol outside the wall.

So not the easiest of impossibilities to pull off. The Hunter shrugged. *Still, could be worse.*

He didn't necessarily need to flee out the city gate. At least not immediately. There were entire sections of the city uninhabited, which offered plenty of hiding places for the liberated *Umoyahlebe*. Perhaps they could even escape the way he, Kodyn, and Aisha had entered: over the wall.

Especially if someone creates a big enough distraction. That brought a smile to the Hunter's face, and he reached up to touch the scimitar hilt jutting up over his shoulder. The more men the

450

Order and Consortium threw at him, the more time it would buy the Spirit Whisperers to find their way to freedom.

He found Aisha where he'd left her, still crouched within the shadows of the empty building facing the domed structure housing the captive *Umoyahlebe*. As he told her what he'd witnessed, rage burned on her face and the blue-white sparks dancing in her eyes brightened to a glowing inferno.

"The plan is simple," the Hunter growled in a low voice. "We hit the whoresons right in the teeth and don't stop until they're dead."

Aisha's bared, snarling teeth shone fierce in the darkness. "Now that's my kind of plan!"

Chapter Thirty-Three

"Oi! This one of yours?"

The Hunter's shout drew the attention of all nine Ordermen guarding the southern entrance to the domed building that served as prison for the *Umoyahlebe*. At the sight of the Hunter, clad in Consortium armor, and the young Ghandian woman he roughly shoved along before him, half their number advanced toward them with leveled weapons.

"I have not seen this one," came the answer from beneath one mask. The voice belonged to a woman and bore the unmistakable accent of Vothmot. "She belongs with the laborers."

The Hunter didn't slow his advance. "That thing she did, setting little sparks dancing around her hand, nearly burned down half the scaffolding." He gave Aisha a particularly rough shove. "Pretty sure that makes her one of yours, aye?"

The masked woman exchanged glances with the three Ordermen who'd stepped up to confront the Hunter alongside her. That moment's hesitation was all the Hunter needed.

"Falchion next," he said, his tone dangerously casual.

One moment he was striding calmly toward the Ordermen, the next he was moving in a blur of motion. His right hand darted forward, snatching up the short-handled spear tucked into the back of Aisha's belt. In one smooth movement, he pulled it free, raised it high, and drove it straight into the throat of the woman who'd spoken. He released the spear in an instant and drew Soulhunger, sending the dagger slashing across the throats of the two nearest Ordermen. They fell back, gurgling and clutching at the crimson bubbling from the gaping wounds in their neck.

The Hunter's attention spun toward the two Ordermen off to his left—the ones nearest him and Aisha. He slid both hands beneath his cloak, seized the grips of his handheld crossbows, and unsheathed them. Even as he raised them and thumbed the trigger mechanism to extend the metal arms from the stock, he followed Aisha from the corner of his eye. He saw her tear the spear from the throat of the woman who'd spoken and hurl herself at the last of the four who'd advanced. The masked bastard never had a chance to raise their falchion before Aisha's already bloodstained spearhead slid through one of the mask's eyeholes.

That left just four for the Hunter to attend to. He brought both crossbows around to sight on the two Ordermen to his left. A caress of the trigger sent two thumb-sized bolts hurtling through the darkness toward the pair he'd chosen as targets. Even before he heard the missiles *thunk* home and felt the mechanisms in his crossbows reloading, he spun to take aim at the last two standing. One actually drew in a sharp breath, no doubt intending to raise the alarm. The bolt from the Hunter's right-hand crossbow punched into their throat, ending their cry in a hissing, choking cough. The other foolishly tried to raise their spear to ward off the bolt. The

452

frantic swing met empty air and the bolt from the Hunter's left-hand bow vanished into the eye behind the mask.

A succession of *thumps* echoed loud as the bodies hit the ground. A few faint gurgling, choking coughs persisted as the Ordermen drowned in their own blood. The Hunter had no time to let them die in misery. Holstering his crossbows, he drew a stiletto and sent the survivors to the Long Keeper's arms with quick, vicious thrusts.

It was over in a matter of seconds. Aisha's snarl and the wet, sucking sound of her spear being pulled free told the Hunter how her battle had ended. When he glanced her way, she stood over the Orderman's corpse, the falchion lying in the mud a dozen feet away where she'd kicked it.

"Come on!" the Hunter hissed. "We need to get these bodies out of sight fast."

He and Aisha had chosen their moment with caution. A quarter-hour after his return, six of those on guard duty outside the domed building had departed—two to fetch food, another pair to bring wine, and two more to answer the call of nature. That left just eight to eliminate, and they'd done so with deadly efficiency. With luck, the six would dawdle and dally enough the Hunter and Aisha could be long gone by the time they returned. But if not, the Hunter would deal with them in turn.

While Aisha set to work opening the double doors into the domed building, the Hunter grabbed two of the Ordermen by their tunics and slung the corpses over his shoulder. The last thing he wanted was to leave scuff or drag marks to alert the dead men's companions.

The moment the doors opened, a wall of stench assaulted the Hunter with near-physical force. The reek of human filth, urine, and ordure nearly overpowered him. He had to fight not to recoil from the stink of too many people cooped up in an enclosed space with no clean clothing, fresh water, or latrines.

In the light streaming in through the open door, the Hunter caught sight of dozens of haggard, emaciated, and hungry-looking faces peering back at him with wide eyes and fearful looks. No bruises or fresh blood from beatings, at least none he could see. But the *Umoyahlebe* were suffering no less from their confines and the Order's abuse of their magical abilities.

Fortunately, he had the task of hauling bodies to buy him a few more breaths of fresh air and a chance to acclimate his sensitive nostrils to the stench. It took him four trips and two minutes to haul the eight corpses inside while Aisha kept watch. The Mistress' fortune favored them; not a single Orderman or Consortium slaver appeared from the darkness.

"Shut it," the Hunter ordered as he carried the last two bodies inside. "But leave it just open enough we can hear them coming." And to let in enough fresh air he didn't suffocate from the enclosed smell.

Aisha obeyed, pushing the door shut until only the tiniest crack remained to allow the torchlight from outside to enter. Not that she needed a torch or lantern. Turning, she summoned sparks to her hand and the head of her *assegai*. The blue-white light of her power sufficed to illuminate the domed building's interior and its nearest occupants.

At their entrance, the *Umoyahlebe* within the makeshift cage had shrunk back in fear. They'd stared in wide-eyed, slack-jawed surprise and horror at the Hunter as he carried the corpses inside and dumped them into a bloody pile out of sight of the door. Yet at the sight of Aisha's power, the sounds emanating from inside the cage turned from fear to joy. The Spirit Whisperers recognized one of their own.

Within seconds, dozens of men, women, youths, and even children were crowding against the chains and columns that served as their prison. Their words came so fast and frantic the Hunter wouldn't have been able to understand them even had he spoken their language. Yet Aisha understood. She spoke in a voice of quiet urgency, her face set in a determined cast.

The Hunter wasted no time examining the prison. A single chain stretched from column to column at waist height did not a grand obstacle make. The moment Aisha explained to them the plan the two of them had concocted for their escape—racing toward the darkened, seemingly abandoned section of the camp to hide until the Hunter dealt with the patrols and got the gates open—they could simply duck under the chain and be free.

While Aisha spoke, the Hunter bent to examine the dead Ordermen. Their masks proved surprisingly difficult to remove—a series of straps and malleable, supple fabric he'd never before encountered held them securely in place, and the interior appeared to have been carved specifically to match the wearers' features. But once the masks came off and he finally glimpsed the faces beneath, he was struck by how ordinary the six men and two women appeared.

In death, the servants of the Order of Mithridas were no different than anyone else the Hunter had killed. As slack-featured, pale-faced, and glassy-eyed as a Consortium slaver, poison-maddened Tefaye, or battle-scarred Buhari *amaqhawai*. Nothing at all remarkable about them. No tattoos or markings he could see. No odd ritualistic scars or deformities. Just…people. Dead people as human as those poor souls their companions had slaughtered at the base of the Bondshold.

They had no identifying marks as to their origin, either. As he'd suspected, the woman who'd spoken had the tawny gold skin of a Vothmoti. Another of the men looked enough like her that the Hunter guessed they were siblings, perhaps cousins. The other woman could have been either Praamian or Voramian. Three of the remaining men had the dark-haired look of Drashi, one bore a walrus moustache evocative of the Nyslian style Sir Sigmund had favored, and the last definitely came from the Kurma Empire. A collection as motley as the Vassalage Consortium. Men and women gathered from every corner of Einan to serve the Order of Mithridas in their efforts to…what? What was their ultimate objective?

Their current labors to break open *Ukuhlushwa Okungapheli* couldn't be the sum total of the organization's endeavors. Otherwise, why would they have given two wet shites about Lord Chasteyn? There was no visible connection between the demon masquerading as a largely unimportant nobleman and this massive undertaking half a continent away.

No, everything the Hunter had seen and heard of the Order of Mithridas spoke of some grand stratagem, some lofty aim far larger than one city, empire, or even one Serenii tower. Their presence here—their efforts to free *Nuru Iwu*—was just a stepping-stone toward a much greater objective.

The Hunter had no more time to consider the matter, for at that moment, his keen ears detected voices coming from outside. Instantly, he was on his feet and darting toward the tiny crack Aisha had left in the door.

"Quiet them down!" he hissed at Aisha.

She had no response for him, but must have heard, for her words grew urgent and she began to gesture for the imprisoned *Umoyahlebe* to lower their voices. To the Hunter's relief, they complied. The blue-white light emanating from Aisha's hands and spearhead faded, plunging the building's interior into darkness. That suited the Hunter just fine. He had no fear of being spotted as he pressed one eyeball to the opening and scanned the darkness for the source of the voices.

There! Thirty paces to the southeast, four masked figures marched their way. Their arms were laden with loaves of bread and clay jugs bearing a Nyslian vintner's mark. The Hunter's

454

heart sank. The Ordermen who'd gone to fetch food had returned far faster than he'd anticipated.

His mind whirled, scrambling to figure out the best plan of attack. It took him but a moment to settle on caution and patience as the indicated course. He'd need to time his actions just right if he wanted to pull this off.

Adrenaline coursed through him, setting his heart hammering against his ribs. His pulse thundered so loud in his ears he could barely make out the quiet conversation of the approaching Ordermen.

"…paid a fortune, and the pissants have the gall to complain about having to stand half-day watches?" A man's voice, edged by the harsh accent of a Voramian, drifted toward the Hunter. "I swear these Consortium cunts have never put in a hard day's work in their lives."

"Ain't that kind of the point of signing up with an outfit like that?" came the response, a woman's voice, markedly Malandrian. "Don't take much skill to crack a whip or swing a club at a chained prisoner. Now the fellas off marching, that's a different story. Battle comes and they'll…hey!" Her words cut off abruptly.

The Hunter identified the woman speaker by the way she stopped first and looked around in confusion at the empty space surrounding the domed building.

"Nynish?" she called out, her eyes darting back and forth.

"Nynish!" shouted one of the men carrying bread. "Rickett?"

"Something ain't right," growled the Voramian who'd spoken. "No way they'd leave their post unguarded. Not Nynish."

"Aye," agreed the woman. "Bask, Thorne, spread out and—"

She never got to finish barking that order.

From the moment the woman had stopped, the Hunter had suspected the jig was up. As soon as they looked ready to drop their cargo and reach for weapons, he moved. With his left hand, he shoved the door in front of him open, and his right hand reached for his holstered crossbow. Even as he brought the weapon up to take aim, he thumbed the mechanism that extended the collapsible arms. The thumb-sized bolt hissed toward the masked woman and buried in her eye.

The Hunter had no time to re-holster the crossbow, so he merely dropped it and reached for the throwing knife concealed in his belt. But as his right hand flashed toward his waist, his other came up and loosed the third and last bolt in his left-hand crossbow. To his dismay, he knew his aim was off the instant he squeezed the trigger. He'd loosed too early, and the bolt buried into an enemy's leg, just above the knee.

In desperation, the Hunter hurled his drawn throwing knife into the same masked enemy's neck. He had to silence the inevitable holler of pain before it alerted everyone within earshot. The force of his throw drove the long, thin blade straight into the Orderman's throat. His cry ended in a whistling, wheezing gurgle, and his hands flew to his throat. The jugs he'd been carrying crashed to the ground in a thunderous cacophony of shattering clay shards and gushing wine.

Yet the clangor worked in the Hunter's favor. The two Ordermen remaining made the foolish mistake of glancing toward the broken jugs, and as their eyes fixed on their slumping, bleeding comrades, surprise rendered them immobile for the space of two heartbeats. In that time, the Hunter's arms pumped like the bellows of a forge, drawing four throwing knives from his belt and the folds of his cloak and sending them spinning toward the masked Ordermen.

Razor-sharp steel found new homes in unarmored chests and bellies, and the two fell to the wine-soaked ground to join their companions in bleeding out.

Keeper's teeth!

The Hunter raced out of the domed building and, in three great strides, crossed to where the first two Ordermen lay dead and dying. With strength borne of necessity, he hoisted the bodies off the ground and carried them into the building to drop them onto the pile of their fellows. The last two joined them a few moments later, and he needed but a moment to gather up his dropped crossbows and shut the door once more.

But even as he did, he knew they were out of time. The spilled wine jugs and fallen loaves would be a dead giveaway. Not even the blindest fool could miss the blood spatter that now stained the dirt, or the deep gouges in the earth carved by one dying Orderman's heels. The moment the last two Ordermen returned from doing their business, the alarm would be raised.

"Time's up!" the Hunter hissed at Aisha, collapsing and holstering his now-empty crossbows. "We need to get everyone out and moving, now!"

"We can't." She had once more summoned the sparks of blue-white light to dance around her palm, and the glow splashed across her face revealed an expression partway between panic and fear. "We can't leave, not yet!"

"The bloody hell does that mean?" It took all of the Hunter's self-control not to roar the words. He crossed to the nearest column in two strides, seized the chain, and pulled with all his strength. The chain was neither steel nor iron, but made of dimercurite alloyed with some other metals he did not know. It snapped beneath the force of the Hunter's might as easily as if it was made of rotting wood.

He rounded on Aisha. "This is all that's standing in their way. They're as free as—"

"No!" Aisha's jaw set in a stubborn clench. "You don't understand! My father and sister aren't here. And *I* won't leave without them. I can't!"

Chapter Thirty-Four

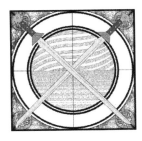

Not here? The Hunter's gaze darted around the nearly three-score imprisoned *Umoyahlebe,* seeking…what? How could he begin to identify Aisha's father and sister from among so many? And if she'd insisted they weren't here—

Then he remembered. *Could it be?* His mind flashed back to the five Ghandians who'd been hauled to the base of the Bondshold and set to do the Order's bidding assaulting the tower's huge stone doors. Had the white-haired man been Aisha's father? One of the young girls her sister? He hadn't looked closely at the time, hadn't paid attention to their facial features. Yet there was one—the only one unharmed by the younger man's violent overload of power—who could have borne a resemblance to Aisha.

He cursed under his breath. "How long will they be gone?"

Aisha gave him a blank look. "I…don't know."

"Ask *them!*" The Hunter jabbed a finger toward the Spirit Whisperers clustered around the chain that served as their pitiful prison. "This can't be the first time some of their number have been hauled away by the Order." The efficiency with which the masked men had set to the task of killing the ill Ghandians, clamping the dimercurite chains onto the five *Umoyahlebe,* and directed their magic against *Ukuhlushwa Okungapheli* made it clear they'd been at the effort a while. Days, perhaps even weeks. "How long are those taken usually gone?"

Understanding dawned in Aisha's eyes. She spun back to face the captives and spoke in her own language, doubtless relaying the Hunter's question.

The Hunter tried to pay attention to their answer, but his incomprehension of their tongue and the urgency of the situation stole his focus. His eyes went to the corpses of the Ordermen. Perhaps he could don their clothing, masquerade as one of them. Keeper knew he'd spent time enough behind masks that he'd have little trouble fitting into the role.

But how long would the ruse last? The remaining two Ordermen would return at any moment. If they saw *only* the Hunter and none of the others known to them, his façade would crumble the instant he spoke.

Still, he thought, *it's better than the alter…*

His thoughts cut off the moment he bent for a closer look. The corpses he'd dropped atop the pile had leaked blood onto the others below, staining their dark grey tunics and trousers. Unless one of the bodies at the bottom of the stack had somehow avoided the crimson droplets, the Ordermen's clothing would be useless to him. The sight of wet blood was far more attention-commanding than a lone Consortium slaver standing guard.

Still, the Hunter wasn't ready to abandon the attempt. He lifted the first body off the pile and tossed it roughly aside. When he went to move the second, however, the tunic ripped in his hands, revealing umber-toned skin beneath. The dead man was likely Ghandian, though from which tribe, the Hunter couldn't tell.

He was about to toss the corpse aside when something caught his eye: a knot of light-colored scar tissue on the man's left breast, directly above his heart. The sight only stopped the Hunter because it reminded him of his own scars. With every demon he'd killed, the mess of tangled, raised scar tissue over his heart had grown uglier and larger. It alone remained on his flesh even after the others had mysteriously vanished—first on the day he'd left Voramis, then again the day he'd pursued the Sage out of the tunnels beneath Kara-ket. Somehow, his body had erased the scars, all save those of the Abiarazi who'd met their grim ends on Soulhunger's blade.

Something about the scar tissue struck the Hunter as deliberate. It appeared like three intersecting lines—three perfectly measured cuts of a knife. Far too clean and neat for a battle scar. But it was more than that. The flesh had raised far more than was to be expected from a regular wound.

Almost as if there's something beneath it.

Curiosity inflamed, he stretched out a hand to touch it. Though the corpse was not yet cold, the skin had begun growing clammy. The sensation sent a shiver down the Hunter's spine. Nonetheless, he forced himself to press his finger against the scar. Sure enough, he felt something just under the skin. Whatever it was, it couldn't be larger than the small knuckle on his pinky finger, yet it was hard and unyielding.

Frowning, the Hunter turned to examine the first body he'd moved. He'd found no identifying marks on the Ordermen, yet if they *all* bore this scar...

Aha! The moment he ripped open the dead man's shirt, he had his answer. This one was pale, likely Malandrian, and the scar tissue appeared pink against his white skin. Yet it, too, bore the same pattern—a horizontal line bisected with two diagonal lines slashing right and left—and appeared equally neat. The *something* hard beneath the skin was present, too.

What in the fiery hell could it be? The thought spun through his mind as he checked two more of the Ordermen corpses at random. Again, he found the raised scars marked in the same pattern.

Two men with similar wounds, he could accept as coincidence. But *four*? And all in the exact same spot depicting the same intersecting lines? The Hunter couldn't be sure, but he'd wager a small fortune that whatever had been pushed beneath the skin was virtually identical in size.

There's no bloody way it's a coincidence. Triumph surged within him. *Which means it's an identifying mark they all share!*

His elation proved short-lived. He had no idea what the markings meant and no way to ascertain their true purpose—without capturing an Orderman and demanding an answer, that was. He could, however, find out what it was the scars concealed. Those strange hard objects beneath the skin *had* to be something important. He reached for one of the throwing daggers he'd retrieved from the dead Orderman; he had no qualms about desecrating these bastards' bodies if it got him answers about—

"What are you doing?" Aisha's question was tinged with more than a little horror.

The Hunter looked up, found her staring wide-eyed at him. He opened his mouth to answer but never got the chance.

"It doesn't matter!" She gave a dismissive wave. "I asked them like you said, and they didn't know how long my father and Nkanyezi will be gone for. But even if they were here, we could not leave. Not while they still wear *those*."

The Hunter looked closer at the imprisoned *Umoyahlebe* and found that every one of them wore the same bands of dark metal around their wrists, ankles, and neck.

"What are they?" he asked.

"*Ubukathaki!*" came the answer from one of the nearby Ghandians, a young girl who couldn't have been more than ten years old, with mud-stained features and an unhealthy pallor to her face. She looked halfway feverish and on the verge of collapse. Yet when she spoke, words poured from her lips in a frantic torrent.

"Some manner of sorcery they do not understand," Aisha translated. "All they know is that while they wear them, they cannot commune with the *Kish'aa*. They are deaf and blind to the spirits. But somehow, the *Amadodabi*—the masked devils—can command them to absorb the *Kish'aa*, even if they cannot see or hear them. The bands of metal give the masked devils power over them. To control them and compel them to use the power of the *Kish'aa*. But that is not all."

She asked the young girl something, and more than a few of the Ghandians clustered around answered. When she turned back to the Hunter, her face was grim. "If they leave this place, if they step outside the circle of this chain, they will die. The bands will tighten around their arms, legs, and necks, crushing them slowly."

The Hunter's eyebrows rose. "That's what they said?" It sounded far-fetched.

Aisha nodded.

"And they've seen it happen?"

Aisha relayed the question to the imprisoned Ghandians. Even before she translated their answer, the Hunter understood the shaking of their heads.

"They have not. But the *Amadodabi* have told them it is so, and they will not risk it being true. Not after everything that has been done to them. They fear the wrath of the *Amadodabi*."

The Hunter growled low in his throat. To his ears, the Order's threat sounded impossible. Yet these people had witnessed firsthand what the Ordermen could do with their dimercurite alloy chains—commanding the *Umoyahlebe* to unleash their power even to the point of burning out and killing themselves—which should have been equally impossible. Whether that claim proved true or a fabrication to terrify them into compliance, the Hunter couldn't fault these men, women, and youths for their fear.

Unfortunately for him, that made their escape plan exponentially more difficult.

He racked his brain for an alternative approach. "You said they feared leaving the circle of chain, yes?"

Aisha nodded. "Let me guess. You're thinking of bringing the chain."

The Hunter didn't need to answer; he'd already stepped toward the nearest metal column and seized the chain. With a hard yank, he tore it free of the ring securing it in place.

"And what of the noise?" Aisha hurried after him as he raced to the next column, and the next. "So many people will already make a lot of noise as they move, and you think of adding the chain on top of that?" She stopped speaking just long enough for him to rip the chain free once more. "Surely the better plan would be to remove the bands!"

"You're welcome to try," the Hunter called back. "But I got a look at them, and I saw no key-hole or latch to unlock." He continued on, but Aisha raced ahead of him and got between him and the next pillar. "Aisha—"

"You know there's no way it works." She shook her head. "Not like this."

"Of course I know that!" the Hunter hissed. "Just like I know there's no way you'd leave without your father and sister." He leaned closer, looming over her. "But what do you expect me

459

to do? Sit still and wait around until we're discovered? I've got no better course of action, and we don't have the time to—"

"Just give me a moment!" Aisha held up a hand. "I need to think about this." Her brow furrowed. "There has to be some way. Something I learned in the Night Guild that would work, or—" Her eyes lit up. "My powers!"

The Hunter narrowed his eyes. "You're going to burn off the manacles? Without burning the people beneath?"

"No. Yes. Maybe. I don't know!" Aisha threw up both hands. "But I can at least give it a try."

The Hunter stepped back. "You're welcome to try." He swept a gesture toward the captives. "Meanwhile, I'm going to keep working at this on the off-chance it'll actually—"

His words cut off in an instant as the sound of a creaking door resounded through the domed building. For the breathless space of a heartbeat, he thought it came from behind him, from the southern entrance where he'd left the corpses piled. If the last two Ordermen had returned from doing their business and found the others on guard missing, it was only a matter of seconds before they raised an alarm.

Yet the sound *didn't* come from the southern entrance. Instead, it came from the north end of the building. Another set of doors creaked open and lantern light spilled into the domed building. The clank of chains and the tromp of heavy feet echoed from outside.

The Hunter and Aisha threw themselves into the shadows, crouching to hide behind one of the huge metal pillars supporting the domed roof. The *Umoyahlebe* nearest them shrank back, wide-eyed and once more terrified. Fortunately, they were far enough back from the northern entrance those entering had no chance of seeing them.

"Get in there!" came a rough shout. A few shouts and cries in the Ghandian tongue were accompanied by the sound of bare feet scuffing on hard-packed earth.

"You five!" The same voice again. "You're up."

The Hunter risked poking his head out from behind cover, just enough he could see the Ordermen unlocking the door and hauling out a group of chained Ghandians—including a shrieking, wailing child, a girl who couldn't have been older than ten or eleven.

Every fiber of the Hunter's being longed to spring to his feet, to hurl himself at the armed men who had come to drag away more *Umoyahlebe* for their grim labor. They had children, for the Keeper's sake, and wouldn't hesitate to push them to the edge of their limits and beyond, just like the adults. How many more would join the young man in the dirt, burned from the inside out, turned to smoking corpses by the power over which they had no control?

The four who'd survived the ordeal outside the Serenii tower were herded back into the cage—or, in the case of the one who'd fallen unconscious, *dumped* roughly with a heavy *thump* of her limp body striking the dirt floor.

At this, the older *Umoyahlebe* who'd accompanied her turned and shouted at the Ordermen in his own tongue. The Hunter didn't understand the words, but the man's defiance earned him a clubbing blow to the head. The blow knocked him to the ground, where he lay in a dazed heap.

A young woman sprang to her feet and shouted at the masked man who'd struck the older *Umoyahlebe*. The Hunter's gut clenched as the Orderman turned to her, his club rising again. It took all his willpower to remain motionless, yet what choice did he have? It would be foolishness to spring into action when so many *more* lives hung in the balance.

He gritted his teeth. *Now is the time for caution, stealth,* he told himself. *The moment will soon come when—*

At that moment, a shadow streaked past him. Little more than a blur of motion in the darkness, silent as a wraith. Yet there was no mistaking the burning heat radiating off the figure or the blue-white sparks blazing to brilliant life around her hands.

Aisha was gone before the Hunter could stop her, barreling through the darkened building toward the Ordermen.

With a curse, the Hunter sprang to his feet and broke into a mad dash. He couldn't stop her—she was as unstoppable as a firestorm, a whirlwind of fury that he had little chance of leashing—but at least he could stop her from getting herself killed.

Chapter Thirty-Five

Aisha tore into the Ordermen with the force of a charging *zabara*. A blast of blue-white lightning erupted from her outstretched left hand and ripped through the Ordermen standing over the unconscious young woman. The three of them flew backward as if struck by a giant hand and crashed into the exterior wall in a cacophony of pulping flesh and pulverized bone. They fell hard onto their masked faces and though their bodies twitched, they did not rise. Didn't so much as move a muscle. Smoke wafted up from holes the power had burned through their grey clothing, and the stink of charred meat thickened the air.

Even as the first trio fell, Aisha turned her attention toward the four standing in the open doorway. Another blast of power sent them flying a dozen feet to land in crumpled heaps in the dirt. This second barrage had lacked the ferocity of her first, and the Hunter saw her steps falter. The life force she'd managed to gather from the Ordermen they'd just killed was running out.

That's my cue! Jaw set in a grim clench, the Hunter drew his watered steel sword and Soulhunger and poured on the speed. Aisha was fleet-footed and driven by her rage, but the sapping of her strength slowed her. And she could never hope to outrun a Bucelarii.

The Hunter overtook her in the space of two heartbeats and charged past. Straight into the knot of Ordermen visible beyond the building. As he'd guessed, there had been an equal number of masked men stationed to guard both northern and southern entrances. Only *this* group hadn't had their numbers reduced by the call of nature, hunger, or thirst. Beyond the seven Aisha had taken down, nearly a dozen remained. All carried weapons—sheathed or resting on the ground, yet within easy reach—and surprise only paralyzed them for a moment before they responded to the threat. Well-trained and alert despite the shock of this sneak attack from within the building they guarded.

Every instinct urged the Hunter to loose a battle cry, a wordless roar to intimidate his enemies. Yet he restrained himself with great effort. The last thing he wanted was to call any more attention his way. A few one- and two-storied buildings obstructed them from the view of the myriad slavers, slaves, and Ordermen at the Bondshold. At the first shout or an over-loud clash of steel, the alarm would be raised and any chance at escape would vanish like mist before the midday sun.

Still, he could not resist the urge to bare his teeth and unleash a low, guttural snarl. He wanted all eyes on *him* now. The more weapons directed his way, the more time Aisha would have to breathe and gather her strength—both magical and physical.

His ploy worked. Eleven masked faces turned toward him, stances shifted in his direction, and weapons were drawn and raised. A tidal wave of dark-clad men and women closed in around him with murder gleaming in the eyes visible beneath the snarling obsidian beast facades.

Had this been any other battle, the Hunter would have met them with a blurring wall of steel. He had nothing to fear—not one carried iron—and could endure the pain of wounds inflicted by the few weapons that would inevitably slip past his guard. But rather than stand firm like a rocky cliff before the surging crest of a wave, the Hunter fought with the slippery grace of an eel.

Twisting, turning, spinning, darting backward and forward, sword and dagger flashing in all directions. He dared not cross blades with his foes—the ring of steel on steel would be far too loud—and thus had to rely on his superior speed, strength, and agility to carry the day. With the speed of a serpent, he drove his sword tip into unarmored bellies, legs, groins, chests, and throats. Each strike precisely placed, each feint an intent to lure his enemies into overextending themselves or overcommitting to a chop, thrust, or slash. He kept Soulhunger close, hidden from sight, only using it when he drew close enough to open a vein or pierce an eye. No sooner had his blow landed than he was moving on, dancing to the side or backward, eternally disengaging and altering directions too quickly for his opponents to comprehend.

And still he was too slow. He knew it with utter certainty. No matter how fast he killed, there would always be the *one* who had the presence of mind to step back just long enough to raise a cry of alarm. The moment that happened, the battle would grow urgent in a hurry.

He fought with every shred of skill he possessed, keeping his strength in reserve and utilizing his speed and innate agility. Slipping beneath hacking swords, dodging swinging axes, twisting out of the path of darting spears. Not always successfully. Searing hot lines burned in a dozen places around his body from where he'd failed to evade his enemies' weapons. He could feel himself slowing, smell his blood joining that of his dying foes. Warmth trickled down his back, his left leg, his right arm, his side.

Yet still he fought on. Silent as the grave, not even the sound of his breathing shattering the darkness. The only noise came from ripping flesh, shattering bones, dripping blood, and the agonized gasping of dying men and women. Jaw set and face hard, determined to hack down every one of the Ordermen before they recovered wits enough to remember they were surrounded by allies and call for help.

Two fell, then three, then five. The Ordermen pressed tight around him, attempting to trap him, lock up his weapons with their own. Another died taking a thrust of the Hunter's watered steel blade to the eyeball, yet as the masked Orderman fell, his weight dragged on the Hunter's sword arm. He stumbled forward, off-balance. Searing agony exploded through him as something struck him in the spine. His legs gave out and he fell to his knees. Only sheer stubbornness kept him from falling onto his face, and he recovered in the space between heartbeats.

Yet that split-second was all it took. He saw a look of realization sprout in one pair of eyes, and the masked Orderman stepped back. Their chest expanded with a sharp intake of breath, filling their lungs in preparation to give voice to the shout that would shatter the near-silence.

The Hunter gathered his strength, prepared to hurl himself the three steps he'd need to tackle the Orderman to the ground. Too slow, he knew it. Yet he had to try!

He had just dug his toes into the ground and braced his legs, heedless of the pain coursing through his lower body, when a brilliant flash lit up the night. The heat of a smith's blast furnace blew past him, accompanied by a searing bolt of blue-white so bright it nearly blinded him. Though the light faded in a moment, the afterimage remained, burned into his eyeballs.

Fear tightened like an iron vise around his lungs. He could not see his enemies, and so could not avoid their weapons. His only hope was to accept the wounds *without* defending himself. Their axes, spears, and swords striking his flesh would make far less noise than would result if he tried to fend off their weapons. Gritting his teeth, he lowered his sword and braced himself for the pain. He had to hope the Consortium armor would at least lessen the impacts and turn aside the worst of the strikes.

Yet no attacks came. No stabbing, searing pain of weapons crashing into his armor or piercing his body.

He blinked, desperate to clear away the light dancing before his eyes. Slowly, the world darkened to normal, the blinding blue-white glow fading until the Hunter could finally see once more. And in the glow of the two nearby, he beheld the truth of the battle. It was over.

The last Ordermen were down. Some lay twitching and writhing, the lightning still coursing through their bodies. Others lay still, little more than smoking piles of charred meat and scorched cloth. Only one had not fallen onto their back or face. The masked enemy who'd been about to cry out was on their knees, staring wide-eyed at the smoking stumps at the end of their wrists. Their hands and fingers had been burned away—or simply blasted off, the Hunter didn't know. The overwhelming torment of the injury had all but shut down their brain, rendering them paralyzed and mute.

The Hunter didn't give the bastard a chance to find their voice. Three quick steps brought him within striking range, and his sword flashed out. Once, twice. Blood flew where steel met flesh. So sharp was the watered steel blade the Orderman's body didn't so much as jerk as the tip tore through. Twin lines opened. The one on the chest leaked only a small trickle, but the one across the front of their neck gushed crimson.

Gurgling, gasping, the Orderman attempted to stanch the flow of blood from their torn throat. Hard to do without hands. The cauterized stumps where once they'd had hands did little to stop them from bleeding; if anything, it only hastened their demise, opened the wound further.

The Hunter placed his boot onto the dying Orderman's chest and shoved. It took little strength to send the masked enemy toppling backward. They lay on their back, eyes wide and staring up into the night as they choked to death on their own blood. The Hunter had no pity to spare. Nor any time. Even as the Orderman thrashed their last, the Hunter sheathed Soulhunger, knelt beside the dying enemy, and drove his left hand into their chest. Right into the cut his sword had made through the flesh and scar tissue over their heart.

His questing fingers found something hard and round amidst all the blood and muscle. He ripped it free without hesitation. The Orderman made no complaint; their last gasps were wasted trying to gurgle out something unintelligible even to the Hunter's keen ears.

The Hunter stared at his crimson-soaked prize. A stone, though what color it was beneath all the blood, he could not tell. But it was a stone, knuckle-sized and multi-faceted.

A quiet *thump* came from behind the Hunter, causing him to spin around. His eyes widened as he spotted Aisha fallen to her hands and knees in the domed building's opened doorway.

His heart leaped into his throat and he raced toward her, heedless of his aches and pains, his grisly trophy still in his crimson-stained hand. He was about to throw himself to his knees at her side, to help her rise so he could get a closer look at her wounds, when she managed to lift her head.

"I'm...fine!" she gasped, her voice breathy. Sweat dripped down her forehead and her face had lost most of its color. "Just over...exerted myself. Too much...power!"

Worry gnawed at the Hunter's gut as he knelt beside her, though the movement sent twinges coursing down his spine and legs where he'd been struck. He'd seen what could happen when an *Umoyahlebe* unleashed the magic of the *Kish'aa* in excess.

"You sure?" He scanned what he could see of her in the faint light of the lanterns. He found no blood, no sign of shattered bones.

"I am." Aisha nodded, albeit weakly. Then her eyes flew wide. "Father!" She staggered to her feet and whirled around but swayed so violently she would have fallen had the Hunter not caught her. "Help me! Please, I need to make sure he's alive."

The Hunter followed the line of her gaze and her outstretched hand to where the white-haired elder lay sprawled on the ground just within the inner circle of columns. Blood leaked from his forehead and he did not stir, despite the young woman kneeling at his side and attempting to coax him back to consciousness.

The reasoning behind Aisha's precipitous action suddenly made sense. The man was her father, which meant the one attempting to awaken him—

"Nkanyezi!" Aisha called out the name in as loud a whisper as she dared. She repeated the name, following it with more words in the Ghandian tongue.

The young woman's head snapped up, and her eyes went round. Her jaw fell slack and for a moment, she stared at Aisha as if at a ghost.

Aisha tore free of the Hunter's grip and rushed to her sister's side. Nkanyezi recovered from her shock in time to rise to her feet and throw her arms around Aisha. The two embraced, clinging to each other with a ferocity that could only exist between loved ones reunited after years spent apart. Tears streamed down Nkanyezi's cheeks, and judging by the trembling of Aisha's shoulders, she, too, wept.

Their reunion proved terribly short-lived.

A dark shadow coalesced in the darkness of the domed building, moving at a blurring speed. The Hunter had half-raised his sword to strike before he recognized Kodyn. The young Praamian was breathless and sweating hard.

"We have to go!" he hissed. "There's close to sixty Consortium guards and half as many Ordermen coming this way. If we want *any* chance of getting everyone out, we've got to make like ghosts and vanish right bloody now!"

Chapter Thirty-Six

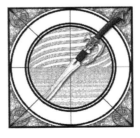

The Hunter's mind spun. "How is that possible? There's been no alarm raised, no indication anyone has detected us here."

Kodyn threw up his hands. "No clue. I only knew you were here because I spotted you through the window of the office I was rifling through. But if I saw you…"

"How far are they?" the Hunter demanded. "How much time do we have?"

Kodyn's face darkened. "Minute, maybe two. I got here as quickly as I could without being detected, but they're not far behind me."

The Hunter cursed under his breath. "Then we've got to move!"

Aisha, who had by now broken off the embrace with her sister, looked between the Hunter and Kodyn and the sixty or so *Umoyahlebe* staring wide-eyed and uncomprehending at them. "There's no way we can get those bands off all of them in that time. Even if we had the keys!"

A questioning look appeared on Kodyn's face, vanishing a moment later when his eyes darted to the heavy metal bands on Nkanyezi's wrists. He advanced on her, hurriedly speaking in Ghandian. To her credit, Nkanyezi didn't retreat, didn't cower as so many others in her position might have done. Instead, she braced her feet and squared her shoulders the same way Aisha did when faced with a challenge. The Consortium and their masters of the Order of Mithridas had chained, imprisoned, and compelled her to do their bidding, but they had not yet broken her.

In response to Kodyn's words, Nkanyezi extended her right arm. Kodyn studied the metal band through narrowed eyes. The Hunter took that opportunity to get a closer look at Aisha's younger sister.

Side by side, the resemblance between them was clear. Nkanyezi had less of her mother's leonine cheeks and jawline, but the eyes were the same. So, too, was the spark of defiance burning within. Her cloth wrappings were stained, filthy, and hung in tatters from her emaciated frame, yet she carried herself with a warrior's pride. There was something else, too, a ponderance to her facial expressions and stance that mirrored Aisha's yet was not present on their mother. The weight of the *Umoyahlebe* gift.

Nkanyezi had to be three or four years younger than Aisha—of an age with Hailen, likely—and like Hailen, she emanated an air of insight despite her youth. That explained why she'd appeared older at first glance. Though the dimercurite alloy bands currently cut her off from the *Kish'aa*, the Hunter had no doubt she had seen and heard a great deal over the last few weeks or months since she discovered her abilities. Even her scent—a mixture of aloe, starfish lily, labdanum, and mahogany—hinted at deep reserves of inner strength. Given her mother's martial nature and the way her father had defied the Ordermen, that should have come as no surprise.

"Damn it!"

Kodyn's curse snapped the Hunter's attention toward the young man.

"Whoever made these is bloody clever." Kodyn's face twisted into a scowl. "I've only ever heard about this sort of design before, but never actually seen it built. The mechanism is housed within the band itself, and can only be opened using a lodestone chosen specifically for this metal." He shook his head. "Without that lodestone, there's no way to get it open. And any attempts to break them off will only cause them to clamp down harder until it cuts off the circulation or snaps the bone beneath. They're called Amputator Manacles for a reason."

The Hunter growled low in his throat. "Is there any link between them and that?" He pointed to the lone chain that encircled the *Umoyahlebe's* prison. "Any reason to believe that the bands will tighten if they step foot outside this building?"

Kodyn's eyes snapped in the indicated direction, and his expression grew pensive. He spent a moment looking between the band and the chain before giving an uncertain shrug. "If the locking mechanisms are moved using a lodestone, it's *possible* the self-tightening mechanisms could be, too." He held up a hand. "It's just a theory here, but if the chain contains some magnetic properties, there's a chance it's the only thing keeping the bands from constricting."

Frustration rippled through the Hunter. *So what in the fiery hell are we supposed to do?* He looked from Kodyn to Aisha to Nkanyezi to the rest of the Spirit Whisperers. No way they'd have time to vanish before the Ordermen and slavers Kodyn had spotted reached the building. And even if he could somehow rip the chain off the columns and gather it up, its clatter and the footfalls of nearly seventy fleeing *Umoyahlebe* would draw the approaching enemies straight at them.

But what was the alternative? He couldn't bring himself to even contemplate it. They'd come all this way, risked so much. There was no way he would accept—

"You must go." The words came from Nkanyezi, quiet yet spoken with the determination the Hunter had seen reflected in her mother and sister both. The young woman turned toward Aisha and spoke in her tongue, her jaw set and stubborn.

"No!" Aisha shook her head. She reached for her sister, clearly trying to reason with her.

Nkanyezi stepped back and moved to kneel at her father's side. Though the Hunter did not understand her words, the look in her eyes and the way she cradled her father's bloodied head made the meaning plain.

She would not leave, but she wanted Aisha to.

Aisha threw herself to her knees in front of Nkanyezi and gripped her sister's shoulders in both hands. Her tone shifted between imploring, wheedling, demanding, and insistent all in the space of a few words. For a heartbeat, Nkanyezi's face lost its hardened edge. She was once again the youthful girl staring into the eyes of the sister she had not seen for years. A sister who had come all this way to free her from the cruelty of her captors.

Then her father stirred. A weak moan escaped his lips and his eyelids began to flutter. Nkanyezi and Aisha both turned to the white-haired man, bending over him and speaking to him as if to hasten him to consciousness.

The Hunter never heard their words.

"Get in there, now!" a strong voice roared in the distance. "And for the love of all the gods, get your arses around to the north side!"

The Hunter's heart leaped into his throat as the door on the southern end of the domed building creaked open and lantern light spilled across the captive *Umoyahlebe*. He stuffed the blood-covered stone he'd torn from the dying Orderman's chest into a hidden pocket deep in his cloak and drew Soulhunger. Now that they'd been discovered, he could abandon stealth in favor of the ruthless savagery needed to fight their way free of so many enemies.

Kodyn sprang to Aisha's side and gripped her shoulders. "Aisha—"

Nkanyezi moved, too. She released her father's head, turned, and placed both of her hands on Aisha's chest. With a mighty heave, she pushed Aisha up to her feet and stumbling backward. Her face hardened and she snapped a few words in her native tongue. A thrust of her finger toward the still-open northern doorway made the meaning plain enough.

Aisha stood paralyzed, torn between desires, anguish etched deep into her features. On the one hand, she *had* to know the smart move was to vanish before they were discovered. Yet had the Hunter been in her place, he couldn't have compelled himself to leave, either. Not this close to rescuing her father and sister.

Fortunately, Aisha had no need to make the decision. Kodyn had been caught off guard by the force of Nkanyezi's push, yet her action and words had reaffirmed what he'd already known to be true. He darted toward Aisha, seized her by the arm, and hauled her bodily out of the building. Her feet stumbled and dragged, weighted down by hesitation and uncertainty, yet she did not pull against him. She put up no resistance at all, but allowed herself to be pulled along after Kodyn.

The Hunter spun to follow the pair, yet could not help but pause for a moment to stare down at the young woman who had chosen her sister's safety over her own freedom. "We will return," he promised. "You will be free."

She gave him a nod and said something in her own tongue, then repeated it in Einari. "*Kish'aa* be with you."

And then the Hunter was racing on, dashing in pursuit of Kodyn and Aisha. His battered body protested the effort, but he ignored the twinges. He had no time to let pain slow him down. The sound of heavy boots approached from the south, Ordermen or Consortium slavers hastening to do as the commanding voice had instructed and cut off their escape.

Fortunately for him, they were too slow. By the time the first torch-carrying guard came into sight along the domed building's western edge, the Hunter was already diving into the shadows between a pair of single-story dwellings.

Kodyn led a barely-cognizant Aisha deeper into the darkness, wending his way eastward and south, circling toward the warehouse-sized smithy. The shouts from behind them grew louder, and the Hunter thought he heard a young woman's voice crying out in pain and fear. His heart ached for Nkanyezi. *So young and so brave.* A lump rose in his throat. *So much like Hailen. And like her sister.*

At that moment, Aisha managed to find her feet and ran on unaided. Kodyn hung on to her arm just long enough to make certain she was following, then relinquished his grip and focused his attention on the darkness ahead. Whether or not he had a direction in mind didn't much matter; they merely needed to put distance between themselves and the guards swarming around the domed building. It wouldn't be long before they discovered no trace of those they sought—only chained and terrified *Umoyahlebe*—and they'd fan out to search the camp. But that would take time. Time enough for the Hunter, Kodyn, and Aisha to be long gone.

As they drew near the smithy building, a pair of Ordermen hurried around the corner. Their clothes were rumpled, their black masks askew, and they were in the middle of tucking their shirts into their unfastened belts. Their eyes flew wide at the sight of the three figures racing toward them and their hands reached for their weapons.

Too slow. Kodyn was on them in a heartbeat, his sword flashing through the darkness in a blur of steel. The first took a thrust to the heart and died on their feet. The second stumbled backward as Kodyn's follow-up slash carved a deep furrow along their sword arm. The grip on their belt slackened and their trousers fell to their ankles. The man, for a man it turned out to be, got tangled up in his own clothing and toppled backward, landing hard enough to *crack* his head against the hard ground. Kodyn skewered him through the eyehole of his mask without missing a step.

Aisha slowed, but only for a moment. Just long enough to extend her left hand toward the two bodies. Sparks of blue-white light materialized around her fingers, and when she continued on, she moved more easily, the burden on her shoulders lightened a fraction.

The Hunter sneered at the corpses as he raced past. He recognized them as two of those who'd left their post guarding the southern entrance to the domed building. They'd claimed—loudly—that they had to answer the call of nature. Just not the call of nature their companions had expected. These fools had learned the hard and fatal way that certain pastimes were better reserved for off-duty hours. He had no pity to spare for them. Not after what he'd seen their comrades doing to the *Umoyahlebe* they held captive and the thousands of slaves laboring around the base of the Bondshold and the cliffs below.

He slowed in his dash just long enough to look over his shoulder. No sign of pursuit, at least not yet. No torches or lanterns bouncing in his direction. No shouts or orders growing louder in the night. He wouldn't stop running until he was *certain* they had gotten away undetected, but they would not have to run for much longer. There would soon be plenty of dark, empty buildings where they could hole up and strategize.

In his mind, he reaffirmed the promise he'd made to Nkanyezi—and, through her, to all the Spirit Whisperers. *I will return,* he vowed. *And when I do, there will be no mercy for the bastards who hold you prisoner.*

Chapter Thirty-Seven

Keeper's icy balls, they moved fast!

A grimace twisted the Hunter's lips as he stared at the line of lantern, lamp, and torch-wielding foes standing guard along the volcanic stone wall barring his escape from the camp. They clustered in groups of twos and threes, easy pickings on their own, but stationed at thirty-pace intervals all along the wall's inner perimeter and well within sight of each other.

"Small bloody chance we're getting out the way we came in," Kodyn muttered from where he crouched in the shadows next to the Hunter.

The Hunter wished he could argue, but the young man's assessment was correct. Their enemies had been clever in the arrayal of their forces. The moment even *one* Consortium guard or masked Orderman spotted the Hunter and his companions, the cry would echo down the line and every armed man and woman spread out to the east and west would converge on their position. They'd be under fierce attack long before they managed to scale the wall.

Which left him just the small bloody chance Kodyn had mentioned. The Hunter didn't particularly like the only route that currently lay open to them, but at the moment, there was no other option.

"Come on." He backed away, receding deeper into the shadows between the empty buildings along the southern edge of the plateau. Only once he'd slipped out of sight of the guards watching the wall did he turn away.

His body had mostly healed from the battering he'd endured during his fight, leaving his mind free to work at the problem. Not even a quarter-hour had elapsed since they'd fled the domed building, and they'd spent most of that time running through the darkened streets. Yet somehow the Consortium and Ordermen had not only reached the wall ahead of them, but spread out and taken up stations. That seemed an impossibility.

Yet could it be any less unlikely than the fact that they had been discovered? If someone had spotted them killing their way to the *Umoyahlebe*, the guards would have taken greater pains to pen them inside the domed building. But the slow, ineffectual response by the slavers and Ordermen didn't sit quite right with the Hunter.

Could something else be going on here? He couldn't begin to imagine what, yet couldn't shake the notion that the Order, in particular, would have responded far more decisively and violently if they'd suspected their prized prisoners were at risk of being freed. It was only *after* the Hunter, Kodyn, and Aisha had fled that they would've discovered the masked corpses—both those piled inside the building's southern entrance and lying in the dust outside the northern entrance.

The Hunter could find no answer to the question twisting in his mind. Yet.

He led the way into the single-story brick building they'd chosen as their temporary hideout, Kodyn on his heels. Neither of them made noise as he entered, not even the squeaking of door hinges. Aisha materialized from the shadows a moment later, lowering the spear she held poised to strike.

Kodyn shook his head. "Not gonna happen." He spoke in a low voice; it was less likely to carry than a harsh, sibilant whisper, proof he understood the art of stealth. "Too many around. We try to climb, they'll be on us like Jarl on a Maiden's Day feast."

Despite the grim circumstances, the Hunter couldn't help cracking a smile. The image that sprang to his head proved amusing—and likely correct. One didn't grow to the size of the burly Hawk without eating their fair share, and then some.

His mirth faded quickly, squelched beneath the iron-hard boot of their dire predicament. "The gate's our best chance."

Your best chance, he amended mentally. His plan involved playing bait to pull the guards away, buying Kodyn and Aisha a chance to escape. But he'd keep that detail to himself for the time being. The two youths had proven themselves far too noble to go through with a scheme like that unless they had no other choice. Which, the Hunter had to admit, appeared more likely with every passing heartbeat.

"We can't wait long," he said. "They've got the wall guarded, so it's a safe bet they'll begin searching house to house soon enough. Maybe half an hour. Maybe less."

He purposely avoided looking at Aisha as he spoke these words. She appeared on the verge of collapse—fiery hell, she *had* collapsed after over-drawing on her *Kish'aa* power during their last clash with the Ordermen. Though she'd absorbed the spirits of the pair they'd killed in their escape, she'd be running on limited strength. Every use of what energy remained to her— both magical and physical—would only hasten the inevitable. She couldn't keep exerting herself like this.

To his relief, she appeared to come to the same realization. "Just give me a few minutes to catch my breath." Her every word was labored, ponderous. "I'll be fine."

The Hunter nodded. "A few minutes, we can spare." He'd delay as much as he could, but it wouldn't be long before they'd be forced to move on. *Let's just hope it's enough.*

Aisha slumped onto the building's lone cot and leaned her head back against the wall. It was too dark to tell if she closed her eyes or merely sat to regain her strength. Either way, he left her alone. They might very well have need of her strength for what lay ahead.

With a nod of his head, he gestured for Kodyn to follow him to the far side of the room. It wasn't exactly a vast distance—no more than six long steps separated them from the cot—but at least it gave him a chance to speak to the young man without being right in Aisha's ear.

"You find anything useful?" he asked.

Kodyn nodded. "Useful? Aye." The moonlight streaming through the room's lone window illuminated his grinning face. "I found the duty roster for the Consortium. A full head-count of the thirteen hundred men sent here."

The Hunter let out a low whistle. "Thirteen hundred? That's a bloody lot!"

"Whatever they're doing here, it's big." The young man's face sobered. "There are records of thousands of cartloads of supplies being hauled in from the northeast. All the way from the Kurma Empire and Odaron. And not cheap."

The Hunter narrowed his eyes. "Anything out of the ordinary? Beyond the usual foodstuffs, building materials, tools, and so on?"

"Like what?" Kodyn's brow furrowed.

"I don't know." The Hunter shrugged. "I found a smithy with a blast furnace, and evidence that they were smelting the dimercurite and alloying it with other metals. But which, I couldn't tell just by looking. I'm no smith."

Kodyn rubbed his chin. "I didn't see anything, but I can look again." He patted a thick bulge under his cloak. He'd brought the satchel he'd stolen from the Consortium offices in *Indawo Yokwesaba*—empty, of course—for precisely this purpose. "Took everything I could get my hands on."

"Good thinking. Anything else?"

"You mean like who's at the top of the Consortium food chain, or who in the Order of Mithridas is calling the shots?" Kodyn shook his head. "Chances are good there's something of use in here—especially once I compare and contrast with everything else I snatched before—but I didn't have the time to go over much. I'd just stolen into the third office when I spotted the group headed your way. Figured it was best to bring warning, so I grabbed what I could and got out of there fast."

The Hunter ground his teeth, frustrated. His annoyance wasn't directed at Kodyn—the young man had been right to warn them of the approaching enemies—but at what felt like *another* failure. Sure, he'd located the captured *Umoyahlebe* and had at least an inkling of the Order's true intentions with *Ukuhlushwa Okungapheli*. Yet they'd been forced to flee before they could liberate the captives or done anything to slow the Order, much less stop them.

He controlled himself with effort, drawing in a slow, deep breath through his nostrils. "You did good," he said, clapping Kodyn gently on the shoulder. "I've no doubt that your efforts will yield something of value."

Kodyn endeavored heroically to keep the proud smile from his face—and failed. "First chance I get, I'll pore over everything—"

The Hunter cut off the young man with a sharp hiss and dragged Kodyn out of sight below the window. A flicker of light had caught his eye, and when he peered over the windowsill, he found the orange glow of a torch streaming through the buildings three streets to the north.

Keeper take it! he cursed mentally.

They'd run out of time.

Aisha was already on her feet—evidently she'd kept her eyes and ears open while resting—and slipping toward them. She didn't look much better than a few minutes earlier, but they could afford to wait no longer. Without a word, the Hunter led the way out the building's lone door and into the darkness.

They left the torchlight behind quickly, long before the distant voices coalesced and became audible. But whoever approached from the north did not come alone. More lights appeared in the darkness. The Consortium and their Order masters had commenced the city-wide search. If there'd been any doubt that the enemy was inside the camp, the presence of more than two dozen masked corpses would've dispelled it like snow in the Advanat Desert. Now, thirteen hundred Consortium slavers would be spreading out to hunt them down.

Thirteen hundred? Something about that number sat poorly with the Hunter for some reason he could not put into words. He had no time to think about it either; he was too busy dodging the torch-carrying companies of guards and navigating the shadows on a steady path toward the gate set into the volcanic stone wall.

There would be no retreat, no hiding, no stealthy escape. Just a bloody battle to fight their way to freedom. Aisha and Kodyn would have no choice but to go along with his plan. The only alternative was certain death.

472

Despite the night's chill, sweat streamed down his back and pricked on his forehead. His heart pounded a furious tattoo against his ribs and his breathing grew louder in his ears with every step. The ever-increasing fear of discovery mingled with the rising thrill of the battle to come. The fingers of his right hand trembled as if aching to close around *Ibad'at Mutlaqa's* hilt, to draw the steel and feel the bloodlust overwhelm him. After the cruelty he'd witnessed this night, he could slaughter every Orderman and Consortium slaver without compunction or hesitation.

When finally the gate came into view at the far end of the darkened street, the Hunter was on the verge of drawing his blades and charging into battle. Only the presence of Kodyn and Aisha at his back kept him from precipitous action. Their lives depended on his next move.

To his surprise, the gates stood *open*. The Hunter blinked. That made no sense at all. *Why, if the camp is up in arms and searching for us, would the gates be—*

Then he saw them. Kneeling in the dirt just inside the volcanic stone wall, hands bound behind their backs, three umber-skinned figures were barely visible between the ring of nearly two-score Consortium guards that stood surrounding them. Every one of the slavers had their greatknives drawn and pointed at their captives. Among them stood a trio of black-masked Ordermen, arms folded over their chests and weapons sheathed. Yet it was clear who was in charge here. At a wordless nod from one Orderman, a slaver drove a clenched fist into the face of the centermost of the kneeling figures.

"Speak!" the man shouted, his Voramian accent harsh and his voice strident. "Tell us how many more of you there are, and we will grant you a quick death." He slammed another punch into the same figure's face. "Silence will only earn you a slow, agonizing death."

When no answer proved forthcoming, the Voramian stepped back and looked to the three Ordermen as if questioning what to do next.

A gap opened up through the ranks of armed men surrounding the three captives, and recognition stole the Hunter's breath.

He knew those three! Knew the shining silver piercings, broad shoulders, and the fibrous cloth battle-wrappings that marked them as Issai warriors. But not just any *amaqhawai*. The thickly-built one on the right was Naledi, while the slighter-framed, wild-haired one on the left was Cebile, the warrior who'd fed him the Ghandian lion pepper soup.

But it was the woman in the middle, the one suffering under the slaver's beating, who drew the Hunter's eye—and earned a muted gasp from Aisha. "Siyanda!"

Chapter Thirty-Eight

The Hunter felt Aisha tense at his side. One heartbeat more, and she'd likely charge into the fray as she had when her father had been the one receiving the blows. He couldn't let that happen.

He spun toward her, gripped her arm tight. "Don't!" he snarled.

She opened her mouth to protest.

He cut her off with a shake of his head. "Stay here and be ready to move on my signal."

To his relief, she did not give voice to the argument forming on her lips. Perhaps it was her exhaustion, or perhaps she saw the logic in his words. Whatever the case, she merely nodded in response.

The Hunter relinquished his grip on her arm, but not before shooting a stern look at Kodyn. Hopefully, the young man could keep Aisha in place long enough for the Hunter to execute the plan that had sprung to his mind. When Kodyn tilted his head in acknowledgement of the unspoken command, the Hunter turned away and marched out of the shadows with all the confidence of one who belonged.

For in truth, he *looked* as if he belonged. He wore Consortium armor and the harsh, scarred features he'd used countless times over the years as Voramis' most feared assassin. The face that had set grown men quaking in their boots and soiling their undergarments appeared right at home among the cruel, whip-wielding slavers.

Straight toward the crowd gathered around the three kneeling Issai the Hunter marched. He put a bit of swagger into every step, kept his advance slow and steady. Just one more of the thirteen hundred armed men dispatched here by the Consortium.

He closed on the ring of slavers, reaching the rearmost just in time to hear one of the masked Ordermen snap, "Make them talk."

"With pleasure." A leering sneer twisted the face of the Voramian slaver who'd been pounding at Siyanda. Turning, he drew a long, single-edged curving dagger from his belt and held it up before the three captive Issai warriors. He grinned as he ran a finger across the blade, looking between Siyanda, Cebile, and Naledi. "Question is, which one of you will prove more fun?"

The slaver stepped up to Naledi, the broadest of the bunch. "Bigg'un like you'll be tough at first, but once I get cutting, you'll crack easy." He leaned lower and laughed in her face. "Especially when I start removing fingers and toes."

Naledi gave no indication she'd heard or understood; her strong face remained impassive, her eyes staring straight ahead.

The Hunter slid through the ranks of slavers, careful to remain out of the line of sight of the three Issai. No sense drawing unnecessary attention to himself yet.

"As for you," the Voramian said, strolling past Siyanda to wave his dagger in Cebile's face. "You've got the look of old leather about you. Tough as hide, just as inflexible." He clucked his tongue. "No, you'll die before you talk. Which leaves *you.*"

He spun on his heel toward Siyanda. "Young as you are, you probably think you can endure." He bent at the waist to speak into Siyanda's ear in a low voice. "You've not yet lived enough to know just how bad things can get f—"

His words cut off in a terrible, wet *crunch* as Siyanda twisted her head and slammed her forehead straight into the bridge of his nose. With a cry, the slaver staggered backward, reeling drunkenly. He clapped a hand to his face but could not stanch the flow of crimson gushing from his shattered nose.

"You bidch!" the Voramian roared. Tears of pain streamed down his face, but rage blazed in his eyes. "You'll bay for thad!"

Raising his dagger, he advanced on Siyanda, fully intending to carry through on his threat. Yet he got no more than one step before his feet faltered, stumbling. His upraised arm wavered, wobbled, and sagged to his side. The hand holding his nose fell to his side, and bewilderment sprouted on his bloodied face as he felt the hilt of the throwing knife buried between his ribs.

"Whad?" With that eloquent final word, he crumpled like a dropped sack of rocks and sprawled in a lifeless heap on the ground before the three kneeling Issai.

For a breathtaking moment, the entire circle of Consortium slavers and their three Order masters remained utterly motionless, paralyzed by confusion. The Hunter had drawn the throwing knife from his belt and hurled it in a motion so smooth and swift none of the men around him had seen where the dagger had come from. They'd been so consumed by the prospect of watching the Voramian torture the three Issai they'd barely paid attention to their surroundings. Not a single one of them had noticed the Hunter sliding through their ranks, until he stood just behind the foremost of the slavers holding their swords leveled at Siyanda, Cebile, and Naledi.

Thus, none were prepared when the Hunter unleashed a whirlwind of carnage on them. He did not draw the Sword of Nasnaz—he could not risk losing control now—but Soulhunger and his watered steel blade whispered from their sheaths to carve devastation through the slavers. Half a dozen Consortium men and women fell within the space of two heartbeats as the Hunter spun a full circle, hacking, slashing, chopping, and gutting with all the might of his Bucelarii muscles.

Even when those first died, he did not stop. He merely vaulted their falling bodies and hurled himself at the next enemies within his reach. Killing one with a sword thrust to the chest, opening another's throat with Soulhunger's keen edge, hamstringing a third in the same up-slashing stroke that severed the spine of a fourth. He was a blur of steel and fury, carving through the ranks of Consortium slavers, inflicting wounds both mortal and disabling. He did not need to *kill* them all—he merely needed to cut down their numbers enough to open the way to freedom.

"Now!" he roared, though he doubted it was necessary. Kodyn and Aisha couldn't have missed the sudden eruption of violence and would be on their way at that very moment.

Through the screams of agony, the clashing steel, and the rush of adrenaline pounding in the Hunter's ears, he heard a shout. "Get those Keeper-damned gates closed!"

His head snapped in the direction of the gates. Three Consortium men were running toward what appeared to be a gatehouse, doubtless to carry out the order. The Hunter changed directions, carving through a pair of greatknife-wielding slavers who barred his path. Yet even as they fell, three more charged him from the side, forcing him to turn to meet their blades. They did not stand long against him—one fell with a deep wound in his thigh, another missing a hand, the third clutching at a gaping tear in his throat—but in those few precious seconds, the guards had almost reached their destination.

Keeper take it! The Hunter sprang in pursuit, only to find himself blocked off once more. Five Consortium slavers and two of the masked Ordermen had seen his intent and moved to intercept.

Worse, more reinforcements were arriving by the second. The sound of battle had alerted every guard stationed within earshot along the wall's inner perimeter. Every one of them would be on their way at that very moment. If the guards got that gate closed, the Hunter, Aisha, Kodyn, and the three Issai warriors would be trapped and surrounded.

Desperation lent strength and fury to the Hunter's blows. He chopped through upraised swords and outstretched sword arms alike, his thrusts piercing armor, cloth, and exposed flesh with terrible efficiency. Yet he could not cut his way through. The two Ordermen facing him fought with skill enough to keep him from overwhelming them as he did the slavers who died around them. The third masked man, the one who'd given the order to torture the Issai, now shouted commands and rallied the guards to the defense of the gate.

The Hunter's mind raced. He couldn't win like this. The time had come to abandon restraint in favor of—

Brilliant blue-white light streaked past him, a trio of blindingly bright spears that punched into the backs of the three guards running toward the gatehouse. They fell and lay in twitching, smoking heaps on the ground.

At the same instant, a ululating war cry rose from the three kneeling Issai—who were kneeling no longer. They had found their feet and gotten free of the ropes holding them bound. Raising high bloodied greatknives taken from their fallen captors, they hurled themselves onto the last of the slavers between them and the gate. Behind them, Kodyn hurled the dagger that had severed their bonds at the third Orderman. The masked bastard never even saw it coming; it buried to the hilt in the side of his neck, turning his strident shouts into horrible choking gurgles.

Hah! The Hunter's spirits soared, and he tore into the Ordermen before him with renewed intensity and a fierce, reckless abandon. He purposely took a thrust to the meat of his left shoulder, accepting the pain of steel scraping against bone as a fair exchange for trapping his enemy's blade long enough to bring his own sword crashing into the mask. Had it been made of a scale pried off one of the freshly killed slashwyrm corpses, the mask might have held, perhaps even offered some mere protection from his blade. But this mask was weak, brittle, akin to those worn by the Ordermen the Hunter had encountered on the road to Malandria. It shattered beneath the force of the impact and watered steel carved a terrible path through the Orderman's face, skull, and neck. The top of their head flew away into the night.

A spin to his right tore the dead Orderman's sword tip from his shoulder and brought him face to face with the last masked enemy. The Hunter saw the widening of the eyes behind the black, snarling beast façade, and a grim smile twisted his lips. "Rot in hell, you whoreson!" he snarled.

A quick high feint brought the Orderman's blade up, and the Hunter twisted his wrist at the last moment to drive his own sword tip downward. Razor-sharp steel punched through the flesh and gristle of the man's throat, just beneath the edge of his mask. Whipping his sword outward, the Hunter tore open the side of the Orderman's neck. He didn't even bother evading the wild, desperate attack aimed at him—the blow flew wide as his dying enemy lurched backward and fell to lie bleeding in the dirt.

Aisha seemed to materialize at the Hunter's side, eyes aglow with the blue-white light of the *Kish'aa* and the end of her *assegai* stained with blood. "Come on!" she shouted. "Time to go!" She punctuated her words by sending a short burst of sparks straight into the eyes of an onrushing slaver. The woman fell screaming and battering at her face in a vain attempt to put out the magical fires consuming her skin and eyeballs.

The Hunter wasted a single moment staring down at the fallen slaver. The woman writhed on the ground in terrible agony, and the smell of scorched flesh rose from her burning face. The Hunter had just pity enough to silence her shrieking with a quick sword thrust to the heart.

"Kodyn's going for the gatehouse." Aisha's words pierced the roaring of the Hunter's heartbeat. "If he can sabotage the gates—"

At that moment, the young Praamian burst out of the gatehouse at a dead sprint. "*RUN!*" he shouted at the top of his lungs. A terrible squealing of metallic mechanisms echoed from behind him and the huge metal bars of the gate's portcullis gave an ominous rumble.

476

Neither the Hunter nor Aisha needed further encouragement. In unison, they broke into a mad dash toward the open gate. Only a pair of slavers stood between them and freedom, but they were too confused and disoriented to do more than raise their swords at the sight of the charging pair. Aisha blasted one out of her path with a surge of lightning and the Hunter cut down the other on his way past. Five long strides brought him to the gate-sized opening in the volcanic stone wall, where Cebile, Naledi, and Siyanda fought side by side.

Time slowed to a crawl as the heavy portcullis began to fall. The Hunter's gaze tracked the movement of the sharpened tips of the grating on its path toward the heads of the three Issai. He could almost *feel* those metallic spikes punching into the warriors' flesh and crushing them beneath their immense weight.

Oh, no, you bloody don't!

He hurled himself at Naledi and Cebile, arms spread wide to wrap around them in a flying tackle. Kodyn and Aisha both did likewise with Siyanda, bearing her backward between them. The Hunter's shoulders collided with the two Issai warriors' muscled torsos and the force of his impact brought them all to the ground. They hit the ground hard, jarring the breath from the Hunter's lungs. A heartbeat later, a thunderous *BOOM* echoed behind them and the very ground jolted beneath the force of the portcullis slamming shut.

The Hunter didn't waste time glancing back; he merely sprang to his feet, dragged Naledi and Cebile upright, and set off running. Yet the muffled, barely audible curses hurled over the wall told him that Kodyn's plan had been successful.

There was no way the slavers could catch them now.

Chapter Thirty-Nine

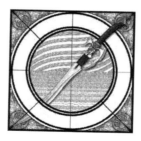

Had it been up to the Hunter, they wouldn't have stopped running until they reached the rocky depression a quarter-league from the wall where they'd concealed the horses earlier than night. But within a few hundred paces, it grew quickly apparent Cebile was in no shape to run.

She'd begun stumbling and limping shortly after leaping over the hidden tripwire chain. Only after she'd fallen a third time did the Hunter finally insist on stopping. She tried to wave him away, but neither he nor Aisha would be dissuaded. Even after Aisha pressed the warrior to a seat, Cebile would yield not an inch.

"It is no pain," she said in thickly accented Einari. The tension lines around her eyes, the clench of her jaw, and the thick streams of sweat pouring down her bloodied and bruised face belied her words. She continued speaking in the Ghandian tongue, but Aisha answered back in a sharp tone that sounded suspiciously like her mother's commanding voice.

The Hunter's gut twisted as he got a good look at Cebile's right knee. "Keeper's teeth!" he muttered under his breath. The joint was swollen to four times its size, the kneecap shifted out of place, and the flesh around it was mottled dark purple.

"Cebile!" Aisha gasped. Her eyes went from the injured knee to the *amaqhawai's* face. She asked a question in Ghandian—including the word for "walk"— and Cebile answered back with a shake of her head.

"You keep walking on that leg," the Hunter said, "and you might *lose* it. I'm no healer, but that knee looks bad. I'm surprised you can even stand."

"It is no pain," was all Cebile would say, a defiant look in her eyes.

"Cebile!" Naledi's voice cracked like a whip. She barked a few words edged with reproach, and the younger *amaqhawai* grumbled some response the Hunter did not understand. The larger warrior turned back to the Hunter. "All Issai are tough, but some are thick like *chipekwe* skulls." She rapped her knuckles against the crown of Cebile's head. "She cannot run much farther. But cannot stay so near the *Gcinue'eleku awandile.*"

"Then I will carry her." The Hunter sheathed his weapons and stepped toward the seated woman. "I can bear her weight and run long enough to—"

Naledi stepped into the Hunter's way with a sharp click of her tongue. "Issai will carry Issai." She thumped a fist against her broad chest. "*Amaqhawe for amaqhawe.*"

The Hunter looked the solidly built warrior over. She hadn't walked away from the Consortium encampment unscathed. Blood trickled from her split lip, and her arms, chest, torso, and legs were covered with the welts and gashes where her captors' weapons had struck her. It would've taken five or ten slavers to take her alive; she wouldn't have submitted to being bound and dragged through the gates without a struggle.

478

Her warrior's pride bore bruises to mirror those mottling her body. She'd done much to assuage the insult of her capture by fighting back and killing those who'd dared to lay hands on her. But she—and, no doubt, Siyanda and Cebile—would want nothing that so much as *hinted* at weakness. That much, he understood. He'd likely have done the same in their place.

Raising his hands in a gesture of surrender, he stepped back. "Of course."

Aisha turned to Siyanda, who had remained silent thus far, too busy gasping for breath to find words. "Are you—"

"I'm fine!" Siyanda snapped. She straightened immediately, laboring to hide her winded state. "But Naledi's right. We can't stay here. We have to leave before they get the gate open and come out searching for us."

"We know a good place to lay low," Kodyn put in. "We've got the horses stashed out of sight, someplace the *alay-alagbara* won't find them." He shot the Hunter an anxious look. "And the others should be meeting us there soon."

The Hunter nodded. "Probably already waiting for us and wondering why we're dawdling." He had to hope Kiara and Tarek's efforts had yielded fruit. They needed at least one victory tonight. "Let's move." This, he directed to Naledi and Cebile.

With a nod, the broad-shouldered warrior bent down to help her companion stand, then wrapped one thickly muscled arm around her shoulder. Aisha seemed to think the Hunter's acceptance of Naledi's insistence didn't include her, for she moved to stand on Cebile's other side and slung the woman's arm around her shoulder. If Naledi had intended to say anything, the intense glare Aisha shot her way sufficed to squash protest.

The Hunter was struck by how strong a resemblance Aisha bore to her mother. Not just in her facial features, but in the way she carried herself with an air of authority unusual for one so young. A far cry from the Aisha he'd met in Praamis, even the Aisha who'd accompanied him on the road to Khafra.

She's come a long way, he thought. His eyes strayed to Kodyn. *Both of them have.*

The young man's growth was subtler, yet the Hunter could see it in his bearing. Kodyn no longer hovered around Aisha as if trying to protect her. Though his strength was far subtler, it proved more than a match for hers. She was the raging flood that ripped up trees and boulders, he the fast-flowing river that carved a path through mountains and canyons.

The thought flashed through his mind and was gone in a moment. Their current circumstances demanded his full attention.

"Kodyn, lead the way," he instructed. "Keep an eye out for any more traps or tripwires. Last thing we want is for our enemies to know which way we've gone. If they can't follow us, they'll likely give up pursuit." No matter how furious the Consortium and their Order masters, thirteen hundred men was far from sufficient manpower for more than a cursory search extending a few miles out from the camp. With *Indawo Yokwesaba* a few leagues to the south, the foothills to the west, and a series of rocky canyons spreading east from *Isigodi Umlilophilayo*, there would be too much land to cover while still keeping a tight rein on the captives and holding the gates against possible attack.

Kodyn nodded and set off at a loping run in the direction of the hollow they'd established as their rendezvous point. Siyanda hurried to follow, with Aisha, Naledi, and a limping Cebile between them. But the Hunter had seen the way Naledi and Siyanda's faces had tightened when he mentioned traps and tripwires.

Is that how they got captured? he wondered as he ran at the rear of their small column. *That would explain a great deal.* After a moment's thought, he amended, *hell, it's the only explanation that makes sense!*

The Issai, like all the Ghandian tribes, had spent their entire lives roaming lands much like these. The Hunter had been impressed by their stealth as they crept up on the Buhari camp; they'd made *him* sound noisy by comparison. No way the heavily armored, torch-carrying Consortium patrols could have crept up on the warrior women unawares. Indeed, the Hunter had little doubt the trio could have evaded the *alay-alagbara's* notice altogether.

Unless they'd stumbled on the tripwire. Such a construction would be unfamiliar to them, which made it all the more effective a hidden defense.

The Hunter hadn't heard any manner of alarm, but it was possible the chain had only tripped some *smaller* bell or claxon, possibly within the gatehouse or one of the barracks where the Consortium guards were housed. Most likely the former.

Kodyn's explanation of the dimercurite bands and chains imprisoning the *Umoyahlebe* flashed through his mind. If the Order or Consortium possessed the ingenuity to craft such devices in miniature, it was no great stretch to imagine it built on a larger scale. He'd made enough traps and snares of his own that he could easily picture the schematic of a tripwire and lodestones that would respond when the chain shifted beneath unwary feet.

He made a note of that for when they returned. They could easily avoid the tripwire now that Kodyn had pointed it out. Yet a part of him mulled over ways to turn the Consortium's defensive mechanism—and *all* their fortifications—against them. He'd learned long ago that even high walls, bastion-like mansions, and an army's worth of guards could go from protection to prison in seconds. Every strength could be turned into a weakness with the right planning.

That thought—and contemplating their next course of action—consumed him so thoroughly he only paid nominal attention to his surroundings. His mind was adept at filtering out the important and unimportant details around him—a flicker of light, a sudden ripple of movement, a shifting of shadows, the faintest hint of sound—to indicate the presence of enemies. There were none. As he'd hoped, the Consortium patrols had been so fixated on the sport of torturing and interrogating their captives they'd abandoned their posts outside the wall. For the time being, all of their enemies were trapped within the gates.

It took them the better part of an hour to reach the rendezvous point. They were forced to slow when their path cut through boulders set so close together they could only pass two abreast. The way beyond was narrow and meandering, descending into the hidden, rocky hollow where they'd left the horses.

The Hunter's gut tightened when they found the five horses but no sign of Kiara or Tarek. *It's still early,* he told himself, glancing up at the stars. Midnight had only just passed. He wouldn't start worrying until sunrise.

Elivast and Ash perked up at the Hunter's approach, and they trotted over to greet him. The Hunter rubbed their noses and whispered a few reassuring words into their ears. They seemed as concerned as he, nickering softly, and darting glances in the direction Kiara had gone.

"They'll be back soon," he murmured, though the words felt intended to convince himself more than the horses.

Siyanda and Naledi helped Cebile to sit, and the two Issai women crouched over their companion to examine the wounded knee. Kodyn hurried to his and Aisha's horses and, after a few moments spent rummaging through his saddlebags, produced a clay jar and a bundle of bandages.

"Here," he said, offering them to Naledi. "This will help with the pain, and you can use this to splint the knee."

"*Ngya'bona,*" Naledi said, tilting her shaven head in thanks. She took the jar but recoiled with a loud protest in her native tongue when she opened it.

"*Gokulah* unguent," Kodyn said, as if answering a question. "Stinks like the rotting hell, but trust me, it works like the Bright Lady's tears."

The smell reached the Hunter a second later, and even the musk of his horses could not drown it out. His nostrils curdled at the stench, familiar though it was. Tassat had offered him the stuff on the road out of Praamis. It had done wonders to heal the bruises Mak had sustained in their scuffle with Lord Chasteyn. All the same, the Hunter determined to stay at least a dozen paces away from Cebile unless otherwise unavoidable.

Movement from off to one side of the hollow caught the Hunter's eye. Instead of going to help Cebile, Aisha had slipped away from the knot of Issai women and Kodyn. Now, she stood alone a dozen paces away, her back turned to her companions.

The Hunter frowned. He couldn't be certain, for the tall cliffs blocked out the moon's pale glow and only the stars illuminated the hollow, but it looked as if her shoulders were shaking. Was she…crying?

The Hunter glanced toward where Kodyn was helping Naledi and Siyanda tend to Cebile. The young man hadn't noticed Aisha's separation or the turmoil consuming her.

With a grunt, the Hunter pushed Elivast's nose out of the way and strode past Ash toward Aisha. As he approached, the quiver of her shoulders grew more pronounced. The sobs shook her whole body, down to her clenched fists and her wide-planted legs.

The Hunter placed a hand on her shoulder. "Aisha—"

His words cut off in a curse and he yanked his hands away. Her bare flesh was searing hot to the touch.

She rounded on him then, and the brilliant blue-white light blazing in her eyes spoke not of sorrow, but fury so all-consuming it set an inferno of magical energy raging inside her.

"I had her!" Aisha hissed through bared teeth. "I had my sister, had her right in my arms. And I had to let her go!"

Chapter Forty

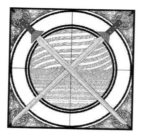

The Hunter sprang backward as a blinding azure corona exploded outward from Aisha. Searing hot wind buffeted him with ferocity enough to singe his skin. He threw up a hand to shield his face, but the light and burning energy diminished in the space between fearful heartbeats.

When he lowered his hand, he found Aisha had fallen to her knees and now bent double, face near to the ground. She drove her balled right fist against the ground once, twice, three times. Again and again, relentless and furious. Every strike sent sparks flaring from her knuckles to dance and sizzle across the rocks beneath her.

"Aisha!" Kodyn's cry came from behind the Hunter.

"Stay back!" Without turning away, the Hunter threw up one hand behind him to halt the young man's inevitable approach. He recalled only too clearly what had happened the last time Aisha's fury had been thus unleashed. Only his innate healing abilities had kept him from suffering permanent damage. "Just give her a moment."

He recognized the inferno raging within her. One much its like had nearly consumed him in the wake of Farida's death, and again after he watched the First drive Soulhunger through Bardin's chest. He'd felt it upon seeing Il Seytani's dagger drawing Hailen's blood and Master Eldor draw in his final breath in the darkened tunnels beneath Kara-ket.

Rage, sorrow, the anguish of loss, and, worst of all, the terrible feeling of helplessness all melded together into one agonizing, seething knot of white-hot torment. *He* had butchered the Bloody Hand, slaughtered Il Seytani's *Mhareb,* and carved through the Sage's Elivasti in an effort to quell the fire raging within him. The bloodshed had given him an outlet, physical targets upon whom to unleash his fury, yet it had not eased the pain.

But for the moment, Aisha needed this. Needed to let out the pent-up emotions before they burst out from her in a wave of destruction she could not control. When he'd lost his grip on himself, he'd slaughtered scores of enemies in cold blood. But her power was enough to decimate entire armies—or kill everyone she loved.

"Aisha." He spoke quietly, doubting she could hear him but determined to try and get through to her anyways. "Aisha, you have not yet failed her. You hear me?" He moved toward her, heedless of the sparks flying around his feet. "She is not yet out of your reach. We can go back for her. For all of them. We can still free them. This is just a setback. Come nightfall—"

Aisha's head snapped up, and her eyes—blazing blue-white with the light of the *Kish'aa*—fixed on him. "They'll kill her!" Her voice, amplified by a power far beyond mortal strength, resounded off the surrounding cliffs and set the ground beneath the Hunter's feet trembling. "They'll kill all of them. Don't you see? They'll want retribution for the ones we killed, and they'll take it out on the only ones they can. On my sister." She pounded a fist against her chest, and every thump sent spears of lightning crackling outward. "*My* father. My fellow *Umoyahlebe*."

"They'll want retribution, sure enough." The Hunter twisted to avoid one blast of power. Almost too slow. A red-hot line seared along the left side of his stolen Consortium studded vest. Gritting his teeth against the pain of his scorched flesh, he forced himself to take another step toward her. *Toward* the simmering fury blazing ever brighter around her. "But think of all the effort they've expended to capture, identify, and transport the *Umoyahlebe* here. They *need* them. Need their power to break through the door guarding the Bondshold. And if what your mother said about your sister is true, that her stone glowed nearly as bright as yours, then it means they *have* to keep her alive."

His mind cast back to what he'd witnessed at the base of *Ukuhlushwa Okungapheli*. "And your father," he hurried on before she could raise her voice in protest or her power in anger, "I saw him wield his power. None of the others had any semblance of control, but he did. He channeled the *Kish'aa* with precision and restraint."

The blaze surrounding Aisha did not dim, yet it did not brighten further. For a moment, she seemed frozen in place, paralyzed by the power that now seemed to glow in every vein, leak out her pores, crackle off the ends of her long, dark hair.

"The Order are cruel, but they are not foolish enough to throw away the lives of their most powerful captives." Even as the words left his mouth, the Hunter winced at how callous that logic sounded. But that made it no less logical. "They will keep them alive as long as possible, because they are the ones who will have the best chance of actually doing what they were brought there to do."

Though he knew it was a risk, he took the chance anyway and stepped closer to her. Close enough he could place both hands on her shoulders. "They will live!" he said, gritting his teeth as the flesh of his palms burned from the contact. "They will live at least a while longer. And while they live, they are still within your reach. You can still get to them and get them out."

It might have been his imagination or merely wishful thinking as the pain built in his hands and face, but he almost imagined the fire burning within her diminishing.

"The moment to unleash this power raging within you will come, and soon, this I swear." The Hunter forced his fingers to squeeze her shoulders, though his nerves screamed as they burned. "But not yet. We've found them, learned what our enemy intends with them. Now we plan how to get them all out and burn to the ground everything the bastard *alay-alagbara* have built here. And we need you for that. We need you, Aisha. You are the only one who can save them."

Throughout his speech, Aisha had remained kneeling, her eyes fixed on him. The Hunter had no idea if she could even hear him through the inferno of magically amplified emotions coursing within her. He'd spoken only out of the hope his words could get through to her.

Yet as he said his last, the fire within Aisha dimmed. Just a fraction, yet it was enough that she no longer glowed through every pore. Her eyes returned to their usual *kaffe*-brown.

"I…can't!" She spoke through gritted teeth. The power muffled and amplified her words in a strange cacophony, making it sound as if multiple people spoke through her. "Too…much! Too…many!"

"Focus!" The Hunter released his grip on her shoulders and, though his hands were nothing more than raw, searing misery, he reached down to grip her bloodied knuckles. "Focus on me. On my voice." He dragged her bodily off the ground, and her legs straightened by instinct to hold her upright. "You are the Spirit Whisperer, Aisha. *You* are in command. The *Kish'aa* answer to you."

Aisha's face contorted, shifting from a rictus grin to a grimace of effort to a flat, deadpan expression and back again, all in the space of a heartbeat. Sweat streamed down her forehead and evaporated in hissing puffs of steam all around her.

"Remember what I taught you!" The Hunter gripped her hands tight, not bothering to be gentle. He needed to give her something to focus on—pain, sounds, sights, anything to anchor her in her mortal body, to give her an edge in her struggle with the spirits within her. "The most important thing to remember is that you are in control of your mind. Believe you have the power to silence the voices, and use that conviction to drive them back."

Aisha's face ceased its twisting, and she gritted her teeth. "Build...the...wall...in my mind!"

"That's it!" The Hunter's voice rose to an eager shout. With those last three words, she'd gained greater control over her mind. "Keep fighting. Keep building that wall. You have the power to silence them. No matter how many or how powerful they are. *You* rule your mind. Not them. Never them."

"Never them!"

The Hunter felt Aisha's hands pulling away from his, and for a moment he had the urge to keep a tight hold on her. Only when his eyes fell to the glowing pendant at her neck did he understand her intention. No sooner had he released her than both of her hands darted to the *Dy'nashia* and wrapped around it so tight her knuckles whitened.

The next instant, the light winked out as abruptly as a candle submerged under the ocean's surface, it felt as if all the searing air around the Hunter had been sucked away. The sudden absence of power radiating off Aisha left him staggering, weak. The night seemed terribly cold, and the gentle breeze gusting all around them drove icicles into the Hunter's seared palms.

Yet the Hunter had just enough presence of mind to reach for Aisha. He caught her as her legs gave out, though his, too, proved oddly weak. For long moments, he stood there, uncertain whether he held her upright or she him. His heart seemed to have frozen between beats, his lungs unable to draw breath.

"Hun...ter?" Aisha's voice was harsh, ragged, barely above a whisper.

"Yes?" he managed to croak out, though it sounded to his ears like the rustling of dried papers, the voice of some long-desiccated corpse.

"Did I...hurt you badly?"

The question shattered the paralysis holding the Hunter spellbound and rooted in place. Strength and warmth coursed once more through his veins and his muscles once more responded to his mental commands to hold him upright. But with the return of vigor came pain. Searing, stabbing agony lanced both palms, his fingers and thumbs, and the flesh of his wrists, arms, and face.

He looked down, turning his palms upward. "Not too badly." It was a lie, and she knew it. How could she not, staring at the blackened, bubbling flesh?

"I—" she began.

"Don't." The Hunter willed the scorched fingers of his right hand to ball into a fist, all except the index finger, which he shook under her nose. "My flesh will heal. What matters is that your spirit and mind remain unbroken."

She turned her face up to him, and moisture glimmered around her eyes. Eyes filled with shame, guilt, and pain. "I'm sorry!" she said, her voice cracking. "I shouldn't have lost control like that. I shouldn't—"

"Don't," the Hunter repeated. He smiled, and it was genuine, though the scorched skin on his face protested as it pulled. "I, as much as anyone, know that pain. Which means I know just how much strength it takes to regain control of yourself the way you did."

"I—"

Aisha's words were interrupted as a dark shadow flew past the Hunter and wrapped arms around her. "Aisha!" Kodyn's embrace mirrored a shred of the desperation echoing in his voice. "Are you hurt?"

"No, I'm not." Aisha wrapped one arm around Kodyn, returning his hug, but her face tightened. "But the Hunter—"

"Is no worse for wear." The Hunter winked at her. "Nothing a few hours of rest and a drink of water can't cure." Already, his face had begun to heal.

Kodyn pulled back. "Was it the *Kish'aa?*" he asked. "Did you absorb too many? Or were their wills too powerful?"

Aisha nodded. "Their rage." Her expression turned grimmer still. "So much rage. And hate. So much of it directed at themselves. At the wickedness of their own actions. I've never felt anything like it. It…" She shuddered. "It was difficult to control them, especially when my own anger burns as hot as the midday sun. Seeing what they did to my sister and father…" She shook her head. "They overwhelmed me. Together. But—"

A gasp cut her off. "*Ohloni'zwayo!*"

The Hunter, Aisha, and Kodyn turned toward the speaker. Naledi hadn't risen from where she'd been kneeling and tending to Cebile, but by the wide-eyed look on her face, it was clear she'd witnessed Aisha's power firsthand. Likely for the first time. Though she'd been among the captives freed from the Consortium camp, the fighting had been frenzied enough she could have missed it.

But now, she'd beheld Aisha's true might with her own eyes, from close enough she'd likely felt the searing hot wind blowing past, been half-blinded by the arcing lightning and dancing sparks. Color had drained from her strong face and a look of utter amazement filled her eyes.

"*Ohloni'zwayo!*" She repeated the unfamiliar Ghandian word, then lowered her other knee and bent her face to the ground. When she straightened a moment later, she touched her right hand—her spear hand—to her heart, her lips, then her forehead.

"*Ohloni'zwayo!*" Cebile repeated. Though she could not rise nor bow, she, too, repeated the reverent gesture, touching heart, lips, and forehead.

Siyanda, however, did not mirror the movement. She had risen to her feet and now stood staring with Aisha. But the look on her face held not a shred of wonderment or respect. Only scorn.

"Of course! Blame it on someone else." A snort burst from Siyanda's nose and her upper lip curled into a sneer. "That has always been your way, has it not, *um'zala?* Better to lay the fault at the feet of another than accept your weakness!"

The Hunter tensed. He'd only just calmed Aisha down, and now Siyanda would stoke the fires once more?

"Siyanda!" Naledi's strong, deep voice cracked like a whip. She snapped some words in the Issai tongue—among them "childish" and "show respect"—her tone unmistakably scolding.

Siyanda did not tear her eyes away from her cousin.

"Aisha—" Kodyn began in a low voice. Evidently, he'd come to the same conclusion the Hunter had.

"No." Aisha cut him off before he could say anything. "You want to do this, *um'zala?* So be it." She pushed Kodyn gently aside and strode toward her cousin. "Let us have it out between us here and now."

Chapter Forty-One

The Hunter had expected anger from Aisha, yet he was struck by how composed she appeared. Her calm contrasted starkly with the fiery inferno that had consumed her only moments earlier.

She moved to stand directly in front of Siyanda and planted her feet, spreading her arms wide. "Here I am, Siyanda. If you have something to say, speak plainly as befits an *amaqhawai*. Do not hide your tongue behind your teeth, as *Okadigbo* did to *Nuru Iwu*."

Siyanda's face creased into a snarl and she spat in her native tongue. "I will speak—"

"No!" Aisha's voice cracked like a whip and she stabbed a finger at her cousin's face. "You treat me as *alay-alagbara,* an invader come to destroy our people. Then speak your accusations in the *alay-alagbara* language, for I will not have your words sully the tongue of my mother and father, and their mothers and fathers before them."

Siyanda sneered. "So you will have it, *um'zala."* She spoke that last word like a curse. "I will make certain to speak slowly and clearly so there is no misunderstanding between us."

The Hunter saw Aisha's shoulders tighten, her spine stiffen as she lowered her arms to her sides. Beside him, Kodyn looked ready to intervene or interrupt. The Hunter stopped the young Praamian with an upraised hand. It had become readily apparent that Aisha needed this. *Both* women needed this, in truth. The bad blood between them could not continue. The only way forward now was to lance the boil and drain the rot to prevent further festering.

And what if this breaks them irrevocably? The question flashed through his mind. And how could it not, seeing the naked hatred and fury burning in Siyanda's eyes? One wrong word could take the matter too far, open so wide the chasm between them that it could never be breached.

But Aisha had no more backed down from this fight than any other in the weeks they'd traveled together. If she was willing to take the risk, then the Hunter and Kodyn both had to respect her decision.

Siyanda lifted her head, trying to stand taller than Aisha despite her inferior height. "You speak of *our* people. You call yourself Issai. And yet, you defy your *nassor* to come here. To risk yourself on what you know to be a fool's errand."

Aisha's face hardened. "This *fool's errand,* as you call it, has revealed to us more about our enemy in one night than you have been able to discover in months."

"Because I was doing what I could to keep our people alive!" Siyanda spat. "While our *amaqhawe* was captive, only I and Zalika remained to shoulder the burden of protecting the *ekhaya,* leading the hunt, watching for our enemies, and attempting to survive. There was nothing more I could have done. Nothing!" That last word rose to a shout that, to the Hunter's ears,

487

sounded far more desperate than angry. As if she were attempting to persuade herself as much as Aisha.

"*I* did not come here to accuse *you*, Siyanda." Aisha's voice held no scorn, merely iron-hard determination. "As to my defiance of our *nassor*, which *nassor* do you speak of? Do you know who leads the Tefaye these days? For with your own lips, you banished me from the tribe into which I was born, cursed me to be outcast."

Siyanda's mouth, open to snap some angry retort, remained agape but no sound came out. Aisha's words had clearly caught her flat-footed.

"I defied no one, Siyanda." Aisha's hands balled into fists. "I have acted in the best interest of *all* Ghandia, not only the Issai. You are merely angry that I did not beg you nor my mother for permission to do what I deemed necessary for the salvation of our people. And our family! Or have you forgotten Nkanyezi and my father already?"

Siyanda growled an ugly-sounding Ghandian word that had Kodyn blanching and Aisha's fists coming halfway up to fighting stance. Shocked looks sprouted on Naledi and Cebile's faces.

Siyanda filled the momentary silence with further vitriol. "And what of your orders?"

Aisha frowned, confused. "Orders?"

Triumph shone on Siyanda's face, as if she'd just trapped Aisha in some deceit. "You return to our people in the company of *alay-alaghara*—one who is *Okanele*, another you call your *oqinywe*. And the one who you serve, this *Hallar*, he is no Issai." She leaned closer, her eyes blazing. "Though you wear no chains or collar, do you deny you are still slave to an *alay-alaghara*?"

At that, even the Hunter's jaw dropped. Aisha had made mention of Hallar—and of the agreement she'd forged with the long-dead Bucelarii to guard the Serenii machinery in Shalandra—long ago. Thinking back on that night, he recalled Siyanda's derisive reaction all too clearly.

Aisha recovered from her surprise in a heartbeat. "Yes, I deny it!" she hurled back into the teeth of her cousin's accusations. "It is not my fault you do not understand what I have done, how much larger my actions are than just our people. Just as it is not my fault that you know nothing of the world beyond the borders of our small slice of the *amathafa* because you have never had the courage to leave the *ekhaya!*"

The Hunter winced. That had been a low blow by any standard.

But Siyanda only grew more incensed. "Never had the courage?" She looked ready to throw a punch, and both Kodyn and Naledi—like the Hunter himself—appeared ready to restrain the two women should things turn violent. "You speak of courage? *You!?* The child who was caught by the *Gcinue'eleku awandile*, unable to protect herself."

This time, it was Aisha who appeared on the verge of punching Siyanda for the remark—*again*. Only through great effort of will did she control herself.

Siyanda just took Aisha's restraint as admission. "How fitting that *you* should be the one to suffer for your actions, rather than someone *innocent* pay the price!"

Aisha sucked in a breath. "You speak of Enanela?" Pain twisted her expression at the name.

"So you admit it!" Siyanda crowed. "Your mother told you of Enanela, and now, after all these years, you can finally admit your guilt in the matter?"

"My mother spoke of your sister." Aisha's words came out clipped, her expression tight. "She also spoke of your father."

Siyanda recoiled as if punched. The mention of her father clearly had struck a nerve. She recovered quickly, however. "Admit it, then!" Her eyes blazed. "Admit you are to blame. Admit

488

that had it not been for you, my sister would not have ended up as hyena food, and my father lost to the *amathafa?*"

"How could I be to blame?" Aisha did not quaver before Siyanda's fury. "I was but a child. I knew nothing. I could have done nothing."

"And yet—"

"And yet *nothing!*" Aisha's voice thundered off the rocks. "You can no more fault me for your sister's death than you could fault yourself!"

Siyanda's eyes flew wide, and she drew in a deep breath, preparing to shout right back. Yet in that moment, the way her face had drained of color revealed the truth to the Hunter.

Of course. It made terrible sense suddenly. *That is the source of the fester.*

Apparently, Aisha came to the same realization. "*That* is why you have come to hate me all these years, Siyanda? Because it is easier to hate me than yourself?"

Aisha's words had an instantaneous effect on her cousin. The violence that Siyanda had held at bay all this time unleashed, and she swung a punch that thundered into Aisha's jaw. Aisha's legs wobbled and she staggered backward, falling hard to the dirt.

Kodyn made to lunge forward, but the Hunter threw out a hand, stopping the young man in his tracks. "No!" he hissed, his voice pitched for the Hawk's ears only. "She has seen the truth of it."

Indeed, he was right. The instant after her attack against Aisha, the air seemed to have gusted from Siyanda's lungs, and she stood frozen, as if paralyzed by the accusation.

Aisha picked herself up from the ground, but instead of anger, only sorrow showed on her face. "Oh, *um'zala!*" She spoke in a voice of such deep concern and empathy that even the Hunter felt it. "Tell me that is not true!" She took a step toward her cousin. "Tell me you have not carried this burden all these years! That you have not believed it is *your* fault what happened to Enanela."

"N-No." Siyanda tried to summon her anger, but it came out hollow, a fragile shield that had already begun to show cracks. "Of course it is not my fault. It is yours. You are the one who—"

"Siyanda." Aisha stepped close and seized her cousin's shoulders. "Look at me. Look me in the eyes and tell me you truly believe that we are to blame for what happened. Me, a child, barely four summers old, and you, a girl of seven." She gripped Siyanda tight. "You cannot believe it."

Siyanda's body went suddenly stiff, rigid, her movements jerky as she tried to pull free of Aisha's grip. In vain. Siyanda struggled harder, but Aisha held her fast.

"Say it!" Aisha insisted. "Say the words, Siyanda. Speak them and be free!" She pulled Siyanda close and wrapped her arms around her cousin's back in a wrestler's embrace.

That touch shattered the last of Siyanda's façade. As if Aisha had suddenly crushed the life from her lungs, her entire body sagged, her shoulders slumped, and her arms fell to her sides.

"It was my fault!" The words poured forth from her lips in a torrent of bone-deep anguish, pent up over more than a decade. That broke the dam. Tears streamed from Siyanda's eyes and she buried her face in Aisha's shoulders. "My fault. I was the older sister. I should have protected her. I should have known where she would go to play! But when my father asked me where you two might have gone, I did not know. It is my fault. My fault." She repeated the words over and over like some terrible, grim mantra.

Aisha tightened her grip on her cousin with her right arm, and reached her left hand up to clasp the back of Siyanda's neck.

489

"We were children," she said, her voice firm yet gentle, soothing. "As *nassor*, would you hold a child responsible for their sibling's actions? Or the actions of wild animals?"

Siyanda blubbered something Hunter could not understand but her violent head shake made it clear she would not.

"Then do not blame the children we were before." Aisha pulled her cousin close until their foreheads touched. "For they deserve the same love and understanding you would give any child now."

The Hunter wanted to turn away, wanted to wipe his burning eyes, but he could not look away from the tableau. Like twin statues, one etched with the sorrow of a thousand years, the other strong as stone and gentle as velvet. It was all he could do to swallow the lump rising in his throat. He had not seen such raw grief in a long time. Hadn't felt it himself since the night he cradled Farida's body on the lip of the Midden.

How long the two stood like that, the Hunter didn't know. Time seemed to hold no meaning within the rocky hollow. All else faded around him—the cool night breeze, the pain in his still-healing hands, Kodyn and the two Issai, the horses, even the beat of his own heart—until nothing remained but Aisha and Siyanda.

Aisha's lips moved now, her voice a whisper so quiet the wind nearly carried it away. Only the Hunter's keen Bucelarii ears enabled him to overhear what was spoken.

"For what happened to you, to your sister and father, I am so sorry, Siyanda. But the fault lies with no one. She was but a child. As was I, and as were you. You cannot take this burden on yourself. It will drag you into the darkness, and as long as you carry it, you will never be free. Trust me, I know this better than anyone."

Siyanda answered with incoherence, her words muffled by her sobs.

"For years," Aisha continued, stroking her cousin's hair with a gentle hand, "even after I was freed from the *Gainue'eleku awandile*, I blamed myself for what was done to me. I believed I was too weak, too afraid, that I should have done more to stop myself from being captured, drugged, and treated like an *alay-alagbara* whore. It took the wisdom of many people to help me see the truth. Even now, there are days when I struggle. But I look at those around me—at the women who freed me and took me into their House, at my *oqinywe* who stood by me through everything, at my friends who fight at my side—and I am reminded that the child who was taken is not the woman who stands in my boots today. That the daggers of my past do not have to inflict wounds on my future."

She wrapped both arms around Siyanda once more and squeezed her cousin tight to her. "I was afraid to return and look my mother in the face, for I felt weak, undeserving of being her daughter. But here I stand nonetheless. And here you stand, too. Despite everything. We are who we have become because of what happened to us."

"I couldn't save her!" Siyanda wept, her voice hoarse, barely above a whisper. "I couldn't save her. Just like I couldn't save you."

"It was not your place to save me," Aisha murmured. "Or her. You were a child, innocent of all guilt. She would not blame you. Take it from one who has spoken with *Kish'aa* by the hundreds. Enanela would no more hate you for not being there on her last day as I would hate you for not being there the day I was taken. For if you had been there, you would have been dead or captive, too. And our people would have suffered for it."

Siyanda buried her face in Aisha's chest, hands clasped over her face like a child weeping in the arms of her mother.

"You were right, you know?" Through her tears, a smile blossomed on Aisha's face. "There was nothing more you could have done—not for Enanela, for me, or for the *ekhaya*. Our people are still alive because you bore my mother's burden when they needed you to. And for that, I and every other Issai still breathing today will forever be grateful."

She rubbed Siyanda's back with a strong hand. "I have always admired your strength, *um'zala*. Through all my long months of captivity, I told myself, 'Siyanda would not cry. Siyanda would not beg. Siyanda would not break.' And so, I did not cry. I did not beg. I did not break." Her voice cracked, and she had to swallow before speaking again. "I am here because of you. Because you showed me the meaning of courage when you bulled your way onto the search party to locate your father, even when my mother wanted to refuse."

Siyanda's tear-stained face turned up toward Aisha. "You…remember?"

"I do." Aisha nodded. "I had forgotten that day, but the memory returned when my mother told me of what happened. I remember that you nearly died from starvation and thirst because you were relentless in your hunt for your father. Until Duma finally spoke to you, dissuaded you from your search."

Siyanda straightened, and in that moment, seemed to regain a measure of her iron will. "I searched for you, too." She wiped tears from her face with a strong hand. "As soon as we learned you were missing, I joined your mother and the *amaqhawe* in the hunt. Though I was but *unkgaliwe*, I would not be refused."

Aisha's eyes widened. "Truly?"

Siyanda nodded. "We traveled to Khafra, but the *Gcinue'eleku awandile* had disappeared. Still, I did not want to abandon the search. I convinced your mother to travel the lands of the Dalingcebo for a full turn of the moon. Village after village, always hoping, always disappointed. Until finally we had no choice but to return."

Her face now glowed with a new light: the light of determination called to the fore by the memories she shared. "Still I did not want to go. I begged your mother to let me keep searching. And so she did. She said it was to be my *uhambo loguquko*. That I was to return only once I had found you—or myself."

"Oh, Siyanda!" Aisha gripped her cousin's hands. "Why did you not tell me that before?"

"Because I did not like what I found." Siyanda's face hardened. "Everywhere I went—to Odaron, to Drash, even to faraway Nysl—I saw only the evil and cruelty of the *alay-alagbara*." She shuddered at a painful memory.

The Hunter himself had seen the depravities and excesses of which humans were capable. It came as no surprise to him that Siyanda's time spent outside Ghandia had led her to conclude all outsiders were malicious.

"Worst of all, I failed to find *you.*" Sorrow pooled in Siyanda's eyes. "Though I was welcomed home upon my return, always I have believed I gave up too soon, and so did not truly complete my *uhambo loguquko*. I tried to blame you—for being so weak you could be taken, for not leaving a trail I could follow, and for being taken so far away I would never find you—but that did not help. No more than blaming you for Enanela's death." She shook her head. "Then I tried to tell myself that I had found my purpose in defending the *amathafa* from wicked men like the *Gcinue'eleku awandile*. But that has felt like a lie, too." Her shoulders slumped. "And even in that, I have fallen short. I was not there to fight beside my sisters when our *nassor* and the *amaqhawe* were taken captive. I failed them, too! Just as I failed the *ekhaya* in the Tefaye attack. It took you and your *Okanele* to do what I should have done."

"No." Aisha shook her head. "You did not fail. Our warriors are free, our people whole. And the battle for the *amathafa* is not yet over, not unless you give up the fight." For the first time, she looked away from her cousin, and her eyes sought out the Hunter and Kodyn, who had stood motionless and silent all this time. "And we are far from done fighting, isn't that right?"

"Too bloody right!" the Hunter growled.

"Until we can no longer swing a sword or kick our enemies in the teeth." Kodyn grinned. "Even then, I've got a good pair of teeth."

Aisha chuckled. "See?" She turned back to Siyanda. "The *Kish'aa* have brought us back together again after all this time. Not as we once were, but who we are now. You, a courageous *amaqhawai*, even *nassor* of the Issai for a short time. Me, an *Umoyahlebe*." She brought her cousin's hands to her chest. "Look me in the eyes, *um'zala*. Speak the word you know in your heart to be true."

Siyanda lifted her gaze. The moment her eyes alighted on Aisha's face, pain, sorrow, and shame twisted her features. Tears slipped down her face once more. When she spoke, her voice was quiet, heavy. *"Ingani."*

A smile lit up Aisha's face as bright as her blue-white light had only minutes earlier. *"Ingani!"* Heart-sister, in the Ghandian tongue.

She leaned her forehead against Siyanda's, and Siyanda leaned against her. For a moment, the two stood there silently, a lifetime of unspoken love and kinship passing between them. Siyanda moved first, but not to break off. Instead, she wrapped her arms around Aisha's shoulders and pulled her close.

The Hunter couldn't help a smile breaking out on his face—a face that seemed suspiciously wet, and which stung as salt seeped into the cracks in his burned flesh. He brushed the moisture away and noticed Kodyn doing the same. Even Naledi and Cebile appeared moved by the moment. The two Issai warriors exchanged beaming grins, Cebile's pain seeming momentarily forgotten.

"Hunter!"

The shout from behind him shattered the moment like a crossbow bolt through a crystal glass window.

The Hunter recognized the voice—and the scent of leather, steel, trumpet lilies, and peonies that accompanied it—instantly.

Even as he spun toward her, Kiara's cry came again, sharp and edged with desperation. "Hunter, help me!"

Chapter Forty-Two

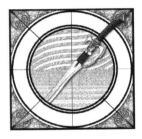

Kiara's cry nearly stopped the Hunter's heart. He braced himself mentally, afraid of what he'd see. Mere weeks had passed since he nearly lost her; he didn't know if he could endure that pain again.

The moment he laid eyes on her, the reason for her urgency became apparent. It was not *she* who needed help, nor apparently Tarek. Instead, it was the stranger staggering between them.

"He's in bad shape!" Kiara visibly struggled beneath the weight of her cumbersome burden—which turned out to be a man with the dark umber skin and tight-curling hair and beard of a Ghandian, though from what tribe, the Hunter could not tell, for the man wore only a filthy loincloth that hung off his emaciated frame in tatters. "We couldn't risk stopping and tending to him, but if we don't—"

"Let us," Aisha broke off from her embrace with her cousin and darted forward with arms outstretched toward the trio. Siyanda was right behind her.

Kiara was about to say something, but when her gaze fell on Siyanda, confusion twisted her face. It only deepened when she spotted the powerfully built Naledi rising from Cebile's side to join Aisha and Siyanda in taking the Ghandian from her and Tarek.

"Siyanda?" She blinked. "Naledi?" She looked to Cebile but seemed not to know her name. She turned back to the two Issai. "How are you here?"

"The *nassor* sent us," Naledi said, kneeling to lower the Ghandian man onto his back on the rocky ground.

"When it was discovered you had all left, Davathi was concerned for her daughter." Siyanda looked at Aisha, but her face held none of the malice or enmity that had darkened it earlier. Only relief and love shone in her eyes. "It was she who believed you had come here. To seek Aisha's father and sister, and for *that* one—" She gestured to Tarek, who, once relieved of his burden, had run toward where Nayaga stood next to Elivast and Ash. "—to locate the plant he believed would save the Tefaye."

The Hunter reached Kiara at that moment. "Are *you* hurt?" he asked, fighting hard to keep the worry from his tone. When he found no visible wounds, his gaze shifted to Tarek. "Either of you?"

Kiara laid a calming hand on his arm. "We are well." Her reassuring smile faded quickly when the Ghandian man lying on the ground gave a weak, moaning cough. "He is the one in need of healing."

"I could bring only the barest healing essentials with me." Tarek raced back toward them, clutching a sizeable leather pouch in his hand. He dropped to one knee beside the unnamed man, tore open the pouch flap, and rummaged within. "I believe I have something that will quell his pain. But alas, I fear I can do little for him."

At those words, the Hunter looked more closely at the Ghandian. What he saw brought acid rising in the back of his throat. The man's wasted body was a mess of weeping sores, blackened veins, suppurating purple boils as large around as a silver half-drake, bubbling blisters, even patches where the skin had burned a terrible, stark white. The flesh of his belly, chest, and thighs was carved to ribbons, as if he'd been raked over a dozen sword edges. How he still lived was a mystery and miracle both. Yet one look at the man told the Hunter he wouldn't live long.

"Hush!" Naledi flung up a hand. "He speaks!"

All of them froze, even Tarek, who had withdrawn a small glass bottle from his pouch and prepared to pull the cork stopper. They all watched the man's lips moving, though no sound came out even the Hunter's keen ears could detect. Naledi lowered her head to within a finger's breadth of the man's mouth and listened for long seconds.

The Issai warrior's eyes widened. "He is Bheka!" She looked up at Aisha and Siyanda. "I can make no more sense of his words, yet this I know."

"Bheka?" Siyanda glanced at Aisha. "Did not Jumaane say—?"

Aisha nodded. "The Bheka vanished months ago." She looked down to Naledi. "What else is he saying?"

Naledi listened again, then shook her head. "Nothing that has any meaning to me. He speaks of awakening. Or one who awakens." A scowl twisted her lips. "I cannot understand him."

"Let me." Siyanda waved the older warrior aside and dropped to her knees, bending low to listen to the man's moanings. But only for a moment. Her expression darkened and she rose upright once more. "He will speak no more."

Sure enough, the Ghandian's groans had fallen silent, and the shallow rise and fall of his chest had stilled.

Tarek, who held the still-corked bottle, seemed surprised. He placed two fingers to the man's neck to feel for a pulse. Slowly, he shook his head and replaced the bottle in his pouch without a word.

The Hunter spared a moment of pity for the Ghandian. His end had come unnoticed by all. No drastic last gasps, no dying words or final pleas. Merely a quietening as silent as the setting of the sun. Only he would not see another day. He had gone to his ancestors. Or so the Hunter hoped.

"Who is he?" the Hunter asked, turning to Kiara.

"I do not know." Kiara shrugged. "We found him on our way out of the Valley of Living Fire."

"*We* didn't find him. You did." Tarek rose to his feet, his shoulders drooping and his expression set in a grim mask. "Though how you heard or saw him tucked in that cluster of rocks thirty paces off in the pitch black, I'll never know. You've got keener eyes and ears than me, it seems."

Something strange flashed across Kiara's face at those words. It made no sense to the Hunter—was that *guilt?* It was gone so quickly he almost thought his mind had conjured it. He couldn't understand what Kiara would possibly have to feel guilty over. Perhaps it was that they'd failed to save the Bheka man. One look at him made that difficult to believe. They *had* to have known he was dying; fiery hell, Tarek had said as much.

So what then? The Hunter studied her expression, which had gone studiedly neutral. *What could she—*

A gasp and shudder from Aisha snapped him from his thoughts. She had remained standing over the dead Ghandian, yet now she took a staggering step backward and reeled as if beneath the thunderous assault of an invisible hand.

"Aisha!" Kodyn and Siyanda both sprang toward her.

"Wait!" She threw up one hand to stop them. "Do not—" Her words cut off in a groaning gasp, and she staggered again. Light sprang to life around her fingertips and her eyes glowed a luminous blue-white. Her body went instantly rigid. She stood frozen like a statue, yet ablaze with that eerie, mystical power of the *Kish'aa.*

"Aisha?" Siyanda ventured. "Are you—"

The Hunter stepped between Siyanda and Aisha. "Give her a moment." He had an inkling of what might be happening. "Let her gain control of the spirit."

Siyanda's eyes flew wide and her face paled. Her gaze darted from the Hunter's face to Aisha, then dropped to the nearby corpse.

"Two weeks." The words dripped from Aisha's lips in a terrible moan. "Two weeks he endured. Such agony. The stone, killing him. Slowly, rotting from the inside out. Yet he could not lay down and die. Not until his message was delivered."

"Message?" This time, it was Kodyn who spoke. He stepped up to stand next to the Hunter and stared at Aisha. "What is his message?"

"Not yet!" Aisha's head snapped back, her spine arched, and her arms flew out wide. "We must hear. We must see. We must do whatever can be done to stop them!"

"Hear what? See what?" Kodyn pressed on. Concern echoed in his voice and darkened his face. "What do we have to stop?"

"You cannot stop it!" Aisha's voice rose in a shout, yet her voice was not her own. It resonated with the deep, masculine timbre, like the rumbling of distant thunder. "You cannot, must not! For if he is not awakened, all will be desolation. The time of the destroyer must come. But it must be the awakener who opens the way. It must be the awakener!"

Her voice rose in one final shriek, like the dying lamentations of a madman, then the light in her eyes and dancing around her hands went instantly dark. The invisible strings that held her arching body upright severed, too, and her legs crumpled beneath her.

The Hunter was already moving toward Aisha as she fell. He caught her in his arms and held her, just long enough for Kodyn and Siyanda to reach them.

"Aisha!" the two cried in unison. Their expressions were a mirror, concern and fear for her wellbeing etched into every line on their faces. The Hunter passed Aisha's limp form to them and stepped back to let them lower her gently to a seat on the ground.

She awoke a moment later. Her eyes flew open, her body jerked, and she sucked in a sharp, gasping breath.

"Aisha?" Kodyn cupped her cheek in one hand, the other cradling her lower back. "Aisha, can you hear me?"

"I-I hear you." Her voice came out weak, hoarse. "I could always hear you. But the spirit..." A shudder set her body trembling like a leaf in a fierce breeze. "He was so powerful. His will...I've never felt anything like it."

She scrubbed a hand over her face, blinking as if to clear sleep from her eyes. "He was determined. He would not die until *someone* heard the message he'd fled to deliver."

"What message?" Kodyn repeated his earlier question. "About the awakener?"

Aisha nodded her head slowly. "Yes. But that is not all."

She attempted to rise, but Kodyn and Siyanda both held her back.

"Aisha, take a moment, catch your breath," Kodyn insisted.

Siyanda said something in the Issai tongue, doubtless echoing Kodyn's urgings.

"I'm fine." Aisha pushed their hands away. "His spirit is gone. He fulfilled his purpose and passed on to the ancestors. It was just the abruptness of his departure, after the force of his will. I am unharmed."

To prove her point, she gathered her legs beneath her and stood. With a slight wobble at first, causing both Kodyn and Siyanda to reach out and steady her, but she quickly regained her balance and waved them away. She concentrated her attention on her legs until they held her upright. Only then did she look up at the Hunter, Kiara, and the others.

"His name was Tundeneyenin." Aisha spoke in a solemn voice, each word heavy and pronounced. "*Indaba* Tunde, they called him. His name was a gift bestowed upon him by the *Umoyahlebe* of the Bheka tribe. For he was a living memory. A walking, talking story."

The Hunter frowned. "What does that mean?"

Aisha turned a sharp look on him. "You'll find out, if you'll hold your questions and be patient." She tapped a finger against her forehead. "Everything I saw and heard and felt—his memories, thoughts, feelings, fears, and hopes—it's all still a bit of a jumble. It will take me a moment to make sense of it."

The Hunter raised his hands in a placating gesture. "Here I am being patient and holding my questions, then."

Aisha shot him a wry grin, but it faded quickly when her legs began to wobble. This time, she didn't refuse Kodyn and Siyanda's help. Instead, she permitted them to help her over to sit on a nearby knee-high boulder. Once settled, she spent a moment gathering herself before continuing.

"What those not of the Bheka do not know is that their people have always lived in these lands." Her brow furrowed in deep contemplation. "They have always considered the shadow of *Ukuhlushwa Okungapheli* to be a blessed place, a place reserved for them alone. While other tribes avoid this place, even fear it, the Bheka believe themselves to be the guardians of the ancient power residing here."

The Hunter wanted to speak—her words brought to mind myriad questions—but he'd promised he'd hold his tongue and so he did.

"For thousands of years," Aisha went on, "they have been caretakers of *Ukuhlushwa Okungapheli*, watching over *Nuru Iwu's* prison and guarding against *Okadigbo's* return. This is a truth known to few—only the oldest and wisest of the *Umoyahlebe* know of it. Yet always the *Indaba* of the Bheka have kept this knowledge written on their hearts. For it is they who heard the admonitions of Ingwe All-Father who told them of what would befall these lands on the day when *Nuru Iwu* escaped and *Okadigbo* attempted to destroy his brother."

A conversation with Aisha from a few days earlier flashed through the Hunter's mind. The Issai belief in the ultimate "fate of the *amathafa*" had been burned into his memory.

Aisha continued speaking without pause. "Always the Bheka have sought peace with their neighboring tribes and endeavored to avoid strife. For their battle was not one for land or resources, but to remember the sacred duty entrusted them by Ingwe All-Father. To watch over *Ukuhlushwa Okungapheli* and make certain that none interfered with the endless struggle between the twin brothers. That was a battle to be waged by *Nuru Iwu* and *Okadigbo* alone. Any interference could tilt the scales in the wrong direction, and all of the *amathafa* would pay the price."

But which way is the "wrong direction"? the Hunter couldn't help but wondering. Which of the brothers did the All-Father—whoever or whatever he *truly* was—intend to win the millennia-old feud?

"And now, the last of the *Indaba* has gone to their ancestors." Aisha's voice was grim, as grave as if she'd just pronounced the death of all things. "With his passing, the truth will be forgotten, and the time of great strife begins."

Chapter Forty-Three

To the Hunter's surprise, it was Kiara who interrupted Aisha first. "But this truth *won't* be forgotten. You said it yourself, Tunde clung to life because he needed someone to hear what was known only to the *Indaba*." Her gesture included the people gathered around Aisha—Siyanda, Kodyn, the Hunter, herself, Tarek, and Naledi—as well as Cebile, who had scooted closer despite being unable to stand on her injured leg. "We all heard. We all will remember."

"Yes, we will." Aisha nodded, as did the rest of those Kiara had indicated. "But according to Tunde, it was when the last Bheka *Indaba* died that this 'time of great strife' begins." Her face darkened. "He did not know what was to come, but in his final moments, I caught glimpses of his imaginings. I saw the plains drowning in rivers of blood, fires rampaging through every *ekhaya,* and disease and pestilence consuming everything in its path."

The Hunter frowned. *Was that some sort of prophetic vision, or merely imagination?* Many cultures around Einan believed that some people were gifted glimpses into the future by whatever gods—or spirits, in the case of the Ghandians—they worshipped. The Hunter himself had never put much stock in such things; he'd always seen those in Voramis who practiced divination for the charlatans and fraudsters they were. Yet given everything that had happened to him over the past few years, he found he was far less quick to scoff and disbelieve.

Perhaps these *Indaba* possessed some ability akin to those of the *Umoyahlebe.* He had no time to ask, however, for Aisha continued.

"*That* is what kept Tunde alive for two weeks when any other man would have died in days." Aisha shuddered. "I felt his pain. Relived his agony condensed into one terrible moment, and it nearly broke me. What he endured—" Her voice cracked and a tear slid down her cheek. Long seconds passed before she could speak again.

"For almost a year, he and his people have been captive to the *Gcinue'eleku awandile.* When the Consortium and their masters—he called the Ordermen 'stone-faces'—first arrived at *Ukuhlushwa Okungapheli,* they came with flattering words and offers of wealth. But when the Bheka turned them away, they returned with swords, whips, and chains. They were set to build the wall blocking off the plateau, to raise the camp where the *alay-alagbara* brought thousands more over the last months. Cold and hunger and thirst and beatings they endured, but always they kept the secret from their captors. Even as the *Indaba* died off, as the Bheka *Umoyahlebe* succumbed to the Unshackling or were killed by the power of the *Kish'aa,* they guarded their tongues. Guarded their tongues and their secrets."

Her shoulders rounded and her eyes turned inward, no doubt reliving the Bheka's grim final months.

"One by one the Bheka fell—to the whips and fists of their captors, to exhaustion, to starvation, or sacrificing themselves to take their secrets to the grave. Five times now, the

498

Gcinue'eleku awandile's efforts have opened a way into *Ukuhlushwa Okungapheli*. Five times the Bheka have given their lives to make certain the way was blocked and impassable."

The Hunter's mind raced. *Of course!* That explained the purpose for the scaffolding descending the cliffs beneath the Bondshold. *The Order haven't managed to break open the tower's front doors, so they're attempting to enter it from below.*

The masked bastards wouldn't be the first to have that idea. Taiana had labored for years to dig tunnels into the Keeps around Enarium, and Lord Apus had carved out a passage adjoining his mansion in the heart of Malandria to the Monolith.

Before he could contemplate the matter further, Aisha's words commanded his attention once more.

"Until Tunde alone of his people remained. When he realized his death would soon come, when he saw others succumbing to dimercurite poisoning, he knew he had to find a way to pass on his story. His chance came when a sixth way was opened. He led the workers through earth and stone to reveal the passages beneath, but before they could alert their captors, he hurled himself into the opening and brought it crumbling down behind him. In darkness he wandered, trusting to the stories passed down by the *Indaba* through the centuries to guide him. Through deep waters and across vast gulfs, over fields of glittering ice, serpents of earth, and forests of sharp stone. Until finally he felt the sun on his face once more."

The thought of the Bheka clawing his way through subterranean passages brought back memories from the Hunter's own past—awakening after leaping into the Midden, fumbling his way out of the tunnels beneath Kara-ket—and sent a shudder down the Hunter's spine.

"He dragged himself through *Isigodi Umlilophilayo,* refusing to die until he found someone to hear his truth." Aisha turned her eyes on Kiara and Tarek. "The Bheka are no more, yet the last of the *Indaba* is at peace with the ancestors because of you." She pressed a hand to her heart and bowed from the waist.

Kiara flushed, and again the strange expression flashed across her face. "We only did what anyone else would," she protested just a little too quickly.

"Wait, wait!" The excited edge in Kodyn's voice drew all eyes toward the young Praamian. "You said Tunde got from the scaffolding to the Valley of Living Fire through tunnels beneath the tower?"

"Yes," Aisha said.

An eager light shone on Kodyn's face. "You said you saw some of Tunde's memories, right? Including, just maybe, the memory of how he found his way through the tunnels?"

Aisha sprang to her feet, all traces of fatigue forgotten. "Yes! It's a bit of a jumble, but…" She squeezed her eyes shut in concentration and a frown twisted her lips. But only for a moment. Her eyelids flew open and excitement brightened her *kaffe*-brown eyes. "I believe I can see it. Or more like *feel* it. So much of it is darkness, but I think I can find the way back."

"Hah!" Kodyn laughed in triumph. "Well done."

The Hunter looked between the two youths. "Am I missing something?" He narrowed his eyes.

Kodyn spun toward him, his words coming fast and eager. "We've got a back way in now. A way in that doesn't involve us climbing over the wall."

The Hunter waved the words away. "Yes, I understood *that*. Move among the captives working on the scaffolding, maybe even stir up a bit of trouble by breaking their chains and killing any slavers we find."

Kodyn nodded.

"Just one problem." The Hunter held up a finger. "Tunde said the way was blocked." He turned to Aisha. "That he collapsed the tunnel behind him so the *alay-alagbara* couldn't get at the Bondshold from beneath."

"He did."

The Hunter turned back to Kodyn, half-expecting to see the young man deflate. But instead of disappointment, Kodyn's expression revealed only resolve, determination.

"Sure, so there's a small obstacle in our path." He shrugged as if a collapsed tunnel was no grand challenge. "But what you don't know is that I spent a great deal of time with Jarl, one of my mother's Pathfinders. He told me all about how my mother earned her place as the Guild Master by breaking into Lord Auslan's vault, and how it was *he* and his crew of Grubbers who made it possible by digging up from beneath."

The Hunter's eyebrows rose. He'd heard of Lord Auslan's vault—it had been the talk of Voramis for years, the envy of every nobleman who wished for some means of protecting their fortunes that didn't involve leaving them in the money-grubbing hands of the Coin Counters Temple—but never that it had been broken into. His already-high estimation of Master Gold rose farther still.

"Part of my training with the Foxes was to spend time working with Jarl widening the underground ways beneath Praamis." Kodyn grinned. "It's no exaggeration to say I know my way around a pick and shovel. With a few strong hands, we could clear a way out sure enough. Hit the Consortium from behind and turn their own captives against them."

The Hunter couldn't help tilting his head in acknowledgement. "A clever plan."

Tarek had remained silent all this time, listening in reverence to Aisha's recounting of what Tunde had imparted to her. He spoke up now. "We saw it, you know. Their digging."

"It's a project on a massive scale," Kiara said, backing up the young Elivasti's words. "The scaffolding descends over half the cliff's height and circles the entire base of the Bondshold, at least what we could see. We didn't get close enough to count, but we guess there must be at least four or five thousand people there."

Tarek nodded his agreement.

The Hunter did quick calculations. "That means easily three thousand captives, maybe more. All turned loose against the ones who've kept them in chains for weeks or months." A grim smile twisted his lips. "I'd say pity the bastards who face that, but after seeing what the Order and Consortium have done, I'm inclined to laugh and enjoy the bloody show. They more than deserve what's coming to them."

Naledi let out a low growl and snarled something in the Issai tongue, which Cebile and Siyanda both echoed. The hard looks on the three warriors' faces made it clear they shared the Hunter's sentiments.

"This way, we don't have to worry about trying to sneak our way through a camp on high alert or an army of—"

"Army!" The word burst from the Hunter's lips before he realized it.

In that moment, he understood what had struck him as off about the encampment surrounding the Bondshold. Kodyn's words had brought the doubt that had nagged at the back of his mind springing to the fore.

"There's no bloody army!" Even as he breathed the words, he cursed himself for not realizing it sooner. He spun on Kodyn. "Tell me, as you moved among the Consortium camp, did you come across anything *close* to the thirteen hundred men your duty roster mentioned?"

The question, coming on the heels of the Hunter's interruption, caught Kodyn by surprise. He frowned in contemplation but didn't have to think long. "No," he said, shaking his head. "There couldn't have been more than two or three hundred all throughout the city. Plus however many were overseeing the work at the scaffolding."

The Hunter's thoughts spun. He'd found it odd coming across so many empty furnished dwellings—nearly *half* of the city had been abandoned—and there'd been precious few armed men on patrol. Even after the alarm had been raised and the Consortium sent out to guard the walls and search the city in force, the enemy had been far too sparse.

"Two or three hundred," the Hunter repeated. "So where in the fiery hell are the rest?"

Silence was his only answer. All around him exchanged bewildered glances. Only the Hunter and Kodyn had known the count of armed men at the Consortium's disposal; to the rest of their companions, even Aisha, this was the first they'd heard of it.

That was when the Hunter recalled snatches of the conversation he'd overheard while crouching in the domed building that served as the *Umoyahlebe's* prison.

"Don't take much skill to crack a whip or swing a club at a chained prisoner," the Vothmoti Orderwoman had said. *"Now the fellas off marching, that's a different story. Battle comes and they'll..."* Her words had cut off, yet she had clearly spoken of battle and marching.

Marching! The memory of another conversation, this one between himself and the slaver Rhodd, flashed through his mind. *"Seems like you're just the sort who'd be marchin' out with the rest,"* the man had said.

The answer to his own question solidified in his mind with a terrible crystalline clarity. He knew where the rest of the Consortium had gone.

Marching to battle...with the only enemy strong enough to threaten them. His heart sprang into his throat. *The united tribes of the Issai and Buhari!*

Chapter Forty-Four

The Hunter wanted to be wrong. He wanted it *desperately,* with every fiber of his being.

But what were the odds that some other enemy existed on the Ghandian Plains that would demand an army a thousand strong to defeat? One who had dealt devastating blows to the plans of the Order of Mithridas and their Consortium hirelings, or who threatened to resist or even interfere with the operations underway here.

Had it been the Hunter sitting behind those high walls and receiving reports of the attack on the camp within *Indawo Yokwesaba* and the liberation of their captives, his first move would have been to dispatch the men at his command in an overwhelmingly superior force to utterly crush any opposition before it could gain strength. The Issai *amaqhawe* was vastly reduced, the Buhari warriors divided, and the other tribes far removed and showing no signs of involving themselves in the affairs of the *alay-alagbara.* Now would be the perfect time to strike, while the combined Issai and Buhari were traveling and far from safety.

As briefly and quickly as he could, the Hunter explained what Kodyn had uncovered in the stolen documents and voiced aloud the conclusion he'd reached. "On our journey here from the southeast, we saw no sign of the *Gcinue'eleku awandile's* forces." He looked between Naledi, Siyanda, and Cebile. "Did you?"

The three Issai warriors exchanged glances.

"None." Naledi's broad face creased into a scowl. "At Duma's counsel, we traveled through *Indawo Yokwesaba* to see if our enemies had attempted to rebuild what was destroyed. The ruins remain empty and silent, nothing but ash and the lingering stench of death. Nor was there any indication an army had passed that way."

"Which suggests they marched east first, traversing the forest's edge." Siyanda frowned. "But why? The Tefaye found our *ekhaya* at the *kopje,* far to the east. If their masters sent them there to hunt us down—" Her voice cut off in a gasp and the color drained from her face. "They march against the Buhari. It is they who hold the lands immediately east of *Indawo Yokwesaba* and beyond."

"And the Buhari *amaqhawe* is not there to defend their lands." The Hunter's heart sank. "Their *ekhaya* is vulnerable."

Grim silence settled over the rocky hollow. None of them needed to voice aloud what would happen when a thousand armed slavers descended upon the far smaller force of warriors left behind to guard the Buhari's camp. Those the Consortium did not slaughter outright would find themselves clapped in chains and dragged back here to join in the efforts to burrow into the Bondshold from beneath.

Kiara broke the silence. "Then it falls to us." Her gaze shifted from face to face, her eyes filled with the same certainty that echoed in her voice. "We must do everything in our power to turn the tide of battle—or prevent battle altogether."

Hesitation flashed across Aisha's face. With good reason. She'd come all this way to find her father and sister—and to free them if possible. They'd gotten close enough that she could embrace Nkanyezi and kneel at her father's side. And now they were simply prepared to ride away?

Kiara must have seen it to, for she stepped up to Aisha and rested her hands on the young woman's shoulders. "We must," she said quietly. "Jumaane and his *amaqhawe* march beside your people, and because of that, *his* people are at risk. We seven may be the only ones who can reach the Buhari in time to bring warning—and if not, to avenge the fallen and free the captive."

Emotions flashed across Aisha's face, revealing the war raging within her. Her gaze darted to the northeast, in the direction of the Bondshold, though it and the camp were hidden behind the cliffs encircling the rocky hollow. The Hunter could all but feel her pain, longing, and dismay—had he been in her place, could *he* have ridden away? Had she the strength to turn her back on her own family for the sake of helping the tribe that, until mere days ago, had been enemy to her people?

"Is not seven." This came from Cebile, who was stubbornly struggling to rise. "Is eight."

"No, Cebile—" Aisha began, but her words were cut off a moment later.

"Cebile!" Siyanda's voice cracked like a whip, and though she spoke in her native tongue, the command in her tone was unmistakable. In that moment, she sounded a great deal like Davathi—like a *nassor.*

Cebile put up a fierce argument, but soon Naledi joined in, then Aisha a moment later. Cebile shook her fists at the three of them and railed at full volume. To no avail. Naledi was as immovable as her size suggested, Aisha had proven herself doggedly tenacious, and Siyanda's determination was written plain on her face. The way they pointed time and again to Cebile's bruised and bandaged knee, there was no doubt in the Hunter's mind their argument proved well-founded.

While the four Issai women argued, the Hunter turned to Tarek and Kiara. "Tell me your search of the Valley of Living Fire turned up more than just one dying Bheka."

Tarek nodded solemnly. "We found it. Spite-fern, I remember the name now." He gestured toward Nayaga. Next to his horse sat the satchel he'd taken to the caldera. It had gone into the Valley of Living Fire empty but now was full and bulging. "I believe we've got enough for all the tests I need to run, with plenty left over to craft the cure for the Tefaye and all those affected by dimercurite poisoning."

"Excellent!" The Hunter beamed and clapped the young man on the shoulder. "One step closer to ripping out our enemy's heart."

At that moment, the nearby argument ended—the only way it possibly could.

"Pah!" Cebile spat, throwing up her hands and snapping something curt-sounding in her tongue. She lowered herself onto a nearby boulder and folded her arms over her chest. Her face twisted into a sullen, angry glower, but she raised no further argument.

Naledi, Siyanda, and Aisha turned back to the others with satisfied looks on their faces.

"She will remain here and keep watch on our enemy." Naledi gestured to herself and Siyanda. "But we run with you to help our allies."

"We will not arrive in time if we run." Kodyn stepped up between the Hunter and Aisha. "The only way we have any chance of gaining ground is on horseback. Which means you *must* ride."

Siyanda's face once again began to harden, take on that stubborn look she'd gotten all those days ago when Aisha first spoke of riding.

"*Um'zala.*" Aisha placed a hand on her cousin's shoulder. "He is right."

The look froze on Siyanda's face, then slowly melted away. "I know." She let out a frustrated breath. "Only I do not know how to ride."

After watching her bouncing like a sack of flour in Nayaga's saddle, the Hunter couldn't argue that statement.

"Issai warriors are fleetest on their own feet," Naledi added with a grim shake of her head. "We are born to run, not to sit and let a beast do the running for us."

A grin sprouted on Kiara's face, and she gave the broad-shouldered Issai a friendly nudge of her elbow. "Once you've felt the wind blowing in your face and see the *amathafa* rushing by, I think you'll feel quite differently."

Naledi crossed her thick arms over her chest, clearly unconvinced. Yet she put up no further protest.

"You will ride with me, *um'zala.*" Aisha squeezed Siyanda's shoulder. "As for Naledi..." She frowned and looked between the Hunter, Kiara, Kodyn, and Tarek as if trying to figure out whose horse would best be volunteered to the cumbrous and heavily-muscled warrior.

The Hunter made the decision for her. "She will ride Elivast. Kiara and I will ride Ash."

Kiara raised an eyebrow. "Think you'll get into my saddle, just like that?" A wicked look sparkled in her eyes.

The Hunter winked back at her. "Pretty much." He made a show of looking her up and down. "Now, if I can just figure out what's the best part to hold on to while—"

His words cut off as Kiara threw a half-hearted punch into his chest. "Scoundrel!"

The Hunter accepted the blow with a theatrical "Oof!" far too exaggerated to be real. Inwardly, though, he was grinning. Kiara had a knack for lightening even the dourest mood and lifting his spirits out of the deepest depths. Only *she* could crack a joke at a grim moment like this.

Her playful spirit and laugh proved contagious, for smiles sprouted on the faces of all around—all save the scowling Cebile.

The humor faded quickly, however, banished by necessity. Kiara set to the arduous task of explaining to the stout Naledi the basics of riding, and Aisha did likewise with Siyanda. Tarek and Kodyn busied themselves strapping their satchels—Tarek's bulging with spite-fern, Kodyn's heavy with the documents he'd stolen from the Consortium's offices—behind their saddles.

The Hunter considered removing the stolen Consortium studded leather vest and trousers. He'd travel more easily clad only in the Buhari woven armor and Issai robes. After a moment, he decided to leave the vest on. He might need the disguise when they caught up to the army marching on the Buhari.

His gaze was drawn to where Cebile sat watching. A scowl darkened her face and her shoulders hunched in morose anger.

He strode over to her, and the moment she spotted his approach, she sat up straighter.

"Here." The Hunter bent and from the tops of his boots drew out a pair of long, curve-edged daggers. These, he held out to her hilt-first. "They are no replacement for your *assegai,* but they will serve you well in a fight."

Cebile eyed him and the blades warily. "No fight." She shook her head, pointing to her knee. "Naledi orders."

The Hunter grinned. "Always be prepared, right?"

A slow smile spread across the warrior woman's face. "Prepared." With a nod, she took the daggers. She flipped them over and over in her hands, testing their weight and balance. "Good," she said, with a grunt of approval.

"Very good." The Hunter tilted his head. "Fine Voramian steel."

Cebile's eyebrows rose. She looked down at the daggers once more and rattled off what sounded like a question in the Issai tongue.

The Hunter stared at her, uncomprehending. He'd heard the words *Okanele* and "weapons" but understood nothing else.

"She asked if these are *Okanele* weapons." Siyanda's voice echoed behind the Hunter, followed a moment later by the young woman herself. She came to stand beside Cebile and looked down at the daggers in her fellow warrior's hands. "Like your sword and that of your *ibhubekazi.*"

"Ahh." The Hunter touched *Ibad'at Mutlaqa's* hilt, jutting up from behind his right shoulder. "No, they are mortal weapons. *Alay-alagbara* weapons."

Siyanda relayed his words to Cebile, who appeared disappointed, but only for a moment. She swiped at the air with the two daggers and snarled something fierce-sounding.

"She says so long as they spill *alay-alagbara* blood and open *alay-alagbara* throats, they will suffice," Siyanda translated.

"That they will," the Hunter said chuckling. He'd recognized the words for "blood" and "throats"—he was picking up the Ghandian tongue faster than he'd excepted. He half-turned, but stopped. "That word, *ibhubekazi*?" He'd heard it from Davathi's lips in reference to Kiara. "What does it mean?"

For the first time since they'd first met, Siyanda actually smiled when speaking to him. "*Ibhubekazi* is our word for the queen lioness." A mischievous twinkle much like Aisha's brightened her dark eyes. "The one who rules the pride. From the *nassor,* it is a great compliment."

The Hunter glanced over to where Kiara endeavored heroically to help Naledi drag her corpulent bulk into the saddle of a protesting Elivast. "Accurate, too." His *lioness.* He liked that. For all his strength, it was she who held their little tribe—their *pride,* including the young lion Evren and Hailen the cub—together.

Siyanda and Cebile bid each other farewell quietly, pressing their foreheads together. But the parting was to be brief. Siyanda allowed Aisha to help her into the saddle, and sat rigid, her arms clutching Aisha's waist tightly and her legs clamped on the horse's ribs.

With that, they set off on what promised to be a mad ride, a race against time to do the impossible.

Chapter Forty-Five

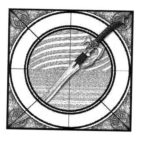

They rode through the night without stopping. Even when Naledi's grunts and harsh breathing rose to rasping growls at the pain of the continuous bouncing and jostling, even when Siyanda swayed in the saddle—and would have fallen had Aisha not snapped out a hand to catch her—they barely slowed. The knowledge of what they raced *toward* kept them moving as fast as the horses and their tired bodies could manage.

Their ride carried them past the Valley of Living Fire, past the petrified trees with their leaves and branches of stone, their twisted trunks frozen forever in time. Beyond it, the terrain grew barren and rocky, descending into a series of canyons and along dried-up riverbeds. However, by the time the sun rose and bathed the world in the golden brilliance of morning, the world once more leveled out, and harsh, stony earth gave way to the gentle rolling waves of grassy plains.

They reached the eastern edge of *Indawo Yokwesaba* shortly after midday. Before turning south, however, they paused to rest their weary mounts. Naledi tried with all the stubbornness of her warrior nature to hide the agony coursing through her, but even the iron-hard woman could not stifle a groan of relief as she collapsed onto the soft grass beneath the shade of a twisted acacia tree.

Siyanda hadn't fared much better, even riding behind Aisha. Her jaw remained permanently clenched and she hissed as she poured a splash of water over the visibly chafed skin on her inner thighs.

From within his pouches, Tarek produced a small vial of what he called *haax,* a healing unguent he claimed the warriors of the Hrandari Plains used to treat saddle sores. Even from ten paces away, the stink of it curdled the Hunter's stomach. He'd thought the Night Guild's *gokulah* unguent the worst-smelling remedy he'd encountered, but the *haax* proved him terribly wrong.

While Kiara laid out a sparse meal, Kodyn saw to his and Aisha's horses, and the Hunter tended to Ash and Elivast. The desert pony was exhausted from carrying the weight of two riders, but the powerfully built Naledi had been no lighter burden for Elivast. Unfortunately, they could afford no more than an hour or two for the horses to rest. They had a lot of ground to cover if they wanted to gain on the Consortium's marching army.

The respite passed in near-silence. Exhaustion dragged all but the Hunter into sleep. Naledi had simply dozed off where she slumped against the acacia tree, overcome by the unfamiliar exertion of riding. Siyanda managed to eat before curling up in the grass beside Aisha. She fell asleep listening to Aisha's explanation as to who Hallar *really* was and why his oath to the Serenii mattered to her. If Siyanda's nodding off bothered Aisha, she didn't show it. She merely smiled down at the arm Siyanda draped across her lap as she slept, as if she feared breaking contact would shatter their newly reforged bonds of sisterhood.

Aisha settled back with one arm draped over her cousin's shoulder, the other holding on to her *assegai*, and her head pillowed on Kodyn's arm. Soon, she, too, was fast asleep. Nearby, Tarek sat with his spear resting across his lap and his chin resting on his chest. Kiara dozed with her back pressed against the Hunter's, soft snores rising into the quiet air.

The Hunter felt a curious sense of peace in that moment. Strange, considering what they had just left behind and what lay ahead. Yet for a few tranquil minutes, he managed to clear all worries and anxieties from his mind and simply sit to enjoy the whispering of the wind and the rustle of the tall plains grass surrounding them.

His worry soon returned in force. Half an hour after they resumed their ride, following Naledi's direction to head southeast from *Indawo Yokwesaba* toward the Buhari lands, they spotted the first signs of the Consortium army. Or, more accurately, the marks of their heavy boots imprinted in the muddy banks of the small creek they crossed.

The Hunter and Tarek slid down from their saddles and knelt to study the marks. Naledi looked as if she wanted to dismount but dared not for fear she'd be unable to force herself back into the saddle once more. Siyanda merely bent to the side, clinging to Aisha to steady herself, and frowned down at the muddy bootprints and the deep ruts left by iron-rimmed wheels.

"No way to get an accurate count," the Hunter said. "Too many bootprints overlapping. But I'd say at least a few hundred." He glanced to Tarek, who nodded.

"No fewer than four, easily twice that number," the young Elivasti agreed. "At least six wagons or carts, too."

The Hunter looked at Siyanda, half-expecting her to contradict them. But she merely nodded in assent.

"At least we *know* we're on the right track," Kiara said from atop Ash's back. "We know they came this way, and in the last day or two, right?"

The Hunter touched a hand to one bootprint. The mud had long ago hardened and dried. "Definitely two days." He ran some quick calculations based on what he'd learned about large-scale troop movements—much of it from drunk and belligerent former Legionnaires moaning about the rigors of military life in The Brawling Trooper. "Given that, I'd say they're ten, maybe fifteen leagues ahead of us."

"Meaning we can catch up with them well before dawn tomorrow if we push hard," Tarek said. He couldn't help glancing toward the horse carrying Aisha and Siyanda, though he had the good sense to keep his eyes from straying to Naledi. "Though we'll arrive too tired to do much in the way of fighting."

The Hunter grunted, gnawing at the inside of his lip. "Problem for later," he decided. "First, we need to at least get eyes on them, then we figure out what to do."

None of his companions voiced opposition or dissent. By the looks on all their faces—even Kiara's, though she hid her emotions better than most—they were equal parts uncertain and nervous about how their ride would end. The Hunter could see the question swirling through their minds: *what can just the seven of us do against an army of hundreds?*

There was an answer, he knew. One which, more likely than not, involved him wading into his enemies wielding the Sword of Nasnaz and Soulhunger. But that possibility, he kept to himself for the time being. Accepting that he might have to cede control of his mind to the scimitar's magic and stating it as a given fact aloud for all to hear were two different matters entirely. He'd keep that as a worst-case scenario.

Though the morning had dawned warm, the afternoon brought clouds enough to keep the sun from beating down mercilessly on their backs. That, combined with the gentle terrain, made for easy going, and they made good time crossing the grassy plains.

Naledi proved even more stubborn than the Hunter had expected; she clung to her horse with the unshakeable tenacity of a swamp leech, though Elivast's gait bounced and jolted her with every rolling step. By contrast, Siyanda proved herself an adept student of horsemanship. Even Tarek appeared impressed by how quickly she mastered riding behind Aisha.

The tracks of the marching Consortium slavers grew broader and more easily visible with every league they covered. By sundown, the occasional bootprint or wheel rut in the mud had broadened to a ten-pace-wide trail of trampled grass that cut a straight line southeast toward the Buhari lands. Even when the sun began to set and darkness descended on the plains, they had no trouble following the signs. Hiding such a sizeable force on the plains would have been nearly impossible, and this army had taken no pains to conceal their movements.

That suggested to the Hunter that the Consortium was confident in their plans. Perhaps they had the Ujana running scout for them, which meant they'd known the bulk of the Buhari forces were off in Issai lands. They had no fear of being spotted or caught unawares by an enemy because they knew that enemy's location.

Circumstances conspired to force them to rest. Burdened as he was beneath the weight of two riders, Ash began to stumble, his pace slowing. Aisha's horse, too, showed signs of fatiguing. The Hunter tried to push on for as long as possible, to cover ground while there was still light to the day, but finally he was forced to call a halt for their mounts' sakes.

Supper consisted of hard trail rations left from their journey to Ghandia and the last scraps of food collected from the Issai's celebration feast. Naledi was in too much pain to do more than lie back and fall asleep—though she managed to gulp down her sparse meal first. Siyanda and Aisha sat talking quietly to each other in their own tongue, for all the world looking like sisters reliving past memories and whispering of secrets. Kodyn took up position a short distance away to give them privacy. He sat with Tarek, each young man silently sharpening their own weapons, filling the air with the rasp of whetstone on steel.

After finishing his meal, the Hunter strode a short distance southeast of the camp, a few dozen paces farther along the trail left by the marching slaver army. He sniffed the air, attempting to catch his enemies' scents. Their passage had left spoor aplenty imprinted on the ground—the stink of sweat, the mustiness of well-worn leather, and myriad unique aromas marking the hundreds of individuals comprising the army—but he sought any fresh odors on the wind. Anything to tell him how much farther they had to ride.

Nothing reached him, as expected. Though the wind blew in from the southeast, the Consortium force had to still be leagues away.

The soft *shuff* of boots moving through grass caught his ear. He did not turn, however, for his keen Bucelarii hearing recognized the stealthy step. Kiara tended to drag the toe of her right boot just before lifting it off the ground to take a stride, but only when she was truly weary. That sound alone told him a great deal about the state of his companions.

"Nice night for brooding, isn't it?" Kiara's voice came soft, edged with a hint of mischievous humor.

The Hunter chuckled. "Not brooding. Searching." As she moved around his right side, he made a show of lifting his nose to sniff at the air like a hound. "We're still far off. But we're closing on them. I'm sure of it."

"I've no doubt." Kiara slid both her arms around his right arm and leaned her head against his shoulder. "You want to tell me what's going through your head? You thinking about what happened back there or what's to come ahead?"

"Neither. Both." The Hunter shrugged his left shoulder so as not to disturb her comfort. "Plenty of grim in both directions."

He told her of what he'd seen in the Consortium camp: the blast furnace used to forge the dimercurite chains, the use of those chains to compel the *Umoyahlebe* to turn their magic against the Bondshold's door, and how the Ordermen had slaughtered their own captives in the name of creating more *Kish'aa* energy.

"Keeper's tits!" Kiara hissed through her teeth. "The old priest was right to fear them. Whatever their ultimate aim, anyone capable of doing *that* falls into the category of 'bloody evil cunts' in my books."

"No argument from me." The Hunter drew in a long breath. "Until last night, I had only small cause for enmity against them. For what they did to Brother Solicitous and Brother Penurius, and to the knight apprentices." He ran a hand over his face. "And, in truth, because Father Reverentus was so adamant that they were a threat to our world. I felt like I owed it to him, after…" His words trailed off. Even after all these weeks, he had not shaken the memory of *his* blade driving into the old priest's chest.

Kiara stroked his arm gently, love and empathy tangible in the warmth of her touch. "But now you've seen it for yourself. Seen what they're willing to do."

"Aye." The Hunter nodded. "Like you said, it proves the priest right. And cements in my heart the certainty that they've got to be stopped. To be eradicated once and for all."

"Yet *another* impossible mission for you to take on, yes?"

The Hunter looked down at Kiara, surprised by the mocking tone of her voice. He found her staring up at him with a sharp grin. "What's that supposed to mean?"

Kiara chuckled. "I'm just saying, you've already got the weight of the world in your hands. And I mean that literally. Killing to sustain Kharna, hunting down demons, collecting enough souls to defeat the Great Devourer. No small feat, even for a Bucelarii."

The Hunter narrowed his eyes. What was she driving at?

"Then there's the little matter of the daughter you'd never met until she murdered a man right in front of you," Kiara continued. "You've got to somehow find her with no true idea of who she is."

"And?"

"And now you want to add destroying a millennia-old secret organization that not a soul in the world knows anything about, but who keep popping up and sowing chaos and destruction everywhere they appear?" Kiara snorted. "Your dance card is full enough already."

The Hunter's eyebrows rose. "So, what, you expect me to simply ignore the threat they pose? To leave them for someone *else* to handle?"

"Of course not!" Kiara gave him a look as if she believed him mad. "You've never met an impossibility you didn't want to prove wrong. It's just who you are." She ran a hand down his arm and pressed her chin into his bicep, staring up at him. "It's who I fell in love with, the man who believes he can do what no one else can—and because of that belief, continues to do precisely that time and time again."

Her voice softened, and worry darkened her eyes. "But I do expect that you won't try to do it all on your own. That you won't take on the weight of the world *alone*."

Her words surprised the Hunter. "What makes you—?" he began, but stopped when she pressed a finger to his lips.

"Because I know you, Hunter." She released his arm and moved around to stand in front of him. Her face grew suddenly solemn. "And, because I can *feel* it. In here." She pressed her other hand to the pit of her stomach. "And I don't mean it in some abstract way, like I know you well enough to understand what's going through your head. This isn't that."

She drew in a breath, seemed to hesitate. But only for a moment. The familiar look of determination blossomed on her beautiful face and she forced herself to speak.

"This may sound utterly mad, but it's true. I can feel it. Feel you twisting up inside because you're afraid that you're going to have to unleash the Sword of Nasnaz against the Consortium to keep the rest of us safe. Feel you brooding because you're worried that we'll arrive to find the Buhari *ekhaya* utterly destroyed. Feel every little thing going through your mind and heart. I feel it in here." She tapped her stomach once more. "And looking back, I think I've been able to feel it ever since the Zamani Falls."

Chapter Forty-Six

The Hunter searched Kiara's face for any hint that she was toying with him, though admittedly it was far from her usual jests. But she spoke utterly in earnest, he knew it at a glance. She truly meant it.

"What...do they feel like?" The question felt foolish, yet it was the first thing that had sprung to his mind. He tried to clarify with, "My feelings." Which only sounded *more* foolish to his ears.

"It's the strangest thing." Kiara's face scrunched up—not in ridicule of him, but in contemplation. "It's like a fire in the pit of my belly, but every feeling burns differently. Some hot as molten lava, others like a candle's flame, others like ice." She shook her head. "It starts out as just the burning in my stomach. But after a moment, it travels up to my mind and it's like I can feel exactly what you're feeling. The good, bad, and ugly. In here." She tapped her temple.

The Hunter stared at her for a long moment. "You're right," he said quietly. "That *does* sound mad."

Her eyes flew wide and a scowl twisted her face. But only for a moment. He couldn't stop a wicked grin from tugging his lips upward.

"Bastard!" She slapped his arm, a bit too hard to be entirely playful.

The Hunter laughed. "Sorry, I couldn't help myself."

"Next time, *help* yourself!" Kiara pulled back from him, scowling and folding her arms over her chest. "Here I was thinking that after all of the madness you've told me about, you would understand—"

"I understand!" The Hunter pursued her, sliding around to wrap his arms around her from behind. "I mean, I don't know if I *actually* understand, but I don't think you're mad." He placed a gentle kiss in the crook of her neck and shoulder. "Mad beautiful, but not mad."

Kiara snorted. "Flattery won't save you this time." Despite the scorn in her tone, she leaned her head back against him. "You'll have to work extra hard to make it up to me next chance we get."

"Deal." The Hunter kissed her neck again, but didn't continue downward, much as he wanted to. He doubted either of them had much room on their minds for romance, given everything else. Instead, he squeezed her tighter, hoping she felt the reassurance in his strength. "You said you've been feeling this way since Zamani Falls, right? So why wait until now to mention it?"

"The truth?" Kiara asked. "I only realized it last night. I've been feeling off for a while now—you've seen it for yourself, like the night of the Issai feast." She took one of his hands in hers and slid it down to place on her belly. "When it felt like I was on fire from the inside."

The Hunter's shoulders knotted with worry. The flesh of her stomach emitted heat enough to rival the aura of power that had enveloped Aisha the previous night and charred his palms. Though they'd healed well enough, the memory of the pain remained fresh.

He fought the urge to pull his hand away. "You think that might be a part of the magic? That it doesn't just absorb *Kish'aa* magic like you believed, but it also lets you feel the emotions of others?"

"It makes sense, doesn't it?" Kiara turned in his arms to face him. "Emotions are their own sort of energy, in a way. When you're angry or embarrassed, you feel hot. When you're afraid, you feel cold." Her face adopted the same look it often got when she pored over some book of lore or attempted to unravel some ancient legend. "So what if *that* is all the shard of crystal inside me is doing? Sensing the energy emitted by the emotions of others around me, and I can understand the way the energy resonates inside my body because I feel them the same way."

Her use of the word "resonate" brought to the Hunter's mind the resonator stones that had opened the Keeps in Enarium. The Lectern in Vothmot had spoken of "vibrating at a certain frequency" which elicited from other similar stones when they drew within a certain proximity. It was why Soulhunger's gemstone—and perhaps *all Im'tasi* gemstones, come to think of it—could serve to open the Serenii's locking mechanisms.

Thoughts of gemstones led him to think back to the Zamani Falls, the night she'd nearly died pierced through by that gleaming golden crystal. A crystal identical to those formed by the droplets of Indombe's blood. Indombe, who'd manipulated the emotions of his prey—the Hunter himself, Kiara, and Tarek—to lure them to their doom.

His breath caught in his throat. "A piece of Indombe burns within you!"

Kiara's nose wrinkled up. "What?"

He told her of the origin of those glowing aureate shards, and her eyes went wide.

"So you're saying those stones, *these* stones—" Her hand went once more to her belly. "—they're formed from Indombe's blood?"

The Hunter turned his palms upward. "I only know what I saw, and what I saw was the droplets of Indombe's blood—gold blood, mind you—hardening into the same crystals we pulled out of you." His mind churned, working at the idea. "So, if those stones are formed from Indombe's blood, it means a piece of him burns inside you. Perhaps even conferring to you a small measure of his power. Not enough to *control* the emotions of others—"

"But enough to sense them!" Kiara finished. Wheels turned behind her eyes, an excited look on her face. "That would explain it. I mean, it offers *an* explanation, one there's no real way to verify without paying our serpent friend a visit." She shook her head. "Which I have no bloody intention of doing in the near future."

"That makes two of us." The Hunter had nearly died *and* nearly lost her that night. Not a chance he'd risk it again unless the fate of the world hinged on it. Which it one day would—Indombe's life force could tip the scales of power in Kharna's favor—but not anytime soon.

"That could explain why I've been so tired ever since." Kiara's face sobered, her expression turning pensive. "As we traveled through Khafra, I wrote it off as nothing more than the after-effects of my wounds. Then, when it was just the five of us traveling alone, it felt like nothing more than the occasional spark, which I worried was due to the heat of the plains. But every time Siyanda looked at Aisha, I felt what she was feeling. All the pain and sorrow and grief transformed into anger. I didn't think much of it—it wasn't like Siyanda made much effort to hide it—even when I felt all the emotions of the people we freed from the Consortium camp. How could I not be affected, seeing their suffering?"

512

The Hunter had no rebuttal to that. Even *he* had been enraged by the sight of the Consortium's mistreatment of their captives.

"After that, I just wrote it off as tiredness, because we were traveling and fighting virtually nonstop." Kiara spoke at a full gallop now, as if she were coming to some great realization. "But the night after the Tefaye attack, when the Buhari and Issai were united and the *ekhaya* was prepared to celebrate, it nearly broke me though I didn't understand what was happening. Sleep was the only escape I could find."

"You had me bloody worried," the Hunter growled.

"I know." Kiara placed a hand on his chest, directly over his heart. "Worried me, too. But it wasn't until last night, when I found Tunde, that I realized the truth. Because I didn't see or hear him. There was no way I could. He was silent, unconscious. I only knew he was there because I felt him. Felt the determination that kept his heart beating and his lungs drawing breath long after he should have died."

She drove on, barely pausing for breath. "And then, on our way back to camp, I could feel Aisha. Feel her pain and anguish at leaving her sister and father behind after holding them in her arms after all these years."

The Hunter fought to keep his jaw from dropping. He hadn't told her those details; they hadn't had the time to speak on the matter in their haste to pursue the Consortium. Yet her words rang with unshakeable certainty. She'd *known*. She'd felt not only the pain, but the reason for that pain.

"Then Aisha and Siyanda both," Kiara continued, her voice dropping low to prevent their companions from overhearing. "So much anger, but I knew that was just a mask for what lay beneath. For the guilt and shame and remorse. For her grief and the feeling of loss that has haunted her all these years."

Her face broke into a beautiful smile. "But I felt the love that passed between them. The love that bound them so many years ago, and which now binds them again." She looked beyond him, toward the two young women. "Their wounds will need time to heal, but heal they will."

The Hunter smiled down at her. "Seems like this newfound power of yours isn't all bad."

Kiara's head snapped back toward him. "Not all bad? What makes you say that?"

The ferocity of her question caught the Hunter off guard. "I-I mean, you can feel the love between them. You can feel the positive emotions—the love, the joy, the hope—not just the negative ones."

Kiara stared at him for a long moment, her face unreadable. Then she slowly reached a hand up to cup his right cheek. "Silly man." She smiled softly. "Of course this power isn't all bad. Being able to feel the emotions of others can be overwhelming, certainly, but because of it, I have the ability to see what lies beneath, to strip away the masks behind which people hide and know the truth of who they are and how they feel." She cupped her other hand on his left cheek. "I've always prided myself on being able to read people just by looking at their faces. This is just taking it to a whole new level."

"So, what? You can feel *everything?*" The Hunter cocked his head. "Like you can feel when they're hungry, or tired, or when they're...feeling other things?" He made a show of pulling her close and running a hand down her back.

"I always knew that last one with you." Kiara slapped his chest playfully. "You're about as transparent as Voramian crystal to me, especially when it comes to 'other things'." A mischievous smile twisted her lips. "But no, that's not how it works. Those are sensations. I feel *emotions*. The stronger they are, the more I can feel them."

513

She turned him around to look back at their camp. "Take Kodyn, for example. Even from here, I can feel just how much he loves Aisha. It's written in every fiber of his being."

The Hunter chuckled. "Don't need magical snake-blood powers to know that."

She chose to ignore him and instead continued. "Aisha's feeling a lot of things right now, most of them involving Kodyn, and of course her father and sister. Plenty of rage at the Consortium and Order barely restrained beneath the surface. But having Siyanda back—the Siyanda she'd hoped she would be reunited with, not the one we met all those days ago—is enough to push all that back for the moment. Once we close with the army, though…" She shrugged.

"What about Tarek?" the Hunter asked. The young Elivasti sat calmly sharpening his spear, a neutral expression on his face.

"Worry." Kiara's eyes narrowed. "A lot of it. Mostly about the *maistyr* he's been sent here to find—and the fact that he hasn't found anything yet."

The Hunter started at the mention of *maistyr*. He'd been so wrapped up in what he'd witnessed in the city built around *Ukuhlushwa Okungapheli* he'd all but forgotten his hunt for the Abiarazi rumored to be here. He cast his mind back to his time moving among the Consortium and Ordermen. He'd detected not so much as a hint of the ancient rot and decay that marked a demon. Had it crossed his path, it would have leaped out at him, no doubt about it.

Before he could wonder further about it—about *where* this thus-far-elusive *maistyr* might be found—Kiara continued.

"But he's also worried about letting his people down. Letting the Second Blade down." Kiara fixed him with a meaningful look. "And letting *you* down."

The Hunter raised an eyebrow. "Me?" He frowned. "What's he worried about my opinion for?"

"He looks up to you," Kiara answered gently, rubbing a hand up his chest. "I can feel it every time he glances your way. He's hungry for your approval. He never knew his father, remember?"

The Hunter nodded. "I remember." He felt the young Elivasti's pain—he had no memory of his own parents—but had never considered himself an aspirational figure for anyone. He'd done his best with Evren and Hailen, true, yet still felt uncertain about his place in their lives, how they saw him.

"Naledi's an interesting one, though." Kiara continued speaking as if she hadn't just dropped a profound and critical revelation on him. "I feel her pride, the deep-rooted sense of duty to her people, her love for the *amaqhawe*. It's as if her warrior sisters are everything to her, the only family she's had in—"

But the Hunter was no longer listening. His head snapped up and his face turned toward the wind. For the last gust of night breeze had brought to him a familiar scent. The scent of steel, leather, pack animals, and fire.

The scent of *humans*.

Chapter Forty-Seven

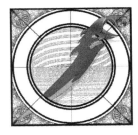

The Hunter hushed Kiara with a finger to her lips. "There's someone out there," he hissed.

"Out where?" came Kiara's whispered response.

The Hunter lifted his nose into the air and sniffed again. Sure enough, the wind brought him the scent again. Only the wind wasn't blowing from the southeast. It had changed directions, and now blew from the south*west*.

He lifted his finger and pointed into the wind. "There." He scanned the darkness, but saw nothing. "Somewhere, though I see nothing." He tapped his nose. "But I smell them. I smell fire, and the smell of armed men."

"From the southwest?" Kiara's nose crinkled as she frowned. "That's—"

"The wrong direction, I know!" The Hunter scanned the darkness of the plains all around him. He could see for at least a league in every direction, but the pale light of the moon and the few stars visible through the last of the cloud cover revealed nothing but empty grasslands dotted with the occasional tree. Not so much as a flicker of light indicating the presence of a fire.

His mind raced, but only for a moment. Only one course of action lay before him.

"Come on," he said, turning back toward the spot where their companions sat. "I need to check it out."

"*We* need to, you mean?" Kiara said, her voice sharp.

"No. *I.*" The Hunter stopped her with a hand on the arm, his expression solemn. "If they're Consortium, as I suspect, I can get in close without raising suspicion." He gestured to the studded leather vest he'd taken off the dead slaver. The bloodstains of those he'd killed back in the encampment around the Bondshold might raise a few eyebrows, perhaps elicit a few questions, but nothing he couldn't handle. "And I'm the *only* one who can."

Kiara looked down at her own armor, and a frown twisted her lips. "I'm still coming with you. I'll be close enough to lend a hand if things turn ugly."

The Hunter grinned. "I'd expect no less."

Every one of their companions—even the exhausted and miserable Naledi—proved as determined as Kiara. Within minutes, they were all mounted and riding, this time veering sharply to the southwest rather than continuing to follow the trail leading to the southeast.

The Hunter rode in the lead; he alone had the nostrils keen enough to pick up and follow the scent carried on the wind. More than once, the wind shifted directions—blowing first from the southeast, then from due west—and every time the Hunter's worry mounted. They were heading *away* from the path they knew would lead them toward the Consortium's army, trusting to his Bucelarii sense to lead them to…what?

What awaited them in the darkness ahead? A handful of deserters fleeing before battle? Yet *another* convoy of slaves carted from beyond Ghandia? A couple of fools who'd gotten separated from their comrades and lost in the plains? There existed the possibility that their endeavor now would be a colossal waste of time. But the Hunter had to be certain. He had to know there wasn't another enemy force lurking in the darkness. *One* consolidated army, he could figure out how to deal with. Multiple smaller companies spread out would prove problematic. He could only commit his full attention and strength to an attack once he knew without a shred of doubt he and his companions were at no risk of being taken unawares from the rear.

Relief bathed him like a cool breeze on a hot day when, half an hour later, he *finally* caught the faintest flickers of firelight in the distance. His keen eyes made out a handful of torches, a lantern, and a small campfire. Though they were still a full league away, he slowed his pace. Sound tended to carry across the plains; better not to alert those ahead to the approach of multiple riders.

Without a word, Kiara slid from her place on Elivast's back behind him. She made no protest about his going alone, for she'd understood the rationale behind his plan. Yet the look in her eyes made it clear she'd be watching and ready to ride in at a moment's notice.

"Get as close as you can," the Hunter told them. "But above all, stay quiet. A lone messenger will draw far less attention than a group." He'd given thought to the best ruse to allay the Consortium's suspicions—if, indeed, it turned out those he'd scented were slavers. Judging by the light coming from ahead, it was a small company—no more than a dozen or so. Few enough he could deal with them alone. With one backup plan, of course. "Any of them looks ready to bolt, you ride them down." This, he directed at Tarek.

The young Elivasti nodded and tightened his grip on his spear. None of the others could match his horsemanship, and Nayaga was the freshest of their mounts.

With that, the Hunter rode on. He let Elivast set the pace—the horse was tired from bearing Naledi's weight—and made no attempt to conceal the noise of his approach. On the contrary, he endeavored to make as much noise as possible. The louder he was, the less he'd have to worry about the slavers ahead overhearing his companions slipping along stealthily behind him.

His efforts proved successful. The figures, who had been sitting around their small campfire or lounging on the seats of their carts, sprang to their feet and turned toward him with weapons drawn. Again, the Hunter experienced a momentary surge of relief as he spotted the studded leather vests and curved-bladed greatknives that marked them as belonging to the Consortium. Rear guards, the Hunter determined, left to watch over the supplies loaded onto the eight carts circled around their camp.

A nasty grin split the Hunter's face at the realization. Every military strategist knew that an army marched on its belly. *If only they hadn't left their bellies so poorly guarded,* he thought.

He loosened his watered steel sword in its sheath and did a quick headcount. Twenty-five was a larger force than he'd anticipated, but too few to cause him much trouble. Soulhunger's bloodlust would be sated tonight.

"Ho, there!" he called out when he drew within shouting range of the rear guard. "Whose pricks did you lads have to suck to earn such a soft assignment?"

His insult had the desired result. The suspicion visible on the faces of every slaver waving bared steel in his direction shifted instantly to ire.

"Sod you!" snarled one, a large fellow with a massive black beard that hung down to his waist, all but obscuring the studded leather vest he wore. He stepped toward the Hunter and stabbed a warning finger at him. "Best watch your tongue, out here all on your lonesome, otherwise someone might rip it out of your head!" The tip of his sword, however, dipped toward the ground.

The Hunter grinned inwardly as he reined in before the circle of firelight. They'd suddenly become too angry to remember their suspicion. At least for a few moments, long enough for him to give explanation as to his presence out here.

"Easy, easy!" He held up a hand in a placating gesture. "Just taking the piss."

"Well, take your piss elsewhere," snapped another, a fellow who had a face terribly akin to a rabbit, all twitchy nose and buck teeth. He even *smelled* leporine, his unique odor thick with carrot, dewy grass, and loamy earth. "'Ent nothing for you here..." He began to frown, which did unfortunate things to his already less-than-pleasant features.

"Hardwell," the Hunter offered, "one of Rhodd's company." In a force of such size, comprised of men and women from all corners of Einan, it was far from uncommon to encounter strangers even in your own corps. "Up from Praamis."

Black Beard grunted. "Don't care who y'are or where you're from. Just—"

"Oh!" The Hunter pushed past the big, bearded fellow—who reeked of boot black, burned metal, and the bacon that stained his face—to stride into the circle of wagons. "Bloody hell, that's good." He made a show out of sighing and extending his hands to the small campfire, then turning to warm his rear. "Swear I've never been hotter and colder, all in the space of the same day. How do you lads put up with it?" He snatched up a clay wine jug one of the guards had set down in their haste to welcome him. "Ahh, this'd explain it, eh? Full bellies and a sip of summat tasty always makes things better."

His confident movements and the familiarity of his tone left the slavers wrong-footed and at a loss for words. That was something the Hunter had learned long ago. One simply had to act as if they belonged, and only the sharpest of mind and fastest of wit would ever think to question it. None of the rear guards around him appeared particularly sharp or fast in any way that mattered.

Not that he gave them time to collect themselves. "Shame I've not got time to stick around and teach you lads how a proper Praamian drinks." He sloshed the wine around in the jug, plastering a wistful look on his face. "Rhodd would have my hide if he knew I'd stopped this long." With his other hand, he patted his cloak, as if checking his pocket to reassure himself something of immense value was still where it was meant to be. "Message he gave me can't wait. Not even for a sip of—" He sniffed at the wine. "—a fine Nyslian red like this!" He gave a theatrical groan and set the jug down with all the reluctance of a starving beggar turning down a king's feast. "Now, which of you lads can point me to where Elmat's posted?"

Blank looks met his gaze.

"Elmat." The Hunter spoke the name again, then repeated it louder as if that would somehow facilitate understanding. "Elmat! You know, big fellow, ugly as a bear and about three times as hairy." He mimicked the fictional man's size with his arms. "Has a habit of scratching his arse crack and sniffing his fingers after?" He glanced between them, expectant. "Boots bigger than a boat and hands the size of an infant? Four front teeth browner'n shite and breath about as bad? Moustache that looks like someone plucked a goat's tail and pasted it onto his lip with mud?"

He couldn't help a moment of delight at seeing the slavers' confusion deepen at his ever-more-ludicrous description.

"Keeper's teeth!" The Hunter threw up his hands. "Never mind that. Just tell me where everyone's at, and I'll find him among the crowd myself." Again, he patted the pocket bearing his imaginary message. "I've orders to get this delivered by sunrise. I don't, it'll be me sent to march into battle with nothing but my prick in my hands."

"'Ent no battle no more." Rabbit Face regained enough of his wits to give the Hunter a nasty, self-satisfied smile. "Way we heard it, it was done and dusted hours ago."

The Hunter's blood ran cold. Had they arrived too late? Outwardly, he forced himself to calm. "That so?"

Black Beard planted his corpulent frame in front of the Hunter. "Aye, that's so!" He gestured to one of his companions, a pale-faced, nervous-looking fellow with no more than a dozen hairs clustered at each corner of his mouth, a single bushy eyebrow, and a drastically receding hairline. "Ossie here told us everything. We're just waiting for word that the last stragglers have been rounded up, then we're to bring in the food."

The Hunter looked to the aforementioned Ossie. "Battle was easy, then?" He gave the young man a nasty smile. "The savages' camp put up even less of a fight than expected?"

"C-Camp?" Ossie looked confused, but shook his head. "N-No. Not c-camp. P-Plans changed w-when we g-got word of the a-army marching b-back this w-way." He swallowed and tried visibly to rein in his stutter, with only limited effects. "T-Took them by surprise, w-we d-did." He beamed. "C-Captured them a-all. Even the ch-ch-chiefs! C-Come dawn, their h-heads will be o-off, and the s-savages w-won't be p-problem no more."

Chapter Forty-Eight

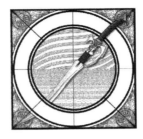

The Hunter kept his face a mask of calm, when inwardly his mind was racing. "That'll be the end of it, eh?" He plastered on a cruel grin. "Back the way we came, neat and tidy?"

"Not afore we finish what we started," Black Beard spoke up. "T'ain't done until it's done and every one of 'em's in chains or the ground."

"With most of their warriors sent to the Keeper," added Rabbit Face with a smile as maliciously gleeful as the Hunter's, "'ent much to do but surround their camp, clap every one of the darkies in irons, and march 'em back. That'll earn a bonus from the maskies, sure as my name's Craind."

Craind, eh? The Hunter decided his appellation suited Rabbit Face better and promptly forgot the name.

"Well, ain't that grand?" he made a show of grinning at all the slavers surrounding him. By now, they'd seemingly forgotten his slight and lowered their weapons. "Just point me at 'em, Ossie, and I'll be off sharpish. Maskies—" He suspected this was their less-than-respectful name for the Ordermen. "—don't like to be kept waiting. 'Specially when their message is marked 'top priority'." He grunted. "As if we ain't got better things to do than ride through day and night, eh?"

The moment he said the words, he *knew* they'd been wrong. Black Beard's eyes narrowed and a frown twisted his lips.

Rabbit Face looked to Elivast, suspicion darkening his face. "Where'd you say you was from?" He took a step toward the Hunter's horse. "Face like yours, easy to forget. But a beast like this..." He glanced back at the Hunter. "No, I'd remember him, seeing as I'm the one assigned to tend to all the horses. Ours and the maskies' al—"

His words cut off in a spray of blood as the Hunter's hurled dagger drove through his open mouth and punched out the back of his brain. The Hunter's left hand reached for his second belt dagger, drew it, and threw it with such swiftness Black Beard never had time to move before the razor-sharp tip buried in his eye. The men around him gasped in shock and fell backward as their burly companion staggered like a drunken ox. Black Beard's big hands fumbled at the hilt protruding from where his eye had once been, finally closing around the sharp steel. Yet it did him no good. In that moment, he toppled backward and crashed into the fire, showering those nearest him with glowing embers.

But the sparks flying in the air were the least of the slavers' problems. In the three heartbeats they'd stood staring at their comrades—one dead, the other dying on his feet—the Hunter had drawn his weapons. Now he tore into the Consortium without mercy, watered steel sword in his right hand and Soulhunger in his left.

519

With a single slash, he hacked Ossie's leg off at the knee, then spun and drove Soulhunger into the chest of the next slaver in line. But now, he did not pull the dagger free. He left it embedded deep in his enemy's chest to let its blood magic activate.

The man's screams echoed loud in the night, and brilliant crimson light flared from the dagger's gemstone. Power rushed through the Hunter in a crackling torrent that drove all fatigue, hunger, and thirst from his body in an instant. Even as the magic coursed in his veins, imbuing him with fresh vitality, he sprang upon the next slaver within his range of attack and drove his knee into the man's face. Nose, lips, teeth, and jaw *crunched* beneath the force of the impact and the man's head snapped backward. His spine gave a terrible, audible *crack* and the man crumpled in a limp heap.

Even as the man fell, the Hunter was flying past, his sword hacking to the right and left in great, sweeping blows. One sheared through a neck to send a head spinning away, blood spraying in a terrible mist from the decapitated stump. The other opened a throat and tore off another enemy's nose before carving out their right eye.

The instant his boots struck the ground, the Hunter dropped low into a crouch and spun. His movement brought him beneath the wild strike of the only slaver who'd regained his wits enough to attack. As the greatknife whistled high over his head, the Hunter drove the tip of his watered steel blade up into the man's groin. His left hand dipped for one boot knife, only to come away empty as he recalled he'd given the blades to Cebile. He refused to waste the movement, however, but seized the ankle of another slaver within reach and heaved upward with all his strength as he stood. The man flew into the air, spun once, and fell to land on his face. His spine gave a sickening snap as his body bent double.

A shout of rage—or was it pain?—echoed behind the Hunter. He spun, bringing up his watered steel blade in a cross-body blocking slash. His sword knocked aside the greatknife that had aimed for the back of his neck and removed his enemy's arm at the elbow. The man staggered backward with a scream. His heel caught on Rabbit Face's corpse and he lost his balance, toppling onto Black Beard's smoldering, smoking body. Three more quick slashes ended four more lives, the slavers too dull-witted and shocked to raise their weapons. Their bodies fell to join their comrades in quick succession.

For two long heartbeats, the Hunter stood alone and silent amidst the carnage. The surviving Consortium guards stared at him open-mouthed, pale-faced, and wide-eyed, seeming incapable of understanding the evidence of their eyes. And how could they? They, who had never seen *true* battle. Who had been stationed here, well away from the fighting. Who had likely never raised a sword against an armed enemy, but merely wielded fists, clubs, and whips against chained slaves.

No, these were not blooded men. Not true soldiers, nor warriors, not even *fighters*. These were brutes, who, for all their outward strength, lacked steel where it mattered most: in their souls. They would not stand and face an enemy who could match them in skill or training. What chance did they stand against the Hunter of bloody Voramis?

And so they broke. Like a puddle beneath the impact of a dropped stone, the cowardly little water droplets fled outward with all the speed they could summon. Fear lent wings to their feet, and they raced in every direction of the compass. Alone, the Hunter knew he could never chase them down, even mounted on Elivast.

But he was not alone.

The sound of galloping hoofbeats echoed from the north, a sound from the darkness that filled him with cruel delight—and his enemies with fear. The Hunter saw the figures materializing, like the famed *Mhareb* of Il Seytani, said to ride the whirlwinds and race on shadows. Four mounted on horseback, raising drawn swords and bared spears. Two more running toward the fleeing slavers with terrible swiftness and surety.

The Hunter lowered his watered steel sword. He did not need to give chase. He did not even need to watch as Tarek rode down those fleeing to the west, Aisha and Kodyn galloped after those racing north, and Siyanda and Naledi bore down on those attempting to escape to the east. Only two fled south, deluding themselves into believing they'd find safety in their army. They wouldn't get more than a few hundred paces before Kiara caught up to them. More souls to feed Deathbite.

Save for the crackling of the disturbed campfire and the hiss of Black Beard's burning flesh, the only sound still audible in the Consortium camp was a pitiful whimpering weeping. The Hunter had no great difficulty pinpointing its source. Ossie had managed to drag himself all of five paces along the ground, clawing his way toward a break in the circled wagons. Perhaps he hoped he could find shelter and safety in the tall grass; a fool's hope, given the thick crimson trail of blood dripping from his severed leg.

The Hunter stalked after the man, pausing only long enough to tear Soulhunger free of its victim's chest. The gemstone had already gone dark and translucent once more, but the Hunter could feel its endless appetite throbbing in the back of his mind. Or perhaps that was merely a trick of his mind, a manifestation of *his* disgust, anger, and hatred of the slavers and everything they represented.

He caught up to the crawling Ossie in five strides and kicked the man in the wounded leg. Pain sapped the strength from the slaver's arms and he fell to his face. The long grass did little to muffle his anguished howls. The Hunter could summon not a shred of pity.

Seizing the back of Ossie's studded leather vest, he lifted the slaver off the ground and hurled him backward. Ossie fell hard onto the body of one of his companions. His hand, covered with his own blood, landed on his comrade's belt, and his fingers closed around the still-sheathed hilt of the dead man's greatknife. But he did not draw. He could not, coward as he was. Indeed, he scrambled to retreat, as if the *weapon* was the true threat, not the dagger-wielding man gliding toward him like shadowy death.

"I give you one chance," the Hunter snarled, leveling Soulhunger to point at Ossie's throat. "Tell me where I will find your army. Tell me where the battle took place and—"

"V-Valley!" Ossie shouted the words so loud the Hunter suspected they could be heard all the way back in Voramis. The acrid stench of fear and urine drowned out his scent of camphor, mint, and white sage. "I-I d-don't know n-name. S-Some p-place w-with r-rocks a-all b-black and w-white!" Fear increased his stutter and made him all but incomprehensible. "I-I c-can t-tell you h-how t-to g-get th-there. J-Just, p-please, d-don't k-kill me—*ahh!*"

The Hunter didn't let him finish; he drove Soulhunger into Ossie's chest, piercing his studded leather vest and snapping ribs with the impact. Ossie's screams rang out high and shrill, his eyes filled with the terror of certain death and the agony of Soulhunger's magic devouring his life force.

It didn't matter that Ossie was far from the sort one would expect to find in a group of armed slavers—far too young, nervous, and callow compared to his companions. He wore the Vassalage Consortium's armor and carried out their orders. Whatever had led him to this place, whatever hunger or poverty or hardship had caused him to join their ranks, join he had. He'd taken the Consortium's gold, followed their commands, perpetrated their suffering on the people of the plains. His life had brought misery, but with his death, Kharna received much-needed sustenance. There could be no more fitting end for a man like him.

Through the power rushing in his veins, the Hunter's ears detected an answering scream coming from behind him, to the south. He tore his eyes from Ossie long enough to spot Kiara, her face illuminated in the crimson light shining from Deathbite's gemstone. A few score paces west of her, Tarek was withdrawing his long spear from the back of the slaver he'd ridden down.

The Hunter turned back as Ossie's screams faded and the light of Soulhunger's gemstone began to dim. As he stared at Ossie, the ritual words Master Eldor had taught him rose to his lips, but he swallowed them. No man of the Vassalage Consortium or Order of Mithridas would receive that final kindness from him. They would go to join the Abiarazi he'd sent to the deepest, darkest hell, unmourned, unremembered.

A ululating war cry from the east snapped his head up, in time to see Naledi and Siyanda racing toward him with their weapons—greatknives stolen from the encampment at the Bondshold—raised high and stained with blood. Hoofbeats came from the north, and Kodyn and Aisha rode toward the light of the campfire still burning beneath Black Beard's lifeless corpse.

"All down," Aisha called as she drew within earshot. "None of them have escaped to bring word of our presence to the rest of their army." She reined in Elivast—who she'd apparently mounted while Naledi ran into battle on her own two legs—right outside the circled wagons and studied their contents. "Supplies for the main force?"

The Hunter nodded and rose to his feet, pulling Soulhunger free. "Which, according to this one—" He waved his dagger's tip toward Ossie's corpse. "—has already won the battle."

"Battle?" Color drained from Aisha's face and Kodyn's eyes flew wide. "You mean—?"

The Hunter recounted what he'd learned from the slavers, loud enough that the approaching Naledi and Siyanda could hear it. About the "army marching back this way", taking them by surprise and capturing them all, and the proclamation that their heads would be off by dawn.

"No!" Aisha's free hand rose to her mouth. "No, it can't be!"

The Hunter shrugged. "All I know is what I heard." His expression darkened. "But the way these were boasting, they were pretty certain they'd won." Eight hundred or more slavers against fewer than two hundred Buhari and Issai warriors. The odds were heavily weighted against Aisha's people.

"It's not over yet." The Hunter glanced skyward. "Midnight's still far off, which means we've got a few hours until dawn. Time enough"—he hoped—"to get close enough to see things for ourselves."

Ossie had spoken of the battle being over "hours ago" which meant he couldn't have traveled *too* far to return to the rear guard and the wagons. Any mind smart enough to take the combined Buhari and Issai armies by surprise in their own lands had to be clever, indeed, and wouldn't make the foolish mistake of stationing the food and water their army would desperately need in the aftermath of a battle too far away.

"Get close to where?" Siyanda asked as she raced into the circle. "Where did they say this battle took place?"

"He didn't know." The Hunter shook his head. "But he said something about a valley with rocks of black and white."

Siyanda's eyes flew wide. "He said that, you are certain?"

The Hunter nodded. "You know it?"

"*Isigodi Zabara!*" Aisha gasped out the word.

"There can be no other," Naledi said, her tone doleful and her expression dark. "And if our enemy has them captive in the Valley of the Zabara, there is no way for us to reach them before it is too late."

Chapter Forty-Nine

Four hours after midnight, the Hunter caught his first glimpse of *Isigodi Zabara*. One look was all he needed to understand why Naledi's prediction had been so dour—and so accurate.

The Valley of the Zabara itself wasn't deep—perhaps twenty or thirty paces at most—bordered to the north and south by cliffs of the white-and-black-striped layered strata from which its name had been derived. Along the valley's bottom wended a river barely wider than a creek, all that remained of what must have once been a waterway mighty enough to carve such a furrow into the earth. Unlike the Unathi River, the banks of the river were wide and smooth, making for easy passage of the Issai's herd of *raya*. With the cliffs to hide them from watching eyes on the plains above, it would allow them to travel the plains undetected on their way to the Buhari lands.

Except there was no way through. A massive pile of boulders now utterly obscured the valley between the cliffs, blocking off passage farther east. The Hunter suspected that had been recently done; the Issai would not be foolish enough to trap themselves in a valley, knowing there were enemies on the *amathafa*. Which suggested the Consortium had *known* they would travel that route and brought the cliffs down upon them. With their way of escape cut off, the combined forces of the Issai and Buhari would have been forced to fight or surrender.

Had it been *only* the two tribes' *amaqhawe*, the Hunter had little doubt Davathi and Jumaane would have led their people into bloody battle without hesitation. Yet the *ekhaya* and the herd traveled with them—the Issai's true wealth. For all her courage, Davathi wouldn't be foolish enough to risk her tribe's extinction as long as some other possibility lay open to her. Based on his knowledge of Aisha, her daughter, the Hunter suspected the Issai's *nassor* had chosen surrender over the slaughter of children, youths, and elders. Her time in captivity had doubtless shown her what the Consortium truly wanted: slaves to put to hard labor, not corpses to bury.

From where the Hunter and his companions lay flat on their bellies at the crest of the last small hill before the edge of *Isigodi Zabara's* northern cliff, he could not see Davathi or Jumaane. A handful of the Issai and Buhari warriors were visible from his vantage point, all bound with ropes or wearing heavy chains around their wrists. There were simply too many for the marching army to carry shackles enough for all. The Consortium clearly trusted in their superior numbers to dissuade any attempt at flight or resistance.

And the numbers *were* visibly on the side of the *alay-alagbara*. Nigh on a hundred figures in studded leather armor stood barely five score paces from where the Hunter lay, all with their backs to him, faces, swords, and torches turned toward their defeated enemy in the valley. The shouts of hundreds more echoed up from below, accompanied by inaudible shouts and the cacophonous clanking of chains. The battle had been over for hours, but disarming and binding nearly four hundred people was no small task. The slavers would be at it all night and well into the following day. Especially if, as Ossie had said, they took the time to execute Davathi and Jumaane.

Where the two *nassors* were, the Hunter didn't know. But he damned well intended to find out.

"I'm going down." He spoke in a voice pitched low enough that it wouldn't carry on the wind. "I'm going to see if I can find your mother and Jumaane. See what state the warriors are in and figure out what to do."

Six grim faces regarded him silently. All had seen him in battle, yet even with his skill, ferocity, and nigh-invulnerability, the odds were far outweighed against him. And that was *without* knowing that among the slavers ahead were at least a handful of iron weapons. The Hunter had picked up the foul scent on the wind within minutes of his arrival, but hadn't told even Kiara. Their situation was already dire enough.

Kiara was first to speak. "We're coming with you, and don't bother arguing."

By "we", she meant herself, Kodyn, and Tarek. All four of them had taken studded leather vests from the dead rear guards, knowing full well they could use the disguise. The Hunter had tried to dissuade them then, just as he wanted to now, but Kiara had yielded to his arguments no more than ocean cliffs gave way before the gentlest tides. Indeed, in the moments he'd spent debating with her, Tarek and Kodyn had followed her example. Now, the three of them, like him, wore Consortium armor, even carried greatknives on their belts.

The Hunter seriously entertained the idea of wasting his breath on another attempt to dissuade her—he trusted his abilities to handle subterfuge and deceit far easier on his own—but gave it up after a moment. In truth, the more of them they could get in position near the Issai and Buhari *amaqhawe*, the greater the chance they could free enough of the warriors to take up arms to fight back. Three additional swords might not be many, but given that one was Deathbite, one had been trained by the Second Blade of the Elivasti and the Soaring Hawk Clan, and one had been schooled personally by the foremost assassin and Master of House Serpent, the Hunter tried to convince himself they could make a difference.

At the end of the night, however, it would come down to *him*. He touched *Ibad'at Mutlaqa's* hilt for reassurance. Kiara, Kodyn, and Tarek all knew that if it came to battle, their primary task would be to keep the Issai and Buhari as far away from the Hunter as possible. When the blood-frenzy overtook him and he lost control to the scimitar's magic, he was as likely to slaughter friend as foe. He could not let that happen.

"And what of us?" Naledi asked, her expression hard. "We will not sit by and do nothing. It is our people below, our *nassor* to be executed come dawn."

The Hunter fought the urge to glance at the sky. The sun would rise far too soon; better not hasten daylight's arrival.

"Naledi is right." Siyanda's jaw muscles clenched, her strong shoulders knotting and relaxing from the tension coiling her corded frame. "Let us draw the attention of the *alay-alagbara*, let them see us running free of their chains. Perhaps we can pull even a few score away to give chase."

"It will do us little good." The Hunter shook his head. "On the contrary, it will remind the Consortium that there are still others on the plains who may see them as foes. If they believe there are enemies in the night, their increased wariness and suspicion will make it that much more difficult for us to talk our way through their ranks."

"Besides," Kodyn said, casting a worried look between Siyanda and Aisha, "if something happens and you get captured—"

Siyanda gave a snort so loud and derisive the Hunter feared it would catch the attention of the slavers guarding the cliff's edge. "You do us insult if you believe there is even the slightest possibility an *alay-alagbara* can catch an Issai on foot." A scowl twisted her lips. "We are fleet as the wind and can run for hours without—"

"That's it!" Aisha sucked in a breath, her eyes suddenly flying wide. She rolled onto her side to look at Siyanda. "We are near *Ichibi Legolide*, yes? My father spoke of its waters often, and of—"

"Of course!" Siyanda's expression suddenly mirrored Aisha's. "The *Uhamaji!*"

The Hunter's mind raced. He'd heard that word before…but where? He could not recall its meaning or when Aisha had used it.

"We must hurry!" Aisha and Siyanda both scrambled backward on their bellies down the hill until they could leap to their feet and run. They sped off without looking back, without offering explanation.

Naledi took a moment longer to understand their meaning, and in the half-second it took her to move, the Hunter managed to call out. "Where are they going?"

The broad-shouldered Issai woman called something back in her own tongue and vanished into the darkness.

The Hunter looked to Kodyn. "What did she say?"

Kodyn blinked. "I did not understand." A confused frown on his face. "At least, I do not think I did." He looked at the Hunter. "I swear it sounded like she said 'We hunt for *Nuru Iwu's* children'."

The Hunter held the young man's gaze for a long moment. He'd understood "hunt" and "children". The name *Nuru Iwu*, too. But it made no more sense now that Kodyn had explained it. Kiara and Tarek's faces appeared equally blank and devoid of answers.

Nuru Iwu's children? He racked his brain, but the only thing that sprang to his mind were Tunde's words from two nights past. The *Indaba* had spoken of the Bheka as being the tribe living nearest *Ukuhlushwa Okungapheli*. Perhaps they believed *they* were descended from whatever *Nuru Iwu* had been, similar to how the Elivasti were sired by the Serenii. But the Bheka were enslaved by the Consortium and laboring to dig their way into the Serenii tower.

When, after a full minute of contemplation, he could make no sense of her words and none of the others had any explanation to offer, the Hunter gave up the effort. He trusted Aisha; she would not turn her back on her mother and her people unless she truly believed it was the best course of action.

He spent a few moments longer studying the Consortium forces arrayed along the clifftop. None of the slavers so much as glanced over their shoulders. Victory here had made them confident. Secure in the knowledge they had defeated the *only* true threat against them, they had grown lax, heedless to everything except their new prisoners.

Which gives us the perfect opening to exploit, the Hunter thought, as a hard smile spread across his face. *Arrogant as they are with their enemies defeated, they'll be too blind to see the dagger before we bury it in their bellies.*

* * *

"Ho, there!" the Hunter called out as he crested the shallow hill mere minutes later. "Looks like you lads have things well in hand. Didn't save none of the fun for us, did you?"

His words immediately had the desired effect. Half of the hundred or so stationed atop the cliff spun toward him, tightening grips on their swords. They squinted in his direction, too night blinded by their own torches to spot him in the darkness. He made things easy for them by spurring Elivast to ride straight down the hill in their direction. Behind him, Kiara, Tarek, and Kodyn followed in tight formation.

Confusion sprouted on the faces of the slavers the moment he rode into the range of their torchlight.

"Who goes there?" shouted one, a thick-necked fellow with the flaming red hair and beard of a Praamian to match his accent.

The Hunter reined in Elivast before the line of slavers who had moved to intercept him and made a show of patting the pocket of his cloak. "Messenger." The charade had worked well enough on the rear guard, and had a decent chance of getting him within striking range of whoever commanded the Consortium's small army. "Orders from the maskies." He laughed as if at some great jest and shot a glance over his shoulder at Kiara. "Y'hear that, Stilla? Orders from the Order!"

"Hilarious," Kiara said, her tone dry and her expression sour as lemons. "Missed your calling, you did, Hardwell. Jokes like that belong in a grand king's palace." She cast a tired glance at the torch-wielding slavers as she reined in beside him. "As far away from us as possible."

A few wry grins appeared on their faces, including the red-bearded fellow's.

"What orders?" the Praamian demanded. With every word, he breathed out noxious clouds of garlic accentuated by the stink of rotting teeth and the white sores dotting his tongue.

"Dunno." The Hunter shrugged. "One of them maskies just handed it to me and said get this delivered. Not the chattiest fellow. Didn't even offer his name, just barked his order and expected it obeyed."

The slaver grunted. "Typical!" He shook his head. "Love to boss us around, they do. As if we're their bloody servants."

Agreeing murmurs rose from a handful of the nearby Consortium men and women.

"Aye, and it's gotten far worse since all of yous marched off to have your fun." The Hunter thumped a hand against his chest. "Us as had to stay back been taking the brunt of things. I swear they've gotten worse ever since—" He pretended to swallow his words, stammering out, "Er...I mean..."

"Since what?" The red-bearded Praamian stepped closer, an eager look in his eyes.

"N-Nothing," the Hunter said, allowing his face to redden as if he'd just spilled some dire secret.

"Since what?" growled the Consortium man, moving his torch in an almost threatening gesture toward Elivast.

"Ugh!" Kiara grunted and threw up one hand. "T'aint nothing, but Hardwell here thinks if he talks, they'll take his tongue the way they did with Evrett."

"Take his...?" The red-bearded slaver's eyes went wide. "They laid hands on us? And Garrick just let it happen?"

"Oh, no." Kiara shook her head. "Garrick fought it tooth and nail. Had him spitting blood, the maskies did. But that did Evrett no good." She clucked her tongue as if checking that it was still attached. "Poor sod bled out before they finished arguing."

The Praamian growled a furious curse, and shot dark looks at his companions.

That particular element of the story had actually been Kodyn's idea. During his exploration of the encampment, he'd overheard a few of the slavers griping about the Ordermen. There had, in fact, been an Evrett who'd fallen afoul of the "maskies", and his punishment—a week spent on latrine duty—had him moaning loudly enough for Kodyn to overhear.

"All that to say," the Hunter said, pretending to wipe sweat from his forehead, "best I don't talk about what's been going on. Not until *after* I deliver this, leastaways." This time, when he touched his pocket, it was a more nervous gesture, like he attempted to reassure himself he still possessed the important missive. "Just point me in the right direction to go, and I'll be out of your hair."

The red-bearded slaver exchanged a look with his companions, and for a moment, the Hunter feared the man would ask more questions or scrutinize his story more closely. But his and Kiara's charade had sufficed to explain their presence, distract, and disarm the man's suspicion. The *pretense* of camaraderie, especially in an organization as large as the Consortium's, almost always worked. Doubly so when those being deceived had something of greater interest to draw their attention.

"Hundred paces west, there's a switchback that heads down into the valley." The man pointed with his torch to a place where twenty or thirty Consortium slavers clustered at the cliff's edge. "It's tricky going, but your horses look sure-footed enough to make the trip down."

"My thanks!" The Hunter doffed an imaginary cap in gratitude. "We meet in the ale line, your next drink's on me."

That earned him a broad, friendly grin. "I'll be taking you up on that!" the Praamian called after him as he rode away.

Sure enough, the narrow trail descending into the Valley of the Zabara was right where the man had said it would be. The slavers clustered around the trail head gave him the same suspicious look as the others had, but word quickly passed down the line that the Hunter and his companions were messengers to be let through. The torch-wielding men moved aside slowly, almost reluctantly, but that seemed more out of an unwillingness to take their eyes off the spectacle unfolding below than out of any suspicion of the Hunter.

And a spectacle it was, grim and terrible to behold. As the Hunter began his descent of the narrow switchback trail, he got his first true glimpse of the scene in the valley bottom. The corpses drew his gaze first. Easily a hundred or more, some piled in a haphazard heap at the edge of the creek-sized river, the rest laid out in neat rows in the shadow of the black-and-white-stone cliffs. Even now, nearly three-score slavers were hard at work tossing the slain Buhari and Issai warriors in the former and carrying their own dead toward the latter. The Ghandians had given as well as they'd got—perhaps even better, judging by a quick count of the fallen—yet in the end, the battle's outcome had been decided by weight of numbers.

The living far eclipsed the dead. The Hunter did not know the true count of the Issai's *ekhaya*, but the number of elders, children, herders, and women among the captives suggested that the casualties among the tribe's non-martial population had been kept to a minimum. The herd of raya had been herded against the cliffs and the boulders blocking the river's eastward flow, and a group of hungry-looking slavers eyed the cattle in anticipation of a great feast.

Of the Buhari's *amaqhawe*, at least three-quarters still lived to kneel and endure the ropes and shackles of the *alay-alagbara*. The Hunter counted at least fifteen of the twenty-odd Issai warriors who'd returned whole from their captivity, along with half of the *unkgaliwe*. A bloodied and beaten Duma knelt among the young and untested warrior women. His leopard-skin cloak had been stripped away, his huge sword taken, and his body was a mess of cuts and bruises. His face wasn't much better, and judging by the way he hunched to his right, he nursed at least two broken ribs. None of the warriors still living had emerged from the battle unscathed. They had fought until they had no choice but to throw down their weapons.

A mighty bellowing roar drew the Hunter's attention toward a spot where the river bent northward to flow around a twenty-pace-wide patch of high ground. There, he spied a towering figure with a great black beard and hair cropped close to his scalp. Jumaane raged and growled his fury as he struggled against his bonds. Manacles had been secured to his wrists and neck, and three slavers held the end of each chain. More slavers poked and prodded at the huge Buhari *nassor* with the long spears taken from his own defeated and slain warriors. Jumaane bled from more than a score of wounds, some minor yet painful, others grave-looking, yet he swatted at the spears thrust at him.

The sight sickened the Hunter. It reminded him of bear-baiting, a cruel sport favored by many of the Voramian nobility. Only once had he witnessed the bear break free of its chains, to disastrous consequences to the fops within range of its paws. Every other spectacle had ended with the death of a mighty beast of the forest. Doubtless a similar end was intended for Jumaane.

Nearby, an enraged Davathi snarled curses in her own tongue at the slavers tormenting her fellow *nassor,* but they fell on deaf ears. She could do nothing to come to Jumaane's aid or raise her hands against the casually cruel blows directed her way time and time again. Her hands were bound behind her back, with more ropes around her neck, waist, and ankles binding her to stakes driven deep into the ground.

But it was the man who stood watching the spectacle, cheering and shouting encouragement to the slavers, that drew the Hunter's attention most of all. A man with skin as dark as Davathi's, robes as bright as those worn by his Issai captives, and the armor and greatknife of the Consortium. A man with scars on his cheeks and chin, cruel humor echoing in his laugh, and malice sparkling in his dark eyes.

The same man the Hunter had met on the road from Zamani Falls, who had stared down at him with the look of a hungry lion preparing to feast on a kill.

Gwala!

Gwala

Chapter Fifty

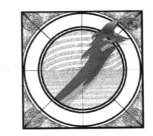

Anger burned in the Hunter's belly, and his hands gripped the reins so tight the leather creaked. It took all his willpower not to clap his heels to Elivast's flanks and send the horse barreling down the path. He'd killed two of Gwala's companions in *Indawo Yokwesaba* and ached to send the bastard himself to follow them into the eternal suffering he hoped awaited the cruel.

Yet he dared not. As the red-bearded Praamian had warned him, the switchback path was barely wide enough for Elivast to keep from falling, the rocks underfoot treacherous and the earth prone to crumbling. Charging down the trail would do nothing but kill Elivast and put the rest of the Hunter's companions at risk.

And so, though fury seethed like molten lava in the core of his being, the Hunter forced himself to remain calm, to maintain his slow, steady descent down the precarious trail. He would do no one any good if he was discovered now. Best he bide his time and wait until the moment counted most.

The Hunter quickly reached the first switchback and was forced to turn away from the grim scene surrounding Gwala. His gaze roved over the rest of the slavers filling the valley—four or five hundred of them, many bloodied and wounded, some gravely—and that was when his gaze fell on the umber-skinned figures standing armed beside the Consortium. The Ujana held their spears, bows, and jagged-toothed, round-tipped swords, their faces twisted in masks as cruel as the slavers. They, too, reveled in the mistreatment of the captive Issai and Buhari.

The Hunter had only seen the tribe from afar, the distance too great to make out much detail about them. Now, however, he had a clear view of the Ghandians who had aligned themselves with the Consortium against their own people. Torchlight gleamed off deep red armor, bracelets, collars, earrings, and anklets. Their adornments clacked loudly every time they shook their weapons in the air or stamped their feet to cheer on the *alay-alagbara*.

Behind them and farther west along the valley, two distinct groups of Tefaye hunkered in the shadows just within the circle of the slavers' lit torches. One cohort stood as still as statues, a strangely unnatural rigidity to their postures, eyes staring straight ahead into emptiness. All carried weapons and wore the dark wooden armor, unlike those which sat in a haphazard cluster across the river from them. These, the Consortium had not cut free of the fibrous ropes used by the Issai and Buhari to restrain them after the battle at the *kopje*. No longer did they rave and howl, however. Like their armed tribesmen, they sat stiff, silent, and vacant-eyed.

The Hunter fought to keep a snarl of disgust from curling his lip. The papers Kodyn had discovered detailing the tests perpetrated upon the Tefaye had mentioned "high suggestibility". One command from whoever led the Consortium's army could have sufficed to imprison the Tefaye within their own bodies. The cruelty of that bondage only heightened the Hunter's loathing of the slavers.

By the Watcher in the Dark, he vowed silently, *I will see them destroyed root, branch, and stem.* He didn't care that the god he'd invoked didn't truly exist; only his intention mattered. And he

531

bloody well intended to butcher every one of the slavers who'd brought their singular brand of wickedness to Ghandia.

He had seen a great many evils in his life. Years as the Hunter of Voramis had exposed him to the worst and darkest secrets of the worst and darkest people of all: the nobility who used their wealth to do whatever they wanted with no consequences. He'd watched Voramis succumb to the Bloody Hand's poison and wickedness over the years, until it was firmly under their thumb. He'd held Farida's mangled body, watched Bardin die at the First's hands, and been bathed in the blood of Elivasti butchered at the Warmaster and Sage's orders.

Yes, the Hunter knew of the evil that lurked in the shadows of Einan, all too well. What he beheld here sickened him as much as anything else he'd encountered. The Vassalage Consortium's deeds set them in parity with the worst Abiarazi and humans who had crossed his path and fallen to his blades. They had earned the fate that awaited them. Perhaps not tonight, but one day soon. The slavers *would* taste the wrath of the bloody justice he meted out.

Again, the narrow trail doubled back, and the Hunter was turned away from the enthralled Tefaye and the cheering Ujana to once again face the captive Issai and Buhari. Jumaane still roared and fought, but even his mighty limbs had begun to tire from effort, loss of blood, and fatigue. Crimson dripped from his heavily muscled frame, spattering the ground around him, speckling the slavers who held his chains and stabbed at him. Sheer stubborn defiance alone kept him from succumbing to injuries that would have killed a weaker man.

Davathi was shouting, straining against her bonds. More stakes had been driven into the ground around her, and the slavers were hauling at her ropes, pulling her arms and legs wide. A sick realization washed over the Hunter. He'd seen prisoners staked out and eviscerated, left to the sun and carrion. Davathi would die a cruel death—beneath the claws and teeth of predators, if she was fortunate, or succumbing to delirium and dehydration if not.

The Hunter's eyes darted toward the sky. He had no more than an hour before daybreak, perhaps less. And that was *if* Ossie's prediction that the *nassors* would be executed at dawn proved accurate. Judging by the treatment of Davathi, the Consortium's commander intended to make a spectacle of their deaths.

But who is the commander here? the Hunter wondered. *Who leads this army?*

His first instinct was to scan the ranks of slavers for any black-masked figures. The Order of Mithridas pulled the Consortium's strings, so it made sense that one of their ranks would lead the battle. Yet he saw not one. Not a single slashwyrm scale mask with the carved, horned demonic face.

Of their own accord, his eyes drifted back to the men who stood watching the torment of Jumaane and the staking-out of Davathi. Gwala, in particular. For the minute it took Elivast to reach the next switchback, the Hunter studied the scar-faced Ghandian clad in Consortium armor and bright-colored robes.

By the end of that minute, the Hunter knew the truth. He'd spent a lifetime assessing situations at a glance and taking measure of his enemies. From the ghastly scene playing out in the Valley of the Zabara, he knew with an iron-hard certainty that Gwala commanded the Consortium here.

It was evident in every minute detail. The way the slavers poking spears at Jumaane and cracking their whips at the bound and kneeling Ghandians looked to Gwala like eager pups seeking the approval of their masters. The steady stream of armed men moving toward Gwala with questioning looks and, at his answers, hurried away with purpose in their steps. Even the confidence in Gwala's stance and the way he watched the torment with the relaxed air of a king safe in his palace.

It made a strange sort of sense. Explained how the *alay-alagbara* had managed to catch the Issai and Buhari *amaqhawe* by surprise. Davathi and Jumaane hadn't been defeated by the Consortium. The battle had been lost to a Ghandian turncoat.

As the trail forced the Hunter to turn his back on Gwala, he called to mind every detail he could recall of the man from their brief meeting. He'd heard no accent, seen no details identifying which tribe he'd originally belonged to. His robes were cut in the style and sewn from the colorful fabric favored by the Dalingcebo and the populace of Khafra. The scars on his cheeks and chin were unique; neither the Issai nor Buhari warriors had displayed similar markings, nor had the Nyemba or Mwaani who'd been freed from the Consortium labor camp. The Bheka, perhaps? Tunde's face had been too disfigured by char and rot and pustules for the Hunter to know for certain.

That might explain how the Consortium and their Order masters found out about the Bondshold, the Hunter reasoned. If so, it only made Gwala's treachery worse. His own tribe had been enslaved, the last of the Bheka *Indaba* slain.

Whatever Gwala's origin, the Hunter knew only one thing: the man deserved to die. This very night, if the Hunter had his way. Killing their leader would throw the Consortium's forces into disarray—or, at the very least, create confusion enough for Kiara, Kodyn, and Tarek to free Davathi and whatever of the Issai and Buhari's warriors were bound with ropes. The chains binding Jumaane and a portion of the captives would take more time to remove, time the Hunter could not spare. He'd have to move fast and fight like a Keeper-damned Abiarazi to keep the slavers and their Ujana allies from slaughtering their prisoners of battle. And if the order was given to the Tefaye to join the fight…

No! The Hunter clenched his jaw. *I cannot allow myself to think about "what ifs". All I can do is fight the fight in front of me and trust those at my back to do likewise.*

The end of the switchback trail approached, and the ground ahead flattened as it reached the valley floor. The Hunter had just a matter of seconds before he would be among the slavers hustling to lay out the bodies of their dead. He had to make the most of it.

"Kiara, Davathi," he called over his shoulder, making certain to keep his voice low for her only. "Kodyn needs to be ready to free as many of the *amaqhawe* as he can, and Tarek needs to stay near the Tefaye, kill anyone who tries to order them into battle." His fists tightened around Elivast's reins. "I'm going for Gwala."

A grunt was all the answer he got, but he knew Kiara would be relaying his message to the two young men.

The battle plan forming in the Hunter's mind was simple: Gwala died first, then the six slavers flanking him—more than likely what passed for his cadre of officers. After that, the Hunter would turn his attention on the bulk of the Consortium men to the west and leave any to the east for Kiara, Kodyn, and Tarek to deal with. He'd have his hands full wrestling to keep *Ibad'at Mutlaqa's* magic from transforming him into a feral, mindless beast of slaughter. His willpower *would* eventually crumble as the scimitar's power amplified with every death. When that happened, he could only hope Aisha returned in time to stop him in his tracks with a blast of her *Kish'aa* magic. Otherwise…

He pushed the thought from his mind. No sense contemplating worst-case outcomes. The situation was already dire enough; better he kept his attention fixed on what he could control.

Starting with his features. He turned his mind inward as the Sage had taught him, focused his will on the muscles, bones, and cartilage of his face. Lightning crackled through his head as he compelled his flesh to shift. He gritted his teeth against the searing pain and forced his body to complete the transformation. It was a minor change—thickening his nose, sinking his eye sockets deeper, elongating his forehead, and adding a few moon-shaped pox scars in honor of Tassat's memory—but when he finished, he trusted Gwala would be unable to recognize the Hardwell of Praamis encountered on the road to Khafra what felt like a lifetime ago.

With his new disguise intact, the Hunter adjusted his cloak, sat straighter in his saddle, and spurred Elivast toward Gwala—and the inevitable bloodshed that would begin the moment the bastard tasted Soulhunger's steel.

Chapter Fifty-One

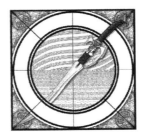

Eyes turned the Hunter's way as he rode through the ranks of slavers on a direct course toward the cleared stretch of riverbank where Gwala stood. A few suspicious glances followed him, but none thought to raise their voice or sword to bar his progress. What need had they? He wore Consortium armor and rode boldly through the Consortium army with an unhesitating confidence.

The Hunter grinned privately. Armies, like mobs, could be bewilderingly wool-headed. Those accustomed to obeying orders unquestioned rarely thought beyond their immediate sphere of influence and responsibility. All around him, the Hunter saw the same thought flash through the men and women who glanced their way: if the guards stationed at the clifftop had thought to let these riders pass, surely they belonged.

Thus, when Kiara, Kodyn, and Tarek turned their horses away from the path the Hunter followed, no one questioned. Concentrated as they were on their efforts to deal with their comrades and enemies fallen in battle, guard their prisoners, and enjoy the spectacle being made of Jumaane, the slavers had little mind for anything else.

Besides, the Hunter made a show of barking curses and shouting impatient commands to any who got in his way. It was more than just a critical part of his façade of a messenger delivering an urgent missive; it kept the attention fixed on him, leaving his three companions free to dismount, melt into the shadows, and lose themselves in the Consortium's ranks surreptitiously.

The Hunter fought the urge to track Kiara, Tarek, and Kodyn's movements. He had to trust they'd be in place when the time came. And come it would, all too soon. He carried no message from the Order of Mithridas. He brought only death into the Valley of the Zabara tonight.

The shouts and jeers hurled at the embattled Jumaane grew louder as he approached. So, too, did the curses Davathi snarled at Gwala. Though the Hunter did not understand them, the blazing fury, hatred, and loathing on Davathi's leonine face communicated with crystal clarity to all *alay-alaghara* who beheld her. The vehemence in her tone was a language as universal as laughter and tears.

Gwala, however, just laughed, clapped his hands, and stamped his feet as if in time to some music only he could hear. Davathi's words had no effect on him; his dark eyes sparkled as he watched his men prodding at the heaving, panting, blood-covered Jumaane.

By now, the Buhari *nassor* was on the verge of collapse—from exhaustion and blood loss both. The men holding his chains barely had to struggle to keep him restrained. The great, bearded warrior could barely stand, his legs trembling with the effort of holding him upright. When the sharp spears darted for his flesh, he had no strength to evade.

Just hold on a little longer, the Hunter urged the man mentally. *Your battle is not yet over*.

"Ho!" the Hunter shouted with all his might. His words rang out through the valley, resounding off the black and white cliff walls, audible even over the cheers and cries of the slavers. Just for good measure, he shouted again. "Ho!"

Scores of pairs of eyes turned his way—among them, the men baiting Jumaane with spears. The lull in the torture bought the Buhari a brief respite, and he collapsed to his hands and knees, great chest heaving as he dragged in one labored breath after another.

The call drew Gwala's attention, too. The Ghandian's smile wavered not an inch, the cruel humor still shining bright in his dark eyes, but a look partway between curiosity and suspicion flashed across his face.

The Hunter reined in Elivast a few paces away from the circle of slavers ringing Jumaane. He dismounted lightly, his strength replenished by the lives Soulhunger had consumed mere hours past. Yet he made a show of groaning, rubbing his rear, and stretching his back as if wearied by a long ride.

"Just give me a moment," he protested to no one in particular, raising one hand as he leaned on his knees with the other. Every second's delay bought Kiara, Kodyn, and Tarek more time to slip unseen through the ranks of slavers and take up their assigned places. "Bloody back's been misery for the last day and night."

He muttered curses loudly enough to fill the near-silence that filled the valley. The slavers nearest him were busy eyeballing him, and even a handful of those set to guard the captive Issai and Buhari glanced his way.

When, finally, the Hunter straightened, a series of loud *pops* and *cracks* of loosening joints echoed from his spine. "Ahh!" he breathed, relief audible in his voice. "Much better." He looked to the men and women around him in search of sympathy. "I swear the dumb beast took every opportunity to make the trip an utter misery. The day he ends up in the stew pot can't come too soon, eh?" He chuckled at his own joke.

Not one of the slavers so much as cracked a smile. His arrival had proven an unwelcome diversion from their cruel sport, earning their annoyance and keeping their attention fixed on him. Precisely as he'd intended. All eyes on him meant fewer watchers guarding the prisoners or taking note of the three newcomers slipping through the ranks.

Again, he began the charade that had brought him this far. "Got a message here." He patted the pocket of his cloak with the tenderness of a mother caressing her beloved child. "The maskies who gave it to me—"

"Ware your tongue!" snapped one of the slavers, a thick-set fellow with a belly only slightly less wide and outthrust than his chest. His clean-shaven face bristled into an angry glare. "Such disrespect toward our employers will not be tolerated."

The Hunter mumbled a hasty apology. Likely he was what passed for a sergeant or mid-ranking officer in the Consortium ranks, the type of man as free with his punishments as his scowls and shouts. Not a popular fellow, to say the least, yet a necessary evil for the operation of any sizeable force of men.

"No disrespect intended," the Hunter grumbled. "But aye, I'll watch my tongue. Just let me deliver what I've been sent to, and I'll be on my way." He gestured toward Gwala. "Message is for him."

The sergeant-type fellow looked as if he wanted to step into the Hunter's path and keep barking at him until he groveled in submission, as such men were wont to do. Fortunately, Gwala saved the Hunter from that particulate fate.

"Let him through, Trammet."

The order halted the thick-set slaver in his advance. After a moment spent lavishing his finest scowl upon the Hunter, Trammet stepped out of the way. The slavers around him did likewise.

The Hunter marched through the opening in the Consortium's ranks, past the men holding their forgotten spears still pointed at the kneeling Jumaane, and across the cleared stretch of ground separating him from Gwala and the six at his back. He took advantage of his approach to study the first of his many foes.

Gwala himself was much as the Hunter remembered him. Striking of feature, cheekbones and chin finely chiseled, nearly as tall and broad as Jumaane, his expression pleasant, almost friendly, save for the vicious humor dancing in his dark brown eyes. The colorful robes he wore contrasted sharply with the metal-spiked vest beneath and the curved greatknife that hung at his belt. The man's scent of citron and myrtle pepper were barely detectable beneath the potent stink of iron rising from the gloved metal hand, the thumb of which he'd tucked into his belt to give him an almost casual air. Yet for all his outward relaxation, the Hunter got a sense that the man was likely the most dangerous enemy he'd face this night.

Four of the slavers at his back were largely unremarkable by comparison. Hard-looking men and women from every corner of Einan, all showing the first signs of greying, marked by the occasional scar, missing a finger or two, yet standing straight-backed and wary-eyed. These, clearly, had been hardened by whatever battles they'd fought over the years.

The fifth member of his cadre was Slant, he of the lopsided smile. That disfigured expression was fixed on the man's face as he looked impatiently from the Hunter to the kneeling, chained Jumaane, visibly eager for the torment of the Buhari *nassor* to resume.

Finally, there was the diminutive Djineza with her enormous sword. Only now she carried it unwrapped from its concealment and gripped in her hand. The two-handed weapon was planted between her feet, its flame-shaped blade of deepest black visible for all to see.

Shalandran steel? The Hunter fought to keep the surprise from showing on his face. It was well-known that the Shalandrans guarded the secret of forging the weapons wielded only by their Keeper's Blades with a ferocity to rival that of the Secret Keepers. The Hunter himself had invested a significant fortune in the effort to procure a blade and wound up empty-handed and poorer for the attempt. Yet here was one, not five steps from where he stood, carried by a woman nearly shorter than the sword itself.

Anger flared anew within the Hunter. It took all his willpower to keep from drawing his weapons and springing at the three slavers he'd first met weeks ago on the road to Khafra. Of the five who had ridden at the head of the convoy transporting the villagers of Nkedi to the labor camp in *Indawo Yokwesaba*, they alone drew breath. There had been more—at least twenty—but the Hunter knew only the faces and names of Gwala, Slant, Thrax, Djineza, and Ahmoud. By sunrise, the world would have forgotten them all.

But not yet, he told himself. *Not until the time is right.*

He stopped just in front of Gwala, just out of striking range, and forced himself to grin at the slaver. "Some victory, eh? I'll bet the bastards never even saw the trap until it was sprung. I've got to know, what made you decide *this* was the place to take 'em?"

He'd put the pieces together as best he could. The Consortium's forces had been marching due southeast toward the Buhari *ekhaya,* only to deviate hard to the west toward *Isigodi Zabara* once Gwala had received word—like from the Ujana who'd made fine scouts—of the combined Issai and Buhari traveling through the valley. That was the simplest, most logical explanation, and nothing he'd seen in the last hours contradicted it.

"Simple." Gwala thrust a finger toward the striped cliffs bordering the valley. "I knew this was where it narrowed, thus would be easiest to block off." He waved a hand toward the pile of boulders obstructing the way east. "As you can see…"

The Hunter beamed. "Impressive! Truly a—"

"What is your name?" Gwala's words cut him off. The Ghandian's smile had gone hard, his eyes fixed on the Hunter's face.

"Elmat, sir." The Hunter ducked his head in mimicry of a military bow. He couldn't risk using the name *Hardwell* on the off-chance Gwala recalled it from their chance meeting weeks ago.

"Elmat." Gwala repeated the name as if tasting it on his lips. "A good name."

"Thankee, sir." Again, the Hunter ducked his head. "Named after my grandpap—"

Gwala's sword cleared its sheath so quickly any *mortal* man might not have seen it. Even to the Hunter's razor-honed instincts, the movement was nearly a blur. It took all of his willpower not to respond until *after* the tip of the curved blade rested against his throat. He let a full second pass before recoiling and gasping in wide-eyed surprise.

"I know the faces and names of all those under my command," Gwala snarled. His scarred face transformed into a mask of cold fury. "There is no Elmat."

Slant and Djineza moved then, springing forward to seize the Hunter by the arms and hold him fast.

Gwala's striking ebony features hardened and he leaned closer, pressing the tip of his sword into the Hunter's throat with just force enough to break the skin. "So tell me, who are you *really?* I would know before I remove your head what manner of man would be foolish enough to—"

But the Hunter was no longer listening. Beyond the harsh dissonance of Gwala's voice, his keen ears heard the innocuous sound for which he'd been waiting.

"Achoo!" The sneeze was echoed by another a moment later, then a third after a brief pause.

A grin twisted the Hunter's lips, and he made no attempt to hide it.

The signal had been given. The time to strike had come.

Chapter Fifty-Two

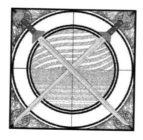

Gwala had moved fast, but the Hunter exploded into motion with such speed even the Ghandian was caught utterly flat-footed. A quick twist of his upper body tore his right arm free of Djineza's grip, and his right hand snapped up to slap Gwala's sword away from his throat. With the same twisting movement, he used his shoulder and left arm to pull Slant forward. Right into the path of Gwala's sword. The disfigured grin morphed into a horrified gasp as the greatknife's curved tip tore a gaping slash in his throat. Slant's grip on the Hunter fell slack and the slaver staggered backward, gurgling and clutching at his neck. His desperate pawing did little to lessen the blood pouring in hot, warm sheets down his front.

Free of his captors, the Hunter reached for the weapons concealed beneath his dark cloak. Soulhunger and his watered steel sword slid free of their sheaths and came up in a vicious disemboweling slash. Gwala's studded leather armor could do little to deter those twin blades on their deadly trajectory toward his flesh.

Luck alone saved the Ghandian slaver's life. Caught off guard by the Hunter's sudden movement, he'd reacted too slow to pull back his greatknife. He'd stumbled backward a half-second too late—the damage to Slant's throat had been done—and his eyes flew wide upon seeing his companion falling. That startled, awkward retreat brought him just beyond the reach of the Hunter's sword. Watered steel *whooshed* through empty air where Gwala's gut had been the previous instant. He twisted the missed blow into a spin that brought Soulhunger driving around point-first at the man's face.

But the near-miss had cleared any vestiges of surprise from Gwala's mind. The impact shivered up the Hunter's forearm as his vambrace *clanged* off the Ghandian's upraised greatknife. Gwala turned the block into a savage slash that curved up and over the Hunter's arm, tearing toward his throat. The Hunter was forced to backpedal to evade the strike. A gap opened between him and the Ghandian, but before he could close, the four slavers who'd heretofore remained frozen and gawking now came to life in an eruption of steel-edged violence.

Four greatknives assailed the Hunter in a full-front attack that drove him back first one step, then two, then a third. At this last, he dug in his heels and willed his muscles to respond faster. Any farther and he'd be within range of the spears that had been used to torment Jumaane. From the corner of his eye, he could see the spear-wielding slavers recovering their wits and gathering their courage.

With a shout, the Hunter batted aside two of his enemies' weapons and hurled himself at the slavers, accepting two weaker strikes in the bargain. One glanced off his stolen Consortium vest with little more than a dull *thump* of impact. The second, however, carved a line of fire down the side of his face and neck, barely missing the Hunter's jugular.

But then he was among the slavers, and there was no stopping him. His outthrust sword drove into one's belly, a kick shattered the knee of another, and Soulhunger opened a third's throat on its path to burying in the last woman's chest. Her screams echoed loud and shrill in the night, higher even than the moans of the other wounded and dying. The light flaring to life from Soulhunger's gem bathed him in a deathly glow the same crimson as the blood gushing from his enemies.

The Hunter basked in the power, in the rush of battle, in the hot warmth spattering his face, hands, and neck. He threw back his head and howled a terrible, savage cry. The call of a predatory beast that had finally closed with its quarry.

The rush of power from Soulhunger's gemstone began to fade, but the Hunter tore it free and buried it to the hilt in the abdomen of the man whose knee he'd shattered. Again, the screams brought the dagger's magic to life, and the fire rushed through every fiber of his being. Every shred of fatigue and pain was driven away, all hesitation and uncertainty with it. He was the Hunter, and every one of the Keeper-cursed slavers surrounding him were his prey.

Releasing his grip on Soulhunger, he tore the watered steel sword from the slaver's gut. Blood sprayed in a wide arc across the cleared stretch of ground where he stood, joining the pool of crimson beginning to form in the dust at his feet. The Hunter's eyes snapped toward Gwala, who was scrambling backward, wide-eyed with horror. The Ghandian's gaze was locked on both the Hunter's snarling face and the still-gleaming gemstone devouring the life from his dying subordinate.

The Hunter wasted no breath on curses, insults, or promises of agonizing death. He hadn't the time. The army surrounding him would regain their wits at any moment. When that happened, he'd be in for the bloody fight of his life.

He sprang toward Gwala, watered steel sword extended before him. The sword's tip aimed at the slaver's heart, a thrust the Hunter knew would strike true.

Only to have it turned aside a moment later as steel *clanged* loudly on steel. A massive flame-shaped blade bashed aside his outthrust sword with such force the Hunter nearly lost his grip on his hilt. Only by reflex did his fingers tighten their hold at the last minute. As it was, the impact knocked his sword wide, nearly sending him flying with it.

He sucked in a breath as a dark sword nearly as long as he was tall swung a deadly arc through the air on a direct course to his neck. The Hunter's blood ran cold at the sight of the razor-sharp Shalandran steel blade hurtling toward. The metalworkers who forged the metal used minerals zealously guarded. The result, however, was undeniably superior to virtually every rival steel on Einan. Only Odarian steel matched it. And, the Hunter had to hope, the watered steel crafted by the Elivasti using techniques known only to their ancestors.

But he could not bring his sword up in time. The attack that had knocked his blade wide had been turned into this decapitating blow. Still off-balance from his leap, the Hunter had no chance of interposing his blade. So he did the only thing he could: he threw up his left arm.

His vambrace had been forged by one of Voramis' finest smiths, yet even that steel could not stand against Shalandran steel. Agony exploded through his forearm as his enemy's heavy flame-shaped blade tore through his armor. Only the fact that he was using his vambrace to deflect rather than block saved him from losing the limb. Still, when the sword tore free, the Hunter's arm hung limp, the bone shattered and half the muscles torn.

The Hunter did not fight the pain; he gave in to it. He embraced it, let it wash over him, spur him to greater ferocity. A roar burst from his lips as he brought his watered steel back on-target and unleashed a flurry of savage blows at Djineza.

To her credit, she was good. Bloody good. She did not swing the sword about as a larger man would, but instead used it to weave an unbreakable guard of black steel that always managed to get between the Hunter's attacks and her armored body. Her gauntlets were forged of the same Shalandran steel, the Hunter saw, and served to both fortify her grip on her weapon and repulse every swing aimed to sever her fingers or snap her wrists.

The pain of his ruined arm drove the Hunter near to distraction, and only years of training kept him from giving in to the torment that throbbed up and down the entire left side of his body with every jarring impact of his sword against hers. Yet he knew he couldn't afford to remain entangled with Djineza for long. Every second that passed locked in combat was a second his companions would be in danger.

"Behind you!"

The bellow snapped the Hunter's attention to a threat from his rear. His body reacted as he'd trained it to, spinning to the side and swinging his sword around in a wide arc behind him. Only when he felt his sword tip carving a deadly path through flesh did his mind comprehend the true danger. The spear-wielding slavers who'd been tormenting Jumaane had closed on him, intending to run him through with their longer weapons. Only the *nassor's* bellow had saved his life.

The Hunter could not stand against the spears on one side and the Shalandran steel sword on the other. Loath as he was to abandon his efforts to butcher Gwala, the choice was made for him by his wounds. The slaver who'd died with Soulhunger driven into his chest lay between the Hunter and the onrushing spearmen.

With a roar of fury and frustration, the Hunter turned his back on his *true* target and the greatest of the threats and leaped toward the spears stabbing toward him. Not *at* them, but below them. His forward dive carried him beneath the upraised polearms. He landed hard on his ruined arm, snapping the last remaining shards of bone and sending lances of searing fire ripping through the limb, but even as the scream ripped from his lips, he dropped his watered steel sword to reach for Soulhunger's hilt. The dagger tore free of its last victim's chest in a spray of blood and the Hunter rolled to his feet in the midst of the six slavers.

Their spears might have given them the advantage of reach when they were closing with him, but up close, the long weapons were a death sentence. The slavers wielded their stolen spears with the clumsiness of unfamiliarity. They put up little more than a paltry defense as Soulhunger carved its way through their ranks. Throats opened beneath the dagger's razor-sharp edge, spraying blood. Muscles and tendons gave way as easily as if the Hunter slashed at strings of gossamer. And when he finally drove the Soulhunger into the last spearman's chest, the other five were too busy dying or screaming to stop him.

Again, the rush of power cascaded through his veins, only this time the anguish it brought nearly drove the Hunter to his knees. He could not help but cry out, howling into the night, all but blinded by the pain of his healing arm. He felt every muscle re-knitting, the bones re-forming, the sheared flesh closing. A torment worse than anything he'd felt since the night he lay on the Warmaster's torture table. It left him gasping, tears blurring his eyes.

Still, he fought through the agony. He ripped Soulhunger free of the dying slaver's breast and spun toward the next, a fellow whose sword arm he'd carved to ribbons. The Consortium man's sword lay at his feet in a puddle of his own blood. Before he could lift his gaze to the Hunter, Soulhunger drove down into the space between his shoulder bones and pierced his heart.

That death, and the vitality it infused into the Hunter, drove away the last of the pain in his arm. Diving forward, he scooped up his dropped sword and hacked off the head of the only spearman left standing. The man's decapitated corpse fell with the stolen Buhari weapon still clutched in his lifeless hands.

The Hunter braced himself for the next attack, but when it came, it was little more than a clumsy attack from a pair of slavers who'd abandoned their grip on Davathi's ropes. The Hunter knocked their blades aside with a single swipe, killed the first of the two on the backstroke, and disarmed the second with a trio of contemptuous, lightning-fast strikes. Even as the man stared dumbly down at his severed hand and the sword it still gripped, the Hunter drove Soulhunger to the hilt in the slaver's chest.

The energy coursing through the Hunter set his blood boiling and his pulse roaring. Yet it was not only his own heartbeat that filled his ears; from all around him, ululating war cries rose from the throats of the Issai and Buhari.

In that moment, the battle around the Hunter diminished for a heartbeat, and for the first time he looked around. The Valley of the Zabara was awash with blood. Dozens of Issai and Buhari warriors wrestled with the Consortium men and women who had, only moments earlier, held them captive at sword-point.

The battle was desperate, the odds weighted heavily in favor of the *alay-alagbara*. But the Ghandians had surprise and desperation on their side. The Consortium had been caught off guard by the Hunter's attack on their commander, and the sudden savagery of the warriors Kodyn had surreptitiously freed.

Now, the Hunter thought, turning his attention back to the place where he'd last seen Gwala, *time to cut the head off this serpent!*

Chapter Fifty-Three

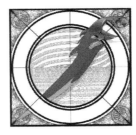

The Hunter's two enemies stood alone at the river's edge.

Gwala had his sword out and held at guard, his eyes assessing the battle raging within the valley. For all his earlier surprise, his face revealed only the cold, confident assurance of one who believed he knew the battle's inevitable outcome. He was actually smiling—*smiling!*—as he watched the handful of freed Issai and Buhari fighting for their lives.

Djineza stood between her commander and the tumult, but she had eyes only for the Hunter. Her golden-skinned features were hard and determined, her great two-handed flame-bladed sword raised to strike.

For a heartbeat, the Hunter's spirits soared. Only one foe stood between him and the bastard who commanded the Consortium's forces here. Those two deaths would tilt the battle heavily in his favor. Even well-trained armies broke when their leaders fell—and the *alay-alagbara* were a far cry from the disciplined ranks of soldiers that marched in the Legion of Heroes.

He gathered his strength and sprang into a charge toward Djineza. For all her skill with her huge blade, she was just *one* human. Mortal and fallible. She could not match him in speed, strength, or sheer savagery.

Djineza saw him coming and began to swing. Her sword sliced the air on a blurring path toward the Hunter's neck. Just as he'd known it would. She *had* to know she was outmatched; her only chance of survival lay in ending the battle before he got within range of her longer, heavier blade.

The Hunter ducked beneath the swinging sword, preparing to drive his own into her belly as he closed within range. Before he could begin the thrust, however, a shrill, harsh sound from his right drew his attention. A half-scream of pain, half-shout of fury he knew all too well.

Kiara!

The Hunter followed through on his attack but could not stop himself from shooting a glance in Kiara's direction. She stood not five paces from him, laying about her with great sweeping blows of her sword. At her side, Davathi wielded a sword she'd plucked up from a dead foe. The severed ends of the ropes used to stake the Issai *nassor* to the ground spun and twisted like wild serpents dangling from her wrists, ankles, and throat as she fought.

The crimson light from Deathbite's gemstone illuminated the ground around the two women for a dozen paces and highlighted the blood spattering both of their faces and bodies. It also glittered off the edge of the greatknife driven a hand's breadth into the meat of Kiara's left shoulder.

Fear coiled like a serpent in the Hunter's gut. There were easily a dozen enemies surrounding the pair, but in this battle, that was far too many. Kiara had learned to fight in cramped alleys and narrow side streets, while Davathi was accustomed to wading into her enemies with spear and shield. There was no way to retreat, and at any moment, the Hunter knew they could be overwhelmed and cut down.

In that moment, the Hunter's sword struck its target. But the moment of distraction cost him. Instead of punching through Djineza's leather vest, it rebounded off a metal spike. The sudden change of direction wrenched the Hunter's wrist. Pain shot up his arm, momentarily slowing his movement, preventing him from turning the failed strike into a follow-up slash.

And then the Shalandran steel sword came for him once more. The woman who wielded it followed through on the missed swing and used the momentum to bring the sword up and over her head for a downward strike backed by force enough to cleave the Hunter's skull. With his attack thwarted and his sword arm momentarily slowed, he had no choice but to dart out of the way. He could not close with his enemy for fear of getting entangled. The delay of a few seconds might very well be the difference between Kiara's life and death.

A growl of fury burst from his lips as he broke off from Djineza and sprinted toward the spot where Davathi and Kiara fought together. His feet moved in a blur, his every step quickened by the sight of the Consortium pressing the two women from three sides. Yet even with all his inhuman speed, he nearly arrived too late.

He saw the greatknife driving in a low thrust toward Kiara's left side. She was too caught up in parrying an attack from her right and driving Deathbite's tip into an enemy's throat to see the danger coming for her. Davathi's eyes widened as she recognized the danger but could do nothing to help. She was barely holding her own against the three enemies hammering at her guard, too busy fighting to stay alive to bring her stolen blade around in time to block or deflect the killing blow aimed at Kiara.

The Hunter launched himself forward into a desperate dive. His sword flashed out, carving a bloody red line across the legs of the slaver striking at Kiara, severing hamstrings and tendons all the way to the bone. The man collapsed with a scream and his thrust struck only empty air. The Hunter struck the ground hard, sending pain jarring up his left shoulder, but rolled to his feet in time to hack open the fallen slaver's throat. In the same movement, he buried Soulhunger into the back of one of the enemies battering at Davathi. The man's entire body stiffened as the force of the strike lifted him up onto his tiptoes. When he screamed, agony turned the sound shrill and harsh.

The sudden brightening of crimson light from behind diverted the attention of three slavers. That momentary distraction bought Davathi a reprieve from the desperate—and losing—battle she'd been fighting. She managed to knock aside a strike aimed at her eye and finish off the lone enemy who'd kept his attention fixed on her. The Hunter, meanwhile, made quick work of the trio who'd gotten distracted. His sword cut them to bloody ribbons in four lightning-fast slashes. Deathbite collected a grim harvest of those surrounding Kiara. Within the space of five heartbeats, the fight was over and the three of them stood alone.

"I had it...in hand!" Kiara called out to the Hunter, though her gasping, labored breaths marred the confidence of her tone. "Bastards...were right...where I wanted them."

"I know." The Hunter shot her a grin as he ripped Soulhunger from the fallen slaver's back. "But—"

His words were drowned out beneath a deafening lion's roar. He spun, weapons in hand, to where Jumaane still stood in chains. The spearmen who'd been baiting the Buhari were dead, their weapons fallen in the blood pooling around their corpses, but more slavers had encircled the huge *nassor* with bared swords. Gone was any thought of torturing their prisoner; they came to kill. Jumaane had regained strength enough to whirl his chains about like weapons, crushing one skull, shattering an arm, caving in the chest of one slaver who drew too close. Yet there were simply too many. He could not stand for long.

The Hunter wasted a single heartbeat searching for Gwala—a curse tore from his lips as he spotted the Ghandian and Djineza wading across the shallow river, surrounded by nearly two-score slavers with drawn swords and murder in their eyes—before charging toward the embattled Jumaane. Kiara and Davathi raced along at his side, and the three of them tore into the slavers like a thunderbolt from the heavens. Only two managed to turn to face their rush, but could not bring their greatknives up to defend against the Hunter's watered steel sword. The rest died without ever seeing the swords that ended their cruel lives.

Yet they were not the last enemies to face. The bulk of the Consortium's forces had been stationed farther to the east, but now flooded westward, hacking their way through the freed Issai and Buhari, reinforcing their comrades. The Ujana fought beside their *alay-alagbara* allies, hacking with the ugly, jagged-toothed swords and driving their spears into the unarmored bodies of their fellow Ghandians. A handful had ascended partway up the switchback and now sent a stream of long-shafted arrows down into the valley.

The Hunter put his back to the chained Jumaane and faced east toward the hundreds of foes awaiting him there. "Get those chains off him!" he shouted over his shoulder, cutting an arrow from the air and gutting the first of the slavers to reach him with a vicious thrust. "We need him in the fight."

Davathi must have come to the same conclusion. No sooner had those words left his lips than the *clang* of steel striking steel echoed loud behind him.

Kiara, however, appeared at the Hunter's side, Deathbite held in a firm grip, her face resolute. She laid into the slavers with ferocity that would do even a Bucelarii proud. Her sword moved nearly at the same speed as his, darting, thrusting, slashing, and hacking through exposed flesh and armor alike. Though she had not his strength, she wielded a weapon of the Serenii, an *Im'tasi* blade forged with arcane secrets long ago lost to time. No mundane leather, studded or boiled, could withstand Deathbite's keen edge.

But as they fought side by side, the Hunter noted the way Kiara favored her left side. The wound to her shoulder was far from the worst. She'd taken an ugly gash to her left thigh, and the blood sluiced down her leg, splattering the dusty ground around her every time she took a step. The sight drove a dagger of worry into the Hunter's gut. Yet he had no time to stop and tend to the wound; there were simply too many enemies to face.

How long the battle lasted, the Hunter did not know. Minutes seemed to stretch into days as he lost himself in the chaos of blood and death. Screams surrounded him on all sides—screams of pain, terror, and rage, rising from the throats of friends and enemies alike. Hot, metallic warmth splattered his face, soaked up his arms, filled his mouth. The stink of bile, sweat, and bowels loosening in death hung so thick around him he could scarcely draw breath. The enemy seemed endless, coming at him in a tidal wave of sinew and steel that threatened to wash away him and the woman who fought at his side.

The urge to draw the Sword of Nasnaz grew stronger with every gasped breath, every labored beat of his heart. Yet he could not unleash the scimitar's magic, not while he stood shoulder to shoulder with Kiara, or while the Issai and Buhari fought so near him. Not until he *knew* Kodyn and Tarek would not find themselves in the path of his bloodstained blade as he tore into his foes.

His plan to fight the bulk of the Consortium's forces alone had gone up in smoke the moment battle began—as all such plans tended to—but that left him in an impossible situation. Though Soulhunger reinvigorated him and mended his wounds with every life he claimed, he could not simply keep fighting as he was. Every second he spent locked in this interminable fight put those he cared for in greater danger. Yet he could not unleash the power of *Ibad'at Mutlaqa* against his enemies for fear *he* would be the danger to his friends and allies.

He was trapped, condemned to fight a battle he knew *he* could survive, but which might very well leave every one of his allies lying broken and dead in the mud.

Chapter Fifty-Four

A mighty roar pierced the din of battle filling the Hunter's ears, and a massive figure hurtled past him to smash into the ranks of slavers. Manacles still clasped Jumaane's wrists, throat, and ankles, and an arm's length of heavy steel chain dangled from each band. Yet the Buhari *nassor* fought as if the metal weighed nothing. He tore into the Consortium's forces like a man possessed.

No, the Hunter decided, as he saw the huge man rip out one man's throat with his teeth and shatter another's head with his bare hands. *He fights not like a madman, but a lion.*

Though his hands were empty, his armor stripped away, and blood streamed from scores of wounds where his tormentors' spears had pricked him, Jumaane thundered through the ranks of enemies like a one-man stampede. His leonine roars and bloody, ferocious mien startled the Consortium so much that they fell back, crying out in fright at the terrible sight. But Jumaane did not relent, did not allow them to retreat. He snatched up a pair of slavers, crushed their necks with the strength of his fingers alone, and used the limp bodies to club his foes senseless. A dozen fell to his savage onslaught in the space of three heartbeats.

The Hunter saw the slavers faltering, their courage wavering. Adding his own full-throated roar to Jumaane's, he hurled himself upon his enemies with flashing blades. Steel carved devastation through flesh, shattered bones, rent armor, sheared off limbs and heads. Torrents of blood misted in the night and turned the ground beneath his feet to mud. The screams of agony rose in a chorus so loud Soulhunger's gemstone flared to life even with no souls to feed on. But the Hunter fed it souls aplenty. His sword opened a path through his enemies' guard and the dagger drove in again and again to sate its endless appetite on too many foes to count.

Deathbite's glow shone on his left, Kiara fighting to keep pace. She could not, he knew, nor did he want her to. For he followed Jumaane into the heart of his enemies, wading in among them until he was pressed from all sides. Only there, surrounded, could he truly unleash the full might of his fury.

Watered steel wove a blurring whirlwind of death all about him as he spun, hacked, chopped, lunged, and thrust. Not once did he attempt to evade; there were simply too many about him, arrows lancing down from above, greatknives striking at him from all directions.

He felt the blows land—against his back, opening his sword arm to the bone, carving a deep furrow along his forehead, nearly hacking off his right cheek and ear, crunching into both legs, pummeling his belly—yet there came no pain. His mind had no space to register such mundane sensations. Only the power coursing through him in a never-ending stream of crackling, searing energy ripped from the hearts of the slavers who died on Soulhunger's razor-sharp blade. No sooner had the dagger finished consuming one soul than he tore it free and found another to serve as its feast.

A terrible, bestial roar rose above the shouts, commands, and ringing steel. The sound came from his own lips, some dim part of his mind realized. Wordless snarls like that of a bloodbear in heat, hurling his fury into the teeth of those fool enough to stand before him. The fear that blossomed in the eyes of his enemies when he did not die, despite their best efforts, only amplified the thrill of battle rushing in his veins.

He carved a deadly swath through the Consortium's ranks, wading into the tightly-packed foes with relish, basking in the blood washing over him. And then, suddenly, he was staggering out the other side. There were no more enemies. At least none within striking range. The slavers still filled the valley, still fought a battle to regain control of their freed captives, but the Hunter stood amidst an empty patch of ground at least twenty paces in diameter. Only a handful of bodies lay scattered around him. All were Issai and Buhari. Prisoners of battle who had risen up in defiance of their captors and fought back.

Something slammed into the Hunter's shoulder with the force of a giant's fist. The impact sent him staggering backward a step, then another as he was struck again. But not by a fist, he realized. Ujana arrows.

The stink of iron rose a heartbeat later from behind him—from the arrowhead protruding out the back of his shoulder and right leg. He felt no panic, felt nothing at all, merely hacked off the shafts sticking out the front of his shoulder and leg with a sweep of his watered steel sword. He did not bother pulling the remnant free; he hadn't the time. In this crucial moment, with the battle balanced on a knife's edge, he could ill-afford to let the iron's poison slow him.

He broke into a run, clearing the distance to the nearest enemy—a spear-wielding Ujana locked in battle with two Issai hunters and a Buhari warrior—and drove Soulhunger into the man's back. A scream rose from the dying enemy, and the Hunter felt the rush of power blazing through his veins, purging the iron from his blood.

But he did not pull the dagger free as the Ujana succumbed to its magic. Instead, he twisted the blade, digging it deeper until it felt it lodge between two of the man's vertebra. With his sword hand, he gripped the Ujana by the back of the red armored shirt he wore and lifted him bodily off the ground. The man was beyond pain; Soulhunger had done its work quickly. He merely hung limp in the Hunter's grip.

That suited the Hunter's purpose just fine. He broke into a run, charging straight toward the switchback ascending to the clifftops above. Arrows hissed down toward him but *thunked* home into the lifeless flesh of his meat shield. The Hunter howled a hideous laugh and sprinted up the trail. Right into the ranks of Ujana.

Some turned their eyes from the battle in time to see him coming, bearing before him the grisly trophy of their dead comrade and filling the night with his terrible mirth. They shouted their fury at him in their own tongue and abandoned their bows to raise their round-tipped swords. Yet they stood no chance at all. The Hunter barreled into them without slowing. Like a Legionnaire fighting from behind his shield, he drove his shoulder through the dead warrior to crash into the Ujana who faced him. He didn't even bother trying to kill them; he merely hurled them off the switchback trail to the ground below.

The first few who fell landed largely unharmed, though surprised, and joined their comrades in attempting to regain control of the Buhari and Issai. But the higher he raced up the trail, the longer their falls and the louder their screams. Their arrows could not stop him, and any who attempted to plant their feet to meet his charge head-on discovered what it meant to come face to face with a Bucelarii. Every one of the Ujana on the trail plummeted to the valley below. Many met a sharp end on the rocks below; those who survived fell beneath the fury of the Ghandians they had turned against.

When the last of the Ujana bowmen had been hurled from their perch, the Hunter raised high the arrow-riddled corpse that had shielded him from his enemies, roared his triumph, and threw the corpse down into the melee below. For the space of two long heartbeats, the Hunter scanned the battle raging in the valley.

To the east, the Tefaye still stood rigid as statues, eyes staring straight ahead and ears deaf to the screams, shouts, and clangor around them. A dozen Consortium bodies lay scattered face-down about the immobile ranks of Tefaye, cut down from behind. The Hunter caught sight of a dark shadow twirling and leaping between the handful of slavers still standing. Tarek fought with skill to rival any Hrandari warrior. Somehow, impossibly, he'd managed to keep the Consortium from speaking whatever command brought the Tefaye to life and unleashed their savagery.

The Hunter wanted to go to the young Elivasti, but he could not. For though Tarek fought a ferocious battle, the Issai and Buhari fate appeared far more precarious. Kodyn had managed to cut enough bonds that the captive warriors could join battle against their guards, sweeping up the weapons that had been taken from them and piled nearby. Kodyn joined the Ghandian warriors in battle, long sword in one hand, dirk in the other, both weapons dripping blood. The Issai and Buhari fought together as if they had always been allies, their ferocity and relentlessness despite the odds awe-inspiring. For tonight they battled for their lives, their families, their friends, their very survival.

But even including Kodyn among their ranks, the combined *amaqhawe* numbered fewer than one hundred and fifty men and women, facing off against easily twice that count of slavers. Only the Ghandians' unpredictable, athletic combat style, replete with leaping, darting, and swirling movements the slower-moving *alay-alagbara* could not match, kept them from being overwhelmed.

Yet it was only a matter of *seconds,* the Hunter saw. The Consortium forces were pressing the Buhari and Issai warriors backward, driving them toward the black-and-white-striped southern cliff face. The Issai hunters and herders had brought down the few enemies set to guard the raya cattle, cutting off any risk of rear attack. However, their choice to protect the livestock left the elders, children, and others of the Issai *ekhaya* undefended.

Duma alone stood between the Consortium and the noncombatants. His huge, flat-tipped sword swung in deadly arcs, cleaving skulls, shattering limbs, crushing chests, opening great bleeding wounds. He fought with impressive speed and agility despite his advanced age, but unlike the women of the *amaqhawe* and *unkgaliwe,* he battled with his feet planted and legs braced. His martial style bore greater resemblance to the *alay-alagbara* than his own people.

He, too, would be overwhelmed within moments. Nearly a score of slavers were circling around the embattled Issai and Buhari, intent on surrounding the civilians. If they held the Issai's *ekhaya* captive, the warriors would have no choice but to throw down their weapons. And if the Issai surrendered, the Buhari could not hope to fight on alone.

A flash of crimson light brightened the darkness, drawing the Hunter's attention to where Kiara and Davathi fought to reach Jumaane. The Buhari *nassor* had driven too deep into the ranks of slavers and the Ujana who joined them in battle. He was surrounded, and only the sheer savagery of his flying fists had kept him from being borne to the ground beneath the Consortium's crush. But he was tiring, and fast. His attacks grew wilder and more frantic with every beat of his mighty heart. For all their effort, Kiara and Davathi could not hack their way through the ranks of enemies and reach him in time.

For a heartbeat, indecision held the Hunter paralyzed. Too many enemies to defeat at once. Too many lives hung in the balance. Whatever choice he made, whichever fight he joined, *someone* would die.

Acid rose in his throat. It was like Tassat and Sir Benoit all over again. He'd *tried* to make the right choice, save the right person, but what had the outcome been? Both men had died—one by his own hand, the other giving his life to save Angdra, Kiara, and the Hunter himself.

So who did the Hunter choose to die now? Did he sacrifice Tarek, Hailen's half-brother, and risk the slavers reaching the Tefaye and sending the poison-twisted outcasts into the fray? Did he abandon Kodyn and the warriors of the tribes he had sworn to protect? Did he go to Duma's aid and protect the noncombatants, or did he lend his strength to save Jumaane, Davathi, and Kiara?

A roar from above the Hunter shattered his momentary paralysis. His head snapped to the right in time to see a hundred Consortium slavers barreling down the switchback trail toward him. The men stationed atop the cliffs were about to join the fight.

But a shout from the other direction and far below caught the Hunter's attention, too. He knew that voice—Gwala's, calling encouragement to the reinforcements racing down into the fray. The Hunter sought its source, scanning the furious melee until he found the one man wearing brightly colored robes and standing with his golden-skinned, greatsword-wielding Shalandran shadow.

Gwala waved his greatknife over his head, directing the reinforcements to hurl themselves upon Tarek and join the battle against the Issai and Buhari warriors. His eyes locked with the Hunter's for a moment. A sneer twisted his lips as, without looking away, he pointed his curved blade toward Kiara and Davathi. With a grim nod, Djineza hefted her sword and sprang to obey her commander's wordless order.

Piss on you, you bastard!

The Hunter had no time to descend the switchback trail the way he had earlier, winding back and forth. The reinforcements were nearly upon him, and only ten paces separated Djineza from her target. Kiara and Davathi had managed to keep the enemy from circling around behind them, keeping the river at their backs. Yet that river was so shallow it failed to reach the diminutive woman's knees. In a matter of seconds, Djineza would come upon Kiara from behind, and that great black flame-bladed sword of fine Shalandran steel would put an end to the woman the Hunter loved.

A furious roar burst from the Hunter's lips and he sprang off the path's rocky edge. Straight down he dropped, a full ten paces to land hard on the switchback below. The impact jarred all the way up his spine, snapping his teeth with an audible *clack* and sending pain flaring through his legs. Yet he would not allow the pain to slow him. Not with Kiara's life on the line. He leaped off the path's edge once more, and this time landed on the shoulders of three Ujana circling around the horde encircling Jumaane.

The Hunter's weight bore the warriors to the ground, and Soulhunger made quick work of them, severing throats and piercing through eyeballs. He was on his feet before the last one died, not giving the dagger time to consume their souls. He broke into a mad dash, wading eastward with the river's flow in the desperate hope of reaching Kiara in time.

The cruel grin on Gwala's face widened. Djineza's grip on her sword tightened, her steps determined. In that moment, the Hunter knew he would never make it.

"Kiara!" he shouted at the tops of his lungs. "Kiara! Look out behind you!"

But his voice was drowned out by the shouts of the slavers, the ululating war cries of the Issai, the lion roars of the Buhari, and the tumultuous clash of steel that resonated through the Valley of the Zabara.

He abandoned his attempt to draw her attention, poured every shred of willpower into urging his legs to move faster. Yet the water and the muddy river bottom slowed his movements.

Slavers and Ujana got in his way, and he could not cut them swiftly enough. Kiara might as well have been across the Frozen Sea, for all he could reach her.

Panic and fear welled within him. His every effort would fail Kiara. He could not reach her before that Shalandran steel sword cut her down from behind. She would never see her killer. Never get to say a final farewell to the Hunter, Tarek, Kodyn, or Aisha. She'd die here, half a world away from her boys.

The realization broke the Hunter's heart, threatened to steal the strength from his limbs. For all his Bucelarii strength and speed, he could do nothing to forestall the death that stalked toward her, inevitable, unstoppable.

Time slowed to a crawl. He could only watch, helpless, powerless, as Djineza waded out of the shallow river and raised her huge sword high overhead in a blow that Kiara had no hope of stopping.

And that was when the thunder began to rumble.

Djineza

Chapter Fifty-Five

The Hunter saw no flash of lightning, yet the thunder struck with such force it set the riverbed beneath his feet trembling. His surprise doubled when the rumbling did not fade as thunder was wont to do. Instead, it grew louder. No, he realized, it came from nearer, rising in volume as the invisible storm bore down on the battle raging in the Valley of the Zabara.

He was not the only one to hear the sound or feel the ground's heaving. Djineza froze, her sword only just begun its downward arc at Kiara's back, and turned to scan the skies to the east.

The Hunter seized that moment of the Shalandran woman's inattention and, in a desperate attempt to save Kiara, hurled his sword. Only a fool threw swords, he knew. The balance was all wrong, the weapon far too long and unwieldy to fly true. Yet he dared not relinquish his grip on Soulhunger. And he did not care what part of his watered steel blade struck Djineza, only that it prevented her attack.

Fortune smiled on him. His precipitous cast sent the Elivasti-forged weapon spinning end over end to carve a glimmering path through the night and buried a hand's breadth into Djineza's upraised left arm. The impact shattered her elbow, hurled her backward, and knocked the flame-bladed sword from her hands. She cried out and staggered backward. Her arm flailed, limp in the middle, and the Hunter's sword slipped free of her flesh.

But the damage had been done. Djineza's cry must have reached Kiara, for she spun toward the foe at her back and hacked out with her sword. Though Deathbite missed Djineza by the width of a single finger, the blood dripping off the *Im'tasi* blade's edge sprayed across the Shalandran woman's face, momentarily blinding her. She fell back, landing with a loud splash in the thick, crimson-colored water of the river.

All that transpired in the space of two heartbeats, and in that time, the rumbling grew louder, the trembling of the earth beneath the Hunter's rushing feet increasing. Then came a new sound: a wild trumpeting, as if a hundred Legion buglers blew their blaring horns.

That sound had a startling and instantaneous effect on the battle. All throughout *Isigodi Zabara*, Ghandian heads turned toward the east. But their eyes did not search the sky as the Hunter's had. Their gazes locked on the boulders blocking the river's flow downstream.

The Buhari were the first to react. *"Chipekwe!"* came the roar from among the ranks of warriors battling against the slavers. The word echoed from two hundred throats, including those of the Ujana. Instantly, the Issai and Buhari retreated from their foes and pressed their backs against the cliff walls toward which the Consortium had been herding them. The Ujana fighting among the ranks of the *alay-alagbara* turned and sprinted toward the switchback trail as if a horde of Abiarazi pursued them. Some even hurled down their weapons in their haste to disengage and flee.

The sudden shift in the battle's currents staggered the Consortium. They froze, confused, staring at the empty ground between them and the warriors who had only moments earlier been fighting savagely to hold their lines. Even those surrounding Jumaane stopped hacking and slashing at the towering *nassor*. They, too, had heard the thunder and trumpeting, but unlike the Ghandians, did not know its meaning.

"Run, you fools!" Gwala's scream rose above the thunder. "You cannot stand before the—"

With a deafening *BOOM,* the boulders blocking the valley suddenly exploded inward, and a colossal creature barreled through the opening. The beast stood easily three times the Hunter's height, its skin a wrinkled, leathery purplish-grey utterly devoid of hair, its four legs thick as tree trunks and its heavy body bigger than five oxen combined. Beady black eyes were set deep in its head between two enormous fan-like ears that flapped outward, and a long, red horn jutted five paces up from just above the sinuous serpentine trunk that raised high in the air and emitted a deafening trumpet's blast.

But it was not alone. Behind it came more—three, four, six, ten, dozens—all of the same immense size and lumbering upstream at a galloping pace that should have been impossible from a creature so gargantuan. The ground heaved and buckled beneath the force of their mighty feet, and the clangor of their blaring calls resonated off the black-and-white-striped cliffs of the valley.

From the corner of his eye, the Hunter saw Davathi's lips move, forming a word he did not understand. The Issai *nassor* took a single step toward Kiara, planted one hand against her shoulder, and shoved with all her strength. Kiara flew to the side—right into the Hunter's outstretched arms. Instinct shrieked at the Hunter to do as all the Issai and Buhari had. Clutching Kiara to his chest, he sprinted toward the northern cliff wall and pressed their bodies flat against the multi-hued stone face.

Not a moment too soon. The dust, stone shards, and water kicked up by the stampeding behemoths slammed into the Hunter's back, and the wind of their passing all but threatened to knock him from his feet. Soulhunger still in hand, he dug his fingers deep into jagged fissures in the cliff and clung on with all his strength. His body was all that stood between Kiara and the monstrosities barreling through the valley with the unstoppable force of a flash flood.

Sound assailed him from all sides. Screams of panic, terror, and agony. His own shouts, accompanied by Kiara's, wordless—at least to his ears—but ringing with the visceral fear bubbling up at the display of such immense power. The rumbling of the earth protesting beneath the mammoth hooves—or feet, or paws, the Hunter did not know—of the four-legged hairless giants.

Then he heard it: a familiar yappy, high-pitched barking, a sound partway between a horse's whinny and a hyena's laughter. His eyes, pressed tight against the flying dust and shards of stone, snapped open and his head whipped to his right. The blood froze in his veins as he saw the stream of enormous equine beasts with stubby tails, short manes, and coats of mingled white, black, and brown stripes.

The Uhamaji! The meaning of that word flashed through the Hunter's mind at the sight. He recalled the morning he'd awoken to watch the herd of magnificent beats swimming across Nsukeja Lake. Aisha had spoken of the "the *zabara's* migration", making mention of stampede.

And what a stampede! The *zabara's* immense height, nearly twice that of a mid-sized horse like Elivast, made them nearly a rival for the towering horn-headed trumpeting beasts. Indeed, the fan-eared, hairless giants seemed terrified by the *zabara* barreling through the valley behind them. With good reason, for the *zabara* herd numbered easily in the scores, perhaps even a hundred—it was impossible to tell, between the dust and water kicked up by their passage, the ear-splitting yapping, and the confusing striped patterns of their bodies. The same pattern mirrored in the cliffs.

Laughter echoed in the Hunter's ears, and he realized it came from his own lips. How could he *not* find mirth in such a display of raw power? At such a critical moment, too! The arrival of the *zabara* and the single-horned behemoths had saved Kiara. There was no doubt in the Hunter's mind that any who attempted to stand in the way of the stampede would fall beneath those flashing hooves and enormous bodies.

Kiara, too, laughed against his chest. Her arms wrapped around him and squeezed him tight. "We bloody did it!" she howled, and even then her words were all but drowned out by the tumult of the herd barreling past mere paces away. "At the very least, we survived!"

How long they stood there like that, pressed against the cliff wall, the Hunter clinging to the stone and Kiara clinging to him, they did not know. It felt like hours, but must have only been mere minutes before the thundering began to diminish, the earth beneath the Hunter's feet settling. Clouds of dirt and dust swirled in the air, obscuring the Hunter's view of his surroundings, but the tumult of the stampeding beasts receded as they raced westward along the valley.

Screams soon filled the momentary silence. Raw and ringing with agony, they resounded off the cliff walls with force that nearly rivaled the pandemonium of the stampede itself.

The Hunter released his grip on the cliff wall, but held on to Kiara for a moment.

"I'm fine," she said, though the tightness of her voice and the pain lining her face belied her words. She bled freely from a dozen wounds now, and her entire left leg was soaked in crimson. Yet she stood steady and raised Deathbite with a determined look on her face. "At least fine enough for us to finish this."

The Hunter didn't bother arguing with her. It would do no good, and for all his worry for her, he had greater concerns at the moment.

Still, he couldn't help insisting, "Stay behind me." He tightened his grip on Soulhunger. He'd nearly lost her far too many times for one night; if anyone wanted to get at her, they'd have to contend with him first.

The agonized screams filling the valley grew louder as the dust settled. When the air finally cleared, the Hunter couldn't restrain a sharp intake of breath at the sight before him.

Where there had been ranks upon ranks of Consortium slavers, now only carnage met his eyes. The *alay-alagbara* had been too slow to respond to the threat—one they could never have predicted, for they were not of the *amathafa*—and failed to move out of the path of the stampede. Flying boulders, lumbering horned giants, and flashing *zabara* hooves had wreaked terrible havoc. Crushed skulls, shattered limbs, pulped muscle and flesh, and caved-in ribs. The herd had slammed into the Consortium forces at full run, and against such immense beasts, the studded leather vests could offer no more protection than a blade of grass.

The fortunate had died instantly; the screams of agony filling the Valley of the Zabara rose from the throats of those men and women unlucky enough to survive the trampling. The wreckage of their bodies littered the river, their blood splattered the walls, and their ripped-off limbs lay abandoned in ever-growing puddles of crimson mud.

A glance toward the switchback revealed nothing but empty trail. The quick-thinking Ujana had escaped, and the hundred or so Consortium reinforcements with them. But they alone of the *alay-alagbara* would live to see sunrise. Gwala's warning had come too late for the bulk of his forces.

Gwala!

555

The Hunter's eyes darted farther east, to where he'd last seen the Ghandian turncoat before the dust and flying debris of the stampede had obscured him. Any hopes of seeing the bastard's corpse lying mangled and crushed were dashed when his gaze found only bare rock. Gwala alone had recognized the danger, understood the warning shouted by the Buhari, and had gotten out of the way.

Worse, he'd used the confusion as cover to flee.

The Hunter searched the darkness to the east. The stampede had broken through the boulders that obstructed the river, opening the way for the river's bloody red flow. And, the Hunter suspected, for Gwala himself. The shadows of night obscured the valley, making it impossible for even the Hunter's keen eyes to see more than a few dozen paces eastward. His nostrils filled with the stench of blood, death, and terror, any trace of Gwala's scent utterly drowned out. The screams of the dying *alay-alagbara* rang off the cliffs, far too loud for the Hunter to have any hope of overhearing the sound of the Ghandian's footsteps splashing downstream or racing along the rocky riverbank.

Yet he knew, with a certainty as solid as the stone wall behind him, that Gwala had lived. Lived, and *escaped*.

Chapter Fifty-Six

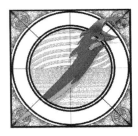

The Hunter was determined to pursue the fleeing Ghandian. He wanted nothing more than to run down the man responsible for so much death, so much suffering. It didn't matter that the battle had ended; the war wouldn't be truly won until the Consortium and their Order masters were utterly driven out, their labors at the Bondshold stopped forever, and the land restored fully to the tribes to whom it belonged.

While Gwala lived, the Consortium's forces here would still be directed by a mind that understood their enemies, who knew the ways of the *amathafa*. The Order of Mithridas hadn't marched into battle; they hadn't even left their stronghold. Their focus was on whatever they intended with the Serenii tower, and it was Gwala who commanded the rest of their operations. He who razed villages, transported captured slaves to join the labor, who would once again lead the *alay-alagbara* into battle against the Ghandians.

His death wouldn't truly end the troubles faced by Aisha and her people, but it would put a great big bloody dent in the ongoing efforts.

But the Hunter's pursuit was stopped cold when Kiara rushed past him.

"Davathi!" Her eyes fixed on the spot where the Issai *nassor* had been standing only moments earlier, panic and fear imprinted on her face. She got just one step before her wounded leg gave out beneath her and she sagged to the hoof-churned, blood-darkened mud.

The Hunter spun back toward Kiara and was at her side in a heartbeat, reaching down strong hands toward her.

"Leave me!" Kiara struggled to rise, to push herself to her feet, but her leg refused to hold her upright. Still, she pushed him away. "Find Davathi!"

The Hunter tore his gaze from Kiara, just long enough to scan the wreckage of bodies trampled beneath the stampeding *zabara*. His heart sprang into his throat. The screams came from the valley's edges, nearer the cliff walls, but none of the fallen nearer the river so much as moved a muscle.

"Kiara—" the Hunter began.

"No!" Kiara gripped his arm, digging her fingers painfully into his muscles. "No, don't you dare say it! Don't you bloody say she couldn't have survived that."

The Hunter swallowed the words that had been forming on his lips. She knew him too well.

"She's alive!" Kiara's voice came out in a hiss edged with desperation. "You hear me? She *has* to be!"

The Hunter stared down at her for a long moment. Her wounds were grave—that much was immediately evident by the pallor of her face and the weakness keeping her from rising—but she'd never let him see to her until she knew for certain what had befallen Davathi. The Issai *nassor* had shoved Kiara out of the stampede's path and effectively saved her life. Kiara needed to know her savior's fate, however grim.

"So be it." He released his grip on her. "But you hold pressure on that wound until I get back. I'm not losing you now that the battle's over!"

"Go!" Kiara pushed him away with her right hand, clamping her left down hard on her bleeding leg. "Find her!"

The Hunter did as she'd instructed, wading across the shallow river—now turned a hideous muddy crimson, slowed to a mere trickle from all the bodies clogging its flow—and into the pile of corpses brought down where he'd last seen Davathi.

The mess was unlike anything he'd encountered in his lifetime. Not even during his slaughter of the Bloody Hand had he laid eyes on such a grim scene. Hundreds of slavers had died beneath those trampling hooves, their bodies turned into something that bore more resemblance to some monstrous pudding than human flesh. He could barely distinguish individual limbs or heads amidst the carnage; there was just so much blood, mangled flesh, shattered bone, shredded leather, and unidentifiable bits of torn skin. The stink of it brought acid rising in the back of his throat, and the stench was only made worse by the thick, swampy sucking sound of his boots with every step.

By the Keeper! Chills ran down the Hunter's spine, set his hands trembling. *Where in this bloody hell do I even begin?*

He had seen death aplenty, turned enemies beyond counting into corpses, and even now was covered in the blood of those he'd slain in battle. But even *he* recoiled at the thought of reaching his hands into the grisly meat soup sloshing around his ankles to search for the Issai *nassor.*

"Find her!" Kiara's shout echoed through the valley, louder than the screams rising from the wounded slavers.

The Hunter gritted his teeth and, drawing in a deep breath through his mouth, began to search.

"Davathi!" he called out as he kicked at headless corpses and arms devoid of hands and shoulders. "Davathi, can you hear me?" He dug his bare hands into messes of intestines and fought the urge to vomit at the feel of yielding, still-warm guts and sharp fragments of shattered bone intermingling beneath his fingers. "Davathi, call out if—"

"Graahh!" A hand suddenly burst up from the puddle of corpses not five paces from where the Hunter stood. Only the Hunter's iron will kept him from startling; even still, his heart hammered a furious gallop, nearly tearing free of his chest.

Yet he recognized the hand. It was the same hand that had clamped down hard on Kiara's shoulder to hurl her out of the path of danger.

"Davathi!" The Hunter's disgust was instantly forgotten, replaced by relief. He raced toward the upthrust hand, his boots barely touching the pulped bodies carpeting the valley floor. Seizing Davathi's hand, he hauled with all his strength. The Issai *nassor's* head emerged from beneath the pile of corpses with a gasp moments later. With the Hunter's help, she clawed her way free of the press and fell to her back, panting for every breath.

The Hunter stared down at her, wide-eyed. She was a mess of crimson, covered head to toe in the blood of her enemies. Yet she was alive. Impossibly, despite the Hunter's certainty to the contrary, she had survived.

"How?" He blurted out the question before he could stop himself.

"Bodies," Davathi said around a wet cough and labored breaths. "Shielded…me. And Jumaane!"

The Hunter spun toward the hole that remained where she'd dragged herself out from the corpses. "Where?"

The question proved unnecessary. No sooner had the words left his lips, than a pile of mangled flesh two paces to his right heaved and surged upward like a great bubble forming on the surface of a lava flow. Limbs, mangled torsos, crushed heads, and other bits of flesh the Hunter couldn't begin to identify flew outward as the enormous chieftain of the Buhari rose like some monstrous blood phoenix.

The Hunter was at Jumaane's side in a heartbeat, looking the huge man over. He bled in thirty different places, perhaps more, but the Hunter could see no mortal wounds.

"I live still, *Umzukeli.*" Jumaane turned to him with a grin made all the more ferocious for the blood dripping from his thick face and great beard. "I live, and my enemies lie dead. Thanks to the *zabara* and the great *chipekwe.*" He thumped a fist against his crimson-stained chest—a chest that bore nearly a dozen slashes and piercing wounds where the spearmen had stabbed him—then did likewise against the Hunter's chest with no more gentleness. "And thanks to you."

The Hunter, caught off guard by the gesture, had just time enough to brace himself against the *thumping* impact of Jumaane's mighty fist. He managed to keep his balance—barely— but returned the man's gratitude with a grim nod. "The credit goes to your *amaqhawe* as well. They proved themselves truly worthy of the lion's spirit this night."

"Hah!" Jumaane's roared laugh sounded oddly out of place amidst the carnage—and yet, it was the most welcome sound the Hunter had heard all night. "The *Okanele* may become Buhari yet."

"After all he has done, you insult him so?" This came from Davathi, accompanied by a sharp smile. "Becoming Buhari is no great feat. One merely needs to have a larger spear between his legs than a brain between his ears. Now, becoming Issai, now that is a legendary accomplishment for an *alay-alagbara,* indeed."

Jumaane did not take offense at Davathi's good-humored jest. On the contrary, he laughed all the louder, mirth sparkling in his dark eyes. "He needs merely overestimate his cleverness, intellect, and skill in battle, yes?" He accompanied his words with an outstretched hand to help Davathi rise. Grinning, she accepted his offer and pulled herself to his feet.

The Hunter couldn't help a grin of his own. "Something all people of the *amathafa* seem to share is that they believe everyone wants to be one of them, eh?"

"And why would they not?" Jumaane turned to him, clapping him heartily on the shoulder. "Where else can you find such courage, cunning, and comeliness in such measure?" He gestured to his bearded and bloodied face as if to illustrate his point.

"Certainly not among the Buhari," Davathi said, winking at the Hunter.

The Hunter smiled to himself. Apparently the two *nassors* had become far friendlier since last he'd seen them. It was almost hard to believe their tribes had been enemies a fortnight earlier.

"Hunter!" a familiar voice called to the Hunter from near the valley's northern cliff face.

The Hunter spun to find Kodyn stumbling toward him, a tired but relieved look on his handsome features.

Relief washed over the Hunter at the sight. "Kodyn!" When had he grown so attached to the young man that merely seeing him alive brought tears of joy to his eyes? Swallowing the rush of emotion, the Hunter stepped toward Kodyn and caught the exhausted, swaying young man. "All that Night Guild training paid off, I see."

"Seems like." Kodyn gave him a wry grin, marred by pain. He held his sword gripped in his right hand, though he'd lost his dirk and pressed his left hand against his side. "Though Errik would be furious to see just how many times I failed to heed his lessons."

The Hunter's pulse quickened. "How bad is it?" He released his grip on Kodyn, knelt by the young man's side, and pulled his hand away just enough to see the wound. A curse escaped his lips. "Fiery hell, Kodyn, that's—"

Kodyn grimaced. "Not great, I know." Moonlight turned his face even paler, revealing just how much blood he'd lost in the fight. "But I take comfort in knowing that if the organ or blood vessels had been truly damaged, I'd be dead right now, not just in a whole bloody mess of pain."

"Easy," the Hunter said, helping the young man to sit. "Keep pressure on the wound. I'll see if Tarek has something to help with—"

He snapped suddenly upright. *Tarek!*

Thoughts of the young Elivasti brought him whirling around to scan the valley to the west. The last of the *zabara* herd had disappeared long ago, not so much as the dust of their passage visible in the night. The only evidence of their passage was the utter desolation they had inflicted on the *alay-alagbara* too slow-witted or startled to get out of their way.

But the Consortium weren't the only casualties. The place where the Hunter had last seen Tarek, fighting among the statue-still ranks of Tefaye, had become an abattoir. Blood, limbs, and bits of flesh spattered the cliff walls fifty paces to the north. At the command of their masters, the Tefaye stood utterly frozen in place, even as the *zabara* and the hairless horned beasts—*chipekwe,* Jumaane had called them—bore down on them. They had obeyed and remained motionless to their final moments.

A handful of Tefaye, those fortunate enough to be stationed at the edges of the valley, remained standing. Covered in the blood of their fellow tribesmen but dull eyed as if they hadn't just witnessed the carnage surrounding them. But the bulk of the Tefaye, every single one who had stood in the path of the stampede, had been trampled into the dirt.

And, the Hunter feared, Tarek with them.

Chapter Fifty-Seven

"Tarek!" The Hunter broke into a mad dash, racing toward the unmoving corpses that were all that remained of the hapless Tefaye. "Tarek!"

Bodies torn apart by *zabara* hooves hampered his progress, their guts and mangled flesh clinging to his legs like swamp mud. Time and time again, the Hunter's booted feet slipped on a severed arm, coils of intestines, a crumpled face, or a greatknife fallen from lifeless fingers. Yet always he dragged himself upright and continued on. Desperation and worry for Tarek spurred him onward.

His eyes scanned the carnage, seeking any sign of movement and finding none. His voice rang out through the valley, all but drowned out by the screams of the wounded and dying, calling for Tarek louder and louder as the fear rose within him. Panic sank icy claws in his mind as he reached the first Tefaye corpses without so much as an answering cry or whisper from Tarek.

Keeper take it, Tarek, where are you?

The Hunter bent to dig among the corpses—though he had no idea where Tarek might have been when the stampede hit—but a flicker of motion from among the unmoving Tefaye drew his attention. A single blood-soaked figure lifted itself off the ground with a groan and struggled to rise. The Hunter could not see their face, for they had their back turned to him, but he recognized the long spear gripped in one trembling hand. Spears much like it had threatened him and Hailen on the Hrandari Plains years earlier.

"Tarek!" The Hunter raced to the Elivasti's side, his spirits soaring. "Bloody hell, lad, you had me worried there for a moment."

A wry smile sprouted on Tarek's face. "Not my first stampede," he said, his voice tight with pain. He lifted his free hand to press against the side of his head. The Hunter hadn't even seen the wound amidst the Tefaye blood that drenched him. "Though the horses on the Hrandari Plains weren't half so big as those damned things."

The Hunter couldn't help chuckling, more out of relief than mirth. "Good to see you didn't get the humor kicked out of you by a *zabara* hoof."

"Bloody close thing," Tarek muttered. He removed his hand from the wound and glared down at it, as if angered at the sight of his blood. "I should have heard them coming. Should have gotten out of the way fast—"

The Hunter cut him off with a slashing gesture of his hand. "Don't waste your energy on should haves. Focus on what you *did*." He stabbed a finger toward the sixty or so Tefaye who'd escaped the stampede unscathed. "You kept them out of the fight. That made all the difference in the world, and don't you forget it."

It was impossible to tell if Tarek blushed beneath the crimson dripping from every part of him, but he ducked his head and an awkward smile blossomed on his face. "Had to give the rest of you a chance, didn't I?"

"Aye, and so you did." The Hunter clapped the young man on the shoulder, albeit gently, so as not to jostle him. "Everyone still standing owes you their lives, in a way." He fixed Tarek with a proud smile. "Some might even call you a hero."

Tarek's smile mirrored the Hunter's own.

"Just don't let it go to your head," the Hunter said with a chuckle and twinkle in his eyes. "Otherwise that split in your forehead'll grow even bigger, and then you'll be a right mess."

Tarek laughed. "I'll be sure to keep that in mind."

"Seriously, though." The Hunter sobered quickly. "You did good, keeping the slavers from turning them loose. Battle could've—"

He had to stop to spit blood from his mouth and wipe clean his eyes with his right hand—a hand, he realized, that no longer held his sword. He fought the urge to glance back to where he'd last seen it, at Djineza's feet. First, he'd make sure Tarek was in shape enough to see the dawn, then he could hunt for his blade—and the Shalandran woman who'd nearly killed Kiara.

"Battle could've turned against us," the Hunter finished once he'd cleared the gore from his mouth. "Things only worked out the way they did because of you."

"I just cut down anyone who opened their mouth and looked like they'd try to say something." Tarek tried for a nonchalant shrug, but he was fairly glowing beneath the Hunter's praise. "Best I could figure it, there had to be some sort of code phrase or verbal trigger. Even just a straight order, given what we found about their high suggestibility."

"Quick thinking." The Hunter clapped the young man on the shoulder. "Now, that healer's bag of yours will be mighty needed for a while. Starting with Kodyn." He gestured to where the Praamian thief sat atop a pile of fallen enemies. "He's taken a bad wound to the side. I didn't see anything serious, but best you give it a closer look, just to be sure. Kiara's leg is in grim shape, too."

"I'll see to them." Tarek nodded, a determined, resolute look on his face. He slung his spear strap over his shoulder, sliding it around onto his back, and reached beneath his blood-spattered cloak for the bag of alchemical and herbal ingredients he carried everywhere.

A confused look appeared on his face when his hands came away empty. Then he cursed. "Ancestors take it!" He raised his hands to cup around his mouth and shouted, "Nayaga!" He accompanied his horse's name with a few words in the Elivasti tongue.

An answering whinny echoed from the east, so distant even the Hunter's keen ears could barely make it out over the screams filling the valley. A few moments later, the dark, stocky form of Nayaga raced toward them from the direction the herd of *zabara* had gone.

Relief sprouted on Tarek's face when he caught sight of the horse. He stepped forward to greet Nayaga with open arms and a few words in the Elivasti tongue. The black steppe pony snorted and tossed its head, doubtless put off by the stink of the blood covering Tarek from head to toe, but heeded his call.

Tarek lifted down his healer's bag from where he'd left it strapped behind his saddle and joined the Hunter in hurrying back the way he'd come, toward Kodyn.

"Good to see you in one piece," Kodyn called out with a pained grin at their approach.

"Same." Tarek nodded in response, but when he knelt at Kodyn's side, his expression was severe, his manner all business. "Let me see the wound."

"It's nothing." Kodyn waved dismissively with the hand not pressed against his side. "I've taken worse scratches training with the Serpents."

Tarek gave him a flat look. "Sure." His right hand darted out, caught Kodyn's left wrist, and pulled the hand away. A sharp hiss that sounded like an Elivasti curse escaped his lips. "Scratch, he says!" With a snort and shake of his head, he released Kodyn's arm and set to work opening his healer's bag. "You're lucky to be alive."

"I'll leave him in your care," the Hunter told Tarek. "Don't bother being gentle, so long as you keep him alive." Kodyn opened his mouth to protest, but the Hunter cut him off with a scowl and snarled, "I've got no more desire to be the one to tell Aisha you died than you."

That silenced the young man. He nodded, and allowed Tarek to help him rise and move away from the pile of corpses littering the valley floor. Better to be as far from the blood and death when his wounds were treated.

The Hunter turned and hurried toward the spot where he'd last seen his sword. He found it where it had fallen on the riverbank just a few steps east of the mess of corpses trampled in the stampede. Miraculously, it had escaped the *zabara* hooves and *chipekwe* feet unscathed. Blood still stained its edge where it had pierced Djineza's arm.

Of the woman herself, the Hunter saw no sign. Nor did he find the black, flame-bladed sword she'd wielded.

A low, angry growl rumbled in the back of the Hunter's throat. *She got away, too!* Likely, she'd fled with Gwala and the handful of *alay-alagbara* closest to him.

His eyes roamed the darkness to the east again, and his nostrils sought out the scents of his prey— citron, myrtle pepper, and iron for Gwala; rose, pistachio, chestnut, and the not-quite-right scent he now realized was Shalandran steel for Djineza. Not that he had any chance of finding them at the moment. The stink of blood and death hung so thick in the valley it threatened to empty his stomach. But when the time came—

"*Umzukeli.*" Davathi's voice drew the Hunter's attention to his left, where the Issai *nassor* and Jumaane were helping Kiara to her feet. Davathi's face was hard, her jaw set. "I did not see my daughter fighting at your side, nor Siyanda. Are they—"

"You will not find them among the dead." The Hunter held up a hand. "They did not enter the valley with us."

Davathi's leonine face relaxed a fraction, relief sparkling bright in her eyes. It vanished a moment later, however, replaced by confusion and apprehension. "Then where is she?"

The Hunter never had a chance to answer. No sooner had the words left her lips than a shout echoed from atop the cliffs bordering the valley to the south. The Hunter's head snapped around and his eyes scanned the darkness high above. Davathi, Kiara, Jumaane, and scores of Issai and Buhari followed suit. Tension suddenly thickened the air between the cliffs. Spines stiffened, hands tightened on spears and stolen swords, and warriors braced for battle.

But there was no battle to come. Two figures raced eastward along the cliffs, illuminated by the blue-white glow emanating from the hand the foremost of the pair held raised high above her head.

"*Indokazi!*" The cry roared from Davathi's throat at a volume to rival even Jumaane's mightiest bellow.

"*Umama!*" Aisha's voice thundered through the valley with force equal to her mother's relief and joy.

Davathi released her grip on Kiara and, turning, set off at a lurching run toward the switchback trail. She could not move fast, weighed down by fatigue and slowed by the wounds she'd taken in battle, but Aisha ran as if the power of every *Kish'aa* for a thousand leagues lent her their strength. For indeed, it did.

The fleet-footed young woman sprang down the wending path just as the Hunter had. She seemed not to feel the jarring impacts or notice the waves of blue-white light erupting from beneath her feet with every step. Never once did she slow in her haste to reach her mother. When finally the two met, the collision was thunderous, like the *chipekwe* crashing through the boulders. Only this ended not with death, but a joyous embrace.

Davathi clutched her daughter to her chest, and Aisha's strong arms encircled her mother. For long moments they stood there, tears streaming down their faces, clinging to one another as if neither had expected to see the other alive. And in truth, given the grim scene the Hunter and his companions had encountered upon their arrival, that grim outcome had been all too possible. Yet somehow Aisha had mustered the strength to run *away* from her mother. She'd had courage enough to trust the Hunter, Kodyn, Tarek, and Kiara to keep her people alive while she and Siyanda went to "hunt for *Nuru Iwu's* children."

563

Seeing her now, it suddenly made sense. The stampede hadn't been mere coincidence. Aisha, Siyanda, and Naledi had triggered it. How, the Hunter had no idea—likely it had involved Aisha's *Kish'aa* powers. If her magic could kill a slashwyrm, it could certainly terrify the enormous *chipekwe* and *zabara* into flight.

By the Watcher! The thought sent a chill down the Hunter's spine. He stood, transfixed, unable to take his eyes from Aisha. The magnitude of what she'd done sank home. *We're only standing here because of her.*

Everyone still alive within the Valley of the Zabara owed their lives to her quick thinking and action. To the determination and iron will that had enabled her to make the decision she'd made this night.

But Aisha hadn't made it alone. Siyanda had no *Kish'aa* powers to fortify her, and so was forced to run down the switchback trail like any mortal would. Yet her step was light, the relief evident on her face from a dozen paces away as she beheld the remnants of her people—still stubbornly clinging to life despite impossible odds.

The Hunter saw Jumaane's great body tense, take a half-step in Siyanda's direction, but he stopped himself. Whether he did so to hide his true feelings for the Issai woman or because his strength was all that kept Kiara standing, the Hunter didn't know.

Easy way to find out, the Hunter thought, with a wry grin.

He hurried to Jumaane's side and held out his arms toward Kiara. "I've got her from here."

Jumaane shifted Kiara's weight to the Hunter without argument, and once relieved, turned back toward the switchback trail. Just as Siyanda's bare feet reached the blood-soaked valley floor. She seemed not to mind, never slowing in her run toward where Aisha and Davathi embraced. Which, the Hunter noted, was directly between her and Jumaane.

Again, Jumaane's muscles twitched, propelling him toward Siyanda. Again he stopped himself.

Kiara gave a quiet snort. "Foolish man," she whispered, shaking her head. "He refuses to trust his heart."

The Hunter grinned, but didn't take his eyes away from the hulking Buhari. Jumaane wouldn't have been the first man to grapple with such emotions. His and Siyanda's tribes had been enemies for years, and allies for but a handful of days. Though his feelings were plain, men like him often found their head got in the way. Keeper knew it had done so for the Hunter with Kiara. *She* had been the one to make the first move. It had taken her kissing him in Khar'nath to open his eyes to the possibilities of something between them.

But Siyanda appeared no more confident in herself than Jumaane. The moment her gaze alighted on the towering Buhari, the tension etched into her hard face softened a fraction, and her eyes lit up as bright as the stars twinkling overhead. Yet her steps faltered, and she came to a stumbling stop a few paces away from Davathi, Aisha, and Jumaane.

"Jumaane," she said, her voice tight.

"Siyanda." His response was equally stiff.

The awkward moment dragged on for far too long. Neither could tear their eyes away yet seemed incapable of speaking. The Hunter was tempted to say something to shatter the tangible tension between them. He racked his brain for some good-natured jest.

Sadly, the words no more materialized for him than for the floundering pair. Davathi proved their salvation.

"*Um'shana.*" The Issai *nassor* relinquished her grip on Aisha and stepped toward Siyanda.

"*Nassor.*" Relief—either at seeing her aunt alive or being distracted from her awkward reunion with Jumaane, or perhaps both—sprouted on Siyanda's face as she embraced Davathi.

The hug between Davathi and Siyanda lasted only a brief moment. When the Issai *nassor* pulled back, her face was grim, her eyes dark.

"What is wrong?" Siyanda asked, confusion twisting her lips into a frown.

"I—" Davathi seemed at a loss for words.

That surprised the Hunter, and intrigued him. Keeping a tight grip on Kiara, he moved closer to hear whatever Davathi would say next.

"What is it, *um'akulu?*" Siyanda frowned.

Tears sprang to Davathi's eyes. "I am so sorry, Siyanda." She clutched the younger woman's arm in an almost desperate grip. "I did not know, I swear to you."

"Know what?" Siyanda blinked, looked between Davathi, Aisha, and Jumaane.

"That your father still lived." Davathi appeared to struggle to speak, as if every word cut her to the core and required a monumental effort to voice. "He not only lives; it is *he* who leads the *alay-alagbara* against us."

Chapter Fifty-Eight

Siyanda's eyes flew wide and her jaw fell slack. For long seconds, she could do naught but stare at Davathi in mute surprise.

The Hunter did likewise. He half-expected the Issai *nassor* to dismiss the words as a jest—no, he *hoped* she would. Were it reality, it would be far too cruel.

Yet the look on Davathi's face left no doubt that she spoke true. The Hunter's eyes returned to the still-stunned Siyanda and studied her features more closely. He'd never seen the similarities between the two because he'd simply never thought to look. What were the odds that a Consortium slaver he'd met on an abandoned road hundreds of leagues to the south would be the presumed-dead father of Aisha's cousin? Infinitesimal failed to adequately describe it.

But now he saw her with new eyes. Daggers twisted in his stomach as he realized that, yes, she *did* indeed bear a resemblance to Gwala. It was there in the shape of her eyes and the lines of her jaw. Present, too, in the way her lips had twisted in her fury at Aisha or the hardness of her anger.

Siyanda finally managed to speak. "How?" The single word came out in a hoarse whisper.

"I do not know." Davathi shook her head, her expression grim. "The last time I saw him was the night he refused to return to the *ekhaya*. Even after weeks of finding no trace, he would not give up the search for your sister. He said he would not stop hunting until he had evidence of her. Even if he had to cut it from the bellies of an entire pack of hyenas with his own knife." The *nassor's* leonine face darkened in painful remembrance. "When we awoke, he was gone. We searched for him, but lost his trail in the Unathi River. When he did not return for weeks, we could reach no other conclusion than the *amathafa* had claimed him. That he had gone to join your sister among the *Kish'aa*."

Tears sprang to Siyanda's eyes. "We mourned him." Her shoulders drooped, her posture dejected. "We entrusted his body to the *makalala*. I remember the ceremony still, though it was so long ago."

"We chose to honor him for his bravery and determination." Davathi pulled Siyanda into an embrace, stroking the younger woman's hair. "But had I known..."

"You cannot blame yourself." This, from Jumaane, who had stood by silently, his eyes never leaving Siyanda. Pain—for her—etched his great face, and he spoke in a soft voice. "It is the way of the *amathafa*. You could not have known."

Davathi shot her fellow *nassor* a nod of acknowledgement, but before she could speak, Siyanda pulled away from her aunt.

"You're *certain?*" she demanded, her face hard beneath the tears streaming down her cheeks. "It is him?"

Davathi allowed her arms to fall by her sides. "It is not, and yet it is." A frown twisted her lion-like features. "The Gwala I knew, the Gwala who danced the *Kim'ware* with my sister and leaped highest at any celebration, that man is dead. He died on the *amathafa*. The one who has returned to us is *Gcinue'eleku awandile*. 'Men of gold, blood, and poison', we name them, and though he was once one of us, he is now the embodiment of everything that makes the *alay-alagbara* our enemies. Which makes *him* our enemy, too."

Siyanda flinched as if Davathi had struck her. The Hunter couldn't blame her. Hearing the father who'd disappeared over a decade earlier had returned was shock enough for one night; accepting what he had become was another thing altogether.

Davathi seemed to come to the same conclusion. "Look around you, *um'shana*. See what he has done and know the truth."

Siyanda looked around, and for the first time seemed to truly see the carnage filling the valley. The Issai and Buhari corpses the slavers had piled like refuse, many of them noncombatants merely fighting for their survival. The rows of Consortium dead laid out in once-neat rows, many of them crushed beneath the *zabara's* hooves like the countless others now littering the valley floor, clogging the river, and turning the water flowing downstream a hideous dark red. The Tefaye standing motionless still, unseeing despite the massive losses they had taken in their inability to escape the stampede's path.

All because of Gwala. *His* had been the hand that directed the Consortium here. His mind had conceived the plan to trap the traveling tribes within *Isigodi Zabara* for his men to slaughter. His tongue had doubtless voiced the order to capture the Issai *amaqhawe* weeks earlier and transport the Dalingcebo from beyond the Chasm of the Lost to work the labor camp within *Indawo Yokwesaba* and carry out the labors of the Order at the Bondshold.

She could not deny the evidence of her eyes, her nose, her ears. The bloody mess of pulped flesh. The stink of death that grew thicker and more cloying with every passing heartbeat. The screams, pleas, and cries of the wounded, which ended in agonized gasps and sickening silence as the Issai and Buhari warriors moved among them with bloodstained spears and grim faces.

"I—" Siyanda began, but her words cut off with a croak. Whatever she'd been about to say, she got no further. Her mouth worked but no sound came out. A tremor shivered through her, starting in her hands and working its way up her arms until her whole body quivered. Color drained from her face. She seemed unable to catch her breath.

"Come, *um'zala*." Aisha moved to her cousin's side, wrapping her arms around Siyanda's shoulders. "Let us get away from here for a while."

Siyanda did not protest—could not—but mutely allowed herself to be led away. Aisha guided her back toward the switchback trail and, together, the two ascended the same path they'd descended only moments earlier, albeit far more slowly. Siyanda walked as if in a daze, her steps leaden and her eyes unseeing. Only Aisha's strength kept her from collapsing or simply walking off the edge of the path she did not see.

A clattering sound from the Hunter's feet drew his attention. Looking down, he found his stolen Consortium armor now lay in long, shredded strips at his feet. His enemies' swords had hacked apart the armor—and the flesh beneath, though Soulhunger had healed his wounds—and it had finally fallen to pieces.

The Hunter looked down at the vambrace he'd taken off the dead slaver. Djineza's sword had nearly slashed it in half. He struggled to take it off, and Kiara's efforts to pull the remnants of the snapped-off arrows from his back only made the task harder.

"The Old Cheetah still has all his spots!" Jumaane's voice echoed through the valley.

Glancing up from his efforts to remove the last of his stolen armor, the Hunter found Duma limping toward them. The rangy old warrior leaned on his enormous flat-tipped sword with every step as if it were a crutch, yet that appeared more out of exhaustion than injury. Only a few new shallow wounds marked his flesh.

A tired grin broadened Duma's face. "And the Great Lion's mane is only a little worse for his battle."

Frowning, Jumaane raised a hand to his hair, which was plastered to his skull by the blood of his enemies.

Duma chuckled and reached up a callused hand to tweak Jumaane's beard—a beard which, the Hunter now saw, had been cut crooked on the right side by a slaver's blade. Duma's gesture was oddly friendly and familiar, but Jumaane seemed not to mind. He made a show of looking horrified when he discovered the state of his beard.

Duma's face quickly sobered. "The night is ours, but sunrise will bring no peace." He wrapped both hands around the hilt of his great sword and leaned heavily on it. "Not while the *Gcinue'eleku awandile* still roam the *amathafa."*

"Your words are wise," Davathi said. Her expression mirrored Duma's as she looked around, taking in the sight of the surviving warriors of the Issai and Buhari's *amaqhawe* finishing off the wounded slavers. A handful stood warily eyeing the Tefaye with spears leveled.

Though the Hunter could not hear the discussion passing between them, he could guess its contents.

"Give the order that the Tefaye are not to be harmed," he said, speaking quickly and with confidence. "Our mission to *Ukuhlushwa Okungapheli* proved successful. We may yet have a chance to turn at least *these* enemies into allies, but only if those still standing live to see sunrise." To illustrate his point, he gestured toward the unmoving ranks of outcast Ghandians.

Both Jumaane and Davathi looked in the direction he indicated.

"Go," Davathi said, addressing Duma, "relay *Umzukeli's* words, but with my voice."

"It shall be done, *nassor."* The elderly warrior placed his bloody right hand flat on his crimson-stained chest and inclined his head. He turned to go, but Davathi stopped him with a hand on his arm.

"Once that is done," Davathi said when he looked back at her, "join us above." She nodded with her head toward the clifftops. "Your counsel will be welcome as always as we plan our next move against the *alay-alagbara."*

"You do me honor." Duma again bowed, first to Davathi, then Jumaane before hurrying off.

Jumaane watched him go, a wry smile on his lips. "Once, I believed the tales told among the Buhari of the Old Cheetah to be nothing more than that: tales. But after what I have witnessed here..." He shook his head with an incredulous look on his strong face. "Our people lost a great warrior the day your mother lured him away."

Duma? A Buhari? The Hunter's eyebrows rose. That explained both Jumaane's respect and Duma's familiarity.

Davathi laughed. "She always told me it was her greatest accomplishment as *nassor."* A broad grin brightened her face. "Stealing our enemy's mightiest *amaqhawai* and finding a love to replace what she had lost the day my father went to the *Kish'aa.* Only when I met my Lwazi did I understand that she placed more value on the latter than the former." She clapped the *nassor* on his broad shoulder. "Perhaps one day you, too, will understand, hmm?"

"Perhaps." To his credit, Jumaane kept his eyes from shifting to where Aisha helped the still-trembling Siyanda to ascend the switchback trail. The Hunter could sense the man's inner struggle, the urge to look toward the woman for whom he clearly harbored feelings. Davathi hadn't exactly been subtle—she had glanced pointedly in the direction he'd refused to look—intimating that she doubtless knew, and likely even approved. Yet *something* stopped Jumaane from following his heart. Why the man restrained himself, the Hunter didn't know. A part of him longed to find out.

Perhaps when all this is over, he thought, *I will ask.*

But for now, he had greater concerns to demand his attention. Though the battle tonight had been won—at great cost—the war was not yet over.

"Come on," he told Kiara, tightening his grip around her shoulders. "Let's find Ash and see about you getting a ride up that trail." He held up a hand to forestall the inevitable protest. "And don't even think about arguing. Even a blind man could see you're in pain. And I'm pretty sure you'd rather I didn't throw you over my shoulder like a sack of flour, aye?"

"If you dare…" Kiara rambled off a lengthy list of torments she'd visit upon him in vengeance for the indignity. The Warmaster himself might have been fascinated to learn a few of the more creative tortures she concocted just for him.

"Sounds delightful." The Hunter planted a kiss on her nose, earning a scowl. "Always wanted to try that thing with the—"

"Hunter!" Tarek's voice drew the Hunter's attention away from Kiara's face. He turned to find the young Elivasti hurrying toward him, a bandaged Kodyn moving in his wake. "Want I should take a look at her wounds?"

"Right now, I'd say she's as like to take your eye out as let you fuss over her." The Hunter shot a nasty grin down at Kiara. "But I'd say that by the time we reach that clifftop, she'll be in a far more compliant mood."

Chapter Fifty-Nine

True to the Hunter's prediction, Kiara proved more amenable to having her wounds treated once they finished ascending the switchback trail. Ash's energetic trotting had jolted her with the steppe pony's every bouncing step. The Hunter struggled to withhold his "I told you so" as he helped her to dismount. While Tarek set to work on Kiara's leg—first washing the wound with water to clear away the blood, then applying some astringent-smelling herbs and stitching the torn flesh—the Hunter set Ash and Elivast, who he'd collected along with Nayaga and Kodyn's horse, free to crop the tall plains grass. The horses had earned themselves a feast after so many hours of hard riding.

The first rays of dawn had begun to brighten the eastern horizon as the Hunter joined Davathi, Jumaane, Kodyn, and Duma in gathering in a circle that included the seated Kiara and kneeling Tarek. Aisha had led Siyanda a short distance away, the two speaking in hushed voices too low for even the Hunter's keen ears, but now the pair returned to join the assembled group.

"Forgive me, *nassor,*" Siyanda said, an ashamed look on her face. "Surprise overcame me, but I assure you—"

"There is nothing to forgive, *um'shana.*" Davathi rested her hands on the young woman's shoulders and kissed her forehead with all the tenderness of a mother. "Seeing your father was a shock to me, as well. Doubly so when it became apparent that *he* is the cause of much of our troubles here."

Siyanda's expression darkened and her eyes dropped toward the ground.

"But do not be ashamed of your feelings," Davathi said, gently placing a finger beneath Siyanda's chin to tilt her head upward once more. "For they are what make you a great *amaqhawai.* What make you truly human."

The Hunter didn't miss Jumaane's nod of tacit agreement, or the large *nassor's* stance, his whole body shifted toward her and his great hands twitching as if aching to reach out to take her in his arms.

Siyanda straightened, lifting her head. "Thank you, *nassor.*" She spoke the word with mingled respect and love, as if to her own mother.

Davathi squeezed Siyanda's shoulders once then lowered her hands to her sides. "Now, to the matter at hand." Her smile faded and her expression grew solemn. "I sent Naledi and Cebile to accompany you to *Ukuhlushwa Okungapheli,* yet neither have returned. Explain, *amaqhawai.*"

Siyanda stiffened like a soldier standing straight before her commanding officer. "Cebile remained behind to watch over the *Gcinue'eleku awandile* encampment at *Ukuhlushwa Okungapheli.*

Naledi returned with us, but when we spotted the *alay-alagbara* and the Ujana fleeing the valley, she insisted we come to investigate the outcome of the battle while she pursued our enemies."

"Pursued?" Jumaane's eyebrows rose. "One warrior alone?"

"She is fierce, but not so driven to bloodshed that she would put herself at risk needlessly." Davathi's lips pursed in thought. "Naledi follows them, yes? To see if they flee back to *Ukuhlushwa Okungapheli* or join up with reinforcements?"

Siyanda and Aisha both nodded.

"On that last," the Hunter put in before either of the two younger Issai spoke, "there is no need to fear." He looked to Aisha. "Do you want to tell her what we discovered, or should I?" He knew her answer even before she nodded in confirmation. In truth, he'd hoped she would relay what they'd found—her fellow Ghandians would find it far easier to believe, coming from her lips.

Aisha spoke in a calm, clear voice, detailing everything they had found since the moment they'd departed the *kojpe* nearly a week earlier. She recounted their journey through the empty Tefaye lands and their discovery of Adeola and Ebere's corpses and the information she'd learned from their spirits—that the outcast tribe had been summoned to the Bondshold by the *alay-alagbara* to discuss terms of an alliance. At that, Jumaane and Duma both appeared shocked and more than a little awe-stricken. The Hunter recalled what Aisha had said about the Buhari's dearth of *Umoyahlebe* and their respect for those who spoke with the *Kish'aa*.

She moved on quickly to detailing what they'd seen of the encampment around *Ukuhlushwa Okungapheli*: the towering wall of volcanic stone, the heavy gates, the roving patrols, and the city built within. She also spoke of the thousands of slaves set to working on the scaffolding, and made certain to share what Kiara and Tarek had seen while in *Isigodi Umlilophilayo*.

At mention of the Valley of Living Fire, Davathi's eyes lit up. "Did you find what you sought?" Her words were directed to Tarek, who had by now finished treating Kiara's wounds and stood to join the circle that was their impromptu *Umkhadulu Iwepi*.

"I did, *nassor,*" the young Elivasti replied, patting to the healer's bag he'd slung over his shoulder. "I believe I have collected enough spite-fern to treat the Tefaye and those still weakened by the effects of the dimercurite."

More than two score of the Dalingcebo and Issai who'd been held captive in *Indawo Yokwesaba* were still suffering from the metal's poisoning; they had been too weak to fight or put up much resistance during either battle, and had largely escaped the abuse the Consortium had heaped upon the warriors of the Issai and Buhari.

Tarek held up a hand in a hesitant gesture. "That being said, I do not know for certain it will work. I will use all the knowledge passed down to me by my teacher, but the ancestors alone know what the outcome is to be."

"It is enough that you will try," Davathi said, inclining her head in a nod of respect. "Our people will owe you a debt of gratitude for that alone."

The Hunter didn't miss the way she referred to "our people"—meaning not only the Issai and the Dalingcebo they had taken in, but also the Buhari—or how Jumaane showed no uncertainty or aversion to the notion.

Tarek nodded. "I will need some help. There is a great deal to be done to prepare the spite-fern."

"You will have the assistance of every herb-gatherer, cook, and tanner in the Issai *ekhaya* to aid you," Davathi promised. "And Duma to translate and ensure your instructions are carried out without hesitation."

"Thank you, *nassor*." Tarek pressed his hand to his heart and bowed to Davathi as Duma had in the battle's aftermath.

For his part, Duma just tilted his head in acknowledgement of Davathi's order, his age-lined face fixed in a sage look that bore a strong resemblance, indeed, to a wise old cheetah.

With that matter settled, Davathi turned back to her daughter. "And what of your *true* purpose for making the journey?" Her eyes narrowed. "The reason you left without bidding your mother or *nassor* farewell."

Aisha's face stiffened at her mother's words. Yet the tension did not last long, for unmistakable beneath Davathi's chastising tone, there was genuine concern. And, the Hunter suspected, a measure of hurt, too. He could only imagine how Kiara had felt upon learning Hailen had run off to Shalandra with Evren. Aisha's intentions had been good—as had Hailen's—but the action inflicted no less pain.

"I found them, *umama*." Aisha's eyes shone bright, blue-white light sparkling among the *kaffe*-brown irises. Hope and joy echoed in her voice. In that moment, she no longer spoke to her tribe's chieftainess, but to her beloved mother. "I found *ubaba* and Nkanyezi. They live still, and they stand strong for our people."

Davathi's face lit up, and tears sprang to her eyes. She staggered a half-step and had to throw out an arm to steady herself on her daughter's shoulders. Jumaane and Siyanda both reached toward her.

"They live," Davathi echoed Aisha's words in a whisper that, though faint, echoed with joy and immense relief. "My *kwa'indokazi*. My Lwazi." She gripped her daughter's hands so tight her knuckles whitened. "You saw them? With your own eyes?"

"I did." Aisha seemed to feel no pain from her mother's hands; indeed, her own hands tightened around Davathi's fingers, their strength a match. "I held Nkanyezi. After all these years, I held my sister in my arms and spoke to her."

Aisha, too, was crying now, but there was no sadness in those tears. Though their encounter had been bittersweet, she clearly cherished the memory of those few seconds.

The Hunter hated to shatter their joy, but Davathi and Jumaane needed to know the manner of threat they faced. Their enemies' plans extended far beyond just eliminating any threats to their excavation efforts. Once the Order of Mithridas broke into the Bondshold, they would have the power of the Serenii—and whatever *Nuru Iwu* and *Okadibgo* truly were—at their command.

And so he told them. Of what the Ordermen had done, slaughtering their ill captives to provide *Kish'aa* for the *Umoyahlebe* to absorb and direct at the entrance to *Ukuhlushwa Okungapheli*. Of the chains that not only kept them from escaping, but which put them at the mercy of those who held them bound. And of the cost of over-drawing on their power, of the terrible sight he'd beheld as the young man burned himself alive with the magic of the spirits.

"The *alay-alagbara* who command the *Gcinue'eleku awandile* will not stop before they get what they want," the Hunter said, his tone grim, a weight sinking in the pit of his stomach. "Even if that means every one of the *Umoyahlebe* dies, they will press on. Whatever power they hope to unlock is tempting enough that they would spend vast fortunes on their operations on the *amathafa*. Which means the only way to save the Spirit Whisperers they hold captive is to destroy them completely. Every slaver and Orderman who soils your land with their taint. Only

572

once they are driven out and you rule these lands once more will your people be safe. And even then, they may come back."

"Not if I have anything to say about that." To the Hunter's surprise, it was Kodyn who spoke up. The young man took a half-step forward, as if making certain his presence and words were marked by all. "Twice now, I've gotten my hands on their secret documents."

He gestured toward his horse, which stood cropping grass a few paces away. Slung over its saddle was the satchel he'd stuffed full of the paperwork he'd stolen from the forest labor camp and the main encampment at the Bondshold.

"I have not yet had the time to look through everything, but what I have seen tells me there is more to the Consortium than *just* those dispatched to this enterprise." His expression darkened, a grim look in his eyes. "Their organization wields far more power than we've seen here—likely more than any of us can truly understand. They have powerful backers across Einan, people with deep coffers and vast fortunes, not to mention immense amount of political wealth among the *alay-alaghara*. Defeating them here is but the first step, albeit an important one. We must *crush* them and make such a spectacle of it that they will not dare to return. And even then, it will not be enough. The threat must be neutralized beyond the borders of the *amathafa*. How, I don't yet know, but I intend to find out."

He stabbed a finger toward the overstuffed satchel. "I *know* there is something in all those documents that I can use against them. I have contacts in Praamis and Shalandra who can turn any information I find into a weapon to eviscerate the *alay-alaghara*."

"My people in Voramis and around Einan will aid you in that endeavor," the Hunter said.

He had no doubt that Graeme and the Hidden Circle would seize upon the opportunity to destroy such a powerful organization. The value of the information they'd use to bring down the Vassalage Consortium would be immeasurable to the right people. And, as Liak had told him in Praamis, *knowing* of an enemy's demise before it occurred would open opportunities for savvy investments that could pay off a hundredfold.

Kodyn acknowledged the Hunter's words with a grin. "Then, with the Mistress' luck, we shouldn't have to worry about the Consortium returning. Ever."

"Once we have driven them from our lands, yes?" Jumaane tossed the question into the center of the ring almost casually, yet there was no doubt in anyone's minds of the impossible nature of that particular accomplishment. Expressions all around the circle grew grim, darkening further when he continued.

"The *alay-alaghara* flee tonight, and there is no doubt in my mind that they go to hide behind their walls." Jumaane turned to face the Hunter, Kiara, and the others who'd accompanied Aisha to the Bondshold. "You entered and emerged from their stronghold, and you have seen their strength for yourselves. What are our chances of victory, given our reduced numbers?"

He gestured to the nearby valley, where the remainder of the Buhari and Issai *amaqhawe*— barely numbering one hundred and fifty now—tended to their wounds, finished off the dying slavers, and helped to herd the cattle and the *ekhaya* farther east, away from the place of battle.

"How many enemies await us behind those walls?" the Buhari chieftain asked.

"Too many." The Hunter shook his head. "Too many for us to defeat in battle, that is." A grim smile twisted his lips. "Which is why we're not going to face them in battle." He glanced at Aisha. "We're going to use the memories of a dead Bheka to hit those bastards from behind so hard they'll be spitting blood and choking on their own entrails before they ever see us coming."

Chapter Sixty

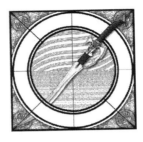

Aisha explained what she'd learned from Tunde's spirit—not only of the route he'd taken to escape captivity in the passages beneath the Bondshold, but also of the Bheka's *true* duties as *Indaba*.

"The *Indaba*." Duma's wrinkled face creased into a frown. "I have not heard them spoken of since I was a youth. Stories given breath and flesh, so my *umkhulu* told me. Great men and women chosen by the ancestors to guard the memories most vital to the *amathafa*."

Davathi looked from the elder warrior to Aisha. "And this Tundeneyenin said he was the last?"

"He did." Aisha's expression grew solemn. "The Bheka have been captive of the *alay-alagbara* from the beginning. Dimercurite poisoning, hard labor, and cruel conditions left only Tunde to remember what was entrusted to the *Indaba*." She folded her hands over her heart. "And now, *I* carry it. As do we all."

Siyanda, Kiara, the Hunter, Kodyn, and Tarek nodded.

"But there is more." A pensive frown twisted Aisha's lips. "Tunde spoke of a 'time of great strife' that was to begin with the death of the last Bheka *Indaba*. For all that has transpired over the last few months, I fear there is worse to come. What, I do not know." She shook her head. "Tunde's spirit had nothing concrete to offer, either. But whatever it is, we must be ready."

"And so we shall." Jumaane folded his great arms over his chest. "Our tribes are united in common cause against the *alay-alagbara,* and when that is over, we will remain united." He looked to Davathi. "The Issai and Buhari will join arms once more. We will be *Ubunye,* the One People, as we were when fighting for our freedom from the Ghandian Empire in days long past."

"My people and I would be honored." Davathi inclined her head to her larger counterpart. "I look forward to the day when we can discuss how best to unite our two tribes. At the moment, however, we have greater concerns." She looked to Aisha. "What the *Indaba* told you, of the *alay-alagbara's* endeavors to free *Nuru Iwu,* did he offer any advice on how to forestall that day?"

"He did not," Aisha said with a shake of her head. "But *Umzukeli's* plan will give us a chance to do precisely that." She glanced at the Hunter, an invitation to speak in that look.

"It's a simple plan, really." The Hunter studied the faces arrayed before him. "The Consortium forces are strong enough to hold their ground, no matter how many warriors we throw at them. We have no siege engines to bring down the wall or break open the gates. After our little visit, I have no doubt they'll be guarding the walls and making sure no one can sneak over the way we did. They'll be confident in their safety."

A grin split his face. "And it's that confidence I fully intend to exploit." He gestured toward Jumaane and Davathi. "Together, you two will march on the walls in the pretense of an attack. No stealth, no subterfuge, just two enraged tribes determined to seek the blood of their enemies in vengeance for what was done to them."

Jumaane's eyes narrowed. "When they see us coming, they will retreat behind their walls and close their gates. As you said, we have no way to get at them."

"From the front." The Hunter's smile widened. "Which they will know. But they'll have no choice but to reinforce their defenses at the walls and gates in case you launch an attack, ill-advised and ill-fated as that would be. And while they are focused on you, we will hit them from behind."

Jumaane's eyes lit up. "Breaking the chains of those they've enslaved and unleashing an army within their own defenses." He nodded. "I have heard of worse plans in my time."

"It will be no great difficulty to climb from the valley floor to reach the scaffolding," Davathi said, a confident smile on her face. "Under cover of darkness—"

Kiara shook her head. "Though the climb will not be difficult, the *alay-alagbara* have torches and lanterns enough that they will see anyone attempting it. And the scaffolding encircles *Ukuhlushwa Okungapheli's* entire base. No, day or night, we would be spotted long before we close with our enemy. We must take another way."

The Hunter gestured to himself, Kiara, Kodyn, Tarek, and Aisha. "Aisha will follow the path Tunde took through the underground and guide us to the tunnel he collapsed. There, we will dig our way out and wreak havoc from behind."

"Just the five of you?" Davathi frowned.

The Hunter had no trouble understanding the true nature of her concern. The *nassor* did not doubt their skill—she'd seen with her own eyes what Aisha was capable of, the ruthlessness the Hunter could unleash, and the capabilities of Kodyn, Kiara, and Tarek. No, the question came from a mother worried for her daughter.

"Six." Siyanda stepped forward quickly. She stood tall, head held high, jaw set. "I will accompany them."

"*Um'zala—*" Aisha began, but Siyanda cut her off by whirling toward her, stepping close, and gripping her cousin by the shoulders.

"Please, *um'zala.*" Siyanda spoke the words with an earnest seriousness so intense it set her body quivering. "I cannot lose you again." She slid her right hand down to rest her palm on Aisha's chest, over her heart. "We are not just bound by blood; we are *ingani.*"

Aisha's eyes lit up, and a dazzling smile broke out on her face. She swept Siyanda into a fierce embrace. "*Ingani.*"

Davathi and Duma exchanged knowing grins. Kodyn's face shone nearly as bright as Aisha's; he'd known how much Siyanda's hostility had hurt the young woman he loved, and understood the significance of those words. Kiara's hand tightened on the Hunter's, and when he looked down at her, she winked up at him. Even Jumaane failed to conceal his delight, though he quickly looked away as if embarrassed to be privy to this intimate moment between the two women.

The hug lasted a long moment before Siyanda pulled free. She did not release Aisha, however, but moved to stand at her side, linking arms.

"The six of us, then." The Hunter looked to Davathi. "We are all that can be spared from the army. If you are to pose any true threat, you will need to make it look as if you are truly intent on laying siege to their walls."

"And if my father is among them," Siyanda said, her grin fading, replaced by a grim tension at the corners of her mouth and eyes, "he will look for you among the Issai *amaqhawe*."

"You are right. He will seek me out, and if he does not see my face among our ranks, he may suspect something amiss." Davathi let out a long sigh and her mighty shoulders drooped slightly. "Though I am loath to let my beloved *indokazi* leave my side, again, especially knowing what she will face, it is the price I must pay as mother and *nassor.*" She forced a smile to her face. "But it settles my heart to know a true Issai *amaqhawai* travels with her."

Siyanda blushed, but glowed beneath the praise.

"I won't lie," the Hunter said, filling the momentary silence, "under any other circumstances, such shite odds would give me pause. We're exhausted. Our numbers are reduced to a fighting force far too small to defeat our enemies. But we *have* to move now. The *alay-alagbara* cannot be allowed to gain access to the power they seek." Both the Serenii mechanisms within the Bondshold and *Nuru Iwu*. "We have no choice but to fight no matter how impossible the battle."

"I do not fear the impossible battle." The smile that appeared on Jumaane's broad face was fierce, predatory, like the snarl of the lion whose mane he wore into combat. "I merely wish to know so I can plan how best to fight it."

"On this, we are of a mind." The Hunter couldn't help liking—and admiring—the man. He'd been a heartbeat from death only hours earlier, yet now stood eager and ready to fight. He was warrior born, as strong of spirit as of flesh. The mantle of *nassor* suited him well.

"We are, indeed." The big man thumped a fist against his chest. "Your plan is clever, brazen, and daring. Like a Buhari. You have the heart of a lion."

The Hunter saw Davathi's lips begin to move, though whether in smile or preparing to utter some jest, he didn't know.

Jumaane continued before his fellow *nassor* spoke. "But you are right on one count. My warriors will follow me, no matter how daunting the battle, but they cannot fight exhausted as they are. They need rest. All our people need rest. We must take the day to mourn our fallen and recover our strength, and when the sun next sets, we march." He looked to Davathi, who nodded agreement.

The Hunter considered arguing. But only briefly. In truth, he had no idea how close the Ordermen were to opening the door to the Bondshold—for all he knew, they could have already blasted through the heavy stone portal and gained entrance or opened a new tunnel to the passages beneath the tower. Whatever danger they faced, be it some ancient spirit freed from its prison or Serenii power like he'd witnessed in Enarium and Malandria, he could not face it alone.

At mention of rest, even Kiara seemed relieved. She and Kodyn had both sustained wounds more serious than they'd admit aloud, and Tarek hadn't escaped the battle unscathed. Davathi and Jumaane had been on the verge of death. Even Aisha and Siyanda had run Keeper-knew-how-far to find the *zabara* and trigger the stampede. He alone had Soulhunger to feed him, to renew his strength.

The Hunter inclined his head. "Come nightfall tomorrow, we march."

"I will send ten of my *amaqhawe* to accompany your *ekhaya* to my own," Jumaane told Davathi. "They will relay my commands to my *ekhaya,* see your people are given space to camp and grass for your cattle to graze. But no more than ten can be spared if we are to prove a true challenge to the *alay-alagbara.*"

"Your ten and my *unkgaliwe* will suffice," Davathi said. "Together with the men of the Dalingcebo, they will suffice to protect the herd and bear the wounded. But first, let us mourn our dead and prepare the fallen to go to the *Kish'aa*. Come, let us walk side by side among our united peoples. Let them see us grieve the brave souls fallen in battle and hold our heads high in defiance of the *alay-alagbara*. The sight will restore their heart and strengthen their spirits for what is to come."

"A wise plan." He looked at the others around the circle, and though his eyes lingered on Siyanda for just a moment longer than the others, he did not address her directly. Instead, he merely followed Davathi from their little huddle and joined her in descending the switchback path and into the blood-soaked valley below. Duma and Tarek followed, too, off to muster the help needed to brew the spite-fern into the alchemical remedy that might very well free the Tefaye from the grip of the Consortium's poison.

Siyanda did not depart with her *nassor*. Instead, she turned to Aisha. "Speaking of *Kish'aa*, after tonight's battle, there must be many spirits you can gather?"

"Yes." Aisha's eyebrows rose, as if surprised the thought hadn't occurred to her already. "Given the mission ahead, we can use all the power we can get."

"Come." Siyanda gestured toward the edge of the cliff. "From up there, surely it will be easier to see and speak to those who linger, to summon them to you."

"Indeed." Aisha shot a sidelong glance at her cousin, more curious than suspicious, but Siyanda's expression was utterly innocent and devoid of malice. After a moment, she looked to Kodyn. "Will you—"

"I'll be just fine." He waved her away. "Bleeding's already stopped, and Tarek's poultices should keep away infection. A few hours of rest and I'll be back on my feet and ready to fight."

"We'll find somewhere quiet," Aisha promised. "And some food," she added as her stomach gave a loud rumble.

"Abso-bloody-lutely." Kodyn's grin was tinged with pain. "But go. The *Kish'aa* await."

Aisha strode to the cliff's edge, toward the spot Siyanda had indicated. Her cousin followed a few steps behind.

"What do you think that was about?" the Hunter whispered when the pair passed out of earshot. Aisha hadn't been the only one to notice Siyanda's odd demeanor.

"Just watch," came Kiara's whispered response.

The Hunter glanced down, found her beaming, her eyes alight and brimming with tears. His eyebrows rose, but before he could raise the question, a shout from the cliff's edge snapped his attention toward the two young Issai women.

Aisha stood looking down into the cliff with her arms outstretched, fingers extended toward the battlefield below—and the spirits there. A nimbus of blue-white surrounded her and sparks danced around her hands. Beyond her, the eastern sky grew lighter with the promise of the coming sunrise, but the power of the *Kish'aa* shone brighter still.

Siyanda stood at her cousin's side, her back turned to the Hunter, her voice ringing through the Valley of the Zabara. "*Issai!*" she roared. When she continued, it was in her own tongue.

The Hunter thought he understood the words, but after all that had passed between the two young women, he found it almost impossible to believe. If he hadn't heard the reconciliation for himself…

Beside him, Kodyn sucked in a sharp breath as she spoke, his eyes going wide in surprise—and delight. A moment later, a thunderous wave of cheers rose from the valley, washing over the two young women with force enough to stagger Aisha. When she turned, shocked surprise stained every line of her face. She and Siyanda spoke only a few words though the roaring of the warriors all but drowned out their voices. Their conversation ended in a fierce embrace, which only caused those below to shout louder.

The Hunter looked down at Kiara, and the tears that had formed in her eyes now slid down her cheeks. She pressed a hand to her heart as if to stop it bursting from the joy evident in the cries and shouts of the Ghandians, in the enormous smile blossoming on Aisha's face.

"What did she say?" the Hunter asked, turning to Kodyn. He wanted to be certain he hadn't misheard.

The young thief, too, was beaming, and moisture glistened in his eyes. "'Issai, raise your voices and lift your spears,'" Kodyn translated, though he had to swallow hard and clear his throat. "'For this, your sister, was taken from us, yet now returned a true Issai. Through her courage and action, she has saved us all. Witness the power of your *Umoyahlebe,* voice of our ancestors, guardian of the *amathafa.* We welcome you back into our hearts, Aisha, pride of the Issai.'"

As if summoned by magic, the sun chose that moment to peer over the horizon. Glorious golden daylight bathed the two cousins—*ingani* once more—and lit up the heavens in vivid display. The coming of dawn burned the tableau into the Hunter's mind and lifted his spirits.

"She reversed Aisha's banishment," Kodyn said, scrubbing roughly at his cheeks, which flushed as if the show of emotion embarrassed him. "She is Issai once more."

The Hunter beamed. He'd understood the words aright, then. "She is truly home."

Chapter Sixty-One

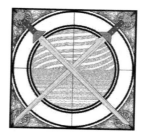

The Hunter's first order of business was to find Kiara someplace to rest—preferably far enough from *Isigodi Zabara* that she could sleep undisturbed by the inevitable tidal wave of grief. He still didn't fully comprehend her curious new ability, but he didn't need to understand it to know she'd never recover if she was assailed all day long by the emotions of the Issai, Buhari, and Dalingcebo mourning their losses.

Unfortunately, the landscape north of the valley was utterly barren. Save for the tall sawgrass blowing gently on the rolling hills, there was not a shrub, tree, or plant in sight, certainly nothing tall enough to offer Kiara shade from the approaching heat.

Kodyn proved himself resourceful once more by collecting four of the long spears the Ujana had dropped in their flight and using them as poles to rig up a makeshift tent using his spare blankets. Together, he and the Hunter erected the shelter at the crest of the hill that had served as their vantage point to watch the Consortium the previous night. The young man put up some resistance when the Hunter suggested he join Kiara in the shade to rest and let his wounds heal. Pain or no, he would not lie abed while others worked.

It was Kiara who finally got through to him.

"Listen," she said in that tone that always seemed to work on Hailen and Evren, "I'm about two minutes away from falling asleep, either in the shade or standing on my feet. The Consortium may be gone, but I'm not taking any chances they catch me dozing. So, you sit yourself down and act as my eyes and ears to keep watch while I sleep."

Kodyn, raised by two strong women and head-over-heels for a third, never stood a chance. "I'll just go fetch the horses first," he told the Hunter and Kiara. "There's enough food in our packs to make a half-decent meal for two. And keeping them away from the smell of blood will keep them calm." With that, he limped off down the hill in the direction of where Elivast, Ash, Nayaga, and his and Aisha's horses stood grazing near the cliff's edge.

The Hunter watched the young man go. He knew what Kiara was doing—by insisting Kodyn keep watch over her, she'd compel him to sit still. Perhaps long enough that fatigue and exhaustion would overcome him and drag him into the sleep he desperately needed. His Night Guild training and innate fortitude could only sustain him so long.

The Hunter turned to Kiara. He was about to say, "I'll get Davathi to send someone to stand nearby so he can sleep, too." But the words forming on his lips were cut off by a sniffling cry from Kiara.

She buried her face in her hands, but the Hunter had seen the look on her face and the tears streaming from her eyes.

He dropped to one knee at her side. "What's wrong?" he asked in as gentle a tone as he could manage. "Is it all the grief? Can you feel them mourning their dead? We can move—"

"No." Her hands muffled the words, but failed to conceal the sob in her voice. "It's not that at all."

"Then what?" The Hunter studied her, racking his brain for anything that might explain the sudden sorrow he felt emanating from her. He could think of nothing—that was to say, nothing beyond the countless lives lost and the seemingly endless suffering they'd witnessed over the last few weeks.

Kiara lifted her tear-stained face from her hands. "Seeing Davathi reunited with Aisha," she said, her words edged with a sadness that emanated from the core of her being. "And Siyanda and Aisha finally making peace. So much love, Hunter. So much love. I miss that. I miss…" Her voice cracked and she had to swallow, wiping tears from her face. "I miss my boys. I miss hugging them and hearing their voices and knowing they're close at hand."

The Hunter took her in his arms. "I miss them, too."

And in truth, he did. More than he'd allowed himself to realize. *Months* had passed since last he'd seen Hailen's nose and brow wrinkled in contemplation, his violet eyes light up with the understanding of some complex problem he'd resolved, or that beaming, innocent smile break out on his lips. Months since last he'd trained with Evren and felt his strength, of flesh and will both, or looked over his shoulder to see that hard, determined expression on the young Vothmoti thief's face as they raced across the rooftops of Voramis.

A lump rose to his throat, but he did not try to banish it. Instead, he allowed the feelings to linger, to expand within him. Despite the pain and sadness he felt from missing them, he welcomed the emotions. For they were accompanied by happy memories. Welcome memories of moments spent together.

He held Kiara tightly and she curled into him, tucking her arms before her, her clasped hands serving as a pillow between her cheeks and his chest. For long moments, they sat in that strange, silent bubble. Neither spoke but no words were needed. The Hunter could feel the emotions radiating from her—as surely as he'd felt the waves of heat washing off Aisha—and he knew she could feel his emotions in return. Bound together by their shared love of the two boys they'd been raising as their own for three years. United in their longing to be reunited as the strange family they had become.

"Thank you." Kiara whispered the words so quietly the Hunter nearly missed them. Would have missed them if not for the sensation of her jaw, pressed against his chest, moving as she spoke.

"For what?" the Hunter answered equally quietly.

"For letting me feel." She didn't sit up, didn't lift her eyes to his, but her voice grew stronger. "I've been so consumed by the emotions of others around me I've forgotten my own." A little sigh escaped her lips. "It's exhausting. Overwhelming."

"I can imagine." The Hunter could think of nothing better to offer than those words, empty as they might feel.

"It nearly broke me," Kiara said, still speaking as if each word required great effort. "Just before the fighting began. I felt it all—your rage, Gwala's hatred, Davathi's fury at seeing her sister's husband betraying their people." She scrubbed a hand over her face and nuzzled closer against his chest. "I don't regret having this ability, you know? But sometimes…"

"It can be a lot." The Hunter blew out a breath. "Aye, I know that one. Was that way with Soulhunger for a long time. Only got worse when one voice became two." He shrugged, though gently, so as not to disturb her. "Not exactly the same, I know. But no matter how bad it gets, just remember I'm here. Anything you need."

"I know." Kiara removed one hand from beneath her cheek and stroked his chest gently. "That's why I'm not more terrified of the power than I am. I know you've got my back, whatever happens."

The Hunter smiled. How strange it was to hear those words from her lips. Not because of the words themselves—they were as true as if she'd stated the sun would rise or the grass would grow—but because of who they were directed at. At *him*.

Not four years ago, the two of them had been enemies. She the Bloody Hand, he the defiant assassin who refused to bow to the might of the demon she served. Had the Hunter believed in such things as fate or the gods, he'd have ascribed this strange turn of events to them. Yet he did not, for he knew the truth of the Serenii the Einari worshipped as deities, and no fate or destiny or pre-ordained events would govern his life. And so, with no one to blame or praise for the outcome, he could only be glad things had taken this exact turn and brought them together. His life had improved markedly since she came into it.

"You should go." Kiara began to push off his chest, to sit up. "There's much to be done befo—"

"No." The Hunter held her tighter, locked his arms around her. "Not yet."

She must have sensed the emotions churning within him, for she relented and snuggled up against his chest once more.

"*I nearly lost you. Again.*" The words formed on his lips, but he did not give them voice. He knew she could feel them—she'd been able to sense his true emotions long before the crystal formed of Indombe's blood was lodged in her flesh—and understood his need to hold her. Just a little longer.

Seconds turned into minutes, and soon the Hunter felt the steady rise and fall of Kiara's shoulders as she breathed deeply into his chest. Sleep was coming for her, and he would not hinder it.

Hugging her to his chest with one hand, he leaned his other on the grassy ground, twisted his torso, and lowered her to her blankets as gently as he could. She stirred as he laid her down, her eyes fluttering open and her voice rising in a drowsy murmur.

"Rest." The Hunter pressed a kiss to the top of her head.

"Mmmkay," Kiara said. Her eyes closed once more, and she blew him a sleepy kiss.

The Hunter rose smoothly and ducked out from beneath the shelter they'd built for her. As if on cue, Kodyn strode up the hill with the horses in tow. Judging by the awkward look on the young man's face, he'd been surreptitiously keeping an eye on them and waiting for the right moment to approach.

"Thank you." The Hunter gave the young man a grateful nod.

Kodyn flushed. "Of course. I'll keep watch over her."

"I've no doubt she's as safe under your care as if Evren or myself guarded her."

Kodyn's eyes lit up, though he managed to keep his grin from showing too much delight. Ducking his head, he hurried up the hill and took his seat under the shade, a respectful distance from the sleeping Kiara.

The Hunter smiled as he descended the slope toward the cliff's edge. Kodyn had spoken highly of Evren, so he'd accept the comparison as a favorable one. Precisely as the Hunter had intended.

He's a good man, he thought, glancing over his shoulder. Kodyn had already accomplished a great deal in the last few months alone—including, apparently, foiling a political coup, stopping a riot, saving Hailen and Evren's lives, and ridding Shalandra from a bloody Abiarazi! *Keeper alone knows what more he will do or who he will become, but whatever the outcome, it will be something great.*

Chapter Sixty-Two

The Buhari did not mourn their dead as the Issai did. This, the Hunter discovered when he descended the switchback trail into *Isigodi Zabara*.

The *makalala* had come with the rising sun, drawn to the scent of carrion. The enormous winged creatures circled high above the valley, shadows gliding through the brightening sky, waiting, waiting, waiting. Twice the size of crows and hungry for the feast that awaited them below. Unlike crows, however, they did not fill the air with their ravenous caws. The Hunter could well understand where legends of silent corpse-eating wraiths had originated—the circling beasts made no more noise than the wind beneath their wings.

The Issai and Dalingcebo had carried their dead westward, upstream from the place of battle. Now, the ranks of fallen warriors, hunters, women, elders, and children lay in neat rows upon the shallow river's banks, which had been trampled to mud by the stampeding *zabara*. The living removed their colorful robes and laid them across the faces of the dead, a final gift to see them to the embrace of the *Kish'aa*. The weeping did not last long, but soon gave way to a mournful song taken up by all the Issai.

At Davathi's command, the dead Tefaye, too, had been arranged for the *makalala*. There had been protests among the Issai—all had witnessed the savagery of the outcast tribe, and many had lost loved ones in their first raid on the *ekhaya*—but the *nassor's* will was carried out nonetheless.

The Hunter couldn't suppress a grimace at the sight of the ranks of Tefaye still standing utterly motionless. None of the outcast tribe so much as twitched a muscle. Their eyes remained glassy, staring off into empty air, as if they had no more mind than a carved marble effigy.

The Consortium dead remained where they had fallen in battle or crushed beneath the hooves of the *zabara* and *chipekwe*. The only *alay-alagbara* to be moved were those whose bodies lay atop those of a fallen Buhari or Issai warrior. They would feed the *makalala* like the rest, but the Ghandians cared not where their spirits went—be it to the *Kish'aa* or the Long Keeper's arms or some deep, dark forgotten hell.

The Hunter knew the truth, though. The souls of the dead—or their "life force", as the Serenii named it—had been absorbed by Aisha. Even from a hundred paces away, the Hunter could see the *Dy'nashia's* glow, so bright it rivaled the rising sun. In her work of carrying the dead Issai, the pendant had slipped free from beneath her tunic and she hadn't bothered to replace it. Or she'd *chosen* not to. Such magic on full display would enhearten even the most despondent or fearful of her people.

The Buhari, however, did not lay out their dead for the *makalala*. Instead, every living warrior drew their belt knives and set to work cutting the hearts free of their dead comrades. The hearts were then collected into a grisly pile, while a second pile was formed of the butchered bodies and covered with stones—akin to a funeral cairn. The spears of the dead were collected and, after the heads had been cut free, the shafts were broken and set in a pile around the excised hearts. A spark was lit, and soon the smell of charred meat hung thick in the valley.

Unlike the Issai, the Buhari did not weep or grieve, at least not that the Hunter saw. Every warrior with strength to remain on their feet stood in a broad circle around the bonfire of burning hearts, laughed and slapped their comrades and kin on the back, each trying to outshout the other. Soon, the merrymaking gave way to raucous singing, then howling and roaring. As one, the red-painted warriors dropped to all fours and cavorted around the blaze like the lions whose furs, manes, and pelts they wore.

The Hunter found he could not take his eyes off the funeral ritual. He'd never seen its like before. There was something utterly bewildering and extraordinary about the way the Buhari honored their dead—not with grief, but celebration.

Jumaane alone did not participate in the celebration. He stood in the heart of the ring of warriors, so close to the fire the Hunter feared he would catch alight. Yet never once did the towering *nassor* flinch or recoil from the heat or the occasional spark. He stood his ground, staring firmly into the blaze, watching the hearts of his warriors turn to ash with a face as hard as the stone cliffs around them.

The dancing did not last long—perhaps a quarter-hour—and when it was over, the ring of warriors closed around their chieftain and the still-burning flames. Every one of them repeated the same gesture: thumping a fist against their chests, clawing a hand down each side of their faces—a few actually drawing blood—and spitting into the fire. When they filtered away from the fire, all trace of their earlier joy had vanished, and they were once again the exhausted, beaten, and bloodied *amaqhawe* that had fought a desperate battle only hours earlier. Those with the strength set to work helping the other tribes hauling their dead, but many ascended the switchback trail to, the Hunter hoped, rest and prepare for the evening's march.

All throughout, Jumaane had not moved. Even when he stood alone, he continued staring into the flames, wreathed in the noxious smoke rising from the burning hearts.

Before the Hunter realized it, his feet carried him close to where the *nassor* stood motionless. He stopped himself before he could interfere on Jumaane's contemplation or silent honoring of the dead. After a moment, he began to depart as quietly as he could. There were others in the valley who could use his—

"Join me, *Umzukeli.*" Jumaane's voice rang out behind him.

The Hunter froze. "Forgive the interruption, *nassor.* I did not mean to intrude on your funeral."

"There is no interruption." Jumaane sounded oddly calm for a man engaged in watching the cut-out hearts of his warriors burning to cinders before his eyes. "In fighting beside us, you earned the right to stand witness to the passing of the brave."

The Hunter hesitated, but only for a heartbeat. The Buhari had fought well and died hard. If Jumaane was inviting him to participate, he owed the warriors who'd fallen in battle the honor of a few moments' time.

He moved to stand beside Jumaane, but the *nassor* never took his eyes off the flames. "Your *alay-alagbara* rituals are much different from ours, yes?"

"In part," the Hunter said, with a small smile. "We bury our dead—" He jerked a thumb toward the cairn of stones piled over the corpses. "—though they go into the ground with their organs still intact." After a moment, he amended. "For the most part." He'd heard of Shalandrans scooping out the innards of their dead, but had never been told the reason why.

"But how do their ancestors know the true measure of their hearts?" Jumaane asked. Still, he did not look toward the Hunter.

"I…don't really have an answer to that." The Hunter shook his head. "The *alay-alagbara* believe there is a divine spirit"—that was his best way to explain "god" to one unfamiliar with the concept—"who judges the living and dead. Those who he deems worthy are taken to the Sleepless Lands. Those who are not…" He shrugged. "Well, we don't talk much about what happens to them. Something to do with a place of eternal torment to atone for their sins."

Jumaane nodded his great head sagely. "We, too, have a place much like your Sleepless Lands. It is called *Pharadesi,* a place of great joy, where great deeds are done, and great songs sung forever."

"Sounds like my kind of place," the Hunter said, with a chuckle.

"All are welcome." A hint of a smile twitched at Jumaane's lips, though he did not turn his face to the Hunter. "Even *Okanele.*"

The Hunter snorted a laugh. "Then you'd be the first people to be so welcoming. To us, the demons, as we call them, come from that place of eternal torment, and it is back there they are sent after their death."

"And you believe *you* will return there?" Jumaane asked.

The question stopped the Hunter short. He'd never given it even the faintest measure of consideration.

"Don't really know." The Hunter tried to keep his voice nonchalant. "Not sure I'll ever find out."

"Every man dies. Even *Okanele.*"

"No argument there. Though we *Okanele* die a lot harder than most."

At that, Jumaane laughed aloud. A single, great chortling guffaw, but it lit up his face—a face he still did not turn away from the fire. "I have seen as much for myself. But surely even you will one day take the journey to *Pharadesi,* too?"

"Maybe." The topic of discussion discomfited the Hunter. He'd always simply assumed that because he couldn't be killed, he wouldn't ever die. "Hope I don't have to find out anytime soon."

"That is the hope of all men and women," Jumaane said solemnly. "But if the day should come when finally you go to join the *Kish'aa,* I would be honored by the knowledge that you faced death like a Buhari."

The Hunter raised an eyebrow. "Including the heart-cutting-out part?"

Jumaane nodded. "That is the most important part of all!" He raised a hand from where it hung at his side and gestured to the fire. "The greater a man's courage, the stronger his heart, and the stronger his heart, the darker the smoke as it burns." His finger traced the smoke ascending into the brightening morning sky. "When the *Kish'aa* see the smoke, they will know the measure of your heart."

The Hunter's eyes followed the dark grey pillar upward. "I like that," he said quietly.

"But that is not all." Jumaane lowered his hand once more to his side. "You must have brothers-in-arms to celebrate you. To tell stories of your life, to laugh at your expense, and to honor you with the memories they guard in their hearts. For when their hearts burn, a measure of your courage will be passed on to them, and you, in turn, will see them and know it is time to escort them from this world."

So that's what they were doing, the Hunter thought. Where other cultures wailed, wept, gnashed their teeth, and mourned, the Buhari shouted and laughed.

"And the dance?" he asked. "Evoking the spirit of a lion or something?"

"Yes." Jumaane nodded. "The Buhari live their lives as the lion does, master of the *amathafa*, primal hunter, passionate lover." A low chuckle rumbled from his lips. "We call upon the spirit of *Zuona,* First Father of All Lions, to run at their side one last time."

Speaking of lovers...

The Hunter considered how best to bring up the question that had been burning into his mind from the moment Siyanda had been reunited with Jumaane after the battle. Delicacy was never his strong-suit, and in truth, he doubted dancing around the issue would be Jumaane's preferred method of approach. And so, he barreled straight in as he always did.

"I've seen how you and Siyanda look at each other. Hell, anyone with even *one* eye has probably seen it. But the way you're both so awkward, it's pretty clear neither of you has actually voiced aloud the way you feel." He folded his arms over his chest. "My question is: why the bloody hell not?"

For the first time, Jumaane shifted his gaze from the fire. Only for a moment, just long enough to glance to where Siyanda and Aisha joined the Issai in mourning their fallen, before looking resolutely back into the blaze. Yet the Hunter hadn't missed it. Hadn't missed the longing in the big *nassor's* eyes, either.

"Matters between us are...complicated," Jumaane said, his words as stiff as his rigid spine.

"Why?" The Hunter cocked his head. "Because you are Buhari and she is Issai?"

Jumaane said nothing. His silence was acknowledgement enough.

"That stopped mattering a week ago when you pledged to join the Issai in their fight against the *alay-alagbara.* If the tribes are to be united..." The Hunter let the words hang in the air. No more was needed.

Jumaane's great face twisted into a frown, his expression growing solemn. "I cannot." His broad shoulders slumped almost imperceptibly.

"Why not?" The Hunter stepped up beside Jumaane, joining him in the searing heat of the fire and the column of noxious smoke. He bit back a cough and fought to ignore the stinging in his eyes. He needed to be close enough to say what needed saying for the big *nassor's* ears only. "I would never accuse you of being a coward. But I've been afraid of being hurt, too. Nearly cost me everything, more times than I can count. Might be you take that risk for your heart's sake, no matter how much your head insists it's a terrible idea."

"No." Jumaane shook his head. "When I say I cannot, it is not because of the fear that turns my belly to water every time I consider what would happen if she says no."

"Not likely that'll happen." The Hunter snorted. "You should've seen how furious she got when she thought you might have been among the Buhari dead."

Jumaane's breath hitched so subtly the Hunter only noticed it because he stood a hand's breadth from the man and was staring right at him.

"I cannot, because it would dishonor the dead." The Buhari raised both hands in a gesture both imploring and indicating the burning hearts. "As *nassor,* it is my duty to carry on the memory of the fallen even after the ceremony is over. I alone remain standing and watching, never turning my eyes away, until the hearts are turned to ash. After that, I gather up the ash and spread it across my skin. Until the smell of smoke is gone and my skin is clean of the last speck of ash, I am forbidden from washing myself, drinking any strong drink, eating any sweet fruit, or touching any woman not yet married."

"Ahh." The Hunter nodded, understanding. "Your customs are as they are, and you are right to honor them."

Jumaane's muscles relaxed, but only a fraction. Tension still stiffened his mighty frame and rendered his spine as straight as the spears that burned beneath the hearts. He struggled to keep his expression blank, but the Hunter recognized the turmoil within the man.

"Your warriors deserve to be memorialized and honored for their sacrifice," the Hunter said in a quiet, gentle voice. "But if I may offer a piece of advice from one hardheaded warrior to another?"

"You may." Jumaane couldn't quite keep the wry smile from his lips.

"This battle was neither the last nor the fiercest we will fight. Tonight, we march against the *alay-alagbara,* a foe who vastly outnumbers us and has the strength of walls and fortifications on their side. None of us can predict the outcome, nor know who will next go to the *Kish'aa.*" The Hunter leaned closer. "Your heart will burn darker for your courage in speaking to Siyanda. No touching needed, but if there is any chance she feels as you do"—and the Hunter knew almost for a certainty the Issai woman did—"might be best you say what needs saying before it's too late for one of you."

He patted Jumaane's great shoulder. "Give it some thought."

"I will." Jumaane nodded.

The Hunter turned to go, but he'd gone only a few steps before the *nassor's* voice rang out behind him. "You are wise, for an *Okanele.*"

The Hunter chuckled. "I've always thought so, but I'd love it if you repeated that someplace where Kiara could overhear."

His departure was accompanied by Jumaane's laughter ringing through the valley behind him.

Chapter Sixty-Three

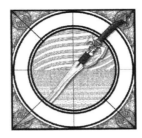

Any good humor brought on by the Hunter's exchange with Jumaane died quickly as he took in the grim state of the survivors. Every single warrior of the Issai and Buhari had sustained wounds—many minor, but more than a few grievous, some even mortal. By noon, a dozen more had succumbed, with another score on the verge.

The noncombatants, too, had sustained casualties. More than a few of the Dalingcebo and the Issai herders had taken up arms in the fight against the *alay-alagbara*. Even some of the white-haired men and women too old to lift a shield or herd the cattle had pitched in. Their lives had not been spent cheaply, given in the defense of the tribe's youth.

Between lending his skills to the care of the injured and brewing his potion in the largest cookpot the Issai could provide him, Tarek spent the day running. The Hunter wanted to order the young man to rest—he looked on the verge of collapsing where he stood—but he knew the Elivasti well enough to understand his words would go unheeded. Tarek could not stop until his labors were completed. That much, he shared with Hailen.

Whatever he'd added along with the spite-fern into the boiling water, the smell was enough to turn the Hunter's stomach. It reminded him of the vats of chemicals that had filled Nashat al-Azzam's workshop or the tanneries that concealed Graeme's home in Voramis. The Hunter didn't know which was worse: the stink of Tarek's brew or the rotting *alay-alagbara* corpses.

Jumaane's warriors led the efforts to clear the trampled bodies from the river. Its flow would be contaminated for weeks yet, gobbets of flesh and torn limbs floating downstream before they could be collected. In truth, between the Buhari burial cairn and the section of cliffs the Consortium had collapsed, the Valley of the Zabara would be forever marked by the battle that had taken place here. So, too, it would be marked in the mind of every man, woman, and child who'd survived the grim night.

As the Hunter surveyed the activity, uncertain where to pitch in, he spotted Duma directing the *unkgaliwe* among the Ujana corpses. On his approach, the Hunter realized they were stripping the deep red armaments and ornaments worn by the tribe that had fought on the Consortium's side.

"What is the purpose of that?" the Hunter asked Duma. "Do you do it to spite your enemies for their treachery?" He'd noticed more than a few of the young warriors snarling down at the Ujana corpses, though none wasted spit—precious in the *amathafa* where water was scarce—on the dead.

"In part, yes." Duma's aged face wrinkled into a thoughtful frown, and he leaned heavily on his flat-topped *nkemba* sword, weary from the night's battle and day's labors. "For any tribe, losing their armor, weapons, and adornments is a dishonor." He gestured to the silver earrings in his ears, the cheetah fur once more wrapping his shoulders, and the gleaming, patinated bracelets clasped on his wrists and ankles. "The loss of their *iznyovu* is no less than they deserve for turning their back on our people."

"And the other part?" The Hunter cocked his head.

Duma shrugged. "*Iznyovu* is valuable to the *alay-alagbara*. In the markets of Khafra, this would buy us much bronze and steel, many cattle." He called a command in the Issai tongue to one of the *unkgaliwe* and held out a hand. In response, she handed him a sheathed dagger with a handle carved from the red material that had comprised the Ujana's armor and jewelry. Duma passed it to the Hunter, who unsheathed it and found, to his surprise, the entire dagger was carved from the same material—one which felt a great deal like actual *bone*.

"This *iznyovu*, what is it?" the Hunter asked, running a finger down the ornamental whorls and lines carved into the flat of the jagged-toothed blade.

Duma raised an eyebrow. "You do not know?"

The Hunter shook his head. "Never encountered it before. It feels like wood, yet not."

"You saw the *chipekwe*, yes?" Duma spread his hands wide, mimicking a great beast.

"The odd-looking giants running at the head of the *zabara* stampede?" the Hunter asked.

Duma nodded. "Giant though they may be, they are largely gentle creatures. They only ran because they no more wished to be trampled by the *zabara* then the *alay-alagbara*." A wicked smile tugged at the old warrior's lips.

The Hunter chuckled. "Unfortunately for the *alay-alagbara*, they are not as fast as the *chipekwe*." His grin mirrored Duma's. "Or, apparently, as smart, because they did not think to get out of the way."

Duma threw back his head and laughed, and for a moment, a glimpse of the great man he must have been in his youth shone through the age lining his face.

"You have the wit of an Issai, *Umzukeli*." He tilted his head. "Almost."

"I'm honored," the Hunter said, grinning. "Almost."

Duma laughed again and though his smile lessened, his dark brown eyes sparkled with mirth as he continued. "The *iznyovu* is made of the *chipekwe's*...how do you say?" He placed his hand in front of his nose and thrust out two fingers like a spear.

The Hunter thought back to his glimpse of the great purplish-grey beast. "Horn?" His eyes went wide. "It is *chipekwe* horn? Like ivory?"

"Yes." Duma nodded. "Like ivory, but more valuable still. Stronger than tusk of elephant. More beautiful, too."

Looking down at the dagger in his hand, the Hunter couldn't disagree.

"The markets of Khafra always have demand for *iznyovu*," Duma explained. "It is used for artwork, carvings, weapons, many things of great value."

The Hunter extended the dagger to him. "The Issai will be wealthy after all this haul."

Duma held out an open palm to reject the Hunter's offer. "That is yours, *Umzukeli*. For it is you who slew the Ujana who carried it." His expression grew solemn. "In truth, all the *iznyovu* of the fallen Ujana is yours to claim. Should you desire it—"

Now it was the Hunter's turn to raise his hand in rejection. "I do not desire it. I have wealth enough with this." He lifted the beautifully carved *iznyovu* dagger in a gesture akin to a swordsman's salute. "Divide the rest amongst yourselves as you see fit. The Dalingcebo will need wealth to rebuild their homes, and those who escort them south will need supplies. Whatever is left, I am certain the *nassors* will know how best to use it to strengthen the united tribes."

590

Duma placed his hand on his heart and bowed low, as he had to Davathi. "My people's debt to you grows greater by the day."

The Hunter waited until Duma straightened to clap the elder warrior on the shoulder. "You owe me nothing. I am simply doing as my *isithembiso* to Aisha demands."

Duma's eyes darted to where Aisha, Siyanda, and Davathi were helping Tarek tend to the wounded while four Issai women stirred the contents of the cookpot. His expression grew thoughtful.

"The child of a rat is a rat," he said in a slow, measured voice. "And the child of a lion is a lion. But what is the child of a *nassor* and *Umoyahlebe?*"

The Hunter grinned. "Something truly special, indeed."

Duma regarded him carefully, then tilted his head in stoic acknowledgement of the Hunter's words. If he'd had an answer to that, any further elucidations or thoughts, they were never spoken, for in that moment, a shout rose from among the women stirring the cookpot.

Duma's shoulders straightened and he lifted his heavy *nkemba* to his shoulder once more. "It is ready," he said.

Stowing his newly acquired treasure of *iznyovu*, the Hunter joined the elder Issai warrior in hurrying toward the cookpot. The two of them reached the spot only a few moments after Tarek, Aisha, Siyanda, Davathi, and every Buhari and Issai within range of the women's shouts. Hundreds of eyes stared in suspicion, wonder, curiosity, and eagerness at the bubbling liquid within the cookpot. It was far from an appetizing brew, dull brown in color and reeking of strong herbs. But it was the sting that burned the Hunter's sensitive nostrils and set him coughing that surprised him most of all.

"Is that…lion pepper?" he asked, covering his nose with his arm and breathing through the sleeve of his Issai robe as if that could somehow diminish the fire.

As if in answer, a dozen or more of the bright-colored peppers broke the surface of the brew and floated on the top for a few moments before they were stirred back down by the ever-moving wooden and brass spoons of the women tending the pot.

"Bloody genius, isn't it?" Tarek's eyes shone and his face glowed with an eager light. "I'd never have thought of it myself, but Onaedo here—" He gestured to the oldest and stoutest of the cooks. "—suggested it. Said it would amplify the effects of the spite-fern and *okhafi* they found growing a few miles up the valley."

The woman in question rattled off a few words, which earned smiles and laughter from every Ghandian around.

"Onaedo says you will never make a suitable bride," Aisha translated through her own laughter, "not cooking like this."

A grin broke out on Tarek's face. "Funny, Kanna said the same thing."

The Hunter had no trouble envisioning the sharp-tongued old Elivasti healer scolding a younger Tarek for some careless blunder or moment of inattention.

Tarek turned to Aisha. "I'll need some form of cup or bowl to transport it, something I can use to pour it down their throats." He shook his head. "I've got none of my usual tools, so we'll have to make do with whatever they can come up with."

Aisha translated his request, and within seconds, a vast assortment of cups, bowls, and even a few small pitchers appeared, offered up by the women of the Issai tribe. Tarek spent a few moments examining each one before finally selecting a vessel that bore a strong resemblance to the saucière the upper-crust of Voramian nobility used to serve sauces and gravies at their fine

591

feasts, albeit made from simple clay pottery rather than delicate porcelain or pristine Praamian crystal.

Tarek held the vessel out for one of the women tending the cookpot to fill. Cradling it gently in his hands, he turned and strode carefully toward the nearest of the statue-still Tefaye.

"Wait!" Davathi called, her voice sharp, commanding.

Tarek stopped gradually, never spilling a drop of his foul-smelling brew, and looked to the *nassor*.

Davathi barked a few words in her own tongue—orders to set a dozen of the Buhari and Issai warriors hurrying to Tarek's side. "A precaution," she said in Einari. "To ensure the Tefaye understand the value of compliance."

Though the warriors appeared on the verge of collapse, exhausted from the night's ordeals and hours spent tending to their dead and wounded, they moved with purpose and determination in their step. To them fell the task of protecting their people from the outcast tribe that had nearly slaughtered them *twice*.

"Of course." Tarek turned away and resumed his careful walk. He had not far to go—he'd had the cookfire set up twenty or so paces from the foremost rank of Tefaye—and headed straight toward a slim, wiry-looking woman with dirt-matted hair and grime-and-bloodstained features. He waited until his warrior escort surrounded the Tefaye with leveled spears before drawing near.

"Here goes nothing," he muttered under his breath, though the Hunter's keen ears overheard.

Cautiously, he lifted the brew to the Tefaye's lips. Then stopped with a frown. The woman's mouth remained firmly shut and her face staring straight ahead.

Tarek glanced over his shoulder. "Uhh, can you ask them to help me with her?"

Aisha and Siyanda both hurried toward Tarek, and joined the warriors in tilting the woman's head backward and squeezing her jaw open. The Tefaye put up no resistance—at least none the Hunter saw—but offered no compliance, either. Whatever the Consortium's alchemy had done left her in a catatonic state.

With her mouth open, Tarek had no trouble pouring a stream of the brew past her lips. At his direction, Aisha massaged the woman's throat to encourage her to swallow, then together they righted her to her feet and released their grip on her, stepping back to open way for the warriors to surround the Tefaye woman once more.

All eyes fixed on the Tefaye, and hundreds of Issai, Buhari, and Dalingcebo waited with bated breath.

The seconds dragged on, fast approaching a minute. Then two.

The tension filling the valley air thickened to mud as all watched, waited.

And waited, and waited.

Yet still, nothing happened.

Chapter Sixty-Four

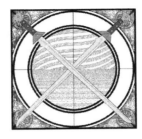

Tarek frowned, glanced down at the vessel in his hand. He shook it to slosh around the liquid within. His brow furrowed, and he turned to look over his shoulder at the cookpot and the women tending to it.

"You're sure—" he began, but was cut off by a loud, sharp gasp.

It came from the Tefaye woman.

She blinked, sucked in a great shuddering breath, then another. She shook her head as if trying to clear away a thick fog within. A twitch of her right hand, mirrored in her left, and both of her arms began to quiver. Her legs wobbled and gave way beneath her. She fell hard, landing on the blood-soaked ground with a cry of pain. Yet when she looked up and her eyes fixed on Tarek, a question blossomed on her face and she rattled off what sounded like a question in her own tongue.

Tarek stared down at the Tefaye woman, wide-eyed and uncomprehending. Aisha was the first to break the silence. She did not raise her spear in visible threat, but instead answered in Issai and extended her hand—a hand, the Hunter knew, that could either help the fallen woman to stand or unleash a blast of *Kish'aa* magic powerful enough to stop her heart.

The Tefaye stared up at Aisha's outstretched hand with a mixture of scorn, bewilderment, and anger. Her face creased into a snarl as she spat something at Aisha. At her words, the Issai and Buhari ringing her raised their spears.

"Stop!" Aisha shouted in the Issai tongue. The command in her voice stopped the warriors cold. None took their eyes off the Tefaye woman on the ground, but they made no move to attack.

Aisha crouched before the woman. The calm tone of her voice and the serenity of her expression contrasted sharply with the bared weapons and carnage surrounding her. Yet she took no notice of it; her attention fixated entirely on the woman, and what the Hunter had no doubt was her attempt to explain the situation.

Not that it needed much explaining. The Tefaye tore her eyes from Aisha and stared at the people around her, both the warriors leveling spears at her and her own fellow tribesmen standing rigid as stone, eyes unseeing.

Two figures strode past the Hunter—Davathi, once more clad in the flowing colorful robes she'd worn during the revelry, and the towering Jumaane, adorned in his lion's mane headdress and covered head to toe in the ashes of his dead warriors' hearts. The warriors surrounding the Tefaye opened a gap wide enough for the pair to enter, then closed behind them.

The Hunter understood enough of the words spoken to piece together the exchange. The Tefaye woman got one good look at the enormous Jumaane and cringed away, retreating as far as her still-weak legs could carry her before encountering the lowered spearpoints at her back. The Buhari *nassor* said nothing, merely planted his tree trunk-thick legs and folded his huge arms over his barrel chest. His presence at Davathi's back was ample threat even without the circle of warriors. A few words out of Davathi's mouth—explaining the situation in which she found herself, offering mercy if she cooperated—was all it took to have the woman nodding with visible eagerness.

At Davathi's command, the encircling warriors stepped back, clearing space for Aisha to help the Tefaye to rise. The woman rose slowly, her knees trembling, pain evident on her face. The blood had pooled in her feet after so many hours standing motionless, and circulation resumed slowly. But when she finally managed to stand, leaning heavily on Aisha, she raised a hand and pointed toward one of the men among the ranks of statue-still Tefaye. "Baako."

Davathi turned to Tarek. "He is what passes for *nassor* among the Tefaye. He must speak for his tribe."

All this time, Tarek had remained unmoving, his gaze roving between the Tefaye woman and the clay vessel in his hands. Davathi's words seemed to snap him from a trance. He startled, the abrupt movement splashing a few droplets of the foul-smelling potion over his hands. Yet he nodded hurriedly. "O-Of course."

Jumaane barked an order, and half of the warriors encircling the Tefaye woman broke off to accompany Tarek. The Issai and Buhari surrounded the frozen Baako with leveled spears. Two stepped forward to help Tarek tilt back the man's head and open his mouth. Only when the Tefaye once more stood upright did they rejoin their comrades.

Again, all within the valley waited with bated breath. Tarek leaned forward, every fiber of his being aquiver with that youthful energy the Hunter had noticed the first time they'd met. The vessel in his hands trembled with the force of his eagerness as he watched and waited. Waited. Waited.

Yet this time, when Baako gasped and sucked in a sharp, loud breath, all were ready for it. Two broad-shouldered Buhari were there to catch the Tefaye *nassor* as his legs gave out and lower him to the ground. They took no pains to be gentle yet did not harm him.

Baako lay on the ground, laboring for each breath. His frame had likely once been thick with muscle, but now the bones of his ribs, shoulders, and elbows jutted sharply beneath his skin. The Consortium had not taken care to ensure the wellbeing of those they commanded. The man's face was sallow, heavy bags beneath his eyes, and his thick beard and braided hair were matted with dirt, grime, mud, blood, and worse.

Leaving the Tefaye woman in the care of two Issai warriors, Davathi and Jumaane marched the ten paces toward Baako lying on the ground. Again, Jumaane loomed large and imposing, Davathi's voice firm and commanding. Baako recovered more slowly than the woman, but it did not take long for the nature of his situation to become plain. He merely needed one look at the unmoving ranks of his fellow outcasts and the warriors who surrounded him with leveled spears to understand the value of cooperating.

Aisha and Siyanda joined the conversation, but no one seemed to pay attention to Tarek. No one but the Hunter. He was looking at Tarek as the young Elivasti turned and stumbled back toward the cookpot containing his brewed potion. He noticed the tremor in Tarek's hands, the stagger in his steps, the pallor creeping into his face. A few quick steps brought him to Tarek's side in time to catch the young man as he fell.

"Easy, easy." The Hunter cradled the clay vessel in one hand, lowering Tarek to the ground with his other. "Are you wounded?" He scanned the young man's body for any sign of injury. Tarek was a mess of cuts and bruises sustained in battle, but outwardly, he appeared otherwise unharmed. But the Hunter knew internal damage could be far more life-threatening than even savage wounds to the flesh.

"N-No," Tarek stammered. His eyes wobbled and he swayed drunkenly. "Just…tired. So tired."

"Too bloody right you are." The Hunter shook his head. "Way you've been pushing, I'm surprised you haven't collapsed a dozen times already."

"I-I'll be fine." Tarek tried to push the Hunter's hand away, but with no more success than if he'd tried to push the ground from beneath him. "I just need to make sure the others are—"

Duma's voice came from behind the Hunter's left shoulder. "Your work here is done." The elderly warrior himself appeared a moment later. His leathery, sun-darkened face creased into a stern frown, and his words echoed with a force of command to match Davathi's. "We will see to the rest of the Tefaye, once the bargain is struck." He took the clay vessel from the Hunter and held it reverently in his strong hands.

"Is there any chance they won't join forces with us?" the Hunter asked.

Duma shook his head. "When they learn what the *alay-alagbara* have done to them, the outcome is all but certain." He glanced toward Davathi and Jumaane. "Especially if the *nassors* heed my counsel and offer the Tefaye a place among our people once more."

The Hunter raised an eyebrow. "Even after whatever crimes got them cast out in the first place?"

"The threat we face is greater than any crime," Duma said, his expression solemn. "We must consider the good of all on the *amathafa*. Unity is the only path to salvation from the *alay-alagbara*."

The Hunter inclined his head. "There is wisdom in that perspective. I trust the *Kish'aa* will lead your *nassors* on the path that is best for all your people."

"As do I." A smile broke out on Duma's wrinkled face. "But go, take the young *amaqhawai* to rest. He has earned it."

Tarek put up no real protest as the Hunter lifted him to his feet and led him up the switchback trail. The climb was slow going—Tarek nearly collapsed half a dozen times, and only the strength of the Hunter's arms kept him moving—but the Hunter wanted to get the young Elivasti away from all the blood and death.

"It worked," Tarek muttered to himself over and over, as if trying to burn the thought into his sleep-muddled mind.

Nayaga whickered eagerly as the Hunter and Tarek approached the spot where he and the other horses stood grazing near their shelter. The Hrandari-bred pony nuzzled against his master, and Tarek ran a sleepy hand over the horse's long nose.

"Later," the Hunter told the horse. "He needs sleep first."

He led the young man toward the makeshift shelter of spears and blankets. A smile touched his lips at the sight that greeted him. Kiara remained where he'd left her, sleeping on her side, her head pillowed on her clasped hands. For all his insistence that he'd remain awake, Kodyn had joined her in slumber. The stolen Consortium documents he'd been studying lay in a neat pile next to his splayed-out legs, his long dirk—recovered in the aftermath of the battle—

serving as a paperweight to keep them from flying away in the breeze. The parchment he'd been studying before dozing off lay crumpled beneath his face.

The Hunter chuckled. *Looks like that plan worked.* No matter how interesting the contents of those documents, the exhaustion following a battle was irresistible and inexorable. Tarek's current condition only served as further proof. The young man had driven himself hard—riding southeast from the Bondshold with scant hours of rest, fought with every shred of strength and skill to keep the Consortium at bay, tended to the wounded, and brewed the potion that had already begun to liberate the Tefaye from the grip of dimercurite poisoning. As Duma had said, he'd earned his rest.

As the Hunter lowered Tarek onto the blanket next to Kodyn, Tarek's drooping eyelids fluttered open. "It worked," he murmured once more.

"It did." The Hunter spoke in a quiet voice so as not to awaken the others. "Kanna would be proud."

The muttered words came again. "It worked." But Tarek's eyes did not flutter closed. His hands gripped the Hunter's arm and clung to him fiercely. "It worked!"

The Hunter nodded. "Yes."

"It could have worked for *her,* too." Pain creased Tarek's face. "It could have saved her."

The Hunter didn't need Kiara's gift to feel the anguish roiling within the young man. There was only one *her* to whom Tarek could be referring.

"Yes, it could have." He knelt beside Tarek, placing a hand on the young man's forehead much the same way Kiara had done to comfort Hailen when he'd fallen ill with fever a few months past. "And that knowledge can either tear out your heart or lift your spirits. If you cling to the thought that you might have been able to do something, you'll never be free of the guilt. But knowing that you've just found a cure for an entire tribe of people—and for your own people, if ever they're poisoned by dimercurite again—that will give you strength to move forward."

He squeezed Tarek's head gently. "Your mother is with your ancestors, Tarek. But you're not. So live *this* life while you still can. Be free of the past, and your future will be better."

Words bubbled up from the depths of the Hunter's soul, forming in his lips. *Now* was the time. He knew it as surely as he knew the sky above was blue and the grass surrounding him was green. Tarek had spent so long looking back—at the lack of a father, at the pain of his mother's death and the guilt it brought—that he was struggling to keep moving forward. The mission to hunt and eradicate *maistyrs* could only drive him so far before his strength would give out. He needed a reason to keep fighting, to keep living.

His half-sister, Risia, was one such reason. Because of her, he'd accompanied the Hunter all this way, faced countless threats and joined a war he should have no business fighting.

So if one sibling could motivate him, how much better would it be to know he had *two?*

The Hunter was about to speak, to tell Tarek about Hailen, but was cut off by a quiet snore rising from the young man's lips. Looking down, he found Tarek's eyes had fallen shut and his chest rose and fell in the deep rhythm of sleep.

The Hunter swallowed the words. *There will be another opportunity later,* he told himself. *For now, he needs rest.*

Heaving an inward sigh, he removed his hand from Tarek's forehead and rose to his feet, backing out of the makeshift shelter without disturbing the blankets or the spears propping them upright. He turned south, heading back to the valley, but got only *two* steps before a voice rang out behind him.

"H-Hunter, wait!"

The Hunter glanced over his shoulder. Kodyn was rising, his eyelids heavy with sleep and face wrinkled from where it had been pressed against the crumpled parchment. He now held the parchment in his hands and waved it high above his head in a triumphant gesture matched by the smile blossoming on his drowsy face.

"I found it!" he hissed, his voice an exhilarated whisper. "I found the key to bringing everything the Vassalage Consortium has built crumbling down and putting an end to their operations for good."

Chapter Sixty-Five

"Look," Kodyn said, stumbling half-asleep toward the Hunter but waking up more with every step, "it's all right here." He thrust the parchment into the Hunter's face.

The Hunter took the proffered document and read it over. He frowned at the contents. "Some sort of ducal charter?" He looked up at Kodyn. "One granting them the right to operate as a 'trading entity' within the borders of Odaron." The words "trading entity" left a sour taste in his mouth, knowing what exactly they traded. "And to offer such services as are required of them." Services like hiring themselves out as muscle for the Order of Mithridas' operations and providing a workforce of enslaved Ghandians to carry out their excavation of the Bondshold.

"Yes." Kodyn nodded, excited. "But look who signed it!"

The Hunter read the name at the bottom. "Duke Lorenz von Althaus." The name sounded oddly familiar, though he had no idea why. He raised an eyebrow. "Someone important, I take it?"

"To say the least." Kodyn gave the Hunter an incredulous look, as if incapable of understanding why he didn't know. Fortunately, he elucidated without needing further prompting. "Odaron is controlled by a Cabinet made up of the five ruling Dukes, the Grand Steelmaster who runs all the guilds in the kingdom, and the Arch-Guardian of the Odarian Temple of Whispers." He gestured toward the name signed on the bottom of the document in the Hunter's hand. "It's well-known that of the Cabinet members, the current Duke von Althaus wields the most power. Indeed, the other Dukes are either direct relations of his, all subservient to his house, or under his thumb through blackmail, bribery, or back-dealings. He is also married to the Grand Steelmaster's sister. Even the Arch-Guardian himself is said to have close ties with him, though what they are, we haven't yet learned."

"We?" The Hunter cocked his head. "The Night Guild has interests in Odaron?"

"The Night Guild has interests everywhere." Kodyn gave him a sly smile that reminded the Hunter a great deal of the woman who currently occupied the role of Master Gold. "My mother's encounter with Odarian steel when planning the break-in of Lord Auslan's vault piqued her interest and showed her the value of such a commodity. She has spent the last five years establishing networks in Odaron, and many other cities besides."

Including Malandria, the Hunter thought. Tassat's link to Angdra had opened enough doors there that the Night Guild's name was known in Malandria.

"So the fact that this Duke von Althaus has signed the Consortium's charter means?" the Hunter asked, cocking his head.

"It means the Vassalage Consortium brings a great deal of clout to any negotiation table, with Duke von Althaus' name at their back." Kodyn produced another document and held it out to the Hunter. "This is a message for Gwala, promising to send further gold and reinforcements 'once the talks with the Princeps of Sundran and Lord Apus of Malandria are concluded to our satisfaction'."

The Hunter looked down at the document. It was signed and dated nearly two months ago—prior to his little detour to Malandria, which had ended with disastrous outcomes for the Abiarazi mentioned therein.

He looked up at Kodyn, frowning. "I'm getting the sense you're going somewhere important with this. Mind skipping right to the part where we bring the Consortium down?"

"Right." Kodyn gestured to the documents that still lay in a neat pile beneath his dagger, beside the place where he'd been falling asleep. "I've only got a limited amount of information to go on, but I've spent enough time working with Darreth, my mother's aide, to have a decent idea of the big picture."

Mention of "Darreth" conjured to the Hunter's mind the memory of a fussy-looking bespectacled fellow with twitchy fingers, darting eyes, and a "put-upon" look forever stamped on his features.

"Based on what I've found in all that," Kodyn continued, "I've got a better idea as to why Indigo was so certain they were a threat to be feared. The organization has been around for a few decades, long enough for Lorenz, father to the current Duke Gaufrid von Althaus, to put his name to their founding charter. With his backing, they've got clout enough to give them real power in any negotiation. After all, no one is going to want to go against the Consortium if their founder is also the same von Althaus who wields a heavy hand in the Odarian Cabinet. A word from him could cut off the supply of Odarian steel, which, as you know, is highly coveted everywhere on Einan."

The Hunter nodded. "So that's how the Consortium has grown so powerful in such a short time? With this Duke von Althaus' backing, they've established connections with the wealthiest and most influential everywhere—including the Sage, the Bloody Hand, and, they hoped, the Malandrian Magister of Rectitude, Lord Apus." That last deal would never be struck.

"Connections which are made even stronger with the promise of low taxes and cheap transportation and processing rates unrivaled by any competitor." Kodyn's face creased into an angry snarl. "Backed by slave labor and trade, as we've seen here."

The Hunter nodded. "So you've explained how they've come to be so powerful. Now tell me how we cut off their balls and burn the bastards to the ground."

"Simple." Kodyn gestured to the document he'd first held out to the Hunter. "We get their ducal charter revoked."

The Hunter looked down at the parchment. "What good would that do? They've already got their hooks in all around Einan."

"That's just the start!" Kodyn's eyes gleamed with the same ferocity that shone in Aisha's when speaking of wielding the power of the *Kish'aa*, or Kiara's when talking of myths and legends. For all his skill at arms, it was clear he loved the thrill of the subtler, more cunning art of destroying his enemies through subterfuge and guile. He was, in that sense, his mother's son.

"We start off by revoking their ducal charter," Kodyn said. "And we do that by bringing evidence of their operation here." His words came out faster and more excited as he warmed to the topic. "As you know, slavery is proscribed in Odaron just as in most other nations around Einan. So, if the current Duke von Althaus receives irrefutable proof that his father's pet Consortium, one which doubtless provides him with a significant portion of his wealth and influence in Odaron, is trafficking in slavery and dealing with the likes of the Bloody Hand of Voramis and the Sanguinaries of Malandria, a gang said to run wishleaf and—"

The Hunter held up a hand. "I've met the Sanguinaries. Had the pleasure of putting an end to their operation in Malandria." He grinned savagely.

"Good." Kodyn was far from finished. "Once that proof is laid out before the Odarian Cabinet, Duke von Althaus will have no choice but to utterly reform the organization from the ground up or simply condemn their actions altogether. Which is likely to be the cheaper and easier choice in the long run. He simply proclaims publicly they're mad dogs who have slipped their leash, and once the scandal blows over within a year or two, his hands are clean of the whole enterprise."

The Hunter had to admit that despite his age, Kodyn had a keen understanding of politics—keener even than he, perhaps.

"Meanwhile," Kodyn continued, "while the Vassalage Consortium has no Duke von Althaus at their back, the already shaky ground they're on will turn downright tremulous." He gestured to the stack of documents he'd left behind. "While Duke von Althaus backs them politically, he is also their largest creditor. The majority of their earnings go to pay off the debt owed to him. Which, of course, forces them to take out loans from other sources to defray operating costs. Costs like marching thirteen hundred of their men into the Ghandian Plains, not to mention the housing, feeding, and paying of all those men."

The Hunter frowned. "Isn't the Order of Mithridas footing that bill?"

"They *are*, but haven't yet." Kodyn grinned. "Among those documents, I found a letter ready to dispatch to the Consortium's headquarters in Odaron complaining that the Order of Mithridas has once again delayed payment. Only a fraction of the gold promised to the Consortium has been delivered, and the operation here is running on nothing more than copper bits and empty promises. The one who wrote the letter—a fellow by the name of Casper— warned that morale among the Consortium forces was dangerously low, and he'd already heard whispers of cutting bait and marching away rather than continue to work without payment."

The Hunter raised an eyebrow. "That would make things a whole bloody lot easier for us!"

"Indeed," Kodyn said. "And we can *hope* it does, but still be prepared for a fight anyway. After all, the Consortium will be afraid for their lives, knowing the tribes are coming for their heads in vengeance of what they've done here."

The Hunter sighed theatrically. "Just once, I'd love it to be easy!"

Kodyn chuckled. "We might not have a stroll in the park here, but I've got high hopes that once the battle's over, the Consortium's troubles will be just beginning." He gestured to the ducal charter still held in the Hunter's hand. "Duke von Althaus will be forced to take away his political backing and support of their organization, but he won't walk away without collecting on his debts. Which, of course, the Consortium won't be able to pay. And even if they could, that's just the first of the debts to be called due."

A wicked twinkle shone in the young man's honey-colored eyes. "My mother has a special...relationship with Grand Reckoner Edmynd of Praamis. One that involves him doing anything she asks for because he knows that saying no could have disastrous consequences for him."

Oddly, that came as no great shock to the Hunter. He wouldn't be surprised to learn that she regularly shared a cup of wine with King Ohilmos of Praamis or debated strategy with General Aravon of the Princelands.

"She'll convince him to reach out to every Coin Counter's Temple around Einan and call in all of the Consortium's debts at once," Kodyn went on. "There's no way they'll be able to pay, which means the organization will go bankrupt in a matter of days. How many of these slavers will stick around when no one's lining their pockets with gold?"

"Not enough to continue operations en masse." The Hunter thought for a moment. "And certainly not enough to put up any real resistance when the Odarian authorities come to arrest them for breaking the laws against slavery."

Kodyn nodded. "Precisely."

The Hunter noted the way the young man's smile wavered. Just a fraction, and only for a moment, but it was enough to recognize the hesitation.

"I sense a 'but'." He narrowed his eyes. "What's the problem?"

"The problem lies with the Coin Counters." Kodyn frowned, rubbing his sleep-wrinkled cheek with one hand. "Grand Reckoner Edmynd will cooperate, but his urgings will stir up displeasure within the various Coin Counters' Temples around Einan. After all, they will lose significant sums when the Vassalage Consortium fails to pay off their debts. There is a possibility that *some* of the Grand Reckoners would rather turn a blind eye than accept the loss of what they consider to be 'the Apprentice's holy coins'."

The Hunter scowled. He'd never been fond of the priests who worshipped Garridos the Apprentice, god of coin and ventures. Not just because they were obsessed with counting and tracking every golden imperial like a miser guarding his hoard, but because they used that gold to gain power and influence. It felt un-priestly, using the worship of the devout as a political tool. For that reason—and countless others—he'd refused to place so much as a copper bit in their care.

"There is one thing that could sway them, though." Kodyn spoke the words with the same caution as a man dancing barefoot across broken glass. "No Grand Reckoner would be able to justify ignoring the call of righteousness if there was something to help balm the wounds of their losses."

The Hunter narrowed his eyes. "Why do I already not like where this is going?"

Kodyn gave him a tight smile and a shrug. "The Apprentice's priests understand just one language: coins. If my mother can bring Grand Reckoner Edmynd the promise of vast quantities of coins being deposited—not just in Praamis, but in every Coin Counter's Temple that stands to lose by calling in the Consortium's debt—it will make them far more compliant." He gestured to the Hunter. "Yours, specifically."

The Hunter growled. Yes, he *definitely* didn't like this idea.

Kodyn held up his hands in a placating gesture. "I know what it sounds like, and I swear to you that this isn't some ploy for the Night Guild to get their hands on your wealth." His expression turned apologetic. "I just know that if my mother walks into the Coin Counter's Temple with the promise of depositing even half of the wealth amassed by the Hunter of Voramis himself, let's just say the outcome will be far more certain."

The Hunter studied the young man. He saw no deception in the handsome face staring back at him, and from what he knew of Kodyn, he expected no underhandedness. Yet he *was* his mother's son. Master Gold had been far from shy about insisting he pay—and handsomely—for the help she'd dispatched in the form of Tassat, Jarl, Mak, and Bover. He'd been more than willing to compensate the Night Guild for their assistance; they'd proven invaluable. So why should he not be willing to do likewise if his actions could bring down the Vassalage Consortium? Keeper knew he had gold enough for two lifetimes, even *his* lifetimes.

He opened his mouth to agree, but Kodyn spoke first.

"I assure you, once I explain the situation to my mother, she will not charge you a single copper bit." The young man actually looked embarrassed, his face flushed. "She will do this because I ask her to, and because it will help Aisha and her people. And because it's the right thing to do." His cheeks colored a deeper red. "She and Ria both taught me that being a thief doesn't mean being scum. Even we of the Night Guild know the difference between right and wrong. My mothers made sure of that."

"On that, I have no doubt." The Hunter clapped Kodyn on the shoulder. "And have no fear on my account. I know your heart is true." It wasn't a lie. He *had* known; it had merely been skepticism developed over decades of seeing the worst of humankind that had given rise to his doubts. "Your plan is a good one. If my gold is what is needed to bring an end to the Vassalage Consortium once and for all, you will have it."

"Y-You're sure?" Kodyn seemed genuinely surprised by the Hunter's acquiescence.

"I am." The Hunter handed back the ducal charter. "You don't live as long as I have and fail to recognize a good investment when you see one. And you, Kodyn, have proven yourself a damned good one."

Kodyn straightened, glowing so brightly from the praise his face lit up nearly as bright as the midday sun.

"Well done, lad," the Hunter said, gripping Kodyn's shoulder firmly. "Because of you, because of what you've learned from your mothers and everyone else in the Night Guild, you've figured out not just how to put a dent in the Consortium, but rip the bastards out root, branch, and stem. That's something to be bloody proud of, indeed. A damned good investment, says I."

Chapter Sixty-Six

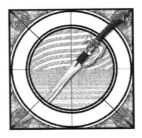

The rest of the day passed in a frenzy of activity.

Kodyn's discovery left him too animated to return to sleep, but he settled back into the shelter to continue studying the stolen documents with the promise that he'd see what else he could find to use against the Consortium and keep an eye on the sleeping Tarek and Kiara. The Hunter left the three of them there and hurried back down the hill toward the Valley of the Zabara.

By the time he descended the switchback trail and reached the valley floor, the treatment of the Tefaye had progressed significantly. Under Duma's watchful eye, a handful of Issai women moved among the unmoving Tefaye, while another group distributed it to those who had been exposed to the dimercurite during their imprisonment with the Consortium. The freed captives accepted the foul-smelling brew with grateful nods, which seemed to work marvels to restore their strength and mitigate the lingering effects of their dimercurite poisoning. The Issai and Buhari *amaqhawe* had to help force-feed Tarek's brewed remedy to the Tefaye, however, and Jumaane, Davathi, and Baako were ever nearby to speak to those coming out of their paralysis.

A few of the outcast tribe looked ready to put up a fight, others to flee, but many simply collapsed where they stood, borne to the ground by the truth of what had been done to them. But at the offer to fight, their faces hardened and they reached for their sickle-shaped swords, spears, and shields in tangible demonstration of their willingness. Duma's prediction held true. Once told what the *alay-alaghara* had done to them, they had no hesitation in throwing off old enmities and taking up arms against the invaders.

The Hunter couldn't help noticing the way a handful of the Tefaye eyed the Issai women moving among them or the Buhari warriors standing warily watching them. How many of the outcasts had once belonged to those tribes? What sins had earned their banishment from the lion warriors or the cattle herders?

Thoughts of banishment drew the Hunter's mind toward Siyanda and Aisha. In the hours since Siyanda's sunrise proclamation, the pair had been inseparable. They moved among the Tefaye in lockstep, offering food, drink, and tending to wounds left to rot by the Consortium. Despite their grim surroundings, the Issai corpses laid out and the droves of *makalala* swooping low to feast, the pair appeared happier than the Hunter had ever seen them. Siyanda no longer carried herself with the tension of a spring stretched to breaking point. Aisha stood straighter and moved easier, like one freed from a heavy burden.

The Hunter smiled at the sight. It did his heart good to know that no matter what else had happened, how many others had been lost, at least some people could find a measure of happiness.

Within an hour, every one of the eighty-six Tefaye who'd survived the stampede had received Tarek's potion. Many were weak from dehydration, hunger, and exertion. The Consortium had treated the outcast tribe with the same cruelty as their slaves. The Hunter suspected they would have run the Tefaye into their graves if it served their purpose. Every time one of the newly liberated warriors collapsed or had to be helped to eat or drink, the Hunter's anger grew.

A part of him felt guilt for what he'd done to the Tefaye. But he could not bring back those he'd killed in defense of the Issai *ekhaya;* all he could do now was make certain every Consortium slaver and masked Orderman in the encampment paid the ultimate price for their cruelty.

He lent the strength of his shoulder in helping the weaker Tefaye ascend the trail, and aiding the Issai *ekhaya* prepare to travel. The herders had kept the raya cattle cornered in the valley a few hundred paces downstream of the site of battle, and the rest of the noncombatants gathered what supplies and belongings had escaped the Consortium's ambush and prepared to travel on deeper into Buhari lands. True to his word, Jumaane chose ten of his *amaqhawe*—the walking wounded who could still hold a spear but would not endure the long run to *Ukuhlushwa Okungapheli*—and dispatched them to aid the Issai in their preparations.

The rest of the warriors prepared to march.

At Davathi and Jumaane's orders, the combined forces of the Tefaye, Issai, and Buhari rested in shifts. Half were set to sleep and recover their strength, while the other half saw to the sharpening of weapons and the inspection of rattan, wooden, and lion-hide armor. Partway through the afternoon, the sleepers were awakened to exchange places with their comrades.

The Hunter noted that Siyanda and Aisha got no rest. Nor did Duma, Jumaane, Davathi, or Baako. Though their faces were lined with fatigue—Duma's most of all—they were tireless in their efforts to direct their united *amaqhawe* and cobble some semblance of order among the three tribes that had, until only recently, been enemies.

But as the sun began to set, the Hunter knew he had to say something. He started with Siyanda and Aisha. The latter could continue on for a while—she had the power of the *Kish'aa* to fortify her, as Soulhunger's magic did for him—but the former did not. Knowing Siyanda, the only way to get her to acquiesce to a few hours of rest was to convince Aisha of its importance.

Fortunately, she had evidently noted her cousin's visible exhaustion. When the Hunter spoke to them—quietly, so as not to risk embarrassing them before their fellow warriors—Aisha understood the significance of the glance the Hunter cast in Siyanda's direction. Before her cousin could raise protest, she dragged Siyanda off toward the makeshift shelter where Kiara and Tarek slept and Kodyn pored over the documents.

The others, however, proved far less compliant.

"A lion does not rest while the pride gathers for the hunt," Jumaane said, though his insistence was marred by the yawn he had to stifle while the words left his lips.

"There is too much to be done," Davathi replied with a shake of her head that set her tightly-curled hair flying about. "I will find the time to rest later."

Duma just gave a weary sigh and shrugged his broad shoulders. "I am not so old that I cannot run with the *amaqhawe.*" A wry grin tugged at his lips. "Yet not so young that I can ignore the ache in my bones and the weight in my muscles for long before I suffer." Despite that, he did not go to rest, merely remained seated for a few moments before returning to his feet and resuming walking among the warriors, calling out encouragement and offering advice.

The Hunter couldn't blame them. Had he been in their position and it was *his* people preparing to march off to battle, he'd have been the last one to sleep. Rest never came easy for him at a time like this. He thrived on action, and these minutes of inactivity before battle always grated on him. He'd much prefer to meet the danger head-on than sit and wait.

But he had no choice. He was not alone, and could not push his companions beyond their limits.

The Hunter filled his and Kiara's waterskins with fresh water a few hundred paces upstream from where the battle had taken place. His, he used to scrub off the remnants of blood from the battle. Kiara's, he laid beside her sleeping form so she could wash when she awoke.

Once clean—as clean as he could be without a proper bath, that was—he donned the light Buhari armor of supple woven vines. Next, he settled on the grass a short distance away from the makeshift shelter and drew his whetstone and set to work tending to his many weapons

Neither Soulhunger nor *Ibad'at Mutlaqa* needed sharpening, yet he ran the stone along their edges out of habit rather than necessity. The action calmed his nerves and settled his mind.

When he examined the *iznyovu* dagger gifted him by Duma as "spoils of battle", he was surprised to find the blade held a keen edge. Backed by his strength, the sharp, sturdy tip could pierce even the woven-vine shields of the Issai or the Buhari armor. He suspected it would have no more difficulty with the slavers' studded leather vests.

He spent more time laboring over the watered steel blade and the various knives he still possessed. He'd given the two from his boots to Cebile, but there were plenty more edged implements secreted around his person that needed tending to. The sword that had been a gift from Master Eldor required a bit more attention. It had lost its edge during the repeated battles, and the Hunter had to smooth out a pair of nicks near the tip. He quickly lost himself in the repeated movements and the rasping of stone on steel.

Only when a shadow fell across his face did the Hunter look up. Kiara stood over him, sleep still on her face but her eyes alert as ever. She'd washed off most of the blood; only a few streaks on the backs of her legs and right shoulder remained. Rest had restored the brightness to her smile and a lightness to her spirit. Without a word, she drew Deathbite and her own whetstone and settled onto the grass at his side to join him. Together, their work filled the air with a steady, grinding rhythm, a grating-yet-familiar music he'd missed greatly over the last few weeks. They hadn't simply sat and enjoyed each other's presence without discussing matters of great importance since before the Zamani Falls.

The simple moment together felt like a balm to his soul. For a few minutes, he could forget about their past troubles and put off dwelling on the difficulties to come. It felt as if they were once again in their little underground stronghold beneath the vintner's shop in Voramis. Or sitting on the rooftop where she'd created his secret garden, watching the sun set. Peace, fragile and short-lived, yet all the more valuable for it.

He had just started work on one of his push-daggers when he spotted Davathi ascending the hill toward them. The *nassor* looked even more exhausted—she clearly hadn't stopped moving—but she moved at that loping, easy run that allowed the Issai warriors to cover leagues without tiring.

But what surprised the Hunter most was that Davathi approached alone. Jumaane stayed back among the warriors preparing for battle, though he cast occasional longing glances their way. Duma was nowhere to be seen—down in the valley, the Hunter guessed, helping the *ekhaya* in their final preparations.

"Nassor." The Hunter inclined his head respectfully, but did not stop his work.

"*Umzukeli.*" Davathi came to a stop in front of him. "*Ibhubekazi.*"

Kiara grinned at the name. "What can we do for you, *nassor?*"

"Join me, if you would."

The Hunter raised an eyebrow. "Join you in…?"

Davathi merely smiled and gestured toward their shelter.

The Hunter and Kiara exchanged glances and, shrugging, they both stood and fell in beside Davathi as she marched farther up the hill to Kodyn's makeshift tent.

There, the Hunter found his sleeping companions had awakened. Tarek appeared as fresh as if he'd slept for four days, not four hours. Kodyn had stowed all of his stolen documents once more in their pack and sat sharpening his long sword as the Hunter and Kiara had done. Aisha and Siyanda were tending to their weapons, too—Aisha her dirk and *assegai*, Siyanda her *assegai* and one of the woven vine shields she'd recovered from an Issai *amaqhawai* fallen in battle.

It was Siyanda who spotted their approach first. She nudged Aisha as she hurried to climb to her feet. Kodyn, Tarek, and Aisha did likewise, and the four of them emerged from beneath the canopy of the spread-out blankets.

"*Umama?*" Aisha shot her mother a curious glance. "Is there something wrong? Is it about the *ekhaya*? Or the Tefa—"

"Peace, *indokazi.*" Davathi shook her head, her voice gentle. "There is nothing wrong."

Aisha's shoulders relaxed a fraction, but when her mother's expression remained solemn, she frowned. "Then what is it?" She looked from Davathi to the Hunter and Kiara.

"Don't look at me." The Hunter held up his hands. "She just asked us to join her."

"For what?" Aisha's head snapped back to her mother. "What is this, *umama?*"

But Davathi ignored her. Instead, she turned her attention to Siyanda. "*Nassor* you once were, and *nassor* you may one day be." She held out a hand to the empty air at her side. "Join me."

"Of course, *nassor.*" With a reverent bow, Siyanda broke away from Aisha and moved to stand beside Davathi. When she turned, her face was equally solemn. Yet there was something strange and indecipherable in the gaze she fixed on Aisha. Far from the enmity that had burned there mere days earlier, but what, the Hunter couldn't yet figure out.

"Kodyn, as *oqinywe* to Aisha of the Issai, join me." Davathi gestured to her other side.

The young Praamian appeared utterly taken aback, but managed to stammer out, "O-Of course, *nassor.*"

When Kodyn stood flanking Davathi, the woman turned her gaze to Tarek. "Tarek, son of the ancients, join me."

Tarek looked as surprised as Kodyn, but didn't stammer out his response and hurried to join her.

Aisha now stood alone, and her face creased into a scowl. "What is this, *umama?* What's all this—"

"Do not speak, Aisha of the Issai!" Davathi's voice cracked like a whip. "Unless your *nassor* gives you permission to do so."

Aisha's eyes widened at the sudden intensity of her mother's voice and the abrupt shift into what sounded a somber, ceremonial tone. Yet she had the good sense to hold her tongue.

Davathi's voice rang out in the momentary silence. "Aisha of the Issai, you stand before your *nassor* as *unkgaliwe*. Untested, uncertain, unblooded."

The Hunter saw the retort forming on Aisha's lips. Not *one* of those words came even close to describing her. She had been tested beyond anything most full-fledged Issai warriors would endure in a lifetime. Over the last few weeks, as her *Umoyahlebe* gifts developed, she had

606

become as certain and sure of herself as anyone in her position could be. And she had spilled blood aplenty.

Yet she held her tongue. Like the Hunter, she must have sensed the ritual nature of the words. They weren't merely about *her;* they were the words spoken by all *nassor* to their *unkgaliwe.*

"As for all *unkgaliwe,*" Davathi continued, her words growing louder and stronger, "to you fell the task of proving beyond any doubt that you possessed the courage, strength, and will of a true *amaqhawai.*" She made a show of looking around the empty tent and unoccupied hillside behind Aisha. "Who will speak for this *unkgaliwe*? Who will bear witness?"

No sooner had the words left Davathi's lips than Siyanda stepped forward. "I will, *nassor!*" She spoke in the same confident tone to match her aunt. Moving to stand at Aisha's side, she stamped her right foot hard against the grass. "I bear witness to her courage." "For what else but courage could compel this *unkgaliwe* to run not toward her family in danger, but run away from it knowing that it was their only hope of salvation?"

Siyanda stamped her left foot now. "I bear witness to her strength. For what else but strength could bear her through the darkness and past the snapping jaws of the *imvubu* to the place where the *zabara* and *chipekwe* slumbered peacefully?"

She thumped both fists against her chest. "I bear witness to her will. For what but the will of an *Umoyahlebe* could unleash such power that the mighty *zabara* themselves feared and fled before it?"

One last thump, and Siyanda dropped her hands to her sides once more. "I will speak for this *unkgaliwe* and proclaim for all the *amathafa* to hear that she is true and worthy of being *amaqhawai.*"

Davathi nodded once, a satisfied look on her face, and turned back to Aisha. "Long your *uhambo loguquko* kept you away from your family, your *ekhaya.* Yet now you have returned. Your *uhambo loguquko* is complete, and you are home once more. Your people are honored to welcome you, Aisha, and—"

"Mother, wait." The words, though spoken quietly, cut into Davathi's proclamation with the force of a razor-sharp dagger.

Davathi stood frozen, mouth open mid-sentence, a perplexed look on her face. "Aisha—" she began.

"No, Mother, listen to me." She did not address her mother as *umama,* the affectionate term, but the more formal "Mother". "I need you to listen and to understand."

Davathi's brow furrowed. "Understand what, *indokazi?*"

Aisha's gaze darted between her mother and Siyanda, who appeared equally confused, then to the Hunter, Tarek, Kodyn, and Kiara. When finally her eyes settled on her mother, she drew in a deep breath and spoke with all trace of hesitation and uncertainty absent from her voice.

"I am honored. Truly." She reached a hand to Siyanda and gripped her cousin's forearm, fixing her with a smile full of love. "Both of you, you have to know how much this means to me. I have dreamed of it since I was but a girl, dreamed of being an *amaqhawai* and standing by your side as a true warrior." Her eyes went back to her mother. "But before you say the words, you must know I am not yet ready."

"Not yet ready?" Davathi seemed surprised at the words. "*Indokazi,* after all you have endured, all you have become—"

"I know, *umama.*" A sad smile touched Aisha's face. "I know how far I have come, what I have endured. But somehow, I feel it, in here"—she tapped her chest above her heart—"as if every *Kish'aa* on the *amathafa* are screaming it into my mind, that my *uhambo loguquko* is not yet complete. That there is more I must yet overcome, more I must *become,* before the words can be spoken."

For the first time, Davathi seemed utterly at a loss. She could only stare wide-eyed at her daughter.

"Please." Aisha moved toward her mother, though she did not release her grip on Siyanda's arm. "Please, *umama.* Trust me in this. I will know when my *uhambo loguquko* is complete, when I am ready." She looked to Siyanda. "And on that day, there is no one I want by my side more than you two. But this is not that day. Not yet."

Davathi stared at her daughter for long seconds, her mouth working though no sound came out.

It was Siyanda who broke the silence. "You honor us with your truth, *unkgaliwe.*" She moved to stand beside Davathi and Aisha, and the three of them formed a small circle, Aisha's hand on Siyanda's arm, Siyanda's hand resting lightly on Davathi's shoulder. "When the day comes, we will stand by your side. We will bear witness."

"And we will be as proud as any *nassor* has a right to be," Davathi said. At those words, it was as if a dam shattered and tears flowed from her eyes. Yet they were not tears of sorrow, but of joy. Of pride. She wrapped one strong arm around Aisha's shoulders and pulled Siyanda close with the other. "Proud as only a mother can be."

Strangely enough, the Hunter couldn't help feeling a fair share of pride, too. She had changed a great deal since their paths first crossed in Khafra. Keeper alone knew where the rest of her journey would lead, but the Hunter found himself oddly compelled to remain by her side so he could bear witness to what he knew she could become—what she *would* become once her *uhambo loguquko* was complete.

Chapter Sixty-Seven

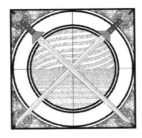

The united armies of the Issai, Buhari, and Tefaye marched with the setting sun.

United, but greatly reduced, the Hunter noted. Barely more than two hundred had survived the carnage in *Isigodi Zabara*, a number roughly equal to the Consortium and Ujana forces who'd escaped.

Had they been marching toward a proper pitched battle, the outcome would have been all but a foregone conclusion. But things were far from certain. For both sides. The *alay-alagbara* had their walls and gates to shield them from their enemies. Yet Davathi and Jumaane's alliance had secret weapons of their own: the Hunter and Aisha.

And so it was with fatigue-heavy limbs yet light spirits that they marched north toward the eastern edge of *Indawo Yokwesaba*.

In truth, it was not so much a march as a run. The Hunter had heard Legionnaires complain in their cups in The Brawling Trooper ad nauseum about forced double-time marches, spurred onward by their officers to reach some advantageous or defensible position in anticipation of battle. Their pace would have been laughably slow by comparison to the swiftness of the Ghandians.

The warriors of all three tribes ran with a loping, ground-eating gait, barely lifting their sandaled, pelt-wrapped, or bare feet from the grass, their strides long and sure. They appeared not to notice the weight of their armor or weapons—which were, admittedly, far lighter than the heavy chainmail and full-sized shield outfitting a Legionnaire. They ran with fleetness nearly a match for the horses the Hunter and his companions rode.

Nearly. The Hunter was forced to keep Elivast to a jog-trot so as not to leave behind the Ghandians. Nor could he push the pace too hard, for Kiara and Kodyn were still recovering from their wounds. Tarek's ministrations had done them good, and they rode with only the occasional wince or grimace of pain, but they were not yet at full strength. The wound in Kiara's leg left her stiff, making it difficult to absorb the impact of Ash's jolting step. Kodyn couldn't quite sit up straight but rode with a slight hunch as if to protect his injured side.

Despite their injuries, the two proved themselves a stubborn pair. They kept pace with the Hunter, who rode a few paces behind the running Davathi and Jumaane. Tarek, who rode Nayaga at the rear of their small group, just ahead of the remainder of the Issai, Tefaye, and Buhari warriors, cast occasional concerned glances Kodyn's way but otherwise kept his face fixed on the rolling grasslands ahead.

Aisha had chosen to run with the Issai. She kept pace with Siyanda, her gait seeming as effortless as her cousin's and the rest of the *amaqhawe*. The Hunter suspected that had a great deal to do with the *Kish'aa* power she'd absorbed. The spirits of so many dead men and women within the Valley of the Zabara provided an immense source of magical energy—energy which the Hunter had seen her instinctively channel into her movements. He did not glance her way, but he felt confident that if he looked closely, he'd see sparks of blue-white light flying from beneath her feet with every step. Nothing else could explain how she ran so easily despite years away from life on the *amathafa*.

Every one of the warriors were visibly exhausted, none more so than the Tefaye, yet they still set a punishing pace. They did not stop until the first rays of morning sunlight brightened the eastern horizon and illuminated the dark shadows of *Indawo Yokwesaba* to the west. When finally Davathi and Jumaane called a halt, all but the stubbornest of the warriors—among them Aisha, Siyanda, and the two *nassors*—appeared grateful for the rest.

Jumaane and Davathi went straight to Baako, who'd run in the midst of his Tefaye. They spoke in voices too quiet for the Hunter to hear, seemingly debating a matter of great importance—perhaps forging the plans for the battle they would soon be facing.

The Hunter dismounted to stretch his legs, but noted that Kiara and Tarek remained in their saddles. Kiara was occupied flexing and relaxing the muscles of her wounded leg. Tarek, however, sat stiffly, his gaze fixed on the grasslands to the northwest.

The lands that stood between him and the Bondshold, the Hunter realized.

He stalked over to stand beside Nayaga. "Seeing him again?" he asked quietly.

Tarek jerked, startled. His hand darted toward the spear strapped beside his saddle but stopped when he recognized the Hunter. "Aye." He nodded and gestured with his left hand into the far distance. "Right there."

The Hunter looked in the direction the young man pointed. A part of him hoped he'd see the twin-bearded, two-horned horse with eyes and hooves of gleaming ruby red. *Nuru Iwu's* apparition was a thing of beauty, of raw strength. A reminder that the spirit himself had once roamed these plains with the freedom of the wind.

Yet another part of him was relieved when he saw only empty plains. He'd been visited by ghosts and dead things enough for one lifetime.

"What's it saying?" the Hunter asked.

"Still the same." Tarek didn't remove his eyes from the spot where the horse-creature manifested to his eyes alone. "Entreating me to free it. Begging me to give it my strength so it can finally throw off its shackles."

"You cannot!"

The utterance came from Kiara, so forceful it surprised both Tarek and the Hunter. They turned in unison to look at her.

"You cannot," she repeated, shaking her head. "The consequences for the *amathafa*—and, indeed, the world beyond—will be dire."

The Hunter stared at her, speechless. "What do you mean?" He frowned. "How do you know this?"

"Because he speaks to me." Kiara lifted her hand and pointed in the same direction. "The Bleeding One."

The Hunter's eyebrows shot up. "*You* see *Okadigbo*?" He'd wondered whom the spirit of the monstrous serpent creature visited once it no longer came to him.

"I do." Kiara's jaw muscles clenched and her fists tightened around her reins. "For a week now, every morning with the sunrise, I see him. He comes to me and begs me to leave. To turn away and take you with me. For he fears you. He fears what you are. *Okanele*. More than that, he fears you have come to free his prisoner."

610

The Hunter chewed on those words. "And what does he tell you will happen if *Nuru Iwu* is freed?"

Kiara shuddered. "Death. Bloodshed and destruction on a scale this world has never before seen. If he is freed—" She froze, her words cutting off suddenly. Her entire body went rigid and her breath came in shallow gasps.

A chill ran down the Hunter's spine. "Kiara!" He sprang to her side and gripped her uninjured leg, shaking it hard. "Kiara. Kiara, can you hear me?"

He tried to keep his voice from rising—no sense drawing the interest of the nearby Ghandians—but had to fight to stop the panic swelling within him. She looked for all the world as the Tefaye had been only hours earlier, her mind trapped and her body firmly held in the thrall of something the Hunter didn't understand.

She came out of it with a gasp only a few moments later. A tremor passed through her body and the color drained from her face. For a heartbeat, she reeled in her saddle and nearly fell. The Hunter caught her by the arm and held her upright.

"Kiara?" He kept his voice low but firm. "Talk to me!"

"I-I'm fine." Kiara shook her head to clear it. Her fists clenched and pressed hard against her thighs, as if they would support her weight and keep her from falling. "Just need a few seconds to recover."

"Recover?" The Hunter stared up at her, his heart hammering in his chest. "From what? What in the fiery hell happened, Kiara?"

Kiara looked to him, and though her cheeks were pale, the shadows in her eyes were dark and deep. "He spoke to me. But not in the way he has before. I didn't just get that same sense I've gotten all these days. I *heard* it. In here." She tapped her temple. "I heard it as clear as I'm hearing you. But I *felt* it, too. I felt his fear. He's no longer afraid of you. At least, you're not what scares him the most. He's afraid of them!"

"Them?" the Hunter asked. Understanding dawned a moment later. "Of the Order?"

"He doesn't know who they are, but he can feel them getting close." The words poured from Kiara's lips in a torrent. "They're so close he can feel them shaking the ground. He's afraid that they'll reach him soon, and when they do, He Who Is Nameless will be freed!" She clutched the Hunter's hand, and her eyes lit with a panic he'd never seen in her before. For in truth, it was not *her* fear, but *Okadigbo's*. "He's begging me to hurry. To reach him before it's too late! We have to hurry. We have to ride now and find our way through Tunde's underground passages to get to him and stop them from freeing *Nuru Iwu*. Because if we don't—Keeper, Hunter, I don't even want to imagine what has him so terrified!"

The Hunter stared at her. He didn't know what to say or do—he had no doubt she'd heard *Okadigbo's* voice and felt the spirit's panic, heightened by her newfound abilities. But could they believe anything The Bleeding One told them? According to Aisha's story, the spirit had used deceit and trickery to lure his brother into a trap. Was this just one more lie? The spirit could easily be manipulating them by preying on the very human fear of wholesale destruction.

Or, it could be telling the truth. Tunde had warned them of what would happen on the day *Nuru Iwu* finally broke free of his prison. *Okadigbo* would finally attempt to destroy his brother, with potentially disastrous consequences for the *amathafa*. Ingwe All-Father himself had warned the Bheka of the importance of keeping others from interfering in the struggle between the two. It was a battle meant to be waged by *Nuru Iwu* and *Okadigbo* alone.

Aisha's words rang in his mind. "*Any interference could tilt the scales in the wrong direction, and all of the* amathafa *would pay the price.*"

That settled it in the Hunter's mind. He might not know which of the two spirits to believe—the one begging to be freed, or the one guarding the prison—but he knew that the cost of inaction would be high. The Order of Mithridas would not stop until they broke into the Bondshold and got their hands on the Serenii power within. If, in their efforts, they released *Nuru Iwu* from his prison, they would tilt the scale as Tunde had feared. It fell to the Hunter and his companions to restore the balance.

"So be it." He turned to Tarek. "Pass the word to Kodyn and Aisha. We ride out now."

Tarek hesitated. "Hunter—"

"I know what *Nuru Iwu* is saying to you." The Hunter gritted his teeth. "I heard it, too. Heard him begging to be freed. And if what *Okadigbo* is telling Kiara is true, he almost is free. But you were there when Aisha passed Tunde's final message to us. This battle between the brothers *must* end without interference from us. Or from the Order or the Consortium. I won't be the one to decide whether *Nuru Iwu* breaks free or *Okadigbo* finally destroys him—that's no more my place than it is yours or anyone else's beside the two of them. But I'll be damned if I sit by and let those bastards unleash something terrible on the world because they're so consumed by the promise of Serenii power to understand the dire consequences of their actions."

Tarek's face tightened. He *had* to know the true power his ancient ancestors had once possessed—he'd spent his entire life living within their shadow, battling against their curse, and suffering beneath the yoke imposed upon them by the Abiarazi because of an oath sworn in fear. Yet something gave him pause. Perhaps it was Nuru Iwu's entreaties or uncertainty over their course of action. He did not spring to action, but looked ready to argue.

"Tarek." Kiara's voice was soft, yet firm. "You know he's right. We *have* to stop them before it's too late."

Tarek's resistance crumbled like a straw dummy beneath hurricane winds. "Of course." He sat straighter in his saddle. "My ancestors' power can't fall into the wrong hands. And if the Order is willing to go to such great lengths to get their hands on it, then we need to stop them. No matter what." With a nod, he dug his heels into Nayaga's flanks and rode toward the spot where Kodyn had dismounted and sat on the grass chatting amiably with Siyanda and Aisha. The three of them sprang to their feet at his approach, their expressions growing serious to match his.

The Hunter didn't wait to see the outcome of their conversation. It was already a given. They had already decided that they would follow Tunde's path through the underground to break out and attack the *alay-alagbara* from the scaffolding, freeing the slaves along the way. Now, it was just a slight adaptation to their plan, but the end-goal remained the same.

Passing Elivast's reins to Kiara, the Hunter ran over to Davathi, who still stood talking with Jumaane and Baako. Jumaane spotted him first and, at a word from him, their conversation cut off and they turned to face him.

"What is it, *Umzukeli?*" the huge Buhari *nassor* asked. "Your face tells me you bring dire news."

"I don't have anything concrete," the Hunter said, shaking his head. "But I believe the *alay-alagbara* will soon be doing something that could have disastrous consequences for all on the *amathafa*. In their efforts to gain access to *Ukuhlushwa Okungapheli*, they may inadvertently release *Nuru Iwu* from his prison and unleash *Okadigbo's* wrath." He didn't have time to explain it—fiery hell, he didn't understand it himself—so he chose the most straightforward explanation.

Baako's face grew confused, and he spoke to Davathi in his own tongue. At her answer, the Tefaye threw back his head and laughed. The mockery in the sound was unmistakable.

The Hunter ignored the man's derision. "I don't have time to explain how I know or why I'm so certain. I just need you to trust me."

Jumaane looked at him through narrowed eyes. "Trust an *Okanele?*"

The Hunter met the chieftain's gaze steadily. "You know what manner of *Okanele* I am. Have you any cause to doubt me?"

"None," Davathi answered without hesitation.

The Hunter shot her a grateful look. "Then believe me when I say this is important. I'm not exaggerating when I say that all of your fates—all of *our* fates—may very well hinge on what we do next."

To his surprise—and relief—Jumaane nodded. "As you say." He spread his hands wide. "What do you need from us?"

"Nothing." The Hunter shook his head. "My companions and I will be departing now, and—"

A shout from one of the warriors behind him cut into his words. Again, the word for "Attack!" At the call, more than two hundred warriors sprang to their feet and raised their weapons.

The Hunter, Jumaane, Davathi, and Baako spun toward the one who'd shouted. Duma stood east of the pack of warriors, his broad-bladed *nkemba* held in a tight grip and his free hand pointing toward the horizon.

Where, the Hunter saw, scores of dark shapes bore down on them at tremendous speed.

Chapter Sixty-Eight

Within a minute of sighting the approaching army, the united armies of the Issai, Buhari, and Tefaye stood ready for battle. As the most numerous, Jumaane and the Buhari claimed the center, where they would bear the brunt of an enemy's charge. Baako and his Tefaye stood to their left, while Davathi and her Issai held the right flank.

Siyanda stood at Davathi's left hand, Aisha at her right. Though both held their spears like the other women of the *amaqhawe* around them, all had witnessed Aisha's power and knew the devastation she would unleash when their enemy closed ranks.

That left the Hunter, Tarek, Kiara, and Kodyn. Kodyn had tried to insist on joining the Issai, but Davathi had dissuaded him, stating his *alay-alaghara* fighting style would only hinder their *amaqhawe*. He had taken the statement without bristling, merely accepting her words and his designated place. That response did him credit and showed his true measure. A more prideful man would have insisted or demanded a place of honor. After all, his actions had played a more-than-significant role in recent events. Yet he demonstrated a measure of humility that matched the intelligence and astuteness he'd displayed thus far.

Kiara and Tarek stood beside Kodyn. The Hunter wanted to join them—better he fight as close to the still-recovering Kiara as possible, keep an eye on her—but instead took his place beyond the Tefaye's left flank. The moment battle was joined, his place would be wherever the fighting proved thickest. He'd carve his way through the enemy ranks from the left while Aisha unleashed her *Umoyahlebe* magic on them from the right. Between the two of them, they had better-than-even odds of turning the tide in favor of the exhausted coalition following Jumaane and Davathi.

A cry went up as the approaching army closed the distance. Yet it was not a cry of anger or hostility, but delight. The Tefaye around the Hunter stared in confusion, but every one of the Buhari and Issai down the line raised their weapons high over their heads and cheered. Their voices rang out across the rolling grasslands with a joyous ululation that rivaled the merrymaking of the celebration they'd shared at the base of the *kopje* nearly a week earlier.

The Hunter hurried toward Jumaane, who roared loudest of all, shaking his huge sword high in the air with one hand and beating his other fist against his chest.

"What's going on?" the Hunter asked, though he had to shout to be heard over the clamor.

"There will be no battle this day." Jumaane turned a beaming grin on him, his dark eyes shining bright in the morning sunlight. "The Nyemba and Mwaani are not our enemies."

The Hunter's eyebrows rose in surprise. Behind him, Baako repeated the same question to Jumaane in his own tongue. But the Hunter barely heard the Buhari *nassor's* triumphant answer. He was busy drinking in the sight of the reinforcements streaming toward them.

Even with hundreds of paces separating them, the Hunter recognized the Mwaani who had spoken in the *Umkhadulu Iwepi*. The venerable man's grey-streaked hair flew wild as he ran, his battle-scarred face creased in a broad grin as he and the warriors around him echoed the shouts coming from the Issai and Buhari. He and a few others wore no helmets, preferring to let their hair loose, but all of the Mwaani wore armor of multiple plates of some beautiful, bright-gleaming green, red, and blue material joined by leather cords. The plates were neither painted wood nor dyed bone. Indeed, for a moment, the Hunter believed they were the scales of some bright-colored slashwyrm.

But as they drew closer, he realized that what he'd first believed were helmets were, in fact, turtle shells fashioned into protective headgear. When he looked again at the armor, he suddenly understood their true origin: they, too, were fashioned from the shell of some turtle, but judging from the size of the plates, beasts large enough to rival a full-grown destrier. The blades of their weapons—a motley assortment of hand-axes, hunting spears, tridents, and something akin to a thresher's flail set with jagged teeth in one end—were also fashioned from tortoise shells sharpened to a keen edge.

So astonished was the Hunter by the sight that he barely looked at the Nyemba until barely a hundred paces separated them. The Nyemba wore cloaks that, at first glance, bore a resemblance to the furs of a black bear. Yet no bear the Hunter had ever seen bore bright patches of silver along their backs, nor paws ending in what could almost pass for human fingers rather than claws.

The Nyemba warrior's words from the council echoed through his mind. *"Our amaqhawe hunts the great kitaka apes of the Mthokozisi Mountains or drives off the packs of wild dogs that dwell among the Nhlanhla foothills."*

The Hunter sucked in a breath. If, as he believed, those furs had come from the great kitaka apes, beasts said to stand twice the height of humans with thrice a fully grown man's strength, the Nyemba *amaqhawe* were no less fierce than the lion-clad Buhari or the ferocious Issai.

The armies collided with thunderous force, yet no clash of weapons or screams of pain echoed in the morning. Instead, the air rang with joyous cries from both sides, accompanied by the Buhari's leonine roars, the ululating calls of the Issai, and a cacophony of chest-pounding from the Nyemba and clacking of the Mwaani's armor as they clasped hands and embraced their fellow Ghandians.

It took the better part of half an hour to bring order to the chaos. At first, the Tefaye stood outside the revelry, but at shouted words from Davathi and Jumaane, the Mwaani and Nyemba greeted them with only marginally less enthusiasm than the others. Finally, Jumaane, Davathi, and Baako led the chieftains of the two newcomer tribes—a white-haired Mwaani woman who Davathi introduced as Khairi, and Zuberi, a whip-thin, sharp-faced Nyemba who Jumaane greeted as a respected friend rather than a former enemy turned ally by circumstance.

"Raizi, tell us what you do," the Mwaani *nassor* said in thickly accented Einari. She gestured toward the greying warrior and stomped her foot hard. "Mwaani fight *alay-alagbara*."

Zuberi added something in his own tongue, and a cheer went up from among the Nyemba *amaqhawe*.

The Hunter and his companions stood silently while Davathi and Jumaane spoke with their three fellow *nassor*. Watching the interaction, there was no doubt in the Hunter's mind which of the tribes would lead the charge. Davathi spoke with an air of unquestioned authority, and Jumaane towered head and shoulders above his fellows. The Nyemba and Mwaani *nassors* had their pride, made certain their tribes' voices were heard, but in matters of the battle to come, they clearly deferred to their more martially inclined neighbors. Baako spoke little, seeming relieved just to be included and treated with respect despite his tribe's status as outcast.

The deliberation did not last long—in fact, the conversation ended so quickly Kodyn didn't even have time to translate what was said before Davathi turned to the Hunter. "Come, *Umzukeli*, we must depart. If what you say is true and the *amathafa* is in danger from the *Gcinue'eleku awandile*, there is a need to hurry. We have many leagues to cover if we are to reach *Isigodi Umlilophilayo* in time."

The Hunter cocked his head. "We?" He looked between Jumaane and Davathi. "What do you mean, we?"

"The Issai *amaqhawe* fights at your side." Davathi pronounced the words with the same note of finality and confidence with which she'd addressed her fellow *nassors*. There was no question, merely a statement and command. "Where you go, we go, even if that means we walk through the halls of *Ukuhlushwa Okungapheli*, where no mortal feet have trod since the days of the *Ukujiswa Okhulu*."

The Hunter frowned. "But are you not needed at the wall? Will Gwala not look for the Issai among his enemies? For *you*, specifically?"

"He will." Jumaane's face split into a broad grin. "And he will find only death." He thumped a fist against his great chest. "At the hands of the Buhari."

"He will look for me," Davathi said, "but by the time he realizes I am not among the enemy outside his walls, my spear will be at his back."

With those words, the *nassors'* intention became plain. "You will join the attack against the *alay-alagbara* on the scaffolding."

"You'll free those held captive and turn them loose on the camp from within," Kiara added. She, too, had apparently deduced Davathi and Jumaane's tactics.

"Our enemies have high walls to hide behind," Jumaane said, his smile growing brighter and more ferocious. "But those walls will do them no good if they are thrown open." He clapped a huge hand to Davathi's shoulder. "None are as fleet of foot as the Issai, nor so fierce at close quarters. They will create chaos, and within chaos, opportunity."

The Hunter contemplated the plan. It was a good one, he had to admit, but placed an immense burden of responsibility on the greatly reduced Issai *amaqhawe*. The Hunter had spotted Sizwe among the Mwaani warriors. Evidently after Aisha's abrupt departure from the *kopje*, the plan laid out in the *Umkhadulu Iwepi* had changed. Sizwe had gone with another of the Issai warriors, one whose name the Hunter didn't know, to recruit the Mwaani and Nyemba to the cause while Naledi, Cebile, and Siyanda were dispatched to follow Aisha and learn what they could of the *alay-alagbara*.

With Sizwe and her companion returned, the Issai numbered fourteen, plus Davathi and Siyanda. Adding Naledi and Cebile, wounded as she was, put their ranks at eighteen. Eighteen fighters. Fierce and brave, unquestionably, but would they suffice?

Davathi seemed to read his mind. "We will do what must be done." Her expression hardened and her fist tightened around the haft of her *assegai*. "There is no question of 'if', only 'how'." She looked to Aisha, who had joined them along with Tarek and Kodyn. "And with my *indokazi* and her *oqinywe* at our side, I believe our chances are good."

Kodyn straightened, beaming proudly. "I would be honored, *nassor*," he said, with a little bow.

Aisha smiled at her mother. "We will find *ubaba* and Nkanyezi together, *umama.*"

Davathi's face twisted, for a moment revealing the pain she had hidden so well all this time—the pain of a woman whose husband and daughter had been ripped from her arms, held captive, and tormented, who could do nothing to aid them without abandoning her people. It passed quickly, but the Hunter had seen it. And, apparently, Kiara had *felt* it. She swallowed hard and turned her face away to hide the tears brimming in her eyes.

"Meanwhile," Davathi said, her voice tight with the emotion she visibly struggled to bottle up, "you, *Umzukeli,* and your *Ibhubekazi* will see to *Nuru Iwu* and *Okadigbo.*"

At her words, surprised expressions sprouted on the faces of Baako, Zuberi, and Raiza. If Davathi noticed, she paid them no heed.

"I do not know how you are certain of this thing," the Issai *nassor* continued, "but I will no more ignore your warning than that of the Bheka *Indaba* who spoke through my daughter. If all is as you say, the fate of the *amathafa* rests in your hands as much as those of who fight the *alay-alagbara.*"

The Hunter bowed. "I will do my best not to disappoint." He tried for a flippant tone, but he could not deny the burden that her words placed on his shoulders.

Thus far, he had merely acted because of a promise he'd made to Aisha to fight for her people. And because, at every moment of decision, the correct course of action had been abundantly clear in his mind. He would never sit by idly and allow cruelty to run rampant when he could do something about it. The Consortium had made him their enemy the day they took up the slave trade. Father Reverentus' words had set him against the Order of Mithridas, for the sake of peace and safety for the people the Hunter loved.

Yet now, this went beyond just him. He hadn't come to Ghandia intending to stop some ancient spirit from being unleashed or forestalling some "time of great strife". He was merely a killer, a man willing to spill blood when needed.

But I suppose if ever there was a time that a killer like me was needed, it's now, he thought. *Because neither the Order nor the Consortium will be stopped any other way, that much is clear.*

And so, he would follow the order he'd been given—and bear the burden as he had when vowing to Master Eldor and the True Descendants that he would aid them in eradicating the maistyrs, and when he'd sworn to Kharna that he would find another way to sustain him in his fight against the Great Devourer that didn't involve the death of hundreds of thousands of people who'd suffered a lifetime in Khar'nath. He would do as he'd always done: fight to his last breath to destroy those who, through their actions, had made themselves his enemies.

"Let us make ready to depart." Davathi's words pierced the chaos in the Hunter's mind. She turned to Jumaane and clasped his hand. "Until we meet again, Great Lion. Either in this life or among the *Kish'aa.*"

He gripped her arm tightly in his and he answered in a voice too low for the Hunter to overhear. Whatever it was, Davathi's leonine face creased into a broad grin and she let out a raucous laugh.

As Davathi moved among the other *nassors,* Jumaane turned to Siyanda. His face turned bright red and he suddenly looked like an awkward schoolboy as he shuffled from foot to foot. Words tumbled from his mouth in a rush, his huge hands gesturing with almost frantic emphasis.

Siyanda's eyes widened, her spine going suddenly rigid. Aisha, too, appeared surprised. Yet she recovered before her cousin and pushed the frozen Siyanda away from her. Siyanda half-stumbled, and Jumaane's arms snapped out to catch her. She managed to right herself, though, before his fingers made contact with her skin. He quickly drew back, as if afraid to touch her.

No, not afraid. The Hunter recalled Jumaane's words as he stood over the burning pile of his warriors' hearts. Ash still stained his skin; indeed, he was more grey than the vermillion red of the rest of his *amaqhawe*.

Yet still, the Hunter couldn't help smiling. Jumaane had heeded his words. Perhaps it was the fact that they were to be parted, or he'd merely needed an entire day to pluck up his courage. Whatever the case, he'd finally *done* what he'd wanted to all along.

"Is that what I think it is?" Kiara whispered into the Hunter's ear.

The Hunter nodded, then broke out into a quiet laugh as Jumaane reached up a hand to snap one of the lion's teeth off his headdress. With a tenderness that bordered on reverence, the giant Buhari *nassor* held the tooth out to Siyanda. She took it hesitantly, and he all but dropped it into her hand as if it were a red-hot ember. Yet there was no denying the light that broke out on *both* their faces as Siyanda closed her fist around the tooth.

"Damned right it is." The Hunter slung an arm around Kiara's shoulder and pressed a kiss to the side of her head.

"Looks like there might be a happy ending for at least *two* people," Kiara said.

At her words, the Hunter felt a sinking in the pit of his stomach. Much as he wished them only good, he'd learned the hard way that reality tended to be cruelest in the face of the greatest joys. Their happy ending would only come *if* they both survived the ordeal that lay before them.

Chapter Sixty-Nine

The Hunter's group rode out a quarter-hour later, with the Issai *amaqhawe* leading the way. Behind them, Jumaane's loud voice rang out across the plains as he ordered the Tefaye, Nyemba, and Mwaani about. He'd have his work cut out for him attempting to integrate the three forces with his own. But if anyone could do it, Davathi had insisted, it was him.

The Hunter noted the way Siyanda's eyes lingered on the Buhari *nassor*. Her fist remained closed firmly around the lion's tooth, her expression grave. Yet she was among the first to join her aunt in setting off at a loping run ahead of the Hunter and his companions.

All through the rest of the day they rode, pushing the horses as hard as they could without pulling ahead of the running Issai. To their credit, Davathi and her warriors set a tireless pace. Jumaane hadn't exaggerated when he claimed none were so fleet of foot as the Issai. The women seemed to glide over the grassy hills, their feet barely touching the ground and leaving hardly a trace of their passage.

Even Duma, who had insisted on accompanying them, ran without visible sign of strain. He wore his *nkemba* sword strapped to his back, his hands empty save for his shield. For all his age, he ran at Davathi's back and never once stumbled, his legs carrying him swiftly and surely across the rolling landscape. The name "Old Cheetah" proved apt indeed.

For the first few leagues, Aisha ran beside her mother and cousin. But after their first rest break shortly after sundown, when Kodyn noticed she appeared more winded than her fellow Issai, he quietly talked her into joining him on horseback.

They journeyed through the night with only what rest proved absolutely necessary, and when morning dawned, the brightening sun shone on the rocky canyons that hid the petrified forest surrounding *Isigodi Umlilophilayo*. In the distance, the midnight black structure of *Ukuhlushwa Okungapheli* rose high above the cliffs, a dagger of night thrusting upward into the cloudless blue skies.

At the sight, the mood of their group grew somber. During their few rest breaks, the Issai women had shared quiet conversations, even laughter, over the sparse meals. Now, the tense silence that hovered over them all was only broken by the occasional snort from one of the horses, the rustle of the plains grass blowing in the breeze, or, finally, the order to resume their journey.

They continued on, traveling until noon before taking another rest. When they resumed, however, their journey did not last long. They'd covered no more than half a league wending through the rocky canyons when a figure appeared through a gap in the stone walls ahead. Tall, broad-shouldered, armed with a Consortium blade yet clad in colorful Issai robes. Naledi.

Davathi had sent the warrior to scout ahead the night after the battle. Now, the Issai warrior raced in their direction at full speed, urgency in every step. Within minutes, the Hunter's group and the lone woman met in the middle of a narrow wash where once a creek had flowed, but now only cracked, barren earth remained.

"*Nassor!*" Naledi shouted upon seeing Davathi. Words in her own tongue poured from her lips in a torrent, a grim look on her face. The Hunter heard the Issai word for "hundred" and *alay-alagbara,* as well as "gate". Angry hisses arose from among the Issai warriors, and Kodyn and Aisha both muttered curses.

"I'm not liking the sound of that." The Hunter glanced toward the two youths who understood what was being said. "Tell me the bad news."

"Reinforcements," Kodyn said, his expression darkening.

"By Cebile's count, at least four hundred more *alay-alagbara,*" Aisha translated Naledi's words. "They came two nights after our departure, only to find the gates would not open for them. They were camped outside the walls until only last night, when finally the gates were opened and they could enter."

"Hah!" Kodyn shot them a sly grin. "Looks like my trick worked. I couldn't break the mechanism completely—it's far too large for that—but a few well-placed blows knocked some critical pins and gears loose." He nodded. "Four days is even better than I'd expected."

"Shh!" Aisha gestured for Kodyn to be silent, straining to hear Naledi's report to her mother. "The army we attacked returned last night." She held her breath for a moment, then sighed and shook her head. "Gwala was with them."

That much was clear from the dark look Naledi shot toward Siyanda.

The Hunter let out a snort. "Men like Gwala die hard. More roaches than men, really. You put them down *hard,* or they get right back up and keep crawling around the dung pile."

"Colorful," Kiara said, chuckling. "And here I thought Graeme was the prosaic one."

The Hunter shot her a scowl, which only caused her smile to broaden.

"The gates were shut behind them and have not been opened since," Aisha continued translating Naledi's words as if there had been no interruption or side conversations.

Now it was Davathi's turn to speak.

"My mother asks if the *alay-alagbara* suspect a counter-attack," Aisha said. "Gwala will be expecting retaliation, though he cannot know for certain, or when it will come."

Naledi shook her head and answered in the Issai tongue, with Aisha relaying her words.

"We have not gotten close enough to find out. We believed it prudent to watch and wait until the gate was shut, and then I was to bring word to you while Cebile kept watch on our enemies." Naledi's eyes roved over her fellow *amaqhawe* behind Davathi. "By your presence here, I take it our answer to the *alay-alagbara* will soon be heard?"

Davathi clapped the warrior on one immensely powerful shoulder. "It will."

Aisha stopped translating and looked to the Hunter. "She's telling Naledi of our battle plan—Jumaane's attack on the walls, our intention to slip in through *Isigodi Umlilophilayo*—and of the arrival of the Nyemba and Mwaani."

Naledi's face lit up and she raised her stolen Consortium greatknife high over her head in a triumphant shout that needed no translation. A battle cry was unmistakable in any language.

Davathi allowed Naledi her celebration, a smile on her leonine face, waiting until the warrior lowered her weapon to continue speaking. She did not speak for long but ended with a gesture for Naledi to join the rest of the Issai warriors. When she turned and found the Hunter's eyes fixed on her, Davathi strode toward them.

"He knows," Aisha said before her mother could speak. "I translated Naledi's report to him."

Davathi nodded. "Good." She came to stand before the Hunter's horse, planting her feet solidly and staring up at him. "The arrival of the *alay-alagbara* reinforcements complicates matters, but it does not change the plan."

"No, it doesn't." The Hunter touched a hand to Soulhunger's hilt. "A few hundred more slavers at the wall will make little difference when attacked from behind by their own captives." Casualties among the freed Ghandians would be higher, certainly, but the odds were still weighted heavily in their favor. "But Jumaane needs to know nonetheless."

"On this, we are of a mind." Davathi's expression grew pensive. "His strategy will remain the same, but he must be aware that our enemies are greater in number than previously believed. His forces must be prepared for a fiercer battle."

"So, who's the lucky warrior who gets to bring him word?" The Hunter cocked his head. "Who can be spared, and who is best-served at Jumaane's side?"

Davathi's shoulders tightened. "There is only one I would trust with this task." With those words, she turned to her warriors—and one in particular. "It must be you, Duma." She spoke not in her own tongue, but Einari, as if what she was about to say needed to be heard and understood by the Hunter and his companions more than her own warriors.

The tall, grey-bearded warrior stiffened. "*Nassor*—" he began, also speaking the *alay-alagbara* tongue.

"I do not do this as an insult, Duma."

Davathi stepped up beside the man, who stood half a head taller than her, though she was broader in the shoulder. She reached for his right hand, which held his *nkemba*. He released the sword, leaning it against his hip, and allowed her to cradle his hand in hers and lift it between them.

"You came to my mother's tent when I was not much older than my *indokazi*. I hated you, then. I hated my mother for replacing my father. But over the years, I have come to understand that I was a fool." She spoke the words quietly, yet they rang with sincerity and a depth of emotion the Hunter had only seen directed at her family. "For twenty years, you have offered me nothing but love, respect, and the gift of your wisdom. The day I took the mantle of *nassor* after my mother's passing, do you remember what you said to me?"

Duma's age-lined face crinkled into a smile that bore a strong resemblance to the cheetah that was his namesake. "However far the river flows, it does not forget the spring that gave it life."

"I did not understand it at the time." Davathi inclined her head. "But I do now." She gripped his callused, strong hand in both of hers. "You said it to remind me that though my father and mother were with the *Kish'aa,* they were still within me. Guiding me as they had while they stood at my side."

"And they have guided you true," Duma said with a little bow. "The Issai have not known a better *nassor*—and I say that as one who loved the *nassor* before you."

Davathi smiled. "It is good for both of us she is not alive to hear those words from your lips."

Duma chuckled. "Very good."

Davathi's smile faded, her face once more growing sober. "But it was not just the voices of my mother and father who guided me. Your voice has been ever present, ever welcome, ever needed." She pressed his hand to her heart. "There is no one who I trust more to do the same with Jumaane. To guide him in this battle, to see that he lives beyond tomorrow's sunrise. For it is *he* who will lead the *Ubunye*. The *Kish'aa* have whispered this in my mind. His strength will be needed to lead us all now."

Duma's eyebrows rose. "Davathi." He spoke the word with a tenderness to match hers, a familiarity never before displayed between them. "You are the greater *nassor* by far. Surely—"

"I am *nassor* of the Issai, and Issai I will always be." Davathi shook her head. "But I am also a woman who has had two children taken from her, whose husband even now suffers in *alay-alagbara* chains." Her great shoulders drooped slightly and the pain of a grieving mother and sorrowful wife flashed across her face. "I will lead the Issai as I have all these years, but it will take a younger, stronger spirit to guide the *Ubunye*." She squeezed Duma's hand. "And that young, strong spirit will require the wisdom of an Old Cheetah beloved by his once-ungrateful *ala'indokazi*."

Tears rose in Duma's dark eyes, and one slipped free to track down his weather-lined face. "It would be my honor, *nassor*." His voice, usually so strong, grew hoarse with emotion. He bowed to Davathi, respect evident in the way he bent so deeply. When he straightened, he did not pull his hand free of her grasp. Instead, he stepped forward and pressed his forehead to hers. "Until we meet again, *ala'indokazi*."

Once Naledi and Siyanda gave him instructions on how to find Cebile upon his return with Jumaane's army, Duma set off at a fast, loping run back the way they'd came. A single jubilant cheer rose from the warriors around Davathi. He'd clearly earned the respect and devotion of many of the Issai *amaqhawe*—not least among them the *nassor* herself—and had proven his value in every battle they'd fought. Watching him go, the Hunter had no doubt Duma would relay the message to Jumaane and see Davathi's order carried out.

They did not wait for Duma to vanish among the rocks. No sooner had the cheer trailed off than they set off again with all haste. They had no choice *but* to push the pace if they wanted to reach *Isigodi Umlilophilayo,* the Valley of Living Fire, by nightfall.

Chapter Seventy

Of all the dark and dreary places the Hunter had visited over his long life, none inspired so much dread and foreboding as the petrified forest surrounding *Isigodi Umlilophilayo*.

Perhaps it was the smell. Where forests typically smelled like trees, decaying leaves, and green life, the air here was thick with a stink the Hunter could only describe as rotting stone. An impossibility, he knew. Stone did not rot, but crumbled to dust. Yet to the Hunter's keen nostrils, it seemed as if the petrified trees were on the verge of collapsing and spewing some horrible ichorous ooze.

Or it could have been the silence. The forest was unnaturally quiet. No birds sang among the myriad branches gone to stone. No deer, hares, or foxes skittered amongst the trees that refused to sway in the breeze. The few leaves still clinging to the branches could have been carved from rock, for all they moved. Most, however, lay scattered on the ground in a carpet that crunched underfoot and sent dust billowing up around the Hunter's legs.

The deepening shadows of dusk cast the world around him in a truly eerie light. Not for the first time since dismounting and leaving the horses tucked into a hidden hollow near the forest's edge a quarter-hour earlier, the Hunter found himself wishing they could have made the crossing during full day. The vanishing sunlight left only encroaching darkness. But not the darkness to which the Hunter was accustomed, which he embraced and welcomed as cover. No, this felt ghastly, unnatural. Almost as if the monolithic *Ukuhlushwa Okungapheli* consumed the day's last fading rays, leaving only a gaping nothingness in its wake.

Fool, he cursed himself. *It's just your mind playing tricks.*

Yet he was not the only one to feel the uncanny sensation. All around him, the Issai warriors cast fearful glances through the forest, eyes darting about as if expecting ghosts or monsters to leap out at them from behind the unnaturally motionless trees. To them, this was a place of evil. Not even Davathi, for all her courage, proved immune. More than once, the Hunter caught the flicker of her jaw muscles as she clenched instinctively at an overloud *crunch* of stone leaves collapsing beneath the Hunter's boots. Her great shoulders rippled with tension and her strong hand held her *assegai* in a grip that stopped just short of white-knuckled.

The Hunter's companions, too, seemed warier and more unsettled than he'd ever seen them. Kiara had Deathbite out, as if the solid feel of the hilt in her hand offered some measure of comfort. Something tangible to ground her amidst the aberration through which they moved. Tarek's eyes darted about like a thief in the market square finding themselves surrounded by angry guards. Kodyn's hands twitched nervously toward his belt, as if aching to draw his weapons and strike down an invisible enemy lurking in the shadows.

Only Aisha showed no sign of fear or nervousness. She led the way through the petrified forest with a surety that surprised the Hunter almost as much as the calm air she exuded. She

623

followed Tunde's memories, the Hunter knew. Perhaps she drew on the Bheka *Indaba's* courage as well.

"There." Kiara's whisper came quietly from the Hunter's elbow. She pointed with Deathbite's tip toward a pile of rocks that bore an uncanny resemblance to a tree canopy, complete with shattered branches and cracked leaves formed of stone. "That's where we found him."

The Hunter nodded; he did not know what else to say, nor had any wish to break the cloying silence that hung thick about them.

Kiara must have taken his silence for encouragement, for she continued. "I almost ignored it, you know. I wanted to. Or more like, I didn't want to feel his pain any longer. I wanted to get far away so I didn't have to suffer like he was. But I couldn't. I couldn't leave him to die alone."

The Hunter understood, then. She talked to fill the silence and repel the fear roiling within her. That wasn't his way—he retreated inward, built walls to shield himself—but he didn't begrudge her. Everyone coped in their own way.

"I'm worried," she said, her voice barely audible even in the deathly quiet.

When she did not continue, the Hunter prompted her. "Worried?" Hearing his voice echoing hers served to help dispel her anxiety. "About what?"

"That it'll always be that bad." Her brow furrowed and shadows darkened her eyes. "Once I realized what was happening and started paying attention to the feelings, it just got worse. Well, not always worse. There've been moments of happiness I've been glad to feel." At this, her gaze flitted to Siyanda. "But there've been so many more bad. And I can't help wondering how much worse it can get."

The Hunter's gut twisted into knots. It could get *worse*? Worse than her being so overwhelmed by the emotions of others that she'd all but fallen unconscious to escape the maelstrom? Worse than feeling the agony of the dying Tunde? He could do nothing to help her when—not *if*—it did.

Yet she hadn't voiced her concerns aloud just for him to say he could do nothing. She didn't want empty platitudes, but what else did he have to offer her?

"Whatever happens," he said, though the words felt hollow, "I've got your back."

To his utter amazement, she smiled. "I know you do." She nudged him gently with her shoulder. "Worse it gets, the more I know I can lean on you and you'll hold me up."

The Hunter couldn't help smiling back. It was a tight, strained smile—it felt wrong to experience anything akin to joy or mirth in the eerily silent petrified forest—but genuine. The sight of her spirits lifting did wonders for his own. He stepped easier, the tension in his shoulders easing a fraction. Suddenly, it seemed as if the ghastly shadows retreated, and the last remaining rays of sunlight brightened.

However, even that faint light soon vanished. Darkness settled like a stifling blanket over the forest. Night had fully fallen by the time they emerged from within the petrified trees and gazed out across *Isigodi Umlilophilayo*.

On his last visit to *Ukuhlushwa Okungapheli* days earlier, the Hunter hadn't truly gotten a proper look at the Valley of Living Fire. The plateau upon which the Bondshold sat had blocked his view into the caldera, and he'd been so focused on moving unseen through the Consortium encampment that he'd barely glanced eastward.

Now, however, he had an unobstructed view of *Isigodi Umlilophilayo*, and what he saw sent a ripple of anxiety through him.

The Valley of Living Fire was aptly named. The valley's stone floor was ridged and uneven, threaded through with fissures—some dozens of paces across, others hair-thin—that belched a noxious steam and a brilliance from the fires glowing deep underground. Only this wasn't the typical red-gold light of magma, even the bright yellow of burning flames. The light seeping up from the ground was a sickly, acidic green.

Odder still was the absence of heat. The Hunter had never ventured close to a volcano—at least not in this lifetime he could remember—but every book he'd read described temperatures high enough to char flesh from bone and turn grown men to ash in a matter of seconds. Yet the air within *Isigodi Umlilophilayo* was merely warm. It reeked of the fumes rising through the cracks in the earth, so thick he found it hard to breathe, but far from the simmering torridity he'd expected.

Beside him, the Issai muttered curses and raised their eyes to the starry sky. The Hunter heard more than one beseeching the *Kish'aa* to shield them from whatever evil they believed lurked within the caldera or the Serenii-built tower looming over it.

The Hunter's gaze roved across the Consortium's scaffolding. As Kiara had said, the maze of ladders, ropes, pulleys, boards, and metal framework descended at least one-third of the cliff's height—close to two hundred paces, unless he missed his guess. Hundreds of torches, lanterns, and lamps shone on every level, illuminating the thousands of chained slaves working beneath the stern eyes and cracking whips of the *alay-alagbara*. The sight sent anger flaring through the Hunter's gut.

A whuff of breath from beside him drew the Hunter's attention away from their objective. His eyes settled on Aisha at his side. Her face had lost a measure of its calmness, lines of tension formed at the corners of her mouth and eyes. Her breath came hard and loud through her flaring nostrils.

Sensing his eyes on her, she turned to him. "Tunde's memories of this place are consumed with pain," she said in answer to the questioning look he gave her. She gestured to the nearest rivulet of bright, glowing green bisecting a plate of rock easily twenty paces across and thirty wide. "He was terrified of what would happen if he fell into one of those."

The Hunter grunted. "Best we don't find out, then."

"Seems like the smart plan to me, too." Aisha nodded. "Come on. No sense dawdling here." She sounded as if she were trying to convince herself. With visible effort, she drew in a deep breath, squared her shoulders, and strode down the short hill that descended from the forest's edge toward the valley's rocky floor.

The Hunter followed close at her heels, Kiara and Kodyn right behind him. Davathi and Siyanda were the first of the *amaqhawe* to move, but Naledi and the others did not delay. The Hunter couldn't help but admire the Issai. They remained resolute, moving with determination despite their visible unease. He did not know if he could ever face his own fears so staunchly.

The caldera stretched nearly a full league from east to west, curling around the plateau to form a horseshoe shape. Fortunately, the distance between the petrified forest's edge and the southern edge of the cliff upon which the Bondshold stood was less than half that. The Hunter estimated they could make the crossing in under two hours at a steady pace.

Provided none of us slips or falls into one of those cracks Tunde so feared.

His stomach tightened as they approached the first fissure in the earth. A hiss of steam greeted them, accompanied by a fresh waft of the sulfur-heavy stench rising from far below. The Hunter stopped just at the edge and peered down into the crack. Far beneath the rock upon which he stood flowed a river of what appeared to be glowing green acid. Not fast like running water, nor sluggish like the labored flow of molten stone. It seemed to flow as if in time with the beat of some great heart, rhythmic, measured. Its light, too, brightened at every pulse.

Almost as if it's the blood of some living, breathing thing, the Hunter thought.

According to Aisha's legend, the valley was once home to a creature named *Ugunkubantwana,* said to be firstborn of Ingwe All-Father. He'd fallen into darkness during the calamity that had created the Chasm of the Lost—the battle between the Serenii and the Great Devourer, the Hunter knew from his communion with Kharna in Enarium—and this flowing, pulsing river of green was believed to be his fire-blood. Not molten lava or magma, but something else. Something…alive.

After his encounter with Indombe, and seeing the crystals formed of the great serpent's blood, he couldn't deny the possibility. That only added to his unease.

Grimacing, the Hunter swallowed as if to push down his anxiety and forced his legs to propel him over the first fissure. It was no great effort—the seam in the earth was barely two hand-spans wide, easy enough to hop—but in the half-second the Hunter hung in the air, he tensed as if expecting some invisible force to ensnare him. If *Nuru Iwu* and *Okadigbo* could reach out to him from across vast distances, could they wield more power here, so close to their prison? Power enough to reach up and drag him down into the depths?

Yet his foot landed on solid ground a moment later, and the others made the crossing with no difficulty. Only a few steps later, when the crack was well and truly behind him, did the Hunter realize he'd been holding his breath. He blew it out as quietly as he could. No sense letting the others see his anxiety. They all had worries enough occupying their minds.

The Hunter tore his eyes from the next glowing crack in the earth, just a dozen paces ahead, and fixed his gaze on the cliff in the distance. It suddenly seemed a great deal farther than it had before he stepped foot in *Isigodi Umlilophilayo.*

Keeper's icy tits! he thought, shaking his head. *This is going to be a long night, indeed.*

Chapter Seventy-One

Aisha led the way across the Valley of Living Fire, guided by Tunde's memories. Memories which, it turned out, were far from flawless.

The cracks separating the rock plate upon which they stood from the next were wider by far. The Hunter could make the jump with ease, his powerful Bucelarii legs propelling him across in a single bound that felt almost effortless. Aisha, too, managed the crossing, her leap empowered by the *Kish'aa* power coursing in her veins. The others, however, needed a running start to span the two-pace-wide gap.

The Hunter frowned as he watched the Issai leaping across the fissure. *No way Tunde could have made that crossing in his condition,* he thought, calling to mind the wreckage of the *Indaba's* body. The man had barely been able to keep his feet with Kiara and Tarek carrying him. Even a crack a hand-span across could have proven his undoing.

That was when the Hunter felt it. As the last Issai made the leap, the ground beneath him shifted. It was barely perceptible, so slight he would have missed it had he not been staring at the crack in the earth. But he'd seen it grow wider by the width of a finger, perhaps two, the light emanating from the depths below brightening a fraction.

They're shifting, he realized. Kneeling, he pressed a hand to the surface of the rock plate. It felt solid to the touch, without so much as a vibration or tremor running through it. Given its immense size, that was no surprise. Yet the certainty grew as he studied the fissure they'd just crossed. The light *was* growing brighter, the distance between the two rock plates wider. The shift, though slow, appeared continual. *Almost as if the entire valley is made up of huge chunks of rock floating on that bright green river of whatever it is.*

"Hunter?"

The sound of his name drew the Hunter's attention. Kodyn and Tarek stood looking his way, and beyond them Aisha was leading the rest of their group deeper into the valley.

"What is it?" Kodyn asked, cocking his head. "You feel something?"

The Hunter glanced down at his hand, still touching the rock. "No." He rose smoothly to his feet. "Nothing."

"Then what?" the young Praamian persisted.

Tarek just stared at him with a curious expression.

"The rock plates are shifting," the Hunter explained. "Minutely, but still shifting. Might make the way across a bit harder to navigate." He hurried past the two young men, running to catch up with the women who had pulled farther ahead. Kodyn and Tarek kept pace with him, and were present when he repeated the explanation to Aisha, Davathi, Kiara, and the rest.

627

"Tunde's memories may prove unreliable. We've got to be prepared to backtrack or search for another way across if the gaps are wider than he remembered."

Aisha nodded. "Understood." Her face tightened, shoulders knotting as she set off once more.

The next few crossings proved a simple matter. The first fissure was barely as wide as two of the Hunter's fingers, the second no broader than the length of his sword, and the third so narrow that the two rock plates scraped against each other. The rock plates were larger, too—easily two or three hundred paces across—allowing the Hunter and Aisha to set a swift pace.

However, they were soon forced to slow when the terrain grew rougher, the flat stone giving way to harsh volcanic rock. Again, the memory of Tunde's grim condition sprang to the Hunter's mind. He had no trouble picturing the dying Bheka dragging his weakened body over these rocks, leaving his flesh mangled and sliced to ribbons.

He couldn't help a flicker of admiration. *By the Watcher, the man had a will more unbreakable than the finest steel!* Tunde had clung to life long after a less determined man should have succumbed. *He truly believed in the duty passed down to him, and it sustained him until he was able to pass it on.*

However, he had little time to dwell on the matter further. The approach of the next fissure pushed all thoughts from the Hunter's mind. Their company slowed as they reached the edge and stared at the five-pace-wide gap that separated them from the next rock plate. Steam rose in a thick wall from the river of acidic, glowing green flowing far below, filling the Hunter's nose with a potent sulfuric stench.

He felt eyes on him, and turned to find Aisha looking his way. "What now?" her expression asked, though she did not voice the words aloud. The surety that had guided her path through the petrified forest appeared to have eroded since reaching the Valley of Living Fire.

"Tarek, Kiara, head north." The Hunter pointed in the direction indicated. "Kodyn, you're with me." He beckoned for the young man to follow him southward along the edge of the crack, then looked to Davathi. "We'll see if we can find a narrower crossing this way. Send a couple of your most agile warriors to backtrack and look for another way if we come up empty."

To her credit, Davathi didn't bristle or take offense at the Hunter giving her orders. She merely turned to her *amaqhawe* and issued orders of her own. Two of the younger Issai warriors ran back the way they'd come a moment later.

The Hunter and Kodyn moved south, following the edge of the fissure and circling the rock plate upon which they stood. The gap widened in parts, stretching to nearly ten paces across at one point, but never did it narrow enough to be easily crossed.

"Kind of kicking myself for not bringing more Night Guild supplies from Praamis," Kodyn said, his brow furrowing. "I've got my rope and a few essentials, but nothing that'll work to rig up a safe enough crossing here."

The Hunter shrugged. "It's not on you. At least, not *only* on you." He shot the young man what he hoped was a reassuring grin. "We're all figuring this out together. And we will."

"I know." Despite the words, Kodyn sounded far from certain. His expression remained doubtful. "Things worked out in Shalandra because all of us brought something different to the table." He shook his head. "But it could have gone wrong at any moment. And there's this voice in the back of my mind that tells me something *will* go wrong."

The Hunter couldn't help chuckling at that. "The lives we've lived tend to bring out the fatalistic in us, eh?"

Kodyn's eyebrows rose.

"What?" The Hunter grinned wider. "Surprised? Thieves and assassins tend to have a fair few things in common." He twitched his cloak. "And not just our peerless fashion sense and affinity for sharp things."

Kodyn nodded, a thin smile of his own appearing. "Strange to think about it. All my life, I've been around men and women who'd kill without compunction, who made a living from it. Yet never in a thousand years did I compare myself with the Hunter of Voramis."

"Give yourself a few decades until your legend's as grand as mine," the Hunter said with a wink.

"All due respect, but I don't think I'm cut out for your kind of life." Kodyn's smile wavered. "Or my own, for that matter. I came out here to get away from the Night Guild. To see who I was away from the shadow of my mothers and the darkness in my past."

"From what I've seen, you've more than found your place." The Hunter looked pointedly Aisha's way. "A place where you're both needed and welcomed. Seems like you could do worse than—"

His words were cut off by a triumphant shout from Kiara. The Hunter and Kodyn spun about to find her and Tarek both waving their arms in the air, gesturing toward the spot they'd found for easy crossing.

The Hunter turned back to Kodyn. "Word of advice. The man you were raised to be and the man you become don't have to be the same. Choice is yours, end of the day."

"Aye," Kodyn said, nodding gratefully. "I'll remember that."

Together, they hurried toward the spot where Kiara and Tarek had already leaped over the fissure—barely a pace-and-a-half wide—and the Issai women were preparing to do likewise. By the time the Hunter and Kodyn crossed, the two warriors Davathi had dispatched returned and vaulted across the crack in the earth.

Their journey continued, heading steadily north across the Valley of Living Fire toward the base of the cliff upon which the Bondshold stood. They had not gone far, however, when the earth beneath them began to tremble. Faintly at first, but soon the tremors grew so fierce even the agile Issai warriors found it difficult to stay on their feet.

Then the rumbling began. Deep-throated booms that echoed up from the cracks, accompanied by pulsing waves of steam.

"Not loving this!" Kiara had to shout to be heard over the growing tumult.

No sooner had the words left her mouth than the first gout of acid-green liquid burst up from the ground. It erupted from a crack fifty paces to the Hunter's right, like the burp of some great giant spewing glowing vomit high into the air. When it finally crashed to the ground ten breathless seconds later, it was no longer glowing liquid, but hardened stone that rained down with the clatter of giant hailstones.

That was all the encouragement they needed to break into a run. Aisha raced in the lead, flanked by her mother and Siyanda, Naledi and the other Issai behind them, with Tarek and Kiara at the wings and the Hunter and Kodyn bringing up the rear. With every step, the tremors grew, as if their continued advance angered the earth itself, and more spouts shot up all around them. Some thick as the great trees in *Indawo Yokwesaba*, others thin as a spear shaft, yet every one of them brought torrents of glowing green liquid streaming up from far beneath the valley floor to spray into the night sky.

The Hunter could almost feel the pressure building far beneath the surface. Like some great cauldron simmering on the edge of a boil, the glowing green rivers began to rise. The air grew hotter, the light brighter, the stench of sulfur thicker. The tremors worsened, too. The rock plates across which they ran bucked and heaved with the ferocity of a wild mustang.

A sudden urge to run faster seized the Hunter. He could outpace his companions by far and reach the cliff—and, safety, he hoped—before the river of glowing green rose or a torrent of liquid hurled high into the air rained down on their heads and buried them in stone.

Yet he forced himself to maintain his pace, though his heart hammered a furious beat against his ribs and his mouth was as dry as the stones raining down all around the Valley of Living Fire. He could not abandon Kiara, nor Tarek, nor Kodyn and Aisha, nor Davathi and her Issai. He was a great many things—ruthless, possessed of a bloodlust that often proved impossible to control, and fiercely savage in his execution of vengeance—but he would not be a coward.

He refused to heed the instinct shrieking in his mind, fought to ignore his legs' compulsion to run faster. In stubborn defiance of his own fear, he fell back a step farther, allowing Kodyn to draw just far enough ahead of him that he could keep an eye on the young man and lend a hand in case he fell.

Which was why he had a clear view of the ground crumbling away to dust behind Issai warriors, opening a hole into which two of the rearmost *amaqhawe* plummeted with a shout.

Chapter Seventy-Two

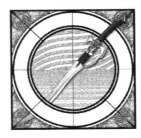

The earth heaved and bucked beneath the Hunter's feet, cracking with an audible *BOOM* of shattering stone. A fissure split the rock plate just five paces in front of him and the force of the roiling tumult far below the surface expanded the newly formed crack in the earth a full pace across in the space between heartbeats.

The two Issai warriors running at the rear of the pack had no time to react before the solid stone beneath their feet vanished and the very air seemed to swallow them. A hissing wall of steam obscured them from the Hunter's view but failed to drown out their terrified cries.

But the Hunter knew where they had been standing, and where their forward momentum would carry them even as they fell. Summoning all the strength he could muster, he dove forward, arms outstretched, hands reaching into the pillar of steam for the women.

His right hand closed around something solid—*an upraised arm!*—and his fingers instinctively tightened. His left hand, however, grasped only empty air.

His dive ended in a graceless sprawl on his belly, and his own momentum sent him sliding straight toward the edge of the newly made fissure in the earth. The weight of the woman he held dragged him inexorably on. Digging his toes into the rock would do nothing to slow his slide. Unless he acted fast, he'd be pulled head-first into the crack after her.

He'd been prepared for precisely this, however. Even as pain flared through him and the air whooshed from his lungs, driven out by the force of his body slamming into the rocky ground, the Hunter dug his right elbow into the ground. His slide slowed, only for a heartbeat, but he was ready for it. His right foot kicked off the hard rock, spinning him around on the ground so he went over the edge feet-first rather than head-first. He extended his legs forward as hard as he could to drive them into the opposite edge of the fissure. The impact slammed his back against the near edge, and his powerful muscles tensed, holding him in place.

For a single terrifying moment, the Hunter was suspended above the abyss, his strength and stubbornness the only thing keeping him from following the Issai woman into the depths. Waves of searing steam rose to scorch his back and the stink of sulfuric steam thickened the air around him. Yet he did not fall. Nor did the woman whose arm he clutched.

A single surge of his powerful Bucelarii muscles hauled the woman bodily upward and hurled her forward. Just far enough her upper body collapsed onto the rock plate. Her hands scrabbled at the rough stone, feet kicking furiously. By the time the Hunter managed to climb to his feet, she had dragged herself fully up onto solid ground. There she lay gasping and clutching the stone as if it was her only lifeline.

Behind the Hunter, a woman screamed. Terror and agony rang in that sound. Spinning, the Hunter found the second Issai hadn't plummeted into the abyss as he'd feared when his hand grasped only steam. In mirror of his own reaction, Kodyn had dived for her and managed to clutch her arm. But though the young man had stopped her from falling, it was all he could do to keep from sliding over the edge himself, much less haul her up. He hadn't the Hunter's strength, and he'd caught the heavier of the two warriors.

The Hunter was at his side in a single step. Bending, he seized the dangling Issai by the wrist and hauled her upward. He had her on solid ground on the far side of the chasm a moment later. Yet what he saw sent horror writhing in his gut.

The woman had hung in the fissure for a few seconds longer than her fellow *amaqhawai*. In that time, the glowing green river had risen enough that it reached her where she dangled. Now, molten stone encased her legs all the way up to mid-calf. Her frantic efforts to scrabble backward and scrape her heels against the rocky ground did her no good. By the time Kodyn gained his feet, the glow had already begun to fade, the liquid hardening to a solid.

The Hunter cast a glance backward. The river had continued rising, bubbling upward toward the surface. "We've got to run!" he shouted. Within the space of ten, perhaps twenty more seconds, it would reach them.

"But she can't!" Kodyn protested.

The Hunter thrust a finger toward the Issai warrior he'd saved. "Get her up and running." He stepped toward the woman screaming and fighting in vain to free her stone-encrusted feet. "I've got her."

The Issai looked up at him, terror in her eyes, and words poured from her mouth in a torrent too fast for the Hunter to decipher.

"Just hold on!" the Hunter shouted. "I'll get you out of here."

He ducked underneath her wildly waving arms, gripped her by the waist, and hauled her onto his shoulders. She roared in fury, beating at his back with powerful blows of her fist, but he ignored the pain and set off at a run. They had no time for her indignation. Better her warrior's pride suffer than meet an untimely end encased in stone.

The blows stopped quickly. At a shout from the woman, the Hunter risked a glance backward. Another gout of glowing green liquid burst upward from the place where they'd been only moments earlier. Had he not picked her up, ignominiously or no, she would have been blown into the air by the fury of that eruption.

After that, the warrior gave him no more trouble. She growled and snarled what could only be curses, but clung to him as if her life depended on it. Which it did. She could not walk in her condition. The Hunter had no idea just how much damage the molten stone had done, but if he put her down, she'd be too slow to escape the flood of glowing green seeping and bursting up from the ground to fill the valley.

The Hunter ran for all he was worth, fighting to keep his feet despite the ground twisting and writhing beneath him and the geysers of molten stone exploding upward all around him. Kodyn and the other Issai, blessedly unharmed, managed to keep pace. Soon, they caught up to the others as they leaped over yet another fissure in the valley.

Some of the Issai glanced back, and a few—Naledi and Davathi—among them even slowed as they spotted the Hunter carrying their companion.

"Go!" the Hunter roared, waving them onward. "We've got to get out of here before this whole valley is flooded."

They needed little convincing. Already, Kiara, Aisha, Tarek, and the Issai farther in the lead were desperately dodging right and left to avoid thin geysers and holes in the rock where the glowing green river bubbled upward. The air was dangerously hot and thick with the choking, sulfuric stench and steam. The very rocks beneath them seemed to crack and break apart like the ice floes in the Frozen Sea shattering beneath the sun. Only destructive force now came from beneath. Churning, seething, bubbling, spouting, and pulsing with the steady rhythm of a great heartbeat.

No, the Hunter realized, breath freezing in his lungs. *Not one heartbeat. Two.*

He knew it, somehow. Perhaps it was something Kharna had implanted in his mind during their communion in the Monolith of Malandria when first he'd seen the Bondshold, or some remnant of the phantasms who had first appeared to him the day he crossed the Chasm of the Lost.

It was *Nuru Iwu* and *Okadigbo.* The brothers were at war, and the power they wielded set the world around them at odds.

The very idea boggled the Hunter's mind. *What manner of creatures are they to command the very earth itself?* The Ghandian legends had called them great spirits, youngest sons of Ingwe All-Father. Some beings older even than the Serenii, perhaps? In Enarium, Kharna had spoken with reverence of the Creators, those who had given life to Einan and the beasts and humans who inhabited it. Any entity—or *entities,* in this case—capable of shaping an entire planet could surely summon the forces of nature to battle at their command.

If that is true, the Hunter couldn't help thinking, *how could anything we do possibly affect the outcome of this battle?*

He had no time to consider the question at greater length, for in that moment, a geyser of acidic green erupted not five steps in front of him, sending a great gout of glowing liquid fifty paces into the air. The Hunter poured on all the speed he could muster. He needed to be as far away as possible before the droplets hardened to stone and rained down on him and the Issai woman he carried.

She howled, whether in pain or fear or fury, the Hunter didn't know. He could barely hear her above the thunderous booming of the earth beneath him and the rush of blood in his ears. His eyes focused solely on the way ahead, seeking a safe path across the increasingly unsteady landscape. A landscape that was even now being submerged by the rising river of shining green.

Then came a sound that filled him with hope. "There!" Aisha's shout rang out above the cacophony, her voice amplified by the power of the *Kish'aa.* Her right hand thrust forward and sent a trail of blue-white light streaking toward the cliffs.

Hope blossomed within the Hunter at the sight. He'd been so focused on his run that he'd barely noticed the distance covered. The cliffs were just a hundred paces away. More than that, the light Aisha sent flying toward the cliffside illuminated an opening carved into the rock a full ten paces above the level of the valley floor. Only a few cracks seeping living, moving stone separated them from the steep incline that rose toward what looked like the mouth of a tunnel or cave.

Even as his eyes lighted on what promised to be their salvation, something hard and heavy struck his back leg. Little more than a glancing blow, barely enough to scratch the skin of his calf. Yet the impact sufficed to knock his foot off-course as he brought it forward. His knee and ankle gave a sharp wrench, accompanied by a horrible *pop.*

Lances of fire shot up the Hunter's leg, searing pain rippling up to his hip. It was all he could do to keep from losing his footing as the leg threatened to buckle beneath him. Only the promise of certain death at his back kept him moving. A howl akin to that of a wounded beast ripped from his lips as he stumbled onward. Slower now, so slow he feared the rising river would engulf him. Indeed, shining green fingers seeped across the rock plate toward him, reaching for his boots with the inexorable hunger of a fire devouring a forest.

The Hunter fought with every shred of willpower to continue running. One step at a time, one foot in front of the other. Every time he placed his weight on his injured leg, the sharp, shooting pain threatened to drain the strength from his muscles. Yet he knew that if he stopped, if he fell, he would die.

Somehow, impossibly, he made it. He half-toppled across the last fissure separating him from the incline—had it been any wider than the breadth of his hand, he might have fallen into its depths, so treacherous was his injured leg—but before he realized it, he was stumbling up the steep hill with the lurching gait of a drunkard.

Only when he reached the top and staggered into the mouth of the tunnel ahead did he finally slow. Just long enough to set down his burden and drop onto his back. There he lay for a moment, gasping, struggling to breathe through the pain coursing through his leg.

But his pain was quickly forgotten at the sound of a cry. "Akosia!"

So sharp and high-pitched was the sound it pierced the Hunter's agony. His eyes snapped open and he looked toward the woman he'd been carrying. She lay on the ground, three of her fellow warriors kneeling at her side. Her eyes were open and staring into the empty air over her head.

Only then did the Hunter realize her screaming and cursing had stopped. He hadn't heard a sound from her since...

His heart sank. *Since whatever it was struck me and nearly knocked me off my feet.*

He sat up, though the movement sent torment lancing through his injured leg. In the light of the night stars and the distant glow of the green molten stone that now engulfed the Valley of Living Fire completely, the Hunter saw the ground beneath her was wet with blood. Far too much of it. As her fellow *amaqhawe* turned her onto her side, the Hunter saw the spot where something heavy—likely a stone falling from the sky—had crushed her skull.

Acid rose in the back of the Hunter's throat and roiled in his stomach. He'd carried her all this way, only for her to die so near to safety. *Just a few seconds longer...*

Even as the grim thought formed in his mind, his gaze fell on her legs. Her upper calves and knees, just above where the stone had encased them, were a horrifying mess. Bubbling blisters, skin burned black and white, blackened veins snaking up her bared thighs.

The Hunter had seen that once before. On Tunde. The Bheka *Indaba* had born similar signs of rot among the myriad wounds and injuries he'd sustained in his escape. Judging by the extent of the damage visible on Akosia, the woman wouldn't have lived through the night.

Her death, though untimely, had been merciful.

Chapter Seventy-Three

The Issai quickly surrounded their fallen comrade. Some knelt to touch their hands to her forehead, while others, Naledi among them, spread their arms wide and turned their faces up to the sky to speak quiet words into the night. Davathi knelt beside the warrior, bent low, and kissed the woman's forehead. Siyanda placed Akosia's spear on her chest and crossed her hands over the weapon.

Aisha alone remained standing. She seemed frozen in place, as if she could not bring herself to join the others in their momentary mourning. Guilt lined her face and filled her eyes with dark shadows.

Her lips moved, but unlike her fellow Issai, she spoke in Einari. "I am sorry." The words were whispered so quietly the Hunter barely heard them over the tumult echoing through the valley below.

Davathi rose to her feet, but paused at the sight of her daughter's face. Gently, she took Aisha by the hand and pulled her forward to join the circle of warriors kneeling around Akosia. Aisha did not resist as her mother placed her hand on the dead warrior's forehead. At the touch, Aisha's head fell forward, her eyes closing.

"Akosia's fate is as the *Kish'aa* willed it." Davathi rested a hand on Aisha's shoulder. "You are many things, *indokazi,* but not even you can know what is to come. Akosia knew the risks of coming here as well as the rest of us."

"I know." Aisha lifted her head, and blue-white sparks danced in her dark eyes. "She has told me as much." She removed her hand from Akosia's forehead, and a hint of the same light shone from beneath her open palm. Her gaze roved around the circle of warriors, now one fewer, all that remained of the Issai *amaqhawe,* before returning to her mother. "Yet when I set out to return to my people after all these years, never did I expect I would lose so many in such a short time."

Davathi rose smoothly, gracefully, and pulled Aisha to her feet. "It is the way of the *amathafa,* Daughter. The *Kish'aa* call us when they call us." She pressed a hand to Aisha's chest, over her heart. "It is our place to accept and be glad for what time we had on this earth. And to make the most of it." She stretched her other hand toward Siyanda. "To gather those we love about us and keep them close, to celebrate every joyous moment and allow room for sorrow and grief. For *all* are reminders that we lived, and lived well."

Siyanda took Davathi's hand in hers, and the *nassor* wrapped an arm around her shoulders. Siyanda pulled the next warrior in line—Sizwe—into a similar embrace, and on it went down the line until all seventeen of the Issai women stood in a circle around Akosia, arms linked and faces turned toward each other.

Davathi spoke a few words in her own tongue, and the women around her repeated it. Aisha joined in on the second repetition, lending her voice to the chorus and the strength of her arms to her mother on her left and Naledi on her right. Every one of the warriors bore wounds—skinned knees from where they'd fallen on the hard stones, scratches on their faces where flying rocks had struck glancing blows, injuries and lacerations from their battles, still-fading bruises from their time in captivity—yet they stood fast, strong, proud. Joined together by common purpose and bound by love of their tribe and each other.

Five times they repeated the ceremonial words, each time raising their voices louder, until on the last, their cry resonated through the open mouth of the nearby cavern and echoed off into the darkness. Yet though they fell silent, they did not break their circle of linked arms. Instead, they looked as one to Aisha

"We follow you, *Umoyahlebe.*" Davathi spoke the words in a strong voice. "The *Kish'aa* guide you, and through you, they lead the way. We are the strong shield at your side and the sharp spear in your hand."

Siyanda spoke in Issai. "Through darkness and danger." She fixed Aisha with a fierce smile, the love in her eyes as intense as the loathing that had gleamed there upon their first encounter. "Beyond death itself. We are yours, honored *Umoyahlebe. Ingani.*"

Sizwe, next in line, took up the words. "*Umoyahlebe. Ingani.*"

Around the circle they went, each repeating the words. Naledi, last in line, wrapped her powerful arm tight around Aisha's neck and squeezed her close to her broad side with such force Aisha could barely catch her breath. Yet there was a smile on Aisha's face and tears of joy filling her eyes. The glow she emanated for once had nothing to do with the power of the *Kish'aa* coursing through her.

"*Ingani.*" She echoed the word, looking at each of her fellow Issai warriors in turn. *Heart sisters,* every one of them.

A quiet snuffle from beside the Hunter drew his attention to Kiara. She wiped moisture from her own cheeks and made no attempt to hide it. The Hunter didn't blame her. Even *he* could feel the emotion emanating from the circle.

Kodyn stood beside Kiara, beaming so broadly his face nearly split in half. Even Tarek was grinning at the sight.

"Come, *Umoyahlebe.*" Davathi released her grip on her and Siyanda's shoulders, and as one, the rest of the warriors lowered their arms. The *nassor* gestured toward the nearby opening in the cliff. "We follow you."

Aisha's confidence, shaken by the uncertainty of their route and the loss of Akosia, returned at her mother's words. She lifted her head and squared her shoulders, visibly lighter now. Raising her hand high over her head, she turned toward the mouth of the tunnel. The blue-white light that blossomed from her fingers illuminated the way ahead and dispelled the shadows. With a newfound certainty, Aisha guided them on their descent into darkness.

The Hunter climbed to his feet in time to join Kiara, Tarek, and Kodyn in bringing up the rear of their small party. The few minutes of rest had done his leg good; already, his ankle had stopped throbbing, and only the occasional twinge shot through his knee. He didn't waste energy accelerating the healing process. His body would see to the damaged tissue on its own.

Light sprang up just ahead of the Hunter. Kodyn held up one of the two alchemical "beamer" lanterns he'd brought from Praamis. It cast only dim light—*thief's light,* Graeme would call it, just enough to drive back the shadows without drawing attention overmuch—but together with the blue-white glow emanating from Aisha's upraised hand, it sufficed to illuminate the tunnel down which they marched.

636

"That chant, the one they repeated five times." Kiara spoke quietly from the Hunter's side, her question aimed at Kodyn. "What were the words?"

Kodyn thought for a moment before speaking. "'Where love shines, darkness cannot take root. While memory lives, none are ever truly gone. And when one warrior's strength fails, the strength of the *amaqhawe* will bear them up.' Something like that."

"Wise words," the Hunter said, nodding.

Kiara shot him a sad smile. "Sounds like the sort of thing Father Reverentus would have said."

It did, indeed. The memory of the Beggar Priest twisted a dagger in the Hunter's belly. Days had passed since last he'd thought about Father Reverentus—not just his death, but the subsequent falling out with the Cambionari that resulted from it—but now, it all came rushing back.

He had no desire to dwell on the matter, and so forced it roughly from his mind. Easier said than done. The image of Father Reverentus' slack, waxy features haunted him nearly as much as the knowledge that *his* daughter was the one wielding the knife. *His* knife, too.

In an effort to banish the memory, he studied the passage down which they marched. Not that there was much to study. The tunnel lacked the precision that marked the handiwork of the Serenii. Instead, it was rough-hewn and uneven, as if formed from the strange glowing green river as the magma cooled and hardened. Its steep angle of descent certainly lent credence to that notion. Even molten rock followed the path of water and flowed downhill.

That thought was followed by a grimmer one: what if the opening had been carved from the rock by some great beast that feasted on stone? No such creature existed to his knowledge, and if it had, he suspected Kiara would have made mention of it. Or one of the Issai, if the creature was mentioned only in Ghandian lore and legend, like *Ugunkubantwana,* the *Okanele,* or *Nuru Iwu* and *Okadigbo.* The Hunter's encounter with Indombe had proven such beings *could* exist.

For a moment, he was tempted to hurry to join Aisha at the front, to push through the ranks of Issai warriors at her back. They had no idea what dangers lay ahead. Better he be at the front to face them first. After all, he had the best chances of survival.

If she can take down a slashwyrm single-handed, he thought, *she's more than capable of dealing with anything hungry lurking in the darkness ahead. At least holding them off long enough for me to join the fight.* Just to be certain, he checked his weapons to ensure they slid free of their sheaths.

The thought rang more than a little hollow. He instinctively glanced over his shoulder, up the rising incline toward the mouth of the cave. Brilliant green light lit up the darkness beyond, and the thunderous tumult from *Isigodi Umlilophilayo* echoed down the passage, washing over them with deafening force. Any creatures or entities that could cause such upheaval in the very earth itself could be well beyond even the power she'd demonstrated.

Yet still, he held himself back. For in the moments the Issai had gathered beside her, the Hunter had come to understand the truth: the time had come for Aisha to lead. On her own. Not just because she alone knew the way through the passages, following the trail left by Tunde's memories.

From what the Hunter had learned of the *Umoyahlebe,* theirs was a position of respect and authority within the tribes. Aisha had already done much to earn the respect of her people. Davathi's proclamation that they followed her lead went a long way toward imparting authority. But she would need to prove herself worth following. The Hunter placed no stock in such things as destiny or fate, but even a blind man could see that Aisha was meant for greater things than just breaking heads for the Night Guild's brothels or wielding a spear in some pointless tribal battle.

Perhaps this is what she meant when she said her uhambo loguquko *was not complete,* the Hunter thought. *She is not yet who she is meant to be.*

Once the thought lodged in the Hunter's mind, he could not shake it. Indeed, it took root and grew larger with every step he took. Somehow, he knew with a certainty he could not explain, that whatever she'd face ahead would be necessary for her to complete the transformation that had begun the day she was first taken from her people. He'd watch her back, as would Kiara, Kodyn, her mother, her cousin, and everyone else following her into darkness.

But ultimately, it was *her* battle to fight. The final trial she had to face on her own.

Chapter Seventy-Four

The thundering of *Isigodi Umlilophilayo* diminished as the Hunter and his companions descended deeper into the bowels of the earth, but tremors still shook the ground underfoot and the walls of the tunnels around them.

The Hunter felt foolish, marching down the steep rocky slope when they should have been *ascending* toward the Bondshold above. The rough volcanic stone would offer sufficient hand and footholds that even the Issai, accustomed to running the flatlands of the *amathafa,* could manage it. Were it not for the risk of being spotted, of course. Kiara had been right in her assessment: the scaffolding descended half the distance from the plateau above, encircling the entire base of the Serenii-built tower. They'd be spotted climbing long before they reached the lowest level. Losing the element of surprise would make the battle to come virtually impossible.

Had the Hunter been attempting it alone, he might have chosen that route nonetheless. But he was not alone. There would be danger aplenty to come without taking unnecessary risk before they ever closed with their foe. The army under Jumaane's command would even now be making their presence seen around the Consortium's camp and pulling all focus in their direction. They'd keep the *alay-alagbara* occupied long enough for the group following at Aisha's back to strike at their enemy's unguarded underbelly. Tactically, it was the smartest play for all involved—the warriors of *both* Ghandian forces.

And still, the Hunter could not help but wonder, *Will we make it in time?* The Valley of Living Fire had been utterly silent and lifeless the night he'd slipped through the Consortium camp; this was no ordinary tumult. The twin spirits of *Nuru Iwu* and *Okadigbo* warred for dominance. No telling how long entities thousands of years old could do battle—hours, days, weeks?—but with every quake, the Hunter felt the urgency growing within him.

Fortunately, he was not alone in feeling the need to hurry. Aisha led the way down the sloping stone path at a pace just short of a run. Tunde's memories had proven flawed already once this night. The Hunter suspected that the uncertainty of what lay ahead kept her from moving faster.

Her caution proved their salvation. They had gone but a few hundred paces downhill before the path leveled out and opened into a broad cavern with the roof rising to nearly twice the Hunter's height overhead. The trail they followed, however, ran straight across a chasm that stretched into the darkness to the left and right far beyond the circle of Aisha's *Kish'aa* light. A bridge of stone formed the way across, but it spanned less than half a pace at its widest section.

Aisha skidded to a halt just at the edge of the chasm, the Issai stopping at her heels. The warriors hesitated, muttering among themselves as they eyed the pitch blackness on either side of the far-too-narrow path of stone that was their only hope of advancing.

"Across vast gulfs." Aisha's voice rebounded from the stone ceiling echoed off into the vast depths. She lifted her head high, squared her shoulders. "If Tunde could cross it in his condition, what have we to fear?"

She led the way onto the bridge, stepping with caution, arms outstretched for balance like an acrobat walking a tightrope. Tension knotted her shoulders and her spine was stiff, yet her fear did not slow her. One foot in front of the other, she made the crossing—little more than twenty paces—and stepped onto solid stone on the far side of the chasm.

"Easy!" she called back, a smile on her face.

The Hunter didn't miss the slight shake in her voice, though. Anyone would be afraid of such a crossing. Fiery hell, even *his* belly knotted at the thought of plummeting off the narrow bridge to an agonizing death Keeper-only-knew-how-far below. But that made her courage all the more impressive. Only a truly brave soul could swallow their fear as she had.

The source of that courage became readily evident as Davathi made the crossing next. She, too, kept her pace steady though her steps were sure, her posture upright. Aisha could not have become anything other than she was after growing up around one with the strength and fortitude that the Issai *nassor* possessed in abundance.

Naledi made to go next, but Siyanda was the quicker. She sprang out onto the narrow bridge and raced across it with the speed any oryx would envy. The Hunter's breath caught in his throat when one of her feet landed a hair too close to the edge, but the stone beneath her held fast and bore her weight. With a breathless laugh, she darted onto the solid ground at the far end and fell into the arms of her aunt and cousin, basking in their cheers and those rising from among her fellow *Issai*.

With that, the tension was broken. For a few moments, the loss of Akosia was forgotten as the Issai warriors turned the crossing into a contest to see who could brave the chasm with the most graceful feat of agility and reach the far side fastest. All but Sizwe and Naledi. Heavily-muscled Naledi was far from the swiftest, but her steps proved most certain. Warriors like Sizwe did not live long if they allowed themselves to be swept up by acts of daring. She made the crossing with an almost solemn reverence for the perilous depths on either side of her and strode calmly onto the ground beyond to join the rest of the *amaqhawe*.

"Guess it's our turn, then." Kodyn gave the Hunter a broad smile and wink. "Always loved the heights of the rooftops in Praamis, running along the Hawk's Highway. Picked up a trick or two."

Turning, he took two long steps and sprang high into the air. His legs tucked into his chest and his body spun about twice before he landed on the tiptoes of one foot, his other foot outstretched to the side. The gasps that earned from the Issai turned to raucous cheers as he flipped once more and walked the rest of the way across on his hands with the ease of one who'd mastered the tumbler's art. He reached the far side and stood to raucous shouts from the Issai warriors and hands clapping his back.

Kiara chuckled. "I'd call him a show-off, but by the Watcher, he bloody earned the right to show off with skills like that."

"Aye." The Hunter nodded, a grin finding its way onto his face as well. "Almost makes me wish I'd crossed first, because my walk will look bloody boring by comparison."

Kiara jabbed a finger into his chest to hold him back. "You wait your turn." She turned to make the crossing. "And don't think for a minute I don't know you're watching my ar—"

Her words cut off in a panicked gasp as she stumbled into Tarek. The young Elivasti, who'd stood watching Kodyn's display with only a faint grin, had made to cross at exactly the same moment as her. They'd collided and Kiara had been caught off-balance. Her outstretched foot struck only empty air and she had toppled forward.

The Hunter reacted with speed that should have been impossible, even for him, borne entirely out of the necessity to save one dear to him. He darted forward and snatched at her wildly windmilling arms. His fingers reflexively tightened around her vambrace and he planted his feet hard, driving his heels into the stone underfoot and bracing his legs to support her weight.

For the space of a single heartbeat, she dangled over the chasm, one heel grounded but the other supported by nothing, one grasping hand clawing at the empty air. Then the Hunter hauled hard, pulling her back toward him so forcefully she collided with his chest. He wrapped his arm around her and held her tight. Her arms encircled his torso, squeezing so hard his ribs protested. Her breath was shaky and he could feel the furious gallop of her heart beating even through her armor.

"I-I'm so sorry!" Tarek stared wide-eyed, his face utterly devoid of color. Horror stained his expression and his arms seemed to be grasping for her, though he had to know he would have been too late. "I-I didn't—"

"It's okay." Kiara reached a hand for the young man, though the Hunter noted the faint tremble of her fingers as she gripped his outstretched forearm. "I'm fine. I'm fine. See?" She pushed off the Hunter a bit more forcefully than might have been necessary, and her jaw clenched tight as she stood on her own and spread her arm wide. "No one got hurt."

Tarek's eyes dropped to his feet and he seemed unable to stop shaking his head, his words coming out in a murmur unintelligible to even the Hunter's ears.

"Tarek." Kiara stepped toward the young man, took him by the scruffy-bearded chin, and lifted his face to a level with hers. "No one got hurt. That is all that matters now."

Tarek's face flushed a deep red, and his eyes flashed with anger. Doubtless directed at himself for his clumsiness. He would beat himself up for that mistake, the Hunter knew, much as he'd done after leaping into Indombe's pool, though the fault had not been his.

"Come on, Lad." The Hunter clapped Tarek on the shoulder, giving him a smile that he hoped hid the racing of his own heart. "No one blames you. Best we get on with getting on. Night's not getting any younger."

"Aye." Tarek gave a jerky nod of his head, turning away to hide the shame on his face. He made the crossing without ever lifting his eyes from the narrow stone bridge. The cheers and shouts that greeted him on the other side sounded halfhearted to the Hunter's ears, but the Issai and Kodyn slapped him and shouted encouragement in their own tongue.

"You good?" the Hunter asked in a voice pitched low for Kiara's ears only.

"I am." She turned her face up to meet his, and the Hunter saw the glimmer of fear that had not yet faded from her eyes. "Bloody close thing, though."

He'd half-expected her to make some joke—scolding him for coming to her aid when she clearly had it under control. The fact that she *didn't* told him just how afraid she'd been. And with good reason.

"If we were in one of Graeme's Taivoro romances, I'd say something witty and poetic here, something like, 'I'll always be there to catch you if you fall.'" The Hunter leaned down and pressed a kiss to her lips. "But that's not me. I'm just the fellow who nearly had his heart ripped out, and is damned relieved to see you on solid ground."

Kiara smiled, and with that, her fear dissipated further. "Never needed a romantic hero." She rose on her tiptoes and kissed him back. "More than happy with the fellow I've got." A gentle shove propelled him toward the crossing. "You go first. I'll follow once you're across."

The Hunter wanted to refuse. No, he wanted to *insist* that they cross together. That way, he could cling to her hand, to hold her up as she made the crossing. But he didn't. And she didn't need him to.

He made the crossing with no difficulty, though he couldn't help marveling again at Tunde's fortitude. Crossing that narrow span in darkness in his condition was a feat even the Hunter himself would find hard-pressed to match. The *Indaba's* stubbornness could rival that of any Bucelarii or Abiarazi.

Or Kiara herself. The woman strode across the narrow stone trail as calmly as Sizwe, with a bounce to her step nearly as light as Siyanda's. Almost as if she hadn't just nearly fallen over the edge.

The Hunter's heart swelled at the sight of such courage—feigned or real, it made no difference. *Keeper's teeth, how I love that woman!*

Chapter Seventy-Five

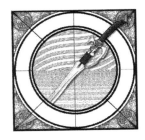

Aisha led the way deeper into the tunnels that wended through the stone far beneath *Ukuhlushwa Okungapheli*. Beyond the chasm, the passage grew so narrow they had to walk in single file. Within the cramped space, the broadest-shouldered of their group—Davathi, the Hunter, and Naledi—could not walk straight on, but had to twist to avoid scraping against the stone walls. As the tallest of the group by a good measure, the Hunter had to stoop slightly or else his head would have struck the low-hanging ceiling.

A dozen paces later, they reached a spot where the tunnel broke off into four branches. Without hesitation, Aisha led them down the left-most passageway. She moved with more confidence than before. Perhaps Tunde's memories had grown clearer or she merely pretended certainty. Whatever the case, the rest of them followed her without question. She was their best hope—perhaps their *only* hope—of navigating the underground maze and finding a way out.

They traveled in relative silence. Between the narrow confines, the rumbling of the ground underfoot, and the growing anxiety over the battle to come, none of their small company seemed in a talkative mood. The only sounds filling the passage were the shuffling of bare and booted feet, the steady breathing of the warriors, and the wooden *clack* or metallic *clink* of their weapons striking the stone walls.

But not for long. A new sound soon filtered toward them. At first, the Hunter mistook it for the earth's quaking, which hadn't stopped since they'd begun their descent. Or, perhaps, the rush of his pulse in his ears. Yet as it grew steadily louder, he recognized it for what it was: fast-flowing water.

Within minutes, the way once more opened up before them. They strode into a cavern shorter and narrower than the one containing the chasm. Where the last might have been hollowed out by a collapse, this chamber had clearly been carved from stone by the river that cut through it. Indeed, there was little more to it than a narrow ledge on either side of the river's edge, and the openings where the river flowed out of the cavern's western mouth and vanished into the stone to the east.

There, their advance ground to a halt. The Issai warriors murmured amongst each other, and the Hunter did not need to understand their Issai tongue to recognize the apprehension in the glances they cast at the river. And with good cause. Its flow was fast, the surface broken here and there by sharp-tipped rocks that churned the water around them white. The crossing would not be easy.

Fortunately for them, a solution was not too difficult.

"You got that rope?" Aisha asked Kodyn.

"Aye." The young man untied the length of finger-thick cord he always wore wrapped about his waist.

The Hunter took the rope and slid through the group of warriors milling about the river's edge. The river's flow was fast—dangerously so—but it was not overly wide. Perhaps ten paces wide at the narrowest point. Too broad for even his powerful muscles to cross in a running leap. Yet he could swim across and anchor the rope for an easy crossing.

He presented his plan to Aisha and Davathi—more out of politeness in front of their warriors than any real need for their permission—earning their assent. It proved a simple matter to uncoil the rope and pass one end to the burly Naledi. The other, he took for himself. But before he could tie the rope to his belt and leap into the water, Tarek appeared from among the Issai warriors and marched straight up to him.

"Let me." The young Elivasti held out a hand for the end of the rope the Hunter held.

The request surprised the Hunter. The fast-flowing river would not be easy to swim, even for his powerful muscles.

"You can swim that?" Kiara asked, brow furrowing.

Tarek nodded, confident. "No problem."

The Hunter understood Kiara's confusion. Since Indombe's pool, Tarek had made clear he didn't know how to swim. Yet now he was intent on making what amounted to a surprisingly challenging crossing?

But even as the Hunter opened his mouth to pursue the line of questioning, movement on the opposite side of the river drew his attention. No, he realized as his eyes darted in that direction, not beyond the river. *Above* it.

Light sprang into existence in the air just above the water's frothy, foam-churned surface. It was not the blue-white light of the *Kish'aa,* nor the glowing green of the burning river that had risen up to swallow *Isigodi Umlilophilayo.* Instead, it shone a brilliant red, like sunlight glimmering through the finest ruby.

And it came from a pair of horns, four hooves, and two burning equine eyes.

The Hunter took an instinctive step backward as *Nuru Iwu's* horse-creature materialized not five paces from where he stood. Always before, they had manifested at a vast distance, yet now the spirit beast was close enough he could all but reach out and touch it. So close the crimson glow it radiated nearly blinded him.

But *Nuru Iwu* was not alone. No sooner had the horse sprung into life before him, *Okadigbo* followed. The sinuous, reptilian form emerged from the fast-flowing river without so much as a splash or droplet of water. Its massive jaws opened wide to reveal row upon row of razor-sharp teeth. Huge dark eyes fixed on the brilliant white horned stallion and its bony frill stood straight up as the monstrosity flew through the air toward *Nuru Iwu,* mouth wide to bite off its head.

Nuru Iwu reared up in a truly horse-like motion, and its ruby fore-hooves slammed into the underside of *Okadigbo's* wide-open jaw. The impact felt like a thunderclap and sent a wall of power exploding outward with such force the Hunter half-expected to be blown from his feet. Yet it did not strike him down. Indeed, he barely felt a rustle of breeze against his face, so faint it could have been kicked up by the river's flow.

In the split second when he instinctively blinked, the creatures vanished. One moment they were there, *Nuru Iwu's* light brightening the cavern and *Okadigbo's* serpentine form lashing at the water; the next, they had disappeared, and the cavern fell dark once more.

Surprise held the Hunter rooted in place for two full seconds. Time enough for Tarek to snatch the rope from his hand and dive head-first into the river.

The Hunter tried to grab for the young man, but his hands met only empty air. His fear proved needless, for a moment later, Tarek's head and arms broke the surface. He surged toward the far end of the river with impressive strength, his strokes swift and powerful. The current had only time enough to carry him a few paces downstream before he reached the other side and scrambled dripping-wet onto the rocky ledge beyond.

A cheer rose from the Issai, and the warriors stamped their feet and slapped their knees hard as they chanted—no doubt praising Tarek for his bravery. Tarek turned back to them with a calm look on his face, but the Hunter knew the young man well enough to recognize the façade of bravado. In truth, he couldn't blame Tarek. After nearly knocking Kiara off the ledge, it made sense he'd risk his own neck to earn back a measure of his companions' esteem. Such was the folly of youth to believe that a single accident could cause the foundation of trust and respect his actions over the last weeks had built to crumble to dust.

Foolhardy or not, Tarek had done well. Between him and Naledi, they held the rope firm enough for Aisha to make the crossing with minimal difficulty. She pulled herself hand over hand along the rope, kicking her legs to propel herself forward and upstream against the current. Once across, Aisha lent her strength to Tarek for Siyanda to make the crossing next. One by one, the Issai warriors hauled themselves hand over hand across the river. Though it was slower going than the Hunter would have liked, it was better than risking a swim.

By the time Kodyn made the crossing, only the Hunter, Naledi, and Kiara remained behind. All throughout, Kiara had watched the growing group on the far side of the river with a thoughtful expression. Though the frown on her lips and furrow in her brow were so slight as to be barely noticeable, the Hunter knew her well enough to recognize the look. One might even call it a "brooding" look if one was so inclined. For all her teasing, she was as prone to brooding as he.

"Go," he told Naledi, who had stood solid as a rock, legs braced against the weight of her fellow warriors. "I will anchor the rope, then make the crossing last."

Naledi nodded, and what *might* have been relief flashed through her eyes. She had far too much of a warrior's pride to show just how exhausting the effort of supporting her comrades' crossing had been.

The Hunter wrapped the rope twice about his waist and braced his legs against the stone. Naledi leaped into the river and hauled herself across, her massive arms making quick work of the task despite the powerful current.

But the Hunter didn't watch her go. Instead, he shot a glance at Kiara. "Odd, isn't it??" He spoke quietly, though he needn't have made the effort. The rushing of the river drowned out all save the loudest of the Issai's cheers at Naledi's safe crossing.

Kiara looked at him sidelong. The corners of her eyes crinkled and fine lines appeared around her mouth as she pursed her lips. "Could be nothing."

The Hunter raised an eyebrow. "Could be something."

"Maybe." Kiara twitched her right shoulder in a shrug. "The way Tarek always stayed close to the shore back at Nsukeja Lake, or how he flopped around in Indombe's basin, I would've sworn he couldn't swim."

The Hunter's gaze snapped back across the river toward where Tarek now stood near the mouth of the tunnel leading deeper into the underground, having been relieved of the task of anchoring the rope by Sizwe and three of her fellow *amaqhawe*. The young man had his back turned to the others and stared off into darkness, his posture intent, wary of danger.

"He can't." The Hunter frowned. "Told me so himself that night at the falls."

Kiara shot the Hunter a curious look. "Learned fast, then."

"I'll say!" The Hunter stared at Tarek. There couldn't have been many opportunities for him to practice. Perhaps Kodyn had given him some pointers during their time in the marshes of *Indawo Yokwesaba?*

Kiara made a sound partway between a snort, grunt, and snuff of air. "Thought it was odd. Might be I'll ask him about it, once this is all over." She dismissed the notion with a wave and a shake of her head.

The Hunter nodded. "Aye." He pushed the thought aside for later. "Get yourself across." He gestured to the river with a thrust of his chin. "I'll be right behind you."

Kiara made the crossing with little difficulty, and once she was on dry stone, the Hunter prepared himself to swim the river. He took a running start and sprang as far out as he could. He flew nearly half the river's breadth before hitting the water.

For a brief moment, as the current carried him downward, he caught a glimpse of something below him. Dots of golden light shone like pinpricks so far beneath the water's surface they could have been stars in the sky. The Hunter's heart clutched at the sight. He knew the color of that light all too well. He'd never forget it. Crystals that emitted the same glow had nearly killed Kiara at Zamani Falls.

The sight sent the Hunter swimming toward the far riverbank with all the strength he could muster. The river's fast flow was far from the greatest threat he imagined within the watery depths. He had no idea how far down the river cut into the stone, nor any desire to find out. Better he was out of the water long before he discovered whether some waterway deep, deep underground connected this place of the Serenii with Indombe's fathomless pool.

Chapter Seventy-Six

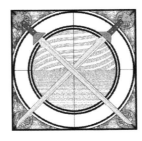

Beyond the river, the tunnel began carving a sinuous path through the earth, like the loops of a great serpent wending its way through stone. *Or,* the Hunter thought, *like Okadigbo's monstrous form.*

Were it not for the rough, unhewn walls and uneven floors and ceilings, the Hunter might have believed them cut intentionally by human hands. Yet it could simply have been formed by water from the underground river wending its ever-widening way through naturally-encountered fissures in the stone.

He had little time to consider the matter further, for within a few hundred paces, they reached another chamber. Its height was far from impressive—the stone ceiling sloped gently downward nearer the center—nor its breadth, barely fifty paces wide. But it was the *depth* that stole the Hunter's breath. And what rose from it.

They had no need of Aisha's magical light, for the entire cavern was aglow with a blue-green light as familiar to the Hunter as the briny-and-floral scent that hung thick in the air.

Intambelu!

A gasp rose from among the Issai warriors. Aisha had spoken of *Uhumi Wolandle,* the cavern behind the waterfalls, as "the ocean's last gift to Ghandia." Yet the vines that had grown there seemed paltry in comparison to this place. The chamber descended into a pit that appeared at least a hundred paces deep, and glowing *intambelu* sprouted from every nook and cranny, grew in a mess so dense that no stone remained visible. Some of the vines farther down appeared to be as thick as the ancient trees growing in *Indawo Yokwesaba.* Every one of them emitted that same gentle light, yet their abundance and majesty filled the Hunter with a sense of awe far grander than he'd felt in *Uhumi Wolandle.*

Reverent whispers passed among the warriors, and even Davathi was rendered speechless by the sight. All of the Issai stood staring spellbound at the natural beauty that spread out before and below them as far as the eye could see.

Only Tarek appeared unmoved. He strode toward the edge of the cliff and stared down. "Looks like the climb shouldn't be too hard. The vines will make for easy hand and footholds, and they're thick enough we'll have little trouble making the descent."

The sound of his voice seemed almost irreverent given the hush that had fallen over the Issai. Yet he wasn't wrong. The Hunter, too, peered over the edge and found the young Elivasti's assessment correct. In truth, he could make the climb down blindfolded and with both arms tied behind his back. The vines grew so thick and large from the stone walls that even a toddling babe could navigate them.

"I'll lead the way." Without waiting for acquiescence or argument, Tarek stepped off the edge and dropped three paces to a vine easily twice as thick as both of his legs together. From there, he slid down the sloping length of the vine and sprang to another. But instead of landing on his feet, he merely caught the vine in his hands, dangled for a moment, then dropped to another vine below.

Well, that's one way to do it, the Hunter thought wryly. The young man's eagerness did him credit. He had the right of it, the Hunter supposed. For all the beauty in the chamber, they had greater concerns to drive them onward. They could enjoy the view *and* keep moving at the same time.

He followed Tarek down the wall of tangled vines. As the young man had predicted—and demonstrated—the descent proved a simple matter. The *intambelu* grew so thick the Hunter had little doubt they could bear up under thrice his weight. With his powerful Bucelarii muscles to absorb the impact, he could drop ten and twenty paces at a time. He reached the vine-covered floor at the base of the cliff wall a full five seconds ahead of Tarek.

If the young man took umbrage at the Hunter's showing him up, he kept it to himself. His expression was tight, but he gave the Hunter an amiable nod as he leaped down beside him.

But the Hunter had intentionally hastened his descent. While the Issai, Kiara, and Kodyn occupied themselves climbing down, he wanted a moment to talk to Tarek alone.

"Everything good, Lad?" the Hunter asked, his voice quiet enough only Tarek could hear him.

"Of course." Tarek gave him a curious look. "Why wouldn't it be?"

The Hunter frowned. Truth be told, he had no reason to suspect otherwise. Yet *something* about the lad struck him as off. He couldn't quite put his finger on what, though.

"Not sure," he said, shrugging. He racked his brain for some valid reasoning or excuse to offer. What he came up with felt lame, but it would have to do. "All that back there with the Valley of Living Fire nearly burning us up, it's enough to set anyone on edge. Just wanted to check in and make certain you're solid."

"Close call, more than once, I'll admit." Tarek gave him a tight smile. "Shook me up, sure. But I'm over it."

The Hunter stared at the young man, trying to get a measure of what was going on in his head.

Tarek met his gaze levelly. "Truth be told, I'm just eager to get on with the battle ahead. Or, to put it honestly, get the battle *over* with. Been fighting and running without stop for a long time." He rubbed the bridge of his nose with two fingers. "I feel like I could eat a whole *zabara* and sleep a week. And that's just to start with."

The Hunter chuckled. "Aye, I know how you feel there." He allowed himself to relax. There was no sign that anything was amiss. Tarek was just reaching the edge of his limits, as were they all. "With luck, we'll be out the other side of this soon enough. And I don't just mean this whole odd underground maze." He gestured to the vine-covered pit surrounding them. "I'll be glad when the Consortium and the Order are put in the ground for good, and this whole mess is behind us. Likely I'll join you for a feast of roast *zabara*." He held up a finger. "On second thought, might be I'll stick with raya stew. *Zabara's* like as not to be tougher than horse."

That earned a grin from Tarek. "Wait until you try it the way Soaring Hawk Clan makes it. Soaking it in mare's milk does wonders to soften up even the stringiest hock. And what that doesn't mask, the spices do."

The Hunter raised an eyebrow. "Next time I pass through the Hrandari Plains, I'll have to give it a try."

If he'd wanted to say more or press the matter further, he never got the chance. Kodyn and Aisha dropped lightly to a nearby vine, followed by Siyanda, Davathi, and a few of the more agile Issai. Kiara joined them soon, until only the bulky Naledi remained clinging to the wall. Much to the delight of her smaller companions. The Issai warriors called up in their own tongue—what *could* have been shouts of encouragement, but equally likely were jests and good-natured insults. More than likely the latter, given Naledi's growled answers.

Soon enough, however, even Naledi reached the bottom, earning a definitely mocking round of applause from her fellow *amaqhawe*. To the Hunter's surprise, even Davathi joined in. Not even the seriousness of their mission could fully suppress the Issai's natural exuberance and joyousness in living. Indeed, as they wended their way across the field of vines, one of the warriors—a woman whose name the Hunter didn't know—took up a song. Trilling notes and a lighthearted melody echoed from the cavern ceiling high above. One by one, the rest of the Issai joined in, clapping quietly and stamping their foot with every fourth step.

The Hunter had to admit that though it was far from the stealthiest sneak attack he'd carried out on an enemy position, it certainly was one of the most entertaining. And he supposed Aisha would have hushed her fellow tribeswomen had there been any risk of being overheard. Tunde's memories likely told her they still had a long way to go before they reached their destination.

Something odd caught the Hunter's attention. The vines around the singing Issai seemed to ripple, pulse, and flow in time with the music. At first, he thought it was just his mind playing tricks on him. Yet the more he watched the *intambelu* beneath the warriors' feet, the more convinced he became. The vines weren't just alive as all plants were; they responded to the song.

Then the vines began to shift in earnest. Like serpents—*serpents of earth, as Tunde called them!*—the *intambelu* writhed and squirmed. The Hunter instinctively reached for his sword, ready to draw and hack his way free if the vines threatened to ensnare him. Yet there was no need. The vines did not reach up to wrap around their feet. Instead, they shifted underfoot like the tide rolling in sea's edge. Only the tide that stirred them was the Issai's *song*.

His eyes widened as the vines squirmed into two familiar figures. One, a horse-like creature with twin horns rising from its forehead and a goat-like beard. The other, a serpentine figure that swirled and writhed around it. *Nuru Iwu* eternally swirled through the pattern with the swiftness of the animal he chose as his avatar, *Okadigbo's* monster ever seeking to ensnare it. In vain. Indeed, everywhere the Hunter looked, he could see the distance between the two growing greater. *Nuru Iwu* gained ground on *Okadigbo*. The vines depicting *Okadigbo* doubled and tripled in number, growing like a tidal wave of pulsing blue-green. Yet the horse-creature outpaced it.

The Hunter felt the thrumming in his belly. The battle between the twin brothers had begun during their crossing of *Isigodi Umlilophilayo*, yet it had not diminished. Indeed, from what he saw, the balance had tipped in the younger twin's favor.

He didn't know what to make of that. A part of him felt relieved—a creature as repulsive as the reptilian monstrosity *Okadigbo* had chosen for his form spoke of a spirit as vile as the phantasmal flesh. Yet Tunde's admonition rang in his mind. If the Order of Mithridas was unnaturally tilting the scales in favor of *Nuru Iwu*, the consequences to all on the *amathafa* could be disastrous.

The images vanished a moment later. Though the vines continued twisting, swaying, and writhing in time to the Issai's song, they no longer depicted the combat between the two brothers. But the Hunter couldn't shake the sense of urgency that had taken root within him and grew larger with every step across the field of vines.

649

"Tell me you're seeing it, too."

The Hunter jumped, startled by the voice at his elbow. Turning, he found Kodyn staring at him with a look of mixed wonder, alarm, and dread.

"It?" he asked, caught off guard by the question.

"The figures." Kodyn's vague gesture encompassed the entire pit with all its myriad vines. "The horse and the serpent."

The Hunter sucked in a breath. "You see them?"

Kodyn nodded. "I do. And I'm not the only one."

The Hunter glanced around him. The Issai had not abandoned their song, but a few voices had trailed away, and those women now stared around them with a look much like Kodyn's. Aisha, too, was staring, though Siyanda looked at her with a confused expression. Kiara's face had taken on that same seriousness that had gripped her when she'd spoken of *Okadigbo's* entreaties the morning after they'd marched away from *Isigodi Zabara*.

His eyes went wide. "All of them?"

"I heard them whispering to each other," Kodyn said. "They wonder if they are going mad, or if they truly are seeing the spirits of *Nuru Iwu* and *Okadigbo*."

"Definitely the latter." The Hunter's gut clenched. "And if more than just a few of us are seeing them, it means either we're getting closer, or *they're* growing stronger."

If, as the Hunter suspected, it was the latter, that meant *Nuru Iwu* might soon very well break free of his prison, and the *amathafa's* "time of great strife" would truly be upon them.

Chapter Seventy-Seven

At the Hunter's urging, their group picked up the pace. The vines settled once more to their gentle pulsing as the Issai's song fell silent, no longer moving or squirming underfoot, making for faster going. However, they did not get far before the Hunter felt a chill in the air. Barely noticeable at first, little more than a whisper of cold, but growing more and more pronounced the deeper they went. Soon, the Hunter's breath misted in the air before him and the bite of ice against his still-damp skin and sodden clothing set his skin prickling.

His companions, too, seemed to feel the cold. The Issai had left their brightly colored robes behind with the horses and now wore only their thin fibrous cloth battle-wrappings around their torsos and loins. The coverings and their skin were damp from the river crossing, and the icy chill in the air set their teeth clacking.

The Hunter was too cold himself to make some remark about the benefits of being *alay-alagbara*. Even Kodyn and Kiara, both of whom had endured harsh winters in Praamis and Voramis, pulled their cloaks tighter and hunched their shoulders against the chill. Only Aisha, warmed by the power of the *Kish'aa* burning bright within her, remained unaffected. Tarek also seemed to barely feel it. No surprise, given the cold winds that blew across the Hrandari Plains, not to mention the icy heights of Shana Laal, the mountain peak where the Elivasti made their home in the shadow of Kara-ket's twin temples.

They soon reached the source of the biting cold. The *intambelu* began to shrink, diminishing in size from thick tree trunks to no more than the width of the Hunter's leg, then to his wrist, and finally no larger in diameter than his little finger. Until eventually, the vines ended altogether. The Hunter and his shivering companions found themselves stepping off vines withered by the cold and onto hard stone. Within a few steps, the ground turned slick, covered by a thin coating of frosty rime. Even the Hunter found it difficult to keep his footing.

The air continued to grow icier with every breath. A few of the Issai began muttering amongst themselves, and more than one glanced over their shoulders toward the vines. The Hunter couldn't blame them for considering turning back. If the cold continued to intensify, the wet, lightly clad Ghandians could be in serious peril. The Hunter had seen the effects of frostbite for himself. Legionnaires loved comparing battle scars, and many who'd fought in the southernmost edges of the Fehlan continent near the frozen-over Sawtooth Mountains had shown off their collection of missing fingers and toes in The Brawling Trooper.

To her credit, Aisha was the first one to raise the concern—not for her own wellbeing, but that of her companions. "We could turn back," she told her mother, who shivered as fiercely as Siyanda, Naledi, and the other warriors. "Perhaps *Isigodi Umlilophilayo* has settled, and the way out is clear."

Davathi gave her daughter a hard look. "W-Would y-you t-turn b-back, t-too?" she asked through chattering teeth.

Aisha's expression flattened. "I would."

"A k-kind l-lie," Davathi said, snorting, "b-but a l-lie nonetheless."

Aisha threw up her hands. "I cannot allow you and the others to risk yourselves. My *uhambo loguquko* beckons me onward." She turned to look deeper into the thickening field of ice. The cavern before them was thick with fog that obscured all view of what lay ahead. "I must continue on."

"Then s-so do w-we," Naledi growled. Her huge muscles bunched with the effort of trying to fight the shivers wracking her frame.

"Y-You w-were al-lone for y-years already." Siyanda gripped Aisha's shoulder hard. "Y-You w-will not c-complete y-your *uhambo l-loguquko* alone."

If Aisha had any intention of arguing, the look on the faces of the Issai warriors silenced her. Despite the vicious chill, they straightened their shoulders and endeavored to still the clacking of their teeth.

"So be it." Aisha, too, lifted her head, squaring her shoulders. "But if we are to venture deeper into the cold, you must allow me to offer you what warmth I can."

At her insistence, all gathered around her—the Hunter, Kodyn, Kiara, and Tarek, too—and touched their cold hands to her warm flesh. Closing her eyes, Aisha summoned the power of the *Kish'aa*. The pendant at her neck began to glow. A flicker sprang to life, accompanied by another, and still more. The sparks danced around her head, along her arms, and swirled around her torso in a brilliant blue-white aura. Gasps echoed from among the Issai warriors as the power radiating outward from Aisha pushed back the chill.

The Hunter had felt the heat emanating from her before—it had burned him badly on two separate occasions. Always it had been born from powerful emotions swirling within her, its intensity burning beyond her control. Yet she had control of it now. The warmth did not sear his flesh, did not so much as set his skin prickling. Instead, it felt like the sun rising over the *amathafa* to drive back the night's chill. Before that power, the air lost its bitter bite, and all around Aisha breathed easier. The chattering of teeth fell silent, and only the rumbling of the ground underfoot broke the silence.

Aisha sustained the surge of power for just a few moments, long enough for her fellow Issai to regain some warmth. Finally, she cut off the flow of her magic with a gasp and clung to the warriors around her for support. She breathed heavily and sweat dripped down her forehead despite the chill in the air.

Davathi and Siyanda moved to support Aisha, bearing her up between them with the pride of an honor guard set to escort a royal dignitary. Aisha shot them grateful smiles and leaned on her mother and cousin as, together, they led the way deeper into the ice.

The cold worsened, as the Hunter had feared, but Aisha's efforts had restored some of the Issai's resilience. No longer did they shiver or tremble in the cold, but they moved with purpose, their steps across the ice-slick floor far more certain. They used the sharpened tips of their *assegai* like walking sticks to support their balance. Though none were immune from the occasional slip—not even the Hunter himself—they made good time.

Or so the Hunter hoped. He could see little beyond his immediate surroundings, the icy fog obscuring his view.

Aisha led the way, once more summoning the *Kish'aa* to illuminate her upraised hand. She served as the light to guide them forward and the beacon that kept them from straying.

The Hunter felt a soft, warm hand slip into his. Kiara's. He gripped the hand tight, and with his other hand, held Tarek by one shoulder. The young man, in turn, placed his hands on the shoulders of two of the Issai, and they on the shoulders of those beside and ahead of them. Thus, they remained together. The deeper they went, the closer their small group drew to each other—both for warmth and to stay within eyesight and earshot of each other in the dense haze.

Then a new sound reached the Hunter through the fog. A distant hissing, faint yet sharp. Angry. Like some enormous serpent he could not see lying in wait for them ahead. Indombe herself? Or some reptilian cousin who dwelled in this impossibly frigid underground clime?

His stomach clenched as the sound came once more. But not from the same spot where he'd heard it first. Closer now, off to his left. A third time, farther again, to his right. After a breathless pause of ten hammering heartbeats, the hissing ripped through the fog yet again. It came from behind. So close the Hunter could almost feel the invisible beast breathing down his neck, its breath stinging and cold.

The Hunter spun, released Kiara's hand, and drew the Sword of Nasnaz in one smooth motion. Yet as he raised the scimitar, he found no serpentine eyes burning at him through the haze. No rustling of metallic coils that had marked Indombe's movements. Only…nothingness.

He sheathed the sword quickly, before its magic could twist the fear coursing through him, use it to unleash his innate demonic bloodlust. But he drew the watered steel sword, just to feel the solid comfort of steel in his fist.

Another hiss echoed from just beyond the front of the group. The Hunter spun, just in time to see a pillar of white shoot up not five paces ahead of Aisha. With it came a gust of wind so frigid it threatened to freeze their entire group where they stood. Shards of ice, some nearly as large as Soulhunger's blade, rained down around them moments later.

Keeper's teeth! he cursed. *It's like the bloody eruptions in the Valley of Living Fire, only ice instead of molten rock.*

What had begun as just an occasional hiss grew more and more frequent, until it sounded as if an army of furious serpents surrounded them. The biting chill, too, increased as every eruption filled the cavern with a gust of impossibly icy air.

Tunde had mentioned "fields of glittering ice," but the Hunter couldn't imagine how the *Indaba* had survived this cavern. In his weakened state, the cold would have killed the already-dying *Bheka* a dozen times over.

Unless it wasn't this fierce when he crossed it, the Hunter thought. *This is the work of Nuru Iwu and Okadigbo's battle.* Just as the twins' struggle had brought the Valley of Living Fire to life, so, too, it was affecting whatever deep pockets of cold had caused this chamber to freeze over.

As if summoned by his thoughts, the two spirits sprang to life before his very eyes. Not as he'd seen them so many times in their forms as horse-beast and serpentine monstrosity. No, they were part of the mists, swirling, churning, rolling over each other as if blown about by some invisible wind. But it was no wind, the Hunter knew. Whatever power they possessed seemed to command the very elements. They could affect the fog just as they had caused the vines to twist and form into their shapes.

The Hunter saw no distinct outlines or forms, yet he somehow sensed that *Nuru Iwu's* spirit was growing stronger as it neared its freedom. *Okadigbo's* efforts increased in tandem, and grand banks of fog rose like towering storm clouds to crash down on the thinner wisps of mist that attempted to seep away. For a moment, it appeared as if the odds had evened out. *Nuru Iwu's* mists were swallowed, only to reappear seconds later. Ever attempting to flee, his power waxing as his twin's waned.

This time, there was no doubt that the rest of his companions saw the same thing. Gasps and muttering echoed among the Issai. Pointing fingers followed the seething battle played out in the fog. Their progress slowed as the Ghandians—even those who had not seen the twin spirits depicted in the vines—watched the battle.

The longer they watched, the thicker the fog began to grow. The Hunter felt his ears begin to ring, pressure growing, and even his lungs struggled to draw breath. He did not know if it was one twin's doing, both, or merely a side effect of being caught in the eddies of their power. Yet he knew that if they stayed, if they stopped, they died. From the cold, the icy geysers erupting all around them, or when the mist itself clawed its way down their throats.

"Move!" he tried to shout. The words came out in an inaudible gasp. His lungs clutched, the air within freezing cold. Covering his mouth with his hand, he drew in a single desperate breath and tried one more time. "Run!"

His words seemed to shatter whatever spell had taken hold of their group. The swirling fog fell suddenly still, the twin figures of *Nuru Iwu* and *Okadigbo* vanishing. Those paralyzed—by awe, fear, or the cold itself—were freed. Sharp, harsh breaths echoed from those around him, and their motionless figures began to move.

Then came a new sound. A loud *crash* like a wine glass shattering on stone. One, then two, then five, then dozens, then scores. The tinkling sound echoed from directly ahead of the Hunter, underscored by a fresh rumbling from the ground underfoot.

In that moment, the fog around them dissipated as if blown away by a giant, and the way grew clear.

Clear enough for all to see the hailstorm of razor-sharp icicles raining down toward them.

Chapter Seventy-Eight

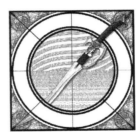

With the fog gone, the Hunter had a clear view of the cavern roof a hundred paces above his head. It was covered in the same ice that carpeted the ground underfoot, but in places the ice had melted enough to drip down only to be re-frozen into spear-tipped stalactites. Some were barely the length of the Hunter's finger, others as large around as the great trees of *Indawo Yokwesaba*. Yet every one broken free by the cavern's trembling plummeted toward the Hunter and his companions with lethal force.

"Run!" The Hunter's shout rang throughout the high-ceilinged cavern with thunderous force. He could not heed his own words instantly—he had to wait until Kiara, Kodyn, and Tarek responded. The minute they set off, he broke into a mad dash. His boots skidded on the ice for a heartbeat before finally finding purchase enough to send him hurtling forward. The others around him suffered similar setbacks, but the rain of razor-sharp icicles proved motivation enough to propel them forward.

Even before his shout fully stopped echoing off the distant ice-covered walls, their entire group was running full-tilt. Where, they did not know. Nor did they care. Forward was the only direction they could go, and so forward they went. All that mattered now was finding shelter until the danger had passed.

All around them, the *crash* of icicles shattering on the hard floor resounded in a deadly chorus. Louder and louder the cacophony grew, until it consumed everything, drowned out every thought. Only instinct propelled them forward. Run or die, every one of them knew.

The Hunter ran with one eye fixed on Kiara, Tarek, and Kodyn, who ran directly ahead of him, and the other roving the air above their heads. His heart sprang into his throat as he spotted a wrist-thick icicle dropping straight toward Kiara's back. In desperation, he whipped his watered steel sword from its sheath and lashed out with all the force he could muster. The crack of his blade against ice set the steel ringing but shattered the falling icicle into a thousand tiny shards. Little more than powder and fine crystals remained to rain down on Kiara.

Ahead of him, flashes of blue-white light gleamed brilliant against the frozen expanse of white. Aisha unleashed the *Kish'aa* against the falling danger, shielding her fellow Issai from the deadly rain, yet somehow managed to keep her feet and run on.

"There!" came a shout from the head of their pack. Siyanda, her voice high-pitched with fear and hope. She thrust one finger toward a single patch of darkness amidst the sea of ice. An opening the Hunter saw. The way forward—and out of this bloody frozen hell.

His spirits soared, only to plummet a heartbeat later when one of the Issai ahead of him suddenly tripped and fell hard. She rolled over and over, nearly taking down three of her fellow warriors in the process. When finally she slid to a halt on the ice, she lay still.

"I've got her!" the Hunter shouted. Doubtless the fall had dazed her. He did not know her name, but it did not matter. She was Issai, his companion in this mission. If his inhuman strength and agility could save her from an icy death, so be it.

He raced toward her, darting around the Issai who'd barely managed to stagger out of her way. Yet as he reached her side, acid rose in his throat. The ice around her was no longer pristine white. A halo of crimson had already begun spreading across the frozen ground. It took one glance for the Hunter to realize the grim truth: the wrist-thick icicle jutting up a hand's breadth from her flesh had slid between the bones of her shoulder. The too-dark blood leaking from her wound told him it had pierced her heart.

Still, he swept her up in his arms and raced on, clutching her to his chest. He had no need to look over his shoulder to know her body left a trail of bloody droplets behind him. The mournful wail rising from among the Issai at his back told him as much. But he would not leave her behind. The ice would not claim her body.

All around him, the rain of icicles continued, the cacophony of their impact rattling the ground underfoot and echoing off the walls of the cavern. The Hunter risked a single glance behind him, eyes scanning the expanse of white for Kiara. Blood leaked from a cut in her cheek and another in her arm, yet she ran on, heedless of the pain. She had drawn Deathbite and held it in a firm, confident grip. A look of resolve was etched plain on her face. With that *Im'tasi* blade, she would defend herself and Kodyn and Tarek running at her side, and the rearmost of the Issai a step ahead of them as he had done for her.

Her determination buoyed his spirits. Returning his attention forward, he gritted his teeth and ran on. Through the hail of icicles, around the hissing geysers of burning ice erupting from the ground on all sides. The dark opening ahead beckoned to him. It promised safety, shelter from the peril that threatened to kill those who mattered most to him. He merely had to reach it before anyone else died and—

The ground before him exploded. One moment it was solid ice; the next a pillar of blinding white clawed up toward him. Razor-sharp crystals carved a deadly path through the air and the blast of cold slammed into him with full force. The impact lifted him from his feet and hurled him backward. Every instinct screamed at him to relinquish his grip on the dead Issai, to save himself, yet he only gripped her tighter to him. He had not carried her all this way to abandon her now.

Then he was falling. Slowly at first, his body seeming to hang suspended. But something hard and sharp struck into his chest with the force of a giant's fist and slammed him down into the solid ice. Pain exploded through him, searing, blinding, wrenching. The air burst from his lungs and darkness wavered in his vision.

He tried to move but could not. Tried to sit up, to roll over, anything. Even to draw in a single gasp of air. Nothing happened. His body refused to heed even the slightest command.

He floated in darkness for what felt like an eternity. The pain faded, drowned in blackness. The cold, too, relinquished its grip on him. His flesh seemed to melt away, until nothing remained but a familiar void.

It was in this place, this endless empty expanse, where he had first spoken to Kharna. And where he had last spoken to Taiana.

The thought brought a glimmer of warmth to his heart. No, he had no heart here. No body. Only his soul. The life force that flickered through him, the energy tethering him to the realm of the living. Yet still he felt the heat coursing through him at the memory of his last conversation with the woman he had crossed a world to find. The one who had been his first true love. Mother to his daughter—the daughter he'd never met until the day she murdered Father Reverentus, his *friend*, with his own dagger.

That memory should have brought him pain. Did bring him pain in the world of flesh, he knew. Yet here, it merely *was*. One more thing the void swallowed. Just as it reached toward him. Like the ravenous, boundless hunger of the Great Devourer, the empty expanse came for him. It sought to drag him into its eternal depths. All pain and heartache forgotten, all joys and hopes left behind. Here, in this place where nothing existed. Nothing. Forever.

But then he was falling. Hurtling upward. Flying backward. Flung forward by an invisible hand. Battered around like a cat toying with a mouse. Agony coursed through every fiber of his being. A scream tore from his lips.

And echoed in his ears.

His eyes flew open, and he bolted upright. Which he instantly regretted. The world blurred around him and dark spots swirled in his vision. He reeled, once again feeling battered about by an invisible force. Yet strong hands held him upright.

"...ter?" A voice. Familiar, distant, worried.

He blinked, tried to focus. The blur refused to leave. He attempted to lift his hand to rub his eyes. Nothing happened. His fingers did not move. Nor did the arm to which it was attached.

"Hunter?" The voice again. He knew it now. Kiara's.

His eyes finally stopped their spinning, the world slowed down, and the formless blur before him coalesced into a beautiful face. A face etched with worry.

"Hunter!" Kiara's lips moved—how he loved those lips. Soft as velvet, sweet as honey. He wanted to kiss them, to—

CRACK!

His head spun, the world once more spinning dizzily around him. Yet the slap served its purpose. The wool filling his mind cleared and he could once again think straight, albeit with some difficulty.

He opened his eyes, found himself lying on hard stone. Gone was the white expanse. The cacophony of falling icicles had faded to a distant chorus.

"What happened?" he tried to say, but his tongue, like his arm, refused to heed his command. His words came out garbled, sounding more like "Wr'mbbnd" than anything coherent.

"He's coming back!" Another face appeared beside Kiara's. Umber-skinned, with strong features, and a sagacity in her eyes that belied her apparent youth. He blinked, and recognition dawned a moment later. Aisha.

"Took your bloody time, didn't you?" Kiara glared daggers, but the Hunter heard the relief beneath her outward anger. "And here I thought you Bucelarii were supposed to be tough!"

Aisha shot Kiara a surprised look.

Kiara ignored it. She had eyes only for the Hunter. "If I'd known something as minor as an icicle to your head was enough to put you down for that long, I might have tried it myself last time I needed a break from all your yammering."

The Hunter stared at the razor-sharp spear of ice she held up before his eyes. In truth, it was as long as her forearm, three-quarters of its length stained with blood. *His* blood.

"What...?" This time, his tongue cooperated, though it proved clumsy even with that simple word.

"What happened?" Kiara clucked her tongue. "You got hit full in the face by one of those exploding ice geysers. Were it not for Neema, you might be in a lot more pieces back there."

Back there? The Hunter tried to turn his head, which proved terribly difficult given the pounding in the top of his head. Yet he managed, and found himself staring back through the open mouth of the stone tunnel toward the icy cavern where the rain of icicles continued, though much-abated.

The rest of her words sank into his sluggish mind. He turned back to her. "Neema?"

Kiara's scowl faded, turned into a solemn, sorrowful frown. "I suspect she was already gone when you got to her." She glanced farther down the tunnel.

Following her gaze, the Hunter found the Issai warriors—all save Aisha, who knelt with Kodyn beside Kiara—gathered in a somber circle around a body. He knew that body. He'd been carrying it when—

It all came rushing back to him then. He struggled upright. "She took the brunt of the blast?"

Kiara nodded grimly.

"But how did I—"

"Get here?" Kiara finished his question. She placed a hand on Aisha's shoulder. "You've got this one to thank for that."

Aisha blushed and tried to dismiss the matter with a wave. "It was nothing, really. I just—"

Kodyn cut her off. "Just risked yourself to drag the Hunter and Neema all this way, danger or no." His tone turned chiding. "Don't downplay your actions, Aisha. They were the actions of a true *amaqhawai*. You have every right to be proud of your courage. I know your mother and every other warrior here is."

Aisha's color deepened further, but she did not raise further protest.

"He's right." Kiara turned to face Aisha fully. "You're capable of things that few alive today could even dream about. That's something to take pride in." She took the young woman's face in her hands and pressed a kiss to each of her cheeks. "You're a woman any mother would be proud of."

Chapter Seventy-Nine

By the time the Hunter regained strength enough to rise to his feet, the Issai warriors had finished bidding Neema farewell. Aisha had gone to join them. She'd knelt between her mother and Siyanda, spoken quiet words over the fallen warrior, and absorbed the power of her spirit into her pendant.

The Hunter's legs proved annoyingly uncooperative. He had to lean on Kiara to steady himself while his mending brain attempted to regain full control over his limbs. The ache in his head slowly lessened, though a persistent throbbing settled behind his eyes and stubbornly refused to dissipate.

He made no mention of it, however. Though Kiara appeared outwardly calm, he could feel the worry brewing beneath the surface of her composure. They'd yet to come face to face with their true enemy and already two of their companions had gone to the *Kish'aa*. More than that, she'd nearly died and the Hunter had been badly injured. Everyone in the group sported some cut, bruise, or injury—some from the rough river crossing, others from the hailstone of rocks flying in the Valley of Living Fire, even a few from where the falling icicles had lanced their flesh.

The Hunter covered her hand with his own, squeezed it firmly. She returned his gesture with a smile that failed to conceal her growing apprehension.

He wanted to offer some measure of reassurance, but she wasn't the sort to be mollified by empty words. Nothing he said would make any difference. Neither of them knew what lay ahead, what dangers remained to face. She needed no reminder that come what may, he had her back. That went without saying. With nothing to say, he merely squeezed her hand once more and winked at her.

"Best we get a move on," he said quietly.

"Aye." She nodded and removed her hand from his arm. "You good?"

The Hunter spread his arms wide and took an exaggeratedly large step as if demonstrating some jaw-dropping new skill.

Kiara chuckled. "Fool!" She slapped his arm playfully. Though the smile that brightened her face was small, it held genuine mirth.

Together, they moved up the stone tunnel to where Davathi, Aisha, and the Issai stood a respectful distance from Neema's body.

The Hunter stared down at the fallen warrior. The icicle that had driven into her shoulder and pierced her heart had been removed—or melted away. There was no trace of the ice shards that had shredded her chest, torso, or the entire left side of her face as the geyser erupted in front of them.

Kneeling, the Hunter placed a hand on the woman's forehead and the other on her chest, over her heart. *May your ancestors take you into their arms and guide you into Pharadesi.* He could only hope the Ghandian afterlife was as peaceful and joyful as the Sleepless Lands to which the Einari believed the Long Keeper sent those judged worthy. It was certainly better than what he'd just encountered—the empty void, the utter absence of light, the vast nothingness that stretched on to eternity. If that was the death that awaited him, he'd cling to life with every shred of tenacity he possessed.

When he rose, he found Davathi, Naledi, Siyanda, and a fourth Issai warrior he didn't know standing before him. The unnamed woman stepped forward and spoke to him in her own tongue.

Though he understood some of what was said, he was grateful for Davathi's translation.

"Tawia says you showed great honor by attempting to save Neema, even at the risk of your own life. For that, she owes you a debt, for Neema was her *ingani* and *oqinywe* both."

The warrior, Tawia, lifted a necklace fashioned of supple intertwined strands of brightly colored twine from around her neck and held it out to the Hunter.

"This was woven by the hands of my heart-sister," Tawia said through Davathi. "Beyond my spear, it is the most precious thing I possess. It is yours, *Okanele,* a token of gratitude for giving me the chance to bid my beloved farewell."

The Hunter looked down at the necklace. It was crafted with care, each knot and braid precisely placed, the weaving intricate. Yet it felt wrong accepting it.

"I do not wish to offend her," the Hunter said, glancing at Davathi. "But I cannot take it."

"And why not?" the Issai *nassor* asked, without translating his words to Tawia.

"Because I will never value it as much as she does." The Hunter saw the tightening of Davathi's expression, mirrored on Naledi and Sizwe's faces, and he hurried on. "Not because it holds no worth to me. The gesture alone makes it a treasure equal to the finest *iznyovu.*" He turned his attention back to Tawia. "But that was crafted for you by your *oqinywe,* a token of her love for you, as boundless as the *amathafa* and as fierce as a mighty lion. Keep it, and cherish it, as you cherish the memories of the time you had together. And let it be a reminder to you that when you, too, are called to the *Kish'aa,* she will be waiting for you."

The tension faded from Davathi's face, and she gave the Hunter an approving nod before translating the words. Tears rose to Tawia's eyes as she closed her fingers around the woven twine necklace once more. Holding it to her chest, she gave the Hunter a respectful bow before turning away to rejoin her sisters. Naledi went with her, but not before offering the Hunter a grunt he took as acknowledgement of his gesture.

Sizwe eyed him for a long moment, saying nothing, her expression flat. Yet she, too, nodded her respect—a single long, slow inclination of her head that touched her chin to her chest.

"Your words were well spoken," Davathi said quietly.

"Truth be told, I've no idea where they came from." The Hunter let out a wry chuckle. "Never been the poetic sort before."

"Don't sell yourself short." Kiara nudged him with one elbow. "Keep talking like that, and who knows, you might be the next Taivoro."

The Hunter rolled his eyes. "Keeper forbid!"

"Wherever the words came from," Davathi said, her expression shifting between amused at their banter and solemnity given the reason for their delay, "know that they were well-received." She looked as if she wanted to say more, but seemed to think better of it. She merely tilted his head to him and said, "An Issai *amaqhawai* does not soon forget such gestures."

Heat rushed to the Hunter's face. He tried to find words to respond, but none came. He'd done it simply because it seemed like the right thing to do. Saying as much felt foolish, though. Only the truly pompous and pious spoke of "the right thing", trumpeting their goodness aloud for all around them to see.

The abrupt reappearance of *Nuru Iwu* and *Okadigbo* spared him from further groping for an answer. The twin spirits materialized for only a few heartbeats—just long enough for their turmoil to set the ground underfoot rumbling and the walls shaking—before vanishing again. Yet in those seconds, the Hunter could see that *both* spirits were growing worse for the wear. *Nuru Iwu's* glossy white coat bore deep gouges from *Okadigbo's* claws, and *Okadigbo's* scaly, serpentine body had been gored by *Nuru Iwu's* horns in multiple places, leaking black ichorous blood.

That was all the urging they needed to set off once more. Aisha and her *Kish'aa* light led the way, flanked by her sisters, with the Hunter, Kiara, Kodyn, and Tarek in the rear. They moved at a brisk walk, driven onward by the mounting urgency and the growing tension that every one of them clearly felt thickening the air.

The farther they moved from the cavern of ice, the warmer the air grew. Sweat soon trickled down the Hunter's spine and seeped down his forehead, but it came as much from the anxiety gnawing in his belly as in the heat filling the tunnel. The battle between the twin spirits would soon come to a culmination. And when that happened…

What? The Hunter wondered. *What will the outcome be?*

He couldn't begin to imagine. He had no idea what *Nuru Iwu* and *Okadigbo* even were. Spirits? Beasts enormous enough to shake the ground? The Serenii who had built this tower? The Creators of Einan revered by the Serenii? A fissure in reality where the Great Devourer attempted to break through to destroy their world? Or something else entirely, something even his wildest imaginings couldn't conjure?

The lack of certainty only added to the dread coiling in his belly. His step quickened, hastened by the need to come face to face with…whatever the fiery hell was happening ahead. Tunde's warning, *Nuru Iwu's* entreaties, and *Okadigbo's* desperate pleas swirled in his mind. Whatever was happening felt beyond him. Something far greater and grander than one steel-wielding Bucelarii could begin to affect. Yet he *had* to. At the very least, he had to try. But first, he needed to see, to understand. Only then could he even attempt to figure out a possible course of action.

Within a few hundred paces, they reached a fork in the tunnel. Two paths, one to the right, the other curving to the left. All this time, Aisha's confidence hadn't once wavered, not even though the fog blinded her, or the darkness pressed in thick around the faint light of the *Kish'aa* emanating from her upraised hand. Yet here she stopped. Not a faltering step or hesitant pause. She came to a firm stop in front of the left-hand tunnel and turned to face the warriors at her back.

"This is the way you must go." Certainty rang in her voice and her eyes shone a brilliant blue-white. "Up here, you will find the passage that Tunde collapsed behind him. There, you can dig your way through and emerge onto the scaffolding to strike at our enemy. But I cannot come with you."

"What?" Davathi's eyes flew wide. "*Indokazi*—"

"*Umama.*" Aisha turned her radiant eyes on her mother. "The *Kish'aa* cry for me. I hear their voices, and I must answer them. For it is there I will find *ubaba* and Nkanyezi." She gestured to the right-hand tunnel, and looked to the Hunter. "And there, I believe you will find *Nuru Iwu* and *Okadigbo.*"

The Hunter inclined his head. "Then I follow you, *Umoyahlebe,*" he said, his tone respectful, almost ceremonial.

"Aisha—" Davathi began.

"Please, *umama.*" Aisha's face twisted with sorrow as she turned back to her mother. "My *uhambo loguquko* took me away from you before, and now it calls me away again. Though I wish it were not so, that we were not to be parted once more, I cannot ignore what I know I must do."

"Nor would I ask you to." Davathi squared her shoulders. "It is the duty of every *amaqhawai* to follow their *uhambo loguquko* to its end. For only there will you find who you truly are." She reached for her daughter and pulled Aisha into a hug.

Aisha embraced her mother, holding her close. For a moment, Davathi clung to her daughter with a fierceness that bordered on desperation. Her powerful muscles bunched as if they could shield Aisha from the perils that had plagued her life thus far.

When, finally, she pulled away, the Hunter saw her visibly struggling to school her expression. "Go, *indokazi*." She cradled Aisha's face in her hands and kissed her daughter's forehead. "Complete your journey. And bring your father and sister home to me once more."

"I will, *umama*." Aisha squeezed her mother's hands.

Davathi released Aisha and turned to go, but Siyanda stepped up to block her way.

"No, *nassor*." Siyanda shook her head. "Your place is with your family."

Davathi's eyes widened. "*Um'shana*, what is—"

"She speaks true." Naledi, too, moved to stand beside Siyanda, her muscular frame between Davathi and the left-hand passage. "You have given much for our people. Let us give this for you."

"Naledi—" Davathi began.

Her words faltered as the rest of the warriors fell in place behind the two, led by Sizwe. Not all of them understood what was spoken—fewer than half spoke Einari—yet they all stood in solidarity with Siyanda, Naledi, and Sizwe.

Uncertainty flashed across Davathi's face. Her eyes darted between the left-hand tunnel, the way she *should* go, and the right-hand tunnel, the way her heart clearly *wanted* her to go. In that moment, the Hunter caught a glimpse of the Davathi beneath the commanding *nassor* exterior. The mother who had grieved for one stolen daughter for years, only to have her other daughter stolen by the same enemies. The wife whose husband had been taken from her. The woman who carried the weight of her tribe on her shoulders, all the worries, cares, and concerns of leadership; a burden great enough to crumble even the mightiest of mountains.

"Please." Siyanda stepped forward, took Davathi's strong hands in hers. "Let us do this. We will see to the battle. You watch Aisha's back, help her make your family whole."

Tears sprang to Davathi's eyes. She caught Siyanda's face in her hands as she'd done to Aisha and pressed a motherly kiss to her forehead. "You do me proud, *um'shana*."

Chapter Eighty

The farewells were said quickly. Davathi gathered her warriors about her and spoke to them solemnly, relaying last-minute instructions to guide them in the battle to come. All save Siyanda. The young woman and Aisha moved a short distance up the right-hand tunnel. They stood with foreheads pressed together, each clasping the other's neck, speaking in whispered voices too quiet for the Hunter to overhear had he intended to listen in. Which he didn't. There was no telling what adversities lay ahead. No way to know for certain if the two would ever see each other again.

He couldn't help a small smile at the sight. A sad smile, accompanied by a bittersweet thought. *It's good to know that if this is the end of the road for one of them, they at least found their way back to each other.*

It had been that way for him and Taiana, in a way. His wife wasn't truly dead, but he would not be reunited with her for five hundred years, until the *Er'hato Tashat* once again empowered Enarium sufficiently for the magic of the Serenii-built Chambers of Sustenance brought her back to the realm of the living.

But before she'd fallen to the Sage's wicked blade—one now wielded by Kiara, in a terribly ironic twist of fate—the love they'd lost to the ages had been rekindled. Taiana's efforts to protect their daughter had separated them for nearly five thousand years. Yet he'd been able to forgive and move past that. Learning the truth about Kharna had opened his eyes to the importance of her mission. A mission that he now pursued in her stead.

He would see Taiana again, he knew. Centuries from now, long after Kiara was gone to the grave, they would be reunited. He could only hope Siyanda and Aisha's reunion took place far sooner.

Siyanda came hurrying down the tunnel a few moments later, her fist closed tight around the lion's tooth Jumaane had given her. She nodded to him as she passed, mirroring the gesture to Kiara and Tarek. To Kodyn, however, she spoke a few words in Issai, her tone sharp. From the occasional glances she cast Aisha's way, the Hunter had no doubt as to the meaning of her words.

For his part, Kodyn answered with the same confidence he'd exuded from the first day the Hunter had met him. He gripped Siyanda's arm with a warrior's strength, head held high. He needed no admonition to watch Aisha's back; he had accompanied her halfway across the world to stand at her side through the fiercest of her trials. It felt fitting, at least to the Hunter, that he would be there at the end of her "journey of awakening". For despite her courage and indomitable spirit, she had largely made it this far because of him. Just as Kiara shored up the Hunter's weaknesses and complemented his strength, so, too, was Kodyn for Aisha.

With one final brave smile for Aisha and Davathi, Siyanda marched resolutely down the left-hand tunnel. The remainder of the Issai *amaqhawe*, fourteen proud, strong warriors, marched at her back.

Aisha led the way down the right-hand tunnel, hand upraised to light the path ahead with the blue-white glow of the *Kish'aa*. Davathi strode at her daughter's side, and Kodyn took a place opposite her. The Hunter had taken note of how the young man watched her, moving at the head of the Issai, and the way he'd consciously hung back. It did him credit, knowing that his place was to wait behind, to let her lead.

For the Issai were *her* people. She was daughter of *nassor* and *Umoyahlebe* both. To her would one day fall the burden of leadership. No one who looked at her now could doubt that she *would* lead—if not as the chieftain of the Issai, then in some other form none of them yet knew. To do that, she would need the respect of the tribe's warriors. Kodyn had chosen to remain in the shadows so her light would shine all the brighter. That demonstrated a maturity far beyond his years.

The Hunter, Kiara, and Tarek brought up the rear. The Elivasti had been uncharacteristically quiet since their conversation in the chamber of the *intambelu*. His steps seemed ponderous, his shoulders burdened, his gaze downcast. One moment, his face was lined with the effort of marching onward; the next, his face seemed to go slack, listless.

The Hunter didn't know if it was merely fatigue or nervousness over what lay ahead. Whatever the case, he watched the young man from the corner of his eye. Tarek had been right; they truly *had* been pushing themselves beyond the edge of exhaustion. If he was on the verge of cracking or collapsing under the strain, the Hunter needed to know. The last thing they needed was Tarek to crumble at a crucial moment.

Worse, the Hunter's headache refused to fade. On the contrary, it seemed to take root deeper, grow stronger, like some foul parasite fed by his exhaustion. Healing himself twice in the last few hours—once from wounds that should have been fatal—had sorely depleted his energy reserves. He needed rest nearly as badly as Tarek apparently did. Or, barring that, a victim to feed to Soulhunger. The dagger's magic would feed him power enough to wipe away the exhaustion that wormed its way through his limbs and set his head throbbing viciously.

How long their small group marched through the darkness, the Hunter didn't know. The pounding in his skull consumed what little of his attention was not dedicated to keeping an eye on Tarek and watching the way ahead. He paid no heed to the stone passages through which they marched beyond scanning the uneven ground for obstacles that could trip him up.

Soon, however, the tunnel exited into another cavern, this one unlike any through which they'd passed thus far. The walls rose five paces to his right and left, and the path sloped down a gentle incline that led through a maze of stalagmites that sprouted like a hedgehog's spikes from the ground. Similar teeth of jagged rock dangled from the ceiling twenty paces overhead.

"Forests of sharp stone," Aisha said in a subdued voice.

The Hunter's gut clenched. He half-expected the massive spears of rocks to fall atop his head as the icicles had in the cavern of ice. It was foolish, he knew—this was not water melted and refrozen, but solid stone formed over countless eons. But he couldn't help seeing Neema's lifeless body lying in a widening pool of crimson on a pristine white expanse.

The tremors running through the earth did little to ease his anxiety. The ground hadn't ceased its trembling though they'd traveled at least a league away from *Isigodi Umlilophilayo*. If anything, the quakes had begun coming at greater frequency, setting shudders rippling through the stone underfoot.

Fortunately for them, this particular cavern was far from the largest they'd encountered. Just fifty paces away, beyond the army of stalagmites, another opening beckoned to them.

Drawing in a deep breath, the Hunter steeled himself and marched down the shallow slope.

No sooner had they crossed between the first stalagmites, nearly as tall as the Hunter himself, than the tremors running through the ground doubled in intensity. The stone beneath the Hunter's feet thrashed so violently it took all of his Bucelarii agility to stay upright. Davathi and Aisha in the lead fell hard against the stalagmites. Kodyn stumbled, but managed to keep his feet until Tarek skidded down the shallow slope and crashed into him from behind. The two young men fell in a tangled heap. Kiara was thrown against the Hunter and clung to him as the earth bucked and heaved.

Nuru Iwu and *Okadigbo* appeared before them once more. Their phantasmal bodies reflected the ferocity of the battle that raged between them. One of *Nuru Iwu's* long ruby horns had snapped off, embedded deep into *Okadigbo's* reptilian throat. *Okadigbo's* maw was missing dozens of razor-sharp teeth, while many more were shattered or blunted. The bony frill on the back of his neck had been crushed or twisted in multiple places. Bright white light leaked from scores of wounds on *Nuru Iwu's* haunches, flanks, and elongated neck. Black ichorous blood stained the goat-like beard that hung from his long horse-like face.

Okadigbo opened its maw and from its throat erupted a deafening scream. The sound resonated not through the Hunter's mind as it had in the past, but it ripped through the cavern with force to match the earth's quaking. The Hunter screamed and clapped a hand over his ears, yet he could not drown out the monstrosity's fury.

The ache in the Hunter's head increased a hundredfold, sending him to his knees. Tears blurred his eyes and his vision wavered. It was all he could do to retain his grip on consciousness when the agony hammering in his skull and the tumultuous cry issuing from *Okadigbo's* open mouth threatened to shatter the very core of his being.

The cry was answered a moment later by a voice of equal ferocity and magnitude. Through the haze covering his eyes, the Hunter saw a vague shape of brilliant white and glowing ruby rear up and spring toward the nebulous darkness before it. *Okadigbo's* scream turned from rage to agony. The power of that cry set the Hunter's consciousness flickering.

But as suddenly as it had come, the chaos in his mind vanished. The ache in his head evaporated like the morning mist before the rising sun. He could see again, the blurring of his vision sharpening to crystal clarity. He could hear, too—hear the thundering of the earth, the cries of fear from those around him, and his own ragged screams echoing through the cavern. Strength returned to his limbs in a flood of fire.

His gaze snapped to the place where he'd seen the two embattled spirits. The cave was empty, save for the silent stone. They would be back, he knew. And when they did—

"Hunter!" Kiara's face materialized at his side. She was trembling—no, the earth's shaking was rippling through her body—but she had managed to keep on her feet. "Hunter, we have to hurry! The battle, it's—"

Her words cut off in a terrible gasp. Her eyes flew wide, color drained from her cheeks, and a look of horror sprouted on her face. Her jaw fell slack and her lips moved, but no sound came out.

A moment later, the Hunter saw it: a bloody, sharp steel tip jutting two fingers out from between her ribs. Crimson trickled from the wound, slithered like grim serpents down her Issai armor of woven vines.

The steel disappeared, pulled free from behind. As if that was the only thing holding her upright, Kiara sagged to her knees. Her hands pressed at the wound, fighting in vain to keep the blood from gushing out.

The Hunter stared, uncomprehending. Watching her bleed out before his very eyes. Dying an arm's length from where he knelt.

Then his gaze lifted to the one who held the bloody blade. Not a sword or knife, but a spear. A long-shafted spear from which dangled the brown feathers of a Hrandari kite hawk.

"Tarek?!"

Chapter Eighty-One

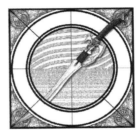

The Hunter's mind reeled from the evidence before his eyes. He simply couldn't comprehend what had just happened.

Tarek had just stabbed Kiara. Stabbed her! Driven his spear into her back.

Instinct screamed at him to move, to react, to do anything that might stop Kiara from dying at his feet. Yet surprise held him rooted in place as surely as if one of the icy geysers had frozen him solid.

The world slowed to a crawl in that moment. Kiara toppled slowly onto her side. Tarek, still carrying his bloodstained spear, spun and dashed off between the stalactites, leaping over the fallen Aisha and Davathi.

The Hunter could not move. His body simply refused to heed his commands—or he merely could not decide which command to give it.

But only for a heartbeat. Everything suddenly sped up and he broke into blurring motion. Two steps brought him to Kodyn's side. "Help her!" he shouted down at the young man still picking himself up off the ground.

Then he was racing on. Sliding between Aisha and Davathi, who'd risen and now stared dumbfounded at Kiara, as paralyzed as he'd been seconds earlier. Sprinting through the maze of stalactites, his booted feet flying across the stone. Carrying him straight toward the fleeing Tarek.

Tarek moved with the fleet-footed swiftness of an Elivasti, one trained to run and ride on the Hrandari Plains. Yet the Hunter caught up to him in ten strides and bore him to the ground in a flying tackle. Head over heels the two tumbled, but the Hunter kept his head as he fell, twisting his body so he rolled to his feet between Tarek and the way out.

"Give me your healer's bag!" Desperation set the Hunter's words ringing. He reached a hand toward the young man. "I don't know what the fiery hell you just did, but there's still time to save her."

He'd acted on pure instinct alone and only come to consciously understand his actions while he gave chase. Yet there was no doubt in his mind: Kiara's only hope of survival lay among the alchemical remedies and healing poultices in Tarek's bag.

Tarek merely bared his teeth in a snarl and thrust his spear at the Hunter. So fast was the attack the Hunter barely had time to slap aside the bloodied spearhead before it tore a hole in his belly. Though the weapon swung wide to pierce only empty air, Tarek recovered quickly, pulling back and spinning it around to slash at the Hunter's throat.

"Tarek!" The Hunter ducked beneath the swing, leaping back out of reach of the young man's spear. "Cease this madness!"

"Stand aside!" The voice that boomed from Tarek's lips held far more power than should have been possible. Deeper, more resonant, echoing off the walls and ceiling of the stone cavern with thunderous force. "You will not stop me."

Tarek charged, his spear weaving a blurring wall of steel and wood as he attacked. The Hunter was forced to give ground. Every step carried him farther away from where Kiara lay. He risked tearing his eyes from Tarek for a single moment, just long enough to see Kodyn and Aisha tending to Kiara. Davathi, however, stood behind Tarek with her *assegai* and shield held at the ready.

"No!" the Hunter shouted. "Stay back!" He didn't fully understand what had come over the young man, but he'd never figure it out if the Issai *nassor* killed Tarek where he stood.

His words were drowned out by a fresh thundering from the quaking earth. He staggered, momentarily off-balance as the ground shook under his feet. Tarek seized that moment to dart forward and drive his spear toward the Hunter's gut. In that moment, Davathi sprang upon Tarek from behind. Her *assegai* thrust straight toward his lightly armored back.

With impossible speed, Tarek spun and brought his longer spear whipping around. The steel head and wooden shaft crashed into the side of Davathi's head with a thunderous *crack* and force enough to send her hurtling away. She slammed into a stalagmite and collapsed to the ground in a limp, unconscious heap.

Tarek rounded on the Hunter, spear poised for another attack.

"What are you doing, Tarek?" The words tore from the Hunter's lips. He could make no sense of the young man's actions.

For answer, Tarek merely bared his teeth and attacked. The Hunter retreated, ducking and evading the thrusts of the young Elivasti's spear. In vain. Tarek moved with impossible speed, the attacks of his long weapon too fast for the Hunter to fully avoid.

More than that, his style had changed. The Hunter had sparred with the young man dozens of times over their weeks of travel from Malandria and learned to recognize many of the patterns and sequences of his blows. After all, he had learned many of the same in his training with Master Eldor, albeit for swords or empty fists instead of spears. But the way Tarek fought now reminded the Hunter more of the Issai's leaping, agile style, blows that appeared wild yet struck with precision. His strength, too, far surpassed what the Hunter remembered from the hours they'd spent training together.

The Hunter let out a growl of rage and pain as the spear punched into his right shoulder, sank into the meat of his left thigh, carved a deep gash down his chin. He sprang backward to put himself far beyond Tarek's reach.

Yet the young man came on, a look of furious determination on his face and a dark light that bordered on madness shinning in his eyes.

"I am doing what I must." Tarek spoke once again in that too-powerful voice. A voice that grew deeper and more guttural with every word from his lips. "I will not be stopped. Not when I am so close to my freedom!"

With those words, the terrible realization sank home. Tarek's words were not his own, no more than his actions. *Nuru Iwu* had the young man in his thrall. How, the Hunter didn't understand. Perhaps the spirit possessed the same magic that had given Indombe the power to coax Tarek to leap into its pool, or some other means of dominating Tarek's mind. But the Hunter knew without a shred of doubt. The spirit who had visited Tarek every morning for days had finally sunk its fangs into the young man's mind and seized control of his body.

How better to explain his sudden ability to swim fearlessly and capably where only days before he'd been terrified of water, or the fact that the usually nimble warrior had made the foolish blunder that nearly sent Kiara plummeting to her death? *Nuru Iwu* had wanted her dead badly enough he was controlling Tarek's mind and using his body to carry out his will!

"Release him, *Nuru Iwu*," the Hunter snarled. "Release him now, and I will consider *not* carving you into tiny pieces and pissing on every one."

Guttural laughter rumbled from Tarek's throat and resounded through the cavern. "Your threats have no fangs. You are as nothing to me. I am the mightiest—"

A blast of blue-white light suddenly slammed into Tarek from behind. The impact lifted him from his feet and sent him hurtling straight at the Hunter. The Hunter had just time enough to throw himself to one side before the young man careened past to land hard on the stone floor. Yet the fall seemed to faze him no more than an ant's bite. He was on his feet in a heartbeat, spear held at the ready.

The Hunter spun to find Aisha had risen from Kiara's side and now stood with spear extended toward Tarek. Blue-white light blazed in her eyes and danced around the head of her *assegai*.

"Don't!" The Hunter threw up a hand to stop her from unleashing another blast. "It's not Tarek."

Aisha faltered, her gaze darting to him.

"*Nuru Iwu* has taken command of his mind." The Hunter spoke quickly; any more delay only increased Kiara's chances of dying where she lay. "He's not in control of himself. But I can get to him!" He hoped. At the very least, he could get the healer's bag Tarek carried on his back.

Aisha didn't back down, but she didn't unleash the pent-up *Kish'aa* magic, either.

The Hunter spun back to Tarek. He half-expected the young man to leap upon him with renewed fury, or to turn and continue his escape. No, the Hunter realized, not escape. He had been running toward *Nuru Iwu*. The spirit had summoned him. Perhaps it needed a mortal body to inhabit, or it wanted Tarek's strength in its fight against *Okadigbo*, or something else entirely. Whatever the case, it had called Tarek to come to him, which is why he'd run off after stabbing Kiara rather than sticking around to finish her off or kill the rest of his companions.

Yet Tarek had not moved. He remained in his fighting stance, spear held level, showing its bright head stained red with both the Hunter's and Kiara's blood. The light that shone in his violet eyes had grown darker still, until it seemed as if shadows consumed him from within.

"Can you hear me, Tarek? Are you still in there?"

"The one you call Tarek is dead," came the guttural response from the young man's mouth. "I feasted on his mind and savored the dregs of his fading consciousness." He licked his lips in a sickening gesture of delight. "Even after all this time, it is a singular and wonderful pleasure. Far greater than anything I ever believed I could experience."

The Hunter's heart sank. During his communion with Kharna, he'd seen just how much power the Serenii commanded. Even with his body trapped in the Chamber of Sustenance, there had been no doubt Kharna could have ripped his mind to shreds had that been his intention. A spirit or entity with power enough to set the very earth shaking would surely have power to rival even that of the Serenii.

"What do you want?" the Hunter asked.

"The same thing I have wanted for six thousand years." Tarek's lips pulled back from his teeth in a bestial snarl. "Freedom! And tonight, I will finally have it."

"Marvelous!" The Hunter held out his hand. "Give me the bag he wears on his back and I will help you break free." The lie came easy. He had no intention of doing any such thing, but he'd say or do anything to save Kiara's life.

669

"I need no help from you!" *Nuru Iwu* roared through Tarek. "But do not attempt to interfere further. I will have this vessel kill you where you stand as he killed the vessel of my enemy."

The Hunter fought the urge to glance over his shoulder. Though he ached to see how Kiara was faring, he dared not take his eyes off Tarek.

"Behold!" the guttural voice from Tarek's mouth proclaimed. "Bear witness to my victory!" The young man's arms spread wide, and in the air above him, the two phantasmal figures of *Okadigbo* and *Nuru Iwu* materialized.

The battle had raged fierce and both creatures suffered greatly. *Nuru Iwu's* broken horn had shattered further, nothing but a jagged shard of ruby jutting from its equine skull, and blood trickled from myriad wounds around its powerful form where *Okadigbo's* jaws had bitten deep.

Okadigbo fared far worse, however. Only stumps remained where its bony frill had been torn away from its back, and its scaly body was gored in countless places. The horn embedded in its flesh had been driven deeper into its rippling serpentine body. An eye had been gouged out, and two of its six stubby legs had been shattered.

Worst of all, a deep wound in its speckled white underbelly gushed black ichor. The Hunter's eyes were drawn to it and he could not tear them away. Somehow, he knew: that wound was twin to the one in Kiara's back. She was The Bleeding One's vessel, and *Nuru Iwu* had struck at his enemy through her.

The reptilian monstrosity thrashed and struggled, but even the fierce snapping of its jaws had grown weaker. It turned its lone eye on him, and in that look, the Hunter felt all the force of its consciousness begging him to help.

"Hunter!" Aisha's voice echoed behind the Hunter. "Hurry! We need that bag *now*."

Even as the words rang in the air, a broad smile twisted Tarek's face. *Nuru Iwu* reared up on its hind legs above the squirming *Okadigbo*. Its glowing ruby hooves clawed at the air, and a deafening cry ringing with triumph roared from his lips.

Tarek slammed the butt of his spear against the stone beneath his feet, and in the same instant, *Nuru Iwu* struck. Its one remaining horn sank into Okadigbo's sole eye. The scream that ripped from the monstrosity's mouth set the cavern shaking and resounded off the stone with such force it drove the Hunter to his knees. He clapped his hand to his ears but could not drown out the sound of terrible agony washing over him.

Long moments passed before *Okadigbo's* scream finally faded and the pressure on the Hunter's eardrums lessened. Yet as he pried his eyelids open, his heart sank as he took in the mangled, limp form of the reptilian monster lying motionless at *Nuru Iwu's* hooves.

The dark gleam in Tarek's eyes brightened as Aisha's cry of "No!" echoed through the cavern.

And in that moment, the Hunter knew the truth. Even before he looked over his shoulder and saw Aisha and Kodyn cradling Kiara's limp, blood-soaked body between them. He knew it with the certainty of a dagger driven into his belly.

Okadigbo had lost the battle, and as his vessel, she had paid the price.

Chapter Eighty-Two

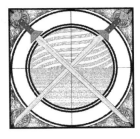

Rage flared to life within the Hunter. A red haze washed over his vision, turning the world to a gory mess. Every fiber of his being ached to unleash the rising tide of fury and bloodlust erupting within him. Not icy like the geysers that had killed Neema, but blazing, searing hot, hotter even than the volcano that had carved the Valley of Living Fire from the ground.

His hands moved of their own accord to his weapons, finding solace in the solid steel in his hands. He wanted nothing more than to draw Soulhunger and *Ibad'at Mutlaqa* and let their magic consume him. To forget about the ache gripping his heart with icy claws, the pain that had not yet fully sunk in at the loss of Kiara. He longed to lose himself in carnage, to tear into *Nuru Iwu* until nothing but gobbets of shredded flesh and shards of shattered bone remained.

But he couldn't. Not when it was *Tarek* he faced. Though *Nuru Iwu* had told him nothing of the Elivasti remained, the Hunter's refused to accept what his mind feared was true.

Indecision paralyzed him, prevented him from giving in to his rage and unsheathing his weapons. Though giving into his rage might hurt *Nuru Iwu*, it would kill Tarek—his flesh, if nothing of his mind remained. There would be nothing left of the Elivasti to bury, to mourn.

And so, he swallowed it. Swallowed the fury threatening to shatter his restraint, the grief that would sap his strength, the anguish taking root deep within his heart. He pushed it all down deep, until nothing remained of it but a red-hot coal glowing in the core of his being. Not truly gone—far from it—but for the moment controlled. He could not give in to the fire; he needed cold, calculating calm if there was to be any chance of emerging from this without suffering even greater loss.

For it would be a loss. The Hunter's mind cast back to a night much like this, in a place much like this. A dark, unlit passage of stone deep beneath the earth, where he stood facing a man he'd loved and been forced to kill. Master Eldor had given him no choice. He'd fought *knowing* he had to die. The First Blade had sacrificed himself for the sake of the Hunter, Hailen, and all of his people.

But tonight…tonight, things were different. The voice was in Tarek's head, manipulating his body, speaking through his mouth. This was not a matter of honor or duty, but of control. And if the Hunter lost his control, he would never have a chance to do for Tarek what he'd failed to do for Master Eldor.

With that thought lodged in his mind, his will firmly in control of his actions, he drew steel. Soulhunger slid free of its sheath with barely a whisper. Though it no longer spoke to him as it once had, he knew it was eternally ravenous. It did not distinguish between friend or foe. It cared for neither—it simply wanted *all*. The dagger's magic would consume *every* living soul until it fulfilled its purpose and fed Kharna power enough to defeat the Great Devourer. Tarek's death could still serve Kharna. And with *Nuru Iwu's* life force devoured, Tarek's flesh would remain intact. A body he could give some semblance of a burial even if it could not be interred in the Elivasti Hall of Remembrance.

At the sight of the blade, Tarek's face broke into a mocking grin. "As I said before, your threat has no fangs." He tapped a hand against his chest. "You will not harm this one. He means much to you. I have seen it in his memories."

That froze the Hunter in place. "You…saw his memories?"

"Every last one." Tarek's expression turned leering, scornful, a look utterly unnatural on his usually serious face. "So much sorrow and misery within him. So much pain, so much loss. Delicious!" He smacked his lips again, spraying spittle. "But though I savored the delicacy of his anguish, his thoughts revealed—"

His voice cut off abruptly and his face shifted back to a semblance of normalcy. Just for a moment, there and gone again so fast the Hunter wasn't certain he'd seen it.

"—much of value. Many feelings about you." Tarek's gaze slid past the Hunter to rest on Kodyn, Kiara, and Aisha. "All of you. Once he understood what I meant to do through him, he fought. A valiant effort—*Okadigbo's* vessel holds much affection in his heart—but futile."

He threw back his head and roared toward the cavern's stone ceiling. "For six thousand years, I have wrestled against my accursed jailor. For six thousand years, I have grown strong. One weak mind, human as it is, could no more stand against me than all the others who have succumbed to my commands over the eons."

"But if you saw his memories, then you know who I am. *What* I am." Slowly, he drew his watered steel sword and leveled it at Tarek—at *Nuru Iwu*. "And you know what I have done to those who harmed the ones I love."

"Love!" *Nuru Iwu* sneered the word. "Such a pitiful *human* conceit. The weakness of all your kind."

"My kind." The Hunter nodded. "You speak of our weakness, but tell me this, oh mighty *Nuru Iwu*." He spat the words with unmistakable contempt. "Why do you inhabit one of our weak forms?"

"Because it serves my purpose!" Spittle sprayed from Tarek's lips, his face twisting into a mask of frenetic rage. "For while this body stands against you, you will not—"

Again, his words cut off mid-flow, and his features shifted. From the leering, enraged face of *Nuru Iwu* to a look that was all Tarek. Terrified, horrified, an unspoken plea in his violet eyes. The look shifted so quickly the Hunter would have missed it had he not been staring directly at Tarek. Yet he had *seen* it.

"—raise your hand against me for fear of harming him!" *Nuru Iwu* finished his roared, mocking words, seeming not to notice the interruption. His face once more took on that maddened, furious, animalistic look. "I need only delay you until—"

The Hunter's roar drowned out the last of *Nuru Iwu's* words. He threw himself forward, watered steel sword leading the way. He brought the long blade swinging toward Tarek's torso with all the power of his mighty muscles. Not to cleave flesh, for that would only serve *Nuru Iwu's* purpose. No, he needed the thing speaking through Tarek off guard and off-balance. For in those moments where *Nuru Iwu* had wavered, the Hunter had understood.

The bastard lied. He'd said Tarek "means" something to the Hunter. Not "meant". He'd held no fear of Soulhunger, either, *knowing* the Hunter wouldn't strike him down. Which suggested a possibility he'd scarcely hoped to entertain, yet clung to with every fiber of his bring. *Tarek still lives!*

As expected, *Nuru Iwu* fought off the Hunter's attack through sheer instinct more than any desire to preserve the human flesh under his command. The long Hrandari plainsman spear batted aside the Hunter's attack and carved a deadly arc through the air on a course toward his head. But the Hunter ducked smoothly and rose with a vicious uppercut that caught Tarek beneath the jaw. Had he struck with full force, the blow would have snapped Tarek's neck. Yet he'd pulled his punch. He just needed to stagger Tarek—and in so doing, hopefully loosen *Nuru Iwu's* grip on his consciousness.

Tarek stumbled, his legs watery from the tremendous blow. He reeled like a drunken man but quickly shook off the attack. *Nuru Iwu* had full control over his mind and manipulated his flesh with a mummer's skill. Even before the Hunter fully recovered from the mighty blow, Tarek was on him again, spear whirling through the air. His movements seemed erratic, a series of leaps and quick, darting steps. But the Hunter recognized the style now. It was akin to the Issai—perhaps the ancient forerunner of their current fighting mannerisms.

And that, he'd faced before. He was prepared for Tarek's lightning fast thrust, the shuffling movement that carried him to the Hunter's right before darting left for a spinning slash of his long spear. The Hunter didn't even bother to block; he merely stepped inside Tarek's guard, caught his arms, and drove a series of punches into Tarek's gut. Air whooshed from Tarek's lungs and he stumbled again. The Hunter finished with yet another blow to Tarek's chin, backed by force enough to render the young man unconscious.

In that moment, *Nuru Iwu's* grip on Tarek's mind weakened. Tarek's eyes lost their darkness and became once again the same deep violet characteristic of his Elivasti people. He gave a pitiful moan, doubling over in pain. Yet he managed to gasp out a single whispered plea.

"Help…Hunter!"

No sooner had the words left his lips, than *Nuru Iwu's* voice roared from his mouth. "No!" He straightened, driving his spear at the Hunter's belly. So fast and unexpected was the attack that the Hunter never saw it coming. He tried in desperation to twist out of its path. Too slow. The spear drove into his gut, ripping its way through his organs before exploding out his back.

Searing agony lanced the Hunter's torso. His legs wobbled, the razor-sharp steel head scraping against the bones of his spine.

Again, Tarek's face rippled, his expression shifting from bestial fury to stunned surprise. "No!" This time it was a gasp of horror as he saw what he had done.

Nuru Iwu regained control in a heartbeat, and Tarek's arms tensed as he prepared to rip the spear free of the Hunter's belly.

Piss on that! The Hunter dropped his sword and dagger and seized the shaft of the spear piercing his belly in both hands. The fire tearing through his belly grew blinding when Tarek hauled on it, yet somehow, impossibly, the Hunter found strength to hold fast. Again and again, *Nuru Iwu* attempted to withdraw the spear. But the Hunter would not let him.

Confusion twisted Tarek's features and uncertainty filled his dark eyes. The Hunter bared his teeth and barked out a sharp laugh. "I'm not so weak as you might think, you whoreson!"

Nuru Iwu recoiled, his eyes going wide. For a moment, surprise weakened his grip on Tarek's body—and the spear in his hands. The Hunter hurled himself forward, driving the spear clean through his belly. The movement sent a fresh flood of anguish coursing through him. His legs gave out, but he was close enough to Tarek that he seized on to the young man's frozen arms and held himself upright.

"Tarek, listen to me!" The Hunter shouted into Tarek's face. "You have to fight him. You're strong enough to break free."

"I'm...not!" Tarek's voice came out, echoed a moment later by *Nuru Iwu's* guttural roar. "No, he's not!"

"You, shut up!" The Hunter punched Tarek in the jaw again, in the same spot, for the third time. That staggered the young man enough that the Hunter saw *Nuru Iwu's* hold on his mind weakening. His expression shifted between beast and youth, the shadows flickering in his eyes, receding and gaining ground like the ocean's waves on a sandy beach.

"Fight him, Tarek!" the Hunter urged. The words came harder, his lungs tightening as blood gushed from the wounds in his back and belly. His strength was fading but he refused to fall. "You can do it. This is *your* body. Your mind. You know it better than he ever could. Find the strength within yourself and use it to fight free of his gri—"

The Hunter's words were cut off in a gasp as Tarek's right hand shot up to grasp his throat. The next instant, Tarek's left hand grasped his own right wrist, as if trying to break its hold on the Hunter.

"Can't—" Tarek panted.

"You. Will. NOT!" *Nuru Iwu* roared through Tarek's lips.

The Hunter felt the hand tightening about his throat, crushing his windpipe. He used what little strength remained to him to grip Tarek's right hand and press on the vulnerable point just behind the thumb. The grip broke and he fell to the ground. His legs could no longer hold him upright, he'd lost too much blood.

He crashed to the ground, and the jarring impact against the spear tore the hole in his belly even wider. The Hunter groaned, torment coursing through his entire body with every beat of his heart. Yet he summoned one last surge of strength and raised his eyes to Tarek. The young man still clutched his right hand in his left, but that hand had already begun reaching for the shaft of the spear, once again intending to pull it free and strike the Hunter down.

"Here's something to fight for." The Hunter seized upon the one thing he *hoped* could finally reach Tarek, could give him strength enough to triumph against *Nuru Iwu*. "You have a brother. A half-brother, born to your father and the sister of the Bright Spear and Second Blade. His name is Hailen, Tarek. Hailen."

The words had an instant effect on the young man. Tarek froze, one hand still outstretched.

"You want to meet him? Then you have to fight!" the Hunter shouted. "Fight for the chance to meet the brother your father died protecting."

Tarek's entire body remained utterly immobile, save for his eyes. *Violet* eyes, free of shadows. They locked with the Hunter's, and in those eyes, the Hunter saw Tarek once more. All the young man's pain over his losses, the absence of his father, the hardships he'd endured, the struggles that had hardened him into the warrior worthy of being sent on this mission.

"You can do it, Tarek!" the Hunter whispered. "For the love of the ancestors, for the love of your sister and all your people, fight. You are the only one who can defeat him now!"

Chapter Eighty-Three

Tarek began to twitch. The tremor started in his face, at the corners of his mouth and eyes, but soon it spread down his neck to his arms and even his legs. Not the jerking, writhing spasms that had wracked Hailen's body in the grip of the Elivasti's inherited madness. It appeared more as if his entire form warred with itself. His mind wrestled against the demon's for control.

"Yes!" Hope surged within the Hunter. He coughed again, groaning at the tearing sensation in his shredded belly. But the sight of the young man fighting heartened him, pushed back the pain a fraction.

"Do you remember what I told you that night at the Zamani Falls? What it was that grounded me and kept me from leaping into the pool?"

"No!" *Nuru Iwu's* guttural roar burst from Tarek's lips, ringing off the cavernous ceiling, echoing in time with the quaking earth. "You will not—"

Tarek's face twitched, his features smoothing, and the violet in his eyes brightened. "I…do!" The words came out in a faint, rasping whisper, so quiet the Hunter barely heard it over the lingering reverberations of *Nuru Iwu's* shout. "Find…people…who…matter."

"That's right!" The Hunter struggled to his feet, but his legs refused to hold him upright. The spear had torn his spinal cord, and though his body would heal, the damage prevented him from doing more than rising unsteadily to his knees. "Think about everyone who matters to you. Your sister, Risia. You came all this way because of your love for her. Because you felt as if you owed me a debt for saving her from the *Irrsinnon*. You crossed half a world because of how much she means to you. Hold her in your mind, make her your power, your strength."

Tarek's right arm reached for the Hunter's throat, but his left hand caught the wrist, held it firm. His facial muscles writhed in the way the demons' flesh did when shifting their features, so violent was the war raging within him. Yet the Hunter did not abandon hope. Every moment spent fighting was one more moment where Tarek had a chance to triumph.

"Think about how much the people around you have come to mean to you," he pressed on, his words flowing faster now. "You've risked your life over and over to help them, to fight at their side. You can't tell me they haven't become your friends over all this time. Think of them, of all you've endured with and for them, and let that fortify your resolve. Picture them fighting beside you now. Because they *are* beside you."

The Hunter glanced over his shoulder, though the movement twisted his spine and set the bone scraping against the spear shaft transfixing his belly. Kodyn and Aisha did not look his way—their attention was fixed on Kiara's limp form lying on the blood-soaked floor between them—but the Hunter had no doubt they would have lent their strength and encouragement had they heard him.

"You…will…NOT!" roared *Nuru Iwu.* Tarek's right hand broke free of his left hand's grasp and reached again for the Hunter's throat.

The Hunter slapped the hand aside but used Tarek's arm to haul himself to his feet. There he stood, legs still watery but his will hard as steel.

"He bloody well will!" he shouted back. "Because it's not just him fighting you. It's him, and everyone he cares about, and everyone who cares about him."

He gripped Tarek's collar and held tight. "Fight for your sister, Tarek. For your friends. For your people. For your brother."

Tarek's face swam, finally settling into a look of incredulity and amazement. "Is it…true?" Again, his voice was soft, faint. "My father…had another son?"

"He did." The Hunter nodded. "And I swear to you that when this is all over, I'll tell you about him." He'd always intended to anyway. "Fiery hell, I'll take you to meet him!" He shook Tarek hard. "But that only happens if you win this bloody fight."

Tarek shook his head. "He's so strong!" Sweat streamed down his forehead from the effort of resisting *Nuru Iwu's* will. "More powerful than Indombe. I-I can't!"

"Yes, you pissing can!" the Hunter shouted. "Beat him, Tarek. Drive him out, and take back control of your mind and body!"

"Y-You have to k-kill me!" Tarek stammered, a look of panic and fear in his eyes. "It's the only way—"

"Don't you dare say that!" The Hunter slammed a foot down on the ground hard enough to shatter stone. "You've proven yourself again and again. You've shown me—all of us—what you're capable of. This is just one more enemy to defeat. Remember what the First Blade taught. Remember the *Elohas id'Arzaian.*"

Tarek's eyes widened a fraction at mention of what Master Eldor had called "the path upon which all warriors and leaders must walk, the rules that govern their lives, the code which they must inscribe upon their hearts and minds." Even after the Sage and Warmaster had attempted to suppress the Elivasti culture, the True Descendants had still passed it on to their young warriors—warriors like Tarek.

"*Failure exists only in death or surrender,*" the Hunter quoted the twelfth and final tenet of the Way of the Hunt. "*Fight to your last breath, and you will never know true defeat.*"

Tarek's face spasmed again, the shadows once again invaded his eyes. His hands came up to clasp the Hunter's throat and squeezed with terrible strength far beyond anything he could possibly possess.

Yet the Hunter did not fight back. Nor did he release his grip on the young man. He needed Tarek to see his face, to look him in the eyes, for that would give him strength to fight the spirit seeking to control him.

"Fight to your last breath!" the Hunter repeated the words, though they came out in a rasp, difficult to form around the hands choking the life from him. "No surrender!"

Bestial, snarling fury blossomed on Tarek's face and his lip curled. "I. Am. Inevitable!" He punctuated each word by shaking the Hunter's body, sending pain lancing through the tear in his belly. "There is no—" His eyes suddenly flew wide in surprise. "NO!"

The sound reverberated off the cavern walls, pitched high with surprise—and, the Hunter noted, a measure of fear.

"No, that cannot be!" *Nuru Iwu* screamed through Tarek.

That was when the Hunter saw it. The tiniest flicker of movement ran through the phantasmal corpse of the reptilian monstrosity that was the manifestation of *Okadigbo*. What started as a tremor, barely a twitching of its long, scaly tail quickly spread along its sinuous body.

"Come on!" Kodyn's voice rang out behind the Hunter. "Don't you die on us now!"

Tarek's hands fell away from the Hunter's throat, and he dropped to the ground, gasping for breath. Fresh fire lanced through him as his fall jostled the spear piercing his body. But instead of coming for him again, Tarek stepped back, the look on his features—*Nuru Iwu's* features—a mixture of shock and dismay.

"No!" *Nuru Iwu* roared through Tarek's lips. "I killed you!"

Okadigbo's eyes flickered open, and its serpentine head slowly lifted. Though it still leaked ichorous blood from scores of wounds, it coiled its great body beneath it and rose high into the air.

Tarek turned fully to face the beast, reaching for a weapon but finding none. For his spear was still embedded in the Hunter's body.

Okadigbo's enormous maw opened and its broad head darted forward. The instant its jaws snapped shut around Tarek's head, it vanished entirely. Tarek crumbled to the ground in a limp heap and lay on the rocky floor gasping, eyes wide and staring up at the stalactites high overhead.

"Tarek?" The Hunter reached for the young man. "Are you—"

Tarek turned his head to face the Hunter. "It's me." A wild light shone in his eyes, but his features were smooth, unlined by the savagery that had twisted his face when *Nuru Iwu* had possession of his body. "I—"

His lips moved soundlessly, but no words came out. He appeared utterly speechless.

A shout rang out from beyond the fallen warrior. Davathi rose, her head bloody and step unsteady. But at the sight of Tarek on the ground, she raised her *assegai* and leaped toward him.

"No!" The Hunter took a single lurching step that carried him over Tarek and interposed his body between the young Elivasti and the Issai *nassor*. "Do not harm him!"

Davathi's eyes widened, surprise etched on her leonine features. That surprise doubled when her gaze fell on the bloody spear in the Hunter's belly.

"He was not himself," the Hunter explained, though he had to grit his teeth against the pain to keep from losing consciousness. Loss of blood left him dizzy and darkness wavered at the edge of his vision. Words proved suddenly difficult. "*Nuru Iwu*...had control of him."

Davathi did not lower her spear, but she did not try to move past him to strike the young man.

Behind the Hunter, Kodyn's voice rang out again. "Hang in there, Kiara!"

"Hunter!" Aisha called. "We need that healer's bag, now!"

The Hunter lifted his gaze to Davathi. "I'm going to need...your help," he gasped, gesturing to the shaft of Tarek's spear. "Pull...this damned thing...out!"

The Issai *nassor* gaped, but only for a moment. This wound, though grievous, was far from the worst she'd seen him survive this night.

She set her *assegai* on the ground behind her—well out of Tarek's reach, the Hunter noted—and moved around behind him to grasp the end of the spear with both hands. "This will hurt," she said, lifting a foot to place against his back.

"Already...bloody does!" The Hunter balled his fists and clenched his jaw until his muscles creaked. "Do it!"

He'd braced himself, yet nothing could prepare him for the blinding, searing agony that tore through his body as she yanked out the spear. He'd driven the weapon deep, and his flesh had begun to heal around it. The snapped wooden shaft had to tear away from newly-mended organs, skin, and muscle to pull free.

He must have passed out at some point, for when his eyes opened, he found Davathi kneeling at his side, holding his body off the floor.

"Take me...to her!" the Hunter gasped, his voice terribly weak. "I have...to see her. Have...to help her!"

Davathi half-carried, half-dragged him across the cave to where Kiara lay, pausing only long enough to pull the healer's bag off Tarek's back. The young man put up no resistance nor offered any help. He seemed too dazed and confused to do more than lie on the ground and stare wide-eyed into empty space. His lips continued moving, but if they formed words, the Hunter could not hear them nor understand their meaning.

When he was but a few steps away, the Hunter lunged free of Davathi's grip and dropped to his belly at Kiara's side. "Kiara!" The cry burst from his lips, tinged with relief at seeing her eyes once more open and her chest rising and falling. But her breaths were weak, her skin pale and clammy. The hand she reached for him was stained with dark heart's blood and gripped his arm with far too little strength.

"Did...you...save...him?" Kiara's question came out weak, every word a supreme effort of will.

"I got through to him!" The Hunter nodded, though the movement set his head swimming. "He pushed *Nuru Iwu* out. With your help." He wrapped both hands around hers, clinging to her desperately. "Now it's your turn to fight. Fight to stay alive, Kiara. Please!"

"Trying...my...best." Her smile was tight with pain, but a hint of humor still sparkled in her eyes. "Seeing you...helps." Even as she spoke, her eyes began to roll up, her eyelids fluttering.

"Kiara!" The Hunter shook her. "Stay awake!"

Her eyes returned to normal, but though she tried to speak, her voice was too weak to form words.

"I don't know what to do!" Kodyn's voice rang with a note of panic.

The Hunter tore his eyes from Kiara, looked over to find Kodyn pawing through Tarek's bag of healing remedies.

"I don't know what any of these are!" Fear and worry darkened the young Praamian's his face. He lifted his eyes to the Hunter. "I don't know how to save her," he whispered.

A hand gripped the Hunter's arm with desperate strength. The Hunter turned back to find Kiara pulling on him, dragging herself up toward him, her eyes filled with determination.

Her lips moved again, forming a single word. "*Kish'aa!*"

Then her eyes rolled back in her head, and she collapsed to the stony ground once more.

Chapter Eighty-Four

Confusion twisted in the Hunter's mind. *The Kish'aa?*

What had Kiara meant by that? She had seen the effects of Aisha's power for herself, witnessed its true destructive potential. But never had it been used to mend wounds, especially one as grievous as hers.

The Hunter looked to Aisha. "Can you do something? Anything!"

Color drained from the young woman's face and her expression turned grave. "What I did before, I just burned away the poison. But this…" She shook her head. "This is beyond my power."

The faint glimmer of hope within him died, snuffed out by her words like a candle flame extinguished in hurricane winds. The reality of the situation came crashing down on him with the force of a falling mountain. Suddenly, it seemed as if he could not draw breath. The sight of Kiara lying motionless beside him sent chills flooding through him. His very heart stopped beating, frozen to ice by the knowledge that he could not save her.

He had endured much in his lifetime. Sustained countless wounds and recovered from them all. Danced along the edge of death far too many times only to find a way to cling to life. Lost his wife for five thousand years, been separated from the infant daughter he'd never had a chance to meet. Watched loved ones ripped from the world before his eyes—Farida, Bardin, Master Eldor, hell, even Father Reverentus.

Every one of those pains had fractured his spirit, and though the fractures had healed, he was never truly whole. He'd never wanted to admit it, yet a part of him had always known the day would come when *something* broke him. Some loss, some suffering, some pain that would strike him at precisely the vulnerable spot in the armor he'd built around his heart and set him crumbling to dust.

This felt like that day.

As he stared down at Kiara's limp form, a feeling of utter helplessness gripped him in iron claws. Despair sank deeper with every labored breath, every sluggish beat of his aching heart. He could not speak, couldn't even move his lips to form words, to beg Kiara to hold on, to keep fighting for life. He longed to reach for her, to clutch her in his arms and will his strength into her, but the weight on his heart bound his limbs in place as immovably as bands of steel.

He could do nothing but watch. Watch in horror as the color drained from her face and her breaths grew shallower. As the last of her life seeped from beneath the rolled-up shirt Aisha pressed against the wound in a vain attempt to stanch the bleeding. He watched until the tears filled his vision and drowned the world around him in a blurry haze.

The Hunter fought to summon the last of his strength to turn his head. To rip his eyes from Kiara and look for Tarek. If the young man had recovered enough, he might know what to do. If *anyone* could help her, it was him. He had saved her once before, had dragged her back from the edge of death with his healing remedies and knowledge imparted to him by Kanna. That night, as she lay dying, her body pierced by the crystal formed by Indombe's dried blood, he had—

Blood! The Hunter sucked in a sharp breath as realization slammed into him with the force of a stampeding *zabara*. *Of course!*

He'd been so blinded by his fear for her and the grief over losing her that he'd given up on her prematurely. She'd told him exactly how to save her life, and he'd been too busy drowning in his sorrow to understand.

Cursing himself for a fool, he scrubbed the tears from his eyes and pushed himself up onto his arms. "You can save her!" He gripped Aisha's arm. "The *Kish'aa* can save her, through you!"

Aisha, too, was crying, and she shook her head. "It won't—"

"Yes, it will!" Words tumbled from the Hunter's mouth in a rush, driven by his desperation. "What you said before, about there being something within her that felt like fire, fire that burned hotter than the power of the *Kish'aa*. Kiara believed that a shard of the crystal remained embedded in her body, and rather than being destroyed by the power you used to burn away the poison, it absorbed it." He thrust a finger toward her. "You said it yourself! The power made it burn brighter and hotter. It made her stronger, as if it was a part of her."

Aisha's eyes widened, and the Hunter saw understanding dawn in her eyes. Understanding, and a measure of hopefulness. She didn't reject the notion outright, but considered it. That only served to buoy his own belief in the possibility.

He gripped her arm hard. "That night at the *kopje,* she told me she believed the shard of crystal inside her might have some sort of magical properties, something that interacted with your *Kish'aa* power. Sort of like how your *Dy'nashia* pendant absorbs the spirits, so, too, she thought the crystal could absorb a bit of your power. Maybe enough that her body could use it to heal her!"

Aisha's expression grew thoughtful. "But that's—"

"Bloody madness? I know!" The Hunter shook his head. "I told her the same thing when she first mentioned it. But what other choice do we have?" Desperation tinged his voice. "Even if it *might* kill her, doing nothing is certain to. We've got to try it! It's what she wanted."

Aisha hesitated, but only for a moment. Her eyes flickered once to Kiara's pale, slack features, and that sight, combined with the earnestness in the Hunter's voice, sufficed to convince her.

"Tell me what to do."

Tears of relief sprang to the Hunter's eyes. Suddenly, he felt as if he could draw breath. Warmth and vigor flooded his limbs, and when he pushed himself up to his hands and knees, his body responded. Indeed, it seemed as if the gaping wound in his belly had already begun closing, the pain receding. Whether he truly was recovering, or his body merely mirrored the hope surging within him, he didn't know or care. All that mattered now was giving Kiara a fighting chance at life.

He lifted Kiara's leather armor and the padded jerkin beneath to expose her belly, and pointed to the spot where she'd placed his hand that night at the *kopje.* The place where he'd felt the feverish heat emanating from within her.

"Right there." He forced himself not to lose hope at the lack of movement in her chest, the silence where he should have heard the sound of even faint breathing. "Direct a bit of power into it. Start with just a spark, but if it feels like she'd absorb more—"

Aisha shot him a hard look. "I've got this." Her expression had gone from sorrowful and surprised to confident. She was once again the calm, composed *Umoyahlebe* fully in command of herself. "You'll want to let go of her."

The Hunter followed the line of her eyes, found his left hand had clamped down hard on Kiara's wrist as if his grasp alone could keep her from slipping into the Long Keeper's arms. He released her quickly and shuffled back to give her space.

Aisha placed one hand on Kiara's belly, right where the Hunter had indicated. She closed her eyes, her expression smoothing to a mask of stone, and drew in a deep breath. Her hand began to glow. Faintly at first, a single spark dancing along the back of her knuckles, but more blue-white light sprang into the air around her fingers. Aisha's face tensed, lines appearing at the corners of her mouth, and the power was suddenly sucked out of the air. Not to vanish, or draw back into Aisha, but propelled downward. Into Kiara.

Then came a sound that filled the Hunter with hope: a faint gasp, a whispering intake of breath. Kiara's chest rose and fell. Just once, but it was enough.

"Yes!" The Hunter's shout echoed through the cavern. "Keep going!"

Aisha didn't open her eyes or look his way; indeed, she gave no indication she had heard him. But again, the blue-white light of the *Kish'aa* sprang into existence around her hands.

A moan pierced the blood rushing in the Hunter's ears. Beyond Aisha, Tarek was stirring. All this time, he'd lain sprawled on the ground, eyes wide and unstaring, his mind doubtless reeling from *Nuru Iwu's* assault. Now, however, he had climbed onto his hands and knees, head hanging down between his arms.

"No, no, no!" he groaned. "No!"

A moment later, a low growl rumbled from his lips. *Nuru Iwu's* voice, wordless and guttural.

A dagger of ice twisted in the Hunter's belly. He wanted to go to the young man, to help him, yet he dared not leave Kiara's side. If *Nuru Iwu* regained control, he'd need to stand between the possessed Tarek and Aisha. The spirit had wanted Kiara, *Okadigbo's* vessel, dead. The bastard would have a bloody fight on his hands before the Hunter let him lay another finger on Kiara.

But the growl quickly cut off, and again Tarek spoke. No longer in a groan, though. "Get out!" he snarled. His voice was strong, commanding. "Get. Out!"

Again came *Nuru Iwu's* guttural tone, yet it was faint, more a whimper than roar.

Tarek planted one foot on the ground, then the other. His hand reached for his spear—still stained with the Hunter's blood—and lifted it from the ground. He straightened, his face twisted in a mask of strain, but he raised the spear high overhead and drove it butt-first into the ground with one last shout. "GET. OUT!"

A shockwave shuddered through the cavern, invisible yet with a force that set the Hunter's skin prickling. Tarek stood gasping, sweat streaming down his face, but a triumphant look brightened his face.

Aisha's gasp snapped the Hunter's attention toward where she hovered over Kiara. A brilliant halo of blue-white light gathered around her hands, setting the air around it crackling with searing heat and snapping sparks. Yet her whole body had gone rigid, and her expression tightened with visible strain. The blue-white light shining in her eyes darkened, and the shadows that had filled Tarek's violet eyes flooded in. A low growl ripped from her throat.

The Hunter's breath froze in his lungs. *No!*

Nuru Iwu had lost his grip on Tarek, and so sought a new host. He'd latched on to Aisha and sought to gain mastery of her mind.

The Hunter's thoughts raced. *If he controls her powers—*

Suddenly, Aisha's eyes flared so bright the Hunter had to throw up an arm to avoid being blinded. From her mouth thundered a voice amplified by the might of a hundred spirits. *"BEGONE!"* The word resonated off the stone cavern with skull-splitting force, setting the Hunter's ears ringing and the very ground beneath them trembling.

Yet as her voice faded, the Hunter felt a sudden absence in the air around him, a cessation of pressure that had been subtly building since the moment they stepped foot in this cavernous chamber.

A grin twisted his lips. *Bastard chose the wrong mind to possess.*

Nuru Iwu's might had been shattered by Aisha's *Umoyahlebe* power and he'd been driven away. How far or for how long, the Hunter didn't know. But it didn't matter.

For in that moment, as Aisha regained control over the *Kish'aa* and sent the power streaming downward, Kiara's eyelids fluttered open, and her dark eyes focused on the Hunter.

The smile that brightened her bloody lips was the most beautiful thing he'd seen in a long time.

Chapter Eighty-Five

The Hunter nearly wept with relief. "Kiara!" His overjoyed shout echoed off the high ceiling, loud enough to bring a pair of stalactites crashing down near the cavern's entrance. He paid the danger no heed; he had eyes only for the woman awakening on the floor before him.

He reached for her, only to freeze when Aisha snapped, "Wait!"

The Hunter looked toward the young Ghandian. More light had appeared around her hands, mirroring the glow in her eyes, and a simmering heat radiating from the aura surrounding her set the very air dancing.

"Not yet." Aisha's face was tight with concentration, her shoulder tensed from the struggle to control the *Kish'aa*. "If you want her back on her feet, it will take more power to finish mending her wounds."

"Do it," the Hunter said without hesitation.

Kiara smiled weakly and turned her gaze to Aisha. She could not speak—yet—but she managed a little nod.

Aisha's brow furrowed. "Fair warning: this will hurt."

For answer, Kiara just gritted her teeth and nodded again.

This time, when Aisha directed the power downward, Kiara's body arched, rising on heels and shoulders, going rigid as the lightning crackled through her. Her screams rang terribly loud in the Hunter's ears. A sound of pure torment that tore at his heart.

He bit his tongue so hard he tasted blood. If he did not, he knew he would insist Aisha stop. And the choice was not *his* to make. He had to trust Kiara and Aisha both understood their respective limits. He could only clench his fists so hard his forearms shook and cling to the hope that both women could endure.

Finally, Aisha cut off the flow of power, and Kiara fell to the ground, her body limp, her breath coming in great, ragged gasps. But when Aisha made to pull back, Kiara's right hand reached out to clamp on her wrist.

"More!" she cried in a horse rasp. "More power!"

Aisha looked to the Hunter, worry written in every line of her face.

The Hunter longed to tell her to stop—he could not bear to see Kiara suffering so—but he merely nodded. "Do it." Kiara had made her choice.

When her screams rose again, he forced himself to watch her. To bear witness to the agony racking her body as Aisha poured a torrent of *Kish'aa* magic into her flesh. He could not see what the lightning did to her—was it even now roasting her from the inside out as it had the

683

slashwyrm—but the last time he'd heard sounds of such terribly anguish, they had issued from the mouths of the Warmaster's victims. *His* mouth.

Please! he begged silently, digging his fingernails into his palms. *Please let her survive this.* Who he entreated, he didn't know. There were no gods to listen, and he knew nothing of the spirit who called himself *Okadigbo* who had chosen Kiara as his vessel. But in lieu of holding her hand and physically willing his strength into her, it was all he could do.

Kiara's body began to jerk and twitch, her eyes rolling up into the back of her head. The Hunter, terrified that she was pushed beyond her limits, reached out to Aisha to stop her.

But before he could speak, Aisha cut off the flow of power with a labored breath. Her shoulders slumped and her head bowed.

"I...can do...no more," she said, every word heavy with exhaustion.

The Hunter turned to Kiara, and found her gaze fixed intently on him. Her hand reached for his and he took it. Wrapped his fingers around hers and clung fiercely to her hand. He could feel the heat coursing through her—no longer contained to her belly, it felt as if every fiber of her being burned. Judging by the torment twisting her face, she had to feel the heat, too. Such terrible pain had to be all but unbearable. Yet she endured it with teeth gritted and brow furrowed. Not only endured it, but somehow found the strength to speak.

"Tell me." Her voice came out almost in a snarl. "Tell me...how you do it."

The Hunter stared at her, eyes wide and mouth agape. "Do...what?" Confusion twisted within him. Had the magic that threatened to burn her alive from within also stolen her senses?

"Use...the magic!" Kiara clawed at his arm, used it to pull herself up off the stone ground until her face was on a level with his. "To heal...yourself. So I...can, too!"

The Hunter sucked in a breath. For a moment, he could do nothing but stare in dumbfounded amazement.

"Tell me!" she cried again. Lightning sparked in her mouth and shot from her lips with the words. She had absorbed so much power—perhaps too much—that it now leaked from every fiber of her being.

Yet with that sight, the Hunter understood. He'd always considered the healing abilities he'd inherited from his Abiarazi ancestors to be mere physiology, something as natural as the color of his hair or the shape of his nose. Queen Asalah and the Sage had shown him the truth. They'd shown him that *he* controlled his own flesh and bone. That he possessed an innate power to command his body to obey his will and change to suit his desires.

Kiara had called that power "magic". Was that magic inherent in the Hunter's blood so very different from Aisha's *Umoyahlebe* powers, the ability to control the *Kish'aa*? Or Indombe's ability to control the minds of its prey? And if so, who was to say that it could not be replicated?

Precisely as Kiara believed she could do now.

The Hunter could have wasted an eternity considering the matter—after all, hadn't countless philosophers and scholars debated such conceits since mankind first discovered the Serenii and their arcane mastery of Einan? But doing so would serve no one's benefit here. He had only to act...and to trust that Kiara understood what she was asking him. She *had* to have given it a great deal of thought in the days since she first came to understand what Indombe's crystal might do to her.

The words he'd first heard spoken by Queen Asalah now poured from his lips. "Turn your thoughts inward. Search for the part of yourself that is more than human." He frowned. That didn't sound right. "Feel the power coursing through you. That fire burning within you, the swirling storm of energy you just absorbed. And now find the center of that storm. The shard of crystal that keeps the power from burning you up, but which draws the power to it. Can you feel it?"

He had no idea if his words came even close to correct—Queen Asalah's instructions had taken into account *his* Bucelarii abilities, and this was something new. Kiara's nod encouraged him, filled him with hope. He hurried on; she needed to either put the power to use or purge it from her body before she lost control or suffered serious damage.

"Feel your body," he continued, still relaying the Abiarazi's instruction. "Feel every fiber of muscle, every length of bone. Focus on that part of your body where you were wounded. On the soft tissue of flesh and muscle, the torn organs and shredded skin."

As he spoke, Kiara's eyes closed and her face scrunched up, nose crinkling in concentration.

"Exert your will on that part. Command it to mend. Tell it what you want it to do, what you want it to look like. The power of the *Kish'aa* can harm your body or heal it. Set it to your purposes. Will it to heed your orders."

Again, he had no idea if what he told her would work. He was so far into uncharted territory he felt like a blind man fumbling in the heart of the Advanat Desert. But he had no choice but to *try*. It was her only hope.

For what felt like an eternity, nothing happened. Kiara remained motionless on the stony ground, face twisted in concentration and body utterly unmoving save for the rise and fall of her chest. Her labored breaths echoed loud in his ears, rasping through her lips at a pace to match the hammering of his heart. Every part of him focused entirely on her—watching, listening, hoping.

Then he saw it: sparks of blue-white light coalescing beneath her skin. Rivers of power ran through her veins, setting her glowing from within. The brilliance was accompanied by waves of heat that scorched his flesh. But he refused to back away. He clung to her hand, feeling his own skin sizzling, yet hers remained utterly smooth and untouched beneath his fingers.

The power flowed through her, not wild and tempestuous like lightning, but controlled, directed. Compelled by the force of her will to heed her commands. Countless rivulets of gleaming magical energy mingled together into a single thick stream that flowed through her belly and to the wound in her side.

The Hunter sucked in a breath as her flesh began to glow, too. Sparks danced around the open wound, hissing where they struck fresh blood. Yet everywhere the light touched, the blood dried up and flesh began to mend. The look on Kiara's face spoke of her pain inflicted by the lightning dancing through her body. Yet she remained firmly in command of the power. Channeled it where it needed to go, and willed it to heal her torn flesh.

Slowly, doubtless excruciatingly, the broad tear in her ribs began to close. Threads of flesh conjoined before the Hunter's eyes, skin pulling together, mending the damage. From a gaping wound to a long laceration to a deep cut to a scratch, until finally the wound fully closed. Utterly gone, with only the dried blood caking her skin to mark its presence. The light, too, faded, but in its wake left skin once more healthy and pink with color.

Kiara's breath rushed from her lungs in a gasp, and her body, rigid with pain, went suddenly limp. The Hunter's heart sprang into his throat, but his fear for her died in a heartbeat when her eyelids popped open. Gone was the pain, the suffering. Fatigue remained, sweat sliding down her blood-streaked face, but she gave him a smile so dazzlingly bright it rivaled the glow that had only moments before suffused her veins.

"Well," she croaked, "it's not exactly Graeme's scientific method, but I think it worked."

Chapter Eighty-Six

The Hunter tried to protest when Kiara insisted he help her to rise, but relented at her stubborn refusal to heed his admonitions. She proved surprisingly steady for someone who had been within the Long Keeper's reach only minutes earlier.

"Hah!" She spread her arms out to either side, flexing and relaxing her fingers to test her muscles. "Would you look at that?"

The Hunter released his grip on her arm, but kept a wary eye on her, ready to catch her if she began to topple. "How do you feel?"

Kiara grinned. "I'd be lying if I said I've never felt better, but all things considered, I could be a whole bloody lot worse." She gave an experimental twist of her upper body. "Pain's gone. Most of the heat, too." Her smile turned to a look of disappointment. "Pity, really. I was hoping I could test my abilities, see if I could do as Aisha does and unleash a bolt of lightning or two."

The Hunter rolled his eyes as she thrust her hand forward in the same manner Aisha did when channeling the power of the *Kish'aa* to blast her enemies.

"If you'd like," came Aisha's voice from beyond Kiara, "we could try it again later." The young woman was rising, too, though she leaned heavily on Kodyn and her mother. Exhaustion lined her face and her shoulders sagged from her sustained effort of directing her magic into Kiara. "After a bit of rest, of course."

"Of course." Kiara lowered her outstretched arms and, stepping past the Hunter, moved to embrace the young woman. "Thank you. Truly."

Aisha returned the hug with a broad, albeit tired, grin. "You're welcome." Happiness sparkled in her *kaffe*-brown eyes. "I'm always glad when my *Umoyahlebe* abilities help to save lives, not only take them."

"That's twice now I owe you my life," Kiara said, pulling back. "I'll find some way to settle that debt, I swear."

Aisha dismissed the words with a wave. "There is no debt between us." She looked from Kiara to the Hunter and back again. "After what you both have done, there could never be."

"All the same, don't think I'll forget it!" Kiara waggled a finger in Aisha's face. "Not a lot of people in this world who can claim the privilege of saving me. Puts you in quite the exclusive circle, you know." She laughed, and Aisha joined in.

The Hunter could only stare at the pair. Not five minutes ago, Kiara had quite literally *died*. Only Aisha's ministrations had brought her back from the Long Keeper's embrace. Now, she was cracking jokes and laughing. Laughing!

The magic she absorbed must have done her more good than either of us could have anticipated.

A whole myriad of possibilities now lay open before them. They were venturing into territory well beyond unknown, at least to him. Whatever abilities the shard of Indombe's blood-crystal imbued upon her had yet to be explored. She might very well be the *first* person alive to have received them. Their full extent and limitations were a complete and utter mystery.

A mystery, it turned out, that would have to wait a little longer to investigate.

The ground beneath the Hunter's feet gave its most violent shudder yet, bucking and heaving with the fury of a wild *zabara*. Tarek, who had stood statue-still all this time, collapsed to one knee, knocked off-balance and seemingly drained of strength.

The Hunter reached for the young man instinctively, intending to catch him before he fell onto his face, but Tarek managed to plant the butt of his spear on the ground. There he leaned, supported only by the sturdy wooden shaft, bloodstained as it was, his head bowed.

Kiara dragged in a breath, a shudder coursing through her body. Her smile faded and tears sprang to her eyes. Her entire face drooped in the same way Tarek's shoulders hung low. For a moment, the Hunter feared she was on the verge of collapse, her strength drained away. Only when she began to move toward Tarek did he realize the truth. The emotions on her face mirrored those burdening the Elivasti warrior.

Tarek flinched when Kiara laid a hand on his shoulder. When he lifted his gaze from the ground, his expression revealed such depth of anguish the Hunter could feel it even without Kiara's empathic gifts. Tears sparkled in his violet eyes and though his mouth opened, the guilt etched into every line on his face rendered him mute.

"No." Kiara's voice was firm, commanding. No anger or resentment, merely a quiet insistence. "Look at me, Tarek."

With effort, Tarek raised his eyes to meet hers.

Kiara bent low. "Do not blame yourself. The fault is not yours."

"But—" Tarek began.

"Listen to me." Kiara placed both hands on the sides of his face, a maternal, comforting gesture. "I know what you are feeling right now. It's guilt and shame doing the talking. It's the voice in your head that tells you that you aren't good enough, that you never will be. But that is not the truth, Tarek. And it's a lie. A trick of your mind that has no foundation in reality." She bent to place a gentle kiss on his forehead. "Get that out of your head. I do not blame you for what happened here."

"None of us do." The Hunter couldn't help himself; he recognized the young man's anguish, for he'd felt it himself countless times in the past. Every death laid at his feet, every loss for which he'd believed himself culpable had added to the weight on his soul until it threatened to break him. He could not let Tarek labor under the same burden. "We all know the truth. We all heard *Nuru Iwu* for ourselves." He stepped up and rested a hand on the kneeling Tarek's shoulder. "You were simply unlucky enough to be the one he chose to control."

Why, the Hunter didn't know. *He* had been visited by the spirit of the horse-like beast during his early days in Ghandia. Yet *Nuru Iwu* and *Okadigbo* both had stopped appearing to him. Perhaps they had deemed him unsuitable as their vessel, and thus chosen new ones. *Okadigbo* had claimed Kiara, and *Nuru Iwu* Tarek.

Tarek turned his eyes on Aisha. "But...he tried for you, too. Why—?"

"Because of the *Dy'nashia*." Aisha's hand went to the pendant at her throat. "There were so many souls stored within that *Nuru Iwu's* voice could not take hold of my mind. I had the *Kish'aa* to fortify me." A kind smile brightened her face. "But you defeated him on your own."

"Pretty bloody awesome the way you did, too," Kodyn added. He mimicked Tarek's actions of planting his feet and driving an imaginary spear butt into the ground. "Get. Out!"

A hint of a smile wavered on Tarek's lips, and the shadows retreated from his eyes. Yet when his gaze fell on Davathi—and on the blood trickling from the spot where his spear had struck her in the head— his expression once more sobered.

"Davathi—"

The Issai *nassor* clucked her tongue loudly and fluttered her hand. "I have taken harder blows in my training with Duma and Naledi. This?" She pointed to her forehead. "This is but a scratch."

Tarek's frown softened. "All the same, I am sorry."

"Waste no strength on apologies." Davathi stepped close to the kneeling warrior and held out her hand to him. "Instead, put it to use fighting our enemies."

Tarek lifted his hand to clasp her outstretched arm, rising as the Issai *nassor* pulled him to his feet.

"You have taken *Nuru Iwu's* measure," Davathi said in a somber tone, "and you have defeated him. But more than that, you have shown us what he is truly capable of, and where his limitations lie. Whatever lies ahead, you have given us an advantage over the one who has revealed himself to be our foe."

"Even the fiercest predator can be killed," the Hunter recited the words first spoken to him by Master Eldor, "the hunter simply needs to know their vulnerability."

At the words of the Way of the Hunt's sixth tenet, Tarek's shoulders lifted and his face brightened. "And we know *Nuru Iwu's*." He rubbed his head as if trying to wipe away the memory of the spirit taking control of him. "When he was in my mind, I felt it, a fear so powerful it has consumed him for thousands of years. He is afraid of his captor. Afraid that if *Okadigbo* regains his strength fully before he breaks free, he will be destroyed forever."

His eyes widened, as if at a returning memory. "But I felt his confidence, too." He blinked fast, words tumbling from his mouth. "His strength is returning. His prison is weakening. That is why he was so insistent on stopping *Okadigbo's* vessel from going further." His gaze shifted to Kiara. "If you get to The Bleeding One before the shackles holding *Nuru Iwu* bound are broken, there exists a chance his plan will fail, that he will remain captive."

"Sounds like we'd best hurry and do exactly that, then!" Kiara said, a fierce grin on her face.

As if to underscore her words, the ground beneath their feet gave another mighty quake and shards of stone rained down from the stalactites hanging from the ceiling above.

A phantasmal figure flickered into existence over Kiara's head. *Okadigbo*, his scaly, serpentine body shredded and bleeding in countless places, legs and back spines broken, black ichor dripping from its mangled eye-socket. Its lone eye turned on them, and the Hunter had no need of Kiara's words to understand its silent plea.

"We have to hurry!" Kiara shouted. "The prison is all but broken. *Nuru Iwu* is almost free!"

The Hunter raced over to where Soulhunger and the watered steel sword still lay on the floor, in the drying pool of his own blood. Kodyn snatched up Tarek's healer's bag and tossed it to the young Elivasti, who caught it with a nod of thanks. Aisha wasted a single moment fussing over her mother's forehead, only for Davathi to swat her hand away and wave her off. But the delay lasted only a few heartbeats. Within seconds, they were running through the trembling cavern toward the mouth at the far end.

The stone passageway beyond was identical to every other tunnel they'd traveled, save for one thing: it curved around to the right and sloped sharply upward. The Hunter pictured the spiraling staircases of a keep tower, only instead of stairs, the ground was formed of rough, uneven volcanic rock.

The steep ascent set his legs burning, and the labored breathing of his companions sounded loud in the Hunter's ears, even over the rumbling of the ground shaken by *Nuru Iwu* and *Okadigbo's* struggle. But the urgency thrumming within him—doubtless within all of them—kept them racing as fast as they could up the jagged stones.

The Hunter led their group, but the light of the *Kish'aa* shining from Aisha's hand illuminated the way ahead. Yet they had only climbed for no more than five minutes before reaching an intersection of three passages. Uncertain of the way to go, the Hunter slowed.

Aisha and Kiara, however, charged ahead without hesitation. "This way!" the two of them shouted at the same time. Aisha was called by the power of the *Kish'aa*, and Kiara summoned by the weakening *Okadigbo*.

Now the blue-white light emanating from Aisha's hand led the way, always upward, ascending and winding around and around in a spiral so dizzying the Hunter's head spun.

Though it felt like hours, it couldn't have been more than ten minutes of running before the spiraling passage abruptly straightened out and they entered a narrow passage that ran just ten paces before reaching a set of stone steps that rose farther still.

The Hunter's hopes soared. *This must be it!* No other reason he could think of for a staircase so far underground.

The instant the Hunter's foot touched the first step, a breeze wafted from somewhere far above, a whisper of wind so faint he barely felt its passing. Indeed, he might have missed it were it not for the smell it carried.

For it was a smell he knew far too well, one which filled him with fear, hatred, disgust, and anticipation in equal measure.

The stench of rot and decay, ancient and timeless. The scent of an Abiarazi.

Chapter Eighty-Seven

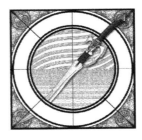

The Hunter's stomach tightened. *After all this time.*

He'd journeyed for weeks in the direction opposite the one he'd wanted to travel. Rather than heading south from Malandria toward Shalandra, there to be reunited with Hailen and Evren, he'd come north to Ghandia, crossing wild and hostile lands. Not out of any personal desire, but because of a vow he'd made to Master Eldor and the True Descendants. A vow to hunt and eradicate the *maistyrrah* wherever they hid amongst humans. For it was the only hope the Elivasti had of retaining the freedom he'd purchased for them—and which they'd purchased for themselves, paying in their own blood and death—with the deaths of the Warmaster and the Sage.

Yet despite the warning of Itan, Second Blade of the Elivasti, they had found no trace of Abiarazi. Until this very moment. The Hunter drew in a deep breath, filling his nostrils with the foul stench and relishing it. For finally, at long last, he had found the *true* threat that lurked in Ghandia. The demon that had led the Order of Mithridas and their flunkies of the Vassalage Consortium to come all this way.

The Hunter experienced a strange warring within him. On the one hand, he couldn't shake the exhilaration and eagerness at the promise of what was to come. The demon *had* to be the head of the snake, and severing it would throw his enemies into disarray. When he finally removed the Abiarazi from the equation, the odds of their carrying the battle to come would tip heavily in their favor.

Yet he couldn't help a measure of dread, even fear, for he knew how fierce the Abiarazi could be, and how much power they wielded. He'd never killed one without a bloody fight, often coming within a hair's breadth of death himself. And now, after the promise he'd made to Kharna, he had to find some way to take the bastard alive and *keep* them alive, at least long enough to lock them in a Chamber of Sustenance to sustain the Serenii in his fight against the Great Devourer.

Let's just hope this Serenii tower is akin to all the others and has a Chamber or three close at hand when I finally come face to face with the demon.

All this flashed through his mind in the time it took for him to push himself up to the next step. He reached ahead to grab Aisha by the shoulder, stopping her, and raised his hand to halt those behind him.

"Demon," he said in answer to Aisha's questioning look, thrusting his chin toward the stairs above him. Even as her eyes flew wide and she inhaled a sharp breath, the Hunter turned to regard his companions below. He locked gazes with Tarek. "The *maistyr* awaits us above."

Every muscle in Tarek's body went rigid, and his grip on his bloodstained spear shaft tightened. The tightness of his expression made his thoughts plain. His people were sworn to serve demonkind, yet he'd come all this way to see it dead. How he intended to make that happen once he came face to face with the *maistyr,* that remained to be seen. Perhaps even he did not know. Yet he gave a curt nod, nonetheless, a gesture the Hunter took to mean, "*When the time comes to join battle, I will find a way to fight.*"

The Hunter turned to Davathi. "Ahead of us, there is an *Okanele.* One with power surpassing even my own." He didn't know that for certain—Lord Chasteyn had been far from mighty as far as demonkind went, and the Hunter had no idea what manner of creature lay ahead—yet only a fool underestimated an unknown threat. "There is no question of your courage or your skill at battle, but for the sake of your husband and daughter who you have come to save, let me deal with the demon and you see to your family's freedom."

Davathi's jaw clenched, but the Hunter's words softened any possibility of offense. "It shall be so, *Umzukeli."*

"You won't face it alone." Kodyn lifted his head, and from among the myriad weapons he carried hidden around his person—as a good thief should—he drew a pair of long daggers with blades of dark grey metal. "Shalandra taught me to always be prepared."

The Hunter's nostrils curled at the stench of iron. He stared at the young man for long seconds. All this time, Kodyn had been carrying the poisonous metal unbeknownst to the Hunter. The fact that he'd kept them sheathed and concealed until this very moment spoke volumes about his character. From the very beginning, he'd been fully truthful when saying they were on the Hunter's side and willing to aid in the quest he'd taken up for Kharna—and had begun training Evren and Hailen to carry on at his side.

He tilted his head to the young men, imbuing the movement with a great deal of respect. The gesture from a warrior or soldier to an honored comrade. An equal. For that was, in a way, what Kodyn had become. Just as Aisha and Tarek had, too. Despite their youth, the three of them had proven invaluable assets, demonstrating skills and capabilities that together had gotten them this far. None of what they'd achieved so far could have been accomplished without each of them. For that, they had the Hunter's admiration, something he did not give easily.

He turned back to Aisha. "I will lead now," he said in a cold, hard voice. "If there is a demon ahead, it is I who must face it first."

Aisha looked as if she wanted to protest—indeed, the glance she shot at her upraised hand, still glowing with the light of the *Kish'aa,* made clear her belief that she had more than power enough to face a demon—but at the Hunter's stony expression and commanding tone, she stepped aside to let him pass.

He climbed two steps above her, then stopped, unslung his pack, and began to rummage within. Digging through the items he'd carried with him all this way until he came to the cloth-wrapped bundle that lay on the bottom. Pulling it out, he unwound the strips of fabric that concealed its contents: two short swords of identical size, length, and heft. Simple, practical weapons, free of gilt-work or fanciful adornment. The Swordsman's blades.

He lifted the first of the two blades, feeling his skin crawl at the nearness of the iron through his gloves. The pain no longer bothered him as it had the first night he'd held the relics given him by Father Reverentus in his fight against the Demon of Voramis. He'd grown accustomed to it over the long months of his journey to Enarium, and though the swords had spent much of the last three years locked in the Cambionari vault, they were nonetheless as familiar to him as Soulhunger or the watered steel blade.

Slowly, he turned and held the blade out to Kiara. She arched an eyebrow, but took it without further question. The Hunter offered no explanation. And in truth, none was needed. He had already armed her with *Kükhliin Khazalt*, the *Im'tasi* blade she'd named Deathbite, twin to his own *Thanal Eth'Athaur* in power, if not form. But she could not turn the sword's magic against an Abiarazi no more than he could allow Soulhunger to consume the demon's life force. With the iron blade, she stood a fighting chance when she faced the threat at his side. For she *would* stand at his side. He knew that as certainly as he knew the sun would rise and the ocean's tide would recede. Fiery hell, it would likely be *him* trying to keep her from charging into the fray.

The second of the iron blades, he slid into his belt behind his back, within easy reach for when the moment came to draw it. Once more he donned his pack, drew Soulhunger and his watered steel blade, and resumed the ascent at the head of their small group. Jaw clenched, resolve hardening, he marched up toward battle and bloodshed.

The smell of demon grew stronger with every step. It filled his nostrils, seeped beneath his skin, permeated his lungs with its taint, and set his stomach roiling.

Yet something about it seemed…off. He didn't know quite how to explain it, nor any notion of what, precisely, struck him as strange. The scent of rot and decay, though familiar, was not quite right. As if the demon's stink was somehow altered.

That made no sense, at least none he could understand. Yet. His grip tightened on his weapons and his step quickened. He'd find out the answer soon enough. And when he did…

His thoughts cut off as his eyes caught the speck of light above and ahead of him. At first, he thought it might have been nothing more than the glow of the *Kish'aa* reflecting off stone. Yet it was not blue-white light that met his gaze. Instead, it was a soft mixture of blue and green that he'd encountered *twice* now.

The glow of the *intambelu* vines.

A few more steps, and he could see the way ahead was lit by vines crawling along the ceiling and walls of the passage. They burst from the very stone like weeds, snaking downward in thick tendrils toward the staircase.

And in their light, the Hunter saw a glistening wetness staining the stone steps ahead of him. But this was no water, no underground river following the path of least difficulty downhill. No, it was far too dark. The Hunter had seen death enough to know that particular shine could come from nothing but spilled blood.

His stomach clenched as he approached the bottom-most stair bearing a dark stain. It was little more than a thread that had run down the stone from the step above, already dry and turned to a crust. But there was more blood around it, more rivulets of hideously dark wetness that glowed deep as black in the light emanating from the *intambelu*.

The Hunter held up his hand to halt his company. It might have just been the blue-green glow of the vines, but every one of them—even Davathi—appeared to have gone pale. They'd seen the blood, too, and recognized it for what it was.

Kneeling, the Hunter touched one of the glistening rivulets. Thick, as he'd expected. A metallic smell arose from the stone. Under the slick wetness, however, was a layer of crust. Dried blood beneath the fresh.

He glanced back at his companions, but he did not need to speak. He merely shook his head and continued climbing.

The blood thickened with each step he climbed. Soon, his boots splashed and sent dark droplets spraying every time he placed his foot down, accompanied by the loud *crunch* of the dried layer crusted onto the stone. The stench of death grew so thick in the air it was all the Hunter could do to keep drawing breath. The smell did not drown out the scent of demon, but layered atop it, somehow compounding the fetor that threatened to bring up the contents of the Hunter's stomach.

So focused he was on the blood that he only noticed the *intambelu* when they brightened the air around him with a light so brilliant it lit up the stone staircase to near-blinding. The glow faded quickly, diminished once more to its usual dim radiance. Yet nearly a full minute later, the brightness came again.

The Hunter studied the vines sprouting from the stone. They were unlike any other vine he'd seen before, no mere plant matter that simply dangled inert from the ceiling. No, these appeared more like serpents, far more alive even than the *intambelu* he'd seen in *Uhumi Wolandle*. Much like the vines that had come to life in the chamber through which they'd passed less than an hour earlier, in fact. At the next pulse of light, an image sprang to the Hunter's mind. Somewhere within the mountain beat a great heart, and the *intambelu* served as its veins.

Was *that* where the blood had come from? The Hunter frowned, staring closer at the vines creeping down the wall and ceiling. Every one of them ended just at the edge of the blood staining the stone steps. No, not at the edge, he realized. Just *within* the flow.

At the next pulse of light, the sickening truth became clear.

The *intambelu* did not release blood like the veins that suffused the body of a human—or Bucelarii—with life. No, they *consumed* the blood on the floor. They fed on the blood, and the power they absorbed was fed back to whatever magical "heart" caused the light to pulse.

Chapter Eighty-Eight

The Hunter's stomach twisted at the cloying stench of blood, both fresh and long-ago dried, and the squirming of the hungry vines slithering along the wall like serpents. Every time his boot splashed in a gory puddle, he felt his gorge rising.

He had witnessed death aplenty—and caused more than his fair share—but the sight of the crimson tide flowing down the stairs felt somehow more hideous, more monstrous than anything he'd done. Not mere carnage, but *butchery*. Like an abattoir following the slaughter of an entire herd of cows.

His companions, too, appeared equally sickened. Kiara and Davathi bore up the best, yet the tightness of their expressions revealed their internal struggle to tamp down their own nausea. Tarek had gone green around the gills and his mouth pressed into a tight line. Aisha was pale, and Kodyn's upper lip curled in disgust with every step upward.

A small part of the Hunter hoped that climbing the stairs faster would get them beyond the worst of it. Yet it only served to send blood droplets spattering those moving behind him, and the vine-covered wall at his side. The *intambelu* drank as greedily as Soulhunger's gemstone. Where they absorbed the blood, specks of light shone bright for a moment before being sucked along their twisting, squirming lengths, vanishing in the stone no doubt to be devoured by whatever served as the "heart" they fed.

The higher they climbed, the brighter the light emanating from the vines grew, until they no longer needed the *Kish'aa* to illuminate their way.

How long the ascent lasted, the Hunter did not know. He had no way to gauge how deep they'd descended into the bowels of the earth beneath the plateau upon which the Bondshold stood. He only knew that the muscles in his legs burned with the exertion. His breath came harder and his lungs begged for fresh air.

"Wait!" Aisha's gasp rang out through the stone stairway.

The Hunter turned to find the young Ghandian woman leaning heavily on the wall, one hand pressed against a bare patch of stone amidst a throng of squirming vines. The color had all but drained from her face and she reeled like a drunkard.

"Just…give me…a moment," she said, holding up her other hand.

Kodyn was at her side in an instant, taking her by the arm and lending her his support. "What's wrong?" Worry clouded his expression.

"Dizzy." Aisha waved a hand in front of her face as if trying to summon a cool breeze. Not that it would do much good; only the occasional whisper of wind descended from above to break the stale, reeking air around them. "Need a second…to catch…my breath."

Davathi joined Kodyn at her daughter's side. "Are you certain, *indokazi?*" A frown deepened her face. "You are unharmed?"

"Yes, *umama*." Aisha turned a tired smile on her mother. "I think…" She had to pause to draw in two ragged breaths before she could continue. "I think I drew…too hard on the *Kish'aa.*"

The Hunter and Kiara exchanged glances. If Aisha had harmed herself trying to save her—

Aisha must have seen the look that passed between them, for she hastened to reassure them all. "I will be fine. Already…I am recovering my strength." The hitch in her breath belied her words, though no one made mention of it.

Not that the rest of them were much better off. Though Kodyn lent his arm to support Aisha, he used the other to wipe away the rivers of sweat sheeting down his forehead. The collar of his cloak was soaked. Davathi surreptitiously pressed the heel of her spear hand against the wound on her temple as if to massage away a headache. Tarek, too, leaned on his knees and gulped air greedily. However, after a moment, he straightened, removed his healer's bag, and began rummaging through its contents.

"Here." The Elivasti produced a small pouch, from which he drew out a pair of dark green leaves. "Chew on these." He passed the two to Aisha, then one more each to the rest of them. "Tastes awful, but it'll keep you on your feet for a few more hours." He glanced upward. "Long enough to face whatever's waiting for us ahead."

The Hunter could see nothing above them but more stairs dripping blood, more vine-covered walls and ceiling. But there *would* be an end to the staircase, eventually. And when they finally reached it…

What? The Hunter's mind raced. *What will we find?*

A demon, he knew as much from the stench filling his nostrils. The prison that held *Okadigbo* and *Nuru Iwu*, whatever in the fiery hell they were. Death aplenty. Aisha had said the *Kish'aa* called to her from above, which meant that *someone* had died. Recently, as the blood beneath their feet made that plain. Yet much of the blood appeared as old as stones and the *intambelu* vines that fed on it.

Too many unknowns, too many uncertainties. The Hunter tightened his grip on Soulhunger and his watered steel sword. *Whatever it is, we face it head-on.*

A gasp brought the Hunter spinning around. Kiara staggered as if struck by an invisible hand, her face going pale, eyes wide. She toppled backward and would have fallen if not for Tarek reaching out to catch her. She trembled in his grip, her arms and legs shaking like a leaf in a hurricane.

"No!" The word hissed from her lips. Her eyes fixed on something on the stairs above. "It cannot be!"

The Hunter followed her gaze, and his heart lurched at the appearance of the phantasmal serpentine form of *Okadigbo*. The monstrous creature lay on the staircase, its legs splayed in the air above its bulky, misshapen body, a body that had been shredded to ribbons, great patches of scales torn away. Its head lolled limply as if its elongated neck had been snapped and involuntary spasms set its long tail jerking, twitching, splashing in the blood. Every one of its teeth had been ripped free of its mouth, leaving only red gums and empty sockets.

Its lone eye fixed on Kiara, and it let out a hideous, pitiful moan. The sound resounded down the stairs toward them, stretching on for what felt like an eternity—an eternity made all the longer by the anguish audible in its tone. But when that single note faded, the great broad-snouted head fell still and its serpentine tail stopped twitching.

696

Only a flicker of light remained burning in *Okadigbo's* eye. Barely more than a spark in the heart of an ocean's storm. It grew steadily weaker, fading, fading, until…

The breath rushed from Kiara's lungs and her legs gave out fully. In the same moment, the light glowing within every *intambelu* vine within the staircase was suddenly extinguished, and the Hunter and his companions were plunged into the utter darkness only possible deep beneath the earth. The ground, too, ceased its trembling entirely. Breathless silence crushed on the Hunter. The absence of noise proved deafening after the rumbling that had persisted since they began crossing *Isigodi Umlilophilayo*.

A moment later, the blue-white glow sprang once more from Aisha's upraised hand, pushing back the shadows. In that light, the Hunter saw the tears spilling down Kiara's face, soaking her cheeks. She turned her gaze up to him, and in her eyes, he saw the anguish that had, only moments before, emanated from *Okadigbo's* phantasmal form.

"It's too late." The words poured from her lips in a half-groan, half-sob. "They've killed him!"

The sight of her pain twisted at the Hunter's heart. He didn't know if it was truly *her* pain or a lingering fragment of *Okadigbo's*, but it did not matter. She was the one weeping. He reached for her to comfort her.

"No!" She pushed him away. "No, there is no time. You must go!" Her voice rose, grew strong despite her tears. She regained strength enough to raise an arm and stab a finger toward the stairs above. "You have to stop them. The Bleeding One is dead, but He Who Is Nameless cannot be allowed to go free!"

The Hunter's eyes widened. He froze, uncertain what to do.

"Hurry!" Kiara's shout rang off the walls with terrible force. "Hurry, before it is too late and the evil he struggled against for so many millennia is unleashed!"

The Hunter was turning and running before he realized it. Perhaps it was something in Kiara's voice—a desperation and terror he'd never heard before—or her words, but he found himself compelled to move. To race up the steps two and three at a time, heedless of the blood splattering with every step.

"Go!" Kiara called after him. "We will follow as we can, but you must stop them! Run as if our very lives depend on it!"

And so he did. He fairly flew up the stairs, arms and legs pumping, heart hammering in his chest, lungs burning with the effort. Beyond the circle of *Kish'aa* light and into the darkness, his steps driven by the urgency and terror in Kiara's voice.

For a few anxiety-inducing heartbeats, he stumbled blindly along the pitch-black staircase, unable to see yet unwilling to slow. Only his inhuman agility kept him from falling to his face or shattering a limb as he raced up the steps, yet he knew he could not sustain the mad dash for long without light to guide him.

As if summoned by his thoughts, the *intambelu* around him pulsed. Barely a flicker of light, so faint it was little more than a spark. Yet in the impenetrable gloom deep beneath the earth, it was enough. Enough to see the next steps. His feet splashed through the blood, spraying gruesome droplets in all direction. And again the vines flared to life. Again, he could see the stairs ahead, though only a few.

The Hunter did not question how—how the vines that had seemingly died with *Okadigbo* still had life enough to guide his way—for he was too busy driving his body to run with all the haste he could summon. The memory of Kiara's expression and voice urged him onward. The woman had faced down thugs, assassins, demons, and even Indombe without flinching. The fear

697

that had gripped her must have been a lingering fragment of *Okadigbo's* dying emotions, yet if they were strong enough to shatter even her composure, the spirit must have been truly terrified.

The ascent seemed interminable, though it could merely have been the thrumming of the Hunter's taut nerves at the mounting danger, the thickening stench of death, the growing possibility of a misstep that could end in disaster. The strobing, pulsing glow flickering from the *intambelu* was his only means of marking the time, for he could not trust his galloping heartbeat, the pounding of his blood in his ears, or his laboring breath.

But then he saw it. Far, far above him, little more than a spark of light at first, but growing steadily brighter and larger as he climbed. The brilliance above lacked the greenish hue of the *intambelu,* and the searing blue-white of the *Kish'aa* that streamed from Aisha's fingers. Instead, it was a blue so deep it rivaled the finest sapphires the Hunter had ever seen. A blue he knew all too well, one he'd seen inside the Keeps of Enarium and the Monolith of Malandria.

The light of Serenii magic.

For a moment, the Hunter feared the slaves laboring under the Consortium's whips had managed to break through into the Bondshold. Though he'd seen no sign of their passage, he could think of no other reason for there to be an opening into the Serenii tower.

Then he spotted the wide fissure through which the azure light streamed. No human hands had carved that aperture. It was the *intambelu* that had wormed their way into the dark grey stone, shattering the rock and forcing wide a crack in the gemstone-like crystal that characterized the Serenii structures.

It was through this crack the Hunter ran, weapons held at the ready, his muscles tensed and braced for battle.

But nothing could have prepared him for the scene of horrendous, unholy carnage that greeted him within *Ukuhlushwa Okungapheli.*

Chapter Eighty-Nine

The circular chamber was fifty paces across, a massive pillar of midnight black at its heart. To the Hunter's eyes, the crystalline stone was identical to the tower's exterior. When the Hunter had first seen it, the Bondshold had appeared to constantly shift the way an Illusionist's optical illusion did, setting complex patterns of spots and sparks dancing in his vision. Now, however, the pillar had gone dark, inert. Gone was the strange magic the Hunter had felt emanating from it before. No longer did it consume the light or set his head aching. It appeared almost…dead.

The Hunter blinked, staring at the pillar, and at the blue-glowing walls etched with Serenii runes. But only for a moment. He had no time to wonder at the meaning of the runes, or the purpose for the bottom-most room of the tower—which, unlike the Monolith in Malandria or the Illumina in Enarium, held neither a Chamber of Sustenance nor stone altar-like console.

For his attention was consumed by the bodies that littered the floor. Hundreds of them. Here piled high like corded deadwood, there scattered like leaves blown in the wind. Throats slashed, hearts pierced, bellies hacked open, heads and limbs severed. Like a corpse-strewn field of battle, only these had not died fighting. They had died on their knees. Many still wore the chains, ropes, and cords that prevented their fleeing or resisting. The blood pouring down the stairs had prepared the Hunter for butchery, but this…this was something far worse. Something utterly *inhuman*.

The Hunter's feet faltered, his steps coming to a halt a hand's breadth away from the body nearest the fissure in the wall. His mind boggled at the gruesome scene laid out before him.

What had done this? He wanted to believe it was the Abiarazi whose scent he'd first detected far below him—and which now lingered in the air—yet there was no way a *single* creature, even a demon, could have killed so many alone. For all the savagery of the scene, the killing blows had been precise, intentional. Not the mindless, frenzied carnage of a monster consumed by bloodlust, but dispassionate and calculated. The wounds left by sharpened weapons rather than talons or claws. This had been an execution en masse.

A terrible *cracking* sound echoed from off to the Hunter's right. He spun, raised his weapons in anticipation of a fight. None presented itself. Instead, the sound had come from a chunk of the blue gemstone wall crumbling away to crash on the ground and shatter into a hundred fingernail-sized shards. Beyond, a network of *intambelu* seeped through the dark grey stone of the plateau. Only the vines now hung limp, inert save for the occasional pulse that had lit the Hunter's way up the stairs.

Some small part of the Hunter's mind understood what had happened. The vines, sensing the blood, had burrowed through stone and shattered the very walls of the Bondshold itself to feed. That was how the crack had formed and the way into the Serenii tower opened. But the aperture had to be brand new. Otherwise, whoever had executed all these poor bastards would have seen it and investigated the staircase into the earth—one of the many secret passages characteristic of the Serenii structures.

Yet all of that faded into the back of his thoughts as his gaze rested on a pile of corpses that lay apart from the rest. All were bound, their copper-skinned bodies battered and bruised even before death. All wore the deep red bone-like ornaments, armor, and weapons that marked them as the warriors of the Ujana. Perhaps the same who had fled the battle within the Valley of the Zabara. Executed for their cowardice or merely slaughtered along with the rest of the captives?

For, indeed, the rest of the corpses littering the floor had once been among those working on the scaffolding to carry out the Order of Mithridas' task of digging a way into this very place. They still bore the marks of their labor: dirt crusted beneath their fingernails, deep whip wounds on their backs, the gaunt, emaciated features of men and women worked beyond starvation and exhaustion.

Many, too, showed signs of dimercurite poisoning. The wasted limbs, bruise-like circles around their eyes, and the black, swollen lips and gums. A few bore no wounds, suggesting they'd succumbed to the dimercurite's effects before their executioners' blades fell. The majority, however, had been dispatched with the same bloody efficiency as the rest.

A new sound drew his attention to the far end of the circular chamber. The sound of booted feet and grunting men coming from somewhere beyond this abattoir, drawing closer with every breath.

For the first time, the Hunter saw past the crimson-stained walls and gore-splattered floors to spot a staircase much like the one that he'd descended to speak with Kharna at the base of the Illumina or ascended to leave Father Reverentus' corpse behind in the bottom-most chamber beneath the Monolith.

He was moving toward the staircase before he realized it. The promise of approaching danger had shattered the horror that rooted him in place. He slipped through the corpses, his boots barely making a sound as he stepped lightly through the blood puddling on the floor. Reaching the stairs, he pressed himself against the wall beside it and waited.

The two figures came into view a moment later. Though he could not see their faces behind the black *slashwyrm* scale masks they wore, their grunts of effort had distinctively masculine depths to them. So, too, did the curse that issued from one's lips as his foot slipped on a bit of blood and nearly slid out from beneath him.

Between them, the two men carried a limp, heavy burden. The corpse of a woman. Young, perhaps in her twenties, as suggested by the slenderness of her frame. It was impossible to tell from her face, though…or what remained of it. Where her eyes had been were now only two pits of blackened, ruined flesh. Her lips had burned away, as had half her right cheek and the entire left side of her face. Even her arms, which dangled limply beneath her, bore the marks of deep burns through the veins and arteries that ran from her shoulders down to her hands.

Yet the burns had not been left by any fire. The Hunter had seen countless victims of torture—the Bloody Hand had not been shy with their measures for cowing Voramians into submission—and he'd seen the worst red-hot irons and alchemical acids could inflict.

No, the only time he'd seen damage like this was the night he'd watched the *Umoyahlebe* unleashing their power at the enormous stone portal that guarded the entrance to this very tower.

Disgust, fury, and hatred roiled within the Hunter at the sight of the two Ordermen and the young woman who had died to carry out their whims. Rage boiled in the pit of his stomach and set fire coursing through his limbs. Seizing that fire, he sprang into motion and charged the masked enemies.

700

The first Orderman died without ever seeing his killer. The Hunter's watered steel sword punched into the back of his neck, tearing through his spine, severing his jugular vein, and laying open his throat. With a savage snap of his wrist, the Hunter ripped the blade out the side of the man's neck. The Orderman fell soundlessly in a spray of blood and landed in a limp heap atop an Ujana corpse.

The second Orderman was caught off guard by the violence and the sudden unevenness of the burden he carried. As his companion fell, the corpse in his arms pulled him downward. Instinctively, he kept his grip on the young woman's legs and bent to maintain his balance. That foolish reaction left him entirely vulnerable to attack. He was a dead man; the killing blow just hadn't yet struck.

Every fiber of the Hunter's being longed to drive Soulhunger into his chest, to let the dagger drink deep of his heart's blood, to watch the eyes behind the mask go wide and hear his scream of terror ring out. He wanted the Orderman to suffer. To feel the inexorable certainty of his impending fate and know without a shred of doubt that nothing he did could stop it. For those final moments of his life to be spent in the excruciating anguish of feeling his essence consumed by Soulhunger's magic.

It took all his effort *not* to give in to that urge. To keep his left hand firmly at his side and strike out with the sword in his right. He could not risk the man's dying screams alerting anyone within earshot of the Hunter's presence.

The tip of Master Eldor's watered steel blade punched into the man's chest, puncturing his lungs, grating along his spine, and burst out his back. The force of the Hunter's lunge knocked the man back a step, and he dropped the corpse he'd been carrying. The Hunter followed through on the blow, moving close enough that the man's scent of hemp, anise, and costus oil flooded his nostrils, close enough to reach up with his left hand and rip off the Orderman's mask. Beneath, the features of a Voramian stared back at him wide-eyed, mouth agape. Though his lips worked, nothing but blood came out.

"Shhh!" The Hunter shook his head. "No one will hear you here."

The Orderman tried to speak, or perhaps to scream, yet he could not draw sufficient breath around the Hunter's sword.

"You're dying." The Hunter spoke in a quiet, almost soothing tone. "How you die is up to you. Quick and painless, or…"

He applied the tiniest bit of pressure on the hilt of his sword to twist the blade within the man's chest. The Voramian gasped at the pain but the sound was choked off by a spray of blood droplets.

"Way things stand," the Hunter said, "you'll spend the next hour or two fighting for every bit of air, and you'll get just enough that you'll feel the exquisite torment of drowning in your own body. Or, you give me what I want, I pull this blade out, and you go easy into the Long Keeper's arms." He tapped a finger against the sword hilt. "Choice is yours."

The Orderman clawed at the Hunter, desperation etched into his pain-lined features.

"One question's all I've got." The Hunter stared down into the man's olive-green eyes, eyes which were round and wide as saucers and filled with panic. "All this." With a nod of his head, he indicated the corpses littered around the circular chamber. "You the ones who did this? The Order of Mithridas?"

The dying man's mouth worked, but as the Hunter had said, he barely had breath enough to cling to life, much less offer whatever pathetic excuse or plea formed on his lips. Finally, he gave a weak, jerky nod.

The Hunter's lip curled into a sneer. "Then every one of you deserves what's coming."

701

He twisted the sword, hard, and drove it upward with all the force of his powerful muscles. The watered steel sheared through bones, muscles, flesh, and organs to burst out between the man's shoulder blades. Agony twisted the man's features and tears sprang to his eyes. He fell to his knees, his mouth forming a scream that his lungs had no breath to voice aloud. For long seconds, he remained there, his hands twitching, his entire body quivering from the effort of staying alive as his blood flowed out to join that of the Ghandians he had killed. When, finally, he toppled onto his side, his eyes remained open, tears still flowing.

The Hunter met the man's eyes calmly. A cold, cruel smile twisted his lips. Death would claim the Orderman, but he'd spend his last moments in pure agony. A fitting fate for one who'd had a hand in such an atrocity.

Life had not yet fled the man when the Hunter turned away and strode toward the staircase. The Order of Mithridas had killed countless innocents in their efforts to break into *Ukuhlushwa Okungapheli*. He'd see to it that every one of the masked whoresons paid for their cruelty and evil this night.

Chapter Ninety

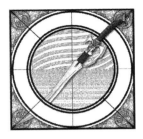

The Hunter ran up the winding staircase with all the silence of a wraith. Without the ground's rumbling to obscure the noise of his passage, he had to move with all the stealth he could muster while still hurrying as fast as he dared.

"Run as if our very lives depend on it!" Kiara's words rang in his ears, fear in her eyes burned into his mind. Even the few moments he'd spent questioning the Orderman could make all the difference in the world.

He noted the blood encrusting the stairs—mostly dried, but here and there a fresh trickle—and his gut clenched. Would he find *more* bodies above? How many lives had the Order of Mithridas extinguished this night in their pursuit of the power within the Bondshold?

Despite the urgency thrumming within him, the Hunter slowed as he reached the top of the stairs, stopping just out of sight of the chamber beyond. Like the Illumina and the Monolith, the Bondshold had another circular chamber at ground level similar to the one far below. At its center stood the enormous pillar of midnight black gemstone, terribly inert and lightless.

Somewhere out of his line of sight, the Hunter knew he'd find another staircase ascending toward the tower's pinnacle dozens of floors above. What he'd encounter as he climbed remained to be seen—he'd discovered the Illumina's purpose in housing scores of Chambers of Sustenance, built by the Serenii to collect power to aid Kharna in his battle against the Great Devourer, but hadn't had a chance to investigate the Monolith's interior, and thus had no way to ascertain its purpose.

That remained a problem for *after* he dealt with the ten Ordermen who occupied the chamber.

Like those who'd been stationed outside the domed building that served as the *Umoyahlebe's* prison, the masked men stood with wary postures and hands on their weapons. They stood with their backs to him, and never once glanced over their shoulders at the staircase down which two of their comrades had carried the dead Ghandian woman. Instead, their attention fixed on the doorway ten paces tall and twenty wide, with the vast doors of dark grey stone. Doors that stood wide open to reveal darkness and a starry night sky beyond.

The Hunter's gut clenched. *Looks like the bastards' efforts finally paid off.* The Order of Mithridas had broken into the Bondshold. *The question is, how many of Aisha's people died in the doing?*

From his vantage point low on the descending staircase, the Hunter could not see the plateau through the open doorway. But the Hunter had little doubt there would be more Ordermen stationed to hold the tower from without. Or, if the "maskies" were lacking in manpower, they would have their lackies of the Consortium on hand.

Though, judging by the way they're watching the door, the Hunter thought, *it doesn't look like they much trust their subordinates, either.*

The Order of Mithridas was known to guard matters close to their vest. It wouldn't surprise the Hunter if they stationed the Vassalage Consortium well away to keep their doings here secret. Which worked out nicely in his favor. Had they been more trusting, there might be more than *ten* foes between him and his target.

The Hunter's gaze roamed the crystalline walls next to the enormous stone doors that opened into the Bondshold, and a smile touched his lips. *Perfect!*

He sprang into motion, leaping up the last stairs in two great bounds and sprinting toward the Ordermen. The first pair never even heard him coming, and he cut them down from behind as he raced past. The unmistakable meaty *crunch* of steel carving through flesh and shattering bone caught one's attention, but too late to spare their life. The Hunter's long sword tore open the exposed flesh just beneath the black *slashwyrm* scale mask and sent blood spraying in a gory, hot mist.

The Hunter unleashed two more vicious strikes as he rushed through the next pair of Ordermen. His watered steel sword shattered one's spine, while Soulhunger punched through unarmored flesh, slipped between ribs, and tore through the heart and lungs of another. The dagger caught on bone for a moment, nearly slipping from the Hunter's hand. The Hunter had a split second to choose—leave Soulhunger embedded to consume the man's life essence, or slow his rush long enough to pull the blade free.

It was no choice at all.

Skidding to a halt, the Hunter shifted his grip on Soulhunger's hilt and yanked with all the strength he could muster. So surprising was his attack the Orderman hadn't yet registered the mortal wound. Yet his scream rang out loud and high as the Hunter's pull on Soulhunger splayed his ribs outward and ripped through muscle and skin.

The Hunter had poured too much strength into the effort—or underestimated the resilience of his enemy's bones—and Soulhunger's sudden freedom left him just enough off-balance that he could not resume his run for the open door before the fastest of the Ordermen reacted. The masked foe drew a long, thin rapier and executed a perfect fencer's lunge that skewered the Hunter straight through the chest.

A needle-thin finger of fire burrowed a burning hole through the Hunter's torso, and he gasped at the sudden rush of pain. Yet the shock of it did little to slow him. His watered steel sword came up in a vicious blow that shattered the rapier just above the hilt. A finger-length of his enemy's blade spun away, while the rest remained embedded in his flesh.

The Orderman gaped down at the broken sword; the Hunter imagined a look of stupid amazement and shock on the face behind the mask. With a snarl, the Hunter drove his own sword into the Orderman's chest in an exact mirror of the fencer's lunge that had skewered him. Only *his* watered steel sword had a blade as thick as three fingers, and both of its double edges had been honed to razor-sharpness. The Orderman let out a gurgling cry as the Hunter's blade tore open their heart and shredded their lungs.

Pulling his sword free, the Hunter ran on, ducking beneath a blow from another enemy that had closed in from his left and parrying a strike coming at him from his right. The impact jarred the length of steel transfixing his chest, but the Hunter only growled at the pain and refused to let it slow him.

He burst through the last of the Ordermen and sprinted toward the enormous opening in the tower's eastern wall. As he'd suspected, another dozen masked assailants stood guard on the muddy ground outside. Yet they had their backs turned to him, their faces turned toward the plateau where the Consortium slavers herded the thousands of emaciated, beaten men and women away from the tower. Whatever the Order of Mithridas was doing, they were keeping it secret from the Consortium. Fortunately for the Hunter, the *crack* of their whips, wailing cries of the slaves, and roared orders created just enough confusion to drown out the screams of his latest victims.

The Hunter had no time to worry about what the Vassalage Consortium intended to do with all their surviving captives now that the Order had succeeded at breaking into *Ukuhlushwa Okungapheli*. He'd have to leave that up to the Issai and the warriors marching at Jumaane's back. To him fell the task of stopping whatever had brought the Order of Mithridas all this way to Ghandia.

He sprinted straight toward the spot where he'd seen the fist-sized, transparent square gemstone set into the crystalline walls. With all the agility of his Bucelarii heritage, he slid to a halt just before crashing against the wall, and brought Soulhunger up to place its gemstone against the one in the wall.

Instantly, the tower responded. The enormous stone doors began to rumble shut, slowly at first, but picking up surprising speed as the mechanisms that controlled them kicked in. The shouts of surprise and alarm from the Ordermen outside the tower were cut off as the doors slammed shut with a deafening *BOOM* that shook the very ground beneath the Hunter's feet.

The Hunter lowered Soulhunger from the resonator stone—a stone said to vibrate at a similar frequency to the *Im'tasi* blades, according to a Vothmoti Lectern—and turned to face the remaining Ordermen.

All five had weapons now—two long swords, a pair of hand axes popular among the Fehlans, a hunting spear, and a flail with a viciously spiked head—and held them level at him. Yet disbelief, and more than a little fear, shone in their eyes. Two darted surprised glances toward the now-shut door, as if they couldn't understand how he'd undone something in seconds that had taken them *weeks*—or even months—to accomplish. The rest merely stared at the shattered rapier blade protruding from his chest.

The Hunter allowed a vicious smile to spread on his lips as he slowly, calmly raised his own weapons. "Good night to die, isn't it?"

Whatever he thought of the Ordermen, he couldn't fault their courage. They'd just watched him whittle down their ranks by half in the space of seconds and shrug off a rapier thrust to the chest. Yet in defiance of the near certainty of their deaths, the five enemies closed in on him from all sides.

The Hunter met them head-on. His sword knocked aside the thrusting spear to send it stabbing into the upraised arm of the flail-wielder. On his backstroke, he hacked through the axeman's right hand and knocked his left-hand weapon free. The hatchet spun end over end, its shaft slamming into the face of the swordsman who'd moved a hair slower than the rest. The impact didn't shatter the black slashwyrm scale mask, but staggered them nonetheless. In the time it took them to recover, the Hunter had buried Soulhunger in the second swordsman's chest and hacked off the spearman's head.

The screams of the dying swordsman brought crimson light flaring from Soulhunger's gemstone, and power raged in a fiery torrent through the Hunter. With his now-free left hand, he ripped the rapier blade from his chest and, while the wound healed, drove the needle-like blade through the eyeholes in the first swordsman's mask.

The axeman was the last one standing—or, *kneeling*. Blood gushed from the stump of his wrist, and his left hand hung at a terrible angle, shattered by the Hunter's disarming blow. The

Hunter was tempted to let the man live. Live, and suffer in agony. But only a fool left enemies alive behind him. With a contemptuous flick of his sword, he opened the dying enemy's throat.

The Hunter wasted no time gloating over his fallen foes. He paused only long enough to let the quivering, twitching swordsman's body go slack before pulling Soulhunger free. The glow from the dagger's gemstone turned the blue light that bathed the Bondshold's interior to a deep, angry violet. A suitable match to the Hunter's mood.

Flicking the blood from his watered steel sword, the Hunter raced toward the stairs that led toward the tower's upper levels. To his surprise, these stairs, too, were crusted with dried blood. Dark blood, black as night. The Hunter's keen nostrils detected the hint of acidity on its metallic edge.

And with the strange scent, the reek of demons. The Abiarazi was *above* him. The one he believed had brought the Order of Mithridas here awaited him somewhere. He'd search every damned chamber in the tower to find the *true* threat he'd crossed half a world to eradicate.

Whoever you are, wherever you are, he promised silently, tightening his grip on Soulhunger's hilt, *you cannot hide from me any longer!*

With the doors to *Ukuhlushwa Okungapheli* sealed, the demon was trapped in the Serenii tower. The only way out now was through the Hunter.

Chapter Ninety-One

The Hunter rushed up the winding staircase, taking the steps three at a time. He'd barely ascended halfway to the first level when he spotted a trio of masked Orderman barreling down toward him, doubtless drawn by the clash of steel and the screams of their dying comrades.

The three faltered at the sight of the Hunter. Their feet skidded on the dark blood crusted onto the crystalline stone of the staircase. The Hunter was among them before they could fully regain their balance or raise their weapons. His sword flashed in a blur, blood sprayed, and three bodies fell behind him as he ran on.

Like the Sage's temple in Kara-ket, *Ukuhlushwa Okungapheli's* exterior was built from marvelous Serenii glass that appeared opaque from the outside, but so transparent as to be nearly invisible from within. As he climbed, the Hunter had an unobstructed view of the world surrounding the Bondshold. His eyes roamed *Isigodi Umlilophilayo,* which still seethed and churned with the acidic green river, though much had hardened to stone to fill the deep fissures spanning the valley.

At the base of the tower, the Hunter could *just* make out the uppermost levels of scaffolding erected by the Consortium to excavate beneath the Serenii tower. Captives by the hundreds—perhaps even *thousands*—clogged the structure, herded up to the plateau in a seemingly endless line by whip-wielding slavers. The labor might have ended the moment the Order of Mithridas gained entry into the Serenii tower, but the laborers still needed to be seen to.

Of Siyanda, Naledi, and the Issai, the Hunter saw no sign. Not that he had much time to look. The winding staircase curved around the inside of the circular tower's outer wall, and his vantage of the land surrounding the tower changed with every step upward. Soon, his circuitous journey up the staircase brought him around to a view of the makeshift city built upon the plateau west of the Bondshold.

There, he saw the long lines of captives being herded by scores of slavers deeper into the city, likely to be confined within their enclosures until their fates were decided. The strongest might be kept alive and marched to slavery elsewhere on Einan. The ill and weak, however, likely wouldn't live many more sunrises before the Consortium decided their fate. Given the corpses littering the chamber below, the Hunter suspected that fate would be far from kind.

His eyes strayed toward the towering volcanic stone wall at the far edge of the camp. The gates were barred and the moving lights of torches and lanterns marked the presence of patrols. Jumaane hadn't yet been sighted—perhaps not even arrived—otherwise there would have been chaos as the men stationed there prepared for a fierce fight.

The Hunter couldn't help a moment of worry. Their battle plan had counted on sufficient time for the Issai to dig their way free of the tunnels and kill enough enemies that the slaves on the scaffolding would summon courage enough to turn on their captors. For that to happen,

Jumaane *had* to make his presence known, drawing the bulk of the slavers' forces and their full attention toward their defenses.

But time had run out. The Order of Mithridas had gained entry to *Ukuhlushwa Okungapheli*. The plan to drive the Consortium from Ghandia had to take second place now. The Hunter *had* to stop the bastards from freeing *Nuru Iwu* from his prison. Whether Tunde's warning was the mad ravings of a dying mind or a terrible truth, the Hunter didn't know. But what was abundantly clear was that he couldn't allow the Order—the Abiarazi that led them—to gain access to or control of any power capable of terrifying a being as ancient as *Okadigbo*.

The Hunter's keen ears detected the sound of enemies approaching long before the group of six Ordermen appeared around the bend in the winding staircase. He was ready for them, hurling himself up the stairs at a mad dash to unleash a flurry of lightning-fast strikes. He'd smelled no demon among them—the tainted scent came from all around him, but grew no stronger as he closed with his foes—and waded into their ranks with full confidence and unbridled ferocity.

The six of them fought well and died hard. Two had made the foolish mistake of carrying polearms—a halberd and a glaive—into the tight confines of the staircase, and they did little more than hamper their comrades' attacks. The Hunter accepted a slashing wound to his side for the sake of trapping the halberd's axe-head under his arm, and a savage twist of his upper body tore the weapon from its wielder's grip and slammed the sturdy shaft into the two masked enemies at the man's side. In the same motion, the Hunter buried three fingers of watered steel into the Orderman's throat. The three of them fell in a heap, one dying, one knocked senseless, the other merely stunned.

A sword stroke caught the Hunter a glancing blow to the back of the head, sending him staggering forward to crash into the stairway's left-hand wall. He felt something *crunch* beneath his boots, and the dazed Orderman he'd knocked down howled at the agony of a shattered sword arm. The Hunter ducked beneath a decapitating blow from behind and rammed Soulhunger into the kneeling man's unarmored chest in a single smooth motion. Even as the man's scream brought the dagger's gemstone flaring to life, the Hunter was already spinning and bringing his sword up to block the strike of a heavy double-bladed axe.

Power rushed through him in a searing tidal wave that set his veins ablaze and his muscles crackling with renewed vigor. With a roar, the Hunter seized the upraised axe in his left hand, cut off the hands holding it, and swung the weapon in a vicious arc that split the sword-wielder from the crown of his head halfway down his spine. The two severed halves of his mask fell away to reveal the bloody, dumbfounded features of a Drashi. The Hunter kicked the dead man hard into the path of the glaive-wielding Orderman. The flying body tangled the long shaft of the polearm between the man's legs, and he could do nothing but gape wide-eyed as the Hunter drove his sword through the slashwyrm scale mask, shattering it, and into his open mouth. Gurgling, gasping, the man slumped to his knees and toppled sideways into the pool of his comrades' blood.

The Hunter finished off the hand-less axeman with a swift thrust to the heart and stamped down hard on the neck of the one he'd knocked unconscious. By the time he pulled Soulhunger free, he alone remained alive within the stairwell.

Instinctively, he reached up to touch the back of his head where the sword had struck him. His fingers came away wet with blood but no trace remained of the wound. Not so much as a flicker of pain, either. Soulhunger's magic had done its work.

He leaped lightly over the corpses and continued his ascent at a run. Soon, he reached the first level—which, in truth, was little more than a landing that continued on to the next set of stairs. Where in the Illumina each level had held Chambers of Sustenance, the Bondshold seemed to contain *only* the pillar at its heart—and, of course, whatever the Hunter would find in the towertop chamber.

On he ran, only slowing once when a group of ten Ordermen attempted to bar his path. They proved a more challenging fight—one had a crossbow, another the short horse-bow favored by the tribes of the Hrandari Plains, and a third hurled spiked stars with efficiency that would have been deadly to anyone else. Yet they could not truly stop him, a fact they seemed to understand only too late. The last two turned to flee, doubtless to bring warning to those above, but the Hunter cut them down before they made it up two dozen steps.

As he ripped Soulhunger from the lifeless corpse of the last Orderman to fall, a memory flitted through his mind. He'd been in a place much like this, fighting a similar battle, facing enemies who, too, followed a demon's orders. The Sage's Blood Sentinels had attempted to slow him and Taiana down and died just like the masked Ordermen barring his path now. A spark of longing blazed within him. But only for a moment. He extinguished it quickly. Now wasn't the time to dwell on such things.

For in that moment, through the blood rushing in his ears and the hammering of his heart against his ribs, he heard the first of the screams. High-pitched, ringing with terrible agony, echoing off the gemstone walls all around him. The sound of immense, all-consuming, mind-shattering suffering.

The Hunter broke into a run, his strength replenished by Soulhunger's magic. The screaming rose in pitch and intensity, until it seemed the entire tower vibrated from the force of that pain. Then it cut off abruptly, replaced by utter stillness. A shudder ran down the Hunter's spine, and dread twisted in his belly.

He passed three more landings before encountering the descending Ordermen. The two masked enemies had their weapons sheathed, their hands full with the lifeless body of a Ghandian. A young man this time, his shirt burned away by the power that had melted his face like a lump of wax and seared the flesh from his palms. Another dead *Umoyahlebe*.

The Hunter butchered the Ordermen with cold, calculated efficiency. They died before they had a chance to drop the body and reach for their weapons. The Hunter raced on without ever slowing a step.

The screams renewed. No longer one voice, but *many*. Rising in ferocity, a symphony of anguish and terror. The sound twisted a dagger in the Hunter's belly. He had no need to imagine its cause—he'd seen the burned-out bodies, not just here, but the night he'd watched the *Umoyahlebe* attempting to break open the Bondshold with the power of the *Kish'aa*.

The Hunter abandoned any attempt at stealth and ran with all the strength he could demand from his body. His feet fairly flew, boots crunching on the blood crusted on the stairs. His pulse roared in his ears and adrenaline amplified by Soulhunger's magic coursed through his veins. Yet the icy dagger of fear twisted deeper into his belly with every step. The Order of Mithridas was compelling the *Umoyahlebe* to draw so much *Kish'aa* power it burned them from the inside out. What were they doing up in that towertop chamber? What could they possibly need with—

CRACK!

The deafening sound rang out so loud it nearly shattered the Hunter's ears. A terrible shudder ran through the tower, setting it trembling with such force the Hunter was thrown against the inner wall. He caught himself, barely managing to remain upright, yet the sight that greeted him stole his breath. The midnight black pillar at the heart of the tower had broken. A fissure as thick as his finger ran through its core, disappearing below. Judging by the tremor he'd felt, it had rippled all the way down to the tower's base.

Keeper's teeth! Horror and amazement drove the Hunter into motion once more. He charged up the stairs at a dead sprint. Not since he'd stared up at Indombe's immense form had he felt terror akin to the one now coursing through him. The power it must have taken to do that, to damage the Serenii structure that had stood for countless millennia! His mind could scarcely even begin to comprehend it.

A shout rang out from above him, but this one held no trace of fear or pain. No, it rang with triumph.

"At last, He Who Is Nameless awakens!"

Chapter Ninety-Two

A savage wave of heat blasted the Hunter full-on as he raced into the towertop chamber. The searing intensity scorched his skin and turned his mouth dry as a desert in a heartbeat.

The source of the heat was unmistakable: thirteen chained Ghandians knelt in an inward facing circle, and from their outstretched hands streamed cracking, sizzling waves of blue-white light. Behind each stood a masked figure, with dark chains of dimercurite alloy linking the Ordermen to the *Umoyahlebe* under their control. Beyond them, pressed against the walls by the drawn weapons of half a dozen more Ordermen, eight *Umoyahlebe* wearing the dimercurite collars, bracelets, and anklets stood watching their fellows wide-eyed—no doubt waiting until one of the thirteen in the circle burned out from within and they were summoned as replacements.

The power streaming from the kneeling *Umoyahlebe* was directed at the black pillar that rose to roughly waist height from the floor at the heart of the chamber. The stone drank in the torrents of blue-white light streaming toward it, and all around its circumference, arcane runes glowed blindingly bright. Atop the pillar, sat what the Hunter recognized to be a Chamber of Sustenance, yet one unlike any he'd had seen before. Thrice as wide and twice as long as those in Enarium, this was carved from the same midnight-hued gemstone that formed the tower's exterior and its central column rather than white stone. The open lid was not a gentle, glowing blue, but glass of an acidic green as bright as the rivers flowing beneath *Isigodi Umlilophilayo*.

But it was what *emerged* from the Chamber that commanded the Hunter's attention.

Something that might have been a hand clung to the lip of the Chamber. Claws as long as the Hunter's forearms sprouted from its seven many-jointed fingers, and the flesh appeared both like pale grey leather wrinkled by the sun and green scales dappled with leprous spots of white.

At a shout, the Ordermen holding the *Umoyahlebe's* chains tightened their grips, and the flow of power cut off. All eyes were fixed on the stone casket atop the pillar. Even the Ordermen keeping the waiting *Umoyahlebe* under control couldn't keep from gawking at the thing within the Chamber.

The hand muscles clenched, claws sinking into the black stone, and heaved. The rest of its body emerged, slithering serpent-like over the edge of the Chamber to collapse onto its hands and knees on the floor. The shape of its skeletal frame suggested it was bipedal, yet its spiny back was bent and its bone-encrusted shoulders stooped by its millennia spent trapped within the casket. Like its hand, the rest of its body was a mixture of mottled, leathery flesh and green of scales with white spots. Its entire left side and the length of its left-hand claws were crusted with the same hideous dark matter that seeped down the black pillar and snaked along the floor in a trail that led toward the descending stairs.

The Hunter had found the source of the blood. And, he realized with dawning horror, the source of the smell.

It seemed impossible. His mind struggled to comprehend the evidence so plain before him. Yet the moment he looked into its eyes—all *four* of them—he knew the truth. He had no need to draw in a breath to confirm it. He'd seen similar creatures in his nightmares, his memories, faint as they were, of the War of Gods.

This thing, this twisted, emaciated, deformed horror, had the depthless, empty black eyes of an Abiarazi.

It cannot be! The Hunter stared slack-jawed. *Nuru Iwu...is a demon?*

The discovery set him reeling, froze him in place for a long moment. Just long enough for the thing that had been called "He Who Is Nameless" to draw itself up to its full height—nearly twice the Hunter's own—reach out a clawed hand, and snatch up one of the kneeling captives, a fellow with snow-white hair and a wispy beard. The Orderman holding the *Umoyahlebe's* chain was yanked forward so hard his arm tore from its socket with a hideous *pop*. The white-haired Ghandian had no time to scream before his head was sheared clean off and the creature of nightmare closed its jaws around its still-twitching body.

That was all it took to snap the Hunter from his momentary stupor. For all his horror and shock at seeing this *thing*, this grotesque monstrosity far worse than anything he might have imagined, the knowledge of what he had to do pushed everything else to the back of his mind.

He sprang from where he'd been standing just within the staircase and rushed toward the Abiarazi feasting on human flesh. He struck out with sword and dagger as he passed between two of the Ordermen holding the *Umoyahlebe's* chains, and the pair fell with severed spines. In the time it took the others nearby to register the *clank* of the chains slipping from lifeless fingers, the Hunter had bounded over the kneeling Ghandians and brought his watered steel sword whipping around to hack off the demon's head.

For all its apparent weakness, the thing moved with impossible speed. The Hunter had just begun his attack when something struck him with the force of a charging ox and hurled him backward. His vision wavered, the world going black, then exploded in sparks as agony flared along the entire back half of his body. Air whooshed from his lungs and he found he could not draw breath.

The Hunter blinked in a frantic effort to clear the darkness from before his eyes. He must have lost consciousness for a moment, for when he came to, he found himself pressed to the floor by a heavy weight. When the blurring finally cleared from his vision, he recognized the bodies atop him. One was headless, its blood still gushing from the stump of its neck. The other still squirmed and writhed, howling like a maddened animal as he fought to keep the last strips of flesh tethering his arm to his shoulder from snapping.

The Hunter's jaw dropped. The demon had *thrown* the dead Ghandian—and the Orderman chained to him—with no more effort than if he'd tossed a pebble into a lake, but with such force it had thrown the Hunter clean across the room. Few Abiarazi had shown such strength—Lord Apus, the Warmaster, certainly, perhaps the one who'd called himself the Third of the Bloody Hand—but the feat should have been impossible from a creature that looked more dead than alive.

Keeper's teeth! Panic sank icy claws into the Hunter. He'd managed to retain his grip on his weapons, but weighed down by the two bodies, he couldn't raise them in his defense. He'd be utterly vulnerable to the Abiarazi's follow-up attack.

Every shred of strength went into struggling free of the weight atop him. His efforts set the Orderman howling again. The caterwauling only stopped when the Hunter finally made his way out from beneath, only to find his foe had passed out from the pain of having his shoulder torn the rest of the way off.

He spun to face the Abiarazi, weapons coming up and muscles braced to defend himself. A few of the Ordermen in the chamber had turned toward him—particularly those guarding the *Umoyahlebe* standing against the wall—but the demon seemed to have forgotten about him. Its attention was consumed entirely by the two shattered, mangled Ghandian corpses that dangled limply from the end of its forearm-length claws. Its enormous maw split open both vertically and horizontally, revealing four rows of sharp teeth, which it sank into *both* of its victims at the same time. Blood sprayed as it tore massive chunks of flesh from one's shoulder and another's thigh.

The two Ordermen tethered to the dead *Umoyahlebe* by dimercurite chains frantically endeavored to unclasp their bracelets, their faces wide in terror. The rest of the Ghandians kneeling around the pillar were attempting to scramble backward, and their captors were either too stunned, horrified, or—in more than a few cases—elated by the grisly display to stop them.

Acid rose in the back of the Hunter's throat at the sickening sight, and from the blow to his head. Yet he swallowed it hard and clenched his jaw to stop his head from spinning. He had no time for hesitation, uncertainty, or weakness. Not in the face of such...such...

Evil. That was the only word he could think of to describe the monstrosity before him.

Though it went against every instinct, the Hunter turned his back on the Abiarazi feasting on human flesh, on the masked foes charging toward him with drawn weapons. A single step brought him to where the now-armless Orderman lay unconscious atop the Ghandian the demon had hurled at him. The Hunter drove a vicious kick into the man's uninjured side, striking hard enough to shatter ribs. The pain snapped the Orderman awake and renewed his howls.

Howls that grew even louder as the Hunter buried Soulhunger into his unarmored chest. The gemstone in the dagger's pommel flared instantly to life, filling the towertop chamber with its brilliant crimson light. Searing, sizzling heat rushed through the Hunter. The fiery torrent set his heart racing, adrenaline coursing in his veins, and energy crackling through his muscles. The pain in his head and back evaporated. Gone was his fatigue, his hunger and thirst. He felt only *power.*

He let the dagger drink only long enough to restore him, then tore it free of the shrieking Orderman and spun to face his charging foes. Three of the masked enemies who had kept the chained *Umoyahlebe* huddled against the wall now lunged for him with raised swords. The Hunter cut down the first one to reach him with a savage slash, gutted the second, and disarmed the third by slicing open his forearm from wrist to elbow. Quick as a striking serpent, he darted forward and drove Soulhunger into the stunned enemy's chest.

His nostrils filled with the dying man's scent—tar, spruce, and bridle leather, a mixture he remembered all too clearly—and agonized screams set the Hunter's ears ringing. Again, crimson light flared in the towertop chamber. A tidal wave of power seared through every fiber of the Hunter's being. He bathed in the blood and the screams of the dying Orderman. Laughing with the joy of it, the thrill of battle, the rush of watching his enemies—pathetic, *human* enemies—die in droves. His mouth opened of its own accord, baring his teeth, preparing to bite down on his prey's neck and tear flesh from bone. Saliva flooded his mouth at the promise of fresh meat and warm, hot blood. For millennia, he had not had such a rich feast as—

No!

The Hunter drove his forehead into the Orderman's masked face. The impact did little to his enemy—the man was well beyond feeling as Soulhunger devoured his life force—but pain exploded in the Hunter's face as his nose shattered against carved slashwyrm.

With agony, came clarity of mind. Freedom from the thoughts that slithered like serpents into his consciousness. His gaze darted to the demon and found all four of its empty black eyes fixed on him.

"Stay out of my head, you bastard!" the Hunter roared, wiping blood streaming from his broken nose.

The demon's head twisted to the side at a terribly unnatural angle, its eyes never leaving him as it took another crunching bite from the dead corpse impaled on its claws. The Hunter felt its scrutiny boring into him, its attention now fully bent to the task of examining him. No, attempting to gain control of him. He could feel the iron grip once more closing in around his skull, squeezing, squeezing, pushing all other thoughts from his mind.

In desperation, the Hunter tapped into the primal fury and the animalistic instinct that had driven him to survive so many times before. A barbaric roar tore from his lips. *"GRAAHH!"* He could find no other words—the demon's grip on his mind rendered him no more eloquent than a beast of prey. Yet like a beast of prey, he was not without fangs.

The demon could attempt to gain command of his thoughts, but the Hunter still had mastery of his body. His right arm came up and whipped forward with all the strength and speed he could muster. His sword flew end over end on a direct path toward the demon's face. Fear and necessity guided his throw, and the sword buried to the hilt right between the Abiarazi's oversized black eyes.

Instantly, the grip on the Hunter's mind lessened, and he was free. Loosing another roar, he charged straight toward the demon. His right hand reached beneath his cloak to grasp the hilt of the Swordsman's iron blade, and his left tightened around Soulhunger.

He'd promised Kharna he would capture Abiarazi rather than kill them outright. The Serenii needed the demons' vitality to sustain him in the battle against the Great Devourer. Yet his vow meant little if he died in its execution. Kharna would have to understand why the Hunter had been forced to kill this demon, for it was far beyond anything he'd—

Two steps were all he managed before a blast of blue-white lightning struck him full in the chest.

Chapter Ninety-Three

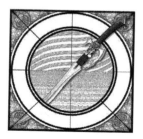

Agony ripped through the Hunter. It was as if the sun itself exploded within him, the heat so intense it scorched every fiber of his being. He felt himself being hurled through the air, flying clear across the chamber to slam into the wall, but there was no pain on impact, only a jolting sensation that did nothing to diminish the fire cracking through his nerves, racing along his muscles, devouring his bones.

He screamed. The sound was ripped from his lips by the blinding torment consuming him for what felt like an eternity—but could only have been mere seconds.

The brilliant light vanished, the flow of power cut off. The Hunter found he could draw breath—the fist of iron that had closed around his heart and lungs loosened its grip—and he sucked air greedily. He managed only the tiniest gasp before his body seized up again. Spasms shook him, the lightning still crackling through his muscles and nerves, setting him twitching and jerking.

And somehow, the pain grew worse. What he'd felt from the lightning blast had been bad, yet the power had overwhelmed his mind, burned his nerves so he could only register *some* of the pain. But now he felt *everything*. Every agonizing twitch of muscles convulsing dozens of times per second. He lay on the floor of the chamber, beyond sensation, beyond control, lost in a sea of torment. He could not even summon the strength to scream now.

His eyes rolled around in his head, the world spinning dizzily before him. He caught bare snatches of reality through the waves of darkness that crashed down on him and receded like the ocean's tide. A masked Orderman thrusting a hand toward him, the other hand gripping the chain connecting his wrist to the collar of an *Umoyahlebe*. A young girl with features he *knew* should be familiar, if only he could marshal his thoughts through the anguish wracking him.

The blue-white light flared to life again, and a fresh surge of coruscating power tore through the air. A bolt of searing hot lightning speared the Hunter again. His jaw clenched so tightly he feared his teeth would shatter, and his bones groaned at the strain of muscles locked up stiff as steel bars by the *Kish'aa* magic.

Through the blinding torment, through the blood hammering against his eardrums with the force of a smith's mallet, came a low, guttural growl. Forceful, commanding, inhuman in its ferocity. Yet the lightning stopped and the Hunter experienced a moment of blessed relief as his body relaxed. He dragged in one ragged breath, then another. Unclenched his jaw, forced his fingers to uncurl, gasping, struggling to regain control of his body.

His relief proved horribly short-lived. The blackness had barely retreated enough for his vision to clear when the demon's monstrous form darkened the air above him. It was thicker now, muscles bulging beneath its patchwork scale-and-leather skin. Feasting on human flesh had restored a measure of its strength. Though far from the mighty beast it could once have been, even in its reduced state, the Hunter had little doubt its strength rivaled that of any Abiarazi he'd encountered before.

Gone was the Hunter's sword; the bastard had pulled it free and hurled it away, and barely a trickle of blood marked where the blade had pierced his face. Four endless black eyes stared down on him. Not a shred of pity existed within those inky voids, only hunger unconstrained. A long, serpentine tongue flicked from its mouth to lick the blood off its face. The sound that grated from its lips echoed with the rumble of satisfaction at its meal. Yet it was far from satiated. Indeed, looking into the dark pits of its eyes, the Hunter saw the truth: the thing would *never* be satiated, even if it devoured every man, woman, and child alive on Einan.

But its hunger differed from that of the Great Devourer. The Great Devourer was a being of pure chaos, a thing that longed to unmake all of reality until only nothingness remained. Entropy was its natural state, and it simply consumed for the sake of survival. This creature merely longed to consume. Not because it truly hungered or needed to survive or even feared for its existence. It devoured for the sake of devouring. For the sheer pleasure of ripping the life from a living creature and snuff it from existence in the most monstrous form possible.

And the bastard had chosen the Hunter as its next meal. Again its jaws hinged open like the petals of some horrible nightmare flower, and its forked tongue slithered between its innumerable teeth, loosening gobbets of flesh and sending flecks of blood dripping onto the Hunter's face. It prepared to feast.

The Hunter struggled to regain control of his body. To will some semblance of strength into muscles utterly drained from the spasms that had contracted them to the point of tearing.

To seize command of limbs that lay limp at his side, not so much as twitching or jerking as the last of the lightning burned away. To rise, to fight, even to flee. *Anything!*

To no avail. The Hunter could barely draw breath, much less power his body. The blast of *Kish'aa* power had rendered him utterly motionless. Helpless. Shattered like Farida. Powerless, like Bardin in the Sage's unyielding grip. As trapped within his own flesh as Master Eldor had been within the confines of his oath and honor.

The demon reached for the Hunter. Its predator senses had to know that its prey was utterly at its mercy, for where it had moved with blinding speed before, it took its time stretching out its mottled, white-spotted hand with terrible slowness. Mocking him. Mocking his frailty and impotence. Like a greatcat toying with a deer with broken legs, unable to fight or flee from certain death.

Panic clawed with razor-sharp talons at the Hunter's mind. He had faced death countless times before—in combat, from the Beggar Priests' poison, even risking a fall from terrible heights—but never like *this*. Never had he been unable to resist. To put up even a token fight, whether it be against superior foes or his own body.

No, this cannot be how I end! a voice shrieked in his mind. Whether it was his own, the animal part of him that eternally fought to survive, or the inner presence summoned by his fear, he didn't know. All he knew was that it filled him with a terror he had never *truly* felt until this moment. The terror of facing imminent death with no way to stop it. He'd seen it in the eyes of his victims countless times, but now, experiencing it for himself, it was far worse than anything he might have imagined.

Something—be it the surge of fear, the cresting wave of panic, or his body's innate healing ability—gave him just strength enough to lift his right arm. To unleash a single blow at his enemy. His sword was gone, the Swordsman's iron blade blasted from his grip by the lightning, so he clenched his fingers and struck out with his fist. A pitiful blow, he knew, yet it *had* to be enough. He would not die without a fight.

It did no good. His knuckles struck the demon's bony leg and rebounded off its scaly hide with pitiful force. The demon didn't even glance down; it merely lifted its legs and stamped down hard on the Hunter's right wrist. Bone crunched beneath the impact and pain shot up the Hunter's arm. A scream bubbled up on his lips, but he seized control of it, turning it from a pathetic cry into a defiant shout, one into which he poured all his desperation and fear.

The sound rolled over the demon with no more effect than the Hunter's blow. It stared down at him, its expression never shifting, the hungry look still plastered on its face. Both of its hands moved toward the Hunter now. Long, razor-sharp claws reaching for him.

The Hunter felt the moment they pierced his chest. Slowly, agonizingly, the demon drove them deeper, deeper, tearing through the smoking hole the lightning blast had torn in his Buhari armor. Peeling back flesh, slicing into muscle, digging past the bones toward the soft organs beneath. The Hunter roared at the blinding agony, far worse than anything the Warmaster had inflicted on him. Yet, as with the Warmaster, he could do nothing but lie there, rendered helpless by the power of the *Kish'aa* and the impossible, overwhelming strength of the creature carving him open.

Memories flashed through his mind. Faces, familiar and beloved. Kiara, smiling at him with a look of such love shining in her eyes. Hailen, fast asleep on his little wooden desk, his head pillowed on a stack of parchments given to him by Father Reverentus, his snores resounding through the small room he shared with Evren. Evren, grinning in triumph at a blow he'd landed on the Hunter during their sparring. Graeme, with that squinting look on his bespectacled face as he bent over his latest Taivoro novel.

Tears sprang to his eyes. He could not bring himself to say goodbye to the ones he'd come to love—and who, despite his best efforts, had come to love him, too. In their own way.

More faces followed. Faces of those who awaited him in the Long Keeper's arms. Farida, her cheeks still smudged with the sap of her fresh-cut roses. Bardin, his eyes no longer wandering, but bright and cheery. Master Eldor, the frown gone from his face, his features smooth and relaxed, an arm draped around Kanna's shoulders. Father Reverentus, standing straight and proud, a book held in the hand he could now uncurl freely, no longer withered or gnarled. Tassat, ever-eager to lock blades and feel the rush of battle. Jak and Karrl, hands clasped, arms intertwined. Old Nan, but no longer old or bent by age.

Taiana. Not as she'd been the day he last saw her, pale, lifeless, on the verge of death. No, the strong, confident, beautiful Taiana he'd fought beside on the field of battle five thousand years earlier.

I'm sorry, he told the memory of his wife. *I'm sorry I will not be there when you awaken years from now.*

Jaia's face followed. Not the face he'd seen—expression twisted by scorn, stained with Father Reverentus' blood—but a softer, kinder face. One he *wished* was truly real though he knew it had to be a fiction of his mind. A fiction created by his desperate hopes that Jaia had gotten the best of both him and Taiana and somehow found a better life.

Forgive me, Jaia. Forgive me for failing you before you were ever born, and failing to find you all these years.

Her face remained etched in his mind as the darkness claimed him. His screams grew distant, the pain receding, but still he clung to her. Fighting to keep her at the forefront of his final thoughts.

Cool, soothing blackness enveloped him. Wiping away the pain, the fear, the anguish at knowing he would not live to bid farewell to the ones he loved. The void came to claim him, and he did not fight it. Could not—and, in truth, had no desire to. There was a strange calm to it. A cessation of struggle, a yielding of control that suddenly seemed very peaceful.

That was it. *Peace* was what awaited him in the void beyond the edge of life. In the comforting darkness where he would never again know the agony of—

Consciousness slammed into him with terrible force, sending a torrent of pain racing through him. Pain and power both. White-hot, impossible to ignore, growing stronger with every beat of his heart.

"GRAAAHH!!" the scream tore from his lips.

His eyes flew open, and he looked up toward the creature looming large above him. Yet it was no longer the *demon* standing over him. Gone were the claws ripping at his flesh, the hungry jaws preparing to snap around his head and tear into his heart. Instead, he saw a familiar strong figure dressed in the colorful, flowing robes of the Issai. Her tight-curled hair flew wildly about her head, and her face was twisted into a mask of rage and exertion.

Aisha stood at his side, feet planted, arms thrust forward, and from her hands streamed a torrent of brilliant blue-white light.

Chapter Ninety-Four

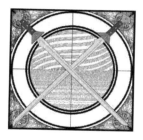

In the blinding blast of *Kish'aa* magic, the Hunter saw the demonic creature flying through the air, hurled by the lightning Aisha unleashed. Its corpulent frame crashed into the black gemstone wall with a terrible *crack*. Limbs snapped, the spines on its back crumpled, and it collapsed to the floor in a limp heap. Where it had struck, spidery cracks appeared in the midnight-hued crystal of the tower's exterior wall.

The Hunter's mind boggled at the ferocity of Aisha's power. To not only blow the monstrosity off him, but with force enough to shatter the virtually indestructible handiwork of the Serenii.

Yet he could spare only a fraction of his attention for her. His mind was consumed by the torrent of energy crackling through him like a river of fire. Suddenly, he had strength enough to lift his head, and his eyes found the flesh of his chest mending, the torn skin and muscle knitting, bones snapped by long demonic claws once more fusing. The vitality rushing in every fiber of his being could only have come from one place.

Kiara appeared a moment later, her face lit up by the crimson light of Soulhunger's gemstone. "On your feet and back in the fight!"

Her shout was drowned out by a fresh scream from the dying Orderman whose soul even now fed the dagger's magic. It was one of the three who'd remained to guard the *Umoyahlebe* not joined in the circle of power. The Hunter's eyes widened at the sight of Soulhunger's shining gemstone embedded deep into his unarmored chest. Somehow, Kiara had managed to retrieve his dropped weapon and hurl it across the circular towertop to bury in the Orderman's flesh. No doubt the sight of the demon crouched atop him and tearing him apart had sharpened her already excellent aim. The Hunter could only bless her bravery and skill while heeding her command to find his feet.

A groan escaped his lips as he rose. The worst of the damage inflicted by the demon's claws had healed, but he was not yet fully recovered. Blood still trickled from wounds on their way to closing, slowly now, as the light from Soulhunger's gemstone faded, the Orderman's life force extinguished completely.

Despite the pain, he had sufficient presence of mind to scoop up his watered steel sword from where it had been hurled, its blade still red with the demon's blood. The thing called Nameless—"He Who Is Nameless" proved far too clunky for him to think, much less say aloud—lay in a limp heap where it had fallen, rendered unconscious by the force of Aisha's power. Yet it was far from dead, the Hunter knew. And when it rose, he'd best be ready to face it or—

"Kill her!" came a shout from somewhere off to his left.

718

The Hunter's eyes snapped to the source of the sound. The voice had come from the far end of the chamber, where one of the Ordermen had turned to stab a gloved finger at Aisha. His other hand, however, gripped the chain tethering his wrist to the collar of the *Umoyahlebe* he'd been controlling. When the young girl turned to heed the command she could not ignore, the Hunter saw the *Umoyahlebe's* features clearly, and a dagger of ice twisted in his belly.

Nkanyezi's eyes were wide, filled with fury and fear and horror. Her face convulsed with visible effort, yet for all her struggle, her hands rose nonetheless and from her outstretched palms streamed two crackling spears of lightning—aimed straight at Aisha.

The Hunter had a split second to act. He spun, dove, and tackled Aisha around the waist, bearing her to the ground. Not a heartbeat too soon. Twin streams of hissing, sparking blue-white power streamed above him, so close he could feel the heat singeing the backs of his legs. He tucked into a roll as he landed, pulling Aisha up to her feet along with him.

A shove sent her stumbling out of the path of yet another blast of *Kish'aa* power unleashed from another *Umoyahlebe*. Her father, Lwazi, his face caked with dried blood and eyes ringed with dark circles of exhaustion. Yet he could no more ignore the commands of the Orderman holding his dimercurite chain than Nkanyezi could. And his blasts, though smaller and backed with less power than his daughter's, were far more controlled. When his first strike missed Aisha, he cut off the flow of magic abruptly and shifted his hands to adjust his aim.

"No!" The roar of rage came from the entrance to the chamber. Davathi stood framed in the doorway, her face illuminated by the blue-white light of the *Kish'aa* still crackling in the air. She roared something in her own tongue, her words aimed at her husband.

Lwazi's head snapped toward his wife, and his face lit up. But only for a moment. His spine suddenly went rigid, and his body moved like a marionette jerked on tight strings, gaze shifting back to Aisha. The Orderman holding his chain snarled a command too low for the Hunter to hear and blue-white light once more brightened in Lwazi's palms.

Again, lightning shot forth from the *Umoyahlebe's* outstretched hands. With the speed of a loosed arrow, the bolts of searing-hot power light up the towertop with blinding force, carving a deadly path through the air straight toward Aisha.

But the blast did not strike her chest nor her head. Aisha had recovered her balance, and managed to spin to face her father and raise her spear. The power of the *Kish'aa* reached crackling fingers toward the metallic spearhead as if drawn to a lodestone. Down the wooden shaft it traveled, burning a course toward Aisha's hand gripping the weapon. The instant the blue-light white touched Aisha's hand, it did not set the skin sizzling or roast her flesh. Instead, it seemed to wink out completely.

It took the Hunter's mind a second to understand what had happened. Only when he saw the light streaming from her eyes did he comprehend the truth. She had *absorbed* the power of the *Kish'aa* into herself.

No, he realized as he spotted the blinding glow emanating from beneath her shirt. *Not into herself. Into her Dy'nashia.*

Indeed, the Serenii pendant shone bright as the morning sun after the darkest night, brighter than the Hunter had ever seen it. From where he stood three paces away from her, he could feel the power humming within its depths. The word "Dy'nashia" meant "repository" in the Serenii tongue. All of the magic channeled at her by her father now resided within that stone, joining the *Kish'aa* she had already collected— doubtless including those the Hunter had killed on the stairs ascending the tower.

He'd had no idea she could do that. Judging by the surprise etched into her face, neither had she. A discovery she'd made in the heat of the moment, driven by desperation and the will to live.

A moment later, Nkanyezi directed another blast of light at Aisha, joining her power to her father's. Aisha's other hand snapped up just in time to catch the searing lighting on her outstretched palm. A growl escaped her throat as the energy scorched her flesh on impact, yet even as the power burned her, it repaired her. Restored her as it had restored Kiara. Whether she'd *always* been able to do such a thing or had merely applied his instructions to Kiara, the Hunter didn't know. Nor did he care. All that mattered now was that Aisha *had* somehow found a way to survive that onslaught of power.

But for how long? Even now, the rest of the *Umoyahlebe* within the chamber were turning to face Aisha, hands rising at the command of the Ordermen holding their chains. The Hunter had no way of knowing just how much power Aisha could absorb before it burned her alive from within.

It fell to *him* to act now while all eyes were fixed on her.

He spared a single glance for Nameless. The hideous four-eyed monstrosity lay where it had fallen, not so much as a twitch from its scale-covered, leathery-skinned body. It would not be out of the fight for long—demons were impossibly resilient, bloody damned difficult for even *him* to kill—but for the moment, it remained unconscious or dazed.

Keeper take it! The Hunter knew it was folly to leave such an enemy alive. Yet he had no choice but to turn his back on it. For Aisha's sake. Until Nameless awoke, it was the lesser of the threats she faced now. Already, the *Umoyahlebe* had begun gathering their power; at any moment, a barrage of lightning would spear Aisha from all sides.

The Hunter raised his voice and shouted with all the strength he could summon. "Break the chains!" He had no time to see if Kiara or Davathi heard him—he was already racing toward the nearest of the *Umoyahlebe.*

The woman couldn't have been older than thirty, but the haggard look on her face from months of imprisonment and Keeper-knew-how-many days of channeling the *Kish'aa* with too little rest made her look on the wrong side of sixty. Her eyes flew wide at the sight of the Hunter barreling toward her. She faltered, only for a moment, just long enough for her left hand to shift away from Aisha to point toward the Hunter's chest. Blue-white light streamed from the blackened flesh of her palms in a wild spray of crackling, searing-hot energy.

The Hunter gritted his teeth and dove *through* the firestorm. Heat washed over him, burning his face, his hands, every bit of exposed flesh. Yet the concentrated force at the center of the blast missed him by a hand's breadth, spearing the air above his back.

And then the Hunter was beyond the worst of it. Landing just beside the Ghandian woman, rolling to his feet, coming up behind her. His sword flashed in a vicious upward chop backed by all the force of his inhuman muscles. Watered steel parted links of dimercurite alloy with the ease of a red-hot knife cutting gossamer strings, then traveled on to hack through exposed flesh and bone beneath. The Orderman hadn't even the time to cry out in fear before the Hunter's sword sheared up through his neck and out his crown. His masked face and the top of his head spun away to land in the oversized, black gemstone Chamber of Sustenance resting atop the pillar. His scent—of sea grass, coriander leaf, and boot black—filled the Hunter with a grim satisfaction.

The Hunter didn't glance back at the *Umoyahlebe* he'd just freed; he just sprang toward the next chained pair without waiting for the first corpse to fall. His sword darted forward with the speed of a hissing serpent and the razor-sharp tip punched through the right eyehole of the next

Orderman's slashwyrm scale mask. Ripping the blade free, he swung it up and brought it down hard on the dimercurite chain connecting the now-dead man to the *Umoyahlebe* he controlled—Aisha's father, Lwazi.

The instant the link was severed, the flow of power from Lwazi's hand cut off. He fell to his knees with a strangled cry, too exhausted to stand. He shouted something in his own tongue the Hunter couldn't hear through the pounding in his ears—a plea to Nkanyezi and the other *Umoyahlebe* still attacking Aisha, a joyous greeting to Davathi, or something else? The Hunter had no time to wonder, for he was already wading into the next Orderman in the circle.

The masked enemy had seen him coming and somehow managed to get their *Umoyahlebe* in place to block the Hunter's advance. But only for a moment. Fool as the Orderman was, he still relied on the power he commanded through his chain to save his life. The Ghandian, a man who looked to be older even than Duma, of an age with Master Eldor or Kanna, raised his hands with a cry of panic, age-lined expression etched with terror. Doubtless he expected a sword thrust to the heart.

The Hunter thrust, but his sword slid past the Ghandian's shoulder to punch into the Orderman's throat just beneath the bottom of his snarling beast mask. The eyes behind the black mask went wide, and crimson gushed from the ruins of the Orderman's neck. The Hunter pulled his sword free just as the Orderman slumped to his knees, gasping, choking, gurgling out a final pathetic effort at remaining alive. The Hunter darted around the stunned Ghandian man and chopped the dimercurite alloy chain in half to free the *Umoyahlebe* before the weight of the toppling Orderman dragged him to the ground.

He had just begun moving on to the next Orderman in the circle when Kiara's shout rang out through the towertop chamber.

"Behind you!"

Chapter Ninety-Five

The Hunter spun, raising his sword to defend himself from the inevitable rear attack.

Only to strike empty air. The shout had not been directed at him, but at *Aisha*.

Too late, the Hunter spotted the monstrous form moving at blurring speed toward the place where Aisha even now struggled to absorb the power of the *Kish'aa* directed at her from the *Umoyahlebe* not yet freed from their chains. Aisha's face was a mask of concentration, her jaw clenched, sweat streaming down her forehead. So intent she was on the threat of her own fellow Ghandians that she could not spare a glance for the doom flying toward her from behind.

The Hunter broke into a mad dash, but even as he took the first step, he knew he'd be too late. Nameless moved far faster, his demonic limbs powered by both its innate magic and strength that surpassed the Hunter's by far. Its grisly feast of human flesh had restored much of its immense musculature. Its powerful legs propelled it across the room in a single bound that carried it directly toward Aisha.

The Hunter acted on instincts honed over decades of fighting. His left hand darted toward his belt, seizing one of his throwing daggers and hurling it at the demon without slowing in his run. An attempt both desperate and fruitless, he knew. The finger-length blade was forged from the finest Voramian steel. Not a speck of iron that could do any lasting damage to the Abiarazi. Indeed, though the dagger buried to the hilt in one of the demon's four eyes, the impact did nothing to slow Nameless, much less knock it off-course. The nightmare creature hurtled toward Aisha with claws outstretched. Glee filled its empty black eyes at the promise of feeding on the flesh of the two-legged creature that had hurt it.

No! the Hunter wanted to shout, what little good it would do. Aisha would never see coming the slash that would remove her head from her shoulders.

Brilliant blue-white light suddenly split the air all around the Hunter. Instinctively, he tensed his muscles, bracing for the surge of pain. Yet the lightning did not strike him. It carved a searing path *past* him, missing him by a hair's breadth, and slammed into Nameless' flying body.

The demon let out a shriek as the *Kish'aa* power punched through his scale-and-leather skin. One fiery spear struck it dead center, another its neck, a third its torso, a fourth its leg. A fifth bolt, the smallest and densest concentration of magic, ripped through its outstretched arm. The power burned the limb away just beneath the shoulder and sent the arm flying across the room.

Nameless' claws had been knocked away from Aisha, but the power had not stopped his momentum. His hulking frame crashed into Aisha and the two of them fell to the crust-covered stone floor in a sprawl.

Right at Davathi's feet. With a howl of rage and fear for her daughter, the Issai *nassor* drove her *assegai* into the demon's neck, just beneath the base of its misshapen skull.

Impossibly, Nameless managed to twist his hulking body just enough that the spear carved a deep furrow into the side of his neck rather than severing his spine as Davathi had intended. His lone remaining hand struck out toward Davathi, claws tearing a path toward her belly.

The Hunter skidded to a halt and attempted to change course, but his boots skidded through on the crust covering the floor, failing to find purchase for a heartbeat. Before he could break into a run again, however, a shout echoed from beside him, and two more lightning bolts hissed through the air toward the demon. Both struck its uninjured arm with force enough to shatter the limb and burn the scaly, leathery flesh away to the bone.

That alone saved Davathi's life. She'd seen the attack coming and attempted to evade, but even her warrior's speed could not hope to match that of a demon. But with the damage inflicted to Nameless' arm, the slashing claws slowed just enough that her dodge carried her out of striking range. Almost. Two shallow wounds opened on her belly where Nameless had scored flesh.

The demon attempted to rise, but the barrage of power did not stop. Lwazi strode toward Nameless, hands outstretched, pouring more and more *Kish'aa* power into the writhing, shrieking monstrosity.

The Hunter spared a single glance for his surroundings. Kiara had freed four more *Umoyahlebe*, butchering the Ordermen holding their chains, but Nameless' attack on Aisha had momentarily halted her advance. Indeed, she had halfway turned as if intending to join Davathi in freeing Aisha from beneath the demon momentarily incapacitated by Lwazi's power. Deathbite would make quick work of even one as powerful as Nameless.

Of the Ordermen who'd been present when he first arrived in the chamber, three remained standing. Those guarding the unchained *Umoyahlebe* were down, killed by their captives the moment their backs were turned. The only ones still alive cowered behind the *Umoyahlebe* whose chains they still held—including Nkanyezi's.

The Hunter's gut twisted as Nkanyezi and the two bound *Umoyahlebe* turned toward Lwazi and began raising their hands. The horrified look on Nkanyezi's face notwithstanding, she could not stop herself from unleashing a blast of *Kish'aa* power at her own father.

Keeper take these Order bastards!

The Hunter's mad dash had carried him close to the Orderman who'd died to restore his strength, and he paused only long enough to tear Soulhunger from the corpse's chest before turning and sprinting across the chamber toward the still-chained *Umoyahlebe*.

Too slow. Even as he vaulted over the first of the corpses between him and his targets, the blue-white glow sprang to life in Nkanyezi's outstretched palms. She gave a strangled cry of horror and anguish as the power burst from her and carved a searing path through the air toward her father.

A cry of pain ripped through the towertop—it came from behind the Hunter—but the Hunter reached Nkanyezi in that moment. He ducked beneath the arcing lightning, slid around her, and brought his sword down hard on the dimercurite chain binding her to the Orderman. Even as the metallic links gave way with a loud *snap*, the Hunter felt the flow of power shut off, the heat behind him diminishing a fraction. Snarling, he drove Soulhunger into the Orderman's chest. As he did, he caught the man's scent: lavender, satin, and crabapple. The Voramian nobleman who'd barked at him like he was a dog. Fury blazed within the Hunter and, with a snarl, he lifted the masked man off the ground and hurled him bodily away. The Orderman screamed as he flew through the air.

Crimson light flared from Soulhunger's gemstone and power flooded the Hunter. He sprang toward the next pair, adrenaline coursing like fire in his veins, and in two fluid motions hacked the chains in half and cut the Orderman's head free of his shoulders. With a shout, he barreled toward the last of the Ordermen and drove his sword through the side of his skull before the masked bastard could turn his way.

All of his happened in the space of two heartbeats, the Hunter's movements so fast his human prey had been unable to see him, much less stop him.

Two heartbeats, however, was also far too much time to give an Abiarazi.

The Hunter ripped his sword free of the dead Orderman's head, pulling bits of brain and bone with it, and spun as the body collapsed. Just in time to see Nameless surging to his feet and springing toward Lwazi.

Lwazi was on one knee, breathing hard, his muscles still twitching from the power Nkanyezi had sent blasting at him. Nameless' right arm was gone, his left arm barely hanging on by threads of scorched flesh, but its enormous maw was agape, monstrous jaws bared.

A roar from Davathi drew her husband's attention upward, and his eyes went wide at the sight of the demon barreling toward him. Through a supreme effort of will, he managed to raise his hands and unleash a blast of *Kish'aa* power into Nameless' open mouth. Too little, and far too late.

Lwazi was slammed to the ground by the enormous demon, and a terrible crunching, ripping sound echoed in time with his shriek of agony.

The Hunter hurled himself toward the demon. It didn't matter he no longer held Soulhunger, or that the iron dagger lay somewhere out of his reach. He only knew he needed to reach Lwazi before Nameless devoured him completely.

For all his speed, he was not the first to strike.

An *assegai* flew through the air to punch into the demon's back. The shining steel spearhead drove through a gap between its spines and half its length buried into his flesh. In the same instant, twin blasts of *Kish'aa* magic ripped past the Hunter, and lightning bolts of dense power speared Nameless in the back of the head.

The abrupt burst of power lacked Lwazi's control, and the force of it cracked the air around the Hunter's head. It set his eardrums ringing and staggered him. He managed to keep his feet, though the world blurred and spun dizzily for a long moment, bringing acid rising in the back of his throat.

He shook his head to clear away the disorientation. In the same moment, a bestial shriek ripped from Nameless' mouth and the demon's head snapped around. Blood and gobbets of flesh dripped from its teeth where it had savaged Lwazi. Its four black eyes—for the one had healed around the Hunter's dagger—fixed on the source of the lightning blasts. Nkanyezi.

The young Ghandian woman screamed in her own tongue and advanced on the demon with palms outstretched. Tears streamed down her cheeks. Anguish was etched deep into every line of her young face, but she poured blast after blast of lightning into Nameless.

The first bolt struck the demon square in the face, eliciting another shriek. The second lanced his chest, the third his belly, but the fourth missed altogether. For the demon had the innate resilience of his kind, and the taste of human flesh had restored his strength. Nameless' clawed toes dug into Lwazi's legs, tearing skin and muscle as it gained purchase and leaped to avoid Nkanyezi's next blast. The lightning bolt seared through empty air where it had been.

724

With impossible speed, Nameless sprang off the chamber's gemstone exterior wall, leaped onto the odd-shaped Chamber of Sustenance atop the pillar, and flew toward Nkanyezi. Already it arms had begun to re-grow, once more forming its hands and the long claws that tipped its seven many-jointed fingers. These it extended toward Nkanyezi with a bestial shriek of pain and rage.

Nkanyezi could not shift her aim in time to match the demon's speed. She barely even saw it coming, her eyes flying wide at the sight of the monstrous creature hurtling toward her.

The Hunter did the only thing he could: he threw himself into the demon's path.

Claws punched through his skin as easily as a crossbow bolt pierced a leaf. The Hunter screamed as agony ripped through him, his organs shredded and torn to pieces by the razor-sharp talons. Yet he embraced the pain just as he threw his arms wide to embrace the demon.

The instant Nameless struck, the Hunter wrapped his arms around the creature's monstrous neck. Though the demon's bulk bore the two of them to the ground, the Hunter launched himself backward and to the side with the fall, using Nameless' own momentum to send them flying away from Nkanyezi.

The world spun wildly around for long seconds, darkness flickering at the edges of the Hunter's vision as he and the demon tumbled over and over, head striking stone and bony flesh and sharp spines. White-hot fire raged within his belly, dragging him first toward unconsciousness, then ripping him back from momentary relief. Grimly, the Hunter hung on for dear life, tightening his grip around Nameless' neck, squeezing, squeezing. Choking every shred of air from the demon's lungs.

Nameless thrashed in the Hunter's grip. The movement drove the spines deeper into the Hunter's belly, tore screams from his lips. The demon's half-formed arms clawed at him until his stomach, sides, chest, and face were little more than ribbons of mangled flesh. He could feel blood gushing from his body like a fountain to pool warm and thick on the stone floor beneath him. Yet still he squeezed. With strength borne of desperation, he tightened his grip.

He felt it the moment the demon began to panic. Felt the thrashing grow wilder, more frantic. The demon's primitive survival instincts took over, its own desperation and fear augmenting its already immense might.

The demon's arms twisted at a terrible angle, its claws raking down the Hunter's spine. Razor-sharp talons struck *below* the nerves that controlled the Hunter's arms, but his legs convulsed, numbness rippling down from his hips to his toes. The pain in his belly slowly vanished, too. Fear thrummed within the Hunter's chest. He knew the danger that threatened the moment his muscles gave out. If the Abiarazi got free, he would be helpless to do anything but lie there and watch his companions die.

And so, the Hunter clung on for dear life. Nameless shrieked its fury, and the Hunter answered with a roar of his own. He summoned all the rage burning within him, every pain coursing through his body, tapped into the reserves of his iron resolve and unyielding determination. All of this he poured into his muscles, willing them to expand, to flood with power and strength.

"Die, you demon bastard!" the Hunter shouted. The tendons in his arm began to snap beneath the strain, yet still he heaved on the demon for all he was worth

Nameless howled once, fear and panic now ringing in its voice. Then, abruptly, the demon's monstrous form went limp, and his cry cut off with a terrible *crack* of his neck snapping.

Chapter Ninety-Six

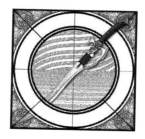

The instant Nameless ceased moving, the Hunter released his grip on the demon and fell back to the floor with a gasp. He could do nothing but lie there, struggling to breathe through the agony overwhelming him. Again and again, darkness swept over him to drag him into unconsciousness, only to recede a moment later when a fresh wave of pain coursed through his mangled body.

"Hunter!" A familiar voice came from far away, so faint he almost believed it imaginary until it came again. "Hunter, talk to me!" Louder this time. Closer, too.

With an immense effort of will, the Hunter pried open eyelids that felt far too heavy. He blinked until his eyes focused on the face looming above him. Kiara's.

"Just...need a moment...to catch...my breath," he croaked out.

Kiara's eyes widened. "Or scoop your guts back inside where they belong?"

The Hunter summoned strength enough to lift his head and look down at his body. Though Nameless' motionless form still lay atop him, his side had been torn open, and pinkish-red coils of intestines spilled out onto the floor.

"Aye...that, too." He cracked a smile, but despite her jest, Kiara was *not* amused. Worry darkened her eyes and twisted her mouth into a frown. Her hands hovered over him, as if she had no idea where to begin tending to him or how to help him.

"Just get...this thing...off me!" the Hunter growled. His voice had regained a measure of strength—or, at least, he hoped it had—as his body began working to repair the damage *again* inflicted by the demon's terrible claws. "Things will...heal...on their own."

Kiara glanced down at the unmoving Nameless. "He's not—"

"Dead?" The Hunter shook his head. "Snapped...his neck. Only thing...will finish him...is Soulhunger or Deathbite." He coughed, spattering her face with blood. "Preferably...Soulhunger."

Kiara needed no explanation as to why. She'd already killed an Orderman to repair similar wounds not minutes earlier. Yet still, she had to ask, "And Kharna?"

The Hunter shrugged, a decision he instantly regretted. The twitch of his shoulders pulled on the flesh pierced and torn by Nameless' claws and a fresh wave of pain washed over him. The world grew dizzy and his head light. "Have to...make do...without one more."

The blurring before his eyes cleared and Kiara's face swam into view just as she nodded. "So be it." She began to rise.

"Wait!" The Hunter reached a hand up to stop her. "Pull his claws...out first." He coughed again, hacking up a gob of crimson phlegm, his breath wheezing in his torn lungs. "Give me...a chance to mend."

Kiara hesitated, but only for a moment. She bent to wrestle Nameless' unmoving bulk off the Hunter. The Hunter tried to help, but his arms refused to heed his commands, the muscles and tendons torn by his exertion. He couldn't help growling out a stream of curses as Kiara's struggle sent new agonies coursing through his mangled body. The numbness in his legs had begun receding, but that only compounded his misery, more nerves to register the terrible torment the demon had inflicted.

He nearly passed out twice—probably did once—but managed to keep a tight grip on his screams, until finally a sweating, struggling Kiara managed to roll Nameless off him.

The Hunter rolled onto his side, curling up around his wounds, clutching the coils of intestines spilling from his belly. "Stomp in...his head...for good measure," he hissed through clenched teeth. "Keep him...docile."

A fierce snarl twisted Kiara's lips. "Gladly." She disappeared from his sight as she stepped over him. A moment later, the Hunter heard a series of satisfying *crunches* of her boot crushing Nameless' skull. The injury would not stop the demon for long, but it merely needed to keep him down long enough for Kiara to retrieve Soulhunger.

The Hunter's oath to Kharna would have to be set aside for this one demon. Nameless was an enemy far greater than any Abiarazi the Hunter had met. Not a demon reduced to human form, their power diminished as a means of hiding themselves from the gods—the Serenii—they feared. Nor a Stone Guardian turned into a mindless beast by Serenii magic. No, this thing was as far above the demons the Hunter had faced as they were above the humans they so disdained. Much too powerful to leave alive.

"There!" Kiara gasped, and stepped over him once more. Her right boot was covered in blood aplenty, along with bits of bone and grey matter. "He won't be healing from that in a hurry."

"Don't be...too sure of that." The Hunter's voice was tight with pain, and it was all he could do to remain conscious against the inferno of agony raging within him. "Better be quick...about killing the damned thing... just in case."

"Aye." Kiara paused for just a moment, staring down at him with a look that failed to fully conceal her concern for him. That concern didn't stop her from turning away and hurrying to retrieve Soulhunger from where the Hunter had left it embedded in the Orderman who'd been holding Nkanyezi's chain.

From where he lay curled on the floor in a puddle of his own blood, the Hunter had a clear view of much of the towertop chamber. The recently freed *Umoyahlebe* stood in various states of shock, horror, relief, and bewilderment. Months of captivity had ended so abruptly and violently they reeled from their sudden liberty. Overusage of the *Kish'aa* had also taken a visible toll on their bodies. Many of them leaned on each other or held up comrades struggling to keep from collapsing. They had gathered in a huddle on the far end of the room, staring wide-eyed at their dead captors and their rescuers with looks of confusion and astonishment etched into their gaunt, sallow features.

All save Nkanyezi. In the seconds since she had been freed, the young Ghandian had rushed to her father, and now knelt beside him, cradling his body in her arms. Tears streamed down her cheeks and dripped onto the blood spattering Lwazi's features. His eyes were bright with pain, and the color had drained from his face. As to be expected given the wounds

Nameless' horrible maw had inflicted. Lwazi's chest and belly were a mangled ruin worse even than the Hunter's. Nkanyezi's near-frantic efforts to stanch the bleeding proved fruitless.

On the opposite side of the pillar from where the Hunter lay, just within his line of sight, Davathi was helping Aisha to rise. A nasty bruise had already begun forming on Aisha's forehead where the demon's heavy frame had crashed into her, and she reeled, unsteady as a drunken sailor after a night spent in The Iron Anchor near Voramis' docks. She bled, too, from a dozen cuts visible on her face and hands, though most were minor.

Davathi cast longing glances at her husband and younger daughter, yet she did not release her older daughter's hand. She gripped Aisha tight and helped her to rise. Only once Aisha proved truly steady on her feet did Davathi begin helping her limp to where Nkanyezi cradled Lwazi's bleeding body.

"No."

The single word commanded the Hunter's attention instantly. His gaze snapped to where Kiara stood on near the corpse where she'd gone to retrieve Soulhunger. She held the dagger, her right foot stretched out before her, yet she'd frozen in mid-step. Her muscles had gone rigid and her eyes were not on him, nor the demon lying behind him. She looked toward the Chamber of Sustenance atop the black gemstone pillar.

"No." She repeated the word again, shaking her head. "No!"

The Hunter's eyes widened. *Could she be hearing—*

He never finished the thought. Kiara moved suddenly, not as if compelled beyond her control, but as if she'd been suddenly freed from a prison of ice. She took a single wobbling step forward, and her eyes snapped toward him.

"He Who Is Nameless cannot die." The words were spoken in her voice, and yet *not*. They resonated through the towertop chamber with a force impossible for any human throat. "To kill him would shatter the balance, and unleash devastation beyond anything this world could imagine."

A chill ran down the Hunter's spine. "*Okadigbo* told you that?"

Kiara nodded.

"But he…died!"

"He did." Kiara's face twisted into a solemn mask, and from her lips came the tremendous, powerful voice once more. "And yet, our kind does not experience such things as yours do."

The Hunter's jaw dropped. For a long second, he could do nothing but stare up at Kiara, as if that would somehow reveal the being that spoke through her. A being of such power it could transcend death.

A shudder ran down Kiara's spine, and she blinked, shook her head. "He Who Is Nameless *must* be imprisoned once more." She glanced down at Soulhunger, her brow furrowing. "We cannot kill him. I can't explain why—I don't even know, in truth—but I just *feel* it. In here." She tapped her free hand against her head, then her chest, over her heart. "And in here."

The Hunter wanted to argue—it would be foolish to leave the demon alive—yet who was he to deny *Okadigbo*? With a groan, he placed one hand on the floor pushed his shoulders up. His other hand had to clutch the guts spilling from his torn stomach and side, and the mere movement sent pain lancing through him. He struggled anyway. "Better…get up…and help…you drag him over."

Kiara shook her head. "There is no need." She knelt and slid Soulhunger across the floor toward him, then turned and sprang lightly into the Chamber of Sustenance atop the central gemstone pillar. "Turns out the *Im'tasi* have more than one use."

To the Hunter's astonishment, she drew Deathbite high above her head and drove it downward. Instead of metal *clinking* against stone, the Hunter heard a *thunk* of steel piercing flesh.

Flesh? The Hunter's eyebrows shot up as he realized what she'd done. She had *stabbed* Okadigbo!

No scream issued from within the Chamber of Sustenance, and so Deathbite's gemstone remained inert.

Kiara's gaze sought out the two figures limping across the chamber toward Nkanyezi and Lwazi. "Aisha!"

Aisha stopped at the sound of her name, glancing back.

"I have need of your power," Kiara said, her expression somber.

Aisha's eyes went wide as she took in the sight: Kiara atop the Chamber of Sustenance, Deathbite's blade and hilt jutting up from within. If the request confused her, she did not show it. She merely glanced over to her father and sister with a look that spoke clearly of her desire to reach them. Before it was too late.

"Please." Kiara reached a hand toward Aisha. "If you do not, everyone in Ghandia dies, and that's just the beginning of sorrows." Again, her voice rang out with that unearthly power, rising in volume to set the walls of the chamber trembling. "Heed me, Awakener. The fate of our world rests on your shoulders now."

Aisha cast another look in the direction of her father, whose struggles had begun to weaken, and her sister, whose efforts grew more frenetic. A look of immense anguish twisted her features. The Hunter did not need Kiara's gift to know that every fiber of her being ached to go to the loved ones from whom she had been separated for so many years.

And yet, when she moved, it was *away* from her father and sister. Away from her mother, to stand on her own two feet. Shoulders squared, head held high, she took two steps until she stood in front of the Chamber of Sustenance.

When she spoke, her voice was hoarse with the strain of fatigue and her emotions, yet her words rang out clearly in the towertop chamber. "Tell me what I must do."

Chapter Ninety-Seven

Kiara's fingers moved deftly across Deathbite's hilt. The Hunter frowned; was she caressing the weapon? His confusion shifted to dumbfounded amazement when she gripped the *Im'tasi* sword's gemstone and twisted it. There was no strain of effort, but the stone affixed into the pommel turned as smoothly and easily as a well-oiled hinge. The Hunter's keen ears picked up the faintest *click* of some intricate mechanism within the sword.

What in the fiery hell? He stared at the sword wide-eyed.

Before he could find words, Kiara straightened, backed away from Deathbite, and lifted her gaze to Aisha. "Send as much power as you can into it." She raised a finger. "The *blade*, mind you. The steel is designed to act as a conduit."

Aisha had to be curious—as curious as the Hunter himself—but she merely nodded and raised her right hand, leveling her *assegai* at the sword jutting up from within the Chamber of Sustenance. Her brow knitted tight and her jaw clenched as she gathered the power of the *Kish'aa* to herself.

"How much?" she asked, darting a glance at Kiara.

"As much as you can summon," Kiara said, her voice ringing with the unnatural force once more. "All you can give me."

Nodding, Aisha raised her left hand, too, and from her palm and outstretched spears streamed twin spears of lightning. The blue-white bolts carved a blinding path through the air and struck Deathbite's blade just below the crossguard. Instantly, runes flared to life all along its length and light streamed from its gemstone.

But it was not the bloody crimson glow that had brightened his own *Im'tasi* blade, Soulhunger, for as long as he could remember. From the gemstone issued a brilliant, cool blue light—the same azure as the Keeps of Enarium, and every other Chamber of Sustenance the Hunter had seen before this one.

The shining runes on the sword's blade drank the blast of *Kish'aa* magic as eagerly as it devoured the blood of its victims, but there was something different about it. Waves of light streamed down the blade and vanished from the Hunter's sight. It took him a moment to understand the truth: Deathbite was not absorbing the power, consuming it, but *channeling*. As Kiara had said, the blade acted as a conduit to direct the flow downward. Straight into *Okadigbo*.

The Hunter's jaw dropped. *How is this possible?* He tore his eyes from the sight, looking down to where Soulhunger lay just within arm's reach. He did not reach for the dagger, though. He stared at it as if seeing it for the first time. The weapon that had been at his side for his entire life, which had accompanied him for five thousand years, was suddenly unfamiliar to him.

730

Questions swirled in a confused tangle through his mind. Could *Thanal Eth'Athaur* do as *Kükhliin Khazalt* had? Could Soulhunger's magic, too, be altered? If so, how had he never learned about it? And how had Kiara known about it?

His gaze snapped up to where she stood, one foot on the edge of the Chamber of Sustenance, one foot within. She stared at the brilliant azure light streaming from Deathbite's gemstone. A rapt look etched on her face, but not a shred of surprise or astonishment. Merely certainty. The same certainty that had guided her movements as she twisted and manipulated whatever mechanisms lay concealed within or had rung in her voice as she spoke with that unearthly power.

Okadigbo had told her.

Since entering the towertop chamber, the Hunter had been so consumed by the demonic Nameless that all thoughts of The Bleeding One had fled his mind. Yet now he couldn't help wondering what manner of creature *Okadigbo*—who had appeared to him in the monstrous form, who even now spoke through Kiara—was. Something *worse* even than the demon he'd imprisoned?

He struggled to rise, fighting to keep a lid on his groans of anguish. He managed to push himself up to one elbow and push his spilling guts back where they belonged before his arms gave out and he fell back to the floor. His body was on the mend—already he could feel the wounds in his belly closing, the muscle and flesh re-knitting—but loss of blood and pain left him weak. He hadn't the strength to rise and see the creature within the Chamber of Sustenance for himself.

Yet as he lay on the floor, he found Kiara's calm confidence reassuring. The Hunter knew her better than anyone alive, and had no doubt that if she'd believed *Okadigbo* worth resisting, she would have fought with every shred of the immense stubbornness she possessed. She had the strength of mind to triumph—she'd proven as much the night she refused to heed Indombe's compulsion at Zamani Falls. He had to trust that she knew what she was doing.

A groan from Aisha drew the Hunter's attention to the young woman. She was visibly tiring, sweat streaming down her brow, her arms trembling with the exertion. "How...much...more?" she grated through clenched teeth.

As if to answer her question, the black gemstone pillar beneath the Chamber of Sustenance flickered to life. A pulse of blue light rippled downward and vanished into the stone floor. *Ukuhlushwa Okungapheli* gave a mighty shudder beneath the Hunter.

"More!" Kiara shouted, her voice ringing off the chamber's circular walls with deafening force, drowning out even the hiss and crackle of the lightning streaming from Aisha's hands.

Aisha's jaw muscles worked and her powerful shoulders knotted. The power arcing out from her brightened, thickened, but only for a moment. Her eyes widened and a cry of pain ripped from her lips. She collapsed to one knee, hands falling to her sides.

"I can't!" she gasped. Her head hung down so low her chin rested on her chest.

"It is not enough!" thundered the unearthly voice from Kiara's lips. "You must give me more, Awakener!" Her words rang not with anger, but desperation, even a hint of fear.

Aisha somehow summoned the strength to raise her face. The blue-white light shining in her eyes revealed twin tracks of blood and tears streaking down her cheeks, and the smell of charred flesh accompanied the smoke rising from the hands hanging by her sides.

"I have...no more...to give!" She spoke in a mere whisper, so faint and weak the Hunter barely heard it. "Any more...and I...will die."

"The cost may be great," *Okadigbo* spoke through Kiara, voice booming, "but the cost to your world will be far greater."

"No!" Davathi's voice rang out from behind Aisha. The Issai *nassor* moved to stand between her kneeling daughter and Kiara. "Surely there is another way!"

Kiara peered down at Davathi, and behind her eyes, the Hunter saw a depth of knowledge and wisdom thousands of years old. "She is the Awakener. What must be, will be."

Davathi opened her mouth to speak, but stopped as Aisha closed a hand around her wrist.

"Help me rise, Mother." Aisha's voice was tight, yet determination shone on her face.

"You cannot mean to—" Davathi began, swiveling to her daughter.

"Please, *umama*!" Aisha's expression turned pleading. "Help me."

Emotions twisted Davathi's leonine face. "*Indokazi*—" she began, but her voice cracked, cutting off her words.

"Listen to me, *umama*." Aisha's hand tightened on her mother's wrist. "For all the years we were apart, I tried to live a life that would make you and *ubaba* proud. To emulate your strength and courage, and *ubaba's* wisdom. In that way, I carried you with me everywhere I went. It was your voices that guided me through the darkest nights, that bore me through the greatest challenges."

She unclenched her right fist, letting her *assegai* clatter to the floor beside her, and reached up to take her mother's other hand in hers. "It is because of you that I have become what I am. I can stand to face what is asked of me because I have seen you do the same every day that you led our people. I do not fear death because your courage has never faltered."

She swallowed, and now tears streamed down her face. "Please, *umama*. I need your strength, now more than ever. Help me to rise. Help me do what must be done. I cannot do it without you."

Davathi, too, was crying. With a surge of strength, she hauled Aisha to her feet and wrapped her powerful arms around her daughter. Her great muscles squeezed as she crushed Aisha to her chest.

"No daughter has ever made a mother as proud as you have made me," Davathi said, stroking Aisha's hair. "Let my love for you guide you into whatever awaits you, *indokazi*. Beloved of my heart."

Aisha summoned strength enough to return her mother's hug. But she broke off quickly, wiping the tears and blood streaking from her cheeks. She cast a glance over her shoulder to where Nkanyezi still struggled to keep their father from bleeding out.

"I will tell her," Davathi said, clasping a hand to Aisha's cheek. "She will sing the song that guides you to the arms of the *Kish'aa*."

Aisha swallowed hard and nodded. She stepped forward, her legs quivering but firm, striding past her mother to stand directly before the Chamber of Sustenance. She raised trembling hands but did not yet summon the power. Instead, she looked up at Kiara, then to the Hunter.

"Make sure Kodyn knows—" Her voice cracked, and the tears flowed anew.

The Hunter found his own cheeks were wet, his voice coarse with emotion. He could barely grate out the words, "I will."

"Hurry, Awakener!" The Bleeding One thundered through Kiara once more. "Every moment you delay—"

Aisha's roar drowned out even the spirit's booming voice. The power that sprang to her hands glowed with such brilliance the Hunter had to shield his eyes with one arm to avoid being blinded. Even still, sparks danced before his vision, and the entire towertop chamber grew bright and hot as if the sun itself shone within the gemstone walls.

The Hunter could not see, but he could *feel* the energy streaming from Aisha into Deathbite. The Bondshold shuddered once, twice, three times. Each time, a scream ripped from Aisha's throat. Her voice rang with pain, but she did not cut off the flow.

Gritting his teeth, the Hunter lowered the arm shielding his face. Though the light seared into his eyes and the heat scalded his cheeks, he forced himself to watch. To bear witness to Aisha's final act of bravery.

The flesh of her hands melted first. Like wax dripping from a candle, the skin sloughed away from her fingers, vanishing in dark puffs of smoke as it was consumed by the super-heated lightning. The flesh of her face began to bubble and blister. Tears streamed from her eyes, only to evaporate the instant they touched her cheeks. Her hair curled back from the heat, and the very fibers of her clothing began to wither.

And still she poured *more* power into Deathbite. Power far beyond anything the Hunter had believed possible, beyond what *should* have been possible, even for her. For all her control and mastery of the *Kish'aa,* she was still human, with all the mortal limitations to her flesh. She could only unleash the spirits she had absorbed into herself and stored in the *Dy'nashia* pendant. Once those had been expended, the only source remaining at her disposal was her own life force. That was what now streamed from her hands, through the *Im'tasi* blade, into Okadigbo and the heart of *Ukuhlushwa Okungapheli.*

The Hunter cried out as Aisha fell to one knee. He reached a hand toward her, heedless of the searing heat ravaging his skin or the agony in his still-healing belly. Davathi stood a few paces behind Aisha, and she, too, looked as if she wanted to reach for her daughter. Yet she held her ground, fists balled so tight her hands were white, shoulders squared in determination. Her expression revealed the anguish and sorrow twisting within her, yet the pride shining in her eyes glowed nearly as bright as the magic crackling through the chamber.

A shout from Aisha drew the Hunter's gaze once more. He willed his eyes to pierce the blinding aura of blue-white surrounding her, to see her as she raised her hands high and loosed another blast of magic into Deathbite.

He saw her face, then. Not twisted in pain nor marred by fear. Her expression was peaceful despite the inferno of magic raging around her.

A serene smile brightened her features and, tilting her head to the heavens, she gave her last shred of strength in service of her people.

Chapter Ninety-Eight

The Hunter's throat tightened at the sight of Aisha's final sacrifice. He braced himself for the inevitable moment when the flow of power cut off and her smoking corpse toppled lifeless to the blood-encrusted floor of the towertop chamber. The thought of it nearly shattered his heart, for he had come to care deeply for the young woman, far more than he'd anticipated or even realized until that very moment.

Suddenly, the one figure within the corona of blue-white light split into *two*.

The Hunter blinked, trying to clear the blinding spots from his eyes. Was he imagining it?

No, he wasn't. The two streams of magic pouring from Aisha's hands had suddenly become *four*.

The Hunter squinted into the light, straining to see. He sucked in a breath as he recognized the one kneeling at Aisha's side. Younger, slighter, yet with features akin to Aisha's own.

Nkanyezi! She had left her father's side to join her sister, to lend her strength. Indeed, the fourth stream of blue-white light slackened a moment, and through the brilliance, the Hunter saw Nkanyezi turn to rest a hand on Aisha's shoulder. Instantly, Aisha's crumbling body straightened, her shoulders lifted, and her eyelids snapped open. Her lips moved, but the sound was lost beneath the crackling of their combined magic. Magic that streamed toward Deathbite's rune-etched blade, to be absorbed downward into the black gemstone pillar.

The great pulsing light shot through the midnight stone, then again, and again. Slow, like the ponderous heartbeat of some creature as vast as the mountains. Yet as the two *Umoyahlebe* poured more power into the tower, *Ukuhlushwa Okungapheli* began to come to life.

The floor beneath the Hunter hummed. The sound grew louder, the vibrations more forceful. The walls of the chamber began to glow, lending their light to the brilliance surrounding the two young women and the Chamber of Sustenance. The air around them crackled and the pressure built in the Hunter's ears.

Then came another stream of power. From the far side of the chamber, thinner and far less controlled than either Aisha's or Nkanyezi's, but no less bright. A middle-aged woman with deep circles around her eyes and a haggardness to her emaciated frame broke away from the pack of *Umoyahlebe* huddled against the wall. She strode toward the heart of the room, her hands spraying bursts of *Kish'aa* magic.

Another *Umoyahlebe* joined in. A young man, likely Nkanyezi's age, his face still unmarred by the first hints of beard. He appeared barely able to stand, yet he, too, lent his power to the effort.

The rest of the *Umoyahlebe* followed suit, until all those who'd survived their captivity and Nameless' hunger stood once more in a circle around the pillar in the heart of the room, as they had when the Hunter had first entered the chamber. The dimercurite alloy collars remained around their necks and the bracelets still clasped their wrists, yet they were free of the chains binding them to the Ordermen. This, they did of their own free will.

Ukuhlushwa Okungapheli responded immediately. The humming beneath the Hunter's feet shook him to his marrow. The pressure mounting within the room threatened to burst his ear drums, crush his lungs in a fist of iron. The power crackling in the air set every hair on his body standing on end. Brighter and brighter the pillar at the heart of the chamber shone. Faster the pulses rippled down its length to vanish into the floor.

The Hunter felt the moment the Bondshold came alive. The air around him *popped,* the pressure on his ears releasing, and the floor beneath him gave one final violent shudder before settling once more to a low murmur, as if something shook the earth at its very root. Yet it was not the angry tremor that had caused the earth to buck and heave as The Bleeding One wrestled with He Who Is Nameless. Instead, it was the smooth, steady thrum of some arcane mechanism the Hunter couldn't begin to understand being activated.

In the same instant, the flow of power from the *Umoyahlebe* cut off, like a cork being thrust into a bottle's mouth to seal it up. All around the chamber, Ghandians collapsed. Some fell to their knees. Others staggered backward and dropped to their seats or toppled onto their backs. One merely crumpled where she stood. All of them ended up on the floor, pale-faced and unconscious.

Only Aisha and Nkanyezi remained upright.

Nkanyezi's shoulders slumped and her breath came in heavy, loud gulps. Yet she had the strength enough to stay on her knees, one hand still outstretched toward Deathbite, the other resting on Aisha's shoulder.

Aisha, too, was on her knees. Her arms hung limp at her sides, her spine drooped, and her head hung low. For a breathless moment, she seemed frozen in place, unable to move save for the quiver passing through her muscles.

Finally, she turned toward her sister and, somehow, found the strength to lift her blistered, burned face. A smile broke out on her lips and tears of joy filled her eyes.

"Told you…I'd return."

With those whispered words, her strength gave out and she collapsed into Nkanyezi's arms.

"Hunter!"

The sound of his name pierced the ringing in the Hunter's ears. Though he could barely bring himself to do it, he tore his eyes away from Aisha and Nkanyezi and turned toward Kiara.

She remained standing within the Chamber of Sustenance atop the gemstone pillar, staring not at the collapsed *Umoyahlebe* around her, but at Deathbite's still-glowing gemstone and rune-etched blade. Her hand hovered a finger's breadth from the sword's hilt.

"We must hurry!" Kiara called to him without looking his way. "*Okadigbo* cannot survive long without *Nuru Iwu.* Their souls are linked, as their minds and bodies were for more than six thousand years. We must get He Who Is Nameless into his prison once more before it is too late."

The Hunter glanced toward Davathi, the only other person in the chamber still on her feet. She, too, seemed frozen, torn between going to her dying husband or her two daughters. One of whom might very well be dead even now. She would be no help to them at this moment.

Which meant it fell to *him* to do what must be done.

The Hunter pushed himself upright, and this time, actually succeeded in climbing to one knee. In the last few minutes, his wounds had healed enough that he could rise without succumbing to the pain. He no longer needed to clutch his intestines to keep them from spilling out of his torn-open belly. He still bled freely, and every movement sent fresh waves of fire coursing through him, but he had the strength to collect Soulhunger and push himself up to his feet. He wobbled a little, dizzy, and had to reach out to catch himself on the transparent gemstone wall.

As his vision cleared, his eyes fell on the plateau to the west of *Ukuhlushwa Okungapheli*. Hundreds of warriors raced through the stronghold built by the Vassalage Consortium. Battle swirled in every street, knots of men fighting in close quarters, wielding sword, spear, axe, trident, flail, and club. Everywhere the Hunter looked, Ghandians wearing the lion furs of the Buhari, the turtle shells of the Mwaani, and the white-backed pelts of the Nyemba hurled themselves against their *alay-alagbara* foes with terrible ferocity. Among their ranks were hundreds of unarmed men and women still bearing the chains and whip marks of their captivity.

The Hunter's spirit soared. *By the Swordsman, they did it!* Siyanda and Naledi had gotten free of the tunnels and turned the captives loose. Jumaane had gotten into the *Gcinue'eleku awandile* city. The battle was far from won, but the Consortium no longer had walls to hide behind.

"Hurry!"

Kiara's words snapped the Hunter's attention away from the battle raging below. He turned back to find her pulling Deathbite—its glow fading, its blade once more going dull—from the Chamber of Sustenance. She hopped down and hurried toward the still-prone Nameless.

"Time is not on our side," she said, worry twisting her face as she sheathed Deathbite.

The Hunter needed no convincing. Looking down, he found the demon's skull had already mended itself, bone closing around its brain, the flesh all but restored. He lifted his boot high and drove it down onto Nameless' neck with force enough to *snap* the bone.

"That ought to buy us a minute or two," he said with a grim smile.

Kiara shook her head. "It's not *him* I'm worried about." She jerked a thumb toward the Chamber of Sustenance. "*Okadigbo's* voice is growing weaker already. The two of them have been conjoined for so long that he cannot survive without *Nuru Iwu's* strength."

The Hunter frowned. "I don't under—"

"It will make sense once you see," Kiara cut him off. "But I don't have time for an explanation. We must get him into the Chamber, now!" With that, she bent to seize one of Nameless' immense arms. It was so thick Kiara could barely close both her hands around his wrist. Strong as she was, she could never drag the corpulent Abiarazi the fifteen paces to the Chamber alone.

And so, though every movement sent ripples of fire lancing through the Hunter, he sheathed Soulhunger, bent, and seized Nameless' other wrist. He nearly passed out as he straightened, the torn muscles in his belly convulsing. Only sheer stubbornness kept him conscious and on his feet. A low growl rumbled in his throat as he set to the task of dragging Nameless toward the Chamber of Sustenance.

Even with their might combined, he and Kiara made slow progress. He'd lost enough blood to kill any mortal man, and his body struggled to compensate. The pain didn't help. Every pull on the demon's heavy frame drained what little strength he had regained. He gasped for each breath, his lungs burning, sweat streaming down his face. More than once, his fingers lost their grip on the demon's wrist merely from exhaustion alone.

Every time, Kiara urged him to hurry, casting worried glances over her shoulder toward the Chamber of Sustenance. The Hunter did his best, but his depleted body betrayed him with each step. He hadn't even the strength to break Nameless' neck or kick in his skull; Kiara had to see to ensuring the demon remained incapacitated while the Hunter swallowed great lungfuls of air and tried not to collapse.

Nkanyezi's tearful shouts didn't help. "Wake up!" the young girl shouted in the Issai tongue. "Please, Aisha. Wake up!"

The Hunter turned his attention away from the effort of Nameless' body just long enough to look over to where Nkanyezi knelt beside her sister. Aisha lay on the blood-encrusted floor, as limp and motionless as the demon the Hunter and Kiara dragged. Beneath the blisters, her face had lost much of its color. Her hands, though, bore no sign of charring, only pinkish, raw skin. However, all of Nkanyezi and Davathi's efforts to revive her—which included beating on her chest to get her heart pounding and shaking her by the shoulders—were in vain.

A lump rose in the Hunter's throat and tears blurred in his eyes. He tapped into the wellspring of anger burning in his chest, used it to fuel his muscles. Growling, grunting like an animal, he heaved on Nameless' body with all the strength he could summon. Moving faster now, legs pumping, arm and back muscles straining with the effort.

"Almost...there!" Kiara gasped from beside him.

The Hunter brushed the moisture from his eyes and found they had drawn within mere paces of the pillar at the heart of the room. Close enough that, had he been at full strength, he could have lifted Nameless and hurled him bodily into the Chamber of Sustenance that had been his prison for six millennia.

And close enough to see the thing that lay within.

His eyes widened as he caught sight of *Okadigbo*. Not the reptilian, many-legged monstrosity he'd seen racing across the plains or begging for his aid in the tunnels below, but a being he'd seen carved into onyx in the twin temples of Kara-ket, and again in his vision with Kharna. A two-legged creature with bi-articulate arms that reached its knees, the rope-like musculature of a predator but the high-sloped forehead that displayed its intelligence, and unnaturally elongated, too-many-jointed fingers that bore no claws.

A Serenii!

It shouldn't have surprised him. Indeed, he felt foolish for not coming to the realization sooner. *Ukuhlushwa Okungapheli* was unmistakably Serenii handiwork from pinnacle to foundation. So, too, was the Chamber of Sustenance that was the "prison" wherein *Okadigbo* had entrapped *Nuru Iwu*, despite its differences in shape and material than those the Hunter had seen in Enarium and Malandria.

Yet somehow, the notion that *Okadigbo* was Serenii came as much as a surprise as the revelation that *Nuru Iwu* was Abiarazi. *Twins,* the lore had called them. Beings as old as the *amathafa* itself, descendants of Ingwe All-Father. The Hunter had expected—even *hoped,* perhaps?—that he'd find something else when finally he came face to face with the two "spirits".

The meaning behind *Nuru Iwu's* name remained a mystery to the Hunter, but the origin of *Okadigbo's* became instantly apparent. "The Bleeding One" was an apt moniker; blood of a violet so dark it was nearly black dripped from deep wounds in the Serenii's belly. Inflicted by Nameless' claws, the Hunter knew without a shred of doubt. Layer upon layer of ancient dried blood crusted the bottom of the cradle in which the Serenii lay, covering nearly half its face. The fresh blood that even now seeped from its torn flesh drained out through a crack in the Chamber and dripped in a slow trickle onto the floor around the gemstone pillar that served as its base.

The sight boggled the Hunter's mind. How long had *Okadigbo* lain here bleeding? The thick layer of blood crusting the towertop chamber, descending the spiral staircase, and out through the fissure in the lowermost room in the tower to the stone steps they'd ascended could only have built up over *millennia*.

"Hunter!" Kiara's voice pierced the Hunter's astonished thoughts. "We've got to get him—"

"I'm coming!" A shout rang up the staircase, accompanied by the rush of booted feet on stone.

The Hunter and Kiara both spun toward the chamber's entrance in time to see Tarek bursting into view. The young Elivasti was breathless and wide-eyed, spear held in one hand. He skidded to a halt and his gaze darted around the chamber, taking in the details at a glance.

"Tarek?" Kiara snapped. "What are you doing here? You and Kodyn should be guarding the entrance, not—"

"You didn't call me?" Tarek's violet eyes darted between Kiara and the Hunter, still covered in his own blood. "But I heard you!" Confusion twisted his face. "I heard you, Hunter. Shouting for me to come help."

"Me?" The Hunter scowled. "I didn't—"

Tarek's gasp cut off the Hunter's words. All the color drained from the young Elivasti's cheeks as his gaze fell on Nameless' monstrous form. "By the ancestors!"

A sudden, terrible realization slammed into the Hunter, freezing the breath in his lungs. It hadn't been *his* voice Tarek heard. Nameless had been playing dead all this time, lulling the Hunter and Kiara into a false sense of security, buying time for his ploy to succeed.

Keeper's teeth! The Hunter spun toward the demon, reaching for Soulhunger.

Too late.

Chapter Ninety-Nine

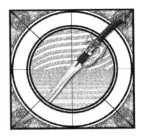

Fear blossomed within the Hunter as Nameless' muscles bunched in his grip. His fingers hadn't yet closed around Soulhunger's hilt when he felt himself lifted bodily off the floor. He caught a glimpse of Kiara flying away, before he, too was hurled across the chamber with no more effort than if he'd been a child's stuffed ragdoll.

Instinctively, the Hunter tucked in his head and curled his body inward. He slammed into the wall, but the impact that could have shattered his neck merely sent agony rippling through his shoulders and upper back where they collided with the solid, smooth gemstone surface. Air exploded from his lungs, and he collapsed face-first onto the floor.

His body reacted of its own according, muscles propelling him to his feet. The pain coursed through him a moment later, sapping all strength from his limbs, freezing him in place. Only pig-headed refusal to die kept him from crumbling once more. He could barely draw breath, and his legs refused to move him a single step. Yet he compelled his arms to move. His fingers to form fists and pull his weapons free of their sheaths. Soulhunger in his left hand, *Ibad'at Mutlaqa* in his right.

He barely registered the needle-prick pain in his finger, paid no heed to the crimson runes that brightened along the scimitar's curving blade. His eyes were fixed on the demon he *knew* was even now coming for him. With no other weapons at hand, the Hunter had no choice but to risk using the Sword of Nasnaz. Its magic gave him the best fighting chance against Nameless' immense might and impossible resilience.

Horror thrummed within him as he saw the demon moving in a blur—not rushing at him, but in the opposite direction. Bearing down on Kiara, who lay in a dazed heap at the far side of the chamber. She'd struck the wall with force enough to momentarily put her out of the fight. She had no way of raising Deathbite or protecting herself against the demon rushing toward her.

The Hunter pushed himself off the wall, pouring what little strength he could summon into his limbs. Knowing even as he did so he'd never reach her in time to stop Nameless' razor-sharp talons from tearing her to pieces.

But before Nameless could cross half the distance, another figure sprang between the demon and Kiara.

"Back!" Tarek shouted, leveling his spear at the onrushing demon.

To the Hunter's astonishment, Nameless *obeyed*. Checked his rush and came to an abrupt halt just beyond reach of Tarek's upraised spear.

"Take another step, and I'll gut you where you stand!" Tarek waved his spear in Nameless' face.

Nameless did not recoil from Tarek's spear—a spear with a head of *steel*, no true threat to an Abiarazi—nor did he advance. He merely stood, still as a marble statue, head still lolling at a terrible angle on its shattered neck. The demon's back was turned to the Hunter, so he could not see the expression twisting its monstrous face or the look in its four, empty black eyes. But if its scrutiny unnerved Tarek, the young man did not show it.

"Back with you!" Tarek thrust his spear toward Nameless' belly.

Again, the demon *obeyed*. It took a step backward, docile as a newborn lamb.

So surprised was the Hunter that he failed to notice the corpse lying in his path. His front foot struck the lifeless body and he went down, hard. A hoarse rasp burst from his lips as his still-torn belly crashed atop the slashwyrm scale mask on the dead Orderman's face. The pain loosened his grip on his weapons and both Soulhunger and scimitar went skittering across the blood-encrusted floor.

The Hunter gritted his teeth against the torment rippling through his torso and forced himself upward. Slowly, struggling, yet knowing that he had to reach Kiara and Tarek before—

A furious roar echoed through the chamber. Nameless' immensely muscled arms spread wide then swept inward toward Tarek. The young Elivasti was ready for it, leaping backward to evade, yet nothing could prepare him for the demon's speed. He barely managed to get out of the way of the slash and throw up his spear to block the blow. Seven monstrous talons sheared through the thick wooden shaft with no more difficulty than a scythe through a blade of grass.

Tarek retreated farther still, not yet realizing he held a now-headless spear.

In desperation, the Hunter staggered to his feet. He tore his eyes away from Nameless just long enough to seek out Soulhunger. The dagger lay in a pool of blood spreading outward from another mask-wearing corpse. A single lurching step brought the Hunter close enough to retrieve the dagger. The simple act of bending set the world spinning wildly and nausea roiling through his stomach. All his effort went into swallowing his rising gorge and forcing his legs to carry him toward Nameless.

The distance between them couldn't have been more than forty paces, but in the Hunter's condition, it felt endless. He dared not throw Soulhunger—it was a long way to hurl a dagger, and the bony spines on Nameless' back would deflect the blade—so he did the only thing he could.

"Hey, ugly!" he shouted. "I've got what you want right here!" He waved Soulhunger before him. Every demon he'd met had lusted after *Thanal Eth'Athaur*, for the *Im'tasi* blade offered vast power. More than the Hunter had realized, if it could be altered as Kiara had altered Deathbite.

But his words had no more effect on Nameless than a snowflake striking a brick wall. Nameless continued his slow, relentless advance. Tarek yielded ground until he could yield no more, stopping a single pace in front of Kiara. There he planted his feet and, brave fool that he was, raised the severed shaft of his spear. A weapon entirely useless against the monstrosity that loomed two full heads above him.

For the first time, Nameless' voice echoed through the room. "Stand aside." His voice was guttural and grated with the sound of rubbing bones, yet his words rang with a force as primal as his immense form.

"Not a bloody chance!" Tarek set his jaw, his expression going hard. "You want her, you're going through me first."

A harsh, crackling sound rang out—the demon's *laughter*, the Hunter realized. "No great difficulty."

740

The Hunter's heart sprang into his throat. He willed his legs to work harder, his feet to propel him faster across the chamber. Forty paces became thirty, then twenty-five. Again he shouted, and again Nameless paid him no heed. The demon merely took another step toward Tarek to loom large over the young Elivasti.

"But I have seen a better way." He tapped a claw against the side of his misshapen head. "A more delicious way. I have seen what you fear most, son of Esanne. The terror that even now turns your belly to water. A vow, sworn by your people, millennia past."

Tarek froze as if encased in a block of ice. All color drained from his face and the spear shaft quivered in his hands.

"Kneel to your *maistyr.*"

The Hunter felt those words as much as heard them. There was power in those words—if not some ancient demonic magic, the power of unshakeable certainty. Nameless *knew* without a shred of doubt what Tarek would do.

Tarek's jaw muscles trembled, his legs quivering. Even from twenty paces away, the Hunter saw the anguish etched into the young man's face, the fear and horror gleaming in his violet eyes.

"Don't do it!" the Hunter shouted, knowing it was futile.

Tarek's head began to bow, spine bending beneath the weight of the Elivasti oath to the Abiarazi. His right leg bent at the knee and his spear lowered.

The pain that coursed through the Hunter had nothing to do with the grievous wounds his body had suffered. Fire burned in the backs of his eyes, tears threatening. Tarek's fears had come true, and the Hunter's with it. After all this time traveling together with Tarek, fighting together, enduring every hardship their journey had thrown at them, *this* was how it ended. Tarek turning on the Hunter and Kiara in obedience to a master he had no desire to worship. Yet he had no choice. The vow of his ancestors compelled him.

Time slowed to a crawl as the Hunter watched Tarek bend the knee, grief twisting his belly, knowing what came next. It was Master Eldor all over aga—

Tarek exploded upward in a rush of movement. Legs straightened, head snapped up, and arms extended with all the force of his powerful warrior's frame.

"No!" the roar burst from Tarek's lips as he drove the spear straight into the demon's face. "NO!"

Nameless' claws had sheared away the spearhead, but the shaft punched out the back of its skull in a spray of blood, bone, and brain. The demon staggered backward, screeching and shrieking its pain, claws slicing the air on a deadly path toward Tarek's head. Tarek dropped into a crouch barely in time to avoid the wild strikes. Then surged upward to drive his shoulder into Nameless' belly. The force hurled the already off-balance demon backward, sent him stumbling.

Right into the Hunter's headlong charge.

With a savage snarl, the Hunter drove Soulhunger into the demon's back, just between its bony spines. Nameless let out another terrible screech and batted at the Hunter with one hand, the other slashing at the spear embedded in its eye. Its agonized screams brought Soulhunger's gemstone flaring to life, but before the dagger could drink deep of the demon's blood, one of its wildly flailing hands struck the Hunter a glancing blow that knocked him away. The Hunter hadn't yet released his grip on the dagger's hilt, and so it was torn free of Nameless' side.

Yet even that small amount of power consumed by the dagger's magic had done wonders for the Hunter. Though the blow hurled him five paces away, the Hunter landed lightly and rolled to his feet in a single fluid motion. Fire coursed through his veins, vitality infusing every muscle. The flesh of his belly closed, the bleeding stopped, and his heart no longer labored with every beat. Though pain aplenty remained, the Hunter was no longer on the verge of collapse.

"Come on, then!" He flexed the muscles of his arms, dropped into a low fighting stance. "Time you were back in your prison, *Demon!*"

Nameless unleashed a roar, but pain mingled with his fury, blood dripped from the ruins of the eye impaled by Tarek's spear. He tore the weapon free, spraying black ichor, but another howl ripped from his lips as another spear—this one with a short handle—buried in his chest.

Someone slipped up beside the Hunter, and he knew without a glance who it was. Drawing the *iznyovu* dagger from his belt, he handed it to Davathi without a word. He could feel the pain radiating off her, yet it did not stop her from joining him in battle against the demon.

Together, they sprang at Nameless. Their daggers were far from the most effective weapons for this particular fight—much too short against the forearm-length claws sprouting from the demon's seven-fingered hands—yet like the Hunter, Davathi knew what would happen if they did not fight. Already, she'd lost a husband to Nameless' savagery, and Aisha…Keeper, the Hunter didn't know if Aisha still lived or had gone to the *Kish'aa!* He'd be damned if anyone else died here.

He was faster than Davathi, and so reached Nameless a step ahead of her. Ducking beneath a wild slash of the demon's claws, he carved a gaping wound in Nameless' left side and darted out of reach behind him. Opening the way for Davathi to do likewise on his right side. Though the wounds were far from mortal, Nameless howled at the pain, and his three uninjured black eyes turned on them.

That gave Tarek an opening to attack from behind. The Elivasti drove two daggers into the demon's back, just between two bony spines. When Nameless whipped around to slash at him, Tarek was ready and sprang back out of reach. The Hunter seized the opportunity to bury Soulhunger into Nameless' side.

The demon screamed in agony, and the dagger's magic sprang to life. Again, power bathed the Hunter, driving away his fatigue, dissipating the last of his pain, fueling his muscles with vigor. He tore the dagger free before it could consume Nameless' life force entirely and darted backward to evade the demon's wild attack. *Okadigbo's* words, spoken through Kiara, remained burned into his mind.

"Okadigbo cannot survive long without Nuru Iwu. Their souls are linked, as their minds and bodies were for more than six thousand years. We must get He Who Is Nameless into his prison once more before it is too late."

Another yowl ripped from Nameless' lips as Davathi sliced open the tendons above its right knee. Caught mid-step, the demon fell hard, and the Hunter aided its collapse by severing the muscles on the arm it threw out to catch itself. Its great form crashed onto the floor with a thunderous *BOOM* that shook the tower beneath the Hunter's feet.

The Hunter and Davathi darted back out of striking range, evading the desperate slash Nameless aimed at them.

"Go for its head!" the Hunter shouted, leaping forward to carve a deep furrow into the demon's uninjured arm. The limb fell limp, only for a moment, but long enough for Davathi to dart in and drive her dagger into the crown of the demon's misshapen skull.

The injury *should* have stopped Nameless—a blade to the brain had stopped Abiarazi before—but instead seemed to enrage the demon. It surged upward in a tangle of flopping limbs, propelled by inhuman savagery and fury. The Hunter and Davathi could not backpedal in time to escape the slashing blows aimed at their heads.

742

Then the towertop chamber suddenly blazed with light so bright it blinded the Hunter. He staggered backward, throwing up an arm in a vain attempt to shield his eyes. He braced for a blow, knowing the demon could strike at him even if it could not see.

Yet prepared as he was, nothing could prepare him for the voice that resounded through the chamber with the force of a thunderclap.

"BE STILL!"

Chapter One Hundred

The Hunter knew that voice. Knew it better than his own, truth be told. He'd heard it every day for the last four years—speaking words of love, offering advice, urging him to do what was right, pushing him relentlessly to seek the best parts of humanity within himself. He'd come to love that voice, every sharp retort and ribald jest, every scolding and whispered enticement.

It was Kiara's voice...and yet it was not. *Okadigbo* spoke through her. Her words boomed with the ancient Serenii's power and the sound set the very ground beneath the Hunter quaking.

The light faded slowly. Slower still the blinding spots dancing in the Hunter's eyes. He brought Soulhunger up to guard position, ears searching for even the faintest sound of movement that could alert him to attack.

Yet none came. He heard only a single pair of footsteps crunching across the blood-encrusted floor. Kiara's, moving in his direction at a slow, measured pace.

The Hunter blinked until his vision cleared. His jaw dropped as he saw Nameless standing a single pace away. The claws of one hand had stopped just short of shearing off his head, the other a finger's breadth from opening Davathi's throat. The Issai *nassor* still held an arm up to shield her face; she hadn't yet seen the death she'd so narrowly avoided.

Yet Nameless' huge body was utterly rigid. His mighty muscles bulged beneath his mottled scale-and-leather skin as if straining against an invisible hand. In vain. The demon's eyes were the only part still moving, darting about wildly, a light of panic shining there as he stared at Kiara.

Kiara advanced on the demon with Deathbite gripped firmly in both hands, sword held out before her with its tip pointed at Nameless' head. From its blade and gemstone again shone the brilliant azure glow. The light surrounded her in a halo of power no less tangible than Aisha's *Kish'aa* magic. Though the towertop chamber had no windows, an invisible wind swirled around her, setting her hair blowing and sending heat rushing in a spinning vortex around the circular room.

In that light, the Hunter saw the strain in Kiara's face. Her hands trembled around Deathbite's hilt, the sword tip wavering, and sweat streamed down her cheeks to drip from her clenched jaw.

"We can't...hold him...much longer!" Kiara snarled through gritted teeth.

The sound of her voice—and her use of the word *we*—snapped the Hunter from his momentary, startled stupor. This was not of her doing; she was merely the vessel through which *Okadigbo* channeled his power.

Without hesitation, the Hunter sheathed Soulhunger and sprang toward Nameless. In the same moment, Davathi's arm dropped and, after recoiling from the sharp-tipped claws

744

dangerously close to her throat, seized Nameless' wrist. The demon was nearly immovable—his weight immense, and his monstrous strength bent to the task of resisting whatever magic *Okadigbo* worked to restrain him—and the Hunter and Davathi struggled mightily to drag his rigid frame toward the Chamber of Sustenance. A moment later, Tarek was there to lend his strength.

Between the three of them, they managed to haul the demon's hulking frame two steps closer to the Chamber. Two steps, no more. Nameless' clawed feet dug into the stone, and the Hunter felt the demon pulling against him. Desperately struggling to break free of both their grip and *Okadigbo's* hold on him.

"Can't...hold...on!" Kiara shouted. Desperation rang in her voice. "He's...too weak!"

The "he" in question wasn't Nameless. Though the Abiarazi had spent six thousand years trapped in the Chamber of Sustenance, the millennia wasting away its powerful frame, the demon's strength seemed to grow with every beat of its monstrous heart.

No, the one growing weaker was *Okadigbo*. If the Serenii was anything like Kharna, his life force would be bound to *Ukuhlushwa Okungapheli,* powering the tower's magic as well as drawing from it. But if *Okadigbo* had also tied his life force to Nameless, to keep the demon under his control in the Chamber of Sustenance, it might explain why he was dying. Both of the twin temples of Kara-ket had been necessary: one to gather power from the earth, the other to siphon that power back into the earth to maintain balance. Without Nameless, a critical connection was missing. The scales imbalanced. As Tunde had warned, all of the *amathafa*—and, perhaps, the world—would pay the price.

Not if I've got anything to say about it! The Hunter clenched his jaw, planted his feet, and bent all his will and strength to the effort of wrestling Nameless toward the Chamber of Sustenance. *I'll get this bloody bastard into that damned thing even if it kills me!*

As if hearing his thoughts, Nameless' struggles intensified. The arm within the Hunter's grasp began to thrash about with strength so great it was all the Hunter could do to hang on. Davathi cried out as one of Nameless' claws scored a furrow along her upper arm and its twin along her cheek. Tarek grunted from the effort of trying to push the feet Nameless had planted firmly against the blood-encrusted floor.

"Losing...control!" Kiara shouted, her words hissing out in great gasping breaths. "Have to..."

Suddenly, she staggered backward as if from a great blow. Deathbite fell from her hands, its azure glow fading in an instant. The air around the Hunter's head gave an audible *snap* and Nameless' wrist tore free of his grasp. The Hunter reached for it, desperate, but Nameless towered a full head even over him. The arm rose high, claws pointed downward toward him, and a vicious smile blossomed on the demon's monstrous face.

"Die!" it roared in its guttural, grating voice. It slapped Davathi aside, knocking her backward out of the Hunter's line of sight, and sent Tarek flying to crash against the gemstone wall. Then the claws came for the Hunter's head. He threw up both arms to stop them, knowing even as he did it would be futile. He felt the moment the razor-sharp talons pierced flesh, punching deeper to grate against bone, but before they could shear through, a wailing shriek burst from Nameless' lips. The Hunter was dragged forward a step before Nameless' claws pulled free of his flesh. Even as pain lanced his arm, his jaw dropped at the sight of the demon howling, staggering backward, and clawing at his head.

What in the Keeper's name?

The thought had barely formed in the Hunter's mind before he caught sight of Kiara. Whatever invisible force had staggered her had now retreated. She stood straight, feet planted, arms stretched out to turn her empty palms toward the demon. Her face was a mask upon which myriad emotions appeared—rage, hatred, disgust, fear, panic, grief, love, hope, desperation, despair, sorrow, and more—only to vanish again into the maelstrom.

"For centuries, you brought suffering," she roared in a voice all her own, yet amplified nearly to match *Okadigbo's* power. "Inflicted pain untold, instilled terror into the hearts of your victims. You savored their emotions, fed on their power, and with it, grew strong."

She took a step closer, and drove her empty palms forward to strike at the air between them. Nameless' howls redoubled in ferocity. He clawed at his face and head so violently he raked deep furrows into his own flesh, all but gouged out two of his eyes.

"Now it is your turn!" Kiara shouted. "Feel it all, *Demon,* and know that your days of supremacy have come to an end."

Nameless' screeching rose in pitch and intensity, and he staggered backward, driven by whatever power Kiara unleashed toward the gemstone pillar in the heart of the room. One step, two, then a third. Farther and farther, until the bony spines on his back scraped against the sides of the Chamber of Sustenance that had been his prison.

Kiara's voice boomed through the chamber once again. "This day, the world is rid of you forever, as it should have been when you were condemned to this prison six thousand years ago!"

Nameless screamed, piercing his own skull with his claws, tearing off his ears, gouging out his eyes. His mighty body trembled and his knees began to give way beneath him.

The Hunter saw his moment. Saw what Kiara had intended all along. He broke into a dash, barreling toward the demon at full tilt. Kiara had done the work of herding Nameless back against his prison. Now, it fell to him—and him alone—to accomplish the final task of lifting the demon's immense frame into the Chamber of Sustenance. *Okadigbo* and the Serenii's construction would do the rest.

He'd taken just two steps when Nameless loosed a final, terrible scream and drove the claws of both hands into his brain. But rather than killing him, it seemed to sever whatever part of his mind was under assault by Kiara's power.

"Nooooo!" Nameless shrieked, his voice garbled and slurring, yet ringing clear with panic. "I will not be imprisoned again!"

The Hunter braced himself for an attack, ready to lunge between Nameless and Kiara, to draw Soulhunger and finish the demon off. But to his utter astonishment, Nameless did the one thing he'd *never* expected nor imagined he'd see: the demon fled.

Like a whipped hound, Nameless scrabbled backward, tearing his claws free of his own head to scrabble at the Chamber of Sustenance—the only thing between it and freedom. The thick coils of transparent tubes snaked upward from the Chamber, but Nameless was too fast, springing away before they could latch serpent-like on to him.

Before the Hunter realized it, much less made a move to intervene, Nameless vanished in a howling, screeching blur through the entrance.

The Hunter sprang toward the staircase, but by the time he reached it and peered down, Nameless was gone. The only sign of his passage were the deep furrows his claws had gouged in the gemstone wall and the trail of reeking ichor that had dripped from his torn head.

Keeper's teeth! He spun back toward Kiara. She had fallen to one knee and leaned heavily on her bent leg, visibly drained from whatever she had just unleashed against the demon. He'd bloody well find out exactly what that *whatever* was later; now, however, he just needed to make certain she was unhurt enough that he could leave her behind to pursue the demon.

The Hunter rushed toward her. As he went, he caught sight of Davathi. The Issai *nassor* was attempting to shake off the effects of Nameless' blow, which had sent her flying to land next to her husband. Lwazi still lay where the demon had borne him to the ground, surrounded by a pool of his own blood. Impossibly, his eyes were open, his chest rising and falling weakly. How he still lived was beyond the Hunter.

Lwazi stretched out a hand, and the Hunter saw he reached toward his daughters. Nkanyezi had both arms wrapped around Aisha's shoulders, and though tears stained her cheeks, her face was set in a determined mask as she dragged her unconscious sister toward where Lwazi lay.

As Davathi found her feet, her gaze went to the Hunter, by the stairway, and her eyes widened with the realization that the demon had fled. But before she could take a step in his direction, she saw her two daughters. Saw Nkanyezi struggling to drag Aisha's limp form toward their father.

Sensing his approach, Kiara lifted her head. She appeared pale, exhausted, yet the only blood the Hunter saw was a small trickle leaking from where she'd knocked her head when the demon had flung them both across the chamber.

"Go!" she shouted, waving him away. "I'll watch over him."

Her eyes darted to the side, and the Hunter's gaze followed. Tarek lay on the ground where he'd fallen, though his eyes were open and already he'd begun to rise. With luck, he'd sustained no broken bones, no serious injury to his head.

"I'll watch over all of them," she said, looking at the unconscious *Umoyahlebe* lying scattered around the towertop chamber. "Just get the bastard back here!"

The Hunter scanned the chamber floor for his weapons. He could not stop Nameless with Soulhunger alone—too great a risk of *killing* the demon. To his relief, he spotted both his watered steel sword and the Swordsman's iron dagger lying side by side five paces away.

As he ran to retrieve the weapons, Nkanyezi's cry rang out. "Help me, *umama!*"

The Hunter glanced over in time to see anguish blossoming on Davathi's face, tears springing to her eyes. Just as the Hunter knelt to scoop up his weapons, Davathi reached her daughter's side, strong hands gripping Aisha's arms. "No, *indokazi!*" she cried, her voice raw with emotion. "I cannot lose you aga—"

"*Umama!*" Though Nkanyezi's cheeks were wet, her voice rang with determination. "She is not yet gone from us. It's not too late!"

Davathi's expression grew puzzled, but her daughter's entreaties goaded her to action. She lent her strength to Nkanyezi and helped carry Aisha to Lwazi's side.

The Hunter stood, sword and iron blades in hand, but couldn't bring himself to leave. Not yet. He knew he had to pursue Nameless, yet for all the urgency pulling him away, a sense of duty held him rooted in place. He *had* to know whether Aisha would live or go to the *Kish'aa.* Had to know whether he would return to mourn her death or rejoice at her survival.

Lwazi's face lit up the moment his fingers touched his daughter's limp wrist. He gripped Aisha's hand tightly and, with a superhuman surge of strength, pulled himself up to a sitting position. Heedless of his own injuries, of the blood pooling around him, he reached a trembling hand up to rest on Aisha's cheek.

"*Bindazi.*" His voice came out so faint even the Hunter's keen ears barely heard it. Tears streamed from his eyes and dripped onto her pale, unmoving face. Yet he smiled. It was a thing of utter beauty and boundless joy. Tenderly, Lwazi leaned forward and whispered to Aisha, "To you, my heart."

A hint of blue-white light blossomed on his lips as Lwazi placed a kiss on Aisha's forehead. The spark was faint, there and gone again so fast the Hunter would have missed it had he not been looking. Yet he hadn't missed it. Nor did he miss the moment when it leaped from Lwazi's lips to the pale flesh of Aisha's forehead.

The spark sank into Aisha's skin, light momentarily rippling outward like a stone dropped into a pond. Where the light touched, color returned to Aisha's face. Her eyes fluttered open and her chest rose as she drew in a deep breath.

The Hunter felt a cry of joy ripped from his throat, joining those bursting from Davathi's and Nkanyezi's lips. Yet as their voices rang out, Lwazi breathed his last, a faint whisper of air slipping quietly from his lungs. Slowly, the white-haired *Umoyahlebe* toppled to one side to lie with his hand still resting on Aisha's cheek.

In that moment, the Hunter understood the truth, and the realization set tears burning in the backs of his eyes.

Like *Indaba* Tundeneyenin, Lwazi had stubbornly clung to life until the moment when he had been most needed. The spark of life passed to Aisha had been *his*. A father's final gift to his beloved daughter.

Chapter One Hundred One

The Hunter turned away before the threatening tears could flow and blur his vision. He had to turn his back on the grim scene as Davathi cried out in elation at seeing Aisha alive while shedding tears over her fallen husband. He couldn't watch Nkanyezi frantically dragging at her father's robe, hear her sobbing for him to wake up.

Still, the lump was thick in his throat as he rushed from the towertop chamber and raced down the stairs in pursuit of Nameless. Mere seconds had passed since the demon fled; he couldn't have gone far.

The Hunter's feet flew, taking the steps three at a time. He descended the spiral staircase at a sprint, leaping over the masked corpses he'd left strewn there on his way up. The vitality Soulhunger had stolen from Nameless flooded his veins and set his muscles burning. No pain remained, his wounds mended, and the anger coursing in his belly only amplified the energy crackling through his limbs.

Every time he passed a landing, he risked a glance through the crystal-clear outer wall to survey the scene below. Fighting still gripped the Consortium's city, and he hadn't the time to stop and survey the battlefield to assess the Ghandian's progress against the *alay-alagbara*. He could only hope their battle plan and the combined forces of the united tribes carried the day.

If not, he thought grimly, *I will personally deal with every surviving Orderman and slaver myself.* None would live through the day if he had his say.

As he ran, he drew in deep breaths through his nostrils, searching the air for Nameless' scent. It was unmistakable. The stench of rot and decay hung cloying and thick in the staircase. The signs of Nameless' headlong flight were everywhere. Bloody claw prints on the walls, stairs, and the central pillar marked his descent, and the fear that spurred him on. The spoor leading unerringly downward. Not that there was any other way for the demon to flee.

The Hunter pushed aside the worry gnawing at his belly. *I sealed the front entrance behind me. No way the demon could have gotten through without a resonator stone.*

All the same, he ran faster, leaping down the stairs at a blurring speed, heedless of the danger to himself. If Nameless hesitated for even a few moments in the ground-level chamber—trying to find a way out or merely attempting to batter the enormous dimercurite doors open—the Hunter had a chance to catch up with him.

And when I do, there will be no escaping me this time.

The Hunter tightened his grip on the Swordsman's blade and watered steel sword. The longer weapon would keep the demon's claws away long enough to slip inside his guard and drive the full length of sharpened iron into his chest. In the moments the demon clawed at the blade, Soulhunger would find a new home in its flesh. This time, he wouldn't pull out the dagger until Nameless was on the verge of death. He'd take no chances with the demon, not when the fate of so many hung in the balance.

Three levels above from the ground floor, something caught the Hunter's gaze. The claw marks began to shift, the furrows in the stone growing shallower, the blood left not in the shape of Nameless' monstrous foot. No, they shrank, shortened, transforming into something more akin to a human footprint in dark crimson.

No! Horror twisted in the Hunter's belly. *It can't be!*

The sight that greeted him as he reached the ground floor sent a chill down his spine, stole the strength from his legs. His feet skidded on gore- and ichor-slick stone, boots crunching through a finger-thick layer of crust formed over millennia of blood flowing down the stairs from the imprisoned Serenii above. Yet he barely noticed it. His eyes were fixed on the huge dimercurite doors that barred entrance to the Bondshold.

Or the mound of rubble where the doors should have been.

Few things existed on Einan with the destructive power capable of such devastation. In Voramis, he'd destroyed one of the Bloody Hand's slave ships, the *Gladiator,* by setting alight barrels filled with Serenii fire. The blast of the igniting alchemical mixture erupted a hundred paces into the sky and consumed the entire ship in a matter of seconds.

The dimercurite doors looked to have been destroyed by a similar blast. Only there were no quick-igniting pots or barrels within the circular chamber. Corpses aplenty, all that remained of the Ordermen the Hunter had carved to pieces on his ascent, but not so much as a scorch mark or singed thread.

No, this had been no fire. *Nameless* had broken those doors. The demon had barreled through the stone, his inhuman strength amplified a hundredfold by the same terror that had spurred him to flee from the towertop chamber—from whatever Kiara had done to him. The Hunter could only stare in stunned amazement at the heap of stone that marked the remains of the huge stone doors. The rest lay in enormous chunks and fist-sized pieces scattered for dozens of paces in a wide arc around the outside of the tower.

The Hunter's gut clenched. *By the Keeper, no!* Though dismay and despair threatened to root him to the ground, he willed his legs to move, his feet to propel him forward. One lurching step turned into two, then three, until he was once more running toward the ruined entrance to the Bondshold.

A groan from his left brought him skidding to a halt and spinning around. His eyes snapped to the figure struggling to rise, and he brought his swords instinctively up to guard.

His hopes that somehow Nameless *hadn't* escaped died as the figure climbed to his feet and shook his head.

"Bloody hell!" Kodyn murmured, shaking his head as if to clear it. "Who in the Keeper's name was that man?"

"Not a man," the Hunter growled, his heart sinking. Kodyn's words had confirmed his worst fears. "It was a *demon."* A demon, changed into a form human enough the young man had mistaken him for a man.

Kodyn jumped at the sound of the Hunter's voice, but even startled, he still had good instincts. He had a dagger out and on its way toward the Hunter in an instant. The Hunter's sword came up in time to deflect the weapon, sending the blade skittering away across the blood-crusted floor.

"Hunter?" Kodyn's eyes widened with recognition. "What are you—" His gaze darted toward the staircase, and he sucked in a breath. "Watcher's teeth, does that mean—?"

"They live." The Hunter turned away from the young man. He had no time for further explanation. "But the thing that came through here, the demon, he did this?"

"Aye. Giant of a fellow, came so fast I never even got a look at him. One moment all's quiet in here, the next I'm hit by something bigger and stronger than Jarl by far."

The Hunter's heart sank. Still, he refused to give up. There still existed a chance he could find Nameless. He clung to hope, though it felt weak, the most tenuous of threads.

He forced his legs to carry him toward the newly made entrance to the ancient Serenii tower. The tumult of battle drifted through the shattered opening: the clash of steel on steel, shouted commands, screams of agony, ululating war cries, feet splashing through mud, wooden weapons and bared fists striking flesh, and countless more besides. The stink of human rot, illness, and old, dried blood joined the stink of fresh wounds and death that hung in a thick miasma, tainting the air with a stench that curdled the Hunter's nostrils. Worse, it drowned out the foul odor of demon.

The Hunter scanned the blood-soaked ground beyond the tower's base, seeking anything that could indicate the demon's path of flight. Claw marks in the mud. Bodies torn up by bestial fangs and claws. Perhaps even the bastard himself, stopped long enough to feed on the fallen, or tearing his way through the embattled humans.

His hope proved vain. He found a single deep footprint leading away from the Bondshold—a foot too large to be fully human, with a claw extending from the heel.

At that sight, the truth settled over him with an unshakable certainty: Nameless had escaped.

A torrent of curses poured from his lips, each more furious and horrible than the last. Since swearing his vow to Kharna, he'd known that capturing demons *alive* would prove a monumental endeavor. Even the weakest Abiarazi he'd encountered—a distinction that fell to Lord Chasteyn—surpassed him in strength.

Yet Nameless...Nameless had been something else entirely. A being far more powerful than any he'd encountered. Stronger than the Warmaster. More resilient than Tane, the Third of the Bloody Hand. More savage and ferocious than Lord Apus. His subtle means of manipulation—taking the form of a beautiful, majestic beast that so belied his true nature, drawing Tarek up to the towertop chamber by making him *think* he'd heard the Hunter's call, and in so doing, distracting his foes long enough to gain the upper hand—rivaled even the Sage's cunning. His skill at controlling the minds of those under his thrall surpassed Garanis'. He'd taken possession of Tarek's very body from across a vast distance, and there had been no use of any magical pendants or Illusionist Cleric tricks.

And now he was free out in the world.

The Hunter's jaw clenched. *Which means I've got my work cut out for me, hunting the bastard down.*

In that moment, the tower beneath him gave a shudder. The humming from far, far below began to weaken. The Hunter knew the truth even as he looked at the central black gemstone pillar and saw the light flickering: *Okadigbo* was dying.

The Serenii needed Nameless. Without the demon's power, it could not survive long.

With that realization, a great weight settled on the Hunter's shoulders. He had failed *Okadigbo*. He had failed Kharna, too. The Serenii entombed in Enarium had somehow *known* its fellow was in peril, even from across half a world, and dispatched the Hunter to Ghandia for this very purpose.

751

He'd failed Aisha, too. He'd promised to help her rescue her family. Now, Lwazi lay dead in the towertop chamber above, savaged by the very demon the Hunter had been sent to defeat. Because of him, Aisha would never have the joy of being reunited with the father she had traveled all this way to see. She would never hear him speak, never feel his arms around her, never introduce him to Kodyn.

Kodyn. The Hunter's gaze strayed to the young man. Already, a dark bruise had begun forming on Kodyn's cheek—courtesy either of Nameless' blow or the hard wall he'd collided with. Only sheer luck had kept the young man from being torn to shreds by the fleeing demon. Had Nameless not been so terrified by Kiara, he might have paused to feed on Kodyn as he had with the captive *Umoyahlebe* above.

And Kiara. He'd nearly gotten her killed far too many times over the course of this journey. At Zamani Falls when she'd followed him to rescue Tarek. In the battles they'd fought, so many he'd lost count. Crossing the Valley of Living Fire. Attacked by Nameless through Tarek as the demon sought to gain his freedom.

Tarek, too, had journeyed at his side because Itan had ordered him to help the Hunter eliminate the *maistyr* that had been rumored in Ghandia. Now, all the Elivasti might soon suffer because of the Hunter's failure to kill or imprison Nameless.

More faces flashed through his mind. All people he'd failed. Tassat. Father Reverentus. Brothers Penurius and Modestus. Garnos. Master Eldor and the True Descendants. Those he'd lost in Voramis, chief among them Bardin and Farida.

The weight atop the Hunter's shoulders grew heavier with every beat of his heart. A fist of iron tightened around his lungs, squeezing tight, stopping him from drawing breath. The world began to spin, darkness closing in at the edges of his vision. Pain lanced up his legs, jolted his spine, jarring his neck. Yet he barely felt it. He felt only a cold numbness closing in around him. Dragging him deeper and deeper into a void from which there was no escape.

"Hunter!" Kodyn's shout seemed to come from across a vast distance.

The Hunter tried to speak, but no words came out. His mind could not summon any. Could no more think than compel his paralyzed lungs to suck in the merest whisper of air. He knew nothing beyond the crushing weight atop his chest, the burden that threatened to flatten him. Despair had him in its grip. He'd believed it behind him long ago. Believed himself free of it, as he'd been free of the demonic voices that shrieked in his mind. But there was no escaping it. It was as relentless as it was patient. The feeling of utter hopelessness surged up like quicksand to swallow him, as it nearly had so many times before.

"Hunter!" Kodyn's shout came again. A dark shape hovered before the Hunter's eyes, but he could not make it out. "Are you hurt? What's—"

Kodyn's voice cut off suddenly in a gasp. Surprise and a hint of pain resonated in that sound. The dark shape before the Hunter's eyes disappeared. Replaced by the bright sunlight streaming in through the ruined opening in the Serenii-built tower.

Light. Color. Golds and blues and oranges of morning splashed across a cloudless sky. The Hunter grasped at it. Like a drowning man clutching a thrown rope, he grasped at it with every fiber of his being. Straining to claw his way from the cold, icy depths of despair in a desperate attempt to reach a warmth he sensed but could not feel.

The darkness around him receded. The cold, too. The numbness seeped from his limbs, replaced by heat. The Hunter tilted his face up to the sun he knew shone just outside the tower in which he stood.

Suddenly, he felt as if he could draw breath. A great, shuddering gulp of air filled his lungs to bursting, driving back the darkness completely. Sensations washed over him: the rush of wind, the stench of battle, and the clash of steel.

Steel? The Hunter's mind was still numb, not yet free of the crushing despair, yet he recognized the sound he knew all too well.

A tiny voice screamed in the back of his mind. His survival instinct, activated by the promise of danger. In an instant, the Hunter was fully on the alert. Somehow, he was on his knees—had he fallen?—so he sprang to his feet, hands reaching for his swords. His eyes took in the scene in an instant.

Kodyn, who had stood over him a moment earlier, was now locked in combat just beyond the far side of the rubble pile that remained of the great stone door. A pair of men in studded leather vests attacked him with curving greatknives and snarling curses. The two of them could not break through his guard, could not push past him into the Serenii tower, yet beyond them, the Hunter spotted more. A dozen, at least. Perhaps twenty.

And in their midst moved a familiar umber-skinned figure clad in both the bright robes of a Ghandian and the Consortium armor.

Gwala!

Chapter One Hundred Two

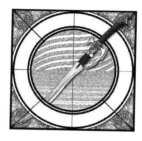

The Hunter's anger blazed white-hot at the sight of the Consortium's leader. Crimson flecked his scar-etched cheeks, stained his colorful robes and the studded vest beneath, and dripped from the *assegai* he carried in his right hand. Gone was the glove covering his left hand, revealing a clenched fist forged of metal. From the iron knuckles jutted a spike nearly as long as his forearm. It, too, dripped the blood of his fellow Ghandians onto the muddy ground beside him.

The diminutive Djineza marched at his side, an ever-present shadow. She did not wear her enormous Shalandran steel greatsword—the bandage on her arm was wet and dark where the Hunter's dagger had pierced it and shattered the bone beneath—but the whip curled in her fingers bore fresh blood.

The Hunter had a single moment to decide. He longed to leap over Kodyn's head and cut down the Consortium slavers between him and Gwala. Yet the whoreson had survived *two* battles now. He was slippery and clever enough to vanish into the chaos, ditch anything that marked him as *alay-alagbara,* and slip unseen among the Ghandians flooding the camp. Few would recognize him on sight, and fewer still would pay attention enough in the midst of the fray to question his movements.

I'll be damned if I let him escape, too.

He darted forward, but instead of leaping over Kodyn's head, he seized the young man by the collar and dragged him back and to one side. As he did so, he unleashed a blood-curdling scream of terrible agony.

So surprised was Kodyn that he put up no resistance. Not that it would have done much good. The Hunter's grip on the young man was hard as iron, his strength exceeding Kodyn's by an immense margin. Two steps carried him and Kodyn both out of sight of the astonished slavers who'd suddenly found themselves without an enemy. He threw himself to the floor and dragged Kodyn down with him.

"Play dead," he hissed into Kodyn's ear. "Wait for my signal."

Kodyn was either too surprised or had too much good sense to resist. He lay utterly still at the Hunter's side, his breathing nearly silent even to the Hunter's keen ears.

Good enough, the Hunter thought. He moved just enough to turn his head and cover most of his face with his hood, leaving a crack between the hem and the blood-encrusted floor that one eye could peer out. From his prone position, he had a clear view of the entrance.

The Consortium slavers had been caught off guard by Kodyn's abrupt disappearance, but the Hunter *hoped* the scream sufficed to explain it. The slavers would be reeling and off-balance from the chaos of battle all around them. Their minds would be muddled by bloodshed and death, sufficiently confused they might very well believe their lone opponent had truly fallen.

His gambit paid off. Mere seconds after he and Kodyn hit the floor, a tide of Consortium slavers flooded into the Bondshold's ground-floor chamber. All carried greatknives, more than a few blades stained with blood, and a few wore on their belts the whips with which they'd driven the slaves to labor. Some sported wounds. Most, however, had escaped the battle unscathed.

Thus far. The Hunter set his jaw grimly. None of those who entered here today would leave alive. He'd make bloody damned certain of it.

Every one of the armed men and women spilling into the chamber gawked. At the black gemstone pillar, now dark and lifeless, at the heart of the chamber. At the transparent walls that gave an unrestricted view of the world beyond the Bondshold while concealing everything within. At the thick layer of blood that crusted the floor, and the fresh blood pooling around the corpses of the Ordermen who'd fallen to the Hunter's fury.

"Keeper's hairy balls!" cursed a slaver, raising the fingers of his free hand to make the sign to ward off the god of death. "What the bloody hell happened in here?"

"The maskies," cried another, a woman with the flaxen hair and freckled skin of a Fehlan. She gripped her greatknife tighter and turned back toward the tower's entrance. "They're dead. Every last one."

"Check them to be certain," snapped Gwala's voice. "Widdar and Samtor, too." The man himself strode into view a moment later, Djineza a half-step behind him. He surveyed the Hunter's handiwork and a sneer curled his upper lip. "Randan, Atrias, get upstairs and see what the bloody hell Ranuld is up to."

The Hunter's stomach tightened as the flaxen-haired Fehlan woman moved in his direction, crouching at each masked body to check if they still lived. At the same time, two more of the slavers spread out in the opposite direction, and another pair broke off from the group to charge up the spiral staircase.

But the Hunter didn't bother watching them go. He had eyes only for the tower's shattered entrance. Watching, waiting until the flow of slavers slackened. Only three men—all with the dark, sun-tanned miens of the Twelve Kingdoms—entered behind Gwala. They kept their gazes fixed on the way they'd come in. Gwala's rear guard. The last of the slavers he'd gathered to his side.

A cold, hard smile spread across the Hunter's face. *Perfect.*

He sprang to his feet and lunged for the Fehlan woman in a blur of motion. His watered steel sword whipped out and opened the side of her neck in the same movement. Blood misted in the air around her head and she fell without a sound, but the Hunter raced on without ever slowing.

Three great strides brought him within striking range of the three slavers holding the entrance. The first never even saw death coming; the Hunter hacked off his head with a single blow. On his backstroke, he opened the face of the second slaver in the line, carving a deep furrow along his nose and ripping out his left eye. The last of the guards halfway turned toward him, his greatknife barely beginning to rise, before the Hunter drove Soulhunger deep into his chest. A savage twist of the dagger's hilt tore a terrible, raw scream from the dying man's lips.

Crimson light brightened the air around the slaver, bathing the Hunter in a savage, bloody brilliance. That was the sight that met the eyes of Gwala, Djineza, and every one of the still-living slavers as they spun toward the source of the sound.

The Hunter raised his sword and leveled the dripping crimson blade at Gwala. "Ranuld's busy giving answer to the Long Keeper for the suffering he's caused. I wonder, Gwala, will the *Kish'aa* welcome you into *Pharadesi* after what you've done?"

Gwala's eyes blazed, but the sneer never left his face. "I do not fear the *Kish'aa.*" He twisted his mouth to the side and spat. "No more than I fear you, whoever you are."

The Hunter grinned. "I am your death."

The words had no effect on Gwala, or Djineza. A few of the slavers, however—those with clean blades and free of wounds—blanched and cast nervous glances at their fellows.

Gwala snorted. "Kill him," he commanded with a contemptuous flick of his *assegai.*

Six of the slavers responded to the order. Six men, ferocious-looking and strong of arm, all carrying bloody greatknives. They closed in on the Hunter in a rush, hemming him in on all sides. Swords flashing, faces alight with disdain and contempt. All six died before they drew within striking range of the Hunter.

The life force Soulhunger had stolen from Nameless had restored him to full strength. The slaver that now lay dying at the Hunter's feet pumped even more vigor through the dagger and into the Hunter's muscles. He was a blaze of power and fury, darting forward and hacking through his enemies so fast they had no time to register the attack before death claimed them. Even as the six fell around him, the Hunter had returned to his place and original stance, bloody sword pointed at Gwala. To anyone who *hadn't* been standing immediately in front of him, it almost looked as if he hadn't moved.

"Come now," the Hunter scoffed, his smile widening. "Surely you can do better than that."

Besides Gwala and Djineza, the only slavers left standing were those who'd escaped the battle unscathed. And not for their skill in combat or their courage. To a man—and one woman—the five turned ashen, eyes going wide, and their legs gave out beneath them. Swords clattered to the ground and they fell to their knees. The sound of their blubbering and begging rang out through the circular chamber.

"Cowards!" Djineza snarled. Her uninjured arm rose and snapped her whip forward, silencing one of the craven slavers' wails in a spray of blood. She drew her arm back to strike again, but her fury turned into a shrill cry of pain as the black hilt of a dagger suddenly sprouted in her upraised forearm. Another followed a moment later, burying in her chest. She stumbled backward as a third lodged in her throat.

The Hunter glanced to the side just in time to see Kodyn hurling his fourth throwing knife. The sharp, thin blade flew straight and true, driving point-first into Djineza's open mouth. Her cry of pain cut off in a harsh, rasping gurgle. She tried to claw at the dagger hilt protruding between her teeth. In vain. Kodyn's throw had severed the tendons in her uninjured arm. She toppled to the side and lay wide-eyed on the floor. Her legs jerked and twitched; death claimed her slowly.

Gwala spun toward Kodyn, *assegai* coming up to block another blade. None came. Kodyn did not release his grip on the dagger, but merely held it ready to cast. His gaze went to the Hunter, a questioning look in his eyes.

The Hunter shook his head. "This one is mine."

"No!" A strong, commanding voice boomed through the chamber. "He is mine."

Gwala spun toward the source of the sound—the spiral staircase that descended from the towertop chamber. Davathi stood two steps from the bottom, her face stained with tears and blood but her expression a mask of fury. With a snarl, she hurled two lifeless corpses at Gwala's

756

feet. Randan and Atrias, the two who'd been dispatched to investigate above. One's neck had been snapped, the other died from a terrible wound to the throat. Inflicted by the spear that Davathi now drew from behind her back.

Aisha's spear, the Hunter saw. Forged by Praamian smiths in an *alay-alagbara* imitation of the Issai weapon, utterly free of the bright beads, feathers, and leather cords with which Davathi and her fellow *amaqhawe* adorned their weapons. Yet its head was sharp and strong. That was all that mattered now as Davathi advanced to stand before Gwala.

"Why?" The single word rumbled from Davathi's throat with thundering force. Anguish and rage burned in equal measure in her *kaffe*-brown eyes, the intensity of her hatred terrible to behold.

"Does it matter?" Gwala sneered. He wore a brave face, but a hint of fear darkened his eyes, and he shifted back a step so he didn't lose sight of the Hunter and Kodyn while watching Davathi.

"To me, it does." Davathi's face and voice were as hard as the stone upon which the tower stood. "To your daughter, it does."

Gwala's right eye twitched, just for a moment. "I have no daughter!" he snapped. "One I left behind the day I turned my back on our people, the day I saw the truth of how weak we truly were, living here in our little secluded corner of the world. The other died because of *your* daughter."

A cruel light shone in his eyes, and he reached up to touch the necklace of finger bones dangling from around his neck. His *daughter's?*

"Tell me, Davathi," Gwala sneered, "did you feel the pain I felt? When you understood that your beloved *indokazi* had been taken from you as mine was, did you suffer, too?"

Davathi gave no answer to that, but a flicker of residual pain flashed through her eyes.

"*I* did that!" Gwala thumped his iron fist against his chest, and blood from the metal spike spattered his studded leather vest. "I led the *alay-alagbara* to find her. I made certain that she was taken along with the rest. Because if I was to have my daughter torn from my side forever, you deserved to have yours taken, too."

"Oh, Gwala." Davathi shook her head. "Lwazi was right about you. All those years ago, when you asked his father for Hasana's hand, he said the *Kish'aa* revealed the *Okanele's touch* on your spirit. That you were corrupted. We did not want to believe."

"How is my brother-in-law?" Gwala's voice dripped acid. "I trust Ranuld and the others have treated him with the respect due an *Umoyahlebe?*"

Davathi's jaw hardened. Her feet shifted into an attack stance.

Gwala saw it, and his eyes brightened. "Come, *nassor*." He sneered the words like an insult, brandishing his *assegai*. "Let us see if your devotion to your people has made you stronger than me. We both know that you could never beat me when we trained with Duma."

Davathi merely shrugged. "Those days are long behind us." From her belt, she drew the *iznyovu* dagger the Hunter had given her and dropped into a fighting crouch.

A part of the Hunter felt guilty standing here; the distance between him and Nameless grew greater with every moment's delay. Yet he couldn't bring himself to leave. After all Gwala had done, the Hunter would not move until the bastard paid for his crimes. The hunt for the Abiarazi could wait a few moments.

Davathi began to circle left, then, when Gwala imitated her, darted right so suddenly the slaver was forced to change directions too quickly. Off-balance, he barely had time to bring up his *assegai* to knock aside Davathi's thrust. Her dagger scored a long gash down his left arm before she darted backward out of range of the metal spike he punched at her.

Growling, Gwala imitated her martial stance, weaving and bobbing in the agile style of the Issai. But for all his heritage and his features, he was Issai no longer. Not truly. He wore Consortium armor, carried out Consortium orders, and within his heart dwelled the wickedness that made men capable of enslaving another. Davathi, on the other hand, fought with the precision that had earned her the title of *nassor* and the respect of even great warriors like Naledi, Jumaane, and Duma. Her blows struck with the force of her fury, empowered by the wrath that drove her to vengeance.

Gwala stood no chance at all.

Davathi disarmed him with a sharp blow to the wrist that snapped the bones of his fingers. When he tried to follow up with the iron spike, Davathi met the attack with the *iznyovu* dagger, driving it deep into his forearm. Screaming in pain and rage, Gwala tried to dart backward, to open space between them in a desperate attempt to flee. Davathi pursued with the characteristic Issai fleetness and knocked his legs out from beneath him with a swipe of her *assegai*. Gwala fell hard, and Davathi sprang atop his back. Twin slashes of the spearhead severed the tendons behind his knees, crippling him and earning a wail of agony.

Gwala's attacks grew frantic, wild. He landed a backward elbow strike in Davathi's side that knocked the air from her lungs with a grunt, but she caught his next blow on her arm and, almost casually, shattered his two lower ribs with a vicious punch. Gwala had vastly underestimated her skill and strength—or overestimated his. So confident he'd been in the strength of his *alay-alagbara* army that he'd never believed he could be defeated. That arrogance was his downfall now.

Davathi took her time breaking him. His legs had already been rendered useless, but she shattered his knees anyways, following up with his elbows. Her muscles bunched as she hauled his left arm out straight, his efforts to resist her futile. She lifted her bare foot and stamped down hard on the dagger still embedded in the meat of his forearm. A sickening *crack* echoed through the chamber as the ivory snapped both forearm bones. The sharpened blade all but cut his arm away entirely.

Gwala's screams grew louder and louder, underscored by the horrible chorus of torment as Davathi shattered him. Until finally, he could scream no more. He lay gasping, blood pooling around him, joining the crimson puddles spreading outward from his slain companions. The five *alay-alagbara* who hadn't been killed stared horrified at their commander from where they knelt beneath Kodyn's watchful eye and the long sword with which he threatened them. None of them had the courage to aid Gwala, and even if they had, the action would have been futile.

With a vicious kick, Davathi rolled Gwala onto his back. He gasped and gurgled, every breath labored. The wetness told the Hunter his ribs had punctured his lungs. He would drown soon enough, choked by his own blood.

Yet that was not to be his end.

Davathi knelt over Gwala, her face a mask of rage. "Hasana would be ashamed of you. As I am." She pulled the *iznyovu* dagger from his nearly severed forearm and dragged the sharp blade across his face, mangling his scars. His cries cut off in a choking cough, spraying blood.

Davathi did not wipe the spatter from her face; she merely straightened, spat on Gwala, and turned her back on her fallen enemy. Her gaze met the Hunter's.

"The *Kish'aa* will not take him." She flicked her hand contemptuously toward Gwala. "I give him to your *Okanele* blade."

The Hunter grinned. "It'd be my pleasure."

Bending, he tore Soulhunger from the dead slaver's chest and strode over to stand over the shattered slaver. Gwala stared up at him with hatred blazing in his eyes and fear staining his mangled face.

The Hunter knelt—careful to stay well away from Gwala's iron hand—and held the dagger up before the man's eyes. He could taste the acrid stench of terror and urine mingling with the man's scent of citron, myrtle pepper, and iron. It brought a smile to his face.

"Rot in the darkest hell, you bastard."

He drove Soulhunger into Gwala's chest, and the traitorous Issai found the strength to scream one last time.

Chapter One Hundred Three

No sooner had the Hunter ripped Soulhunger from Gwala's corpse than Kodyn's voice rang out.

"Aisha!"

The Hunter glanced up from the dead slaver and found a pale-faced, exhausted-looking Aisha struggling to stay upright as she and Nkanyezi descended the stairs side by side.

Kodyn hurried toward the staircase, stopping just short of the bottom step. "Are you—"

"I'm fine," Aisha said, in a voice hoarse from both exhaustion and sorrow. Tears still glistened among the blood flecking her cheeks. "But my father..." Her voice cracked and her eyes dropped to the limp figure she and Nkanyezi carried cradled in their arms.

"Keeper!" Kodyn reached a hand toward her. "I'm so sorry, Aisha."

She seemed not to hear the words. Her eyes remained fixed on her father's pale, lifeless features.

Davathi moved toward her daughters. "Come, *indokazi.*" Gone was the warrior's fury that had consumed her moments earlier; in its place was a mother's concern and wife's grief. She stood in front of both Aisha and Nkanyezi, her powerful shoulders drooping visibly as she joined them in staring down at her husband. "He is at peace," she whispered, her voice quiet. "He is with the *Kish'aa* now."

Sobs burst from Aisha and Nkanyezi's throats, and they bent their heads, weeping into their father's body and their mother's arms.

Above and behind them, more Ghandians appeared on the staircase. The surviving *Umoyahlebe* were bloodied and haggard, some barely with the strength to stand. Between them, they carried the bodies of their dead fellows.

Davathi lifted her head and, seeing the people waiting on the stairs, ushered Aisha and Nkanyezi to one side of the circular chamber. There, they set down Lwazi's body and knelt around him. The rest of the *Umoyahlebe* did likewise with the corpses they carried.

A lump rose in the Hunter's throat. He turned away; the Ghandians had endured torments and horrors beyond imagining, and had earned the right to mourn their fallen in privacy.

As he moved, his gaze fell on Kodyn. The young man looked utterly torn. He wanted to go to Aisha, that much was visible in the way his entire body turned and leaned in her direction. Yet the uncertainty in his expression made it clear he wanted to give Aisha's family a moment to grieve.

The Hunter strode toward the young man, taking Kodyn by the shoulder. "Go," he said when Kodyn looked over at him. "She will be glad you are close, even in this difficult moment."

Kodyn hesitated, but only for a moment. He gave the Hunter a grateful nod and hurried over to stand behind Aisha. She did not turn toward him, did not rise, but she reached a hand behind her and gripped his leg. Kodyn stood, still and silent as an honor guard, lending her the comfort of his presence.

The Hunter turned and marched toward the ruins of the great dimercurite door. As he approached the entrance, the tumult of the battle beyond seemed to grow louder. Shouted orders. The roaring of the Buhari and the Issai ululations. A strange, bestial grunting and a sound that reminded the Hunter of fists beating chests. The sharp clashing of steel on steel. The meaty *thumps* of wooden spears striking flesh. Screams of agony and fury and terror.

Gwala and his lieutenants were dead, the Ordermen who'd freed Nameless sent to their graves, but the fighting beyond still raged hot.

The Hunter glanced over to where the five captive slavers lay face-down on their bellies. To his surprise, all had been bound wrist and ankle. He'd been so focused on Davathi's battle with Gwala that he'd missed Kodyn's swift movements. The restrained men and women appeared utterly unwilling to put up resistance or fight against their bonds. Any shreds of courage they might have once possessed had vanished with their commander's death.

The Hunter fought back the urge to open their throats and be rid of them. Or to drive Soulhunger into their armored backs one by one. Their cruel actions had earned them a cruel end. But there was killing aplenty awaiting him outside *Ukuhlushwa Okungapheli's* walls.

All the same, he slipped toward the five bound *alay-alagbara* and bent low to growl at them. "Any one of you so much as moves a muscle, I'll cut you apart so slowly your commander's death will be a mercy by comparison."

Jerky nods and gibbering, tearful pleas were hastily offered.

Satisfied, the Hunter turned and strode toward the ruins of the heavy stone door. The sooner he put an end to every slaver fighting on the plateau, the sooner he could be off tracking down Nameless. He could ill-afford any delay; the demon's speed and stamina far exceeded his own. It would take all of his strength to catch up to the fleeing Abiarazi.

Before he reached the door, however, a voice called out his name.

"Hunter!"

Turning, he found Aisha striding toward him. Tears still streamed from her eyes and deep lines of anguish etched her face, yet she moved with confidence and certainty in her step, her head held high and fists clenched.

"I'm going with you," she said. "We're putting an end to this once and for all."

"Aisha—" he began.

His words cut off abruptly when her eyes flared a brilliant blue-white. Her aura crackling with the power of the *Kish'aa* she was even now absorbing from the corpses strewn around her.

"The time for mourning is *after* the battle ends," she said, with a look that dared him to raise further protest. "I will not weep while my people fight for their lives, for their very future." She raised clenched fists—somehow *healed,* like the rest of her flesh that had melted away— around which danced a torrent of searing-hot sparks. "No more will die today while I draw breath."

"While *we* draw breath." Nkanyezi moved up to stand beside her sister and, reaching out, she took one of Aisha's clenched fists. Gently, she pried Aisha's hand open and intertwined her fingers with her sister's. "We do this together."

761

Fresh tears streamed from Aisha's eyes, but mingled with her sorrow was a measure of joy and delight. She tightened her grip on Nkanyezi's hand, and a torrent of light streamed down her arm to flow into her sister. "Together," she whispered.

Hand in hand, the two of them strode through the ruined entrance of the Bondshold and into the brightening morning beyond.

Davathi slipped up beside the Hunter. She held Aisha's *assegai* and the *iznyovu* dagger—both stained with Gwala's blood—in a firm grip. "Come, *Okanele*. My daughters have grown beyond even a mother's greatest hopes, yet still they have need of me. Join me in guarding their backs."

The Hunter grinned. "With pleasure."

He and Davathi marched after Aisha and Nkanyezi. Kodyn moved to follow, but first stopped to pull his daggers from Djineza's corpse. Glancing over his shoulder, the Hunter caught a glimpse of the young man's frown, and for long seconds, Kodyn seemed to remain motionless, studying the dead Shalandran's face. However, by the time they exited the Serenii tower, Kodyn was at their back.

In unison, the three of them fell in behind Nkanyezi and Aisha, ready to ward off the blades and fury of any slaver who dared to strike at the two *Umoyahlebe*. It proved unnecessary. With every step they went, they gathered to themselves more of the *Kish'aa*, more souls of the myriad dead that had fallen in battle. Brighter and brighter they glowed. Wind swirled around them, warm at first, but growing so hot none could draw near without being burned. Even the Hunter fell back before the intensity of the power they radiated. The streams of lightning they unleashed together sent foes flying by the dozen and burned skin and bone to ash in a heartbeat.

The Consortium never stood a chance.

* * *

"*Umoyahlebe*." Jumaane bowed his great head to Aisha and Nkanyezi when they came face to face with him and a group of thirty Buhari warriors in the heart of the Consortium camp. The *nassor* was covered head to toe in crimson—some of it his own—and his great *nkemba* was so stained the Hunter could no longer see the steel beneath. He'd lost his lion's mane headdress, yet standing there, bathed in sweat and the blood of his enemies, he appeared the embodiment of the beast itself.

When the giant warrior straightened, a ferocious snarling grin broadened his face. "The battle is won. Our enemy is routed, all save that coward, *Gwala*." He twisted his mouth to spit on the ground. "I received word he was sighted fleeing through the gates. I've already sent ten of my best to catch him, but—"

"That was not Gwala." Davathi snarled the name of her former brother-in-law. "Gwala lies dead among the *Gcinue'eleku awandile*, a fate he earned the moment he turned his back on our people."

She made no mention of the fact Gwala had been the one who'd led the Consortium slavers to capture Aisha years earlier, the Hunter noted. Though whether to spare her daughter further pain at the memory or to let the matter die forever, he didn't know. Nor did he care. Gwala would trouble neither the living nor dead again.

"What you saw was an *Okanele* who took on Gwala's form," the Hunter said. "A true dark spirit of *Inzayo Okubi*, one who must have seen his own evil mirrored in Gwala's soul. Your men will return empty-handed." That, he knew for a certainty. "And it is better for them the *Okanele* flees. No disrespect to your *amaqhawe,* but that is a foe far beyond their skill."

During the battle, he'd spotted drag marks leading into a back alley, and broken off from guarding Aisha and Nkanyezi to follow them. He'd found a few gobbets of flesh and a foot still adorned by a lion's-tooth anklet, the only remnants of Nameless' meal. The Hunter knew little about the habits of Abiarazi—*true* Abiarazi, the bestial creatures they had been before they gave up their power to hide from the Serenii—but if the demon was anything like the other predators on Einan, he'd be sated from his meal and soon begin looking for someplace to rest and digest.

To the Hunter's relief, Jumaane took no offense. He merely nodded. "Then the battle is over. The day is ours. Thanks in part to you, *Umzukeli.*" He looked from Aisha to Nkanyezi. "But chiefly because of the both of you."

"The credit belongs to your warriors," Aisha responded, her voice as solemn as her expression. "It is the courage and skill of our united *amaqhawe* that has carried the day."

Jumaane burst into a hearty, full-throated laugh. "I can see much of you in this one, Davathi," he said, clapping his Issai counterpart on the shoulder, leaving a bloody handprint. "She has your strength and wisdom."

Davathi turned a tearful smile on her daughters. "And her father's spirit." She reached out to take Aisha's free hand, and Aisha took it, squeezing firmly. They were among the few who knew how true that was, in more ways than one.

Davathi's gaze shifted to Nkanyezi. "They both do."

"This is the *kwa'indokazi* of whom I have heard so much?" Jumaane turned to Nkanyezi and gave her a bow of respect from one warrior to another. "If even half of what your mother has told me of you is true, then I am honored that the *Kish'aa* saw fit to guard you among the living."

Nkanyezi blushed, but managed to tilt her head to the towering—and handsome—*nassor.* "If half of what Siyanda has told me of the Buhari's fiercest warrior is true, then I would say the same."

To the Hunter's surprise, Jumaane flushed, too. His eyes shone with a sudden excitement. "Your *um'zala* spoke of you to me. Er...I mean...spoke of me to you?"

Nkanyezi's face brightened, and her resemblance to her mother grew unmistakable. "A great deal." She reached up and mimicked twisting a key between her lips. "But what words are spoken between sisters in the dark of night must remain always secret."

Jumaane's expression tightened, and he darted a nervous glance at Davathi. "Speaking of your *um'shana,* is she—?"

Davathi shook her head. "I do not know." Her expression grew grim. "My *amaqhawe* and I parted ways in the tunnels below."

"I saw her at Naledi's side when they opened the gates for us." A frown twisted Jumaane's lips, his eyes darkening. "But I lost track of her in the battle. We were separated—"

"Jumaane!" A familiar voice echoed through the streets toward them.

The Hunter, Davathi, Jumaane, Aisha, Kodyn, Nkanyezi, and all of the Buhari warriors spun toward the sound. Davathi and her daughters drew in sharp inhalations of relief, and a cry of joy burst from Jumaane's lips. His huge legs propelled him up the street in the direction of the blood-soaked woman marching toward him.

Siyanda threw out her arms to him, and Jumaane swept her up in a passionate embrace. She clung to him with a ferocity to match his.

The Hunter exchanged grins with Davathi, Aisha, Nkanyezi, and Kodyn, then joined the Buhari warriors in flocking toward their *nassor*. By the time they reached Jumaane and Siyanda, the giant had once more set the young woman down on her feet, but neither seemed eager to release their grip on the other. The Hunter knew that well—fear at the near-certainty of losing the one they loved had given way to an almost desperate relief and elation at being reunited. He'd felt it himself far too often of late.

A spike of fear pierced his belly. His eyes darted instinctively toward the midnight tower that loomed over them all. So consumed he'd been with keeping Aisha and Nkanyezi safe and finishing off the *alay-alagbara* that he'd given Kiara no thought. He had no idea where she was, or how she'd fared in the battle.

But his concerns for Kiara vanished a moment later when Naledi, Tawia, and four other Issai warriors marched into view. All bore wounds, but it was not their injuries that made Jumaane cry out in anguish or sapped the strength from Davathi's limbs.

Now, it was Aisha and Nkanyezi's turn to hold up their mother, and Siyanda's turn to offer comfort to Jumaane as the two mighty *nassors* wept over the broken, limp body cradled in Naledi's arms.

Duma, the Old Cheetah, had gone to the *Kish'aa*.

Chapter One Hundred Four

The Hunter hurried through the streets of the Consortium city. No longer empty as they had been the night he, Kodyn, and Aisha had snuck in; now, the mud was churned by boots and dark red with drying blood, every narrow alleyway and side street choked with corpses. The *alay-alagbara* had fought hard, but Jumaane's warriors had given no quarter. So determined they were to be rid of the scourge of the *Gcinue'eleku awandile* that they'd killed even those who'd thrown down their weapons and attempted surrender.

After everything the slavers have done to these people, the Hunter thought grimly as he took in a line of dead corpses with empty hands, their greatknives lying in the mud before their bent knees, *they deserve no less.*

The Vassalage Consortium had destroyed villages, slaughtered hundreds of Ghandian warriors and noncombatants, twisted one tribe into mindless killers using dark alchemy, and eradicated two more entirely. Not to mention what they'd helped the Order of Mithridas compel the *Umoyahlebe* to do, or the countless victims who had succumbed to dimercurite poisoning because of them.

No, their fate here today had been well-earned. And that was just the beginning of their woes. Thanks to everything Kodyn had found, the Vassalage Consortium's downfall was all but certain.

But all that came later. First, the Hunter had to see for himself that all those who mattered to him had lived through the day. Seeing Duma's body had reminded him of the *two* people he'd left in *Ukuhlushwa Okungapheli.* His hasty steps led now toward the Serenii tower in search of Tarek and Kiara.

He found Tarek standing lone vigil over the corpses of the *Umoyahlebe* laid to rest on the floor of the ground-level chamber. Dried blood crusted his face where it had trickled from a nasty-looking cut to his head—courtesy of Nameless' final desperate struggle—and he stood with the slight sway of a man fighting against dizziness. Yet his spine was straight and his expression solemn. He'd planted the butt of his spear between his feet in a stance reminiscent of an honor guard.

The Hunter breathed an inward sigh of relief upon seeing the young man—*mostly*—unhurt. "Nothing cut that won't heal, or broken that won't mend?" he asked, trying not to let the worry show on his face.

"I've got something in my healer's pack that'll have me solid as a rock," Tarek said, his expression hardening. "I'll be ready to ride come noon."

"Ride?" The Hunter cocked his head. "You going somewhere?"

"Aye, *we* are." Tarek's eyes narrowed a fraction. "Unless you found *Nuru Iwu's* corpse among the Consortium dead out there?" He gestured through the shattered door toward the battlefield of the city beyond.

The Hunter's jaw clenched. "No such luck." He ran a hand through his hair, and his fingers came away with what looked like bits of bone and shredded flesh among all the blood. "He slipped out the gate in all the confusion. He'll be long gone by now."

"The question is: where's he gone *to?*" Tarek's face darkened, and visible worry knotted his shoulders.

"Probably someplace quiet," the Hunter said, trying to sound more confident than he felt. "He's gorged himself and will need to rest, use the food to restore his body."

"Then we'd better ride out now, while there's still time to catch up."

The Hunter studied the young man. He could see Tarek's pain—a pain he, too, had felt earlier, when he'd discovered Nameless had fled. It was the pain of failure. The sting that came from *knowing* he'd fallen short, and that because of him, more people would suffer. It had nearly broken the Hunter, and only the threat to Kodyn and Gwala's appearance had snapped him out of it. Tarek, too, was clearly laboring under that stifling burden. The Hunter owed it to the young Elivasti to help him come out the other side, but he'd come to know Tarek well, and got the sense his words would fall on deaf ears if he spoke now.

Later, he promised himself. *We'll have plenty of time to speak as we ride in pursuit of Nameless.*

First, he had to make certain Kiara was safe.

"Any sign of Kiara?" he asked. "Any idea which way she went, or how long ago?"

Tarek shook his head. "She won't leave him."

The Hunter blinked, confused. But only for a moment. Even before Tarek's eyes darted upward, the Hunter understood which "he" the young Elivasti referred to.

The climb to the towertop chamber seemed both shorter and longer than the Hunter remembered. Without fear and need urging him onward, he ascended the winding circular staircase at a slow, steady pace. Yet with every step, he was keenly aware of just how quiet the tower had grown. Gone was the faint humming of vast Serenii mechanisms, and the light that had once pulsed within the enormous black gemstone core had gone dark.

Okadigbo had died, and *Ukuhlushwa Okungapheli* with him.

He found Kiara sitting on the edge of the Chamber of Sustenance, her feet resting on the empty stone cradle where Nameless' body had once lain. She'd wiped the blood off her forehead, though the flesh around the wound had begun to darken and bruise. She appeared exhausted, leaning heavily on her left elbow, which rested on one knee. In her right hand, she held Deathbite point-downward inside the Chamber. She did not look up as he entered, nor when he spoke her name softly.

"Kiara?"

When no answer was forthcoming, the Hunter slipped around the masked corpses littering the floor and approached the central gemstone pillar upon which the Chamber of Sustenance sat. As he drew closer, he saw the tears streaking the blood spatter on her face. Her eyes, too, were red and puffy from crying.

"I couldn't leave him," she said in a hoarse voice, never taking her gaze off the lone corpse within the Chamber. "After everything he's endured for so long, it felt…wrong to let him die alone."

For the first time, the Hunter had a clear view of *Okadigbo's* body. He'd only seen Serenii twice before—once carved in onyx within the Warmaster's temple of Kara-ket, and in the visions

766

Kharna had implanted in his mind. The similarities between the ancient beings and the Abiarazi, who Kharna had called "relatives", was evident in their long, many-jointed limbs and the power inherent in their musculature, a leaner build than the hulking demonkind.

Okadigbo, however, appeared like a withered root, so shrunken over countless millennia that his skin—a curious mixture of light grey with hints of lavender and cerulean—had stretched like parchment over his bones long ago gone brittle. Any remnants of his arcane power that had survived six thousand years of imprisonment with Nameless was now gone, his body as still and silent as the very human corpses that lay scattered around the chamber that had served as his prison for eons.

"Funny." The Hunter gave a mirthless chuckle. "When he said 'our kind doesn't experience death as yours do', I almost believed him. Almost expected he might somehow be strong enough to cheat death. Yet look at him now. He's as gone as anyone I've put down."

"He is," Kiara said, nodding slowly. "And yet, he is not."

The Hunter raised an eyebrow. "That sort of cryptic horse shite's for the priests, Kiara. Either he's dead or he's not. No two ways about it."

Kiara smiled, though it was more sad than amused. "I don't pretend to understand it any better than you. But in his final moments, before the life fled this body, I felt a strange energy rippling through the tower. And in my head, I saw this image." She tapped two fingers against Deathbite's hilt. "An image of the *intambelu* vines spreading throughout the ground beneath the tower, and all throughout Ghandia."

The Hunter frowned. "He's alive in the vines?"

Now Kiara lifted her eyes from *Okadigbo's* corpse and met the Hunter's gaze. "The *intambelu* were a part of him. He created them, sent them questing out into the earth in order to gather to himself the power he needed to keep *Nuru Iwu* in here. *Ukuhlushwa Okungapheli* was created to gather the power of the sun, and the energies churning far beneath the Valley of Living Fire. But it was not enough. Nameless was too strong, his will too great for *Okadigbo* to fully dominate on his own. So he created the *intambelu* to gather more power from every corner of the world. Spreading outward, seeping through the land, seeking pockets of arcane magic not yet vanished from the world. In the end, though…" Her eyes dropped once more to the dead Serenii.

The Hunter's mind struggled to comprehend the amount of power required to create such a vast network of vines. The *intambelu* not only wended deep beneath the earth, but extended all the way to *Uhumi Wolandle* scores of leagues to the south, and the Keeper alone knew where else in the Ghandian Plains. Even for a Serenii, over thousands of years, such a feat had to be immense.

A question sprang to his thoughts—one he'd contemplated since he'd first realized who and what had been dwelling within the Bondshold. "Is that *really* his name? *Okadigbo*?" His brow furrowed. "I've no idea what kind of names the Serenii had, but that's…not how I imagined it."

"Once he chose his fate, to be imprisoned here, his name ceased to matter." Kiara shook her head. "He gave it up the day his people laid him to rest alongside He Who Is Nameless."

The Hunter's eyes widened. "Wait, he *chose* this?" He looked to the dead Serenii, disbelieving. "He *chose* to spend six thousand-odd years imprisoned here, with a bloody Abiarazi as cellmate?"

Kiara gave a slow, grave nod of her head. "He did." She shifted forward to kneel beside *Okadigbo*, and reached a hand forward to rest on the dead Serenii's hairless cranium. "When those we call demons first came to this world, there was one among them so cruel and terrible that even his own kind feared him. All of the Abiarazi's worst traits distilled into a single being of pure evil. The demons abhorred and reviled him, but they could not stop him, for his evil made him stronger than any ten of them combined."

A shudder ran down the Hunter's spine. He could well believe it. He'd faced Nameless in a pitifully reduced state, wasted away over thousands of years, and the demon had come damned close to killing him half a dozen times over. The thought of confronting the Abiarazi in his prime brought fear surging in his belly.

"The Abiarazi sought aid from their cousins, the Serenii," Kiara continued, never taking her eyes off *Okadigbo*. Her hand stroked the dead Serenii's head with maternal tenderness borne of the sorrow welling within her. "The one we now call *Okadigbo* was renowned even among his brethren, for though his body was no match for others—including those we call Kharna and Deneen, the Swordsman—none could rival the powers of his mind. And it was his mind that would be needed to keep the Abiarazi's evil at bay. This place was created for just that purpose."

Kiara drew in a deep breath, and silence hung heavy in the towertop chamber for a long moment before she continued. "The Abiarazi imprisoned here was stripped of his name, for his own people demanded that he was to be forgotten. With no name to summon him, the power he held over the Abiarazi and the early humans upon whom he preyed would be shattered."

"*Nuru Iwu*," the Hunter said quietly. "He Who Is Nameless."

"That name was born over the millennia, spoken by the *Indaba* who passed down the memory of the Bondshold's true purpose from generation to generation." Tears welled in Kiara's eyes. "They alone remembered the sacrifice made by the Serenii who abandoned every part of himself to protect the world from a being of purest evil."

"Until Tunde, the last of the Bheka *Indaba*." The Hunter felt a sinking in the pit of his stomach, and the burden once more settled on his shoulders. "And until we failed to lock Nameless back up in his prison." He slammed a clenched fist onto the edge of the chamber. "He is dead, and the sacrifice he made over six thousand years means nothing because of us. Because of *me.*"

Chapter One Hundred Five

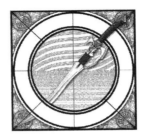

A wave of despair welled within the Hunter, once more washing over him with overwhelming force. The numbness began to return to his limbs, a slow, steady seeping that he could not resist. And why should he? After his failures—

"Stop that!" Kiara's voice cracked like a whip.

The Hunter blinked, drew in a breath around lungs that felt sluggish and tight. He managed to raise his eyes and found Kiara had turned on her knees to fix him with a hard stare.

"That's not you talking, not really." Kiara clenched her jaw muscles, her eyes narrowing. "I felt it, too. When Nameless fled the Bondshold, that overpowering rush of despondency, it threatened to steal my strength and leave me helpless, powerless to do anything." She shook her head. "But that was no more me than it was you. It was *him*." She turned back to face the dead Serenii. "Those were *his* final moments of melancholy, *his* wretched last thoughts."

The Hunter's eyes widened. Strange to think such an ancient and powerful being could know such depths of despair. It was an emotion far too *human* for the logic-driven and largely emotionless Serenii. But perhaps if there existed a vast difference in temperament among the Abiarazi, it was the same among their cousins. Some might feel more strongly than others— hope, fear, desperation, need, and pain. No doubt *Okadigbo* had felt that last keenly over millennia spent imprisoned with Nameless.

Kiara turned to face him. "But you did not fail him. *We* did not fail him."

"Oh?" The Hunter cocked his head. "He's dead because we couldn't get Nameless back into his prison."

Kiara nodded slowly. "That is so. And yet, it is as it was meant to be."

The Hunter frowned. "What in the Watcher's name does that mean?"

"I'm not certain." Kiara shrugged. "It was his final thought. After the despair passed, just before his consciousness dissipated and passed into the *intambelu,* I heard that thought in my mind, clear as if it had been my own." She raised a hand to tap her temple. "Exactly those words, too. *'It is as it was meant to be.'*"

The Hunter threw up his hands. "Then why the fiery hell did we fight so hard?" Anger ripped the words from his lips in a ringing shout. "Why did Lwazi and all the other *Umoyahlebe* die if Nameless was *meant* to escape?"

"I don't know the answer to that any more than you do." Kiara's tone was patient, calming. Always keeping a level head when he exploded. "I can only tell you what I felt, and what I saw."

"And what was it you saw?" the Hunter asked, his brow furrowing. He'd seen a great deal during his first communion with Kharna in Enarium, then only snatches and glimpses when the Serenii had spoken to him in the Monolith.

"Not much more than I've told you," Kiara said. Now it was her turn to frown. "I've heard his voice for a while now, but it wasn't until I planted Deathbite into his flesh that I truly *saw* anything. Almost like his memories imprinted on the sword, and passed through it into me. That's how I knew about Nameless, about what he was before all this, and how *Okadigbo* ended up here."

Her expression grew pensive. "I've also got flashes of what might be memories from over the thousands of years he spent imprisoned here. His body was trapped, most of his mind dedicated to keeping Nameless comatose, but there was enough of his consciousness left to at least get glimpses of the waking world. He felt it when all of Einan shook, and when the Chasm of the Lost was opened. For in that same cataclysm, the perfect tower he had built was damaged. That was when Nameless began to awaken."

The Hunter's eyebrows shot up. "During the War of Gods?" He whistled through his teeth. "That was five thousand bloody years ago!"

"Yes," Kiara said simply. "After a millennia trapped and kept dormant, Nameless awoke and began to fight. Though *Okadigbo* was far stronger, Nameless was not without his own strength. Over the centuries, he shifted his body, cell by cell, driving his claws relentlessly into his enemy."

The Hunter glanced down at the puncture wounds in the dead Serenii's belly. From them had issued blood enough over thousands of years to stain the towertop chamber and the stairs descending far below the earth. Only the Serenii's innate resiliency—and the power it absorbed from the sun and Einan itself—had kept it alive.

"*Okadigbo* bled, and Nameless consumed that blood, using it to regain his strength. But the more blood he consumed, the more of *Okadigbo's* mental abilities he absorbed into himself. Until the day he grew strong enough to reach out from his prison and speak directly into human minds."

That explained how Nameless had been capable of doing what no other demon could. Not even Garanis with all his Illusionist Cleric tricks had possessed such power. For it was not innate to the Abiarazi. It was a *Serenii* gift, and like a leech, Nameless had stolen it from his captor. Through his blood.

A thought occurred to the Hunter. "Could that be how the Order of Mithridas knew of their existence when it was a secret guarded by the Bheka *Indaba* alone?"

"Perhaps." Kiara twitched one shoulder in a shrug. "*Okadigbo* did not know how far and wide Nameless' reach expanded, only that his mind was growing beyond his ability. He grew desperate, and so, too, sought out humans to aid him in his fight."

"You," the Hunter said.

"You first," Kiara corrected. "But when he delved deeper into your mind and saw your kinship with his prisoner, he knew he needed another. And that was when he found me. He chose me...for this." Her hand went to her belly.

The Hunter's pulse sped up until his heart galloped like a herd of stampeding *zabara*. He stared open-mouthed at her, trying to decide how it was possible, and if she truly was—

Oh, Keeper take me for a fool! She spoke not of her womb, but of the crystal formed of Indombe's blood embedded deep within her body.

He fought to keep the flush from rising to his cheeks or letting her see his efforts to compel his heart to quit racing. They'd never explicitly spoken on that particular subject, and now seemed far from the best time for such a discussion.

"He sensed it inside you?" he asked, as much to cover his reaction as out of genuine interest.

"He sensed *something* inside me. I don't think he knew what it was at first, only that it *was*." Kiara's expression grew pensive. "In truth, I believe it was only when I struck my head and he was able to speak directly through me that he came to understand its true purpose." Her hand flattened against her stomach, her fingers probing the skin gently, as if exploring some new growth. "He did something to it. I don't know how to explain it, but while he was in my mind, he did something to the crystal. Fused its power to my soul, that's the best way I can think to put it. And in doing so, he gave me the ability to control its power, not just *feel* it. Which is how I could turn it all against Nameless. Somehow, I just *knew* how to do it. I think he implanted the knowledge in my mind."

"Damn!" The Hunter's gaze slid sideways to the dead Serenii. "Kinda wish he'd have lived long enough to implant the knowledge of how to harness the power of the sun and earth in my mind." He shot Kiara a wry grin. "Would make the matter of hunting down Nameless a whole lot easier, me being able to lift my hand and blast a bit of sunlight at him like Aisha with her lightning or you with your…feelings."

"Watch it, you!" Kiara slapped him playfully on the arm. "Unless you want to spend the next few hours curled on the ground in a weeping mess, you guard your tongue."

The Hunter raised both his hands in a defensive gesture. "Point taken." He chuckled and was surprised to find it felt natural. Strange, given that he stood in a place stained by so much blood and death. Yet perhaps it was in places like this where mirth held the greatest value.

His smile faded slowly. "In all seriousness, you think you can repeat that? Wielding emotions like a weapon the way you did against Nameless?"

"I…think so." Kiara's face scrunched up into a frown. "I didn't do it alone. I felt *Okadigbo's* touch on my mind, bringing the stone to life. But I think I might be able to do what he did. Maybe. With a great deal of practice."

"Fortunately for you, we'll have plenty of time for that." He told her of Tarek's insistence on pursuing Nameless, and his intention of helping the young man. "I owe him that much, after all he's done. And after the oath I swore to the True Descendants—"

"I know." Kiara placed a hand on his shoulder, her touch gentle and reassuring. "Just give me a moment here. One final farewell before I can leave him."

The Hunter glanced past her to the creature within the blood-filled Chamber of Sustenance. He'd never truly understand what passed between *Okadigbo* and Kiara—the Serenii had only appeared to him, while it had spoken to her, taken control of her mind and body for a time—but he could give her what she needed.

"Sure." He nodded, and his gaze fell on the dead Orderman he'd killed to free Nkanyezi from her chains. "I'll be ready when you are."

Kiara turned away from him and once more knelt before the dead Serenii. She placed one hand on the creature's hairless head, the other over where it's heart might have been—who knew with Serenii?—and bowed her head to speak words the Hunter could not hear. Nor did he want to. They were for her and the Serenii's spirit, wherever it was, alone.

His attention focused on the task of first searching the towertop chamber for any mechanisms that could be used to bring it back to life. As he'd learned in Enarium and Malandria, each of the Serenii-built towers had been crafted to harness the magical energies of the world. They were controlled and activated by the altar-shaped, rune- and gemstone-encrusted consoles the Sage had attempted to use to turn the Illumina against Kharna, and which Jaia had somehow known to use to turn on the Monolith.

But this particular structure had no controls. At least none he could find. The bottommost chamber in the tower had been empty, and this room in the towertop contained only the gemstone pillar at its heart and the Chamber of Sustenance resting atop it. Almost as if it had been built to remain eternally functional and forever feed The Bleeding One the power needed to keep Nameless imprisoned. The damage to the tower caused by the breaking of the world during the War of Gods had been responsible for *Nuru Iwu's* eventual freedom.

The Hunter felt a sinking in the pit of his stomach. This tower wouldn't be sustaining Kharna in his fight against the Great Devourer. Then again, it had been built long *before* Kharna's entombment, so it might never have been intended for that purpose. Whatever the case, he'd failed Kharna's mission. That thought weighed heavily on him.

He set about collecting his weapons, then searched the Ordermen for any additional hints as to where they might be found. Nashat al-Azzam's message had sent him here to investigate the link between the mysterious masked men and the slashwyrms that provided the scales they utilized. Unless he found something on these corpses, he'd leave Ghandia no closer to finding anything real about the bastards than when he rode out of Malandria.

He went around the chamber, removing each mask and studying the corpses' faces. They were a motley bunch, from every corner of Einan—Drashi, Voramians, Praamians, Vothmoti, men and women of the Twelve Kingdoms, even a few with the features of the distant Kurma Empire far to the northeast. None bore any tattoos or identifying marks. A few bore the scars of those trained to the art of fighting, but all the sort inflicted by ordinary weapons.

No, beneath the masks, the only thing they shared in common was the strange knot of scar tissue on their chests. The Hunter cut into two Ordermen at random, and sure enough, both corpses yielded the same stones. He spent a moment wiping away the blood on the dead men's cloaks, revealing knuckle-sized, multi-faceted stones of a deep violet hue. Darker even than Elivasti eyes, though not so dark as *Okadigbo's* blood.

Magical? The Hunter frowned down at the two stones. *If so, what manner of magic?*

"I am ready." Kiara's voice cut into the Hunter's thoughts.

Looking up from where he knelt beside a dead Orderman—the Voramian nobleman who'd smelled of lavender, satin, and crabapple—the Hunter found Kiara climbing down from the Chamber of Sustenance atop the gemstone pillar. She sheathed Deathbite and turned toward him, raising an eyebrow at the two stones in his hand.

"Anything interesting?"

He shrugged. "Not sure yet." He moved toward her and held out the stones. "*Okadigbo's* memories got anything to say about these?"

She studied the pair for a moment, then shook her head. "Nothing that springs to mind."

The Hunter grunted in annoyance, though it didn't surprise him. "Plenty of time to examine them later," he said, stuffing them into the same hidden pocket of his cloak that held the first one he'd cut from an Orderman corpse. "Lots of nights on the road ahead of us. Nameless won't make it easy to catch him."

Kiara nodded. If she had any thoughts as to what they'd do when they caught up to the fleeing demon, she kept them to herself. The Hunter knew he had to discuss the matter with her, though. *Okadigbo's* death complicated matters. The Chamber of Sustenance here wouldn't suffice to imprison him, not without the Serenii's mental abilities to keep him dormant. Which left...what? Imprisonment in Enarium? Death? The Hunter didn't know, but at the moment, he hadn't the energy to try and figure it out. As he'd said, they had plenty of nights on the road ahead of them.

Something compelled him to stop just before he and Kiara descended the stairs. He doubted he'd return to this place; there was nothing left for him in *Ukuhlushwa Okungapheli*. And so, he looked one last time at the ancient Serenii who had sacrificed himself for six thousand years to imprison an evil so terrible even Abiarazi feared it.

"It is at it was meant to be." Kiara spoke the words softly at his side. "I understand now."

The Hunter looked down at her.

"What Tunde said." Kiara met his gaze calmly, all trace of anguish or sorrow gone, replaced by serenity. She repeated the *Indaba's* words. "'*If he is not awakened, all will be desolation. The time of the destroyer must come.*' He knew. He knew what was going to happen here. Today. Long after he was dead."

The Hunter frowned. "You know how I feel about anything that remotely resembles 'prophecies'. No less horse shite than 'fate' or 'destiny'."

"I do." Kiara took his hand in hers, not caring that it was stained with blood. "But sometimes, these things are bigger than how we feel about it. And look at this." She gestured with her other hand to the towertop chamber. "Look at this place, and tell me you don't feel it, too. What happened here today *had* to happen. And somehow, we had to be a part of it."

She doubtless meant it to be reassuring, but in the Hunter's mind, that realization only made recent events all the more burdensome. Whether or not it had been foretold, Nameless' survival meant that countless humans—most of them innocent and defenseless—would suffer.

An ancient evil had been awoken here. Keeper only knew what manner of darkness it would spread across Einan.

Chapter One Hundred Six

By the time the Hunter and Kiara descended to the ground-level chamber, Tarek no longer stood lone vigil over the fallen Spirit Whisperers.

The rest of the surviving *Umoyahlebe* had come to bear the bodies of their fellows outside, to join those laid out for the *makalala*. Aisha and Nkanyezi carried their father between them, Davathi holding her husband's head to keep it from dangling. An honor guard of warriors from every tribe stood in a line before the entrance to the Bondshold—lion-clad Buhari next to Nyemba in their *kitaka* ape furs, the dazzlingly bright and multi-colored giant turtle shells of the Mwaani beside the filthy, haggard Tefaye and those few Dalingcebo who had come to fight. The eight Issai warriors who had survived the battle marched at the head of the column, Siyanda and Naledi guiding the procession through the enormous doorway and out into the bright noon light.

The Hunter made to follow, but something caught his eye. Frowning, he moved over to stand over the lifeless, slack-featured corpse that had once been Djineza, Gwala's lieutenant. One of Kodyn's throwing knives had driven through her studded leather vest and buried in her chest. Yet *that* hadn't been the dagger that killed her. The knife thrown into her open mouth had done the final deed.

And now, looking closer, the Hunter saw why. Kodyn's knife hadn't pierced her heart. Instead, it had struck off the gemstone embedded in her chest.

The gemstone was gone—torn from her flesh when Kodyn drew out his dagger, perhaps?—but the tangled knot of scar tissue over her heart was unmistakable. He'd seen its match marring every Orderman in the towertop chamber.

Djineza...belonged to the Order of Mithridas? The Hunter's mind raced. She'd worn Consortium armor, carried a Consortium weapon, and heeded Consortium orders. *Or was that just a role she played?*

A thought occurred to the Hunter. He hurried to cut open Gwala's vest, exposing his chest. Scars aplenty marred his flesh—no less than expected for a warrior who, like all Issai, had once fought lightly armored or wearing nothing but fibrous cloth battle-wrappings—and Soulhunger's keen edge had carved a broad wound on its way in and out of his breast.

But no tangled mess of flesh. The Hunter frowned. *No gemstone?*

"Hunter?" Kiara's question came from behind him, but he ignored it. "Is everything—" She cut off in a sharp intake of breath. "What are you doing?"

"Confirming a theory," was all the Hunter had to offer for answer. Kiara's footsteps crunched across the blood-crusted floor toward him, and she cast a shadow over Gwala's corpse. Yet she merely watched in silence as the Hunter sliced open Gwala's chest with a few quick flicks of Soulhunger's razor-sharp tip.

"Nothing." He cursed quietly. "No gemstone."

"You expected one?" Kiara asked. "He was Consortium—"

"So was Djineza." The Hunter gestured to the Shalandran's corpse. "But she has the scars on the chest like the rest of the Ordermen."

Kiara padded over to confirm with her own eyes, then turned back to the Hunter with a curious expression. "You think she was an Order plant? Set to ensure the Consortium followed commands and heeled like obedient hounds?"

"I don't know what to think." The Hunter rose to his feet with a shake of his head. "All I know is that there *should* be a gemstone in her chest, and the only one who could have cut it out—other than Djineza herself—is Kodyn." He glanced through the tower's massive doorway in the direction of the procession marching slowly away from the Bondshold. "On our way out, he stopped over her body—to retrieve his knives, I thought, but he had time enough to cut the gemstone free and pocket it."

"You think he has any idea what it is?" Kiara asked. "Surely you can't suspect he has anything to do with the Order of—"

"No, nothing like that," the Hunter said hurriedly. "But there's got to be some reason he cut that gemstone free. If it's nothing more than a born-and-bred thief spotting something of value worth selling, so be it. But if there's more to it…"

"Not sure he'll be in much of a talking mood for a while." Kiara's face darkened. "Lwazi wasn't exactly his father-in-law yet, but it was just a matter of time. He'll want to be there for Aisha, too."

"I know." The Hunter let out a breath. "I'll see if I can catch him alone on our way out, or draw him away from the others for a quiet word. I'll need everything he's got on the Consortium, too."

Kiara nodded. "Put an end to their outfit once and for all."

"Aye." The Hunter's jaw muscles worked. The documents Kodyn had stolen from the Consortium offices were more than enough to rid Einan of the slave trafficking enterprise. The shattering of their power here was just the first of the many miseries the Hunter intended to inflict.

"I'll go fetch the horses." Tarek's voice interrupted the Hunter's thoughts.

The Hunter glanced over to find the young man staring at him with an impatient look in his violet eyes, a frenetic energy quivering through every muscle in his body. It was more than just the impetuousness of youth; Tarek was driven by the *need* to bring down Nameless, to put an end to the threat the *maistyr* posed to his people. The demon had seen the truth of the oath in Tarek's mind, and knew the young Elivasti—and all those descended from the Serenii—were compelled to bend the knee to his command. Tarek had refused, perhaps the first of his people in millennia to do so, but that didn't mean other Elivasti the demon encountered around Einan would do likewise.

He looked at Kiara. She was pale-faced, dark circles ringing her eyes, and her shoulders were stooped by exhaustion. She was in no shape to ride.

"Kiara—" he began.

"Will be just fine," she said, shooting him a sharp look. "Go." She nodded to Tarek. "We'll be ready when you return."

"Bring Aisha and Kodyn's, too," the Hunter said. "He's got the documents we need to bring down the Consortium. We'll be ready when you return."

Tarek raced out of *Ukuhlushwa Okungapheli* and vanished from sight in the bright daylight beyond.

"How long do you think we have?" Kiara asked quietly.

The Hunter considered the question. "An hour. Maybe two. He's got at least a league-and-a-half to run back to where we left the horses last night. Chances are, the fatigue'll hit him hard before he gets there."

"Worried he'll crumble?"

The Hunter shot a sidelong glance at Kiara. She was staring at him with a look far too piercing for his liking. "You read thoughts now?" He scowled. "Because *crumble* is exactly the word that came to my mind."

Kiara gave him a grin that was part-amused, part-chagrined, and part-triumphant. "No, for your information, I *can't* read thoughts. Yet." Mischief sparkled in her eyes as she slipped her hand into his. "I just know you better than anyone else walking Einan these days. Probably better even than you know yourself."

The Hunter's scowl gave way to a wry smile. "No argument there." He squeezed her hand tightly in his. "I worry he'll push himself too hard, ride into a danger he's not prepared to face."

"Which is why we're going with him," Kiara said. "Tired or not, we've got to look out for him. Hailen can't lose a brother before he gets the chance to meet him."

The Hunter nodded. That had been his line of thinking, too. "Any thoughts on what to do with that hour or two we've got, then?"

"Yes." Kiara nodded, but there was no humor in her eyes now. "We say what needs saying to the people who need to hear it." She leaned her head on his arm. "Odds are good we'll never see them again."

* * *

As the Hunter had expected, they found Kodyn in the thick of the crowd gathered around the fallen *Umoyahlebe*. He stood arm in arm with the rest of the Issai, Tefaye, Nyemba, and Mwaani in a long line that stretched out behind the Spirit Whisperers laid out for the *makalala*. But the bodies of the dead were not yet to be commended to the spirits. First, the Issai would commemorate their lives as only they could.

Davathi stood at her husband's head, arms linked with Aisha and Nkanyezi's. Though tears streaked their cheeks, their voice rang out in song as loud and joyous as those who celebrated beside them. They bounded so high the Hunter half-expected them to float away and join the *makalala* in the bright blue, cloudless sky above.

Beyond the fallen *Umoyahlebe,* the rest of the Tefaye, Issai, and Nyemba fallen in battle had been equally arrayed for their journey with the *Kish'aa* to the Ghandian afterlife, *Pharadesi*. Every one of the Nyemba lay atop the great *kitaka* ape furs they had worn in life, their long spears snapped in half and placed on their chest. The Tefaye mimicked both the Issai and Nyemba—for doubtless many of their number had once hailed from those tribes—and laid the bronze hand axes and long spears beside the warriors, who they had stripped out of their dark wooden armor.

The Mwaani celebrated death in their own way. Their fallen warriors were laid atop the scaffolding, which was then destroyed to send the bodies plummeting hundreds of paces into the depths of *Isigodi Umlilophilayo*. What that signified or why they chose that method, the Hunter didn't know. He wasn't one to judge how anyone honored or mourned the fallen. Keeper knew his own methods hadn't ever been much to talk about. Mostly brooding and self-remonstration accompanied by heavy bouts of guilt.

Deeper in the city, the Hunter spotted the column of smoke rising into the sky, and the smell of charred flesh reached his nostrils. Jumaane and the Buhari burning the hearts of their fallen warriors, no doubt. They'd already brought the domed building where the *Umoyahlebe* had been held crashing down atop the bodies of their dead to form a burial cairn of sorts.

To the Hunter's surprise, Jumaane appeared marching up the street long before the smoke thinned and the fire died. He came alone, his head bare of its lion's mane headdress, his hands empty, his body utterly bare save for his sturdy loincloth. With a bowed head, he moved into the center of the knot of leaping and singing Issai.

He moved to stand before Davathi, then dropped to one knee.

At the action, the chorus of Issai voices fell quiet, and the gamboling ceased in moments. A pregnant hush descended over the hundreds of men and women who stood gathered over the fallen *Umoyahlebe* and the warriors of the Issai, Tefaye, and Nyemba tribes. Everyone, even Aisha and Nkanyezi, took a step back, leaving Davathi standing alone before the kneeling Jumaane.

"*Nassor* Davathi of the Issai," the Buhari's great voice boomed out in the silence, "I come to humbly request a favor of you." He spoke in the tongue of his people, but the Hunter had come to understand enough to comprehend what passed between them.

"Ask, *Nassor* Jumaane of the Buhari." Despite her sorrow, Davathi's voice rang out clear and true, as mighty as the kneeling giant's.

Jumaane lifted his face, his eyes meeting hers. Yet there was a strange hesitation in his expression. Was he *afraid* of voicing his question aloud for fear of what she'd say?

The Hunter noted the way Jumaane's gaze flicked to Siyanda. *Ahh,* he thought, nodding to himself. *So that's what this is about.*

It was certainly a strange time for such things, in the midst of a funeral. But perhaps that was not the case here in Ghandia. Einari funerals tended to be a far more solemn affair—at least until after the body was consigned to the ground and the drinking began. The Issai revelry, however, showed a spirit of celebration rather than pure mourning.

Siyanda met Jumaane's eyes, and she gave him an encouraging nod. The gesture visibly bolstered him, and he drew in a deep breath to speak.

"I would ask for the honor of commending the heart of the Old Cheetah to our fire," Jumaane's voice rang out.

The Hunter startled. That was not at all the request he'd expected from the Buhari *nassor.*

"Though he is of your people," Jumaane said quickly, "and he was your *iza'ubaba,* he was once Buhari, and within his heart beat the spirit and strength of the lion. It was *he* who held the gate against the *alay-alagbara* long enough for our *amaqhawe* to enter the city, and his courage served as an example to every warrior who saw him fight. He gave his last breath defending his fellow Issai—" At this, his gaze shifted to Siyanda. "—including his daughter's *ingani.* I would honor him in the way of our people, who were once his people, too. But only if you permit it."

Davathi's gaze shifted to where Duma lay among the fallen Issai warriors—including the young Cebile and the aged-yet-fierce Sizwe. His cheetah pelt had been placed around his shoulders, his *nkemba* sword, shield, and spear lying at his side. Sorrow twisted her face and tears flowed anew.

Even without Kiara's gift, the Hunter could feel the *nassor's* pain. She had lost two of the great loves of her life—her husband and the man who had been like her father—both in a single night. Even she, who had borne the mantle of leadership upon her broad shoulders for years, would feel that weight. Weight enough to bring her crumbling to her knees.

Yet she did not face it alone. As one, Nkanyezi and Aisha moved up to stand beside their mother, taking her hands in theirs. A shiver passed through Davathi, but at her daughters' touch, she regained a measure of her strength and lifted her head. She gave Aisha and Nkanyezi a smile and a squeeze of her hand in turn, then returned her gaze to Jumaane.

"Your request is granted." Her voice cut through the silence, heavy with emotion yet ringing with strength. "But only if you grant me one request in return."

Jumaane's eyes widened a fraction, his expression growing curious. "Anything."

"Allow me the honor of carrying out the ritual." From her belt, she drew the *iznyovu* dagger Duma had given the Hunter, and which the Hunter had given to her in the Bondshold. "And standing at your side as you commend his heart to the fire."

Jumaane placed his hand over his heart and bowed low. "Your request is granted, *nassor.* The Buhari welcome our Issai sisters and brothers." He spread his great arms wide and looked at the crowd gathered around Davathi. "All are welcome to stand before our heart-fire!"

Chapter One Hundred Seven

The Hunter *finally* managed to catch Kodyn's attention. No easy task, given that Kodyn marched a step behind Aisha, who, alongside Nkanyezi, followed Jumaane and Davathi toward the column of smoke that marked the Buhari's heart-fire.

Fortunately, the Hunter stood out from the throng—one of the three paler-skinned figures among the Ghandians—enough that Kodyn spotted him. Curiosity blossomed on the young man's face when the Hunter indicated with a nod of his head to follow him down a side street, away from the procession. It took some effort, but the young man finally managed to push free of the crowd. Aisha didn't notice him slipping away; she was focused on her mother, who struggled under the weight of her grief. Only the presence of her daughters at her side bolstered Davathi's strength and kept her steps sure and steady as she marched alongside Jumaane, cradling Duma's heart in her hands.

"You're leaving, aren't you?" Kodyn asked when he, the Hunter, and Kiara finally stood alone, a few streets away from the procession.

The Hunter nodded. "We have to. Nameless is my problem—"

"Our problem," Kiara corrected.

"—to deal with," the Hunter finished, jaw muscles clenching. "Tarek's already gone to fetch the horses. When he returns, we ride out."

"So this is farewell, eh?" A sad look twisted Kodyn's face. "Aisha will be disappointed she didn't get to see you off."

"No less disappointed than we are not to have one last chance to see her," Kiara said, the sorrow in her eyes mirroring Kodyn's. "But Aisha has greater concerns at the moment."

"As do we." The Hunter's words came out harsher and more gruff than he'd intended; the feelings swirling within him turned his voice rough. Easier to speak curtly and quickly than let emotions stop him from speaking altogether. "What you found in Djineza's chest, was it one of these?"

Kodyn's eyes widened as the Hunter produced from his pouch the violet gemstone he'd cut from the dead Voramian. "Yes!" His brow furrowed. "How did you know?"

"All the Ordermen have them." The Hunter watched that sink in, and the young man's expression shifted from surprised to confused.

"But Djineza was..." He cut himself off, the wheels behind his eyes turning. "A plant? Someone the Order of Mithridas installed among the Vassalage Consortium to keep an eye on their hired thralls?"

The Hunter had to admit Kodyn was sharp. He'd clearly inherited at least a measure of his mother's intellect. "That was my thought. But I needed to see the gemstone to confirm."

For an answer, Kodyn rooted around within his own cloak—nearly as riddled with hidden pockets as the Hunter's own—and produced a gemstone identical to the one the Hunter held. "Wouldn't have seen it there had my dagger not struck it dead center. Chipped the steel good, but as you can see, the stone's utterly unblemished."

Sure enough, the gemstone's myriad facets showed neither crack nor chip. No indication that it had been struck by a thrown dagger.

"At first," Kodyn said, "I thought it was a chunk of shalanite, embedded in her body. But it ain't. No idea what it is, truth be told. You know what they're for?"

The Hunter shook his head. "Not a clue." He looked to Kiara, who shrugged. "Not much chance of us finding out, now that we've cut down the only link to the Order we've found here."

"Oh, of course!" Kodyn's eyebrows shot up, and he shook his head. "Fool that I am, I totally forgot." He reached for something stuffed into one of his hidden pockets. A stack of neatly folded parchments, which he held up before the Hunter. "When I spotted the Buhari carrying their dead into that domed building, I figured I'd best search it quickly, see if I could find anything the Order left behind. There wasn't much, just these few documents. I know there's got to be more elsewhere in the city. I just haven't had the time to search for—"

"What did you find in those?" the Hunter asked, pointedly glancing toward the papers Kodyn held. The young man wouldn't have mentioned them had they been unimportant.

Kodyn's face fell. "Not much, truth be told. In truth, everything here is written in some unfamiliar language or a code I haven't even begun to attempt to crack. It's not Secret Keeper script, that much I know. Nor thieves' script or beggar's cant, either."

The Hunter took one of the parchments and scanned their contents. As Kodyn had said, the writing, though Einari, appeared utter gibberish, a mess of letters, numbers, lines, and symbols that he could no more decipher than Serenii runes.

The sight brought back a memory of the nights the Hunter had spent recovering in Bardin's tent. The madman had *loved* ciphers and hidden codes. Had he been here, he might have an idea as to the scribblings' meaning. An Illusionist Cleric might recognize it. Not that the Hunter could ask them. The priests of the Illusionist wanted his memory scrubbed as they believed their god had ordered. Until his death, Father Reverentus had been the only thing keeping the madmen clerics at bay. Now…

"But?" Kiara's question dragged the Hunter's attention out of his thoughts, returned his attention to Kodyn.

"But look at the parchment." Kodyn gestured with his free hand to the document in the Hunter's hand. "After what nearly happened to my mother years ago, she *insisted* I learn not only to recognize handwriting, but also identify various types of parchment, paper, vellum, and papyrus from every corner of Einan."

The Hunter couldn't help wondering what, exactly, had happened to the Master of the Night Guild, but kept the question to himself.

"I'd recognize this parchment anywhere." Kodyn's expression grew triumphant. "It's Shalandran. I saw a lot of the stuff scattered around Arch-Guardian Suroth's office. I've a…" He hesitated a moment. "…a contact in Shalandra who could tell you more about it, but I know for *certain* that it comes from the City of the Dead."

The Hunter frowned. "As did Djineza."

"Coincidence?" Kiara voiced aloud the question the Hunter had been thinking.

"I don't know yet." Kodyn shook his head. "Fiery hell, until I find whatever building the Order of Mithridas was using as their base of operations and search it thoroughly, I can't tell you much more than that." His expression soured. "But there's something else. About Djineza. Her sword, specifically."

The Hunter and Kiara exchanged glances. "We're listening," Kiara said.

"Issa told us about the flammards crafted for each of the Keeper's Blades." Kodyn's eyes flicked to Deathbite, once more sheathed at Kiara's hip. "They're not exactly *Im'tasi* blades, but similar."

The Hunter's eyes flew wide. "*What?!*" The question burst from his lips. The idea of hundreds, perhaps *thousands,* of magical blades crafted by the ancient Serenii in the hands of an army of Shalandrans sent a chill down his spine. It couldn't be possible!

"They don't have anywhere near the same magic as real *Im'tasi* weapons," Kodyn said, his words coming out in a hurry. "But they're all forged after the Blade of Hallar, which *is* an actual *Im'tasi* blade. A great two-handed sword, which once belonged to the Bucelarii who founded Shalandra. But in order to be accepted into the Keeper's Blades, every Shalandran youth takes a test—a trial by combat first, then a trial of blood. Testing to see if they are descendants of Hallar. And if they are, they're given one of those swords and recruited into Shalandra's elite."

The Hunter's mind spun. "Descendants...of Hallar." He could barely form the words. "You mean every one of the Keeper's Blades—"

"Has a bit of Bucelarii blood in them," Kodyn finished the thought. "I don't pretend to understand it—any more than I understand how Hailen could have Serenii blood in him—but the flammards are forged specifically for each new Keeper's Blade. Which means there are only two ways Djineza could have gotten her hands on one."

The Hunter worked at that problem. He'd been unable to procure one of the Shalandran steel greatswords for himself, sparing no expense. Bar that, the only other possibilities were...

"Either she stole it," the Hunter said, "or she was once a Keeper's Blade herself."

Kodyn nodded. "And I'm pretty sure the second is the far worse of the two options."

The Hunter considered that. In the Valley of the Zabara, Djineza had fought with a skill and speed far surpassing the vast majority of the foes the Hunter had faced. But she'd died almost *too* easily in the Bondshold. When she was separated from her sword and whatever magic it imbued upon her or activated within her. It could have been mere happenstance—both the Order of Mithridas and the Vassalage Consortium were comprised of a motley assortment of men and women from every corner of Einan, even from Fehl across the Frozen Sea—but the presence of Shalandran-made parchment near a Shalandran-born Orderwoman wielding a blade forged exclusively for Shalandra's elite warriors was far too many links to be true coincidence.

"Look," Kodyn said, holding up a hand, "I understand your wanting to ride out, but if you give me a few hours, I'll have a chance to search the city, see if I can find anything else that might point you in the direction of the Order." Anger and disgust twisted his expression. "After everything they've done here, I'd love nothing more than to send you off armed with the knowledge to rip those masked bastards a whole new mess of arseholes."

The Hunter shot a questioning glance at Kiara. Much as he wanted to ride off in pursuit of Nameless, the idea of departing with no concrete means of tracking down the Order of Mithridas left a bitter taste in his mouth. It was because of *them* the ancient and terrible demon now roamed Einan. *Theirs* had been the hand to orchestrate all the chaos, suffering, and bloodshed that had infected Ghandia for over a year now. Were it not for them, Father Reverentus would still be alive. He owed them a far greater bounty of misery than what he'd inflicted on them here. Their suffering had just begun, and he wouldn't stop until every Orderman hiding around Einan was sent to the darkest, deepest hell, their souls devoured to sustain Kharna.

Before he could respond, however, the sound of hoofbeats echoed through the city. All three of them turned to find Tarek riding up the street at the front of a column of horses—among them Ash, Elivast, and Aisha and Kodyn's mounts. The young Elivasti's head constantly turned, his eyes scanning the streets in search for them. Upon spotting them, he turned Nayaga's head and rode in their direction.

"Ready?" he called, an impatient look etched on his scrubby-bearded face. A face that seemed more haggard and lined than before. He'd aged years in the space of the last few weeks—hell, in the last *hours,* by the looks of it.

The Hunter let out a long breath. "Aye." He turned to Kodyn. "Conduct your search, and anything you find, send word through the Hidden Circle." He quickly explained to the young man about the secret network of alchemists and information-brokers, including how to locate them, identify their establishments through the interlocking rings symbol, and the true nature of coin with which they bartered. "I'll stop in at every city I pass until I hear from you."

Kodyn opened his mouth to protest, but the Hunter drove on quickly. "And everything you've got that I can use against the Consortium, I'll need it. I'll send it off—"

"No." Kodyn cut him off with a shake of his head.

The Hunter raised an eyebrow, but the young man was unfazed.

"Look, I know you're determined to see the Consortium eliminated, and I'm right there with you." Kodyn lifted his head, square jaw clenching. "But for there to be a *real* chance of ripping the slavers' organization to shreds, we've got to do this right. And by right, I mean the Night Guild way."

The Hunter narrowed his eyes. "The Night Guild way?"

A hard grin broadened Kodyn's handsome face. "I told you, my mother's got the in with Grand Reckoner Edmynd. *He's* the one who'll put the financial squeeze on the Consortium. And when she hands King Ohilmos evidence of their misdeeds here, I guarantee he'll sit up and take notice. Not just that, he'll actually *act.* Because five minutes after my mother learns of what we discovered here, she'll figure out a way to use it to the Night Guild's advantage and strengthen the King of Praamis' political clout in Odaron. She'll know just how to apply the right pressure and twist the screws so tight on the Consortium's balls they'll be shrieking like a *castrati* when she and the king are done with them."

The Hunter couldn't help chuckling at that particular—and pleasant—mental image.

"Leave it with me," Kodyn said, his voice and expression filled with confidence. "First thing I do after we're done here is ride to Obrathe and send everything downriver to Praamis. Two weeks from now, my mother will have everything I've found—and everything I hope to find as I search the rest of the city for anything else. Once it's in her hands, the Consortium is as good as done for."

The Hunter had no trouble believing that. His encounters with Master Gold had left him impressed with a great many things about her—from the way she ran her organization to the loyalty of her people to the ferocity with which she attacked her enemies.

He glanced at Kiara and found her already nodding. "So be it," she said, confirming the Hunter's opinion aloud. "But if there is anything you need from us to see it done—"

"I'll send word through the Hidden Circle," Kodyn said, nodding. He looked from the Hunter and Kiara to Tarek, who remained still in his saddle, impatience radiating from him in tangible waves. "No way I can convince you to delay a little long—"

"No!" Tarek snapped, his voice as taut at his spine. "Already, we've delayed too long."

"Okay, but will you at least give me *five* minutes?" Kodyn held up his hands in a pleading gesture. "I swear, five minutes. Just enough time to get Aisha here. She'll be furious if I let you ride out without saying goodbye."

Tarek opened his mouth, but the Hunter spoke first. "Five minutes, we can do."

"Great!" Kodyn's face lit up, and he took off at a sprint in the direction the funeral procession had gone.

Tarek shot the Hunter a glare, his teeth grinding. The Hunter ignored it. He wanted to say goodbye to Aisha, in truth. He'd grown terribly fond of the young *Umoyahlebe* over the last few weeks, as proud of who she'd become as he'd be of Evren and Hailen were they in her circumstance. The thought of riding away and never seeing her again saddened him.

The Hunter and Kiara waited standing in the street, Tarek never moving from his saddle. Time seemed to drag—slowed by the Hunter's reluctance to depart without making the proper farewells to the people he'd come to care about—but when five minutes became ten, he could feel Tarek's impatience swelling. When a full quarter-hour had passed and still Kodyn did not return, Tarek snarled, "Enough! We need to leave, now. Every moment wasted here increases Nameless' lead on us."

The Hunter wanted to argue, wanted to insist they give Kodyn a few more minutes, but he knew Tarek wouldn't be dissuaded. The Elivasti *would* ride out, alone if he had to. His odds of tracking the Abiarazi down on his own were better than average, but there was no way he'd survive coming face to face with the demon on his own. The Hunter owed it to Tarek to help him—and not only for the sake of the oath he'd sworn to the True Descendants. He'd come to regard the young man highly, too. He couldn't stand around to leave Tarek to ride off alone to face near-certain death—or, worse, have his mind seized once more by Nameless' mental abilities.

With a sigh, the Hunter swung up into his saddle. Kiara did likewise, but halfway up, she let out a little groan and sagged back to the ground.

"Kiara!" the Hunter swung a leg over his saddle to dismount.

"I'm fine, I'm fine." She waved him away, but when she turned to give him a smile, it was shaky, and her face had gone a bit pale. "Just a bit dizzy."

The Hunter didn't dismount, but he didn't slide his leg back into his stirrup either. "You look exhausted." His brow furrowed. "You overexerted yourself with *Okadigbo*, didn't you? And now you're about to collapse."

"Of course not!" Kiara's retort lacked any real strength. She wavered slightly where she stood, clinging to the saddlehorn with a white-knuckled grip. "Just…have to catch…my thoughts."

"That's it," the Hunter said, dropping from his saddle and moving toward her. "You're making no sense, and that's proof you're too tired to ride out now." A part of him was glad; better they wait until Tarek cooled off enough that he would not go riding straight into danger.

Kiara fixed him with a pointed look, then with her eyes, indicated Tarek. "I'm fine to ride," she said, her jaw clenched, her voice filled with determination. "Someone has to keep the two of you out of trouble."

The Hunter scowled. He knew she meant keep Tarek out of trouble, but still…

"That settles it then," Tarek said, impatience audible in every huffing breath and curtly spoken syllable. "We ride."

The Hunter raised a questioning eyebrow, and Kiara answered with a shrug, as if to say, "What choice do we have?" Knowing Tarek as they did, it wasn't a far stretch to imagine the young man riding off on his own. And the Hunter couldn't let that happen. Tarek would pursue Nameless' trail even if it led right down the demon's gullet.

With a sigh, he pulled himself into his saddle. "As you say."

This time, when Kiara mounted, she managed to make it all the way into the saddle. The instant she was seated, Tarek turned Nayaga's head and set off toward the gate.

The Hunter and Kiara didn't ride immediately. Instead, they glanced around, taking in the city, the Bondshold, and the rising smoke of the Buhari funeral one last time. Saying silent farewells to the people who they might never see again once they left this place behind.

The city seemed strangely quiet as the trio rode toward the gates. Tarek led them through on a path that kept them far from the domed building where the Buhari mourned their fallen, doubtless intending to avoid delays and farewells. Yet the Hunter was surprised that he couldn't hear even the slightest sound of singing, chanting, stamping feet, or slapping hands. Had the funeral already ended and the Ghandians departed?

Then the city wall came into view, and the Hunter's jaw dropped. Between them and the gates was formed a line of men and women. Every warrior of the Issai, Buhari, Tefaye, Nyemba, and Mwaani who had survived the battle stood there. Silent as statues, weapons drawn, faces set. At their head were Jumaane and Davathi, flanked by Siyanda, Naledi, Aisha, Nkanyezi, and Kodyn. A mischievous light shone in the young man's eyes. This was *his* doing.

Tarek reined in a few paces before Davathi and Jumaane, and the Hunter and Kiara slowed their mounts beside him.

"Ghandia!" Davathi's shout shattered the silence.

A roar rose from the lips of all the warriors. Hundreds of bare feet stamped against blood-soaked earth, setting the ground trembling beneath the hooves of the Hunter, Kiara, and Tarek's horses.

"Ghandia!" Jumaane echoed.

Weapons rose high in the air, and a chorus of war cries echoed from every pair of lips in the line before them.

"Ghandia!" Jumaane and Davathi's voices rose in unison.

The shout that rang out rolled across the Hunter with ear-splitting force, a wall of sound that resonated to the core of his being. The clamor did not die down quickly, but rose in intensity and pitch as every man and woman in the line lent their voice to the cry. The clank and clatter of weapons, the stamping of feet, and the slapping of hands against thighs and chests added to the tumult, amplified by the towering stone wall rising behind them.

Emotions swelled within the Hunter. Heat pricked at the backs of his eyes and a lump thickened in his throat, making it difficult to swallow. For in the warriors' shouts echoed every shred of their defiance, resilience, ferocity, and elation. Not the hatred or disgust to which he'd grown accustomed. They did not fear or revile him. They did not look at him as if he were a monster as so many others had. They *welcomed* him, recognized the warrior within him, and in that, found kinship. With him, an *alay-alagbara* and *Okanele*.

Davathi and Jumaane's right arms shot up in unison, raising sword and spear high overhead. The chorus of shouts quelled in the space of three heartbeats.

"Our people owe you a debt, *Umzukeli*," Davathi said. Her gaze lingered on him only for a moment before shifting to Kiara. "And you, *Ibhubekazi*." Her eyes finally moved to Tarek. "And you, *Isbindi*."

The Hunter startled at that last. He recognized that word, *isbindi*. It meant valor, courage. Values prized highly among the Issai—and, doubtless, all the Ghandians.

"Please," Jumaane said, stretching out his empty left hand toward them. "You have faced our enemies with us, grieved our fallen alongside us, and spilled your blood with ours. Do us the honor of staying one night to celebrate with us now."

The Hunter knew what his answer would be. Kiara's, too. He had but to look into Aisha's smiling face to know he'd love nothing more than to stay longer, to bid proper farewells, to snatch even a few more moments together. There was much he wanted to say to her, if he could bring himself to put into words the emotions swirling within him.

But the choice wasn't his alone. Nor Kiara's. The Hunter turned his head to regard Tarek. He could see by the young man's expression that Tarek was torn between desire and duty. Between the burden of guilt and the ties of friendship he'd formed. He wanted to stay, but the feelings that he'd failed his people compelled him to leave.

And in that moment, the Hunter knew what he had to do. He glanced at Kiara, and she nodded her understanding of what he intended. That was all the confirmation he needed.

He turned back to Davathi and Jumaane and bowed in his saddle. "The honor would be ours, *nassors*," he said in the Issai language, though the words felt clumsy on his tongue. "We will stay the night."

The roar from the assembled warriors did not drown out Tarek's sharp intake of breath. The young man shot him a glare.

"You'd risk Kiara's life?" the Hunter hissed back. "You saw how drained she was!" He leaned closer to the Elivasti. "You cannot defeat Nameless without her, and you know it."

Tarek's glare sharpened, but he did not argue. The Hunter was right, and they both knew it. With a scowl, he turned Nayaga's head sharply and rode back the way they'd come.

The Hunter watched Tarek ride away from the cheers for a few moments, then looked to Kiara. She gave him a nod. She agreed with his decision. Despite his words, the choice to stay had been made not for his own sake, nor hers, but for Tarek's.

Chapter One Hundred Eight

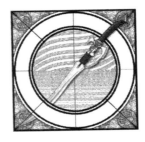

The celebration took place beyond the walls of the Consortium city. And what a celebration it was!

The Hunter had joined the bulk of the Ghandian forces in spending the day dumping the *alay-alagbara* bodies into *Isigodi Umlilophilayo* under Jumaane's command, while Davathi had led a full two-score warriors to hunt game for a great feast. Siyanda had gone with them, but Aisha remained behind to tend to Nkanyezi and the surviving *Umoyahlebe*. Tarek lent his healing skills to the task, Kiara helping as she could. Months spent in captivity and over-utilizing their abilities left them weak, half-starved, and dehydrated. Their road back to health would be long, but according to Kiara, Tarek was optimistic most would make a full recovery. Especially once he taught them the alchemical formula to mix up the brew that had cured the dimercurite's effects on the Tefaye and those exposed in the Consortium camp in *Indawo Yokwesaba*.

The smoke of the Buhari's heart-fire died just before sundown, but it was quickly replaced by a great bonfire over which roasted the warthogs, gazelle, and eland the hunters had brought down. The rich, heady scent of Ghandian spices filled the night sky. A handful of steel cauldrons were discovered among the Consortium's buildings, and soon bubbled merrily with a plethora of stews as varied and colorful as the united *amaqhawe* gathered around.

Singing and laughter rang out loud in the night. Warriors wrestled, sparred in bouts of friendly combat, or attempted to best each other in feats of strength. Shouts, cheers, jests, and boasts echoed off the stone walls that stood between the place of celebration and the city that was filled with death. For a few hours, the sorrow of battle was forgotten, and all of the tribes shared in the joy at their triumph. The *alay-alagbara* were gone. Ghandia was once more theirs.

When the food was finally served, it proved to be as delicious as the Hunter remembered from the Issai feast. Except now, every tribe had added their own unique mixtures of spices and herbs to the melange. The Hunter had never tasted such bold combinations. Einari fare seemed suddenly bland and boring by comparison to the rich, piquant, and aromatic feast in which they all partook.

The Hunter sat with Kiara, Tarek, Kodyn, and Aisha, basking in the revelry swirling around them. Only Tarek appeared immune to the merrymaking; he sat with his shoulders hunched, hands twisting the hem of his cloak over and over. The dour look on his face wasn't the result of any physical wound he'd endured. The bandage he'd wrapped around his head was clean and free of blood. No, this was an *internal* strife, that much was plain for even the Hunter to see.

Time and time again, when the Hunter wanted to speak to the young man, Kiara shook her head. She could feel his emotions, though it didn't take her gift to see how Tarek was struggling. Now was not yet the time.

"Umzukeli!"

At the sound of his name—a title, he'd come to learn, meaning "Reaver," which he found oddly appropriate—the Hunter looked up from his bowl of spiced and roasted eland meat.

Siyanda strode toward him with a bowl of soup in her hands. "For you," she said, offering him the food. "I recall from our last feast that you particularly enjoyed this soup."

The Hunter's stomach, already half-filled from the abundance he'd consumed, rumbled eagerly at the smell rising from the bowl. Oh, yes, he knew the scent of that particular vegetable stew all too well.

"Thank you," he said, inclining his head to her and taking the bowl. "It is good to know that despite our initial differences, we will part ways as allies."

Siyanda's lips twitched, but she mirrored his gesture.

"To your health." The Hunter lifted the bowl. "To the Issai, and all of Ghandia."

He brought the soup to his lips and drank deep, draining the bowl in a single long pull. The liquid had cooled to just below scalding, and his taste buds reveled at the richness of flavors dancing across his palate.

His tongue caught fire a moment after he finished his first swallow. The Ghandian lion pepper's bite hadn't lost its fury—if anything, the heat of the stew and the spices added only reinforced the feeling of an inferno raging in the Hunter's mouth.

A howl of laughter echoed through the night, accompanied by the sound of meaty hands slapping against even meatier thighs. The Hunter lowered the bowl to see Naledi standing a few paces away, roaring with mirth, watching him and awaiting the moment he broke into choking, hacking coughs from the lion pepper's heat.

But the Hunter merely smiled and raised his bowl to her first, then Siyanda. "Hmm, could use a bit more spice, truth be told." He spoke loud enough that his words carried to Naledi.

The huge warrior's laughter died for a moment, then redoubled as she understood. She hurried toward him with an enormous smile on her broad face.

"You gave him the right bowl, yes?" she asked Siyanda.

"Of course!" Siyanda said. Her expression held a mixture of amusement, confusion, and surprise.

"Where I'm from, it's believed many of the *Okanele* are born in a fiery hell." The Hunter grinned at the two Issai warriors. "What is the burn of a little pepper by comparison?"

Naledi roared even louder now, slapping the Hunter's back. Siyanda, too, grinned even broader. They couldn't possibly know the Hunter had smelled the lion pepper in the soup and deadened the nerves that told him his mouth was on fire. That particular Bucelarii trick, he'd keep to himself.

"Cebile could not be with us tonight." Sorrow flickered in Siyanda's eyes, and even Naledi's smile grew slightly sad, tears springing to her eyes through her laughter. "So we honor her in the way she would like best."

"To Cebile." The Hunter raised the empty bowl. "May she find many more in *Pharadesi* upon whom to pull this prank."

Both women's smiles brightened once more. With another hearty slap of the Hunter's shoulder, Naledi hurried away, proclaiming loudly she was off in dire need of good, strong meat. Not surprisingly, the powerfully built warrior gathered a procession of eager-looking men on her way to the cookfires.

Siyanda, however, didn't depart. Instead, she took a seat beside Aisha, near enough to reach out and touch her cousin, squeezing her shoulder. Aisha smiled and leaned toward Siyanda, and for a few minutes, the two sat like that, sharing a quiet moment of closeness as they once had so many years ago.

The merrymaking was interrupted a short while later. Singing and laughter gave way to curious murmurs, and the dancing ceased, the ranks of warriors parting to reveal a figure marching determinedly toward where the Hunter and his companions sat.

A fresh coat of grey ash darkened Jumaane's skin, but he'd once more donned his lion's mane headdress and trimmed his beard. He had even taken pains to wash as much of the blood off his Buhari armor as he could. He had abandoned his shield and great spear, wearing only his *nkemba* hanging from his back. Yet even lightly armed, he appeared imposing, commanding, regal.

He strode straight toward the Hunter, stopping in front of where Siyanda sat at Aisha's side. A flush rose to his cheeks, barely discernible beneath the ash staining his face, and once he cleared his throat, his voice rang out strong and clear.

"Siyanda of the Issai, I come to you tonight not as *nassor,* nor *amaqhawai,* but as a man."

Jumaane's spine was stiff, his great shoulders knotted, his fingers clenching and unclenching at his side. His eyes shone with a burning intensity all too familiar. The giant was head over heels in love, and he'd finally plucked up the courage to proclaim it aloud. For all his skill and strength as a warrior, in this, he was as uncertain as any other man alive—and the Hunter included himself in that number.

"The day we first met, I knew I would never find another your equal. Though I feared it could never be possible, I hoped." Jumaane placed a clenched fist against his huge chest. "In my heart, I hoped that the *unkgaliwe* fierce enough to slay a lioness alone in her enemy's land would someday see the lion's spirit within me, too. That though our tribes have been enemies, that *we* would not have to be. Like Falakhe and Jabhile of old. That somehow, the *Kish'aa* would guide us to a place where we could be together. And now they have."

Siyanda's eyes were wide, her lips parted slightly, and she sat utterly frozen.

"Up!" Aisha hissed, pushing an unresistant Siyanda to her feet. There the woman stood, staring at Jumaane with a shocked expression on her face. Yet her silence did not diminish Jumaane's confidence, not a whit.

The *nassor* lifted his head and continued. "Today, a great battle has been won. We have rid ourselves of the *alay-alagbara* curse and reclaimed *Ukuhlushwa Okungapheli,* a place your people believe to be among Ghandia's greatest treasures. But to me, there is no greater treasure in all of Ghandia than you, Siyanda."

Excited gasps and whispers rippled among the crowd that had now gathered around the towering *nassor* and the cleared space where Siyanda stood leaning on Aisha and staring wordlessly at him.

"All my life," Jumaane went on, his voice rising so loud it seemed to set the volcanic stone walls ringing, "I have given all that I am in the name of my people. And now, if you are willing, I would give all that I am in your name, too."

The huge *nassor* looked to the two warriors at his side, and as if at some invisible signal, they produced a lion's pelt. No, the Hunter realized, a *lioness'* pelt.

Jumaane took the pelt and turned back to Siyanda. "You are my heart, Siyanda. I now offer you mine, if you will—"

"Yes!" The word burst from Siyanda's lips loud enough to be audible for a league in every direction. "Yes, yes!" She looked ready to launch herself at him, but only barely stopped herself. Indeed, her muscles quivered with a sudden energy, her hands reaching out for Jumaane yet her feet pushing her away. She appeared torn between desire to wrap her arms around Jumaane and respect the Buhari tradition of mourning their dead.

Until, finally, she spun to Aisha and threw her arms around her cousin's neck, squeezing with all the pent-up emotion consuming her. Her eyes never left Jumaane's, though. "My answer was always yes," she cried.

At the proclamation, a deafening roar rose from the crowd, and hundreds of warriors stamped their feet, slapped their thighs, and clanged their weapons against their shields.

An enormous grin blossomed on Jumaane's face, bright despite the ashes, and Siyanda's eyes shone brighter than even the bonfire burning nearby. All around them roared and cheered, and many of Jumaane's warriors thronged their *nassor* with well-wishes and congratulations.

Aisha extracted herself from Siyanda's grip—with effort—and moved to take the lioness pelt from Jumaane, careful not to touch him. She bore the gift back to Siyanda with a beaming grin "For shame, *um'zala!*" She had to shout over the tumult. "He went through all the effort of putting together that speech. The least you could have done is let him finish."

Siyanda threw her arms around Aisha again, crushing the fine pelt between them. Tears of joy streamed down her face as she held a hand toward Jumaane. The giant Buhari mirrored the gesture, and though a half-dozen paces separated them, there was no doubt in anyone's mind that they were joined in that moment—and for every moment thereafter.

Beneath the raucous cheers and roaring, the Hunter's keen ears heard Aisha's whisper, "I'm so happy for you."

"And you," came Siyanda's whispered reply. She broke off and held Aisha out at arm's length. "Don't pretend like you won't be next."

Aisha flushed a deep red, earning a laugh from her cousin.

Siyanda turned to Kodyn, who had climbed to his feet behind Aisha. To everyone's surprise, Siyanda held out her arms to embrace Kodyn, too. No one seemed more taken aback by it than he, and he could barely respond as she hugged him. It was brief, but when she pulled back, she gave the young man a broad smile. "After Aisha was taken, I swore I would hate every *alay-alagbara*. But I'll admit, you're not as bad as I expected."

Kodyn chuckled. "I'll take that as a compliment, I guess?"

"If my *um'zala* intends to truly choose you as *oqinywe*, she could do worse." Her smile broadened. "But first, we must make a proper Issai out of you."

"How, exactly?" Kodyn asked.

"You shall see," Siyanda said. She clapped him on the shoulder. "I will make certain the *amaqhawe* goes easy on you. Though perhaps not *too* easy. You must prove yourself truly strong if you are to stand at her side." The sharp glint in her eyes promised either mischief or torment—or perhaps both in equal measure.

Chapter One Hundred Nine

"What, exactly, did she mean by, 'set you to dance atop the *imvubu'?*" Kodyn asked Aisha, a worried look on his face.

Aisha gave him a consoling pat on the shoulder. "I'll explain it to you later. But don't worry. I've seen you run across the Hawk's Highway. You've got fancy footwork enough to avoid all those snapping jaws."

Visible alarm blossomed on Kodyn's expression. With good reason, the Hunter knew. The thought of being anywhere near the barrel-bellied *imvubu*—said to have a bite powerful enough to crush a full-grown horse—was enough to unnerve even him.

Amidst the crowd, the Hunter spotted Davathi and Nkanyezi moving on a direct course toward them. The *nassor* paused long enough for them both to congratulate Jumaane and Siyanda—who now wore the lioness' pelt draped over her shoulders—but broke off quickly and slid through the throng of jostling, shouting, cheering Buhari in their direction.

Aisha and Kodyn must have spotted her, too, for they both turned toward her with expectant looks on their faces.

"Walk with me," Davathi said, gesturing to the darkness beyond the ring of firelight. "All of you. There are matters best discussed in private."

Something in the *nassor's* eyes or the gravity of her tone set the Hunter's stomach twisting into knots. *That can't be good.*

He and Kiara joined Kodyn and Aisha in following Davathi and Nkanyezi through the throng. When Tarek didn't follow, the Hunter stopped, turning back to beckon the young man to join them.

Only to find the space where Tarek had been sitting empty. Frowning, the Hunter scanned the crowd. Tarek had been at his side only a few minutes earlier. Had he returned to the cookfires to refill his bowl? Joined the Ghandians who had once again taken up dancing? He spent a full half-minute searching, but found no sign of Tarek.

Where in the Keeper's name has he gotten off to now? the Hunter couldn't help wondering. An image of Tarek's scowling, gloomy face sprang to his mind. *Lad's likely off brooding somewhere.* He sighed inwardly, shaking his head. *Best I find him and talk to him sooner rather than later.*

He turned to follow Davathi and the others—he'd hear what the Issai *nassor* had to say, then hunt down Tarek after—only to find his path blocked by a looming figure. Jumaane, towering a full head taller than the Hunter in his lion's mane headdress, a burning look in his eyes.

"*Nassor.*" The Hunter gave the big man a respectful nod. "You have my sincere congratulations. I wish you two—"

"There is a debt between us, *Umzukeli*." Jumaane's words came out in a growl. A frown tugged his lips downward, knitting his brow. "The blood of my *amaqhawe* that you spilled." He leaned down until his huge face hovered a hand's breadth from the Hunter's. "Do you recall what you told me, the day we spoke of your actions—and their consequences?"

The Hunter's stomach twisted. He'd thought this particular matter put behind them— Swordsman's teeth, they'd just fought side by side against the Consortium, and Ghandia was rid of the *alay-alagbara* because of him. Yet one look at Jumaane's expression made it clear that the deaths of his warriors, his brothers-in-arms, had no more been forgotten than forgiven.

He called to mind his conversation with Jumaane, and repeated his words from that day, what felt a lifetime ago. "When the *alay-alagbara* are destroyed and these lands are once more yours, you and every *amaqhawai* who has cause to hate me will be free to take up spears and seek my blood."

"That is as I remember it, too." Jumaane straightened, the powerful muscles in his chest and shoulders flexing, his hands clenching into fists. "It is the way of the *amathafa*. The matter must be settled between us once and for all. Between you and me, and every warrior who lost a friend or comrade to your blades."

The Hunter tensed, suddenly keenly aware that scores of Buhari had now turned his way, dark eyes fixed on him, hands hovering near the hilts of their *nkemba*.

A sick sensation settled in the pit of the stomach. *Really?* He met Jumaane's gaze, glaring his defiance. Though he said not a word, his eyes spoke volumes. He had no desire to raise his hand against those who had joined him in battle, but if Jumaane pressed the issue, he would not lie down and die. It was not his way. Besides, he had greater concerns than some blood debt between him and the Buhari.

"Buhari!" The roar burst from Jumaane's lips, so suddenly the Hunter's hand dropped to the hilt of his sword. Jumaane's enormous *nkemba* rose high over his head.

"BUHARI!" The answering roar was deafening. The sound rumbled from every Buhari mouth, and every *nkemba* in the crowd surrounding the Hunter rose, too.

"Buhari!" Jumaane shouted again, thrusting his *nkemba* into the sky once again.

"BUHARI!" The ground rumbled beneath the force of their shout.

"Buhari!" Jumaane called a third time, and a third time the answering cry washed over the Hunter with ear-splitting force.

As one, the Buhari threw back their heads and loosed a leonine roar into the air. None roared louder than Jumaane. His great arms spread wide, the powerful muscles beneath his arm constricting with the intensity of his cry.

But when Jumaane's roar trailed off and he lowered his face, a beaming smile broadened his lips. He lowered his *nkemba* to the ground and clapped the Hunter's shoulder with his free hand. "I give you a gift, *Umzukeli*, I and all my people, in gratitude for what you have done for us." He lifted a finger to point at the Hunter's face. "That gift is your head."

The Hunter couldn't help a snorting laugh. "You are too kind, great *nassor*." He'd said those same words last time they'd spoken on the matter, too. As with that day, Jumaane just laughed. The rest of the Buhari joined in. More than a few cast respectful nods the Hunter's way, but most merely turned back to their food, drink, and dancing.

As the revelry resumed, Jumaane stepped closer and spoke in a voice pitched low for their ears only. "I understand the message you were sent by *Inzayo Okubi* to deliver, *Okanele*." He placed his free hand over his heart and inclined his head in what passed for a bow for the big man. "I will heed its wisdom until I draw my last breath."

The Hunter's jaw dropped. Before he could regain his wits, before he could think to ask what message Jumaane had understood, the *nassor* was gone, once more swept up in the celebration of his warriors and the woman he loved.

* * *

The Hunter was still shaking his head in confusion over Jumaane's mystifying final words when he finally caught up to the others.

Kiara, Kodyn, and Nkanyezi stood around Davathi and Aisha. The *nassor* gripped her daughter's hands firmly, an earnest look on her face. "...know it is a great deal to ask of you," she was saying. "You have only just returned to me, and it pains me that we will be apart once more. Yet I know in my heart that it is what must be done."

For an answer, Aisha merely swept her mother into an embrace. The two of them held each other, Aisha's hands wrapped tight around Davathi's back, Davathi stroking her daughter's tight-curling hair.

"What'd I miss?" the Hunter whispered to Kiara.

"Jumaane and the Buhari will be staying to protect the Bondshold," Kiara whispered back. "Siyanda's joining them, obviously. And she asked Aisha to stay, too."

The Hunter frowned. "Why?"

"Because of Tunde." Aisha's words drew the Hunter's attention. She had half-turned toward him, though she still had one strong arm wrapped around her mother, as if unwilling to lose her again so soon after their reunion. "What the *Indaba* guarded for thousands of years, the truth of *Nuru Iwu* and *Okadigbo*. That must not be forgotten, nor the power within *Ukuhlushwa Okungapheli* left unguarded."

"The tower appears to be dead," Kiara said, her expression solemn. "But you know as well as I do that when it comes to the Serenii, appearances can be deceiving."

The Hunter considered the meaning behind those words. "You think *Okadigbo* will somehow find a way back to life? Collect the consciousness he spread out into the *intambelu* and what, wake up again?"

The lack of surprise on the faces around him told the Hunter that Kiara had filled them in on much of their conversation in the towertop chamber—including the fate of the Serenii and the purpose behind the Bondshold.

"Perhaps." Kiara shrugged. "Either way, none of us believe it's worth taking a chance the wrong people get their hands on it."

"Who better to defend Ghandia's greatest treasure than its fiercest tribe, or its most powerful *Umoyahlebe*?" Nkanyezi stepped toward Aisha, gripping her sister's free arm and leaning her head on Aisha's shoulder. "My sister."

Aisha tilted her head to rest atop Nkanyezi's.

Davathi beamed at her two daughters, pride glowing on her face. "I must return to the Issai, and my *kwa'indokazi* with me. There is much that must be done to restore our tribe. But what is begun here will grow. Already, Jumaane and I have spoken with Baako of the Tefaye and Naeem, she who leads the last survivors of the Bheka and Ujana held prisoners here. They have agreed to remain, to transform this place from one of sorrow to one of safety for all who wish to dwell here. When I return to the Issai *ekhaya*, I will speak to them on the matter, too. As will Khairi and Zuberi when they are once more among their people. The *amathafa* will know peace and harmony between the tribes. We will be *Ubunye*."

Ubunye. The One People. Tribes united by a common cause—once, fighting for their freedom from the Ghandian Empire that was; now, defending their *amathafa* from those who would mistreat and enslave them as the *alay-alagbara* had.

"But for that to happen," Davathi reached her arm for Aisha, pulling her into a hug once more, "I must give up my daughter. For a time, at least."

Aisha returned her mother's embrace, and Nkanyezi joined in, wrapping her arms around both Davathi and Aisha.

When Davathi broke off, tears streamed down her face. "Oh, my brave, beautiful, beloved *indokazi.*" Joy mingled with the sorrow etched into her strong, leonine features as she reached up to cup Aisha's face in her hands. "For years, I feared I would never see you again. Yet the *Kish'aa* led you home to us. Your *uhambo loguquko* was long, but wove you into something far stronger than anything your father or I could have hoped for." She pressed a kiss to her daughter's forehead. "You are the best of both of us." She reached a hand to cup Nkanyezi's face, kissing her younger daughter, too. "You both are. And I know how proud he was of you, how much he loved you."

Tears flowed down Aisha and Nkanyezi's faces, too, though their smiles never wavered.

"You are more than I ever dreamed you could be. *Amaqhawai* and *Umoyahlebe.* Strength and spirit." She pulled her daughters close to her. "No mother could be prouder."

The Hunter felt his own cheeks grow wet, too, and he looked away quickly to brush off the moisture. He caught Kodyn and Kiara both doing likewise, and chuckled to himself.

When Davathi finally broke off, she turned to Kodyn and took his hands in hers. "I trust you will look after my *indokazi.* And know that if you fail in your duty, you will answer to the both of us." She gestured to herself and Nkanyezi.

To illustrate the threat in those words, Nkanyezi summoned blue-white sparks to dance around her fingers, which she waggled menacingly in Kodyn's face.

Kodyn merely laughed and bowed to the *nassor.* "I swear to you, upon my mothers' souls and the love I bear for your daughter, I will give my life in defense of hers. My blood, sweat, and tears will be shed in the pursuit of her goals, and every shred of my strength will go to supporting her wherever and however she needs me."

The words rang with a formality that, in any Einari hall of nobility, might have belonged in any official betrothal ceremony. Beneath the stars, they merely felt…right.

"Well, then." Davathi clapped Kodyn on the shoulders. "I suppose it's only right to welcome you to the family."

Nkanyezi grinned broadly and threw her arms around Kodyn. "If you weren't officially my sister's *oqinywe* before, you definitely are now."

Judging by the smiles shared between Kodyn and Aisha, the two youths didn't seem to mind that particular outcome much at all.

Chapter One Hundred Ten

Davathi and Nkanyezi did not tarry long. The *nassor,* wise as always to her surroundings, seemed to understand that the Hunter and Kiara needed a few moments to bid farewell to Kodyn and Aisha.

She clasped the Hunter's forearm with a respectful nod. *"Okanele."*

"Nassor." The Hunter mirrored the gesture.

To Kiara, Davathi smiled and said, "May the *Kish'aa* watch over you wherever your path leads."

"And you, *nassor,*" Kiara said, bowing.

Nkanyezi offered similar farewells, then joined her mother in leaving them alone— though not before extracting a promise from Aisha to come find her once they had finished.

The four of them watched mother and daughter stride away arm in arm, laughing and joking as they returned to the celebrations.

"Listen—" the Hunter began when they were finally alone.

"Hunter—" Kodyn started at the same time.

"I know—" Aisha added.

"Well, this is—" Kiara's voice joined the fray.

They cut off with a laugh, though the Hunter found himself feeling suddenly awkward. He'd *wanted* to say goodbye properly to the two youths, but now that the moment was upon him, he had no idea what to say.

"You go first," Kodyn said, nudging Aisha.

"You sure?" Aisha shot a questioning glance at the Hunter. "What you've got to say—"

"Can wait." The Hunter swept his hand in a dismissive wave.

When Aisha glanced Kiara's way, Kiara just nodded and said, "We're listening."

Aisha shot a nervous look at Kodyn.

The young man gave her an encouraging smile and nudged her gently. "Say it."

Aisha drew herself up, taking in a deep breath. "I know our journey got off to a rocky start." Once she began, the words tumbled from her mouth in a rush. "But in the weeks since then, I've come to think of you both as more than just companions. More than just friends. Sort of…yeah…sort of like family." A blush rose to her cheeks, but she bulled on. "Like Ria, Master Phoenix, who was among those who freed me from the Consortium in Praamis, who took me in and gave me a home. She's the reason I met Kodyn." She reached out and took Kodyn by one hand. "I'm here largely in part because of her. But I wouldn't be here without you, too."

Her gaze went to the Hunter. "Without your advice, I would never have learned to keep the *Kish'aa* from overwhelming me with their emotions and desires and pleas. I've only gained what control I do have because of everything you taught me. More than that, though, what you *showed* me."

The words surprised the Hunter. He'd shown her nothing, at least not that he could remember.

"After that first battle against the Buhari, Kiara told us about the Sword of Nasnaz," Aisha said, flicking a finger of her free hand to the hilt of the scimitar jutting above the Hunter's right shoulder. "About what its magic does to you. Every time we faced a battle, it would have been so easy for you to just give in to its power, to draw the blade and lose yourself in the bloodlust. *Kish'aa* know I've wanted to many times over. Seeing my people suffering, my sister and father in chains, I wanted nothing more than to loose every bit of power I could summon against them."

A determined light shone in her *kaffe*-brown eyes. "I watched you, you know. Every battle, every fight, I watched you. And I saw you fighting against that desire to give in to the power. Knowing that it might cost you—not just your own blood, but the lives of those you love—you *still* made the choice to resist. Seeing you do that, it's what gave me the strength to resist, too. To not lose myself to the anger and hatred and sorrow, but to hold on to myself. My sanity." A wry smile twisted her lips. "Funny to think it was a half-demon who showed me how important it was to fight for my humanity."

The Hunter couldn't help laughing. "A bitter irony, indeed." Yet the words came hard; he had to force them around the lump that thickened his throat. His treacherous eyes had begun to sting, too. His attempts to swallow the rising emotions could not stop the moisture from forming at the corners of his eyes.

"Staying means I won't be able to keep the promise I made to Hallar," Aisha said, her expression clouding, "but after what you told me, about what Kharna revealed to you about all the Serenii towers, I know that task is in good hands."

The promise she'd made to Hallar. To reactivate the Serenii towers around Einan, all to sustain Kharna in his fight against the Great Devourer. Now that the Hunter knew the purpose of those towers, that did, indeed, feature heavily into his future.

"I'll do my best," he said with a wry grin.

"And you." Aisha turned to Kiara. "That first night we spoke, when I told you of Evren and Hailen, I didn't just see your love for them. I *felt* it. Like a soft blanket or a warm summer breeze, something entirely real and tangible. You reminded me of my mother in all the best ways."

She stepped closer and took Kiara's hands. "I thought Hailen and Evren were some of the luckiest people in the world, to have someone who cared for them with every fiber of her being, who would give *anything* to make certain they were safe. But I know now that I'm as lucky as they are. Because I see and feel that same love from you now. I'm fortunate enough that my true mother is alive, but if ever there was another who could take her place, it's you."

"Oh, now!" Kiara threw her arms around Aisha and hugged her tight. Tears streamed down her cheeks, but her smile lit up the night brighter than the moon.

When they broke off, Kiara held Aisha out at arm's length. "I've watched you along this journey. This *uhambo loguquko* of yours. I've seen everything you've been through in just these last few weeks, and all that on top of everything else from your past. And I've been utterly amazed by your strength and spirit. I have no doubt you'll continue to become a truly spectacular woman."

She hugged Aisha tight to her again, and their tears renewed. Even the Hunter couldn't keep his cheeks fully dry.

"So, yeah." Aisha stepped back, her expression suddenly awkward once more, her cheeks coloring. "I just wanted to say that. To thank you both for everything. And to make sure you know that if you're ever in Ghandia again, I expect you to stop in for a visit. Actually, scratch that." She waggled a finger at them. "If you *don't* stop in for a visit, I'll be bloody furious. And we all know how miserable I can make your life if I am."

To illustrate her point, blue-white light brightened around her hand and a pair of sparks shot out toward the Hunter and Kiara. The flicker of *Kish'aa* power flooded them with a heat that stopped *just* short of painful.

"Message received!" the Hunter said, throwing up his hands like a shield between them.

The four of them broke into laughter, and the tension drained away, replaced by the warmth of the camaraderie they'd developed as a result of everything their recent ordeals had heaped upon them.

"Your turn now," Aisha said, turning to Kodyn. "Tell them what you—"

"Wait." Kiara's voice cut in. "First, I need to give you something."

All eyes turned to her, watching curiously as she drew something from her pouch. The Hunter's eyes widened as he recognized the object: a small necklace formed of small, tarnished brass links, bearing a crudely fashioned pendant that might have been a star or sun. He'd considered asking about its meaning in the past, but held back for fear of causing her pain.

"This was my daughter's," Kiara said, her voice quiet, heavy with emotion. "I've carried it with me since the day I laid her to rest." She stared down at the necklace with tears in her eyes. "Told myself I'd never be parted from it. It's all I have left of her. It'd be here, even after my memories of her faded."

She lifted her eyes to Aisha, and a sad smile formed on her lips as she stroked the pendant with one thumb. "Her name, Beyla, it's a word from the Twelve Kingdoms. Means 'shining light' or 'spark'." She held the necklace out to Aisha. "Seems fitting, given what you can do."

Aisha's eyes widened. "Kiara, I can't—"

"Yes, you can, and you will." Kiara pressed the brass necklace into Aisha's hands and curled her fingers around it. "Beyla's memories aren't going anywhere anytime soon. Got 'em locked up tight in here." She tapped a finger against her temple. "But she's not the only spark in my life now. I've got this one, brooding storm cloud though he is most of the time." She elbowed the Hunter in the ribs, earning a good-natured growl. "Hailen and Evren, too. And now the both of you." She removed her hand from Aisha's and reached up to cup the young woman's face in her hands. "I may have lost my child years ago, but I'd be honored to say I've found another one in you."

Aisha wrapped her arms tight around Kiara, holding her with the same ferocity with which she'd clung to her mother.

"And you," Kiara said, reaching one hand toward Kodyn.

He took her hand with a beaming smile. "Got two mothers already. A third can't hurt."

Kiara laughed, a sound ringing with the purest joy and unfettered emotion. Hearing it and seeing the light in her eyes filled the Hunter's heart to bursting. Before he realized it, *he* was stepping forward.

"Here," he said, his words roughened by the maelstrom of emotions swirling within him. His fingers fumbled with his buckles, pulling free the belt that supported the watered steel sword in its sheath. "You'll need this to guard her back." He thrust the weapon into Kodyn's arms.

Kodyn's eyes flew wider even than Aisha's had. He stood, staring open-mouthed, frozen by surprise.

"Not many finer blades in all the world." The Hunter spoke quickly to keep his voice from cracking. "Watered steel, forged by one of the greatest living Elivasti smiths for the last of the Elivasti blademasters. A man who took me in alongside his own son, who taught me everything I know. Made me much of what I am."

At the memory of Master Eldor—from their reunion to everything they'd shared to the First Blade's final sacrifice for him and Hailen—the Hunter couldn't stop his own tears from flowing. Yet he brushed them away roughly and drove on.

"He crafted it for his son, Aerden, but never got the chance to pass it on. Gave it to me. It's served me well. Now it's time it serves you well, too."

"B-But…" Kodyn stammered, but no more came out. His eyes dropped from the Hunter's face to the sword now clutched in his unmoving arms.

"Holds an edge better than the best Voramian steel, but weighs far less." The Hunter forced a smile. "Way you fight, should be just the thing to give you an edge next time you cross blades with an enemy. Keep it in good shape, and it'll last you a lifetime."

"Th-Thank you." Kodyn's voice held a note of awe, his expression filled with disbelief.

"Won't you need it?" Aisha asked.

The Hunter glanced over at the young woman, who stood next to Kiara, staring at Kodyn and the Hunter's gift with astonishment etched on her strong face.

"Got plenty of other swords," the Hunter said, shrugging. "This one…" He smiled. "This one's special, but I suppose that's what makes it worth the giving."

From the proud, approving look Kiara gave him, the Hunter knew his actions, though unplanned, had been right.

That filled him with a warm glow. "Can't think of a finer young man to give it to." He clapped Kodyn on the shoulder. "Wield it in defense of those who need your strength, and you'll do right by the sword and everyone else who carried it before you."

"I will," Kodyn said, with a firm nod. He removed one hand from the sword and thrust it out toward the Hunter to shake. "I'll do my utmost to honor both the blade and its former bearer."

Chapter One Hundred Eleven

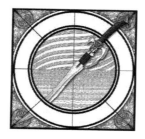

"Well," Kiara said, beaming and wiping the tears from her eyes, "that's got me done." She shot the Hunter a mock scolding look. "Had this whole grand speech planned for Kodyn, too, along with this." She drew out a fine dagger, one of her prized throwing knives. "But, no! Someone had to go and steal my thunder."

The Hunter raised his hands defensively. "Can't help it if I give better gifts than—*oof!*" This last was far more theatrical than necessary, for Kiara's punch to his ribs didn't *truly* sting quite as much as he pretended.

Kodyn and Aisha laughed, and even Kiara couldn't keep up the pretense of annoyance for more than a few seconds.

"My turn," the Hunter said when the laughter died down. "Feel kinda foolish now, saying what I need to say after all those kind words and gifts." He scowled. "But I s'pose I oughta just come out with it." Drawing in a deep breath, he turned to Aisha. "I need your help. Yours and every *Umoyahlebe* you can train."

"What manner of help?" Aisha cocked her head.

"You know what I've sworn to do for Kharna, aye?" the Hunter asked, to which Aisha and Kodyn both nodded. "Way I've been going about it, one demon at a time, I'll be at this long after everyone alive today is dead and gone. A million souls is a bloody damned lot." He glanced at Kiara. "Even if we somehow imprisoned Indombe and every other mythical beast still roaming Einan today within one of those Chambers of Sustenance, still might not be enough."

Aisha's eyes narrowed. Then widened suddenly. "You want us to...?"

The Hunter tilted his head in acknowledgment. "Best plan that comes to mind, truth be told."

The idea had occurred to him sometime between first seeing the *Umoyahlebe* pouring power into the Chamber of Sustenance to free Nameless at the Order's behest and watching Aisha and Nkanyezi tear through the last of the Consortium. They wielded the magic of the *Kish'aa,* which came from the souls—or spirits or life forces, depending on who was speaking— of the dead. Many of those dead had been intentionally made by the Order and Consortium. Captives slaughtered specifically to power up the *Umoyahlebe's* reservoirs.

The look of disgust that rose to Aisha's face startled the Hunter. Then he understood. "No, no!" He shook his head vehemently. "I've no intention of following in the Order's footsteps with this. No mass executions or butchery, I swear."

Aisha's expression shifted from revulsion to confusion. "Then how do you—"

"Like you did in Shalandra!" This came from Kodyn. The young man's eyes had gone wide and bright with excitement. "All of the spirits of the dead you absorbed from the Keeper's Crypts. His plan is for you to do that, but on an even grander scale." He turned to the Hunter as if for confirmation. "Souls collected from every corner of Einan, until you've got the million needed to sustain Kharna."

"That's the thought," the Hunter said, turning his palms up. His gaze shifted from Kodyn back to Aisha. "Question is, do you think that you can pull it off?"

Lines furrowed Aisha's brow, and her lips pressed together in thought. "A million is a bloody awful lot." She tugged at her lip with one hand, the other toying with the skin of her elbow. "Hard to even think about that many. Much less try to store them all. That many voices, things tend to get chaotic, you know?" She tapped her temple. "In here."

The Hunter's heart sank. "So it's not possible?" Disappointment settled like a burden that dragged his shoulders downward.

"Didn't say that." Aisha waggled a finger at him, then went back to worrying at her lip. "I didn't exactly keep count, but in the battle, I'd say between Nkanyezi and me, we probably absorbed a good two hundred or so."

The Hunter's eyebrows shot up. "Two hundred?!"

"Apiece."

The Hunter's jaw dropped. His mind ran quick calculations. A dozen *Umoyahlebe* had emerged from the towertop chamber, not counting Aisha and Nkanyezi. But if they were the most powerful of the Spirit Whisperers—

"I'm not saying it's a done deal," Aisha said, her frown deepening, "but maybe, *maybe,* we could work our way up."

Hope surged within the Hunter.

"No promises!" Aisha shot him a sharp, hard look. "But I will say that when I first began to use my abilities in Shalandra, I could barely keep my head straight with one spirit. Now, I can hold my own against a few score. My will is stronger. Add in this—" She tapped the *Dy'nashia* pendant hanging at her neck. "—and hundreds isn't too hard a stretch. Within a few more months, or years, even, and who knows how many I'll be able to handle."

"And the others?" the Hunter asked, his spirits soaring. "Nkanyezi and the rest? Think you can train them? Teach them how to control their powers? Share the tricks I taught you, help them gain mastery over the voices, too?"

"Aye." Aisha nodded. "But that won't solve the big problem. Without this—" Again, she tapped her pendant. "—if they try to hold too many, they'll burn out as if thrown in a bonfire. Or the *Kish'aa* will claim them, as they did my father, and they will become Unshackled, their minds cast adrift from their bodies."

With those words, reality came crashing down on the Hunter. What a fool he was to get his hopes up. Of course Aisha would have the *only* Serenii-crafted pendant in existence that would—

"Until we figure out how to use the collars, that is."

"The collars?" The Hunter sucked in a sharp breath. "You mean the ones the Ordermen used to control them? Keep them trapped in that circle of chains?"

Aisha nodded. "The same." Her lips twisted into a grimace. "Truth be told, I don't understand it. Haven't given it a test. No real desire to. But Nkanyezi swore that they worked."

"Worked?" Confusion thrummed within the Hunter. "What do you mean by that?"

"Like I said, I don't understand it, exactly." Aisha turned her palms upward, shrugging her shoulders. "But according to Nkanyezi, something about the metal—the mixture of dimercurite alloy, steel, and whatever else was melted in with it—gave her some measure of control over the *Kish'aa*. Silenced their voices, kept her from being drowned by their entreaties. Only when the one holding the chain *willed* it did they have access to their power, and then it came flooding out of them in a torrent that only the strongest could resist."

The Hunter couldn't begin to understand the nuances of her *Kish'aa* abilities, but he *could* understand the peace that came from being shut off from voices in his head. Iron had done that with Soulhunger's voice long ago. It hadn't rendered the dagger any less potent, hadn't sapped its powers, merely blocked it so it could not speak in his mind.

Or so he'd *believed* at the time. In truth, he didn't quite understand what was reality and what was his mind's manifestation of the imperative implanted by Kharna. All he knew was that his head was free of the voices, and he was bloody well glad for it.

"There's too much we don't understand about dimercurite still," Aisha said. "But the way the door to the Bondshold resisted so much *Kish'aa* magic for so long proves that there's *something* there. Something that we might be able to use to create our own version of the *Dy'nashia*. It'll take time to experiment and sort it all out, but by the grace of the *Kish'aa,* I think we've got a decent chance at making it work." A sad smile blossomed on her face. "It certainly worked for my father."

"How?" Kiara asked. Her expression mirrored Aisha's—a mixture of joy and sorrow the reason for which the Hunter couldn't quite fathom. "How did it help him?"

"My father was lost to the *Inkuleko* long ago." Aisha's eyes darkened at a painful memory. "He delved too far into the realm of the *Kish'aa,* and the spirits claimed his mind. When last I saw him, before I was taken, he was barely conscious, didn't even know I was trying to speak to him. He spent his nights wandering the *ekhaya* and talking to the dead. I've lost count of how many times my mother set me or Siyanda to watch him, to make certain he didn't wander off and lose himself in the *amathafa.* He was all but gone."

Her smile brightened. "But Nkanyezi told me that once he was brought here and the collar placed around his neck, the *Kish'aa's* hold on his mind was loosened. He was himself again, for a time. Because of him, Nkanyezi and the others had strength to endure. For he was a powerful *Umoyahlebe* and had spent decades communing with the spirits. With his mind restored, he was able to share what he had learned with those who were so brutally forced to utilize abilities they had only just discovered. Those who live today only do so because of him."

Moisture welled in her eyes, and again her face took on an expression of grief mingled with gladness. "He saved my sister. And he saved me, too. He recognized me, at the end. He saw me, remembered me, though we had not seen each other for years. When he touched me, I felt all the love I had thought lost when the *Inkuleko claimed him."*

The tears flowed freely down her cheeks now, but she did not wipe them away. "That is why, despite everything, all that our people have lost, I cannot help but feel grateful. Because though his body is gone, his spirit remains with me." Her hand rose to touch the *Dy'nashia* pendant. "He will be with me always, close to my heart, watching over his beloved *indokazi.* If ever I feel his absence, I can always hear his voice in my mind."

She wrapped both her hands around the pendant and closed her eyes. Though the tears did not dry up, a small smile stretched her lips. Perhaps even now she spoke to the fallen *Umoyahlebe* who had given the last spark of his life to save hers.

Neither the Hunter, Kiara, nor Kodyn spoke. None of them dared shatter the silence for fear of interrupting Aisha's communion with her father.

Finally, Aisha's eyelids opened, and the blue-white light that shone in her eyes slowly faded, returning to her usual *kaffe*-brown. She wiped away the tears and straightened her shoulders.

"I set out to return home hoping to help my sister and all the *Umoyahlebe* of Ghandia," she said, her voice strong and sure. "My *uhambo loguquko* showed me that there are many more touched by the *Kish'aa* than any of us knew. The *alay-alagbara* came with cruelty and torment, but they leave us with hope that we may yet find more *Umoyahlebe* among all the tribes. That is why I will remain here. To administer the test to any who would wish it, to discover as many Spirit Whisperers as I can, and train them all. To share with them what I learned in Shalandra, the remedies to keep the Unshackling at bay. And, most of all, to turn the evil that was visited upon my people to good."

She gestured to the Hunter. "And I believe it is the will of the *Kish'aa* to aid you in your efforts. So yes, Hunter of Voramis, *Umzukeli* and *Okanele,* you will have our help." A brilliant crown of blue-white light flared around her head. "As you have kept your oath to me, so you have my oath that when you call, I and every *Umoyahlebe* willing will answer."

Chapter One Hundred Twelve

"Well, I guess that just leaves me, then," Kodyn said when Aisha had once more withdrawn the magic into herself. "No way I can top any of that. No gifts or promises, no fancy words of gratitude. Fiery hell, I can't even thank you properly for this." He patted the watered steel sword cradled almost reverently in his arms. A wry smile twisted his lips. "I feel like the last Hawk to scale the Perch or the last tyro in the gruel line."

Aisha chuckled. "Quit stalling and tell them what you found." She nudged him with an elbow, giving him an encouraging smile. In the space of a few heartbeats, she'd lost the air of power and authority that came with her mastery of the *Kish'aa,* and once again become a young woman. One burdened by greatness and a duty to her people, perhaps, but still fierce, exuberant, even, in the right company, playful. "Might not be world-shattering, but it's got value aplenty. Just like you." She shot Kodyn a sly grin and a wink.

Kodyn flushed but returned the wink without hesitation. The sight brought a smile to the Hunter's lips. There was no denying that the pair was perfect for each other. It took just one look at the two of them together to make that clear. They had differences aplenty, but they complemented the other in all the right ways.

The day comes these two tie the knot properly, the Hunter thought, *there won't be a damned thing on this world that can tear them apart.*

"Spent the day searching the city for any trace of the Order," Kodyn said, "or to see if I could find anything else that could be used to rip apart the Consortium. On that last, I came away with plenty to show for it. Came across a few more offices with Consortium paperwork. Bits and pieces, mostly, but enough to bring them down once and for all. A few contracts with the wrong people here, a handful of complaints over promissory notes that never got paid out there, and more besides." He nodded. "By the time the Night Guild's done with them, there won't be a Vassalage Consortium left standing. Those that don't end up in prison will spend the rest of their lives running from the law."

His face fell. "But that's all I've got in the way of good news."

The Hunter raised an eyebrow. "Couldn't find the Order's lair, or is everything you found in that same code?"

"You guessed it." Kodyn reached into a pocket and drew out a small stack of folded parchments, which he held out to the Hunter. "Bastards weren't polite enough to leave a cipher key around for me to find, so it's all just gibberish."

The Hunter unfolded the parchments and, together with Kiara, scanned their contents. As Kodyn had said, utterly incomprehensible.

"Except for this." Kodyn held out another parchment, this one only half-filled. "My guess is someone started decoding it and got interrupted a few lines in. Not much there, but what there is…"

The young man's dour expression surprised the Hunter. He'd expected Kodyn to be excited by the prospect of finding something—*anything*—on the Order of Mithridas. So why did he look like someone had just kicked him in the fork of his legs?

The Hunter read the paper's contents aloud. "In the name of Amhoset Nephelcheres, Pharus of Shalandra, Servant of the Long Keeper, Word of Justice and Death, I hereby order the delivery of—" He frowned and looked up. "That's it?"

Kodyn nodded. "That's it." His lips twisted into a scowl. "But I swear, there's *no* way that the Pharus of Shalandra has anything to do with the Order."

The Hunter raised an eyebrow. "And you know this how?"

"I—" Kodyn caught himself, then threw up his hands. "Well, I don't, exactly. I didn't come out and ask him about the Order of Mithridas, because I had no idea of their existence last time I stood in the Pharus' court."

The Hunter exchanged a glance with Kiara. "Not quite a convincing argument there."

"I'm with Kodyn." Aisha stood tall, shifting close until her shoulder nearly touched her companion's. "We both spent enough time around the Pharus and Lady Callista that we got a pretty damned good sense of who they were. And I'm telling you—we're *both* telling you—I can't see the Pharus being involved in this. He's a just ruler, a good man."

The Hunter sighed. "Seen plenty of 'good men' do all sorts of terrible things." He shook his head. "Being good on the surface makes it easy to hide the darkness beneath. Everyone has their secrets, most of them ugly. Some uglier than others."

"I won't argue that." Kodyn's tone grew determined, his square jaw clenching. "But I'm telling you, when the Pharus found out that there was a demon hiding among his own people, he was downright horrified. Fought the damned thing with his own two hands. Nearly got himself killed in the process. But he stood fast and did his best."

Still doesn't mean he's not secretly a conniving bastard, the Hunter thought. *Keeper knows I've met more than my fair share who wear one face in public, but it's naught but a mask. Hell, I've been the one in the mask more times than not.*

And yet, looking at the two youths, the Hunter had no cause to doubt their sincerity. They truly *believed* that this Pharus Amhoset Nephelcheres, with all his fancy titles and honorifics, was a legitimately decent sort. Never mind the fact that he was carrying on correspondence with—and issuing *orders of delivery* to—the Order of Mithridas.

"What else aren't you telling us?"

Kiara's question surprised the Hunter. He'd been studying Kodyn's face carefully, but he'd seen no sign of deceit, only stubborn insistence.

Kodyn's eyes darkened. "What makes you think I'm—"

"Kodyn." Kiara's tone was flat, calm. "I can feel it." She tapped the spot on her belly above the shard of crystal embedded deep within her flesh. "There's something you know you need to tell us, but you're worried about what'll happen when you do." She cocked her head. "The question is: who are you worried for?"

Kodyn's eyes slid away from Kiara's, meeting Aisha's for a moment.

"She read you," Aisha said simply. "Might as well spit it out like I told you that you ought to."

With visible reluctance, Kodyn reached into a pocket of his cloak and drew out a pair of stones. "I found these among the Order's things."

The Hunter stared at the two stones. They were darker than dimercurite, a midnight black as dark as the Serenii-built Bondshold itself. Yet the closer the Hunter looked, the more he could see the subtle differences between them. One had a smooth, flat surface, but the other appeared to glint in the moonlight. Not quite the same as the stone that had gone into the construction of *Ukuhlushwa Okungapheli,* which even now, after the power that had kept it alive for six millennia had died with *Okadigbo,* still sparkled as if embedded with a thousand thousand stars.

"What are they?" he asked, tearing his eyes from the stones to look up at Kodyn.

"This one's shalanite," Kodyn said, holding up the one with the flat surface. "Saw some of the raw ore during our time in Shalandra. This one, though." He pointed to the other and shook his head. "Never seen it before."

The Hunter drew out the chunk of dimercurite he'd carried with him since the battle in *Indawo Yokwesaba.* Sure enough, the difference between it and the two specimens Kodyn held were visible at a glance. The dark grey dimercurite couldn't come close to matching the deep obsidian of the other two. One of them *might* have been the same stone used in the construction of the *Dolmenrath,* the standing stones scattered around Einan by the ancient Serenii.

"Shalanite," he repeated the name Kodyn had spoken. "From Shalandra."

Kodyn's expression fell, but he nodded. "Like Djineza and her Keeper's Blade, and the parchment used to write these messages on."

The Hunter looked to Kiara. "Impossible to ignore evidence like that."

"I know," Kodyn said, his face glum. "But after what I found linking all this to the Pharus…" He trailed off.

The Hunter understood the look on the young man's face. "You expect me to go riding hard for Shalandra to rip some answers out of the Pharus you believe is a 'good man'."

"Will you?" A spark of defiance shone in Kodyn's eyes, and his fingers twitched toward the hilt of the watered steel sword.

"Kodyn," Aisha warned.

"What?" The young man rounded on her. "You know him as well as I do. The Pharus we met—"

"The Pharus we met did seem like a good man." Aisha spoke calmly, but her voice was firm. "But the Hunter we've spent the last weeks fighting beside is, too."

The words were quiet, but struck the Hunter with the force of a thunderclap.

Aisha turned a serene look on him. "You've got information pointing you in this direction, but that doesn't mean you're just going to run off and start butchering people. Because despite what everyone believes about you, the reputation you've built for yourself as the Hunter of Voramis, *you're* a good man." Her eyes hardened a fraction. "Or am I as wrong about you as you think I am about the Pharus?"

She had him there, the Hunter had to admit.

"I give you my word that I'll ask questions first, spill blood *after,"* the Hunter told Kodyn. "If he's linked to the Order, I'll find out. But if this is all just a misunderstanding—"

"Or treachery!" Kodyn's eyes suddenly lit up, and he spun to face Aisha. "This could be Groebus!"

Surprise flashed on Aisha's expression. "You think?"

"Groebus?" Kiara asked, eyes narrowing. "Wait, is he the hunchback you told us about? The one who set those cultists—Hallar's Warriors, you called them—to pour that alchemical concoction into the Heartspring?"

The Hunter sucked in a breath. He'd forgotten all about the name, but Kiara hadn't. She'd evidently been paying much closer attention to the details of Kodyn and Aisha's story than he. He'd been so concerned about Hailen and Evren at the time he'd missed some things—including this one very important thing.

"That's him!" Kodyn nodded vigorously. "Coward fled while the city was preoccupied with the Stumblers, and when we left, Invictus Tannard and a few of his best were off to hunt him down." He spoke quickly, excitedly. "He's someone I can absolutely see caught up in all this. He was working for one demon—"

"The Iron Warlord, you called him, right?" the Hunter asked.

"—and after what he did to his own people, I've no doubt he'd be more than willing to condone the mistreatment of strangers a world away." Kodyn's face twisted into a snarl. "Fiery hell, maybe everything he did in Shalandra, that was all for the Order of Mithridas."

The Hunter's stomach twisted. "Then finding him will be high on our list of priorities. Right below finding Nameless, but well above questioning the Pharus." He tried for a wry grin to pass it off as a joke.

Kodyn was not amused. "This *has* to be Groebus." He spoke the words without a shred of doubt. "I can't believe the Pharus is actually in on the Order's schemes. I won't."

Aisha nodded her agreement.

The Hunter held up his hands in a placating gesture. "If the two of you say he's not, I'll trust you on this. Innocent until proven guilty, I swear it."

That seemed to mollify them both.

"Look, take these." Kodyn pressed the two stones into his hand. "When you get to Shalandra, seek out Arch-Guardian Ennolar of the Secret Keepers in the Temple of Whispers. Tell him I sent you. If that doesn't get you in, you can go through Councilor Briana. No way Ennolar can refuse her."

That surprised the Hunter. The notion that the young man would have any kind of clout with a Secret Keeper—and an *Arch-Guardian*, no less—was surprise enough. But last he'd seen this Briana girl, she'd been a terrified, pale wreck, freshly liberated from captivity by the Gatherers. Now she wasn't just a Councilor, one of the highest-ranked officials in Shalandra, but could bend that very same Arch-Guardian to her whims.

"Is this the same Briana who Evren's taken a shine to?" Kiara asked.

The Hunter's head snapped around. "When was *that* mentioned?" He really *had* missed important details.

"Girl talk," Kiara said, patting him gently on the hand. "Aisha filled me in on the details. Which I'll fill *you* in on. Later."

The Hunter didn't quite know what to make of that. He'd always known Evren was mature for his age—the same as Kodyn and Aisha—but somehow he found it hard to wrap his head around the young thief he'd spent the last year training "taking a shine" to anyone. It had simply never entered into his mind. To him, Evren had always simply been…Evren.

"Arch-Guardian Ennolar can tell you about the shalanite and whatever that one is." Kodyn gestured to the unidentified stone. "And if there's been any word on Groebus' whereabouts, he's the one who'll have it."

"And you can also go through Evren and Briana to talk to Issa," Aisha added. "She'll know if Invictus Tannard and the Keeper's Blades sent by the Pharus found anything. And she might be able to help you figure out who Djineza was and how one of the Keeper's Blades wound up working with the Vassalage Consortium for the Order of Mithridas."

That name, Issa, the Hunter recognized and remembered well enough. "Aye, we'll do that."

"And say hullo to Hailen for us, too." Aisha's eyes lit up with a fond familiarity. "Tell him we've missed him terribly all these weeks. And if he ever wants to visit, he's more than welcome. Evren and Briana, too."

The Hunter nodded. "We'll do that."

"Oh!" Aisha said. "Actually, while you're talking with Hailen, see if he's uncovered anything else about the *Dy'nashia* and the other Serenii artifacts he was studying." She tapped a finger against the stone hanging at her neck. "He was working with Ennolar to decipher them. Maybe he's found something I can use to figure out how the dimercurite collars work. The Order wasn't polite enough to leave any written records, or any instructions on what elements went into the dimercurite alloy, so it'll be a lot of guesswork for the time being. Anything he's got that could help me understand the *Dy'nashia's* construction and the magic that makes it work the way it does might just be the key to solving my problem of preventing over-absorption of the *Kish'aa*. Which would get me one step closer to preparing the *Umoyahlebe* to help you with your problem."

"We will, I promise." Kiara spread her arms wide. "And I'll give him a big hug from the both of you."

Aisha accepted the embrace first, while Kodyn gripped the Hunter's hand in the manner of Praamians and Voramians. He held on for just a moment longer than necessary, studying the Hunter's face as if searching for any sign the Hunter wouldn't keep his word regarding the Pharus. But when he broke off with a nod and turned to accept a hug from Kiara, the Hunter knew the young man trusted him.

Strangely, that made him *want* to keep his word. If only to prove that he deserved the trust Kodyn—and Aisha, who embraced him as warmly as she had Kiara—placed in him.

Aisha pulled back from him and, to his surprise, wiped a tear from her eye. "Sad to think that after all we've shared these last few weeks, it'll be a long while before we see either of you again."

"Or Tarek." Kodyn's brow wrinkled. "Speaking of, I figured he'd show up to say farewell before he rode off." His eyes slid past the Hunter and searched the shadows behind him. "Where is he, anyway?"

Chapter One Hundred Thirteen

As the Hunter had expected, they found Tarek sitting by the horses. Elivast, Ash, and Nayaga stood saddled and ready to ride. Tarek sat stiffly, with his back to the distant merrymaking, staring off into the south. In the direction Nameless had fled.

At the sound of their approach, Tarek sprang to his feet and spun around. "Finally!" he snapped, a look of impatience infiltrating the gloom that hung over him like a thundercloud. "Thought you'd be all night, but hopefully Kiara's finally recovered enough to—oh!" He trailed off when his eyes fell on Kodyn and Aisha marching between the Hunter and Kiara.

"Really, Tarek?" Kodyn's voice echoed with a mixture of surprise, outrage, and hurt. "You don't think we deserve a proper farewell? After all this time?" He rolled up his right sleeve to expose his forearm which he held up before Tarek's eyes. "After *this?*"

Guilt blossomed on the young Elivasti's face, and his eyes slid away. He muttered something, but the Hunter barely heard the mumbled words. He had eyes only for the halfway-healed lines carved into Kodyn's flesh. He recognized the Serenii runes instantly—he'd know them anywhere—but their meaning escaped him. The sight left him blinking, stunned. When had Kodyn done *that* to himself? He'd known the two young men were growing close, but to etch the Serenii rune into his flesh signified more than just a bond of friendship.

Kodyn waved his rune-carved arm like a club to menace Tarek. "This was *your* idea!" He leaned forward. "Tell them, Tarek. Tell them what this means."

Tarek looked as if he wanted to melt into the ground on the spot. Though he was a few years Kodyn's senior, he wilted before the anger directed his way and could barely mutter a few inaudible words.

"What was that?" Kodyn snarled.

"*Chy'ianest,*" Tarek said more loudly, a flush rising to his cheeks. "Brothers-in-arms."

"And what kind of brother-in-arms rides off without a single word?" Kodyn raised an expectant eyebrow.

For answer, Tarek just dropped his gaze.

"Listen to me, Tarek." Kodyn's tone grew suddenly gentle. He stepped closer, until he and the Elivasti stood face to face. "I'm not going to pretend I understand everything you're feeling. It's never been *my* people in the kind of danger yours are facing now. But I do understand feeling like you failed those who were counting on you. I understand it because it happened to me, too."

Tarek's eyes widened slightly, but he didn't look up.

"Back in Praamis, when the Gatherers were carrying out their ritual murders, they took one of my fellow Hawks. An apprentice, Sid. Someone *I* was supposed to be watching over."

Kodyn's gaze slid to the Hunter; they'd both been in Praamis and seen what the Long Keeper's cultists had done to their victims. What they'd *planned* to do to Sid and would've done had the Hunter and the Night Guild not slaughtered them just in time.

"I blamed myself for nearly getting him killed." Kodyn shook his head. "Truth be told, I still do. Every time I think about it, I wonder what might have happened if I'd just been there, if I'd had my sword at hand when they took him, or if I'd have been able to do anything to stop them."

He leaned in until his forehead hovered a hand's breadth from Tarek's. "But that does me no good. Just like you twisting yourself into knots over what happened here is going to do you no good." He spoke firmly, but his voice held a fraternal warmth and kindness. "You did everything you could, Tarek. You faced down the *maistyr* and fought back. That's—"

"Don't you see?" Tarek's shout cut Kodyn off. His words rang with a frantic desperation that bordered on panic. "I fought back!" Tears sprang to his eyes. "I broke the oath my people swore to the Abiarazi. When I return home—*if* I return home—and tell them what I've done, I'm as good as dead."

"You believe your people will kill you for breaking your oath?" Aisha asked from behind Kodyn, surprise etched plain on her features.

"I don't know!" Tarek's tears slid free now, and the stiffness that had held him rigidly upright seemed to shatter, his body slumping as if beneath an immense burden. "I don't know what's going to happen. All I know is that I was sent here to destroy the *maistyr* before he could be a threat to our people. Now, I've not only failed to do that, but I've as good as signed my own death warrant."

He spun to face the Hunter. "You heard him yourself! He *knows* about the oath that binds my people to his kind. Ancestors alone know what else he saw while he had control of my mind." He brought a hand up to strike the side of his head with a clenched fist, as if seeking to punish himself. "If he found out about Kara-ket, everyone is in danger. My sister, Risia. Itan. All the True Descendants. My people cannot—"

"Stop that!" Kodyn's voice cracked like a whip, and his left hand darted out to seize Tarek's right wrist before the young Elivasti could hit himself again. "Yes, they're in danger. Yes, you're in a situation. But beating yourself up over it isn't going to help anyone."

Tarek's arm muscles tensed, and for a moment, the Hunter thought he'd try to tear his wrist free of Kodyn's grip, to resume his self-chastisement. Instead, he merely went limp, his arms falling to his sides, his shoulders drooping, his head hanging down so low his chin rested on his chest.

"What does *Elohas id'Arzaian* tell you about this?" Kodyn asked. "What's that twelfth and last tenet?"

Again, the Hunter couldn't help a moment of surprise. Evidently the two young men had shared a great deal with each other over the last few weeks.

When Tarek did not speak, Kodyn supplied the answer for him. "*Failure exists only in death or surrender,*" he quoted. "*Fight to your last breath, and you will never know true defeat.*"

The words seemed to fall on deaf ears, for Tarek did not lift his head nor straighten his spine. At first. But as Kodyn let the silence drag on, Tarek began to recover. His fists clenched at his sides, his shoulders squared, and, finally, he looked up. Though tears still sparkled in his eyes, a measure of gratitude shone from amidst the darkness of despair clouding his expression.

"Haven't died yet," he said in a quiet voice. "And I've no bloody intention of surrendering."

"That's the spirit!" Kodyn broke into a smile, clapping the young man on the shoulder. "What's happened here has already happened. Best you can do now is figure out the way forward and start down the path with your head held high. Because regret and guilt can drag you down faster than quicksand. Eyes clear, face forward, that's the only way you can live your life."

"Eyes clear, face forward." Tarek straightened. "Easier said than done, you know."

"I damned well do!" Kodyn nodded. "Still gotta try, right?"

"Right," Tarek said. His tears had dried, and his voice grew stronger with every word. "It doesn't matter that my pact with the Abiarazi is broken. What matters now is that my people know about this new *maistyr,* and we're prepared for whatever comes our way."

The young Elivasti turned to the Hunter. "The gift you gave us, the knowledge of the *opia* and its ability to cleanse us of the *Irrsinnon,* it gives us a chance. Even if we have to depart Karaket and Enarium for a time until the *maistyr* is eliminated, we will not be yoked ever again."

"I swear to you that I'll do everything in my power to keep my oath to the True Descendants." The Hunter held out a hand to Tarek. "We follow the damned thing until we cut out his heart and send his black soul to the forgotten hell. Your people *will* be free, Tarek."

Tarek clasped his forearm. "My people will be free."

* * *

The sun hadn't yet begun to rise by the time the Hunter, Kiara, and Tarek departed, but dawn's first light threatened over the eastern horizon. Kodyn and Aisha had ignored Tarek's desire for a quick farewell, and insisted he share one last meal with them.

"Gonna be a bloody long time before you return to visit us—" Kodyn said.

"Or we come to visit you," Aisha put in.

"—so best we do this right," Kodyn finished as if she hadn't interrupted him. He produced a small clay bottle and held it out to them. "Found this tucked away in one of the Consortium's offices. Figured it's enough for a farewell toast."

When the bottle of Nyslian red was drunk and their bellies full, they had lingered with the goodbyes, embracing each other one final time. The Hunter was surprised by the reluctance he felt at departing. A strange contrast to the *last* place he'd ridden away from. He'd all but fled Malandria—not only to escape the inevitable Cambionari pursuit, but to outrun the guilt over the deaths of Father Reverentus, Tassat, and others. Now, however, he felt the urge to stay, and only duty compelled him to depart.

But depart they did. Kodyn and Aisha stood arm in arm, waving farewell until the darkness concealed them and the terrain rose to block them from view. The Hunter cast one final glance up at the Bondshold, which towered high into the night sky. Even without its magic, the ancient Serenii-built tower was still a marvel. Its shimmering surface still played tricks on the Hunter's mind, but no longer did it cause his head to ache or fill him with a sense of foreboding. The evil that had lain dormant there for six millennia was gone. And with it, perhaps the land would one day be cleansed.

That thought lifted his spirits. He felt the same burden of failure that dragged on Tarek—Nameless had escaped *his* blade, too—but even that weight could not erase all the good that they left behind. Aisha had been returned to her family, her bond with her cousin rekindled and her sister restored to her. She had a purpose, one that might someday help the Hunter fulfill his oath to Kharna. The Ghandian Plains would know peace, for at least a time. Harmony and an end to inter-tribe bloodshed was certainly a hopeful outcome.

And so, though the greatest threat facing the world lay ahead of him, he could ride away today knowing that because of him, Kiara, and Tarek, at least one small corner of Einan was a little bit better.

Chapter One Hundred Fourteen

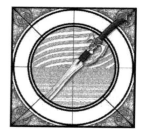

For days, they followed Nameless' trail across the Ghandian Plains.

The Hunter had no trouble tracking the demon's scent at first. Even after nearly a day, the stink of ancient rot and decay marking the Abiarazi proved impossible to miss. The spoor led due southward, straight toward the northern edge of *Indawo Yokwesaba*.

The marshy forest's myriad scents made it harder to track by smell alone. Fortunately for them, Nameless had made no attempt to conceal his passage. Ripped tree limbs, torn-down vines, and crushed saplings marked the demon's path through the dense foliage clearly enough for even a blind man to follow.

Shortly before sunset, they came upon a scene that sent the Hunter's heart springing into his throat. A slashwyrm, or what remained of it, lay gutted and torn apart far from its watery home. Deep claw marks gouged its scaly hide, and the top of its skull had been bitten off, its brains consumed. Its guts, too. Only stringy muscle and tough bone remained behind.

"No maggots yet," Tarek said with a grimace, waving his hand to clear away the flies buzzing around the corpse. "Means it was killed no later than this time yesterday."

Anxiety gnawed at the Hunter's belly. The demon had regained a great deal of its strength just from feasting on the flesh of humans. How much stronger had it grown after sating its hunger with a meal of slashwyrm?

They pressed onward, but didn't get far. The sun set quickly in the jungle, plunging them into utter darkness. Not willing to risk the horses, they made camp in the hollow of a vine-choked tree. The dark, cold night was made all the worse by the knowledge that Nameless might even now be lurking somewhere, watching them. With its returning strength came clarity of thought and an increase of cunning. The demon could have switched from flight to evasion and ultimately to hunting them.

The Hunter had never been so glad to see a sunrise. They pressed on as fast as they could on foot; the marshy forest was too thick to ride, and they couldn't risk one of the horses stumbling in a hidden hole or breaking a leg on some submerged root.

An hour later, the demon's trail led toward what looked suspiciously like a nest. Drag marks that stretched for five hundred paces ended at another half-eaten slashwyrm carcass that lay beside a natural shelter formed by the roots of three enormous *kapok* trees. The hollow beneath the trees was large enough to accommodate a fully grown bloodbear—or an Abiarazi gorged on human and slashwyrm flesh. Around the carcass were strewn the bodies of four *makalala* who'd dared to steal from Nameless' kill.

The Hunter, Kiara, and Tarek rode on without stopping.

From that point onward, Nameless' path no longer carved through the forest like the wreckage of a charging *chipekwe*. Despite the scant trail, between the Hunter's nose and Tarek's skill at tracking, they managed to follow the demon all the way to the waterfall that concealed the entrance to *Uhumi Wolandle*. From atop the cliff, they had a clear view of nearly two score *crocodylus* and *umvubu* corpses Nameless had left in his passage.

"Keeper's teeth!" the Hunter gasped, a chill seeping into his limbs. "That's…"

"Terrifying," Kiara finished.

To reach the river below, they were forced to travel far to the east, then descend the foothills until the land once again flattened out and they could circle back westward. They picked up Nameless' trail in the soft mud beside the river where the Consortium had built a dam of rocks to divert the flow into Tefaye land. The scent was faint, for they'd lost half a day on Nameless, but the demon's enormous, claw-toed footprints were unmistakable.

Day turned to night, forcing them to rest again. Every day brought a fresh sense of fear and uncertainty. Was *this* to be the day Nameless doubled back and came for them, like a lion stalking those warriors daring to hunt him? Or the day they lost his trail altogether?

Fortune guided them along their journey south. Past Nsukeja Lake, where they had to circle the enormous body of water until they found the spot where Nameless had emerged after swimming across. Past the field where the Watcher's Bloom grew, which the demon had gone out of his way to avoid. Though his scent all but died, growing so faint the Hunter couldn't be certain it wasn't just his imagination guiding him, and his footsteps became all but invisible in the hard-packed earth of the dusty plain, *somehow* they managed to keep on Nameless' trail.

It led them right to the edge of the Chasm of the Lost, a half-day's ride east of Imperial Khafra. While Tarek and Kiara rode a quarter-league to the east and west to search for any hint of Nameless' passage, the Hunter stared down into the enormous fissure gouged into the earth by the Serenii's struggle to imprison the Great Devourer in what the Einari called the War of Gods, and what the Ghandians called *Ukujiswa Okhulu*. He alone had eyes keen enough to see the minute details that marked the demon's path of descent: a shattered rock here, claw marks in the stone there, snapped roots and deep gouges that had dislodged dirt clinging to the cliffside.

The Hunter's heart sank. *Keeper take it!* No way he could follow Nameless into the Chasm of the Lost, much less Kiara and Tarek. The demon had found the *one* place he could not pursue. Where it intended to go while traveling in the canyon's shadowy depths, the Hunter couldn't begin to fathom.

He'd known this moment had been coming. He'd known it from the instant he laid eyes on the wreckage of the door Nameless had destroyed to escape. The demon was an apex predator of the highest magnitude, far above the Abiarazi who had sacrificed their innate powers to remain hidden among mortals. Nameless had been imprisoned *before* the war between the Serenii and demonkind, and thus had his full capabilities, now restored by his feast of human, slashwyrm, *crocodylus*, and *umvubu* flesh. No matter how hard they'd pushed the horses, it had only been a matter of time before they lost the demon. He was too swift, too cunning. It had been a toss-up over whether he'd turn on his pursuers or simply flee someplace they couldn't follow.

In truth, they were lucky it was the latter. Had it been the former, and had the Hunter let Tarek ride out alone as the young man had wanted, he'd have been at Nameless' mercy. A lone straggler far too easy for a mighty Abiarazi to kill. *That* was why he'd agreed to stay one extra night, and insisted Tarek did likewise. He'd made the choice for the young man's sake more than his own.

Still, he dreaded telling Tarek the truth. The young man had been on the verge of crumbling the night they parted ways with Kodyn and Aisha. Over the last few days, he'd been dogged, determined, driven. More than once, the Hunter had been prepared for Tarek to argue when he called a halt to rest. The young man had wanted to push on until he ran either himself or the horses into the ground.

But when the sound of hoofbeats told him of Tarek's return from the east, the Hunter knew he had no choice. He owed Tarek honesty. He'd have to deal with Tarek's reaction as best he could.

"He's gone," was his answer to Tarek's questioning glance. With a hand, he indicated the Chasm of the Lost. "No way we can follow him down."

He braced himself for an outburst—of rage, frustration, guilt, or Keeper-alone-knew what other reaction. He had to be prepared to talk the young man out of attempting to descend into the Chasm, weather Tarek's fury and blame, or help him see that it was not *his* fault. No human, even one descended from the Serenii themselves, could stand against an Abiarazi alone. He'd already proven himself stronger than most of his kind by refusing to kneel, oath or no.

Yet as the Hunter fumbled for the words he hoped would keep Tarek from cracking, the Elivasti surprised him by responding not with anger or accusations, but calm acceptance.

"I knew this was coming," Tarek said. Though disappointment echoed in his words, his face held only a serene stoicism. "I was arrogant to think we had *any* chance of catching up to him once he fled in earnest. I was so determined not to fail in this mission that I overestimated myself. And, worse, underestimated the *maistyr*. I'm sorry for taking out my shame on you, Hunter. You've done nothing but right by me and my people."

The apology left the Hunter utterly speechless. He could only stare slack-jawed at the young man.

"Kodyn reminded me of the *Elohas id'Arzaian*." Tarek's lips pressed together into a firm line. "The sixth tenet warns us, *Don't react, respond*."

"Reacting is emotional," the Hunter said, completing the words of the Way of the Hunter, "but responding is emotional *intelligence*."

Tarek nodded. "Right now, my reaction is to be furious and fearful. But I know better than that. My response is to do the only thing I can do: return to my people and warn them of this new threat."

"It might not be a threat," the Hunter said, "not in the way you think."

"What does that mean?" Tarek's brow furrowed.

"Think about it. The Abiarazi trapped Nameless in a Serenii prison. A prison where he absorbed into himself a great deal of Serenii blood." The Hunter raised his eyebrows. "It could be argued that he's no more a *maistyr* than I am. He's a half-blood, too, in a way."

Tarek's eyes widened. "I hadn't thought of that."

The Hunter tilted his head. He'd only had the thought a few hours earlier himself. "It could also be argued that if he was banished and cast out by his own people, the oath your ancestors swore to serve all Abiarazi doesn't include him."

"That...could actually hold water." Tarek's expression grew musing. "I will do my best to convince my people that either of those are true. But if not..."

"If not, you'll have to leave Kara-ket," the Hunter said. "Go into hiding until I can put Nameless down."

"Exactly," Tarek said. "I know there will be some of us who won't want to leave Kara-ket, but many of us have come to understand that place for what it is. It's a prison. Comfortable and safe, certainly, but no less confining than an iron cage. Now that we are free of the

Warmaster and the Sage, we can be free of that place, too. Especially if it means our people have a chance of surviving and living unshackled until Nameless is eradicated."

The Hunter couldn't help marveling at the new steel in Tarek's spine. The young man hadn't only *not* crumbled as he'd feared; he was rising to a challenge none before him had ever faced. A *maistyr* with abilities far beyond anything the Elivasti—or the Hunter himself—could even begin to imagine, one who knew that an entire race of people had sworn to be his servants. A threat that might compel the Elivasti to leave the place where they had hidden from humanity for millennia to wander Einan once more in search of safety and shelter from an enemy with the power to destroy them.

"Itan will have people waiting for me just outside Khafra," Tarek went on. "I'll get word to him about everything that happened, and he'll talk with the rest of the True Descendants, figure out what to do. He'll also make sure every contact we have around Einan is keeping an eye out for Nameless. When the demon surfaces, and I've no doubt he will, I'll make sure you're first to know."

"I'll tap into my own network, too," the Hunter promised. "Anything I find out, I'll pass along. And if I hear from your people that he's popped up, wherever I am, whatever I'm doing, you have my word I'll come running as fast as I can." He spoke the words without hesitation; he meant them with every fiber of his being. "You've stood up for your people in a way few others ever have. Not even Master Eldor was strong enough to openly defy the Abiarazi. I promise you that no matter what your people say or do, you won't stand alone."

A slow smile spread across Tarek's scruffy-bearded face, and his violet eyes lit up. "Means more to me than you know, Hunter." He swung down from Nayaga and strode toward the Hunter. But instead of offering his hand to shake in a fond farewell, he took a seat on the grass and looked up at the Hunter. "Before we part ways, though, please, will you tell me of my brother?" He leaned forward, an eagerness in his eyes. "Tell me about Hailen."

* * *

"*Melechha?*" Tarek's eyebrows shot up. "You're certain?"

The Hunter's gut tightened. "Aye, I'm certain." His fists clenched of their own accord, his shoulders knotting. He was keenly aware of how the Elivasti felt about those said to have only pure Serenii blood in their veins. Hailen's mother and father—*Tarek's* father—had died protecting their infant son from his own people.

"Seen him do marvels with my own eyes," the Hunter said, forcing his jaw to relax, his voice to lose the growl. "Anyone who'd spent two minutes with that boy would be a fool to call him an abomination." His fingers twitched as if aching to reach for his sword, just in case. *And will have me to answer to.*

"*Melechha.*" Tarek repeated the word, though to the Hunter's surprise, his voice held a note of reverence, not revulsion. He grinned suddenly. "Kanna always told me stories of the *Melechha.* Said she'd only ever heard of them, never had a chance to meet them. Yet for her, for all of us, they are the *truest* of our ancestors' descendants. And it turns out my *brother* is one!" He whistled. "Risia will be thrilled to hear about it."

The tension drained from the Hunter's body. "Hailen'd be tickled pink to know Risia was his half-brother's half-sister." He grinned. "Grew fond of her during the time they spent together. Was sad to leave."

"Then we'll have to make sure to get them reacquainted," Tarek said, beaming. "I'd like a chance to meet him, too."

813

"You tell me where and when, and I'll introduce you." The Hunter found a smile breaking out on his face, too. "Or, you get a chance, you follow us to Shalandra. That's where we're off to now. Got to sort out this mess with the Order. Find out what the connection is to Shalandra."

The Order of Mithridas had somehow learned about *Ukuhlushwa Okungapheli,* the secret of *Nuru Iwu* and *Okadigbo* known only to the Bheka tribe. Perhaps it had been Gwala who'd told them, or they'd found out some other way. However it had come about, they'd expended immense effort and monumental sums of gold into their operation to break into the Bondshold. No way they'd simply let Nameless run free now that they had liberated him.

Though it would take time for the Order to learn about the fate of their agents in Ghandia, or discover that their efforts to release the demon from his Serenii prison had succeeded, once they did, they'd doubtless bend all their power to the task of tracking him down. There were simply too many connections between the Order and Shalandra to believe it mere coincidence. If Nameless had reached out to them mentally from the Bondshold, he might even now be traveling in their direction, seeking their aid in whatever a monstrosity like him intended to do with his liberty. The Hunter gave it at least even odds that once the Order found Nameless, they'd bring him to Shalandra.

And if not? Anything that led the Hunter one step closer to unmasking the Order of Mithridas, learning their true intentions and uncovering their true source of power, was a step in the right direction as far as he was concerned. Too many people had suffered and died at their hands for him to leave off hunting them now.

But there was one more reason to pay Shalandra a visit: it would reunite his little "family". To see Hailen and tell him about his half-sibling. To meet this Briana who had caught Evren's eye. He knew Kiara would be overjoyed at being able to see their boys, too.

"One day, perhaps," Tarek said. "My people must come first."

The Hunter's smile faded, replaced by an apologetic frown. "Should've told you about Hailen earlier, I know. But—"

Tarek dismissed the words with a wave. "I understand why you didn't. Way you talk about him, it's clear you care about him like he's your own. Were that me in your place, I'd have done much the same." His eyes brightened. "I'm just glad you did."

"As am I," the Hunter was about to say, but was interrupted by the sound of approaching hoofbeats. He and Tarek scrambled to their feet and spun about to find Kiara riding back toward them. She'd gone west, in the direction of Imperial Khafra. Judging by the look on her face, she had found some form of trouble—or it had found her.

"Consortium!" she shouted, reining in a steaming Ash five paces away.

The Hunter's gaze slid past her to search the terrain behind her for racing men or the dust of fast-moving horses. In the same moment, his hand dropped toward his watered steel sword.

Only to find his belt no longer held the weapon. He'd given it to Kodyn as a parting gift.

Fortunately, the land behind Kiara revealed no sign of pursuit. "Where?" he asked, looking back to her. "How far behind you?"

"On the bridge." A wicked light shone in Kiara's eyes. "Waiting politely for us to ride up and slit their bloody throats."

The Hunter recalled the night they'd crossed the stone land bridge spanning the Chasm. They had no other means of returning south—and from there, along their respective journeys—

814

which meant they had no choice but to face the slavers taking their toll from every traveler or caravan making the crossing.

A prospect which he more than relished.

"Thirty of them?" he asked, a cold smile on his lips.

"Give or take a few." Kiara tapped a finger against Deathbite's hilt. "Still shite odds, against the three of us."

The Hunter chuckled. "Might be we tell them about the fate of their fellows at the Bondshold, do the honorable thing and give them a chance to run."

"Aye," Kiara said, nodding. "The honorable thing." She knew as well as he that men accustomed to strong-arming docile peasants and traders into submission tended to overinflate their skill at arms and the fear their reputation bred.

The Hunter turned to Tarek. "What say you? One last fight, for old time's sake?"

"It'd be my pleasure." The young man sprang lightly into Nayaga's saddle and loosened his spear from where it hung sheathed against his horse's side.

The Hunter was already mounted and setting Elivast trotting after Kiara. The burden of responsibility sat heavy on his shoulders. The trouble stirred up by the Order of Mithridas was far from over. Eliminating them here was akin to excising a lump of infected flesh, but the rot spread deep beneath the surface. No telling how far or wide their influence spread, but the power and influence they wielded was immense. They were an enemy not easily defeated. Worse, an enemy few even knew existed. And the priest who might have been his staunchest ally in the fight against them lay dead, and the entire Cambionari order would be coming for his head.

Then there was the matter of Nameless. An evil so great even the Abiarazi had feared him, now unleashed upon the world. Until the Hunter personally cut out the demon's black heart and fed his life force to Soulhunger, he had no doubt the monstrous creature would wreak havoc and leave a trail of death and destruction across Einan. The Elivasti would be unable to stop Nameless—indeed, if, as Tarek feared, the demon knew of the oath they'd sworn, the Hunter might find himself facing off against the Serenii's descendants once again. Nameless had to be stopped, for the sake of all mankind.

The Abiarazi was too powerful to be imprisoned in a Chamber of Sustenance without a Serenii as mighty as *Okadigbo* to keep him under control. That left only one possible fate: death by Soulhunger's ravenous blade. The demon's soul would sustain Kharna in his fight against the Great Devourer.

As always, the Hunter's oath to the Serenii weighed on the Hunter. It influenced *everything* he did, drove every action, consciously or unconsciously. For he knew without a shadow of doubt that if Kharna lost his battle, reality would be unmade and everything he cared about destroyed forever.

But such concerns were far greater than he could resolve in a single day.

Come, Soulhunger. He drew the dagger and felt its ravenous appetite—or his own— thrumming in the core of his being. *What say we give these Consortium bastards a taste of their own bitter draught?*

The road ahead was long, his enemies numerous, and the ordeals awaiting him no doubt arduous. For the moment, however, he could revel in a bit of wanton bloodshed.

End of Book 6

Thank You All! Please Read!

What an exciting journey! I've been *dying* to explore Ghandia since I first made mention of it in *Thief of the Night Guild (Queen of Thieves #2)*. I barely got to scratch the surface with Ria, then again explore a little more through Aisha's story in *Heirs of Destiny*. So I'm incredibly excited to finally journey into this fascinating corner of my world—and I hope you were just as excited as me.

I am so grateful to you, the reader, for taking a chance on this story. It's not often we read about a "villain" who is the "hero" in this way, so it makes it all the more wonderful that you gave it a shot—and, I hope, loved reading the Hunter's journey as much as I enjoyed writing it.

Your support is what makes it possible for me to sit down and put these tales to paper (or Word document), and your thoughts, opinions, comments, and involvement is incredibly valued.

To that end, *PLEASE* consider rating and reviewing *Darkblade: Awakener* on Amazon or any of your other favorite book sites and social media platforms. With many thousands of books published every day—most in the USA—there are so many authors vying for spots on your digital and physical bookshelf. We need all the help we can get, and you, wonderful reader, can make an enormous difference! Reviews are your way of showing others why they should read a book, and it's what helps one story like *Darkblade: Assassin* to stand out from the millions of other stories around.

If you'd like to share your thoughts or comments, want to ask a question, or simply yell at me for killing off all those characters so cruelly, my contact email is <u>contact@andypeloquin.com</u>.

Once again, thank you, and see you on the next step in the Hunter's journey!

Your biggest fan,

Andy Peloquin

Book 7 Available for Pre-Order

The seventh book in the *Darkblade* series is available for pre-order, so make sure to reserve your copy now.

Go preorder *Darkblade: Reckoner* on Amazon!

Made in the USA
Middletown, DE
25 September 2023

39369042R00453